Praise for *The Dictionary of Imaginary Places*

"A book no self-respecting dreamer should be without."

—*The Economist*

"Presented with mock solemnity and written with grace and wit, the book is a genuine work of scholarship that is also a pleasure to read."

—*Newsweek*

"References to Tolkien and García Márquez abound in this fanciful travel guide to pretend lands in literature....The comprehensive citations are entertaining."

—*Chicago Tribune*

"There is a great deal to excite and delight in the book."

—*Times Literary Supplement*

"A very satisfying work. No small part of the fun derives from its 150 maps and 100 illustrations [which are] models of their type....Witty and stylish."

—*The New York Times*

"This tourist guide to literary lands maps out Narnia, Oz, and Middle-earth along with lesser-known fantasies, like Dadist Tristan Tzara's city of Fluorescente, notable for the three-story piles of fruit and invisible dogs."

—*U.S. News & World Report*

"I myself have squirreled away for wintery afternoons the new edition of *The Dictionary of Imaginary Places.*"

—*The Washington Post*

THE
DICTIONARY
OF
IMAGINARY
PLACES

NEWLY UPDATED AND EXPANDED

THE DICTIONARY *OF* IMAGINARY PLACES

ALBERTO MANGUEL & GIANNI GUADALUPI

Illustrated by Graham Greenfield
With Additional Illustrations by Eric Beddows
Maps and Charts by James Cook

A HARVEST BOOK
HARCOURT, INC.
San Diego • New York • London

For information about permission to reproduce
selections from this book, write to Permissions,
Houghton Mifflin Harcourt Publishing Company,
215 Park Avenue South, New York, New York 10003.

The Dictionary of Imaginary Places was originally published by
Macmillan in 1980, then was substantially expanded for the
paperback edition published by Harcourt in 1987.

Additional art on pages iv, 5, 60, 135, 375, 413, 431, 434,
441, 455, 460, 524, 550, 570, 663, and 756 by Eric Beddows.

Italo Calvino entries slightly adapted and reprinted from *Invisible Cities*
by Italo Calvino, translated by William Weaver, by permission of
Harcourt, Inc. Copyright © 1972 by Guido Einaudi Editore S.p.A.;
English translation copyright © 1974 by Harcourt, Inc.

Library of Congress Cataloging-in-Publication Data
Manguel, Alberto, 1948–
The dictionary of imaginary places/Alberto Manguel &
Gianni Guadalupi; illustrated by Graham Greenfield;
maps and charts by James Cook.
p.   cm.
"The newly updated and expanded classic."
Includes index.
ISBN 0-15-600872-6
ISBN 978-0-15-600872-3
1. Geographical myths — Dictionaries. 2. Imaginary places —
Dictionaries. I. Guadalupi, Gianni. II. Title.
GR650 .M36 1999
809¢.93372—dc21   99-046994

Text set in Ehrhardt
Designed by Ivan Holmes
Printed in the United States of America

For Alessia, Alice Emily, Giulia, Rachel Claire, and Rupert Tobias
What seas what shores what grey rocks and what islands

FOREWORD

Professor Summerlee gave a snort of impatience. "We have spent two long days in exploration," said he, "and we are no wiser as to the actual geography of the place than when we started. It is clear that it is all thickly wooded, and it would take months to penetrate it and to learn the relations of one part to another. If there were some central peak it would be different, but it all slopes downwards, so far as we can see. The farther we go the less likely it is that we will get any general view... You are all turning your brains towards getting into this country. I say that we should be scheming how to get out of it." "I am surprised, sir," boomed Challenger, stroking his majestic beard, "that any man of science should commit himself to so ignoble a sentiment... I absolutely refuse to leave until we are able to take back with us something in the nature of a chart."

SIR ARTHUR CONAN DOYLE, *The Lost World*

In the winter of 1977 Gianni Guadalupi, with whom I had collected an anthology of true and false miracles for a Parmesan publisher, suggested that we prepare a short Baedecker or traveller's guide to some of the places of literature—he was thinking at the time of a guided tour of Paul Féval's vampire city, Selene. Excited by the idea, it did not take us long to compile a list of other places we felt we would like to visit: Shangri-La, Oz, Ruritania readily sprang to mind.

We agreed that our approach would have to be carefully balanced between the practical and the fantastic. We would take for granted that fiction was fact, and treat the chosen texts as seriously as one treats the reports of an explorer or chronicler, using only the information provided in the original source, with no "inventions" on our part. Personal comments would be included only if the description called for them, and then only to the extent that one would expect in a normal guidebook. With this intention, we based the design of the book on a nineteenth-century gazetteer— the relic of a time when travelling in the real world was still exciting and adventurous.

But as the project developed, our list of entries kept growing, threatening to become endless. Given the vast scope of the imaginary universe, we had, for practical purposes, to establish certain limits. We began by deliberately restricting ourselves to places that a traveller could expect to visit, leaving out heavens and hells and places of the future, and including only those on our own planet. We decided to exclude places such as Proust's Balbec, Hardy's Wessex, Faulkner's Yoknapatawpha and Trollope's Barchester, because they are in effect disguises, or pseudonyms, for existing locales, devices to let the author feel free when talking about a city or country otherwise lumbered with reality.

But here our definition of "imaginary" grew diffuse. Why include Conan Doyle's Baskerville Hall, haunted by a hound finally explained, and not Dickens' Satis House, with its gloomy spinster in her decaying bridal robes? Perhaps because Dickens' stones and mortar belong to the realm of what is possible, while Baskerville's gravel path—with its footprints of a man walking not on tiptoe but running madly for his life—belongs to the world of nightmares. Why include Crusoe's Island, which was based on historic facts? The reason, we venture to suggest, is that it has drifted out of its confinement and become forevermore a symbol of something undefined, something vaguely linked to escape and dream-like solitude and white sand beaches. Why include so many places from children's literature, and not Pooh's turf or Watership Down? Our excuse is that these exist, that they can indeed be visited and are mapped in the real world, that the authors looked upon real landscapes and installed on these landscapes their visions: the characters, the actions, were imaginary—not the places.

Similarly, Frankenstein's monster staggers around old towns and Arctic plains solidly bound within Rand McNally's atlas, whereas Dracula, despite the efforts of the Rumanian Tourist Board, has no irrevocably fixed domicile. Neither Atlantis nor Ophir, tentatively adopted by the followers of Schliemann, have yet been secured for reality; neither have the many castles, forests, fields and mountains roamed by King Arthur and his valiant knights—all these appear in our dictionary. Seemingly obvious candidates were *Metropolis, News from Nowhere, Looking Backwards*—all, alas, in the future, and therefore excluded. Tolkien, C.S. Lewis, Burroughs, Ursula K. Le Guin, Lloyd Alexander, occupy many pages; so do Bensalem, Meccania, Utopia, less entertaining but important as forbears to an imaginary architecture without which the worlds of Gulliver, of Dr. Moreau, of Oz, would perhaps never have been built.

But for some entries we can present no convincing excuse. Ultimately we admit to having chosen certain places simply because they aroused in us that indescribable thrill that is the true achievement of fiction, places without which the world would be so much poorer. We will not denounce them, and hope that the reader will not mind their intrusion.

Over a period of more than two years we visited some two thousand places, many of which were almost unknown, many of which proved unacceptable, so that in the end a little over half that number were included. The imaginary universe is a place of astonishing richness and diversity: here are worlds created to satisfy an urgent desire for perfection, immaculate utopias such as Christianopolis or Victoria that hardly breathe; others, like Narnia or Wonderland, brought to life to find a home for magic, where the impossible does not clash with its surroundings; yet others, like Dream Kingdom, built to satisfy travellers bored with reality; or travellers who long to practise dark, unorthodox arts, as on Noble's Island.

And many places dreamt up by forgotten chroniclers are perfect in themselves and require no justification whatsoever, places like Frivola, the land of tenuous marvels, where horses are so flimsy that no one can mount them; Capillaria, inhabited by gigantic blonde women who devour the small, defenceless *bullpops*, creatures in the shape of male sexual organs; the Isle of Odes, where the famous roads of the world take their holidays but are savagely attacked by the notorious Road-bashers; London-on-Thames, inhabited by Henry the Eighth, an old gorilla, and his ape-wives, who live in an African-cum-Tudor residence; Pauk, an empty room of which the sole inhabitant is a gigantic spider; X, so difficult to reach, infinitely surrounded by vast circles of classified rubbish; Nimpatan, where the most wonderful products of the human spirit are stored, like the complete works of Jacqueline Susann and the wardrobe of Pierre Cardin; Malacovia, a city of iron in the shape of an egg, the stronghold of ferocious Tartars on bicycles.

We hope that our dictionary will awaken readers' interest in these places, and in many cases provide a text when the original can only be found on the shelves of La Bibliothèque Nationale or the British Library. Readers who have thoroughly explored the realms of Tolkien and Ursula K. Le Guin will be able to refresh their memories and perhaps compare those forests and hills, cities and islands with the landscapes that have risen in other imaginations.

To help in these excursions, we have included both maps and illustrations. An article in the *Sunday Times* led us to the Graffiti Gallery in London, where we discovered Graham Greenfield and asked him to join us in the project; the revealing detail of his drawings is matched by the maps of James Cook which follow the routes laid out in the entries and graphically explain the setting of many stories.

As a work of reference our dictionary is necessarily incomplete and other travellers will certainly have explored many realms unknown to us. We take this opportunity to ask our readers to inform us of any suitable places that have escaped our notice. With their help we hope to prepare a supplement or revised edition of this book, thereby including omissions from the past and newcomers from the future, thereby turning the reader into author, the traveller into chronicler.

A.M.
Milford, May 1980

AUTHORS' NOTE
TO THE REVISED EDITION

In 1923, a group of young sappers was surveying an inaccessible part of Africa. At the end of a hard day's work under the tropical sun, a single hill remained to be plotted onto the plane table. The men were eager to return to base; it occurred to one of them that it was only a little hill and could easily be filled in, by the eye of faith and a little imagination, in the drawing office. The suggestion was approved. The inventive gentlemen cut out a picture of an elephant from a magazine, fixed it to their map, and drew around it, creating form lines for the hill they had not surveyed. The elephant-shaped hill may still be seen today in the north-west corner of sheet 17 of *Africa (Gold Coast)* in the British 1:62,500 map series.

This victory of the imagination (or common sense) over duty, over the restrictions of factual truth, is of course rare. The world we call real has deadlocked boundaries in which the long-established principle that two bodies (let alone two mountains) cannot occupy the same place at the same time is rigorously observed. Our dictionary, however, deals with a more generous geography in which there is always room for one more town, island or kingdom.

Since its publication in 1981, readers have kindly pointed out the many places not included. Some fell outside the limitations we set out in our foreword (no heavens or hells, no places in the future, none outside the planet Earth, no pseudonymous places such as Wessex or Manawaka); some did not arouse our curiosity; a few we were unable to track down. But in many cases the suggestions were useful and instructive, and we are profoundly grateful to our readers for their collaboration. There are still, of course, many gaps; the imaginary world keeps growing, and countless continents of the mind are born between book covers every year. "We carry within us the wonders we seek without us," said the wise Sir Thomas Browne. "There is all Africa and her prodigies in us."

No book, especially no dictionary, is complete without its readers. We therefore wish to acknowledge this co-authorship—Gianni Guadalupi and myself on this side, you on that side of the page.

Alberto Manguel

ACKNOWLEDGEMENTS

We wish to express our deepest gratitude to David Macey, who with such care and intelligence read the greater part of this book's original sources; to Louise Dennys, who believed in the book even before the first entry was written, and whose skill and dedication guided it to its completion; to Marilyn Wachtel, for all her help and patience, and for the sound advice of the best of friends; to Giampaolo Dossena, for his many useful suggestions.

We also wish to thank Malcolm Lester and our agent, Lucinda Vardey, for supporting the project with such enthusiasm for so long; the researchers, Michel-Claude Touchard, Olivier Touchard, Cynthia Scott, Trista Selous, Margaret Atack, Christine Robinson, Gillian Horrocks, Andrew Leake, Dorothea Gitzen-Huber, Sean, Michael and Han Wachtel; Gena Gorrell, our copy-editor; the suppliers of useful clues, Marie-Noëlle and Charles-Edouard Frémy, Ann Close, Didier Millet, Rudolf

Radler, John Robert Colombo; Professor Harold Beaver of Warwick University, Professor Hallstein Myklebost of Oslo University; Lin Salamo, Senior Editor of the Mark Twain Papers, University of California, Berkeley; Victor Brewer for his meticulous checking of maps and charts; Nick Bernays for his invaluable technical advice; Zoë Chamber for two years of hard typing.

We further acknowledge the assistance of the staff of the British Library, London; the Bibliothèque Nationale, Paris; the Metropolitan Library, Toronto; La Biblioteca Ambrosiana, Milan; the Goethe Institute of London; the National Film Theatre Archives, London; the Nobelsbibliothek, Stockholm; the New York Public Library.

We could not have compiled our dictionary without the fundamental book by Pierre Versins, *Encyclopèdie de l'Utopie, des Voyages extraordinaires et de la Science-Fiction*, Paris, 1972, and Philip Grove's *The Imaginary Voyage in Prose Fiction*, New York, 1941. Though many other bibliographies were consulted, these two proved to be essential and we hereby acknowledge our debt to both.

Finally our gratitude goes to Polly Manguel for delving in libraries, for reading sources, writing out entries, correcting the typescript and sharing two years of nomadic existence from Shangri-La to Ruritania.

THE
DICTIONARY
OF
IMAGINARY
PLACES

A

ABATON (from the Greek *a*, not; *baino,* I go), a town of changing location. Though not inaccessible, no one has ever reached it and visitors headed for Abaton have been known to wander for many years without even catching a glimpse of the town. Certain travellers, however, have seen it rising slightly above the horizon, especially at dusk. While to some the sight has caused great rejoicing, others have been moved to terrible sorrow without any certain cause. The interior of Abaton has never been described, but the walls and towers are said to be light blue or white or, according to other travellers, fiery red. Sir Thomas Bulfinch, who saw the outline of Abaton when travelling through Scotland from Glasgow to Troon, described the walls as "yellowish" and mentioned a distant music, somewhat like that of a harpsichord, coming from behind the gates; but this seems unlikely.

(Sir Thomas Bulfinch, *My Heart's in the Highlands,* Edinburgh, 1892)

ABBEY, THE (sometimes known as the ABBEY OF THE ROSE, though this name is a much later denomination), the ruins of a large Italian abbey high on the top of a range of mountains, above two small villages which are now deserted. The abbey was destroyed by fire in 1327, and of its magnificent constructions only scattered ruins remain. Ivy covers the shreds of walls, columns and the few architraves that are still intact; weeds have invaded the grounds on all sides, obscuring the places where vegetables and flowers once grew. Only the location of the cemetery remains recognizable, because some of the graves still rise above the level of the terrain. Of the church door there are only a few traces, eroded by mould, but half the tympanum has survived and the traveller may still see, dilated by the elements and dulled by lichens, the left eye of an enthroned Christ, and something of a lion's face.

Even in its days of glory the abbey was not as majestic as those of Strasbourg, Chartres, Bamberg and Paris. It resembled those built in Italy throughout the thirteenth and fourteenth centuries, with scant inclination to soar dizzyingly towards the heavens. Its base was set firmly on earth and was surmounted, like a fortress, by a sequence of square battlements. Above this storey rose another construction, not so much a tower as a solid second church, capped by a pitched roof and pierced by severe windows. Two unadorned columns flanked an entrance which opened, at first sight, like a single great arch; but from there two embrasures surmounted by multiple arches led the gaze, as if into the heart of an abyss, towards the door. The doorway itself was crowned by a great tympanum, supported by two imposts and by a central carved pillar which divided the entrance into two apertures with metal-reinforced oak doors. The sculpted stone within offered an unforgettable vision of a throne set in the sky, and a figure seated on the throne. The face of the Seated One was stern and impassive, the eyes wide and glaring; majestic hair and beard flowed around the face and over the chest like the waters of a river, in streams symmetrically divided in two. The crown on his head was rich in enamels and jewels, and the purple imperial tunic with its rich embroideries was arranged in broad folds over the knees. The left hand rested on one knee and held a sealed book, and the right was uplifted in token of blessing or admonition. Four awful creatures were arranged around the Seated One: an eagle, wings outstretched and beak agape; a winged and haloed lion and bull, each clutching a book between his forefeet; and a man who looked both handsome and kindly but was frightening in an unexplainable way.

The Aedificium, the first welcoming sight to meet travellers before the fire, is now all rubble except for the ruined south wall, which seems to stand and defy the course of time. The two outer towers, which look over the cliff, appear almost untouched, but inside the traveller's eye runs to the open heavens through a breach of the upper floors, and everything that is not green with moss is still black from the smoke of centuries ago.

In its heyday the Aedificium was an octagonal construction that from a distance seemed to be a tetragon, the perfect form which expresses the sturdiness and impregnability of the City of God. Three rows of windows proclaimed the triune rhythm of its elevation, and each corner included a heptagonal tower, five sides of which were visible on the outside. Each of these holy numbers represented a subtle spiritual significance: eight was the number of perfection; four was the number of the Gospels; five was the number of the zones of the world; seven was the number of the gifts of the Holy Ghost.

The most notable of all the abbey's buildings was the library housed within the Aedificium. Entrance to the library was possible either through the Aedificium itself, whose gates were jealously guarded by the head librarian, or by a secret passage through the ossarium. The architecture of the library itself was that of a labyrinth, full of stairs that led nowhere and rooms that reflected other rooms; mirrors, dead-end corridors and blind doors helped heighten the confusion. It has been claimed that the anonymous architects sought their inspiration in the plans of the library of BABEL.

Of all the treasures the library housed, the greatest was Aristotle's long-lost treatise on comedy. It was to preserve the world from the knowledge of this work—thought to encourage the oblivion of God—that an aged monk is said to have committed a series of atrocious murders here which culminated with the destruction of the abbey itself.

Travellers interested in the history of the abbey are referred to *Le Manuscrit de Dom Adson de Melk, traduit en français d'après l'édition de Dom J. Mabillon,* by a certain Abbé Vallet (Aux Presses de l'Abbaye de la Source, Paris, 1842). There are further references to Adso's original in Milo Temesvar, *On the Use of Mirrors in the Game of Chess,* Tbilisi, 1934.

(Umberto Eco, *Il Nome della rosa,* Milan, 1980)

ABDALLES, KINGDOM OF THE, a large country on the North African coast, bordering on the Kingdom of the AMPHICLEOCLES.

Legend has it that the people are descended from and named after Abdalles, an offspring of the sun god and Phiocles, the first woman. (Phiocles is reputed to have been conceived when a sunbeam struck a serpent, and to have been brought up by a vixen after the serpent died. Phiocles also had relations with Abdalles' brothers Tumpigand and Hor-His-Hon-Hal; her union with the latter gave birth to the first of the Amphicleocles.) Like their legendary ancestor, the Abdalles' skin is blue. The Abdalles believe in the existence of a universal being, Vilkhonis, Father of Light, who created the world.

Many of the laws and customs of the Abdalles may seem cruel to the novice traveller. In a highly popular form of entertainment known as *Lak-Tro*

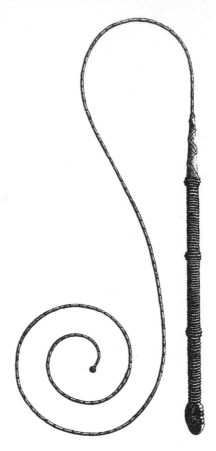

An iron-tipped whip used for juridical torture in the Kingdom of the ABDALLES.

Al Dal, four naked men insult each other, then come to blows and are finally whipped by a fifth, much to the amusement of spectators. Then all four turn on their tormentor and beat him to within an inch of his life. Next, they place him on a stool to which four cords are attached. By jerking the cords, they cause him to jump into the air and fall back onto the stool, a game which goes on for about an hour. He is then flung out of a window to the crowd below, who maul him severely before burying him up to his neck in the ground; keeping him in this position, everyone urinates on his head. The other four men are placed in the stocks and their hair is pulled out in handfuls. A similar cruelty can be seen in a form of juridical torture called the *Gil-Gan-Gis,* now rarely used. The victim is whipped with iron-tipped whips until he is almost on the point of collapse. He is then revived with the most delicious viands before being whipped again. The process continues until death. The flogging is administered by four executioners, whose chief, the *Goulu-Grand-Gak,* has the right to claim the victim's skin. The skins of executed criminals are tanned by being soaked in urine and are then sold to fashionable ladies as exquisite dress material.

But the most feared punishment is the *Kirmec,* a kind of *lettre de cachet.* It consists of the leaf of a tree—symbolizing the authority of the *Kirzif* or prime minister—which grows in a pot surrounded by an iron barrier. Only the king has a key to this barrier. When he wishes to imprison someone for misconduct, he tears a leaf from the tree and presses it to his own face. The imprint of the royal face remains on the leaf, which is then delivered to the victim of his displeasure. The victim is lowered into a deep pit known as the *Houzail* with enough food and drink for three days. According to those travellers who have visited the *Houzail,* the bottom is strewn with skulls and bones. Very few, however, actually reach the bottom safely—most fall from the frail basket used to lower them to their deaths.

The marriage customs of the Abdalles give great importance to the *Ab-Soc-Cor,* the representative of the groom. The day before the wedding he visits the bride; at dusk he is locked with her in a darkened room where he instructs her in the sexual and physical duties of a wife and ascertains that she is indeed a virgin. At sunrise he goes to the groom, greeting him with the words "The child is sleeping"; to this the groom replies "Let us go and wake her." Only then do they go to the temple for the marriage service itself.

Funeral rites are characterized by the great respect shown to the deceased. The corpse is washed, dressed in its best clothes and questioned as to why it died. If there is no answer, it is placed upright in a *Tou-Kam-Bouk,* a tall, deep coffin, and given a needle and thread to mend its clothes should they be torn. The *Tou-Kam-Bouk* is filled with aromatic herbs to preserve the corpse and is hung up in the deceased's bedroom. If the deceased is rich then *Guer-Ma-Ka*—women who get drunk in order to entertain the corpse—are employed.

The Abdalles consider it offensive to point with the finger. Only the king and the divinity are indicated by this gesture. All other objects are indicated by pointing with the elbow.

At present the Abdalles are ruled by King Mocatoa—the *Houcais,* to give him his official title. Unlike the rest of the population, Mocatoa is white, the son of a white mother. When he was born, his father immediately assumed that his mother, Nasildae, had been unfaithful to him and issued a *Kirmec* against her. Nasildae and Mocatoa were lowered into the *Houzail,* but survived the descent and lived at the bottom of the pit for many years. Here they met Lodai, a minister who had been sentenced to death years earlier. To their surprise, they discovered that it was possible to live in the caves and that they had access to the open air through a tunnel leading out on to a mountainside. The underground realm in which they found themselves was strangely beautiful, with shimmering torrents of mercury, blazing lakes of fire and swift rivers of rose-coloured liquid flowing across golden sand beneath mountains of sulphur and bitumen. They also discovered the Stream of the Universal Remedy, a golden liquid which cures all ills and wounds.

In the meantime, Mocatoa's father began to persecute all white-skinned people in the kingdom, and it was only after many years that he was finally convinced of his wife's innocence and descended into the *Houzail* in search of her; he was never heard of again. A relation of his second wife seized power and immediately began to massacre the supporters of the legitimate dynasty. Mocatoa returned to his country and his legitimate claim to the throne was at once recognized by the people. The kingdom is now rich and flourishing, thanks largely to the efforts of Lamekis, the son of an exiled Egyptian high priest who found refuge in the cave leading to the *Houzail* when he was shipwrecked on the coast.

Travellers should note that the most typical tree in the Kingdom of the Abdalles is surprisingly tall, with broad tapering leaves. The fruit is the size of a melon and so light that it bounces when dropped; its transparent juice is intoxicating, and its flesh tastes like rice-bread, resembling flour when dried. Huge carnivorous birds are sometimes seen off the coast, where they nest on isolated cliffs. Even the young are the size of a bull and are quite capable of carrying off sheep and cows.

(Charles Fieux de Mouhy, *Lamekis, ou les voyages*

extraordinaires d'un Egyptien dans la terre intérieure avec la découverte de l'Isle des Silphides, enrichi des notes curieuses, The Hague, 1735)

ABDERA, a walled Thracian city by the Aegean Sea, notable for the curious mental processes of its inhabitants. Many tales have been told about the people of Abdera's strange use of logic. For example, when the city was divided into an Eastern and a Western District the people in the west complained that they had lost "their Eastern District"—while their counterparts to the east lamented "their Western District."

Abdera is also known for its enormous horses. The city's finest temple is devoted to Arion, the horse that Neptune expelled from the sea with a blow of his trident. Houses, ships and columns are decorated with horse-motifs, and stables are considered part of the house and are decorated with simple frescos. Some horses, however, aspire to a higher degree of luxury. One mare, who had demanded some mirrors for her stall, tore them out of her master's own bedroom with her teeth, and then kicked to pieces some panelling that was not to her taste.

A famous incident in the history of Abdera was the renowned horse rebellion, when the city's horses, endowed with a sort of aberrant intelligence, reared up and sacked the city. They killed men and mules, violated women and only surrendered when the hero Hercules came to rescue the citizens of Abdera.

(Anonymous, *Physiologus Latinus,* 4th cen. BC; Christoph Martin Wieland, *Die Abderiten,* Munich, 1774; Leopoldo Lugones, "Los Caballos de Abdera," in *Las Fuerzas extrañas,* Buenos Aires, 1906)

ACAIRE, a vast forest in POICTESME surrounded by a low red wall. Within the forest, the ground rises to a mountain with three peaks. The two outer peaks are densely wooded but the middle one, the lowest, is bare. On it stands the castle of Brunelbois, overlooking the waters of a perfectly still lake which is fed by underground springs and has neither tributaries nor outlets. The castle is entered through two pointed arches, one for pedestrians and one for horsemen. Above these arches is an equestrian statue in a niche, and a large window with a stone tracery of hearts and thistles.

Brunelbois was the court of King Helmas, once famous for being the silliest monarch in the world. But prophecy told that he would gain perfect wisdom when a young sorcerer brought him a white feather moulted in the forest of Acaire by the Zhar-Ptitza bird. The bird, the oldest and wisest creature in the world, is not in fact white; it is purple, with a golden neck and red and blue tail-feathers. But Helmas did indeed receive his white feather, from a former swineherd, Manuel, destined to become ruler of Poictesme. It was in fact a very ordinary feather, but Helmas accepted it as that of the fabled bird and was immediately recognized by the people as being possessed of infallible wisdom. In celebration, All Fools' Day was struck from the calendar.

In later years Helmas quarrelled with his daughter Melusine, and she caused him and all his court to fall into an enchanted sleep from which they have never awakened. Travellers will find him sitting on his throne in his scarlet and ermine robes at the side of his queen Pressina. Pressina is one of the water-folk, and in sleep the bluish hue of her skin and the green tint of her hair have become quite obvious. Melusine herself has immortal blood, but has been suitably punished for her actions: every Sunday her legs turn into a fishtail and remain like that until Monday.

A number of interesting monsters inhabit the forest of Acaire. These include the black *bleps,* the crested *strycophanes* and the grey *calcar,* as well as the tawny *eale* with its movable horns, the golden *leucrocotta,* and the *tarandus* which takes on the colour of its surroundings. Each of these creatures is unique and therefore very lonely, and their ferocity has been greatly overestimated by those who have strayed into the forest.

(James Branch Cabell, *Figures of Earth. A Comedy of Appearances,* New York, 1921; James Branch Cabell, *The High Place. A Comedy of Disenchantment,* New York, 1923)

ACRE OF THE UNDYING, see Land of the GLITTERING PLAIN.

ADAM'S COUNTRY, in the jungles of Borneo, where disciples of Proudhon, Fourier and Cabet created a colony towards 1850. The colony is thought to be as large as a third of France, but it is probably not larger than Borneo itself. The capital consists of vast, comfortable houses with hot and cold running water, electric light, central heating and phonographs (which the pioneers invented before Edison). The rooms are decorated with orange tiles, the floor is of opaque glass and the ceiling is concave and coated with stucco. Each house has bow windows with a fine view of the streets. There is a Ministry of War, a Ministry of National Aesthetics and a Palace of Pleasure for the weekly group love-making of all law-abiding citizens.

On arrival, the pioneers took to the mountains to protect themselves from the natives. Slowly they grew confident and ultimately they became the masters of the entire population. Because their ideal was an egalitarian social State, they suppressed all opposition so that there would be only one opinion. In Adam's Country, individual welfare is subservient to the welfare of the nation. The State decrees what is agreeable or useful, and everyone must accept this ruling as law. The State religion is the Religion of Natural Harmony, and in its honour the Ministry of National Aesthetics organizes a yearly parade of young and beautiful virgins. There is no money, because the State provides everything; however, nothing can be bought, sold or given away. Individuals considered to be a threat to the National Ideal are sterilized. Criminals are sent to the army, where they are guarded by flying bombers (which the pioneers invented in 1860). Children belong to the State and are brought up according to national guidance. Artists must refrain from expressing personal emotions and must produce works that reflect the communal ideal. The motto of the colony is: "Knowledge is Pleasure; Production is Honour; Destruction is Shame."

Visitors are advised that alcoholic drinks and tobacco cannot be brought into the country and are confiscated by the customs authorities.

(Paul Adam, *Lettres de Malaisie*, Paris, 1898)

AEPYORNIS, an island in a swamp some ninety miles to the north of Antananarivo, also called Tananarive, Madagascar. The island is famous for being the only known habitat of the *aepyornis*, a curious species of bird. The salt water around the island contains a substance which smells like cerusite and keeps things from decaying, protecting the eggs which the birds lay in the water.

An *aepyornis* and its hatchling on AEPYORNIS Island.

The eggs, one and a half feet long, taste like duck eggs. Once opened, they show a circular patch about six inches across one side of the yolk, with streaks of blood and a white mark, like a ladder. The *aepyornis* embryo has a large head and a curved back; it develops into an adult fourteen feet high, with a broad head—similar to the end of a pick-axe—and two huge brown eyes more like a man's than a hen's, with yellow rims. Its plumage is fine, at first a dirty brown with a sort of grey scab that falls off at an early age, finally becoming a handsome green; its crest and wattle are blue.

There are four species of *aepyornis: vastus, maximus, titan* and *vastissimus*, in increasing size. Visitors are advised that though these birds can learn to talk more fluently than parrots, they are likely if contradicted to attack their trainer.

No European has ever seen a live *aepyornis*, with the doubtful exception of Macer, who visited Madagascar in 1745, and of a certain Mr. Butcher who was stranded here in 1891. It has been suggested that the *aepyornis* is connected with Sinbad's roc. (See also ROC ISLAND.)

(H.G. Wells, "Aepyornis Island," in *The Stolen Bacillus and Other Incidents*, London, 1894)

AFFECTION, see TENDRE.

AGARTHA, an ancient kingdom in Sri Lanka (although some travellers say it is located in Tibet). Agartha is remarkable mainly because visitors are known to have crossed it without ever realizing it. Unaware, they have probably gazed on the famous University of Knowledge, Paradesa, where the spiritual and occult treasures of humanity are guarded. Unaware, they have walked through Agartha's royal capital, which houses a gilded throne decorated with the figures of two million small gods. Perhaps they have been told (and now cannot remember) that this divine exuberance holds our planet together. If a common mortal ever angered any of the two million, the divine wrath of the gods would be immediately felt: the seas would dry up and the mountains would be powdered into deserts.

It is probably useless to add (again, visitors will have seen them and forgotten) that Agartha holds some of the world's largest libraries of stone books and that its fauna includes birds with sharp teeth and turtles with six feet, while many of the inhabitants have forked tongues.

Forgotten Agartha is defended by a small but powerful army, the Templars or Confederates of Agartha.

(Saint-Yves d'Alveydre, *Mission de l'Inde en Europe*, Paris, 1885; Ferdinand Ossendowski, *Bêtes, Hommes et Dieux*, Paris, 1924)

AGLAROND, or the **GLITTERING CAVES,** the extensive grottoes and caverns beneath the mountains around HELM'S DEEP. Originally the caves were simply used as a place of refuge and storage by the Rohirrim, the men of ROHAN; their true extent was only discovered during the battle of the Hornburg.

Gimli the dwarf, one of the defenders of the Deep, was the first to realize the great beauty of these natural caverns with their fantastic gems and veins of precious ores, and their fluted and twisted pillars of white, saffron and pink that support the roofs and are mirrored in the still pools of Aglarond.

History has it that at the end of the War of the Ring, Gimli settled here with some of the dwarves of the LONELY MOUNTAIN and became known as "Lord of the Glittering Caves." Under his guidance, the dwarves pursued and developed their traditional skills. Among other services to the men of GONDOR and Rohan, they forged the new steel and *mithril* gates of MINAS TIRITH.

(J.R.R. Tolkien, *The Two Towers*, London, 1954; J.R.R. Tolkien, *The Return of the King*, London, 1955; J.R.R. Tolkien, *The Silmarillion*, London, 1977)

AGLAURA, a city of unknown location. Little can be said about Aglaura beyond the things its own inhabitants have always repeated: an array of proverbial virtues and of equally proverbial faults, a few eccentricities, some punctilious regard for rules. Ancient observers, whom there is no reason not to presume truthful, attributed to Aglaura its enduring assortment of qualities, surely comparing them to those of the other cities of their times.

Perhaps neither the Aglaura that is reported nor the Aglaura that is visible has greatly changed since then, but what was bizarre has become usual, what seemed normal is now an oddity, and virtues and faults have lost merit or honour in a different code of virtues and faults. In this sense, nothing said of Aglaura is true, and yet these accounts create a solid and compact image of a city, whereas the haphazard opinions which might be inferred from living there have less substance. This is the result: the city that they speak of has much of what is needed to exist, whereas the city that exists on its site, exists less.

Today Aglaura is a colourless city, without character, planted at random. But this is not entirely true, either: at certain hours, in certain places along the street, travellers see before them the hint of something unmistakable, rare, perhaps magnificent; they would like to say what it is, but everything previously said of Aglaura imprisons their words and obliges them to repeat rather than say something new.

Therefore, the inhabitants still believe they live in an Aglaura which grows only with the name Aglaura and they do not notice the Aglaura that grows on the ground. Even experienced travellers, who would like to keep the two cities distinct in their memories, can speak only of the one, because the recollection of the other, in the lack of words to fix it, has been lost.

(Italo Calvino, *Le città invisibili*, Turin, 1972)

AGZCEAZIGULS, a mountainous, desert country in the far north of Chile, on the Bolivian border. Travellers who wish to visit Agzceaziguls must cross a narrow mountain pass called the Gates of Dawn, some two thousand feet above sea level, through which runs a small stream on a yellow and pink bed. The name of the pass is derived from the fact that the sun seems to rise at its farthest end. The traveller will enter a deep semicircular valley, and then, through a cleft in the rock, a sombre tunnel will lead him straight into Agzceaziguls.

The country is inhabited by an ancient tribe, said to be descended from the Incas and from the sun god himself. Their underground temples are fabulously rich. But in spite of the temples' wealth, the people are desperately poor and cannot cure their herds of llamas of disease. They believe that their animals are ill as a result of a curse put on them by white men. According to a legend, the inhabitants will one day be visited by a couple of white men who will atone for this injustice: the animals will be cured, springs will appear in the desert and miraculous harvests will grow on the rocks.

Travellers who manage to find their way to Agzceaziguls are advised to visit the holy city of Gunda, ringed by mountains and full of pink palaces. Gunda houses the royal tombs in a huge, underground crypt, filled with precious stones, and guarded by twenty golden statues with emerald eyes. No missionaries have ever reached Agzceaziguls, and the inhabitants continue to practise an ancient religion which includes human sacrifice and unspeakable rites.

(Charles Derennes, *Les Conquérants d'idoles*, Paris, 1919)

AIAIA, an island in the eastern extremity of the Mediterranean, though some believe it to be in the Black Sea. It is almost uninhabited, except for Circe the Sorceress and her servants who live in a house of polished stone, surrounded by thick bushes and trees in the midst of a large valley. Travellers are warned that a visit to Aiaia may change their outlook on life, as Circe usually transforms her guests into wolves, lions and pigs.

(Homer, *The Odyssey*, 9th cen. [?] BC)

AIOLIO, a floating island usually found in the western extremity of the Mediterranean. It consists of naked rock surrounded by an indestructible bronze wall. Here, in the centre of the rock, Aiolos Hippotades, King of the Winds, has built a magnificent palace for himself, his wife, six daughters and six sons, all of whom currently practise incest. Visitors who for some reason please the king are given large ox-skin sacks filled with violent winds which might otherwise spoil their journey home. These sacks are best left unopened.

Travellers to RUACH can see the wind given by the king to Ulysses, preserved there like the Holy Grail.

(Homer, *The Odyssey*, 9th cen. [?] BC)

AIRCASTLE or **AMAUROTE**, capital of UTOPIA.

AIRFOWLNESS, a remote part of western Scotland; its exact location remains unknown. Airfowlness is a gathering place for seabirds, who meet here before flying north to their summer breeding places. Visitors will be able to observe immense flocks of swans, geese, eider ducks, smews, gossanders, divers, petrels and gannets, outnumbering those seen anywhere else in the world.

Before the arrival of the great migrating flocks, the ness is visited by thousands of hooded

An ox-skin sack for winds from AIOLIO.

crows, who come here for their annual caucus. At this great yearly parliament, the crows boast and brag of all they have done the previous year, and, inevitably, they bring one of their number to trial. As an example, a young female crow was tried one year for not having stolen any grouse eggs, a favourite food of the species. She pleaded that she did not like grouse eggs, could get by quite well without them, dared not steal them for fear of gamekeepers and had not the heart to eat the eggs of such pretty birds. All this was to no avail; she was pecked to death. The local fairies, however, took pity on the poor crow and, giving her nine new sets of feathers, they transformed her into a bird of paradise and sent her to the Spice Islands to spend her new life eating delicious fruit.

The only human inhabitant of Airfowlness is the keeper, who looks after the grouse. He lives alone in a turf hut thatched with heather, with great stones slung across the roof to protect it from the winter gales. His main interests appear to be his Bible, his grouse and the knitting of stockings on winter nights. He also collects the feathers and down left by the migrating seabirds. After cleaning them he sells them to the southerners, who make feather beds from them.

Apart from the migrant seabirds and the crows that visit it annually, the ness supports a large colony of puffins who mostly nest in rabbit holes.

(Charles Kingsley, *The Water-Babies: A Fairy Tale for a Land-Baby*, London, 1863)

AKKAMA, a vast country to the north-west of FINGISWOLD. The southern parts of Akkama are a sandy desert, rising to the high tablelands of the centre and the north. The climate is bleak and wintry. Akkama supports a small population of barbaric nomads and woodmen. The only town of note is Pissempsco, the capital, which stands on top of a high cliff. There appears to be little or no settled agriculture in the country, though pigs are widely kept and are sometimes called "the cattle of Akkama." These pigs are notoriously fierce and the normal punishment for criminals is to be treated as pearls.

(E.R. Eddison, *Mistress of Mistresses, A Vision of Zimiamvia*, London, 1935; E.R. Eddison, *The Mezentian Gate*, London, 1958)

ALALI, a village of gigantic women in the heart of the impregnable Great Thorn Forest, Africa. The village is reached through a narrow sandstone gorge eroded by the elements into the capricious architecture of a dream, with grotesque domes set among miniature rocks. Half a mile from the entrance of the gorge is a circular amphitheatre, its precipitous walls pierced with numerous caves.

Alali society is entirely dominated by women. Because the women cannot admire the males over whom they hold dominion they cannot love them either, and they treat them with brutality and contempt. Girls are suckled for only a few months and then cast away to look out for their own food. Boys are kept penned up until they reach the age of fifteen or seventeen and are then chased into the forest. There they become legal quarry and can be hunted by any members of the tribe, including their own mothers. Older males are killed with bludgeons, kept as slaves or used for mirthless procreation.

(Edgar Rice Burroughs, *Tarzan and the Ant Men*, New York, 1924)

ALASTOR'S CAVERN, somewhere in the Caucasus, amid crags and whirlpools, discovered by the dreamer Alastor after he left his home to seek strange truths in undiscovered lands. Travellers who have dreamt of a similar place are advised not to seek it, as the whole region seems to have the property of bringing despair and disappointment to those who reach it.

The windings of the cavern lead eventually back into daylight and on to a whirlpool. The waters in the whirlpool raise boats up to an opening in the rocky bank where the waters overflow and surround a patch of grassy quiet. A soft, smooth stream flows away from the abyss amid trees and yellow flowers; farther on, the trees meet over the water, and in the base of crags that form the banks dark caves gape at the traveller. As the forest grows deeper, oak, beech, cedar and, higher up, ash and acacia, can be seen. Beneath the trees are lawns of herbs; one particularly dark glen boasts musk-rose and jasmine. The rivulet continues through a varied landscape—through ravines, over moss and stones, through plains and mountains and tall windlestraw, knotted with the roots of ancient pines growing in the sparse soil. On one of these mountains is a nook known as Alastor's Tomb, a

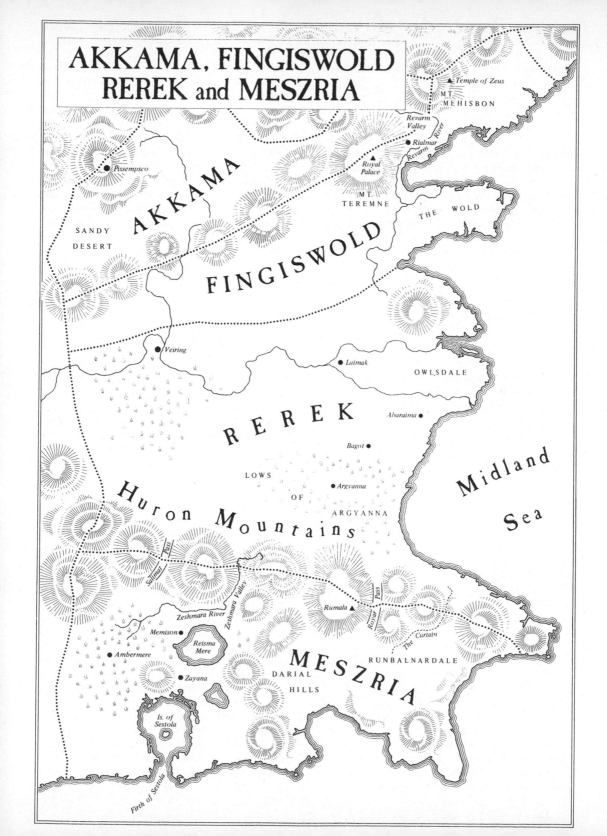

AKKAMA, FINGISWOLD
REREK and MESZRIA

Temple of Zeus
M.T MEHISBON

Revarm Valley
Rialmar
Revarm
River

Royal Palace

Pissempsco

AKKAMA

M.T. TEREMNE

THE WOLD

SANDY DESERT

FINGISWOLD

Veiring

Laimak

OWLSDALE

R E R E K

Abaraima

Bagot

Midland

LOWS

OF

Argyanna

Sea

ARGYANNA

Huron Mountains

Salimat Pass

Rovar Pass

Rumala

Zeshmara River

Zeshmara Valley

Memison

Reisma Mere

The Curtain

Ambermere

RUNBALNARDALE

M E S Z R I A

Zayana

DARIAL HILLS

Is. of Sestola

Firth of Sestola

quiet recess amid the roots and fallen rocks, overgrown with creeping ivy.

(Percy Bysshe Shelley, *Alastor or The Spirit of Solitude,* London, 1816)

ALBINO LAND, a small country of ill-defined borders somewhere in central Africa. The inhabitants are albinos with features similar to those of the Negroes in the surrounding countries. Their eyes are like those of partridges and their white hair is like very fine cotton. In stature, they are smaller than the nearby population and they are also physically weaker than their neighbours. The albinos are few in number and nothing is known of their social or political life.

(Voltaire [François Marie Arouet], *Essai sur l'histoire générale et sur les moeurs et l'esprit des nations depuis Charlemagne jusqu'à nos jours,* Geneva, 1756)

ALBRACA, the fortified capital of Galafrone's kingdom, in the eastern extremity of Cathay. Angelica, Galafrone's daughter, who drove Orlando to madness and made so many of Charlemagne's knights fall in love with her, took refuge here from the King of Tartary. The king besieged the city and was killed by Orlando.

(Matteo Maria Boiardo, *Orlando innamorato,* Milan, 1487; Ludovico Ariosto, *Orlando furioso,* Ferrara, 1516)

ALBUR, the largest state on PLUTO, the underground world in the centre of the hollow globe of the earth. Like everything on Pluto, things in Albur are much smaller than their equivalents on the surface. Despite its apparently reduced size— merely one hundred and twenty leagues long by seventy-five leagues wide—the country has four hundred towns and supports a population of forty-five million. The people of Albur are about two feet tall, white-skinned and among the most highly developed of this miniature world. Their agriculture is sophisticated and the use of bronze tools and weapons is common.

Visitors will find that all towns in Albur are built to the same pattern. The capital, Orasulla, is distinguished from the provincial centres by its size. Orasulla is walled and built on a circular ground plan. One league in circumference, it has a population of one million. The streets radiate from a central piazza in which stands a great pyramid, the centre of the country's religious life. Being so large—by Alburian standards—Orasulla is divided into sub-districts, each with its own piazza and pyramid. The houses—all four storeys high—are painted yellow and have green doors.

Albur is a hereditary monarchy in which the king is regarded as the representative of the nation and its rallying point. Society is based on a hierarchy of orders, each distinguished by the colour of its clothes. The king wears red and is the only person to do so in the country; ministers, priests and magistrates wear blue, with coloured belts to indicate their function and rank; poets and writers wear white. These orders form the aristocracy of Albur—the first group by right of birth. Poets, scientists and writers can be ennobled if they are awarded the Crown of Green for service to the country, but their titles are not hereditary. Labourers and merchants wear dark and light green respectively; doctors, miners, cooks and gravediggers wear black; artisans wear grey. Valets, the lowest stratum of the hierarchy, wear yellow. The wives of ministers, priests and magistrates wear pink and those of ennobled poets and writers wear white. Wives of members of the other orders wear the same colour as their husbands, but in a lighter shade. The queen wears white with a red belt.

The king is the supreme authority and is advised by a council of twelve ministers elected by the free orders of Albur. The king's entire life is sacrificed to the government and welfare of his people and country. He is held responsible for all the actions of the government and can be deposed if either he or the government appears to be acting against the will or traditions of the nation.

Under the terms of a law passed by King Brontes, no praise may be addressed to a reigning monarch and no monuments or statues may be built to him during his lifetime. The coins of the realm bear the image of the previous king—provided he was a man of virtue. The same is true of all medals issued in Albur.

Those who oppose government policies are never persecuted. If their ideas seem useful or valuable they will be discussed and sometimes adopted. The authors of accepted projects are given a state pension and the Crown of Green and are admitted to the nobility. Ideas and projects which are not useful are simply ignored.

Both men and women wear clothes similar to

those of the ancient Greeks. The simplicity of dress is largely the result of laws passed by King Brontes. According to these laws, only old and ugly women may wear make-up, adopt elaborate hair styles, or wear jewellery. As a result, all other women consider themselves to be young and beautiful and the custom of artificially enhancing their natural charms has completely died out.

All visitors to the capital are required to wear the local costume and to conform to accepted moral customs. They must also accept a prohibition on the eating of meat and fish, originally imposed out of respect for the god of Pluto. To the foreign palate, the food tastes plain, but it is nourishing. The local wine (although comparatively low in alcohol content) is rich and mellow. Meals are normally eaten every six hours.

Visitors are warned that the laws of Albur are rigorously enforced. Under them a murderer is punished by being shut up with the body of his victim for nine full days. His name is then removed from all civic records and he is branded on the forehead before being sent to work in the mines for life. Most other crimes are punishable by periods of work in the mines. For instance, those who eat meat are sent to the mines for five years. Visitors who contravene the law are usually deported.

The fauna of Albur includes elephants little bigger than calves, used to draw carriages and as mounts for soldiers. The largest animals in the country are the *lossine*, lizards which grow to a length of six feet. The *lossine* appear to like men and are often kept as watchdogs by the richer farmers. They are also used to protect people who stray into the forbidden zone around the country's only volcano. Although the volcano has not erupted for many years, it is forbidden for anyone to build in the vicinity or to venture onto the higher slopes. The *lossine* kept in the forbidden zone have been trained to carry those who stray across the ditch to safety on their leathery backs.

Visitors are advised to attend one of the many Alburian funeral ceremonies. The bodies of the virtuous dead are cremated and their ashes are kept in bronze globes housed in the temple. Criminals are not cremated, they are buried. It is considered a fitting punishment for their bodies to decompose in the earth.

Marriage in Albur is a matter of personal choice. Young people who wish to marry must inform their parents eight days before the ceremony, but parents can only prevent the marriage if the proposed partner has committed a crime or has a dishonourable reputation. Bachelors over thirty are deprived of many of their civic and political rights, and those who die celibate are buried, not cremated.

In Albur, the children of the poor are merely taught to read; any further education is the responsibility of their parents. The children of the rich attend school until they are eighteen. Both sexes receive the same education. Up to the age of twelve their education concentrates on physical development through dancing, sports and the rudiments of self-defence. The children also begin to learn domestic skills and the first elements of their future professions. At twelve they begin to study drawing, writing and the dead languages. The latter include Nate, from which the modern Alburian tongue has developed. Nate is still used by some savants in conversation and in formal speeches, but it is never written. Only when they are fifteen do children study religion, moral philosophy, history and education.

The cultural and artistic life of the nation is centred on the Academy of Orasulla. The Academy has only twelve standing members, who are appointed to study the language of the country and to examine all linguistic innovations. Only by their consent can new words be officially recognized. All poems, novels and other literary productions are read by members of the Academy, who correct any faults of grammar or vocabulary they may find and who censor works which are deemed immoral in any way. Records of the events of the year are kept by a body of fifty historians, each of whom writes his own account of the facts. Their texts are submitted anonymously to the Senate where they are all read; only the two most accurate accounts are printed and sent to the public libraries; the remainder are unceremoniously burnt.

The capital's remarkable museum consists of four buildings surrounding a square. The first contains sculptures. The second houses the national collection of paintings, including a delightful series of 120 agricultural scenes. The third building is devoted to historical exhibitions and houses a collection of medals. The fourth shows displays of recent inventions, together with examples of the costumes and arms of the past. A garden in the central square is adorned with the statues of virtuous kings and great men of old. A brief summary of each hero's life is inscribed on the plinth. All the inscriptions are in the modern vernacular so that as many people as possible can read and learn from them.

Albur was discovered in 1806 when a group of English and French sailors, shipwrecked in the Arctic Ocean, eventually found their way to Pluto via the north polar entrance in the IRON MOUN-TAINS. They were well received, but later told to leave when it was discovered that they had eaten meat. Before leaving, they visited the BANOIS EMPIRE, travelled through several of the countries of Pluto and finally returned to the surface of the earth via the southern polar entrance.

(Anonymous, *Voyage au centre de la terre, ou aventures de quelques naufragés dans des pays inconnus. Traduit de l'anglais de Sir Hormidas Peath*, Paris, 1821)

ALCA or **PENGUIN ISLAND**, a republic in the English Channel, now attached to the coast of France. High mountains loom over a pleasant green land covered with a certain kind of salt grass, willows, fig and oak trees. To the north is a deep bay; to the east a rocky coast, uninhabited, called the Coast of Shadows, which the people of Alca believe is the home of departed spirits; to the south is Divers' Bay, surrounded by orchards. The south is also the site of a church and monastery built by the venerable Mäel. Legend has it that Mäel was sent by the devil to a deserted island in the Arctic Ocean where he decided, being a naïve and generous man, to baptize the sole inhabitants—the penguins. The Archangel Raphael changed the penguins of Alca into men and made the island drift until it reached the northern coast

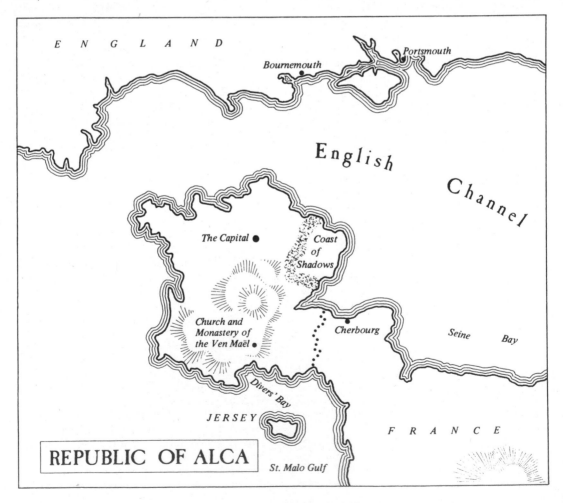

REPUBLIC OF ALCA

of France, where it attached itself to the mainland. The penguin-men went through all the stages of civilization, discovering first their nudity like Adam and Eve, then the sense of property and social class. Early Alca history is chronicled in the famous *Gesta Pingouinorum*. Alca reached its golden age under Emperor Trinco, who conquered half the world and founded the Penguin States, later abolished. Nowadays Alca is a republic of more than fifty million inhabitants, and the once green meadows have been taken over by large factories and office buildings.

It is also said that while it was drifting the island of Alca reached the East coast of Latin America and was claimed for Britain by Sir John Narborough during the reign of Charles II. But of this there is no proof.

(Anatole France, *L'Ile des pingouins*, Paris, 1908; Daniel Defoe, *A New Voyage Round The World, By A Course never sailed before. Being A Voyage undertaken by some Merchants, who afterwards proposed the Setting up an East-India Company in Flanders*, London, 1724)

ALCINA'S ISLAND can be found, according to some travellers, near the coast of Japan; according to others, in the Caribbean. A large island, the size of Sicily, its flora is abundant: woods of laurel, palm, cedar, myrtle and orange shade the low hills and the meadows. The fauna is scarce: hares, rabbits, deer, goats and a few monsters. The political situation is somewhat complex. Upon the death of the previous king, his legitimate daughter, Logistilla, became rightful heiress to the throne. The

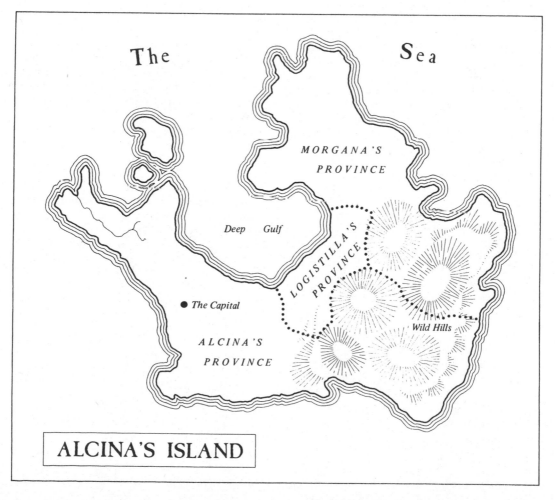

ALCINA'S ISLAND

king, however, had two other daughters by another woman, Alcina and Morgana, both knowledgeable in the science of sorcery. Alcina and Morgana fought against Logistilla and left their half-sister a small strip of land between a large gulf and a wild rugged hill. This state of affairs was reversed by Ruggiero, a knight of France, to whom we owe the only description of the island, as well as of Alcina and her customs. According to Ruggiero, Alcina would satisfy her lust by bringing to the island innumerable lovers whom she would later transform into plants or stones. She commanded an army of male, female and hermaphrodite monsters—centaurs, cat-men, ape-men and dog-men—and with her magic art built a splendid city, capital of Alcina's Island, surrounded by a towering wall of gold, and a palace, probably the most beautiful and joyful in the world. Struck at first by the beauty of Alcina, Ruggiero became her lover, but thanks to a magic ring he soon discovered that the sorceress was in fact old and ugly. He escaped to Logistilla's small kingdom while yet another sorceress, Melissa, re-transformed Alcina's previous lovers into men. Leading her monster army, Alcina went into battle against her half-sister but was vanquished by Ruggiero, thanks to an enchanted shield with the power of dazzling and striking down its opponents. Since the departure of the knight nothing is known of Alcina's Island, which probably should not be called Alcina's since the sorceress no longer resides there.

(Ludovico Ariosto, *Orlando furioso*, Ferrara, 1516; George Friederic Handel & A. Marchi, *Alcina*, first performance London, 1735)

ALDERLEY EDGE, a high sombre hill in Cheshire, six hundred feet high and three miles long. A road runs along the foot of the hill, with fields on its far side. Tall beeches extend right down to the road but despite the trees there are no birds. Many caves, tunnels and shafts from old copper mines puncture the hill, creating an intricate system of caverns, some with high curving walls that form cathedral ceilings. At the foot of Alderley Edge is a stone trough into which water drips from an overhanging cliff. High in the rock is carved the face of a bearded man, underneath which is engraved:

> *Drink of this*
> *And take thy fill*
> *For the water falls*
> *By the wizhards will.*

Legend has it that on Alderley Edge there is a narrow tunnel, concealed by a great rock and guarded by iron gates, which leads deep into a cave known as FUNDINELVE where one hundred and forty knights in silver armour lie in enchanted sleep. These are the Sleepers, guardians of the world, warriors pure in heart and brave in spirit who were chosen to fight the evil Spirit of Darkness.

(Alan Garner, *The Weirdstone of Brisingamen*, London, 1960)

ALEOFANE or **GEM OF TRUTH**, an island of the RIALLARO ARCHIPELAGO in the southeast Pacific. Its coastline consists of cliffs and quicksand beaches. Inland, on the banks of a river, stands the capital. Numerous palaces with marble steps and landing stages line the river, rising from the banks in great terraces; around the city lie miles and miles of squalid slums and hovels.

Aleofane, originally populated by the hypocrites exiled from LIMANORA, is a monarchy, with a very complex social hierarchy. The artisans and the country people are virtual slaves to the upper classes.

The Church is a State institution and is headed by a minister responsible to the government: ecclesiastical officials are poorly paid and have to rely on charity. No one enters the priesthood voluntarily. Criminals are given the choice between entering the Church or becoming journalists, as journalism and the Church are very closely linked. The people of Aleofane say that those who influence people become State servants and that journalism is simply the Church in writing.

The Bureau of Fame is a State department with a monopoly on all advertising and employs the best poets, writers and artists of Aleofane. Fame can be bought by individuals, ranging from whispered rumours to public demonstrations. The highest prices are paid for the creation and maintenance of a reputation as a truthful, generous or clean-living citizen. The charges vary—for example, a journalist pays more for a reputation for truthfulness than a peasant.

Travellers in this region should observe some of the social customs of Aleofane. The *fallallaroo*, for instance, an entertainment which consists of turning cartwheels around a room to the sound of fast music, is a fashionable practice among the elite, and marriages often result from meeting at such gatherings. Only men smoke pipes; they inhale via the nostrils the smoke produced by the leaves of the *kooannoo*, which exudes a nauseating aroma claimed to be a discipline for the mortification of the body. No wine or fermented drinks are available on Aleofane; alcohol is termed *pyrannidee*, the same word used for "devil," and is sold only for medical reasons. Moral rules are very strict, especially for girls, and those who break them are expelled from their homes.

The language of Aleofane is tonal, and meanings vary according to intonation and facial gesture. Opposites are often signified by the same word (as in BRODIE'S LAND), the difference being indicated by gestures; even the dropping of an eyelid or the raising of an eyebrow have entire grammars and vocabularies associated with them. Hyperbolic forms of address are frequent, such as "Your noblest highness in the whole universe," "Your most beautiful ladyship upon earth," etc.

(Godfrey Sweven, *Riallaro, the Archipelago of Exiles*, New York & London, 1901; Godfrey Sweven, *Limanora, the Island of Progress*, New York & London, 1903)

ALIFBAY, a country of uncertain location, is the site of the saddest city on earth, a city so ruinously sad that it has forgotten its own name. Factories in the city's northern districts manufacture sadness which is then packaged and sent all over the world. The city is divided according to the wealth of its citizens: skyscrapers for the super-rich; concrete houses with pink walls, blue balconies and lime-green windows for the middle class; and, for the poor, tumbledown shacks made of old cardboard boxes and plastic sheeting glued together by despair. The super-poor have no homes at all, and sleep on pavements and in the doorways of shops. The city stands by the Mournful Sea, where glumfish are caught. These fish constitute the inhabitants' principal diet, but visitors are warned to refrain from eating them; they make people belch with melancholy even though the skies are blue.

Many places in Alifbay are named after the letters of the alphabet. Because of the limited number of letters and the almost unlimited number of places, many places share the same name, and travellers must make certain that the one they are visiting is indeed the one they want to see. Among the Alifbay sites worth visiting are the Valley of K, where the weather is said to be fine and where the visitor can explore fields of gold and mountains of silver, with their ruined fairy castle, and the beautiful lake known as Dull, a name inspired by Dal Lake in Kashmir. Around the lake are pleasure gardens built by the ancient emperors, whose spirits still fly about the fountains and terraces in the guise of hoopoe birds.

(Salman Rushdie, *Haroun and the Sea of Stories*, London, 1990)

ALKOE, a volcano on the edge of the territory of SAS DOOPT SWANGEANTI. The name also applies to the mining and trading settlements on the lower slopes of the mountain, now a colony of Sas Doopt Swangeanti.

The colonization of Mount Alkoe was largely the work of Peter Wilkins, an Englishman, who came to Sas Doopt Swangeanti after residing for many years in GRAUNDVOLET. Very little is known of the history of Mount Alkoe before his arrival, although prior to its colonization, Mount Alkoe was a society based on slavery. Slaves worked the mines and frequently died there amid the volcanic fires that still burn deep inside the mountain. The slaves responded enthusiastically to Wilkins' overtures, especially when he promised them freedom if they joined him in overthrowing their oppressive rulers. Slavery was abolished and the mines are now worked by men who are paid for their labour.

MOUNT ALKOE, the southern face.

The people of Sas Doopt Swangeanti formerly shunned Mount Alkoe, regarding it as the abode of evil spirits. According to their legends, the volcano's earliest eruption occurred when two murderers, Arco and his wife Telamine, were flung into a cleft in the rocks. Arco had been persuaded by his wife to kill his father and the couple were condemned to death. But as they were cast into the cleft, flames appeared and have burned there ever since. For seven thousand years Arco and Telamine lived in the flames inside the mountain before gnawing their way through the rock to emerge at the foot of the volcano where their children founded a new race of miners and cave dwellers.

(Robert Paltock, *The Life and Adventures of Peter Wilkins, a Cornish Man. Taken from his own Mouth, in his Passage to England, from off Cape Horn, in the ship "Hector." By R.S., a Passenger in the "Hector,"* London, 1783)

ALLALINA, see Isles of WISDOM.

ALLALONESTONE, a sea stack in the North Atlantic, the home of the last surviving *gairfowl,* or great auk, a bird hunted to extinction long ago. The last *gairfowl* sits on this remote rock, crooning old songs it learnt in its far-off youth.

Visitors will find the *gairfowl* quite willing to tell its sad story to anyone who comes onto the rock, provided that the visitor has no wings. The *gairfowl* is a flightless bird, and clearly regards wings as something of a vulgar and pretentious innovation.

(Charles Kingsley, *The Water-Babies: A Fairy Tale for a Land-Baby,* London, 1863)

ALLIANCE ISLAND, see ENNASIN.

ALPH RIVER, see XANADU.

ALQUALONDE, see AMAN.

ALSONDONS, EMPIRE OF THE, located in the Southern Seas, far to the north of ANTARCTIC FRANCE. It is a small subterranean empire, one and a half leagues by six, situated in a huge cavern crossed by a wide river. Waterfalls upstream and downstream make the empire virtually inaccessible.

Above the capital, Tentennor, is a vault supported by rock pillars seamed with gold. Many of the houses are dug out of the rock; others are built on flat ground. The straight streets of the city are lit by oil lamps.

Originally a gold mine, the area was sealed off by an earthquake, and the miners—criminals condemned to spend their lives underground—became the founders of the new State. The Alsondons are commonly known as "gnomes," and speak the Gnomic language.

Of particular interest to the visitor is the temple built to the sun god, Grondinabondo. It is a circular building reached through a labyrinth of corridors, with a domed roof of polished gold pierced at the top. The sun can be glimpsed through this opening, and to a people accustomed to living by the light of oil lamps the sight of the sun is a miracle, a true manifestation of their god, especially when the light is reflected on the gold ceiling and mirrored walls.

The Empire of the Alsondons was first discovered by a certain Grégoire Merveil, who was rescued by the Alsondons after his boat was swamped by a waterfall. He was well treated and during his stay introduced various innovations: he improved lighting, built locks to overcome the dangers of the waterfall and taught the Alsondons the art of mechanical clocks. Visitors however may prefer the old method of measuring time, in which a young bare-breasted girl stands on a pedestal in the main square and a youth places his hands on her breasts, counting her heartbeats out loud, each beat being the equivalent of a second.

(Robert-Martin Lesuire, *L'Aventurier Français, ou Mémoires de Grégoire Merveil,* Paris, 1792)

ALTA PLANA, a land of wild peaks and glaciers, east of GREAT MARINA. After the fall of Great Marina, Alta Plana became a place of refuge. Many small monuments and the Tomb of the Heroes commemorate the war against the Chief Ranger of MAURETANIA.

(Ernst Jünger, *Auf den Marmorklippen,* Frankfurt, 1939)

ALTRURIA, a large island-continent in the Southern Ocean. Its exact location is not certain. According to Altrurians, their country represents the kingdom of Heaven upon earth.

Altrurians are a strictly Christian people, whose origins date back to the time of the first Christians immediately after the death of Christ. When the Christians were dispersed, one of them was shipwrecked on Altruria on his way to Britain. He established the Christian faith and set up a commonwealth of peace and goodwill which was, however, short-lived. His rule gave way to a long period of economic and civil war, during which even religion appeared to be on the point of extinction, the strong overpowered the weak and a system of absolutism emerged. But the new system was overthrown by a popular rebellion and a prosperous, wealthy republic developed. Known as the Period of Accumulation, this was an industrialized and ultimately destructive system in which huge labour-saving machines became monsters that devoured men, women and children. The whole country became a slave to the great centres of commerce and industry, dominated as they were by vast monopolies. Periods of prosperity alternated with periods of poverty, inflation, unemployment and even severe starvation. Opposition to the Accumulation originated among the proletariat, which started to use its vote and its political power to voice its aspirations. Parliament began to re-establish the powers it had once had and to take on new ones. Land, transport and mines were nationalized and the power of Accumulation began to weaken. The Accumulation, which in fact represented very few people, was out-voted again and again by the vast majority of the people. Through this bloodless "evolution," the Commonwealth of Altruria was at last founded on the same principles as its first primitive community.

In the early days of the Commonwealth, nations from the north attempted an invasion. They were met at the frontier by the entire population, in arms, who chose to negotiate rather than to fight. During the negotiations the invaders were persuaded to join political and social forces and to become part of the Commonwealth. Since then, Altruria has known nothing but peace. In accordance with its Christian, pacifist principles, even the old coastal defences have been entirely abandoned.

After the "evolution," the big, centralized towns began to decline. Most people now live in villages within sight of one another and the industrial cities have been destroyed. Their former sites are now the homes of poisonous reptiles and wild beasts; travellers are warned not to attempt to cross them.

For administrative purposes, the country is divided into four regions, each with its own capital. The regional capitals are built in a circle and are linked by the Great National Highway, which is supported by tall white pillars inscribed with the names of famous citizens. Although the capitals are administrative centres they also house universities, theatres and museums, and serve as artistic centres for the neighbouring villages. The capitals are connected with the villages by a radial system of electric railways, with trains travelling at up to a hundred and fifty miles per hour. The villages themselves are connected by road. The old railway system has been abandoned and the tracks turned into country roads, planted with fruit trees and flowering shrubs. Horse transport has also been abandoned because of the filth it caused in the capitals, which are now served by electric trolleys. All transport is free.

Most Altrurians live in small houses built around grassy courtyards. Much of their life is collective and meals are usually taken communally in refectories. However, the privacy of the family is guaranteed and respected.

The force of collective opinion can be seen in the treatment of the few criminals who exist in Altruria. Judiciary assemblies meet in marble amphitheatres and their rare verdicts of "guilty" are greeted by public expressions of sorrow and of hopes for the sinner's redemption; the only punishment is the remorse felt by the offender himself. The crime rate dropped greatly after the abolition of private property, since there is no need for criminal activity in a commonwealth which provides its citizens with all they need.

The Altrurians eat frugally and are vegetarians; they drink very little. Hospitality is informal and is offered on impulse. They wear brightly coloured clothes, so that groups of people seen from a distance resemble bunches of flowers. Their language is Greek in origin, but has been greatly simplified and is no more difficult to learn than English. The title of the national anthem sums up much of Altrurian culture: "Brothers All." On Evolution Day all the people of the different regions meet in the regional capital for celebrations. Once every five years they visit the national capital.

The climate of Altruria is warm and pleasant, and has been modified by human efforts. In former times, the south-east coast suffered almost Antarctic winters, as a peninsula prevented the equatorial currents from reaching it. The peninsula was cut off and the area now enjoys a Mediterranean climate all year round.

The Commonwealth keeps spies and observers in other countries to monitor their development. The first emissary to openly visit the outside world was Aristides Homos, who spent several months in the United States in 1893–94 and eventually returned to Altruria with an American wife. Nowadays Altruria has more contact with the outside world and its emissaries travel openly. Access to Altruria is not easy; Homos is known to have reached the United States via Europe, but the details of his route are not known.

(William Dean Howells, *A Traveller from Altruria*, Edinburgh, 1894; William Dean Howells, *Through The Eye of the Needle*, London & New York, 1907)

AMAN, also known as the **BLESSED REALM**, the **DEATHLESS LANDS** and the **UNDYING LAND**, to the west of which lies only the Outer Sea; beyond it are the Walls of the Night. To the east lies Belegaer, the great sea of the west, on whose eastern shore lies MIDDLE-EARTH. Aman includes the great realm of VALINOR, the home of the Valar or Angelic Powers who chose to enter the world in order to realize the vision of its Creator, Ilúvatar. No one, not even the Valar, knows the full extent of Aman. Along the north, east and south boundaries of the country runs the crescent-shaped mountain of the Pelóri, originally raised by the Valar as a defence against Melkor, or Morgoth (who set himself in opposition to the Creator, and so brought into existence the qualities of Evil and Disharmony) when they first settled in this land after the creation of Middle-earth and the battles against Morgoth that took place there during the First Age.

On the eastern shore lies the bay of Eldamar or Elvenhome, a region settled by the Teleri, or sea elves, from TOL ERESSËA. Their main city is Alqualondë, the Haven of the Swans, with halls and mansions of pearls. The beaches before it are strewn with the precious gems given them by the Noldor, the elves who later lived in LINDON. The great harbour is reached from the sea through an arch of rock, a natural gateway carved out by the sea itself. Here the Teleri built their swan ships, fabulous vessels in the shape of swans with golden beaks and eyes of jet and gold.

To the south of Eldamar, between the sea and the eastern fringe of the Pelóri, lies a narrow strip of land. This is Avathar, land of the darkest shadows in the world. Avathar was once the home of Ungoliant, a foul being of unknown origin who took the shape of a great spider. It was she who wove the monstrous webs that covered her domain with darkness. Ungoliant is thought to have come from the darkness beyond the known world and to have been corrupted by the evil of Melkor, finding in Avathar a place where she might be subservient to no one's will, but perhaps drawn there too by the light of Valinor, though she hated it. Wherever she moved she surrounded herself in the darkness that came to be known as the Unlight of Ungoliant. She helped Melkor poison the Two Trees of Valinor that had brought light into the world, and subsequently fled from Aman to Middle-earth. Here she settled in the mountains of Beleriand, the region which was engulfed by the sea at the end of the First Age. Ungoliant herself escaped the inundation and is said to have travelled south, although her ultimate fate remains unknown. It is believed that the great spiders of MIRKWOOD and even Shelob, the giant spider of SHELOB'S LAIR on the boundary of MORDOR, are her descendants.

After the destruction of the kingdom of Númenor on ELENNA, Aman and Tol Eressëa were moved far away, out of the reach of man; their precise location is therefore unknown.

The fauna of Aman includes all the creatures ever known in the world, with the exception of the evil beings created by Melkor.

(J.R.R. Tolkien, *The Return of the King*, London 1955; J.R.R. Tolkien, *The Silmarillion*, London, 1977)

AMAUROTE or **AIRCASTLE**, capital of UTOPIA.

AMAZONIA, known too as **FEMINY**, somewhere between the Caspian Sea and the Thainy River, bordering on both Albania and Chaldea. Amazonia is an empire of women who do not tolerate the presence of free men within their territory. Their only contact with the opposite sex is at an annual festival designed to ensure the reproduction of their race. To this celebration they invite a few gullible males from across the sea. Once in Amazonia, the males are dispassionately used and then either transformed into eunuchs and kept as slaves or expediently disposed of. Only the female children conceived during these festivities are kept by the Amazons; the boys are sent away.

The Amazons are brave warriors and cut off one of their breasts in order to be able to draw their bows with greater ease. Though their empire is rich in gold and precious green stones, nothing is known of their cities or of how they use their wealth. (See BRISEVENT, also NEOPIE.)

(Sir John Mandeville, *Voiage de Sir John Maundevile*, Paris, 1357; Sir Walter Raleigh, *The Discoverie of the lovlie, rich and beautiful Empyre of Guiana with a relation of the great and golden City of Manoa (which the Spanyards call El Dorado) And the Provinces of Emerria, Arromania, and of other countries, with their rivers, adjoyning. Performed in the year 1595 by Sir Walter Ralegh, Knight, Captaine of Her Majesty's Guard, Warder of the Stanneries and Her Majesty's Lord Lieutenant of the Countie of Cornewalle*, London, 1596)

AMIOCAP, an island in the KORSAR Az of the underground continent of PELLUCIDAR. Amiocap is long and narrow, with a coastline heavily indented by coves and bays. At one point the bays are so deep that from a distance they seem to cut the island in two. The shore is fringed with green hills which rise to the high tablelands of the interior. The plateaus are clad with waving, waist-high grass; elsewhere the tropical vegetation is typical of that found throughout Pellucidar.

Amiocap has comparatively few of the animals found elsewhere in this subterranean realm and life is consequently more peaceful than in other areas. The *tarag* or sabretooth tiger and the *ryth* or cave-bear are found in the higher hills, but present little threat.

The dominant species on lower ground is the *tandor* or mammoth, hunted by the Amiocapians for food as well as for its ivory tusks. The Amiocapians normally hunt the *tandor* in groups. While some of the men make a lot of noise to attract the attention of the huge beast, others creep through the undergrowth to within striking distance. They attack the *tandor* with axes and then dispatch it with spears and arrows. The key to this art is the ability to strike so quickly that the *tandor is* crippled almost before it realizes it has been attacked. A hunter who fails to do this stands little chance of escaping alive.

The Amiocapians are a handsome race, with regular features and a naturally dignified bearing.

They live in small communities, each ruled by its own chief. The Amiocapian villages are grey clusters of thatched huts surrounded by a type of fence peculiar to the island: a fibre rope is suspended between the trees around the village perimeter; wooden poles hang from the rope, some four feet from the ground, and the lower end of the poles is pierced to take pointed stakes of hard wood which protrude horizontally in all directions. These fences are constructed for protection against the *tandor* rather than against human enemies; as the great beasts try to demolish the fence with their trunks the stakes swing to and fro, threatening their eyes and lacerating their trunks.

Amiocap is also known as the "Island of Love" (not to be confused with FIGLEFIA) as its tribal life is based primarily on love and kindness. Harsh words and ugly quarrels are almost unknown on the island, whose people often seem effeminate to visitors. Amiocapians consider love the most sacred gift of the gods and they practise free love without any kind of restrictions. It is by no means unusual for girls to declare their love for a man without feeling shame or embarrassment; this would be unthinkable in the rest of Pellucidar. Relations between men tend to be quite friendly and gay—not the deadly rivalry seen in many areas. Despite their cult of love the Amiocapians are excellent warriors, feared and respected by the men of neighbouring Hime, who nevertheless occasionally make raids on the island and try to carry off the Amiocapian women. The Amiocapian cult of love does not normally extend towards strangers and captives, who are burnt at the stake to the accompaniment of music and dancing, or tied to poles and left to appease the Buried People of Amiocap.

The Buried People or Coripies are a type of troglodyte who live in deep caverns beneath Amiocap. They are bipeds, but there the resemblance to human beings ends. The feet are flat, with nailless, webbed toes; the arms are short and armed with three heavy claws. The naked body is hairless and has the sickly pallor of a corpse. The head is the most repulsive of all their features. They have no external ears, simply two small orifices in their place. The mouth is large, and when the lips are drawn back two rows of heavy fangs are revealed. Two small openings above the mouth serve as nostrils and a pair of ugly, bulging protuberances as eyes without eyelids or eyelashes.

The Buried People maintain a crude tribal

organization and can communicate in a rudimentary language. Relations between the different groups are bad and cannibalism is frequent. Their usual food consists of lizards and toads, and fish from their underground lakes, supplemented by the carcasses of animals they find on their occasional expeditions to the surface. They crave warm-blooded flesh and eat any humans who fall into their clutches. There are very few recorded cases of anyone escaping alive from the caverns beneath Amiocap.

The maze of tunnels and galleries between the various caves appears to be very ancient. Many of the tunnels have been hewn from the limestone; the natural passageways appear to have been artificially enlarged and widened. As the Buried People have no implements, it must be assumed that the tunnels were excavated with their claws throughout many dark and forgotten centuries.

(Edgar Rice Burroughs, *Tanar of Pellucidar*, New York, 1930)

AMNERAN HEATH, an extensive area of moorland in POICTESME, on both sides of the River Duardenez. Much of the area is desolate, covered in brambles and other thorny plants. The heath is the haunt of witches and should be avoided by travellers, especially on Walburga's Eve, when the voices of invisible creatures are heard in the air. It is advisable to wear a cross when venturing onto the Heath.

Perhaps the strangest feature of the Heath is the large cave beneath it. Centaurs have been seen in this area and when Jurgen, one of Poictesme's celebrated heroes, ventured into the depths of the cave he saw the bodies of the many women he had loved in his life lying on tombstones. Deeper still within the cave he found Guenevere, the daughter of Gogyvran of CAMELIARD, who had been stolen away by Thragan the Troll King. She had been placed in an enchanted sleep and was watched over by the Troll King himself, an old and villainous-looking man in full armour.

The entrance to the cave is lit by lamps on tall iron stands, but lower down there are no more lights and the floor is covered in white dust. Finally the cave opens into a chamber lit by a kettle of burning coals suspended from the roof by chains. At the far end an aisle leads to a wooden door which in turn opens into a room lit by six lamps representing the power of Assyria, Nineveh, Egypt, Rome, Athens and Byzantium. Six other cressets stand by them, but these have yet to be lit. This is the abode of the mysterious and deathless Koshchei—also known as Ardnari, Ptha, Abraxas and Jaldalaoth—whose true name is known by none.

(James Branch Cabell, *Jurgen. A Comedy of Justice,* New York, 1919)

AMORPHOUS ISLAND takes its name from its lack of shape—it is rather like soft, amoeboid or protoplasmic coral, with trees similar to the horns of snails.

Amorphous Island is an oligarchy, ruled by six kings. The first king lives on the devotion of his harem. At one time, in order to escape the justice of his parliament (which acts only out of envy), he crawled through the sewers until he reached a monolith in the central square of the island. He gnawed away at it from the inside, so that all that remained was a thin crust. Like Simon Stylites, he lives inside the column, working, eating, drinking and making love on a tall ladder in the centre. The ladder is also used for giving banquets, and selected visitors are invited to sit on the rungs. Not the least important of this king's inventions is the tandem, which extends the benefits of the bicycle to quadrupeds.

The second king, well versed in halieutics, lives off his railway lines, which resemble river beds. Being of an age at which they know no pity, the trains chase the fish and upset the ecological balance.

The third king has rediscovered the language of paradise, which had become unintelligible to the animals themselves. He has also manufactured electric dragon-flies and numbered the innumerable ants of the island by counting up to three and starting again.

The fourth member of the oligarchy is chiefly remarkable for his hairless face and for the extremely good advice he offers visitors on how to spend their spare evenings and gain recognition through public institutions.

Puppetry is the pastime of the fifth monarch; his puppets mime the actions of human beings. The king has only retained the upper parts of the puppets' bodies so that everything the government does is seen as pure-minded.

The last of the kings is the author of a great work celebrating the virtues of the French. Nothing else is known of this worthy ruler.

(Alfred Jarry, *Gestes et Opinions du Docteur Faustroll, Pataphysicien. Roman Néo-Scientifique*, Paris, 1911)

AMPHICLEOCLES, KINGDOM OF THE, in North Africa, bordering on the kingdom of the ABDALLES.

The people are said to be descended from Hor-His-Hon-Hal, the third son of the sun god, who was flung to earth with his brothers for plotting to overthrow his father. Hor-His-Hon-Hal fell in love with the first woman, Phiocles, kidnapped her and hid her away in a cave; together they founded the race of the Amphicleocles. In order to prevent any contact with the Abdalles (a race founded by his brother), Hor-His-Hon-Hal erected a high wall around his kingdom. For many years, the Amphicleocles remained in total isolation. But an earthquake destroyed much of the wall, laying open the country to the rest of the world.

All male Amphicleocles are red-skinned, like their legendary ancestor: the women, however, have inherited the white skin of Phiocles.

The country is a monarchy, governed by a king or queen and a high priestess. They are advised by the Council of Seven (a body of unknown origin), which has the power to declare war and call an assembly of the Estates General. During an interregnum, the Council rules under the general leadership of the high priestess. It is composed of elders who have rendered outstanding service to the State. They take an oath of loyalty to the *Ki-Argouh*, an effigy of the king which they wear around their necks. If one of their number is found guilty of an offence punishable by death, all members of the Council are executed.

Visitors are advised to see the Amphicleocles' most precious treasure, the royal crown—a tall cap, six feet high, spun from spiders' webs. It is the colour of dawn and is surmounted by an image of the sun, which turns on a pivot. The crown is worn only when the king mounts the high throne in the temple, which normally happens on just one occasion during his reign. Once he is seated on the throne, he drops the *Tak-lak-lak*, a golden ball symbolizing royal privilege, signaling a general amnesty for prisoners. For a brief period the right of primogeniture is abrogated, debts are cancelled, divorce is allowed, widows may remarry if they so choose and old men are allowed to die in the minor temples of the kingdom. At this time too, the

The *Ki-Argouh* or effigy of the king, from the Kingdom of the AMPHICLEOCLES.

people are permitted to enter the main temple (normally they are made to remain in the courtyard) and oracles and other pronouncements are inscribed on brass balls and thrown to them by the priestesses.

Like their neighbours the Abdalles, the Amphicleocles worship the god Vilkhonis. In former days they worshipped a deity known as Fulghane, represented as a huge man and said to be the creator of all things. The cult of Fulghane was used by the priestesses to maintain a degree of political power: the idol in the temple was hollow and the divine oracles it gave were spoken by the high priestess. The deception was discovered when Ascalis was proclaimed princess.

Ascalis was the daughter of Indiagar the Great, the seventy-third king of the Amphicleocles. It was she who rebelled against the ancient custom that royal children be brought up without ever meeting their parents and that they marry in accordance with traditional laws. By tradition, all children born at the same time as a royal infant were brought up in the temple so that the prince or princess could choose a spouse from their number when he or she reached maturity. Ascalis refused to accept this imposition and succeeded in seeing her father. Natural affection overcame tradition and the unnatural laws were abolished. The high priestess was strongly opposed to this and maintained that Ascalis was not the legitimate heiress to the throne. During a confrontation in the temple, the deceit practised by the priestess was discovered and the people destroyed the idol of Fulghane. Travellers of the school of Nostradamus will know that an ancient prophecy maintained that the cult of Fulghane would end when a princess of the Amphicleocles saw her father.

Ascalis and Indiagar ruled jointly and happily until she was kidnapped by the king of TRISOLDAY. Indiagar traced his daughter to that subterranean kingdom, but died there when he became involved in a plot to overthrow the king. The princess was finally rescued by Mocatoa, Prince of the Abdalles, whom she married. During the absence of the royal couple the cult of Fulghane enjoyed a brief revival, but it has now been abolished.

The royal palace is a strange but magnificent edifice. The façade is totally blank, with no doors or windows. The only entrance is through the roof. Court etiquette requires that no one knock at the door of the royal apartments; those seeking entrance must blow through a hole in the door to attract the attention of a mute dwarf who stands with his ear to the hole. The greatest favour shown to a subject is for the monarch to lay his or her hands on the subject's head. Putting one's finger in one's mouth and holding one's breath is a sign of great respect.

The laws of the Amphicleocles have been collected in a large volume said to have been brought to earth by the *kirkirkantal* or angel of light. It measures eighteen by twelve feet and the laws are written in a combination of dots and commas. The *Book of Laws is* considered sacred; if anyone breaks an oath sworn on it, he is handed over to the priestesses to be tickled to death. It is guarded by the four *Foukhouourkou*, elders who can claim to have had four forbears who served on the Council of Seven. Only they, the high priestess and the reigning monarch may see the book. All others present when it is opened must be blindfolded.

According to the law, those receiving capital punishment are squeezed to death in a large press. Their blood is used in the religious rites and their skin preserved in the temple. A bas-relief records the offence for which they were executed.

In the Kingdom of the Amphicleocles, messages are carried by runners known as *Foul-bracs*. The *Foul-bracs* eat only feathers, spiders' webs and ivy, light substances which help them become nimble and fleet of foot, and they are thus capable of covering up to ten *karies* or leagues in an hour.

(Charles Fieux de Mouhy, *Lamekis, ou les voyages extraordinaires d'un Egyptien dans la terre intérieure, avec la découverte de l'Isle des Silphides, enrichi des notes curieuses,* The Hague, 1735)

AMR'S TOMB, in that area of Wales known as Archenfield, by the Llyead Amr or Stream of Amr. It is the burial place of Amr, son of King Arthur of CAMELOT; for reasons that remain obscure, Arthur slew Amr and buried him here. The tomb has magical properties and its dimensions are never the same on any two consecutive days. On one day it may be six feet long and on the next day it may be nine, twelve or even fifteen feet long.

(Anonymous, *The History of the Britons,* 10th cen. AD)

ANASTASIA, a city in Asia with concentric canals watering it and kites flying over it. Many objects can profitably be bought here: agate, onyx, chrysoprase, and other varieties of chalcedony. Travellers should taste the flesh of the golden pheasant cooked over fires of seasoned cherry wood and sprinkled with a lot of sweet marjoram. The women of Anastasia enjoy bathing in the pool of a garden and sometimes—it is said—invite the stranger to disrobe with them and chase them in the water. However, all this is not the city's true essence; for while the description of Anastasia awakens desires one at a time only to force the traveller to stifle them, when he finds himself in the heart of Anastasia one morning his desires will waken all at once and surround him. The city will appear to him as a whole where no desire is lost and of which he is a part, and since it enjoys everything he does not enjoy, he can do nothing but inhabit this desire and be content. Such is the power, sometimes called malignant, sometimes benign, that Anastasia, the treacherous city, possesses; if for eight hours a day the visitor works as a cutter of agate, onyx, chrysoprase, his labour which gives form to desire takes from desire its form, and he will believe he is enjoying Anastasia wholly when he is only its slave.

(Italo Calvino, *Le città invisibili,* Turin, 1972)

ANDERSON'S ROCK, a barren rock of unknown location. The only person known to have visited it is John Daniel during his ill-fated attempt to return from the moon to PROVIDENCE ISLAND. The rock is bare and precipitous. At the bottom of a deep chasm is an extensive cavern, only a few feet above water level. This is the home of the inhabitants of Anderson's Rock, who live in caves roughly furnished with planks from sunken ships. They are basically human, but their mouths are as broad as their faces and they have virtually no chins; they have long thin arms and legs and webbed fingers and toes. Their legs are covered in scales, their bodies in fur like that of a seal. Damp and cold to the touch, these creatures live entirely on the fish they catch, which they dry in the sun. A certain species, the oil-fish, provides the inhabitants with oil to light their cavern homes.

These curious beings are descended from an English couple wrecked on their way to East Africa in the early eighteenth century. Though they still speak English, they have forgotten how to read and write. They attribute their mis-shapen form to the fact that their mother, Joanna Anderson, received a severe fright when she saw a sea-monster during her pregnancy. The truth is more sinister, as John Daniel discovered when he found a manuscript written by the lady. Her marriage proved childless and, in frustration, she gave herself to the seamonster she claimed had frightened her so badly; the original inhabitants were the offspring of that union. By the time John Daniel arrived on Anderson's Rock the humans were long dead; union between the original twins born to Joanna had given rise to a population of thirty seamonsters.

(Ralph Morris, *A Narrative of The Life and astonishing Adventures of John Daniel, A Smith at Royston in Hertfordshire For a Course of seventy Years. Containing, The melancholy Occasion of his Travels. His Shipwreck with one Companion on a desolate Island. His accidental discovery of a Woman for his Companion. Their peopling the Island. Also, A Description of a most surprising Engine, invented by his Son Jacob, on which he flew to the Moon, with some Account of its Inhabitants. His return, and accidental Fall into the Habitation of a Sea-monster, with whom he lived two Years. His further Excursions in Search of England. His Residence in Lapland, and Travels to Norway, from whence he arrived at Aldborough, and further Transactions till his death, in 1711. Aged 97... Taken from his own Mouth. By Mr. Ralph Morris*, London, 1751)

ANDORRA, a small republic in southern Europe, not to be confused with the Pyrenees country of the same name.

Andorra is a land of narrow valleys and stony fields on steep slopes. The traditional crops are olives and rye; the dry terrain does not allow mechanized farming and grain is still harvested in the age-old manner, cut by hand with sickles. Andorra is not a particularly picturesque country, in spite of the whitewashed houses around the main square in the capital.

Andorrans are proud of their country's traditional Christianity and like to think of themselves as a pious people. Religion is closely allied with politics; when the statue of the Virgin is carried through the streets in procession, it is accompanied by olive-grey-clad soldiers who march with fixed bayonets. On the day of St. George the virgins of Andorra have the traditional task of whitewashing the entire capital.

Although generally a peaceful country, Andorra has always been marked by a certain xenophobia. It is worth noting that Andorrans are known to have at times expressed strong anti-Jewish feelings which they apply impartially to Jews and non-Jews alike.

(Max Frisch, *Andorra*, Frankfurt, 1961)

ANDROGRAPHIA, a country of unknown location where the State is considered a large family and each family a miniature State, with both subscribing to hierarchies of authority and birth. Towns and villages are under the government of a senate composed of magistrates and elders; wives are under the authority of their husbands.

Within this hierarchy, there is equality—all those belonging to a given category of age, trade or sex are equal, yet subordinate to their hierarchical superiors. Villages are subordinate to towns, towns to provincial capitals, provincial capitals to capitals, capitals to the king or sovereign magistrate; within the family, the father's authority is absolute.

Land is divided among the different families, who are supplied with livestock according to their needs and abilities. Parents of large families are highly honoured and marriage is compulsory for all healthy individuals. By the age of eighteen every young man must already support at least two other persons, in preparation for marriage and a family.

Those interested in the written arts will find a visit to Andrographia rewarding, for literature and the theatre are considered honourable professions. Education is strict and no one may marry or enter a trade without first attaining a certain minimum standard of education.

The circular public halls which are built in all the towns are multi-purpose. They are used to store food and as dining rooms for collective meals. Here the *National Gazette* is read aloud on Saturdays, detailing all important news and events, and travellers wishing to know what to do and what to see in Andrographia are advised to attend.

(Nicolas Edme Restif de la Bretonne, *L'Andrographe ou idées d'un honnête homme sur un projet de réglement proposé à toutes les nations de l'Europe pour opérer une réforme générale des moeurs, et par elle, le bonheur du genre humain avec des notes historiques et justificatives*, The Hague, 1782)

ANDUIN RIVER, see GREAT RIVER.

ANDUIN, VALES OF, the area between the MISTY MOUNTAINS and MIRKWOOD, drained by the tributaries of the GREAT RIVER of MIDDLE-EARTH. The Great River itself is crossed by a ford near the great rock of Carrock. Steps carved in the rock lead to the large stone seat on its summit. Much of the surrounding land is grassland, with the exception of an oak forest to the east of the Carrock.

The Vales are inhabited by the Beornings, a rather unfriendly people who do not welcome outsiders. Their task is to guard the Ford of Carrock and keep it safe for merchants and travellers in return for a toll. They also keep the land free of wolves, and of orcs, or goblins, whom they loathe. Otherwise, the Beornings are on friendly terms with all other animals. They do not eat meat: their main dish is a kind of honey cake which visitors are strongly advised to taste.

The precise origin of the Beornings is uncertain, but they are known to take their name from Beorn, their leader during the years before the War of the Ring. Beorn had the uncommon ability to take on the shape of a bear, in which guise he would travel long distances in a very short time. Some say that at one time all Beornings had this ability, and there is speculation as to whether or not they descend from the great bears which once roamed the mountains of this part of Middle-earth. Beorn also had the ability to talk with the animals he kept as servants, who carried out all the normal domestic tasks such as bringing food and setting the table. His dwelling was a long, low, wooden hall set in the oak forest and surrounded by a thorn hedge. It appears that this crude architecture, using roughly fashioned tree trunks, still survives among his descendants.

After the War of the Ring, the Beornings were given the section of Mirkwood that lies between the mountains and the Narrows—the area where the western and eastern fringes of the wood draw together to form a narrow "waist."

(J.R.R. Tolkien, *The Hobbit, or There and Back Again*, London, 1937; J.R.R. Tolkien, *The Fellowship of the Ring*, London, 1954; J.R.R. Tolkien, *The Return of the King*, London, 1955)

ANGMAR, the hostile region to the north and west of the MISTY MOUNTAINS of northern MIDDLE-EARTH. For much of the Third Age, the area was ruled by the Witch-king who overthrew the kingdom of ARNOR. He established a fortress city at Carn Dûm in the far north of the mountains. He peopled the area with hill-men— an evil people who are thought to have come originally from the ETTENMOORS—and orcs, the powerful goblins of Middle-earth. From his fortress, he launched attacks on the three countries into which Arnor had been divided and, in 1974 Third Age, he took Arnor's capital FORNOST. A year later, however, he was defeated and the town was liberated, though it was not again inhabited until the end of the War of the Ring. After the Battle of Fornost, the Witch-king withdrew to MORDOR and the area was gradually cleansed of the last of his evil servants.

(J.R.R. Tolkien, *The Fellowship of the Ring*, London, 1954; J.R.R. Tolkien, *The Return of the King*, London, 1955)

ANIMAL REPUBLIC (see INDIA), on a vast island of unknown location, inhabited by many different species of beasts and birds who have rid themselves of the tyranny of man.

Visitors will find that the island presents many characteristics described by classic poets: the lambs associate with the wolves, the falcons fly wing in wing with the pigeons, the swans have social intercourse with the serpents and the fish swim in the company of the beavers and the otters.

The republic is governed by the phoenix, a

singular bird whose ambassadors are monkeys. Tigers and lions serve as soldiers, geese and dogs as sentinels, parrots as interpreters, storks as physicians and the unicorn (a lonely beast forgotten by Noah during the Flood) holds the function of chief toxicologist in charge of finding antidotes to all sorts of poisons.

Two main religions are found on the island: sun-worship, in which most animals believe, and moon-worship, a sect of growing importance, fostered by the elephants.

Visitors can admire the phoenix's palace, where magnificent spectacles take place, including the "Colour Display" by the birds of paradise.

After stamping out a revolt led by the snakes and the basilisks (probably from BASILISK COUNTRY), the Animal Republic is now again at peace.

(Jean Jacobé de Frémont d'Ablancourt, *Supplément de l'Histoire Véritable de Lucien,* Paris, 1654)

ANIMAS, MONTE DE LAS or MOUNTAIN OF THE SPIRITS, near Soria, Spain.

The mountain used to belong to the Knights Templars, who had been invited by the King of Spain to protect the city of Soria after it was recaptured from the Arabs. The invitation was taken as an insult by the lords of Castile. As a challenge, they organized a hunt on the mountain, thereby disobeying the Templars' express order not to invade their territory. The result was a bloody battle in which both hunters and defenders were slaughtered. The King of Spain declared the mountain to be cursed and instructed that it be left uninhabited from then onwards. The bodies of both friends and enemies were buried together in the chapel built by the Templars, which soon became overrun by weeds and creepers.

Travellers are advised to visit the mountain on the night of All Saints, when a phantom bell is heard tolling in the foggy air. The ghosts of the dead come out of their tombs in torn and bloody shrouds and hunt phantom stags on phantom horses. The wolves howl in fear, the deer leap in terror, the snakes utter frightened, sibilant sounds and the whole mountain rings with the clatter of galloping hooves. On the following morning, the snow will be covered with traces of the hunt. If the visitor is fortunate, he will also see the figure of a beautiful, pale and dishevelled young girl, running on bleeding feet, clutching a blue scarf in her hand, fleeing from the hunt. She is said to be a noble lady of Soria, called Beatriz, who had asked her lover to return to the Monte de las Animas on the night of All Saints, to pick up a scarf she had dropped. He was found next morning, half-devoured by wolves, his face a mask of horror. On awakening, Beatriz found by the side of her bed her lost scarf stained with her lover's blood.

(Gustavo Adolfo Becquer, "El monte de las ánimas," in *Leyendas,* Madrid, 1871)

ANNUMINAS, capital of ARNOR.

ANOROC,

a group of islands in the Lural Az of the underground continent of PELLUCIDAR which takes its name from the largest island. There are dozens of islands, large and small, in this group, and the total population is thought to run into the millions. The people of Anoroc are known as Mezops, a copper-skinned race of fishermen and hunters. They are natural sailors and have traditionally supplied the Pellucidarian navy with many men. Anoroc is now a major centre for shipbuilding and for trade. Iron ore is mined, and gunpowder is manufactured on a small uninhabited island.

The Anoroc islands are covered in thick tropical forests which come right down to the water's edge. The villages are concealed deep in the forests and are built on a pattern peculiar to the islands. In hidden clearings, large trees are cut down to a height of about twenty to thirty feet. Spherical dwellings made from woven twigs and dried mud are then constructed on top of them. Long narrow slits are cut into the walls to give light and ventilation. The trunks of the trees are hollowed out and ladders erected inside them. The size of the houses varies; some have up to eight rooms and are built on two floors, while others are much smaller. A carved image on the roof indicates the identity of the owner.

The forest clearings are large enough also to accommodate well-cultivated fields and gardens in which the Mezops grow their cereals, fruit and vegetables. Most of this work is carried out by the women.

Mezop villages are extremely difficult to find as the visible trails do not lead directly to them. A clear, well-marked trail will suddenly appear to end when in fact it continues beyond the tangled trees; it requires expert knowledge to find the sign indicating where the continuation is. Travellers are advised to climb trees, cross the watercourses or retrace their steps along the trail to try and find the right sign. The nature of these trails makes it extremely difficult to move fast, both for the inhabitants and for visitors, but it also protects the villages from possible enemies. Learning the trails is a major part of a boy's education and a man's status is judged by how many trails he knows on his own island. The layout of the trails is not taught to the women, who rarely leave the villages.

(Edgar Rice Burroughs, *At the Earth's Core*, New York, 1922; Edgar Rice Burroughs, *Pellucidar*, New York, 1923; Edgar Rice Burroughs, *Tanar of Pellucidar*, New York, 1930)

ANOSTUS, a gulf and the farthest point of a large and verdant island beyond the entrance to the Mediterranean. From here onwards there is no return. In Anostus it is neither very light nor very dark, the air being dusky and reddish. There are two rivers in Anostus, the river of Pleasure and the river of Grief, and on their banks grow venerable trees. Those that grow on the banks of the river of Grief bear sorrowful fruit and if a visitor should eat of them he will spend the rest of his life in tears and grief and so die. The fruit on the trees along the river of Pleasure are of the opposite nature, and whoever tastes them is freed from all former desires. If the visitor has loved someone, he will forget his love, and in a short time become younger and younger, live over his former years once again and die a newborn babe.

(Claudius Aelianus, *Varia Historia*, 2nd–3rd cen. AD)

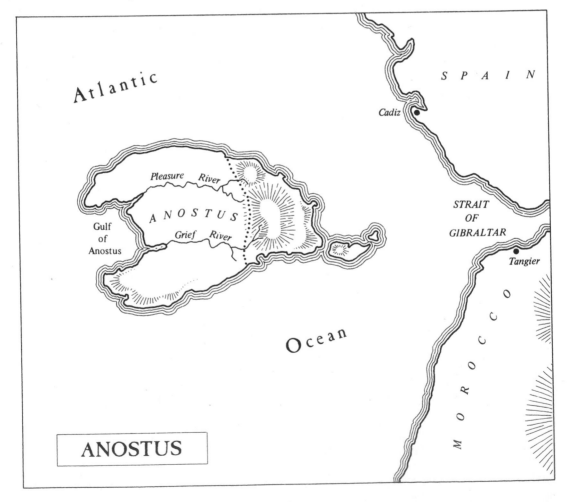

ANOSTUS

ANTANGIL, a vast island-kingdom, some two hundred leagues long with a circumference of 1,060 leagues, which extends 6° north of the Tropic of Capricorn to some 50° from the Antarctic Pole.

Mild summers, harsh winters, pleasant springs and sunny autumns can all be found at the same time in the different regions of Antangil, so that a traveller visiting the kingdom at any time of the year should be properly dressed for all seasons.

To the north, on the Indian Ocean, the coast is abrupt and rocky, with no bays or harbours except at the mouth of two rivers, the Iarri to the east—fast-flowing but navigable—and the Bachir to the west—slow and muddy. To the south, beyond the fertile valleys of the region, rise the tall Sariche or Salices Mountains, inhabited by savage and cruel people. The mountains themselves are rich in many minerals. Also to the south is the Pachinquir Gulf which cuts one hundred leagues into the mainland; the regions round the Gulf are famous for their precious stones and beautiful pearls. In the waters of the Gulf a strange gentle animal can be found, as large as a horse, with the face of a lion, covered half in hair and half in scales; it can swim at great speed but is also found on land and seems to enjoy human company.

Visitors approaching Antangil from the sea will notice the high volcano on Corylée Island, on the south-west coast; in the hours of darkness it shines like a lighthouse, warning sailors of the dangerous sand shoals. The kingdom of Antangil is divided into 120 provinces, each of which boasts a capital city. The capital of the kingdom itself is Sangil, built in the

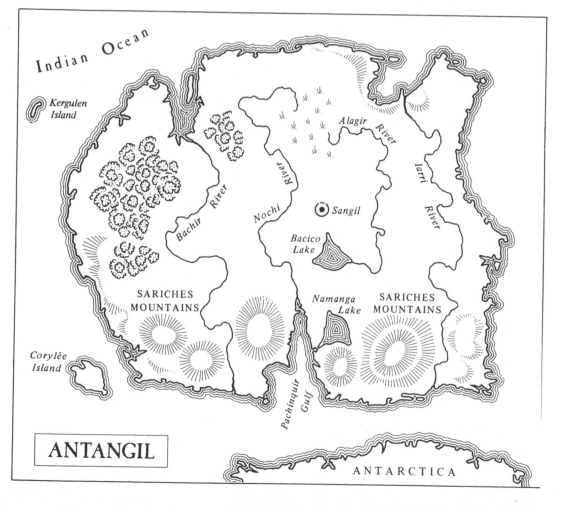

geographical centre of the island. Many centuries ago, the inhabitants of Antangil decided to forget their quarrels and work for the prosperity of a united nation. It was agreed that each city would be divided into groups of ten inhabitants under leaders elected by all ten. These commanders or *dizainiers* would form further groups of ten that would elect *centeniers*. The *centeniers* would elect a king who would make no decisions without the approval of the senate, and would have no say in the finances of the kingdom.

The entire wealth of Antangil belongs to the people, who may decide to increase or reduce private and public taxes. It is also the people who control the army, and all men between the ages of eighteen and fifty-five can be called to serve. The martial laws are strict and any act of plunder by a soldier is punishable by death. The death penalty may consist of either hanging or decapitation, but torture is strictly forbidden.

Only girls of noble families are given any kind of education, and this in proportion to their family fortune. The richest girls—and therefore the best instructed—leave the Academy at the age of twenty-four.

The religion of Antangil is Catholicism, although certain rites such as the keeping of saints' days and the worship of religious symbols are excluded. Fasting is not observed on the days normally prescribed by orthodox Catholic religion.

Travellers will find that all hotels and inns, by law, display the price of rooms and meals. Tipping is forbidden as the inhabitants consider that they should only be paid for their work. Poverty is unknown throughout the kingdom and the unemployed are sent to work in the mines of the Sariche Mountains, thereby keeping idle hands busy and the devil unassisted.

(Joachim du Moulin [?], *Histoire du grand et admirable royaume d'Antangil Inconnu jusques à présent à tous Historiens et Cosmographes: composé de six vingts provinces très-belles & très fertiles. Avec la description d'icelui, & de la police nonepareille, tant civile que militaire. De l'instruction de la jeunesse. Et de la Religion; par I.D.M.G.T.*, Saumur, 1616)

ANTARCTIC FRANCE, a rock-bound peninsula about the size of France and with a similar climate, situated in the Southern Seas. High mountains protect it from cold winds, and the populated area, situated in an enclosed valley, is hidden by the mountains and cut off from the coast by sandy deserts.

The well-fortified capital, New Paris, is a replica of the original, and any visitor familiar with Paris will find his way about easily. The only difference is that the slums of the original Paris have been replaced by fine buildings and the new city is more beautiful than the old. No ports exist in Antarctic France, and apart from New Paris, there are only five or six towns of any size or importance.

The country is a hereditary monarchy, and is traditionally ruled by a beautiful queen whom the inhabitants call Ninon. There has been only one king in the country's history—Grégoire Merveil from the Empire of the ALSONDONS who eventually resigned in favour of his daughter, reestablishing the female reign.

All the arts and technology of Europe—except shipbuilding—exist in this southern country where many customs, such as the wearing of masks at balls, are inspired by those of seventeenth-century France. A good time to visit Antarctic France is during the carnival, a period of celebration and gaiety, of masks and disguises, often marked by the playing of extravagant practical jokes; or during the Feast of Marriages when the prettiest girls are auctioned off in the presence of the queen and her ministers, and the money used to find accommodating husbands for the ugliest. This is an occasion for a great public feast, held in a series of cafés and dance halls.

While male travellers may wish to avoid the Province of the Viragos (women who have failed to find husbands at the Feast of Marriages) where at one time women held all the power and men were sold as slaves, they may find the southern part of the country more interesting. This is the home of a sect of Immortals, who are extremely old but appear to be relatively young; they have spent years in suspended animation (by being buried in a glacier) and periodically go back into that state, sometimes for years at a time, through the use of opium.

(Robert-Martin Lesuire, *L'Aventurier Français, ou Mémoires de Gregóire Merveil*, Paris, 1792)

APE KINGDOM, in Africa, somewhere in the high tree-tops of the tropical jungle, inhabited by large apes or Mangani. Though the apes usually live some twenty-five miles inland, they travel extensively, sometimes remaining for months in a distant locality. They sleep where darkness overtakes them, covered in the leaves of the elephant's-ear plant. This particular tribe of apes is famous for having brought up the young Lord Greystoke after slaughtering his father (see also TARZAN'S ABODE).

The apes have a number of strict laws. Among these, it is useful to know that if an ape-wife is stolen, she may choose between her kidnapper and her husband; if she chooses her kidnapper, she must give her husband one of her daughters in exchange. If a husband beats his wife or his wife is slovenly, the offender can be flogged by one of the older members of the tribe.

Travellers are advised to attend the famous Dum-Dum ceremony. It takes place in a natural amphitheatre—a hollow among low hills—in the centre of which is a drum built especially for this mad and intoxicating revel. Historians say that from this primitive ritual have risen, unquestionably, all the forms and ceremonials of the modern Church and State. For through countless ages, back beyond the uttermost ramparts of a dawning humanity, these fierce and hairy forbears of man danced out the rites of the Dum-Dum to the sound of their earthen drum beneath the bright light of a tropical moon in the depth of their mighty jungle, unchanged today as it was on that long-forgotten night in the dim past when man's first shaggy ancestors swung from a swaying bough and dropped lightly upon the soft turf of the apes' first meeting-place.

(Edgar Rice Burroughs, *Tarzan of the Apes*, New York, 1912)

APE MOUNTAIN, on an island somewhere in the Indian Ocean, so called because of the numerous monkeys that are found here, hardly four inches high, with yellow eyes, black face and a lion's mane. They assault ships that dock in the island's harbour, stealing everything that they can find.

Should the traveller escape the monkeys' clutches, a greater danger awaits him on the mountain slopes. Here stands a castle inhabited by a creature reminiscent of a human being but as tall as a palm tree and black from head to foot, with blazing eyes, tusks like those of a wild boar, a mouth as deep as a well, lips like those of a camel hanging down to his chest, ears like watermelons hovering over his shoulders and nails like lion's claws. His main dish is human flesh, and visitors should therefore avoid all contact with him.

(Anonymous, *The Arabian Nights*, 14th–16th cen. AD)

APES, CITY OF THE, on the coast of the Indian Ocean, where lofty houses overlook the sea. Its name derives from the ape population in the surrounding area. Every night the apes invade the city, sack it and kill every human being they can find. To avoid being slaughtered, the inhabitants leave at dusk through their back doors that open onto the sea and spend the night in small ships which the apes cannot reach. These same apes, however, are also the cause of the city's prosperity, because in the daytime, when the apes retreat into the mountains, the inhabitants follow them with baskets full of stones with which they pelt the beasts; to defend themselves, the apes throw back coconuts. These are collected by the inhabitants of the city and sold for a large profit to the many other cities on the coast.

(Anonymous, *The Arabian Nights*, 14th–16th cen. AD)

APHANIA, a kingdom in Central Europe. The country is renowned for its many bells and steeples, and for the statue of King Rumti who was changed into stone by a good fairy because, in his absent-mindedness, he had forgotten to give alms to a beggar. The present king must pay homage to this statue on the 81st of Blowsy. There are only four months in the Aphanian year—Growsy, Rosy, Blowsy and Snowsy which correspond to the four seasons.

Aphania is a peculiarly literary country. There is a special statute-book for literary offences, and a Court of Letters presided over by six judges who receive immense salaries as compensation for their necessary abstention from literature. Any person found guilty of borrowing from the works of other writers is sent to the treadmill for three years. Adaptations from the French are contraband, and violations of syntax merit capital punishment without benefit of clergy. Anyone presumptuous enough to pen a sentence such as "These laws of grammar, originally promulgated by Lindley Murray, *and which* have been sanctioned by general usage" would be immediately executed. To ensure purity of style, all adjectives are kept at the National Library, and no writer is allowed to use more than a certain number per day without a special licence from at least three of the Judges of Letters. In spite of this stringency, a great number of books are published every year, and most of them are books of worth. With regard to publishing, the regulations of Aphania are specific: for every volume sold, the publisher is allowed to repay himself the cost of paper, type and binding, at a certain rate varying from one to five per cent according to the style in which he brought out the book. As he ought to be, if anything, a better judge than other people of the value of the books offered him, it is decreed that he justly suffer the entire loss of publication if the book is worthless. The writers, on the other hand, receive everything (except this percentage) which the books realize, it being laid down that the success of the work depends entirely on what they add to the paper, as type and binding are common to all books. In case of failure they are held acquitted by the cost of lost time and damaged reputation.

Salaries are paid only to those who do nothing; otherwise it is supposed that those who have real work might be inspired by desire of gain rather than by an innate sense of duty.

History is preserved by the Royal Remembrancer, who must also remind the king of everything. He was first appointed by King Buffo LXI after the monarch had the whole of the top of his head—including the seat of memory—cut off in a combat with the usurping giant Swashdash.

Warfare is frowned upon but it exists, and because drum practice is noisy, a special district called Bootinter was set aside on the sea-coast for the training of the soldiery and the manufacture and trial of big drums. To the scientific traveller, Bootinter is a place of great interest and is invariably visited by all tourists of note who can obtain a pass from the War Department. Spectacular trials take place here: for example, the great contest of "Drums *versus* Cotton Wool" which is particularly worth attending.

(Tom Hood, *Petsetilla's Posy*, London, 1870)

APODIDRASKIANA, see DOTANDCARRY-ONE TOWN.

APRILIS, see NEW BRITAIN.

ARABIAN TUNNEL, an underwater passage connecting the Red Sea with the Mediterranean. It can only be travelled from south to north due to the force of the currents. The entrance lies some fifty metres below the Gulf of Suez and the exit is in the Gulf of Tinah or Pelusio, not far from the submerged ruins of the ancient city of Pelusio.

According to Professor Aronnax of Paris, author of *The Mysteries of the Great Sea Depth*, the tunnel was discovered and used for the first time by Captain Nemo of the *Nautilus*. Captain Nemo discovered the existence of the tunnel by observing that the same species of fish inhabited the Red Sea and the Mediterranean, and deducing that some sort of communication must exist between the two. Because of the different levels, he also deduced that the current must run from the Red Sea into the Mediterranean. To prove his point, he caught a number of fish in the Gulf of Suez, marked them with rings and put them back into the water. Several months later, near the coast of Syria, he found several of his marked specimens.

(Jules Verne, *Vingt mille lieues sous les mers*, Paris, 1870)

ARCADIAN TUNNEL, a subterranean passage from Arcadia in Greece to Naples in Italy, only to be used by unhappy lovers; to cross it, it is best to obtain the services of a guiding nymph. Both the entrance and the exit are infested with satyrs, crystal fountains, sweet-smelling herbs, gentle flocks, loitering nymphs, singing nightingales, loving shepherdesses, solicitous bees, lonely turtledoves, noisy crickets, low-flying swallows, perfumed apples, gentle storms, quiet sepulchres and many-coloured butterflies.

(Jacopo Sannazaro, *Arcadia*, Naples, 1501; Félix Lope de Vega y Carpio, *Arcadia*, Madrid, 1598)

ARCHAOS, a kingdom in central Europe, famous because of its liberal monarchy. Capital: Tremenes, in the province of Onirie. Govan Eremetus, King of Archaos, established the laws of the country by refusing to be drawn into war with the kings of Bilande and Aboree. When these presented themselves with their armies at the Castle of Tremenes, King Govan appeared in his party clothes and asked where the spectacle was to take place. He offered wine to everyone present and finally both kings left Archaos laughing and half drunk.

The laws of the country require that all the inhabitants of Archaos work until the Royal Treasury is full; the king then shares the profits with everyone. Once this is spent, the people go back to work again. Even when famine struck Archaos, King Govan found the right law to keep the country from disaster, and set down law No. 14: "Everything is free." Merchants and shopkeepers could not sell their foods, money became of no use and the goods had to be shared by everyone. Another royal law established that "everyone should do what he likes," which was later, in a fit of formal religious belief, changed to "everyone should do what he likes with the grace of God." Archaosite philosophy explains that the works of love are better than those of riches and wars, that no one should work more than is strictly necessary, that good manners can solve almost any problem. "We pick flowers and play with cats, we thank God for a particularly lovely sunset," say the inhabitants of Archaos.

Worth visiting are the Royal Castle of Tremenes which the king has opened to all women who wish to escape from irate fathers, bad husbands or imposed fiancés; the Institute of Public Necessities, a bordello set up by the king which the king himself frequently visits: and the Convent of Onagre, founded by Princess Onagre, twin sister of King Govan, who was abandoned as a child in the enchanted forest of Feline. The convent is dedicated to the enjoyment of the present and to meditation.

(Christiane Rochefort, *Archaos ou Le jardin étincelant*, Paris, 1972)

ARCHENLAND, a small country to the south of NARNIA, from which it is separated by a high range of mountains. Looking west from Archenland the traveller will observe the mountains rising above pine-covered slopes and narrow valleys, to a range of blue peaks that stretch as far as the eye can see. At one point, however, the mountains dip to a wooded saddle—this is the pass leading into Narnia. The highest peaks in the range are Stormness Head and, much farther inland, Mount Pire. The latter is a double-peaked mountain; it was once a two-headed giant, turned into stone by the legendary Fair Olvin. The story of their combat and of the petrification of the island is recorded in the songs of Archenland.

The southern boundary of Archenland is marked by the Winding Arrow River, beyond which lies the desert that separates Archenland from CALORMEN. Travellers crossing the desert from Calormen to Archenland usually use the double peak of Mount Pire as a landmark.

The seat of the kings of Archenland is at Anvard—a small but many-towered castle nestling at the foot of the northern mountains. A wooded ridge behind it protects it from the north wind. The castle is extremely old and built of a warm, reddish-brown stone. It is defended by a gate and a portcullis, but it is not moated. Green lawns stretch out in front of the entrance gate.

In the Southern Marshes visitors will find the only inhabitant of this area, a hermit who lives in a thatched cottage surrounded by a circular wall of green turf. In his garden is a magic pool in which he can see reflected the events of the world.

The first recorded king of Archenland was the second son of King Frank and Queen Helen of Narnia. Little is known of the history of Archenland before the days of King Lune, who ruled during High King Peter's reign in Narnia. By all accounts, King Lune was a jolly, fat man with twinkling eyes, who often appeared in public in his old clothes, since he had just come from attending to his animals.

In accordance with Archenlander customs, visitors will notice that brothers tend to have similar names; thus pairs of brothers are called Cor and Corrin, Dar and Darrin or Cole and Colin. The origins of this custom are unknown.

Archenland is famed for its wine, so potent that it has to be mixed with water before drinking.

(C.S. Lewis, *The Voyage of the "Dawn Treader,"* London, 1952; C.S. Lewis, *The Horse and his Boy*, London, 1954; C.S. Lewis, *The Magician's Nephew*, London, 1955)

The Castle of Anvard, ancient seat of the kings of ARCHENLAND.

ARCHOBOLETUS, see BRISSONTE.

ARD, capital of ARDISTAN. The original capital was abandoned when the River Suhl dried up, and it became known as the City of the DEAD. Ard stands in a natural basin completely enclosed by mountain ridges, in the centre of which is a meeting-point of four rivers: the Pison, the Gibo, the Tigris and the Prhat, names which are mentioned in the Bible, the Koran and the ancient Vedic texts.

Ard is said to occupy the site of the original earthly paradise and rumour has it that the foundations of the palace of Ard were laid by God. An Ardistan legend says that God commanded the gigantic races known as the Assyra and the Babyla to begin building what was to become the palace of the Mir of Ardistan and that the Christians drove the giants away, continued the work and added their crosses to the spires and dome. The Mir of Ardistan, angry at their arrogance, himself chased them away and had their crosses destroyed.

Whatever the truth behind the legend, the palace is an extraordinary edifice which dominates the whole city both by its size and by its beauty. Its central element is a large dome, flanked at the four cardinal points by towers which taper from their massive bases to slender spires so remarkably high that they seem to disappear into the sky. Between the four towers, descending sets of pinnacles and domes give the impression that the whole building rises from the earth and then descends once more. The interior is richly furnished and dimly lit; all the walls and floors are covered with rugs which deaden the sound of even the heaviest foot. There are no doors. All entrances, apart from the entrance gate, are simply hung with rugs which are easily pushed to one side. At the centre of the palace is the throne room, a large chamber lit from above through coloured glass, with a profusion of scented candles and hanging lamps. The throne room has something of the feel of a church, but the effect is muted by the abundant evidence of earthly riches and vain splendour. Visitors are warned that touching the sacred throne is an act punishable by death.

The houses and gardens of the city spread for miles along the banks of the four rivers, built in a wide range of architectural styles. One feature which is common to all is the sounding-board which hangs by the outer gate, to which a wooden hammer is attached. This serves as a doorbell; everyone recognizes the sound of his own board and comes to the door when he hears it being struck.

Ard is full of churches, mosques and temples belonging to many religions from various historical periods. Nowadays the crosses of Christian churches can again be seen among the domes and minarets, though for many years Islam was the dominant religion in Ard. Buddhism and Lamaism are also well represented.

(Karl Friedrich May, *Ardistan*, Bamberg, 1909; Karl Friedrich May, *Der Mir von Djinnistan*, Bamberg, 1909)

ARDISTAN, a large mountainous country to the south of EL HADD, bordering on TSHOBAN-ISTAN and DJUBANISTAN. Though Ardistan has an extensive coastline, there are no ports and therefore little or no trade. Most of the coastal area is uninhabited and rarely visited, although itinerant merchants from Indochina are known to have landed here occasionally. Inland, the country is fertile and quite rich, especially the area around the new capital, ARD. The former capital was deserted when the River Suhl dried up and for centuries it was known to travellers as the City of the DEAD.

Until recently Ardistan was the realm of a long line of despots or Mirs who oppressed many of the neighbouring lands; their control extended as far as distant USSULISTAN, which traditionally provided the Mir of Ardistan with his bodyguard.

All the Mirs who ruled Ardistan had the peculiarity of dreaming the same dream—a dream in which they were judged for their crimes by their dead ancestors and told that their souls would never be free until one of them agreed to sacrifice himself to expiate their sins. Shedid el Ghalabi, ruler of Ardistan, saw his dream come true in the City of the Dead, where he had been sent by the so-called Panther, a man from Tshobanistan who had seized power and installed himself as Mir only to die during a doomed attempt to invade neighbouring DJINNISTAN. After being judged for his past sins by a tribunal of dead ancestors, Shedid el Ghalabi returned from the City of the Dead as a man of peace, and worked with his neighbours and allies to defeat the evil Panther.

As a number of ancient legends foretold, the return of peace to the area was accompanied by the return of water to the River Suhl, which now flows from Djinnistan to the distant sea that bathes the coast of Ussulistan.

Most of the world's religions have followers in Ardistan, but Christianity, Islam and Lamaism are the most important. Under the early rule of the Mirs the country's Christians were a despised and barely tolerated minority, but after Shedid el Ghalabi's transformation they became both more numerous and more important, and travellers of any creed are nowadays well received in the country.

(Karl Friedrich May, *Ardistan*, Bamberg, 1909; Karl Friedrich May, *Der Mir von Djinnistan*, Bamberg, 1909)

ARGIA, an underground city in Asia. What makes Argia different from other cities is that it has earth instead of air. The streets are completely filled with dirt, clay packs the rooms to the ceiling, on every stair another stairway is set in negative, over the roofs of the houses hang layers of rocky terrain like skies with clouds. It is not known if the inhabitants can move about in the city, widening the worm tunnels and the crevices where roots twist: the dampness destroys the people's bodies and they have scant strength; everyone is better off remaining still, prone; anyway, it is dark.

From above Argia looks deserted; and yet at night, putting his ear to the ground, the traveller can sometimes hear a door slam.

(Italo Calvino, *Le città invisibili*, Turin, 1972)

ARGYANNA, a strategically important town in southern REREK, on an island in the centre of the Lows of Argyanna, an area of fens and marshes which surround the town for ten miles in all directions. Dangerous quicksand between the pools and clumps of reeds makes it difficult for man or beast to cross the marshes. The Lows are the home of numerous waterfowl and of the harriers and owls which prey on them.

The island is some five miles long and three and a half miles wide and rarely rises more than twenty feet above the level of the surrounding marsh, except to the north where the escarpment is almost twice that height. Most of its surface is intensively farmed and covered by small but rich meadows.

The tiny town of Argyanna stands on the highest point of the escarpment and is reached via a causeway of granite across the marshes, the only available access. The causeway is supported by oak piles driven deep into the bog. Argyanna itself is defended by stout walls and encircled by a moat;

two gate-houses guard the causeway. One straddles the road where it reaches the tongue of rock; the second stands astride it where it begins to cross the marsh. Argyanna has its own natural water supply in the form of a small tarn inside the walls.

In times of peace, Argyanna is a hospitable and friendly town. Its gates stand open and all travellers, be they rich or poor, are entertained free of charge and given a night's lodging. Because of its strategic position and natural defences, the town was an important stronghold during the civil war that broke out after the death of Mezentius, the overlord of Rerek, FINGISWOLD and MESZRIA.

(E.R. Eddison, *Mistress of Mistresses, A Vision of Zimiamvia*, London, 1935; E.R. Eddison, *A Fish Dinner in Memison*, London, 1941; E.R. Eddison, *The Mezentian Gate*, London, 1958)

ARIMASPIAN COUNTRY, near the Mountains of the Moon, in Africa. The Arimaspians are a one-eyed race, known to fight with the gryphons, large creatures half-eagle and half-lion. The gryphons are capable of lifting a man and a horse or two oxen at once; their claws are so strong that the Arimaspians make cups from them. They also use their rib bones to make bowls. Gryphons are also found in WONDERLAND, England.

In the grasslands, to the south, live the Mermecolions. This creature has the fore-parts of a lion, the hind-parts of an ant, and sex organs set the wrong way round. It is born from the seed of a lion that has impregnated the egg of an ant. Because of its double nature, it cannot eat flesh (being an ant) nor grains (being a lion). It therefore perishes for lack of nourishment. A similar alimentary difficulty is encountered by the bread-and-butterfly, whose wings are thin slices of bread and butter, its body a crust and its head a lump of sugar. It lives on weak tea with cream in it, which it never finds. So it always dies (see also LOOKING-GLASS LAND).

(Herodotus, *History*, 4th cen. BC; Pliny the Elder, *Naturalis Historia*, 1st cen. AD; Pliny the Elder, *Inventorum Natura*, 1st cen. AD; Anonymous, *Physiologus latinus*, 12th cen. AD; Marco Polo, *Il Milione*, Venice, 14th cen. AD; Sir John Mandeville, *Voiage de Sir John Maundevile*, Paris, 1357; Lewis Carroll [Charles Lutwidge Dodgson], *Through the Looking-Glass, and What Alice Found There*, London, 1871; Gustave Flaubert, *La Tentation de Saint Antoine*, Paris, 1874) *Illus. follows*

A gryphon in ARIMASPIAN COUNTRY makes off with a pair of oxen.

ARKHAM, an old city in Massachusetts, in the United States, crossed by the murky Miskatonic River. Arkham was founded in the first years of the seventeenth century, but has changed very little since then. In the hills around, in the dark valley of white stones nearby and on the uninhab- ited island in the Miskatonic River, terrible cere- monies are said to have taken place since the founding of the city. Many buildings in Arkham are the silent witnesses of dark deeds: the famous Witch House, for instance, inhabited by Keziah Mason who caused an unmentionable scandal dur- ing her trial in 1692.

Miskatonic University, one of the centres of New England culture, has specialized in the occult, and a number of famous scholars—Dr. Ar- mitage, Professor Wilmarth Randolph Carter— have passed through its venerable halls. The li- brary of the university is celebrated for its rare and dangerous books: the *Necronomicon* of the mad Arab Abdul Alhazred, the fragmentary *Book of Eibon,* the *Unaussprechlichen Kulten* by von Junzt, the *Pnakotician Manuscripts,* the *Sussex Fragments* and the *Cultes des Goules* by the Count of Erlette.

The history of Arkham is full of dreadful episodes. Travellers visiting the city do so at their own risk but they are warned that the conse- quences of such a visit may haunt them for the rest of their lives.

(Howard Phillips Lovecraft, *The Outsider and Oth- ers,* Sauk City, 1939; Howard Phillips Lovecraft, *Beyond the Wall of Sleep,* Sauk City, 1943)

ARNHEIM, a region in the United States, created by the American millionaire Ellison, an enthusiast of landscape gardening. The usual approach to Arnheim is by river. The visitor who leaves for Arnheim in the early morning will pass, before midday, a shore of tranquil and domestic beauty. As evening approaches, the river will grow narrower, the banks more precipitous and sombre and the water more transparent. After a thousand turns, the river becomes a gorge, with walls rising to al- most a hundred and fifty feet, so inclined to each other that they shut out the light of day. The water is still as clear as crystal and unblemished by dead leaves or stray pebbles. Suddenly the visitor will be brought into a circular basin, some two hundred yards in diameter, surrounded by hills as high as the walls of the chasm, although of a thoroughly different character. Their sides slope from the water's edge at a forty-five-degree angle and are clothed from base to summit in a drapery of gor- geous flower blossoms. The bottom of the basin is a thick mass of small, round, alabaster stones and the transparent water reflects every detail of the flowered hills.

Here the visitor must leave whatever vessel has borne him so far and step into a light canoe of ivory, which he will find waiting for him, the sides of which are stained with arabesque designs in vivid scarlet, both within and without. On its ermined floor reposes a single feathery paddle of satinwood. But no oarsman or attendant is to be seen and the traveller must steer the canoe himself.

The canoe will advance with a gentle but gradually accelerating speed accompanied by a soothing yet melancholy music of unseen origin. A rocky portico is approached and beyond, above the softer banks, an emerald plateau stretches onwards until it becomes lost in the distance. Floating gently onwards, with slightly increased speed, the traveller will find his progress apparently barred by a gigantic door of burnished gold, elaborately carved and fretted. The door will open and the canoe will glide into a vast amphitheatre, completely enclosed by purple mountains. Here is an oppressive sweet scent and a dreamlike intermingling of colours: tall, slender eastern trees, bosky shrubberies, flocks of golden and crimson birds, lily-fringed lakes, meadows of violets, tulips, poppies, hyacinths and tube-roses, amid a mass of semi-Gothic, semi-Saracen architecture, sustaining itself by a miracle in mid-air, glittering in the red sunlight with a hundred oriels, minarets and pinnacles: this, at last, is the domain of Arnheim.

(Edgar Allan Poe, *The Domain of Arnheim*, Philadelphia, 1847)

ARNOR, the northern kingdom of the Dúnedain, founded in the north of MIDDLE-EARTH. At its height the kingdom included most of the lands between the River Lhûn and the MISTY MOUNTAINS excluding RIVENDELL and HOLLIN. The capital, Annúminas (Tower of the West), stood on the shores of Lake Nenuial, to the north of the area now known as the SHIRE.

The kingdom was founded in 3320 Second Age by Elendil the Tall, who was High King of both Arnor and the southern kingdom of GONDOR. Unlike its southern counterpart, Arnor does not appear to have prospered, and its prestige declined steadily over the next centuries. By 861 Third Age, the capital was transferred to the city of FORNOST. A significant blow was struck against Arnor at the beginning of the Third Age when King Isildur (son of Elendil) and his army were ambushed by a huge army of orcs, or goblins,

from the Misty Mountains. They were all massacred in what became known as the Battle of GLADDEN FIELDS. It was then that the One Ring which was to affect so much of Middle-earth's history was lost.

When the tenth king of Arnor died, in 861 Third Age, the kingdom was divided between his three sons who ruled the areas known as Arthedain, Cardolan and Rhudaur.

Increasingly, all three kingdoms came under attack from the forces of the powerful and evil Witch-king, who was to appear in the later history of Middle-earth as the Lord of the Nazgûl of MORDOR. Some of the Dúnedain survived in Fornost and in areas like the BARROW DOWNS and the OLD FOREST. In 1636 Third Age, a great plague swept through much of Middle-earth and ravaged the remaining population of the northern kingdoms. The groups living on the Barrow Downs were wiped out and the area became inhabited by evil spirits. In 1974 Fornost itself fell to the Witch-king, and its past ruler, King Arvedui, fled north to FOROCHEL where he took refuge with the Snowmen. He died in the wreck of the ship sent to take him to the GREY HAVENS.

Arnor was now almost totally in the control of the Witch-king. A year later he was defeated in the Battle of Fornost, but the kingdom of Arnor did not recover its former position. The few Dúnedain left in the north became known as the Rangers. They had no fixed homes or settlements, but travelled throughout the north, protecting it as best they could from the forces of evil. It is largely due to their work that the Shire knew peace for so long.

The first king of the Reunited Kingdom established after the War of the Ring had been patrolling as a Ranger for many years, using the name Strider. Not until he ascended the throne at the war's end, as Aragorn II (Elessar Telcontar), was it known that he was in fact the heir of Isildur, High King of Arnor and Gondor.

(J.R.R. Tolkien, *The Hobbit, or There and Back Again*, London, 1937; J.R.R. Tolkien, *The Fellowship of the Ring*, London, 1954; J.R.R. Tolkien, *The Two Towers*, London, 1954; J.R.R. Tolkien, *The Return of the King*, London, 1955; J.R.R. Tolkien, *The Silmarillion*, London, 1977)

ARROY, a forested area some eight days' ride from CAMELOT, consisting mainly of oak and beech, and laced with whitethorn. Tangled briars seem to guard it from outsiders. At the centre of the forest is a valley where travellers can see the ruins of an ancient building of unknown origin and purpose on the edge of a stream.

Arroy is the domain of three damsels, aged fifteen, thirty and sixty, whose task it is to lead knights in search of adventures; they travel with the knights for a year and then return to the stream in the forest. It was one of these damsels who led Sir Marhalt to Castle FERGUS where he slew the giant Taulurd.

Sir Ewain, son of King Arthur's sister Morgan le Fay, met the Lady Lyne in this forest. She led him to the Castle of the Rock on the Welsh border, where he defeated the two brothers who had taken it from its rightful owner.

Nearby also, the famed Sir Pelleas first met Nyneve, a young woman responsible for sealing the enchanter Merlin in the cave known as MERLIN'S TOMB. Sir Pelleas had been rejected by the woman he loved, Ettarde. Nyneve cast a spell on Ettarde, making her fall in love with him, and at the same time caused Pelleas to abandon her. Nyneve and Sir Pelleas have lived together ever since.

(Sir Thomas Malory, *Le Morte Darthur*, London, 1485; John Steinbeck, *The Acts of King Arthur and His Noble Knights From the Winchester Manuscripts of Sir Thomas Malory and Other Sources*, New York, 1976)

ARTHUR, PALACE OF, situated high above a city surrounded by a distant chain of mountains. From the top of the palace the visitor can enjoy a panoramic view of the frozen sea that encircles the footings of the city, reflecting its smooth, transparent walls. In the square in front of the palace lies a magnificent garden of ivory flowers and fruit, whose lights and colours are quite wondrous to behold. In the middle of the garden rises a fountain made of ice which will only melt when the sea becomes unfrozen once again.

Outside the windows of the palace are clay receptacles overflowing with flowers of snow and ice. The lighting inside is so intense that a prismatic light escapes the high multicoloured windows and washes the narrow streets, columns and walls. The throne room, which was carved from a block of sulphur crystal, is decorated by a priceless rug, and a talking bird with exotic plumage can often be found at the back of the room. Wide staircases lead from the throne room to the dome, where the king likes

to spend his time. The royal family particularly enjoys a game in which cards covered with mysterious symbols are meticulously sorted, chosen and displayed, and the players then attempt to construct harmonious figures out of the symbols. As the stars shine down through the dome, their light transforms the cards' symbols into living tableaux.

(Novalis, *Heinrich von Ofterdingen*, Leipzig, 1802)

ASBEFORE ISLAND, once part of the Baladar Archipelago and now attached to Europe; it retains, however, its designation as an island. The name of Asbefore has been changed several times: it has been called Trifle Island, Treasure Island, and Leastimportant Island. The archipelago to which it used to belong seems to have disappeared; the Farapart, Jumptoit and Incognito islands can no longer be found, in spite of intense research.

Asbefore is famous for its lack of gardeners, perfume vendors, florists, cooks, judges, bakers and poets. The Town Hall is supervised by a cleaner, Mr. Busybody, who saved the island from an invasion of turkey-hunters sent to Asbefore by the city Bang-Bang-Turkey, in France.

Visitors can still see the ruins of a golden bridge, built after the Asbefore gold rush of the 1950's. For further information, two periodicals can be consulted: *The Gossipmonger* and *The Bang-Bang-Parrot*.

(Jacques Prévert, *Lettre des îles Baladar*, Paris, 1952)

ASHAIR, also known as the **FORBIDDEN CITY**, deep inside the Tuen-Baka volcano in Africa. It is entered through an underground river that leads to the volcano and a beautiful vaulted lake. Ashair is small, walled, and ruled by a ferocious queen who leads an army of saurian men called *ptomes*. These creatures are almost amphibian though they must wear diving helmets when walking on the lake's bed. Only the lion arena and the Royal Palace are worth visiting.

From the Palace itself, however, a splendid underwater realm can be reached. Through the door of the so-called Torture Chamber a number of bolted doors lead to a cylindrical room. Once inside, the doors are closed and new doors open onto other chambers like the first. At last travellers will enter Horus, a city under the lake. Prisoners are sometimes taken here and put in a small circular room without any breathing gear. Then the water is let in and the unfortunate captives drown.

Lions and small *tyrannosaurus rex* haunt the region surrounding Ashair; sea-serpents and dangerous fish swim in the waters of Horus.

Should visitors be tempted to carry off the so-called Father of Diamonds which is guarded in Ashair, they will be well advised to spare themselves the trouble: it is simply a lump of coal kept in a locked box as a sort of bland intellectual joke.

(Edgar Rice Burroughs, *Tarzan and the Forbidden City,* New York, 1938)

ASH GROVE, CASTLE, an ancient Elfin realm in a valley beneath Mynnydd Prescelly, the most westerly mountain in Wales. The kingdom's name refers back to its early history, when its inhabitants did not build houses and simply flew up into the boughs of the ash trees to sleep at night. That custom no longer prevails and, in common with other Elfin kingdoms, Castle Ash Grove has adopted the etiquette whereby only working fairies fly; normally the aristocracy do not take to the wing, as it would mar their dignity. The Elfins of Castle Ash Grove are famed for the matchless mead they brew and for their great traditions of singing. They are good neighbours and are usually tolerant of cows and human children who stray into their realm, contenting themselves with watching them from their trees.

The greatest achievement of the inhabitants of this small thatched castle has been to make the mountain above their valley appear and disappear; sometimes it is there, and sometimes it is not. They first performed this feat long ago, when they still slept in the trees. In those days an old man came to their realm who had travelled from Ireland to St. Bride's Bay on a slab of granite which he had made seaworthy "by faith," as he put it. He explained the nature of faith to the Elfins, claiming that it could move mountains, but said that regrettably it was not for them as they had no souls and were therefore unable to move a pebble, much less a mountain. This injured their pride, and when the old man left to convert the heathen of Carmarthenshire they immediately began to try to disprove his statements, but not a pebble would move. Finally the nephew of the court poet came to the conclusion that if they were to move the mountain, they must do so by the power of singing. A special *Removal Song* was composed to the words "Mynnydd Prescelly, Be thou removed." At first they sang in unison, but spontaneous descants were later added

to the basic melody and glorious choral singing resulted. Much to their surprise, the mountain did remove itself. Careful investigation revealed what happened: Mynnydd Prescelly rose up in the shape of a cloud and travelled to Plynlimon, where it fell as heavy rain for a few days; it then travelled back to its original site, fell once more as rain and solidified into a mountain. The singing and removal of the mountain has become a regular ceremony and humans in the area who notice it disappearing from the skyline take its return as a sign that harvesting should begin.

The Queens of Castle Ash Grove have always been called Morgan and their line includes the notorious Morgan le Fay. Perhaps the most famous singer ever produced by the kingdom was Morgan Breastknot of Music. Her successor was Morgan Spider, so called because of her skill in spinning, under whose reign the Elfins adopted the custom of disguising themselves as mortals and going to Worcester to listen to organ recitals in the cathedral and, later, attending the Three Choirs' Festival in that city.

(Sylvia Townsend Warner, *Kingdoms of Elfin,* London, 1972)

ASH MOUNTAINS, see ERED LITHUI.

ASLAN'S COUNTRY, high up and beyond the End of the World (see WORLD'S END ISLAND). Little is known of this country, but as seen from the World's End, it seems to consist of mountains of extraordinary height, always free of snow, clad in grass and forests which stretch far into the distance. The highest peak, rising near the frontier, is the Mountain of Aslan. From its summit the clouds above the world appear to be small sheep; the ground below cannot be clearly seen.

The water of Aslan's Country has the remarkable property of quenching all thirsts immediately. As to the fauna, it boasts many beautiful multicoloured birds, whose song resembles rather advanced music.

Aslan, creator of NARNIA, usually appears to visitors in the guise of a lion, but has also been known to take the shape of a lamb. Neither appearance should be mistaken for a specimen of the local fauna.

(C.S. Lewis, *The Voyage of the "Dawn Treader,"* London, 1952; C.S. Lewis, *The Silver Chair,* London, 1953)

ASTOWELL, the easternmost island of the EARTHSEA ARCHIPELAGO, sometimes referred to by the inhabitants as **LAST-LAND**. There is only one port on this small island—a creek between high rocks, on the northern shore. Visitors will find that both the port and the town to which the port is attached are made up of crude wattle huts, all of which face the north-west, as though turning towards mankind and the rest of the great archipelago.

There is no wood on Astowell and the only boats are frail coracles woven of reeds. There appear to be no metals either, and the islanders' only weapons are shell knives and crude stone axes. Few ships ever touch on Astowell, as the islanders have no trade to offer and the surrounding sea is rough and dangerous. So primitive is Astowell that it has neither a sorcerer nor a wizard and its people have no knowledge of magic, which is odd, since magic, as most travellers know, is so common in the rest of Earthsea.

(Ursula K. Le Guin, A *Wizard of Earthsea,* New York, 1968)

ASTRAGALUS REALM, high in the Alps, inhabited by Astragalus, king of the snowy regions. Astragalus is attended by the Alpine spirits and is always ready to help travellers in distress. Visitors will find that not only does Astragalus set them on the right path, but he also provides spiritual advice and guides lost souls in their search for the true meaning of things.

(Ferdinand Raimund, *Der Alpenkönig und der Menschenfeind,* Vienna, 1928)

ASTRALIA, see SPECTRALIA.

ATHNE, see CATHNE.

ATHUNT, see FLORA.

ATLANTEJA, an underwater city built by settlers from ATLANTIS discovered by the shipwrecked survivors of the ATLANTIC TUNNEL some one hundred and fifty miles from the coast of Brittany. All that is left of Atlanteja today are the ruins—broken or superbly erect columns, destroyed temples which resemble the wreck of a forest blown by a tempest, houses now inhabited by seaweed and fish, palaces where the debris fills the space once occupied by exquisite furniture. Wide streets, now overgrown by underwater plants, cross the city from east to west and from south to north, trailing on into the underwater horizon. But what enhances, above all, the sublime beauty of these ruins is the phosphorescent bluish light that seems to rain upon the city like a shower of stardust and which gives these ancient places an illusion of life. The light comes from large numbers of medusae and jellyfish that haunt these dark waters. Inside the ruins, thousands of micro-organisms also give out a faint light which, combined with that of the medusae and jellyfish, makes the walls of Atlanteja glitter with a strange and eerie movement.

(Luigi Motta, *Il tunnel sottomarino,* Milan, 1927)

ATLANTE'S CASTLE, in the Pyrenees, between France and Spain, set upon a steep rock pitted

The Castle of ATLANTE.

with caverns and terrible chasms, in a wild and un-cultivated valley. Travellers say that from afar it seems to burn like a raging flame, surrounded by iron walls said to have been wrought by demons in Hell. Here lives Atlante, the wizard. On his hip-pogriff (a species of winged horse, offspring of a gryphon and a mare), he travels through the world kidnapping beautiful young girls of whom he takes great advantage in his castle. Visitors should be-ware Atlante's magic shield, as the wizard is known to use its reflective properties to dazzle his victims into submission.

(Ludovico Ariosto, *Orlando furioso*, Ferrara, 1516)

ATLANTIC TUNNEL, an underwater railway tunnel some 4,700 kilometres long that used to join Europe and America and was designed by the French engineer Adrien Géant. The building of the tunnel started in 1924, at one end of the island of Manhattan. The construction proceeded by placing under water enormous segments of tubes, lined with cement to protect them from the un-avoidable chemical reactions of the metal with the water. Each segment was united to the next by iron bolts covered with rubber so that any leakage of water into the tubes would be avoided. Above

this colossal tube, other workers, as the project pro-gressed, spread a strong iron net to protect it from possible shipwrecked vessels that might fall to the bottom and damage the construction. The tubes were lowered down to their position by steel ropes. Being full of water, they descended slowly to the bottom of the ocean so that the workers could eas-ily put them into place. The tubes were closed at one end only; the open end was placed next to the previous segment and pumps used to get the water out. Once a section was completed, the workers inside demolished the iron wall that closed the end of the previous segment and the tunnel thus pro-ceeded. It is said that all great enterprises are born from small things. The Atlantic Tunnel project suggested itself to Géant as he observed some chil-dren playing in the street with a bamboo cane that consisted of a number of empty chambers sepa-rated from one another by wooden discs.

When the depth of the ocean became exces-sive and the sections could no longer be lowered safely to the bottom, enormous boxes, hermeti-cally sealed, were dropped into the sea and dis-posed in two parallel lines. Between one and the other, large iron cables were laid and the tube seg-ments placed on top. Thus the tunnel became in part a sort of underwater bridge below the At-

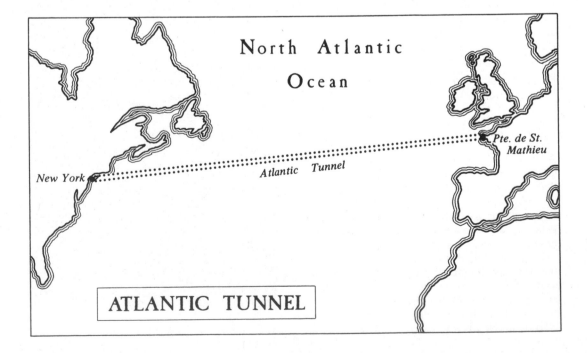

lantic, a massive highway signposted by many gigantic buoys. The European outlet of the Atlantic Tunnel was Pointe de Saint-Mathieu in Brittany, not far from the French city of Brest.

On the day of the inauguration, May 12, 1927, during the passage of the first underwater train, an explosion shook the tunnel and destroyed most of Géant's work. The train remained trapped under water, but the passengers managed to save themselves by putting on divers' helmets and walking back to Europe. On the way home, they had the good fortune of discovering ATLANTEJA, one of the lost cities founded by the people of ATLANTIS. The author of the explosion, a certain MacRoller, is said to have perpetrated this terrorist attempt out of spite, being a rival of Géant both in business and in love, and was fortunately brought to justice. The remains of the tunnel were slowly eroded by the sea and only minor ruins can now be visited. The project was never renewed.

(Luigi Motta, *Il tunnel sottomarino*, Milan, 1927)

ATLANTIS, a vast island-continent submerged under the waters of the Atlantic towards the year 9560 BC; parts of it are still inhabited and can be visited.

The ancient Atlantis had a somewhat elliptical shape, extending 533 kilometres from north to south and 355 from east to west. It consisted of an elevated plateau surrounded by steep mountains that loomed over the sea. On the mountain slopes and in the mountain valleys were a large number of prosperous villages; many streams and rivers rich in fish made the plateau fertile. A precious mineral, *oricalcum,* which the inhabitants regarded as highly as gold, was mined in underground quarries. Industry and art prospered, and the ships of Atlantis called on the ports of Europe, Africa and America. Atlantis' army and navy counted over a million men and granted the country both internal security and dominion in foreign lands. Atlantis had colonies throughout the world and even menaced both Egypt and Greece; it is said that the Athenians repelled an Atlantean invasion and that they were one of the few people to do so successfully.

The capital, also known as Atlantis, was in the very centre of the plateau, surrounded by concentric rings of earthworks separated from one another by deep canals. The central nucleus or the first ring was protected by an *oricalcum* wall 900 metres in circumference, and contained the fortress, the Royal Palace and the Temple of Poseidon, the latter nestled in a small sacred wood; the walls of both the temple and the palace were of silver decorated with gold. The *oricalcum* wall was separated from the second ring by the first canal which was also used as an internal port; the second ring was defended by a stone wall covered in tin. A second canal was followed by the third or main ring, so wide that it held several small forests and numerous buildings: among these were the gymnasium, the barracks, and the horse-racing course—the favourite sport of the Atlanteans. The third ring was protected by a wall of bronze and separated from the fourth by a third canal which lodged the Great Port of Atlantis; the fourth ring contained the warehouses and merchants' quarters. All canals and ports were connected by underwater tunnels, and huge secret grottoes had been built into the rings to hide the large Atlantean triremes.

After the cataclysm that brought destruction to Atlantis, two major sections of the island were miraculously preserved, one some two hundred miles south-west of the Canaries, under the sea; the other, uplifted by the same seismic movement that sunk the rest of Atlantis, in the Sahara desert. The Atlantean descendants in both places have evolved different characteristics but visitors to both will perhaps be able to have some idea of what life in ancient Atlantis was like by recognizing a few common traits.

The Atlantean remains under the sea were discovered in 1926 by Professor Maracot while exploring the ocean depths in a diving bell. He found that the population lives in an immense building presumably constructed before the cataclysm as a sort of ark or refuge. Over the centuries so much silt has accumulated that it can now only be entered by the roof. The original building has been expanded by excavation to provide laboratories, powerhouses and other quarters. Around the building lie the streets of Atlantis and the ruins of a temple that originally stood on the third or second ring. Dedicated to the Lord of the Dark Face it is built entirely in black marble. Above the door is sculpted a Medusa head with radiating serpents; the same design is repeated at intervals on the walls together with scenes of sadistic beauty and bestial lust. On a throne of red marble sits a figure which it is difficult to gaze upon without a profound feeling of disgust: it is said to represent a deity whose name is unmentionable.

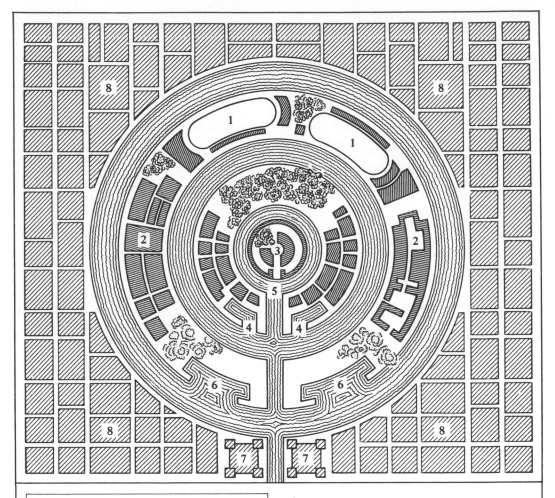

ATLANTIS The Capital

1. Racetracks
2. Gymnasium & Barracks
3. Fortress, Royal Palace & Temple of Poseidon
4. Second harbours

5. Internal port
6. First harbours & Great Port of Atlantis
7. Guards' towers
8. Warehouses and merchants' quarters

The inhabitants of this portion of Atlantis are dark-skinned. They are served by a race of white slaves, probably descendants of Greek captives, who mainly work in the coal-mines. These slaves have preserved the cult of Athena, but the main religion in underwater Atlantis is the worship of Moloch or Baal. Baal's Temple is a square room with golden doors; the walls are decorated with grotesque figures wearing large headdresses. The priest sits Buddha-like on a small seat, surrounded by electric lights; behind him is a small oven into which human victims are thrown, mainly the children of mixed marriages—Atlanteans and slaves—as these liaisons are strictly forbidden.

Their technology is highly advanced. Atlantean scientists have discovered a means of chemically producing wine, coffee, tea and flour with all the same characteristics as the natural substances. They have also managed to preserve their history and traditions by projecting mental images onto a screen, which can then be followed as a film. In this fashion travellers can witness the destruction of Atlantis recorded by the earliest survivors.

The Atlantean underwater language is extremely difficult to learn. In fact it includes peculiar rasping and clicking sounds which are almost impossible for a European to imitate and which cannot be represented by any European alphabet. It is written from right to left on dried fish-bladder; many books are printed on this same substance. The slaves speak a form of archaic Greek.

The fauna of this section of Atlantis is extremely dangerous. Black and white tiger-crabs, as large as Newfoundland dogs, crawl along the ocean bed, and poisonous red eels lurk in the slimy hollows between the rocks. Sting-rays thirty feet long and giant sea scorpions are common, as well as sea serpents, though one species—black and silver and over two hundred feet long—is fairly scarce. Giant flatfish, covering an area of up to half an acre, the *marax* or giant crayfish (*Crustaceus maracoti*), up to thirty inches long, and the *Hydrops ferux*, a small fish similar to a piranha, are all best avoided. However, the strangest beast in this area is the *praxa*, a creature partly organic and partly gaseous, like a greenish cloud with a luminous centre; it preys on human beings to tear out their eyes and eat them.

The other remains of Atlantis were discovered several years earlier, in 1897, by a French expedition led by Morhange and Saint-Avit. After finding some strange inscriptions in a cavern at the foot of the Geni Mountain in the Ahaggar massif these two officers were drugged with hashish by their guides and led deep into the cliffs, where they were astonished to find one of the most beautiful oases in the Sahara desert. A member of their expedition, Dr. Le Mesge, recognized it as part of a long lost Atlantean continent, thereby confirming a theory he had developed after reading the *Travels to Atlantis* by Dionysius of Miletus; Dr. Le Mesge had found the manuscript, mentioned by Diodorus Siculus, in Dax, in the French Landes.

This oasis kingdom is ruled by Queen Antinea whose customs do little to promote tourism. Male visitors are first betrothed to the queen, then put to death and carefully mummified. The mum-

mifying process is different from that of the ancient Egyptians. First the skin is painted with silver salts; then the body is placed in a bath of *oricalcum* sulphate. An electrical exchange takes place and the body is transformed into a statue of solid metal, more precious than silver and rarer than gold. These splendid creations are used to decorate the royal chambers and are placed in special niches of which, at the latest count, there were 120—though only fifty-four have been filled.

(Plato, *Critias*, 4th cen. BC; Plato, *Timaeus*, 4th cen. BC; Pierre Benoit, *L'Atlantide*, Paris, 1919; Sir Arthur Conan Doyle, *The Maracot Deep*, London, 1929)

ATNINI, see KARGAD EMPIRE.

ATROCLA, see ISLES OF WISDOM.

ATUAN, see KARGAD EMPIRE.

ATVATABAR, a vast subterranean country lying exactly under the American continent and stretching from Canada to approximately Ecuador. It was discovered in May 1891 by Commander Lexington White and Captain William Wallace, on board the *Polar King*. The visitor to Atvatabar can reach the country through an enormous cavern to which the North Pole is the entrance. Heat and light are provided by an interior sun which never sets, producing a climate similar to that of the tropics.

The Atvatabarese are handsome and of a golden-yellow tint. They are very inventive: among their creations are rain-making machines, marine railroads and bicycles without wheels.

The government of Atvatabar is an elective monarchy—the king and the noblemen are elected for life. The legislative body, or Borodemy, and the Royal Palace are in the capital city, CALNOGOR. The army and air force are combined: the soldiers fly with the aid of magnetic wings, worked by a little dynamo. When on land, they ride a kind of immense ostrich made of steel, called a *bockhockid*. Steam engines and gunpowder are unknown. Gold is as common as iron.

The Atvatabarese language is extremely complicated. The alphabet is a transposition of the English alphabet: *a* is *o*, *b* is *p*, etc. "Hello," for example, is *Vszzc*. In the words of Master-at-Arms Flathootly, the language of Atvatabar "bates Irish, which is the toughest langwidge to larn undher the sun."

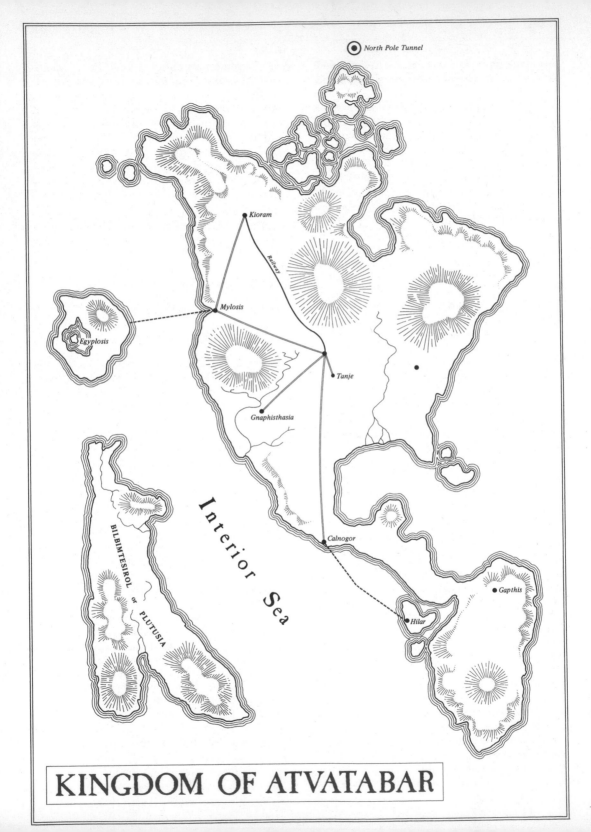

North Pole Tunnel

Kioram

Railway

Mylosis

Egyplosis

Tanje

Gnaphisthasia

Interior Sea

BILBIMTESIROL or PLUTUSIA

Calnogor

Hilar

Gapthis

KINGDOM OF ATVATABAR

The flag of Atvatabar is a pink disc surrounded by a bright green circle on a violet field.

(William R. Bradshaw, *The Goddess of Atvatabar, being the History of the Discovery of the Interior World and Conquest of Atvatabar*, New York, 1892)

AUDELA, the land of all that lies beyond the veil of human sight and sense. The veil can never be lifted, but it is often torn. Men call the gaps in the veil fire.

Audela was formerly ruled by Queen Freydis, who took on mortal form for love of Manuel of POICTESME. She now lives on the island of Sargyll.

(James Branch Cabell, *Figures of Earth. A Comedy of Appearances*, New York, 1921)

AUENTHAL, a village on a river close to the town of Scheerau in Germany. The village is famous for having been the home of one Maria Wuz, organist and schoolmaster, who used to write books using other authors' titles. This custom, and a healthy disregard for anachronism, led him to believe that all books were plagiarisms of his own. The only other book in his possession was the catalogue of the Leipzig Book Fair, which he considered to be a great source of inspiration. It is not known whether the works of Herr Wuz have been published.

(Jean Paul [Johann Paul Friedrich Richter], *Leben des vergnügten Schulmeisterlein Maria Wuz in Auenthal*, Berlin, 1793)

AUËRSPERG CASTLE, in Schwartzwald, northeastern Germany, property of the Auërsperg family.

It was here that Axël d'Auërsperg learnt the arts of black magic in the mid-nineteenth century. The castle is medieval but has probably been restored several times. It has a few notable towers and a stupendous hall in which some of the material used in black magic rites has been carefully preserved: carcasses of long-extinct animals, alchemist's equipment, and books kept on long shelves of black wood. On the walls, together with Saracen arms and shields, vultures and eagles are nailed with their wings outspread. The doors are covered with tapestries, the floor with the skins of bears and foxes. The narrow windows, through which the dark forests of Schwartzwald can be seen, are Gothic. All the furniture carries the coat of arms of the Auërsperg family, held by two

The fireplace in the Large Hall of AUËRSPERG CASTLE, Schwartzwald.

golden sphinxes, with the motto: *AltiUs rEsurgeRe SPERo Gemmatus.*

A vast maze of passages runs beneath the castle, lined with the statues of ancient heroes. In these vaults the members of the family have been buried since time immemorial.

(Philippe-Auguste, Comte de Villiers de L'Isle-Adam, *Axël*, Paris, 1872)

AUSPASIA, a kingdom whose main claim to fame is the talkativeness of its inhabitants. It is said that its capital is the noisiest in the world, even more so than New York. The extremely chatty nature of the people—especially the southerners—may explain why the parliament of the country has become a mere talking-shop. Auspasia is constantly divided into quarrelling factions whipped up by famous orators, and power effectively rests in the hands of a few masters of rhetoric. Great public meetings in huge halls attract immense crowds; speeches are unprepared (as speech is much more important than thought, the art of improvisation becomes all-important). It is quite possible for orators to lead great political careers and amass huge fortunes by rushing from one meeting to the next.

This passion for oratory and the political divisions it produces lie no doubt at the root of the recent civil war that swept through the country. Few details of the conflagration were made public, but it is known that the defeated opposition was exiled to the convict island of Morania; the few prisoners who attempted to escape are reported to have been eaten by sharks.

The national love for the spoken word is also at the origin of the Auspasian enthusiasm for the theatre. So great is the interest in drama that actors, managers and even stage hands are more than ready to offer advice and comments to aspiring authors. It is very uncommon for a play to reach the stage in the form conceived by the author—it is usually completely changed by the people working on the production. (This procedure is known in American publishing houses as "editing.") Auspasia's most important dramatist is the well-known Justin Babilot, renowned for his tragedies.

The National Institute is the main cultural organization of the country. Its distinguished members include Cussac (famed for his research on the snail and for his part in breaking the State monopoly on snail-breeding) and Scrube (who is known for the poisons he invented). Scrube is regarded as a philanthropist, largely because his poisons were used only against the enemies of law and liberty during the last great war. The Royal Company of Moral and Natural Sciences is equally famous and has as its Permanent Secretary the legendary Mascarol, responsible for the introduction of a sense of discipline into Auspasian philosophy and ethics—formerly the traditional quality of the country's enemies.

But perhaps the most noteworthy scientist produced by Auspasia is, paradoxically, almost unknown, even within his own land. Léonard is a quiet, retiring man, much of whose work has been claimed and published by other scientists. After ten years of solitary research, financed by himself, he was able to write his *Rapid Functional Mutations of Differentiated Organic Elements*, a brief but fundamental treatise describing how a living organism can acquire new functions. Despite his attempts to involve more famous colleagues, no one has yet taken any interest in this new and important research, and Auspasia's most brilliant scientist still remains to be discovered.

(Georges Duhamel, *Lettres d'Auspasie*, Paris, 1922; Georges Duhamel, *Le dernier voyage de Candide*, Paris, 1938)

AUSTRALIA, a large island southeast of Java, not to be confused with the continent of the same name. The coastal area is mostly dry and uninhabited.

Australia is divided into two main countries: to the east, SPOROUMBIA, to the west, SEVARAMBIA. Along the coast are a number of rocky islands.

(Denis Veiras, *Histoire des Sevarambes, peuples qui habitent une partie du troisième continent, communement appelé la terre Australe. Contenant une relation du gouvernement des moeurs de la religion, et du langage de cette nation, inconnue jusques à présent aux peuples de l'Europe*, Amsterdam, 1677–79)

AUTONOUS' ISLAND, probably in the Atlantic Ocean. It is fertile and beautiful; the climate warm and equable, storms rare. The fauna includes goats, deer and marine fowl. A lake in the south of the island holds a colony of beavers. Because there are no predators, the beavers build their lodges on dry land rather than in the water. The island is named after Autonous, son of Eugenius, Duke of Orthotinia. Together with his parents he was exiled from the Kingdom of Epinoia—famous for the University of Eumathema—and was shipwrecked on this island where the duchess died.

Five leagues away is another smaller island, where the duke was marooned after being separated from Autonous in an accident. Autonous lived alone on his island for nineteen years, educating himself through the observation of nature. The duke and his son were eventually rescued by a ship from Epinoia.

(Anonymous, *The History of Autonous, containing A Relation how that Young Nobleman was accidentally left alone, in his Infancy, upon a desolate Island; where he lived nineteen years, remote from all Humane Society, 'till taken up by his Father. With an Account Of his Life, Reflections, and Improvements in Knowledge, during his Continuance in that Solitary State. The Whole, as taken from his own Mouth*, London, 1736)

AVALLONË, see TOL ERESSËA.

AVALON, a beautiful lake and rock island, surrounded by deep meadows with orchard lawns and wooded hollows, where no wind blows and where hail, rain and snow have never been known to fall.

On the island is a small church built by Joseph of Arimathea; the rest of Avalon is inhabited by a race of women who know all the magic in the whole world.

A great wonder happened in this place. When King Arthur of CAMELOT was led here by the enchanter Merlin a hand reached out of the water and offered him the sword Excalibur which was to serve him so well during his life. It is said that the hand in the water belonged to the Lady of the Lake.

Arthur, having received the sword in Avalon, was required to return it here at the end of his life. He asked Sir Bedivere to throw it back into the lake; the hand appeared again, caught the sword and brandished it before disappearing.

So it was to Avalon that King Arthur returned to die, and from here he was borne by four queens—Morgan le Fay, the Lady of the Lake, the Queen of Northgales and the Queen of the Wastelands—on his last voyage.

(Anonymous, *La Mort le Roi Artu*, 13th cen. AD; Sir Thomas Malory, *Le Morte Darthur*, London, 1485; Alfred, Lord Tennyson, *The Idylls of the King*, London, 1842–85)

AVATHAR, see AMAN.

AVONDALE, the site of the United Avondale Phalanstery, one of a number of phalansteries established in southern England during the latter part of the nineteenth century. The phalanstery is situated in pleasant countryside and its gardens are particularly delightful. A dancing streamlet runs through a mossy dell, providing an agreeable walk for the brothers and sisters of the community.

The phalanstery is a hierarchical community, governed by the Hierarch and the Elder Brothers, and dedicated to the higher development of humanity. All members see themselves as the stewards of mankind's future. Their religious formula sums up the fundamental beliefs of the community: "The Cosmos is infinite and man is but a parasite on the face of the least among its satellite members. May we act so as to fulfil our own small place in the system of the Cosmos with all becoming reverence and humility! In the name of universal Humanity, so be it." Their beliefs also include a Darwinian view of evolution.

All members of the phalanstery work, but the working day has been reduced to five hours. Each member has a twenty-four-hour respite every ten days—a ten-day period being referred to as a "decade."

The community is mainly agricultural, surrounded by extensive vegetable gardens. There is a sexual division of labour—the majority of unmarried women work as nurses in the communal infirmary.

Visitors will find that within the phalanstery, individual feelings are always subject to the greater good of the community. For instance, permission to marry must be asked of the whole community, and it is granted unless there are reasonable objections to the proposed match. Only when permission to marry has been obtained may the couple kiss.

As the phalanstery is dedicated to the improvement of humanity as a whole, all crippled or deformed children born here are killed, painlessly. This is not considered murder, but as granting the child a release from a life for which it is unfitted. Avondalians explain that such a child would be unhappy within a society of healthy people and would be forced into a state of resented dependence. It is accepted that this may be difficult for the parents, but higher, abstract pity usually overcomes the lower, more concrete emotion. When a crippled child is born, the news is kept from the mother for four decades and a further four are then allowed for physiologists and other doctors to decide whether a cure is possible. If there is no hope, the child is killed with anaesthetics.

There is one recorded case of a mother failing to overcome her "lower" feeling of pity. The child of a certain Olive was born with deformed feet. Olive begged to be allowed to release her child from the world herself, and when she was given permission to do so, she killed both herself and the child.

(Grant Allen, "The Child of the Phalanstery," in *Twelve Tales*, London, 1899)

AVRA, see LONE ISLANDS.

AWABATH, see KARGAD EMPIRE.

AWDYOO, see LOONARIE.

AXEL ISLE, a small rocky island somewhere in the underground LIDENBROCK SEA, named after Professor Lidenbrock's nephew, a member of the famous expedition that travelled to the centre of the earth through SAKNUSSEMM'S CORRIDOR in 1863. The island lies some 620 leagues east-south-east of Iceland and therefore exactly below England. Its shape is that of an immense cetacean.

In the middle of the island rises an enormous geyser where the water is always 163° centigrade. Due to the variations in the pressure of the vapours accumulated in its reservoir, the geyser's spurt is highly irregular.

(Jules Verne, *Voyage au centre de la terre*, Paris, 1864)

AZANIAN EMPIRE, a large island in the Indian Ocean, off the east coast of Africa, separated from the Somali Republic by the Sakuyu Channel. The capital is Debra-Dowa. The Arabs dominated the island, then called Sakuyu Island, for two centuries. In the north lived the Wanda tribe, in irregular communal holdings; in the hills lived the native Sakuyu, black, naked, man-eating, with their herds of puny cattle. The Arabs held aloof from the affairs of both these peoples and built a prosperous town, Matodi, on the coast: great houses with intricate latticed windows and brass-studded doors, courtyards planted with dense mango trees, narrow streets and a magnificent bazaar. One of the Sultan's commanders, a slave's son from Muscat, armed the Wanda, defeated the Sakuyu, changed the name of the island to Azania and became Emperor Amurath the Great. He founded a new capital, Debra-Dowa, two hundred miles inland, and had the French build the *Grand Chemin de Fer Impérial d'Azanie*, from Debra-Dowa to Matodi. For this he was given an elegant ivory sceptre by the President of the French Republic, which together with the golden crown of Azania is the chief treasure of the Empire. When Amurath died, his grandson Seth came back from Oxford where he had received his Bachelor of Arts degree and was crowned as the new emperor. Seth died by poison in the early years of this century.

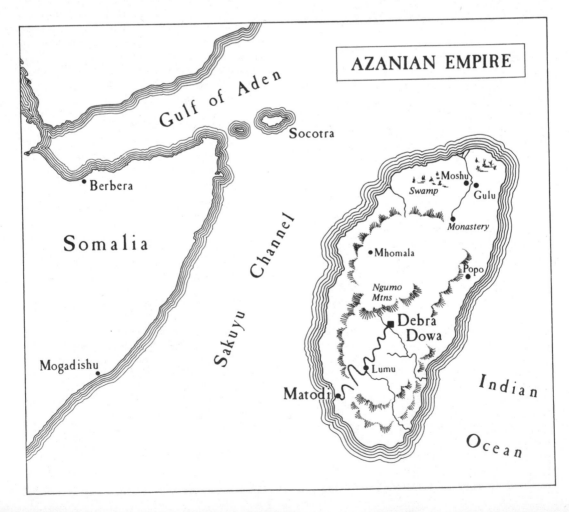

There are many churches in Azania: Anglican, Catholic, Nestorian, all of which have cathedrals in Debra-Dowa—Quaker, Moravian, American-Baptist, Mormon and Swedish-Lutheran. Indians, Armenians, Goans, Jews and Greeks also have their places of worship on the island.

The palace in Debra-Dowa is a stucco villa of French design, surrounded by sheds of various sizes which serve as kitchens, servants' quarters and stables. There is also a thatched barn which is used for state banquets, a domed octagonal chapel and a large rubble and timber residence used by royal guests. The whole is enclosed by an irregular fortified stockade. Outside the walls is a haphazard jumble of shops, missions, barracks, legations, bungalows and native huts.

The army is all-important. The Imperial Guard wear field-grey uniforms. The infantry—in threadbare regalia, puttees wound up anyhow and caps at all angles—were organized by an Irishman, General Connolly. The native tribes are represented by the Wanda and Sakuyu warriors. The Sakuyu wear their hair in a dense fuzz, their chests and arms embossed with ornamental scars. The Wanda have their teeth filed into sharp points and their hair braided into many mud-caked pig-tails. In accordance with their custom, they wear around their necks the genitals of a slain enemy.

The Imperial newspaper is the *Azanian Courier*. The currency is rupees. The inhabitants sometimes indulge in anthropophagous repasts.

(Evelyn Waugh, *Black Mischief*, London, 1932)

AZANULBIZAR, see DIMRILL DALE.

AZAR, a remote valley beyond the Valley of the JUKANS in the underground continent of PELLUCIDAR. Azar is usually avoided by travellers as it is inhabited, like many other regions of Pellucidar, by cannibals.

The so-called Man-Eating Giants of Azar are among the tallest people in Pellucidar, over seven feet in height, and also among the ugliest, with protruding tusk-like teeth. They are one of the more primitive races of Pellucidar, armed only with stone clubs and knives. They have no knowledge of building; their village is simply a palisaded enclosure with no huts, and the Giants sleep on the ground beneath the trees. Their only skill appears to be hunting. Human flesh is their favourite food and visitors who wander into the area are captured for culinary purposes. The victims are

tied to posts inside the compound and fed on fruit and nuts until judged ready for eating. Their bones are then broken with stone clubs and their flesh roasted over a fire in a pit. The Giants of Azar are a savage, cruel race, who do not show any affection even for their own children.

A further hazard in this region is a species of giant ants which often reach a length of six feet or more, their heads nearly three feet above the ground. Their anthills are so large that seen from a distance they seem to be natural hillocks. Travellers interested in entomology will observe that this unique species is highly developed, to the point of cultivating their own crops. In selected clearings, symmetrical rows of plants are carefully tended by worker ants, guarded by heavily-built soldier ants. Travellers who are captured by the ants are taken into the anthills, where they are fattened on a varied diet planned to produce the very best results.

In their turn, the giant ants are preyed upon by a species of giant ant-bear or ant-eater. The ant-bears of Azar are as large as elephants but otherwise very similar to the type found in Latin America.

(Edgar Rice Burroughs, *Land of Terror*, New York, 1944)

One of the giant ants of AZAR captures a wayward traveller.

B

BABAR'S KINGDOM, see CELESTEVILLE.

BABEL, a city of unknown location (not to be confused with the biblical Babel, Genesis 11:1–9) famous for its library. This library—which some call the Universe—is composed of an indefinite and perhaps infinite number of hexagonal galleries, separated by vast air shafts and surrounded by very low railings. From any of the hexagons one can see, interminably, the upper and lower floors. The distribution of the galleries is invariable: twenty shelves, five long shelves per side, cover all the sides except two; their height, from floor to ceiling, scarcely exceeds that of a normal bookcase. One of the free sides leads to a narrow hallway which opens onto another gallery, identical to the first. To the left and right of the hallway are two very small closets: one is for sleeping standing up, the other is a toilet. A spiral staircase and a mirror complete the furnishings. Men infer from this mirror that the library is not infinite (if it really were, why this illusory duplication?). On each shelf are thirty-five books of identical format, four hundred and ten pages long. On each page are forty lines, on each line eighty black letters. Because the orthographical symbols are twenty-five and because the library is infinite, all that can be said in any language is here on a printed page. Everything: the minutely detailed history of the future, the autobiographies of the archangels, a faithful catalogue of the library, thousands and thousands of false catalogues, the true story of every man's death, the translation of every book in all languages. Generation after generation of librarians wander through the library in an attempt to find the Book.

(Jorge Luis Borges, "La Biblioteca de Babel," in *El jardín de senderos que se bifurcan,* Buenos Aires, 1941)

BABILARY, an island in the East China Sea, south-west of Japan. The island is ruled by women. The capital is Ramaja. Its main feature is an octagonal marketplace, some six hundred metres wide. The houses on each side are symmet-rical and in the centre is a statue of Queen Rafalu who built the site in the seventeenth century, surrounded by the statues of famous Babilary women. There are eight royal academies, one on each side of the octagon.

The island fell under women's rule at the Battle of Camaraca, when Queen Aiginu I fought against her weak husband and his army and won by placing the youngest and most beautiful girls in the front line. The men could not resist their charms and the battle was won without bloodshed.

The queen has a harem, mostly of foreigners, from which she chooses her husbands. She cannot keep more than one at a time and whoever she chooses must be her consort for at least one year. The consort must be well behaved and shy and must not even be suspected of immodesty.

The women are not only warriors or pirates, but also musicians and poets. The men receive no education and need only worry about their looks. The women are not too careful about whom they marry because they have the right to divorce, which the men do not have.

A Literary Tribunal, composed of seven women, judges all plays and the queen rewards the best authors. Bad authors are punished and are not allowed to write again. A Fashion Tribunal, composed of men, dictates hair and dress styles.

Babilarian religion has two gods: Ossok for the women and Ossokia for the men.

In the native tongue, Babilary means "To the Glory Of Women."

(Abbé Pierre François Guyot Desfontaines, *Le Nouveau Gulliver ou Voyage De Jean Gulliver, Fils Du Capitaine Gulliver, Traduit d'un Manuscrit Anglois, Par Monsieur L.D.F.,* Paris, 1730)

BACHEPOUSSE, an island of the Chichi Archipelago, full of tropical trees and perfumed flowers. The natives are friendly and welcome visitors with many-coloured blossoms, fruits, venison and honey.

The centre of the island is occupied by three hills and a small volcano; when the latter erupts, the island shakes slightly and streams of fertile lava cover the mountain slopes. Very soon afterwards golden flowers spring from the renovated soil. These flowers are immediately picked by the natives who use them as coinage for food and other goods from neighbouring islands. The natives are lazy but artistic; each of the things they do in their

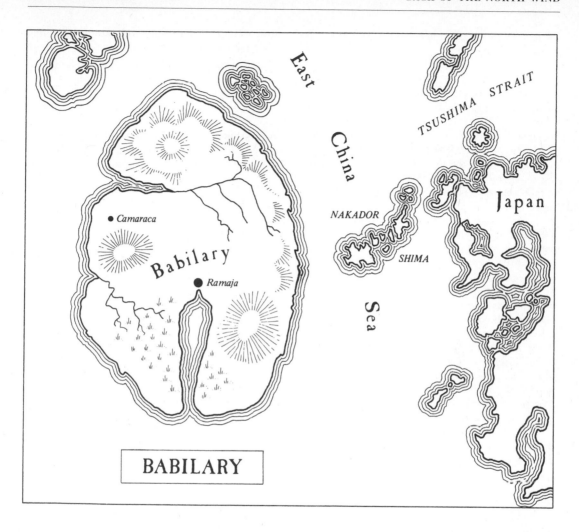

everyday lives is accomplished in a new and exalted way. For instance, the men paint their cattle according to the weather before taking them out to graze: grey during storms, bright blue on sunny days, white and purple when the wind blows. The women do their washing in rose-petal water. The children fulfill their daily bodily functions on square pieces of fine silk. The young girls, at the age of puberty, pierce their nipples with tiny roses which they wear with sensual elegance.

(Robert Pinget, *Graal Flibuste*, Paris, 1956)

BACK OF THE NORTH WIND, reached by walking through the body of the North Wind, who sits at the door of this realm in the Arctic wastes.

Accounts of this land have been given by three different people and vary somewhat. The first account was written by Durante, the fourteenth-century Italian writer. He claims to have entered the land through a door of fire and to have seen a country where everything smells sweetly and it is always the month of May. A gentle breeze blows constantly and a pure brook gurgles through grassy meadows dotted with red and yellow flowers. Durante described the inhabitants as free and healthy, and wearing crowns.

Centuries after Durante, the daughter of a Scottish peasant fell asleep in a wood and awoke in the Arctic realm, from which she returned a month later. She described a land where no rain ever falls and where the wind never blows, a land of light in which there is neither sun nor moon, neither night nor sin.

A more complete account was given in the nineteenth century by a child named Diamond, the son of a London cab-driver, who was carried there by the North Wind herself. He entered the figure of the Wind and found himself in a country free from snow and ice. He saw no sun, but a pure radiant light seemed to issue from all things. A river flowed over the long waving grass. According to Diamond nothing ever goes wrong there but, on the other hand, nothing seems to be quite right.

The people at the Back of the North Wind do not speak; they look at each other and understand without the use of language. Again, Diamond's account differs somewhat from the earlier versions; he agrees that the people looked quite happy but he adds that they were not perfectly so. Diamond thought they looked a little sad at times, as if expecting to be happier some day. It seems that the inhabitants are in fact people the North Wind brings back after sinking their ships. Once established in this country, they can still see those they loved back home by climbing to the top of a particular tree, where they become invisible. The tree is large enough to accommodate all the inhabitants of this curious realm.

Travellers are advised that time passes very slowly at the Back of the North Wind; a week sometimes seems to last a whole century.

(George MacDonald, *At the Back of the North Wind*, London, 1870)

BAHARNA, an important port on the island of Oriab, in the SOUTHERN SEA of DREAM-WORLD, eleven days' sail from DYLATH-LEEN. The quays of Baharna are of porphyry; the city rises behind them in great terraces of stone and steep roads with steps, sometimes roofed by bridges that link the buildings on either side. Notable are the twin lighthouses, Thon and Thal, at the entrance of the harbour and the great canal that crosses the city through a tunnel with granite doors and arrives at Lake Yath, on the shores of which lie the ruins of an unnamed primeval city. Visitors are not advised to spend the night among these desolate remains. If they do so, upon awakening they are likely to find their mounts (usually zebras) bled dry and the imprint of enormous webbed feet on the ground by their side. Visitors

may also find that a few unimportant trinkets have disappeared from their luggage.

(Howard Phillips Lovecraft, "The Dream-Quest of Unknown Kadath," in *Arkham Sampler*, Sauk City, 1948)

BALADAR ARCHIPELAGO, see ASBEFORE ISLAND.

BALBRIGIAN AND BOULOULABASSIAN UNITED REPUBLIC, in Central Europe. The country is noted for the beautiful palace of King Kaboul I of Balbrigia, Emperor of the GREEN ISLES. It stands on a hill, next to the water cisterns. The high rooms are filled with plants as tall as trees, and huge aquariums of goldfish. The large gardens are built on sloping terraces, and orange trees and palm trees grow among fine marble, costly rugs, statues and fountains.

Balbrigia and Bouloulabassia were united by a scullery boy, François Gauwain. When the Bouloulabassians attacked the palace of King Kaboul I, Gauwain drove them away by smoking them out of the royal cellars where they had cunningly hidden themselves. But because King Kaboul refused to give him his daughter's hand in marriage, Gauwain went over to the Bouloulabassians and offered his services to King Bridabatu XXIV. It was then that the king pronounced the historic words: "He who managed to choke my army in a cellar, will surely make it glorious on a battle field!" Gauwain was defeated and taken captive by King Kaboul I, who did not recognize his old scullery boy. Gauwain, however, was able to pour poison into the cisterns and thereby exterminate the entire population of Balbrigia. He married Princess Julia, King Kaboul's daughter, whom he had spared, united both kingdoms and proclaimed the republic.

(Max Jacob, *Histoire du roi Kaboul Ier et du marmiton Gauwain*, Paris, 1971)

BALDIVIA, see INDIAN ISLAND.

BALEUTA, one of the Isles of WISDOM, an extensive but little known archipelago in the north Pacific. Like most of the islands of the archipelago, Baleuta has deliberately based its civilization and culture on a system of ideas gained from the outside world through books. In the case of Baleuta, the system adopted is the political ideal sketched by Plato in his writings.

Baleuta claims to be the only State in the world ever to have put the Platonic ideal into practice. Both State and government are under the control of philosophers trained to rule by the Platonic University; the Baleuta Academy is equivalent to the institution of the State itself. The Post Office, for instance, has recently been placed under the control of the Ministry of Transcendental Ethics, following the discovery that, under the previous organization, eighty per cent of the mail failed to reach its destination.

Socially, the people of Baleuta practise the communal sharing of women and children. This, it is believed, prevents women from interfering in the affairs of the State. Sexual relationships are transitory and incidental; a man's wife can easily be the wife of another man tomorrow. The idea of motherhood is given no importance in itself and the men of the island keep no record of the children they may have fathered. What is termed "love" in other countries is seen here simply as a physical lust connected with the need to procreate; in consequence, it is considered of no importance for the culture of the island.

Men often cannot recall if they have or have not been "married" to a particular woman; they have no means of telling whether their offspring are among the crowds of ill-nourished children that the visitor will see playing in the streets. Nor, it must be admitted, do they particularly care about such matters. It appears that marriage lotteries are held at certain times of the year, but no description of these ceremonies or rites is available.

Health care is organized in accordance with Plato's criticisms of Hippocratic medicine and its concern for prolonging life. In order to prevent the death rate from falling below a certain level, epidemics are allowed—to a certain extent—to run their natural course and doctors refrain from treating all curable diseases. Abortions are also used to control the population. For older women abortion is compulsory, in accordance with Plato's view that parenthood should not be allowed after a certain age. The entire health system is controlled by the Minister for Medical Philosophy, who is said to be completing his major study on the question: "What are men's moral duties towards the bacilli which cause anthrax, with special reference

to the *De Officiis* of Cicero?" The people of Baleuta await the publication of this important work with great impatience.

The strict application of Platonic principles has led to one of the few political conflicts known to have occurred on Baleuta. Following Plato's doctrine, lyric and epic poets are banned from the island. Therefore, when a small anarchist group attracted some attention by demanding the destruction of the present State and the establishment of poetry as the leading social principle, the ringleader was duly brought to trial and sent to the convict island of Krakatume where his poems were destroyed. Despite this example, groups of poets still infest parts of the island, in defiance of the constitution. The repression of such groups is the major task of the efficient and well-trained police force, who have little time to deal with the violence that often breaks out as a result of quarrels over gambling. In general, however, the crime rate has been considerably reduced since the introduction of the Socratic principle "It is better to suffer wrong than to do wrong." The island's tribunals seem never to tire of suffering wrong; the conviction rate has fallen accordingly and the State jail is nearly always empty.

In both pure and applied arts, the island lacks any national artistic tradition and the notion that beauty should be pursued for its own sake is considered an immoral luxury. The architects have resorted to a compromise solution; the visitor cannot fail to notice that though the houses of Baleuta have extremely shabby façades, they are well designed to the rear, away from the street. All public buildings resemble silos or warehouses, except shops, which are often modelled on the Acropolis and the Parthenon.

This dichotomy is most clearly illustrated by the memorial in the central square of the capital, a huge bronze statue of Plato, with Kant standing on his shoulders (in order to demonstrate that Kant's philosophy is totally dependent on that of his Greek forbear). As is to be expected in a State that officially scorns the role of the artist, the figures are grotesque and show no knowledge of the theory of proportion or perspective. In order to symbolize the Kantian theory of antinomies, a public convenience has been built into the plinth of the memorial. It is called a *Heracliteon*, and bears the inscription *panta rhei* or "all things flow." Platonic theory also places limits on the island's achievements in music. Several instruments are banned from Baleuta and those that remain in legitimate use tend to produce a cacophonous sound, especially as all musicians improvise freely during public concerts.

Education on Baleuta is based on the study of the classics, with special reference to Plato. In order to facilitate the teaching of grammar, Homer and Horace are used as textbooks, but the pupils are taught to despise the poetic content of the works and to consider them as grammar manuals. Adult education is available to all in the form of open lectures, such as "Parmenides for barbers" and "An Introduction to Platonic-Socratic ethics for taxi-drivers."

Perhaps the greatest festival of the island is the celebration of the anniversary of the Platonic University, when floats illustrating the lives of the philosophers or important scientific discoveries are drawn through the streets. The anniversary is also marked by the presentation of prizes won in essay competitions. Recent topics have included: "Give a sketch of a gaily illustrated children's fable primarily based upon Aristotelian topics and metaphysics," and "Why was Glaucon, who spoke scornfully in Plato's presence of a pig republic, not executed?"

Visitors to Baleuta will be asked to fill in seven forms on arrival. In addition to all the normal questions, they are asked to state their philosophical convictions. This is done so that the Ministry for Philosophical Affairs can take appropriate measures to encourage or discourage particular persuasions. Visitors are furthermore advised that they will be required to pay for all official hospitality shown them during their stay on the island.

(Alexander Moszkowski, *Die Inseln der Weisheit, Geschichte einer abenteuerlichen Entdeckungsfahrt,* Berlin, 1922)

BALLOON PICKER'S COUNTRY, between the countries of OVER AND UNDER and ROOTABAGA. Balloons are the staple crop here and at the end of the summer the sky is thick with balloons of every colour. Peach, watermelon, rye-loaf and wheat-loaf balloons also flourish, as well as sausage and pork-chop balloons. The balloons are picked by people on stilts. Should they fall off their stilts, the balloons they are holding will keep them floating until they are able to regain their footing. It occasionally happens that one of the pickers sings too happily and becomes so light that

he is carried away by his balloons. When his songs are all gone, his heart will grow heavy and he will drop down to his stilts again.

On the very edge of this country is the place where circus clowns are made. They are baked in a variety of ovens—long ovens for long clowns, short ovens for short clowns. When a clown is baked, he is taken and propped up against a fence, like a white doll with a wide red mouth, until two men approach. One throws a bucket of white fire over him and the second pumps a living red wind into him. The clown immediately comes to life and begins to turn cartwheels in the sawdust-ring by the fence.

(Carl Sandburg, *Rootabaga Stories,* New York, 1922)

BALNIBARBI, an island in the north Pacific, between Japan and California. The capital, Lagado,

The laboratory for experiments in architectural balance, Academy of Lagado, BALNIBARBI.

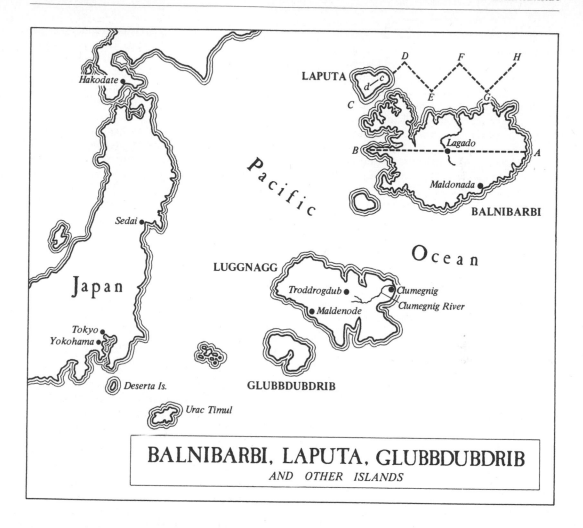

BALNIBARBI, LAPUTA, GLUBBDUBDRIB
AND OTHER ISLANDS

is a major port for trade with the island of LUG-GNAGG. Ships from Maldonada, a port about the size of Portsmouth in England, also sail regularly to Luggnagg.

The capital is roughly half the size of London. All its houses are in bad repair and are built in the most peculiar fashion. The citizens are dressed in rags and rush through the streets with wild, staring eyes. In the countryside, labourers can be seen working with a variety of tools, but it is impossible to tell what they are actually doing. Although the soil is fertile there is no sign of grass or wheat or corn.

The poverty that reigns in Balnibarbi is largely the responsibility of the so-called Projectors. In about 1660, a group of people sailed to LAPUTA and returned after five months with a smattering of mathematics and their heads full of volatile spirits acquired in that lofty region. They immediately began to devise schemes or "projects" for putting everything on a new footing. An academy of Projectors was set up in Lagado; today every city of any consequence has its own academy. The "projects" were designed to enable one man to do the work of ten, to produce buildings that would never wear out and to bring all plants and crops to maturity at any given time of the year. The difficulty is that none of these schemes has yet come to fruition and in the meantime the country lies in waste. Some lords or *Munodi* held out against the Projectors, but they were ultimately forced to destroy their houses and to rebuild them in the modern fashion in order to avoid public hostility and royal displeasure.

One typical "project" involves the extraction of sunshine from cucumbers: the sunbeams are hermetically sealed in phials and then released in inclement weather. In another, an architect has contrived a new method for building houses by beginning at the top and working downwards (as in PHILOSOPHERS' ISLAND), arguing that this is how bees and spiders make their wonderful constructions. In the School of Languages, "projects" are established for the simplification of language by cutting out polysyllables and leaving out verbs and participles, on the grounds that all things imaginable are merely nouns. Another Projector is working on the abolition of words altogether. This, it is claimed, will improve people's health by lessening the corrosion of the lungs. The underlying logic is that since words represent things it would be more convenient for men to carry with them the things that may be mentioned in their speech. It is said that this "project" might have been put into operation had not the women and the illiterate threatened rebellion unless they were allowed to go on speaking with their tongues in the manner of their forefathers. A scheme devised to discover plots against the government involves the examination of the diet of suspects and analysis of their excreta, on the grounds that men are never more serious, thoughtful and intent than when they are defecating.

Although Balnibarbi is itself a kingdom, it forms part of the empire of Laputa, to which it pays tribute.

(Jonathan Swift, *Travels Into Several Remote Nations Of The World. In Four Parts. By Lemuel Gulliver, First a Surgeon, and then a Captain of several Ships*, London, 1726)

BAMBA, see ZAVATTINIA.

BAMPOPO, a British colony in Equatorial Africa, inhabited by a number of tribes, the most noteworthy being the Bulanga, the Bilongo and the M'tezo; the Bumbali, Kubango and Mugwamba are less important. Bampopo is an important diocese of the Anglican church, whose missionaries have been making great efforts to convert the native population to Christianity. They have been successful with the Bilongo who, despite their incorrigible tendency to lie, have readily turned to the new faith. Many of the Bulanga have also been converted, but their conversion does not appear to be permanent; shortly after three hundred of their number were baptized in a single day, others of the tribe killed and ate a Mrs. Richardson, widely regarded as the best lady preacher in the diocese. The M'tezo have resisted all attempts to convert them and still retain their traditional customs of going naked, filing their teeth and eating their superfluous female relatives. The M'tezo are an extremely promiscuous people; some observers claim that they swap wives at every new moon.

(Norman Douglas, *South Wind*, London, 1917)

BANOIC, also known as BENWICK, a kingdom in western Gaul, ruled by King Ban, brother to the great King Bors of GAUNES and father to Launcelot, one of the greatest of all the knights of the round table of CAMELOT.

(Anonymous, *La Mort le Roi Artu*, 13th. cen. AD)

BANOIS EMPIRE, in the subterranean world of PLUTO, in the centre of the earth. The empire borders on ALBUR and there are some similarities between the two countries. The Banois are roughly the same height as their neighbours—rarely more than two and a half feet tall. The language of the Banois resembles that of the Alburians, but appears to have been simplified over the centuries; visitors will find it can now be learned in a matter of weeks. However, unlike the Alburians, the Banois sing instead of speaking. Even the children of the country hum as they cry; adults sing harmoniously every hour of the day.

The Banois are noted for their sociability. They are lively, curious and noisy and much given to extreme bouts of joy and sadness. Their favourite pastime is the telling of riddles, often in verse. Riddle "contests" usually take place in the cafés of the towns and frequently go on until the early hours of the morning.

Although the country is ruled by an emperor, his power is circumscribed by the rigid terms of a constitution which cannot be altered, so that there is little possibility of political change in the country, and it is most unlikely that the emperor would be able to use his position to establish a tyranny.

Like the Alburians, the Banois are vegetarians and will not kill animals, out of respect for their Creator; they do, however, eat fish. It is typical of the tolerance of the country that foreigners arc allowed to eat meat if they kill and prepare it themselves—no Banois cook would touch the flesh of a dead animal. Indeed, foreigners who kill and eat the wild boars of the forest are welcomed, as they help to rid the country of animals that are a great threat to the farmers' crops.

Travellers with an interest in zoology will be pleased to know that dragons are found in the forests of the empire. They are about seven feet long and have membranous, bat-like wings. Their heads are the shape and size of a wolf's and their skins are smooth and leathery. The Banois regard the dragon as a sacred animal.

The Banois Empire was discovered by a party of English and French sailors who reached Pluto via the north polar entrance in the IRON MOUNTAINS after having been shipwrecked in the Arctic Ocean in 1806. They came to the empire after being expelled from Albur for having eaten meat, which is strictly forbidden in that country. After spending some months in the Banois Empire, the group travelled on to FELINIA before finally returning to the surface of the earth.

(Anonymous, *Voyage au centre de la terre, ou aventures de quelques naufragés dans des pays inconnus. Traduit de l'anglais de Sir Hormidas Peath*, Paris, 1821)

BANZA, capital of the Congo (not to be confused with the African state of the same name). Banza is famous for showing the best theatre plays in the whole of Africa and for having the worst theatres. It also houses the most beautiful and least efficient College of Soothsayers in the world.

Banza is governed by the great sultan Mangogoul, 1,234,500th descendant of the same dynasty, established in the year of the creation of the world 1,500,000,003,200,001, and of the founding of the Kingdom of the Congo 3,900,000,700,003.

A deeply religious man, Mangogoul is on excellent terms with the Congolese deities, in particular with the god Cucufa, an old hypochondriac who, not wishing to be bothered by the problems of the world or those of the other gods, sought refuge in the void. Here he could perfect the holy virtues of pinching himself, scratching himself,

boring himself, making himself angry and starving himself to death. He lies in this void, on a bamboo mattress, sewn into a sack, arms across his chest, his head in a hood under which only his beard is visible. He is accompanied by an owl, a few rats that gnaw at his mattress and several bats flying around his head. Cucufa is said to have great powers: with his rings he can become invisible and he can bestow upon ladies' jewellery the power of speech.

(Denis Diderot, *Les Bijoux indiscrets*, Paris, 1748)

BARANKA ISLAND, see ZAROFF'S ISLAND.

BARATARIA, an island somewhere in La Mancha, Spain, in a place whose name does not wish to be remembered, the only island in the world surrounded by land instead of sea.

Barataria is famous for having been governed for a week with honourable rectitude by Sancho Panza, who accompanied the ingenious knight Don Quixote throughout his travels. Sancho Panza abandoned his governorship rather abruptly, after having repelled a fearful enemy invasion, armed only with two wooden tables tied to his waist. (His comments on the island's cuisine were rather unfavourable—he compared it to a prison diet in times of want.)

Should the traveller visiting Barataria be invited to govern the island, it will be useful to bear in mind some of the advice Don Quixote gave Sancho Panza:

> *First fear God; for the fear of God is the beginning of wisdom and a wise man cannot err.*
> *A man should consider what he has been and endeavour to know himself, the most difficult knowledge to acquire.*
> *A man should not be governed by the law of his own whim.*
> *A man should let the tears of the poor find more compassion, but not more justice, than the representations of the rich.*
> *If the scales of justice be at any time not evenly balanced, let it be by the weight of mercy and not by that of a gift.*

It is said that if a governor follows these rules, his days will be long, his fame eternal, his recompense full and his happiness unspeakable.

(Miguel de Cervantes Saavedra, *El ingenioso hidalgo Don Quixote de La Mancha*, Madrid, 1605–15)

BARON HUGHES CASTLE, somewhere in the lowlands of France, a squarish white building with plain turretted battlements and a huge drawbridge. It was made famous in the mid-fifteenth century when it was visited by a couple of envoys from the devil who, instead of fulfilling their commitment and doing the devil's work, were tempted into taking the side of the castle's mortals. In fact the handsome Gilles, one of the devil's envoys, fell in love with the mortal Anne. Both were punished by the devil and transformed into stone statues which can today be seen in the small cemetery behind the castle. However the devil did not succeed in obtaining the absolute silence of death, for deep within the statues' breasts the lovers' hearts can still, to this day, be heard beating.

(*Les Visiteurs du soir*, directed by Marcel Carné, France, 1942)

BARROW DOWNS, a region of broad valleys and smooth, treeless hills to the east of the OLD FOREST in northern MIDDLE-EARTH. On the hills stand the barrows of the long-dead kings and queens of the EDAIN, which give their name to the area. Some of the barrows are surmounted by great stones, like jagged, broken teeth in green gums.

The Downs are a dangerous, sinister place because of the evil spirits who took them over during the Third Age of Middle-earth. These spirits, called Barrow-wights, entice people into the barrows in order to sacrifice them. The only person known to have any real power over these spirits is Tom Bombadil, who sometimes guides visitors.

(J.R.R. Tolkien, *The Fellowship of the Ring*, London, 1954; J.R.R. Tolkien, *The Return of the King*, London, 1955)

BASILISK COUNTRY, in southern Africa, a desert region inhabited by a terrifying serpent, the basilisk, whose stare is so powerful that it has made the area a desert: it can split rocks, scorch grass, poison the streams it drinks from and kill animals with a glance. Only weasels remain unaf-

fected by this creature; it is also said that the basilisk fears the sound of roosters crowing. Keeping this in mind, travellers should provide themselves with a rooster or a weasel when travelling through the territory. Another useful tool for defending oneself against the basilisk is a mirror; its own image will strike a basilisk dead. But trying to kill the monster with a spear while riding on horseback is not recommended: the venom would rise through the spear and kill not only the rider but also the horse.

The basilisk's aspect has never been accurately described; some have seen him as a four-legged cock with a crown, talons like drills, yellow feathers, white thorny wings, and a serpent's tail ending either in a hook or in a rooster's head prickled with darts which he can shoot like arrows, making blood drip from the leaves of trees; yet others describe him simply as a feathered serpent. The basilisk's eggs are hatched by toads in the season of the Dog Star.

Near the coast live the manticores, gigantic red lions, with human faces, a triple row of teeth which fit into each other like those of a comb, a tail ending in a sting like that of a scorpion, and sweet blue eyes. Their voices resemble the mingled sounds of a flute and a trumpet. They are notable for their swiftness and for their fondness for human flesh.

(Pliny the Elder, *Naturalis Historia*, 1st cen. AD; Pliny the Elder, *Inventorum Natura*, 1st cen. AD; Lucan, *Pharsalia*, 1st cen. AD; Gustave Flaubert, *La Tentation de Saint Antoine*, Paris, 1874)

BASKERVILLE HALL, a house in Dartmoor, England. The ancestral home of the Baskerville family, not far from the hamlet of Grimpen, fourteen miles from the great convict prison of Princetown. The great detective Sherlock Holmes and Dr. John H. Watson visited Baskerville Hall from September 25 to October 20, 1888, and solved the problem of a gigantic hound who, according to an odd eighteenth-century legend, haunted the desolate moors around the Hall. Baskerville Hall is now probably in the hands of the National Trust.

(Sir Arthur Conan Doyle, *The Hound of the Baskervilles*, London, 1902)

BASTI, a cave-village of uncertain location, towards the south of the underground realm of

BASKERVILLE HALL, Dartmoor, England.

PELLUCIDAR, not far from the Forest of DEATH. Basti is situated at the end of a narrow, winding gorge between chalk cliffs surrounded by low, rolling hills.

The Bastians are a primitive race of cannibals. Like many of the people of Pellucidar, they adhere to the simple rule of assuming that all visitors are enemies and should be killed on sight. Those who are captured are used as slaves and are forced to excavate new dwellings for their masters. They are given crude stone tools and are savagely beaten if their work is not up to the required standard. The Bastians are not noted for their intelligence and are easily provoked into fits of rage.

(Edgar Rice Burroughs, *Seven Worlds to Conquer*, New York, 1936)

BASTIANI, a large fortress. A massive example of military engineering, which guards the only pass between the TARTARY DESERT and the southern slopes of the steep and uninterrupted chain of mountains that marks the border between the northern and the southern States of an unnamed country.

Bastiani stands alone, almost plastered into the rocks of a plateau. The nearest town, San Rocco, is thirty kilometres away, a two-day ride on horseback. Miles upon miles of wild, impenetrable

mountains loom to the right and left of Bastiani. Despite its military importance (which, with the passage of time, has declined, as there has never been an invasion in that area), the fortress presents an unpretentious appearance. From the central blockhouse—a structure resembling a barrack with few windows—two massive, crenellated walls connect the lateral redoubts, two to each side. In this manner the walls block the entire pass, approximately five hundred metres wide, enclosed on both sides by tall, steep cliffs. To the right of the fortress, just under the mountain's walls, the plateau dips down into a kind of saddle; the old road to the pass goes through there, ending against the walls of Bastiani.

The New Redoubt, a small, detached fort on top of a hill overlooking the Tartary Desert, is a forty-five-minute walk from the north of the fortress. This is the most important outpost, completely isolated, and must give the alarm if any menace approaches.

The rules which regulate the changing of the guard of the New Redoubt are very strict: for example, nobody may enter from north of the fortress, not even well-known officers, if they do not know the different passwords. A complicated system of controls regulates these passwords. Each morning at 5:15, the guards of the New Redoubt leave Bastiani—as an organized detachment, they need a password to leave. To re-enter the New Redoubt before the changing of the guard they use the previous day's password, known only to their commanding officer. Once the guard is changed at the New Redoubt, the new password, also known only to the commanding officer, becomes operative. The new password remains in force for twenty-four hours, until the next change of the guard. The following day, when the garrison of the New Redoubt returns to the fortress, the password has changed. Thus a third password is necessary. The commanding officer must therefore know three: the password to go, the password that will be in use during the tour of duty and the password to return. If something were to happen to the commanding officer during this interval, the soldiers would no longer be able to re-enter the fortress, and if an accident were to delay them, they would not be able to return to the New Redoubt, because the password would have changed in the meantime. Visitors are therefore advised to organize their excursions very carefully.

In military circles in the Southern State, the silver trumpets of Bastiani are famous for their red silk cords and for the crystal clearness of their blare.

(Dino Buzzati, *Il deserto dei Tartari*, Milan, 1940)

BAUCIS, a city in Asia. After a seven days' march through woodland, the traveller directed towards Baucis cannot see the city and yet he has arrived. The slender stilts that rise from the ground at a great distance from one another and are lost above the clouds support the city. He must climb them with ladders. On the ground the inhabitants rarely show themselves: already having everything they need up there, they prefer not to come down. Nothing of the city touches the earth except those long flamingo legs on which it rests and, when the days are sunny, a pierced, angular shadow that falls on the foliage.

There are three hypotheses about the inhabitants of Baucis: that they hate the earth; that they respect it so much they avoid all contact; that they love it as it was before they existed and with spy-glasses and telescopes aimed downwards they never tire of examining it, leaf by leaf, stone by stone, ant by ant, contemplating with fascination their own absence.

(Italo Calvino, *Le città invisibili*, Turin, 1972)

BEAR COUNTRY, an immense realm extending from the mountains south of the WOOD BEYOND THE WORLD to the hills above STARK-WALL, reached through a narrow pass. The grey downland ridges run north to south; nut and berry trees grow on the high lands, but the greater part of Bear Country is covered in parched pasture-land.

The northern and eastern regions are inhabited by a race of half-wild people, tall and with long red hair. The men are grave and solemn and have great shaggy beards, the women are comely. They dress in scanty garments made from sheep- or deer-skins, but elders are distinguished by their deer-skin mantles, gold bracelets and the chaplets of blue stones they wear on their heads. Their only weapons are clubs, flint-axes and spears tipped with either bone or flint. They live in round huts made of turf and thatched with reeds.

Tribal and religious assemblies are called by sending out messengers with tokens to bring the people to the Doom Ring, a circle of standing rocks with a stone throne in the centre. During the *motes* or assemblies an elder chieftain sits on the throne, flanked by two women dressed in war gear.

The Bears' religion revolves around sacrifices made to a goddess believed to have been the mother of the tribe who ruled them before the coming of the first elders. Strangers are not welcomed.

(William Morris, *The Wood Beyond the World*, London, 1894)

BEAR ISLAND, situated off the coast of the United States, near the Island of FORTUNE, and subject to hurricanes and floods. As the name of the island makes clear, bears have become the dominant species. They walk erect, cultivate the land and gather the crops. Men, on the other hand, move on all fours, live wild in the forest and are the bears' slaves or beasts of burden.

When the bears began to walk on their hind legs they also began to suffer from the ills of ursinity—impatience, a desire for constant novelty, and an interminable attention to fashion. The she-bears are no longer content with wearing just fur, they require rich dresses and showy jewels.

Visitors should endeavour to arrive at Bear Island during harvest time, when rural feasts are held. Then the bears dance and sing, elect a queen of the feast and crown her with sweet-smelling roses.

(Abbé Balthazard, *L'Isle Des Philosophes Et Plusieurs Autres, Nouvellement découvertes, & remarquables par leur rapports avec la France actuelle*, Chartres, 1790)

BEAST'S CASTLE, deep within the woods of France, an ancient rambling building with many staircases and dusky courtyards. Lifelike statues of men and bloodhounds decorate vast terraces, and seemingly impregnable doors form arches in the massive walls. Though now uninhabited, the castle used to belong to an enchanted prince who had been transformed into a monstrous beast. A traveller arriving at the castle at that time would be led by invisible hands into a dark corridor, barely lit by candelabra held out by live human arms growing from the walls. A sumptuous meal would appear on a solitary table, guarded by live marble busts on both sides of a huge chimney piece.

The Beast, lord of the castle, would then appear and demand retaliation for any minor infraction committed by the traveller, such as picking a white rose. For this the trespasser would have to pay with his life unless a young girl consented to take his place. It was, in fact, the daughter of such a trespasser who restored the Beast to his former self, by weeping over his dying body and begging him to live on; the Beast answered that if it were a man it would do what she asked, but that poor beasts who wanted to prove their love could do nothing else but lie down and die. Her sorrow broke the spell and allowed him to shed his beastly form and become again the prince he had once been.

A vast fortune of jewels and precious stones lies in the castle vaults, but they are protected by the statue of an archer who will shoot whoever enters uninvited. A celebrated mirror, which allows those who look in it to see any place in the world, is said to lie unused in one of the castle's many chambers.

(Mme Marie Leprince de Beaumont, "La Belle et La Bête," in *Magasin des enfants, contes moraux*, Paris, 1757; *La Belle et La Bête*, directed by Jean Cocteau, France, 1946)

The archer guarding treasure in the BEAST'S CASTLE.

BEASTS, VALLEY OF THE, in Snow River country, Canada. It can be reached by travelling downriver by canoe and then walking through the forests, down across a mountain ridge and into the valley. Here the air is like wine and a sweet delicious sunshine covers the ground. The valley has the desolate grandeur of the mighty spruce and hemlock, the splendour of the granite bluffs which in places rise above the forest and catch the sun.

Here the lust of the hunt, the fierce desire to find and kill, disappears. In the open park-like places where silver birch, sumach and maple splash their blazing colours, and where a crystal stream broken by waterfalls foams past towards a quiet pool, many large animals wander passively. Moose, bears, wolves live in perfect harmony together. Eagles, hawks and buzzards share the tree boughs with the doves. A feeling of compassion, of confidence, a lack of anxiety will overcome the traveller, and even fire will seem to him a hideous modern invention.

It is said that the Valley of the Beasts is looked after by the Great Ichtot, a gigantic Red Indian who may or may not protect travellers, and it is wise not to offend him by any act that might shed blood.

(Algernon Blackwood, "The Valley of the Beasts," in *The Dance of Death and Other Stories*, London, 1927)·

BEAULIEU, a walled town on a river, about forty miles from one of the largest cities in New England, in the United States, is in an area totally free of advertising hoardings and smoking factory chimneys. All cars must stop at the bar-gate of the town, for they are not allowed inside. There is a good garage at the entrance, and a sort of inn and livery stable where one may hire a carriage or saddle-horses, the only means of transport permitted inside the gates. Visitors are advised that entry to Beaulieu is severely restricted, and that unless they are prepared to relinquish the world outside the town walls they should not attempt the journey.

The bar-gate to the town is merely a chain stretched across an arched entrance set into an irregular mass of stone buildings with many mullioned windows and a lofty tower something like that of St. John's College in Cambridge. The rambling grey stone buildings in parts rise sheer from the river's edge and are themselves reminis-

cent of Warwick Castle. They serve many purposes. The octroi here is strict and all goods brought into the town for sale must pay a varying *ad valorem* tax, while the "liberty of the town" is granted to outsiders only on payment of a small fee. No one can stay in the town without a licence, and visitors should note that some things are wholly prohibited: for example, anything that would compete with native products (whether foodstuffs, manufactured goods or crafts), and those articles which the town has prohibited as "useless luxuries." Also at the gate are the town's telephone and telegraph facilities. Like cars, these are recognized as necessities in emergencies, but are considered "useless luxuries" as private possessions and so are forbidden within the walls. There is nothing to prevent a townsman from owning and using a motorcar or private telephone beyond the town walls, if he likes, though this is looked on with disfavour and is unusual.

Over the gate-tower floats the banner of the town, above the arch is its coats of arms emblazoned in colour and gold, and within the gates are always two halberdiers on guard. This is no affectation or wilful medievalism—Beaulieu simply knows the value of symbolism and uses it universally and intelligently.

Passing under the great echoing vault of the bar-gate, visitors will come at once into the town itself. There is, first of all, a small marketplace with closely set stone-built, gabled houses. On one side is the Exchange, a considerable building with an open arcade along its front; it is here that the surplus products of the town, such as cloth, grain and farm produce, are sold, or placed in the hands of the Exchange officials for sale outside the community. The main street leads from the square and curves up a slight gradient. Here the houses are well separated, with garden walls between them, the grated openings in the walls allowing more glimpses of gardens around and behind. As in the old days, these houses are mostly workshops and sale-rooms as well as residences for this is the street of craftsmen of all kinds. The restoration of real crafts has substantially reduced the use of machinery; steam is not used at all. Beaulieu holds that mechanical labour is mentally stultifying if not actually degrading, and it is a moral point with the people of Beaulieu that it should become as unnecessary as possible.

The main street leads to the central square of

the town, a spacious place of great dignity and beauty, surrounded by admirable public buildings in which the simplicity of the houses and shops has given way to considerable richness both in design and colour. On one side of the square is the parish church—in this particular case not unlike Saint Cuthbert's—half hidden by fine trees and surrounded by a green and shady churchyard. On another side is the town hall, also with a lofty tower flying the great flag of the city, while the other sides of the square are taken up with the richly carved façades of the Guildhalls.

Off the central square is the main marketplace, entered through a noble archway between two of the Guildhalls. On the opposite side of the central square the street connects with a pleasure garden; here too is the theatre, the concert hall, the public baths, the principal inn and several cafés and shops, the latter being more specially devoted to those things that are associated with the lighter side of life. In spite of the many theatres and concert halls, films are prohibited. Art museums are unknown, for they are believed to be a contradiction in terms, as all art is part of everyday life.

Beyond these squares are the dwelling places, each house with a garden of at least an acre. No multiple houses of any sort are permitted, and each family must maintain a separate house and garden. The roads here wind pleasantly and are well shaded by trees; niched statues, secular and religious, are quite common. Here also are the establishments belonging to various religious orders, each separated into two: one house for men and one for women. In Beaulieu, the chief monastic institution is Benedictine and it stands on higher land than the rest of the town, a true abbey in both size and official status. There is also a house of Dominican Sisters and one of Canons Regular of Saint Augustine. Where the land begins to drop down again towards the river is the College, with its spacious grounds, groves and gardens, the whole commanding a wide view out across the zone of farms beyond the walls of the town.

In Beaulieu no man is a free burgess unless he is a land holder—the minimum land he can hold is garden land sufficient to supply all the needs of his family, the maximum is that amount of farm land that he can maintain at a minimum standard of productivity. Taxation is almost wholly in the form of rent of land, and the scale is fixed from the moment the land is taken over; it varies between

arable land, forest, orchard, pasture, garden and the land on which a dwelling has been built. If through his own industry a land holder improves any portion of his holding, he receives a rebate on his taxes; if he allows any land to degenerate, his taxes increase. The tax revenue is supplemented by various fees, not very numerous, and by the "gate tax" imposed on those from outside who are admitted to buy or sell within the walls. Public debt is prohibited; by law, the revenue must always meet the annual expenditure, and no bonds secured by public credit may be issued.

Beaulieu has abandoned the old nineteenth-century theory that the vote is a natural right. This privilege is exercised only by land holders and it may be withdrawn for any period of time, for reasons specified in the town's charter. Any man found guilty of a crime or misdemeanour forfeits his franchise, for periods varying from one year to life, depending on the gravity of the offence. The law courts of Beaulieu are very different from the European ones. In the first place, it is a fundamental principle that the object of a court of law is the administration of justice, the defence of right and the punishment of wrong. An appeal based on technicalities is therefore prohibited and any advocate that makes such an appeal is promptly disbarred.

In Beaulieu, the prime object of all education is the development of character, and for this reason education is never divorced from religion. The idea of a rigidly secularized education is abhorrent to the inhabitants of Beaulieu, who attribute to its prevalence in the nineteenth century much of the retrogression in character, the loss of sound standards of value, and the disappearance of leadership which synchronized with the twentieth-century breakdown of civilization. Education is not compulsory, but parents are required to see that their children can read, write and do their sums. There is no effort to subject all children to the same methods or even to make them follow the same courses: quite the reverse—the idea of pushing all children through the same schools to the same point is ridiculed. It is held that beyond a certain stage most children profit little or nothing by continued intensive study. If they wish to continue their studies, they go to the Beaulieu College, which blends something of the feeling of New College, Oxford, with St. John's College, Cambridge. It is perhaps the most beautiful building in Beaulieu, and every intellectual, spiritual and artistic quality is fostered here to the fullest degree. There are many fellowships granted for notable achievements along many lines and a Fellow may claim free food and lodgings for life.

(Ralph Adams Cram, *Walled Towns*, Boston, 1919)

BEAUREPAIRE, a mighty fortress surrounded by ocean and wastelands; to reach it travellers must cross a precarious bridge that will perhaps not support their weight. All the inhabitants of Beaurepaire are exhausted by fasts and long nightly vigils, and misery is apparent everywhere. The two monasteries in the castle (one for distraught nuns, the other for bewildered monks) lack any decoration or colour; the walls are cracked and crumbling, and there are no roofs on the towers.

At night, while you are sleeping soundly, the sobbing of a beautiful, scantily clad woman will waken you, and she will reveal the name of the author of her misfortunes: Anguinguerron, seneschal of Clamadeu des Iles. If you spend the night with her, you will be unable to refuse—if asked—to do combat with her mortal enemy.

(Chrétien de Troyes, "Perceval chez Blanchefleur," in *Le Conte du Graal*, 12th cen.)

BEDEGRAINE or **BEDGRAYNE**, a forest in central England and the site of the defeat of the rebellious lords of the north in the early years of the rule of King Arthur of CAMELOT.

(Sir Thomas Malory, *Le Morte Darthur*, London, 1485; T.H. White, *The Once and Future King*, London, 1939; John Steinbeck, *The Acts of King Arthur and His Noble Knights From the Winchester Manuscripts of Sir Thomas Malory and Other Sources*, New York, 1976)

BEDGRAYNE, see BEDEGRAINE.

BEELZEBUB'S CASTLE, see DEVIL'S GARDEN.

BEERSHEBA, a city of uncertain location. The inhabitants believe that, suspended in the heavens, there exists another Beersheba, where the city's most elevated virtues and sentiments are poised, and that if the terrestrial Beersheba will take the celestial one as its model the two cities will become one. The image propagated by tradition is that of a city of pure gold, with silver locks and diamond gates, a jewel-city, all inset and inlaid, as a maxi-

mum of laborious study might produce when applied to materials of the maximum worth. True to this belief, the inhabitants honour everything that suggests for them the celestial city: they accumulate noble metals and rare stones, they renounce all ephemeral excesses, they develop forms of composite composure.

They also believe that another Beersheba exists underground, the receptacle of everything base and unworthy that happens to them, and it is their constant care to erase from the visible Beersheba every tie or resemblance to the lower twin. In the place of roofs they imagine that the underground city has overturned rubbish bins, with cheese rinds, greasy paper, fish scales and dishwater, uneaten spaghetti, old bandages spilling from them. Or even that its substance is dark and malleable and thick, like the pitch that pours down from the sewers, prolonging the route of the human bowels, from black hole to black hole, until it splatters against the lowest subterranean floor; and from the lazy, encircled bubbles below, layer upon layer, a fecal city rises, with twisted spires.

In Beersheba's beliefs there is an element of truth and one of error. It is true that the city is accompanied by two projections of itself, one celestial and one infernal; but the citizens are mistaken about their consistency. The inferno that broods in the deepest subsoil of Beersheba is a city designed by the most authoritative architects, built with the most expensive materials on the market, with every device and mechanism and gear system functioning, decked with tassels and fringes.

Intent on piling up its carats of perfection, Beersheba takes for virtue what is now a grim mania to fill the empty vessel of itself; the city does not know that its only moments of generous abandon are those when it becomes detached from itself, when it lets go, expands. Still, at the zenith of Beersheba there gravitates a celestial body that shines with all the city's riches, enclosed in the treasury of cast-off things: a planet aflutter with potato peelings, broken umbrellas, old socks, candy wrappings, paved with tram tickets, fingernail cuttings and pared callouses, eggshells. This is the celestial city, and in its heavens long-tailed comets fly past, released to rotate in space by the only free and happy action of the citizens of Beersheba, a city which, only when it shits, is not miserly, calculating, grasping, greedy.

(Italo Calvino, *Le città invisibili*, Turin, 1972)

BEKLA, capital of the BEKLAN EMPIRE, stands on the slopes of Mount Crandor which dominates the surrounding Beklan Plain. The walls of the city are six miles in circumference and rise to the south to enclose the summit of Mount Crandor, crowned by a large citadel, from where the cliffs fall sheer to the ancient stone quarries below. A steep flight of steps leads up the rock face and disappears into a tunnel which emerges in the cellars of the citadel. The only other means of access to this citadel is via the Red Gate in the south wall, a low arch through which a stream flows down to the falls known as the White Girls. The bed of the stream has been deepened, but the builders left a narrow winding causeway of living rock beneath the water. Those who know of this path can find their way through the pool under the arch and into the citadel. The walls of Bekla also enclose large areas of pasture and woodland on the lower slopes of Mount Crandor. A brook flows across the pasture land from a wood east of the citadel to a lake known as the Barb.

Bekla is divided into two sections, the Lower and the Upper cities, separated from each other by stone walls. The only way from the Lower to the Upper City is through the Peacock Gate. Visitors who wish to use this entrance are first admitted to a small chamber known as the Moon Room while the porter operates the counterpoise that opens the Peacock Gate. However, only those who have express permission are allowed into the Upper City. Here the travellers will find both the King's House and the House of the Barons on Leopard Hill, a rise overlooking the Barb to its east. Stone buildings, similar to those found on QUISO, cluster around the lake and the cypress groves that flank it. These buildings are used as residences for the nobility, for delegations from the provinces, and for foreign ambassadors.

The most beautiful sight in the Upper City is Leopard Hill, with its terrace of vines and flowers. Above the gardens rise the twenty round towers of the House of the Barons, with circular balconies projecting like the capitals of giant columns. The height and shape of the marble balconies are all the same, but each one is decorated differently, carved with low relief sculptures of leopards, lilies, birds or fish, and the towers are known by the name of the plant or animal portrayed. They all end in slender painted spires which house the copper bells that summon the citizens of Bekla

to festivals. Surrounding the Royal Palace, the towers themselves look like great lances set against the palace wall. The parapets are carved with lotus leaves and buds, to which the craftsmen who built them have added insects, other plants and drops of water, all much larger than life. In full daylight the palace tends to look severe, but dusk softens the outlines and enhances the beauty of the carvings.

At the foot of the hill stands the so-called King's House, built originally as a mess hall for soldiers but converted for a more sinister purpose after the conquest of the city by the army of ORTELGA. The building is ill-ventilated and ill-lit, the only windows being high in the walls; originally the building was designed to be used mainly after dark. After the Ortelgan conquest, the original arcades were bricked up and heavy iron bars were set into the floor at one end. This closed off the area in which Shardik, the bear once worshipped here as the incarnation of the power of God, was kept. In the far wall visitors can still see an iron gate leading into a deep rock pit excavated for the bear. At the height of Ortelgan rule, the hall became a grim temple filled with trophies captured in the wars, its walls lined with the skulls of Shardik's enemies.

The Lower City is a maze of streets and squares, the heart of a busy trading empire. From the Peacock Gate, the Street of Armourers leads down to the colonnaded Caravan Market, where all goods coming into the city are checked and weighed. On one side of the square stand the city warehouses and the brazen scales designed and built by the celebrated Fleitel, scales strong enough to lift and weigh a cart and two oxen at a time. A tavern called *The Green Grove* is a common eating place for traders and some of the market officials, and can be recommended. In summer travellers can dine in the courtyard with its singing fountain; in winter it is best to avail oneself of the charcoal brazier that burns inside.

One of the great wonders of Bekla was destroyed when the city was besieged by the inspired army that marched on it from Ortelga. The Tamarrik Gate, the north gate of the city, was Fleitel's masterpiece. It was carved with concentric spheres, spirals, faces peering through sycamore leaves, great ferns, lichens, the wind harp, and the silver drum that beat by itself when the sacred doves came down to be fed in the evening. No pictorial record of it has been preserved.

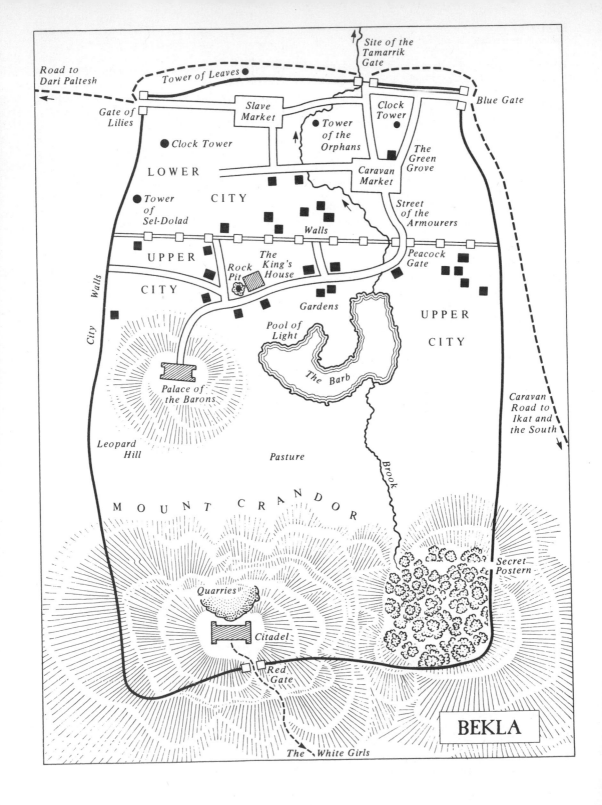

Road to
Dari Paltesh

Site of the
Tamarrik
Gate

Tower of Leaves •

Gate of
Lilies

Slave
Market

Clock
Tower

Blue Gate

LOWER

• Clock Tower

• Tower of the
Orphans

The
Green
Grove

CITY

Caravan
Market

• Tower
of
Sel-Dolad

Walls

Street
of the
Armourers

UPPER

Rock
Pit

The
King's
House

Peacock
Gate

CITY

Gardens

UPPER

City Walls

Pool of
Light

CITY

Palace of
the Barons

The Barb

Leopard
Hill

Pasture

Brook

Caravan
Road to
Ikat and
the South

M O U N T   C R A N D O R

Secret
Postern

Quarries

Citadel

Red
Gate

The   White Girls

BEKLA

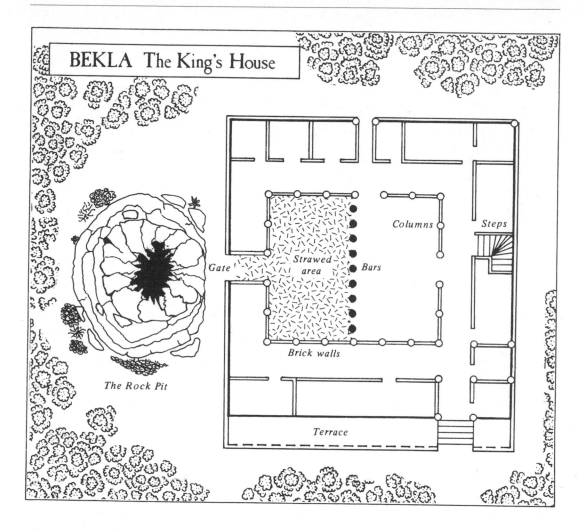

BEKLA The King's House

Columns

Steps

Gate

Strawed area

Bars

Brick walls

The Rock Pit

Terrace

The fall of Bekla to the Ortelgan army resulted in the looting and burning of much of the city. After the breaching of the Tamarrik Gate, the Lower City fell quickly to the invaders, but the almost impregnable citadel held out for a further four months. In an attempt to break the morale of its defenders, the Ortelgans hanged two children within sight of the citadel each day. Finally Santil-ke Erketlis, the Beklan commander, agreed to surrender and was allowed to march his army away unharmed.

It was during and after the fall of Bekla that the original cult of Shardik, as practised in Quiso, began to change. Kelderek, the hunter who had found the bear, now emerged as a priest-king, a figure which had not existed in earlier versions of the cult. Tuginda, the high priestess, saw this and other developments as evidence that the cult of the bear was being altered, if not perverted, for political ends and began to voice her opinions. As a result she was exiled to Quiso.

Bekla remained under Ortelgan rule for several years. During this period, the city became a military stronghold rather than the trading capital it had once been. The changes involved in Ortelgan rule included the abolition of the traditional cult of Cram (of which almost nothing is now known) and the desecration of the temple. The cult of Shardik was omnipresent and provided the basis for an effective and at times cruel dictatorship under the priest-king, known as "The Eye of God."

Only with the disappearance of Shardik himself from the city did any change come. During the annual fire festival—adopted from the older religion and adapted to the cult of Shardik—when fires were lit on rooftops throughout the city, an attempt was made to kill Shardik in the flames. The plot failed and much of the roof of the King's House was destroyed. During his trial, the man responsible for the plot succeeded in flinging a burning coal onto the straw in the bear's cage. In panic and fear, Shardik burst through the iron bars and fled into the town, causing great carnage before finally escaping to open country. Kelderek immediately followed his master and left the city forever. Soon after his departure a revolt broke out, but in the armistice that finally put an end to the wars, Bekla was once again restored to Ortelgan rule and today still retains its status as the capital.

Visitors will find that little is known of Bekla's origins. Architectural evidence suggests that the city may have been built—as legend claims—by craftsmen who erected the structures seen on Quiso. It also seems that in the distant past the city was ruled by Ortelgans before a revolt drove them back to their island in the Telthearna River.

The countryside around Bekla, known as the Beklan Plain, is flat and largely dry. Fierce dust storms sweep across it at intervals. The only farming is cattle-rearing and herding; the only settlements are scattered villages. Several roads lead from Bekla across the plain to the foothills of the GELT MOUNTAINS and to the provincial cities and capitals. Bekla is supplied with water by a conduit which runs from KABIN, and visitors can drink it safely.

(Richard Adams, *Shardik*, London, 1974)

BEKLAN EMPIRE, a vast country bordered by YELDA, Belshiba and Lapan to the south and by TERENKALT to the west. To the north and east, the empire finds a natural frontier in the Telthearna River and the forests of Tonilda. The capital, BEKLA, stands at the heart of the empire, in the midst of the Beklan Plain. In recent times the empire has entered into trading relations with ZAKALON to the east; iron, embroidery and other commodities are exported.

Long ago the whole of the Beklan Empire was ruled by people from the island of ORTELGA.

They were devotees of the cult of Shardik, a huge bear which was believed to be the incarnation of the power of God. Shardik himself remained on the island of QUISO, which attracted pilgrims from all over the empire. This period of Ortelgan rule came to an end when the high priestess fell in love with a slave trader who killed the sacred bear and fled with the priestess to safety. Following these events, a general revolt broke out and the Ortelgans were driven back to their island home in the north. But Bekla was still the capital of the empire and the centre of all military operations. Standing armies were maintained in the field to protect the borders and to ensure that taxes were collected. Initially, patrols went as far as the Telthearna and even to Ortelga, but this custom soon fell into disuse and the army was rarely seen beyond the GELT MOUNTAINS. This may explain the ease with which the Beklan army was defeated after the revival of the cult of Shardik in the north.

Throughout this period, slavery existed in the empire. Some historians, however, maintain that it had always existed and that it was considered normal for defeated soldiers to be enslaved. During the golden age of the Beklan Empire the demand for slaves increased greatly, as estates and trading concerns became bigger and more prosperous; eventually a class of professional slave dealers emerged. At first they were subject to State controls, but gradually they became the powerful and feared leaders of armed bands. Increasing numbers of escaped slaves became a menace to farmers and villagers and opposition to the slave trade grew stronger. Eventually, civil war broke out over the issue. It ended when Santil-ke Erketlis, a Yedashay estate owner, emerged as the most capable general of either side and defeated the strong armies of the southern slave traders before finally settling matters in Bekla itself.

Under the rule of the victorious Heldril or "old-fashioned" party, all slaves who could prove themselves citizens of the empire were freed; but foreign slaves continued to be held. To offset the cost of freeing the slaves, the traditional crafts of masonry and carving were once more encouraged. At the same time, measures were taken to improve the lot of the peasants and small farmers. It was at this time that the great reservoir was built at KABIN.

Some ten years after the conclusion of the civil wars, the empire was invaded by the Ortelgan followers of a bear they claimed to be the reincar-

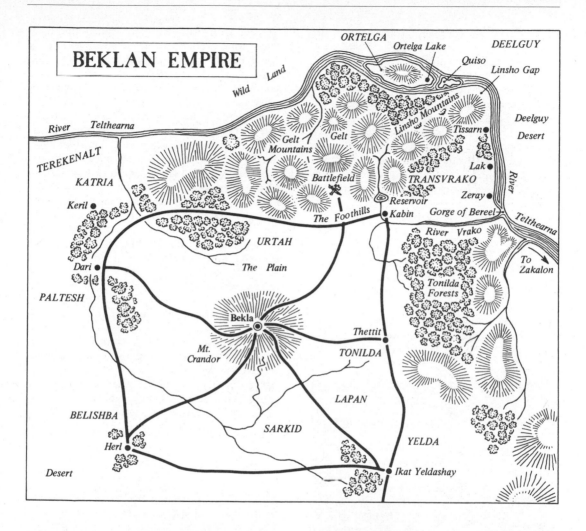

nation of Shardik. The northern provinces and Bekla itself soon fell, and the southern provinces seceded and joined in alliance against the new rulers of the empire. War against the southern provinces continued for years. The Priest-King of Bekla—Kelderek—found allies in those provincial lords who had been opposed to the Heldril party, and gave them important positions. Partly in order to placate them and partly in order to help finance the war, a highly taxed system of slavery was re-introduced; this move also had the effect of strengthening opposition to Beklan rule in the south. It also placed limits on the possible expansion of the cult of Shardik; the bear was seen merely as the god of the slave traders. The slave trade itself became a source of discontent to many people. Licensed traders frequently exceeded their allotted rights, kidnapping people from the settlements on the plain. Quotas were frequently disregarded when it came to slave-children, for whom there appears to have been a great market. Slavers specializing in children were known to mutilate many of their victims so that they could be sold as professional beggars. Other illegal practices included the castration of boys for a specialized market.

Some time later, Shardik escaped from his cage and fled from Bekla, followed by Kelderek, and a revolt broke out in the capital. At the same time the southern armies swept up through the empire, even taking KABIN and effectively isolating the Ortelgan army in the centre of the country.

In the face of the inevitable military defeat, the Ortelgans negotiated an armistice. Slavery was once more abolished and all remaining slaves were freed. The former provinces of Yelda, Lapan and Belshiba became independent countries and Ortelgan rule over Bekla was, under the terms of the armistice, permitted to continue.

Visitors will find that two main languages are spoken throughout the empire, although there are considerable similarities between them. Beklan is spoken in the north and in the centre; Yeshalday in the south. There are, in addition, a number of regional dialects and accents.

The currency of the Beklan Empire is the *meld*.

(Richard Adams, *Shardik,* London, 1974)

BELEGAER, see AMAN.

BELESBAT, an underwater city in the Bay of Biscay just off the coast of the French Vendée, between the towns of Jard-sur-mer and Saint-

Northern section of the underwater labyrinth in BELESBAT, Bay of Biscay.

Vincent. In ancient times, the neighbouring cities knew that Belesbat was rich and opulent, but little more, because no living soul ever left the city. Many curious travellers tried to enter Belesbat but never succeeded. One day, a fisherman sought refuge from a storm in Belesbat's port. To his amazement, he was given a royal reception; all the gates of the city were flung open and splendid balls and sumptuous banquets were given in his honour. Stung by curiosity, he pretended to be tired and asked to be left alone. Unguarded, he discovered a small door behind which he could hear music and joyous laughter. He opened it and found himself in a vast silent labyrinth. He followed long dark walls, crossed deserted courtyards and finally arrived in a large room filled up to the ceiling with severed human members, decomposing bodies and skeletons. He returned in haste, pretended to have left his nets on the beach and asked to be allowed to collect them. They let him go and he escaped to spread the terrible news all over the neighbourhood. The lords of Vendée formed a coalition, besieged Belesbat and killed all its inhabitants, after which a storm rose from the sea and the waves covered the city. Travellers are advised that it is dangerous to visit Belesbat because underwater spirits stand guard day and night over the treasures that it still contains.

(Claire Kenin, *La Mer mystérieuse,* Paris, 1923)

BELSHIBA, see BEKLAN EMPIRE.

BENGODI, a district in Berlinzone, or Land of the Basques (not to be confused with Biscay in the Western Pyrenees), famous for its mountain of grated Parmesan cheese. The mountain's summit is inhabited by people who spend their lives making macaroni and ravioli, which they cook in chicken broth and then send rolling down the mountain for the delight and nourishment of the natives below.

Not far from this landmark, travellers will find a river of wine (similar to that which flows through the Island of the BLESSED) which descends from the noted vineyards of Bengodi. The labourers tie up the vines with sausages, thus enhancing the fragrance of their wine.

Many curious stones can be found in Bengodi. Notable are the heliotrope, which makes whoever wears it invisible, and the local millstones which (if picked before they are holed) can be mounted on rings and are said to grant all the bearer's wishes.

(Giovanni Boccaccio, *Decameron*, Florence, 1858[?])

BEN KHATOUR'S VILLAGE, an Arab village somewhere in Africa. It lies hidden away on the banks of a small unexplored tributary of a large river (most likely the Congo) that empties into the Atlantic. Tarzan's daughter-in-law, the Princess of Cadrenet—daughter of General Armand Jacot—was kidnapped by the village sheik and spent her childhood here, behind the heavy palisade, in a palm-thatched beehive hut.

(Edgar Rice Burroughs, *The Son of Tarzan*, New York, 1915)

BENNET, an island in the Antarctic Polar Circle, latitude 82°50′ south, longitude 42°20′ west. It is low, rocky and about two kilometres round. Hardly any vegetation grows there, with the exception of a species of prickly pear. Its only peculiarity is a singular ledge of rock that projects into the sea, visible to travellers approaching the island from the north and bearing a strong resemblance to corded bales of cotton.

The island takes its name from the co-owner of the schooner *Jane Guy* of Liverpool whose captain discovered it on January 17, 1828.

(Edgar Allan Poe, *The Narrative of Arthur Gordon Pym of Nantucket*, New York, 1838)

BENSALEM, an island in the south Pacific, in the region of the Solomon Islands probably near UFFA ISLAND; several small offshore islands also come under its jurisdiction. Bensalem was thought to be roughly 5,600 miles in circumference; however, it is almost certainly no larger than two-thirds the size of Ireland.

Although long isolated from the world, Bensalem was well known in ancient times, when it was frequently visited by ships from Tyre, Carthage, China and ATLANTIS. In the second millennium BC the island State was itself a powerful trading nation. With the decline in the art of navigation that followed the destruction of Atlantis, Bensalem became increasingly isolated. Its isolation became complete in about 300 BC, when King Solamona of Bensalem decided that the na-

tion was rich and fertile enough to be self-sufficient. Strict laws concerning the admission of foreigners were established and communication with the outside world was forbidden, unless absolutely necessary for the good of the nation. Travel to foreign countries was banned in order to preserve Bensalem's purity. Since then, the island has had little direct contact with the outside world, as few ships have come to its shores. The powerful merchant fleet is now used for fishing, for the transport of goods from town to town and for maintaining contact with the offshore islands. The memory of King Solamona is greatly treasured by the people of Bensalem.

Bensalem was converted to Christianity by a miracle that took place *circa* 50 AD. The people of Renfusa, a port on the east coast, saw a great pillar of light, crowned with a cross, approaching the island. Boats were sent out to investigate, but were miraculously stopped short. Only one of the city's sages was able to approach it, after falling to his knees and praying. As he came closer, the column of light vanished, leaving a cedar ark floating in the water, containing the Old and New Testaments and a letter from St. Bartholomew which explained that he had been commanded by God to commit the ark to the sea and that it would bring salvation to the people of the land where it was washed ashore. Miraculously, Hebrews, Persians and Indians could all read the Gospel and the letter as easily as if they had been written in their own language.

Since that time, Bensalem has been Christian, although there are still groups of Jews whose views are perfectly tolerated. The Jews of Bensalem accept the doctrine of the virgin birth and believe that Christ was more than human, referring to him as the Milky Way, or Eliah. By tradition, they believe that the people of Bensalem are descended from Abraham's son Nachoran and that their laws were handed down to them from Moses in a secret cabbala. When the Messiah comes to rule in Jerusalem, the King of Bensalem will sit at his feet. It should also be noted that there are strong Hebraic elements in the Christian beliefs of Bensalem. The people show a particularly strong veneration for certain biblical characters, such as Adam and Noah, who peopled the world, and Abraham, father of the faithful.

Today, Bensalem still maintains its isolationist policy and continues to send its mission ships around the world. It is still a monarchy, as the

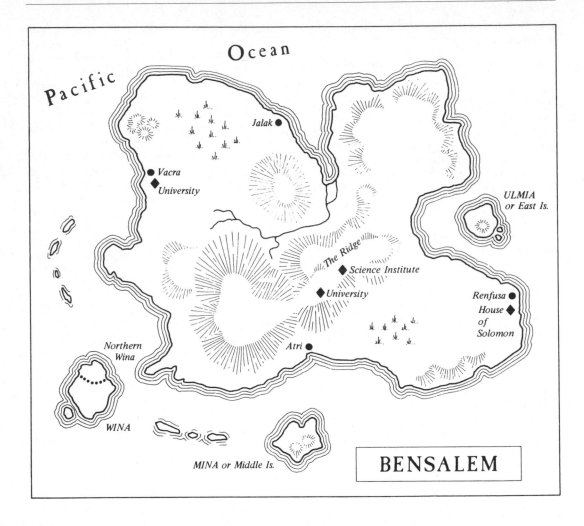

The map shows:

Pacific Ocean

Jalak

Vacra
University

ULMIA
or East Is.

The Ridge

Science Institute

University

Renfusa

House
of
Solomon

Northern
Wina

Atri

WINA

MINA or Middle Is.

BENSALEM

people have great respect for their king or *Radar* and for an institution that is coeval with their history, but the monarch's role is now mostly symbolic. As there are no foreign relations, government is largely a matter of administration carried out by a series of boards and councils. Boards consist of three appointed members responsible for the administration of thirty-nine towns and ten rural districts, as well as for the development of arts, sciences and industries. Each board works in conjunction with a council, which anyone may attend. Overall administration lies with the central board and council. The *Radar*'s only real political function is to appoint the central board, advised by the central council. Any differences of opinion that

arise at any level are submitted to the superior board and council for adjudication.

The natural social unit in Bensalem is the family, ruled by the father, or *tirsan*. Any man who lives to see thirty of his descendants reach the age of three is honoured by the State-financed Feast of the Family, during which he arranges family affairs and appoints one of his sons to live with him; this son is known as the "Son of the Vine," and serves as his father's ensign. At a special ceremony held after divine service, the father is presented with the King's Charter, which contains a gift of revenue and many privileges and exemptions. He is then presented with a cluster of grapes made of gold, one for each descendant of the family. The grapes are enamelled—greenish yellow with a crescent on the top if the female descendants outnumber the male, purple with a sun on the top if the male offspring are the more numerous. Whenever the father appears in public, the Son of the Vine goes before him, bearing the cluster of enamelled grapes. The father of a large family is so honoured that the king himself is said to be in debt to him. The family unit is considered the only suitable environment for the bringing up of children, and the chief defence against sexual promiscuity.

The people of Bensalem are noted for their chastity. There are no prostitutes or courtesans and homosexuality is unknown. Their chastity and self-respect are summed up by two sayings: "Whosoever is unchaste cannot reverence himself" and "The reverence of a man's self is, next to religion, the chiefest bridle of all vices." In marriage, monogamy is strictly observed. Parental consent to a marriage is not a formal requirement, but if it is not obtained, the children of the marriage inherit only one-third of their parents' inheritance. A full month's interval between first meeting and engagement or marriage is compulsory. In order to detect possible physical defects in the couple, friends of the same sex are allowed to watch them bathe naked. This takes place in watering places called Adam and Eve's Pools outside the towns.

The most important institution on Bensalem is the House of Solomon, founded by Solamona and dedicated to the study of the works and creatures of God. The house is named after the Hebrew King and preserves in its library his *Natural History* (referred to in I Kings 4:33) which was long thought to have been lost.

According to Solamona: "The end of the foundation is the knowledge of causes and secret motions of things; and the enlarging of the bounds of human empire to the effecting of all things possible." The House's scientific research has led to the development of submarines and flying machines. Streams, cataracts and windmills are used to provide energy. Caves deep beneath the buildings are used for the production and preservation of metals, while high towers have been built for astronomical and meteorological observations and experiments. Weather conditions can be created experimentally in great halls built for that purpose. "Perspective" houses are devoted to experiments in optical science and to the production of telescopes, microscopes and other optical devices. Acoustic experiments are carried out in the "Sound" houses, which also manufacture musical instruments like the violin-piano and devices to reproduce natural sounds. Research carried out here has made it possible to transmit sound over many *karans* (one *karan* equals one and a half miles) via a system of tubes and pipes, a system which probably inspired a Scotsman, Alexander Graham Bell, in his invention in 1876. In the "Engine" houses, all manner of machines, weapons and fireworks are manufactured, while the "Perfume" houses specialize in the analysis and synthesis of scents. Houses of the deceit of the senses are used for the representation of illusions—similar indeed to the devices found on VILLINGS ISLAND and in KARPATHENBURG. As lying and imposture are loathsome to the people of Bensalem and are also forbidden by law, these illusions are not used to give a false picture of natural objects.

In the biological sciences, the House of Solomon has found methods of crossing animal and plant species and of creating new ones—some plants are even grown now without the use of seeds. Medical research is also thoroughly encouraged. Various healthgiving drinks and medicines are prepared and distributed through a countrywide system of dispensaries. Pools of mineral water, including one known as the "Water of Paradise," are used medically to prolong life and to cure many ailments. The House of Solomon also carries out work on nutrition and has produced foods for specific purposes, such as nourishing people for long periods or strengthening the body to help withstand long fasts. Medical advances have made it possible to eradicate all bacterial diseases. Cancer has been defeated by the discovery of a crab immune to the disease. A serum developed from the crab is used in cancer inoculations given in adolescence. News of this discovery was communicated anonymously to scientific institutes around the world, but was ignored because no source was given for the research. Medical science has led to a great increase in life expectancy; most people now live to be over eighty and some even reach the age of a hundred and ten.

The Fellows or Brethren of the House of Solomon are the only people allowed to leave Bensalem. Every twelve years, six of them set out in two ships to discover the state and condition of foreign countries and to bring back news of scientific and other discoveries. These are two of Bensalem's major imports and those who bring them are known as "Merchants of Light." During their travels, they go under assumed names and nationalities to preserve the secrecy surrounding the existence of their homeland.

The Merchants of Light are known by the following titles: "Depradators," who collect experiments; "Mystery Men," who specialize in the mechanical arts and liberal sciences; "Pioneers," who carry out new experiments; "Compilers," who classify the results of experiments; "Dowry Men" or "Benefactors," who specialize in finding practical applications for new knowledge; "Lamps," who analyze the results of existing experiments and devise ways of improving them; "Inoculators," who carry out those approved experiments; and, finally, "Interpreters of Nature," who translate these discoveries into broader observations, axioms and aphorisms for the instruction of the people.

As well as having its mission ships, Bensalem uses radio to learn what is happening in the outside world. News is printed simultaneously in all towns by a tele-photographic process and is distributed in slim newspapers, often only one sheet. There is no advertising and no editorials.

The scientific research that has made possible the present-day development of Bensalem is carried out in the various institutes from the original House of Solomon. The Science Institute, the University, and the educational establishments, occupy The Ridge, a natural rise behind the seaport of Renfusa. The Renfusa Institute specializes in the inorganic sciences, whereas the Vacra Institute concentrates on the biological sciences. Vacra, a major town on the west coast, also has a zoological park, in which the social organization of animals is studied. It is here that the very first "suturization" experiments (see below) were carried out on monkeys. Nowadays, it is possible to train "suturized" monkeys to sweep up leaves and carry out simple gardening tasks, and much of the maintenance of the parks is now carried out by monkeys. The Jalak Institute specializes in the study of light, while the Atri Institute works on sound.

The people themselves have changed over the past centuries. Their brains and their crania have been enlarged through the process known as "suturization," which artificially delays the process of the occlusion of the brain in childhood and has resulted in increased mental powers, better memory and an improved judgement. The people of Bensalem can, for example, acquire knowledge of any language within a matter of months. The change also led to an increase in psychic sensibility and to more frequent use of telepathy. For reasons which remain obscure, the treatment has also made the people taller: the average height of a man is now six feet; women are, on average, two inches shorter. The effects are not hereditary and have to be induced in every new generation. The introduction of "suturization" also led to the events known as the Separation. Those people who refused to allow their children to undergo the treatment for fear of possible side effects gradually developed into a disinherited class (known colloquially as "small heads"), which was rapidly outstripped in learning and intelligence by the others. The resentment of the "small heads" eventually led to violence and to the outbreak of civil war. In the 1830's an agreement was reached whereby the "small heads" left Bensalem and settled on the various offshore islands, forming independent states of lesser importance.

Should the traveller wish to visit the offshore islands, it is important to note that they have developed in different directions. Their governments are very unstable and they are constantly at war with one another. East Island, for instance, is now known as the Union of Logical Material Idealists, or Ulmia, named after the group that led a successful revolution there. It is their belief that human societies are simply the product of economic factors; their emblem is a pitchfork crossed with a saw and the motto "Things rule men." Initially, Ulmia was a totally egalitarian society which believed that misery for all was preferable to comfort for some. Shortly after the revolution, famine and poverty decimated the population and the leaders now tend to be less dogmatic about their own traditional principles.

Mina, or Middle Island, is a totally militarized society led by a self-appointed dictator. No one is allowed to remain on his own or to join groups of more than five people. All obey their superiors, carry arms—stone clubs and slingshots—and wear identical masks. The sole aim of the nation is to grasp whatever it can. The propaganda is incessant and stresses the supremacy of the State with slogans like "Mina is all, we are nothing" and "Whatever our government says is true, even when it is false." The stress is on ruthlessness; the normal greeting is "Ruthless sir," accompanied by a clutching gesture. The island's emblem is a beehive with a circle of bees and the motto "Sting and Die."

Wina, on the other hand, is a totally haphazard society. The majority of the people work in poverty to support a small leisure class which they consider superior. The towns are dominated by advertising; the seacoast has been ruined by unplanned developments and there is litter everywhere. Road accidents are frequent. Alcohol and drugs are widely used. The people are easy-going, but lack foresight and are extremely superstitious. Nine, for instance, is regarded as an unlucky number, whereas wearing green sprigs on one's coat and "touching green" will ward off ill-fortune. The working day lasts nine hours... yet there are still chronic shortages of everything and unemployment is high. The people of Northern Wina are a dour, thrifty race, accustomed to living in a desert environment. Many of them have moved south and now occupy important positions in Wina.

On Bensalem itself, in contrast, the social system has developed into a society free of all class distinctions. The total population is roughly two million. Birth control has made it unlikely that the number will rise unreasonably. Most couples marry at between twenty and twenty-five and rarely have more than two or three children.

The economic and social systems of Bensalem are based on the availability of unlimited supplies of energy. Until recently, this was provided by hydroelectric power generated from dams built across the mouths of fjords on the north and south coasts, but this has been superseded by sub-atomic power, generated by splitting the atoms of a new element known as "Bensalium." The use of electricity has helped the process of automation, which is held to be the key to liberation and progress. The highly automated factories employ few workers, mostly to regulate the distribution of raw materials and finished products. All factories are clean, pollution-free and almost silent, as all moving parts and joints are cushioned with an elastic material.

Land is publicly owned and its use is strictly controlled. All commodities can now be supplied free of charge and money has disappeared. There is no accumulation for private gain. Automation has meant that the working week—referred to as "Duties"—has been reduced to barely nine hours. The remainder of the time—"Secondaries"—is devoted to gardening, amateur scientific research, literary and artistic pastimes, and so on. "Duties" are organized and allocated by local boards; "Secondaries" are chosen by the individuals. People do not remain in their jobs for life—they frequently change their occupations subject to practicability and with the approval of the appropriate board. Bensalem is so rich in raw materials that the only mineral import, brought back by the mission ships, is copper for the electrical transmission lines. All imports are paid for in gold recovered from seawater by electrolysis. The general principle of the economy is that supply must and shall meet demand. There is no competitive retail trade.

All towns in Bensalem are situated on the coast for health reasons. The coastal location also facilitates communication and offers better natural amenities. The average population of a town is forty thousand, although the capital, Renfusa, has a population of sixty thousand and Vacra fifty thousand. The population density is not a matter of choice; this has proved to be the optimum figure for industrial and social purposes. The towns are linked by a coastal highway and a frequent service of fast boats. The villages, which are usually less than twenty miles inland, are linked to the towns by excellent roads. Transport is by three-wheeled electric cars which move at fifteen miles per hour but which can travel up to one hundred miles on a single charging of their light-weight accumulator batteries. Horse transport is still used. For marine transport, boats the size of river barges are employed. They have short airplane wings, a propeller mounted at the bow and two helicopter rotors. The under-surface appears to move backwards on its "caterpillar tracks" or water banks, slotted tracks which allow it to skim the surface of the water. The boats are built of an aluminum alloy and are capable of moving at speeds of up to a hundred and fifty miles per hour. Yachts are sailed for sport and pleasure.

The towns of Bensalem are beautiful and peaceful. All the roads are treelined and quiet. Walking through them is rather like walking through an extensive park. Houses are only one storey high and, like Roman villas, are built around central courtyards. A roof of flexible glass can be rolled back in warm weather. All houses are centrally heated; rubbish and sewage are incinerated electrically. For purposes of cleaning, powerful air-blasts can be blown across the floor from vents in the walls. Each house is connected to the underground postal–tube system, somewhat similar to that connecting sorting offices in London. All domestic articles and utensils, from cups to chairs, have a grace and simplicity of line recalling early Chinese art. In addition to their town houses, most families have simple log cabins in the countryside, where all roads are surfaced in dark green to make them as unobtrusive as possible.

One of the attractions of the towns of Bensalem is the number of animals that roam the streets at liberty. Deer, gazelles, kangaroos, koalas, monkeys and squirrels all live freely in the towns and are fed from the trough and food bowls provided. The animals are all semi-tame and have been trained not to damage plants. The people of Bensalem believe that man has certain duties towards animals, and hunting, shooting and all unnecessary killing of animals is unknown. Cats are not kept on Bensalem, as no way has been found of stopping them from eating birds. Animals are still used in medical laboratories and the majority of the people continue to eat meat. In Bensalem, food and drink are more nourishing than in Europe. Drinks include several kinds of wine, a type of ale and apple cider.

The countryside has been transformed by applied science. There are no individual farms; instead, large areas are controlled by directors with teams of assistants. All weeds have been eliminated and all boundaries and hedges removed. Fruit and vegetables are often cultivated under large transparent greenhouses built of a substance similar to cellophane and electrically heated by underground wires. Grain plants have been modified to produce strains with very heavy heads and short, sturdy stalks. As the yield is so high, only the best land is cultivated, the majority being reserved for leisure activities.

Fish are intensively farmed in the two great fjords and the food content of the water has been heightened by increasing the plankton through chemical fertilization. Fish are caught by specialized vessels with tanks that open up in the bottom. The fish are attracted to the open tanks by scattered food and the tanks are then closed with sliding panels. This is probably the simplest and most effective method of fishing ever developed. The fishing industry makes an important contribution to the Bensalem diet and yet only employs five hundred men.

Scientific research has not led to any decline in the religious faith of Bensalem. On the contrary, it is said that nature is the language of God and that science is the interpreter of nature. Religious doctrine has been examined rationally and untenable doctrines, like the biblical story of Creation, have been abandoned. There is no strict dogma and the religion of the island is now a harmonious union of philosophy, science and spiritual beliefs. The combination has made the people of Bensalem very planet-conscious, aware, that is, of their place in the universe and able to take a pride in the human race and its achievements. The inscription found in their churches reads simply "Love, truth, energy." The churches are decorated with pictures of the world's religious teachers, not as a sign of acceptance of a multiplicity of faiths, but as a symbol of the achievements of the human personality. There is no professional clergy; preachers are volunteers selected by an appropriate board. Services are punctuated by periods of silence during which telepathic communication produces a real feeling of total spiritual communion.

The religious doctrines of the past are studied by the Institute of Selection, usually known as "The Sieve," because of its emblem. The Institute is on The Ridge behind Renfusa and bears inscriptions of two quotations: "The beginning of wisdom is to unlearn that which is nought" (Antisthenes) and "Let us not make random judgements on the greatest of things" (Heraclitus). The work of the Institute is to systematically examine and classify the knowledge inherited from the past. This inheritance is classified by a tribunal of ten sages, using the following classifications: truths, possible truths, ideas, legends and myths with poetic value, facts relating to the physical, social and psychical sciences, false or meaningless statements. These, with the exception of the last category, are formulated in basic propositions and published in a series of volumes known as *The Gist*. This is constantly revised to prevent its propositions becoming dogma.

Education begins at seven and is divided into three stages. Initially, reading and other basic skills are taught. Pupils then go on to study the natural sciences and metaphysics. Their education is completed by the study of personal conduct and social organization. The latter is subdivided into dramatic history (the topics normally taught as history in other countries) and the science of human experience. This includes all aspects of human experience and knowledge, from economics and politics to climatology and the influence of religion and philosophy. At all stages, the emphasis is on learning to learn. Once the tools of learning have been grasped, the teacher serves as a guide rather than as a pedagogue.

The language of Bensalem is of unknown origin. It sounds vaguely like Rumanian, but there is no similarity in vocabulary. The old script has some resemblance to Amharic, but again there is no etymological connection. It contains more than thirty words for describing various kinds of odours, a fact which is connected with developments in the science of smell and in the practice of manufacturing and blending scents. The people of Bensalem use a particular gesture when they wish to give thanks to God: the right hand is firmly raised and then gently lowered to the mouth.

The men dress in clothes which are vaguely Elizabethan: a shirt with a collar turned down over the coat, knee breeches and loosely cut calf-length coats. No hats are worn except by the Masters of the House of Solomon, who are also distinguished by their black robes—with a white linen undergarment, fastened with a white belt—their peach-coloured shoes, and gloves studded with jewels. In summer, the women wear a garment similar to a sari. In colder weather, hooded capes and coats are worn. Fabrics used to be of a fine cloth woven from goats' hair, but are now probably all synthetic. The men do not shave.

Every year a great festival is held in the Valley of Mironal, near the centre of the island. The valley lies between wooded hills, backed by high mountains. A river flows through it, leaving the valley via a narrow gorge dominated by the ancient castle of the *Radars*. The level floor of the valley is covered with stadiums, race courses and open-air theatres, wooden dining halls and other buildings. The festival, attended each year by half the population, lasts a whole week and includes sports, games, drama competitions and concerts. Scientific exhibitions and agricultural shows combine with musical performances and poetry readings. Chess matches are a very popular attraction. The prizes given to winners are symbolic: a commemorative plaque and a flower from the *Radar*'s garden preserved by chemical means and set on a stalk of gold. Different types of flowers are awarded for each type of event.

Travellers are advised that access to Bensalem is strictly controlled. Under the code laid down by King Solamona, only visitors who have not unlawfully shed blood within a specified period are al-lowed to enter the country. Others who chance to reach the island's shores will be given supplies and assistance but will not be permitted to land.

Travellers with visas are well received and are given generous hospitality at State expense. They are under no compulsion to stay and may leave freely. All visitors undergo a three-day quarantine and are then housed in Strangers' House, a spacious building built of blue brick, with handsome windows of glass or oiled cambric. The Governor of Strangers' House is a priest, his rank being indicated by a white turban with a small red cross on the top. Neither he nor any other official will accept payment for his services. Visitors may not travel more than one and a half miles from the capital without special permission.

(Francis Bacon, *New Atlantis*, London, 1627; Viscount Herbert Louis Samuel, *An Unknown Land*, London, 1942)

BENWICK, see BANOIC.

BERILA, see ENLAD.

BINGFIELD'S ISLAND, somewhere in the East Indies. The island is large and it takes many days to cross it from east to west. The western shore is covered in dense forest, with the trees coming down almost to the water's edge. Inland, the broad river valley is more open. To the east the island becomes a long, narrow neck of land and because of this curious geography, early visitors were led to believe they were on a promontory. The hills gradually descend to the shore where a narrow passage leads through the coastal cliffs. The stone structures found in this area were set up by the cannibals from Barka who occasionally visit the island to perform their hideous ceremonies. Otherwise, the island is uninhabited.

The most remarkable thing about Bingfield's Island is its fauna, which includes the curious dog-bird as well as more normal carnivores and wild cattle. The dog-bird is a great flightless bird covered in long shaggy hair. The head is like that of a greyhound and the tail like that of a pig. It has long legs ending in claws that resemble those of a panther. Although the dog-bird lays eggs, it suckles its young. It is a ferocious and quite fearless creature. It will attack anything, and is capable of killing the great cats of the island, leaping onto their backs and tearing at the flesh with teeth and claws. The dog-bird can be tamed and makes an excellent hunting animal.

Bingfield's Island is also the home of a strange amphibian found in its swampy areas. This creature is larger than an elephant, with a head halfway between that of an ox and that of a horse. The ears are short and close to the head; the neck is as thick and strong as that of a bull.

The island is named after William Bingfield, an Englishman whose boat drifted here after a shipwreck. With two companions, he lived in a small cave for two full years. On one occasion Bingfield saw a party of cannibals come on shore and prepare to kill and eat their victims, and recognized a white woman among them as his fiancée, Sally Morton, from whom he had been separated in England. He succeeded in rescuing her, with the aid of the dog-birds he had trained for hunting. However, Bingfield was then forced to kill one of his companions and badly injure the other when they attempted to rape the unfortunate Sally.

(William Bingfield[?], *The Travels and Adventures of William Bingfield, Esq.; Containing, as Surprizing a Fluctuation of Circumstances, both by Sea and Land, as ever befell one Man. With An accurate Account of the Shape, Nature and Properties of that most furious, and amazing Animal, the Dog-Bird*, London, 1753)

BIRDS, ISLAND OF, a desolate island off the east coast of Canada, the home of Amenachem the Ugly, who has forbidden anyone to set foot on it. Those who do become dreadfully unhappy and are haunted by the island's landscape: trees, flowers and stones the colour of sand.

(Michel Tremblay, *Contes pour buveurs attardés*, Montreal, 1966)

BIRDS, ISLE OF, in the Caribbean, so small it takes only six hours to walk right around it. The many species of birds found here give the island its name, but the Isle of Birds is mainly remarkable for the enormous serpents that inhabit it.

In the eighteenth century, the Comte d'Uffai was shipwrecked here. He met a beautiful woman who had been sent to the island in punishment for disobeying her father's orders, and with her established a pleasant society of primitive innocence, of which very little is known. Their huts can still be seen standing where d'Uffai built them and are available to couples in search of bucolic bliss.

(Eléazar de Mauvillon, *Le Soldat Parvenu Ou Mémoires Et Aventures De Mr. De Verval Dit Bellerose. Par Mr. De M****, Dresden, 1753)

BIRDS, LAND OF, see WAQ ARCHIPELAGO.

BISM, also known as the **REALLY DEEP WORLD**. Bism is deep below the surface of the earth and has rarely been visited. It can be reached via certain chasms which at times open up and provide access to Bism's great River of Fire, a dazzling, brilliant stream of blue, red and green. Even the gnomes who live in Bism cannot survive in this river; the only creatures who can—and who thrive in it—are the salamanders, whose habits are not known in any detail. The salamanders resemble small dragons and are apparently renowned for their eloquent and witty use of language.

Travellers will find the gnomes of Bism friendly, welcoming creatures, who have difficulty in imagining how any being can actually choose to live in the world above ground, a prospect they find both frightening and distasteful. They are all very unlike each other in appearance, ranging from one to six feet in height and possessing a wide variety of facial traits. Some are bearded, others smooth-faced; some have horns in the centre of their foreheads, others have noses like small trunks. All, however, have large, soft feet with either ten or twelve toes.

Gold, silver and precious stones grow in Bism like flowers. The rubies are edible and the diamonds can be squeezed for their juice. According to the gnomes, the so-called mines of the rest of the earth produce only dead gems and minerals.

The land above Bism—still beneath the earth—was once known as the Underland, and is now totally destroyed. The Underland (the gnomes of Bism call it the Shallow Lands) was the realm of the witch who killed the wife of Prince Caspian of NARNIA and spirited away his son Rilian. At the end of a long quest, undertaken by two human children and a Marsh-wiggle at the demand of Aslan, creator of Narnia, the witch's ten-year reign came to an end. This was a great relief to the gnomes who, under her rule, had been forced to dig tunnels to be used in an invasion of the Overworld, thus having to work much too close to the surface for their comfort.

The caves that were excavated here in order to rescue the witch's prisoners are still visible and are a favourite excursion place for Narnians on hot summer days.

(C.S. Lewis, *The Silver Chair*, London, 1953)

BLACK CHAPEL, standing between Salisbury Plain and the sea. After the catastrophic battle on the plain during which King Arthur of CAMELOT was mortally wounded, he was carried to the Black Chapel by Lucan the butler and Sir Girflet. It is said that Arthur accidently killed his butler by embracing him too hard and visitors can see Lucan lying in one of the two tombs in the chapel. The second tomb is said by some chroniclers to be the resting-place of King Arthur himself.

According to eyewitnesses, the dying Arthur was carried off across the sea in a barge holding four black-hooded ladies, and his body was later brought back to the chapel for burial. Others say that he was taken to AVALON and from there borne away in a ship, never to be seen again. The rich tomb in the Black Chapel bears the inscription "Here lies King Arthur who through his valour conquered twelve kingdoms." The inscription on Lucan's tomb simply records the manner of his death.

(Anonymous, *La Mort le Roi Artu*, 13th cen. AD)

BLACK HILL COVE, a small cove and hamlet on the coast of Devon, England, near which stands the *Admiral Benbow Inn*, an isolated hostelry on the Bristol road. Bed and breakfast can be had at the inn.

Visitors should know that it was in this inn that the papers and map giving directions to TREASURE ISLAND first came to light. They were found among the belongings of a seaman known as Bill Bones, who had been with the notorious Captain Flint when he buried his treasure on that island. For some weeks Bones lived at the inn, obviously in fear that someone from his past would find him and kill him in order to get the map. When he finally died of apoplexy, Jim Hawkins, the landlady's son, found the papers and took them to Squire Trelawney, who fitted out a ship to search for the hidden treasure.

Should visitors happen to hear the tap-tap of a wooden stick, they are advised to ignore it, as its owner has long since departed from this world.

(Robert Louis Stevenson, *Treasure Island*, London, 1883)

BLACK HOUSE, a remote ruined mansion in a dense forest. Little of the roof remains and most of the internal walls have crumbled long ago. The floor is lost under a thick carpet of moss and the lower walls are invisible behind their fringe of ferns. The House gives off an air of deadly darkness which has more to do with decay than with night; even by daylight it appears sombre and gloomy. The only creatures to come near the ruin are the animals of the forest—badgers, stoats, squirrels and foxes.

The Black House was chosen as the site for a grotesque celebration by certain people who had met the famous Titus Groan in the days when he wandered the countryside after leaving GORMENGHAST. The leader of the party was one of his ex-mistresses who, like most people, did not believe his claim that he was a lord in his own right. Under her direction, a series of people masqueraded as the figures Titus had described from his past in a cruel, mocking pageant which ended in violence and murder.

(Mervyn Peake, *Titus Alone*, London, 1959)

BLACK JUNGLE, on the island of Raymangal, in the delta of the Ganges, so called because of the closely knit vegetation that shuts off all light and because of the dark horrors that take place deep in its heart. Among the gloomy trees rises the immense sanctuary of the Thugs, the stranglers who worship the goddess Kali. The building is a gigantic pagoda built in granite, some sixty feet high and forty feet wide, surrounded by stupendous columns sculpted with panache. The dome of the pagoda ends in an erect serpent with a woman's head. The corners of the sanctuary show the goddess Trimurti, with three heads, one body and three legs. Inside, visitors will see a statue of Kali herself, and a small white basin full of goldfish by means of which the goddess is said to communicate with the faithful.

Beneath the building runs a maze of low galleries; in these horrible cold, dark, humid places live multicoloured scorpions, poisonous centipedes, furry spiders and several species of cobra.

At just a short distance from the sanctuary is a banyan tree through which an underground passage can be entered; the passage is lined with sharp spears and can be very dangerous for those unfamiliar with the straight and narrow path. It leads into a large cavern of pink granite supported by twenty-four columns with elephant heads; it is here that the Thugs sacrifice virgins to Kali.

(Emilio Salgari, *I misteri della Jungla Nera*, Milan, 1895)

BLACKLAND, the ruins of a city in the middle of the Sahara, longitude 1°40′ east and latitude 15°50′ north, south of the Gao-gao oasis, built by a group of adventurers; their history, rich in tears and blood, lasted barely ten years from 1895 to 1905.

The chief founder of Blackland was a certain William Ferney, better known as Harry Killer, an English kidnapper and murderer who decided to use the fruits of his sinful trade to found a city of crime. It was built on the banks of the Tarfasasset (now called Red River), a river which had run dry until Harry Killer again filled it with water. The city measured exactly two hundred metres from north-east to south-west and six hundred metres from north-west to south-east. The surface was divided into three unequal sections.

The first section of the city, nearest to the river, on the flat land on the right bank, was inhabited by the Merry Fellows, the aristocracy of Blackland and the original companions of Harry Killer. These numbered sixty-six and the figure was never allowed to vary.

The functions of the Merry Fellows were several. Organized in military fashion, with a colonel, five captains, ten lieutenants and fifty sergeants, the Merry Fellows constituted Blackland's army. They made war on the miserable villages that surrounded them, capturing their inhabitants and slaughtering those they did not need. The Merry Fellows were also the city's police and were in charge of the hordes of slaves that were taken to work in the fields. Above all, the Merry Fellows formed the Chief's Guard, carrying out his orders with blind obedience.

The second section, some thirty-one and a half hectares, was occupied by the slaves: 4,196 men and 1,582 women. Their life was not easy. Every morning the four gates in the wall that surrounded their portion of hell would open, and

under the surveillance of armed Merry Fellows they would be taken to their jobs. Many would die from the cruelty of their masters.

The third section, the farthest from the centre of Blackland, consisted only of a semicircular space sixteen hundred metres long and fifty metres wide. This section was inhabited by the so-called Civil Body, the white population who had not been able to enter the first section. Here they waited for a vacancy among the Merry Fellows—never very long in view of the brutal habits of the aristocracy. The Civil Body was considered a sort of purgatory and the Merry Fellows' community a sort of paradise.

These three sections on the right bank of the river were not the whole of Blackland. On the left bank, where the ground rose abruptly, the walls surrounding the city formed a rectangle two hundred metres long and three hundred metres wide. This second area was divided into two by a high wall.

The first half, on the north-east slope, contained the Fortress' Garden, a public park which communicated through its northern end, via the Garden's Bridge, with the Merry Fellows' and Civil Body's sections across the river. The second half, on the top of the slope, contained the so-called vital organs of the city. In the northern corner rose the Palace, the dwelling-place of Harry Killer.

Next to the palace lay two barracks, one lodging the black slaves who constituted the body of servants and the Black Guard, the other for forty white men in charge of the flying engines of Blackland. These flying engines could travel up to five thousand kilometres at four hundred kilometres an hour, thereby giving Blackland's army a ubiquity that its enemies lacked.

Perhaps Blackland's blackest building was the Factory. Rising on the bank across from the Palace, the Factory was an independent entity with a body and a soul of its own, in which the flying engines and many other remarkable inventions were created. The Factory's soul was its director; the Factory's body was one hundred workers of different nationalities, mainly French and English. These unfortunate men and women had been lured to Blackland by very high salaries. In exchange for the money, they were to consider themselves as recluses; they were never allowed to leave the Factory, or to write abroad or receive letters from home. Their passage to Blackland was highly devious. A ship took them from their homeland to one of the Bissagos Islands, near the coast of Portuguese Guinea. Here they were blindfolded and flown to the Esplanade adjoining the Factory. From there onwards, they were prisoners. If they decided to leave, they were promised a safe trip home; in fact they were taken into the desert and slaughtered, their salaries returning to the vaults of Blackland's treasures. Because of all these precautions, Blackland remained unknown for a great many years.

The Factory's director was a French scientist whose genius was close to madness—Marcel Camaret. Camaret had been laughed out of scientific circles by his colleagues after inventing a machine to produce rain. Harry Killer heard about the invention, enlisted his services and used his talents to transform the arid Sahara into a garden. The flying engines, propelled by liquid air, were among his many inventions.

Unfortunately for science—but fortunately for humanity—Blackland was destroyed in 1905. Harry Killer captured the members of the Barsac Mission sent over by the French parliament to investigate whether the natives should be given the right to vote. But when the captured Frenchmen explained to Camaret his master's wicked acts, the scientist lost the little reason he possessed and destroyed all his creations and with them the city. A French rescue team saved the members of the Barsac Mission and arrested the surviving adventurers. Travellers today can only see a few ruins struggling against the sands of the Sahara.

(Jules Verne, *L'Etonnante Aventure de la Mission Barsac*, Paris, 1919)

BLACKSTAFF, a country between PAFLAGONIA and CRIM TARTARY, ruled by the Fairy Blackstaff, whose name derives from her black wand. Fairy Blackstaff is known to visit all important christenings throughout the world, bestowing upon each child the gift of a ring or a rose. Those who receive the ring make happy marriages and lead sober, established lives. Those who receive the rose grow up instead to be consumed by the flames of passion, and end their lives in desperate and ardent love affairs.

(M.A. Titmarsh [William Makepeace Thackeray], "The Rose and the Ring," in *Christmas Books*, London, 1857)

BLANK, a castle of uncertain location. Sir Launcelot, one of the greatest knights of the round table of CAMELOT, was brought here by Sir Bliant (brother of Slivant, lord of the castle), who had found him wandering and raving in the surrounding forests. Launcelot had been driven mad by anger and grief after being tricked into lying with Elaine of ESCALOT and therefore accused of faithlessness by Guinevere, wife of King Arthur and Launcelot's true love. For two years he roamed the forests in a distraught state before being found by Sir Bliant. He was eventually cured of his madness in CORBIN.

The fruit of his union with Elaine was Galahad, destined to become even more valorous than his father and to be one of three knights who saw the Holy Grail at CARBONEK CASTLE.

(Sir Thomas Malory, *Le Morte Darthur*, London, 1485)

BLATHUANIA, see BLITVA.

BLAZING WORLD, an archipelago stretching from the North Pole to near the British Isles, through the Greenland and Norwegian seas. It has a North Pole of its own, thus doubling the cold of those inhospitable regions. Its southern extremity,

One of the many carved thrones in the Imperial Palace, BLAZING WORLD.

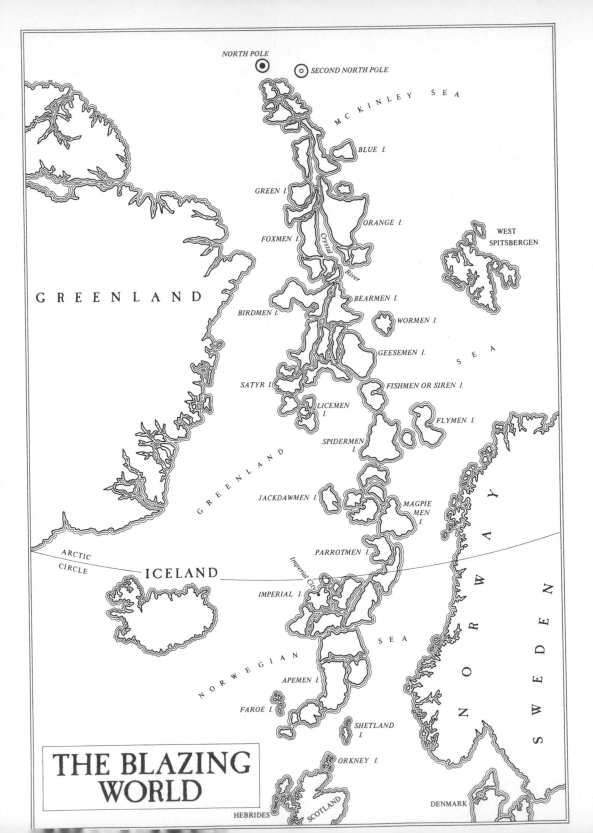

NORTH POLE

SECOND NORTH POLE

MC KINLEY SEA

BLUE I.

GREEN I.

ORANGE I.

FOXMEN I.

Crystal River

WEST SPITSBERGEN

G R E E N L A N D

BEARMEN I.

BIRDMEN I.

WORMEN I.

GEESEMEN I.

S E A

SATYR I.

FISHMEN OR SIREN I.

LICEMEN I.

FLYMEN I.

SPIDERMEN I.

G R E E N L A N D

JACKDAWMEN I.

MAGPIE MEN I.

ARCTIC CIRCLE

PARROTMEN I.

N O R W A Y

ICELAND

Imperial Circle

IMPERIAL I.

S E A

S W E D E N

N O R W E G I A N

APEMEN I.

FAROE I.

SHETLAND I.

THE BLAZING WORLD

ORKNEY I.

HEBRIDES

SCOTLAND

DENMARK

however, is more temperate: the climate here is mild and pleasant. The entire archipelago is governed by an emperor who resides in the Imperial City. The people of the Blazing World believe in one government, one religion and one language; a government of more than one person, a choice of several religions and a medley of different languages, they equal to "a monster with many heads."

From the North Pole a crystal river leads through several islands to a labyrinth of canals, along whose sides stand cities of marble, alabaster, agate, amber and coral. The islands, and in fact the whole of the Blazing World, are inhabited by people of many colours and races: blue, green, orange; bear-men, fox-men, geese-men, worm-men, satyres, fish-men or sirens, bird-men, fly-men, spider-men, lice-men, ape-men, jackdaw-men, magpie-men, parrot-men. Each type corresponds to a different profession: the bear-men are experimental philosophers; the fox-men are politicians; the bird-men are astronomers, etc. Along the river sail many types of vessels suited to the various types of people; some are shaped like fox-traps; others like bird-nests; the emperor's ships are made of gold; the merchants' ships of leather. All vessels are very light, whatever substance they are made of, and float like wood. The Imperial City, also called Paradise, is built in the Roman style, in gold. A series of canals makes it appear as a group of islands, which in fact it is not. The different blocks are united by bridges. The houses are no more than two storeys high.

The Imperial Palace is built on a hill, surrounded by pillars in a four-mile semicircle with a gate every half mile. The First Gate, which leads from the city itself to the palace, has a cloister on either side, mounted on more pillars. The palace, lit and heated by the sun, is built in the shape of a church, one and a half miles long by one and a half miles broad. The roof is arched and also set on pillars. A notable feature is that a throne can be found in every room, for the convenience of the emperor. The Room of State is paved in green diamonds and there are also diamonds in the arches between the pillars. The roof is of blue diamonds with a carbuncle set in the centre to represent the sun. On either side—east and west—are rubies symbolizing dawn and dusk. The entire decoration gives visitors the impression of a rainbow. The emperor's bedroom is black and even the floor is of black marble, but the ceiling is of mother-of-pearl with the moon and stars picked out in diamonds.

The imperial bed is encrusted with carbuncles and more diamonds. Faced with such treasures, the visitor will easily understand the popular saying — that there are more riches in the Blazing World than in all the rest of the planet.

(Margaret Cavendish, Duchess of Newcastle, *Observations upon Experimental Philosophy. To which is added the Description of a New Blazing World. Written by the Thrice Noble, Illustrious and Excellent Princesse, The Duchess of Newcastle,* London, 1666)

BLEFUSCU, a small island separated from LILLIPUT by a channel only eight hundred yards wide. In size and appearance, the people of Blefuscu are similar to the Lilliputians who to most travellers will seem exceedingly small. Blefuscu is the traditional refuge of Big-endian exiles from the neighbouring empire, who were unable to accept the Lilliputian doctrine of opening eggs at the little end.

(Jonathan Swift, *Travels Into Several Remote Nations Of The World. In Four Parts. By Lemuel Gulliver, First a Surgeon, and then a Captain of several Ships,* London, 1726)

BLEMMYAE COUNTRY, in Africa, inhabited by people with no heads, whose faces are on their chests (see also BRISSONTE). This does not seem to inconvenience them greatly, except that they have to turn their whole bodies in order to see about them, not having the advantage of possessing necks. Their staple diet is human flesh, and travellers are advised not to be deceived by their stolid appearance.

(Pliny the Elder, *Inventorum Natura,* 1st cen. AD)

BLESSED, ISLAND OF THE, some five hundred miles long, in the Atlantic Ocean, the home of a people who dress in beautiful purple spider-webs. In spite of being bodiless, they can move and talk as mortal beings. They resemble naked spirits, each covered with a web that gives it the shape of a body.

The island is long and flat, ruled by the Cretan Radamantus. The capital of the island, also called Blessed, is built of gold with walls of emerald. It has seven doors made from a single piece of cinnamon, and the roads that cross the city are of ivory. There are temples to all the gods, built of beryl and containing tall altars made of amethysts, used for human sacrifices: visitors easily frightened by the sight of blood are not advised to attend the ceremony. Around the city runs a river of exquisite perfume, fifty feet deep and easily navigable, seven rivers of milk, and eight of wine, and fountains spouting water, honey and perfume. The city baths are large crystal buildings, heated with cinnamon; the tubs contain both water and hot dew.

Travellers will not find on the Island of the Blessed the darkness of night or the light of day to which they are accustomed. The island is constantly bathed in a twilight, as if the sun had not yet risen. It is always springtime and only one wind, the zephyr, blows here. The country is rich in every species of flower and every kind of plant; the vines give grapes twelve times a year; apple trees, pomegranate trees and others, give fruit thirteen times a year, because in the month of Minossa they give fruit twice. As well as ready-made sheaves, the wheat produces beautifully baked loaves, growing from its tips like mushrooms.

(Lucian of Samosata, *True History*, 2nd cen. AD)

BLEST ISLE OF SAINT BRENDAN, see SAINT BRENDAN'S FAIRY ISLE.

BLIND, CITY OF THE, where no one except the blind is allowed to enter. Anyone else who comes in is struck by the mysterious condition that afflicts all its citizens. After the first case of blindness (a man sitting in his car, waiting for the lights to change), the disease spread quickly, affecting everyone from the ophthalmologist who was trying to find a cure, to young students and housewives. To prevent chaos, the government decided to round up the blind and intern them in a lunatic asylum. As a quarantine measure, all those who had been in contact with them were also imprisoned, in a separate wing of the asylum and under heavily armed guard. In spite of an attempt on the part of the blind to organize themselves as a self-sufficient society, the disease turned into an epidemic and overtook the whole city.

In the City of the Blind, food is scarce and provisions depend on chance. The streets are clogged with rubbish that seems to increase in the hours of darkness—rubbish apparently unloaded from some unknown place where life is still normal. Cars have crashed into shop windows and

rotting corpses sit amid debris and broken glass. The only entertainment consists of listening to speeches by certain blind citizens who feel compelled to extol the fundamental principles of great societies: private property, a free currency market, a stock exchange, taxation, lotteries and more.

The climate of the City of the Blind is extremely unpleasant: the heat is oppressive in spite of torrential downpours, causing toxic vapours to rise from the rubbish heaps. Umbrellas are hard to come by.

(José Saramago, *Ensaio sobre a cegueira*, Lisbon, 1995)

BLIND, COUNTRY OF THE, a valley in the Ecuador Andes, approximately three hundred miles from Mount Chimborazo and one hundred miles from Mount Cotopaxi. At first the valley lay open to the world, and several families of Peruvian half-breeds came here seeking refuge from the tyranny of an unnamed Spanish ruler. However the eruption of the Mindobamba, which darkened the skies of Quito for seventeen days and made the waters boil at Yaguachi, broke off a whole side of the Arauca crest and cut off the valley from the rest of the country.

All the inhabitants of the valley are blind; a disease broke out soon after the eruption and blindness became hereditary. "They forgot many things; they devised many things," says a historian. And they built a city within the valley to fit their requirements.

The valley has fresh water, plentiful pastures for the flocks of llamas and slopes of rich soil with tangles of a shrub that bears excellent fruit. The climate is mild. On one side, great hanging forests of pine hold back the avalanches. Far overhead, on the three other sides, loom vast cliffs of grey-green rock capped by cliffs of ice. The peak of Mount Parascotopetl, "the Matterhorn of the Andes" has yet to be conquered.

The houses are built in a very orderly fashion, along paths paved with black and white stones, and are astonishingly clean. They have doors, but no windows. The walls are coloured with extraordinary irregularity, smeared with some sort of plaster that is sometimes grey, sometimes drab, sometimes slate-coloured or dark brown. Around the city runs a highly developed irrigation system.

The inhabitants speak a rudimentary or archaic Spanish, but all words related to sight have no meaning for them. They are guided by the other four senses and especially by their hearing, which is very keen.

Only one man is said to have visited the Country of the Blind, a mountaineer from the country near Quito, called Nunez or "Bogota" by the natives. He joined a party of Englishmen who were trying to climb Mount Parascotopetl, when one of their three Swiss guides fell ill. The expedition met with disaster and Nunez arrived in the valley by accident. After some time he escaped to tell his story. In spite of its natural beauty, a visit to the Country of the Blind is not recommended.

(H.G. Wells, *The Country of the Blind*, London, 1911)

BLITHUANIA, see BLITVA.

BLITVA or BLITHUANIA, a republic in northern Europe, once part of the Hunian Empire, which achieved independence following the Blato-Blitvinskian treaty. Almost one and a half million inhabitants live in Blitva, and as many again in the State of Blathuania, which also became independent following the same treaty. Eight hundred thousand are still under the Hunian yoke. After the Christmas coup of 1925, war broke out between Blithuania, Hunia, Kobilia and Ingermanlandia, a war which has not yet ended and which makes the whole area extremely dangerous for travellers.

(Miroslav Krleža, *Banket u Blitvi*, Zagreb, 1939)

BLOKULA, a small Elfin kingdom in the far north of Sweden, ruled by a child queen known as Serafica. The castle stands in a mountain pass; it is a squat, rectangular structure built around a central courtyard. A number of wooden statues of men stand in the courtyard; they are much taller than the Elfin inhabitants of the castle and, although very realistic, they are rather badly carved.

Serafica's subjects are known as Trolls. Their only interests are eating, drinking, horseplay and tracing their pedigrees. They drink heavily and their revels are so rowdy that the name of Blokula is synonymous with gross feasting. In the eyes of other Elfin kingdoms, Blokula does not rate very highly.

Serafica is small, almost dwarfish, and appears to be somewhat of a shrew. Although she is the absolute ruler of the court, her power is overseen by her governess, Dame Habonde, one of the famed Lapland witches and the only mortal permanently resident in the castle.

Although remote and difficult to reach, Blokula does have relations with other Elfin kingdoms in Europe. Aquilon, the ambassador from BROCELIANDE and former master of the werewolves in that court, was recently made the official Royal Favourite of Queen Serafica.

(Sylvia Townsend Warner, *Kingdoms of Elfin*, London, 1972)

BLOMBODINGA, capital of PAFLAGONIA.

BLUEBEARD'S CASTLE, somewhere in France; the exact location remains unknown. The castle is famed for its many riches and fine furniture, tapestries and full-length mirrors with frames of gold.

Travellers—in particular female ones—should proceed with caution when visiting the many apartments the castle contains. Upon arrival, visitors are given a small golden key which will let them into the different rooms. Only one room will be forbidden to them; but curious visitors may nevertheless want to see it. They will find this small chamber gorishly decorated with female bodies chained to the walls in various stages of decomposition, and large pools of blood on the marble floors.

Because of the shock the sight will certainly produce, the visitor must avoid dropping the key, so leaving an accusing stain on it which cannot be removed. When interrogated by the castle's owner (the original Monsieur Bluebeard was slaughtered, but the new owners probably continue the guided tours) it is best to flee to one of the towers with the assistance of a far-sighted friend. Tradition requires that the assistant be the visitor's sister whose task it is to look over the parapet towards the horizon to see if help is at hand, so that the visitor may ask, at prudent intervals: "Sister Anne, Sister Anne" (or whatever the assistant's name might be), "do you see something coming?" Help should finally arrive and nothing worse should derive from the experience than the thrill of the chase and perhaps a recurrent nightmare.

Visitors are advised to disregard a certain pretentious guidebook to Bluebeard's Castle and environs written by a well-known Viennese armchair traveller.

(Charles Perrault, "La Barbe Bleue," in *Contes*, Paris, 1697)

BOHU, see TOHU.

BONG-TREE LAND, a year and a day by sea from a country of uncertain location. One of the main charms of the land is the Bong-Tree Wood, which the experienced traveller will see also on the coast of COROMANDEL where the early pumpkins blow, and on the great GROMBOOLIAN PLAIN.

The country boasts a few unspectacular species of fauna, such as turkeys (whose natural habitat is the hills and who are qualified to perform marriages) and pigs, some with rings on their noses. These rings can be purchased for five new pence and are popular as souvenirs.

Bong-Tree Land cuisine consists mainly of delectable combinations of mince and slices of quince, sometimes eaten—*noblesse oblige*—with runcible spoons.

A now famous wedding between an elegant fowl and a beautiful pussy cat was celebrated here.

(Edward Lear, "The Owl and the Pussy Cat," in *Nonsense Songs, Stories, Botany and Alphabets*, London, 1871; Edward Lear, *The Dong with a Luminous Nose*, London, 1871; Edward Lear, "The Courtship of the Yonghy-Bonghy-Bò," in *Laughable Lyrics: A Fourth Book of Nonsense Poems, Songs, Botany, Music, etc.*, London, 1877)

BOOMING ROLLERS, an extensive lake in ROOTABAGA COUNTRY. Its shores are flat beaches of white sand, and pines come down almost to the water's edge. Above the lake, the mist people make pictures in the sky, sometimes grey, blue and gold, but mainly silver. At dawn the shapes of strange animals can be seen moving across the sky. These figures date back to the time when the Makers of the World were experimenting with the shape of the animals they wanted to create to populate the earth. The shadow horse with its mouth open, its ears laid back and its legs thrown in a curve like a harvest moon was their first attempt, but it was found to be a mistake and thrown away. Similarly elephants with no heads and six legs can be seen crossing the dawn sky—they too were mistakes and were discarded, like the cows with horns in front and behind, and camels with one hump larger than the other. Discarded types of men and women can also be observed in the skies above the Booming Rollers.

(Carl Sandburg, *Rootabaga Stories*, New York, 1922)

BOREDOM, ISLE OF, a swampy island of unknown location, always shrouded in mist. All its plants are poisonous and all its animals let off a venomous stench. Travellers are warned that these animals are likely to attack any visitors, tear out their entrails, and then heal them, repeating the process again and again. Those who have visited the Isle of Boredom are not known to have ever visited it a second time.

(Marie Anne de Roumier Robert, *Les Ondins*, Paris & London, 1768)

BOSSARD or **HUMPED ISLAND**, of uncertain location. The birds of Bossard are all humpbacked, lame, one-armed or deformed in some other way. Their mothers refuse to keep them at home for more than seven or nine years—at about that time they simply snip a hair or two from the crown of their heads, mutter a few words to ward off evil spirits and pack them off to RINGING ISLAND where they reside from then on. The Bossards never sing sweetly and constantly curse their relations and friends who have turned them into birds.

(François Rabelais, *Le cinquiesme et dernier livre des faicts et dicts du bon Pantagruel, auquel est contenu la visitation de l'Oracle de la dive Bacbuc, et le mot de la bouteille; pour lequel avoir est enterpris tout ce long voyage*, Paris, 1564)

BOU CHOUGGA, ruins of a city in the Sahara. According to the testimony of many of the inhabitants who live in the vicinity, beneath the ruins lies a large city inhabited by Christians who took refuge there when North Africa was invaded by Islam. The Christians diverted the rivers and streams that once made this area fertile, and now live happily underground. But one day they will water the desert once again.

The large stone well in BOU CHOUGGA.

On the surface, the only remaining trace of Bou Chougga is a large stone well, four to five metres deep. Although the well is now dry, a traveller placing his ear to the stone will be able to hear the underground murmur of the water that once fed it.

(Certeux,—, *L'Algérie traditionnelle,* Paris, 1884)

BOULOULABASSIA, see BALBRIGIAN AND BOULOULABASSIAN UNITED REPUBLIC.

BRAGMAN or **LAND OF FAITH,** an island in the Indian Ocean. The people here live strictly by the Ten Commandments. When Alexander the Great set out to conquer this island, the people of Bragman wrote to him describing the simplicity of their lives and Alexander decided not to trouble them. There are no entertainments on Bragman and a visit is hardly worthwhile.

(Sir John Mandeville, *Voiage de Sir John Maundevile,* Paris, 1357)

BRANDLEGUARD, capital of SAS DOOPT SWANGEANTI.

BRAN ISLE, not far from LACELAND. The island is, in fact, the decaying body of Baron Hildebrand of the Sea of Habundes. It is sterile and desolate, as the baron is putrefying from the brain, bone and marrow outwards.

Visitors will find that birds the colour of writing—presumably black and white—hover around the island. The inhabitants pay daily homage to the decaying baron, finding their way with perfect assurance, although they are blind. They are guided by the cloacal, subterranean lighthouse of the island, as blind as a man who has stared too long at the sun. The lighthouse is fed on pure matter, exhaled from the baron's mouth. Pious travellers are advised to visit the white greybeards, who are building a convent known as the Catholic Maxim Chapel on Bran Isle.

(Alfred Jarry, *Gestes et Opinions du Docteur Faustroll, Pataphysicien. Roman Néo-Scientifique,* Paris, 1911)

BRASS, CITY OF, a dead city in an undetermined region of the Magreb, probably to the west of the Sahara Desert. It was discovered and explored by an expedition organized by the Caliph Abd-El-Melik ibn Marwan, Prince of the True Believers (AD 685–705). The Caliph had heard, during a banquet at his court in Damascus, of a place by the sea where fishermen frequently found bottles of brass sealed with the signet of Solomon, son of David. When the seal was broken, blue smoke would rise to the heavens and a horrible voice would cry: "Repentance! Repentance! O, Prophet of God!" It became known that King Solomon had imprisoned jinns or evil spirits in the bottles which he had then thrown into the ocean. Upon hearing this, the Caliph expressed a great desire to see these bottles and ordered the Emir Moosa ibn Nuseyr to find their place of origin. The Emir, who then ruled the Magreb, consulted the blind wise man, Abd-Es-Samad, a knowing man who had travelled much and was acquainted with the deserts, the wastes and the seas, their inhabitants and their wonders, and the countries and their districts. Under the guidance of the Emir and the blind man, the expedition arrived after a four-month journey at a town on the edge of the sea, surrounded by grass and springs. Travellers are advised to spend the night here.

Somewhat farther on, there stands a palace which should be visited. An open door leads to two wide steps of coloured marble, and above the entrance is a slab with an inscription in ancient Greek concerning the frailty of human things. The ceilings and walls are decorated with gold, silver and precious stones. In the middle of the deserted palace, surrounded by four hundred tombs, is a lofty, domed chamber, its eight sandalwood doors stubbed with nails of gold, ornamented with stars of silver set with various jewels. Inside the chamber is a long tomb, of terrible appearance, on which is a tablet of iron of China, on which is written that Koosh ibn Sheddad ibn Ad the Greater, who possessed four thousand horses, married a thousand damsels, was blessed with a thousand children, lived a thousand years and amassed riches such as all the kings on earth are unable to procure, ended his life in death, and is here buried. Visitors should also note the absence of a splendid alabaster table on which was inscribed: "Upon this table have eaten a thousand one-eyed kings, and a thousand kings each sound in both eyes. All of them have quitted the world, and taken up their abode in the burial grounds and the graves." This piece of furniture was removed by the Emir himself.

Leaving the palace, visitors will arrive after a three-day march at a high hill on which stands a brass horseman. He holds a spear with a wide and glistening head, on which is written: "O thou who comest unto me, if thou know not the way that leadeth to the City of Brass, rub the hand of the horseman, and he will turn, and then will stop, and in whatever direction he stoppeth, thither proceed, without fear and without difficulty, for it will lead thee to the City of Brass." Following these instructions, and continuing the journey across a wide tract of country, the traveller will come upon a pillar of black stone, in which stands a person sunk to his armpits, with two huge wings and two human arms with lion's paws. The hair on his head is like horses' tails, and of his three eyes, two are like burning coals and the third, in his forehead, is like the eye of a lynx. The creature is a jinn, punished in this manner by King Solomon; he will point the way to the City of Brass.

The City of Brass has twenty-five gates which cannot be seen and cannot be opened except from within. The city walls, flanked by two brass towers, are of black stones. In order to enter, visitors should follow the instructions given by the Emir Moosa ibn Nuseyr. A ladder must be made

out of wood and covered with plates of iron, and then fixed against the wall. (Note that the construction of such a ladder will take approximately a month.) Once on the wall, visitors will see, inside the city itself, ten beautiful ladies who will make signs with their hands as though to say "Come to us." They should not be heeded, as a leap from the wall would prove fatal. It is best to walk along the wall to one of the brass towers. The visitor will see here two gates of gold without visible means of opening. However, in the middle of one of the gates is the by now familiar figure of a brass horseman, one hand extended as if he were pointing. Visitors should turn a pin in the middle of the horseman's body twelve times; this will open the gate with a loud noise.

Inside are a number of handsome wooden benches, on which lie a quantity of dead people with elegant shields, keen swords, strung bows and notched arrows hanging over their heads. Visitors should approach the oldest-looking of these corpses and take a bunch of keys from under his garments. These will open the iron gates that lead down into the city with its lofty pavilions and shining domes, and its many mansions set on the banks of crystal rivers. Here, on beds of silk, lie yet a greater number of corpses, all the way into the marketplace. The visitor will find the shops open and the merchants dead. After four such markets—the silk market, the jewellery market, the money-changers' market and the perfume market—the visitor will arrive at a strangely constructed palace with banners unfurled, drawn swords, strung bows, shields hung by chains of gold and silver and helmets gilded with red gold.

In the exact centre of the palace is a great hall with four large and lofty chambers decorated with gold and silver, and in the middle of the hall stands a great fountain of alabaster over which is a canopy of brocade. The first chamber contains gold, silver and precious stones; the second is full of weapons from all over the world; the third is filled with arms decorated with jewels; the fourth contains precious utensils for food and drink. Through a door inlaid with ivory and ebony, visitors will come into a passage paved with marble and decorated with embroidered curtains depicting wild beasts and birds. The passage leads into a room, the floor of which is so decorated with polished marble and pearls that the beholder might imagine that it is made of running water. Inside the room stands a great dome of red gold, covering a pavilion of brocade which is held by birds with feet made of emeralds. Beneath each bird is a net of brilliant pearls spread over a fountain and by the brink of the fountain stands a couch adorned with jewels on which lies a beautiful damsel. Visitors should notice her eyes which were taken out after her death and quick-silver put beneath them. Now, restored to their sockets, they give a truly horrible impression of life. A tablet of gold at the foot of the couch reveals the secret of the City of Brass, and should be read carefully by all travellers with a smattering of Arabic. It relates how during the reign of Tedmur, daughter of the King of the Amalekites, famine and drought struck the City of Brass. For seven years no rain descended from heaven and no grass grew for the inhabitants of the city. After eating the food that was still available, the queen sent out messengers to trade her fabulous riches for something to eat; but they did not find anything and returned to the city with all the treasures. The queen decided to expose her riches to the public, lock the gates of the city, submit herself to the decree of the Lord and starve to death with her people, leaving what she had built and treasured as an eternal monument to the futility of riches.

Visitors will find the treasures of the City of Brass somewhat depleted, because the Emir and his men loaded as many riches as their camels could carry and took them back to their own country, after ultimately discovering, on the Sea of KARKAR, the place of origin of the jinn bottles.

(Anonymous, *The Arabian Nights*, 14th–16th cen. AD)

BRAZIL, an island in the same latitude as southern Ireland. The name may be Gaelic as *Bresail* is the name of an ancient pagan demi-god and both syllables *Bres* and *ail* denote admiration. It consists of a large ring of land surrounding an inland sea dotted with islets. The ordinary mortal cannot see it and only a chosen few have been blessed with the vision of Brazil.

(Angelinus Dalorto, *L'Isola Brazil*, Genoa, 1325)

BREADLESSDAY, a country of unknown location. Many of the birds that live on RINGING IS-LAND come from Breadlessday. Every year, flocks of them migrate from Breadlessday because if they remained at home there would be no inheritance

for them. Although the journey is very long, they are willing to go to Ringing Island, where they are at least assured of a comfortable living. The migrants include those who have not the skill or means to work at a trade, those who are crossed in love or whose businesses have failed and those fleeing punishment for some crime they have committed. Few of them return to their homes once they have left. The inhabitants of Breadlessday are collectively known as the Asaphis.

(François Rabelais, *Le cinquiesme et dernier livre des faicts et dicts du bon Pantagruel, auquel est contenu la visitation de lOracle de la dive Bacbuc, et le mot de la bouteille; pour lequel avoir est enterpris tout ce long voyage*, Paris, 1564)

BREE-LAND, a somewhat isolated community to the east of the SHIRE in MIDDLE-EARTH.

Bree-land is a small area of woods and trees, surrounded on all sides by barren lands. There are only four villages in the area: Bree itself, Staddle, Combe and Archet, the latter on the edge of the Chetwood, the main forest of Bree-land. Of the four, Bree is by far the most important. It stands at the intersection of two ancient roads: the North Road and the East Road. The former, known as the Greenway to the Bree-landers, is little used now, as most of the Northern Lands are uninhabited; the East Road runs from the GREY HAVENS through the Shire and Bree-land to RIVENDELL.

The village of Bree consists mostly of stone houses built against Bree Hill and facing west. Bree is protected by a thorny hedge and a large dyke which forms a loop around its western side and which is crossed by the causeway of the East Road. Both the southern and eastern entrances are guarded by gates which are locked at night. Because of its position, Bree is an important meeting place for travellers and for the exchange of news. "Strange as news from Bree" is still used as an expression for something out of the ordinary in the East Farthing of the Shire. *The Prancing Pony Inn,* a favourite resting place for travellers, can be recommended. It is a great centre for the smoking of pipe-weed, a custom which originated with the hobbits of Bree and which has since spread into the Shire.

Bree-land is unique in Middle-earth in that it is inhabited by men and hobbits, who live together happily and who refer to each other as Big Folk and Little Folk respectively. They all have equal status as Bree-landers. Visitors will find that they are not great travellers, being mainly concerned with the local affairs of their four villages. In the past, however, there appears to have been greater contact between the hobbits of Bree and those of the Shire.

The men of Bree-land are broad and short. They are of a cheerful and independent disposition and are friendlier towards other humans than most of their kind. They claim to be the original inhabitants and descendants of the first people to settle in the area. The Bree men have names such as Rushlight, Goatlife and Heathertoes, and, of course, there are the famous Butterburs, who have kept *The Prancing Pony* since before records began.

The hobbits of Bree claim to be the oldest settlement of hobbits in the world and they say that their land was settled long before the hobbits crossed the Brandywine into the Shire. Indeed, they claim to have done everything before the Shire hobbits, whom they somewhat disparagingly refer to as "colonists." They are a friendly and inquisitive race, living mostly in hobbit holes in Staddle; a few, however, live in Bree itself. Some of them have names similar to those of the men, but most have normal hobbit names which should be familiar to any visitor from the Shire, such as Banks and Underhill.

Visitors in Bree-land will frequently hear an enigmatic phrase: "He can see through a brick wall in time." The meaning has not been determined, but the phrase appears to indicate a certain form of cleverness or wisdom unique to the area.

The currency of Bree-land is the silver penny.

(J.R.R. Tolkien, *The Fellowship of the Ring*, London, 1954)

BRENN, see SEVEN ISLES.

BRIDGETOWN, see MECCANIA.

BRIGADOON, a village in the Scottish Highlands, found on no National Survey map. The countryside is typical of this area; the village lies deep in a glen, surrounded by mountains and pine forests, and the only access to it is across a single-span stone bridge. Brigadoon is made up of small stone cottages built around MacConnachy Square.

Visitors will be interested to know that two miracles have occurred in Brigadoon, the first on May 22, 1753. On that day, the local parson, Mr. Forsythe, horrified by the presence of witches in the vicinity, prayed that the village might be removed from temptation by falling asleep, to awaken on only one day every hundred years (a device reminiscent of that applied to SLEEPING BEAUTY'S CASTLE). The prayer was granted, at the cost of Mr. Forsythe's life, but the condition of the miracle was that no inhabitant could leave Brigadoon or the village would disappear forever; the bridge leading out of the glen is the boundary which no one may cross.

On May 24, 1953, two American tourists, lost in the Highlands, came upon the village on its one day of reawakening in the twentieth century, when an inhabitant, disappointed in love, tried to leave Brigadoon. The villagers had no choice but to give chase and one of the Americans accidentally killed the deserter.

Shocked by what had happened, the Americans left to return to New York, but not before one of them had fallen in love with a local girl. He decided to go back to Scotland in the hope that Brigadoon might reappear. It was then that the second miracle occurred: the village re-awakened for the second time in the century and the American was united with the girl he loved.

Travellers, however, are not advised to wait too long for Brigadoon to come into sight and should instead visit the other, less romantic villages in the Highlands.

(*Brigadoon*, directed by Vincente Minnelli, USA, 1955)

BRIGALAURE, an island of uncertain location, where butchers make sausages from the ears of those sailors who are unfortunate enough to land there. They prefer ears to any other part of the body because they are part flesh and part cartilage—particularly suitable for sausage-making.

(Anonymous, *Le voyage de navigation que fist Panurge, disciple de Pantagruel, aux isles incognues et éstranges de plusieurs choses merveilleuses et difficiles à croire, qu'il dict avoir veues, dont il fait narration en ce présent volume, et plusieurs aultres joyeusetez pour inciter les lecteurs et auditeurs à rire,* Paris, 1538)

BRISEVENT or **MARVELLOUS ISLANDS,** a group of islands in the south Atlantic, inhabited by extraordinary creatures such as centaurs, cyclopes, ape-men. Some look like ordinary men except that they are covered with eyes, others with ears; some are giants; some are so small that their main concern is fighting off insects. The most important island of the group is Amazon Island, where a group of women from AMAZONIA have settled. They govern the island on their own, have established their own economy and have their own police force. Men are kept on the opposite side of a large river that flows through the island. They are sometimes captured by the Amazons, kept for one or two days—or *moons,* in their language—and then sent back. On a neighbouring island, some escaped men have established their own government with the help of their mistresses, whom they keep as slaves in revenge for the treatment received on Amazon Island. These women do anything to please their men: they sing serenades under their balconies; they lie flat on the ground when they pass; they chew their masters' food for them and in winter they warm their beds with their bodies.

(Charles Sorel, *La Maison des jeux,* Paris, 1657)

BRISSONTE, a river not far from the mouth of the Nile. Though its source has not yet been discovered, it is known in Egypt as Archoboletus, which means "Large Waters," indicating perhaps a lake as its birthplace.

Travellers taking a cruise down the Brissonte will see a number of interesting creatures on the islands along its course. For instance, on one small island with pleasant beaches lives a curious tribe called the Epistigi. These natives are seven feet tall and carry in their bodies the several senses which would normally be lodged in their heads, a commodity they lack. On another island lives a group of natives who are born with their feet turned the wrong way round; as a result, they give the impression of coming instead of going, and vice versa.

Finally, travellers are advised to look out for vast herds of a bizarre and beautiful animal, the *celeste,* of which no description has ever been written and no picture ever taken.

(Anonymous, *Liber monstrorum de diversis generibus,* 9th cen. AD)

BROBDINGNAG, an extensive peninsula on the coast of California, in the United States, discovered

Part of the eastern wall of Lorbrulgrud, BROBDINGNAG.

in 1703. The peninsula is six thousand miles long and between three and five thousand miles wide. To the north-east it is cut off by a range of volcanic mountains, some of them thirty miles high; no one knows what lies behind these mountains. The coast is rocky and dangerous. There are no ports and no coastal shipping, so that Brobdingnag remains totally cut off from the outside world. There is no known access from any other country.

The people of Brobdingnag are a race of giants as tall as church steeples. They cover ten yards with a single stride. All things in their country are in proportion—the corn is forty feet high, the rats are the size of large mastiffs and the flies, a great nuisance in summer, are as big as larks. The hailstones are eighteen times the size of those known elsewhere in the world. A normal human being can break his shin simply by stumbling against a snail shell. Huge bones and skulls dug up in various parts of the country suggest that the ancestors of the Brobdingnagians were still larger than the present race, which seems puny in comparison.

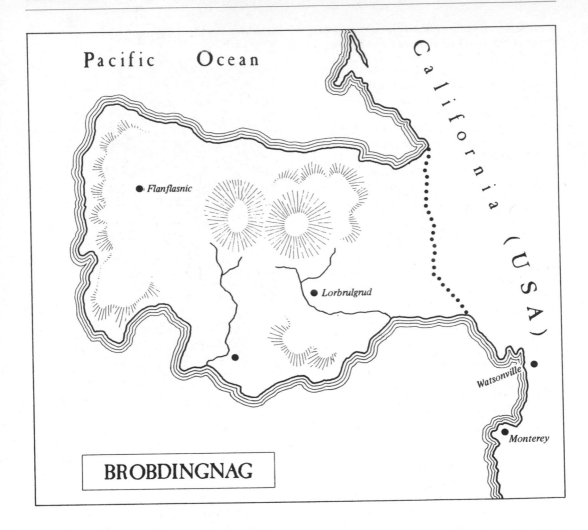

Pacific Ocean

California (USA)

Flanflasnic

Lorbrulgrud

Watsonville

Monterey

BROBDINGNAG

The history of the country is not known in any detail. In the recent past there have been struggles between the king, the people and the nobility, each vying for power. It is also known that there have been several civil wars arising from these struggles, the last one ending with the signing of a general treaty. The monarchy is based on the principles of common sense, reason, justice and lenience; for instance, a farmer who can improve the yield of his land is considered more important than a politician.

The culture of Brobdingnag is limited to morality, history, poetry and mathematics, in which this race of giants excels. They also make excellent clockwork objects. All science is studied solely for its practical applications and there is no concern for abstract speculation or theorizing. Like the Chinese, the giants have used the art of printing since time immemorial. Their libraries are not, however, particularly extensive. That of the king, the largest in the country, contains only one thousand volumes in a gallery 1,200 feet long. The dominant literary style is clear, masculine and pure, avoiding all florid expressions or superfluous words. Building does not appear to be an art in which Brobdingnagians excel. The king's palace in the capital city of Lorbrulgrud, for instance, is an irregular pile of buildings some seven miles in circumference. The king also has a palace at Flanflasnic, about eighteen miles from the sea.

Lorbrulgrud (which may be translated as "Pride of the Universe") stands almost exactly in the centre of the country. It is divided into two al-most equal parts by a wide river. Its most impor-tant and impressive monument is the temple tower, three thousand feet high (which, in relative terms, means it is about the height of the spire of Salisbury Cathedral), with walls one hundred feet thick. It is built of blocks of stone forty feet square and is adorned with marble statues of the coun-try's gods and emperors standing in niches. In ad-dition to the capital, there are fifty-one large, walled cities and some one hundred towns.

The laws of the country are simple and clear. None of them may exceed in words the number of letters in the alphabet (many of them are much shorter) and they must be expressed in plain, simple language. In general, the people are not sufficiently mercurial to interpret the laws in more than one way, and there are correspondingly few cases of civil litigation. Murder is a capital offence and offenders are beheaded.

A large army commanded by the nobility and local gentry is maintained, although the country has no reason to fear invasion from abroad. Disci-pline is extremely good and all manoeuvres are performed in admirable fashion. In all, the army comprises 176,000 infantry and 32,000 cavalry. Gunpowder and firearms are unknown.

The fauna includes the *splacknuck*, a graceful and elegant mammal roughly the size of a human being, and travellers are advised that they could be mistaken for one. Indeed, this may be an advan-tage, since after hearing Captain Lemuel Gul-liver's description of European natives, the king of Brobdingnag concluded that they were "the most pernicious race of little odious vermin that nature ever suffered to crawl upon the surface of the earth."

(Jonathan Swift, *Travels Into Several Remote Na-tions Of The World. In Four Parts. By Lemuel Gul-liver, First a Surgeon, and then a Captain of several Ships,* London, 1726)

BROCÉLIANDE, an important Elfin kingdom in a dense forest in Brittany, the proudest and most elegant of all the Elfin courts of Europe; its inhab-itants regard other kingdoms with a certain dis-dain. For them the prosperous court of ZUY is little more than a gilded grocer's shop, while the English courts such as POMACE and the ancient Scottish realms of ELFHAME and FOXCASTLE are mere provincial backwaters.

Brocéliande claims it has preserved the an-cient traditions of Persia, the original home of all Elfins, but evidence from the PERI KINGDOM does not support the claim. Despite that, the queen of Brocéliande wears a pink turban instead of the normal crown and the royal wand is of cedarwood said to come from the banks of the Eu-phrates; it is so massively encrusted with jewels that a team of courtiers is needed to wave it.

Brocéliande is famed for the rosewater dis-tilled by its ladies-in-waiting and for the peculiar species of cats bred there. It is the only kingdom known to have preserved a belief in the supernat-ural world of the Afrits, creatures of incalculable power. Quarterly ceremonies to appease the Afrits are held, preceded by a round of ritual cockfights after which the victorious cock is sacrificed.

Much of the life of the court is dominated by the fashion of the day, which may be anything from the purification of the language to cat-racing. There are picnics and deer hunts, and expeditions to the coast to watch shipwrecks. At one time the famous Royal Pack of werewolves was used in deer hunting, but they were destroyed after they turned on one of the Lords of the court and killed him; that was the end of the last pack kept in any of the courts of Europe.

Although fashions change continually at court, gambling is a constant preoccupation. Large sums change hands on such questions as which of two hailstones will melt first or which way a cat will jump; all gambling debts are debts of honour, which means that life at Brocéliande can be very expensive. The craze for gambling, and the fact that much of the court's income comes from feu-dal dues and even smuggling, helps to explain why the citizens of Zuy, an important trading centre, view Brocéliande with such scorn. Nevertheless, the kingdom is seen as a delightful posting by the ambassadors from foreign courts.

Spring and winter are celebrated in Brocé-liande by a ritual change of clothes. At the spring festival, the furs and velvets of winter are ex-changed for silks and gossamer. The climate of the moment is not taken into account, which means that courtiers are often dressed in furs during warm springs and in light summer clothes during cold, wet autumns. When this happens they bolster their courage by boasting of the inheritance of the ancient Persians, much to the amusement of visi-tors from less formal courts.

Court etiquette is strict. No aristocratic fairy

in any court will fly unless it is absolutely necessary—flight is considered an activity fit for servants and working fairies—and in Brocéliande the
convention is firmly upheld. At the same time
great interest is taken in the flying abilities of the
lower classes, and a regular programme of race
meetings is organized throughout the year. Again,
vast sums of money change hands. The fervour for
racing is so great that one favourite racing valet
who had the misfortune to break a wing was kept
at stud for some years, producing several winners
before his death.

Not all court activities are frivolous. Brocéliande maintains an official astronomer, and a former archivist named Dando is the author of one of
the standard works on the history of Elfindom, the
Cosmography.

In the past, the most famous site in the kingdom of Brocéliande was a spring called Barenton.
Its water is cold even in the middle of the hottest
of summers, but it never freezes over in winter. A
lady is sometimes seen sitting by it. She is tall and
as stately as a queen, but seems to lead a life apart
from the kingdom. According to the *Cosmography*
of Dando she is one of the indigenous fairies of
Brittany who lived here long before the arrival of
the Elfins. He also claims that the spring is as old
as the stones of Carnac and that it was the original
centre of Brocéliande, the spot where the vagrant
tribe settled when they were driven out of Persia.
The spring has, however, taken on a sinister reputation over the years and is now rarely visited,
though its waters are still used in making the famous *Eau de Brocéliande*. A ceremonial picnic is
held by the pool once every twenty-five years, but
it is usually ignored by the courtiers.

The traditions of Brocéliande require that
each queen who succeeds to the pink turban introduce a new custom of Persian origin. When Me-
lior became queen she decided to introduce
eunuchs. Two young boys were chosen from the
ranks of the changelings, mortal children carried
away by the Elfins, and the castration was performed by a surgeon brought in from Constantinople. For years they served as the queen's
attendants, but were later assigned to the court
astronomer as assistants. They were judged particularly suitable to that task as the astronomer has
dealings with the Afrits, who are known to be particularly strict about virginity; the least suggestion
of infringement in that matter will drive them into
a fury. A further change in their status came when

it was suggested that they enliven the life of the
court by taking part in prizefights; eventually this
led to their being armed with spurs, like fighting
cocks, and to the serious injury of one of them. It
appeared that they had now outlived their usefulness and the queen proposed that they be sent to
the Island of Repose, a small island off the Pointe
du Raz, known to the Bretons as the Island of the
Dead. The proposal aroused protest from the
ladies of the court and murmurs of revolt among
the working fairies, who finally refused to fly and
went about their duties at a walking pace. Sensing
that she was on dangerous ground, the queen
withdrew her suggestion, and a disused hermitage
was refurbished for the two eunuchs who lived
there until they died of old age.

According to certain historians, Merlin the
Enchanter was imprisoned in a hollow oak in the
Forest of Brocéliande by the maiden Vivien, and is
there still. This version is contradicted by those
who affirm that Merlin can be seen sleeping his
eternal sleep in MERLIN'S CAVE; neither theory
has been convincingly disproven.

(Alfred, Lord Tennyson, *The Idylls of the King*,
London, 1842–85; Sylvia Townsend Warner,
Kingdoms of Elfin, London, 1972)

BRODIE'S LAND or **MLCH COUNTRY**,
somewhere in the north of Africa. A report on this
country and its inhabitants was written by a Pres-
byterian missionary, David Brodie, D.D., born in
Aberdeen towards the end of the eighteenth century. The manuscript was discovered by Jorge
Luis Borges, of Argentina, in one of the volumes
of Lane's *Arabian Nights' Entertainments* (London,
1839). Several primitive tribes live in this region:
the Ape-men, the Nr, the Kroo and the Mlch. The
latter were called Yahoos by Dr. Brodie (see
HOUYHNHNMS LAND) who described their
habits in detail.

The Mlch language is harsh and has no vowels. Few individuals have names. In order to address one another, it is their custom to fling a small
handful of mud or throw themselves to the ground
and wallow in the dust. They eat fruits, root-stalks
and small reptiles; they drink cats' and chiropter-
ans' milk; they fish with their hands. While they
are eating, they normally conceal themselves or at
least close their eyes. All other physical habits they
perform in public. In order to gain their wisdom,
they devour the raw corpses of their witch-doctors

Set of four gold favour-pins and a royal bracelet from
BRODIE'S LAND.

their shoulders like a flag or a talisman, to the thick of the fight. In such cases he dies almost immediately under the hail of stones flung at him by the Ape-men.

The queen lives in another cave and wears bracelets of metalwork and ivory which the Mlch consider to be natural. To show royal favour, the queen will sink a golden pin into the flesh of the chosen.

The Mlch have very bad memories, and can hardly remember things that have happened barely a few hours before. Yet their memory runs forward and they can foretell common events with great accuracy, as if they remembered the future.

They have peculiar ideas of Heaven and Hell. Hell is dry and filled with light; it harbours the sick, the aged, the ill-treated, the Ape-men, the Arabs and the leopards. Heaven is marshy and cloudy and is the dwelling-place of the king and queen, the witch-doctors and those who have been happy, merciless and bloodthirsty on earth. They worship a god whose name is Dung, and whom they have perhaps conceived in the image and semblance of their king: blind, mutilated and stunted, and enjoying limitless powers. He is wont to take the shape of an ant or a serpent. They have no notion of fatherhood, and cannot understand that an act carried out several months before bears any relation to the birth of a child, pointing out that all women engage in carnal commerce, and not all are mothers.

Their language is complex. Each monosyllabic word corresponds to a general idea whose specific meaning depends on the context or upon accompanying grimaces. The word *nrz*, for example, suggests dispersion of spots and may stand for the starry sky, a leopard, a flock of birds, something bespattered, the act of scattering or the flight that follows defeat in warfare. Pronounced in a different manner or with other grimaces, each word may have an opposite meaning.

Another of the tribe's customs is the discovery of poets. Six or seven words, generally enigmatic, may come to a man's mind. He cannot contain himself and shouts them out, standing in the centre of a circle formed by the witch-doctors and the common people, who are stretched out on the ground. If the poem does not stir them, nothing comes to pass, but if the poet's words affect them they all draw away from him, without a sound, in great fear. Feeling then that the spirit has touched him, nobody, not even his own

and the royal family. They go about quite naked, the arts of clothing and tattooing being altogether unknown.

Although they have a wide grassy plateau on which there are springs of clear water and shady trees, they prefer to swarm in the marshlands which surround it, as if delighting in the rigours of the hot climate and the general unwholesomeness. The tribe is ruled by a king whose power is absolute, but the true rulers are the witch-doctors. Every male born into the tribe is subjected to a painstaking examination; if he exhibits certain stigmata he is elevated to the rank of king. So that the physical world may not lead him from the paths of wisdom, he is gelded on the spot, his eyes are burnt out and his hands and feet are amputated. Thereafter he lives confined in a cavern called the Castle (*Qzr*), which only the four witch-doctors and two slave women who attend him and anoint him with dung are permitted to enter. Should war be declared, the witch-doctors remove him from his cavern, display him to the tribe to excite their courage, and bear him, lifted onto

mother, will either speak to him or cast a glance at him. Now he is no longer a man but a god, and anyone may kill him.

(Jorge Luis Borges, *El informe de Brodie*, Buenos Aires, 1970)

BROOLYI or **ISLE OF PEACE**, an island of the RIALLARO ARCHIPELAGO in the south-east Pacific. Broolyi is a high island with sheer cliffs and jagged reefs cut into fantastic shapes by the waves. A cape shelters the great harbour and city of Broolyi. Opposite Broolyi lies Kayoss, the Island of Anarchy. Shipments of exiles from Broolyi are landed here but kill each other off in a matter of days. The government of Broolyi is an absolute monarchy and the islanders believe in the ultimate triumph of peace. They maintain that when warfare is brought to perfection, all wars will cease, that the terror of death will be the universal guiding principle and that the cause of peace is best served through war. Broolyi was populated by exiles from LIMANORA, notably the proud and the warlike.

Broolyian religion is quite unique. The temples on the island are worked by machines from a religion factory. Automatic priests, made of wax, perform the services and take part in the processions.

From time to time, the island is affected by plagues which are fatal to the Broolyians but which do not affect their slaves. During plague time, the Broolyians flee to the mountains; for the slaves, plague time is a carnival, celebrated by looting and killing, and it is best to avoid Broolyi during these periods.

(Godfrey Sweven, *Riallaro, the Archipelago of Exiles*, New York & London, 1901; Godfrey Sweven, *Limanora, the Island of Progress*, New York & London, 1903)

BUCKLAND, an outlying region of the SHIRE between the Brandywine River and the OLD FOREST in the north-west of MIDDLE-EARTH.

Buckland is separated from the Old Forest by a thick, tall hedge known as the High Hay. Planted many years ago for protection against encroachment by the Old Forest, the Hay is over twenty miles long, pierced only by Buckland Gate, which gives access to the road leading east to BREE-LAND and to RIVENDELL. Shortly before the outbreak of the War of the Ring, the Hay was attacked by the malevolent trees of the Old Forest. In resisting and throwing back the attack, the hobbits of Buckland burnt trees in an area of the Forest still known as Bonfire Glade. Visitors will notice that even today no trees grow in that area.

Buckland is a thickly populated region. It was added to the Shire when a leader of the Oldbuck family crossed the river—the original boundary of the Shire—and built Brandy Hall, a large *smial*, or hobbit hole, beneath Buck Hill. He changed his name to Brandybuck and became known as the Master of Buckland. Ever since, the head of the family has resided at Brandy Hall. His authority is still recognized by the people of the Marish, the boggy area to the west of the Brandywine. At the end of the War of the Ring, Buckland was officially incorporated into the Shire itself, but it remains relatively autonomous.

The hobbits of the Shire consider those of Buckland strange and eccentric, although the differences between them are minor. One of the peculiarities of the Bucklanders is their fondness for boats, perhaps because of their familiarity with the self-operating ferry across the river. Some of them can even swim and appear to be more adventurous than their Shire cousins.

(J.R.R. Tolkien, *The Fellowship of the Ring*, London, 1954; J.R.R. Tolkien, *The Return of the King*, London, 1955)

BUNBURY, a town in the woods of southern OZ, near UTENSIA. The town and everything in it is edible. The houses are made of crackers, with porches supported by breadsticks, and are roofed with wafers. The soil is composed of flour and meal, the trees are mostly doughleanders and doughderas and produce useful crops of doughnuts in autumn. At one end of the town is a buttermine. Bunbury is inhabited by animated buns, crackers and biscuits. Cinnamon Bunn Esq. claims to be the chief citizen and a member of the town's most aristocratic family, but not everyone in Bunbury accepts his claim. Visitors to Bunbury will not go hungry.

(L. Frank Baum, *The Emerald City of Oz*, Chicago, 1910)

BUNNYBURY, a walled city in the woods of southern OZ, not far from BUNBURY and UTEN-

SIA, surrounded by a high marble wall. The only break in the wall is a concealed grill made of heavy brass bars. This gate is called the Wicket and all visitors are scrutinized through it. Strangers are not normally admitted to Bunnybury unless they carry letters of introduction from Ozma of Oz or her friend Glinda the Good Witch.

The wall conceals the beauties of the town, whose streets are paved with white marble. The houses too are of marble, with delicate slender spires and minarets rising above them. Each house has a clover lawn in front of it. Bunnybury was created by Glinda the Good as a home for all the white rabbits of the forest; they now live here under their own king, but continue to recognize the authority of Ozma.

All the white rabbits dress in rich clothes, usually of delicately coloured silks and satins, encrusted with bright gems. The dresses of the females are even more gorgeous; they wear bonnets with feathers and jewels in them and beautiful gowns. One of their kind can be seen in WONDERLAND and is said to wear a more restrained attire.

The Royal Palace stands in a square in the centre of the city. It is an imposing construction of white marble covered with a filigree of frosted gold.

All visitors to Bunnybury are required to allow themselves to be shrunk by magic until they are the same size as the rabbits; they will be restored to their normal size on leaving the city. No dogs are admitted.

(L. Frank Baum, *The Emerald City of Oz*, Chicago, 1910)

BURNT ISLAND, a low, green island within sight of DRAGON ISLAND. The only living creatures on the island are rabbits and goats, but ruins of stone huts, several bones and broken weapons between the blackened areas suggest that it was inhabited until fairly recently.

Travellers are warned that a sea-serpent has been seen in the waters off Burnt Island. It has been described as an enormous creature with a hide that resists both arrows and swords. Its body is said to be green and vermilion with purple blotches, except where shell-fish cling to it. The head is rather like that of a horse, but it has no ears; the gaping mouth is lined with a double row of sharp teeth, similar to those of a shark; the gigantic body tapers off into a huge tail. Though extremely aggressive and dangerous, the sea-serpent appears to be of low intelligence, and therefore can be easily foiled.

(C.S. Lewis, *The Voyage of the "Dawn Treader,"* London, 1952)

BURZEE, an ancient forest lying beyond the Deadly Desert that marks the western boundary of OZ, close to NOLAND. In the centre of its giant oaks and firs, a fairy ring has been traced on the smooth, velvety grass by the feet of elves and fairies who come here to dance at the full moon.

History has it that one night, bored with dancing, the fairies decided to make something which would benefit the race of mortals; they hit upon the idea of weaving a magic cloak which would instantly grant a single wish to anyone who wore it—provided that it had not been stolen from its previous wearer. The cloak was woven on a fairy loom consisting of a large and a small ring of gold, supported by a pole of jasper. The whole fairy band danced around it, each carrying a silver shuttle, fastening the ends of the thread to the rings and then passing the shuttles from hand to hand as they danced until it was completed. Queen Lulea herself wove the magic thread that gave the cloak its power.

The cloak was a miracle of beauty, sparkling with all the colours of the rainbow, as light as swansdown but so strong that it was almost indestructible. The question of who should receive it was decided by the Man in the Moon, who suggested that it be taken to Noland by one of the fairies and given to the first unhappy person he met. The fairies agreed to this and the cloak was offered to an orphaned girl known as Meg (alias Fluff), sister of the boy who was to become King of Noland due to the peculiar succession laws of that country.

The cloak subsequently became the cause of a war between Noland and its neighbour IX, because of the Queen of Ix's desire to possess it. But the wish she made was not granted, since she had stolen the cloak. Eventually the fairies took back their gift, after granting a last wish to King Bud of Noland, namely that he become the best ruler his country had ever seen. The whereabouts of the cloak remain unknown.

(L. Frank Baum, *Queen Zixi of Ix, or The Story of the Magic Cloak*, New York, 1907)

Three Bustrolian vessels for alcoholic honey-beverage.

BUSTROL, a kingdom on an island south of Madagascar, longitude 60° (east or west?), latitude 44° south. The access to Bustrol is through a large forest of immense oak trees which leads to a lake surrounded by high cliffs. On the other side lies a fertile strip of land some five hundred kilometres long. A species of large otter lives in the lake and the woods are full of the cries of extraordinary large birds that can be roasted like chickens or turkeys.

The inhabitants have organized themselves in perfectly square provinces of fifteen hundred feet per side, and shallow trenches have been dug to separate one from another. The houses are never more than one storey high because the winds that blow through Bustrol are terribly strong. Each province is ruled by a judge who represents twenty-two families before the king, and a priest who is in charge of education and religion, teaching humility and morals. The traditions of Bustrol are seven thousand years old and are the basis of society, entertainment and work. At the beginning of the eighteenth century Bustrol had 8,323,000 inhabitants: the number has not increased very much since. Men do not get married before they are thirty (except the king who marries at twenty-five), nor women before they are twenty. Polygamy is common practice.

Bustrolians are not hard workers. Fruit trees and vegetables grow easily and there is an abundance of apples, pears and nuts in the south–south-east and beans and peas in the north–north-west.

(Simon Tyssot de Patot, *Voyage et Avantures de Jaques Massé*, Bordeaux, 1710)

BUSY BEES, ISLAND OF THE, in the Tyrrhenian Sea, so called because the streets of its city buzz with people running here and there, getting on with their jobs. Everyone works, no one has a minute to spare. No idler or vagabond can be found anywhere on the island. Beggars are discouraged by being offered work and it is extremely difficult to obtain a free meal. However, the fish in the sea around the island are extremely courteous and will provide visitors with any information needed.

(Carlo Collodi, *Le avventure di Pinocchio*, Florence, 1883)

BUTTERFLIES, ISLE OF, see FORTUNATE ISLANDS (1).

BUTUA, a kingdom in central South Africa. Towards the north it borders with the kingdom of Monoemugui, towards the east with the Lupata Mountains, towards the south with the Land of the Hottentots.

The customs of the people of Butua are far more depraved than anything that has been said or written about the fiercest people on earth. Their skin is raven-black; they are short and highly strung; their hair is set in tight curls and they are naturally healthy and well-proportioned, boasting strong teeth and long lives. They indulge in every kind of criminal passion, such as lust, cruelty, spite and superstition. They are wrathful, treacherous and ignorant. Their women are beautifully shaped and almost all have well-kept teeth and sparkling eyes, but are so cruelly treated and so abused by their despotic husbands that their charms barely last thirty years and they rarely live to be over fifty. In Butua, women are considered to be born only for man's pleasure. Each inhabitant can have as many wives as he can afford to nourish; the chieftain of each region, as well as the king, has a considerable harem, usually in proportion to the extent of his wealth. Every month a tribute of about five thousand women is sent to the monarch from every part of the kingdom, from which he chooses the two thousand he prefers. In all, the women kept by the king number some twelve thousand and are constantly changed. These women are divided into four classes: the tallest and strongest are set to guard the Royal Palace; the second class, also called the "Five Hundred Slaves," are twenty to thirty years old and do the menial jobs in the palace, the gardening and much of the hard outdoor work; the third class is made up of girls from sixteen to twenty who are used as sacrificial victims to the gods of Butua; finally, a fourth class consists of the most delicate and beautiful infants up to the age of sixteen, and these are reserved exclusively for the royal pleasure.

In spite of the many crimes in which the inhabitants of Butua tend to indulge they are, as a people, very devout and god-fearing. Each district has a religious leader, under the authority of the king and in charge of a school of priests. In each temple an idol is worshipped, half-serpent and half-human, a copy of the original that stands in the Royal Palace—the people of Butua believe that the serpent created the world. The king alone has the privilege of worshipping in a private chapel in which the sacrifices take place; however, he also attends the services in the main temple in the capital. The governor of each province must send, every year, sixteen victims of both sexes to his religious leader who will then, with the help of the priests, immolate them on certain specific ritual days. The priests are also in charge of healing the sick, for which they employ quite effective balms made from plants. They are paid in women, girls or slaves, according to the social standing of the sick person they are treating. They do not accept food in payment; thanks to the offerings left at the temples, they never go hungry.

The most common food is corn, fish when available and human flesh. Public butchers provide the latter, as well as monkey meat, much appreciated in Butua.

As they are totally devoid of sensibility, these savages cannot imagine that the death of a friend or a relative might be in the least afflicting. They can see others die without showing the smallest sign of trepidation and it is usual for them to hasten the end when someone has no hope of being cured or has reached an advanced age. Their funeral customs consist simply of placing the body at the foot of a tree.

The population of Butua is continually diminishing, not only because of the criminal habits of those in power but also because after giving birth a woman is condemned to three years of complete abstinence.

(Donatien-Alphonse-François, Marquis de Sade, *Aline et Valcour*, Paris, 1795)

BUYAN ISLAND, in the north Atlantic. Visitors will find the weather in Buyan an unpleasant surprise: after sailing around the world, storms, winds, and showers gather here and vent their rage on Buyan. The fauna of the island accords well with the climate: many serpents, among which visitors can, but hopefully will not, find the oldest serpent in the world: crows with prophetic visions which they utter from time to time; a bizarre species of bird with an iron beak and copper wings; snakes of lightning; fowls of storm; and bees of thunder, whose honey—a great Buyan delicacy—tastes of rain.

The famous Alatuir Stone, used in the cruel ancient times as a sacrificial altar, can no longer be seen in Buyan. It was transported to the banks of the Jordan River where a small golden church was built around it, and it is said that it now serves as a chair to tired travelling gods.

(Karl Ralston, "Buyanka," in *The Songs of the Russian People*, Edinburgh, 1932)

C

CABBALUSSA, an island in the Atlantic, of which little is known. Visiting Cabbalussa is dangerous because the island is inhabited by fierce Indian women, who instead of hands and feet have asses' hooves and are known to be anthropophagous. Any traveller unfortunate enough to land in Cabbalussa is first made to lie with the inhabitants, then made drunk and finally eaten.

(Lucian of Samosata, *True History*, 2nd cen. AD)

CACKLOGALLINIA, an island in the Caribbean. The capital is Ludbitallya. Cacklogallinia is chiefly populated by chickens up to six feet tall. Their height and bulk is in fact variable: adversity will reduce a Cacklogallinian to the size of a three-foot dwarf and promotion to ministerial status will immediately cause him to reach a height of nine feet. Other birds occupy inferior positions.

One Englishman is known to have spent some years on Cacklogallinia, a certain Samuel Brunt, who was shipwrecked on the island's shores. At first he was treated as a natural curiosity, but he was finally befriended by the chief minister and made great progress at court, eventually rising to become *Castleairiano* (Examiner of Projects to Raise Taxes) with a salary of 30,000 *spasma*. He later floated a company which financed the first successful expedition to the moon before he ultimately returned to England.

The island is ruled by the Emperor Hippomina Connuferento, Darling of the Sun, Delight of the Moon, Terror of the Universe, Gate of Happiness, Source of Honour, Disposer of Kingdoms. He is also head of the established church. The emperor rules with the assistance of a prime minister and the members of the Grand Council of the Nation (*Bable-Cypherians*). It is, however, no secret that council members are appointed and removed in accordance with the prime minister's wishes. Bribery *of Bable-Cypherians* to ensure that certain matters will be discussed in council is a common practice.

Most laws are drawn up by lawyers anxious only to promote their businesses. All laws are extremely ambiguous, which leads to endless debate as to their true meaning. To make matters worse, a *Caja*, or judge, has the power to interpret the law

as he chooses, regardless of precedent. Judges tend to be appointed, not for their integrity or knowledge of the law but for their obsequiousness towards their patrons.

The Cacklogallinians of old were proud and noble. Trade flourished and the nation was noted for its honesty. Nowadays, the kingdom has fallen into something of a decline, although Cacklogallinians still consider themselves the freest nation in the world and regard all other people as slaves. They fawn upon tyrants, whom they appear to love, and always criticize mild and prosperous governments. The only thing they regard as a disgrace is poverty, and all methods—no matter how dishonest or corrupt—are used to procure riches. At court, the influence of the intriguing *squabbaws*, or courtesans, is all important.

The Cacklogallinians claim to believe in one God, but increasingly the rich mock the very idea of religion. In former times a gold ball, symbolizing eternity, was kept in the temple. It was covered with unintelligible inscriptions to symbolize the inscrutability of God. Theological quarrels began to break out over the form of the image. Some claimed it should be square to symbolize divine justice, others that it should be octagonal in order to symbolize the ubiquity of God. Still others claimed that the image should be formless, arguing that all regular shapes were evidence of superstition. Much of the precious gold was lost in the repeated melting down and recasting of the original image. Eventually it was agreed that small globes could be worshipped at home, provided that the priests continued to be paid to make sacrifices, but this custom eventually died out. The rich are now effectively atheists, and the cult of the golden ball continues to be maintained only by a sect of poor priests.

One religious rite that does survive throughout the country is the cult of St. Danasalio. Legend has it that a goat once damaged the Saint's corn. To commemorate his memory, each Cacklogallinian family piously takes a goat on St. Danasalio's Day, breaks its legs and then flays it alive.

Unlike European hens, Cacklogallinians, live mainly on meat and drink goat's milk. Only the poorer classes eat grain. Ministers and high-ranking officials are often cannibalistic and the poor go about in constant fear of being eaten by their superiors. But at the same time they are so servile that it is not unknown for the poor to come to the houses of the rich, begging them to have their families served up at table. This they consider a great honour.

Under Cacklogallinian law, those guilty of non-capital offences are imprisoned and given purges to make them vomit—the number of purges administered depends on the nature of the offence. Murderers are pecked to death. Military discipline in the large standing army is particularly severe.

For even a trivial offence, a soldier is sentenced to have all his feathers torn out; a corrosive plaster is then applied, which rapidly eats its way through to the bone. Under the inheritance laws, on the death of the father the entire estate goes to the eldest child, other surviving cocks go into the army or trade, and hens are married to relatives or are given a pension for life. Polygamy is illegal, but is nevertheless common among the upper classes.

Entertainments and sports are usually bloodthirsty. The poor are paid to hack one another to pieces on stage for the amusement of the crowd, and brawling is a popular sport among the young. Listening to the song of the cuckoo is a more gentle pastime. Cuckoos are paid large sums by rich Cacklogallinians and are able to build palaces with their profits when they return to their own land.

All funerals are by cremation in the marketplace. The corpse is carried in a hearse drawn by ostriches and preceded by heralds who proclaim his titles and genealogy; professional mourners are also employed. After the funeral, a portrait of the deceased is hung over the door of his house for one whole year. Funerals are extremely expensive and often ruin the heirs of the deceased.

The rich wear doublets and mantles and cover their legs with fine cloth. Medals, bells and ribbons are worn around the neck. Peacock feathers are sometimes added to the tail feathers. The nobility frequently cut off their spurs and replace them with elaborate golden ones.

To show respect to a superior, a Cacklogallinian will throw himself down and hold his beak to the ground until he is told to rise. Another sign of respect is to kiss the golden spurs of a nobleman. When greeting a *squabbaw*, one bows deeply. She will reply by turning her back, raising her tail feathers and allowing her posterior to be kissed: courtiers consider this a very great honour. Newly married couples are inseparable for a week or so after their wedding; after this period, it is considered indecent for married couples to appear together in public. Although they make frequent social visits, Cacklogallinians are not particularly

hospitable; refreshments, for instance, are offered only to formally invited guests.

Transport is by coaches drawn by ostriches or by palanquins carried through the air by uniformed hens at speeds of up to twenty miles per hour.

The flora of the island is typical of the Caribbean. The land is fertile and rich, with flourishing corn fields and rich pastures. The fields are kept in perfect order by hovering hens. The main farm animals are goats and sheep.

Cacklogallinia's relations with her neighbours have been stormy in recent years. A long and costly war was fought when both the Cacklogallinians and the Bubohibonians (owls) sought to nominate a successor to Chuctinio, Emperor of the Magpies. The closest allies of the Cacklogallinians in this war were the cormorants, who dominate trade in the area. They now exert great public influence in Cacklogallinia itself and appear to be intent upon encouraging the young to debauchery and atheism. The war, which ended in victory, was financed by increased taxation, doing much to enrich the already wealthy tax collectors.

Local currency is the *spasma* (equivalent to ten English pence) and the *rackfantassine* (roughly three to the pound). The unit of linear measurement is the *lapidian*, equal to one mile. The standard unit of weight is the *liparia*, equivalent to one-sixth of a pound.

(Samuel Brunt, *A Voyage To Cacklogallinia: With a Description of the Religion, Policy, Customs and Manners, of the Country*, London, 1727)

CAER CADARN, the fortress of Smoit, king of Cantrev Cadiffor, and the largest of the valley Cantrevs or small kingdoms of southern PRYDAIN.

Unlike the strongholds of the lesser nobility—some of which are little more than fortified stockades—Caer Cadarn is a stone castle with strong towers and iron-studded gates. Over it flies Smoit's banner, with the emblem of the Black Bear—the same emblem that appears in the Great Hall of the castle, where Smoit's throne can be seen, carved from half an oak tree in the shape of a great bear with its paws raised on either side of the seat.

The area around Caer Cadarn was once famed for its corn, the best in all Prydain. Agriculture fell into decline during the years when Achren ruled Prydain, when many of the ancient arts were also lost. Even after the defeat of Achren, it did not effectively recover and the constant feuds—usually over stolen cattle—between the petty nobility made it all but impossible for the farmers to work the land.

Throughout the wars between the Sons of Don and Arawn the Death Lord who sought to dominate Prydain, Smoit remained loyal to the House of Don and to High King Math of CAER DATHYL, unlike many of the lords of the southern Cantrevs. The castle did, however, fall into the hands of his enemies on one famous occasion. In the last stages of the war, Smoit was lured out of Caer Cadarn and ambushed by the soldiers of Magg, once steward of MONA but now an ally of Arawn. He was then imprisoned in his own castle. Travelling north from CAER DALLBEN, Taran, Gwydion—war leader of the Sons of Don—and Gurgi, walked into the trap, assuming that the castle was in Smoit's hands simply because his banner had been left flying over it.

The prisoners were ultimately rescued by the Princess Eilonwy, the bard-king Fflewddur Fflam and King Rhun of Mona, with the help of Gwystyl, one of the way postkeepers of the Fair Folk of TYL-WYTH TEG, who provided the royal trio with weapons of Fair Folk origin: eggs which exploded and released great clouds of smoke, and mushrooms which gave out great flames when broken. The attack took place in darkness, and during the confusion caused by the explosive devices the captives were released without difficulty. Caer Cadarn was handed back to its rightful owner, but in the fighting King Rhun of Mona was killed. He lies buried beneath the funeral mound in front of the castle.

(Lloyd Alexander, *The Black Cauldron*, New York, 1965; Lloyd Alexander, *Taran Wanderer*, New York, 1967; Lloyd Alexander, *The High King*, London, 1968)

CAER DALLBEN, a small farm, with a forge attached to it, in the south of PRYDAIN. The white thatched farmhouse is surrounded by an orchard and by cornfields which stretch to the edge of the forest. Caer Dallben is sheltered from the north wind by the hills that rise beyond the Great Avren River.

Although it appears to be an ordinary farm, Caer Dallben was once a stronghold against Arawn the Death Lord who on several occasions threatened the very existence of Prydain. Like CAER DATHYL in the north, Caer Dallben was built by the Sons of Don as a spiritual defence

against Arawn and his allies; even after the fall of the great castle at Caer Dathyl, Caer Dallben remained a shield against evil.

Caer Dallben is associated with many of the major events of the history of Prydain. It was here that Taran worked as an assistant pig-keeper, he who was to become at last High King of Prydain after the final defeat of Arawn. It was here, too, that the great council was held at the beginning of the second stage of the struggle against Arawn, and that the audacious plan was drawn up to steal the cauldron that the Death Lord used to create his undying Cauldron Born warriors. It was also the home of that oracular pig, Hen Wen, who foretold the manner in which Arawn would be defeated.

Caer Dallben takes its name from Dallben, the powerful enchanter who once lived here. In appearance, Dallben was simply an old man; but his powers exceeded those of any other enchanter in Prydain. His origins are obscure, but the three enchantresses who once lived in MORVA claim that they found him as a child, abandoned in a wicker basket in the grim marshes of their domain, and brought him up. It was under their tutelage that Dallben gained his first magical powers. It is said that he accidentally tasted a wisdom potion they were brewing and so began his career as an enchanter. Dallben was given the prophetic *Book of Three* by the three enchantresses, which told much of the future events of Prydain.

Caer Dallben is protected by the old man's magic; it is impossible for anyone to approach it without his permission and visitors are strongly warned not to try to enter against his will. In the past, in order to defend his seemingly humble abode, Dallben raised great storms and caused the earth to tremble. The one limit on his power is that he cannot kill—but it is written that anyone who kills him will perish.

Nowadays, Dallben no longer inhabits Caer Dallben. After the final defeat of Arawn, the enchanter left Prydain with the Sons of Don and returned to his true home in the SUMMER LANDS.

(Lloyd Alexander, *The Book of Three*, New York, 1964; Lloyd Alexander, *The Black Cauldron*, New York, 1965; Lloyd Alexander, *The Castle of Llyr*, New York, 1966; Lloyd Alexander, *Taran Wanderer*, New York, 1967; Lloyd Alexander, *The High King*, New York, 1968)

CAER DATHYL, a citadel in the north of PRY-

DAIN, and seat of Taran, High King of the country.

The present structure stands on the site of the original castle, built by the Sons of Don when they came from the SUMMER COUNTRY to drive the evil forces of Achren and Arawn the Death Lord from that land. Together with CAER DALLBEN in the south, its immense castle became one of the principal defences of Prydain, where the High Kings held their court.

As well as being a fortress in time of war, Caer Dathyl was also a place of beauty and memory, containing many fine examples of the work of the craftsmen of Prydain. It was the centre for the Bardic culture, and the many books and records of the bards were stored here in the great hall.

During the long war that followed against Arawn, Caer Dathyl was threatened by the armies of the Horned King, the dread battle leader of Arawn, who was defeated by the enchanted sword Dyrnwyn. Towards the end of the war, the citadel was again attacked and ultimately razed to the ground by the army of the Death Lord himself— the terrible undying warriors, the Cauldron Born. No trace of the former castle can be seen. Taran, on becoming High King, swore to rebuild Caer Dathyl, and so made it what it is today.

(Lloyd Alexander, *The Book of Three*, New York, 1964; Lloyd Alexander, *The Black Cauldron*, New York, 1965; Lloyd Alexander, *The Castle of Llyr*, New York, 1966; Lloyd Alexander, *Taran Wanderer*, New York, 1967; Lloyd Alexander, *The High King*, New York, 1968)

CAERLEON or **CARLION**, a walled city and fortress on the River Usk in Wales. The city is guarded by great towers which rise above the walls at intervals of two hundred yards, and by four strong gates. Within the walls, crowded streets, minor fortifications and churches cluster around the castle itself. A curious feature of the castle is the flight of 208 steps leading up to the room once used by Merlin the Enchanter.

The court of Arthur of CAMELOT sat periodically at Caerleon, perhaps because it was one of the most easily reached places in all his dominions.

It was here that Arthur massed his forces for the battle of BEDEGRAINE, and here that he celebrated his victory. It was also here that Arthur slept with the wife of King Lot of Orkney, unaware that she was his sister Morgan le Fay.

The favourite pastime of the court is hunting.

Dogs and men are divided into parties and the dogs are set free to drive the stag towards the huntsmen. Great honour falls to the man who slays the stag.

(Sir Thomas Malory, *Le Morte Darthur*, London, 1485; Anonymous, *The Mabinogion*, 14th–15th cen. AD; T. H. White, *The Once and Future King*, London, 1939)

CAFFOLOS, an island in the Pacific Ocean. Friendship is the main concern of the people of Caffolos. When one of their friends falls sick, the natives of Caffolos hang him from a tree, claiming that it is better that the birds, angels of God, eat him, than that the worms of the earth devour him. On a neighbouring island, the sick are smothered by specially trained dogs to spare them the pain of a natural death. To avoid any waste, their flesh is then eaten.

(Sir John Mandeville, *Voiage de Sir John Maundevile*, Paris, 1357)

CAGAYAN SALU, a small, volcanic island in the Salu Archipelago, near the southern Philippines. The natives of the coast are partly Mohammedan, harmless but well-armed. The natives of the interior are an independent tribe, the Berbanangs, and no other natives will go near their village. The Berbanangs are cannibals who are able to throw themselves into a trance and to project their astral bodies to a distance with a loud, deafening noise. This causes both men and animals to die of fear, a process which toughens the victims' meat to an adequate consistency. Visitors are advised, however, that the Berbanangs will not attack anyone wearing a coconut pearl necklace.

Accounts of Cagayan Salu were published by E.F. Skertchley of the Asiatic Society of Bengal (*Journal*, Part III, No. 1, Baptist Mission Press, Calcutta, 1897) and by Henri Junod (*Les Baronga*, Attinger, Neuchatel, 1898).

(Andrew Lang, *The Disentanglers*, London, 1902)

CAIR ANDROS, a long wooded island in the GREAT RIVER, some fifty miles to the north of GONDOR's capital at MINAS TIRITH. The island is shaped like a ship and the river breaks against its northern "prow" with great force.

The island was fortified to protect the surrounding regions from attack. During the War of the Ring, it was briefly captured by forces from MORDOR but was retaken without difficulty. After the final defeat of Sauron, the Dark Lord of Mordor, the ships of the Army of the West anchored here.

J.R.R. Tolkien, *The Return of the King*, London, 1955)

CAIR PARAVEL, capital of NARNIA.

CALAMY, see MABARON.

CALEJAVA, a republic on a small island of unknown location. It was founded towards the end of the seventeenth century by a European doctor, a certain Ava, who was exiled to the island by a despotic king. Visitors to Calejava will find an organized and peaceful civilization. The whole of the republic's economy is communitarian, based on agriculture. Everyone works the land five hours a day, with an hour's interval: all have the right to an equal period of leisure. All the goods produced are shared alike and can be obtained from nationalized warehouses. Political power is achieved through work, mainly by proving one's capabilities in ploughing, sowing and reaping; to make the task easier, all agricultural machinery has been highly developed.

Lodgings in Calejava are not difficult to find, but rooms must be shared with the inhabitants. The food is simple but nourishing and visitors can be assured that they will not be harassed for their political or moral beliefs. However, visitors are advised that Calejava lacks any form of entertainment and should not be considered for a fun holiday.

(Claude Gilbert, *Histoire de Calejava ou de l'Isle des Hommes Raisonnables, avec le Paralelle de leur Morale et du Christianisme*, Dijon, 1700)

CALEMPLUI, an island off the coast of China in the mouth of a large river. It is surrounded by a twenty-six-foot-high marble rampart made up of such perfect slabs that the entire wall seems to be one single piece. The rampart is crowned by a marble balustrade, and behind it travellers will find a vast circle of feminine statues, each with a brass ball in its hand. Beyond this first circle is a second one of cast-iron monsters all holding

hands. A third circle consists of decorated arches; a fourth of orange trees—the only trees on the island. A fifth circle comprises 360 small chapels, each dedicated to a different god and each looked after by a Chinese hermit. Finally, in the centre of the island, the traveller will find a small group of golden buildings similar to Greek temples, the purpose of which is unknown.

(Fernão Mendes Pinto, *Peregrinação*, Lisbon, 1614)

CALIBAN'S ISLAND, see PROSPERO'S ISLAND.

CALLIOPE, see OCEANA (1).

CALNOGOR, the capital city of ATVATABAR, five hundred miles inland. It can be reached from the city of KIORAM by a sacred railroad as well as an aerial ship. All buildings are of fine white marble. The king's palace and the legislative body, called Borodemy, are both in Calnogor, as is the Pantheon or Bormidophia, the largest building in the city. The palace of King Aldemegry Bhoolmakar is a tall, conical building, twenty storeys high, each storey surrounded by a row of windows decorated with pillars. Colossal lions of gold stand on the entrance towers, their claws formed of straps of gold running down the walls and riveted to the lower tiers of stone, giving the impression that they hold together the whole structure beneath. The architecture is a combination of Hindu, Egyptian, Greek and Gothic styles. The palace itself is surrounded by a spacious court enclosed by cloistered walls. A water tank runs through the court and the walls are decorated with lions, elephants, serpents, eagles, mechanical ostriches called *bockhockids*, youths and maidens all carved in stone.

The Pantheon or Bormidophia is a place of worship and the abode of Lady Lyone, Supreme Goddess of Atvatabar. It contains the most extraordinary object in all Atvatabar: the Throne of the Goddess, which consists of a solid gold cone, shaped somewhat in the form of a heart, some one hundred feet high. The throne is divided into three parts corresponding to the various castes of gods and to symbols of science, art and spirituality. The lower section, or scientific pantheon, forty feet high and seventy-two feet in diameter, surmounted by plaster casts of the bodies of the chief inventors of Atvatabar, shows bas-reliefs of their most important creations. The middle section is dedicated to art and its attributes. It is twenty-four feet high and sixty feet in diameter, divided into two sections: the upper, representing the gods of Poetry, Painting, Music, etc.: and the lower, showing the qualities of the soul developed by art, such as Imagination, Emotion, Tenderness. The top section, thirty-six feet high, with a diameter of thirty feet, contains the actual seat of the throne and three further divisions: magic and astrology; witchcraft, prophecy and similar arts; and theosophy, electro-biology and other related sciences. The goddess can be seen on a seat of aloe-green velvet that revolves slowly in the centre of the supporting base—a forest of magnolias, oaks, elms and other such trees—presenting the goddess, during opening hours, to every section of a vast audience of tourists and true believers.

(William R. Bradshaw, *The Goddess of Atvatabar, being the History of the Discovery of the Interior World and Conquest of Atvatabar*, New York, 1892)

CALONACK, a rich island kingdom beyond PATHAN, a paradise for travellers who are keen fishermen. The king of Calonack is entitled to a thousand wives, who are chosen from the fairest maidens of the country and who give him hundreds of children. Local legend has it that, as a reward for the king's obedience in following God's command "increase and multiply," all kinds of fish from all over the world come to the shores of Calonack. Each species comes once a year, staying by the coast for three days before its place is taken by a different species. They come in such numbers that nothing else can be seen in the water and people can catch and eat as many as they wish.

Elephants, called *warkes*, are used in battle and carry wooden castles on their backs; the king himself has an army of fourteen thousand *warkes*. The Calonackian fauna includes many species of snails, some so large that people can live in their shells, and beautiful villages of shellhouses can be seen throughout the island. Dangerous species of serpents are also found on Calonack. One black-headed species, as thick as a man's thigh, is prized by kings and lords as a great delicacy.

(Sir John Mandeville, *Voiage de Sir John Maundevile*, Paris, 1357)

A wooden elephant-castle from CALONACK.

CALORMEN, a large empire, more than four times the size of NARNIA, which lies to the north. The nearest country to Calormen is ARCHENLAND, from which it is separated by a wide tract of desert. To the north, the desert ends on the banks of the River Winding Arrow, the true boundary with Archenland. To the south runs an unnamed river, and Tashbaan, the capital of Calormen, stands on an island in this river. The desert itself is uninhabited, with only one small oasis. Travellers are advised that it is difficult and dangerous to cross. Probably the best route is through a rocky valley to the west of the oasis and then towards the double peak of Mount Pire, at the foot of which flows the Winding Arrow.

The only significant site in the desert is the group of twelve tombs of the ancient kings, northwest of Tashbaan, resembling huge stone beehives or huge people draped in grey robes that cover their heads and faces. There appears to be no order to the placement of the tombs and their origin remains obscure. Superstition has it that they are haunted by ghouls.

Tashbaan, the capital, is one of the wonders of the world. A many-arched bridge leads from the southern bank to the brazen gates of the city surrounded by high walls and always guarded by many soldiers. Horns are blown morning and night to signal the opening and closing of the gates, the only means of access. Inside the walls, the city climbs to the top of a hill, every inch of which is covered with buildings. At the summit stands the palace of the Tisroc and the great temple of Tash, with its silver-plated dome. Visitors will find the city a dazzling sight—a mass of terraces, colonnades and archways surmounted by countless spires, minarets and pinnacles.

The poorer areas, lower down the hill, present a sad contrast to the splendour higher up. The streets are narrow, and there are hardly any windows in the walls that flank them. Piles of rubbish lie everywhere and the whole area is always crowded with people on their way to and from the markets. Progress is further impeded by the passage of the lords and ladies of Tashbaan, who are carried through the streets on litters. Travellers are warned that it is a legal requirement to get out of their way immediately and that the streets are patrolled by the watch.

Higher up, the roads become wider and are lined with palm trees, arcades and great statues of the country's gods and heroes. Arched gateways lead into the richly furnished palaces, which are built around central courtyards or gardens with fountains and citrus trees.

The palace of the Tisroc consists of a series of great halls whose beauty defies description. Visitors must see the Hall of Black Marble, the Hall of Pillars, the Hall of Statues, and the Throne Room with its great doors of beaten copper. The old palace stands in the royal gardens, which descend in terraces to the city wall.

From Tashbaan, travellers can see the masts of ships riding at anchor in the mouth of the river. On either side of the city, the river banks are lined with gardens through which the white walls of innumerable houses can be seen. To the south of the city lies a range of low, wooded hills.

Another town to be visited in Calormen is Azim Balda, to the south of the capital. At the junction of many roads, Azim Balda is an important centre for communications and is the core of the country's postal system. From here, mounted messengers of the House of Imperial Posts carry letters throughout the country, which takes many weeks to cross on horseback.

Other notable places include the Lake of Mezreel, a particularly delightful spot in the south, near the remarkable valley of the Thousand Perfumes.

Calormen is basically an agricultural society, although fishing, crafts and general trading are also important, and salt is mined in the coastal area of Pugrahan. For administrative purposes, the country is divided into provinces, each ruled by a *Tarkaan*, or lord.

In contrast to Archenland and Narnia—the countries to the north—Calormen is strictly hierarchical. The dark-skinned peasants who make up the majority of the population have few or no rights and slavery is common practice here. The *Tarkaans*—whose power is enormous—are themselves subject to the absolute authority of the king; only the most privileged, for instance, have the right to stand in his presence. The lords and ladies dress extremely richly, the men resplendent in their jewelled and sometimes plumed turbans, perfumed hair and dyed beards. Even their horses are decked out in rich apparel, with stirrups and bridles inlaid with silver. Arranged marriages are common among the upper classes.

In contrast with the rich, the poor people of Calormen dress in long, dirty robes and wear wooden shoes turned up at the toe. Like their superiors, they wear turbans.

Historically, Calormen has always been an aggressive country and has frequently sought to conquer and annex the free lands to the north. When Prince Rabadash was refused in marriage by Queen Susan of Narnia, plans were laid to invade both Archenland and Narnia itself. These plans became known to King Lune of Archenland and to the rulers of Narnia, with the result that the Calormen army was defeated at Anvard by a mixed force of Narnians and Archenlanders. After his defeat, Rabadash of Calormen was turned into a donkey by Aslan, the lion creator of Narnia, but was allowed to regain his human form for the annual Autumn Festival. He was warned, however, that if he ever strayed more than ten miles from Tashbaan, he would remain a donkey forever. Chastened by his experiences, Rabadash became the most peaceful ruler Calormen has ever known and gained the title of Rabadash the Peacemaker. More commonly, however, he was known as Rabadash the Ridiculous, by which name he now appears in official history books. In popular speech, anyone who does something particularly stupid is inevitably referred to as "a second Rabadash."

In Calormen, the gods invoked are Azaroth and Tash. Little is known of the former, but Tash is represented as a vulture-headed figure with four arms, a demon god, who requires human sacrifices. The kings of Calormen claim to be descended from the immortal Tash, which may explain why any mention of the king's name is followed by the phrase "may he live forever." Apart from the worship of Tash and Azaroth, it is customary for the maidens of Calormen to offer secret sacrifices to Zardeenah, Lady of the Night, as they prepare for their weddings.

Travellers will find Calormen food extremely rich. A meal served to one of the aristocracy might consist of lobster and salad, snipe stuffed with almonds and truffles, chicken liver with rice and raisins and nuts, followed by melons and gooseberry or mulberry fool, the whole washed down with white wine. A similar taste for luxury can be seen in the Calormen custom of taking perfumed showers or baths in asses' milk.

The Calormen people are much given to quoting instructive lines, full of useful maxims from their poets, such as "Natural affection is stronger than soup and offspring more precious than carbuncles." The art of storytelling is taught to the young as a normal academic discipline.

The local unit of currency is the *crescent*: it costs five *crescents* to send a message by the Imperial Posts.

(C.S. Lewis, *The Horse and His Boy*, London, 1954; C.S. Lewis, *The Last Battle*, London, 1956)

CALYPSO'S ISLAND, see OGYGIA.

CAMELERD, the kingdom of King Leodegrance or Leodagran, somewhere on the border between England and Wales. Harassed for many years by King Rience of North Wales it fell into a state of dilapidation, and the land became overgrown and infested by wild animals. In the words of one observer, "The land was torn between man and beast." Rience was driven out of Camelerd by Arthur of CAMELOT who then married Leodegrance's daughter, Guinevere.

(Sir Thomas Malory, *Le Morte Darthur*, London, 1485; Alfred, Lord Tennyson, *The Idylls of the King*, London, 1842–85)

CAMELIARD, capital of Glathion, a country near POICTESME, seat of King Gogyrvan, who is also Lord of Emisgarth, Lord of Camwy and of SARGYLL. Not to be confused with CAMELERD. His court is renowned for its chivalry.

The main occupations of the courtiers are love-making, hunting and tournaments—in the latter, the only prizes are honour and a chaplet of pearls. The court is also famous as a school of love-poetry which makes extensive use of allegory and metaphor. It is the custom of Gogyrvan never to eat until all those who ask justice of him have been provided with champions to redress the wrongs that have been done to them.

The main room in the palace is the great Hall of Justice, lit by six tall windows in the east and west walls. The throne on which the king sits to hear the plaints of those who come before him is a seat of green rushes covered with yellow satin beneath a canopy.

Cameliard is haunted by two ghosts. One is the ghost of Smoit, the grandfather of the present ruler, who murdered his third, fifth, eighth and ninth wives and became known in his lifetime as the wickedest king ever to have reigned in Glathion. Smoit died shortly before his marriage to his thirteenth wife, when he fell down a flight of steps and broke his neck. Smoit appears in a suit of ill-fitting armour and is usually accompanied by another ghost—his ninth wife, Queen Sylvia Tereu, a pale lady in long flowing robes.

(James Branch Cabell, *Jurgen. A Comedy of Justice*, New York, 1919)

CAMELOT, the capital of King Arthur's kingdom of Logres, in southern England. The court normally sits here, although it occasionally meets at CAERLEON or KINKENADON. It was visited in the year 528 AD by a mechanic from Connecticut, in the United States.

The castle and city stand on Camelot River. The city itself is not particularly impressive; most of its houses are poorly thatched dwellings, there are few stone buildings of any substance and the streets are merely a maze of unpaved alleys. Camelot is dominated by a huge castle built on the peak of a hill above the river.

The main hall in the castle was built by the enchanter Merlin whom visitors can still see asleep in the cave known as MERLIN'S TOMB. The walls of the hall are decorated with sculptures and mystic symbols. Visitors will note that the sculptures can be divided into four main groups, showing beasts killing men, men killing beasts, perfect warriors and angels. The twelve stained-glass windows depict scenes from Arthur's mightiest victories; special attention should be paid to the window at the east end which shows the king receiving the sword Excalibur at AVALON. There are stone-railed galleries at either end of the hall and the floor is of large flagstones laid in black and white squares; the massive fireplace has projecting sides and a hood of carved stone.

The main hall houses the famous round table, at which 150 knights can sit. Although the design was conceived by Merlin, it was actually given to the king by Leodegrance of CAMELERD on the occasion of Arthur's marriage to Guinevere. It is said that the table symbolizes the roundness of the world. It is also the symbol of the Fellowship of the Round Table, composed of the most noble and virtuous knights in the land. For many years the knights of the Fellowship sought the Holy Grail which, it had been foretold, would be shown to certain of their number. Only three proved virtuous enough to see the sacred relic at CARBONEK CASTLE.

Visitors should also see the great hall of justice, a chamber lit by casement windows and decorated with the tapestry of Bathsheba. It is here that justice is normally administered by a plenary court of knights, and cases are adjudicated by the principal barons. The so-called trial by ordeal is often used, but cases may also be decided by combat, as it is presumed that the victor has God and truth on his side. If the accused is female, she may elect a champion to fight on her behalf.

The life of Camelot centres around the great feasts of the Christian year, with particular emphasis placed on Pentecost. Tradition has it that the feast of Pentecost cannot begin until an adventure has been undertaken or a challenge issued. It was at Pentecost that the Green Knight arrived at Camelot and issued the challenge that led Sir Gawain to the distant GREEN CHAPEL; it was also at Pentecost that the quest for the Holy Grail was inaugurated.

According to the code of Camelot, a knight may not ignore the slightest incident which may lead him to adventure. Once a quest or adventure has begun it must be followed through to the very end and an account of it be given to the court. No knight may refuse a challenge made to him by any of his equals.

Arthur established his capital at Camelot when he became king. His long reign was marred by the illicit love of Guinevere and Launcelot, which led to the siege of the castle of the JOYEUSE GARDE to which the guilty lovers had fled. The latter years of Arthur's rule were marked by increasing conflicts which culminated in the disastrous battle on Salisbury Plain, when Arthur was mortally wounded by his bastard son Mordred.

Arthur himself is not buried at Camelot, but visitors can see the tombs of many other heroes and famous personages, such as King Lot of Orkney and the unfortunate Elaine of ESCALOT who died for love of Sir Launcelot.

(Anonymous, *La Mort le Roi Artu*, 13th cen. AD; Sir Thomas Malory, *Le Morte Darthur*, London, 1485; Alfred, Lord Tennyson, *The Idylls of the King*, London, 1842–85; Mark Twain [Samuel Langhorne Clemens], *A Connecticut Yankee in King Arthur's Court*, New York, 1889; T.H. White, *The Once and Future King*, London, 1939)

CAMFORD, a university town in England, famous for its chair of Comparative Anatomy which was held in 1903 by Professor Presbury. Mr. Sherlock Holmes revealed the secret of Professor Presbury's researches—that a man can be transformed into an ape by the simple process of injecting monkey serum into the veins. Professor Presbury's intention of finding a rejuvenating serum failed, as did that of his Scottish colleague, Dr. Jekyll.

(Sir Arthur Conan Doyle, "The Adventure of the Creeping Man," in *The Case Book of Sherlock Holmes*, London, 1927)

CAMPAGNA, a country to the north of GREAT MARINA, from which it is separated by the MARMORKLIPPEN Range. In summer it is hot and misty and in autumn lonely and parched.

The inhabitants are mainly wild and unruly herdsmen who lead a seminomadic life. Their laws are based on an eye-for-an-eye system and their sense of justice is so typical of the region that the lawyers of Great Marina have called this kind of feud "a Campagna case." Despite their rough ways, the inhabitants are hospitable people who have given refuge to lovers, monks and debtors.

The gods of the country have idols made for them, rudely cut from stone or oak, which are set up at the boundaries of private pastures and public crossroads. Libations of melted butter or fat are offered to them, and on the night of the winter solstice, with the charred sticks which have been used in the sacrificial fires, the herdsmen mark the body of any creature about to bear young. One of the most famous of all idols in Campagna is the Coppice of the Red Steer, with red nostrils, tongue and sexual organs, around which grisly rites are rumoured to take place.

(Ernst Jünger, *Auf den Marmorklippen*, Frankfurt, 1939)

CAMPHOR ISLAND, somewhere in the Indian Ocean, so called because of the many camphor trees that grow there. The branches of each tree are so wide-spread that over a hundred people can sit in their shade. Should a traveller wish to obtain camphor from a tree, he must pierce the foliage with a pointed stick; camphored water will run out, becoming as dense as rubber upon contact with the air.

On the island lives a curious beast, the *karkadann*, larger than a camel, which lives on hay. It has a large horn in the middle of its forehead on which the figure of a man can be seen. Should an elephant cross its way, the *karkadann* impales it on its horn and continues on its way without noticing it. The elephant dies and the elephant grease, melting in the midday sun, runs down the *karkadann's* face into its eyes and blinds it. When this happens, the *karkadann* proceeds to the beach where it is caught by a bird called a roc or *rukh*, which grasps the beast in its claws and carries it and the dead elephant to feed the young rocs in their nest (see also ROC ISLAND).

(Anonymous, *The Arabian Nights*, 14th–16th cen. AD)

CANADIAN FLOATING ISLES, a group of islands in Lake Superior, ruled by a vexatious god to whom the Indians pay homage by casting ornaments and tobacco into the water. The islands are full of beautiful trees and flowers, sparkling crystals and melodious birds. However, should the delighted traveller try to approach them, the jealous god who keeps these lands for his own pleasure will cast a fog over them to shield them from the eyes of the curious. No matter how long the traveller keeps searching for them, he will never be able to set foot on the Floating Isles.

(Charles M. Skinner, *Myths and Legends of Our Own Land*, Toronto, 1896)

CANNIBAL ISLAND, one of the Ciacos group, near Isle des Jumeaux, in the Caribbean. The natives prefer to be called *Caraibes* (which means "great warrior") and have some contact with Europeans, mainly trading with them for weapons and spirits. They paint their bodies and live in long huts made of reeds and roofed with palm leaves, though the women and children are kept apart in smaller lodgings. They are governed by a Grand Cacique elected by popular acclaim. Though they hunt with poisoned arrows skilfully carved from beech wood, these are not employed in the pursuit of roosting birds, their main prey, which they hunt by placing glowing coals at the foot of the trees and throwing rubber or pepper on the embers. The thick smoke suffocates the birds, which fall to the ground. Travellers, however, are not advised to attempt this method of hunting as it often results in uncontrollable forest fires.

The Caraibes believe that man has several souls, the main one in the heart. At death, the heart-soul is guided to heaven and the others disperse into the air, causing storms at sea and mischief on land. They worship the sun and the moon and believe in a supreme being who is indifferent to the state of the world. When a Caraibe dies, all relatives are expected to attend the funeral. If anyone happens to be absent, he is compelled to slaughter all those who have attended, the ritual assumption being that they have either killed the dead man or contributed in some way to his death.

The nearby Isle des Jumeaux ("Twin Island") derives its name from two English children abandoned here towards the end of the eighteenth century. They were rescued but later returned to the island to establish a colony under the leadership of Lord Welly.

(François Guillaume Ducray-Duminil, *Lolotte Et Fanfan, Ou Les Aventures De Deux Enfans Abandonnés Dans Une Isle Déserte. Redigées & publiées sur des Manuscrits Anglais, par M.D.***. du M****, Charlestown & Paris, 1788)

CANSAY, see MANCY.

CANTAHAR, an island separated from Saint Erlinique by an arm of the sea, some two thousand leagues from the savage island of Tristar, south-east of the Cape of Good Hope. Cantahar is a near-perfect circle, with a ring of mountains around the coast enclosing a flat interior. A system of canals is used to travel and to transport merchandise throughout the island by means of barges towed by swimming horses. The banks of the canals are lined with trees, the fruit of which belongs by law to any traveller.

For the past ten centuries, Cantahar has been a monarchy, ruled by a *Kincandior* (a portmanteau word meaning "justice, clemency and valour"). The inhabitants are generous, hospitable and jealous in matters of honour. They are all ambidextrous, strong and agile, living to be over a hundred, and extremely fond of gambling. Marriage takes

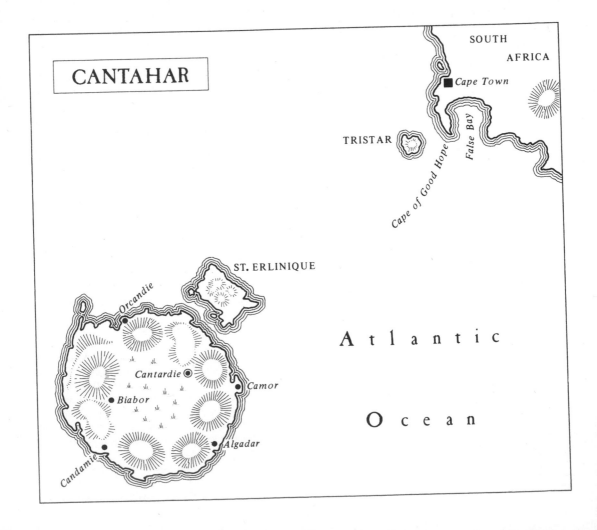

A stone altar in CANTAHAR.

place during an annual feast in which the men select the brides of their choice and make a public statement regarding their riches and health. A rose is then presented to the selected bride, who indicates her acceptance by placing it on her breast. The next day, the couple swear to honour the sun and promise mutual fidelity for life. The sun (Monsky) and the moon (Raka) are the only objects of worship and though other religions are tolerated—provided that they are not discussed in public—it is strictly illegal to introduce new religious beliefs. The inhabitants of Cantahar are convinced that Monsky will punish their evil deeds. He will steal the miser's money, put flies in the fussy man's food, sprinkle the lazy person's bed with crumbs and water down the drunkard's wine. All male children are dedicated to Monsky and all girls—seen as plants that will one day bear fruit—to Raka.

Visitors will notice that the inhabitants of Cantahar are very fond of religious ceremonies. Apart from the usual human sacrifices at their bloodstained altars, the people of Cantahar take pride in celebrating almost any event with unrestrained pomp. Funerals, for instance, are conducted amid military music. The body is dressed in fine robes and surrounded by pretty pictures illustrating the major events of the deceased's life. Then, among great rejoicing, the body is cremated. In another festival, the women celebrate their victory in a seventeenth-century war against Saint Erlinique, when the men of Cantahar had been defeated and the only chance of survival lay in the women's hands. During this celebration, the women wear paper crowns and take command of the towns and citadels for the whole day. Several other festivals are worth attending: in spring, the Cantahar Olympics; in summer, wild animal combats; in autumn, the Water Festival; and in winter, poetry competition.

Criminals are punished by being forced to work for the State and, if unskilled, they are taught a trade by their keepers. Education is free for all, but the children of the wealthy are usually brought up within the family and taught by private tutors.

The capital, Cantardie, is on a large island in an interior lake. Narrow roofs supported by elaborate pillars of jasper protect visitors on the streets from the rain. Similar pillars surround Cantardie's main temple, which houses the great statue of Monsky but can only be visited by the priests. The city contains large public granaries, a palace built in marble and a superb library.

The fauna of Cantahar contains a number of unique species. The *picdar*, hunted for sport, is about the size of a bear, green with white spots, and has the head of a leopard. Travellers are warned that the *picdar* is a very dangerous beast. The *igriou*, or "lazy," resembles a white donkey: it only moves in the presence of dogs and runs away from diligent and energetic people. The *tigrelis* looks like a cross between a horse and a deer, has a striped coat and a white crest between the ears and is used to draw carriages. Its mouth is very tender and a silk cord must be used instead of a bit. The *tigrelis* can cover thirty leagues in a day.

Travellers should know that no alcohol is sold in Cantahar and that people eat and drink in moderation. Clocks, sun-dials and hourglasses are unknown. Time is measured by means of a plant, the *rigody*, each branch of which produces only one leaf that turns very slowly, taking six hours to trace half a circle.

The language of Cantahar is Grondo and because of its difficulty it is advisable that the visitor learn certain signs that will make him understood.

Greetings, for instance, are as follows: to a superior, a hand placed on the chest and then on the ground, meaning that one grovels at his feet; to an inferior, hands placed on the forehead, meaning "I remember you." A woman is greeted by folding one's arms across the chest and a man by tickling his elbow. The Cantaharese currency is the *ropar*, equivalent to four American dollars. Twelve *poc* make one *rati*, and twenty *rati* make one *ropar*.

(De Varennes de Mondasse, *La Découverte De L'Empire De Cantahar*, Paris, 1730)

CANTARDIE, capital of CANTAHAR.

CAPA BLANCA ISLANDS, a group of islands in the Atlantic, belonging to Spain. The capital, Monteverde, is a very ancient town with twisting, narrow streets, barely wide enough to allow a wagon to pass through. Since the upper parts of the houses overhang the street, the people living in the attics can lean out and shake hands with their neighbours on the other side.

The food is good, and Monteverde has a profusion of cafés and restaurants that stay open until very late at night.

Traditional bullfights, which once took place every Sunday, have now been abolished. This was the work of the English naturalist, Dr. John Dolittle, who challenged the most famous bullfighter of the day, asking that bullfights be abolished forever if he was victorious in the ring. Thanks to his unique ability to speak the language of animals, Dr. Dolittle was able to persuade the bulls to chase the true matador out of the ring and then got them to perform a number of interesting tricks. Since that day, there has been no bullfighting in the Capa Blanca Islands.

(Hugh Lofting, *The Voyages of Doctor Dolittle*, London, 1923)

CAPE-VED ISLANDS, see GREENS WHARFE.

CAPHAR SALAMA, an island in the Academic Sea, in the Antarctic zone. It is shaped like a triangle and its perimeter is approximately thirty miles. The island is rich in grain and pastures, watered by rivers and brooks and full of all species of animals: a sort of world in miniature. The famous city of CHRISTIANOPOLIS is situated near the north coast of the island.

(Johann Valentin Andreae, *Reipublicae Christianapolitanae descriptio*, Amsterdam, 1619)

CAPILLARIA, an extensive, submarine country, comprising the ocean bed between Norway and the United States. On average, it lies about thirteen thousand feet beneath the surface. Warm currents make its soil especially fertile so that it nourishes all kinds of plant and animal life. A study of its fauna and geology suggests that Capillarian soil represents one of the most ancient strata of the earth. Millions of years ago, when the majority of the continents were uninhabited deserts, prehistoric fauna in Capillaria had already evolved into many rich and varied forms.

Unfortunately, the inhabitants of Capillaria have no knowledge of history or of recording traditions, so little can be said about the country's past. The inhabitants are a race of beautiful, stately women, all of them over six feet tall, with blonde hair that floats around them like a cloud. Their faces are angelic and their bodies soft, without any definite, angular lines. They are usually clad in flowing cloaks which, when flung back, reveal silky, but translucent skin, hinting at the inner organs with the transparent shimmer of milky glass. The skeleton is visible as a fragile and graceful structure, the lungs as two soft, blue spots and the heart as a rosy area. The alabaster-like skin, the quiet throbbing of the veins, the movement of the blood, all appear as a vision of beauty which might at any moment scatter and fade away, like water in water.

These women are called *Oihas*, a word which can be translated as either "human being" or "perfection of nature." Men are unknown in Capillaria. Their mythology has it that the *Oihas* are descended from the first *Oiha*, a creature similar to themselves, self-impregnated and self-propagating. The original *Oiha* finally eliminated from her body the uncomfortable and ugly organ that had performed the function of impregnation within her. Ever since, that organ has continued to exist as a parasite, living with the eternal but vain desire to be reunited with the body that has cast it out. The male sex is thus considered a primitive creature, expelled from the female body.

This external parasite is the *bullpop*, a small

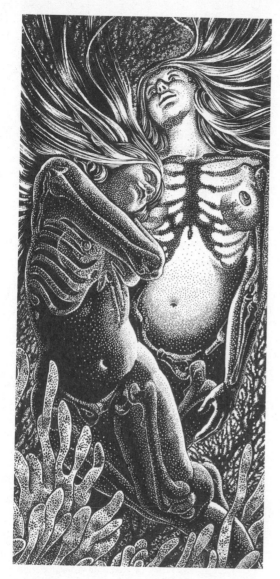

A pair of translucent inhabitants from the watery country of CAPILLARIA.

like seahorses, and are greatly despised by the *Oihas* who eat them, considering their bone marrow a particular delicacy. The *Oihas* believe that the consumption of this bone marrow is in some way linked with their ability to reproduce, as though it were a type of philoprogenitive stimulus.

Their theory contains some truth, as does the myth of the first *Oiha*. The *bullpops* are indeed reproductive organs, reproduced in turn by the *Oihas* themselves. When an *Oiha* is born, a couple of hundred *bullpops* are also expelled from the womb, in the placenta, and others are contained in the excrement of the infant *Oiha*. When the flowing water washes away the placenta and excrement, the tiny *bullpops* cling to branches of coral or mix with the mud of the sea bed. This is the true explanation of the *Oiha* belief that *bullpops* are generated from the slime on the ocean bed.

These two species or races are thus forced to co-exist, although both are ignorant of the bond between them. *Bullpop* attitudes to the *Oihas* vary. Some of them attempt to imitate the *Oihas* in order to please them: they compete for the honour of leaping into the cooking pot, believing that the *Oihas* will eat them because of some personal preference rather than out of physical need. Others adopt an almost religious attitude, watching the *Oihas* with admiration and then painting pictures of them. These pictures are, in fact, pornographic—showing pairs of *Oihas* in various obscene poses. A few *bullpops* inevitably appear in such pictures: this inclusion is seen by their creators as a way to propitiate the divine *Oihas* and win their favours.

All *bullpops*, however, have one thing in common. Compulsively they build immense, circular towers, which spiral upwards from the ocean bed, in the belief that somewhere above the liquid element in which they live a much freer and greater world exists. They believe they will eventually join the divine creatures that live there if only they can build a tower that will reach the surface of the sea. But their efforts are always frustrated by the *Oihas*, who take over the towers once they decide they are tall enough and use them as dwelling places. When they judge the tower to be ready, the *Oihas* invade the building and spray it with a liquid rather like the perfume used by European women, which disinfects the building by killing the *bullpops* working on it. As a result, none of the towers is ever completed.

creature some nine to ten inches long, with a cylindrical body, a human face and a bald, nobbly head. Instead of a nose, it has two curious apertures. The arms and hands are small and thin, but the legs are extremely well-developed and strong, with long toes, nails and fins as well as a pair of rudimentary wings. *Bullpops* swim vertically, rather

The "perfume" used in these invasions has a curious effect on the *bullpops*, who never try to defend themselves. At first it excites them and they begin to circle the intruding *Oiha* at ever-increasing speeds. Then they begin to attack each other and, at times, accidentally bump into the *Oiha*. Other *bullpops*, known as gallants, interpreting this as an attack on the superior *Oiha*, attempt to defend her by killing the others, referred to as *truborgs* or *strindbergs*. A few *bullpops* attempt to defend the towers, but they—the *gonts* or *kants*—are inevitably exterminated by sub-species of *bullpops* known as *goethes*, *wildes* and *dannunzios*, who appear to have a spontaneous hatred of the *kants*.

Not only do the *bullpops* provide the *Oihas* with their towers and palaces, they also supply their clothes. The old, fully developed *bullpop* who has not been eaten or asphyxiated usually pupates, emitting a thin, black thread to weave his cocoon. The *Oihas* treat the cocoons like silkworm cocoons, dropping them into boiling water. The *bullpop* dies and the thread can be unwound and spun into fabric used to make gossamer-thin, silk garments. This substance, excreted by the *bullpop* brain, is the most important raw material in the *Oiha* economy. Chemical analysis shows that it resembles ink, presumably because the favourite food of the *bullpops* is printed paper which floats down from the surface of the sea. *Bullpops* fed on such paper make a particularly prized delicacy for the *Oiha* table.

In the towers constructed for them by the *bullpops*, the *Oihas* lead lives of luxury. Even their furniture is edible, made of chocolate or sugar. Their whole life is centred around pleasure, which in their language is equivalent to "philosophy." "Sensitivity" is the highest quality of life in their culture and is, effectively, synonymous with "sense" or "wisdom." All their senses are highly developed and are tuned in to pleasant stimuli in a heightened manner. The scent and taste of certain dishes, the music of particular instruments, a colour, all produce an almost orgasmic reaction in the *Oihas*. Since birth, all *Oihas* have been surrounded by constantly moving water, which tickles and caresses their sensitive skin; in effect, they live in a state of voluptuousness from birth onwards. Their love-life has nothing to do with the preservation of the species; it is an art existing only for its own sake, which finds expression in the admiration of one *Oiha* for another; like every other area of pleasure, it is so refined that it has virtually become a spiritual experience. It would be impossible to describe

their love-making without being charged with gross indecency. Yet, in the language of the *Oihas* themselves, it represents the purest and most noble ideals, the expression of all that is majestic and lofty—a pure manifestation of the soul contained within the body.

The language of the *Oihas* does not belong to any known linguistic group. There are no words to express abstract ideas, or, indeed, any ideas at all. Words refer only to tangible objects or to things that can be experienced through the senses, but the words do not define the object, they refer, rather, to the feelings and sensuous effect that it produces in the speaker. In short, *Oiha* language consists entirely of interjections and ejaculations. Variety is obtained by changing the pronunciation or inflection of a word. The word *Oiha* itself is basically an ejaculation, an exclamation of joy and ecstasy.

The *bullpops*, in contrast, live in a comparatively complex society, dominated by the need to build their towers. They assemble in a variety of tribes, each organized in accordance with the political preferences of the group. There are monarchies, republics and socialist states, all of which build towers following their particular political lines.

Despite the *Oihas'* opinion of the *bullpops*, they are, in fact, highly developed. Although their bodies are small and have evolved various redundant organs, they are quite capable, for example, of performing the most difficult surgery: changing an eye into a liver, transplanting brains, grafting the gills of a fish into the heart of a *bullpop* with no difficulty at all, and their leaders are versed in every aspect of science and technology.

The more advanced *bullpops* do not accept that the seizure of their towers by the *Oiha* is a natural disaster, a *gonchargo* or even the effect of some supernatural power. They claim that, on the contrary, it is the effect of pathological substances that causes the dissolution of certain atoms. Even so, the wisest of the *bullpops* fail to understand why their towers are constantly taken from them. Some will even deny that the *Oihas* exist, explaining everything in terms of a mass psychosis that affects the nervous system of the more sensitive of their number.

War between the towers is not uncommon. An attempt to create an Empire of United Towers failed when a violent *gonchargo* destroyed three of the towers. One group was accused of having caused the disaster by overbuilding and increasing the concentration of waters above them, thus giving rise to changes in the ocean currents. The resulting war led to huge losses on both sides.

In the initial stages of the war, a dispute arose among the allies of one of the towers, when one group argued that it was in the interests of the *bullpop* society as a whole that the first person singular be erased from the language and be replaced by the first person plural, claiming that governments based on "I" could never be brought into harmony with those based on "we." The triumph of the First Person Pluralists was the outcome, ushering in an era of even greater conflicts over grammatical and other issues. Some grammarians demanded the eradication of the word "mine" and pleaded for its replacement by "ours" in all contexts, easily overcoming arguments put forward by the Conservative Party of Eighteen-Month-Old Babies, who claimed that children use the word "mine" before they learn to use "ours" and that it was therefore of much greater significance. Quarrels also arose as to the best method of building towers: for instance, should work begin with the uppermost storey, given that the aim was to reach the surface as quickly as possible?

All kinds of projects to prevent *gonchargos* were set in motion, many of them relating to language. It was argued that tenses needed reform, so that all actions of the present could be considered as taking place in the future, the assumption being that if the practical results of forecasts for the future were put into application at once, whole centuries could be saved. The party propounding this view—the Party of Futurist Social Rubber Stretchers—achieved power for a brief period, but were forced to yield their position when a sudden outbreak of dysentery (which they had not predicted) forced them out of their tower. Following the downfall of the Futurists, the Society of Freezing Last Year's Snow took over—a group convinced that, as the future was so difficult to predict, it would be preferable to return to the past, with everyone going back to the position he had held 1,640 years ago.

A wide variety of conflicting ideologies and theologies continued to flourish in the *bullpop* society, some arguing over racial and physical types and their respective qualities, others demanding race-purification and race-defence. The final battle, however, arose between the two great races, those of the Mole-on-the-Nose and those of the Protruding-Ear-Lobe. Matters became more complicated when it was realized that some *bullpops* had neither. A new basis was finally found in a return to the commonplace and traditional belief that the *Oiha* represented the common danger and that the *gonchargo* was a punishment of fate. Finally, a Gonchargo Government came to power, founded by the First Gonchargo Cooperative. Their first action was to set up a Consumers' Institute of Gonchargo and a Biochemical Boot Factory. Subsequent developments remain obscure.

Visitors to Capillaria are advised to quickly avail themselves of the artificial gills invented by the *bullpops* which will enable them to breathe underwater. Male visitors should not reveal their sex as this would make them liable to punishment and they would be faced with the choice of being eaten by the *Oihas* or undertaking forced labour among the *bullpops*.

(Frigyes Karinthy, *Capillaria*, Budapest, 1921)

CAPRONA, see CASPAK.

CAPTAIN SPARROW'S ISLAND or ISLE OF DEVILS, in the north Pacific, longitude 5°2'18" north and latitude 123°4'7" east. It was first reported in 1744 by Captain Geoffrey Cooper, of the brig *Good Adventure*. The island is some twenty miles round and has no bays or inlets. It lies remote from other lands in a region which sailing ships dread: the Marquesas Islands are fifteen hundred miles to the south-west; Duncan Island, twelve hundred miles east; and Christmas Island, two thousand miles west. The island is one huge volcanic crater. The southern side is fertile land, with miles of park-like garden-ground bearing fruits of many kinds and many tropical flowers. This area is tended by a number of huge birds *(ruka)*, larger than the cassowaries of Patagonia, some nine feet tall, which the natives employ to weed and prune. To the north is a large swamp inhabited by curious blue pigs somewhat like small tapirs.

As planes cannot land here, the only access to the island is from the sea, through a tunnel on the east coast, at the far end of which is a flight of steps that leads to a high chamber in the rocks. Here can be seen the drawing of a human form with wide stag-like horns, in dull red, the work of an artist for whom man and stag were one; it stands eight feet high with a sword in its left hand. Also in this chamber lies an old brass cannon inscribed *The*

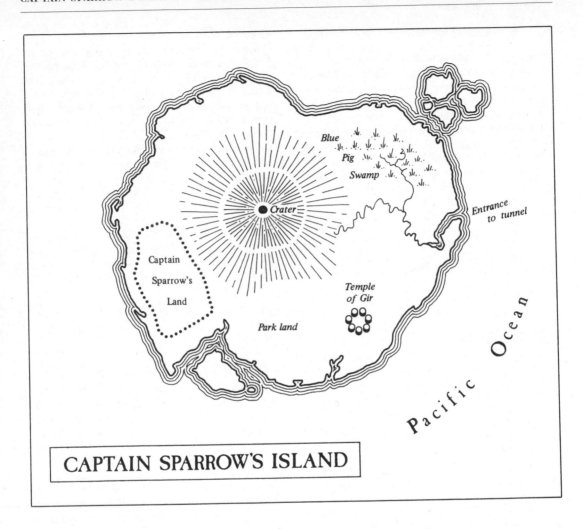

CAPTAIN SPARROW'S ISLAND

Fighting Sue, 1866. Another tunnel leads from this chamber into a smaller one full of serpent-like roots, opening onto the hillside in the interior.

Three tribes inhabit the island. One is a small group of what remains of the original inhabitants, most of whom died infected by European viruses. Though Europeans regard this as a mark of their own superiority, the natives say that it is as though a sewer should boast that it can tolerate garbage. The second group is a race of satyrs. The third is a mixed race of Europeans and satyrs, very much degenerated. These Europeans arrived in the mid-nineteenth century, led by Captain Andrew Sparrow of the pirate ship, *The Fighting Sue,* Captain Sparrow was looking for a place in which his men and their families could

find security. Soon after setting up a small colony on the island, he decided to scour the seas once again in search of new booty. This time, however, he was captured and executed. His people, left alone on the island, continued to carry out his orders. Captain Sparrow had agreed with the priest of Gir, High Priest of the original inhabitants, that his people would not interfere with them; furthermore, his men would be allowed to hunt the blue pigs, but not the monkeys or the *rukas,* and they would be allowed to shoot only one satyr per moon. The Temple of Gir was sacred to the priest's people; the south-west of the island was reserved for the privacy of the invaders. But Captain Sparrow's people mated with the satyrs and this mixed race now dominates the island.

Travellers should pay a visit to the Temple of Gir and carefully ascend the steep and narrow stairs cut in the thickness of the temple walls. It is said that "he would have been a bold man who would have adventured to climb them without knowing the reception to which the next turn might bring him." The walls are stained red, almost purple, with the blood of the original inhabitants sacrificed to Gir. An ancient law decreed that there should only be eighty of their race, no more no less, and the old and the sick were chosen as ideal victims. The temple is neither beautiful nor ugly, except as strength is beautiful.

(S. Fowler Wright, *The Island of Captain Sparrow*, London, 1928)

CARABAS CASTLE, somewhere in France; in fact the Castle of the Ogre, taken over by a clever cat known as Puss-in-Boots. The cat was the only inheritance left to the youngest son of a miller, who at first lamented his meagre share in his father's fortune. However the cat managed to convince the King of France that his master was in fact the Marquis of Carabas, and then drew up a plan to overcome an ogre, lord of a nearby castle. The cat taunted the ogre into transforming himself first into a lion and then into a rat, whereupon the cat ate him up and offered the castle to his master. Seeing the young man in such a rich environment and believing him to be a true marquis, the King gave him his daughter's hand in marriage; the cat became an important personage at the French court.

(Charles Perrault, "Le Maître Chat ou Le Chat Botté," in *Contes*, Paris, 1697)

CARAS GALADHON or CITY OF TREES, the now deserted capital of LÓRIEN and the site of the court of the Lady Galadriel and Celeborn. The capital stands on a green hill crowned by the tallest of the famed *mallorn* trees on Lórien. The city is surrounded by a great wall of green. Outside the wall runs a deep ditch, the outer edge of which bears a road of white stone. A white bridge gives access to the gates of the city. On the top of the hill stands the tree where Galadriel and Celeborn lived, guarded by elf wardens.

In the south of the city there is a walled enclosure where no trees grow. A flight of steps leads down to a green hollow where a silver basin stands on a low pedestal carved in the form of a branching tree, catching the water that streams from a fountain high above. When filled with water, the basin becomes the Mirror of Galadriel. Galadriel would fill the basin and then breathe on the water, and as the water cleared it would reveal strange images of "things that were, things that are and things that yet may be."

Caras Galadhon became deserted at the end of the Third Age of MIDDLE-EARTH when Galadriel left to return west across the sea and when Celeborn went to found a new elven kingdom in that section of MIRKWOOD that became known as East Lórien.

(J.R.R. Tolkien, *The Fellowship of the Ring*, London, 1954; J.R.R. Tolkien, *The Return of the King*, London, 1955)

CARBONEK CASTLE, in which the Holy Grail was once housed. It stands above the stormy waters of the Sea of Collibe and can only be reached by travelling in the Ship of Faith. This magic vessel contains a bed and crown of silk, and a sword, the haft of which is made from the bones of a magic serpent and a magic fish. Travellers are advised that only brave and virtuous persons may draw the sword; anyone else who tries to do so will be wounded by it, as was King Pelles, who was injured in both thighs.

At the end of the long quest for the Grail, Sir Galahad, Sir Bors and Sir Perceval crossed the Sea of Collibe. They passed the lions that guarded the gate and found their way to the tiny chapel of the Grail at the very heart of the castle. Here the three knights saw a vision of Christ, the angels and Joseph of Arimathea, and drank from the Grail. Sir Galahad was then commanded by Christ to take the holy relic away to Sarras, a city of unknown location, where Joseph of Arimathea is said to have converted a pagan king to Christianity.

So travellers today will not see the Grail at Carbonek nor the guardian lions; only the ruined castle and the holy chapel and the ghosts of many brave men.

(Sir Thomas Malory, *Le Morte Darthur*, London, 1485; Alfred, Lord Tennyson, *The Idylls of the King*, London, 1842–85; T.H. White, *The Once and Future King*, London, 1939)

CARLION, see CAERLEON.

CARNAL POLICY, see City of DESTRUCTION.

CARN GAFALL, a curious monument in the Buellt area of Wales, which consists simply of a pile of stones, the uppermost of which bears the imprint of a dog's paw. The print was left by Gafall, a dog owned by King Arthur of CAMELOT, during the hunt for the boar Trwyd. Visitors to the monument have repeatedly tried to carry off the stone bearing the print, but they have never succeeded in keeping it for more than a day and a night. The next morning, it inevitably returns to its place on top of the pile of stones.

(Anonymous, *The History of the Britons*, 10th cen. AD)

CARTOGRAPHICAL EMPIRE, a small country probably on the northern frontier of Mongolia. First described by the Spanish traveller Suárez Miranda in 1658, its main attraction is some ruins in the western deserts, the remains of a vast map that the imperial cartographers had built to coincide point by point with the empire itself. By the mid-seventeenth century the map, neglected by the younger generations, was almost completely destroyed. Nowadays, hordes of wild beasts and beggars roam in the western regions.

(Suárez Miranda, *Viajes de varones prudentes*, Lerida, 1658, in Jorge Luis Borges and Adolfo Bioy Casares, *Cuentos breves y extraordinarios*, Buenos Aires, 1973)

CASEOSA or **MILK ISLAND**, in the Atlantic Ocean, surrounded by milky waters. It is entirely white, of the shape and consistency of a twenty-five-mile-round mature cheese. It is uninhabited, but a temple dedicated to the nymph Galatea was built here and is worth visiting. Vines grow freely, and the grapes when pressed produce not wine but milk.

(Lucian of Samosata, *True History*, 2nd cen. AD)

CASHEEDOORP, see SAS DOOPT SWANGEANTI.

CASPAK, a large island in the far south of the Pacific Ocean. Though its exact location is unknown, Caspak is far enough south for icebergs to appear in the vicinity. Caspak's cliffs rise steeply from the ocean and no landing-places exist. The cliffs are of uniform height, shot with green and brown; the glint of iron pyrites and the verdigris of copper can be clearly seen from the sea. The only known means of access is via a river which flows out below sea level through a winding tunnel in the cliffs. Beyond the cliff barrier, the river surfaces and can be traced to its source in a vast inland lake or sea; twenty miles above the main lake is a smaller expanse of water surrounded by red sandstone cliffs.

Most of the land is covered in dense forest, broken by parklike areas and beautiful rolling downs. The roughly circular plains and forests end at the foot of the steep cliffs that cut Caspak off from the ocean. The climate is warm and humid; the lakes are fed by subterranean hot springs whose vapours add to the sultriness of the air. Important oil deposits have been found on the island.

The physical appearance of Caspak and what little is known of its geology suggest that it is all that remains of an ancient mountain destroyed by volcanic action. Most of its features point to its once having been part of a great land mass which now lies deep below the Pacific Ocean. The only other land known to have survived the volcanic activity is the offshore island of Oo-oh, which lies at some distance from Caspak itself.

The flora of Caspak is similar to that found in other parts of the world in prehistoric times. The plains are covered in tall lush grass, each blade of which is tipped with a brilliant flower from violet and yellow to carmine and blue. In the forests giant tree-ferns are found, many of them over two hundred feet high. A type of giant maize can also be seen, some fifty to sixty feet high, with ears the size of a man's body and kernels the size of a fist. Inland, in the more open areas, eucalyptus and acacia are common.

The fauna is equally diverse. In the rivers and lakes, the dominant species are the reptiles of prehistoric times. Among these are the enormous plesiosaurus, with a neck some sixteen to eighteen feet long, and the allosaurus, a large lizard ten feet high with a huge and powerful tail, vast hind legs and short forelegs; it moves in enormous bounds, somewhat like a gigantic kangaroo. Giant pterodactyls can also be seen. The island's waterways swarm with smaller lizards and reptiles, all extremely savage and dangerous carnivores.

Inland, large herds of antelope and red deer roam the plains, together with the giant woolly

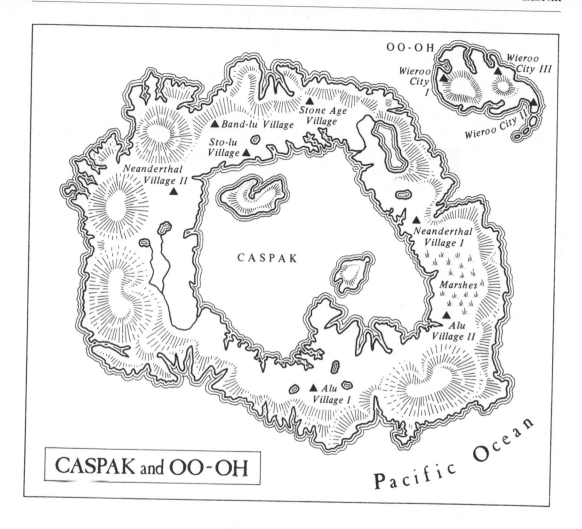

CASPAK and OO-OH

rhinoceros and the bison-like aurochs. At least three species of horse have been seen, the smallest little bigger than a dog and the largest measuring about sixteen hands.

Caspak is inhabited by a variety of races, from ape-men to Neanderthal men to the comparatively highly developed Stone Age men. The various races are distributed according to a definite geographical pattern: the most primitive peoples are found in the south and the more sophisticated in the north. The farthest advanced of all races, the Wieroos, no longer live on Caspak but have migrated to Oo-oh.

The least developed of Caspak's inhabitants are the Holu or ape-men, who fight with their fangs and heavy clubs. The race known as the Sto-

lu represent a higher stage of evolution; they live in man-made caves and are armed with stone hatchets; they appear to have no knowledge of agriculture and live by hunting and gathering. To the north the Sto-lu territory gives way to that of the Band-lu, who wear crude garments fashioned from snakeskins and fight with stone-tipped spears, stone knives and stone hatchets; farther north live the Kro-lu or spear-men. All these people are equally aggressive; all will kill strangers on sight. They all speak variants of the same language; the sophistication of vocabulary and syntax rises as one moves from south to north.

All races found on Caspak share the belief that they originally came from the south and that they will eventually go north; their word for south literally means "towards the beginning." This belief is probably based on the unique and complex pattern of evolution found on this island. No children or babies are ever seen in any of the tribes. Instead, life begins in the warm pools near the Caspak villages. These pools are full of eggs and tadpoles surrounded by a poisonous serum to protect them from predators. The eggs are deposited in the pools and float down towards the sea, developing as they go. Some become reptiles or fish, and some even develop into apes or monkeys. Once this stage has been reached, the individual develops slowly into the higher forms of life, finally reaching the form known as Galu. A few Galus give birth to their young in the normal manner; they are referred to as Cos-ata-lu, which literally means "no-egg-man."

It is believed that Caspak is what remains of the mysterious continent of Caprona, discovered by the Italian navigator Caproni, who followed the route taken by Captain Cook in about 1721. Caproni described a rockbound, inhospitable coast in this area of the Pacific; it stretched, according to his account, for hundreds of miles without a single harbour or beach. He also claimed that it was made of a strange metal which seemed to affect his ship's compasses. He was unable to make a landing, but cruised along the coast for several days before changing course; he never made a proper chart of his discovery. The only people known to have explored Caspak are a group of Englishmen and Americans who captured a German submarine in 1916. Together with their German prisoners they drifted south and eventually reached Caspak, perhaps because the hull of the submarine was attracted by the magnetic rocks in its cliff barriers. The submarine was able to travel up the underground river and reach the inland waters of Caspak. Several of the party died and the survivors had great difficulty in leaving. Travellers would be well advised to establish an escape route at the beginning of their visit.

(Edgar Rice Burroughs, *The Land That Time Forgot*, New York, 1918; Edgar Rice Burroughs, *Out of Time's Abyss*, New York, 1918)

CASTLE, THE, an unnamed fortress belonging to the Count of Westwest, somewhere in Bohemia. It consists of a vast conglomerate of two-storey buildings and several low dwellings set one against the other. Visitors who have not been warned that the edifice is in fact a castle will suppose it to be a small city. The Castle has a single tower, round and almost featureless, in part mercifully covered with ivy, and pierced by a few windows. The tower's battlements seem uncertain, irregular, grasping at the sky like the faltering drawing of a negligent or timid child.

The Castle looms over an oppressive village situated on the banks of a river; no one is allowed to reside or even spend the night in the village without the Count's permission. The inhabitants have strange physical characteristics: their skulls seem flattened by blows and their features seem to portray the agony of these blows.

Winter lasts long in this area and the village is usually covered in snow, sometimes even in summer.

Visitors are warned that access to the Castle is difficult if not impossible. Though invited by the Count himself, they may be made to wait for days on end without crossing the threshold, watching the Castle's outline change shape in the hazy light.

(Franz Kafka, *Das Schloss*, Munich, 1926)

CASTORA, a country of unknown location, ruled by a queen. All men have been banished from Castora and the Assembly of Women has passed a law that no male visitor can spend more than twenty-four hours in the country, after which he will be sacrificed to the goddess Pallas, Protectress of Castora.

The Temple of Pallas should be visited: it is supported by twenty-four marble columns and houses a gold statue of the goddess inscribed with a list of her attributes. The temple is attended by fifty young women from the noble families of Castora. The goddess herself has created a miraculous fountain near the temple site, and those who bathe in it give birth to daughters nine months later. The law states that all women must visit the fountain once a year in order to increase the country's population.

The only means of transport in Castora are chariots pulled through the air by teams of birds. In cases of dire need, teams of rats can also be used.

Castora is surrounded by mountains inhabited by magicians who use the numerous strange plants that grow there for their spells: it is said that Medea obtained her poisons from the mountains of Castora. Travellers should also visit the Tower of Regrets, a grim fortress in which a Castorian princess was exiled for giving birth to a boy. A fairy palace and garden were built next to it to make the place more comfortable; in spite of being invisible it should certainly be visited.

(Marie Anne de Roumier Robert, *Les Ondins*, Paris & London, 1768)

CASTRA SANGUINARIUS and **CASTRUM MARE**, two ancient Roman outposts surviving unchanged by time in the heart of Africa, beyond the Wiramwazi Mountains. Travellers in this region will probably hear about these cities from the native Bagego tribe, who refer to them as the Lost Tribe. Both cities are at war with one another and it is advisable not to speak well of one when visiting the other.

Castra Sanguinarius is reached through a for-

est behind which rises a lofty rampart surmounted by palisades and battlements. At the base of the rampart is a wide moat through which a stream moves slowly; a bridge crosses the moat and leads to a gateway flanked by high towers. The buildings within the city are not, as would be expected in this part of Africa, native huts, but substantial constructions. Those near the gates are one-storey stucco houses, built around an inner courtyard. Shops and other dwellings constitute the centre of the city. Notable among all other constructions is the Castra Sanguinarius colosseum. Arched apertures flanked by graceful columns up to a height of forty or fifty feet enclose this mighty arena which bears a marked resemblance to that of Rome. It is here that prisoners are taken to fight with Roman

CASTRA SANGUINARIUS and CASTRUM MARE

gladiators, savage beasts and members of a tribe of apes (see APE-TRIBE).

Castrum Mare, at a fair distance from Castra Sanguinarius, is built on a small island and is also surrounded by walls. The streets have no pavements and are deep in dust. The houses are built up to the street line and where there is a space between adjacent houses a high wall closes the aperture so that each side of the street presents a solid front of masonry broken only by arched gateways, heavy doors, and small unglazed and heavily barred windows.

Though this might give the impression that Castrum Mare is a prison overrun with criminals, these bars are in fact defenses set up against the possible uprising of slaves or the invasion of barbarians. However, doors are seldom locked, for there are no thieves to break in, nor criminals to menace the lives of the inhabitants. This is because Honus Hasta, who left Castra Sanguinarius soon after its foundation in the times of ancient Rome, decided to establish another city that, unlike Castra Sanguinarius, would be free of criminals and evildoers. He became the first emperor of Castrum Mare and made laws so drastic that no thief or murderer lived to propagate his crime. The laws established by Honus Hasta condemned not only a criminal to death, but also all the members of his family so that there would be no one to transmit to posterity the inclinations of a depraved sire.

Both cities preserve the customs of ancient Rome, in dress, in food, in the arts. Travellers visiting either city are well advised to obtain the services of a loyal slave who will be willing to give up his life in exchange for that of his master, as there is always the danger of foreigners being captured and either slaughtered or made to take part in the bloodthirsty combats in the arena.

(Edgar Rice Burroughs, *Tarzan and the Lost Empire*, New York, 1929)

CATHNE, a walled city built entirely of gold in the Valley of Onthar, Africa. It can be reached from Mount Xarator, a high peak filled with fire and molten rock. Cathne lies between a forest and the bend of a river crossed by the Bridge of Gold. The river itself is extremely dangerous and many travellers have fallen into its boiling waters.

The Temple of Thoos is one of the city's most notable sights, a large three-storey building with a great central dome; galleries run around the interior at the second and third storeys, and the insides of the dome and walls are embellished with mosaics. Directly opposite the main entrance is a large cage built into a niche, and on either side of the cage is an altar supported by golden lions; a row of stone seats faces the niche. At the ceremony of Thoos, in which the king or queen takes part, a young girl is sacrificed to a lion in the cage.

Outside the city is a plain called the Field of the Lions, a sort of arena in which prisoners are made to fight the savage beasts. The arena itself is excavated to a depth of twenty or thirty feet, and slabs of stone arranged upon the excavated earth serve as seats. At the east end of the Field of the Lions is a wide ramp spanned by a low arch on which the royal loges are set.

The citizens of Cathne dress in clothes reminiscent of the ancient Romans. The men wear short tunics and the women scanty skirts with only a band to confine their breasts.

The mortal enemies of the people of Cathne, the City of Gold, are the people of Athne, the City of Ivory, in the Valley of Thenar, twenty-five miles to the east. Once a year a truce is declared and both cities have commerce with each other, buying salt, steel, black slaves and white women.

The best way to travel in this region is by elephant.

(Edgar Rice Burroughs, *Tarzan and the City of Gold*, New York, 1933; Edgar Rice Burroughs, *Tarzan the Magnificent*, New York, 1936)

CATHURIA, see SOUTHERN SEA.

CATMERE, an Elfin kingdom on the reedy shores of Catmere Lough in northern Northumberland, England. The palace of Catmere is far from luxurious and is surrounded by a few strips of cultivated land. The rest of the area is a succession of barren moors and peat bogs.

The Elfins of Catmere live mainly on mutton—pies, broth and enormous lamb chops large enough to fell an ox. Sheep are in fact basic to the economy of the estate; Virtually all the clothes worn here are knitted from the wool provided by the flocks. The winter clothes made in Catmere are particularly well adapted to the harsh winters of the area: cloaks, heavy woollen jerkins, gloves and lambskin-lined boots.

Catmere has not always stood on its present site. The original castle was built by a spring near what became Hadrian's Wall, near Procolitia, the seventh station between the North Sea and the Solway Firth. The Romans were attracted by the excellent natural water supply, but soon began to sense that they were somehow unpopular with invisible local spirits. They resorted to flattery; the spring was sanctified, a small temple was built around it, and Queen Coventina was venerated as its nymph or patron goddess, a tribute she accepted with regal calm.

Some time later, however, a member of her court revealed that a rival cult—that of Mithras—had been established at Borcovicus. Coventina flew into a rage at the idea that she was being put on a par with Mithras, whom she regarded as a mere foreign upstart, and removed the court to its present site in an uncontaminated waste. Catmere is still within sight of the wall and was chosen by Coventina so that she could watch the slow and inevitable decay of the Roman fortifications. She lived to see it abandoned, and talked up to her dying day of returning to her ancestral home. It was expected that her successor Coventina II would carry out her intentions, but nothing came of the plan, as the climate of Northumberland is not conducive to moving house unless it is absolutely necessary.

During the reign of Coventina IV, Catmere began to accept exiles from other Elfin kingdoms. In effect this is a service to other kingdoms who wish to rid themselves of troublesome subjects; the accommodation and food provided for the exile is paid for by his or her country and this asylum service has become an important part of Catmere's revenue. Strict enquiries are made into the background of the exile and rigorous conditions are laid down before any agreement is reached. One stipulation is that exiles be given opiates before their departure, so that they arrive without having any notion of where they are. A signed statement to the effect that the exile has arrived in good condition is given to those who have conveyed him to Catmere. One of the more famous exiles brought here was Sir Bodach, who was exiled from ELFWICK for heresy.

(Sylvia Townsend Warner, *Kingdoms of Elfin*, London, 1972)

CAULDRON, LAKE OF THE, somewhere in Ireland. The lake takes its name from the cauldron that was fished out of it by a gigantic, yellow-haired man. Visitors should note the curious property of the cauldron: if a dead man is cast into it he will be brought back to life, but will never again be able to speak. Men revived in this way are said to make extremely good warriors.

For some time the giant who carried the cauldron served Matholwch, king of Ireland. But the giant, known as Llassur Llaesggyvnewid, his wife and his children aroused great hatred among the people because of the outrages they committed. Finally the people of Ireland constructed a huge chamber of iron, lured the man and his family into it and heated it. Llassur waited until the iron was white-hot and then broke out unharmed. He fled to Wales, where he was well-received. His offspring entered the services of the king but the cauldron itself was returned to Ireland.

(Anonymous, *The Mabinogion*, 14th–15th cen. AD)

CELEBRANT, FIELD OF, an area several miles to the south of LÓRIEN, between the River Limlight, which at the time of the War of the Ring marked the northern boundary of ROHAN, and the GREAT RIVER of northern MIDDLE-EARTH.

In 2510 Third Age the Field was the site of a great battle. The northern army of GONDOR had marched under Steward Cirion against the Balchoth, a tribe of Easterlings from the area round RHÛN who had swept through the area and occupied Gondor's province of Calenardhon. The Balchoth were reinforced by hordes of orcs from the MISTY MOUNTAINS and the northern army was rapidly surrounded. It was relieved by the arrival of the men of the north under Eorl, and the enemy were routed. After this the Balchoth seem to have disappeared from the history of Middle-earth. In gratitude to the men of the north, Gondor allowed them to settle in Calenardhon, which became the kingdom of Rohan.

(J.R.R. Tolkien, *The Two Towers*, London, 1954; J.R.R. Tolkien, *The Return of the King*, London, 1955)

CELEPHAIS, a famous and marvellous city on the shores of the Cerenerian Sea, in the land of Ooth-Nargai, in DREAMWORLD. Coming by sea, travellers will first discover the snowy peak of Mount Aran with its ginkgo trees swaying on the lower slope. Then come into sight the glittering minarets of Celephais, the untarnished marble walls with their bronze statues and the great stone bridge where the Naraxa River joins the sea. Behind the city rise gentle hills with groves and gardens of asphodels and small shrines and cottages, and far in the background the purple ridge of the Tanarians, potent and mystical. Down the Street of the Pillars is the turquoise temple of Celephais, where the high priest worships the great god Nath-Horthath. Visitors will find that other important gods are also worshipped in Celephais and that cats are regarded with as much veneration as cows are in India. Should the traveller wish to visit the rose-crystal Palace of the Seventy Delights, it is best to ask the old chief of Celephais' cats, a grey and dignified being who is usually found sunning himself on the onyx pavement.

(Howard Phillips Lovecraft, "The Dream-Quest of Unknown Kadath," in *Arkham Sampler*, Sauk City, 1948)

CELESTEVILLE, an elephant town, capital of Babar's kingdom, founded by King Babar on the banks of a blue lake where birds bathe and sing, and luscious tropical plants embalm the air. After discovering the beauty of this place, King Babar decided to import the necessary materials for the construction of his capital, and caravans of camels brought all the necessary equipment from abroad. Beautiful gardens were laid out around the Royal Palace; each elephant has his own hut, and a magnificent theatre was built for the entertainment of the population. When the task was completed, Babar gave each of his subjects a present of clothes and toys, and a large party was held to celebrate with a costume ball and a night at the opera.

Celesteville School is in the hands of the Little Old Lady, a friend of Babar's, and lessons are given to both the very young and the older elephants.

Celesteville was named after the famous Queen Celeste, Babar's beloved queen consort.

(Jean de Brunhoff, *Le Roi Babar*, Paris, 1939)

CELESTIAL CITY, beyond the DELECTABLE MOUNTAINS, surrounded by the river known as the River of Death, in CHRISTIAN'S COUNTRY. The waters of the River of Death are bitter to the taste, but once they have been swallowed the bitterness disappears quickly. No bridge spans the river and travellers must wade across it; some will find it very deep, others very shallow.

The city itself—which guards the celebrated Tree of Life—is built entirely of pearls and precious stones, and its streets are of the purest gold. Its approaches are lined with orchards, vineyards and gardens where the shining inhabitants of the city like to walk.

Travellers who overcome the dangers of the long journey from the City of DESTRUCTION to the river receive great rewards for the toils and sufferings they have undergone. They are welcomed by a blast of trumpets and the inhabitants of the Celestial City gather to watch them cross the river. As they enter the city they are clothed with majesty and crowned with garlands of gold. An inscription in letters of gold above the gate reads: "Blessed are they that do His commandments, that they may have right to the Tree of Life; and may enter in through the Gates into the City."

(John Bunyan, *The Pilgrim's Progress from this world, to that which is to come. Delivered under the similitude of a Dream. Wherein is discovered, the manner of his setting out, his dangerous journey and safe arrival at the Desired Country*, London, 1678; John Bunyan, *The Pilgrim's Progress from this world to that which is to come. The Second Part. Delivered under the similitude of a Dream. Wherein is set forth the manner of the setting out of Christian's wife and children, their dangerous journey and safe arrival at the Desired Country*, London, 1684)

CENTRUM TERRAE, a region some nine hundred miles below the surface of the earth, reached through several lakes on the earth's surface. One known entrance is through the MUMMELSEE but there are said to be as many lake entrances as there are days in the year. All passages leading from the lakes meet in the palace of the king who rules Centrum Terrae much in the same way that a queen bee rules her hive. His subjects are a race of water spirits, who are mortal and have mortal souls. They live to be up to three hundred years old and cannot be killed; they simply fade away. The spirits are incapable of sin and do not, therefore, suffer the wrath of God. They are completely free from disease.

Each of the lakes that gives access to Centrum Terrae is ruled by a prince who dresses in similar fashion to the people of the country in which the lake lies, but without any of the pomp normally associated with earthly rulers. The lakes were created for four main reasons: they provide the water spirits with a window on the world; they anchor the seas and oceans of the world, acting, so to speak, as the nails which hold them in place; they provide a network of water supplies; they are an expression of God's will. The function of the spirits who live in and below them is to keep the earth moist.

The water spirits thrive on pearls which have yet to harden and which resemble soft-boiled eggs.

(Johann Hans Jakob Christoffel von Grimmelshausen, *Der abenteuerliche Simplicissimus Teutsch*, Nürnberg, 1668; Johann Hans Jakob Christoffel von Grimmelshausen, *Continuatio des Abentheurlichen Simplicissimi oder Schluss desselben*, Nürnberg, 1669)

CESSARES REPUBLIC, a country on the western slope of the Andes, between Chile and Argentina, latitude 43° or 44° south. The country is surrounded by mountains on three sides and on the fourth it is cut off by a river. Spaniards are refused access and other visitors are warned that whoever reveals the exact location of Cessares is considered a traitor and executed. The republic was established in the seventeenth century by a group of one hundred and fifty Dutch families under the guidance of a certain Alphen, who became their first governor. In three ships—one of which was wrecked while crossing the Strait of Magellan—the Dutch brought some two hundred orphans, seeds, instruments and tools, food for two years in case of a bad crop, clothing, drugs, animals

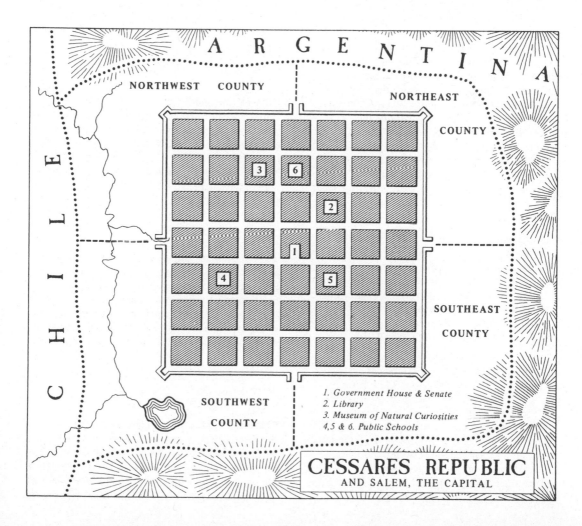

1. *Government House & Senate*
2. *Library*
3. *Museum of Natural Curiosities*
4, 5 & 6. *Public Schools*

CESSARES REPUBLIC
AND SALEM, THE CAPITAL

for meat and labour, arms, and books on crafts, art and science. They also brought with them ten pre-fabricated houses so as to have immediate lodgings upon arrival: two for the men, four for the women and children, and the rest for the supplies.

The capital of Cessares is Salem, a square mile in the centre of the country, set in a fertile field and crossed by several canals that flow from the river down the main streets. The streets are a mile long and thirty yards wide. The houses are clean, very tidy and uniform, each surrounded by a small garden fifty yards wide by a hundred and twenty-nine yards deep, and are all two storeys high. Trees have been planted along the middle of the streets to keep the sun out and to freshen the air. Notable in Salem are the Library, the Museum of Natural Curiosities, the Schools and the Cemetery sown with aromatic herbs to mask the unpleasantness of decomposing bodies.

The laws of Cessares are simple: all citizens are brothers, therefore everyone must work, except widows and orphans, who are taken care of by the State. No man can own more than fifty acres. Excessive feasting is forbidden by law. The governor cannot dictate new laws without the Senate's approval. There are three senators chosen by the people; they must be at least forty years old and are elected for life, but can be deposed in cases of bad conduct. To be considered a citizen, a man must be at least twenty-one years old, Protestant and married. No Catholic can take part in the Government. Torture is forbidden.

(James Burgh, *An Account of the First Settlement, Laws, Form of Government and Police of the Cessares: A People of South America, in nine Letters. From Mr. Vander Neck, one of the Senators of that Nation, to his Friend in Holland, with Notes by the Editor*, London, 1764; Fray Diego de Ocaña, *Relacion del viaje a Chile, año de 1600*, Supplement to *Anales de la Universidad de Chile*, Santiago de Chile, n/d.)

CHALLENGER FIELD, at Hengist Down, Sussex, England, where Professor G.E. Challenger, F.R.S., M.D., D.SC., etc., accomplished his amazing experiment at 11:30 A.M. on Tuesday, June 21, in the last years of the nineteenth century. The nearest station is Storrington, about an hour and a half from Victoria Station, London.

On arrival at Challenger Field the traveller will see the remains of a shaft through which Professor Challenger injured the planet Earth—

which, as everyone knows since this experiment, is a live animal, somewhat like a sea urchin. The most horrible yell ever heard echoed along the whole South Coast and even reached France. Fourteen lift cages that had been sent down for exploration were shot into the air, one of them landing in the sea near Worthing Pier, a second one not far from Chichester. A treacly substance of the most penetrating and nauseous odour—a protective secretion, according to Professor Dreisinger of Berlin, analogous to that of the skunk—shot up into the air, burying an airplane in filth. Every volcano on earth voiced her indignation: Hecla in Iceland, Vesuvius and Etna in Italy (followed by a half-a-million-lire damage suit awarded against Professor Challenger in the Italian courts for the destruction of vineyards), the volcanoes of Mexico and Central America and the whole of the eastern Mediterranean. This experiment has never been repeated.

(Sir Arthur Conan Doyle, *When the World Screamed*, London, 1892)

CHANA, an island near the coast of India, in the Indian Ocean, formerly boasting a great harbour which has now been overcome by the sea. It is said that the king of Chana was once so powerful that he waged war against Alexander. Today Chana is notable mainly for its vast range of religious beliefs. The Chanians worship the first thing that they see in the morning, causing great confusion because of the rapid succession of religions on the island, and as they build idols of the things they worship, numerous new idols are built every day. They have many superstitions. For instance, it is deemed unlucky to see a hare, a swine or a raven in the morning. A sparrowhawk catching its prey in front of an army is a good omen rarely seen.

There are numerous lions on Chana, and rats as big as dogs that hunt side by side with mastiffs. The dead are not buried, but left to rot in the great heat.

(Sir John Mandeville, *Voiage de Sir John Maundevile*, Paris, 1357)

CHANCE, ISLAND OF, situated off the coast of the United States near the Island of FORTUNE, where earthquakes are not infrequent. Here all appears to be left to chance, and all kinds of monsters are produced by a nature which appears to be still in an infantile state of experimentation. On the Is-

A discarded idol from CHANA.

land of Chance people are born with horseshoes instead of hands; they are considered to be as stupid as horses and left in the fields to graze. On the other hand, horses are born with human hands and have established workshops and tailors' shops. They can also play musical instruments, chance having given them the limbs that in other countries have granted man superior status.

A forest to the south of the island is inhabited by a new species of animals whose bodies are chance combinations of organs—two or eight fingers, a vertical mouth, eyes in the back of the head, all in random combinations. Animal species multiply at unpredictable rates. Some years there is a surplus of crocodiles, others a dearth of domesticated animals. However it is believed that chance will eventually lead to a perfect world in which every beast will speak; in preparation for this animals are already being taught to read and write by teachers using sign language.

Visitors will enjoy playing a game in which several eight-sided dice, with letters on each side, are placed in a dice box, shaken, and cast. The winner is the player who, by chance, composes the greatest number of words and sentences. In 1789 an earthquake caused the dice box to fall: the letters on the dice formed Louis XVI's address to the Etats-Généraux.

(Abbé Balthazard, *L'Isle Des Philosophes Et Plusieurs Autres, Nouvellement découvertes, & remarquables par leur rapports avec la France actuelle,* Chartres, 1790)

CHANEPH ISLAND or HYPOCRISY ISLAND, inhabited by all types of hypocrites, male and female, young and old. They are, without exception, hermits, saintly mumblers and bigots, but it is said that it is quite possible for travellers to have a little hypocritical fun with the women of the island.

The people of Chaneph are poor and live on the alms given to them by passing travellers. But, as the island's location is unknown, these are few and far between.

(François Rabelais, *Le quart livre des faicts et dicts du bon Pantagruel,* Paris, 1552)

CHARGES, ISLAND OF, a colony of Attorney-Land, separated from the Island of IGNORAMUSES by a narrow ford. The entire island is covered with curiously formed rocks.

Visitors will find that the only utensils on the Island of Charges are parchments, inkhorns and pens, on which the islanders thrive. Everyone who has business on the island has to pass through the hands of one Fleecem, adept at shaving the crowns in people's pockets. Visitors will recognize him because he wears a short, bright chestnut-coloured coat and a demi-worsted doublet with stained half-sleeves; above the elbow, his sleeves are of chamois leather. He also wears a cockaded cap.

(François Rabelais, *Le cinquiesme et dernier livre des faicts et dicts du bon Pantagruel, auquel est contenu la visitation de l'Oracle de la dive Bacbuc, et le mot de la bouteille; pour lequel avoir est enterpris tout ce long voyage,* Paris, 1564)

CHARIOT, a castle of the enchantress Morgan le Fay, sister of King Arthur of CAMELOT. The castle lies slightly to the north of the almost impenetrable woodlands of Forest Savage. It is built of edible substances in order to lure children into the hands of the enchantress. The castle rises from a lake of milk bathed in a buttery glow, the drawbridge is made of butter strewn with cow hairs, and gives off a sickly sweet smell. Normally only children enter this enchanted castle, but on one occasion Launcelot was imprisoned here under a spell cast by the evil Morgan.

(T.H. White, *The Once and Future King*, London, 1939)

CHARYBDIS, see SCYLLA.

CHATAR DEFILE, an isthmus connecting US-SULISTAN with TSHOBANISTAN, consisting of a narrow water channel flanked by high cliffs on either side which from their outer edges fall precipitously to the sea. At the isthmus' narrowest point a conversation could be held between people standing on the cliff tops on either side; and at its widest it can be crossed in less than fifteen minutes. At the Ussulistan end of the defile the cliffs can be scaled.

The Chatar Defile is said to have been built by a race of giants who threw rocks about like bricks to construct a channel for the river that flows along the isthmus between its walls of rock. At two places the ravine is practically blocked by natural obstacles. Near the northern end the river runs through an enormous boulder; there is only a narrow path on either side of the watercourse. Above the entrance to the tunnel, a carved inscription reads *Fum es Ssacha*, meaning "rock hole" or "orifice"; the author of the inscription is unknown. Farther along, the gorge is blocked by a natural stone wall, with only a long narrow channel at its base.

It is said that the area that is now Tshobanistan was once a large lake, fed by a river and separated from the sea by a wall of rock. As pressure built up in the lake, it burst through the wall, flinging the rocks away to both sides and forming a channel through which the river could flow into Ussulistan. Over the centuries—some say because of the wars waged by the tyrants of nearby ARDISTAN—the lake and river both dried up so that Tshobanistan became an arid desert, while the defile was transformed into a rocky gorge with almost no water in it. Only when peace returned to the whole area did water flow through the Chatar Defile once more.

(Karl Friedrich May, *Ardistan*, Bamberg, 1909; Karl Friedrich May, *Der Mir von Djinnistan*, Bamberg, 1909)

CHELI, a large, fertile and rich island in the Mediterranean, north-east of ENNASIN ISLAND. Also known as the **ISLE OF COMPLIMENTS**. Cheli is ruled by King Panigon, or All-things-to-all-men.

The court is known for its elaborate etiquette and compliments. It is the custom of the country, for example, that the king and his children and courtiers come down to the port to greet visitors. All visitors will be expected to kiss the queen, her daughters and her suite as they enter the castle.

(François Rabelais, *Le quart livre des faicts et dicts du bon Pantagruel*, Paris, 1552)

CHELM, a Jewish town of some notoriety, probably in the former USSR, held by certain authorities to be the offspring of a town in East Poland, with which it no longer has any connection. The inhabitants of Chelm are noted for their unique system of reason, which does not allow reality to interfere with pure logic.

Travellers should visit Chelm's magnificent Town Hall—built with no windows. To compensate for the lack of light the inhabitants brought large buckets of sunshine into the Hall which has, however, made little difference to the darkness inside. It is also useful to know that the centre of Chelm, and for that matter the centre of the world, is in several places at the same time. This is because the inhabitants reason that whatever place is chosen as the centre can be reached from any other place and it would be useless to argue that this is not so. Travellers should not be surprised to see that the people walk in the streets while horses and carts go along the pavements, since, after all, the road is wide and the sidewalk is narrow and the inhabitants believe that a human being is more important than a horse or a wagon and should therefore use the wider path.

The inhabitants of Chelm have an easy and flawless way to tell a duck from a drake. They throw a piece of bread in front of the bird. If he runs after it, it is a drake; if she runs after it, it is a duck.

(Samuel Tenenbaum, *The Wise Men of Chelm*, New York, 1965)

CHIAOHU TEMPLE, west China, where visitors can admire a beautiful jade pillow with a small opening in it. Should a male visitor ask to make a good marriage, the priest will bid him enter the pillow. Creeping through the opening he will see red pavilions and splendid mansions. A high-ranking officer will marry his daughter to him and she will bear him six children; all their sons will become Imperial Secretaries. The visitor will stay there for dozens of years with no thought of return. One day, without warning, as if awaking from a dream, he will find himself back by the pillow. Long will he grieve.

(Anonymous, *Tai-Ping Geographical Record*, 981 AD)

CHICHEN ITZA, capital of UXAL.

CHINA COUNTRY, in the south of the Land of OZ, completely surrounded by a high white wall of china without a single gate in it. The area inside the wall is smooth and flat and shines like the bottom of a large white dish. Around it stand the tiny china houses of the inhabitants, all painted in bright colours. The houses are small; the largest of them only reaches the level of a child's waist.

Like their houses, the people of this city are made of delicate china. They include milkmaids with bright bodices and golden spots all down their gowns, shepherds in pink and yellow striped knee-breeches, princes with jewelled crowns, and clowns in ruffled costumes and tall pointed hats. All the animals in the fields are also made of china.

The china people are all extremely fragile, which may explain why their land is surrounded by a wall. If they are broken they can be repaired, but they never regain their original beauty. In their own country the china people can move about quite happily, although they must take care not to fall and break. If they are taken away from China Country, their joints stiffen and all they can do is stand still and look pretty, which is, of course, all that is expected of them when they are kept on shelves or tables.

(L. Frank Baum, *The Wonderful Wizard of Oz*, Chicago, 1900)

CHING PEH, see MARBOTIKIN DULDA.

CHITA, an island in the Caribbean, one of the Lesser Antilles. It was discovered by the *Ange-du-Nord* in the 1940's and named after the Cuban mistress of the organizer of the expedition. The object of their voyage was to find the treasure of the pirate Edward Lou, described in a document found in a bookshop in Pont-Aven, Brittany. The island is low and pleasant, very green, with a few purple hills and strips of red earth, giving the impression of patchwork. No insects or birds are found here but a species of tree, somewhat like a giant lettuce, is probably peculiar to the island.

Chita is governed by a Chinese executioner who keeps a number of mutilated men as subjects for observation and visitors are advised to be extremely careful.

(Pierre-Mac Orlan, *Le Chant de l'équipage*, Paris, 1949)

CHITTERLINGS' LAND, see SAVAGE ISLAND.

CHRISTIAN CITY, near the Hercynish Forest in the principality of Argilia, considered a place of refuge for all those persecuted for their beliefs. Travellers looking for a respectable and devout life will find Christian City a haven. All kinds of excesses are forbidden in the city and order and discipline are strictly observed. The law is in the hands of the Church, which persecutes crime and any violation against Christian morals.

Because marriage is considered of special importance to the public welfare, a request to get married is treated very much like a request for an honorary office. The couple present their application to four elders in charge of matrimonial affairs. The suitor is investigated and much attention is paid to his physical and mental condition. His intelligence must be adequate and he must be in a position to keep and supervise a wife, children and servants. If discord between a couple cannot be resolved, the matter is put before a marriage tribunal and a special arrangement to split the property by divorce is made with the aim of benefiting the children. Little more is known about this perfect city.

(Johann Michael, Freiherr von Loen, *Der redliche Mann am Hofe, oder die Begebenheiten des Grafen von Rivera*, Frankfurt, 1740)

CHRISTIANOPOLIS, a city on the island of CAPHAR SALAMA founded by an exile from an unspecified country. Beggars, quacks, stage-players who have too much leisure, busybodies, fanatics, drug-mixers who ruin the science of chemistry and

There is also a circular temple with a diameter of one hundred feet. All buildings are three storeys high, with public balconies leading to them, made of burnt stone and separated by fireproof walls. There are abundant springs and flowing water, and fresh air and ventilation throughout the entire city. The moat outside the walls is stocked with fish, so that in peacetime also it may serve a purpose. The open and otherwise unused spaces are inhabited by wild animals.

The whole city is divided into three districts: one to supply food, one for drill and exercise and one for beauty. The first section—called the Farm Quarters—is to the east: it consists of two public storehouses for agriculture and animal husbandry, with seven mills and bakeries adjoining them. Everything, except artifacts made with fire, is produced in this section: paper, beams, wine, etc. A district in the north is devoted to the slaughterhouses, and in the west is the forge for metals and minerals. The most notable buildings in the city are the Temple and the Library. The Temple has a circumference of 316 feet and is seventy feet high. In the half where the gatherings take place, the seats are cut into the rock in such a way that all ears are equally distant from the voice of the speaker. On the stage occupying the other half sacred comedies are shown every three months. The only decoration is a crucified Christ set between two of the many windows. The Library is one of the most complete in the world: every volume man thinks he has lost is here, and every language on earth is fully represented. The houses are not privately owned; they are granted and assigned by the government to individuals. Every house has three rooms and only one door for which the head of the house is responsible. This door leads to the public balcony and from there to the towers or to a spiral staircase. At the rear of each building is a garden. The windows are double: wood and glass. The furniture is scant.

Four hundred people live in Christianopolis. The men do all the heavy work, but this does not alter their sweet nature nor do they become wild and ill-mannered. The women learn to sew, spin, embroider and weave and no woman in Christianopolis is ashamed of her household duties. In church and council hall the women have no voice. The soldiers of Christianopolis are not gluttons, but temperate and well-washed. Every citizen has the same public duties: watching out for enemies, guarding the city walls, harvesting grain and vines,

View of the south-east tower of the city of CHRISTIANOPOLIS.

Rosicrucians are not allowed in. Christianopolis consists of a square, some seven hundred feet across, fortified with four towers and a massive wall. Eight other towers inside the city increase its strength, plus sixteen smaller ones near the centre surround the impregnable citadel. The disposition of the city creates one single public street, two continuous rows of buildings and one marketplace.

working the roads, erecting buildings, draining the sewers and assisting in the factories. In school they learn grammar, oratory, various languages, logic, metaphysics, theosophy, arithmetic, geometry, mystic numbers, music, astronomy, astrology, natural science, history, Church history, ethics, theology, medicine and jurisprudence. All inhabitants are Christians. The chief priest is not a Roman pontifex and is married. Three prayers are offered every day: morning, noon and evening, and no one may be absent from these. Meals are private, but all food is obtainable from the public storehouses. There is no money in Christianopolis, but everyone receives according to his needs. The people of Christianopolis do not consider death a worthy punishment: misdeeds are simply corrected, for they say, "Anyone can destroy a man, but only the best can reform him." No value is set on succession of title or blood. Christianopolis is governed by eight men, each of whom lives in one of the larger towers. They have eight subordinates, distributed through the smaller towers of Caphar Salama. In Christianopolis everyone is happy.

(Johann Valentin Andreae, *Reipublicae Christianopolitanae descriptio,* Amsterdam, 1619)

CHRISTIAN'S COUNTRY, a land of unknown location, famous for its pilgrim route and named after a celebrated traveller, a certain Christian. Travellers leaving the City of DESTRUCTION can reach the CELESTIAL CITY after crossing a number of dangerous but enjoyable places. (See also DELECTABLE MOUNTAINS, Plain of EASE, DOUBTING CASTLE, DEVIL'S GARDEN in Beelzebub's Castle, Slough of DESPOND, Hill of DIFFICULTY, Valley of HUMILIATION, Valley of the SHADOW OF DEATH, VANITY FAIR, ENCHANTED GROUND, INTERPRETER'S HOUSE.)

(John Bunyan, *The Pilgrim's Progress from this world, to that which is to come. Delivered under the similitude of a Dream. Wherein is discovered, the manner of his setting out, his dangerous journey and safe arrival at the Desired Country,* London, 1678; John Bunyan, *The Pilgrim's Progress from this world to that which is to come. The Second Part. Delivered under the similitude of a Dream. Wherein is set forth the manner of the setting out of Christian's wife and children, their dangerous journey and safe arrival at the Desired Country,* London, 1684) *Map follows*

CIACOS GROUP, see CANNIBAL ISLAND.

CIBOLA or **CITY OF FROZEN FIRE,** capital of QUIVERA.

CIRCE'S ISLAND, see AIAIA.

CIRCULAR RUINS, COUNTRY OF, of uncertain location, possibly at the mouth of a river flowing into the southern extremity of the Caspian Sea, where the Zend tongue is not contaminated with Greek. There is a small hill on the island, and brambles and bamboo stalks grow along the muddy coast. The main feature of the country is the charred circular ruins of a primitive temple, crowned by a stone tiger or horse. Here a man can be dreamt and made to live, and the only proof of his unreality will be that fire cannot harm him. Dreaming a complete man takes over a year; dreaming his innumerable hairs is perhaps the most difficult part of the task. Dreamt men act as priests to the fire god in other broken temples whose pyramids survive downstream; others live among normal men, unaware of their own inexistence, and any traveller who wishes to confirm his own reality may do so by withstanding the test of fire, frequent in this country.

(Jorge Luis Borges, "Las Ruinas Circulares," in *El jardín de senderos que se bifurcan,* Buenos Aires, 1941)

CIRITH GORGOR, also known as the **HAUNTED PASS,** the great pass leading into the Land of MORDOR in Southern MIDDLEEARTH. The pass leads through the great cliffs formed by the meeting of two ranges of mountains: ERED LITHUI and Ephel Dúath. Two black, steep

Remains of a primitive temple in the Country of CIRCULAR RUINS.

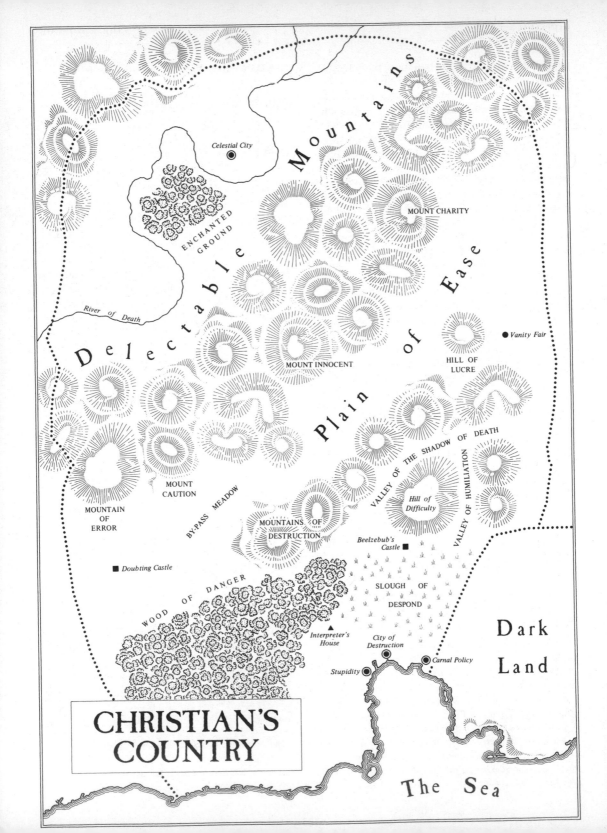

CHRISTIAN'S COUNTRY

hills, bare of vegetation, rise in front of the entrance to the pass. The pass is approached by three roads: one from DAGORLAD, one from ITHILIEN, and a third running along the flanks of Ered Lithui.

At the end of the Second Age, towers were built on the hills to guard against the return of Sauron, the Dark Lord of Mordor, who had been defeated by the Last Alliance. During the Third Age, Sauron did return and the towers, the Teeth of Mordor, became his outposts. Sauron built a stone rampart between the cliffs of the pass. This became known as Morannon, the Gate of Mordor. The gate set in the wall was a massive construction of iron. Patrols constantly walked the battlements and red lights burned high up in the twin towers.

The plain before Morannon, a desolate black land stretching to the DEAD MARSHES, was the scene of the last battle between Sauron and the Army of the West on March 24–25, 3019 Third Age. The army marched from MINAS TIRITH and camped among the many pits and mounds that lie before Morannon. The challenge was issued to Sauron, but his lieutenant rode out from the Tower of Barud-dûr to taunt the allies. With him, he bore the clothes of Frodo, the hobbit who had been appointed to carry the One Ring of power to the Cracks of Doom within Mordor itself to destroy it forever.

The sight of Frodo's clothes, taken from him in CIRITH UNGOL, convinced the allies that all hope was lost and that Sauron's power could never be overcome. Sauron's lieutenant issued the terms on which their surrender would be accepted, but the allies rejected them and the banners of GONDOR, ROHAN and Dol Amroth were unfurled as Sauron's forces poured through Morannon, completely encircling the Army of the West and outnumbering them by ten to one. The great battle against the orcs, trolls and human allies of Sauron began.

Just as the battle appeared to be lost, the crumbling of the Teeth and of Morannon itself was heard; the Ring had been destroyed and Sauron's day was over. The earth quaked and a great shadow covered the sky, like a vast hand trying to cover everything. As it was blown away by the wind, total silence fell. The creatures of Mordor became crazed and the orcs and trolls began to kill each other. Many of the men fell or surrendered, although some fought to the last, so great was their hatred of the West.

(J.R.R. Tolkien, *The Two Towers*, London, 1954; J.R.R. Tolkien, *The Return of the King*, London, 1955)

CIRITH UNGOL, the high pass across the Ephel Dúath, the Mountains of SHADOW—the range that guards the western side of MORDOR. The pass is reached by following the road east from MINAS MORGUL. A gap in the stone wall by the side of the road gives access to a path climbing up the side of the valley; this in turn leads to the Stairs of Cirith Ungol.

Two flights of stairs lead up to the pass itself: the clearly marked Straight Stair—a flight of narrow steps cut into the rock and rising almost as steeply as a ladder—leads to a long dark passage through the mountain which eventually comes out onto a shelf high above the ravine at the head of IMLAD MORGUL; beyond the rock shelf, the secret Winding Stair begins. It winds tortuously across the face of the mountain past yawning chasms, and eventually comes to a path which follows a cleft through the upper slopes. The pass itself is at the crown of this path—it is a cleft in the highest ridge and is guarded by the Tower of Cirith Ungol.

The great watch-tower stands in a boulder-strewn ravine and rises up like an enormous wall. To reach the far side of the tower one must go through caves and tunnels known as SHELOB'S LAIR. On the far side, the land falls away in a series of great cliffs, down to the jagged edge called the MORGAI. The red glow of the fires in ORODRUIN, the mountain of fire, can be seen from here. A road leads down from the tower gate to the valley of GORGOROTH. The main gate is on the eastern side, but there is also a subterranean entrance, the Undergate, which connects with Shelob's Lair.

The tower itself is built in three massive tiers on a shelf of rock, with its back to the cliff. On the lowest tier there is a small courtyard surrounded by a battlement. Inside, long flights of stairs lead up to the flat roof of the third tier, a space about twenty feet across and covered by a small dome. Behind the dome, a great turret rises high above the hills. The tower was originally guarded by the Watchers—two great stone figures seated on thrones. Each had three bodies joined together and three heads facing in three directions to survey all approaches from inside and outside Mordor. They had the features of vultures and great claw-like hands. The Watchers have been destroyed.

The position of the main gate suggests that the tower was originally built to prevent people from leaving Mordor rather than from entering it. Like the towers that once stood before CIRITH GORGOR, it was built by the men of GONDOR to watch over Mordor when Sauron the Dark Lord was defeated by the Last Alliance at the end of the Second Age. When Sauron returned to power, the tower's use was turned against its builders, like so many of the defence works in the area. As Sauron ruled by fear in Mordor it became a check against the possibility of anyone leaving. Under his rule, the tower was guarded by orcs and the Watchers were inhabited by evil spirits.

This was the difficult route taken by Frodo and Sam in 3019 Third Age on their journey to destroy the Ring of power in the fires of Mount Doom. They were led by Gollum, who had once possessed the Ring and hungered to have it back. The choice of route was dictated by the need to avoid better-guarded entrances, but also by Gollum's hope of regaining the Ring by delivering the Ring bearers to Shelob, the last of the giant spiders. He failed, and thus the Ring was successfully destroyed—and Sauron's dark power with it.

(J.R.R. Tolkien, *The Two Towers*, London, 1954; J.R.R. Tolkien, *The Return of the King*, London, 1955)

CITÉ DES DAMES, see City of VIRTUOUS WOMEN.

CITTABELLA, a city of unknown location, probably in Central Europe. Cittabella is also known as "the City of Holes." The ground on which the city is built must be truly unique; not only is it different from that of any other city but it cannot be accurately compared to either a honeycomb—because its holes are not regular—or a Gruyère cheese.

Visitors to Cittabella must first be made familiar with the city's singular topography, that is, its various classes of holes. The most common and least worrying holes are about the size of an ordinary saucepan. They are round, with serrated borders, owing to the sudden collapse of the upper layer—which is the colour of an eggplant—spread on a softer lower layer of dark brown earth. The interior of the "saucepan" is rough and uneven, with small clumps of dirt and pebbles that lie on the bottom and crack and crumble when stepped upon. When it rains, the holes become small slimy puddles and it is not infrequent to find some unfortunate butterfly lying with its poor dead wings in the mud. The inhabitants of Cittabella proceed either by putting their feet right in them and walking in this sloppy fashion, or by taking careful large steps so as not to crumble the uneven borders. The children delight in simply jumping over them.

Next, in order of danger, come certain vast and deep holes that could easily swallow a couple of houses. The visitor will notice at the bottom of these colonies of frogs who live in the water which collects after the rain and which never quite disappears, as well as a few water-lilies and reeds. The borders of these holes are chocolate-coloured and round. Visitors are advised not to fall into the holes as this would disturb the frogs and upset the ecological equilibrium.

The holes in the next category, smaller than the ones before, have the shape of giant apples, pears or oranges cut in half on the previous day. This detail is important in describing them because, having been sliced beforehand, the border of the fruit would tend to shrink and crinkle, as do the borders of this particular kind of hole. It is best to descend by digging one's heels into the walls just above the many whitish stones that line the interior. This exercise, say the inhabitants of Cittabella, is excellent for the muscles of the calves, and gymnastic instructors often take their students to exercise up and down the sides.

The holes in the last group are the most dangerous, in spite of being almost invisible. These treacherous openings seem to be hardly big enough to hold a pin. Dreadful misapprehension! Should a traveller simply come near one of them all the earth around would crumble into its depths; frequently whole coaches drawn by eight or more horses find themselves disappearing forever in those unexpected cavities. This category of holes is particularly annoying to the citizens of Cittabella, because it constantly interrupts the parades and ceremonies of which they are very fond.

An entirely different class of holes, far less common but especially dangerous to one's feet, are those of very little depth; whoever steps into one will find it almost impossible to extricate himself. There are also those holes seemingly covered by a sort of blind or shutter, leaving a thin zigzag opening: whoever falls into one of these will find the shutter closing over his head as if brusquely pulled across by an irate feminine hand.

The people of Cittabella are known for their peculiar gait: they always walk as if looking for something. They do this for several reasons—either because they find themselves in a district of the city with whose holes they are not familiar; or because they are searching (mainly to satisfy their anxious families) for some recently arrived country cousin who seems to have disappeared a couple of days earlier; or because the coachman has lost yet another set of coach and horses. In the latter case it is best to give up the search as soon as possible, as this task is rarely crowned with success.

(Lia Wainstein, *Viaggio in Drimonia*, Milan, 1965)

CITY, THE, see ISLANDIA.

CIUDAD, see ISLA.

CIVILIZATION, ISLAND OF, the most important of the VITI ISLANDS of Polynesia, claimed for France in 1831 by the captain of the *Calembredaine*, the first ship to sight it. The small island is wooded and mountainous, but thick mist often obscures the scenery.

The Island of Civilization is a monarchy ruled by a rosewood king. The king is mechanically operated and can sign up to thirty decrees at a sitting; his signature is beautifully written in English. The advantages of this system are numerous. It avoids all the problems posed by succession and changes of dynasty. It also means that the Civil List amounts to only fifty francs per annum in oil and grease. Only the President of the Council of Ministers is entitled to wind up the king.

Ministers have heavy responsibilities. Each has a slip-knot around his neck and any elector may pull the rope until the minister strangles if the latter is shown to have acted against his charter of appointment. All members of parliament are deaf and dumb, which puts an end to endless debates and significantly reduces the possibility of their being influenced by persuasive arguments. Debates are conducted in sign language.

Under the terms of a law adopted shortly after the arrival of the French, it is forbidden for more than one person to fight a duel. This has put an end to duelling as such.

The island is rich and prosperous. The old railway system has been replaced by a transport

The mechanical rosewood king ruling the ISLAND OF CIVILIZATION.

system using electric fluid. The locomotive, made of metal and known as a "horse-pistol" because of its shape, is attached by an iron ring to a glass carriage in which the passenger sits. The carriage travels at incredible speeds along a thin, metal strip which serves as a conductor. The friction gives off sparks which at night light up a wide area on either side of the track. The system is cheap, easily installed and can be removed if local residents object to it. Unfortunately only one passenger can travel at a time; more than one person in the carriage would greatly increase the risk of electrocution. The system is also used by the postal service. The mail is so quick that one often receives a reply to a letter before it is delivered.

Gas lighting has been replaced by a portable apparatus using *phosphoriculine*, a subtle and inflammable substance discovered by Cucu-Mani-Chou. A long tube is attached to the rectum and genitals. *Phosphoriculine* is extracted from the excreta and flows into a lamp carried on a belt at waist-level. The quality of the light varies in accordance with the user's diet—onions, peas, lentils and turnips produce a particularly clear light. Temperament also has an effect on the quality and colour of the light: a lymphatic temperament will produce white light, whereas a nervous temperament will produce a blue light. Bilious and sanguine people give off yellow and red lights respectively.

Phosphoriculine is also used medically, for the diagnosis, for example, of gastro-enteritis and colic. Doctors usually treat their patients with nothing, as they believe all medicine to be harmful. Dysentery is cured by making the patient put his head to the ground and press it with his hands—a treatment which has never failed to work.

(Henry-Florent Delmotte, *Voyage pittoresque et industriel dans le Paraguay-Roux et la Palingénésie Australe par Tridacé-Nafé-Théobrôme de Kaou't'-Chouk, Gentilhomme Breton, sous-aide à l'établissement des clysopompes, etc.,* Meschacébé [i.e. Mons], 1835)

CLERKSHIP, an island in the Mediterranean, one day's journey from CHELI. Clerkship is a blurred and blotted place and it is difficult to make it out. It is populated mainly by procurators and bum-bailiffs. Visitors are unlikely to be offered hospitality, but will be assured, with an endless string of compliments, that the people are at their service, as long as they pay well.

The peculiarity of the island is that many inhabitants make their living by being beaten. A monk, priest, lawyer or money-lender who has a grudge against a gentleman will send him a bum-bailiff, who will, according to the terms of his brief, insult and abuse him. Inevitably, he will be beaten and assaulted in return, and this is the source of his income, for as well as receiving a wage from his employer, he will receive substantial damages from the man who has assaulted him. The damages awarded in such cases frequently cost a man all that he possesses.

(François Rabelais, *Le quart livre des faicts et dicts du bon Pantagruel,* Paris, 1552)

CLIO, see OCEANA (1).

CLOUDCUCKOOLAND, a city built on air above the plain of Phlegra, Greece. It was founded by an Athenian, Pesithetaerus, towards 400 BC, as a stronghold for birds of all species, and was dedicated to the Persian Prince Cockerel, the God of War of birds. The plans of Cloudcuckooland were

laid by squaring a circle. In the centre was the marketplace and from there the streets led out in all directions. Ruins of the city still exist today, notably the gate in the Great Wall, built of wood by flocks of pelicans.

It is said that from this stronghold the birds claimed the sovereignty of the world, and used the walls as a barrier to stop the sacrifices offered by men from reaching the sky, thus starving the gods into submission.

(Aristophanes, *The Birds,* 414 BC)

CLOUDS, MOUNTAIN OF, in a country six months by sea from Basra, Iraq, probably in the Indian Ocean. Travellers would be wise to bring along a Persian magician with a knowledge of alchemy, as these are the only people who can easily find their way to the Mountain of Clouds. However, as it is their custom to sacrifice their travelling companions to satisfy their alchemical needs, prudence is recommended. A description of the Mountain of Clouds was first given by a goldsmith from Basra, Hasan by name, who had indeed taken with him a Persian magician and barely escaped being murdered.

Once landed, travellers should leave the magician on his own at the foot of the mountain; he will proceed to unpack a copper kettledrum and a silk drumstick decorated in gold, with which he will beat the kettledrum. A cloud of dust will rise from the ground, slowly taking the shape of three fine camels, one of which the traveller is advised to ride. After a seven-day journey, the traveller will see a domed building supported by four columns of red gold, and a large and beautiful palace, inhabited by the daughters of a king. These young ladies will try to make the traveller forget his destination; it is best, however, to continue for yet another eight days. Finally, a host of clouds will be seen spreading from east to west. This is the mountain that the traveller is seeking.

The ascent of the Mountain of Clouds can only be achieved in the following manner: the traveller should kill one of the camels, skin it, place himself inside the skin which he must then carefully sew up, and wait until a vulture seizes him as its prey. The bird will deposit the camel-skin on the top of the mountain; the traveller should then make his exit, frighten the bird away with loud cries (which should be practised beforehand) and explore the mountain at his ease. Here he will find mainly bones and firewood. The Persian magician will shout up to him to throw down the firewood, indispensable for the successful practice of alchemy. But travellers are warned not to do so, in spite of the magician's insistent requests; he would simply abandon the traveller to his fate and leave with his precious sticks. Unfortunately, no easy way of descent can be recommended. Hasan, abandoned on the mountain, managed to get down the other side and was borne by stormy waves to a nearby beach. But his fortunate survival was probably just a stroke of luck.

(Anonymous, *The Arabian Nights*, 14th–16th cen. AD)

COAL CITY, fifteen hundred feet below the surface of the earth, the centre of the New Aberfoyle caverns which extend for miles beneath the counties of Stirling, Dumbarton and Renfrew in central Scotland and contain rich veins of coal. The caverns are natural, although they have been extended by men, and stretch for more than forty miles from north to south, below Loch Katrine and the Caledonian Canal. In some areas the galleries reach beneath the sea and the sound of the waves can be heard above them.

Coal City itself stands on the shores of the huge subterranean lake known as Loch Malcolm, in whose transparent waters swim shoals of eyeless fish. Ducks have been introduced and flourish, feeding on the abundant fish of the lake. The brick-built houses of the miners and their families rise on the banks of the loch, beneath the high dome of the great central cavern. Coal City is heated and lit by electricity. Electric lights hang from the vaulted roof and from the rock pillars and can be switched off to provide a so-called night; all the lights are completely enclosed to prevent a possible methane explosion. A chapel dedicated to St. Giles stands on a huge rock high above the loch.

As well as being a highly productive mine, Coal City has become a major tourist attraction. It is reached via a sloping tunnel entered through a castellated entrance seven miles to the south of Callender. New Aberfoyle is ventilated by tunnels and airshafts, one of which emerges within the ruins of DUNDONALD CASTLE.

The inhabitants of Coal City are more than happy to live in its even, calm climate and disparagingly refer to the outside world as "up

The castellated entrance to COAL CITY.

there," a realm of storms and bad weather. They take great pride in the sombre beauty of their underground realm and rarely venture to the surface.

New Aberfoyle was discovered in the mid-nineteenth century, some ten years after the closure of the Dochart pit, whose coal reserves had become exhausted. One old miner refused to believe that more coal could not be found; he built an underground cottage for himself and his family in the depths of the old mine and for ten years explored the disused workings until he finally found faint traces of seeping methane, sure evidence of more coal. With the help of the former manager of the Dochart he broke through the rock walls and discovered the untapped wealth of New Aberfoyle. Within three years the underground community of Coal City was flourishing. But the development of the town did not go unopposed. Its main enemy was Silfax, the former fireman or monk of the Dochart pit, whose job it had been, swathed in damp garments, to set fire to small deposits of methane before they could build up and become dangerous. Silfax had remained underground after the closure of the Dochart, living in deep shafts known only to him, his sole companions his granddaughter and a great owl which used to go everywhere with him. Silfax came to believe that the wealth of New Aberfoyle belonged to him, and he resisted all attempts made to enter the caverns, even after the settlement of Coal City.

Silfax's most spectacular act of sabotage was to blast away the rocks supporting the basin of Loch Katrine. This had little effect on the underground town, merely raising the level of Loch Malcolm by a few feet. The effects on the surface were much more spectacular; the waters of Loch Katrine were diverted into the chasms and steamboats were left stranded on the mud of the lake bed. After a failed attempt to cause a massive methane explosion, Silfax committed suicide by flinging himself into Loch Malcolm. His great owl can still be seen flitting about the remote outer edges of the central cavern.

(Jules Verne, *Les Indes Noires*, Paris, 1877)

COCAIGNE, an island beyond SARGYLL, the realm of Anaitis also known as the Lady of the Lake, said to be the daughter of the sun and related to the moon. Her mission is to divert, to turn aside and to deflect. She travels widely, showing a special interest in turning ascetics from the spiritual path that leads to canonization. It was she who gave Arthur of CAMELOT his sword and who caused his wife Guinevere to fall in love with Sir Launcelot.

The coast of the island is uninhabited and the only city inland is surrounded by a high grey wall. To gain admission, visitors must knock once or twice. The first people to come to the gateway were Adam and Eve, now represented on the door-knocker. The city is frequented mainly by half-human, half-animal creatures who come here to visit Anaitis.

Inside the city, the Royal Palace is surrounded by a dimly lit park in which indescribable creatures can be found. A narrow path leads to a courtyard of yellow marble beneath many domes and pinnacles. The only ornament in the courtyard is a statue of a god with thirty-four arms and ten heads. He seems greatly preoccupied with caressing one woman while holding a second with his free hands. The

most splendid room in the palace, littered with erotic toys and symbols, is the library. The walls are painted with the twelve Asan of Cyrene and the ceiling is frescoed with the arched body of a woman, her toes touching the east cornice and her fingertips the west. The library contains records of everything man has invented in the way of pleasure, as well as rare manuscripts by Astyanassa, Elephantisis, and Satades. A collection of Dionysian formulas and a chart of erotic postures can also be seen, as well as two most prized possessions, *The Litany of the Centre of Delight* and *The Thirty-Two Gratifications*, truly unique volumes.

There is only one law in this island kingdom: "Do that which seems good to you." Nothing ever changes in Cocaigne and life is an interminable flow of curious pleasures. There is no regret. The trees are always in bloom and the birds sing a perpetual evening chorus. According to legend, time fell asleep here at the most pleasant hour of the day in the year's most pleasant season, and can be seen in a crystal hourglass kept in a small blue chamber in the palace. If two interlocking triangles are traced in the sand from the hourglass, vapours arise forming visions of far-off places.

Guests to Cocaigne are taken into a white room with copper plaques on the walls. Here they are bathed by four girls who give them astonishing caresses with their tongues, fingernails, hair and nipples. Then they are anointed with four different oils and dressed, before being served the typical food of the island: eggs, barleycorn, red triangular loaves and pomegranates, and wine mixed with honey.

(James Branch Cabell, *Jurgen. A Comedy of Justice*, New York, 1919)

COCKAIGNE, a country of unknown location sometimes confused with CUCCAGNA or BENGODI. Cockaigne is famous for its exquisite food which is not cooked but grows like flowers. Sweets and chocolates spring up at the edge of the woods, roast pigeons fly through the air, perfumed wine flows from fountains and cakes rain from the heavens. The Royal Palace is made entirely of icing sugar, houses are made of barley sugar, the streets are paved with pastry and the shops supply goods for nothing. It is said that the gingerbread house found in one of the German forests, and made famous through the exploits of a young brother and sister, comes from Cockaigne.

The inhabitants enjoy a kind of immortality both because war is unknown and because, when they reach the age of fifty, they revert to the age of ten. The inhabitants of Cockaigne are served by a troop of sylphs, gnomes and water-nymphs.

(Anonymous, *Le Dit de Cocagne*, 13th cen. AD; Marc-Antoine Le Grand, *Le Roi de Cocagne*, Paris, 1719)

COCKLEV, see NAZAR.

COIMHEADACH, an island in the north Atlantic. To reach Coimheadach, visitors must travel attentively through Wales and then alone, and very carefully, either up through Scotland or right across Ireland to the farthest coast until they arrive at the other side of the Blasket Islands, Aran or Achill or the Outer Isles—depending on which route is taken. Coimheadach lies out to the west, just over the horizon of the great Atlantic. Neither *Coras lompair Eireann* nor *Macbrayne's* will take travellers there. They must travel out on *St. Ursula,* a bitchy old cattle-boat with four holds and a saloon bar. It is usually rough and always dark for *St. Ursula* sails just after midnight, so that she pitches and screws her way across the race— lurching after last night despite the dawn coming up behind her. The island smashes up the horizon, pointed like a pile of dung; like Skellig Michael or the rocks beyond Aberbach. A monstrous wedge of granite, touched by the rising sun as *St. Ursula* rolls in, Coimheadach has the detached look of the last detritus discarded by the Creating Spirit when Europe was finally finished. *St. Ursula* docks apprehensively, with much churning and bumping and scraping, pointing out of the harbour towards the sea, ready for the return journey.

Jettisoned upon the diesel- and fish-stinking quay-side, visitors will find themselves like Captain Lemuel Gulliver: all out of proportion—their frames too big, their voices too nasal, their consonants too hard. There are no "Bed and Breakfast" signs, no postcards and no trees. Moving into the town, visitors will find the streets paved with the same grey flagstones of which the long, dark houses are built. Of these, some are dwellings and some are pigsties and some are shops selling whisky, barbed wire and tinned peas.

Sitting on sea-warped chairs or slithering knowingly in and out of doorways too low for the common mortal, the islanders will neither greet nor reject the traveller's bright complexion and his coloured clothes, nor should he stare at their unvarying goitres and fishermen's jerseys. They are a small, dark people, the size of those clenched bodies seen in cists in museums, quite unlike classical Rome's bright Gaels, and their quick, deft movements are cramped by the diseases of damp and a diet of too many potatoes. Should travellers stop to ask the way, they should be grateful for even a pointing finger, for in the islanders' language, degenerate Gaelic and appropriated English are so slung together that even familiar sounds slide away into incomprehension.

Following the indicated road, the visitor will find himself hypnotically drawn uphill, towards the great crest of the island which rises to the west—the core of Coimheadach, a height of profligate significance to which the fertile harbour shore is an expediently deployed narthex. Travellers must move first through a multiplicity of small fields, some set to potatoes but most enclosing groups of the small, curly-haired black cattle whose flesh is Coimheadach's wealth. Each field is divided from its neighbours by stone-slab walls whose intricate patterns are as variable and personal as the knitted designs in the coarse family jerseys. Into the structure of the walls are built the names of the builders and, in the repairs, the identities of each successive owner. Then the walls end. The fields die. Up here, at last, is only the granite heart of Coimheadach and the harsh heather on its massive breast. Dye-marked sheep scurry and drift and vanish and there are no gates and no children's voices, and the track, swinging around the western end of the island, runs into an ecstasy of space where Coimheadach Abbey stands.

(Helen Wykham, *Ottoline Atlantica,* London, 1980)

COLONY, ISLE OF THE, not an island but a fertile plain surrounded by mountains, situated on St. Helena. The plain is unknown to the outside world, its only entrance a narrow gap in the steep cliffs. The plain has a surface of about four by six leagues, and comprises cultivated land alternating with meadows and woods. There are numerous fruit-trees and the climate is a perpetual springtime that nevertheless produces continual and abundant autumn harvests.

(Abbé Antoine François Prévost, *Le Philosophe anglois, ou Histoire de Monsieur Cleveland, fils naturel de Cromwell, par l'auteur des Mémoires d'un Homme de qualité,* Utrecht, 1731)

COMEDIANS' ISLAND, see MUSICIANS' ISLAND.

COMMUTARIA, a village on the Portsmouth-Waterloo line in Southern England. Everything a commuter longs for can be found in this village. It was set up by a distant descendant of the English scientist Merlin, to reward tired commuters, especially on Monday mornings. The droopy-eyed, pinstripe-suited commuter gazes out of the dirty second or first-class window. Suddenly the landscape becomes clear, almost dazzling. The train stops quietly, not with a jerk but as if in slow motion. The doors open silently and soft music, reminiscent of third-rate romantic Sunday afternoon films, fills the air. Outside, each commuter finds his secret craving. It may be a white sand beach with soft, wide-spread waves. It may be a comfortable chair by a fire, a glass of excellent whisky, a large yellow dog and a new Agatha Christie novel of infinite pages. It may be the best seat at the World Cup Football Final. A businessman from Woking found a mile-long miniature train track with an assortment of miniature trains. A clerk from Surbiton found a small French garden, already weeded and ready for planting roses. A saleslady from Liphook found the ruins of a large supermarket; threads of smoke were still rising from the charred remains and a beautiful white toga and a Roman harp lay at her disposal. Whenever the passengers wish to leave, the train departs and reaches Waterloo not a second late.

(Elspeth Ann Macey, "Awayday," in *Absent Friends and Other Stories,* London, 1955)

COMPLIMENTS, ISLE OF, see CHELI.

CONCORDIA, the smallest country in Europe, found on very few maps. The population is minimal and the country is entirely dependent on the tourist trade.

Concordia maintains a small army with no cannons. The climate is warm in winter and torrid in summer; the annual rainfall in the capital, also called Concordia, averages three millimetres; a general atmosphere of sleepy indolence prevails.

Time is established by the cathedral clock, installed in 1811 and losing gradually; by now Concordia has lost two entire days. There are 6–7 kilometres of narrow-gauge railway, with another five kilometres under construction since 1912. There are no secondary schools.

Concordia's position—geographically, militarily and horticulturally—is so hopeless that it acts as a magnet to every invader. It has gained independence at least four hundred times, so Concordians regard themselves as cumulatively the most independent people on earth: a different Independence Day is celebrated every day of the year. The English have been there several times, on the pretext that Concordians are unfit to govern themselves; the French have followed the pretext that they are unfit to be governed by the English. The Dutch made them Protestants, the Turks made them Mohammedans.

In 1811, Concordia was threatened by the Albanians and the Lithuanians, who had made a treaty to divide her between them. It was then that the Emperor Thomas the Impossible was assassinated by an Albanian desperado. His son, the boy-king Theodore the Uncanny, married the Infanta Inez of Old Castile, and thus brought Spanish troops to Concordia, who drove out the invaders and imposed Roman Catholicism. Subsequently, Concordia reverted to the Holy Unorthodox Church of its forefathers, to which it adheres up to this day. The Holy Unorthodox Church is headed by an aged bishop, over one hundred years old and very deaf. There are many religious orders—among the most severe are the Mauve Friars, who neither sit nor stand, but go about on their knees, keeping a vow of silence.

Concordia won the last conflagration by declaring war on Germany several hours before the surrender; as a consequence, they were offered six acres of land which did not belong to them. The gift was refused and Concordia is now on good terms with everyone.

The city of Concordia is built around the main square and dominated by the Gothic cathedral built in 1811. Sombre buildings with balconies surround the square; facing each other are the Soviet and American embassies.

Concordia is now a republic, with a proliferation of political parties and splinter groups: the National Iron Fist (NIF) and the Rally of Union Separatist Extremes (RUSE) are two. No one party is at present in power; a dictatorship was declared in 1955 and a coalition government is now in control.

(*Romanoff and Juliet*, directed by Peter Ustinov, UK, 1961)

CONNUBIAL SACRIFICE, ISLAND OF, located somewhere in the Indian Ocean and first described by the famous chronicler, Sinbad the Sailor. The inhabitants of the island, who live in a large and splendid city, are noted for their peculiar funeral rites. When either the husband or the wife dies, the surviving partner is buried as well. The body is lowered by means of a rope into a profound chasm not far from the city; the widow or widower then follows the same route, but is allowed to take into the tomb a small flask of water and a few loaves of bread. Over the mouth of the chasm the funeral *cortège* places a stone slab, thus joining the couple for ever.

In another part of the island lives a savage Negro tribe which welcomes travellers by offering them delectable dishes and coconut milk. However, travellers are advised not to taste these, as they are usually drugged with a powerful hallucinogen which produces a prolonged state of madness. The victims are then used in some of the native dishes, which fall into two categories: cooked and served with heavy sauces which only the king is allowed to taste, or raw—in the style of *la cuisine minceur*—for the rest of the tribe.

(Anonymous, *The Arabian Nights*, 14th–16th cen. AD)

COOK'S ISLAND (not to be confused with the Cook Islands), a small tropical island in the South Seas, of truly unique sandy beaches. The sand seems to change colour as the light shifts—sometimes golden, at other times opal-coloured, contrasting with the green forest that rises behind it up a gentle slope. Travellers are warned that it is not easy to walk through the island, as the undergrowth is thick and the paths are often blocked by curtains of dazzling flowers.

The only settlement on Cook's Island is a village of huts in a forest clearing, the home of a copper-skinned people—the original inhabitants of the island—who are now ruled by a white woman who was once a cook in north London. An ancient prophecy handed down from generation to generation stated that the islanders would one day be ruled by a great white queen who would rise out of the sea wearing a white crown.

The prophecy was fulfilled in strange circumstances. A group of London children came into possession of a flying carpet which granted their wishes. One day they expressed the wish to travel to a southern shore and were carried here—together with their cook, who happened to be standing on the carpet at the time. The natives accepted her as their long-awaited queen. Some time later the children brought to the island a good-natured burglar they had met. He married the cook, or queen, in a ceremony carried out by the Reverend Septimus Blenkinsop, who was brought from Deptford for that very purpose.

Travellers are advised that a visit to Cook's Island is an almost certain cure for whooping cough.

(Edith Nesbit, *The Phoenix and the Carpet*, London, 1904)

COOPERATIVE CITY, in Maine, in the United States, built in the first quarter of the twentieth century by the Cooperative Association of America, an organization founded in 1901 with the stated aim of making the twentieth century the era in which it will finally be possible to practise Christianity by creating "Thy will on Earth as it is in Heaven." The city now has a population of one hundred thousand.

The Cooperative Association was founded by a businessman. Its first purchase was a brick homestead which was converted into a restaurant with social and artistic facilities for members of the Association. Plans for the Cooperative City were first published in *The World, A Department Store*, which outlined how a cooperative system could overcome the evils of the industrial society of the nineteenth century and turn everyday life into heaven on earth.

The life of the Cooperative City is based on the use of coupon cheques, which have now replaced money. Deposits are paid into a member's account in accordance with the Association's valuation of his or her contribution to the Association, thus representing the life and labour of the individual member. These coupons are used for all transactions, and have put an end to money-lending, speculation and stock-jobbing; in doing so it has freed large numbers of people for more productive work. Every human being is considered an

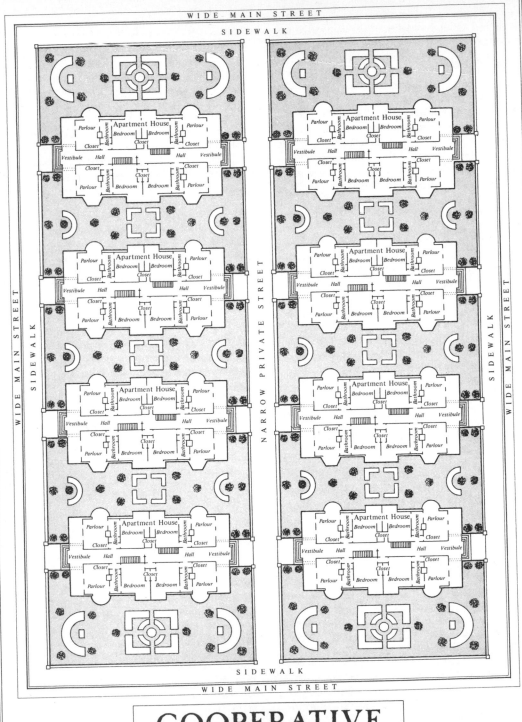

COOPERATIVE CITY

PLAN OF CITY HOUSING BLOCK

investment and accounts worth $120 per annum are opened by the Association for all children born in the city. The amount deposited each year rises as the child gets older and extra credits are given for scholastic achievements. No member has less than $1,500 per annum. No interest is paid on undrawn deposits. The strictest rule of the Association is that no member may, under any circumstances, patronize any outside enterprise.

The cooperative system has led to the abolition of unemployment. In accordance with the principle that "No man eats unless he works" the only form of social charity known in the city is the creation of opportunity. Servants still exist in the Cooperative City, but they are no longer treated as menials; they are regarded as friends and assistants and show no trace of servility.

The city and Association are under the administration of an Executive Board and its various departments, including the Department of Real Estate, the Department of Manufacturing, the Department of Agriculture and the Department of Engineers. They are responsible for production and distribution in their various areas and ensure delivery to specialized stores which cater to the retail trade. All goods are delivered direct from the manufacturing department in question; there are no intermediaries or middlemen. Labour is transferred from one branch of industry to another as required, in accordance with the Association's watchword "Economy." The working day has been reduced to six hours. Nowadays, people do not spend their whole lives at one job, but change their occupations frequently in order to test and develop their abilities. There is no longer any surplus or unnecessary production; goods or lines which cease to sell are immediately discontinued and remaining stocks sold off at reduced prices in popular annual clearing sales.

The city is built on a square grid pattern. Apartment blocks line the streets and are laid out so that all rooms have daylight. Parkways between the blocks replace the dingy backyards of older cities. Each apartment building has a frontage of forty-five to fifty feet, and two suites of apartments on either side of a central hallway. All buildings are three storeys high and have a basement. Individual houses may also be bought and are built to the specifications of the Real Estate and Architecture departments, in accordance with the member's station and means. Parks and open spaces are common. Most public buildings stand in landscaped gardens and are decorated with all that art and skill can produce. They are not overly ornate and are planned to be completely harmonious.

One particular feature of the city deserves special mention: cooking in the home has been done away with and public restaurants have been set up in all areas. Meals can be ordered for take-out or else they can be eaten in the restaurants themselves. All food is prepared to the highest standards by highly trained chefs. All the restaurants open onto three streets and have an entrance in the middle of a wide façade, which leads into a central rotunda with a fountain and a glorious profusion of plants. Reception rooms, parlour and toilets are located on the ground floor. General dining rooms occupy the first and second floors, those on the first floor providing slightly cheaper meals. The third floor is occupied by private dining rooms, which can be hired by small parties or families and, on the fourth floor, banquet rooms capable of seating four hundred guests can be reserved. The restaurants are open from 6 A.M. to midnight. In accordance with the principles of temperance, no intoxicating drinks are sold.

Education and health are under the general control of the Department of Education. Drugstores and patent medicines have disappeared. All citizens undergo periodical medical examinations and are given appropriate treatment if there is any sign of disease. In cases of nervousness, they are sent on vacations. Health is constantly supervised at school, which encourages physical exercise and sport. The classrooms are airy and spacious, with flowers on every desk and never more than twenty-five pupils in a class. Competition is encouraged to promote excellence.

Although the city and Association are specifically Christian foundations, they do not preach any one form of Christianity and no single creed is taught. Services are held in a large central meeting place, which is also used for public meetings and exhibitions and is capable of holding five thousand people. There are no long, dull sermons; addresses to the congregation consist of simple statements believed to be conducive to the public good. Both men and women preach, the only qualification being that they lead exemplary lives. People attending services pay for their seats, just as they would for any public entertainment. All ministers and preachers are closely connected with the work of the Education department.

The countryside has profited greatly from the

development of the city. Improved transport has broken down the old isolation of the farmers, who now live in small townships scattered across the countryside. Electric trains provide public transport both inside the city and in the countryside. Automobiles, complete with attendants, can be hired for private use from stands in the squares and in small country towns; in other cities, these are known as "taxis" or "cabs."

A newspaper, *The Daily American*, is published by the central publishing house, which also prints all books produced in the city; it contains no advertising or sensational headlines. There are no Sunday newspapers.

(Bradford Peck, *The World, a Department Store. A Story of Life under the Cooperative System*, London, 1900)

COQUARDZ, ISLE OF, see FORTUNATE ISLANDS (1).

CORADINE, a country somewhere in Northern Scotland. It consists of a valley among rolling hills beyond which, twenty or twenty-five miles away, rise the high mountains of Elf. The fauna is not remarkable; white bulls with long horns, sheep, horses with long tails and immense manes which give them a bold and formidable appearance, many very tame small birds that hop on visitors, and large dogs with fox-like features, taller than a St. Bernard.

Coradine is notable for its architecture. No roads or avenues lead to the different buildings, each of which stands isolated without gardens or hedges. A typical example is the House of the Harvest Melody. It rises like a rock from the earth and stands alone on its stone platform, five feet above the ground. The sloping sides are covered with ivy, shrubs and many flowering plants. The ceilings are low, and are not held up by any wood or metal-work. The entire building, except the roof, is made of grey stone, richly sculpted. The sloping roof is supported by sixteen huge caryatides on round, carved pedestals. The arched entrance, about one hundred feet long and made of pinkish-brown glass, rises like a cloud on a hill. All the buildings in Coradine are ancient and no new houses are built; the inhabitants compare them to the hills, "whose origins," they say, "are lost in the mists of time."

It is interesting to visit a typical Coradine interior. The visitor enters a lofty octagonal room. The floor is a mosaic of dark coloured stones. The fireplace, of hammered bronze, is fifteen feet wide. One of the walls is covered with bronze bas-reliefs; the remaining walls are of wood, carved very elaborately and combined with a yellow metal, all of which has undergone a petrifying process. A pedestal of polished, dark red stone serves as a table, on which can be seen glass and earthen jars. In the corner stands a statue of a woman on a white bull with gilded horns. Couch-like seats and chairs are scattered around the room. Beside each seat is a small table with a round stone top, beautifully inlaid, on bronze feet. Every doorway in the house, opening directly to the air, has double doors and a coloured window in between, which slide back into the wall. The dormitories or sleeping cells open onto a terrace at the back of the house. Coradine is a matriarchy and therefore the principal room in every house is the Mother's Room, where the head of the family has her quarters.

The women, being the stronger sex, live to be over one hundred. Their foreheads are broader and much lower than normal, the noses larger, the lips more slender and firm. Their mouths are purple-red and their complexions terracotta.

Coradine food is simple. Breakfast and lunch consist of a crust of brown bread, a handful of dried fruit, and milk. A kind of endive, bitter and crisp, bruised brain and pulse, stews and soups with milk, crushed nuts and honey are served for supper. They drink no alcohol, only fruit juices. The people of Coradine produce music through small revolving globes which emit sounds resembling human voices. Their songs, however, have no words. Money is unknown. Communal bathing is a popular entertainment. Giving or taking gifts is a grave offence—something must always be given in return, usually in the way of manual labour; for instance, the gift of a set of clothes requires a year's work in the field. Lying is considered the gravest fault. Their funeral rites are a combination of burial and cremation: a fire is lit upon the grave. The priest's parting words are: "Farewell for ever, oh well beloved son (or daughter)! With deep sorrow and with many tears we have given you back to the Universal Mother, but not until she has made the sweet grass and flowers grow once more on this spot of earth, scorched and made desolate by fire, shall our hearts be healed of their wounds and forget their great grief."

(W.H. Hudson, *A Crystal Age*, London, 1887)

CORAL ISLAND, a roughly circular island in the south Pacific, some thirty miles in circumference and ten in diameter. There are two mountains on Coral Island, one about five hundred feet high, the other roughly a thousand feet; the latter is broken by a number of small valleys, glens, rivulets and streams. The slopes of the smaller mountain are crossed by three valleys, separated by ridges, full of luxuriant tropical vegetation.

The beaches of the island are of pure white sand, completely ringed by a coral reef in which there are three narrow openings. Inside the lagoon the water is perfectly still; outside the reef, the ocean swell never ceases. At one point near the shore, the surf is forced by its own pressure into clefts in the rock and emerges like a great cloud of sea-water steam.

The island was given its present name by three young Englishmen who were the only survivors of the wreck of the *Arrow*. There is no record of the exact date of the wreck; it appears to have occurred in the first half of the nineteenth century. The three were able to survive on the natural resources of the island and on their own ingenuity. Some equipment was salvaged from the wreck itself and made their early days on the island easier. Visitors can still see their names engraved on a piece of wood standing near the shore.

Although the vegetation of the island is rich and varied, the fauna is poor. There are a few wild pigs and a marked absence of reptiles, though lizards have occasionally been seen. The bird life is more varied; parrots, parakeets, pigeons and doves abound in the woods and a variety of seabirds including penguins and waterhens visit the island.

The flora includes breadfruit, coconut palms and banana trees; yams, taro and a type of potato grow wild. One of the more useful species is the ironwood tree, buttressed by what appear to be regular, natural planks. Its wood is remarkably tough and can be used as nails. The nuts of the candlenut tree can be baked and then used as candles; they burn with a steady, bright light. The waters off the island are full of a wide variety of seaweeds that can be cooked like spinach.

The climate of the island is warm and constant, although there are occasional violent storms. There is no twilight; darkness falls with the suddenness typical of the tropics. Tides in the lagoon are very slight; the water is constantly warm and it

is possible for swimmers to stay in the sea for many hours at a time.

In spite of the island's charms, travellers should be wary of the likely attack by both cannibals and pirates. Should the need arise, it is possible to take refuge in an underwater grotto of crystal walls, the Diamond Cave.

(Robert Michael Ballantyne, *The Coral Island*, London, 1858)

CORBIN, a castle of uncertain location, on a hillside above a prosperous village with cobbled streets. On the opposite side of the valley a handsome tower can be seen. The castle is said to be haunted. One room in particular is to be avoided because of the supernatural beings that come through the door and attack anyone sleeping there.

It was here that Sir Launcelot was cured of his madness by the presence of the Holy Grail in a nearby tower; it was also here that Launcelot was tricked into lying with Elaine, provoking the wrath of Queen Guinevere of CAMELOT.

(Sir Thomas Malory, *Le Morte Darthur*, London, 1485; T.H. White, *The Once and Future King*, London, 1939)

CORK, a floating city in the Atlantic Ocean (not to be confused with Cork or Corcaigh, in the Irish Republic). The inhabitants resemble Europeans in their height and their looks but their feet are made of cork—hence their name, the Corkfoots. They do not sink in water and thanks to the substance of which their feet are made they can walk on the sea with as much ease as on land. The city of Cork itself is built on one immense, round, floating piece of solid cork.

(Lucian of Samosata, *True History*, 2nd cen. AD)

COROMANDEL, where the early pumpkins blow, some way from the sunset isles of Boshen. On the coast of Coromandel lived the Yonghy-Bonghy-Bò who once asked the Lady Jingly Jones to be his wife.

Bong-trees grow in Coromandel as they do on the great GROMBOOLIAN PLAINS. Here prawns are plentiful and cheap, and shrimps and watercress—and even milk-white hens of Dorking—are available. Down the slippery slopes of Myrtle, beyond the Bay of Curtle, lives a turtle.

(Edward Lear, "The Courtship of Yonghy-Bonghy-Bò," in *Laughable Lyrics: A Fourth Book of Nonsense Poems, Songs, Botany, Music, etc.*, London, 1877)

COUNT ZAROFF'S ISLAND, see ZAROFF'S ISLAND.

COXURIA, an island of the RIALLARO ARCHIPELAGO in the south-east Pacific. It is inhabited by pygmies convinced that the gods resemble them in shape and size. According to the Coxurians the gods often visit them, and have presented them with a magic cake made from their divine saliva. They maintain that this cake is found only on Coxuria and that it turns everything it touches into something sacred. There are various sects that argue the properties of the cake, and the different theological schools that have sprung up from these opinions are major political forces in Coxuria today. An important argument among the sects is over the question of whether the gods said "fuzz" or "buzz-fuzz" when they came to Earth. The population of Coxuria is regularly augmented by outcasts from other islands exiled for their religious dogmatism.

(Godfrey Sweven, *Riallaro, the Archipelago of Exiles*, New York & London, 1901; Godfrey Sweven, *Limanora, the Island of Progress*, New York & London, 1903)

CRACKED HEADS, PALACE OF, the home of the Queen of Cracked Heads. Her palace is full of goats which walk up and down the stairs and slide down the banisters. The goats eat alarm clocks, first winding them up and then swallowing them. As a result, the alarms ring after they have been swallowed and digested. The goats usually have spare clocks hanging on their horns; tired of waiting, the clocks speak to each other in their own ringing language. The Queen also feeds clocks to her collection of baby alligators. To do so, she sits on a ladder, winding and setting the clocks before throwing them to her pets. A second cousin of one of these may have emigrated to NEVER-NEVER LAND where it can still be heard today.

(Carl Sandburg, *Rootabaga Stories*, New York, 1922)

CREAM PUFFS, a small village in the upland corn prairies of ROOTABAGA COUNTRY, to the west of the Shampoo River. From a distance the village looks like a little hat of the type that might be worn like a thimble on the thumb to protect it from the rain.

The village is as light as a cream puff, hence its name. In the centre, where Main Street runs into the main public square, stands the Roundhouse of the Big Spool which houses a great spool of string. One end of the string is attached to the village and when the wind carries it away, the thread on the spool runs out. When the wind has had its sport, the people of the village wind up the spool and pull the village back to its original site. The winds in the area are very strong.

The village was founded by people from the Village of Liver and Onions who had decided to start a community of their own. Trekking across the high prairies they were trapped in a blizzard and were rescued by five rats with rust on their skin, feet, noses and tails. The rats dug their noses into the snow, leaving their tails sticking out so that the people could take hold of them like handles. The rats then dragged them to the site of their present village. The rescue of the founding fathers of Cream Puffs Village is commemorated by a realistic statue of the rats, erected in front of the Roundhouse of the Big Spool.

(Carl Sandburg, *Rootabaga Stories*, New York, 1922)

CRIM TARTARY, a kingdom on the Black Sea bordering on Ograria, Circassia and BLACKSTAFF, which separates it from PAFLAGONIA. Paflagonia and Crim Tartary are now united by ties of royal marriage but for many years the two countries were involved in a series of costly and bloody wars.

Crim Tartary is notable for its ancient titled families such as the Spinachi, the Broccoli, the Artichoki and the Sauerkraut. Members of these families have obtained some of the highest honours in the country: the Order of the Pumpkin, First Lord of the Tooth Pick and Joint Keeper of the Snuff Box.

Visitors are advised to attend functions at the Imperial Theatre and to admire the work of Tomaso Lorenzo, painter to the king, at the Royal Galleries. Visitors are further advised that they will be required to show loyalty to the members of the royal family; this is done by rubbing one's nose on the ground, and then placing a royal foot on one's head.

(M.A. Titmarsh [William Makepeace Thackeray], "The Rose and the Ring," in *Christmas Books*, London, 1857)

CRIPPLES, ISLE OF, see HOOLOOMOOLOO.

CRISTALLOPOLIS, see ELISEE RECLUS ISLAND.

CROSS-ROADS, the name given to the meeting of the four ways on the western side of the Mountains of SHADOW in the fair province of ITHILIEN. The roads from CIRITH GORGOR in the north, MINAS MORGUL to the east, HARAD to the south, and OSGILIATH in the west meet here beneath a large circle of enormous old trees.

In ancient times, the men of GONDOR erected a large statue of a seated king here. When Sauron the Dark Lord took power in MORDOR on the far side of the Mountains of Shadow, and established his reign of terror there, the statue was despoiled by his forces. The head was knocked off and a stone, with a grinning face and one red eye (Sauron's emblem) scrawled on it, was set in its place. The statue was restored when the Army of the West passed this way as it marched to the battle that effectively ended the War of the Ring and brought peace to MIDDLE-EARTH.

(J.R.R. Tolkien, *The Two Towers*, London, 1954; J.R.R. Tolkien, *The Return of the King*, London, 1955)

CROTALOPHOBOI LAND, a region of north Africa, inhabited by a race of cannibals and necromancers. The region in which they live is so hot that their eyes grow on the soles of their feet. It was here that St. Dodekanus, the patron saint of NEPENTHE, was martyred. The details of his life are uncertain, but he is known to have been born in the city of Kallisto in Crete in AD 450. After performing a number of miracles in his home country, the saint travelled to Africa, and strove, for eighty years, to convert the Crotalophoboi to Christianity, finally achieving some success. His followers, however, reverted to their old practices and killed him at the age of 132. His body was cut into twelve pieces and ceremoniously eaten. A femur was cast aside and fell on a millstone which miraculously carried it across the sea to Nepenthe, where it is now enshrined.

(Norman Douglas, *South Wind*, London, 1917)

CROTCHET CASTLE, in one of the valleys of the Thames, England, is famous for its vast collection of statues of Venus. The name derives from the Roman ruins discovered on the castle grounds, and from the castle's owner, Ebenezer MacCrotchet, Esq., who, eager to conceal his Jewish and Scottish ancestry, used to sign himself E.M. Crotchet, convincing his neighbours that his name was Edward Matthew Crotchet.

Reading in the papers that London magistrates had ordered that no statues of Venus should appear in the streets without petticoats, Mr. Crotchet decided to give them shelter, and filled his home with statues of the goddess. Bathing Venuses, crouching Venuses, sleeping Venuses, rising Venuses and Venuses of every other description now litter the castle gardens, which are open to the public.

The Crotchet coat of arms is as follows: Crest, crotchet rampant in A sharp; arms, three empty bladders turgescent (to show how opinions are formed), three bags of gold pendant (to show why they are maintained), three naked swords tranchant (to show how they are administered), and three barbers' blocks gaspant (to show how they are swallowed).

(Thomas Love Peacock, *Crotchet Castle*, London, 1881)

A corner of the gardens of CROTCHET CASTLE.

CROTCHET ISLAND, see MAZAR.

CRUSOE'S ISLAND or **SPERANZA** (sometimes called **ISLAND OF DESPAIR**), a small island some twenty leagues off the coast of South America near the mouth of the Orinoco, Venezuela, and not midway between the island of Juan Fernandez and the coast of Chile as has been suggested by French geographers. The interior is hilly, divided by a fertile valley. There are several fine beaches and coves, and the mouth of a small river makes a good port in the north-east. The island became known in the early eighteenth century through the chronicle of one Robinson Crusoe of York, who was shipwrecked here on September 30, 1659. The remains of the three camps he built can be visited: one near the mouth of the river, another on a rocky platform towards the north-west, from which a good view of that part of the island can be had, and a third camp in the interior valley. Here Crusoe planted barley, corn and rice which now supplement the indigenous species on the island: thorny fir-trees, iron-trees, tobacco, aloes, sugar-cane, melons, grapes, citrus and cocoa-trees. There are no wild beasts, except a kind of wildcat (now interbred with a domestic species brought by Crusoe) and goats. Many birds live on this island: parrots, hawks, penguins, rock-pigeons, etc. There are also turtles and a few hares. To the south is Friday's Beach, where Crusoe first saw a human footprint, and a little farther to the west stands a pole Crusoe set

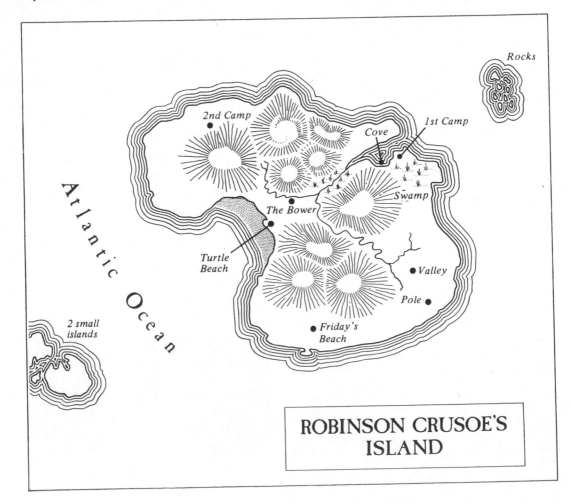

Rocks

2nd Camp

Cove

1st Camp

Swamp

The Bower

Atlantic Ocean

Turtle
Beach

Valley

Pole

2 small
islands

Friday's
Beach

ROBINSON CRUSOE'S ISLAND

up to mark his way. A wooden post that served him as a calendar, with the words "*I came on shore here on the 30th of Sept. 1659,*" can still be seen near his first camp. Towards the south-west, some two leagues away, are a couple of small islands of no major interest. Human bones, the remains of an anthropophagous feast, can be found on Friday's Beach. There are two main seasons twice a year: rainy from mid-February tó mid-April and from mid-August to mid-October; dry from mid-April to mid-August and from mid-October to mid-February. Travellers should bear this in mind and avoid the rainy season. (One of the world's leading authorities on Crusoe's Island, Mr. Gabriel Betteredge, house-steward, has unfortunately not written a book on the subject.)

(Daniel Defoe, *The Life and Strange Adventures of Robinson Crusoe, Of York, Mariner: Who lived Eight and Twenty Years, all alone in an un-inhabited Island on the Coast of America, near the Mouth of the Great River of Oroonoque; Having been cast on Shore by Shipwreck, wherein all the Men perished but himself. With An Account how he was at last as strangely deliver'd by Pyrates. Written by Himself,* London, 1719; Daniel Defoe, *The Farther Adventures of Robinson Crusoe,* London, 1719; Michel Tournier, *Vendredi ou Les Limbes du Pacifique,* Paris, 1969)

CSTWERTSKST, a small town in Poldivia, Europe, famous for its school of Good Souls.

Following the tradition begun by an elderly spinster, Marichelle Borboïe, who gained entrance to Paradise by passing herself off as the local regiment's whore, Cstwertskst teaches its visitors how to prepare their souls for a better world by adopting more convenient occupations. Though giving pleasure to others is regarded as an excellent qualification for entering Paradise (according to the inhabitants of Cstwertskst), other edifying tasks can be chosen as well—for example, evading tax payments in order to prevent the State from becoming too rich and powerful, or stealing jewels from the crowned heads of Europe to later distribute among the more bohemian students on the university campus.

(Marcel Aymé, "Légende Poldève," in *Le Passe-Muraille,* Paris, 1948)

CUBA, see LAMIAM.

CUCCAGNA (not to be confused with COCKAIGNE), a small country not far from Germany; according to some travellers, it is entered through a river. In the middle rises Mount Mecca, a volcano filled with boiling broth. From its bowels spring forth ravioli and other pasta which, rolling down its cheese-covered slopes, fall into a vale of melted butter at the mountain's foot.

In Cuccagna visitors will see monkeys playing chess, the royal family sleeping for three years at a time in a bed of sausage rolls, roast pheasants running about to the sound of trumpets, and showers of capons falling from the heavens. The soil produces truffles as large as houses, the rivers are full of milk or wine. In winter the mountains lie covered with cream cheese, and all year round delicious pastries sprout along the roads. The houses are made of all kinds of Italian food and the bridges are large salami. Coaches run on their own, with no need of horses, and trees bear all kinds of fruit.

A small fountain stands at the disposal of whoever wishes to reduce his or her age by washing in its waters. Women give birth singing and babies walk and talk immediately after being born. He who sleeps most, earns most; he who is found working is taken straight to prison.

(Anonymous, *Capitolo di Cuccagna,* 16th cen. AD; Anonymous, *Storia del Campriano contadino,* 17th cen. AD; Anonymous, *Trionfo del poltroni,* 17th cen. AD)

CUCUMBER ISLAND, off the southern coast of Africa, so called because of the cucumbers that grow on trees. Storms are very severe in this area and usually rip up the trees by their roots and hurl them into the air. These trees, however, have the peculiarity of falling back into place when the storm is over, and everything returns to normal. Only once did a single huge tree not fall back into place—it landed on the king, putting an end to the tyranny that had been the scourge of the island for many years.

(Rudolph Erich Raspe, *Baron Munchausen's Narrative Of His Marvellous Travels And Campaigns in Russia. Humbly Dedicated And Recommended to Country Gentlemen; And, If They Please, To Be Repeated As Their Own, After A Hunt, At Horse Races, In Watering-Places, And Other Such Polite Assemblies; Round the Bottle And Fire-Side,* Cambridge, London & Oxford, 1785)

CUFFYCOAT'S ISLAND, about one hundred miles to the north of New Guinea, covered with dense forests. The fauna includes flying squirrels, kangaroos, and mermaids (possibly related to those of MER-KING'S KINGDOM) that live on the coast in underwater houses of coral. They travel widely and have been seen, for instance, near Sandgate Castle, Folkestone, southern England. Though the mermaids attempt to keep up with western fashion, they find the task extremely difficult as the humidity quickly ruins their garments. To add to the problem, Cuffycoat dressmakers are known to be troublesome and frequently go on strike. Underwater life is reputedly unpleasant. Going home after work involves pushing one's way through a crowd of ill-mannered octopuses, deep-sea monsters that try to devour anything they can find, and obstinate swordfish that keep digging their swords through the cracks in the walls of the houses.

The rest of the island is inhabited by two different racial groups. One is a tribe of Indians who practise cannibalism as part of their religious rites; they eat old men to absorb their wisdom and at the same time pay tribute to their ancestors. They wash down their meals with palm wine and hold their women as virtual slaves. The second group is a tribe of orangoutangs whose level of social organization is higher than that of the natives and who sometimes reduce the cannibals to slavery. They speak a primitive form of English with an American accent, mixed with barkings similar to those of a seal. Phrases like "all right" and "quite well" can easily be made out in their speech.

The island takes its name from a certain Mr. Cuffycoat who was shipwrecked here when en route for Australia. He escaped the cannibals, met one of the mermaids—a certain Miss Waters—and went to live in the forests with the orangoutang tribe.

(André Lichtenberger, *Pickles ou récits à la mode anglaise*, Paris, 1923)

CUNA CUNA, capital of TACARIGUA.

CUTTENCLIP, a sheltered village in Quadling Country, OZ, not far from FUDDLECUMJIG. The village is surrounded by a high wall painted blue with pink ornaments. The only entrance is through a small door which bears the legend "Visitors are requested to move slowly and carefully, and to avoid coughing or making any breeze or draught." This warning is necessary as the village is populated entirely by living paper dolls.

Cuttenclip itself consists of houses and streets cut from coloured paper. The exception is a wooden house in the centre of the paper village. This is the home of the ruler and creator of the community, Miss Cuttenclip. Originally she lived near the castle of Glinda the Good, in the far south of Oz, and made paper dolls, but these were so beautiful that it seemed a pity they were not alive, so Glinda gave her live paper: all dolls and animals cut from it immediately came to life and were able to think and talk. The problem was that the dolls created in this way were blown away by the slightest breeze. Glinda therefore settled Miss Cuttenclip in a sheltered area and built a wall around her domain. She also protects the village from rain, so that there is no danger of the paper people being damaged or dissolved. Miss Cuttenclip is obviously loved by her subjects, who are only too happy to wave their paper handkerchiefs and sing the national anthem, *The Flag Of Our Native Land*.

(L. Frank Baum, *The Emerald City of Oz*, Chicago, 1910)

CYCLOPES ISLAND, somewhere in the Mediterranean. The island is uncultivated but not infertile: wheat, corn and vines grow naturally from its soil, and numerous trips of goats roam the inte-

A cannibal's ornate drinking cup from CUFFYCOAT'S ISLAND.

rior. The name of the island derives from its inhabitants, the Cyclopes, gigantic men with a single eye in the middle of their foreheads. They live in an uncivilized state, in deep caves high in the mountains. They have no notion of sociable living; each family is a society in itself where the eldest has all authority. Among other unpleasant habits, they sometimes eat human flesh and, like *snarks* (see SNARK ISLAND), always look grave at a pun.

(Homer, *The Odyssey,* 9th cen. [?] BC)

CYRIL ISLAND, of unknown location. Seen from a distance, Cyril Island looks like the fire of a volcano or a bouquet of shooting stars. It is, in fact, a mobile volcano, run by strong propellors at each of its four corners.

The blinding redness of the volcano and of the flowing lava make it difficult to see anything on the island; to remedy this, the native children carry lamps to guide the visitors. These children live and die, without ever growing old, in several sections of a worm-eaten barge near the shore.

Inquisitive travellers will notice lampshades scuttling about the bottom of the barge. Farther inland, visiting botanists can admire the island's sleeping umbels.

The island is the home and vessel of Captain Kidd, who can sometimes be seen drinking gin and lighting his pipe on glowing lava.

(Alfred Jarry, *Gestes et Opinions du Docteur Faustroll, Pataphysicien. Roman Néo-Scientifique,* Paris, 1911)

D

DADDY JONES' KINGDOM, a valley on the coast of Finland, to the north of MOOMINLAND. The lower slopes of the valley are formed by round, green hills dotted with trees laden with green and yellow berries. A heart-shaped island lies two miles offshore from the seaward end of the valley. The valley is crossed by a river.

This small kingdom is ruled by Daddy Jones, a somewhat autocratic monarch with a taste for practical jokes. His subjects include a variety of creatures. The *Hemulens* serve as his soldiers, guards and policemen. These are tall creatures with protruding snouts and pink eyes but no ears, those organs being replaced by tufts of blue or ginger hair; they have large flat feet. *Hemulens* are not noted for their intelligence and easily become fanatical about things. For example, they dislike all whistling and all whistlers, simply because they themselves cannot whistle. Beneath the river bed live the *Niblings*, sociable animals who dig tunnels with their strong white teeth. They are good at building things, but visitors may find them difficult to deal with socially—they nibble constantly, especially at unfamiliar objects. For instance, they may chew off the noses of visitors if they consider them to be too long. The *Niblings* are hairy creatures with long tails and whiskers. They have suckers on their feet and leave a sticky trail wherever they go. Their characteristic call is a muffled bellow, as though they were calling through a thin tube.

The kingdom is also the home of the *Bobbles*. Only two *Bobbles* have ever been seen, Edward and Edward's brother, whose name is not known. Edward the Bobble is said to be the largest creature in the world, with the possible exception of his brother. Edward is clumsy and has an unfortunate tendency to kill people by accidentally treading on them. Travellers will be glad to know that when this happens he always insists on paying for the funeral of his unintended victim.

(Tove Jansson, *Kuinkas sitten kävikään*, Helsinki, 1952)

DAGORLAD, a great treeless plain between the DEAD MARSHES and CIRITH GORGOR, fa-

mous for the great battles that have been fought upon it at various times in MIDDLE-EARTH'S history. Towards the end of the Second Age, the Last Alliance—an alliance forged between elves, dwarves and men to defeat Sauron the Dark Lord—were victorious here after a battle that is said to have raged for months. In this battle the leaders of the Last Alliance fought with their legendary weapons; Gilgalad the elf with his spear Aiglos, and Elendil with his sword Narsil.

During the Third Age, Dagorlad became the main route into GONDOR for the invaders from the east who repeatedly attacked that kingdom, and the plain was again the site of great battles. In 1944 Third Age, a great force of Wainriders, so called because they rode to battle in great wagons, was defeated here by the armies of Gondor and totally annihilated. Dagorlad, with its many groves, is slowly being swamped by the Dead Marshes, which are not recommended for any but the most stouthearted travellers.

(J.R.R. Tolkien, *The Fellowship of the Ring*, London, 1954; J.R.R. Tolkien, *The Two Towers*, London, 1954; J.R.R. Tolkien, *The Return of the King*, London, 1955)

DALAND'S VILLAGE, in Norway, famous for being the only known port at which the phantom ship of the Flying Dutchman, the Wandering Jew of the ocean, came to call.

After having tried to double the Cape of Good Hope in a furious gale, the Dutchman, captain of the ship, swore he would accomplish his purpose, even if he had to keep on sailing forever. For this he was condemned to sail until Judgement Day, and only allowed to stop once every seven years so that he might find a woman who would love him faithfully until death. The lady proved to be a certain Senta, daughter of a Norwegian sea captain, who showed her devotion by throwing herself into the sea.

(Richard Wagner, *Der Fliegende Holländer*, first performance Dresden, 1843)

DALE, a city-kingdom of men in the valley of the River Running in the north-east of MIDDLE-EARTH. The city is built on the southern slopes of the LONELY MOUNTAIN overlooking the river which forms a large loop around the southern flank.

Dale was a rich and prosperous town until the great dragon Smaug the Golden came south to the Lonely Mountain in 2770 Third Age. Traditionally friendly with the dwarf-kingdom under the Mountain, the men of Dale had long traded food, cloth and other essentials necessary to the dwarves for works of metal and stone. Smaug's presence and nocturnal forays against Dale in search of prey led to the death of many men; the remainder fled and settled mainly in LAKE-TOWN, and Dale fell into ruins.

Bard, a direct descendant of the last king of Dale, was among those who defended Lake-town when it was attacked by Smaug in 2941 Third Age, and, being a noted archer, he killed the dragon. Acclaimed as the new king of Dale, he led the men who fought alongside the dwarves against a huge army of orcs on and around the Lonely Mountain during the battle of the Five Armies. After the victory, Bard received a fourteenth share of Smaug's hoard and used his wealth to rebuild Dale which once again became a rich town.

During the War of the Ring, the men of Dale joined with the dwarves of the Lonely Mountain in the struggle against the forces of Sauron the Dark Lord. Dale and the Mountain were beseiged by an army from the east but after the defeat of Sauron in the south, men and dwarves sallied out under Bard II and Thorin Stonehelm, King under the Mountain, and broke the siege. Subsequently, Dale has always been in close alliance with GONDOR and remains under the protection of the rulers of the Reunited Kingdom.

Dale is a great trading centre and is the major outlet for the beautiful articles made by the dwarves, especially magic toys.

(J.R.R. Tolkien, *The Hobbit, or There and Back Again*, London, 1937; J.R.R. Tolkien, *The Fellowship of the Ring*, London, 1954; J.R.R. Tolkien, *The Return of the King*, London, 1955)

DARK LAND, see City of DESTRUCTION.

DAY BEFORE, ISLAND OF THE, so named because visitors are unable to fix a point in space from which time can be measured, which makes it impossible to inscribe the island in the present. Visitors intent on travelling to the Island of the Day Before should know that they will not be allowed to land on the island itself, but must content themselves with observing it from a fully provisioned ship, the *Daphne*, anchored in its bay. To the untrained eye the island appears pale, its peak tufted with a patch of wool, since ocean islands retain the humidity of the trade winds and condense it into cloudy puffs. These clouds resemble not the harmonious arrangements of nature, such as snow or crystal, but rather those volutes that architects impose on domes, capitals and columns.

The colouring of the fruits and plants—visible through a telescope or binoculars—has significances opposite to those in the Western world. The mortuary white of a certain fruit guarantees vivid sweetness, whereas more russet fruits may secrete lethal philtres. Trees are strange and dangerous: for instance, on the star-shaped tree, the tips of the star are as sharp as blades. At the centre of the island, tempting in its delicate hues, stands the Tree of Oblivion. Its fruit, if eaten, grants the traveller peace at last.

Birds too are different from those encountered in Europe. Their songs are like the music of a complex orchestra: whistles, gurgles, crackles, grumblings, cluckings, whimperings, muffled musket shots, whole chromatic scales of pecking. Though found on the islands, the Orange-Coloured Bird is said to be originally from the Island of Solomon, because the Song of that great king speaks of a dove rising like the dawn, bright as the sun, with wings covered with silver and feathers glinting with gold. More ordinary are the flying foxes, pigs, non venomous snakes and innumerable lizards. Yet it appears that on this island every form of life has been conceived not by an architect or a sculptor but by a jeweller: birds are coloured crystal, woodland animals are delicate, fish are flat and almost transparent.

In the island's waters there are curious, seemingly two-headed eels—the second head, scientists have noted, is in fact a decorated tail to frighten off enemies—and Beelzebub fish with yellow eyes, tumid mouths and teeth like nails. In the coral reefs live turtles, crabs and oysters of every shape, big as baskets, pots or serving platters.

Visitors should be aware that the island they see may not be the same one others see, since landscape seems to mirror each visitor's own experience of the world.

(Umberto Eco, *La isola del giorno primo*, Milan, 1994)

DEAD, CITY OF THE, the former capital of ARDISTAN on the banks of the River Suhl. When the river dried up the city was deserted and a new capital was built at ARD. For centuries the old capital lay empty, with only one or two buildings being used as prisons. Few people, apart from some of Ardistan's secretive religious leaders, ever visited the city and it has never been fully described.

The Suhl has now begun to flow again, but thanks to the dry climate of the area, the city is perfectly preserved. The eastern section is the old residential quarter, with its houses, churches and mosques still intact. Although the dominant impression is one of desolation and a death-like sleep,

it is not difficult to imagine the former beauty of this great city. On the west bank stands the walled citadel, almost a separate military town. Its western side is built against the slopes of the surrounding mountains, and its walls and towers are so massive that it is considered an almost impregnable fortress.

The City of the Dead contains many important secrets, some of them known only to the high clergy of Ardistan. Some of the prison buildings, for instance, have floors which can be tilted, dropping unsuspecting prisoners into deep underground rooms. Subterranean passages and ancient covered waterways provide hidden means of access to the citadel. To the west of the fortress is the

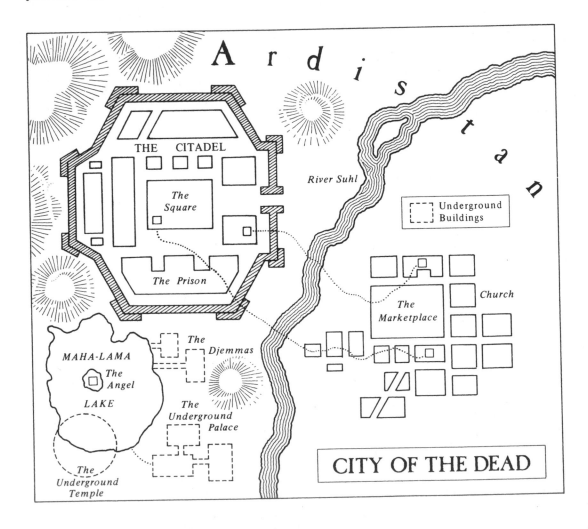

so-called Maha-Lama Lake. The crater which formed the lake is completely surrounded by steep walls of rock. All that can be seen from above is the upper part of the statue of an angel. The area is feared and avoided by the few who have visited the city, perhaps because it is connected with ancient legends of evil. It is said that the lake was created by the devil and than an ancient high priest of Maha-Lama was told by the Devil that he would live for another hundred years if he drowned all those who insulted him in the lake. Although once loved by the people, the Maha-Lama became unpopular. Hundreds were drowned in the lake, and it became so choked with corpses that the Maha-Lama could no longer fulfill his commitment and was finally carried off by the Devil.

The floor of the crater has been dry for centuries, and strange structures have been built into its walls. At intervals, around the walls, pillars and doors can be seen; these doors give access to a vast underground palace with more than three hundred rooms. The doors themselves are inscribed with letters in several oriental languages; they can be opened by turning a metallic image of the sun. Inside, travellers will find many workrooms, storehouses and dwelling quarters, as well as sick-bays and burial grounds.

Perhaps the most impressive building in the crater is the temple hollowed out within the rock. Around its circular walls runs a spiral of seats, climbing from the floor to the highest point of the roof. A balustrade runs along the outer edge of this gently ascending gallery, pierced with hundreds of openings, in each of which is a candle. At the very bottom of the spiral, travellers will see a simple stone pulpit. The acoustics here are such that every word uttered can be heard at the very top of the spiral of seats. Like the other underground buildings, the temple is lit by window openings which slope horizontally to ground level. The windows are made of a kind of mica as transparent as glass.

Built into the rock travellers will also find two *djemmas* or council chambers. One is known as the *djemma* of the Dead because it houses the mummified corpses of the dead rulers of Ardistan. It is a huge room, with a roof supported by gigantic pillars of rock which were left in place when the chamber was excavated. The dead kings and high priests sit here as judges in a court-room. In their parched hands they all hold notebooks in which

the crimes committed during their lifetimes are recorded.

Another secret of the City of the Dead lies beneath the figure of an angel in the centre of the Maha-Lama Lake. Like similar angels in EL HADD and USSULISTAN it marks the site of an underground water supply, in this case a large pool which is supplied by hidden conduits.

Large numbers of clay tablets covered in an ancient script have been found in the City of the Dead; these describe the early history of Ardistan, with particular reference to the period before the rise of the Mirs and the decline of the power of the old religious leaders. Many paintings of past rulers have also been found here, adding much to the knowledge of this ancient kingdom.

(Karl Friedrich May, *Ardistan*, Bamberg, 1909; Karl Friedrich May, *Der Mir von Djinnistan*, Bamberg, 1909)

DEAD MAN'S VALLEY, see TROPICAL VALLEY.

DEAD MARSHES, an extensive marshland on the eastern side of EMYN MUIL, in the south of MIDDLE-EARTH, to the west of the battle-plain of DAGORLAD before the gates of MORDOR.

The Dead Marshes are a dismal area of stagnant pools and bogs, from which an unwholesome smell rises. The ground is often clad in mist. Visitors are warned that it is extremely dangerous to cross the marshes, as there are few reliable paths. Safer tracks do, however, skirt the marshes and eventually lead to Dagorlad.

The vegetation is poor—a livid coloured weed grows on the greasy surface of the water, but other than that, and a few rotting weeds, there are only patches of dead or dying grass. No birds are seen in the marshes; the only living things are the snakes and worms. At its southern end, the marshland gives way to an area of dead, dry peat.

The marshes take their name from the fact that they have slowly extended until they reached the graves of those who fell in battle on the plain of Dagorlad. The marshes nearest to the graves are now known as the Mere of Dead Faces. Here visitors can see the faces of the dead, both fair and foul, rotting deep in the pools. To add to the peculiar atmosphere of the place, mysterious candle-like lights flicker in the stifling air—these are called "candles of corpses."

(J.R.R. Tolkien, *The Fellowship of the Ring*, London, 1954; J.R.R. Tolkien, *The Two Towers*, London, 1954; J.R.R. Tolkien, *The Return of the King*, London, 1955)

DEADS' TOWN, somewhere in the Nigerian bush. No person alive is allowed to enter Deads' Town, and therefore no information is available about either the town's aspect or its customs. It is said to be inhabited by those who have recently died, who suffer neither hunger nor thirst and thus have no need for either bed or board.

(Amos Tutuola, *The Palm-Wine Drinkard and His Dead Palm-Wine Tapster in the Deads' Town*, London, 1952)

DEATH, CITY OF, see City of NIGHT.

DEATH, FOREST OF, a broad forest in the underground continent of PELLUCIDAR, not far from the village of BASTI. The forest is a gloomy place lying in perpetual twilight as the sun filters through the intertwining branches of the tall tropical trees. It is the home of the Gorbuses, a white-skinned people with long white hair, whose appearance is enhanced by the two tusk-like teeth that protrude on either side of the jaw and reach down to the chin. The Gorbuses are cannibals and their main dish is roast human flesh. They are, however, a timid race and prefer to trap their victims rather than capture them in open battle. Once trapped, the bodies of the victims are stored in deep caves until they have decayed sufficiently to be eaten. Live captives are fed on fruit and nuts until they are ready for slaughter.

Nothing is known of the origin of the Gorbuses. Some of their language and customs suggest, however, that they did not originally live in the forest. Their language, for instance, includes words for "cleaver" and "dagger" and their myths speak of another world which they sometimes glimpse through a fog of almost forgotten memories. Basically they are a sad race, despite their grisly habits. All of them know that they have at some time killed someone who was loved by one of their fellows or by members of other races; their

lives are therefore dominated by feelings of guilt, hopelessness, fear and hate. With almost religious fervour, the Gorbuses believe that they are all being punished for something that happened in the distant past of their race. The Gorbuses have never been seen outside their secret, shaded forest home.

(Edgar Rice Burroughs, *Seven Worlds to Conquer*, New York, 1936)

DEATHWATER ISLAND, of no more than twenty acres, to the east of BURNT ISLAND. The island was claimed for NARNIA by Caspian X, its discoverer. It is rocky and rugged with a tall central peak; the vegetation consists merely of perfumed heather and coarse grass. Seagulls appear to be the only living creatures on it.

There are two streams on the island, one of which flows from a small mountain lake surrounded by cliffs—anything dipped into the water of this lake is immediately turned to solid gold. Visitors are advised not to swim in it. The body of one of the exiled lords of Narnia was found in the lake, transformed into a gold statue. It is speculated that he had been bathing, unaware of the powers of the water. The discovery of the corpse gave the island its present name, although Caspian X was tempted, at first, to call it Goldwater Island.

(C.S. Lewis, *The Voyage of the "Dawn Treader,"* London, 1952)

DEBRA-DOWA, capital of the AZANIAN EMPIRE.

DEELGUY, a kingdom of traders and merchants to the north-east of the BEKLAN EMPIRE. The frontiers of Deelguy are a matter of dispute, however it is usually accepted that the territory belonging to the country includes the semi-desert land, known as the Deelguy Desert, lying to the east of the Telthearna River.

(Richard Adams, *Shardik*, London, 1974)

DELECTABLE MOUNTAINS, a lofty mountain range in CHRISTIAN'S COUNTRY, above the Plain of EASE; the river surrounding the CELESTIAL CITY can be seen from their upper slopes. The countryside in this region is very pleasant, covered in fine orchards, vineyards and woods. Sheep are kept on the higher slopes, watched over by the shepherds Knowledge, Sincere, Experience and Watchful.

The mountains are safe for a few travellers, but extremely dangerous for those who transgress the law or whose faith is not strong. Those who err in their beliefs plunge to their death from the steep slopes of the Mountain of Error, while hypocrites will inevitably find their way onto a bypass which leads directly to their perdition. On the slopes of Mount Caution, blind people can be seen stumbling among a number of tombs; they were travellers who turned aside into By-pass Meadow instead of staying on the path across the Plain of Ease, and so fell into the hands of Giant Despair of DOUBTING CASTLE who blinded them.

On Mount Innocent, a man dressed in pure white can be seen by travellers; two others, Prejudice and Ill-will, constantly throw dirt at him, but his garments are never stained. The man in white is called Godly-man and his white robes are said to represent the innocence of his life. On Mount Charity another man distributes clothes to the poor; no matter how many garments he distributes, his bundle is never exhausted.

It is the custom of the shepherds to show something of these wonders to passing travellers.

(John Bunyan, *The Pilgrim's Progress from this world, to that which is to come. Delivered under the similitude of a Dream. Wherein is discovered, the manner of his setting out, his dangerous journey and safe arrival at the Desired Country*, London, 1678; John Bunyan, *The Pilgrim's Progress from this world to that which is to come. The Second Part. Delivered under the similitude of a Dream. Wherein is set forth the manner of the setting out of Christian's wife and children, their dangerous journey and safe arrival at the Desired Country*, London, 1684)

DELIX, see Isles of WISDOM.

DESERT TOWN, a forgotten Roman city somewhere in the Atlas Mountains, inhabited by a tribe of Jews who trade in gold, silver and fabrics. Black jackals haunt the area.

It is said that one of the inhabitants of Desert Town, Abdias—hated because of his wealth, persecuted by his rivals, disfigured by illness and accompanied by a blind daughter—established himself in the arid valley of the Bohemian mountainside where the barren landscape reminded him of his homeland. A flash of lightning restored his daughter's sight, and to please her he transformed the bleak region into a flowery garden. However, his daughter imprudently stepped out into the open air to watch a thunderstorm and this time was killed by a less merciful bolt of lightning. Abdias became insane but lived on in the garden he had created for another thirty years.

(Adalbert Stifter, "Abdias," in *Oesterreich-Novellenalmanack*, Vienna, 1843)

DESPAIRIA, a desolate land, consisting mainly of rock and sand deserts, to the west of JANSENIA. Despairia has no exports. However, it does import, from its neighbour, rope, knives, funeral shrouds, gravestones and copper plaques for epitaphs.

(Le Père Zacharie de Lisieux, *Relation du pays de Jansénie, où il est traité des singularitez qui s'y trouvent, des coustumes, Moeurs et Religion des habitants. Par Louys Fontaines, Sieur de Saint Marcel*, Paris, 1660)

DESPAIR, ISLAND OF, see CRUSOE'S ISLAND.

DESPINA, a city in Asia. Despina can be reached in two ways: by ship or by camel. The city displays one face to the traveller arriving overland and a different one to him who arrives by sea.

When the camel-driver sees, at the horizon of the tableland, the pinnacles of the skyscrapers come into view, the radar antennae, the white and red windsocks flapping, the chimneys belching smoke, he thinks of a ship; he knows it is a city, but he thinks of it as a vessel that will take him away from the desert, a windjammer about to cast off, with the breeze already swelling the sails, not yet unfurled, or a steamboat with its boiler vibrating in the iron keel; and he thinks of all the ports, the foreign merchandise the cranes unload on the docks, the taverns where crews of different flags break bottles over one another's heads, the lighted, ground-floor windows, each with a woman combing her hair.

In the coastline's haze, the sailor discerns the form of a camel's withers, an embroidered saddle with glittering fringe between two spotted humps, advancing and swaying; he knows it is a city, but he thinks of it as a camel from whose pack hang wine-skins and bags of candied fruit, date wine, tobacco leaves, and already he sees himself at the head of a long caravan taking him away from the desert of the sea, towards oases of fresh water in the palm trees' jagged shade, towards palaces of thick, white-washed walls, tiled courts where girls are dancing barefoot, moving their arms, half-hidden by their veils, and half-revealed.

Each city receives its form from the desert it opposes; and so both the camel-driver and the sailor have each a vision of Despina, a border city between two deserts.

(Italo Calvino, *Le città invisibili*, Turin, 1972)

DESPOND, SLOUGH OF, a great marsh lying between the City of DESTRUCTION and the wicket-gate that gives access to the route to the CELESTIAL CITY. The Slough is one of the first and most dangerous obstacles which travellers attempting to reach the Celestial City have to overcome. Many have been sucked into the bottomless marsh and many more have been discouraged from going on with their journey because of their experiences here.

It seems impossible to reclaim the slough and to turn it into good land, so great is the quantity of scum and filth that collects here. For almost two thousand years, attempts have been made to fill it in, but they have come to naught. The workmen sent by the Lord of the Celestial City are still working at the task, but it is far from over. Some workmen who claim to be employed by the lord are in fact deceivers who fling more dung and dirt into the Slough. Travellers should note that there are safe steps through the centre of the Slough, but they are difficult to see because of the shifting mud and murky water.

(John Bunyan, *The Pilgrim's Progress from this world, to that which is to come. Delivered under the similitude of a Dream. Wherein is discovered, the manner of his setting out, his dangerous journey and safe arrival at the Desired Country*, London, 1678; John Bunyan, *The Pilgrim's Progress from this world to that which is to come. The Second Part. Delivered under the similitude of a Dream. Wherein is set forth the manner of the setting out of Christian's wife and children, their dangerous journey and safe arrival at the Desired Country*, London, 1684)

DESTRUCTION, CITY OF, a large and populous city adjacent to the City of Stupidity and the town of Carnal Policy, in CHRISTIAN'S COUNTRY. The City of Destruction is noted for the worldly attitude of its people towards religious matters, and as the home of Christian, a famous traveller who first charted this entire area.

(John Bunyan, *The Pilgrim's Progress from this world, to that which is to come. Delivered under the similitude of a Dream. Wherein is discovered, the manner of his setting out, his dangerous journey and safe arrival at the Desired Country*, London, 1678; John Bunyan, *The Pilgrim's Progress from this world to that which is to come. The Second Part. Delivered under the similitude of a Dream. Wherein is set forth the manner of the setting out of Christian's wife and children, their dangerous journey and safe arrival at the Desired Country*, London, 1684)

DEVIL'S GARDEN, the spacious walled grounds surrounding Beelzebub's Castle, close by the wicket-gate that gives access to the road leading from the City of DESTRUCTION to the CELESTIAL CITY in CHRISTIAN'S COUNTRY.

Travellers are warned that Beelzebub shoots arrows at those who have succeeded in crossing the SLOUGH OF DESPOND and then try to pass the gate. His gardens represent a great temptation to the traveller, as delicious-looking fruit hangs over the wall above the narrow path. However, travellers should note that the fruit is highly poisonous and many have died from eating it. The severe gripes and stomach pains it causes can be cured only by the physician who lives in Watchful's House on the nearby Hill of DIFFICULTY.

(John Bunyan, *The Pilgrim's Progress from this world, to that which is to come. Delivered under the similitude of a Dream. Wherein is discovered, the manner of his setting out, his dangerous journey and safe arrival at the Desired Country*, London, 1678; John Bunyan, *The Pilgrim's Progress from this world to that which is to come. The Second Part. Delivered under the similitude of a Dream. Wherein is set forth the manner of the setting out of Christian's wife and children, their dangerous journey and safe arrival at the Desired Country*, London, 1684)

DEVIL'S ISLAND, in the Aegean Sea, not to be confused with the penal settlement of the same name off the coast of French Guiana. Some prefer to call it Island of Santa Maria, but the more ancient name of Devil's Island is still retained by the inhabitants. In ancient times, Devil's Island was ruled by the giant Bandaguido, who, because of his extraordinary fierceness and strength, subdued the other giants who ruled the neighbouring lands. His wife was a charitable woman who tried to ease the torments that her husband inflicted on the inhabitants and who bore him a beautiful daughter called Bandaguida after her father.

Because the islanders were afraid of the giant's ferocity, no suitors dared approach Bandaguida; so she decided to kill her mother and make love to her father. From their union a creature was born, the likes of which has never been seen again. Its body was entirely covered with hair except for its back, which was covered with scales so tough that no weapon could pierce them. It had immense hands and feet and a pair of long wings, made of black leather, which it used as shields. Its scaly arms were dark and powerful, and instead of fingers it had claws like an eagle. Only two teeth adorned its mouth, each about a foot long, and its eyes were large, brown and red. It could run and jump faster than the mountain deer and it rarely ate or drank. Its only pastime was to kill human beings and other living creatures.

Confronted with such a monster, its father consulted the idols, who imposed upon the parents the obligation of not seeing their son for one whole year. After this period, Bandaguido and Bandaguida entered the child's chamber; seeing his mother, the monster leapt upon her and plunged its teeth into her neck. Trying to save his daughter, the mother of his child, the giant drew forth his sword, but with such ill-luck that he cut off his own leg and died of a dreadful haemorrhage. His son jumped over the bodies and escaped into the mountains, with the result that most inhabitants decided to abandon the island forever. Forty years later, after an epic fight, the monster was killed by Amadís of Gaul who returned Devil's Island to its rightful owner, the Emperor of Constantinople.

(Anonymous, *Amadís de Gaula*, Zaragoza, 1508)

DEVILS, ISLE OF, see CAPTAIN SPARROW'S ISLAND.

DEVILS, LAND OF, see LIMANORA.

DEVIL'S TEETH, THE, a chain of five mountains which stand in a circle in north-east Greenland, their jagged outlines giving the appearance of teeth. They can be reached by a natural basalt bridge one and a half kilometres long, with precipitous sides falling away into a chaos of rock and ice. At one end of the bridge, a cave or tunnel leads through one of the mountains, and at the other a huge cavern with glittering stalactites runs deep into the mountains where subsidiary tunnels and caves branch off at regular intervals. All exits lead to a megalith shaped roughly like a mammoth and

The natural basalt bridge leading to the DEVIL'S TEETH, Greenland.

bearing the runic inscription "Beyond this sacred stone lies ERIKRAUBEBYGD."

(Paul Alperine, *La Citadelle des glaces*, PARIS, 1946)

DIAMOND MOUNTAINS,

DIAMOND MOUNTAINS, on an unnamed island in the Indian Ocean, so called because in the valleys below lie vast quantities of sparkling diamonds. Travellers are warned that these stones are extremely dangerous, being in fact carnivorous creatures who will attack any stranger impudent enough to try to pick them up. The merchants of the island manage to collect them by using the following system: they take a sow, slaughter it, skin it and cut it into small pieces which they throw from the mountain-tops into the valleys. The pieces of fresh meat are attacked by the diamonds; towards the evening, eagles and vultures fly down from the mountains and grab hold of the pieces of meat, with the diamonds still attached, and carry them to their nests. The merchants, who have in the meantime climbed to these nests, frighten the birds away with loud cries. Quickly and carefully they separate the diamonds from the meat, put them in large bags and sell them to unsuspecting jewellers throughout the world. Many an elegant finger is at this very moment wearing what looks like an innocent ring, but is in fact a ferocious beast waiting for its chance to strike.

(Anonymous, *The Arabian Nights*, 14th–15th cen. AD)

DIANA'S GROVE,

DIANA'S GROVE, the ruins of a mansion in Staffordshire, England, within walking distance of Mercy Farm. All that remains of the mansion—said to have occupied a site inhabited since Roman times—is a round hole which disappears into the bowels of the earth.

The hole was the entrance to the lair of the white worm, a monstrous creature which seems to have survived from prehistoric times in the swamps below the china clay levels. Over the centuries, it acquired the ability to take on the shape of a beautiful, slender woman possessed by a lust for blood and a desire to kill, as well as a liking for power. The mansion and the evil spirit that lived in it were destroyed by an Englishman, Adam Salton, who lowered dynamite into the worm's pit. The dynamite was ignited by lightning and the re-

sulting explosion destroyed both Diana's Grove and the nearby Castra Regis, ancestral home of the celebrated Caswell family.

(Bram Stoker, *The Lair of the White Worm*, London, 1911)

DICTIONOPOLIS or CITY OF WORDS,

DICTIONOPOLIS or **CITY OF WORDS,** rival city of DIGITOPOLIS, in the foothills of Confusion, caressed by breezes from the Sea of Knowledge. From this walled city come all the words in the world. They are grown in orchards and once a week a word-market is held where people come to buy the words they need and trade-in those they have not used. For people wishing to make up their own words, individual letters are also on sale. Visitors should know the taste of letters before they acquire any: *A* tastes very good, but *Z* on the other hand is dry and tastes of sawdust. *X* is like stale air, *I* is icy and refreshing, *C* crunchy and *P* full of pips. A French connoisseur has described some letters according to colour rather than taste: *A* black, *E* white, *I* red, *U* green and *O* blue.

Dictionopolis is a constitutional monarchy. King Azaz the Unabridged established a cabinet of ministers who ensure that all words sold exist and are meaningful: the Duke of Definition, the Minister of Meaning, the Earl of Essence, the Count of Connotation and the Under-secretary of Understanding. At one point, King Azaz made his great-aunt Faintly Macabre responsible for decreeing which words were to be used and when. On the principle that "brevity is the soul of wit," Miss Macabre became more and more miserly, keeping more and more words for herself. Sales fell off in the word-market and finally ceased when she put up a sign saying "silence is golden"; she was thrown into a dungeon by the king himself. Dictionopolians today think themselves wise to use as many words as they can and they have become very verbose, speaking in great streams of synonyms, as though they were reading from a thesaurus.

The Royal Palace physically resembles an enormous book standing on its end, with a door in the place usually occupied by the publisher's name. Inside, walls and ceilings are covered with mirrors. Here are held the royal banquets, where the guests are requested to make speeches, listing items of food which immediately appear in the form of words. Then the guests literally eat their words. On special occasions, half-baked ideas are supplied by the Half Bakery. Though tasty, they do not always agree with one and people have been known to swallow some for years on end.

According to the laws of Dictionopolis, dogs are not allowed to bark without a barking meter and it is an offence to sow confusion, upset the apple-cart, wreak havoc or mince words. All visitors must have a reason, explanation or excuse for whatever they do, but failing everything else, "why not" is a good reason. The law is administered by a police force of one, Officer Shrift, who is also judge and jailer. He enjoys putting people into jail for long sentences but does not care about keeping them there. Visitors are also advised that upon mounting the *shandrydan* or wooden wagon that crosses the city, they are to keep silent: the *shandrydan* goes without saying.

The fauna of Dictionopolis consists solely of two insects and a species of watchdog, the latter traditionally known to be ferocious. These watchdogs have to be wound up periodically, but keep good time as long as expressions such as "wasting time" and "killing time" are not used in their presence. Because time flies, these dogs have wings (see also THE DOLDRUMS). The two species of insects mentioned above are only found in Dictionopolis. The spelling bee is an enormous insect which spells out its words letter by letter when it seems useful or necessary. It was formerly an ordinary bee that smelt flowers and occasionally picked up part-time work by nestling in people's bonnets; now it has decided to improve itself by getting an education. Finally, the humbug is a large beetlelike insect, *insecticus humbugium*, that wears a lavish coat, striped trousers, checked waistcoat, spats and derby hat.

(Norton Juster, *The Phantom Tollbooth*, London, 1962)

DIEGO RODRIGO, see RODRIGUE.

DIFFICULTY, a steep hill on the long road from the City of DESTRUCTION to the CELESTIAL CITY, leading down into the Valley of HUMILIATION, in CHRISTIAN'S COUNTRY.

The hill is so steep that travellers often have to climb it on their hands and knees. At the foot of the hill, two paths diverge from the main road, one leading to the great Wood of Danger and the other to the Mountains of Destruction. Although these paths are now barred and bolted some travellers still insist on taking them, as they appear to be much easier than the road over the Hill of Difficulty.

On the slopes of the hill itself is a comfortable arbour but the traveller is advised not to linger in it; many who have stayed there have lost their belongings while they slept.

Above the arbour the road narrows, and is guarded at its narrowest point by two lions. The lions are chained and cannot in fact harm the traveller who walks down the middle of the road; they are kept here solely to test the traveller's faith.

Halfway up the hill is the house of Watchful, the porter, built for the relief and security of travellers to the Celestial City. Here they are lodged in a large room called Peace and are attended by Prudence, Mercy, Charity, Discretion and Piety. The house is a rich store of relics and records of the deeds of the Lord of the Hill and his servants, as well as of the travellers who have passed this way. Visitors are usually given food when they leave: bread, wine and raisins. Some travellers will also be given suits of armour to defend themselves against the dangers they will meet in the next valley.

On the lower slopes of the hill stands a stage, built to punish those who are afraid to go on with their journey because of mistrust or timorousness. Those who try to hinder travellers on their journey are burnt on the tongue with a hot iron.

(John Bunyan, *The Pilgrim's Progress from this world, to that which is to come. Delivered under the similitude of a Dream. Wherein is discovered, the manner of his setting out, his dangerous journey and safe arrival at the Desired Country*, London, 1678; John Bunyan, *The Pilgrim's Progress from this world to that which is to come. The Second Part. Delivered under the similitude of a Dream. Wherein is set forth the manner of the setting out of Christian's wife and children, their dangerous journey and safe arrival at the Desired Country*, London, 1684)

DIGITOPOLIS or **CITY OF NUMBERS**, a small city ruled by the Mathemagician, in the north of the old WISDOM KINGDOM. The main produce of Digitopolis is numbers, extracted from the numbers mine and then polished and exported throughout the world. Numbers accidentally broken are used as fractions. Though the mine also produces vast quantities of precious stones these have no value in Digitopolis. Notable is a staircase said to lead to the Land of Infinity where the biggest, smallest, tallest, shortest, most and least of everything are kept; Infinity is a poor land, as its inhabitants can never make ends meet.

Travel in Digitopolis is achieved through various means: rubbing everything out and beginning again; taking the shortest distance between any two points, drawing a line between them and walking along it; or multiplying oneself to be in several places at the same time. Visitors are advised not to eat in Digitopolis; their famous subtraction stew causes one to become hungrier the more one eats. People begin dining when they are full and eat until they are hungry, and consider this the most logical and economical way of eating.

(Norton Juster, *The Phantom Tollbooth*, London, 1962)

DIMRILL DALE, a valley between two eastern spurs of the MISTY MOUNTAINS of MIDDLE-EARTH, known to the dwarves as **AZANUL-BIZAR**. Dimrill Dale once formed part of the dwarfish kingdom of MORIA or Khazad-dûm. Towards the end of the First Age, Durin, the eldest of the seven fathers of the dwarves, came to the dale and began the construction of Moria beneath the Misty Mountains. Durin gazed into the waters of Mirrormere, known to his people as Kheled-Zâram, and saw a crown of several stars appear as jewels around the reflection of his head—even though it was daylight. It was this that inspired him to found his kingdom here. The spot where Durin stood when he first looked into the lake is marked by Durin's Stone, now cracked and worn; the runes on it are faint and indecipherable.

At the head of the vale, a great torrent cascades over a seemingly interminable succession of falls. Beside the torrent, the road known as Dimrill Stair leads up to the pass of Redhorn Gate, one of the few passages through the Misty Mountains. An ice-cold stream rises in the dale, flowing out to form the Silverlode River, which eventually joins the GREAT RIVER.

The remains of an ancient paved road can still be seen in the lower part of the dale, leading to western Moria.

Dimrill Dale was the setting for the Battle of Azanulbizar, the dwarfish victory that brought an end to the six-year war between the dwarves and the orcs who had occupied Moria.

(J.R.R. Tolkien, *The Fellowship of the Ring*, London, 1954; J.R.R. Tolkien, *The Return of the King*, London, 1955)

DIONYSUS' ISLAND, in the Atlantic Ocean, some eighty days from the Columns of Hercules. Travellers who have seen it describe it as high and wooded. Its name can be explained by the traces left here by the ancient Greek god of wine. For instance, some distance from the coast is a bronze column inscribed in somewhat faded Greek characters: "Up to here travelled Hercules and Dionysus." Somewhat farther inland runs a river of wine, similar to that of Chio, so wide that in certain parts it can be navigated. Following it to its source, one does not—despite one's expectations—reach a fountain, but a small wood of large vines whose rich grapes distil drops of red wine that eventually form the river. The fish in the river have the colour and the taste of wine, and when caught are found to be full of sediment.

All around the island grows another species of vine with large and robust trunks that are women from the waist upwards. These women grow tendrils and clusters of grapes from the tips of their fingers and their hair is made of leaves, stems and tendrils. Some speak Lydian or Hindu but most of them speak Greek. If the grapes are plucked from them they cry out in pain. Travellers are advised not to let themselves be embraced by these arborescent creatures—they will become at once inebriated and fall into a swoon, forgetting family, honour and fatherland. Whoever has intercourse with one of them is immediately transformed into a vine, sprouting roots on the spot.

(Lucian of Samosata, *True History*, 2nd cen. AD)

DIRANDA, a large island in the MARDI ARCHIPELAGO divided into two kingdoms. Arriving at Diranda, travellers will be surprised at the large number of blind, one-legged, one-armed, and generally maimed individuals who inhabit the island. This is due to the custom of celebrating cruel gladiatorial contests in which young people from both kingdoms fight each other. The inhabitants are very fond of this form of entertainment and consider it an excellent occasion to demonstrate their courage, a virtue prized above all others. However, these contests are in fact the method chosen by the two kings who rule Diranda to prevent the excessive growth of the island's population, and travellers are strongly advised not to take part.

(Herman Melville, *Mardi, and A Voyage Thither,* New York, 1849)

DISAPPEARED, an enormous city somewhere under the ocean. From a distance the traveller can see only deep, wind-swept water, but if he dives beneath the surface he will behold a city made of bricks. Towers, bazaars, factories, arches and palaces which once vibrated with the sound of melodious lute music make Disappeared look like a hydra. In the parks, by the royal palace where the queens came to bathe in the nude, visitors can admire the wreck of an ancient cutter.

(Victor Hugo, "La Ville disparue," in *La Légende des siècles,* Paris, 1859)

DJEBBEL ALLAH, a treble volcanic peak on the border between EL HADD and ARDISTAN. The three peaks are known respectively as the Father, the Mother and the Son, the latter being the central cone. A difficult and dangerous path leads beneath the Son to the plateau above El Hadd. Although it is quite broad, the path is treacherous and there are steep ravines on either side for most of its length. Many legends surround the Djebbel, which is a southerly extension of the volcanoes that surround DJINNISTAN. It is said that the Djebbel never vomits ash or rock when it erupts but instead gives off a pure blazing light. Some say that, in antiquity, religious services used to be held on the plateau on the El Hadd side and that on such occasions the peaks glowed with a mystic light. The peak known as the Son shakes to its foundations from time to time and then discharges streams of boiling water, as though it wished to cleanse itself of the filth accumulated on its lower slopes over the years. All three volcanoes are believed to have the power to defend the approaches to El Hadd and to Djinnistan itself and it is said that no evil thing or person has ever crossed them. Evil-doers either stumble into the steep ravines or are destroyed by the volcanoes themselves.

(Karl Friedrich May, *Ardistan,* Bamberg, 1909; Karl Friedrich May, *Der Mir von Djinnistan,* Bamberg, 1909)

DJINNISTAN, a mysterious land to the north of EL HADD. Few people have visited this country, which is extremely remote and very difficult to reach; it is surrounded by volcanoes extending as far south as the DJEBBEL ALLAH. It is said that beyond Djinnistan rise the mountains that surround the original earthly paradise.

Little is known of the country itself, apart from the fact that its ruler, the Mir, has always stood for peace, even when challenged by authoritarian and despotic monarchs from ARDISTAN. It is said that when Ardistan declared war upon Djinnistan, the river Suhl—which rises in this country before flowing into El Hadd—dried up or, as some historians claim, reversed its course and flowed back to paradise. Not until peace was restored to the whole area did the river flow again. Throughout the centuries of drought the Mir of Djinnistan maintained secret supplies of water, essential to those who served the cause of peace during that long, dry period, in what had become the desert of TSHOBANISTAN and on the borders of USSULISTAN. And every one hundred years, the people in places as far away as USSULA watched the distant light of the erupting volcanoes around Djinnistan, eruptions said to symbolize the opening of the gates of paradise to those who sought peace.

In Djinnistan—as in LOOKING-GLASS-LAND—proper names are always perfectly truthful and define the nature, occupation and even profession of their bearers with great precision. For instance a man named Abd El Fadl, which literally means "servant of kindness," devoted his whole life to charity and mercy, as did his daughter Merh-Meh, "compassion." Only the Mir himself is never known by any personal name. His title—an abbreviated form of Emir—simply means "Lord" and perfectly describes his character and function.

The inhabitants of Djinnistan have a custom of veiling their faces when they make an oath, never removing the veil until they have carried out the vow.

(Karl Friedrich May, *Ardistan,* Bamberg, 1909; Karl Friedrich May, *Der Mir von Djinnistan,* Bamberg, 1909)

DJUNUBISTAN, a fertile and rich country bordering on TSHOBANISTAN. Very few outsiders have ever visited it and most of our knowledge has been gleaned from Djunub travellers in neighbouring countries. The wealth of the country can be seen in the clothes they wear, which are ostentatiously decorated with gold and jewels. Their turbans are often studded with pearls.

Djunubistan is a caste society and the caste system dominates much of its life. For instance, food prepared by a low-caste member for a superior must be consecrated by a priest before it can be eaten. Members of high and low castes never eat together for fear of contamination. The people consider themselves to be Buddhists and regard the Maha-Lama as a living incarnation of the True God.

The rulers of Djunubistan attempted to annex both USSULISTAN and Tshobanistan. In order to do so, they tried to negotiate an alliance with the Ussula, claiming that they would drive the Tshobans into their arms, but actually hoping that they would be able to occupy Ussulistan itself. The plan was frustrated when a large force from Djunubistan was trapped by the Ussulas in the CHATAR DEFILE. They were forced to surrender and to negotiate for peace. A number of those captured were sent to work on forest-clearance projects in Ussulistan.

Most neighbouring peoples regard the Djunubs as an arrogant, lazy race whose natural environment is so rich that they take everything for granted. Djunub etiquette requires one to eat very loudly; belches are taken as a sign of appreciation and are a compliment to one's host.

(Karl Friedrich May, *Ardistan*, Bamberg, 1909; Karl Friedrich May, *Der Mir von Djinnistan*, Bamberg, 1909)

DOCTOR MOREAU'S ISLAND, see NOBLE'S ISLAND.

DOCTORS' ISLAND, one of several high islands near Tierra del Fuego, discovered by Ferdinand Magellan in 1520. A rich, prosperous island of unhealthy climate, it is famous for the number of medicinal plants that grow among the mineral springs, and it is inhabited mainly by doctors and apothecaries. The notable features of Doctors' Island are the Doctors' Palace, built of black marble, with walls covered in black velvet, and the vast cemeteries, necessary because of the high number of dead, especially foreigners, who adapt badly to the insalubrious climate. Visitors come mainly from GREEDY ISLAND and spend much of their income here. A legend has it that on Doctors' Island lies the entrance to an underground passage which leads to Hell by the shortest route, but this has not been proven.

(Abbé Pierre François Guyot Desfontaines, *Le Nouveau Gulliver, ou Voyage De Jean Gulliver, Fils Du Capitaine Gulliver. Traduit d'un Manuscrit Anglois. Par Monsieur L.D.F.*, Paris, 1730)

DODON'S KINGDOM, in Russia, not far from the coast. For many years at war with its neighbours, King Dodon tried to find a way of preserving the peace. To ensure that the kingdom was guarded without having to be constantly at war, a wandering magician gave the king a golden cockerel which, perched on the highest steeple of the capital, would alert the people of any danger by turning towards the source, lifting its red comb and ruffling its golden plumes. The kingdom lived for many years in peace while the cockerel stood still on its perch until one day it turned and crowed towards the east. The king sent an army to investigate the supposed threat of war, but the army never returned. He then sent a second army and when this one failed to return, the king decided to see for himself. In a valley between the mountains of the east, he found both armies slaughtered and a beautiful woman sitting in a silk tent. She introduced herself as the Queen of Shemakhan and the king fell madly in love with her. The magician who had given the king the golden cockerel appeared then to claim in return for his gift the hand of the beautiful queen. Furious at the magician's boldness, the king refused and returned to his capital with the queen. However, on the royal couple's arrival, the golden cockerel flew from its perch and attacked the king, leaving him dead by the gate of his palace. The queen of Shemakhan vanished into thin air, the magician was never again seen in the kingdom and the golden cockerel became a gilded weathercock on the top of the capital's highest steeple.

(Alexander Pushkin, *Skazka o zolotom petushke*, Moscow, 1835)

DOLDRUMS, THE, an area in WISDOM KINGDOM where nothing ever happens and nothing ever changes. It is inhabited by the Lethargians, who are difficult to see because they take the colour of whatever they happen to be near. The laws of The Doldrums establish that it is illegal to think, to think of thinking, to surmise, to presume, to reason, to meditate or to speculate. Laughing is also forbidden and smiling is only permitted on alternate Thursdays. Lethargians do nothing all day, which is tiring, so once a week they take a holiday and go nowhere. They live in fear of two watchdogs, large hounds whose bodies have the shape of an alarm clock and who go by the names of Tock and Tick (see also DICTIO-NOPOLIS). Travellers who wish to arrive at The Doldrums must simply drive without thinking.

Near The Doldrums is a small house called Expectations, the home of the Whetherman, whose job is to hurry people along the road whether they like it or not, though they never go beyond Expectations.

(Norton Juster, *The Phantom Tollbooth*, London, 1962)

DOLLS, KINGDOM OF, a delicious world. To reach it the traveller must climb into the large wardrobe that fills an entire wall in President Silberhaus's antechamber in Nuremberg, Germany. A guide named Nutcracker (alias Mr. Drosselmayer) must accompany him.

The wardrobe leads into a meadow. At the end of the meadow is a gallery supported by columns of barley-sugar, and paved with macaroons and pistachios. Farther along is a fragrant forest populated by shepherdesses, huntsmen and huntswomen, all made of sugar, and beyond the forest is Marzipan Village.

To reach the capital, visitors must travel down the Essence-of-Roses River aboard a raft made of seashells and gems, pulled by gold dolphins. Beyond Candy Wood lies the metropolis, Candyburgh, built of glazed fruit sparkling under crystallized sugar. Above the main square stands the Brioche Obelisk, amid reflecting pools filled with Chantilly cream, and fountains running with orange and red-currant syrup. (People who love Chantilly cream may bring their own spoons to dip into the pools, without offending the population.)

The people of Candyburgh believe in metempsychosis and venerate a spiritual leader, called "Confectioner," who they think will see to it that they receive a "better baking" and a more beautiful shape in some future life.

Travellers may be lucky enough to receive an invitation to take tea with the Doll-Princesses of Marie Silberhaus in the Marzipan Palace. The Doll-Princesses are attended by marvellous little pages with heads made of perfect pearls, bodies covered with rubies and emeralds, and feet of pure gold sculpted in the style of Benvenuto Cellini. But all is not well at the Marzipan Palace; the existence of the building is constantly being threatened by the "nibblings" of the giant Hungrymouth, who bites off a tower now and again.

(Alexandre Dumas (*père*), *Histoire d'une casse-noisette*, Paris, 1845)

DOMINORA, an important island to the north of the MARDI ARCHIPELAGO in the south Pacific, the most powerful of the Mardi Islands. Its canoe flotilla strives to maintain this supremacy. To explain the heavy rains to which the island is subjected, the warriors of Dominora believe that even the heavens pay their liquid tribute to their powerful island. Visitors should note the traditional dress of the king: the crown is a sort of helmet surmounted by a large sea urchin, bristling with stings

The helmet of the King of DOMINORA.

and adorned with a hippopotamus tooth; as earrings, he wears a couple of arrows with curved points; from his belt, made of dogfish skin, hangs a small pouch of darts. Upon his chest the king has a map of the archipelago tattooed in blue; on his right arm are written the names of all national heroes; on the sole of his right foot is tattooed the emblem of his traditional enemy, the king of the island of Franko. In this way, the king of Dominora can constantly have the king of Franko under his foot.

(Herman Melville, *Mardi, and A Voyage Thither*, New York, 1849)

DONDUM ARCHIPELAGO, south of SILHA, in the Atlantic Ocean. The King of Dondum is the overlord of fifty-four other islands in the archipelago, all of which pay him tribute. The inhabitants of Dondum are hideous giants, with one eye in the middle of their foreheads, who eat only raw flesh, and seem to be distantly related to the Cyclopes (see CYCLOPES ISLAND). When a parent or friend of one of the Dondum natives is sick, the Dondumite goes to the priest and asks if his parent or friend is to die. The priest then puts the question to an idol and if the spirit in the idol says yes, the sick person is suffocated, cut into pieces and solemnly eaten at a ceremony to which friends and minstrels are invited. The bones are then buried.

To the south of Dondum lie the fifty-four other islands of the archipelago. Notable among them is the island inhabited by people of short stature who have no heads and whose eyes are in their shoulders. Other interesting peoples of the Dondum Archipelago are the tribe with flat faces, no noses and no mouths; the people with lips so great that they can sleep in the sun by covering their faces with their upper lips; the dwarves with no mouths, whose food and drink are taken in through a hole at the top of the head; the people who go on all fours, covered in skins and feathers, and leap from tree to tree like apes; the hermaphrodites (probably a colony of the HERMAPHRODITE REPUBLIC); the people who walk on their knees, and have eight toes on each foot. It is said that all these tribes are descended from the union between women and the devils who came to earth during the reign of the giant Nimrod, builder of the tower of Babylon.

(Sir John Mandeville, *Voiage de Sir John Maundevile*, Paris, 1357)

DOONHAM, a river which marks the edge of the marshes of the vanished land of Antan, to which gods, heroes and poets once went after they had served their worldly purpose. For nine thousand years the princess Evasherah was condemned to live in this river in the shape of a crocodile, for having stolen six drops of the Water of the Churning of the Ocean from her father. This water has the power of bestowing everlasting vigour upon anything it touches; Evasherah's plan was to use it on her lover, but he was drowned by her father before she could reach him. The so-called immortal part of her lover was, however, removed and is still worshipped in LYTREIA.

Travellers to Doonham will see Evasherah reclining on a couch of alabaster covered in green satin and embroidered in gold, with legs made from elephant tusks, beneath a canopy adorned with fig leaves and worked in pearls and emeralds. Sometimes she appears in her crocodile guise, sometimes in her human form, sometimes as a butterfly with dull-coloured wings.

(James Branch Cabell, *Something About Eve*, New York, 1929)

DOOR IN THE WALL, the entrance to a garden of changing location, where everything is beautiful and where everyone feels exquisitely glad.

Through the door, which can be found in many places throughout the world, a long, wide path with marble-edged flower borders on either side leads to a tall, fair girl with a soft, kind, agreeable voice. Visitors will be entertained by her and by many other beautiful people. The fauna of the garden is surprising; spotted panthers, Capuchin monkeys and parakeets are common. In the garden stands a spacious and cool palace, with many pleasant fountains and lovely shaded colonnades.

Travellers who find the door to the garden are usually faced with a choice of keeping an important appointment or entering this realm of delight. However, they must be warned that after a certain number of visits the blissful garden may become their grave.

(H.G. Wells, "The Door in the Wall," in *The Country of the Blind*, London, 1911)

DOORN, see LONE ISLANDS.

DOTANDCARRYONE TOWN, in the state of Apodidraskiana, in the United States. Its inhabitants are people who have run away for different reasons. They look upon Timothy Touchandgo, who owns the local banking firm, as their leader. Mr. Touchandgo, a London banker who disappeared with the contents of his till, is respected by the people for having run away with something worth taking. He is now the owner of five thousand acres of land and prints the town's currency. With his assistant, Robthetill, he lives in a sumptuous villa built by his slaves.

The laws of Dotandcarryone Town are curious. Judges can be physically attacked over points of procedure or drawn into bets about the outcome of the trial. The town is rough and has no sophisticated entertainments. The three most prosperous groups are Methodist preachers, slave drivers and manufacturers of paper money. Volunteer groups of regulators will savage visitors whose character they dislike, until they are forced to leave town.

(Thomas Love Peacock, *Crotchet Castle*, London, 1831)

DOUBLE ISLAND, probably in the Indian Ocean, has the curious habit of emerging and submerging at will. The only existing description of Double Island is that of an Egyptian sailor, who landed there by chance after the sinking of his ship.

For three days the sailor wandered completely alone, eating figs, grapes, berries and seeds, melons, fish and game. On the third day, after digging a pit, he lit a bonfire in honour of the gods. He had no sooner done so than he heard a rumble similar to thunder, the trees began to quiver, the earth trembled and he saw a one-hundred-metre-long serpent, with a beard two metres long, before him. The serpent's body was the colour of lapis lazuli and seemed to be inlaid with gold. While the sailor prostrated himself, the snake rose up in front of him and asked who had brought him to the island. On hearing the tale of the shipwreck, the serpent was touched; picking the sailor up in his mouth, he took him to his lair, where he lived with seventy-five other serpents as gold and blue as himself.

The serpent predicted that within four months a ship would come and find the sailor. On the predicted date an Egyptian ship approached the island. The sailor was rescued, and the island disappeared suddenly beneath the waves.

(George Maspero, *Les Contes populaires de l'Egypte ancienne*, Paris, 1899)

DOUBTING-CASTLE, the ruins of what was once the home of Giant Despair and his wife Diffidence in CHRISTIAN'S COUNTRY. The castle represented a serious threat to those travellers on their way to the CELESTIAL CITY who strayed into his grounds by crossing By-pass Meadow on the edge of the Plain of EASE. All who trespassed on the giant's lands were taken and thrown into a dark dungeon where they were mercilessly beaten and starved. Giant Despair wished to reduce travellers to such a miserable state that they would commit suicide rather than continue to live in such conditions.

Two travellers, Christian and his friend Hopeful, were captured but managed to escape; they erected a sign warning those who came after: "Over this stile is the way to Doubting-Castle, which is kept by Giant Despair, who despiseth the King of the Celestial Country, and seeks to destroy his holy pilgrims." Some years later, the giant and his wife were put to death by a company led by Great-heart, who guides travellers across the country. The company razed the castle to the ground, leaving only the ruins that can be seen today. The head of the giant was affixed to the original sign erected by Christian and Hopeful.

(John Bunyan, *The Pilgrim's Progress from this world, to that which is to come. Delivered under the similitude of a Dream. Wherein is discovered, the manner of his setting out, his dangerous journey and safe arrival in the Desired Country*, London, 1678; John Bunyan, *The Pilgrim's Progress from this world to that which is to come. The Second Part. Delivered under the similitude of a Dream. Wherein is set forth the manner of the setting out of Christian's wife and children, their dangerous journey and safe arrival at the Desired Country*, London, 1684)

DOXEROS, see NEOPIE ISLAND.

DRACULA'S CASTLE, in the Carpathian Mountains, near Bistritz (Hungarian Besztercze), an ancient town of Eastern Hungary, in the county of Besztercze-Naszod. To reach the castle from Bistritz (where the excellent *Golden Krone Hotel* can be recommended) travellers should take the

View from the west side of DRACULA'S CASTLE.

coach which departs every day at 3 P.M. and drives through Jail, Borgoprund, Maros Borgo, Tihucza and on to the Borgo Pass, some twelve hundred feet above sea level. Here a carriage from Count Dracula himself will meet the travellers and will deposit them at the castle by midnight.

The castle is built on the edge of a terrible precipice. Three sides of it are quite impregnable. The western wing, no longer occupied, is more comfortable than the rest of the building. From its windows a deep valley can be seen, with the great jagged mountains in the distance. The chapel, though in ruins, is quite interesting, as it contains the coffins of Count Dracula and other members of his family. These coffins serve as resting-places for the vampires during the daytime and it is not recommended to visit the chapel at night. Visitors are advised to take with them the usual array of silver crosses, strings of garlic and wooden stakes and hammers which have proved successful over so many years.

(Bram Stoker, *Dracula*, Westminster, 1897)

DRAGON ISLAND, to the east of the LONE IS-LANDS, discovered and named by Caspian X of NARNIA in the fourth year of his reign. An inscription cut into the face of the cliff on the bay where he first landed commemorates this event.

The island is mountainous, with deep bays rather like the fjords of Norway, ending in steep valleys, often with waterfalls. What little level ground there is, is covered with cedars and other trees. Though the island is beautiful, it appears uninviting and seems to be uninhabited, with the exception of a few wild goats.

Dragon Island owes its name to the events that took place when King Caspian's party landed here for water. One of the company, a somewhat difficult child named Eustace, wandered off into the mountains, hoping to escape work. In the interior he met a dying dragon, and to shelter himself from the rain, he entered the dragon's cave, found its treasure hoard and fell asleep. Having slept on a dragon's treasure and having spent the night dreaming of it, he awoke to find himself transformed into a dragon, complete with the cannibalistic habits of the species, and proceeded to eat the flesh of the dead dragon. Eustace tried to return to human form by tearing at his layers of scales with his great claws. He was finally restored to his former self by Aslan, creator of Narnia. Aslan peeled off the layers of dragon skin and plunged the boy into a pool of delicious water to soothe his pain. After this second transformation, Eustace became a much more agreeable child.

One of the bracelets found in the dragon's hoard bore a fragmentary inscription attributed to Lord Octesian, one of the seven lords of Narnia exiled by the tyrant Miraz. It is assumed that he was either killed by a dragon or was transformed into one himself.

(C.S. Lewis, *The Voyage of the "Dawn Treader,"* London, 1952)

DRAGON'S RUN, an area of islets, rocks and shoals in the west reach of the EARTHSEA ARCHIPELAGO, to the southwest of SELIDOR. Travellers are warned that Dragon's Run is to be avoided, partly because of the dangerous rocks and partly because of the dragons that frequent the area and give it its name.

The Run itself is a maze of narrow channels running through the shoals and islands. Some of these islands' reefs are half-covered by the waves and by barnacles and sea-anemones, and look like strange seamonsters, wallowing in the blue water. Others rise sheer, like pinnacles or man-made towers and arches. The higher rocks are worn into fantastic shapes—boars' backs and serpents' heads. One great rock, particularly when seen from the south, seems to have the shoulders and head of a man, although from the north it looks merely like a cliff in which a great cave has been hollowed by the surging waves. As the waves rise and fall, the sea near the rock seems to speak. Some travellers say that it pronounces the syllable *ahm*, which in the Old Speech of Earthsea means "the beginning" or "long ago." Others say the sound is closer to *ohb*, which means "the end."

Beyond this rock, the water becomes deeper and the black cliffs of one of the area's highest islands—called the Keep of Kalessin—looms up three hundred feet above the water. The cliffs of Kalessin resemble cylinders or pillars of rock pressed together by great geological forces, giving the whole island the appearance of a huge black tower.

(Ursula K. Le Guin, *A Wizard of Earthsea*, New York, 1968; Ursula K. Le Guin, *The Farthest Shore*, London, 1973)

DREADFUL NIGHT, CITY OF, see City of NIGHT.

DREAM ISLAND, in the Atlantic Ocean not far from the WICKED ARCHIPELAGO, difficult to approach because it always seems to draw away in the distance. Travellers are advised to arrive at dusk. The capital or City of Dreams is surrounded by a jungle thick with gigantic mandrakes and poppies from which hang great numbers of bats known as the "birds of the island." A large river, the Night-Traveller, flows from two sources at the gates of the city. The sources bear the names of Sleep Eternal and Darkest Night. The walls of the city are high and rainbow-coloured. The gates are four: two look towards the Meadow of Indolence—these are made of iron and bricks and through them escape dreams that are fearful, murderous, and sinful; the other two open towards the sea, one made of horn and the other of ivory. According to a distinguished Roman gentleman, who saw two such gates in another country, the one made of horn allows the passage of true dreams, and the one made of ivory, of false ones. Visitors from England will recognize the guardian of the gate of horn, Mr. Sweeney.

Coming from the port, the traveller will find to the right the temple dedicated to the Goddess of Night. Together with the Temple of the Cock, built at the entrance to the port, the Temple of Night is the most popular on the island. To the left is the Royal Palace and a square with a fountain, called the Drowsy Waters, and next to it two smaller temples, those of Truth and Deceit. The inhabitants, known as Dreams, are of diverse aspect; some are long, delicate, beautiful and graceful; others are hard-looking, small and ugly. Some are winged or have an astounding feature on their faces; some are dressed in full regalia, in the robes of a king or a priest.

(Lucian of Samosata, *True History*, 2nd cen. AD; Virgil, *The Aeneid*, 1st cen. BC)

DREAM KINGDOM, a small state of about three thousand square kilometres somewhere in the vast Tien-Shan (Heavenly Mountain) area between western China and Kazakhstan. A third of the territory is mountainous, and the rest a plain with a few hills. There are large forests, a lake and a river that divide and lend character to this small kingdom. Apart from the capital, PERLA, only a few farms and villages are sprinkled throughout Dream Kingdom. There are some sixty-five thousand inhabitants according to the latest official census.

The founder of Dream Kingdom was the rich and extravagant Klaus Patera, who came to this region towards the end of the nineteenth century to hunt the very rare Persian tiger, found only in

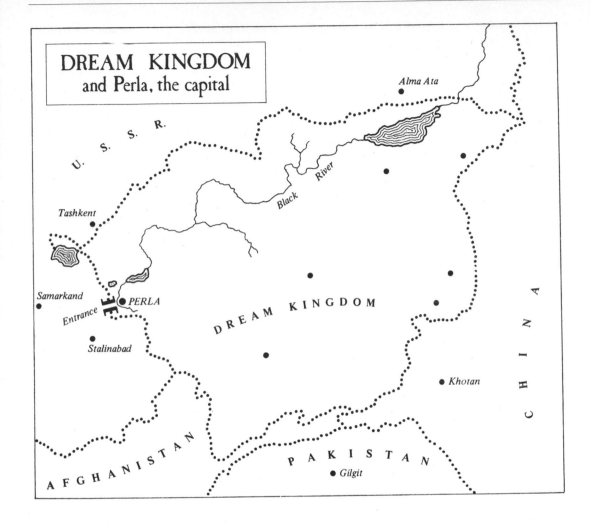

the Tien-Shan. Wounded by the beast, Patera was healed by the chief of a strange and rare tribe of about a hundred members, all of whom have blue eyes and live in isolation surrounded by pure Mongolian tribes. It is said that they practise bizarre and unspeakable rites of which nothing is known. Patera returned to Europe but came back after nine months with a high-placed mandarin and a group of engineers and land surveyors, plus an entire army of coolies, and after buying vast extents of land he started to build Perla.

Because Patera was exceptionally averse to any type of progress, especially in the field of science, he separated his kingdom from the surrounding world by a large wall and defended it against any possible attack by powerful fortifica-

tions. A single gate permits entry and exit and allows an easier surveillance of everything and everyone. In Dream Kingdom, a haven for those dissatisfied with modern civilization, all material needs are taken care of. However, nothing is further removed from the government's will than the simple creation of an ideal society.

Whoever is received into Dream Kingdom has been predestined for the honour either by birth or by a turn of fate. In Dream Kingdom, an exceptional perfecting of the sense organs allows the inhabitants to note the existing interrelations of their individual worlds, which for any common mortal, with certain exceptions, simply do not exist. These so-called "inexistent" interrelations are in fact the essence of the inhabitants' aspirations. Everything is geared towards a spiritualized life; the inhabitants live only for and on spiritual changes. Their entire external existence, which is organized according to their wishes by carefully coordinated work in common, alone furnishes the raw material on which they base their true lives. The inhabitants of Dream Kingdom believe only in dreams, their own dreams. This tendency is nurtured and developed, and to interfere with this belief is taken to be high treason.

The selection of those invited to form part of the community is based strictly upon the ability to believe in dreams. Once invited, the traveller must arrange his own passage to Dream Kingdom. He should travel by caravan from Samarkand to the border, where Customs officials will furnish him with a certain sum of money and a train ticket for Perla. The train station is next to the Customs Hall and the journey to Perla takes some two hours. Travellers should note that it is forbidden to take any new articles into the country; only secondhand articles are admitted.

(Alfred Kubin, *Die andere Seite: Ein phantastischer Roman*, Berlin, 1908)

DREAMS, LAKE OF, the only lake in the world where it is possible, while doing a bit of fishing, to take a general course on the second principle of thermodynamics as applied to biology.

At the Lake of Dreams one can easily deduce, for instance, that bovines are atomical animals that function in the same way as high-performance nuclear generating stations their only waste products are fertilizer, and the energy they use comes indirectly from the sun through the plants they eat. Or, while marvelling at the ingenuity of Nature, one can sing incantations that cause the clouds to assume fantastic shapes: dinosaurs, glyptodons and pterosauruses frolic across the sky.

To reach the Lake of Dreams, the traveller enters the hospital of his choice and sits in an armchair in the waiting-room. There a special syringe is used to inject him inside his own body, and he reaches the mainstream of his blood aboard an erythrocyte or a red corpuscle. Thrown up on a beach of muscles, he may meet such learnèd professors as Father Mendel Morganstern, whose intelligence and knowledge come from the fusion of the respective qualities of Messrs Morgan and Mendel, pioneers in biology and genetics, and Mr. Morgenstern, father of the theories of chance.

Through them the traveller may meet Dame Enzyme, alias Miss Polymerase DNA (deoxyribonucleic acid), who presides over the replication of the genetic code; she is a young woman dressed in Oriental clothes. While the cells are dividing she stands in front of glazed clay tablets, working out three-letter words by using an alphabet of four letters in every possible combination. Any traveller who is willing to listen will receive a most informative explanation of gene-pool mathematics.

Still inside the world of his own body, the traveller will have to climb the rungs of the DNA ladder. Here he will see a large man, no doubt an Englishman, wearing a blazer bearing the crest of Cambridge University, and another rather slovenly person, unquestionably American, wearing tennis shoes with no laces. They are both biologists and will guide the traveller to their "double helix." The nucleus of a cell, as well as its cytoplasmic compartments, can also be visited, by means of a gigantic python known as the DNA messenger which travels in Brownian movements, due to the molecular agitation of colloidal particles in a low-density homogeneous environment.

It is hard to determine how travellers return from the most intimate layers inside their own bodies. Even more inexplicable are the famous people they meet—such as Darwin, who takes pains to let them know that he receives copies of such modern scientific journals as *La Recherche, Scientific American* and *Les Echos de la Mode*. In any case, all travellers are known to have returned safely to the world outside themselves.

Other areas can also be visited. Thanks to a computer, one can journey to the *Country That Can Only Be Seen in the Mind's Eye*. After changing himself into a computer card, the traveller can participate in the analysis of molecules according to the principle of X-ray diffraction. He will then meet the inhabitants of FLATLAND, with whom he can exchange his impressions of two-dimensional worlds.

(George Gamow, *Mr. Tompkins inside Himself, Adventures in the New Biology*, New York, 1967)

DREAMWORLD, a vast, almost unexplored continent in the southern regions. The American explorer Randolph Carter visited several of its wild regions: BAHARNA, CELEPHAIS, DYLATHLEEN, ENCHANTED WOOD, HLANITH, INQUANOK, KADATH, KIRAN, Jungle of KLED,

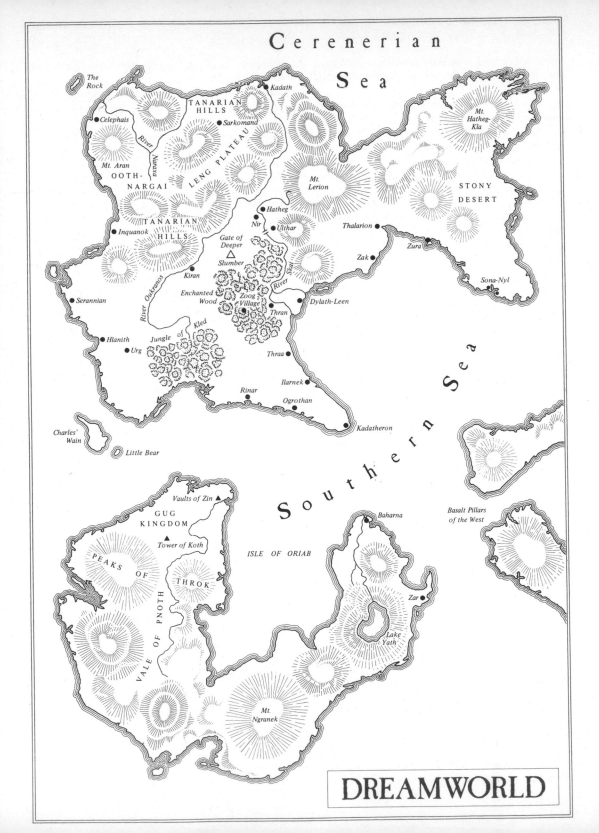

LENG, NGRANEK, PNOTH, SARKOMAND, SOUTHERN SEA, THRAN, ULTHAR, URG.

(Howard Phillips Lovecraft, "The Dream-Quest of Unknown Kadath," in *Arkham Sampler*, Sauk City, 1948)

DREIVIERTELSTEIN, SCHLOSS, a minor Elfin kingdom in Styria. The capital is the castle of Queen Aigle, an out-of-the-way and undistinguished place. In the past the Schloss's great claim to fame was the cooking of Ludla, one of the most famous cooks in the Elfin kingdoms. Visitors to the castle came mainly to enjoy her stuffed goose, eel soup and other specialties. One of her finest dishes was the crawfish soufflé served on Royal Birthdays; the flavouring was a secret and all were banished from the kitchens while it was being prepared. One resident at the castle claimed that eating it was like eating a cloud. Aigle herself showed little interest in the delights prepared for her by Ludla, being more concerned with organizing the quests that took up so much of the life of the court. The objects of these quests ranged from the Toad in a Stone to the Chamois Shod in Silver and the Ring Hung on the Topmost Bough. There was also a twice-yearly contest to find the First and Last Rose of Summer. A few quests for dragons were undertaken but these were abandoned, partly because dragons became out of date, but mainly because a number of questers became lost in caverns and some were never seen again.

The life of the court was disrupted by the arrival of Tamarind, a political exile from TISHK who at once became very popular, especially with the children and servants. His fall from grace began when he took Queen Aigle flying. Under normal circumstances the Elfin aristocracy does not fly, considering it undignified and fit only for servants. During her flight the Queen was slightly injured, and word soon spread that the exile was responsible. Immediately all turned against him, displaying the xenophobia normal in most Elfin realms, and Ludla sought revenge by inserting a bone in a Hunter's Pie. Tamarind choked on the bone but soon recovered and Queen Aigle, who had fallen in love with the exile, straightaway banished her famous cook from court. Shortly afterwards Tamarind was persuaded to leave the Schloss and set off on a tour of Europe. Since the incident of the pie, there have been no quests at the Schloss. Aigle appears to be too preoccupied to

arrange them, and her courtiers have found a new pastime—they have taken to going for walks in the forest, walks that inevitably lead them to the cottage where Ludla has established herself. Here travellers can taste her exquisite cooking for very moderate charges; they are, however, required to bring their own wine.

(Sylvia Townsend Warner, *Kingdoms of Elfin*, London, 1972)

DREXARA, a deserted region beyond the Appalachian Mountains in North America. The area is wooded, mountainous, rich in game and inhabited by wandering bands of Indians. Travellers should be aware that these Indians are considered the most savage of all the indigenous tribes and that they regard human flesh as the most delicate of meats. They are also given to selling their captives to Spanish slavers in exchange for spirits and other commodities.

(Abbé Antoine François Prévost, *Le Philosophe anglois, ou Histoire de Monsieur Cleveland, fils naturel de Cromwell, par l'auteur des Mémoires d'un Homme de qualité*, Utrecht, 1731)

DRIMONIA, a European country of uncertain location, perhaps in the Balkans; to reach it, according to Signor Olindo Lindi, author of the *Traveller's Guide to Drimonia*, one must cross northern Italy, Yugoslavia, and a few other countries.

The practical information in Lindi's guide is scarce, yet it abounds in linguistic considerations. To understand the language, the traveller need only learn two essential expressions. The first is *trunca*, which means approximately "yes," but the literal translation is: "If-thus-be-the-will-of-the-great-and-all-powerful-Oskutchawa-thus-be-my-will-as-well." The curious traveller who enquires who this great Oskutchawa may be will receive several different answers. Nothing is known for sure. Some believe that Oskutchawa is a very ancient idol, the worship of which was abandoned many centuries ago. Others say that he was a prophet devoured by the wolves to which he was preaching a vegetarian diet. According to a more probable hypothesis, he was a tramp who lived towards the end of the thirteenth century, a great drinker and the author of satirical songs. In keeping with the barbaric usage of his time, he ended on the scaffold because of his impartial neglect of the truth.

The second word to learn is *narta*, which is usually translated as "no," but literally means: "As-I-cannot-know-whether-it-will-rain-today-or-tomorrow-I-cannot-pledge-my-answer." Some particularly pedantic philologists will insist on adding to this translation the words "in-spite-of-whatever-I-may-say"; but this nuance is not sufficiently corroborated by the evidence in the classic texts on the subject, and can therefore be discarded.

Experienced travellers will notice a certain similarity with the Entish language (see FANGORN FOREST).

(Lia Wainstein, *Viaggio in Drimonia*, Milan, 1965)

DRUADAN FOREST, a forest on the hill of Eilenach in the Anórien area of GONDOR in MIDDLE-EARTH, some thirty miles to the north of MINAS TIRITH. A beacon tower stands on the summit of Eilenach, and a second to the east of the forest; these are the first of the beacon towers of Gondor.

The forest is inhabited by the Woses or Wild Men of the Woods, descendants of the Wild Men who inhabited the area before the establishment of Gondor. A primitive people, armed with poisoned arrows, the Woses bear some resemblance to the so-called Púkel-men, the great stone figures on the road leading to the fortress of DUNHARROW. They communicate over distances with drums, and speak a crude version of the Common Speech of Middle-earth, referring to Minas Tirith as "Stonehouses" and to its inhabitants as "Stonehouse Folk." The Woses dress simply in grass skirts and have deep guttural voices. It appears that, during the Third Age of Middle-earth, they were occasionally hunted for sport by the warlike Rohirrim, or men of ROHAN.

During the War of the Ring the Rohirrim reached the pine woods on the eastern edge of the forest during their great ride from Rohan to Minas Tirith only to learn that their way was blocked by the orcs. They were approached by Ghân-buri-Ghân, chief of the Woses, who offered to lead them through the forgotten tracks of the Forest on condition that his race be allowed to live in peace in the forests and that the hunting cease. To show his good faith, he walked ahead of the Rohirrim with Théoden, their leader. After the War of the Ring, the forest was given to the Woses. Visitors are warned that it is forbidden for anyone else to enter it without their express permission.

(J.R.R. Tolkien, *The Return of the King*, London, 1955)

DUBIAXO, see Isles of WISDOM.

DULL (lake), see ALIFBAY.

DUNDONALD CASTLE, a ruined building about two miles from Irvine, a small port near the mouth of the Firth of Clyde, Scotland. The castle was for a long time said to be haunted by Fire Maidens, who were believed to appear on its towers on dark nights. At such times jets of flame were seen running along the broken walls or shooting up from the tower. In the mid-nineteenth century these fires caused the wreck of the Norwegian brig *Motala*, bound for Glasgow with a cargo of timber; it seems that the captain mistook a jet of flame for the Irvine light and steered his ship onto the rocks, where she was totally wrecked. An enquiry revealed no trace of human activity in the ruined

The ruins of DUNDONALD CASTLE.

castle and the myth of the Fire Maidens grew stronger.

However, shortly after this mysterious incident, the truth behind the myth was at last discovered: a hidden tunnel connects the canal with the caverns of New Aberfoyle and COAL CITY, and the jets of flame resulted from the combustion of escaping methane.

(Jules Verne, *Les Indes Noires*, Paris, 1877)

DUNHARROW, a fortress in HARROWDALE, one of the major defences of ROHAN. Strictly speaking, Dunharrow refers to the area in general and the fortress itself is called the Hold of Dunharrow, but usage does not always follow this distinction.

Dunharrow was first fortified during the dark years of the Second Age, when Sauron dominated MIDDLE-EARTH, and before GONDOR was established as a kingdom by the men of Númenor. The reasons for its original construction remain unknown. The Hold is built on precipitous cliffs on the eastern side of Harrowdale and is reached by a steep path which winds up the sheer rock face. At each turning in the road—which connects the fortress with EDORAS—the traveller will find huge statues of men sitting cross-legged with their arms folded across their fat stomachs. Known as the Púkel-men, these are believed to have been carved by the original builders of the fortress. The figures have been badly worn by wind and weather and in some cases the eye-holes are the only discernible facial features.

The road winding up to the Hold is wide enough to allow horses and carts to pass, but the clear and unimpeded view from the top makes the fortress virtually invincible. At the top of the cliffs, a cutting through the rock leads out into an area of grass and heath known as the Firienfeld. To the south, visitors can see Starkhorn Mountain and the jagged mass of Irensaga. Between the two looms the peak of Dwimorberg, where a door in the rock gives access to the PATHS OF THE DEAD. One road crosses the Firienfeld and reaches an entrance to the Paths. Another road goes to HELM'S DEEP.

During the great War of the Ring which affected much of Middle-earth, Dunharrow was the gathering place for the Knights of Rohan and for the court of their king, Théoden. During this period, tents and booths lined the access road to the fortress. It was here that Théoden received the Red Arrow, brought by messenger from Gondor, the symbol of a request for aid under the terms of the longstanding alliance between Gondor and Rohan. And it was from here that the Rohirrim, or men of Rohan, rode out to Gondor, leaving Eowyn in command of Dunharrow. Eowyn, a tall fair woman of Rohan, disobeyed her orders, disguising herself as a man and riding with one of the Rohan squadrons. She distinguished herself greatly in the subsequent battles, almost losing her life as a result. After her recovery, she married Faramir, Lord of ITHILIEN.

(J.R.R. Tolkien, *The Two Towers*, London, 1954; J.R.R. Tolkien, *The Return of the King*, London, 1955)

DUNKITON, a town inhabited by donkeys and ruled by King Kick-a-Bray, a few miles down the road from FOXVILLE.

Dunkiton is surrounded by a high, whitewashed wall with very few gates, leaving nothing visible from the outside. Inside, the low brick houses of the donkeys are scattered at random. There are no regular streets and the houses are not numbered; the donkeys explain that they are so wise that they do not need such aids to find their way around. Their town, they say, is prettier than one with regular streets. All the houses are whitewashed, both inside and out, and are extremely clean. Normally they have only one room, and the only items of furniture, even in the Royal Palace, are neatly woven grass mats.

The inhabitants of Dunkiton are convinced that they live in the centre of the world's most highly developed civilization. They are equally convinced that they are the most intelligent beings in the world; in their eyes, the word "donkey" is synonymous with "clever." There are no schools in the town, the donkeys claiming to be so wise that they need attend only the "School of Experience." To keep the young—who would in other countries be at school—out of mischief, they are set to whitewash the houses and walls, using their tails as brushes.

Although they wear no clothing, all donkeys wear hats—pointed caps for the males and sunbonnets for the females. Gold and silver bangles are worn on the fore wrists and bands of various metals on the hind wrists. Usually the donkeys sit and stand upright, using their forelegs as arms and their hoofs as hands. Despite the fact that they have no fingers visitors will find them surprisingly dextrous.

The donkeys are afraid of their near neighbours, the foxes of Foxville. To protect their town from attack, they kick large sheets of metal, hung up just inside the walls, making a tremendous din which helps drive away any would-be intruders.

Apart from meagre repasts of grass, bran and oats, to which visitors must submit, Dunkiton presents one major disadvantage to the traveller in search of peace and quiet; every morning the donkey population assembles and greets the dawn with a chorus of braying, said to be one of the loudest and most unpleasant sounds in the world.

(L. Frank Baum, *The Road to Oz*, Chicago, 1909)

DUNLAND, an area of MIDDLE-EARTH to the west of the MISTY MOUNTAINS. Although the land itself is fertile, it is inhabited only by a race of rather backward herdsmen and hillmen known as the Dunlendings who have their own ancient language and primitive culture. They are the last remnants of the men who once inhabited the regions around the mountains and who were driven out by the Rohirrim, or men of ROHAN, when they settled in that area.

For generations, the Dunlendings were extremely hostile to Rohan, referring to its inhabitants as the "Robbers of the North." The first of the great attacks on Rohan took place in 2598 Third Age when, as Rohan was being assaulted from the east, the Dunlendings came down from the west under the command of a certain Wulf. The second major attack came many years later, during the battle of the Hornburg, in 3019 Third Age. Saruman the White, the great Wizard whose power had become corrupted, inflamed the hatred of the Dunlendings for the Rohirrim and many of them joined forces with his orcs during the attack. Those who survived the battle were surprised to hear that the Rohirrim would allow them to go back to their own lands unharmed if they swore never to cross into Rohan again.

(J.R.R. Tolkien, *The Fellowship of the Ring*, London, 1954; J.R.R. Tolkien, *The Two Towers*, Lon-

don, 1954; J.R.R. Tolkien, *The Return of the King*, London, 1955)

DUN VLECHAN, a high, wooded area in northern POICTESME. Deep in the woods stands a grey hut supported by the bones of four great bird's feet. The corners of the hut are carved into the shapes of a lion, a dragon, a cockatrice and an adder; these are said to symbolize the miseries of carnal and intellectual sin, pride and death. Inside, the walls are covered in ancient frescoes, innocent of both perspective and reticence. In each corner of the room stands an umbrella worked in nine colours and with a handle of silver, similar in design to those used for sacred purposes in the east. The most important object, however, is a pumpkin standing by the door.

This hut is the abode of Misery on Earth, whom some call Beda and others Kruchina. Travellers may summon Misery by placing a candle under each of the umbrellas, making the requisite kind of soup and calling out that supper is ready. A disembodied head will then appear and ask to be let in. Misery is a head of white clay that was left over from the creation of the world. It is said that the fashioning of Misery was interrupted by the coming of the Sabbath; being an orthodox Jew, the Creator would not work on that day and so the world's last creation remained unfinished. All day long Misery goes about, devouring kingdoms and spreading envious reports. At night the head returns to the hut and its work is carried on by a certain Phobetor. Misery is all head and no heart and is therefore quite devoid of pity. His province is life itself; the birth-cry of every infant is an oath of allegiance to Misery. Misery enjoys company, but each day spent with him is the equivalent of a year in the company of men.

Travellers are warned that the forests of Dun Vlechan are haunted by various strange creatures who have invaded Misery's domain and have been driven mad as a result.

(James Branch Cabell, *Figures of Earth. A Comedy of Appearances*, New York, 1921)

DUNWICH, a village in Massachusetts, in the United States. When a traveller takes the wrong fork at the junction of the Aylesbury Pike, just beyond Dean's Corners, he comes upon a lonely and curious country. The ground gets higher, the trees seem too large and wild weeds, brambles and grasses attain a luxuriance not often found in settled regions. At the same time, the planted fields appear singularly few and barren, while the sparsely scattered houses wear a surprisingly uniform aspect of age, squalor and dilapidation. Without knowing why, travellers will hesitate to ask directions from the gnarled, solitary figures spied now and then on crumbling doorsteps or in the sloping, rock-strewn meadows. When a rise in the road brings the mountains into view above the deep woods, the feeling of strange uneasiness increases. The summits are too rounded and symmetrical to give a sense of comfort. Deep gorges and ravines cut across the road, and the crude wooden bridges always seem of dubious safety. When the road dips again, there are stretches of marshland that travellers will instinctively dislike, where unseen whippoorwills cry and fireflies come out in abnormal profusion to dance to the raucous piping of bullfrogs.

It is not reassuring to see that most of the houses along the way are deserted and falling to ruin, and that the broken-steepled church now harbours the slovenly mercantile establishment of the hamlet. A gloomy bridge must be crossed and a faint malign odour will invade the traveller's nostrils with the mould and decay of many centuries. Afterwards, he will learn that he has been through Dunwich.

It was here that a horrible creature was born to a member of the Whateley family, a foul monster said to be the image of his spectral father. Only once was this creature glimpsed—a kind of enormous egg with many legs and proboscises. It was killed when a single bolt of lightning shot from the sky. An indescribable stench hit the countryside; trees, grass and underbrush were whipped into a fury; the foliage wilted to a curious, sickly yellow-grey; and both field and forest were scattered with the bodies of dead birds. The stench left quickly but the stricken countryside around Dunwich was never the same again.

(Howard Phillips Lovecraft, "The Dunwich Horror," in *The Outsider and Others*, Sauk City, 1939)

DYLATH-LEEN, a large and populous city in DREAMWORLD, on the shores of the SOUTHERN SEA, near the mouth of the Skai River. Built mostly of basalt, Dylath-Leen, with its thin angular towers, looks from a distance like a fragment of the Giant's Causeway in Ireland. Its streets are dark and uninviting. There are many dismal taverns near the wharves and the whole town is thronged with strange seamen from every land on earth and a few others.

Travellers will find that it is hard to get any information in the taverns because the traders and sailors confine their talk to whispers about certain black galleys. These galleys arrive at the docks of Dylath-Leen laden with rubies from an unknown port, and the townsfolk shudder even at the thought of seeing them appear on the horizon. The men in charge have mouths a fraction too wide; their turbans are humped up in two points above their foreheads in a particularly disagreeable manner and their shoes are the shortest and queerest in the whole of Dreamworld. However, what frightens the citizens of Dylath-Leen most are the unseen rowers. Each galley has three banks of oars that move too briskly and accurately and vigorously, and the townsfolk believe that it is not right for any ship to stay in port for weeks while the merchants trade, yet to have no glimpse of the crew. Nor do they feel it is fair to the tavern-keepers or grocers and butchers, for not a scrap of provisions is ever sent aboard. In exchange for their rubies, the unpleasant merchants take only gold and stout black slaves; never anything else.

Travellers are advised that the smell that the south wind blows in from the galleys is so bad that only the hardiest seamen, constantly smoking strong *thagweed*, can bear it.

(Howard Phillips Lovecraft, "The Dream-Quest of Unknown Kadath," in *Arkham Sampler*, Sauk City, 1948)

E

EAR ISLANDS, several small islands off the coast of Germany, inhabited by a tribe of fishermen called the Auriti or All-Ears, whose ears are of such abnormally large dimensions that they cover their whole bodies. As a consequence, they are very sharp of hearing and can detect the fish under the sea.

(Pliny the Elder, *Inventorum Natura,* 1st cen. AD)

EAR, ISLE OF THE, see EARTHSEA.

EARTHSEA, an archipelago consisting of hundreds of islands, some uninhabited and others important trading and agricultural communities. Earthsea is roughly circular and has a diameter of some twenty thousand miles. At the heart of the archipelago lies the group known as the Inner Isles, which cluster around the Inmost Sea. To the north of this sea lies HAVNOR, the seat of the King of all the Isles; to the south lies WATHORT, an important post for the trade with the southern islands. ROKE is in the heart of the Inmost Sea and is the centre for the teaching of the magic which is so vitally important to the life of Earthsea. If Havnor is the core of the archipelago's political and commercial life, Roke is its spiritual centre. On the west side of the Inmost Sea lies the cluster known as the NINETY ISLES, small islands which lie amid a maze of channels, shoals and rocks. The Ninety Isles are important to the economy of Earthsea because of their *turbie* fishing industry; *turbie* are small fish caught for their oil, which is exported from here to the entire archipelago. Beyond the Inmost Sea the islands become more scattered. To the west few of the islands are inhabited, and the seas around PENDOR, SELIDOR and the DRAGON'S RUN are shunned because of the dragons found there. Beyond the distant island of Selidor lies nothing but the open sea, the home of the strange Raft Folk who land only once a year, at the LONG DUNE, to refit the ocean-going rafts on which they live.

The South Reach of Earthsea is perhaps the strangest in the entire archipelago. Here the fish are said to fly and the dolphins are reputed to sing.

This may simply be a trader's tale; as the popular saying has it, "To hear a southern trader is to hear a liar." The South Reach is traditionally a rebellious area, with an unsavoury reputation for piracy and slaving. The most famous island in the area is LORBANERY, famous for its silk industry. The southernmost island of Earthsea is the Isle of the Ear, to which no seaman will go.

With the exception of IFFISH, the islands of the East Reach are small and poor. Few ships, for instance, venture as far east as ASTOWELL, a stark and isolated island, or to the twin rocks known as the HANDS. On many of these islands the people have no produce to trade, and live in harsh and primitive conditions. Farther north lie the four great islands of the KARGAD EMPIRE, once the great rival and enemy of Earthsea, although the two are now at peace.

To the north of the archipelago is ENLAD, closely associated with many of the semi-legendary figures of the past and with the ancient kings who ruled on Havnor. Enlad is separated by the Osskil Sea from OSSKIL itself, a bleak island with a somewhat sinister reputation and a magic quite different from that practised in the rest of Earthsea.

The people of Earthsea are mostly red-brown or copper-coloured, although the inhabitants of the extreme south tend to be darker. Colour is one of the main distinctions between the people of the archipelago and the Kargs of the Kargad Empire, who are fair-skinned and fair-haired.

Earthsea includes a wide variety of cultures, ranging from the simplicity of the mountain people of GONT to the sophistication of the people of Havnor, not to mention the inhabitants of Roke, to whom magic is simply a part of daily life. Dress tends to vary considerably. The Gontish shepherds weave woollen clothes which do not bear comparison with the fur-trimmed garments of Osskil or the silks of the south. But the whole of Earthsea is united by a few cultural rites. All the islands, with the exception of the Kargad Empire, celebrate the Long Dance, which is held on the shortest day of the year. On that night the people dance down the roads of their island to the sound of drums, pipes and flutes. As they return, only the flutes are heard. There are of course regional variations—the Raft Folk, for instance, who perform the ceremony on their rafts, do not use an instrumental accompaniment—but the dance itself is universal and, symbolically, it binds together the

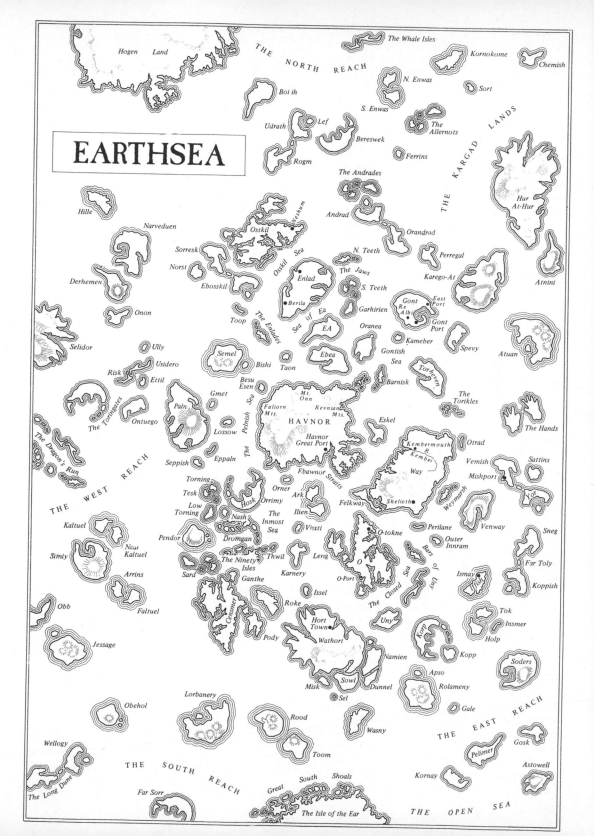

EARTHSEA

THE NORTH REACH

The Whale Isles

Hogen Land

Kornokome

Chemish

N. Enwas

Boi ih

Sort

S. Enwas

Udrath   Lef

The Allernots

Bereswek

Ferrins

Rogm

The Andrades

THE KARGAD LANDS

Hille

Narveduen

Andrad

Orandrad

Hur At-Hur

Osskil   Nesnum

N. Teeth

Perregal

Sorresk

Enlad

The Jaws

Karego-At

Norst

S. Teeth

Atnini

Osskil Sea

Ebosskil

Berila

Garhirien

Gont Re Albi

East Port

Derhemen

Onon

Toop

The Enlades

Sea of Ea

Oranea

Gont Port

Selidor

Ully

EA

Kameber

Spevy

Usidero

Semel

Bishi

Ebea

Gontish Sea

Atuan

Risk

Ettil

Besu Esen

Taon

Barnisk

Torheven

The Torikles

The Tortingtes

Gmet

Paln

Mt. Onn

Faliorn Mts.

Revnian Mts.

The Hands

Ontuego

Lossow

HAVNOR

Eskel

Seppish

Eppaln

Havnor Great Port

Kembermouth

Otrad

The Dragon's Run

Torning

Fbawnor Straits

R. Kember

Vemish

Sattins

Tesk

Hosk

Orner

Orrimy

Ark

Felkway

Way

Shelieth

Weymarsh

Mishport

Yor

THE WEST REACH

Low Torning

Nash

Ilien

Venway

Sneg

Kaltuel

Drumgan

The Inmost Sea

Vissti

Perilane

Outer Innram

Ismay

Wish

Far Toly

New Kaltuel

Pendor

Thwil

Leng

O-tokne

Bars of Uny

Koppish

Simly

Arrins

Sard

Ganthe

Karnery

O-Port

O

Korp

Tok

Insmer

Obb

Faltuel

Censmur

Roke

Issel

Uny

The Closed Sea

Holp

Jessage

Pody

Hort Town

Wathort

Namien

Kopp

Soders

Misk

Sowl

Dunnel

Apso

Rolameny

Obehol

Lorbanery

Sel

Gale

Wellogy

Rood

Wasny

THE EAST REACH

Gosk

The Long Dune

Far Sorr

Toom

Pelimer

Astowell

THE SOUTH REACH

Great South Shoals

Kornay

The Isle of the Ear

THE OPEN SEA

sea-divided lands. The festival of Sun-return, held on the shortest day of the year, is also universally recognized. Usually it involves the singing of the ancient chants and epics in which so much of Earthsea's past is recorded.

Another custom which is observed everywhere is the ceremony of naming a child, closely connected with magic. In infancy a child is named by its mother, and this name is used until he or she reaches the age of thirteen. The child then undergoes the rites of passage, wading through water to receive his or her true name. The true name is given by a witch or wizard and is whispered to the child, and no one but the child and its namer knows it. As the magic of Earthsea is based upon the knowledge of the true names of things, whoever knows a man's true name holds his life in keeping. The true name may be told to a friend — and this is the greatest mark of trust in Earthsea — but it will never be spoken aloud in the presence of a third party. For normal social purposes, a use-name is adopted. To take only one example, the boy who was to become the Archmage of Earthsea was known in his childhood as Duny, the name given him by his mother. At his naming ceremony he received the name Ged from his first master, but became known to the world by his use-name, Sparrowhawk. Only to his closest and most trusted friends was he known as Ged.

Magic permeates every aspect of life in Earthsea. Virtually every village has its witch, who can cast love spells or speak charms to repair broken utensils and tools or cure the most common diseases, and ships frequently carry weatherworkers who have the power to control the winds and the waves. True magic, however, is taught only at the Great School on Roke, where the mages and wizards are trained. Those taught on Roke often spend their careers as sorcerers and advisers to the great princes and lords of the islands. On Roke, magic is not merely a matter of casting spells but of studying and mastering the world itself; ultimately it becomes a philosophy and a form of practical wisdom.

Little is known of the early history of Earthsea, and it belongs to legend rather than true record. The archipelago is said to have been raised up from the sea by Segoy, who spoke the first word. Segoy alone knew all the words and all the names; he alone had a true knowledge of the Old Speech from which modern Hardic developed. In the Old Speech all things have their true names, and he who speaks it can control them. Much of the language has been forgotten and it is now spoken only by dragons, although the mages study it and have more knowledge of it than ordinary mortals. The first recorded king of Earthsea was Eland, who is said to have been drowned in the sea of Ea, to the north of the island of that name. But the best known King was Erreth-Akbe, who was not only a sorcerer but also a dragonmaster, one to whom the dragons deigned to speak. It was he who defeated the Firelord who sought to banish darkness and stop the sun at noon; the flowers known as *sparkweed* are said to have sprung from the ashes that fell from the Firelord when he was at last defeated.

Erreth-Akbe was also responsible for much of the conflict between Earthsea and what is now the Kargad Empire. He is said to have challenged the power of the Kargish high priest and to have been defeated by him. His wizard's staff was broken and his power taken from him; more important, his amulet or ring was broken in two. The ring was of silver and was inscribed on the outside with nine runes of power and on the inside with a wave design, and while it remained broken Earthsea could not be governed by a single king.

After the fall of the centralized monarchy, Earthsea was ruled by provincial lords and by whoever could hold power on his own island. The archipelago, as a whole, was eclipsed by the rise of the Kargad Empire, which became a major threat to many of the eastern isles.

The recent history of Earthsea is dominated by one man, Ged, probably the greatest wizard the archipelago has ever seen — certainly the only dragonmaster known for many years. Ged was born on Gont, where he revealed his magical abilities as a very young man; he was later trained by the famous mage Ogion, and finally went to study on Roke itself.

In an unfortunate incident, Ged unleashed an evil shadow which he had summoned from the dead. The quest to destroy the shadow took Ged across the whole of Earthsea before he finally defeated it by naming it in the waters far beyond the limits of the East Reach. A fortunate side-effect of his quest was the rediscovery of half of Erreth-Akbe's ring on the desolate shore of SPRING-WATER ISLE.

Like many mages before him, Ged travelled in

later years to Atuan, the sacred island of the Kargad Empire, in search of the second half of Erreth-Akbe's ring. But unlike those who had gone before him, he returned to Earthsea in possession of the second half, which meant that the whole ring could be remade and Earthsea reunited. It was after his return that Ged was acclaimed Archmage by his peers on the island of Roke.

The remaking of Erreth-Akbe's ring did not mean that peace had been restored to Earthsea. On the contrary, news constantly came to Roke of the decline of many important towns and islands. Magic was being abandoned; wizards were said to have given up their powers to a greater force; in Wathort drugs had led the population to a state of near-anarchy; the silk industry of Lorbanery had fallen into decline because of the absence of magic. It became clear that some power of evil was at work and rumours spread of someone who could offer eternal life to those who gave up their names and followed him. Ged set out in search of the source of this evil, accompanied by Arren, a direct descendant of Eland himself. With the help of the dragons of the west the evil was traced to its source on Selidor, where Ged and Arren finally overcame the greatest threat that Earthsea had ever known—the force of the Unmaking. Arren became King of all the Isles under his true name, Lebannen, and ruled a reunited Earthsea. According to the *Deed of Ged*, the great mage attended Lebannen's coronation and then left in his legendary boat, *Lookfar*. Lebannen said simply, "He rules a greater kingdom than do I."

The currency used in Earthsea varies from region to region. The Inner Lands normally use ivory counters as money, whereas the islands of the south use trade counters of silver. In Osskil and some other northern lands, the normal currency is gold.

(Ursula K. Le Guin, *A Wizard of Earthsea*, New York, 1968; Ursula K. Le Guin, *The Tombs of Atuan*, London, 1972; Ursula K. Le Guin, *The Farthest Shore*, London, 1973)

EASE, PLAIN OF, a narrow plain between VANITY FAIR and the DELECTABLE MOUNTAINS, in CHRISTIAN'S COUNTRY. The plain is overlooked by the Hill of Lucre, where there is a rich silver mine. Many travellers making their way to the CELESTIAL CITY allow themselves to be tempted by the wealth of the mine and turn away

from their path to dig there. The ground around the mine, however, is extremely treacherous and not a few of them fall into the depths, where they are left to die. On the far side of the plain stands a strange monument in the shape of a woman who appears to have been turned to salt. An inscription on it reads "Remember Lot's wife."

At the edge of the Plain of Ease lies By-pass Meadow, into which many travellers have been tempted to stray, thinking that it was an easier path than the one they should be following. This is an illusion, as the meadow is full of carefully concealed traps for the unwary, and leads to DOUBTING CASTLE.

(John Bunyan, *The Pilgrim's Progress from this world, to that which is to come. Delivered under the similitude of a Dream. Wherein is discovered, the manner of his setting out, his dangerous journey and safe arrival at the Desired Country*, London, 1678; John Bunyan, *The Pilgrim's Progress from this world to that which is to come. The Second Part. Delivered under the similitude of a Dream. Wherein is set forth the manner of the setting out of Christian's wife and children, their dangerous journey and safe arrival at the Desired Country*, London, 1684)

EAST FARTHING, see the SHIRE.

EASTWICK, a Rhode Island town on the Atlantic Ocean. Though today little distinguishes it from many other such towns, in past years Eastwick was the site of strange events linked to the appearance of a new resident known as Darryl Van Horne, said to be an inventor from New York. Van Horne, who apparently had a devilish charm for the women of Eastwick, purchased the famous Lenox mansion. Visitors today can explore this early-nineteenth-century home, with its roof of reddish and bluish-grey slates, cunningly fashioned copper gutters and massive end chimneys like bundles of organ pipes. The house has a forbidding, symmetrical façade with many windows that seem slightly small—especially the row on the third storey, which help illuminate the servants' quarters. Unfortunately, since the house has been turned into condominiums some of its appeal has been lost.

For decades Eastwick hovered between being semi-depressed and semi-fashionable, fitted like an L around its bit of Narragansett Bay. Then as now, egrets nested everywhere and speckled crabs crawled along the beach. In the olden days, downtown business took place around Dock Street, while Oak Street, set at right angles to it, was the site of the town's fine old homes. Dock Street has now been repaved and widened to accept more traffic and Oak Street is a straight thoroughfare, but much of the old arrangement remains, including a reconstructed blue marble trough for watering horses in the very centre of town, where the two streets meet.

Eastwick once had a sinister reputation as a site for the performance of dark arts, but the town is nowadays reputed safe. Visitors will find that the terrifying thunderstorms that once afflicted the town have disappeared since the departure of the mysterious Mr. Van Horne.

(John Updike, *The Witches of Eastwick*, New York, 1984)

EBUDA or **WEEPING ISLE**, in the north Atlantic, beyond the coast of Ireland. The inhabitants are few and savage. They maintain a secular and terrible custom: the daily offering of a young girl to a killer whale in the sea off their coast. This unpleasant celebration goes back many generations. Proteus, keeper of Neptune's herds, one day fell in love with a daughter of the king of the island and left her, pregnant, on the beach. Furious, the king had her put to death at once. In vengeance, Proteus let loose against Ebuda the entire marine fauna: killer whales and sea lions invaded the island destroying both men and flocks, and put the fortified city under siege. The terrified inhabitants consulted an oracle as to how to end his scourge. The answer was that a beautiful girl should be offered every day to Proteus until he should find one who could substitute in his heart for the dead daughter of the king. Proteus does not seem to have taken advantage of the offer; every day the appointed girl, tied to a rock off the coast, is devoured by a killer whale. Even today the inhabitants of Ebuda scour the seas searching for beautiful young girls to offer to Proteus and his beasts.

(Ludovico Ariosto, *Orlando furioso*, Ferrara, 1516)

ECNATNEPER or **NODNOL**, capital of TAERG NATIRB.

EDEN VALE, capital of FREELAND.

EDORAS, capital of ROHAN, a kingdom in the central area of MIDDLE-EARTH, on the River Snowbourn at the foot of the WHITE MOUNTAINS. The city, built some five hundred years before the beginning of the War of the Ring, stands on a hill and is surrounded by a great wall, a dyke and a thorn fence.

Immediately inside the gates, a wide path of hewn stone leads upwards, with a stream flowing down a channel cut to one side of it. The water springs from a stone carved in the shape of a horse's head on the terrace at the top of the hill, splashing into a stone basin before flowing out into the channel. A great stairway leads from this terrace to a high platform before Meduseld.

Meduseld is the Golden Hall of the Lord of the Mark, the hereditary ruler of Rohan. Built in 2569 Third Age, the hall takes its name from its great roof of gold, supported by tall pillars. Inside, it is quite dark, a place of shadows and half-light, lit only through windows set high up in the eastern wall. The hall is richly decorated: the carved pillars and the flagstones of the floor gleam with many colours and are inscribed with runes and curious devices. On the walls hang cloths depicting legendary and historical figures of Rohan's past. Visitors should notice the one depicting Eorl the Young, founder of Rohan, riding south on his great horse Felaróf to the battle of the Field of CELEBRANT. The pose is heroic—the rider, his yellow hair streaming out behind him, sounds his horn; the nostrils of the horse are flared and red as he raises his head in anticipation of the battle to come.

In the language of Rohan, Edoras means simply "The Courts."

(J.R.R. Tolkien, *The Fellowship of the Ring*, London, 1954; J.R.R. Tolkien, *The Two Towers*, London, 1954; J.R.R. Tolkien, *The Return of the King*, London, 1955)

EGGS UP, a village of unknown location. Many years ago, the people of this village decided to construct a skyscraper which would reach to the moon, hoping to be able to go up in its elevator and eat supper there. When their skyscraper was half-finished, they suddenly realized that the moon had moved and that their skyscraper would never reach it. Accordingly they tore down their skyscraper, and built another pointing directly at the moon. Again, they found that the moon moved. Ever since, the people of Eggs Up have spent their nights wondering why the moon moves and trying to find a way to stop it doing so.

(Carl Sandburg, *Rootabaga Stories*, New York, 1922)

EGYPLOSIS or **SACRED PALACE**, a palace on an island in a lake one thousand miles west of CALNOGOR in ATVATABAR. It consists of an aggregation of temples carved out of a block of green marble. The chief building is a Grecian theatre with a dome of multi-coloured glass one hundred and thirty feet above the lowest tier of seats. Egyplosis is built above the Infernal Palace, a group of rock-hewn temples devoted to the occult worship of Harikar, where objects and living things can be created by spiritual power. The Infernal Palace is reached from Egyplosis through a maze of sculptured vegetation.

(William R. Bradshaw, *The Goddess of Atvatabar, being the History of the Discovery of the Interior World and Conquest of Atvatabar*, New York, 1892)

EIGHT DELIGHTS AND BACCHIC WINE, ISLAND OF, a small island of unknown location. Its inhabitants, the Hyperboreans (not to be confused with the people of HYPERBOREA), are mostly fishermen, smallholders and artisans, who live very simply by exchanging their products— money is unknown on the island. Artists and scholars are fed and clothed by the whole community and kept like honey-gathering bees. The Hyperboreans are free of any disease and mortality has been greatly reduced; almost everyone dies peacefully at an advanced age.

    Murder, fraud and robbery do not exist. The only cases the courts have to deal with are occasional petty thefts, slander and adultery. There is a single punishment: to make the criminal wear special clothes and sit to one side during communal assemblies; there he must wait until someone makes an appeal to the judge on his behalf. The criminal is then solemnly dressed in normal clothing, kissed by the governor in the name of the

A selection of twenty utensils from the Island of the EIGHT DELIGHTS AND BACCHIC WINE.

whole community, and his re-integration into society is celebrated with a splendid feast.

    Pagan and Christian religions coexist on the island and their followers are forbidden to make public attacks on one another. It is widely accepted that the fruits of both the inward and outward life are the same for both religions: Christians and pagans have studied each other's beliefs and now share many items of faith. Many Christians (including several Catholic priests) have been initiated to the rites of Demeter. The country's theologians maintain that whereas the pagan religion operates "horizontally," absorbing nature into the divine, Christianity soars upwards, towards infinity. The two intersect like threads on a loom, weaving a divine garment with a pattern of humble goodness and longing for peace. Perhaps the major festival of the year is the miracle of wine, celebrated on January 6, in the Temple of Dionysus.

(Stefan Andres, *Wir sind Utopia*, Berlin, 1943)

EJUR, capital of PONUKELE-DRELCHKAFF.

ELDAMAR, see AMAN.

EL DORADO, a kingdom somewhere between the Amazon and Peru. The name derives from an ancient custom by which once a year the king is covered in oil and then powdered with gold dust, thus becoming *El Dorado*, "The Golden One." In spite of all their riches, the people of El Dorado are not at all greedy and consider their treasures to be superfluous. The only use they have for their gold is as a thing of beauty, to adorn their palaces and temples; otherwise, they regard it as something far inferior to food and drink.

The religion of El Dorado concentrates on the worship of the Creator of the Universe, who is thanked for all His goodness. In His eyes the king and his people are equal, as death will level them all.

Travellers in El Dorado will find that they are well received. Typical dishes can be sampled at the many roadside inns; recommended are the fruit salads, parrot stews and stuffed hummingbirds. Should the traveller be tempted by the number of gold nuggets and precious stones strewn over the countryside, he should not hesitate to pick some up, in spite of the natives' mockery.

The capital of El Dorado is Manoa, founded by the Incas themselves, on the shores of a great lake of golden sand at the head of the Caroin, a tributary of the Orinoco. Everything in the city is made of gold. From buildings to weapons, from furniture to clothing, every object in Manoa glitters like the sun. Manoa has been visited by very few Europeans; one Spaniard, Juan Martin de Abuljar, is said to have been taken here blindfolded. He was not ill-treated, but was confined to the city and not allowed to go into the countryside. Trav-

ellers are therefore advised that, in spite of the welcoming native attitude, their freedom of movement may well be severely curtailed.

There have been reports that on an isolated island, in a river to the north of El Dorado, lives a tribe of fierce red-skinned maidens; little is known of their customs, but it is said that they are a far-flung colony of ATLANTIS.

(Sir Walter Raleigh, *The Discoverie of the lovlie, rich and beautiful Empyre of Guiana with a relation of the great and golden City of Manoa (which the Spanyards call El Dorado) And the Provinces of Emerria, Arromania, and of other countries, with their rivers, adjoyning. Performed in the year 1595 by Sir Walter Ralegh, Knight, Captaine of Her Majesty's Guard, Warder of the Stanneries and Her Majesty's Lord Lieutenant of the Countie of Cornewalle*, London, 1596; El Inca Garcilasso de la Vega [Gómez Suárez de Figueroa], *Comentarios reales que tratan del origen de los Incas*, Madrid, 1609; Voltaire [François Marie Arouet], *Essai sur l'histoire générale et sur les moeurs et l'esprit des nations depuis Charlemagne jusqu'à nos jours*, Geneva, 1756; Voltaire [François Marie Arouet], *Candide, ou l'Optimisme*, Paris, 1759; Paul Alperine, *L'Ile des Vierges Rouges*, Paris, 1936)

ELENNA, an island in the sea between MIDDLE-EARTH and AMAN, the most westerly of all Mortal Lands, being within sight of the Undying Lands. Elenna was given to the Edain—men—by the Valar, the Guardians of the World, for services rendered in the struggle against Morgoth during the First Age, and on Elenna the Dúnedain, or Men of the West, established the kingdom of Númenor at the dawn of the Second Age of Middle-earth.

The Númenóreans became rich and famous mariners and began sending expeditions to Middle-earth, establishing colonies at such places as PELARGIR. Gradually, however, the majority of the Númenóreans began to turn against the Valar. Late in the Second Age, Sauron the Dark Lord was brought here as a prisoner. He soon corrupted Númenor itself, establishing a cult dedicated to the worship of Morgoth and even introducing human sacrifices. Finally he persuaded the Númenóreans to sail to the Undying Lands in the west, which lay tantalizingly close and which had been forbidden to them by a mighty prohibition—the "Ban of the Valar."

In anger, the Valar drowned Númenor in the sea. Only the Faithful survived, those who had never been seduced away from their worship of the Creator and their respect for the Valar. It was they who first founded the kingdoms of GONDOR and ARNOR, the kingdoms of the Númenóreans in exile.

(J.R.R. Tolkien, *The Return of the King,* London, 1955; J.R.R. Tolkien, *The Silmarillion,* London, 1977)

ELFHAME, an Elfin Kingdom beneath a hill near the Eskdalemuir Observatory on the Scottish border. The hill is almost perfectly round and is very steep-sided. On its summit is a small lake, known locally as the Fairy Loch, into which babies suffering from croup are dipped. The loch is free of weeds and has a crystal floor, and serves as a skylight for the Elfin realm beneath. Elfhame is entered through a door in the side of the hill; it opens by legerdemain and leads to a complex system of branching corridors and eventually to the throne room, with its silver wainscotting and its candles in crystal sconces. The room is circular and a gallery runs around its circumference, rather like an ambulatory in a cathedral; this is the centre of the kingdom's life and an important meeting-place for the courtiers, who gather in the gallery to gossip, flirt and gamble.

The inhabitants of Elfhame are neither immortal nor very small, as popular tradition would have it. They are roughly the height of a small human being and are mortal, even though they are very long-lived. That, coupled with the fact that they remain slim and good-looking until they die, has no doubt given rise to the legend of their immortality. Like all the Elfins of Europe they are descended from the Peris, an ancient race who appear to have originated in Persia. The PERI KINGDOM is the only known Elfin realm still in that country; all other Peris were driven out of Persia and settled in numerous places in the west: Elfhame and ELFWICK in Britain, BLOKULA in Sweden and BROCÉLIANDE in France. The culture of these various kingdoms is basically the same, although Brocéliande claims to preserve the most ancient traditions of all. It appears that it is only in Britain that Elfins live beneath hills—a custom which appears barbaric to many of their European cousins, such as the sophisticates of ZUY. Only in Britain are Elfins green but all Elfins can fly and have detachable wings. The aristocracy, however, do not normally use them, and leave flying to working fairies and servants.

One of the peculiarities of the aristocrats is that they rarely have children. They are, however, exceptionally fond of them, and human babies are stolen from time to time and changelings left in their place. The children are brought to the court, where they become pets, fondled and spoilt by all. The arrival of a new child is the occasion for a week of ceremonies. Each day a weasel, which has been starved for some time, is allowed to bite the child's neck and drink its blood for three minutes. The blood is replaced by an equal quantity of a distillation of dew, soot and aconite, which dehumanizes the child, although it cannot totally destroy human nature. (The distillation is no more than an approximation of Elfin blood, which contains several substances which cannot be analyzed; one of them is thought to be magnetic air.) It also gives considerable longevity, and human children treated in this way often live to be 150 (Elfins themselves live for several centuries). Once the child begins to show signs of going grey, it is expelled from the hill and left to make its way through the world of men.

Normally the death of a monarch is attended by portents; in Elfhame the sign is usually the appearance of black swans which fly over the lake for days on end. The queen then names her successor. If no successor is named, divination is used. Larks are caught, ringed and weighed down with lead; each bird represents one of the eligible ladies of the court. At noon the Chancellor, the Astrologer, the Keeper of the Records and the Chamberlain put on black hoods and go in procession to the Knowing Room, a cellar containing a well which is said to be bottomless. One by one the larks are dropped into its waters; the lady whose lark struggles longest before drowning is made queen. The court officials return to the throne room, kiss her hand and drink her health from a loving-cup of spiced and honeyed wine.

Nothing is known of the origin of the language spoken by the Elfins, although the same tongue is used in all the kingdoms, with some local variations. Although it does not resemble any known human language, some scholars have speculated that it may be related to Gaelic. It is a soft language, full of slurred sounds and hushed hisses.

(Sylvia Townsend Warner, *Kingdoms of Elfin,* London, 1972)

ELFWICK, an Elfin kingdom ruled by Queen Gruach in eastern Caithness, Scotland. The Royal Castle stands on the cliffs overlooking the sea. Elfwick is famous for its library rich in the classics which includes a cabinet of books classified as "curious"—treatises by the patristic authors, Jerome, Chrysostom and Origen.

The combination of the sea and the great library recently led to the downfall of Sir Bodach, one of the kingdom's aristocrats. The sound of the waves breaking ceaselessly against the cliffs and the immensity of that body of water caused him to meditate on the question of endlessness. To satisfy his curiosity he entered the universities of St. Andrew's and Oxford and read over the shoulders of mortal students, and discovered the idea of immortality. Sir Bodach also travelled to Germany, where he heard lectures by a certain Master Faustus. But the final conviction that he had an immortal soul came while he was flying high over the sea.

However, Elfindom rejects any idea of the immortality of the soul as being antisocial and subversive, and when the studious Sir Bodach began to discuss immortality in public he found himself condemned for heresy and exiled to CATMERE. During his exile he broke his promise not to proselytize and narrowly escaped execution as a result. After reaching Catmere he became a sailor and was, after a long and happy life, buried at sea.

(Sylvia Townsend Warner, *Kingdoms of Elfin*, London, 1972)

EL HADD, a small but extremely fertile country between ARDISTAN and DJINNISTAN. The mountains facing Ardistan are mostly barren but on the other side they slope down to a fertile plain irrigated by an efficient system of canals and ditches. There are no very large towns in the country, but every valley and hill is inhabited and intensively cultivated. El Hadd is also rich in minerals; gold, silver, copper and iron are all mined in the lower slopes of the mountains.

There are only two ways through the mountains from Ardistan. A hidden pass leads through the DJEBEL ALLAH in the east, but the more normal route is through the Bab Allah or "God's Gate," where the River Suhl plunges down the cliffs in a huge waterfall. The pass is not easy to cross, but tracks lead up along the river-banks and past the falls. North of here, the Suhl flows out of a great lake in a basin of solid rock. Houses line the edge of the basin and a road runs along its lip. Public buildings rise from the water's edge in terraces and at the highest point a large statue of an angel looms against the skyline. Tunnels lead from the foot of the angel to a small artificial island in the centre of the lake. The island has a cistern which houses the mechanisms whereby the flow of water is controlled. For centuries, however, the rock basin was empty and no river flowed out of El Hadd to water the surrounding lands. During those long years the basin appeared to travellers as a gigantic construction built for some indecipherable purpose. The lack of water caused the land behind the mountains to turn into a desert but El Hadd itself seems to have survived by using alternative sources of water. The Suhl only began to flow again when the wars that once tore this area apart finally came to an end and peace was restored.

The lancers of El Hadd ride white horses, saddled and harnessed in the Persian manner. They dress in tightly fitting suits of braided leather straps which look like armour from a distance. Their only weapons are long lances and the knives they wear at their belts; their only real protection is their characteristic helmet made of a light shimmering metal. Sometimes the helmets are covered with light cloths. Those who have seen the lancers of El Hadd on the march claim that they look like the heavenly hosts mentioned in so many sacred books. That impression is heightened by the instruments they use in their fanfares—trumpets and trombones of ancient design.

(Karl Friedrich May, *Ardistan*, Bamberg, 1909; Karl Friedrich May, *Der Mir von Djinnistan*, Bamberg, 1909)

ELISEE RECLUS ISLAND, in the north Pacific near the Arctic Circle, discovered simultaneously by a French and an American expedition, who each claimed it for their own country.

The island is crossed by a mountain chain eight hundred metres high and has a zone of hot springs and geysers that never freeze. The highest peak is the Schrader Volcano. The French expedition stayed on while the Americans moved north, and they were forced to winter on the island. Using minerals and volcanic heat, an expedition member, a former glassblower, constructed a large glass dome on lava columns which he called Cristallopolis. Under the dome he built a number of small dwellings incorporating a natural lagoon and a geyser. Cristallopolis is heated by steam drawn from the hot springs and steam-powered dynamos produce electricity for lighting. The members of the expedition founded a literary journal to avoid boredom and also domesticated seabirds which are now a major part of the food supply. The Americans, on the other hand, established themselves in a city of igloos called Maurelville or Maurel City. In the mountains behind Maurel City a subterranean town, called New Maurel City, was also established by the Americans, and a gold-bearing seam has lately been discovered there. A telephone system—constructed with equipment from the wrecked ship, connected with wire made from aluminum found in the clay of the geysers and supported by pillars of lava—provides a useful communications network for the inhabitants.

(Alphonse Brown, *Une Ville de verre*, Paris, 1891)

ELVENHALLS OF MIRKWOOD, on the banks

of the Forest River in MIRKWOOD, the ancient forest of northern MIDDLE-EARTH. Great beeches come down to the river-banks. The Forest River is crossed by a bridge leading to the huge doors of stone that give access to the cave of the Elvenking. Beyond the doors, a series of twisting passages, lit by red torchlight, lead into the cave itself, an impressive sight with its magnificent stone pillars. The Elvenking holds court here, seated on a chair of carved wood, a carved oak staff in his hand. In spring he wears a crown of woodland flowers; in autumn a crown of berries and red leaves.

From the great cave, passages lead to innumerable other caves and to a wide hall. A stream runs beneath the lowest levels, flowing out from the hill into the Forest River through the watergate. Although the watergate can be blocked by the dropping of a portcullis, it is often open, for the stream is used in trade between the elves and the men of LAKE-TOWN; barrels are floated down the river and poled back up on the return journey.

The wood elves of Mirkwood are descended from those elves of ancient times who did not go to Faerie in the west. They therefore differ from the so-called High Elves who did make that journey and who live in the hills and mountains of Middle-earth. A good and kindly people—if less wise than the High Elves—they have powerful magic and tend to be wary of strangers. They are very fond of

wine and, as there are no vines in the region, it is imported from the vineyards of their kinfolk in the south or from those of men in other areas.

In contrast with the caves inhabited in other areas by the orcs and goblins of Middle-earth, the caves of the wood elves are relatively shallow and the air in them is fresh and cool.

(J.R.R. Tolkien, *The Hobbit, or There and Back Again,* London, 1937; J.R.R. Tolkien, *The Fellowship of the Ring,* London, 1954; J.R.R. Tolkien, *The Return of the King,* London, 1955)

ELVENHOME, see AMAN.

EMERALD CITY, capital of OZ, in the exact

centre of the country, at the point where the lands of the Munchkins, Quadlings, Winkies and Gillikins meet. The area immediately around the capital also comes under the city's jurisdiction and no houses are built here, to avoid spoiling the view and the approaches to the city. The trees found on the smooth green lawns around the city do not grow anywhere else; they have soft leaves fringed rather like ostrich feathers and shimmer with all the tints of the rainbow.

The Emerald City is surrounded by a high wall, with only one gate. This single gate is studded with emeralds and leads into a gatehouse within the wall itself. All visitors are taken into this high arched room before being allowed into the city.

Once inside, travellers will find the Emerald City dazzlingly beautiful. Its streets and pavements are of smooth cut marble, and where the marble blocks meet they are studded with emeralds, as are the curbs. The houses are large imposing structures with many towers and domes. For internal decoration all types of precious stones and metals are used, but all that can be seen from the street are glittering gold and emeralds.

In the centre of the city stands the Royal Palace, the seat of Ozma, ruler of the whole land of Oz. It is surrounded by a wall and by extensive grounds, and is a masterpiece of baroque architecture. Perhaps the most spectacular section is the great Throne Room, a high domed circular chamber. All visible surfaces are encrusted with large emeralds sparkling in the light of a central lamp. High up in the dome is a gallery where an orchestra plays on important occasions; two fountains throw jets of coloured and perfumed water almost to the top of the dome. In the centre stands the magnificent jewel-encrusted throne itself.

Somewhat less ornate, the rest of the apartments in the palace are equally luxurious. Many of the rooms have tinkling fountains and all are thickly carpeted. All suites have marble baths large enough to swim in and golden bedsteads.

Although the city is guarded by a single soldier with long green whiskers (a relative perhaps of LOOKING-GLASS LAND's White Knight), it in fact needs no defences. Above the gate hangs a love magnet which makes all who pass beneath it both loved and loving.

Even the city's prison is a luxurious dwelling. It has a domed roof of coloured glass and the walls are panelled with satin brocade; books and a collection of rare and curious objects are provided for the prisoner's entertainment. None of its three doors is ever locked. Ozma takes the view that anyone who has committed a crime is unfortunate in that he has done wrong and has to be deprived of his liberty. Her reasoning is that the offender did wrong because he was not strong and brave and that he should be imprisoned until he becomes both—and since kindness makes people strong and brave, prisoners are treated with great kindness. The prison has held only one captive.

The citizens of the Emerald City do not have to work for more than half the time and in any case regard work as a source of pleasure. The total population is estimated at 57,318 souls, living in 9,654 buildings.

The Emerald City was built by the famous Wizard of Oz, who ruled the country after the overthrow of Oz's legitimate ruler by witches. Initially all visitors to the city had to wear green glasses, officially to protect their eyes from its dazzling beauty. It seems however that the city appeared green only because of the tinted lenses in the spectacles—but though the custom of wearing spectacles has been abandoned, no visitor has reported a diminishment of the city's celebrated beauty.

(L. Frank Baum, *The Wonderful Wizard of Oz*, Chicago, 1900; L. Frank Baum, *The Marvelous Land of Oz*, Chicago, 1904; L. Frank Baum, *Ozma of Oz*, Chicago, 1907; L. Frank Baum, *Dorothy and the Wizard in Oz*, Chicago, 1908; L. Frank Baum, *The Road to Oz*, Chicago, 1909; L. Frank Baum, *The Emerald City of Oz*, Chicago, 1910; L. Frank Baum, *The Patchwork Girl of Oz*, Chicago, 1913)

EMO, a volcanic island, surrounded by a coral reef, several weeks' sail from CORAL ISLAND. There are two mountains on Emo, both some four thousand feet high, separated by a broad valley whose sides are lined with thick woods. The island has valuable stands of sandalwood.

Emo is inhabited by cannibals who live in settlements of bamboo shelters thatched with pandanus leaves. Many of them consist of little more than a sloping roof, three sides, and an open front. The cannibal society is strictly hierarchical, ruled by a chief whose word is absolute.

The religion of Emo is centred on the notion of taboo. If a man chooses a particular tree as his god, its fruit automatically becomes taboo to him; if he eats it, he is sure to be killed and eaten by his fellows. The chief himself is taboo, so that anyone who touches a living or dead chief becomes taboo as well and has to be killed. The chief wears his hair fluffed out to such an extent that it resembles a turban. This hair style requires a great deal of attention from his barbers, whose fingers—declared taboo—must not be used for normal purposes; the barbers have, therefore, to be fed like babies.

The islanders have other interesting religious customs. One of their gods is an enormous eel kept in a pool of stagnant water. The eel, twelve feet long and as thick as a man's body, appears at the sound of a low whistle from its attendant, who feeds the creature.

The people of Emo usually wear a strip of cloth, called a *maro*, around their loins, although on formal occasions the chief wraps himself in a voluminous garment of cloth made from the bark of the Chinese paper-mulberry. The bodies of the chiefs and leading men are tattooed with complex designs. The tattooing is carried out by specialized artists and the process is long and painful, beginning at the age of ten and not completed until the individual is thirty. The skin is punctured with a sharp piece of bone; a preparation made from the kernel of the candlenut, mixed with coconut oil, is rubbed into the punctures. Visitors are not advised to attempt this form of make-up, as the process causes severe torment and inflammation and sometimes leads to a very painful death.

The sports on Emo include violent forms of wrestling, boxing and surfing. Enthusiastic visitors should practise the latter with caution in view of the many sharks that infest Emo's waters.

(Robert Michael Ballantyne, *The Coral Island*, London, 1858)

EMPI ARCHIPELAGO, in the Atlantic Ocean, not far from the FORTUNATE ISLANDS. It is surrounded by a disagreeable mist of unbearable smell, reminiscent of human flesh burnt on a fire of sulphur, pitch and bitumen. The atmosphere is dark and humid, made worse by a rain of pitch that sometimes covers the ground. Visitors will be surprised by the constant uproar that can be heard throughout the archipelago: from no specific location, there seems to rise a mingling of cries and lamentations, as of many people in pain. Only one of the islands has been explored: it is said to be rocky, infertile, without trees or water. The island is strewn with thorns and naked blades, and is crossed by three rivers: one of dirt, one of fire and one of blood. The river of fire, very long and difficult to cross, runs like water and has waves like the sea. It is rich in fish, some like burning coals, others like fire-brands.

(Lucian of Samosata, *True History*, 2nd cen. AD)

EMPORIUM, capital of OCEANA (1).

EMPTY HATS, a city ruled by a dignified queen. The only inhabitants are empty hats. Fat rats, fat cats and fat bats are sometimes seen in the streets; they too are considered to be no more than empty hats. The few travellers who have visited the city describe it as a terrifying place; they rapidly begin to feel that they as well are empty hats. The Queen of Empty Hats constantly mumbles under her breath: "There is a screw loose somewhere, there is a leak in the tank." No one knows what she means by these enigmatic phrases.

(Carl Sandburg, *Rootabaga Stories*, New York, 1922)

EMYN MUIL, a range of hills on the edge of GONDOR, in the south of MIDDLE-EARTH, to the east of ROHAN and to the west of the DEAD MARSHES. The GREAT RIVER flows through these hills to the waterfall of Rauros, which carries it down to the marshes of Wetwang. The hills of Emyn Muil are grey and stony, and run from north to south in great ridges. To the west, they end in sheer precipices and cliffs, while the eastern slopes are more gentle though scored with great clefts. The upper ridges are completely barren. On the lower slopes the twisted remains of dead trees killed by the cold east wind do little to lighten the landscape.

(J.R.R. Tolkien, *The Fellowship of the Ring*, London, 1954; J.R.R. Tolkien, *The Two Towers*, London, 1954)

ENCHANTED GROUND, a forest near the river that surrounds the CELESTIAL CITY in CHRISTIAN'S COUNTRY. The tracks through the forest are difficult to find and extremely muddy and treacherous underfoot. At times they are almost impossible to follow because of the dense undergrowth. Travellers are warned that at one spot there is a bottomless pit into which they are likely to stumble.

There are no inns or houses in the forest; there are several arbours but they should be avoided, as those who fall asleep in them will never again wake up. It is in fact dangerous to fall asleep anywhere in the Enchanted Ground. Because thieves and monsters are sometimes seen in these parts, travellers should go about armed.

The forest is under the spell of the witch known as Madame Bubble, also known as the Mistress of the World, who claims to make all men happy. She is a tall, attractive woman who tries to stop pilgrims on their journey, speaking gently and smiling at them; those who surrender to her beauty are as good as dead and will never reach the goal of their travels. Madame Bubble wears a great purse at her waist and is constantly fingering the money in it as though it were her heart's delight. She is particularly interested in wealthy travellers, usually scorning the poor ones. Madame Bubble has convinced some people that she is a goddess and she is worshipped as such in some places. She is fond of feasting and can often be seen at banqueting tables. Her promises are empty and though she has told many travellers that she will give them crowns and kingdoms if they will listen to her advice, she has in fact destroyed thousands by appealing to their lusts and ambitions. She sows discord between rulers and subjects, man and wife and even, it is said, between the flesh and the heart.

(John Bunyan, *The Pilgrim's Progress from this world, to that which is to come. Delivered under the similitude of a Dream. Wherein is discovered, the manner of his setting out, his dangerous journey and safe arrival at the Desired Country,* London, 1678; John Bunyan, *The Pilgrim's Progress from this world to that which is to come. The Second Part. Delivered under the similitude of a Dream. Wherein is set forth the manner of the setting out of Christian's wife and children, their dangerous journey and safe arrival at the Desired Country,* London, 1684)

ENCHANTED WOOD, beyond the Gate of Deeper Slumber, in DREAMWORLD. Travellers are advised that it is best to set off with the formal blessing of the priests who dwell in the surrounding area.

In the tunnels of that twisted wood, whose low prodigious oaks extend their groping boughs and shine dimly with a phosphorescence of strange fungi, dwell the furtive and secretive Zoogs who know many obscure secrets best left untold. Certain unexplained rumours, events and disappearances that have taken place in both Europe and America are said to be the responsibility of the Zoogs.

The Zoogs are small brown creatures who prefer to remain unseen, living in burrows or the trunks of great trees. Though they feed mainly on fungi it is said that they have a taste for human flesh, and few who have entered the Enchanted Wood have ever left it.

(Howard Phillips Lovecraft, "The Dream-Quest of Unknown Kadath," in *Arkham Sampler,* Sauk City, 1948)

ENGLAND, a vast theme park built on the Isle of Wight—not to be confused with the country of the same name—containing everything that is deemed essentially English. The brain-child of the visionary tycoon Sir Jack Pitman, it is open to the public and has proved so popular that it threatens to overtake the other England, known now as "Old England," in prestige and importance.

Among its attractions are Wembley Stadium with its twin towers, a White Horse cut in a chalky hillside, a half-size Big Ben, Shakespeare's and Princess Di's graves, the White Cliffs of Dover, a realistic London fog complete with beetle-black taxis, Cotswold villages full of thatched cottages serving Devonshire cream teas, a National Gallery full of reproductions, Brontë country, Jane Austen's house and Stonehenge. Expert topiarists have

trimmed Great Scenes from English History on the west-facing clifftop. Beefeaters serve Great English Breakfasts and a band of Merrie Men accompany Robin Hood on his excursions. A Royal Shakespeare Company performs regularly. An unconfirmed rumour has it that the Royal Family has agreed to relocate to the replica of Buckingham Palace, but this seems doubtful. In the meantime, visitors will meet Elizabeth I, Charles I and Queen Victoria as they tour the site.

Visitors are well looked after. There are luxuriously carpeted hotels decorated with potted trees, in the style of the Dorchester and the Savoy, and golf courses on Tennyson Down, as well as shopping malls and sheepdog trials.

(Julian Barnes, *England, England,* London, 1998)

ENLAD, an island in the north of EARTHSEA, separated from OSSKIL by the narrow waters of the Osskil Sea. The main port is Berila, also known as the City of Ivory, on the west coast. Enlad is a peaceful country of pleasant green hills; its main activity is sheep-farming, and on New Year's Day the shepherds' wives come into Berila bearing the first lambs of the year. They are sprinkled with incense, and spells are pronounced over them by the court sorcerer in order to ensure the increase of the herd. Enlad is also a centre for trade in sapphires, ox-hides and tin with the islands of the West Reach.

Enlad is the oldest principality of all Earthsea and its lords trace their ancestry back to the legendary hero Eland himself.

(Ursula K. Le Guin, *A Wizard of Earthsea,* New York, 1968; Ursula K. Le Guin, *The Tombs of Atuan,* London, 1972; Ursula K. Le Guin, *The Farthest Shore,* London, 1973)

ENNASIN or **ALLIANCE ISLAND,** a triangular island, of approximately the same shape and location as Sicily. The people resemble red-painted Picts, except that their noses are all shaped like the ace of clubs.

All the inhabitants are related to one another by both kinship and marriage, a fact of which they are extremely proud. Degrees of kinship are so complex and the people so intermarried that it is impossible to find anyone who is not mother, father, son-in-law, aunt, cousin or nephew to someone else. Visitors to the island will be surprised, for instance, to hear an old man call a little girl of three or four "father," while she calls him "daughter." Couples use a wide variety of curious endearments when addressing one another: "octopus," "porpoise" and "hatchet" are typical examples.

Marriages between the most unlikely partners appear to be the main pastime and amusement of the Ennasians, but visitors are seldom invited to join in.

(François Rabelais, *Le quart livre des faicts et dicts du bon Pantagruel,* Paris, 1552)

ENTELECHY, an island kingdom of unknown location. The main port is Mataeotechny, or "Home of Useless Knowledge."

Although the queen of the island is commonly known as "The Quintessence," her true name is Entelechy, like the island itself. The name was given her by Aristotle, her godfather. Travellers will see the queen as young, fair and delicately built, but in fact she is more than two thousand years old. The queen has the ability to cure all diseases simply by playing a tune chosen according to the nature of the complaint the patient is suffering from; she does not even have to touch the patient. The instrument on which she plays her miraculous music is a curious object: its pipes are made of cassia sticks; its sounding board, of guaiacum; its stops, of rhubarb; its pedals, of tussock; and its keyboard, of scammony. A tune played on this instrument will immediately cure the blind, the deaf, and the dumb, the leper and the apoplectic.

The queen herself only cures "incurable" diseases; less serious complaints are dealt with by her officers: the *abstractors, perazons, nedibins, calcinators* and others, who cure by other means than music. Venereal disease is cured by touching the dentiform vertebra three times with a piece of a clog; fever, by hanging a fox's tail on the left side of the patient's belt. The endemic penury of friars is cured by relieving them of all their debts. Houses are cleansed of pestilential air simply by throwing them up into the air.

One of the members of the royal household has the ability to restore women to their youth by recasting them. Toothless, bleary hags are transformed into attractive, fair-haired maidens of sixteen. This rejuvenator is, however, unable to restore

their heels to their previous state and the recast women are thus shorter than they were in their first youth, which explains why they tend to collapse so suddenly when they meet with men and why they are so easy to throw onto their backs. It is not possible to rejuvenate men in the same way; men must regain their youth by living with recast women. They then catch the fifth, or quintessential, pox— known as the "Slough," or *Aphiasis* in Greek— and they change their hair and skin every year.

Other tasks carried out on the island include the whitening of Ethiopians, the extraction of water from pumice stones, and the gathering of grapes from thorn bushes and figs from thistles. Some members of the court make great things out of nothing and then make great things return to nothing; yet others can be seen making a virtue of necessity.

The sight of Queen Entelechy curing the sick is enough to reduce men to a state of swooning ecstasy, from which they can only be revived by the white roses she always carries with her. Visitors will notice that the queen speaks in a curious manner, using terms drawn from abstract philosophies and logic. Her greeting to honest men, for instance, is in this style: "The probity scintillating on the surfaces of your persons gives me perfect assurance of the virtues latent in the core of your minds. It is for that reason that I, who in the past have mastered all private affections, cannot now prevent myself from saying to you that you are heartily, most heartily, more than most heartily welcome." Although an extremely generous hostess who provides an excellent table for her guests, the queen herself drinks nothing but divine nectar and eats nothing but celestial ambrosia. Her masticators chew everything for her, digesting it in their crimson-lined gullets. Then, when they have chewed it finely, they pour it into her stomach through a funnel of the finest gold. The queen is said to perform all natural functions by proxy.

(François Rabelais, *Le cinquiesme et dernier livre des faicts et dicts du bon Pantagruel, auquel est contenu la visitation de l'Oracle de la dive Bacbuc, et le mot de la bouteille; pour lequel avoir est entrepris tout ce long voyage,* Paris, 1564)

EPHEL DUATH, see Mountains of SHADOW.

EREBOR, see LONELY MOUNTAIN.

ERED LITHUI or **ASH MOUNTAINS**, a mountain range running east to west along the northern border of MORDOR. The Ered Lithui meets the north-south EPHEL DUATH range at the pass of CIRITH GORGOR. The range takes its name from the barren, grey appearance of the mountains.

(J.R.R. Tolkien, *The Fellowship of the Ring*, London, 1954; J.R.R. Tolkien, *The Return of the King*, London, 1955)

EREGION, see HOLLIN.

EREWHON (pronounced in three syllables: E-re-whon), a kingdom probably in central or northern Australia, though its location has been deliberately concealed by travellers who have visited it. Those geographers who have placed it in New Zealand (Upper Rangitata district, Canterbury) have not taken into account the sheer immensity of its land surface.

It can be reached from the sheep-rearing plains that surround it through the gorge of a river that descends from very cold mountains. Most passes on these mountain-tops are glaciered, but the persistent traveller can find one which, though covered in snow, is still practicable. Erewhon shares its frontiers with Erewhemos, a country inhabited by coloured people bearing no affinity to the Erewhonians. Erewhonians resemble Mediterraneans and have magnificent presence. The women are beautiful, courteous and benign. They seem to be a combination of Egyptian, Helenic and Italian races—their noses, for example, are Greek. It should be held in mind by anyone desirous of visiting Erewhon that being blond and blue-eyed is a distinct advantage.

In Erewhon, the traveller will find much the same customs as in Europe. He will be struck, however, by the primitive character of the Erewhonian appliances; they seem five or six hundred years behind Europe in their inventions (but this is also the case of course in many European villages). A few things are unknown in Erewhon: gunpowder and matches, for instance. Tobacco is also unavailable but the needy traveller is advised that a certain sort of wort, found in most private gardens, can be dried and used as a substitute. Food is wholesome. Lunch usually consists of goat's flesh, oatcake and some milk. Children delight in blue barley sugar—not twisted but plaited. Erewhon produces a good red wine.

The Erewhonian countryside is very pleasant. On the country roads can be seen little shrines with statues of men and women of great beauty, depicted either in the heyday of their youth or in distinguished maturity and old age; Erewhonians bow their heads in homage when they pass them. There are a great many rivers, some very wide, which may be crossed by ferryboats. One interesting site, very near the river which gives access to Erewhon, is the Erewhonian Stonehenge. It consists of rude and barbaric figures with superhuman, malevolent expressions on their faces—a mixture of Egyptian, Assyrian and Japanese features. They are six or seven times larger than life and of great antiquity, worn and lichen-grown. Each statue is built out of four or five enormous blocks. In ancient times, the Erewhonians sacrificed the ugly and diseased to these statues, in order to avert such scourges from falling on their own people. When the wind blows through these statues, which are hollow, it produces a melody reminiscent of Handel:

The villages of Erewhon are similar to those in the Alps or Lombardy. The houses huddle together on each side of a narrow main street, with large, overhanging roofs and a few windows, some of which are glazed. Vines grow outside some of the houses; inside, the walls are papered with old issues of *The Illustrated London News* and *Punch*. Inns are indicated by a sign of a bottle and a glass, and can be recommended as clean and comfortable.

Fauna and flora are unspectacular: a small breed of black cattle; sheep with rounded noses and enormous tails; goats; dogs; a certain type of quail reminiscent of a New Zealand species, now extinct. There is a total absence of cats.

There are many towns and cities, and from afar the towns give an impression of lofty steeples and rounded domes. Most towns contain Musical Banks and Hospitals for Incurable Bores: some even have a Museum of Old Machines, like the one in Sunchildston (formerly Cold Harbour) which also boasts a famous prison. Other important towns are Fairmead and Bridgeford. Statues of famous Erewhonians are found in some towns; a jury of twenty-four men decides every fifty years which statues should stay and which should go, according to the dictates of the latest school of art. All others are destroyed.

The capital of Erewhon is magnificent, with great towers and fortifications and lofty buildings that look like palaces. Typical of these is Senoj Nosnibor's house, situated near the outskirts of the metropolis (from here can be seen the venerable ruins of the old railway station, which form an imposing feature from the gardens of the house). The grounds, of some ten or twelve acres, are laid out in terraced gardens, one above the other, with flights of broad steps ascending and descending. On these steps are statues of the most exquisite workmanship beside vases filled with various Erewhonian shrubs. On either side of the steps are rows of old cypresses and cedars, with grassy alleys between them, and choice vineyards and orchards full of fruit trees. The rooms of the house itself open onto a courtyard, as at Pompeii. In the middle of the courtyard is a bath and a fountain.

The only musical instruments in the houses are a dozen large bronze gongs which are kept in the larger drawing room and which the ladies occasionally beat at random, producing a rather unpleasant sound. This music is also used in all mercantile transactions, most of which take place in what is called the Musical Bank. The Erewhonian coinage is entirely silver—gold pieces are very rare—and there are two distinct currencies in Erewhon, each under the control of two different banks and mercantile codes, the exact functionings of which are extremely complicated. The Musical Bank is socially acceptable, but its currency is of no use in the outside world; the other bank is commonly used but not talked about. The main branch of the Musical Bank is on a large central piazza. The building is of strange but noble design and of great antiquity. It does not open directly on to the piazza. An archway in a screen leads from the piazza to the actual precincts of the bank. Passing under the archway one comes upon a green sward, enclosed by an arcade or cloister, while in front rise the majestic towers of the bank and its venerable façade divided into three deep recesses and adorned with different kinds of marble and many sculptures. On either side are quaint but substantial houses of singularly comfortable appearance, situated in the midst of orchards and gardens and beautiful old trees in which nest great numbers of birds. The Musical Bank takes both the imagination and judgement by storm. But if the outside is impressive, the inside is even more so. It is very lofty and divided into several parts by walls which rest on massive pillars. The windows are filled with stained glass depicting the principal commercial incidents of the bank over many ages. In a remote part of the building the visitor may hear men and boys singing: this is the only disturbing feature, as the music is singularly hideous to European ears.

Education is imparted in Colleges of Unreason. Here the principal study is Hypothetics. Erewhonians argue that to teach a boy merely the nature of the things existing in the world around him, and about which he will have to be conversant during his whole life, would be to give him a narrow and shallow conception of the universe, which, they argue, might contain all manner of things not found in it now. To open his eyes to these possibilities, and so to prepare him for a set of utterly strange and impossible contingencies, is reckoned the fittest way of training him for the actual conduct of his affairs in life. Erewhonians believe that life would be intolerable if men were guided in all they did by reason only. Reason betrays men into drawing hard and fast lines and into defining language—language being, they say, like

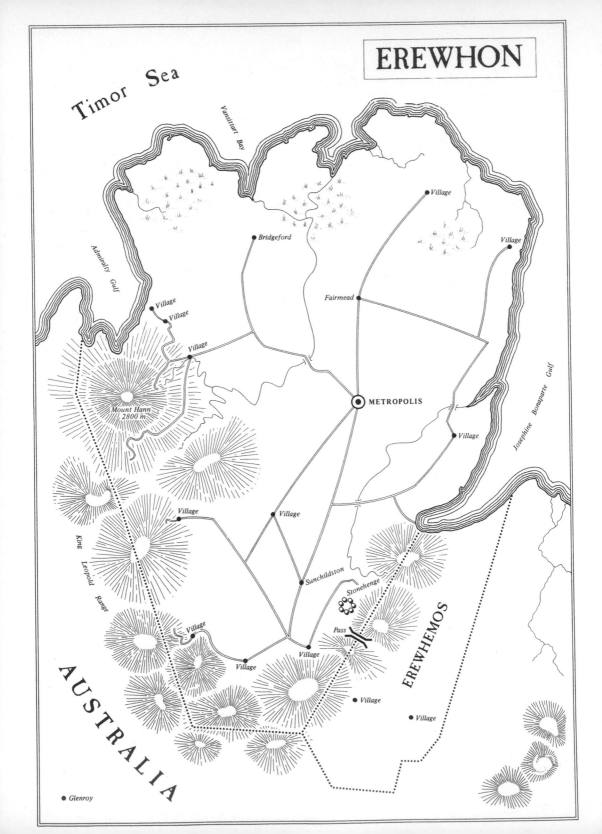

The Erewhonian Stonehenge.

the sun, which rears and then scorches. Erewhonians are taught a hypothetical language, originally composed in ancient times. Fluency in this is the true mark of a scholar and gentleman. Of genius, however, they make no account, for they say that everyone is, more or less, a genius. Some radical professors are members of the Society for the Suppression of Useless Knowledge and the Society for the Complete Obliteration of the Past, but they are minor factions. The study of art is well developed, and students must learn commercial history in order to know the market value of their work. A College of Spiritual Athletics has also recently been established.

The laws of Erewhon are very strict. Illness of any sort is considered highly criminal and immoral, and for catching cold anyone is liable to be had up before the magistrates and imprisoned. However, embezzlement and other such moral misdeeds are seen in the same way that Europeans see illnesses, and are a matter for condolence and curative treatment. They are treated by Straighteners. The office of Straightener is one which requires long and special training. In order to become practically acquainted with the moral ailment he would cure, the student is required to set apart certain seasons for the practice of each vice in turn, as a religious duty. These seasons are called "fasts" and are continued by the student until he finds he really can subdue all the more usual vices

in his own person, and therefore can advise his patients, using the results of his own experience. There are numerous specialists who have practised these exercises throughout their lives and some devoted men have actually died as martyrs to drink, gluttony or whatever vice they choose for their special study. To be poor is also considered criminal in Erewhon. Loss of fortune or loss of some dear friend is punished almost as severely as physical delinquency, and offenders are brought before the Court for Personal Bereavement.

These laws have originated a number of peculiar social customs. For instance, people enquire about someone's temper, as one would, elsewhere, about someone's health. Ill luck of any kind, or even ill treatment at the hands of others, is considered an offence against society, in as much as it makes people uncomfortable to hear of it. Because illness is such a dreadful felony, it is polite, according to Erewhonian etiquette, to say "I have stolen a pair of socks," or in more colloquial language "I have the socks," to mean that one is slightly indisposed. To cure themselves and keep healthy, Erewhonians take a flogging once a week and punish themselves with a diet of bread and water for two or three months a year, under the strict supervision of the family Straightener.

In Erewhon, death is regarded with less abhorrence than disease. Erewhonians argue that if it is an offence at all it is one beyond the reach of the law, which is therefore silent on the subject. Erewhonians burn their dead and scatter the ashes over any piece of ground (which the deceased may choose himself). No one is permitted to refuse this hospitality to the dead. Generally, they choose some garden or orchard which they may have known and been fond of when they were young. The superstitious hold that those whose ashes are scattered over any given land become its jealous guardians from that time on. When anyone dies, the friends of the family send little boxes filled with artificial tears (from two to sixteen, according to the degree of intimacy or relationship), and people find it a nice point of etiquette to know the exact number of tears they ought to send.

The birth of a child is regarded as a painful subject which it is kinder not to touch upon since Erewhonians think it wrong to be out of health—even if good may come of it. All believe in preexistence and that it is of their own free will in a previous state that they come to be born into this world. They say that the unborn are perpetually plaguing and tormenting the married of both sexes, fluttering about them incessantly and giving them no peace of either mind or body until they have consented to take them under their protection. If this were not so (argue the Erewhonians) it would be a monstrous liberty for one man to take with another, to say that he should undergo the chances and changes of this mortal life without any option in the matter. When a child is born, a document is set out in which it is said that the child acknowledges full responsibility for his birth. The guests will harass the child, reprimanding him severely for causing such distress to his parents. When the child cries, it is taken to mean that he shows repentance and a friend of the family will sign the birth document on his behalf.

A notable characteristic of the Erewhonian mind is that when they are quite certain about any matter and avow it as a base on which they are to build a system of practice, they are seldom prepared to criticize it. If they smell a rat about the precincts of a cherished institution, they will always stop their noses to it, if they can.

The Erewhonian notion of time is quite peculiar. They say that we are drawn through life backwards; or again, that we go onwards into the future as into a dark corridor. Time walks beside us and flings back shutters as we advance, but the light thus given often dazzles us, and deepens the darkness which is in front. We can see but little at a time, and heed that little with far less than our apprehension of what we shall see next. Forever peering curiously through the glare of the present into the gloom of the future, we presage the leading lines of that which is before us by faintly reflected lights from dull mirrors that are behind us, and stumble on as we may until the trapdoor opens beneath us and we are gone. They say that there was once a race of men who knew the future better than the past, but that they died in a year from the misery their knowledge caused them.

Erewhonians worship a number of gods openly, but secretly believe in only one. The gods they worship are personifications of human qualities, such as justice, strength, hope, fear and love. They believe that these gods have a real objective existence in a region far beyond the clouds. The gods' interest in human affairs is keen and on the whole beneficial, but they become very angry if neglected and punish the first person they come upon rather than the person who has offended them.

A condolences box from EREWHON.

The gods have a law that two pieces of matter may not occupy the same space at the same moment, a law administered by the gods of Time and Space jointly. So if a flying stone and a man's head occupy the same space simultaneously, attempting to outrage these gods by "arrogating a right which they do not possess," a severe punishment, sometimes even death itself, is sure to follow.

In spite of their idols and temples, this professed religion is only skin-deep among Erewhonians. They really believe in the goddess Ydgrun, whom the priests consider an enemy of the true gods. She occupies a very anomalous position: she is held to be both omnipresent and omnipotent, but she is not an elevated conception and is sometimes both cruel and absurd. Even her most devoted worshippers are a little ashamed of her and serve her more with the heart and in deed than with their tongues. True Ydgrundites seldom speak of Ydgrun, but they never run counter to her dictates without ample reason for doing so: in such cases they override her with due self-reliance, and the goddess seldom punishes them, for they are brave and Ydgrun is not.

There is a small but growing sect who believe, after a fashion, in the immortality of the soul and the resurrection of the dead. They teach that those who are born with diseased bodies and who pass their lives in ailing will be tortured eternally hereafter, but that those who have been strong, healthy and handsome are rewarded for ever and ever.

For a brief period, a religion called Sunchildism took over Erewhon, the result of a visit from an Englishman, George Higgs, whom the inhabitants believed to be of divine origin after his escape in a balloon with an Erewhonian lady.

The visitor to Erewhon should not fail to see the Museum of Old Machines in Sunchildston. The greater part of the Museum contains all sorts of broken machinery: fragments of steam engines, a very old railway carriage, clocks and watches, and the like. It seems that five hundred years ago the state of mechanical knowledge was far advanced. However, a professor of hypothetics wrote an extraordinary book proving that the machines were ultimately destined to supplant the race of man. He convinced everyone and got the law to strictly forbid all further improvements and inventions under pain of being considered a case equivalent to typhoid fever, which Erewhonians regard as one of the worst of all crimes.

It should be noted that Erewhon is a rapidly changing country and that no information has been forthcoming for a number of years. The authors cannot therefore vouch for the exactness of the above description.

(Samuel Butler, *Erewhon*, London, 1872; Samuel Butler, *Erewhon Revisited*, London, 1901)

ERIADOR, an old name for all those lands in MIDDLE-EARTH that lie between the MISTY MOUNTAINS and the Blue Mountains and to the north of the rivers Greyflood and Glanduin. By the end of the Third Age, the only inhabited areas were the SHIRE, BREE-LAND, and the thinly populated RIVENDELL.

(J.R.R. Tolkien, *The Fellowship of the Ring*, London, 1954; J.R.R. Tolkien, *The Return of the King*, London, 1955; J.R.R. Tolkien, *The Silmarillion*, London, 1977)

ERIC THE RED, LAND OF, see ERIK-RAUDEBYG.

ERIKRAUDEBYG or **LAND OF ERIC THE RED**, a settlement in the north-east of Greenland, surrounded by the DEVIL'S TEETH mountains, seventeen days' journey from the coast. It stands on the bank of a river which disappears underground at the rim of the Devil's Teeth. From the foot of these mountains a pine forest interspersed with poplar, sycamore and plane-trees extends to the river, where it gives way to a marsh that can be crossed by an earthen causeway.

Erikraudebyg is in fact what remains of the kingdom of Eric the Red, the discoverer of Greenland in the tenth century. It is known in Eskimo legends as "The Land of the Red-Haired Men" and is the only Viking settlement to have survived the Eskimo conquest of Greenland. The central village consists of several hundred stone or wooden huts with high steep roofs, windows of obsidian and gardens filled with north-European plants and flowers. It is divided into two areas by a central path which leads through a square to the Royal Palace at the foot of a mountain. The palace is a one-storey stone building with about thirty windows, and door posts carved in the shape of dragons; it is decorated with hunting trophies. In the Throne Room are benches placed in front of a dais which supports a ceremonial chair made from mammoth tusks.

Naturalists will find the fauna of Erikraudebyg of great interest. Mammoths abound, as well as huge bears, larger than polar bears and the colour of the grizzly. *Ursus spelaeus*, the cave-bear of prehistoric Europe, lives in the caves of the Devil's Teeth, and a survivor of the Pliocene Age, *rhinoceros tichorhinus*, a two-horned rhinoceros, is found in the salty marshes.

The inhabitants of Erikraudebyg are tall and white-skinned, the men with long red hair and thick moustaches, the women blonde—evidence of their Viking ancestry. The men wear tunics and trousers of reindeer-skin, criss-crossed with leather thongs from ankle to knee, and fur-lined sandals; the women are clothed in long, hooded, fur-trimmed dresses. Soldiers wear armour of chain-mail, with pointed helmets, swords, war-clubs and round shields; the chiefs wear helmets with ivory horns. Their Viking warships are formidable, about forty metres long with a large striped sail, with fifteen oarsmen on each side.

The people speak Nordenne, the guttural language of the Vikings, some sounds of which are similar to modern Scandinavian languages, and they worship Odin as the main god. The government is that of an elective monarchy; the kings usually have a physical resemblance to the colony's founder and take the name Eric followed by a surname (for instance "The Enlightened") on acceding to the throne. Justice, with its trial by combat, is administered by the Halmar or High Priest who has great influence over the choice of king.

The people of Erikraudebyg are anxious to preserve the secrecy of their land, and while Eskimos are their main enemies they will kill anyone they meet on their excursions beyond the mountains. There is a saying that Erikraudebyg will survive so long as no one from beyond the mountains reaches it. Yet tradition has it that someone resembling Eric the Red will come again to rule and will save the city from a great danger. Red-haired, moustachioed travellers should therefore incorporate this knowledge into their plans to visit Erikraudebyg.

(Paul Alperine, *La Citadelle des glaces*, Paris, 1946)

ERSILIA, a city of changing location, where, in order to establish the relationships that sustain the city's life, the inhabitants stretch strings from the corners of the houses, white or black or grey or black-and-white according to whether they mark a relationship of blood, trade, authority, or agency. When the strings become so numerous that one can no longer pass among them, the inhabitants leave; the houses are dismantled; only the strings and their supports remain.

The inhabitants then rebuild Ersilia elsewhere, weaving a similar pattern of strings which they try to make more complex and at the same time more regular than the other. Then they abandon it and take themselves and their houses still farther away.

Thus, when travelling in the territory of Ersilia, a visitor will come upon the ruins of the abandoned cities without the walls, which do not last; without the bones of the dead, which the wind rolls away: spiderwebs of intricate relationships seeking a form.

(Italo Calvino, *Le città invisibili,* Turin, 1972)

ESCALOT, a castle not far from Winchester, in England. Sir Launcelot once stayed here before taking part in a joust at Winchester. While he was in Escalot, Elaine, the daughter of the lord of the castle, fell in love with Launcelot who agreed to wear her colours at the tournament. He did not return her love and it was only by deception that she

managed to sleep with him at Castle CORBIN. The son of their union was Galahad, who was eventually to become the noblest of all knights and to find the Holy Grail at Castle CARBONEK. When Launcelot left Elaine she died of grief and her body floated down the river to CAMELOT carrying a letter which told of her unhappy love. The letter was read aloud to the company assembled in the castle and she was buried at Camelot amid much lamentation and sorrow.

(Anonymous, *La Mort le Roi Artu,* 13th cen. AD; Alfred, Lord Tennyson, *The Idylls of the King,* London, 1842–85)

ESSUR, a kingdom to the west of Phars. A high mountain range separates the two kingdoms. Unlike most of the neighbouring countries, Essur is a land of great forests and rushing rivers, and is rich in game. Its natural wonders include a hot spring close to the capital.

The religious life of the country is dominated by the cult of Talapal, a goddess who has much in common with Ungit, the goddess worshipped in GLOME. More recently the worship of Istra has been introduced; many details of the legends of the goddess are obviously based on the life of Princess Istra of Glome. The images of Istra are plain wooden sculptures housed in temples no bigger than a peasant's hut, built of pure white marble with fluted pillars in the Greek style. Istra is believed to live regally during the spring and summer, and to wander the world weeping in the winter. Towards the end of the harvest season the images in the temple are veiled to symbolize both goddesses' departure.

(C.S. Lewis, *Till We Have Faces. A Myth Retold,* London, 1956)

ESTOTILAND, an island smaller than Iceland in the north Atlantic, crossed by four rivers and with a mountain in its centre. It lies to the north of the island of Drogio, where men eat each other in splendid temples. The people of Estotiland possess every single art in the world, except that of using a mariner's compass.

(F. Marcolini, *Dello scoprimento dell'Isole Frislandia, Eslanda, Engrovelanda, Estotilanda e Icaria, fatto sotto il Polo Artico dai due fratelli Zeno, M. Nicolo e M. Antonio,* Venice, 1558)

ETERNITY, LAND OF, see MAGMELL.

ETIDORHPA'S COUNTRY, an underground region, reached through an entrance in the well-known cave systems of Kentucky, in the United States. Through an archway in a cliff flows a stream which must be followed into a tunnel. At times the water almost reaches the roof of the tunnel and visitors will find it necessary to swim their way through. Eventually a large cavern is reached, with a path leading away from the stream. The darkness becomes less intense, and a peculiar light seems to float in space without a fixed point of radiation. Here the visitor will discover hordes of eyeless subterranean creatures who have developed the ability to see with the whole surface of their bodies. Next, the traveller will reach a cavern of white crystal littered with mounds of glass. The floor of the cavern is the dried bed of an underground lake strewn with small salt crystals. Beyond this lies a deep chasm running for many miles, and on the other side, the path leads steeply down to a flat sheet of water that feeds the Epomeo volcano in Italy. The traveller is now one hundred and fifty miles below the earth's surface.

For those who falter on the subterranean journey there is a chamber called the Drunkards' Den. Here live a race of tiny degenerate beings, once intelligent and now stupid, shrunken and mis-shapen, each with one gigantic hand, leg or forehead. They tempt newcomers, trying to bring them down to their level by inviting them to drink. On earth it is the mind of a drunkard that becomes abnormal; here it is the body. The den is a vast amphitheatre, one thousand feet in diameter, with a stone rostrum in the centre where liquor is fermented in huge bowls. The traveller should resist the pleas of the drunkards who will then disappear to be replaced by a group of beautiful women who come forward dancing to the sound of soft music. The most beautiful of all is the maiden Etidorhpa.

Next comes the Middle Circle, a transparent film about seven hundred miles below the surface of the earth. Invisible to the eye, it is a layer of force which, although weightless, induces or conserves gravity. From here one can enter the intra-earth space by leaping from a rock shelf into the void. Here is the junction of the earth's crust and the inner sphere, also known as the End of the Earth. No description is available of the land beyond this point.

The flora of Etidorhpa's Country consists mainly of giant fungus forests of brilliant white, red, yellow and blue, with geometrically patterned stems and the fragrance of pineapple or strawberry. The colours called "primary" on earth's surface are here more finely subdivided, so that many more shades exist in Etidorhpa's Country. The fauna is scarce: insects, birds and flying creatures somewhat like prehistoric reptiles.

(John Uri Lloyd, *Etidorhpa or the End of the Earth, the Strange History of a Mysterious Being and the Account of a Remarkable Journey as Communicated in Manuscript to Llewellyn Drury who Promised to Print the Same but Finally Evaded the Responsibility which was Assumed by John Uri Lloyd,* Cincinnati, 1895)

ETTENMOORS, an area of bleak fells in the north of MIDDLE-EARTH. The fells lie between a western spur of the MISTY MOUNTAINS and the river Mitheithel which runs almost parallel to the mountain spur before flowing south-west across RHUDAUR where it eventually joins the Bruinen. Visitors are advised that there are no bridges over the river in the Ettenmoors. Like Rhudaur, the Ettenmoors are inhabited by trolls, enormous, stupid creatures who appear to kill for pleasure and who often eat their victims after robbing them. The trolls live in caves and must be underground before dawn, or else they will be turned into stones by the light of the sun. It is therefore best to travel through the Ettenmoors during the day.

(J.R.R. Tolkien, *The Fellowship of the Ring,* London, 1954; J.R.R. Tolkien, *The Return of the King,* London, 1955)

ETTINSMOOR, a vast, lonely moorland on the far side of the River Shribble, which limits the marsh areas of north-eastern NARNIA, beyond which lie the wild lands of the north. There are no bridges across the Shribble, but as it is shallow, visitors will find they can easily ford it. The only sounds that can be heard are the calls of the peewits and the curlews, and a hawk may sometimes be glimpsed.

From the west a shallow stream flows down through a gorge to join the Shribble. The gorge is a favourite haunt of the giants of the north lands, who use it as a street. They can often be seen there, with their feet on the bottom of the gorge and their elbows on its rim, as though they were leaning over a fence or wall.

The best-loved sport of these giants is shying rocks at a cairn. This is one of the few games they are capable of understanding, even though they never hit the cairn; visitors who find themselves in the vicinity when this sport is in progress are advised that probably the safest place to be is by the cairn itself. Such games often lead to quarrels, with the giants hitting each other over the head with great stone hammers. Their skulls, however, are so hard that the blows are more likely to hurt the aggressor than his victim.

Beyond the gorge, the moor stretches on for many miles, a bleak, desolate place frequented only by wild fowl. Its northern edge, a ten–day march from the Shribble, breaks into a steep slope descending into a region of cliffs. The country beyond is full of dark precipices, high mountain peaks and deep, narrow, sombre ravines.

At the foot of the slope, a river rushes noisily through a deep gorge full of rapids and waterfalls. The gorge is spanned by an enormous bridge (its arch as high as the dome of St. Paul's Cathedral), now in poor condition but still serviceable. Each of the stones used to build this bridge is as large as the stones of Stonehenge, all intricately carved with the images of giants, minotaurs, squids, centipedes and dreadful gods whose origin and nature can only be guessed at. From here, the road leads northwards to the ruined city of the giants and to HARFUNG.

(C.S. Lewis, *The Silver Chair*, London, 1953)

EUDAEMON, capital of the island of Macaria (not to be confused with the African kingdom of the same name). Eudaemon is a large, magnificent and happily constituted city. Its inhabitants are highly educated and place the good of their republic before their own interests. Rich and poor, high and low work together for the common happiness. Sumptuary laws are strictly enforced, drunkenness is heavily punished and State officials are deprived of their office for any offence. Blasphemy is punished by cutting out the tongue.

The lower classes are not allowed to vote or to share in the government of the city and a notice in Latin is publicly displayed: *Vulgus pessimus rerum gerendarum auctor est.* In fact visitors will notice that signs throughout the city are always in Greek and Latin, the Greek ones being mainly taken from Euripides' *Hecuba.*

The religion of Eudaemon is evangelical but without superstitious observances. No public disputes about religion are allowed and religious opinions can only be expressed by appointed ministers; troublesome philosophers are banished.

(Gaspar Stiblinus, "Commentariolus de Eudaemonensium Republica," in *Coropaedia*, Basle, 1555)

EUDOXIA, a city in Asia, which spreads both upwards and down, with winding alleys, steps, dead ends and hovels. A carpet is preserved in Eudoxia, in which travellers can observe the city's true form. At first sight nothing seems to resemble Eudoxia less than the design of that carpet, laid out in symmetrical motifs whose patterns are repeated along straight and circular lines, interwoven with brilliantly coloured spires, in a repetition that can be followed throughout the whole woof. But if one pauses and examines it carefully, one becomes convinced that each place in the carpet corresponds to a place in the city and all the things contained in the city are included in the design, arranged according to their true relationship, which escapes one's eye distracted by the bustle, the throngs, the shoving. All of Eudoxia's confusion, the mules' braying, the lampblack stains, the fish smell, is what is evident in the incomplete perspective, but the carpet proves that there is a point from which the city shows its true proportions, the geometrical scheme implicit in its every, tiniest detail.

It is easy to get lost in Eudoxia: but when a traveller concentrates and stares at the carpet, he will recognize the street he is seeking in a crimson or indigo or magenta thread which, on a wide loop, brings him to the purple enclosure that is his real destination. Every inhabitant of Eudoxia compares the carpet's immobile order with his own image of the city, an anguish of his own, and each can find, concealed among the arabesques, an answer, the story of his life, the twists of fate.

An oracle was questioned about the mysterious bond between two objects as dissimilar as the carpet and the city. One of the two objects—the oracle replied—has the form the gods gave the starry sky and the orbits in which the worlds revolve; the other is an approximate reflection, like every human creation.

For some time the augurs had been sure that the carpet's harmonious pattern was of divine origin. The oracle was interpreted in this sense, arousing no controversy. But one could, similarly, come to the opposite conclusion: that the true map of the universe is the city of Eudoxia, just as it is, a stain that spreads out shapelessly, with crooked streets, houses that crumble one upon the other amid clouds of dust, fires, screams in the darkness.

(Italo Calvino, *Le città invisibili,* Turin, 1972)

EUGEA, an island in the Atlantic. Its inhabitants, the Symphytes, are a gentle and courageous people. They colonized the island, cut down the forests, cultivated the land, built houses for their families and proclaimed laws for their cities. The religious rites and principles were established in those ancient times by a wise man who wished that his name be forgotten. The great god Théose was to be venerated sixteen times a year, as "inconceivable author of an inconceivable world." According to the wise man's teachings, the goddess Psycholie—who animated nature and all beings including man—impregnated with her fire the goddess Syngènie, who represents the chemical properties of all matter. Many other gods and goddesses represent the essential forces in this world, forces described years afterwards by Sir Isaac Newton. For instance, the tides are represented by the amorous conflicts of three gods: the God of the Ocean, Hélion the Sun and Ménie the Moon. Polar magnetism is symbolized by the twin gods Axigères. Hélion the Sun is the father of Lampèlie (or light) and Pyrophyse (or heat). Because the Symphytes are guided by the secret principles of the universe they are just and brave and were able to fight off an invasion of the inhabitants of ATLANTIS when the latter fled their country after the cataclysm.

(Népoumucène Lemercier, *L'Atlantiade, ou La Théogonie Newtonienne,* Paris, 1812)

EUPHONIA, a small city of some twelve thousand inhabitants in the Harz Mountains, Germany, considered by some visitors to be a gigantic music conservatory because music is the sole activity of its people. All Euphonians—men, women and even children—do nothing but sing, play an instrument or practise some other activity connected with the musical arts. Some make instruments, others print music, yet others spend their time in acoustical research or studying physical phenomena related to sound.

The city is divided into sections corresponding to the various musical activities. Each voice, each instrument has a street that carries its name and is inhabited only by those concerned with that specific talent.

It would not be fair to say that Euphonia, under its military regime, is a despotic tyranny. Certainly it is governed in perfect order with the result that extraordinary works of art have been created. The German government has done everything within its power to make the life of the inhabitants easier and more agreeable, and in return demands no more than to be sent, two or three times a year, some one thousand musicians to take part in different festivities.

The Euphonians otherwise hardly ever leave their city. Instead, those interested in the musical arts come to Euphonia. A large amphitheatre built for twenty thousand people plus ten thousand artists, receives yearly a huge number of tourists who have to pass severe tests before being elected as part of the public.

Euphonian education begins at a very tender age; children are taught all possible rhythmic combinations, then the study of the scales and an instrument of their choice, finally singing and harmony. Upon reaching puberty—that time of life when true passions begin to be felt—adolescents are taught expression and *bello stile.* Sincerity of expression—that rare quality so difficult to appreciate—is held in the highest regard by all Euphonians and is therefore carefully taught. Those individuals who cannot or will not learn true sincerity of expression are exiled from the city, even if their voices or instrumental skills are excellent; however, such renegades are sometimes allowed to live in the farthest houses, preparing skins for drums or stringing instruments.

All teachers have several assistants who specialize in the different branches of each general subject. For instance, while the teacher gives a general dissertation on playing the violin, the assistants will deal with the secrets of *pizzicato,* velocity, and other aspects of the violin.

The beginning and ending of the hours of work and rest are announced by sounding a gigantic organ on top of a tower that dominates the whole city. This five-century-old instrument works on steam and can be heard almost four leagues away. Instructions and general information are also conveyed by the organ, in a musical code that only Euphonians can understand.

When a new musical work is to be tried out, each part is individually studied for three or four days. Then the organ announces a meeting at the theatre of singers. Directed by the choir master, the singers are divided into groups of one hundred, each forming a separate choir. Breathing pauses are so placed that the mass of breathing singers is never above a quarter of the total number and so no audible interruptions spoil the flow of the music.

The musical works are studied first with the intention of being faithful to the text, then in order to get the right gradations, and finally to achieve the right style and expression. All bodily movements that follow the rhythm of the music are severely forbidden to the members of the choir. To improve their technique, the singers are made to exercise in silence—in such perfect silence that the drone of an insect can be heard or a blind man believe he is alone in the theatre. After such pauses, the singers are made to attack a *tutti* and not a single one misses his or her entry. The same work is carried out by the orchestra, and only when both parts are perfect is their union fulfilled; then the two masses, vocal and instrumental, produce a work of art that the public may finally hear.

A clever mechanism, used in Euphonia for the past several centuries, allows the conductor to indicate the movements of his baton to each musician without being visible to the public. In this way his directions reach the musicians immediately without distracting the public's attention.

The philosophy of music is an important science in Euphonia, and the inhabitants study the laws and historical precepts on which musical evolution is based. One of the professors who specialized in this science was responsible for creating the curious custom of bad music concerts. At certain times of the year, Euphonians are invited to listen to the monstrosities which the rest of the world has admired for centuries and whose defects Euphonians are strongly advised to avoid. These concerts include many of the *cavatine e finali* of Italian early-nineteenth-century music, and the more or less religious fugues for several voices written before the twentieth century.

It is almost impossible for uninvited travellers to enter Euphonia; they are required to have mar-

vellous voices, to play practically every instrument, and to pass personality tests judged very harshly by Euphonian officials.

(Hector Berlioz, *Euphonie, ou la ville musicale. Nouvelle de l'avenir,* Paris, 1852)

EURALIA, two joined kingdoms, West Euralia and East Euralia, each ruled by a king and queen, north of the kingdom of Barodia. The landscape is mostly hilly with a few forests and brooks. An important landmark is the palace of Euralia, with guest rooms named according to the colour of their decorations. The palace gardens, of roses and carnations, are looked after by titled members of the court. The magical past of Euralia has been told in *Euralia Past and Present* by Roger Scurvilegs. Dragons are commonplace and wizards are numerous; good wizards, however, are scarce.

(A.A. Milne, *Once on a Time,* London, 1917)

EUSAPIA, a city in Asia, dedicated to the full enjoyment of life. To make the leap from life to death less abrupt, the inhabitants have constructed an identical copy of their city underground. All corpses, dried in such a way that the skeleton remains sheathed in yellow skin, are carried down there to continue their former activities. Of these activities, their carefree moments take first place: most of the corpses are seated around laden tables, or placed in dancing positions, or made to play little trumpets. But all the trades and professions of the living Eusapia are also at work below ground, or at least those that the living performed with more contentment than irritation: the clockmaker, amid all the stopped clocks of his shop, places his parchment ear against an out-of-tune grandfather clock; a barber, with dry brush, lathers the cheekbones of an actor learning his role, studying the script with hollow sockets; a girl with a laughing skull milks the carcass of a heifer.

To be sure, many of the living want a fate after death different from their lot in life: the necropolis is crowded with big-game hunters, mezzo-sopranos, bankers, violinists, duchesses, courtesans, generals—more than the living city ever contained.

The job of accompanying the dead down below and arranging them in the desired place is assigned to a confraternity of hooded brothers. No one else has access to the Eusapia of the dead and everything known about it has been learned from them.

Geographers say that the same confraternity exists among the dead and that it never fails to lend a hand; the hooded brothers, after death, will perform the same job in the other Eusapia; rumour has it that some of them are already dead but continue going up and down. In any case, this confraternity's authority in the Eusapia of the living is vast.

They say that every time they go below they find something changed in the lower Eusapia; the dead make innovations in their city; not many, but surely the fruit of sober reflection, no passing whims. From one year to the next, they say, the Eusapia of the dead becomes unrecognizable. And the living, to keep up with them, also want to do everything that the hooded brothers tell them about the novelties of the dead. So the Eusapia of the living has taken to copying its underground copy.

But the inhabitants of Eusapia have another theory: that actually it was the dead who built the upper Eusapia, in the image of their city. They say that in the twin cities there is no longer any way of knowing who is alive and who is dead.

(Italo Calvino, *Le città invisibili*, Turin, 1972)

EV, a kingdom to the north-west of the desert that surrounds OZ and to the south of NOMELAND, the realm of King Roquat of the Rocks. Ev is now ruled by a young king, Evraldo XV.

The coastal areas of Ev are covered in thick forest, but the capital was built in a beautiful vale of fruit trees and green fields, dotted with farmhouses. The Royal Palace stands in a park adorned with fountains, marble statues, lawns and flower beds. Close to the palace lies the town of Evena itself, famed as the headquarters of Smith and Tinker, the well-known engineers who built Tiktok the Machine-Man, now a respected citizen of neighbouring Oz.

Evraldo XIV, the father of the present ruler, was a tyrant who beat all his servants to death. Unable to damage Tiktok—who can think and speak when correctly wound up—he shut him up in a cave by the sea, flinging the key into the water. His final action was to sell his wife, his five daughters and his five sons to the wicked king of Nomeland, who transformed them into ornaments for

his underground palace. Evraldo then drowned himself in sorrow and remorse.

As his death left the country without a proper ruler, his niece Langwidere took the opportunity to seize power and moved into the palace where she lived alone with her soldiers and her servants. The people of Ev were at a loss as to what to think of Langwidere, who looked different every time they saw her; she was recognizable only by the ruby key that hung at her belt. The explanation was that Langwidere had a collection of thirty different heads, one for each day of the month, and could change them at will; the key opened the cabinet in which the collection of heads was kept. Langwidere's appearance was not the only thing that changed when she put on a new head; her whole character and mood changed as well, which made her a very unpredictable lady.

Visitors to Ev will find that survival is no real problem, as lunch boxes and dinner pails containing ready-cooked meals grow on trees; they are royal property and each pail is marked with the royal *E*. The only sign of danger is a warning written in the sand—"Beware of the Wheelers"—but it should be ignored. The Wheelers live only in the remoter areas of Ev and, despite their air of ferocity, are quite harmless, if somewhat mischievous. Physically they resemble human beings, except that their arms and legs are of equal length and they end in wheels—their equivalent to fingernails. On level ground, the Wheelers can move extremely quickly, but they are incapable of crossing rough or rocky ground. They can run people over, but cannot grip anything and are unlikely to hurt anyone seriously. In fact, they are quite helpless and can only protect themselves by making others believe that they are really ferocious. The Wheelers dress in bright multicoloured clothes and jaunty straw hats.

(L. Frank Baum, *Ozma of Oz*, Chicago, 1907; L. Frank Baum, *The Road to Oz*, Chicago, 1909)

EVARCHIA, a country in the Balkan peninsula, a kingdom until 1978, when it was taken over by the National Military Government. The islands off the coast of Evarchia were annexed in the ninth century, making Evarchia an empire; the islanders had asked for protection against pirates and the change-over was bloodless. Several of these islands are named after the spices they produce,

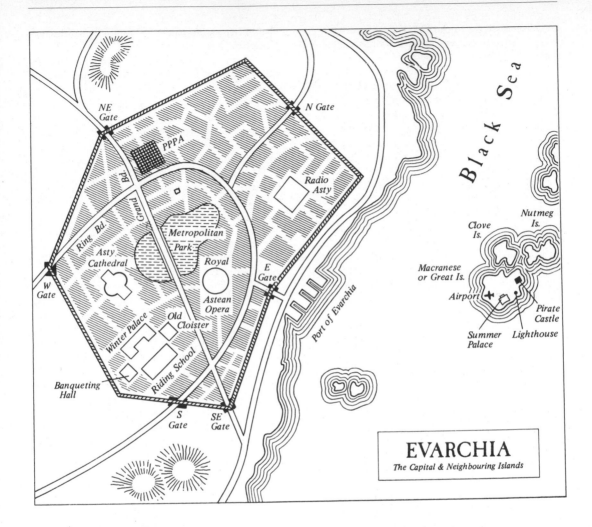

EVARCHIA
The Capital & Neighbouring Islands

like Nutmeg Island or Clove Island. Travellers are advised to visit the Great or Macranese Island, where the airport is located. The Summer Palace can be seen here near the Old Lighthouse, not far from another of the island's main features, the Pirate Castle, partially destroyed in the 1566 earthquake. A typical species of the island fauna, the island finch, can be easily spotted on Macranese Island. Known to the adult islanders as "gaudybird" and to the children as "bobby-dazzler," its breast is green and its spread wings are streaked with scarlet, although giving an overall impression of blue or turquoise. It is the size of a green finch and has a small yellow parroty beak.

The capital is on the mainland and the sparsely furnished Winter Palace, with its beautiful Gothic windows and post-pre-Raphaelite decorations, was built here in 1869. Three other buildings with notable façades surround the palace: the domed Riding School with its rising left end that squares itself off and becomes a clock tower; the Banqueting Hall to the left of the Palace, pilastered, corniced and cartouched; the Old Cloister to the right. The Royal Astean Opera and Asty Cathedral are also worth a visit. The Metropolitan Park lies in the centre of Evarchia, and to the east, in the Asty district, are the famous gardens maintained by the Ministerium for Parks, Ponds, Public Monuments and Culture (PPPC). Two wide and tree-lined boulevards cross the wintry capital: the Grand Boulevard and the Ring Boulevard.

Evarchia has a national radio, Radio Asty,

The clock tower of the Riding School in the centre of EVARCHIA.

and several newspapers and magazines: *The Times of Asty, The Astean Times, The Evarchian Gem-Collector Monthly* and *Red Racket*. Only one great novel has been written in Evarchian; an English translation was published in 1954 by the Grey Walls Press. Most people speak English as well as Evarchian, though islanders and peasants pronounce the *v* soft, as an *f*. According to Catholic and Precanonical Church of Evarchia tradition the major winter festival is Epiphany but visitors are advised that Christmas, though a comparatively minor feast, is also celebrated.

(Brigid Brophy, *Palace without Chairs: A Baroque Novel*, London, 1978)

EVILEYE LAND, a land near the North Pole, inhabited by a tribe of nomadic hunters. Certain of their women possess the evil eye and are powerful practitioners of the magic arts, which they use for the protection of their people in these desolate and barren lands.

Visitors are warned that these women are able to bewitch, or even kill, with their stare. In one eye they have a double pupil, and in the other the likeness of a horse. It has been reported that there are more women of this kind among the Bitiae of Scythia and among another tribe living in the Pontus.

(Apollonius of Rhodes, *Argonautica*, 2nd cen. BC; Pliny the Elder, *Inventorum Natura*, 1st cen. AD)

EWAIPANOMA, the name given to an area around the Coara River, a tributary of the Orinoco. The land is covered in dense jungle and is the realm of the tribe who give it its name. The natives are mighty warriors who have absolute control of their territory; few outsiders have seen them. Those who have describe the Ewaipanomas as possessing eyes in their shoulders and mouths in the middle of their breasts, with a ridge, or train, of long hair growing between their shoulders.

(Sir Walter Raleigh, *The Discoverie of the lovlie, rich and beautiful Empyre of Guiana with a relation of the great and golden City of Manoa (which the Spanyards call El Dorado) And the Provinces of Emerria, Arromania, and of other countries, with their rivers, adjoyning. Performed in the year 1595 by Sir Walter Ralegh, Knight, Captaine of Her Majesty's Guard, Warder of the Stanneries and Her Majesty's Lord Lieutenant of the Countie of Cornewalle*, London, 1596)

EXHAM PRIORY, the ruins of an ancient and noble mansion near Anchester village, Wales. It remained uninhabited for three centuries after a hideous tragedy which struck down the master, five of his children and several servants, casting a cloud of suspicion over the third son. Its architecture comprises Gothic towers resting on a Saxon or Romanesque substructure whose foundation, in turn, is Roman or even Druidic. This foundation is a very singular thing, merging on one side with the solid limestone of the precipice overlooking a desolate valley.

Exham Priory was bought in 1918 and occupied in 1923 by a descendant of the baronial family that had owned the Priory. When the new owner's cats became intensely agitated on hearing certain noises within the Priory walls, the owner and a friend decided to investigate and found their way down a stone staircase into a room completely covered with human or semi-human remains. A few steps further on, they found a twilight grotto of enormous height stretching farther than any eye could see, a subterranean world combining Roman ruins, a sprawling Saxon pile and an early English edifice of wood. But these were dwarfed by an insane tangle of human bones in postures of demonic frenzy—the remains of prisoners kept by the ancient lords of the Priory as fodder for the savage rats that inhabit, even today, these underground regions.

Days later, the new owner of Exham Priory was found crouching over the half-eaten body of his friend like a demon rat, purging with his sin the sins of his ancestors.

(Howard Phillips Lovecraft, "The Rats in the Walls," in *The Outsider and Others*, Sauk City, 1939)

EXOPOTAMIA, a vast deserted country that can be reached in two different ways. The first is by taking a train from Paris to the coast, then a ship, then a train again and finally a rented car or a taxi. It is necessary to reserve seats in advance for the train and for the ship. The latter is usually so full of passengers that it nearly touches the bottom of the sea. Young female travellers are warned that the captain is a dirty old man, much inclined to pinching the bottoms of young girls. Food on board consists mainly of veal fricassee, seafood ripened in the sun and soup.

The second way of arriving in Exopotamia is by taking the 975 bus from the terminus. From time to time the driver becomes insane and, instead of taking the normal route through Paris, joins one of the larger national highways and drives straight on to Exopotamia for no extra charge.

The climate in Exopotamia is very warm; it is never windy and because of the total lack of air the atmosphere seems very healthy. Travellers must be careful when walking on the golden sand, as whoever remains standing is likely to grow roots.

The vegetation is rather poor. Notable is the *scrub spinifex*, a thorny plant that hangs on to the ankles of passersby and can be rather painful. Certain long creepers will tickle the soles of those who walk barefoot in the dunes; if these creepers are cut, a strong smell of resin embalms the atmosphere and thick drops of a sticky substance fall to the ground. In the short green grass small yellow snails can be found, as well as sand *lumettes*. Children amuse themselves by hunting these *lumettes;* eating one, however, can make a child sick. Should one tread upon one of the yellow snails, the shell will crack and a transparent drop of water in the form of a heart will appear.

The most striking characteristic of Exopotamia is the sun, which gives an unequal light throughout this country. Seen from the dunes, the sun appears crossed by light and dark stripes: the parts of Exopotamia illuminated by the light stripes are remarkably hot, those under the dark stripes are cold. If a visitor standing in a light zone extends his hand into a dark zone, it will disappear before his very eyes.

The famous hotel and restaurant owned by Joseph Barrizone, alias Pippo, alias La Pipe, has now disappeared. The railway line crossed the site of the hotel and a large hole swallowed up the entire building.

The population of Exopotamia is, of course, large since it is a desert country; there is lots of room and therefore many people go to live there.

(Boris Vian, *L'Automne à Pékin*, Paris, 1956)

EXPIATION CITY, somewhere in Europe. Built on a wide river that crosses a large plain, Expiation City is surrounded by high walls with only one gate and is divided into the Upper Town, which lodges the government, public buildings and the houses of merchants and craftsmen, and the Lower Town, inhabited by those undergoing expiation. In the suburbs are small houses with gardens and farms, inhabited by those who have completed expiation. The Lower Town, divided into sixty hamlets or regions, is referred to as "the Desert" and is walled within the city walls. The Desert is patrolled by supervisors and soldiers and the hamlets are segregated by sex. Between the Upper and Lower towns are twelve Catholic chapels and a few Protestant churches.

Expiation City was founded for those who need or desire social re-education or for those who wish to atone for their personal moral or spiritual weaknesses. Those who come to Expiation City undergo a civil death. For an initial period, the neophyte is held in a prison called "the Tomb." His former life is abolished and for thirty days he has no name. He is then visited by priests and judges who explain to him the Christian doctrine. The neophyte is given a new name and assigned a residence in the Lower Town. During his entire stay, he must never say why he has come: his past has been abolished and violation of the rule results in a dreadful punishment. The neophyte's lodging is constantly changed to prevent him from becoming attached to his place of residence; this reinforces the idea that nothing in life is stable, that life is a voyage to a land of exile, and that a fixed abode is a reward for exceptionally good conduct. He may write to his friends and family, but his letters will be censored. Finally, after his period of atonement, he may return to his country of origin. Throughout the city, celibacy and silence are observed. The only sounds that can be heard are the morning and evening litanies.

Expiation City is governed by a dictator who alone is responsible to the king of the country. The dictator's residence resembles a gigantic cube of granite, with a broad courtyard in front and gardens in the back, reminiscent of ancient Egyptian architecture. Near the residence is the courthouse, with a single, low, narrow entrance and no windows; the prison is attached to the courthouse. In the Lower Town, the houses are built in the shape of tents, with only one room. The furniture is sparse: a bed, a table, a chair, a lamp, a clock and a copy of the *Christian Manual*. The floor is wooden, the windows barred and the door locked from the outside. The houses are built around three sides of a square that has a fountain and a few fruit trees in the middle; the fourth side is occupied by the superintendent's house. Visitors will notice, throughout the town, statues of those poets and philosophers considered to be benefactors of humanity.

The main building in Expiation City is the moated temple, with no visible gate. Visitors are led here blindfolded. Inside, the ceiling is gilded, the floors are of mosaic and an avenue of columns leads to a huge obelisk. The temple is crowned by a splendid blue dome supported by a circle of caryatides.

Travellers need letters of introduction to visit Expiation City. They will be housed in the city's only hotel and may not go out alone into the streets.

(P.S. Ballanches, *La Ville des expiations*, Paris, 1907)

F

FAIRYLAND, a country of changing locations, which can be visited only by those with a reason for coming—be it known to them or only to the spirits who have charge of them. It is reached via several paths leading through a thick forest. Near the edge of the forest stands a cottage, its corners formed by four great trees whose branches meet and intertwine above the roof. The woman who lives here on the edge of Fairyland has fairy blood, and in the cottage garden, flower fairies can be seen whose outer bodies—the flowers themselves—die when the fairies go away. The trees at the four corners of the cottage are oaks which protect both the cottage and its inhabitants from the evil ash tree which frightens people to death. The forest itself, which must be crossed, is also full of various fairies and more sinister creatures like goblins. The goblins live in an underground realm where no trees or plants grow; their language is incomprehensible to humans. They amuse themselves by rushing together in a heap and writhing like entangled snakes.

The trees of Fairyland are full of strange fruits and nuts, all of which are edible. The beech tree has the form and voice of a woman and protects travellers from goblins. The alder tree is capable of changing appearance in order to lure people to her grotto and deliver them to the ash

The cottage on the edge of the forest in southern FAIRYLAND.

tree. The animals of Fairyland are not dangerous and their speech is comprehensible to humans.

After about a day's walk through the forest, the traveller comes upon a steep, rocky hill. At its foot is a small cave with a bas-relief representing the story of Pygmalion. A further day's walk brings one to a farmhouse already part of Fairyland. Several interesting buildings should be visited here. The House of the Ogre is a long, low hut, built against a tall cypress in a small clearing. Should a traveller open the door of a particular closet in this house, he will find his own shadow which will follow him everywhere.

The white marble palace of Fairyland stands on the banks of a river. By night it shimmers softly in the moonlight which is not reflected in the windows. In the courtyard is a fountain of porphyry. Visitors will find that their rooms, prepared for them by invisible hands, have been made to resemble their own rooms in every detail. In the blue-ceilinged hall there is a pool as large as an underground sea, with wondrous caves and corals of every hue. The library contains books which so absorb the reader that he becomes the traveller in a travel book, the hero in a novel or play; as he reads on, the story becomes his own. Another hall, filled with subdued crimson light, is supported by slender black pillars that intersect against the ceiling, forming a black and white pattern like the skeleton of a leaf. The voice of anyone who is moved to sing here is astonishingly beautiful. Embroidered draperies conceal the entrance to yet another hall with a black ceiling and floor and dark red pillars. Here stand white statues on black pedestals depicting various positions of a waltz, so that a visitor has the impression that the statues have just stopped dancing.

Finally, visitors are urged to visit a cottage on a peninsula which can be reached through several tunnels. As long as the fire is kept burning in the hearth it is always daytime in the cottage. Inside, there are four doors: the door of childhood, the door of sighs, the door of dismay and the door of the timeless. It is possible to return through any of these doors by finding the mark = on the wood.

Money is of no use in Fairyland and fairies are seriously offended if it is offered to them. Time seems longer than in other places; a journey lasting twenty-one days will seem to the traveller to last twenty-one years.

(George Macdonald, *Phantastes*, London, 1858)

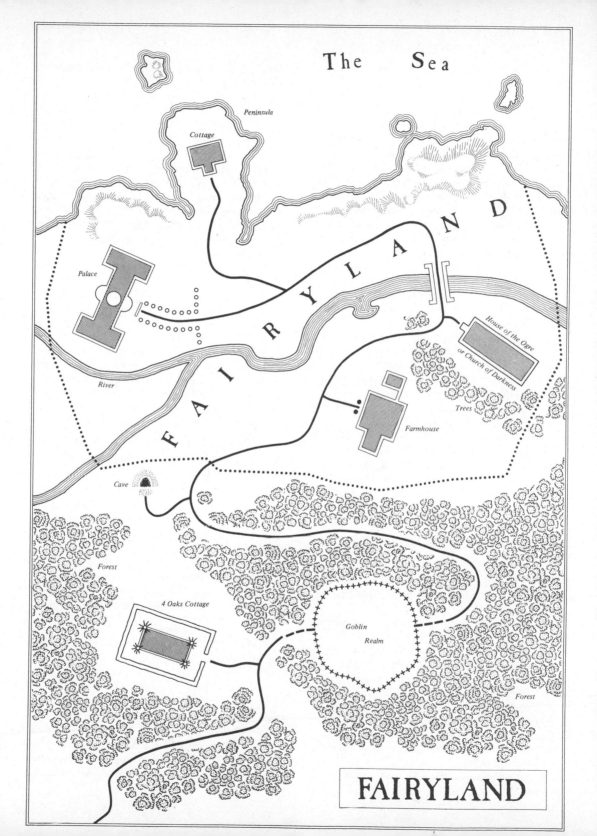

The Sea

Peninsula

Cottage

FAIRYLAND

Palace

River

House of the Ogre
or Church of Darkness

Trees

Farmhouse

Cave

Forest

4 Oaks Cottage

Goblin
Realm

Forest

FAIRYLAND

FAITH, LAND OF, see BRAGMAN.

FAKREDDIN VALLEY, a beautiful valley ruled
by the Emir Fakreddin, between SAMARAH and
the ruined palace at ISHTAKAR. The floor of the
valley is fringed with flowering shrubs and partly
covered by a wood of palm trees; the trees shade a
gracious building crowned with airy domes. Each
of the building's nine bronze doors bears the inscription "This is the asylum of pilgrims, the
refuge of travellers and the depository of secrets
from all parts of the world."

Inside, guests are received beneath a vast concave ceiling illuminated by lamps of rock crystal.
Sherbet is served in vases of the same material, accompanied by a wide range of delicacies, from rice
boiled in almond milk to saffron soup. A thin veil
of carnation-coloured silk masks the doorway leading to the oval baths of porphyry and to the harem.

The valley is a meeting-place for wandering
holy men from all over the Middle East and even
from as far away as India. Cripples and people suffering from every describable affliction also make
their way here, certain that the emir and his attendants will help alleviate their sufferings.

Surrounded by barren deserts, the valley of
Fakreddin is like an emerald set in lead. It is in fact
so pleasant that it is even said that the clouds to the
west are the domes of Shadukian and Amberabad,
the dwelling-places of the delicate peris, gentle
fairy-like beings who direct the pure in mind on
the way to heaven.

(William Beckford, *Vathek*, Lucerne, 1787)

FALUN, open-pit mines measuring almost 360
metres in length, 160 metres in width and 60 metres in depth.

The great Falun Fault has been described as
the "gaping jaws of an apocalyptic vision." The
steep, blackish-brown walls at the entrance to the
mine level out to great heaps of rubble and fallen
rocks. The bottom contains entrance-ways to galleries supported by metal frames similar to those
used in *blockhaus* architecture. No vegetation, no
light; all one finds is a confused pile of rocks and
slag, some ore and suffocating gas. One can easily
imagine Dante encountering a similar entrance at
the gates of Hades.

Nevertheless, a traveller with a pure heart

need not be afraid to follow the miners through
these unfriendly depths. His most magnificent
dreams will become reality as he is overcome by
adoration of the mysterious Queen of Falun. He
will watch as the decor of deformed, petrified
monsters is transformed into a truly celestial vision of paradise; he will see marvellous plants
made of brightly shining metal sprout from the
ground. The ground becomes transparent revealing the plant roots; but more appealing is the sight
of countless intertwined young girls who dally
under the trees and beckon with white arms.
Higher on the metal trees hang fruit, flowers and
brightly sparkling stones.

The queen rewards her intrepid miners for
their diligence by asking the Prince of Metals to
show her where the trap-rock veins and rich veins
of iron are to be found in concentrated amounts,
instead of spread out into threads of selvage.

The powerful and maternal queen draws in
any traveller who has a pure heart and a naive and
melancholy soul, and who turns away from earthly
pleasures running him through with a burning ray
of light to annihilate him in a sea of happiness. But
she will bury alive anyone who keeps in his heart
even a drop of love for someone in the world under
the open sky.

(Ernst Theodor Amadeus Hoffmann, *Die Berg-
werke zu Falun*, Berlin, 1819)

FANATTIA, an island of the RIALLARO ARCHI-
PELAGO in the south-east Pacific, not far from
the island of SPECTRALIA. It is inhabited by mad
quixotists who, convinced that certain foods,
drinks, clothing or gestures are injurious to the
health, devote their energies to bringing about the
abolition of these assorted vices by fighting over
their opinions like scorpions in a bottle.

(Godfrey Sweven, *Riallaro, the Archipelago of Exiles*, New York & London, 1901; Godfrey Sweven,
Limanora, the Island of Progress, New York & London, 1903)

FANGORN FOREST, an ancient forest to the
east of the southern end of the MISTY MOUN-
TAINS. The eastern slopes of Methedras, the
southernmost peak of the Misty Mountains, are
within the forest itself. Fangorn Forest, once part
of the great forest which stretched as far as the

Ered Luin, the Blue Mountains, in the north-west of MIDDLE-EARTH, and which also included the area now known as the OLD FOREST, is a shaggy, overgrown tangle of trees which often gives those who enter it a feeling of great disquiet. Some describe it as airless, dim and stuffy, others say that they feel tension and anger, as if they were being constantly watched. It has the reputation of being an evil and dangerous place and visitors are warned that if they cut any part of a living tree that grows there, they do so on peril of their lives.

In the Common Speech of Middle-Earth Fangorn means "Tree-beard." Treebeard is the guardian of the forest and eldest of the ents, or Onodrim, the tree-herds or shepherds of the trees, one of the oldest living creatures in all of Middle-earth. The ents vary considerably in appearance and resemble different species of trees. Some are like the chestnut, with brown skin, splay-fingered hands and short thick legs; others resemble the ash and have many fingers, long legs and a greyish complexion; some have three toes, others as many as nine. But a feature they all share is the eyes, with a characteristic slow, thoughtful expression and a green flicker. In general they are tall, dressed in grey or brown hides and with long grey or greyish-green beards. Fangorn himself is at least fourteen feet tall, with seven root-like toes on each foot; he has a large head and almost no neck, and a bushy grey beard. His eyes are said to "sparkle with the light of the present," but also seem to have "great depths of past memories and wisdom."

The ents are the oldest inhabitants of Middle-earth. When the elves first awakened in Middle-earth, Yavanna (literally, "Giver of Fruits") summoned the ents to go among the *olvar* (living things which do not move as opposed to living things which can move freely—the *kelvar*) because she was afraid for the safety of her creations, especially the trees. Yavanna had learned of the coming of the dwarves, who would need wood for their crafts.

For countless years the ents walked the forested lands which stretched from Northern Eriador to Fangorn, protecting and tending their herds of trees. Originally, the ents lived and travelled together with the entmaidens and the ent-wives. The latter are said to have been lovely and fleet of foot in their youth, but bent and sunburnt in their maturity. Gradually the ents and the ent-wives began to go their different ways: the ents took to the forests and mountains, where they lived on wild fruit and talked with the trees and the elves; the entwives were drawn to smaller trees and to the meadow-lands outside the great forests. Here they wandered far and wide, commanding the trees and flowers to flourish and creating beautiful gardens wherever they went. Eventually, they crossed the GREAT RIVER and passed on their knowledge of plants to men. During the Second Age of Middle-earth they disappeared, and their gardens, laid waste during the wars, fell desolate and became known as the Brown Lands. The search of the ents for their lost companions is recorded in the songs of the elves, but the ents themselves made no songs and merely chanted the names of the entwives. Nowadays some ents are still relatively lively, but many have become sleepy and tree-ish in nature. Others have awoken and have been found to be thoroughly bad, a legacy of the days of darkness when the shadow of Morgoth lay heavy on Middle-earth. A few bad ents can be seen in the Old Forest, but the majority are in Fangorn, where, in some areas, the darkness never lifted at all.

The ents live in enthouses, which vary considerably in appearance and nature. Treebeard himself usually lives in Wellinghall, at the foot of the Last Mountain and close to the stream of the Entwash, which rises in the mountains above. Two evergreen trees stand as living gateposts, lifting their branches to allow the ent to pass through them onto a level space cut into the side of the mountain. On either side, the rock walls slope upwards to a height of about fifty feet. At the back, an arched bay is hollowed out of the rock. Trees line the walls on either side and their branches meet overhead to provide a partial covering for the outer area. A stream tumbles down the rear wall, forming a fine curtain of spray before the rock bay, and flowing into a stone basin before running out to join the Entwash. The only items of furniture are a stone table and a bed on low legs, covered with dried grasses and bracken. Lighting is provided by two vessels filled with water; when Treebeard places his hands over them, they glow green and light up the recess and the trees beyond it. Even though other enthouses differ in shape and form, all contain running water.

Ents live on *entdraught*, a liquid which tastes like the water of the Entwash but also has the flavour of the forest air. It is a powerful restorative, providing immense reserves of energy and vigour. During the War of the Ring, two hobbits from the SHIRE lived for many days on *entdraught*, and as a result grew remarkably tall for hobbits.

Ents do not die naturally, although they can be killed. Their physical strength is awesome: iron crumples like thin tin at a blow from an ent's fist and they can tear a rock apart with their fingers and toes as easily as if it were a breadcrust. Their thick, tough skin protects them, and arrows and swords cannot harm them. A heavy blow from an axe will wound them, but no man will be given an opportunity to strike a second blow. The ents are, however, extremely vulnerable to fire.

As a race, the ents are wary, cautious and slow of speech, taking a long time to reach any decision, perhaps because of their great age and wisdom and their awareness of the complexity of everything. Their passions are rarely fired. The one thing guaranteed to rouse them is a threat to themselves or to the trees. When such a threat is perceived, the change in them is startling; from being slow, patient and somewhat melancholy they become fearsome and terribly savage.

The same ponderous character appears in their language, which is extremely difficult to learn. It is slow and repetitious; it seems to be devoid of the concept of an object divorced from its context. Thus when Treebeard says his name, it is as though he were telling a story: the name grows as his life lasts longer. The only known written record of Entish is contained in the *Red Book of the Shire;* Treebeard translated his "a-lalla-lalla-rumba-kamanda-lindor-burúmë" as "The thing we are on, where I stand and look out on fine mornings, think about the grass beyond the woods, and the horses and the clouds and the unfolding of the world." The two hobbits who recorded this example of Entish told Treebeard that it simply meant a hill. His reply typifies much of the character of the ents: "A hasty word for a thing which has stood here ever since this part of the world was shaped."

The knowledge of the ents is ancient and immense. They regard themselves as elves in that they are better at understanding other things and less self-centred than men, and as men in that they are more adaptable than elves. Their superiority over both is that they are steadier and keep their minds on things longer.

Fangorn is also the home of the strange and dangerous creatures known as Huorns, who are thought to be ents who have come to resemble trees. They are wild creatures, capable of extremely swift movements and of wrapping themselves in shadows so that they become almost invisible. The Huorns are spread around Fangorn, and in the surrounding dales, where they watch over the trees. With the ents, led by Treebeard, the Huorns fought on the side of men during the War of the Ring, and played an important role.

Since the disappearance of the entwives it is sometimes thought that this ancient race is on the road to extinction. It is foretold, however, that ents and entwives will one day come together again when both have lost everything.

(J.R.R. Tolkien, *The Fellowship of the Ring,* London, 1954; J.R.R. Tolkien, *The Two Towers,* London, 1954; J.R.R. Tolkien, *The Return of the King,* London, 1955; J.R.R. Tolkien, *The Silmarillion,* London, 1977)

FANTASTICA, a land without borders. No precise geographic description of this region can be given, nor is it possible to draw a map of it. The geographic locations of its countries, rivers, seas and mountains—even the directions on its compass—change constantly. Since distances cannot be measured, concepts such as "far" and "near" are completely subjective, as are the times of day and the seasons. Moreover, the latter are determined by different laws than in our own world: one may find a frozen polar landscape right next to a burning desert.

Fantastica has a vast range of features: woods, moors (such as the notorious Moldymoor by Lake Foamingbroth—the homeland of the willo'-the-wisps—and the Swamps of Sadness), mountain ranges (the charming landscape of the Mountains of Destiny, the Silver Mountains and the Dead Mountains), crags and the so-called Deep Chasm, half a mile wide, that almost cuts the country into two halves. It also has a great variety of inhabitants, who are often not on good terms with each other. There are the tinies, for example, who construct their cities on tree branches; their little houses are connected to each other by rope ladders, staircases and slides. In the Howling Forest live the bark trolls, both male and female, who look like tree stumps. The so-called rock chewers live there, too, on a mountain which they are gradually devouring (it is already as full of holes as a piece of Swiss cheese). Beings with bodies made of fire move through the flaming streets of the city of Salamander, while in the Land of the Sassafranians people are born old and die as infants.

A trip to Fantastica should include a visit to the Singing Tree Country, the Glass Tower of Eribo, the Grass Ocean beyond the Silver Mountains and the jungle temple of Muwamath, with its moonstone column swinging in the air. A unique natural spectacle awaits the traveller in Perilin the Night Forest, which changes at dawn into Goab, the Desert of Colours. Botanists should not pass up a chance to see the garden of meat-eating orchids which belongs to Horok Castle, home of the most powerful sorceress in the land, but visitors should avoid meeting her if possible.

One of the largest cities in Fantastica is Spook City, in the Land of Ghosts, with whole districts of great palaces whose façades are decorated with large figures representing demons or skeletons. Spook City is empty and abandoned. Its inhabitants, hypnotized *en masse,* lost all hope and committed suicide by throwing themselves into a growing vacuum called the Nothing.

Another highlight of Fantastica is the Silver City of Amarganth, one of the most beautiful places in the country. It is ruled by its oldest inhabitant, be it a man or a woman. Amarganth is located on a violet-blue lake surrounded by wooded hills. Its houses are built on ships, which means that whenever friends wish to live together (or enemies wish to part) the ships need only be moved to another part of the city. Streets and bridges connect the ships, and the barges bearing the larger palaces. The skiffs on the canals are made of silver, as are the windows, balconies and towers of the houses. Silver was used because the city was once on the Moru (or Lake of Tears) as a defence against attacks, and the lake's water was so salty that it could eat through most materials—such as those used in an enemy's boats and troops—in an extremely short period of time, before a foe could reach the city. Only silver could withstand the effects of the water.

Today the city is a tourist attraction and overflows at times with visitors. A particular attraction is the Amarganth Library, located inside a gigantic silver box aboard a perfectly round ship. On the windowless walls are several storeys of books,

numbering in the thousands—the complete works of the poet Bastian Balthasar Bux.

The residence of Fantastica's ruler, the Childlike Empress, is an ivory tower shaped like a sugar-loaf, with its point in the clouds. It is located on a vast plain that has been made into a maze of flowerbeds, hedges and paths. The tower is twisted like a snail's shell; it is made of the finest ivory carved into gates, staircases and little houses with alcoves, balconies, turrets and domes, all closely fitted together. The main street winds around the tower in a narrowing spiral. Above the houses is the circular throne room, and at the very top, in a pavilion shaped like a magnolia blossom, are the chambers of the Childlike Empress. No path or stairway leads there, and no one who has been there recalls how he managed to make his way up the smooth sides to the top.

No other country on earth is as dependent on tourism as Fantastica. If its visitors ever stayed away, the entire empire would be swallowed up by the Nothing that surrounds it. Fortunately, the arrival of a single traveller is enough to restore Fantastica to health.

Travellers are warned that while Fantastica is an entrancing place to visit, too long a stay can cause the tourist to forget his identity; he will then have to stay in Fantastica forever. Such travellers stay in the City of the Old Emperors, a place where insanity and absurdity reign.

Finally, mention should be made of other prominent visitors to Fantastica, whose traces the traveller may encounter: these range from Homer, Rabelais and a certain Shexpir, to Borges, Tolkien, Lewis, Magritte, Dali, Arcimboldo and many others.

(Michael Ende, *Die unendliche Geschichte,* Stuttgart, 1979)

FANTIPPO, a kingdom in West Africa. The capital of the same name stands at the mouth of the Little Fantippo River which flows into the Bight of Benin some fifty or sixty miles east of the mouth of the Niger. The capital is bright, cheerful and large, almost the size of a European city. It is not, however, considered an important port and only a few ships a year call there.

Fantippo is remarkable for two things: its postal system and its celebration of Christmas, although it is not a Christian country. The postal system was introduced by King Koko, who was so impressed by what he heard of the European postal system that he immediately decided to emulate it. Stamps were printed and letter-boxes were set up at the corners of the streets, but the system initially failed to work since the people believed in the magical power of the stamps and did not see the need for actual postmen. When King Koko realized what was wrong, he remedied matters by importing postmen's uniforms and setting his men to work. The uniforms imported from England proved too hot for the climate and the typical Fantippo postman's uniform evolved: a smart cap, a string of beads and a mail bag. The system began to work and soon became immensely popular. In a sense, its very popularity led to its downfall. Stamps were so sought after that people began to make suits from them; garments of this kind soon became prized possessions. By chance, two European stamp collectors came to Fantippo looking for the rare twopenny-halfpenny Fantippo red (no longer printed because the king found that his picture was not sufficiently flattering). As the two collectors stepped ashore, they saw the stamp they were looking for on the coat of the porter carrying their bags and immediately began to outbid one another for it. King Koko heard of this and, learning of the value given to stamps by collectors, began to print them for collections rather than for use in the postal system. The mail service became badly neglected as Fantippo began to export vast quantities of stamps for the international collectors' market.

The difficulties of the postal service were remedied by Dr. John Dolittle, who visited Fantippo on his return from one of his journeys of exploration. Under his guidance a new system was set up, using birds as postmen. A separate mail service was organized for animals and birds, with its headquarters on a houseboat off NO MAN'S LAND. The overseas service was particularly efficient and rapid, as it used migrating birds as couriers; a letter could be sent to America and a reply received within twenty-four hours.

The introduction of Christmas celebrations was a direct result of the reorganization of the postal services. A Cockney sparrow, who was brought in to organize mail deliveries in the capital, was affronted to learn that the postmen would not receive Christmas presents, as Christmas was not celebrated in Fantippo. He and the other post-birds refused to deliver mail unless Christmas and Christmas presents were introduced. Accordingly, the custom of giving gifts at that time of year was quickly established and has since continued, much to the surprise of the first missionaries to visit the country. The same sparrow was responsible for the introduction of letter-boxes in all Fantippo's houses.

Dr. Dolittle's other major innovation was the setting up of a weather bureau, using high-flying birds as meteorological observers. The system was extremely successful and encouraged the Fantippans to build large boats and to sail farther than they had ever done before, as they had always been afraid of running into storms at sea.

(Hugh Lofting, *Doctor Dolittle's Post Office*, London, 1924; Hugh Lofting, *Doctor Dolittle and the Secret Lake*, London, 1949)

FARANDOULIE, a vast kingdom in Australia, built near the ruins of Melbourne. It was founded by Saturnin Farandoul, a Frenchman who had been brought up by apes on an island near Borneo. Captured by pirates but rescued by other apes, Saturnin Farandoul invaded the state of Victoria in south-east Australia towards the end of the nineteenth century and defeated the British army.

He became Saturnin I and established a kingdom in which the laws of men and the laws of apes were the same and in which creatures with two hands and creatures with four hands could live in peaceful harmony. Though the intention of Saturnin I was to conquer India as well, and liberate the apes of Asia, the vast enterprise collapsed when the British corrupted his army of fifty thousand apes by introducing them to Scotch whisky and English girls.

Visitors today can visit the beautiful capital of Farandoulie built on the blueprints of Melbourne. The latter was destroyed when Saturnin's army attacked the Melbourne Aquarium to rescue a woman with whom Saturnin I had fallen in love and who had been kidnapped by the chief biologist. The true facts of this campaign have not been fully investigated but will certainly come to light when the definitive history of the Australian continent is finally written.

(Albert Robida, *Voyages Très Extraordinaires de Saturnin Farandoul dans les 5 ou 6 parties du monde [et dans tous les pays connus et même inconnus de M. Jules Verne]*, Paris, 1879)

FARGHESTAN, a country lying across the Sea of the Sirtes, opposite ORSENNA. The capital, Rhages, stands on the lower slopes of Tangri, a volcano which was for a long time thought to be extinct, but which has recently shown new signs of activity. Rhages is also the main port of Farghestan and its approach is protected by a line of reefs.

For three hundred years, Farghestan has officially been at war with Orsenna, but as no major interests are involved there has been little conflict of late. The hatred between the two nations stems from Farghestan's pirate raids on its neighbour's southern coast and from Orsennian reprisals. In the past, these reprisals have included the siege and bombing of Rhages, an event which is still celebrated in Orsenna.

The Seal of the Chancery of Rhages is a chimera enclasped with a serpent.

(Julien Gracq, *Le Rivage des Syrtes*, Paris, 1951)

FATTIPUFF and THINIFER KINGDOMS, below the Forest of Fontainebleau. Travellers wishing to visit either of these two kingdoms should go to the Roche Jumelle or Twin Rock, near the Castle of Fontainebleau, where a long staircase descends into the bowels of the earth. This whole underground region is illuminated by large balloons filled with a blue, dazzling gas, which float in the underground sky, allowing a splendid view of the magnificent villas set among the cliffs.

At the bottom of the staircase a narrow quay borders a large gulf. The traveller has the choice of two liners: the *Fattiport*, painted red, and the *Thiniport*, made of glittering steel. The red ship, commanded by a stout captain, leads to Fattiburg, capital of the Fattipuff Kingdom. The steel vessel, under the orders of an authoritarian captain, a dry and bony man, will take the traveller to Thinigrad, capital of the Thinifer Kingdom.

Fattipuffs and Thinifers do not mix. The Fattipuffs are friendly, happy people, who live only for eating and drinking. In their kingdom, everything is round and cushioned, their architecture is rumbustious, their art baroque. The Thinifers instead are frighteningly thin, as hard as nails and as yellow as custard, living in a mad rush, hardly eating, drinking nothing but water and working to exhaustion. They pretend that their life-style has given them the best of all possible worlds and incite all visitors to emulate their ways.

For centuries Fattipuffs and Thinifers have been mortal enemies. In the middle of the stretch of sea that separates the two kingdoms is an island called Fattifer by the Fattipuffs and Thinipuff by the Thinifers. To avoid confusion, it has been suggested that the island be called Pink, and travellers should opt for this last name when speaking of the island to an inhabitant of either of the two kingdoms.

(André Maurois, *Patapoufs et Filifers*, Paris, 1930)

FAY, ISLAND OF THE, a small, round island in a river, near a waterfall, somewhere in the mountains of the United States. The grass is short, springy, sweet-scented, and interspersed with asphodel. The trees are lithe, mirthful, erect, bright, slender, graceful as Eastern figures, with a smooth, glossy and particoloured bark. The eastern end of the island lies in the blackest shade, with many small, unsightly hillocks, supposed to be the green tombs of the Fays, the inhabitants of the island. The lifecycles of the Fays are brief; every time they go from light to shade, it is as if they went from summer to winter.

(Edgar Allan Poe, "The Island of the Fay," in *Tales*, New York, 1845)

FEATHER ISLAND, in the Indian Ocean, discovered in 1784 by the Chevalier de l'Etoile, French philosopher and traveller, who first saw the island from a balloon. Feather Island is surrounded by rocks that protect it from the outside world, and its perfumed air, the scent of its flowering trees and its crystal-clear streams make it a magical holiday resort. The sole inhabitants of the island are women.

Interestingly, the upper classes grow feathers instead of hair—hair, grown only by the lower classes, is considered a vulgar stigma—and social rank is indicated by the colour of the feathers. No one is ever ill on Feather Island; the women remain perpetually young, evaporating into air after a thousand years. The ladies of the higher classes are hatched from the eggs of rare birds. The servants hatch from the eggs of hairy caterpillars, hence the hair on their heads. The queen, called Celeste, is born from a phoenix egg: she is therefore perpetually reborn. The queen always appears to be barely eighteen, with a nymph-like waist, lilac and rose complexion and large dark

An upper-class feather and a royal egg from FEATHER ISLAND.

eyes; yet when the Chevalier de l'Etoile visited the island she was already in her 650th year.

Travellers should visit Celeste's palace, where all the rooms are decorated with feathers arranged to form attractive pictures. Even the doors and floors are covered with feathers, as is much of the furniture. Her room contains an abundance of precious stones. Should visitors encounter the queen, court etiquette requires that they address her on their knees.

When the Chevalier de l'Etoile visited Feather Island, he was taken at first to be a woman because of his long hair, and later to be an incarnation of the Divine Phoenix, in whose honour a temple was constructed. Despite the pleasures of the island, the Chevalier became bored and left after twelve months, which seemed to him five or six years. Time passes very slowly on Feather Island and the inhabitants fall victim to a mortal ennui. The servants find some consolation in the knowledge that the ladies of the court are even more bored than they are.

(Fanny de Beauharnais, *Rélation très véritable d'une isle nouvellement découverte*, Paris, 1786)

FEDERAL HILL, in the western section of Providence, Rhode Island, in the United States, a spectral mound bristling with huddled roofs and steeples enmeshed in the city's smoke.

Travellers are advised to visit the church of Free-Will or Starry Wisdom, bought in May, 1844, by Professor Enoch Bowen, who had returned from Egypt to found a religious sect. In 1846 three citizens of Providence disappeared under mysterious circumstances and rumours began to circulate about an unholy stone called the Shining Trapezohedron. In 1848 another seven people disappeared and stories of blood-sacrifice started being told about the church. In 1853 a cer-

tain Father O'Malley obtained a deathbed confession from Francis X. Feeney, who had joined the Starry Wisdom sect in 1849, in which it was revealed that the Shining Trapezohedron had been found by Professor Bowen when investigating some Egyptian ruins, and that the sect conjured up a mysterious entity that could not exist in the light. The Shining Trapezohedron enabled the members of the sect to see other worlds, and the conjured entity—whom the members of the sect called the Haunter of the Dark—revealed to them some unbearable secrets. In 1869, after the disappearance of an Irish youth, a mob of Irish boys attacked the church. Finally, in 1877, after a further six people had disappeared, the mayor of Providence closed the church.

Only in 1935 did the church come again into public notice. After a series of unexplainable events, including a terrible storm which shook the city, a certain Robert Blake who had tried to investigate the mysterious events was found dead at the site of a terrific explosion. No explanation was given by the authorities but rumours of ancient abominable rites were whispered throughout the city.

(Howard Phillips Lovecraft, "The Haunter of the Dark," in *The Outsider and Others*, Sauk City, 1939)

FELICITY ISLE, in the Aegean Sea, governed by Queen Felicity, also known as Théone. It is protected by a number of natural obstacles—precipitous rocks, raging torrents, savage lions, tigers and panthers, and a serpent in every rose.

If a traveller does manage to enter Théone's kingdom he will find that the island is enveloped in an eternal present where nothing grows older. There are no illnesses, worries or fears and the air is perfumed with the dew of amber, the orange trees temper the heat of the sun, and the streams reflect the many flowers. The fruit is always ripe, the birds do not sing but whisper, and it is always very dark. The island is inhabited by eternally young nymphs, the eldest of whom is barely fifteen years old.

Théone's palace is made of gold. At the entrance, a column bears an inscription warning faithless lovers to stay away; for three hundred years the queen was happy with the man she loved; he left her, and it will take Théone two thousand years to overcome the pain his faithlessness has caused her. Understandably, Théone's palace is closed to visitors.

(Fanny de Beauharnais, *L'Isle de la Félicité ou Anaxis et Théone,* Paris, 1801)

FELIDO, ISLAND OF, see GALLINACO.

FELIMATH, see LONE ISLANDS.

FELINIA, a kingdom bordering on NOLAND and the Empire of the BANOIS in PLUTO, a land at the centre of the hollow core of the earth. As in the other countries of Pluto, everything in Felinia is much smaller than on the earth's surface; the inhabitants are rarely more than two and a half feet tall.

The Felinians are an extremely superstitious people, whose main intellectual interests are theology and the law; it would be impossible to enumerate the books published on these two topics in the country. Great importance is given by the Felinians to the interpretation of dreams which they believe foretell the future and forecast the results of public lotteries—a belief which has resulted in a not inconsiderable number of bankruptcies.

The religion of Felinia is based on the teachings of the prophet Burma. The inhabitants worshipped only birds and animals and lived in spiritual darkness until Burma arrived to enlighten them. His first action was to take an egg and break it, releasing a bird that flew off, thus illustrating the release of the soul from the body by death and the principle of immortality. But the miracle for which Burma is best remembered occurred when he ordered an oak tree to sink into the ground, causing a fountain of pink water to appear in its place, followed by two other fountains—one of blue and one of golden water. A temple was built around them and visitors can still admire, for one hour every day, the coloured waters. Should the visitor be interested in purchasing a sample, bottles of any of the three colours are sold to the faithful by the sixty priests who serve the temple.

Following the miracle of the fountain Burma left, saying that he would return after three days. He was carried to heaven on the back of a winged elephant and returned with the *Sacred Book,* still the basis of Felinian religion. But some of the people remained sceptical. To demonstrate the truth of his teachings, Burma took ten virtuous men to a high, sterile mountain in the south of the country, telling them that he would help them reach heaven. He gave them metallic hats to wear; as soon as they had put them on, the men disappeared, soaring into the skies from where they never returned. These hats can be bought from any of the priests and have become a popular item among amateur suicides.

The cult established as a result of Burma's teaching centres on the worship of the sacred winged elephant and the eagle that guards the doors of heaven. Travellers should visit the major religious site in the country, the Palace of the Sacred Elephant, a sumptuous building on the slopes of an arid mountain. A blue elephant is kept here, said to be directly descended from the one that carried Burma to heaven. Enthusiastic zoologists will, however, be disappointed; closer examination reveals that the sacred elephant is merely a normal specimen which has been painted blue.

Like the sacred elephant hoax, the levitation miracles seem to have a rational explanation. Felinia is situated directly below the south polar passage from the surface of the earth to Pluto. The magnetic force of the nearby IRON MOUNTAINS is such that those wearing the metallic hats are drawn up by it and eventually reach the surface of the earth. It has been suggested that the pygmies seen in Africa and the mountain gnomes of several countries are in fact Felinians who have been attracted to the surface in this manner.

Felinia was discovered by a group of French and English seamen who stumbled across the north polar passage to Pluto after their ship was wrecked in the Arctic Ocean in 1806. After visiting several other countries they reached Felinia and heard of its legends. They soon realized the truth behind the myths and decided to use the magnetic power of the Iron Mountains to return to earth. Large metallic hats were made for them by the workmen of the temple and, as they had expected, they floated up to the surface of the earth, emerging into the mountains around the South Pole. This route is recommended to returning travellers, who will eventually reach the Antarctic Ocean and finally land somewhere in New Holland.

(Anonymous, *Voyage au centre de la terre, ou aventures de quelques naufragés dans des pays inconnus.*

Traduit de l'anglais de Sir Hormidas Peath, Paris, 1821)

FENERALIA, an island of the RIALLARO ARCHIPELAGO in the south-east Pacific, inhabited by bankrupts deported here from LIMANORA. Nothing grows on Feneralia and in order to sustain themselves the inhabitants have become buccaneers. They land on other islands, request loans with good interest, make initial payments and then vanish with the proceeds.

(Godfrey Sweven, *Riallaro, the Archipelago of Exiles,* New York & London, 1901; Godfrey Sweven, *Limanora, the Island of Progress,* New York & London, 1903)

FERDINAND'S ISLAND, a small island somewhere in the West Indies, with forests, meadows, fields and bubbling springs. A flock of sheep and a few chickens will direct travellers to a small house with a thatched roof. It is here that a German sailor spent thirty years after being shipwrecked on the island. For the benefit of future visitors, he left a complete chronicle of his life on the island, laying down reports on climactic conditions, instructions for agriculture and other helpful hints.

In the mid-eighteenth century, the island was colonized by a small group of slaves who had been washed ashore during a storm. Their descendants probably still inhabit the island, where quarrels and strife are unknown.

(Johann Michael Fleischer, *Der Nordische Robinson, oder Die wunderbaren Reisen auch ausserordentlichen Glücks- und Unglücks-Falle eines gebohrnen Normanns, Woldemar Ferdinand, wie derselbige auf eine sonderbare Art nach einer vorhin von einem eintzigen Manne bewohnt gewesenen Insul gelanget, auch sich eine ziemliche Zeit allda aufgehalten, endlich aber nach vielen gehabten Fatalitäten sein Vaterland wieder glücklich erreicht, nebst untermengten merckwürdigen Begebenheiten anderer Personen, zum erlaubten Zeivertreib ans Licht gestellet durch Selimenem,* Copenhagen, 1741)

FERGUS, the castle of Earl Fergus, on a small island in the River Cam which provides it with a natural moat. Because of the depth of the water there is no need for high walls or heavy fortifications, and the castle is light and airy. The drawbridge across the moat is defended by a double portcullis.

The castle and the area around it were once threatened by a giant named Taulurd, a somewhat stupid and childish creature. The land was left untilled as Taulurd ate the horses that were used to pull the ploughs, and the castle was avoided by prudent travellers. During his life Taulurd acquired what he considered to be a formidable treasure but his sense of discrimination was so poor that he collected bits of broken crockery as well as gold, silver and jewels. The giant was killed by Sir Marhalt, one of the knights of CAMELOT, who was led to Castle Fergus by a lady he met in the forest of ARROY. Sir Marhalt was somewhat reluctant to kill the giant, whom he found rather pathetic, but he was left with little option when Taulurd attacked him. No giants have lived in the area since and the castle is now a safe and interesting place to visit.

(John Steinbeck, *The Acts of King Arthur and His Noble Knights From the Winchester Manuscripts of Sir Thomas Malory and Other Sources,* New York, 1976)

FERISLAND, an island in an extensive archipelago off the coast of the continent of GENOTIA in the south Atlantic. It is covered with scrubby trees and inhabited by a bloodthirsty people. In the midst of the island stands a large dome, supported by nine pillars, with a red flag flying over it. Below the dome lies a large underground chamber, reached through a trapdoor, containing an ancient tomb. This is the burial place of Prince Agragantorus, remembered for his skill in black magic. His portrait hangs over the tomb, together with his prophecy that one day a great conqueror will be born among these people. Until he appears the people take no other king but elect a governor to rule over them.

Their method for recognizing this future king should be noted, as otherwise their proceedings might surprise the unwary traveller. The heart of a young foreigner is torn out of his breast and reduced to powder. Whoever can drink this powder, mixed with water, without disgust or hesitation is chosen to marry the most beautiful woman in the world—according to Ferisland standards—and the future king is the child born from the union. Because of this intriguing superstition, the eviscerated bodies of many young men adorn

The ancient tomb of Prince Agragantorus in
FERISLAND.

the island's paths and pirates along the coast conduct a thriving business in selling foreigners to the people of Ferisland for gold and pearls.

No prisoners are kept on Ferisland because the inhabitants believe that they would be poisoned if they had to share with the prisoners the air they breathe. The curious traveller is advised to watch the ritual of the carrying of the governor; he is carried on a throne made of branches, clad in a lion skin and feather head-dress.

(Louis Adrien Duperron de Castera, *Le Theatre Des Passions Et De La Fortune Ou Les Avantures Surprenantes de Rosamidor & de Theoglaphire. Histoire Australe,* Paris, 1731)

FESTENBURG CASTLE, see ZENDA.

FIGLEFIA or ISLAND OF LOVE, an island off the RIALLARO ARCHIPELAGO in the southeast Pacific. It was originally inhabited by the exiled sensualists from LIMANORA who became a promiscuous and debauched race, kidnapping and enslaving women from other parts of the archipelago. Officially they practise monogamy, largely to allow themselves the pleasures of betraying their wives and cuckolding their friends.

On some islands Figlefians are regarded as enemies of the State and their agents are hunted down like vermin. The Figlefians believe that it is their mission to replenish the earth and to renew the human race through cross-breeding and selective sterilization. Their number was greatly reduced by a plague deliberately introduced and spread by slave women from SWOONARIE.

(Godfrey Sweven, *Riallaro, the Archipelago of Exiles,* New York & London, 1901; Godfrey Sweven, *Limanora, the Island of Progress,* New York & London, 1903)

FINGISWOLD, a kingdom to the north of REREK and to the south-east of AKKAMA. Fingiswold is separated from Rerek by the isthmus known as the Wold, a desolate wind-swept area; high, ice-capped mountains separate it from Akkama. Much of the kingdom is mountainous; the ranges to the north of the capital, RIALMAR, are said to be the highest in the world.

The history of Fingiswold has been a violent succession of wars, treachery and broken alliances. Relations with Akkama have always been difficult since a group of rebellious nobles were exiled from Rialmar and established a dynasty there; Fingiswold has been invaded three times by armies from Akkama, and on two occasions the capital has been occupied.

(E.R. Eddison, *Mistress of Mistresses, A Vision of Zimiamvia,* London, 1935; E.R. Eddison, *A Fish Dinner in Memison,* London, 1941; E.R. Eddison, *The Mezentian Gate,* London, 1958)

FIONAVAR, a land of undetermined location. At present, barring divine intervention, Fionavar can only be reached with magical assistance—either from the mages and sources of the Council of Mages, using the skylore they command, or from the priestesses of the Mother Goddess, Dana, tapping into the earthroot (*avarlith*).

Fionavar has an exceptional variety of geographical features to interest the traveller. In the south the benign weather and soil conditions have combined to make the country of Cathal a veritable garden. Nowhere is this more evident than at the Summer Palace of Larai Rigal, where the spectacular walled gardens (designed by the gifted T'Varen in the reign of Thallason) extend for miles and include a variety of flora and fauna found nowhere else in Fionavar. The gardens are divided by streams crossed by nine bridges—one for each of the historical provinces that became Cathal. Near the northern wall of the gardens of Larai Rigal may be found the large *lyren* tree that legend holds to be the site of the first meeting of Prince Diarmuid of Brennin and Sharra, Princess of Cathal, in the last days before the Second War against Rakoth Maugrim.

The traveller with a liking for such things should not leave Cathal without sampling *m'rae,* the celebrated liqueur (best drunk chilled), or tasting the much-praised sherbets of the Garden Country.

Travel northward to the High Kingdom of Brennin must be accomplished by a barge crossing between the coastal cities of Cynan and Seresh. This should not deter the traveller from journeying north from Larai Rigal to view the magnificent coursing of the Saeren River through its gorge. The gorge itself is impassable to all but the most well-equipped and trained mountaineers.

Brennin enjoys a temperate climate (except in certain periods of historical crisis) and has extensive agricultural land under the plough. The largest city, Paras Derval, shares its name with the Royal Palace built on the slope northeast of town. The town itself offers easily the best selection of items for purchase in Fionavar—particularly the wonderfully crafted cloth goods, from table coverings and tapestries to sweaters and outer coats. Paras Derval is also celebrated for its beer, and the number of taverns there is extraordinary. Of these, *The Black Boar* is recommended for its historical associations with Prince Diarmuid and others.

Within the Palace itself the Great Hall (designed by Tomaz Lal) must be seen, with its twelve massive pillars, mosaic-inlaid floor, ubiquitous tapestries and the justly celebrated stained-glass windows of Delevan. Ideally the hall should be visited at sunset, when the play of light on the westernmost window—showing Conary and Colan, the High Kings during the First War against Maugrim (the Bael Rangat)—is most pleasing.

West of Paras Derval lies the Mornirwood, or Godwood, wherein is found the Summer Tree, long bound up with the fate and power of the High Kings of Brennin. Access to the Godwood and the tree is strictly controlled, and the casual traveller is unlikely in the extreme to have occasion or opportunity to go there.

The easternmost province of Brennin, Gwen Ystrat, has long enjoyed a special status by virtue of its ancient connections with Dana, the Mother Goddess, and the priestesses who serve her. The

welcome travellers receive in these parts is likely to depend directly upon whether they are male or female. Men will be expected to give a ceremonial offering of blood to the goddess should they wish to view the temple and its grounds in the town of Morvran, along the shores of Lake Leinan. Uninhibited travellers should note that the Midsummer Eve Festival (Maidaladan) is notorious for the unbridled eroticism associated with its celebrations in Morvran.

East of the town, almost in the foothills of the southern arm of the Carnevon Range, lies the goddess's sacred cave of Dun Maura, shrouded in historical and religious associations. Incidentally, Gwen Ystrat is noted for the quality of its wines, particularly the white.

North of Brennin, running all the way up to the evergreens of Gwynir, lie the vast grazing lands of the Plain, home to the Dalrei (the Riders) and to enormous numbers of the *eltor,* the creatures upon which the Dalrei depend for their subsistence. The fortunate traveller may be permitted to watch a tribe of the Dalrei in their highly ritualized hunting of a "swift" of *eltor,* and, if even more fortunate, may be invited to one of the open-air barbecue feasts that often follow the hunting. Caution is advised with respect to the consumption of *sachen,* the very potent liqueur favoured by the Dalrei.

West of the Plain lies the ancient forest of Pendaran, the Great Wood. There have been reports of a lessening of this sentient forest's antipathy to intruders of all kinds, but pending confirmation of this the traveller is advised to stay well clear of what may still be a very dangerous area. The one exception, for the adventurous, might be to take a sea voyage north from Taerlindel or Rhoden to the Anor Lisen (Tower of Lisen) at the edge of the sea, just at the western edge of Pendaran. The tower itself is off limits to travellers, but this wild, romantic strand was the setting for the reunion of Arthur, Lancelot and Guinevere in the days of the Second War, as well as the place where the beautiful Lisen of the Wood leapt to her death at the time of the First War.

The northern lands of Andarien and Sennett Strand are only now undergoing extensive rehabilitation, after more than a thousand years of lying ruined and desolate. Andarien, for students of military affairs, was of course the setting for the last battle in the Second War, and the site can readily be visited. Farther north, approached with some difficulty through a singular lack of travellers' amenities, may be seen the rubble of the fallen towers of Starkadh, the fortress of Rakoth Maugrim the Unraveller. The traveller who does venture this far will be rewarded with unparalleled views of Rangat Cloud-Shouldered, the magnificent mountain which utterly dominates the skyline. At one time this area was regrettably unsafe, but there have been no reports of the malevolent *svart alfar* (dark elves) for quite some time.

Between Andaricn and Pendaran Wood lies the blurred outline of Daniloth, the realm of the *lios alfar* (light elves). Although no longer known as the Shadowland since the overthrow of Rakoth, the land of the *lios* is not one where travellers may go with impunity even now, and so, barring an express invitation, this too is a place best avoided—despite the lure of sites such as the upward-flowing falls of Fiathal, or the Mound of Atronel whereon sits the crystal throne of the *lios alfar*.

East of the dividing mountain ranges of Carnevon and Skeledarak lies the tragically desolate wilderness of Eridu. In the Second War the evil Rakoth Maugrim caused a genocidal death-rain to fall throughout this land, and as a result the once-magnificent cities of Akkaize, Teg Veirene and Larak are only now being resettled. In the north of Eridu, still keeping much to themselves under the current reign of King Matt Sören (though less so than before), dwell the Dwarves of Banir Lök and Banir Tal—the Twin Mountains in the bowl of which lies the legendary Calor Diman (Crystal Lake). Other than the Dwarves themselves only two people—Loren Silvercloak, once First Mage of Brennin, later counsellor to King Matt; and Kimberly Ford, who came from our own world to briefly become the Seer of Brennin in the days of the Second War—have been permitted to enter the meadow of the Crystal Lake, and neither has offered an account of what they saw there.

Fionavar's prehistory is hazy. Originally there appear to have been only two peoples (aside from the various gods and goddesses) inhabiting it: the Paraiko (Giants) and the Kings of the Wild Hunt. These were followed by the *lios alfar* and the Dwarves; it is a matter of some dispute which race came first.

Many years later Men arrived on the Plain and across the mountains in Eridu, and in the south, in the provinces that became Cathal after unification. The rise of Men as a formidable race coincides with the arrival of Iorweth Founder from over the sea to the west. Legend has it that he was summoned by the god Mörnir to the place of the Summer Tree, and near that wood founded the city of Paras Derval and then shaped the High Kingdom of Brennin.

The epochal conflict in Fionavar's ancient history was the Bael Rangat, fought against the fallen god Rakoth Maugrim the Unraveller. The evil Unraveller, based in his fortress of Starkadh far in the north, was only defeated after very great hardship by an army led by Conary the High King of Brennin and, after Conary's death in battle, by his son Colan the Beloved. The Dalrei, led by Revor, their Aven ("Father"), were instrumental in the battles that led to victory, and as a consequence Colan ceded the Plain to Revor and his heirs forever. Rakoth was captured, but being "outside of time" could not be slain. Instead he was bound in magically forged chains beneath the great mountain, Rangat, and five wardstones were shaped to be given to the people of Brennin, Cathal, Eridu and the Plain, and to the *lios alfar* in Daniloth. The wardstones were designed to give warning if Rakoth ever exerted his powers to attempt to achieve his freedom.

(Guy Gavriel Kay, *The Summer Tree*, Toronto, 1984; Guy Gavriel Kay, *The Wandering Fire*, New York, 1986; Guy Gavriel Kay, *The Darkest Road*, New York, 1986)

FIRE MOUNTAIN, see HES.

FIRST MEN CITY, an underground city in PAROULET'S COUNTRY, inhabited by a race that traces its origin back to Noah's Flood. The people claim that Noah was not the only man to be spared, but that Jalesh, their ancestor, was also commanded to build an ark, which came to rest not on a mountain like Noah's but far below the surface of the earth. The descendants of Jalesh retained the memory of the earth's crust, which they believe to be uninhabited. They refer to themselves as the "First Men" and are governed by patriarchs. They live in peace, have no sense of envy, greed or hatred and will only welcome strangers on condition that they never return to earth. Their language is an early form of Hebrew and their dress is fashioned on the clothes of biblical times. At the waist they wear boxes, studded with rubies, that fire ultra-violet rays; with these they hunt the prehistoric monsters which roam around the city. The boxes are kept in an arms depot and no one is allowed to wear them at home.

The houses of First Men City resemble ancient Hebrew or Egyptian dwellings, with only one entrance and a few windows.

(Maurice Champagne, *La Cité des premiers hommes*, Paris, 1929)

FIXED ISLE, a peninsula, despite its name, linked to a continent (either Europe or Africa) by a narrow strip of land about an arrow's throw in length. Fixed Isle is seven leagues long and five leagues wide and received its name because it seems to be "fixed" to the continent by the short bridge of land. It was discovered and colonized by Apolodion, nephew of the Emperor of Constantinople, who arrived here with his wife Grimanesa, daughter of Siudan, Emperor of Rome. After vanquishing the giant who lived on the island, Apolodion founded a splendid dominion, living here for sixteen years with his beloved Grimanesa.

Upon the death of the Emperor of Constantinople, who had no children, Apolodion was recalled as successor to the throne; but before leaving he put Fixed Isle under a charm which allowed no one but a perfect knight and his lady to become the island's new masters. He left a governor in charge of collecting the rent and guarding the island until such a successor should arrive and prove his authenticity. Apolodion also made the following arrangements: he planted a beautiful garden with trees of every kind, and around it he built a wall with only one entrance, an arch, on top of which he erected a copper statue of a man sounding a trumpet. In the middle of the garden he set up a small building with four richly decorated rooms, and in one of the rooms he placed life-like images of himself and his queen, and next to them a rock of shining jasper. "From this day onwards," reads his proclamation, "none shall pass into the garden who has deceived the sacred principles of love, for the statue you here see shall let out such a terrible sound from its trumpet, spouting forth smoke and tongues of fire, that it shall paralyze the unworthy visitor, who will be taken away as if he were already dead. But should the person entering through the arch be loyal and loving, he or she shall pass without any impediment and the statue will let out a sound so melodious that it will enchant all those who hear it. Because of their virtue, they will be allowed to see our images and behold their names being written on the jasper, without knowing who writes them."

In the room where Apolodion and his queen

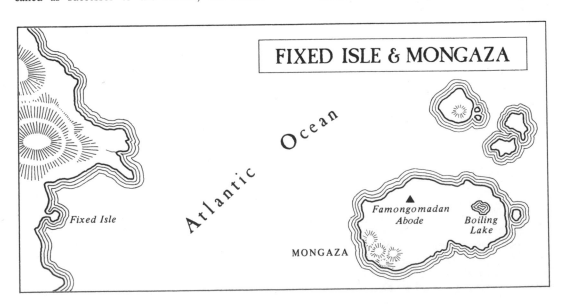

FIXED ISLE & MONGAZA

Atlantic Ocean

Fixed Isle

Famongomadan
Abode

Boiling
Lake

MONGAZA

had experienced the many pleasures of love he placed two columns—one of copper in front of the door and one of stone on the other side of it—and he set a charm upon the room, forbidding entrance to any man who was not a greater warrior than himself or to any woman who was not more beautiful than Grimanesa. Whichever warriors did not manage to pass the copper column were to leave their weapons outside the door; those who were stopped by the column of stone were to leave behind their swords; those who reached beyond the stone column were to leave behind their shields. Finally, those who passed both columns and yet were stopped by the room itself were forced to leave behind their spurs. The ladies only had to say their names, which were then written up at whatever point they had reached. Throughout the years many knights tried their luck, but only Amadis of Gaul succeeded in entering and so became Lord of Fixed Isle.

(Anonymous, *Amadís de Gaula*, Zaragoza, 1508)

FIXIT CITY, in the Bauchi Plateau, Federal Republic of Nigeria. Though not particularly beautiful, Fixit City is a useful place for visitors in need of rebuilding a human body after it has been partially eaten by ants or caught in a shredding machine. Being very clever with their hands, the inhabitants of Fixit City can reconstruct a body from just a few bones or bits of hair.

To reach the city, travellers must follow certain instructions. They will find that the road to Fixit City is lined with open-air stalls, on which half-cooked meals are displayed. Courteously refusing the stall owners' entreaties to taste the half-cooked viands, they should ask them the quickest way to Fixit City. Reluctantly, the stall owners will indicate a narrow path that avoids complicated detours through the jungle and brings travellers up to the city gates. Once these have been passed, the inhabitants of Fixit City will lodge the visitors for one night only. Next morning, they will be requested by their hosts to take the cattle out to graze. Followed by a small herd of short-horned cows and long-horned bulls, visitors should walk until they reach a small forest of *adduwa* trees. After collecting some of the *adduwa* fruits, they should give the ripest ones to the cattle, while eating the green ones themselves. Almost immediately, the largest bull in the herd will

run off to the city and inform the inhabitants that the visitors have passed the test. Without further ado, the inhabitants of Fixit City will now take the bones (or any other remains) submitted by visitors and proceed, with incredible ability, to rebuild the destroyed body. However, it must be noted that the results are not always up to par. It is possible that the visitor may find himself with an armless, toothless or noseless body—which in any case will be better than a small pile of bones and a fistful of hair.

(A.J.N. Tremearne, *Hausa Superstitions and Customs*, London, 1913)

FLATLAND, a land where all objects, animate and inanimate, appear as straight lines. Flatland has no sun, nor other heavenly bodies, but by its own laws of nature has a constant attraction to the south, and this peculiarity serves as a compass.

Most of the houses are built in the shape of a pentagon and are windowless, since light appears mysteriously inside and out, day and night. Each house contains a small door in the east side for women and a larger door on the west side for men. Square and triangular houses are not presently allowed for safety reasons; the lines of inanimate objects being dimmer than those of men and women, the absent-minded traveller might run into them.

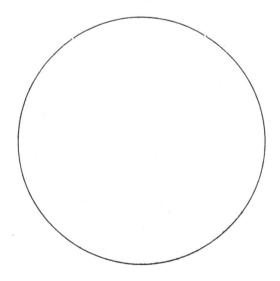

A FLATLAND priest and his wife.

It should be noted however that in some remote and backward agricultural districts the occasional square house can still be seen, a residue of eleventh-century architecture.

The general length or breadth of the inhabitants of Flatland is eleven inches—twelve inches maximum—the size depending upon the age of the individual. Women, at the bottom of the social strata, are straight lines, while the rest of society falls into the following shapes: soldiers and the lowest classes of workmen are isosceles triangles; the middle classes are equilateral triangles; professional men and gentlemen are squares or pentagons; the nobility have six sides or more; while the highest class of all, the priests, are perfect circles. Visitors must remember that since there is no light from above to create shadows, all figures appear as flat as a straight line, like a distant island upon the horizon, or a penny viewed at eye level from the edge of a table.

The student of sociology will note with interest that one of Flatland's laws of nature provides that a male child shall have one more side than his father, so that each generation rises one step in the scale of development and nobility. This rule does not always apply to tradesmen and soldiers, though it is possible through military success, diligent work, or intermarriage to rise in the social scale.

The women of Flatland are noteworthy, for in addition to being all point (at least in two extremities), they possess the power of being able to make themselves invisible and are therefore not to be trifled with. To run up against a Flatland woman could bring absolute and immediate destruction. At the same time they are wholly devoid of brain power and have neither reflection, judgement nor forethought, and hardly any memory.

Despite the identical appearance of all the inhabitants of Flatland, they are able to recognize each other through various means—through the senses of hearing, feeling and inference and, among the higher orders, through sight. On the other hand, the aesthetic and artistic life is somewhat dull. This is to be expected when all landscape, historical places, portraits, flowers, and still life are single lines with no variety except degrees of brightness and obscurity. Yet this was not always so. For a brief period in its history, colour played an important part in the life of Flatland, but the resultant rapid decay of the intellectual arts, and the

confusion in social recognition caused it to be outlawed. Colour is now non-existent.

The pillars and mainstay of the constitution of Flatland are the circles, or priests. Their maxim is "Attend to your configuration," a doctrine which is applied in all areas—political, ecclesiastical, moral—the object being above all improvement of the individual and collective configuration.

(Edwin A. Abbott, *Flatland*, New York, 1884)

FLOATING ISLAND, SUMMER ISLAND or SCOTI MORIA, in the middle of the Thames-Isis Gulf, off the coast of England. A small island, it can be circumnavigated in twenty-four hours. It is divided into four parts or provinces: Christianshore to the north; Turkishore to the south; Pont-Troynovant to the east; and Maidenhead to the west. Since the island floats away in winter and hides in an unknown, narrow bay until the summer, it is sometimes called Summer Island.

The Naiads live in the highlands and play at ninepins there, making a very loud noise that can be heard throughout the land. The people are noted for their sloth. They are too idle to make wine in spite of their luxuriant vineyards and too lazy to cultivate the land however fond they are of green pastures. They speak a lingua franca and smoke a great deal. In the province of Maidenhead is a region called Westmonasteria, the site of an ancient and refined Temple of Apollo.

(Frank Careless, *The Floating Island or A New Discovery Relating the Strange Adventure on a late Voyage from Lambethana to Villa Franca, Alias Ramallia, to the Eastward of Terra Del Templo: By three Ships, viz. the "Pay-naught," the "Excuse," and the "Least-in-Sight" under the conduct of Captain Robert Owe-much: Describing the Nature of the Inhabitants, their Religion, Laws and Customs*, London, 1673)

FLORA, a beautiful peninsula covered in flowers, where winter is unknown. Its inhabitants spend their lives singing, dancing and reciting poetry, and have no use for weapons of any kind. Flora is separated from the kingdom of Athunt by a range of steep mountains.

These blissful conditions have not always existed in Flora. Several years ago two sisters, knowledgeable in the black arts, built a castle on the

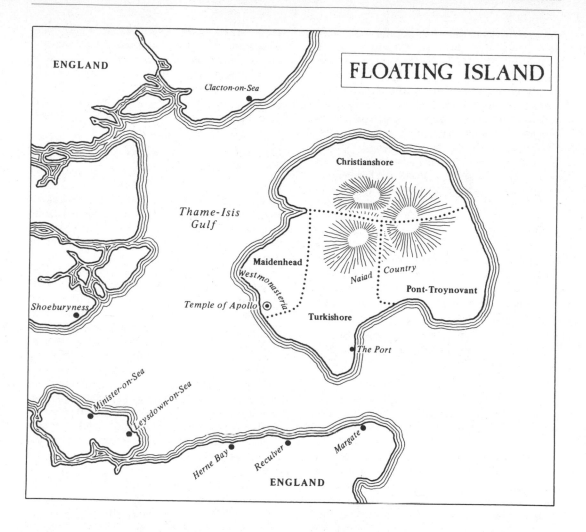

peninsula with fierce lions to guard it, and set out to trample the flowers and kill the inhabitants with poisoned arrows. Flora was delivered by the son of the King of Athunt who managed to kill the witches. In gratitude the Queen of Flora gave him her hand, and the country resumed its peaceful existence.

(Ferdinand Raimund, "Die gefesselte Phantasie," in *Sämtliche Werke,* Munich, 1837)

FLOTSAM, an island in the south Pacific, latitude 10° south and longitude 150° west, within the Pacific earthquake belt. The coast alternates between beaches and cliffs; the inland forest covers the numerous hills dotted with caves. The fauna comprises a small species of deer, foxes, squirrels, panthers and snakes. Although Flotsam was discovered by Captain James Cook in 1773, the interior has not, to this day, been fully explored.

However, a certain Waldo Emerson Smith-Jones left an account describing the inhabitants of Flotsam. They are a primitive people, divided into several tribes that appear to be at different stages of evolution. The most primitive of all is the so-called Bad Men—large, skulking, nomadic brutes covered with hair, who are unable to kiss and who carry clubs as their sole weapons. Another tribe, of no specific name, is somewhat more developed; the people live in caves for extended periods and move only when their chief decides to do so. A third tribe—the closest to civilization—is the Wild Men. They live in thatched huts set on long piles, smoke tobacco and are ruled by the law of the strongest. They explain natural phenomena through certain intriguing legends; for instance, an earthquake is explained as the escape from its underground imprisonment of a large panther called Nagoola. Inside the Wild Men's temple the visitor can see several raised platforms and, at the back, a small cell where victims are kept waiting before they are sacrificed. From the rafters hang many colourful human skulls, as the tribe is renowned for its accomplished headshrinking. Visitors are warned that the greeting customs of the natives are somewhat bizarre: upon meeting, they will call out each other's names, adding the phrase "I can kill you," whereupon they set about proving their point. This system has been useful in retaining the necessary biological equilibrium on the island.

(Edgar Rice Burroughs, *The Cave Girl*, New York, 1913; Edgar Rice Burroughs, *The Cave Man*, New York, 1917)

FLOZELLA-A-NINA, an island of the MARDI ARCHIPELAGO, famous for its beauty. It rises from the sea in three immense terraces covered with flowers and fruit trees, giving the impression of hanging gardens. Its name means "The-Last-Stanza-Of-The-Song" and to this meaning is attached an ancient legend. In years long past there used to live in the Mardi Archipelago, together with the Mardians, winged creatures of a good and kindly nature. These creatures had chosen to live among men but were hated by them because of their kindness. For many years these superior beings responded to hatred with love and continued to show man the virtues of justice and charity. But the Mardians were intractable and chased the winged creatures from one island to another. Finally, one day, the kindly beings opened their wings and flew back to heaven. Without their beneficial influence the Mardians quickly fell victims to feelings of guilt and suffering and became what their descendants are today. However, those ancient Mardians did not know they were bringing themselves misfortune; they believed they had achieved a great victory and rejoiced by organizing banquets and games. The legend says that a poem of celebration was then written, having as many stanzas as there were islands in the archipelago, and that a group of young people, in party dress, went round the entire lagoon in a festive canoe, singing to each island the corresponding stanza. Flozella was the last island they reached and the Queen of Flozella, to celebrate the event, gave her island the name by which it is known today.

(Herman Melville, *Mardi, and A Voyage Thither*, New York, 1849)

FLUORESCENTE, a city where, according to the local historian, "a street-singer puts darkness to a test of silence spread like a pool of red wine"—a phrase that has a profound meaning in its original language, Dada.

The most striking feature is the fruit placed in piles at crossroads throughout the city, some of the piles reaching the height of three-storey buildings.

In the city of Fluorescente, the daily news is broadcast by naval signal flags strung up on ropes. The men of the town cannot speak, and the women can only sing a few meaningless phrases, in limited quantities and according to very strict rules; every Friday these phrases are changed. Sounds are muted by spreading a thin layer of rubber over everything that might make a sharp noise. During peak times for traffic in the streets, packs of invisible dogs are let loose throughout the town.

Travellers in Fluorescente will notice that the townsfolk touch each others' hands in a desire to be polite, but that they never prolong these possibly voluptuous attachments. Travellers may also be fooled by the perfectly made "witness-mannequins" posted at bus-stops. Made of edible products encrusted with pearls, they are the brunt of endless jokes of certain passersby, who insist on paying them their respects.

Finally, travellers should note that in Fluorescente it is forbidden to dream about accosting women in the streets.

(Tristan Tzara, *Grains et Issues*, Paris, 1935)

FLUTTERBUDGET CENTRE, a large town on a hill in southern OZ, almost on the border between Quadling Country and Winkie Country. Like RIGMAROLE TOWN, Flutterbudget Centre is one of the defensive settlements of Oz. Anyone in the country who shows signs of becoming a Flutterbudget is sent to live here.

Flutterbudgets are characterized by their constant worrying over imaginary fears and are obsessed by the disasters that might befall them if such-and-such a thing happened. To take only one example: a Flutterbudget may complain that he cannot sleep because in order to do so he would have to close his eyes. If he closed his eyes, the lids might stick together and he would then be blind for life. He may well agree that he has never heard of such a thing happening, but will immediately add that it would be dreadful if it did and that the very idea makes him so nervous that he cannot fall asleep.

(L. Frank Baum, *The Emerald City of Oz*, Chicago, 1910)

FLYING DUTCHMAN'S PORT, see DALAND'S VILLAGE.

FONS BELLI, capital of VENUSIA.

FONSECA, an island often shrouded in thick clouds; because of this, travellers have mentioned that it appears and disappears as if by magic. The circumstances of Fonseca's original discovery and colonization remain unknown; the earliest references to it are found in the letters of two Turkish sea-captains who visited the island in 1707, and pinpointed its location only a few miles to the east of Bardados.

Fonseca has a white population, mostly of British origin, of less than sixteen thousand, and a slave population of about seventy thousand. Many of the slaves came originally from Africa, especially from Guinea. In order to increase the slave population, the Whites actively encourage promiscuity and immorality among the slaves, although they themselves claim to be Christians.

Visitors will notice that both the Whites and the Blacks appear to enjoy quarrelling, drinking, gambling—at which they cheat—and malicious gossip. The streets of the main town are filthy and no attempt has been made to adapt the houses to the tropical environment. The level of culture and education is very low, and there are not many schools on the island. The only subjects which are taught with any proficiency are reading, writing and bookkeeping. Religion is in the hands of a few hard-working priests.

The basic currency of Fonseca is small pieces of paper with deckled edges, bearing an indecipherable inscription. Given that all commercial transactions are conducted while swearing, it is believed that this inscription is a charm invoking the spirit of discord. Visitors who would rather avoid an argument will find that Spanish silver is also widely accepted.

(Anonymous, *A Voyage To The New Island, Fonseca, Near Barbados. With some Observations Made in a Cruize among the Leward Islands. In Letters from Two Captains of Turkish Men of War, driven thither in the Year 1707. Translated out of Turkish and French*, London, 1708)

FOOLGAR, see LOONARIE.

FOOLLYK or **POETS' ISLAND**, one of several high islands near Tierra del Fuego, discovered by Ferdinand Magellan in 1520. The inhabitants claim they descend from Herosom, an ancient poet, child of the Sun and the Moon. They are very poor, because the poetry trade is not prosperous. They speak in rhyme and within given metres, in an elliptical style as far removed as possible from that of common folk. An annual fair is held here where all sorts of poetical articles can be bought or sold: tragedies, comedies, words for an opera, epic poems, fables, epigrams. Customs officials can prevent some of these articles from being exported.

(Abbé Pierre François Guyot Desfontaines, *Le Nouveau Gulliver, ou Voyage De Jean Gulliver, Fils Du Capitaine Gulliver. Traduit d'un Manuscrit Anglois. Par Monsieur L.D.F.*, Paris, 1730) *Map follows*

FORBIDDEN CITY, see ASHAIR.

FORBIDDEN FOREST, a dangerous wooded area near HOGWARTS School in England, inhabited by unicorns, werewolves and centaurs. Evil beings come to the forest to kill the unicorns and take their blood (which is the colour of silver), because it will grant whoever drinks it protection from death. Those who slay unicorns, having taken a pure and defenceless life to save their own, will have but a half life, a cursed life, from the moment

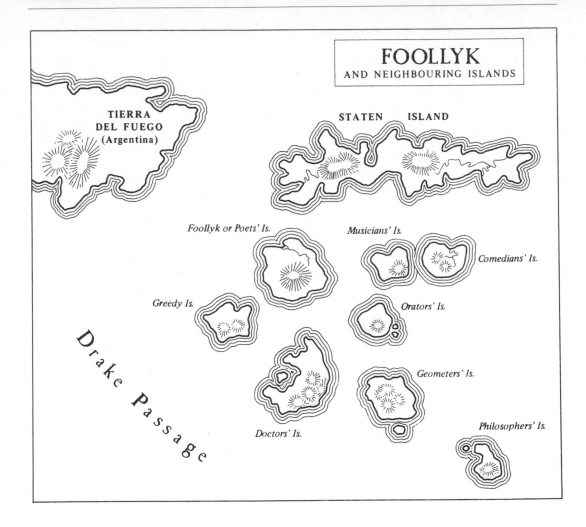

FOOLLYK
AND NEIGHBOURING ISLANDS

TIERRA
DEL FUEGO
(Argentina)

STATEN   ISLAND

Foollyk or Poets' Is.

Musicians' Is.

Comedians' Is.

Greedy Is.

Orators' Is.

Drake Passage

Geometers' Is.

Doctors' Is.

Philosophers' Is.

the blood touches their lips. Visitors are urged to take great precautions before entering this place.

(J.K. Rowling, *Harry Potter and the Philosopher's Stone*, London, 1997 [*Harry Potter and the Sorcerer's Stone*, US])

FOREST, THE, a wooded area of unknown location that feels to its inhabitants like the last forest on earth. The ruler is the witch, an all-powerful creature, sometimes male and sometimes female, who has lived in The Forest since before the world told time, and has cast upon the area a spell that protects it from intruders. Farmers, hunters and seekers of ore have all been known to meet with

terrible accidents in their efforts to enter The Forest, but most of the time the spell works on the intruder's mind, arousing fear and effecting a sudden change of heart. Visitors are therefore warned that travel to The Forest is almost impossible.

Among the inhabitants are creatures of all species—birds and ants, bears and ferrets, pumas and duelling elks, spiders, rabbits and foxes—living in companionable love that crosses barriers of sex and species. Once, during a time of crisis, The Forest fell under the wing of the Great Horned Owl, the witch's old familiar, who imposed a reign of terror over the animals, condemning anything "different," such as all behaviour seen as unusual and all characteristics perceived as foreign. The

Owl's dictatorship came to an end thanks to a resistance movement led by Albertus, an apprentice wizard, and today the rare visitors to The Forest can share in the blissful atmosphere that pervades every aspect of its peaceful life.

(Paul Monette, *Sanctuary*, New York, 1997)

FOREST ISLAND, of unknown location, takes its name from the thick forests that cover most of its surface. Beyond the beaches—dotted with bright flowers—are the almost impenetrable forests. Guarded by a dragon, they prevent visitors from going on into the interior.

However, there is another means of access, via a river which leads deep into the woods. Visitors will be able to identify this river because the central hill of the island, a bare peak rising above the dark trees, can be clearly seen from its mouth.

There is only one settlement on the island, a scattered village of curiously constructed buildings, made of wattles woven between the trunks of the trees. The natives are gentle and hospitable, though in many ways primitive, using only flint or copper weapons and tools; iron is unknown on the island. Travellers will be surprised to find that the people are totally ignorant of the arts of navigation and have little or no contact with other nations. They dress simply, in cotton, but wear ornate gold ornaments. Gold is extremely common on the island and attracts occasional traders.

The island is a monarchy. When the king becomes old and feeble, he is taken to the central hill and killed with a wild root which has narcotic powers but which causes no pain. His body is then carried to a chapel of rough-hewn stones, half-way up the hill, where it is embalmed and hung on the wall. The bodies of many dead kings, still wearing their gold chaplets of office, can be seen here. The king's servants are killed before the death of their master, and their embalmed corpses are kept briefly and then flung into the river.

(William Morris, *The Earthly Paradise, A Poem*, London, 1868)

FORMOSA (not to be confused with Taiwan), a large island in the Pacific Ocean between the Philippines and Ryu Kyu.

In Formosa the natives walk around naked except for a golden or silver plaque covering their sexual organs. Their food consists mainly of serpents which they kill by flogging them with branches; this procedure makes the serpents lose their poison and they can then be cooked in the delicious Formosan fashion. The inhabitants speak a language similar to no other in the world and therefore very difficult to learn.

Formosan religion makes use of human sacrifices; some twenty thousand children under the age of nine are slaughtered every year. The inhabitants hate Christians; when a visitor arrives in Formosa he is presented with a crucifix and asked to hit it. Should the visitor refuse, he is immediately executed, but without wrath or scorn because the Formosans are courteous and sweet-natured people.

(George Psalmanaazaar, *Description de l'isle Formosa*, Amsterdam, 1704)

FORNOST or **FORNOST ERAIN**, known as **KING'S NORBURY** in the Common Speech, the chief stronghold of ARNOR and later the capital of Arthedain. The great northern fortress stands on the North Downs.

The original capital of Arnor was Annúminas on the banks of Lake Nenuial, Fornost becoming the royal seat during the latter part of the Third Age. When Arnor finally fell to the Witch-king of ANGMAR, Fornost was largely destroyed. Although the city was retaken after the Battle of Fornost a year later in 1975 Third Age, when forces from GONDOR and RIVENDELL joined the remnants of the population of Arnor, it was abandoned for many years. It fell into ruins and travellers feared to go near it for it was believed to be haunted—it became known as "Deadmen's Dike." At the end of the War of the Ring, Arnor was reestablished as a kingdom and the stronghold of Fornost was built.

(J.R.R. Tolkien, *The Fellowship of the Ring*, London, 1954; J.R.R. Tolkien, *The Return of the King*, London, 1955; J.R.R. Tolkien, *The Silmarillion*, London, 1977)

FOROCHEL, a cold, barren area on the northern coast of MIDDLE-EARTH, roughly three hundred miles north of the SHIRE. The Ice Bay of Forochel—so called because it freezes over in winter—is the southern inlet of a vast unnamed bay which opens onto the sea. The whole region is inhabited by the Lossoth or Snowmen who are descended from the Forodwaith, the men of the extreme northern area of Middle-earth during the First Age. They live mainly on the Cape of Forochel, on the north-west side of the bay and on its southern shores, beneath the high Ered Luin, the Blue Mountains.

The Lossoth are a poor and primitive people of whom little is known. They build houses in the snow and are said to be able to run on ice, wearing bones as skis on their feet. They are also said to have carts without wheels, reminiscent of sledges.

The Lossoth somewhat reluctantly sheltered Arvedui of ARNOR after the fall of Arthedain in 1974 Third Age. Their reluctance to come to his aid was probably due to their belief that his enemy, the Witch-king (later to be known as the Lord of the Nazgûl, the Ringwraiths of MORDOR), was able to bring about a thaw or a frost at will.

(J.R.R. Tolkien, *The Fellowship of the Ring,* London, 1954; J.R.R. Tolkien, *The Return of the King,* London, 1955)

FORTUNATE ISLANDS (1) (not to be confused with the FORTUNATE ISLANDS at the entrance to the Mediterranean), a group of islands of uncertain location and varying characteristics, fauna and flora. On one of them, green goats with immense ears—finer than velvet—can be found. When the goats grow old their ears are cut off by the men of the island, who use them to make coats. When their ears are removed in this way, the goats are transformed into lovely women.

The fertile Isle of Butterflies is so called because of its enormous butterflies, whose wings are used to make the sails of both ships and windmills. Everything on this island grows to an enormous size: marrows and cucumbers become so large that they are dried, scooped out and used as houses and churches. Roast storks fly through the sky, ready to be eaten—the natives catch them with falcons.

On the Isle of Coquardz, travellers will find a mountain of butter with a river of milk flowing down its side. The river is as wide as the Seine and is navigable. Eels and lampreys up to a league in length can easily be caught in it—pork sausages are commonly used as boats. Upstream is a mountain of fine flour which may be taken and used by anyone; thanks to the existence of this mountain, there is no need for windmills on the island. Near the flour mountain, a fountain gives rise to a river of hot pea-soup which flows across a bed of spicy French sausages. Evergreen trees, taller than a pine, produce more food; the male of the species bears black puddings and the female, Italian salami.

Travellers will also find large fields in which the natives plant eggs. These germinate into pods containing between thirty and forty fresh eggs—the normal diet of the islanders. In one region of Coquardz, pies grow in the fields, spontaneously sprouting overnight like mushrooms, and roast larks fall from the sky every morning. The hedges produce tarts and flans in such profusion that they

A butterfly-rigged sailing ship departs the Isle of Butterflies, one of the FORTUNATE ISLANDS (1).

are used to roof houses, just as slates are used in less favoured countries. The children of the island virtually live on the produce of the hedgerows.

On both Coquardz and the Isle of Butterflics, rivers of delicious wine flow across the meadows, and cups and goblets are found on the river banks. One species of tree produces all kinds of cheeses, while another bears swords and knives which can be used to cut the cheeses. A third species of tree produces a fruit as large as an ass's head, although the tree itself is little bigger than an oak. The fruit contains all kinds of gold coins which are its seeds. Visitors are advised that the fruit never falls until it is completely ripe, which is usually in mid-August. On rare occasions the fruit is attacked by worms, in which case it will contain only silver coins when it falls. The islanders dress in bark taken from the trees; it is whiter and softer than any known cloth and renews itself perpetually.

There are no women on either of these two islands; nature is so generous here that there would be nothing for women to do. When one of the men becomes old and bored with life, he lies down to die in a tub filled with malmsey; this wine is so sweet that he feels no suffering. His body is then dried in the sun and burnt to ashes; the ashes are mixed with egg glaze and remoulded into the original shape of the deceased. Finally, the dead man is reanimated: a friend blows up a straw inserted into his anus until he whistles or sneezes, a sure sign that he has returned to life.

(Anonymous, *Le Voyage de navigation que fist Panurge, disciple de Pantagruel, aux isles incognues et éstranges de plusieurs choses merveilleuses et difficiles à croire, qu'il dict avoir veues, dont il fait narration en ce présent volume, et plusieurs aultres joyeusetez pour inciter les lecteurs et auditeurs à rire*, Paris, 1538)

FORTUNATE ISLANDS (2) just outside the entrance to the Mediterranean, in the Atlantic, off the west coast of Africa. They are said to be inhabited by happy spirits, but common souls can find these islands equally delightful. One traveller has reported that here "the life of mortals is most easy: there is no snow, no winter, not much rain, but the ocean is forever sending cool-breathing breezes to refresh men." In 82 BC some sailors from Cadiz reported having been here but said they saw only two of the islands. According to their description,

the inhabitants are indolent and the land is so fertile that food is produced spontaneously.

A small fishing village on the mainland close by the Fortunate Islands is apparently allowed to exist there because the fishermen are summoned in rotation to perform a singular office. In the dead of night a knock is heard at the door of one of the cottages, and a whispering as of a decaying breeze summons the fisherman whose turn it is to his duty. He hastens to the seashore and launches his boat; when the hull sinks perceptibly in the dusky water he knows that his passengers are ready. He sails to the Fortunate Islands where his passengers disembark, still unseen, and then returns home at once—he is not allowed to spend even one night on the islands.

A partial description of the islands was given by a Druid from Skerr who was ordered by a voice to board a mysterious vessel and sail away for seven days. On the eighth he saw an island beneath the setting sun, with green hills and beautiful trees descending to the shore, its peaks, from which gushed limpid streams, enveloped in bright and transparent clouds. This was probably the island of Ombrios, one of the archipelago. There are five Fortunate Islands: from east to west, Junonia, or Purpurariae; Canaria, or Planaria; Nivaria, or Convallis; Capraria; and Ombrios, or Pluvialia. The learned King Juba of Mauritania named Canaria for the big dogs that roam over the island; Capraria for the curious large lizards that crawl on the rocks near the coast; Ombrios for a pleasant pool that is found in the midst of the mountains; and Nivaria because it is always covered in mist and snow.

(Homer, *The Odyssey*, 9th cen. [?] BC; Marcus Tullius Cicero, *Letters to Atticus*, 68–44 BC; Pliny the Elder, *Naturalis Historia*, 1st cen. AD; Plutarch, *Life of Sortorius*, 1st cen. AD; Ptolemy, *Geography*, 2nd cen. AD; James Macpherson, *An Introduction to the History of Great Britain and Ireland*, Dublin, 1771; Julien-Jacques Moutonnet de Clairfons, *Les Iles Fortunées, ou les Aventures de Bathylle et de Cléobule, par M.M.D. C.A.S.*, Paris, 1778; Sir Walter Scott, *Count Robert of Paris*, London, 1898)

FORTUNE, ISLAND OF, situated off the coast of the United States; its exact location is unknown. The coast is wooded and uninhabited, but beyond the forest lies a broad well-watered plain which is intensivcly cultivated. Here live the inhabitants of the island.

The inhabitants take a great interest in the arts and sciences and are always eager for new information. They worship the sun, whom they regard as Father of the Universe, and they believe in the immortality of the soul, with eternal rewards for the good and eternal punishments for the wicked. Atheists are burned, together with their works.

(Abbé Balthazard, *L'Isle Des Philosophes Et Plusieurs Autres, Nouvellement découvertes, & remarquables par leur rapports avec la France actuelle,* Chartres, 1790)

FOXCASTLE, an Elfin kingdom beneath a hill in Peebleshire, Scotland. From the outside there is little to distinguish the hill from others in the area; like them, it is heather-covered and has peat bogs on its lower slopes. It is perhaps steeper than others and has a flat top, but there is no sign to indicate that it is an Elfin realm. Inside, the hill is a labyrinth of stone-walled halls and corridors. It is veined with springs and streams, some of which have been tapped to give a regular water supply to the kingdom.

The life of Foxcastle is similar to that of other Elfin kingdoms from ELFHAME to CATMERE. The Elfins are fickle and their interests vary constantly. Some train squirrels, some study astronomy, others play the French horn, each individual whisking from one pursuit to another. The queen is more constant than most of her subjects and spends much of her time knitting, an occupation of which she never tires. If she has no more wool she simply unravels her work and knits it up again. Holding her skein of wool is a great mark of royal favour, rarely bestowed.

Foxcastle is one of the few Elfin kingdoms to have been visited by a mortal. James Sutherland, lecturer in Rhetoric at Aberdeen University and a keen scholar of fairy legends, was taken prisoner by the inhabitants of Foxcastle and stayed there for some years. He was never ill-treated, though he was kept bound in cobwebs for some time after his arrival; it seems that the Elfins wished to make precise measurements of all parts of his body for scientific purposes. Some years later he was expelled from the hill, without any explanation. On his return to Aberdeen, Sutherland was taken to be a madman.

It is thought that the name Foxcastle may derive from "Folks' Castle," the castle of the fair folk.

(Sylvia Townsend Warner, *Kingdoms of Elfin*, London, 1972)

FOXVILLE, a city-state close to DUNKITON, inhabited by talking foxes and ruled by King Renard IV, who prefers to be known as King Fox, reserving his official title for State occasions.

Visitors will arrive in Foxville through one of the broad, ceremonial arches on either side of the city, with their brightly painted gates and carved peacock friezes running along the top. In the centre of each arch is a stone head of King Renard wearing his spectacles and his small crown of gold.

All the houses of Foxville are built of marble carved with representations of chickens, geese, pheasants and turkeys—the basic elements of the foxes' diet—and above each door is set a carving of the householder's head. Travellers should visit the Royal Palace with its impressive throne room and stained-glass windows.

Foxville maintains a large army, mainly to frighten its neighbours in Dunkiton. The soldiers wear green jackets and yellow trousers, round caps, high red boots, and red bows tied to their tails; the officers are distinguished from the men they command by the gold braid embroidered on their jackets. The troops are armed with wooden swords with edges of sharp teeth. The civilian population dresses in garments made from multicoloured woven feathers. Large numbers of fowl

An elaborately carved throne of gold in the Royal Palace of FOXVILLE.

are kept in the city to provide food as well as feathers for clothes and mattresses.

In spite of the city's charms, visitors are advised to be on their guard as the nature of the inhabitants is, at best, unpredictable.

(L. Frank Baum, *The Road to Oz*, Chicago, 1909)

FRAGRANT ISLAND, an island where everything is sensitive. It is fortified with madrepores, which retreat into their coralline casemates when anyone approaches the island.

Fragrant Island is a monarchy; the king's main role is to protect the island's gods. One divinity is fastened with three nails to the mast of the king's boat; it resembles a triangular sail or a dried fish brought back from the north. Another god is set above the house used by the king's wives; between the interlaced buttocks and young breasts of two sibyls, the god pronounces the famous double formula of happiness: "Be in love" and "Be mysterious."

When the king walks along the shore and sings or prunes the shoots that disfigure the images of the gods that line the beach, his wives huddle in their beds in fear of the Spirit of the Dead and of the eye of a great porcelain lamp which is always lit in their room. When he is not walking, the king is usually to be found in his boat—stark naked apart from a brindled diadem worn round his hips.

(Alfred Jarry, *Gestes et Opinions du Docteur Faustroll, Pataphysicien. Roman Néo-Scientifique*, Paris, 1911)

FRANCARIA, see MECCANIA.

FRANCE-VILLE, a city on the Pacific coast of the United States, latitude 43°11′3″ north and longitude 124°41′173″ west, founded in 1872 by the French scientist, François Sarrasin.

The construction of France-Ville was financed by the inheritance left to Sarrasin by a great-uncle who had married the Begum Gokool in Bengal. The enormous sum of 527 million francs was divided between the Frenchman and a German scientist, Professor Schultze, who also used his part of the inheritance to found a city, STAHLSTADT. Travellers can reach France-Ville by travelling from White Cape, in Oregon, twenty leagues to the north, across the Cascade Hills in the Rocky Mountains.

By January 1872 the territory was already surveyed, measured, laid out, and an army of twenty thousand Chinese coolies, under the direction of five hundred overseers and European engineers, was hard at work. Placards posted up all over the state of California, an advertisement van permanently attached to the rapid train which starts every morning from San Francisco to cross the American continent, and a daily article in the twenty-three newspapers of that city, were sufficient to ensure the recruiting of the workers. It was not even found necessary to resort to publishing on a grand scale, by means of gigantic letters sculptured on the peaks of the Rocky Mountains, that men were wanted.

The first enterprise of France-Ville's founder was to establish a railway connecting the new town with the Pacific Railroad running to Sacramento. While it was under construction, all plans for the town itself stopped. This was not for want of materials; from the first, America had hastened to load the quays of France-Ville with every imaginable requisite for building. It was merely the difficulty of choice. The founder at last decided that freestone should be reserved for national edifices and general ornamentation, and that all houses should be built of brick—not of common, roughly-moulded, half-baked bricks, but of light, well shaped ones, regular in size, weight and density and pierced from end to end with a series of cylindrical and parallel holes. These bricks, when placed together, allowed the air to circulate freely throughout the walls of the building. This arrangement had, at the same time, the valuable effect of deadening sounds and giving complete independence to each apartment.

The committee in charge of directing the building did not wish to impose a model on the architects. They were averse to wearisome, insipid uniformity and merely gave a number of fixed rules to which the architects were bound to adhere.

Travellers wishing to reside in France-Ville must give good references, be fit to follow a useful or liberal profession and must engage to keep the laws of the town. Idle lives are not tolerated.

From the age of four all children are obliged to follow physical and intellectual exercises calculated to develop the brain and muscles. They are also accustomed to such strict cleanliness that they consider a spot on their simple clothes quite a disgrace.

Individual and collective cleanliness is one of the fundamental precepts of the founder of

France-Ville. "To clean, clean unceasingly, so as to destroy the miasmus constantly emanating from a large community"—such is the principal work of the central government. For this purpose all the drains lead out of town, where the contents are condensed and daily transferred to the fields around the city.

Water flows everywhere in abundance. The streets are paved with bituminised wood and the stone footpaths are as spotless as a Dutch courtyard. The provision markets are subject to strict surveillance, and any merchants who dare to speculate on public health incur the severest penalties. The man who sells a bad egg, damaged meat or a pint of adulterated milk is treated as the poisoner he really is. This necessary and delicate office of being a merchant is confined to experienced men who receive special education for it and whose jurisdiction extends to the laundries and disinfecting rooms. No body linen is sent back to its owners without being thoroughly bleached and special care is taken never to mix the washing of two families.

Because of these simple precautions, hospitals are few and reserved for homeless strangers and exceptional cases. The idea of making the hospitals larger than any other building, and of putting seven or eight hundred patients under one roof so as to make a centre of infection, would not enter the head of the founder of France-Ville. The sick are isolated as much as possible and the hospitals are regarded merely as temporary accommodation for the most pressing cases. Twenty or thirty patients at the most, each having a separate apartment, are put into light barracks built of fir wood; the barracks are burnt regularly every year. Being all on one model, they can be multiplied to any extent and have the advantage of being easily carried from one part of the town to another.

(Jules Verne, *Les 500 millions de la Bégum*, Paris, 1879)

FREE COMMOTS, a region to the south-east of CAER DATHYL in northern PRYDAIN, east of the central hills and stretching to the banks of the Great Avren River. On the edge of the Commots, the Llawgadarn Mountains rise to the peak of Mount Meledin where the MIRROR OF LLUNET can be found.

The Commots are by far the most fertile and attractive area of Prydain, and the region is famed for its sweet grass and its rich soil. But the chief glory of the Free Commots is its craftsmen, whose work is famed throughout the land, surpassed only by that of the Fair Folk of TYLWYTHTEG, with whom the craftsmen are on traditionally good terms.

Unlike the rest of Prydain, the Free Commots are not ruled by feudal lords, and they recognize only the High King of Prydain himself as their overlord.

(Lloyd Alexander, *Taran Wanderer*, New York, 1967; Lloyd Alexander, *The High King*, New York, 1968)

FREEDONIA, a small European country to the north of SYLVANIA. The capital is also known as Freedonia, a small city characterized by its picturesque, steeply pitched roofs and tall steeples. Most of the country is devoted to agriculture.

Economically, the most important figure in the country is the stout and wealthy widow Mrs. Gloria Teasedale, known to cover a lot of Freedonian ground; her fortune is the power behind the government. Because of her financial status she was able to demand the resignation of the administration of President Zandor, insisting that she would lend more money to Freedonia only if the celebrated Rufus T. Firefly were appointed president. Firefly was accordingly made president and at once began to rule in his characteristically flamboyant manner. Although Firefly was immediately popular with the people of Freedonia, his behaviour and attitude led to the resignation of some of his ministers.

Nor was his appointment to the taste of neighbouring Sylvania or its ambassador Trentino. For some years Sylvania had been trying to subvert the economy and politics of Freedonia and Firefly's appointment was seen as an obstacle to these plans, as well as to Trentino's marrying Mrs. Teasedale, as Rufus T. Firefly had offered her a roofus over her head if she became his wife. Attempts to have Firefly seduced by a dancer failed—even though he announced his intention of dancing with the cows until she came home—as did Trentino's attempts to steal certain State secrets. Eventually an exchange of insults between Firefly and Trentino—during which Firefly called Trentino, a baboon, a swine, a worm, and an upstart—led to the declaration of war and the invasion of Freedonia. Although it initially seemed that the victory would go to the invaders, matters changed when Trentino himself was captured during an attack on the Sylvanian headquarters and was forced to surrender after having been sadly humiliated by Firefly.

(*Duck Soup,* directed by Leo McCarey, USA, 1933)

FREELAND, an extensive country in East Africa, stretching from the Kenya and Kilimanjaro ranges westward towards the frontiers of the European colonies in central and western Africa. Freeland now includes the areas that were once known as Masailand and Uganda. The southern boundary touches Lake Tanganyika and, to the north, the country extends to the Mountains of the Moon.

Freeland is an independent State which has its origin in a colony set up by the International Free Society, founded in Europe in the latter part of the nineteenth century with the aim of establishing a nation based on perfect liberty and economic justice, a society which would guarantee the unqualified right of every individual to control his own actions and which would secure for the worker the full and uncurtailed enjoyment of the fruits of his labour. The location for this free community was to be East Africa, partly because of its suitable climate and partly because it had not yet been claimed by any western power. The scheme was first announced at a public meeting and it immediately attracted a positive response from a number of countries. Very soon afterwards, the first drift of pioneers arrived in Africa.

The site of the initial colony was a broad valley high on the slopes of the Kenya range, chosen for its beauty and favourable environment. The valley slopes down to a large lake and a wide area of open parkland; close by, a large waterfall plunges down from the glacier fields on the mountains to the waters of the Dna River. Struck by the overwhelming beauty of the site, the first pioneers called it Eden Vale, a name which has been retained for the capital of Freeland. Within a comparatively short time, Freeland has expanded from a small settlement to a major country of international status. Eden Vale is now linked with the outside world by a fast, sophisticated communications network. A railway line follows the track of the route taken from Mombasa by the original settlers; another line connects with the Mediterranean via the Sudan and the Nile Valley. But Freeland's

greatest achievement is probably the railway link with the Atlantic coast via Lake Victoria and the Congo Valley. Telegram communication lines have also been set up and a fleet of steamships cruises the lakes and rivers of the area.

Eden Vale is a large and populous town, spaciously laid out, each house having ten thousand square feet of garden around it. The architecture is a combination of Moorish and Greek styles and the houses are scattered among gardens with numerous fountains. All the streets are lined with shaded walks. The most impressive building in the capital is the National Palace, an immense construction which has a loveliness normally associated with fairy-tale castles. Built entirely in white and yellow marble, the National Palace is larger than the Vatican and more lofty than the dome of St. Peter's.

Eden Vale is well provided with public buildings, libraries and a magnificent amphitheatre. The city is quiet and wholesome, as all industry has been located in such a way as to avoid pollution. All transport within Eden Vale and the other towns is by *draisne*, a small vehicle whose motor power is provided by a spring wound up by ingeniously converted steam power. Once the spring is wound up the *draisne* will travel for twelve and a half miles before it winds down. The spring can then be replaced by another carried as a spare or by new springs purchased from wayside service stations. The system is pollution free and quite soundless. On the lake below the city, gondolas, propelled by elastic springs, are available for pleasure trips.

The prosperity of Freeland is based entirely on its economic philosophy. The means of production are collectively owned and their use depends solely on the capacity and industry of each individual citizen. The one aim of the economy is the satisfaction of real needs, which means that there is no surplus production and no wasteful competition for markets. Production necessarily rises with the natural growth of consumption and the entire system testifies to the solidarity of the economic interests of the society as a whole. Money has now disappeared. Gold is retained as a measure of value, but all actual transactions are carried out on paper or through the use of cheques drawn on accounts at the central bank. Coinage does exist, but is used almost exclusively for foreign trade. Less than seven per cent of the currency issued circulates in Freeland itself. All buying and selling of goods takes place in large halls or warehouses under the management of the community as a whole. Prices are established partly through the decision of manufacturers, partly by auction.

The sole measure of value, and hence of income, is labour, calculated in terms of hour equivalents. Tax is levied in direct proportion to income. Income itself is equivalent to the net share of total profit due to the individual. Initially taxes were extremely high, because of the need for collective investment in capital goods, but they have gradually fallen. It has been estimated that, thanks to the high productivity achieved in Freeland, average hourly wages are equivalent to the average weekly wage in Europe; the average working week in Freeland is only thirty-five hours.

Those who cannot work are paid "maintenance allowances" by the community in proportion to the income due to the individual. The non-working population includes the sick, the aged, children and women. A single woman receives thirty per cent of the average income and a married woman fifteen per cent. The first three children in a family receive three per cent each; orphans receive twelve per cent and the sick and the aged receive forty per cent.

Women do not normally work in Freeland, unless they are teachers or nurses; these are considered the only occupations fitting to the dignity of women. Both occupations are comparatively well paid by European standards and, in the early years of the colony, the wages offered to teachers were high, as an inducement to attract young female immigrants.

Freeland's industrial success is based on its natural resources, which include coal, iron, oil and many minerals, and also on its ability to use machinery. Given that there is no competition (and therefore no industrial or commercial secrets), improved technology can be introduced without any difficulty for the benefit of all.

In its early days, Freeland was governed by the committee of the International Free Society, which remained in Europe. All decisions were laid before a general meeting of the people, and differences of opinion were referred to an elected board of arbitrators. As the colony expanded, this system became impracticable for very obvious reasons. The committee was subdivided into elected executive boards and the whole country was split into five hundred sections, each electing a deputy to a constituent assembly.

In its early days, Freeland did, of course, have

difficulties with the native population. The first settlers had to fight battles with the Masai tribesmen of the area, but warfare rapidly gave way to a system of alliances. The settlers of Freeland have even succeeded in convincing the Masai warriors to give up their traditional occupations and cultivate the land—although the Masai also serve as a kind of mercenary army and are an important factor in fending off attacks by other tribes. Yet despite its early battles, Freeland has never maintained a regular, standing army. On the other hand, all young men are trained in weapon handling and military drill from an early age. This military training was vital when war broke out between the European powers and Abyssinia and threatened to involve Freeland itself. Freeland's "non-professional" army and superior technology were able to defeat the Abyssinian soldiers who had severely mauled the best trained European units. This, perhaps more than anything else, convinced the European powers that Freeland was more than just a vague ideal.

Education is given a high priority in Freeland; all children attend school between the ages of six and sixteen. Classics are not taught, but otherwise the academic syllabus resembles that of a good European school. What is different is the great emphasis placed upon physical education and, in the case of boys, basic military training. Girls tend to receive less physical training, concentrating rather on domestic subjects and music. At sixteen most boys enter institutes of higher or technical education. These institutes are designed to make sure that all workmen in all branches of industry have a full understanding of the machinery and processes with which they will be dealing in their professional lives. University education is then available for those who display a higher than average intelligence and application. Girls who do not wish to follow the professions of nursing or teaching become pupil-daughters, that is, they enter the households of particularly refined and well-respected women, in order to perfect their domestic and social skills. Pupil-daughters are regarded as being half-way between real daughters and maids of honour. It may be a privilege to enter a well-respected household, but it is also an honour to have a pupil-daughter.

Marriage in Freeland is a simple matter: a declaration of reciprocal intent to live together as man and wife. Mutual affection is the sole guarantee of the sanctity of the marriage bond, yet marriage is regarded with such solemnity that divorce is unknown. No official witness is required for a marriage, but the Department of Statistics is notified so that records are kept up to date.

Life in Freeland is extremely comfortable; all houses are artificially cooled and slightly ozonized. All domestic cleaning is done by machines. Food and service are provided by community associations, thus liberating the individual from a wide range of household tasks and obligations. The arts flourish, thanks to a country-wide system of libraries which also function as cafés and general meeting places. Sales of books and journals are astonishingly high, making this one of the few countries in which the creative artist is assured of making a living. Disease has been reduced considerably and medical care is provided by skilled doctors who are employed as public officials. It must, however, be noted that Freeland is not a communist state. On the contrary, it is dedicated to individualism in the true sense of the word. Absolute equality is not forced on people and the communalism of Freeland ensures a flourishing of individual talents and interests rather than the "levelling" characteristic of communist societies.

Freeland is still under the control of the International Free Society, which maintains offices in Europe, with shipping bureaux in Trieste and Mombasa. Applications for immigration and membership are processed there.

(Dr. Theodor Hertzka, *Freiland*, Leipzig, 1890)

FRISLANDIA, an island somewhere in the North Sea, not far from the Dutch coast and not to be confused with the small Frisian Islands. It was from here that a Venetian captain, Nicolo Zeno, and his brother Antonio set off to discover a number of other islands. Among these were Icaria (not to be confused with the country of the same name), where the governor is a direct descendant of Daedalus and the inhabitants are a race of miniature troglodytes; and ESTOTILAND.

(F. Marcolini, *Dello scoprimento dell'Isole Frislandia, Eslanda, Engrovelanda, Estotilanda e Icaria, fattosotto il Polo Artico dai due fratelli Zeno, M. Nicolo e M. Antonio*, Venice, 1558)

FRIVOLA or **FRIVOLOUS ISLAND**, discovered by Admiral Anton, an Englishman, towards 1750, near the island of Juan Fernandez in the Pa-

cific Ocean. Frivolous Island is ruled by an emperor, called "His All-Elegance," whose palace presides over a large square surrounded by shops in the middle of Spiritual City, the capital. Spiritual City is larger than London, and like London it is divided by a river and has many beautiful gardens.

The main characteristic of Frivolous Island is that everything it contains is light or "frivolous." The trees, for instance, bend easily as if made of rubber, and the fruit they bear is scarcely edible— it dissolves in the mouth like foam. A few wild beasts roam the Frivolous forests, but they are harmless, their teeth and claws are soft and their roar is like the whispering rustle of silk.

The inhabitants breed horses, but these again are useless: they collapse under the slightest weight and are too fragile to be used in farming.

Agriculture on the island is an easy task. The women blow on small whistles and the sound makes the necessary furrows in the light dust. The men then idly cast a few seeds into the wind which gently deposits them in the furrows.

Local currency is the *agatine*, pieces of agate used as coins.

(Abbé Gabriel François Coyer, *A Discovery Of The Island Frivola: Or, The Frivolous Island, Translated from the French, Now privately handed about at Paris, and said to be agreeable to the English Manuscripts concerning that Island, and its Inhabitants. Wrote by Order of A—1 A—n*, London, 1750)

FRIZE, ISLAND OF, see SATINLAND.

FROZEN FIRE, THE CITY OF, or **CIBOLA**, capital of QUIVERA.

FROZEN WORDS, SEA OF, on the edge of the frozen sea of the north. In winter, all words and sounds in the area are frozen; as the milder weather approaches in spring, they begin to thaw out and can be clearly heard. Travellers can pick up the frozen words, which resemble crystallized sweets of various colours.

Crossing the sea in summer, a certain Pantagruel heard the noise of a battle between the Arimaspians (see ARIMASPIAN COUNTRY) and the Cloud-riders—a battle which had taken place at the start of the previous winter.

(François Rabelais, *Le quart livre des faicts et dicts du bon Pantagruel*, Paris, 1552)

FUDDLECUMJIG, a town in Quadling Country, in OZ. The inhabitants of the town are known as the Fuddles, and are among the most curious people in the whole of Oz. Their main peculiarity is that they are made of many pieces, rather like jigsaw puzzles, and literally fall apart when strangers approach or when they hear unexpected noises. They then have to be reassembled by anyone with the skill and patience to fit together the pieces.

Some people in Oz find that putting the Fuddles back together again is a fine amusement; the Fuddles themselves never match up one another's scattered parts, explaining that they are no puzzles to themselves and that the experience would be no fun.

The chief citizen of Fuddlecumjig is the Lord High Chigglewitz, or Larry, to use his first name. His personal quirk is that, for reasons best known to himself, he constantly scatters himself all over the place. Some years ago a fragment of his left knee was lost when he did this and he has walked with a limp ever since. Another prominent citizen is Grandmother Gnit. Her main activity appears to be knitting mittens for a kangaroo which is often in the area.

When fully assembled the Fuddles are a kind and hospitable people. Visitors who want a meal are advised to put the cook together first.

(L. Frank Baum, *The Emerald City of Oz*, Chicago, 1910)

FULWORTH, a seaside village in Sussex, England, situated in Fulworth Cove, a few miles from the cottage to which Mr. Sherlock Holmes retired in 1903 to pursue his interest in bee-keeping. Half a mile away from Holmes' cottage stands Harold Stackhurst's coaching establishment, *The Gables*. Holmes' cottage is now privately owned.

(Sir Arthur Conan Doyle, "The Adventure of the Lion's Mane," in *The Case Book of Sherlock Holmes*, London, 1927)

FUNDINELVE, ancient dwarf-halls situated underground in ALDERLEY EDGE in Cheshire. The Fundinelve is protected by a spell which keeps its sleeping guards from growing old and weak. The heart of this magic spell is sealed within the Weirdstone of Brisingamen, and guarded by the Wizard Cadellin. Should the stone be damaged or destroyed, the spell will be broken and the warriors will age and die.

(Alan Garner, *The Weirdstone of Brisingamen*, London, 1960)

FUTURA, a kingdom of unknown location. Travellers are advised to visit the temple of the king's daughters, built high on a rock above the sea. The route is somewhat long and progress may be slow. On reaching the rock, the traveller must pass through seven doors, each made of a different metal, corresponding to the seven planets. An eighth door, made of gold, is reserved for the king alone and must not be opened. The doors are defended by dragons, flames, giants, winged serpents, sirens and a phoenix.

The name of the kingdom comes from the concern of its inhabitants with the problems of the future. Their speculations on this matter have led them to endless quarrels, despite their evident desire for peace.

(Marie Anne de Roumier Robert, *Les Ondins*, Paris & London, 1768)

G

GAALDINE, see GONDAD.

GALA, a kingdom in Asia, somewhere in the middle of the southern temperate zone, ruled by an absolute monarch more European than Oriental. The mild climate and natural fertility of the land favour a prosperous agricultural system; in addition, nature has enriched Gala with mineral deposits.

The most striking detail of the political system of Gala is the method of taxation. The Galans have discovered the mildest and most secure way to force the inhabitants to pay the taxes which the State needs in order to function. The taxation system is like an obligatory lottery: each adult must, by law, acquire from the State a number of lottery tickets proportional to his income. The winner of a draw receives one-twentieth of the total sum collected. As a result, the Galans pay their taxes with evident satisfaction—even with a kind of unhealthy eagerness.

Another important innovation established in the kingdom of Gala is the suppression of all commercial middlemen: all products are acquired by the State, which puts them on sale through a network of State-owned stores. In this way, the several stages which otherwise increase the price of all commodities is abolished. Visitors will be agreeably surprised by the excellent condition of the roads. The State, with special care, maintains an extensive network of roads which enables all goods to travel easily to their destinations. These roads are the basis of the country's economy.

Thanks to its reforms, Gala is the richest kingdom in Asia—so rich that its foreign policy consists of acquiring its neighbouring States (whenever the King of Gala finds it convenient) rather than conquering them by bloodshed.

(André–François de Brancas-Villeneuve, *Histoire ou Police du royaume de Gala, traduite de l'italien en anglais, et de l'anglais en français*, Paris, 1754)

GALLIGENIA, an island of uncertain location, some twelve by eight leagues. The inhabitants, who now number over one hundred thousand, are all descended from three French exiles who, after being shipwrecked in a storm, took refuge on the island which had just risen from the sea. The three founders of Galligenia were a certain Almont and his son and daughter, who committed incest in order to establish the Galligenian race.

So that the rest of the world should not set a bad example to the Galligenians, Almont and his children did not tell their descendants anything about the outer world. However, on their own, the people discovered the existence of God, whom they worshipped without churches or clergy, and learnt about other countries from travellers and merchants.

The Galligenians have established a republic, governed by the Parliament of Sages, in which everything, even the citizens themselves, belongs to everyone. Every woman is the wife of all men and every man the husband of all women.

All citizens, men and women, work two days a week; this suffices to provide for the needs of the community. The Galligenians show no ambition, no greed, no lust of any kind. But in recent years several groups of dissenters, bored with their impeccable society, have tried to create minor commotions to disrupt the perfect order of the republic. Europeans are not particularly welcome as the Galligenians fear that they will take over the lands and civilize them in the same way the Spaniards civilized the South American Indians.

(Charles François Tiphaigne de la Roche, *Histoire Des Galligènes, Ou Mémoires De Duncan*, Amsterdam, 1765)

GALLINACO, a country of undefined location, originally inhabited by the Long Hand monkeys and now colonized by the Big Foot monkeys from the Island of Felido. After the colonization, the Long Hand monkeys lost their right to climb the banana trees to pick bananas. This became the exclusive right of the Big Foot monkeys, who decided to make bananas their staple trade. They ate as many as they liked, dried the surplus to sell abroad and gave the banana skins to the Long Hand monkeys in exchange for their labour. But the Long Hand monkeys hated the taste of banana skins, in spite of assurances from the Big Foots that the skins were nourishing and they envied them the privilege of consuming them. "If things go on like this," the defeated Long Hands moaned, "our children will have forgotten how to climb the banana trees in search of food, and they will no longer be true monkeys."

It became necessary to post a Big Foot armed with a stone in front of every banana tree, because under cover of night the bananas were being stolen. There were not enough guards, so Long Hands were recruited to fill the gaps; as a reward they were given the right to eat a banana from time to time, in secret. The Long Hands thus recruited felt deeply satisfied and wonderfully important. Both tribes shared the same territory but lived apart, spying on one another among the trees and ferns. Gallinaco, once so joyful and bustling, was enveloped in a melancholic atmosphere, even on sunny days. Hostilities grew into skirmishes, and the situation became grimmer and grimmer.

Eventually the Long Hands won permission to climb ten of the banana trees, allowing them a taste of the bananas. Soon, however, squabbling broke out; everyone wanted a taste but there were not enough bananas to go round, and the Big Foot monkeys refused to increase the quota of trees. Things went from bad to worse as certain unscrupulous Long Hands set up a black market in bananas. Dissatisfaction grew, quarrels multiplied and the Long Hands' dislike of their masters increased even more.

Then Fino, one of the cleverest Long Hand monkeys, called the tribe together, saying that he had a plan. He suggested that he be leader of both the Long Hands and the Big Foots. Fino's plan was approved with enthusiasm and put into effect.

For several months, peace reigned in Gallinaco. Never before had one monkey been the leader of both tribes, and admirers came from everywhere to congratulate Fino and try to understand how he had pulled off such a stunt. Fino kept a modest profile but his victory was quickly going to his head. Yet the lot of the Long Hand monkeys had scarcely improved. They still had only ten banana trees at their disposal, and most of them had to feed on banana skins all year long. At last, Fino convinced the Big Foots to give the Long Hands two more banana trees. The handing-over took place during a sumptuous ceremony, and everyone rejoiced.

At the end of the day, Fino summoned several elders of the Long Hand tribe and assured them that this handing-over was only the begin-

ning. With a little patience, he said, they would recover practically all their lost trees. Then he summoned several elders of the Big Foot tribe and told them that for the sake of peace he would be forced, from time to time, to hand over a few more banana trees, but that these would be few and far between, so as not to damage business in any way.

A year passed and Fino's fame spread far beyond Gallinaco. Now, when he strolled among his subjects, he strutted with an insolent swagger. No one dared address him except in respectful tones and after long reflection, since he no longer accepted any criticism. Yet he lost none of his perspicacity, and he sensed that revolution was simmering among the Long Hand monkeys. One evening, a spy told him that a revolt was in the making.

Fino ordered that the trouble-makers be arrested at once, and assembled his counsellors. The discussion was long and loud. Finally, one of the counsellors had a simple but remarkable idea. Since what mattered most to the Long Hand monkeys was not eating the bananas but simply climbing up the banana trees, he proposed that they be allowed to climb up all the trees that had already been picked bare; they would thus have the impression of having regained almost all their old freedom. Fino approved of this excellent idea, and proposed to call those banana trees "distinct" since only the Long Hand monkeys would be allowed to climb them. It is therefore by the name "distinct society" that the land of Gallinaco is known to travellers today.

(Yves Beauchemin, "The Banana Wars," in *The Ark in the Garden: Fables for Our Times*, Toronto, 1998)

GALMA, an island off the coast of NARNIA, about one day's sail northeast of Cair Paravel.

On his great voyage across the Eastern Ocean, King Caspian X of Narnia stopped at Galma. The event was marked by a great tournament given by the reigning duke. Visitors of plebeian blood should not expect a similar reception.

(C.S. Lewis, *The Voyage of the "Dawn Treader,"* London, 1952)

GANABIN ISLAND, although of uncertain location, is probably situated not far from CHANEPH ISLAND. The island is mountainous, with a double peak that from a distance resembles Mount

Parnassus. Near the top is a fine forest and the most beautiful fountain in the world. The people are thieves and robbers, and travellers are advised to be constantly on their guard.

(François Rabelais, *Le quart livre des faicts et dicts du bon Pantagruel*, Paris, 1552)

GANAKLAND, a region of rolling plains in the underground continent of PELLUCIDAR not far from JA-RU. The area takes its name from the Ganak or Bisonmen who inhabit it. The Ganak have short stocky bodies, but their faces and torsos are covered in long brown hair. Small, heavy horns protrude from their foreheads, and they have tails which end in a bushy tuft of hair. The Ganak use their horns to fight with, charging with lowered heads and trying to gore or disembowel their adversaries. Even though they can speak like the other people of Pellucidar, they often bellow like bulls and when angered they paw at the ground with one foot.

Although vegetarian, they are vicious, sadistic creatures. They keep females slaves, both to satisfy their sexual appetites and to till the fields. When the slaves are too old to work, they are killed. Men are kept as slaves only if there is a shortage of women; otherwise they are killed. If an excess number of slaves has accumulated, the Ganak amuse themselves by torturing them and finally burning them at the stake. This entertainment is usually accompanied by the consumption of "dancing water," a potent spirit which loosens muscular coordination and reduces inhibitions in all those who drink it.

(Edgar Rice Burroughs, *Seven Worlds to Conquer*, New York, 1936)

GANGARIDIA, a kingdom rich in diamonds, on the east bank of the River Ganges. The Gangarides are peaceful shepherds whose vast herds of sheep produce the finest wool in the world. They live in houses decorated with ivory and orange-tree wood and they sleep in beds made of roses. They are vegetarians and consider all animals to be their brothers; killing and eating an animal is an act of murder in their eyes.

The animals here have retained their ability to speak. The fauna includes unicorns—the most gentle and at the same time the most fearsome of animals—which the Gangarides ride. One hundred Gangaridian shepherds mounted on their unicorns are capable of defeating huge armies. Gangaridia is also the home of the phoenix, but there are no longer any thrushes in the country—they were expelled when one of them brought back false news about the Princess of Babylon, who was loved by the King of Gangaridia.

At the full moon, the people gather in cedar temples and give thanks to God for His goodness to them; men and women use separate temples to avoid possible distractions. All the quadrupeds meet on a beautiful lawn for their devotions, and the birds gather in a wood. Some of the parrots are particularly fine preachers.

The King of India once attempted to invade Gangaridia with an army of one million soldiers and ten thousand elephants. The unicorns impaled the elephants on their horns and the men fell to the swords of the Gangarides as easily as rice plants fall to the sickle. The Indian king and six thousand soldiers were captured; the king was bathed in the Ganges and fed on a vegetarian diet until his pulse was steady and his humour less sanguine. Only when the Council of Gangaridia and the unicorns were satisfied were the captives allowed to return home. Since then the Indians have had great respect for the Gangarides.

Gangaridia is currently ruled by a queen. Her son, Aldee-Amazan, succeeded to the throne of Babylon (from which his father had been wrongly deposed) and married the Princess of Babylon.

(Voltaire [François Marie Arouet], *La Princesse de Babylone*, Paris, 1768)

GARAMANTI COUNTRY, in a valley to the east of the Rifei Mountains, on the Afghan side of that mountain chain. The inhabitants, the Garamanti, should not be confused with the tribe of the same name that lives in the Libyan desert south of Sirti.

The Garamanti of the Rifei Mountains are a small group of barbarians who have never been conquered by other tribes, thanks, no doubt, to their natural isolation and to the extreme difficulty of reaching the valley where they live. The first travellers to mention them came from Europe in the sixteenth century. According to their reports, the valley is fertile but sparsely populated. The Garamanti live by farming and animal breeding and are ruled by six laws that regulate their government, religion, dress, family, philosophy and heredity. Nobody is allowed to add other laws to these six: whoever tries to do so is immediately condemned to death.

The rules of Garamanti Country are strictly enforced. All clothing is rigorously uniform, both for men and for women. Every couple is entitled to three children: beyond this limit, any offspring are put to death. Work, property and inheritance are shared equally among all inhabitants. When women reach the age of fifty, they are put to death; this way nobody grows old, depraved or useless to society. Liars are also condemned to death, because the Garamanti believe that a single liar is enough to ruin a population. Travellers are advised that they will not be permitted to worship more than two gods at a time.

(Antonio de Guevara, *Libro llamado Relox de los Príncipes, en el cual va encorporado el muy famoso libro de Marco Aurelio*, Madrid, 1527; Mambrino Roseo, *Institutione del prencipe cristiano*, Venice, 1543)

GARB, see HIME.

GARGOYLES, LAND OF, an underground country reached via the spiral staircase that travellers will find inside PYRAMID MOUNTAIN.

Everything in this land is made of wood—the soil is sawdust and the pebbles are knots of trees. Carved wooden flowers grow in the gardens, where the grass is wood shavings. In those spots not covered by grass or soil, a solid, wooden floor can be seen. Wooden birds fly through the air.

The city of the Gargoyles lies at some distance from the depths of Pyramid Mountain; it is also made entirely of wood. The houses, built like towers, vary in shape: some are square, others hexagonal or octagonal. The best seem old and weather-worn.

The Gargoyles themselves are also made of wood. Less than three feet tall, they have short legs, but extraordinarily long arms. Their heads are too big for their bodies and their carved faces are fantastically ugly. The tops of their heads are decorated with a variety of grotesque designs, combining vegetables with squares and other geometrical shapes. All wear wooden wings attached to their shoulders with wooden screws; these enable them to fly rather than walk, their legs being of almost no use to them. When they sleep, the Gargoyles take off their wings and hang them up. Criminal Gargoyles are punished by having their wings removed and by being imprisoned in a high tower until they mend their ways.

Perhaps the most curious feature of the Land of Gargoyles is the silence that reigns everywhere. The Gargoyles themselves make no sound while flying and communicate by making signs and gestures with their fingers; the cattle of this wooden country do not low and the birds do not sing. Visitors should bear in mind that the Gargoyles are afraid of noise, which is therefore one of the most effective weapons that can be used against these creatures in the case of an attack; the other is fire.

(L. Frank Baum, *Dorothy and the Wizard in Oz*, Chicago, 1908)

GASTER'S ISLAND, not far from the Sea of FROZEN WORDS, seems from a distance to be barren and mountainous. In its centre is a steep, rocky cliff, extremely difficult to climb; at its summit, however, is a pleasant and fertile realm, the seat of the governor of the island, Master Gaster, who is the first Master of Arts in the world. With him lives Dame Penia, or Poverty, mother of the nine muses and, by a former marriage to Porus, mother of Love.

Gaster is a strict and imperious monarch who will not accept arguments from anyone and, being deaf, speaks only in signs. At his command, the sky is known to tremble and the earth to shake. Gaster has invented all the arts, machines and contrivances used on the island and has instructed the island's fauna in the arts denied them by nature: for instance, he makes ravens and jays into poets. He has even found a means of turning his enemies' bullets against themselves: they return on the same trajectory and with their original violence; as a result, they are as dangerous to the firer as to the intended target. He has a violent temper and when angered devours everything, man and beast alike.

Two kinds of courtiers can be found at Gaster's court: the *Engastrimythes*, or "Ventriloquists," and the *Gastrolaters*, or "Belly-worshippers." The former claim to be descended from the ancient stock of Eurycles and cite the authority of Aristophanes, in *The Wasps*, to prove their case.

The *Manduce* idol, GASTER'S ISLAND.

The *Gastrolaters* worship Gaster, claiming that he is the only true god. Despite their differing appearances and humours, *Gastrolaters* have one thing in common: they are all idle and never do a stroke of work, arguing that they are afraid of reducing or insulting their bellies. They wear strange clothes and shell-shaped cowls. Their religious rites involve walking in procession to Gaster, carrying with them a hideous idol known as the *Manduce*. It is a terrifying figure: its eyes are bigger than its belly and its head is larger than the rest of its body. It has wide jaws, well provided with teeth which are made to gnash most horribly by means of a concealed cord. Immense quantities of food and drink of all imaginable kinds are brought to Gaster on feast days. But Master Gaster himself makes no claim to divinity.

Dame Penia is Gaster's regent. When she travels through the land, all courts are closed, all edicts are void and all ordinances are in vain. She is subject to no law. Travellers are advised to flee her; the islanders themselves would prefer to expose themselves to all kinds of danger rather than let her capture them.

(François Rabelais, *Le quart livre des faicts et dicts du bon Pantagruel*, Paris, 1552)

GAUNES, a kingdom in the west of Gaul, the realm of King Bors, uncle of Launcelot. Both Bors and Launcelot became knights of the Round Table of CAMELOT and greatly distinguished themselves in the service of King Arthur. Bors was one of Arthur's allies in the liberation of CAMELERD and his nephew became one of the most famous of all Arthur's knights. Nothing else is known about this kingdom.

(Anonymous, *La Mort le Roi Artu*, 13th cen. AD)

GELT MOUNTAINS, a range of rugged and precipitous mountains between the Telthearna River—which marks the northern frontier of the BEKLAN EMPIRE—and the Beklan Plain itself. The lower slopes of the mountains are clad with myrtle and cypresses. From here, a road crosses the mountains, winding through the rocks. The town of Gelt, high on the summit, is a centre for the iron trade.

(Richard Adams, *Shardik*, London, 1974)

GEM OF TRUTH ISLAND, see ALEOFANE.

GENELIABIN, see TELENIABIN.

GENII, LAND OF THE, see WAQ ARCHIPELAGO.

GENOTIA, a large continent in the south Atlantic, divided into various kingdoms, with numerous islands off its coast. Piracy is not uncommon in the surrounding seas and slavery still exists in some areas. Genotia was known to the Greeks through the tales of Venetian travellers.

Certain countries on Genotia are worth a visit: GYNOPYREA, PANDOCLIA, FERISLAND, NEOPIA ISLAND and PHENACIL (see under XIMEQUE).

(Louis Adrien Duperron de Castera, *Le Theatre Des Passions Et De La Fortune Ou Les Avantures Surprenantes de Rosamidor & de Theoglaphire. Histoire Australe*, Paris, 1731)

GEOMETERS' ISLAND, one of several high islands near Tierra del Fuego. A dry, sterile island with vast, square, silent cities. The inhabitants spend their time drawing figures in the sand.

(Abbé Pierre François Guyot Desfontaines, *Le Nouveau Gulliver, ou Voyage De Jean Gulliver, Fils Du Capitaine Gulliver. Traduit d'un Manuscrit Anglois. Par Monsieur L.D.F.*, Paris, 1730)

GIANT'S GARDEN, somewhere in England, a large lovely garden with soft green grass. Beautiful flowers are scattered here and there like stars over the grass, and there are twelve peach-trees that in the springtime break out into delicate blossoms of pink and pearl and in the autumn bear rich fruit. In the middle of the garden stands the Giant's Castle, with high windows and strong towers. In the farthest corner of the garden, visitors will find a tree covered with lovely white blossoms; its branches are golden and laden with silver fruit. At the foot of the tree lie the mortal remains of the Giant himself, covered with white blossoms.

Though today the garden can be visited without difficulty, many years ago the Giant decided to build a wall around his garden and set up a sign, "Trespassers will be Prosecuted," in order to keep out the children who came to play here. But with the children gone the birds did not care to sing and the trees forgot to blossom. Snow, frost, hail and the north wind took over the garden and spring never came. Then one day, the Giant heard some lovely music, and found that winter had ended. The children had crept back in through a hole in the wall, and brought spring with them. Regretting his selfishness, the Giant took a great axe and knocked down the wall.

Among the children who came that day was a little boy, smaller than the rest, whom the Giant loved best of all. But after that day the little boy never came again, even though the other children came back to the garden every morning. Over the years, the Giant grew old and feeble, and spent his days watching the children at their games. One winter morning, he looked out of his window and saw in the farthest corner of the garden the white-blossomed tree: underneath it stood the little boy he had loved. The Giant ran out into the garden, but when he came close to the child his face grew red with anger, for on the palms of the child's hands were the marks of two nails, and the prints of two nails were on the little feet. The child's voice stopped the Giant's wrath. "You let me play once in your garden," said the child. "Today you shall come with me to my garden, which is Paradise."

(Oscar Wilde, "The Selfish Giant," in *The Happy Prince and Other Tales*, London, 1888)

GIANTS, SEA OF, part of the frozen Arctic Ocean, inhabited by giants and trolls who have taken refuge here. The giants, several of whom are one-eyed (see CYCLOPES ISLAND), have ferocious dogs; they often kidnap and marry maidens from Greenland because—to tell the truth—they are very ugly. The parents of the maidens, in order to get them back, must resort to the arts of the sorcerers, or *Angakok*, who are able to kill the giants by using magic.

Travellers are warned that those who land on these shores at night are attacked by the giants, beaten with cudgels and then devoured. When the terrible nordic winter ends and the ocean, freed by the warmth of the sun, breaks up the strangely shaped mountains of ice that glitter like gems, then the giants, with their long beards and red costumes, climb up onto these icy temples tinted in the light with every colour of the rainbow. With the polar bears, the giants travel on these majestic monuments of crystal through their vast domain, blowing on small reed pipes to provoke storms. Several push on even to the northern shores of Norway. When they speak, they bellow horribly, tearing the trees from the ground with their hands. They are known to dive underwater to catch fish and to hunt wild animals on land with such sure steps that they never slip.

One of the giants, called Hafstraub, often likes to show himself to sailors. Tall, armless and of imposing shape, he rises like a whale from the water. Pale blue, the colour of ice, he wears a helmet on his head; but nobody has ever been able to determine whether the part which remains hidden beneath the sea has the form of a man or a fish.

(Tommaso Porcacchi, *Le isole piu' famose del mondo*, Milan, 1572; Maria Savi-Lopez, *Leggende del mare*, Turin, 1920)

GIPHANTIA, an island in a vast sea of shifting sands, surrounded by the deserts that lie to the north of West Africa. To the traveller arriving in Giphantia, the island presents itself as an immense plain. As one advances, the vegetation becomes taller and taller until finally the trees touch the sky, forming a vast amphitheatre. The air is deliciously cool and beautifully perfumed, so sweet that one never feels tired, only calm and content.

The island is inhabited by spirits who protect human beings from the four elements: air, water, fire and earth. Giphantia is the only place in the world in which nature still has its elemental energy, constantly producing new species of animals and plants. Not all species survive, but the spirits do their best to preserve them and then to distribute them throughout the world. It sometimes happens that the new species cannot find a suitable habitat and so it dies out. When the spirits travel abroad, they become what are known as nymphs, naiads or gnomes. In some places, the spirits of Giphantia are known as *zaziris* (from the Chinese "agent"). They are governed by a prefect, whose face resembles a reflection in murky water.

When in need of purification, the spirits enter a tall, hollow column filled with four elemental essences. Near the purifying column rises a small hill, reached by a staircase of two hundred steps. On the top of the hill is a globe that represents the world, connected through imperceptible channels to every country. The collected information is chaotic, but if the globe is touched with a certain wand it becomes possible to hear what is happening at any given point. A mirror used in conjunction with the globe enables the spirits to see as well as to hear. Near the globe is a grassy hollow, at the bottom of which is a stairway that leads into a large, bare room. Visitors will note here an astonishingly realistic picture of the ocean projected on one of the walls by rays of light. These images are fixed, but can be replaced at will without being damaged, and appeal to all senses at once.

There are three remarkable trees in Giphantia. The first is the Tree of Love. Its leaves are like myrtle, with purple flowers covered in white triangular spots. The tree is never affected by cold or by heat, no matter how extreme. Once, however, it began to wither and although the spirits managed to save it they could not avoid affecting its nature; because of this, human love is now a source of discord, not of union. The second tree has no flowers, leaves or fruit; it consists of an infinite number of very slender tendrils, at the end of which the traveller can see tiny worms. The worms become flies whose sting provokes various unreasonable passions and manias—hence the expression "What's

bitten him?" The third tree is no higher than a man but its branches spread out horizontally, along a rock wall, for three hundred paces in either direction. No two of its leaves resemble one another, and the veins of each leaf show a particular shape—a colonnade, a scientific instrument, a mathematical problem or a machine. When they reach maturity they are blown away and become so fine that they can enter a person's bloodstream through the pores. Once in the bloodstream, the leaves take on their original form and provoke a fever. The brain finally perceives the design on the leaf and, when it does, it produces the corresponding invention.

(Charles François Tiphaigne de la Roche, *Giphantie*, Paris, 1760; Charles François Tiphaigne de la Roche, *L'Empire des Zaziris sur les Humains ou La Zazirocratie*, Paris, 1761)

GLADDEN FIELDS, an area between the MISTY MOUNTAINS and the GREAT RIVER in northern MIDDLE-EARTH. The Fields lie by the confluence of the Great River and the Gladden, to the north of LORIEN.

During the Battle of the Gladden Fields at the beginning of the Third Age, Isildur, King of ARNOR, and his men were attacked and massacred here by a band of orcs from the Misty Mountains. The Kingdom of Arnor never fully recovered from this blow. During the battle, the One Ring was lost in the waters of the Great River, an event that was to completely alter the subsequent history of the whole of Middle-earth.

(J.R.R. Tolkien, *The Fellowship of the Ring*, London, 1954; J.R.R. Tolkien, *The Return of the King*, London, 1955; J.R.R. Tolkien, *The Silmarillion*, London, 1977)

GLATHION, see CAMELIARD.

GLITTERING CAVES, see AGLAROND.

GLITTERING PLAIN, LAND OF THE, near the coast perhaps of northern Scotland. A kingdom of high mountains and sloping meadows, it is reached by a narrow path through the cliffs, guarded by a warden dressed in scarlet, whose duty it is to help travellers coming in and to prevent them from leaving. Visitors are advised that no one is allowed to return from the Land of the Glittering Plain.

Since immortality is conferred upon them on arrival, those visitors who have managed to escape have become drifting ghosts. Although the Land of the Glittering Plain is also called "Acre of the Undying," visitors should keep in mind that use of this name is forbidden. The country should only be referred to as "The Land of the Glittering Plain" or "The Land of Living Men."

The king's pavilion, surrounded on three sides by woods and decorated with embroidered flowers, should be visited. Because weariness is unknown here, most people travel on foot.

(William Morris, *The Story of the Glittering Plain which has also been called the Land of Living Men or the Acre of the Undying,* London, 1891)

GLOME, a kingdom bordering on Phars and Caphad. The capital, also known as Glome, stands on the banks of the river Shennit. The city was originally built far back from the river because of its tendency to flood, but now the Shennit has been deepened and narrowed and barges can be brought upriver to the city gates. The Royal Palace stands on a hill above the city. It is not a particularly luxurious or distinguished building; it is made of wood and painted brick. On the second floor is a small five-sided room which is sometimes used as a prison; this was built as the second storey of a round tower which was never completed.

On the opposite bank of the river stands the main temple, the House of Ungit. Four great stones, twice the height of a man, have been erected here in an egg-shaped ring. The stones are very ancient and no one knows who brought them here or who set them up in this manner. Between the standing stones brick walls have been constructed, and the roof is thatched with reeds. According to the priests, the shape of the temple is symbolic and represents the egg from which the world hatched or the womb in which the world once lay. The goddess Ungit (who is also worshipped in ESSUR under the name of Talapal) is said to symbolize the earth, the womb and the mother of all things and is believed to have forced her way up through the earth itself. In the past the goddess was represented by a shapeless stone which stood in the centre of the temple, but a statue of a woman has recently been placed beside it. The introduction of the statue indicates a Greek influence on Glome's traditional religion. Ungit is regarded as the mother and sometimes the wife of the God of the Mountain, who is believed to dwell on the Grey Mountain above the city. He is held to represent the celestial powers.

The cult of the two gods involves constant sacrifices. These are usually of animals, but when the need to placate the gods becomes pressing, humans may be used. The sacrificial victims are fastened to a barkless tree on the mountain with an iron collar and are left there to be devoured by the God of the Mountain and the legendary Shadowbeast which is said to appear in times of great trouble. The victims are drugged and go more or less willingly to their deaths.

The temple is served by a hierarchy of priests and is defended by its own soldiers, normally subject to the authority of the captain of the king's guard. It is also attended by a number of women who serve the goddess throughout their lives.

Although sacrifices are offered all year round, the main festival is the Birth of the Year, when a masked priest is shut in the house of Ungit from sunset onwards. At noon next day he fights his way out and the year is said to be born. The fight is symbolic—only wooden swords are used and wine instead of blood is poured over the combatants. As the priest emerges, the crowd gathered outside the western door whirl rattles and fling wheat seed into the air. By tradition, the king must spend the night before the birth in the temple with the priest, together with one of the nobles, one of the elders and a representative of the people. The manner in which these are chosen is a sacred mystery, and it is forbidden for a virgin to witness the things that are done in the temple that night.

The wealth of Glome comes from its cattle and its silver mines, the richest of any country in the area. In the past the mines were worked by convicts but the yield was low and many men died. Now there is a new system: young slaves are bought specifically for the mines and can earn their freedom by digging a set quantity of ore. It takes a steady worker roughly seven years to earn his freedom. As a result of this reform, the productivity of the mines has greatly increased.

Glome is a hereditary monarchy. The throne normally passes to the eldest son of the king, but in the absence of a son the daughter succeeds and in fact recent history has been dominated by the daughters of King Trom. By his first marriage

Trom had two daughters, Redival who later married Trunia of Phars, and Orual the present ruler. Trom's second marriage to a princess of Caphad produced a third daughter, Istra; her mother died giving birth. Istra was one of the most beautiful girls the country had ever seen and was initially beloved by everyone. When plagues, rebellions and droughts began to affect the country, she was at first thought able to heal the sick with her touch, but gradually popular opinion turned against her and she came to be regarded as the Accursed, the person responsible for the sufferings of the people. Finally the girl was taken to the Grey Mountain to be sacrificed; shortly afterwards the rains returned.

Orual climbed the mountain after the sacrifice and found that Istra had been taken by the Westwind for his wife, and now dwelt in a magnificent palace he had built for her. The palace was not visible to mortal eyes, but Orual claimed to have had a glimpse of it at dawn. Istra was never seen again, but she has become the object of a religious cult in neighbouring Essur.

Orual herself is one of the most famous monarchs of Glome. From an early age she was convinced that she was extremely ugly and habitually wore a veil in public. She was taught to use a sword and astonished everyone by defeating Argan, leader of a rebellion in Phars, in single combat, restoring King Trunia to his rightful throne. In subsequent years she led the armies of Glome into battle on several occasions, defeating both the Wagon-men who live beyond the Grey Mountain and the armies of Essur. In one incident in the war with Essur she is said to have slain seven men in a single encounter.

In addition to her military achievements, she is celebrated for her many reforms—particularly those affecting the silver mines—and for the rebuilding of much of the capital. Throughout her career she has been advised by the man known as the Fox, a Greek bought by King Trom to bring up his children. The Fox was at least partly responsible for the introduction of certain Greek philosophical ideas into the country, and for the birth of the small palace library which now contains a well-chosen selection of the Greek classics. Thanks to these texts, some of the nobility are beginning to learn to read and study philosophy.

(C.S. Lewis, *Till We Have Faces. A Myth Retold*, London, 1956)

GLOUPOV (from the Russian *gloupy,* "stupid"), now known as Nepreklonsk, built, like Rome, on seven hills. Three rivers run through Gloupov, creating a confused tangle of narrow streets and alleys. The town was founded by the Head-Bangers (so called because they would bang their heads against walls or any other obstacles in their way), a tribe in the north of Russia. After centuries of warfare with their neighbours, the Head-Bangers defeated their arch-enemies, the Askew-Bellies, in a head-banging contest, and having united both tribes, they set off to find a king. After two kings had declined the honour of ruling them, they determined to find the stupidest king in the world.

They finally found a man who accepted their nomination and who appointed the bandit Cut-Purse as his governor. In order to obtain money and thanks from the king, Cut-Purse stirred up rebellions among the people. At first he was successful, but when his excesses became too great he was sentenced to death; however, before he could be hanged, he cut his throat with a cucumber. Two more governors were appointed, with similar results, before the king himself came to the town as ruler. His words "I will flog you to death" marked the end of Gloupov's early history.

Travellers interested in the development of Gloupov should consult *The Gloupov Chronicle,* which traces the story of the town from 1731 to 1825. Twenty-one governors ruled Gloupov during this period. Some were remarkable, like one Simon Konstantinovitch Dvoiekourov (1762–70), who introduced the art of brewing to the town and made the use of mustard and laurel sauce compulsory. Following Dvoiekourov's death, the mustard fields were turned over to cabbages and peas and the habit of eating mustard died out. Governor Borodavkine reimposed the custom in the first of the so-called "Civilizing Wars." The second war was fought over the need to explain to the Gloupovians that houses should be built on stone foundations; the third, over their refusal to plant pyrethrum; the fourth, in an attempt to establish an academy. Borodavkine later realized that he had gone about his civilizing campaign too quickly and launched a series of revolts against civilization, burning down three suburbs in the process; only his death in 1798 prevented him from destroying the whole town.

Borodavkine was followed by Negodiaev, who attempted to teach the people of Gloupov good manners. As a result of his policy of ensuring that the people could stand up to adversity, the town was almost reduced to starvation by the end of his governorship. His successor, Mikaladze, tried to abolish corporal punishment and not to pass any laws; he was followed by Benebolenski, a man with a mad passion for legislation who among other things ordered that everyone was to walk carefully and give appropriate presents. He was arrested on suspicion of Bonapartism when he invited Napoleon to come to Gloupov.

The next governor, Lieutenant-Colonel Prychtch, announced on arrival that he had come to Gloupov to rest and during his rule the town prospered. The people suspected Prychtch of practising black magic; when his head was cut open by a conspiring marshall, they found it to be stuffed with pâté. After that, Gloupov was governed by police-inspectors, whose plot to poison the town dogs—so that they could rob food shops—was foiled.

Ivanov, the next governor, was so small that he could absorb nothing of any great volume, and it is said that he died because he was literally incapable of taking in all the new legislation of the period. Other historians have written that his brain atrophied from lack of use and that he retired to the country where he fathered a microcephalic race.

In 1815, Ivanov was replaced by the Viscount du Chariot, a French adventurer who tried to explain the rights of man and the rights of the Bourbons to the Gloupovians, exhorting them to believe in the goddess Reason and in the infallibility of the Pope. The people began construction of a tower that would reach to the heavens, but it was never completed, for lack of architects. They began to worship ancient Slav gods, corruption and immorality spread, respect for the elderly died out, and the operetta *La Belle Hélène* was performed. Du Chariot was eventually found out to be a woman and was exiled.

Groustilov, who helped himself to the State funds and, to relieve his conscience, wept profusely whenever he saw his soldiers eating rotten bread, replaced du Chariot. However, his belief that everyone who tried could be a parasite and his refusal to see that happiness leads to materialism, brought about his fall. He underwent a religious conversion and resolved to work for the salvation of all, wearing an ascetic hair-shirt and flagellating himself in public. Visitors can still admire his velvet whip preserved and on display at the Gloupov Archives. It was during this period of conversion that Groustilov wrote his *Delights of the Pious Soul*.

Groustilov was succeeded by Ougrioum-Bourtcheiev, who slept on the floor on a stone pillow, kept his wife and children locked up in a cellar for life, and ultimately decided to re-establish discipline in the State of Gloupov. In order to end a particularly long drought, Ougrioum-Bourtcheiev tried to divert a neighbouring river. When the river would not move, he decided to rebuild Gloupov on a new site and renamed it Nepreklonsk. One day, the sun disappeared, the earth shook and the governor vanished as if by magic. *The Gloupov Chronicle*, wherein all this information is contained, gives no explanation for this occurrence. The *Chronicle* was written by one of the last governors of Gloupov, Perekhvat-Zalikhvetski, who entered the town on a white horse, burnt down the school and destroyed all rudiments of science.

(Saltykov-Shchedrin [Mikhail Yevgrafovich Saltykov], *Istoriya odnogo goroda*, Moscow, 1869–70)

GLUBBDUBDRIB, a small island, about one-third the size of the Isle of Wight, England, five hundred leagues to the south-west of BALNIBARBI. The name can be translated as "Island of Sorcerers."

This rich and fertile land is ruled by the governor of a tribe of magicians, who lives in a noble palace, in a park of three hundred acres, surrounded by a twenty-foot wall. The most curious feature of his court is that all the servants are ghosts, called back from the dead by necromancy. The governor has the power to summon up the dead and command their services for a full twenty-four hours, after which he may not summon the same ghost for a period of three months.

Visitors to the island are conducted to a private house from where they are taken to pay their respects to the governor. Should their appearance please the governor he will allow them to command any spirits of their choice to rise from the dead. Visitors may thus enjoy an opportunity to talk with Alexander, Hannibal, Caesar, or some more recent characters. They are warned, however, that certain aspects of the history of the world may be revealed in such a way as to leave them forever disgusted with the human race.

(Jonathan Swift, *Travels Into Several Remote Nations Of The World. In Four Parts. By Lemuel Gulliver, First a Surgeon, and then a Captain of several Ships,* London, 1726)

GLYN CAGNY, a glen in Ireland, near the Cave of the SLEEPERS OF ERINN and GORT NA CLOCA mora The salmon in the pool of the glen are said to be the most profound and learned of all living creatures in Ireland.

The glen is associated with two philosophers who lived in the neighbouring pinewoods with their wives, the Thin Woman and the Grey Woman. The philosophers were so wise that they could solve all difficulties and answer all questions, and were able to communicate with the leprechauns of Gort na Cloca Mora and with the numerous clans of fairies in this region. Caitilin, the daughter of one of the philosophers, was abducted by the god Pan when he visited Ireland, but later married Angus Og and now lives with him in the Cave of the Sleepers of Erinn.

One of the philosophers chose death because he was no longer able to find new things to learn. He cleared the centre of a room in his cabin, removed his coat and boots and stood on tiptoe. He then began to spin faster and faster until his movements became steady and smooth, like those of a top. After a quarter of an hour the movement slowed and he dropped dead with a serene expression on his face. His wife repeated the process, but it took longer for her to die as she was apparently made of sterner stuff. Their bodies were buried beneath the hearthstone of their cabin.

(James Stephens, *The Crock of Gold,* London, 1912)

GNAPHISTHASIA, a city over one hundred miles south-west of CALNOGOR in ATVATABAR. The city is built on a mountain slope leading to a rich valley. The buildings are all of porcelain, adorned with sculpted mouldings. In the centre of the city stands a semicircle of conical towers, gleaming like enormous jewels and connected by sculpted walls. This is the Palace of Art, a haven for all artists, where a megaphone constantly sounds the famous twenty-two Atvatabarese principles of Art.

(William R. Bradshaw, *The Goddess of Atvatabar, being the History of the Discovery of the Interior World and Conquest of Atvatabar,* New York, 1892)

GOAT LAND, a large empire in the Indian subcontinent, that takes its name from the dominant religion: the worship of the *choukaki* or red-bearded billy-goat.

Goat Land is traditionally ruled by a woman, Empress of Goats. When she dies expeditions are sent out to look for her successor, who is regarded as a gift from the gods. It was in this manner that the daughter of a certain Dom Pedro was found on MASK ISLAND and brought to Goat Land to become the empire's ruler, and later unwittingly married her father, then King of England, with tragic results.

(Charles Fieux de Mouhy, *Le Masque de Fer, ou les Aventures Admirables du Pere et du Fils,* The Hague, 1747)

GOAT WORSHIPPERS, LAND OF, a wide plain bordered by a range of mountains in southeast Russia. The plain is partly covered with pine forests and dotted with primitive huts made from branches and reeds, some grouped together in rudimentary villages, others scattered among the pines. The only furnishings in the huts are reed mats.

The Goat Worshippers are primitive and dress in goat skins. However, they use iron-tipped spears and metal axes, which suggests that they

A primitive village in the Land of GOAT WORSHIPPERS, south-east Russia.

have been in contact with more sophisticated races. They are hospitable and friendly, more than willing to share their meagre diet of milk, dried meat and cheese with visitors. When strangers arrive, the heads of families draw lots with black and white pebbles. Those who pick black pebbles from the chief's hat give the strangers a goat to provide them with milk, and send their own wives to sleep with them. It is a serious insult to refuse the favours of these wives; both the women and their husbands would be deeply offended. If visitors stay for a long period, other married women will replace the first ones offered.

The language of the Goat Worshippers is harsh and guttural, something like the croaking of frogs. Happiness is expressed by piercing screams and howls, and similar screams are used as a sign of encouragement and gratitude. When strangers take the wives into their huts, the men gather outside, screaming and shouting in encouragement and happiness. To reply to an expression of gratitude they will spit in their grateful correspondent's face then wipe his face with their beards.

At intervals, the Goat Worshippers march into the forest in procession, led by armed men and followed by four women carrying small children. The children are crowned with leaves, their bodies are painted, and then they are ritually disembowelled in front of a large ram while the people piously kneel and watch.

(Abbé H. L. Du Laurens, *Le Compère Mathieu ou les bigarrures de l'esprit humain*, London, 1771)

GOLDEN ASSES, ISLAND OF, near the island of POLYPRAGMOSYNE. This is where the Wise Men of Gotham, and other people from Polypragmosyne who have meddled with things they do not understand, end their days, having been turned into donkeys with ears a yard long. It is said that they will remain donkeys until, by the laws of natural development, the thistles on the island turn into roses.

In the meantime, the inhabitants comfort themselves with the thought that the longer their ears, the thicker their hides, so a good beating will not hurt them. Visitors can ride the inhabitants at leisure.

(Charles Kingsley, *The Water-Babies: A Fairy Tale for a Land-Baby*, London, 1863)

GOLDEN ISLAND, fertile and welcoming. Visitors are greeted with garlands of fruit and flowers.

The island takes its name from the precious metal that seems to abound here. The women of the island wear radiant golden robes; the men dress in costumes that glitter in the sun. Both sexes wear elaborate ornaments. But despite their wealth, the people know nothing of the arts of navigation. Their rare battles are fought with swords edged with flint, copper or gold, and they have no iron weapons.

In the past, Golden Island was conquered by a neighbouring monarch who demanded a tribute, every five years, of ten maidens and ten youths to be sacrificed in the temple of his kingdom. This depletory custom came to an end with the arrival of the Wanderers, a company which had left Europe in search of the Earthly Paradise, which they were never able to find. Hearing of the barbaric custom that had been imposed on Golden Island, the Wanderers resolved to help their generous hosts and, partly thanks to their superior weapons, were able to defeat the king. (See Island of the WANDERERS.)

(William Morris, *The Earthly Paradise, A Poem*, London, 1868)

GOLDEN LAKE, in the Andes, fed by mountain streams and brooks flowing out into a wide river of great beauty; wild cattle and sheep graze around its banks. Golden Lake is so named because its feeder streams carry gold down from the mountains and deposit it into the lake. Gold is so common in this area that the Indians pay little attention to it and it can be picked up on the shore by the handful.

(Daniel Defoe, *A New Voyage Round The World, By A Course never sailed before. Being A Voyage undertaken by some Merchants, who afterwards proposed the Setting up of an East-India Company in Flanders*, London, 1724)

GOLDEN MOUNTAIN, a hill near the city of Kilemba, Kassongo, in the Saharian province of Kivu. It is famous as the site of a fabulous golden treasure amassed by an Arab sultan, lord of these lands before the arrival of the Europeans. The sultan died in battle and the natives neglected the gold, which had no value for them. An Englishman who discovered the secret treasure was captured and made a prisoner of the Kilemba natives, but managed to get a message to Zanzibar. Several expeditions, anxious to recover the gold, immediatcly sct off for Kilemba but only one, led by a German and a Greek on board one of the first dirigibles, managed to free the Englishman and carry off the treasure.

(Emilio Salgari, *Il treno volante,* Milan, 1904)

GOLDEN RIVER, see TREASURE VALLEY.

GOLDENSTONE, an outcrop of weathered grey sandstone on ALDERLEY EDGE in Cheshire, upon which a *stromkarl*—a young man about three feet high with skin lustrous as a pearl and hair rippling to his waist in green seawaves—sings of old prophecies.

(Alan Garner, *The Weirdstone of Brisingamen,* London, 1960)

GOLDENTHAL, a small but prosperous village in Switzerland, famous for its agricultural produce and its honey.

Travellers who visit Goldenthal today may be interested to learn that the village has not always known this affluence. In the past it fell into decline after lengthy wars and ensuing famines, sinking into lethargy and decadence. The people began to abandon their traditional religion, taking a perverse pleasure in their misery; houses fell into disrepair and both public and private debts became enormous. Drinking developed into a major problem but the authorities, owners of the main inns, encouraged rather than repressed alcoholism and debauchery. For many years the word "Goldenthaler" was a synonym for pauper.

The son of the village schoolmaster, a certain Oswald, returned to the village after seventeen years' absence and found it in this deplorable state. He began teaching in order to influence the local children for the better but was greatly mocked, and rumours about Oswald being a kind of wizard grew within Goldenthal. Finally he convinced the inhabitants that they could become "goldmakers" and prosper if they followed his advice. He established a League of Goldmakers formed by thirty-two heads of families, who swore that for the next seven years and seven weeks they would adhere to Oswald's rules: they would attend church regu-

larly, they would not drink or swear, they would work and not contract any further debts, they would maintain their farms and farm buildings in a state of cleanliness and order, and they would follow a modest and moral code of personal behaviour. Work was found in a nearby city for those whose debts were particularly high and saving accounts were established. Before long matters began to improve, and a public kitchen was set up to free women from domestic labour and to allow them to work in the fields whenever possible. Bees were introduced to Goldenthal, thereby laying the foundations for its later prosperity. Common land, once exploited almost exclusively by the rich landlords, was distributed evenly among the peasants, and the parish debt was gradually repaid by allowing individuals to rent parish land. Pauperism was overcome by providing food and clothing in return for work on the roads and in the forests, and for draining the extensive marshy areas.

Goldenthal became rich once again, and the temptation to use this new-found wealth in frivolous ways was controlled by the passing of sumptuary laws regulating even the style and cost of dress.

(Johann Heinrich Daniel Zschokke, *Der Goldmacherdorf,* Aarau, 1817)

GONDAL and **GAALDINE**, two islands in the Pacific. Gondal is in the north Pacific and its capital is Regina. The north of Gondal is mountainous and contains several lakes: Lake Aspin lies near Aspin Castle, as does Lake Elderno, deep and subject to wild storms. Lake Elnor, surrounded by moors, lies near mountains snowcapped in summer. In the south of Gondal is the famous Southern College. Gondal is divided into several provinces or shires: Alcona, Almeda, Elbë, Angora (in the north) and Exina (in the south).

Gaaldine is a large island in the south Pacific, part of an archipelago discovered and colonized by the Gondalians. Gaaldine is divided into several kingdoms: Alexandia, Almedore, Elseraden, Ula, Zedora and Zalona. Almedore's flag is crimson; Zalona's flag is sea-green.

Information on the history of Gondal and Gaaldine is scarce and piecemeal. The kingdom of Almedore conquered Zalona after a siege and Julius Brenzaida of Gondal became king of Almedore in the mid-nineteenth century. He invaded his native Gondal and, together with his kinsman Gerald, he was crowned joint-monarch. Julius was stabbed in his palace and buried in the mountains of Gondal. Gerald was imprisoned and Gondal fell into the hands of a tyrant. Finally Gondal saw the peaceful reign of Queen Augusta. It lasted eleven years, but after her death the republicans fought the royalists—the outcome of their struggle is not yet known.

(Emily Jane Brontë, *The Complete Poems*, Columbia, 1941; Charlotte and Branwell Brontë, *The Miscellaneous and Unpublished Writings*, London, 1936–38; W.D. Paden, *An Investigation of Gondal*, New York, 1958)

GONDOR, the most important of the kingdoms of MIDDLE-EARTH, lies to the south-west of the WHITE MOUNTAINS that extend from the area around MINAS TIRITH, the capital, almost to the Bay of Belfalas in the west. The mountain range separates Gondor from the realm of ROHAN.

A large and varied country, Gondor includes many provinces which owe allegiance to the crown. Several of these provinces are major population centres, like Lebennin, the home of a mixed race descended from both the wild men who originally inhabited the area and the ancestors of the present men of Gondor. Lebennin, a relatively safe area in time of war, was chosen as the refuge for the women evacuated from the capital during the great

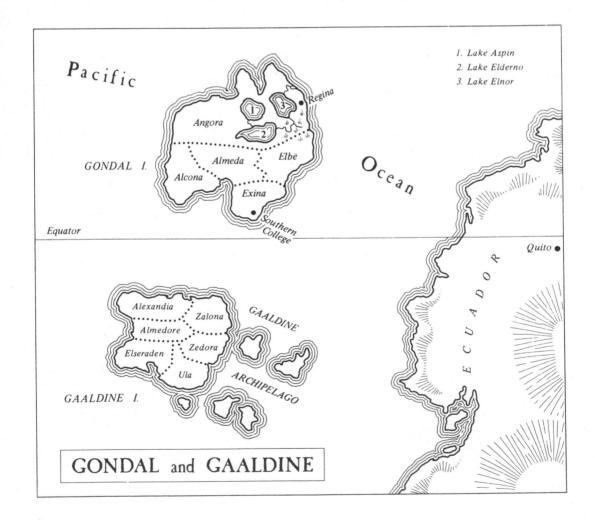

1. Lake Aspin
2. Lake Elderno
3. Lake Elnor

GONDAL and GAALDINE

siege and battle of 3029 Third Age. In contrast to the people of Lebennin, the men of the lands around the Bay of Belfalas are tall, proud sailors with sea-green eyes, who man Gondor's fleets. Major ports are sited at PELARGIR on the GREAT RIVER and on the sea coast at Dol Amroth.

The kingdom of Gondor is the more southerly of the two Númenórean realms-in-exile founded by Elendil the Tall in 3320 Second Age, after he and his house escaped the destruction of Númenor (formerly known as the island of ELENNA, the most westerly of all Mortal Lands), and returned to Middle-earth with the remnant of the Dúnedain, the Men of the West. Although ARNOR, Elendil's North-Kingdom, was the elder of the two realms-in-exile, Gondor soon grew more powerful and more glorious.

In its golden days, Gondor stretched from the Celebrant or Silverlode River (which flows through what is now LORIEN) to what is now HARAD and from the Sea of Rhûn in the east, to the western coast. The kingdom reached its zenith in about 1149 Third Age and then gradually declined.

From its early days, Gondor suffered frequent invasions: attacks from the Easterlings—men from the area around the Rhûn—were common, as were incursions from the south by the tribes of Harad. During the years 1432 to 1448 Third Age, Gondor was torn apart by the Great Kin-Strife—the civil war which broke out between the men of the north and the men of the south when certain groups claimed that the ruling king was not of sufficiently pure blood. The legitimate monarch, Eldacar, was driven out for some years before being able to return with an army and recapture his kingdom. It was during the Kin-Strife that the original capital at Osgiliath was almost burnt to the ground and Minas Tirith became the capital of the kingdom.

An even longer period of strife began when the warlike Wainriders from Rhûn invaded Gondor in 1851 Third Age. Although temporarily defeated on the plain of DAGORLAD, the Wainriders continued to harass the country and were strong enough to capture and hold the province of ITHILIEN for some years. Not until 1944 Third Age was Gondor freed from them completely.

But Gondor was not always the victim of these invasions. When the northern kingdom of Arnor was attacked by the Witch-king, Gondor went to its help and, with the aid of the elves of RIVENDELL, the Witch-king was defeated on the downs to the north of the SHIRE. The Witch-king was in fact Lord of the Nazgûl of MORDOR in a different guise—one of the greatest and most evil servants of Sauron, the evil Dark Lord of Mordor who had launched so many of the earlier attacks on Gondor.

In 2050 Third Age King Eärnur, thirty-third king of Gondor, accepted a challenge from the Witch-king and travelled to Mordor in search of him. He never returned from the journey and the royal line was broken. Not until the end of the War of the Ring was Gondor to be ruled by a king again. In the interim, the land was governed by the stewards of the king. The office of steward was a hereditary one and, in general, the stewards were good rulers. However under their leadership the inhabitants of Gondor became more concerned with building magnificent tombs for themselves than with defending their homeland, and tended to ignore the threat of Mordor, which grew stronger over the years. The population began to decline and Gondor lost much of its ancient splendour.

But at the end of the War of the Ring, Gondor once more came under the rule of a king, Aragorn II, last descendant of the Dúnedain of the North-Kingdom who had been raised in Rivendell and who had, in different guises, fought Sauron and his allies for many long years. It was Aragorn who led the soldiers who finally raised the siege of Minas Tirith and who later led the Army of the West—the joint force sent out by Gondor and Rohan against Sauron. After the final victory, Aragorn took the name Elessar, meaning "elf stone," after the green-coloured elfstone given him by Arwen Evenstar (daughter of Elrond Halfel-ven and Celebrían, and granddaughter of Galadriel—most royal princess of the Noldor of Tirion) who gave up immortality to be his bride. Under Elessar, Gondor entered a lasting period of prosperity and peace.

The emblem of Gondor is a white tree, the Nimloth, which grew in the lost land of Númenor. A sapling seeded from Nimloth was brought to Middle-earth by Elessar's forebear Elendil the Tall and was planted in MINAS ITHIL. The tree was burnt by Sauron when he captured that city, but a seedling was saved and taken to the new capital, where it was planted in the Court of the Fountain. It and its successor died, and finally no sapling could be found to replace it. For many years only a dead tree stood in the court, until, after the end of the War of the Ring, Elessar found a white sapling on the slopes of Mindolluin above the citadel. It is this tree which visitors can see standing in the Court of the Fountain. The leaves of the tree are dark on top and silver beneath, and it bears white flowers.

The Common Speech or Westron, the language most widely spoken among the people of the westlands of Middle-earth, is found in its purest form in Gondor, where it has retained some of its original grace and music.

(J.R.R. Tolkien, *The Hobbit, or There and Back Again*, London, 1937; J.R.R. Tolkien, *The Fellowship of the Ring*, London, 1954; J.R.R. Tolkien, *The Two Towers*, London, 1954; J.R.R. Tolkien, *The Return of the King*, London, 1955; J.R.R. Tolkien, *The Silmarillion*, London, 1977)

GONDOUR, a republic of unknown location, ruled by the Grand Caliph, who is elected for a term of twenty years. Since in fact the ministry and the parliament actually govern the land, the Grand Caliph is always liable to impeachment for misconduct; therefore the length of his term does not affect the quality of his government. This great office has twice been ably filled by women.

The Republic of Gondour has achieved a very peculiar form of democracy through a long process of trial and error. At first the people of Gondour chose universal suffrage pure and simple, but they threw that form aside because the result was not satisfactory. It seemed to deliver all power into the hands of the ignorant and non-taxpaying classes; and, of necessity, the responsible offices were filled from these classes also. A remedy was sought, and people believed they had found it, not in the elimination of universal suffrage, but in its enlargement. It was an odd and ingenious idea. As the constitution gave every man a vote, that vote was a vested right and could not be taken away. But the constitution did not say that certain individuals might not be given two votes or twenty. So a mandatory clause was inserted in a quiet way, a clause which authorized the enlargement of the suffrage in certain cases, to be specified by statute. To offer to "limit" the suffrage might have made trouble; the offer to "enlarge" it had a pleasant aspect. The new law was

framed and passed. Under it, every citizen— however poor or ignorant—possessed one vote, so universal suffrage still reigned; but if a man possessed a good common-school education and no money, he had two votes; a high-school education gave him four; if he had property to the value of three thousand *sacos*, he wielded one more vote; for every fifty thousand *sacos* a man added to his property, he was entitled to another vote; a university education entitled a man to nine votes even though he owned no property. Therefore learning being more prevalent and more easily acquired than riches, educated men became a wholesome check upon wealthy men, since they could outvote them.

Then a curious thing happened. Whereas, formerly, a man was honoured only according to the amount of money he possessed, his grandeur was measured now by the number of votes he wielded. A man with only one vote was conspicuously respectful to his neighbour possessing three. And if he was a man above the commonplace, he was as conspicuously energetic in his determination to acquire three for himself. This spirit of emulation invaded all ranks. Votes based on capital were commonly called "mortal votes," because they could be lost; those based on learning were called "immortal," and they were usually permanent. Because of their customarily imperishable character these immortal votes were naturally more valued than the other sort. However, they were not absolutely imperishable, since insanity could suspend them. Under this system, gambling and speculation almost ceased in the Republic of Gondour. A man honoured as the possessor of great voting power could not afford to risk the loss of it on a doubtful chance.

In Gondour today, to be in parliament or in office is a very great honour; under the old system, such distinction had only brought suspicion on a man and made him a helpless mark for newspaper contempt and scurrility. Officials now do not need to steal, their salaries being vast in comparison with the pittances paid in the days when parliaments were created by hod-carriers (who viewed official salaries from the hod-carrying point of view, and compelled that view to be respected by their obsequious servants). Justice is wisely and rigidly administered, for a judge, after once reaching his place through the specified line of promotions, is permanently installed as long as his behaviour is deemed good, and he is not obliged to modify his judgements according to the effect that they might have on the temper of the reigning political party.

There are numerous public schools and free colleges in the Republic of Gondour. Because a person can make himself powerful and honoured according to the amount of education he acquires, these free schools and colleges require no law to fill them, and visitors will be surprised at the high level of school attendance.

(Mark Twain [Samuel Langhorne Clemens], *The Curious Republic of Gondour,* Atlanta, 1875)

GONT, an island to the north-east of the EARTH-SEA ARCHIPELAGO. Above all, Gont is a land famed for its wizards, many of whom have served the Lords of the Isles of Earthsea. All the villages have their witches, who can weave charms to mend things and brew potions to cause love or jealousy, as the circumstances require. Weather-workers are also common and it is not unusual to see rain-clouds buffeted from one part of the island to another before they are sent out to sea to let their rain fall there.

In general, the witchcraft practised by Gont's witches and weather-workers is of a low order and has little in common with the magic taught and practised, for instance, on ROKE. The people of Gont know little of the principles behind the art they practise and use it mainly towards banal ends. Two Gontish sayings illustrate the nature of the village witches' magic: "Weak as woman's magic" and "Wicked as woman's magic." Travellers in need of magical assistance are advised to address themselves to the magicians of other Earthsea islands.

Probably the greatest magician produced by Gont was Ged, or Sparrowhawk. Ged was brought up in the Gont village of Ten Alders, high on the mountain at the end of the Northward Vale. He was the son of a copper-smith, but soon revealed his talents for magic. In his early youth he picked up some spells from his aunt, the local witch, and he was soon able to summon the birds of the air and weave spells to control the weather or to create simple illusions. It was the latter skill which brought Ged his first fame.

When Ged was a young boy, Gont suffered a raid by a party of soldiers from the KARGAD EMPIRE, who swooped down on the island in their longboats. The port fell to the raiders, who moved inland in search of loot, spreading death and destruction throughout the lower valleys. Eventually they reached Ten Alders. Ged realized that he could defend the village by using his skill at fog-weaving (the art of gathering a dense fog and creating illusions with it). Fog closed on the village, hiding it from the invaders and enabling the local people to counter-attack without being seen. In the confusion, some of the Kargs stumbled over the cliffs above the village and fell into the water below; many others were cut to pieces by an enemy they could not see. Believing the place to be enchanted, the Kargs withdrew in panic, but once back in the valleys they found that the coastal forces of Gont had rallied and burnt the Kargan boats. The Kargs fought with their backs to the sea until the sands of Arnmouth were red with their blood.

This action brought Ged to the notice of Ogion—a wizard or mage from the small town of Re Albi, or Falcon's Nest, some fifteen miles from the capital—who began to train the boy as a true magician. During his apprenticeship, Ged allowed himself to be persuaded by a girl to exceed his powers. An impulsive and proud young man, he accepted the challenge to transform his shape. Using Ogion's rune books, he tried to say the words of the spell, but by mistake called up an evil shadow which was to pursue him for years before he finally destroyed it. He was saved from the darkness he had brought into the world by the arrival of his master, who explained to him that the girl's mother was herself a witch who had, no doubt, caused the book to fall open at the wrong spell. Shortly after, Ged left Gont to train as a true wizard on Roke.

Travellers arriving in Gont will certainly be struck by the unique physical characteristics of the island. Less than fifty miles wide, Gont is, in fact, a single mountain, rising a full mile above the storm-racked waters of the surrounding Gontish Sea. The coastline of Gont is indented with deep, narrow bays opening into the valleys of the island. Though the lower slopes of the valleys are farmed, the arable land soon gives way to the forests of the higher ground.

The town of Gont Port lies on the bay between what is known as the Armed Cliffs; its land gate is guarded by carved dragons. The town is the largest on the island and is an impressive sight, with its great houses of stone and towers, and with the many ships from the Inmost Sea gathering along its quays and wharves. Gont Port was once saved from an earthquake by Ogion. It is said that Ogion spoke to the mountain as one might speak soothingly to a frightened animal and prevented an avalanche that would otherwise have destroyed the town and closed the channel between the Armed Cliffs.

The mountain villages of Gont are very different from Gont Port. Most village houses are made of timber and usually have only one room, with a goat shed traditionally attached to the side of the house. The interiors are quite primitive; a fire pit in the centre of the room often replaces the hearth and chimney found in wealthier houses. In winter, these villages are often cut off by heavy snowfalls.

The people of Gont are mostly goat-herds or fishermen, although in the past the island was famed for its pirates. Despite its small size, Gont is strictly divided into landmen and seamen. Travellers will find that the artisans and herdsmen of the higher valleys are totally ignorant of the sea which they behold every day of their lives, and that the fishermen of Gont have no knowledge of their island's beautiful highlands.

Gont's main export is a silky cloth woven from goat hair. Warm *fleecefells* or sheepskin coats are also exported and are well known throughout Earthsea.

Physically, the people are lean and wiry, with dark, copper-brown skin. In other parts of the archipelago they tend to be nicknamed "goat-herds."

(Ursula K. Le Guin, *A Wizard of Earthsea*, New York, 1968; Ursula K. Le Guin, *The Tombs of Atuan*, London, 1972; Ursula K. Le Guin, *The Farthest Shore*, London, 1973)

GORGOROTH, an extensive plateau in the north-west of MORDOR, stretching from the MORGAI to the ERED LITHUI. The cone of ORODRUIN rises from the centre of the plateau.

The plateau was the site of the Dark Tower of Barad-dûr, the mightiest stronghold of the Age, built by Sauron, the Dark Lord. Construction began in roughly 1000 Third Age and the great Tower was completed some six hundred years later. A chasm surrounded it and was crossed by means of a vast iron bridge. From here, a road led to the Chambers of Fire high on the slopes of Orodruin. The fortress itself was a forbidding mountain of iron with gaping gates of steel and adamant

and many towers, the highest tower of all topped by pinnacles and an iron crown. This was the location of the Window of the Eye, which faced west towards Orodruin—a red light flickered in the tower as the Eye turned this way and that. When the One Ring of power went from the world, and Sauron's power went from him too, the Dark Tower was completely destroyed.

During Sauron's domination of Mordor, Gorgoroth was largely populated by hill trolls. These are taller and broader than men and are covered in close-fitting horny scales; it is difficult to tell if this is their natural hide or some kind of garment. Their gnarled hands are clawed and they carry heavy hammers as their main battle weapons. They bite the throats of those they fell with their hammers. Like the other species of troll found in MIDDLE-EARTH, the hill trolls have black blood.

After the destruction of the Dark Tower, Gorgoroth returned to what is presumably its natural state—a great dreary plain, pitted with holes and craters, with smoke from the fissures in the earth drifting across it.

(J.R.R. Tolkien, *The Fellowship of the Ring*, London, 1954; J.R.R. Tolkien, *The Two Towers*, London, 1954; J.R.R. Tolkien, *The Return of the King*, London, 1955; J.R.R. Tolkien, *The Silmarillion*, London, 1977)

GORMENGHAST CASTLE, hereditary seat of the Lords of Groan, some miles to the east of the sinister Gormenghast Mountain which struggles up from the tangled thorn trees of the Twisted Woods. So dreadful is the castle's aspect that it appears to have been drawn out of the earth as a curse on all those who look upon it. The landscape between the mountain and the castle is bleak and desolate. Much of it is wasteland, broken only by tracts of marshy ground where waders live undisturbed in the reeds; the only dash of colour is the red tips of the rushes. The marshland eventually gives way to a shelving plateau of greenish-black rock—a dreary and deserted spot, below which flows the river that feeds the area's swamps. The only sound that can be heard here is the cry of the peewits and the curlews in the wind.

The west side of Gormenghast Castle is surrounded by a pine wood known as Gormenghast Forest, which shelters a small lake lying silently at the foot of fern-covered slopes. There are no birds on this stretch of water. To the north, lonely wastelands fade away into the distance, while to the south lies a region of quicksand on the shore of a tideless sea.

Seen from the slopes of the mountain, Gormenghast itself looks like an island of stone set in a wild sea far from all known trade routes. From a distance it appears to float lightly, as though its stones were petals, but the impression is deceptive. As one approaches the castle the sheer cliffs and wasted outcrops become apparent. The rambling stones and mortar are visibly crumbling, but it seems somehow as though the grey stone will go on crumbling forever, its destruction outlasting everything else.

In summer the enormous castle lies inert like a sick animal; the ancient masonry sweats and dust lies heavy in the courtyards. Colonies of shining lizards bask on the mouldering stones, and the moat that partially surrounds Gormenghast turns to soup. In winter it may be snow-bound for many months at a time.

Outside the castle, thousands of mud huts and rough shanties spread around the outer walls, sprawling over the rising ground and clinging to the walls like some malignant epidemic. These confused hovels lie scattered along a number of dusty lanes, like so many mole-hills. The lanes themselves are like gullies and the roofs of the huts almost meet overhead. At night, lanterns are hung above the doors. Travellers should note one custom: when two people meet in the pitch-black lanes at night, they place their heads in the light of the nearest door lamp, moving on when they have had a look at one another.

The huts are about eight feet high with coarse glass windows. Inside, they have floors of trampled earth covered with grass matting, and rough plank beds. The people who live here are known as the Dwellers or Bright Carvers, a poor and disease-ridden community whose only pride is in their carving and in their allegiance to the House of Groan. They seem almost to enjoy their grinding poverty; for one of them to leave and seek fame and fortune would be unthinkable, a matter of shame and humiliation.

The Bright Carvers take their name from the age-old craft of woodcarving, which is their only passion. They have little or no contact with the people of Gormenghast Castle, which they enter on only one day each year, the first of June, when they present their best work. The carvings are judged by the Earl of Groan, and the finest are taken and set up in the Hall of the Bright Carvings, a long room in the north wing of the castle. No one ever visits the hall; the masterpieces are simply left there to gather dust over the years. All rejected works are burnt in the courtyard below the earl's chamber. The carvers whose efforts have been chosen are given vellum scrolls and the privilege of walking the battlements above the Dwellings at the full moon of each alternate month. This is their only reward, an honour greatly prized by the Bright Carvers.

There is great rivalry between the different families or schools of carving, which have developed in highly distinctive ways. The most famous of all the carvings stands in the Square of the Black Rider beneath the castle walls. Its creator remains unknown, but all agree that this is the greatest statue ever produced in the Dwellings. It is a highly stylized figure of a horse and rider, repainted each year in its original bright colours. The horse's head is thrown back in an arch, so that it faces the sky and its mane coils over the knees of the cloaked rider like frozen foam. The rider is a sinister figure, with his arms hanging limply at his sides; only the colour of the lips and hair break the deathlike face. None but the most accomplished carvers are allowed to reside in the hovels that surround this square.

Apart from the carvings displayed on the roofs of the huts, there is little colour in the Dwellings. The only plants that grow here are stubby cacti; mangy dogs scavenge in the dusty and crooked lanes.

The Dwellers always eat supper in the open air, sitting at four long tables in the dust beneath the battlements. The elderly sit nearest to the wall; mothers and their children at a table to their left and men and boys at the two remaining tables. Adolescent girls eat separately in a hut of their own, although a few are delegated each day to serve the elderly. The normal diet consists of sliced white *jarl*-root, which is dug up each day from a wood in the vicinity, washed down with sloe wine. Some extra food is thrown down from the battlements of the castle every day. When there is need for further contact between the communities, formalized greetings are used; anyone coming from the castle is addressed simply as "Gormenghast" and will preface his or her reply with the expression "Bright Carvers." This custom was introduced centuries ago by the seventeenth earl.

Traditionally, a pre-eminent carver of fifty or over may choose a bride from among the girls of the community, who have no right to object. The marriage ceremony takes place on Marriage Hill, to the south of the Twisted Woods. A voice calls to the couple through the woods and they join hands, while the woman places her feet upon her husband's. Marriage is very important to the Bright Carvers, as they believe an illegitimate child to be evil, like a witch in embryo. The mother of an illegitimate child is ostracized by the community.

The inhabitants of the castle itself can hardly be said to love their home; they are simply part of it and have no idea of the world that exists abroad. The atmosphere is not especially pleasant; anyone who wanders into the more deserted areas of the castle is struck by the impression that someone or something has just left the place he has entered.

But in fact the Castle is so vast that members of the household may not see each other for weeks. The main building consists of several large wings, although the additions and alterations made over the centuries make it almost impossible to trace the ground-plan. The result is a bizarre collection of buildings; some, like the pavilions, observatories and galleries, have an obvious use; the purpose of others remains obscure. One curious structure, for instance, is an area entirely packed with pillars that are set so close together that it is impossible for a normal man to force his way through them. Another has a stone carving of a huge lion holding the limp corpse of a man in its jaws; the corpse bears the inscription "He was an enemy of Groan."

Many of these experiments in architecture are now in a semi-ruinous state, but the most sinister of all is still the Tower of Flints, in the East Wing. The tallest of the many towers of Gormenghast, it is a time-eaten edifice covered with black ivy and inhabited by death-owls which rise up from the fields of masonry like a mutilated finger pointing blasphemously at heaven. It is associated with the macabre end of Lord Sepulchrave, the seventy-sixth earl of Groan. After a long period of depression, Sepulchrave became convinced that he was a death-owl and began to eat rats which he caught in the subterranean kitchens of the castle. He finally entered the Tower of Flints

itself, taking the present of a corpse with him to give to the resident owls, and was torn to pieces by the savage birds.

The East Wing also houses the library which was badly damaged during a fire and then by a flood. All that remains of the original library is a marble table and a stone gallery that runs around it, fifteen feet above the level of the floor. In the fire, the collection of Martrovian drama was completely destroyed, although much of the poetry collections survived. Sourdust, the old librarian, perished in the fire and his skeleton was found on the marble table in the middle of his old domain.

The major room in the West Wing is the great Stone Hall, traditionally used for meals. It is a long, high building, lined with mighty pillars. The floor of the hall consists of stone slabs. The ceiling is decorated with pale paintings of cherubs, who peruse one another across a flaking sky. The colours have faded over the years to a subtle blend of grey, green, old rose and silver. The cherubs were painted by the seventy-fourth earl with the help of a servant who fell to his death from the scaffold. The hall is always dark, as though it had been built in defiance of the light of the sun. At one end stands the earl's table on a seven-foot-high oak dais.

High up in the central part of Gormenghast is the Hall of Spiders, a gallery surrounded by rotting, mouldering wooden pillars. It takes its name from the vast numbers of spiders found here, spinning their webs across the crumbling woodwork. At one end a great window opens onto a wide expanse of stone-terraced roof with turreted edges. Rainwater collects on the roof and is often several feet deep in places.

Perhaps the most curious part of Gormenghast is, however, the great South Wing, much of which is now uninhabited and practically forgotten by the dwellers of the castle. In some places, the walls tower up high; in others the visitor suddenly emerges into great courts of brick and stone, with rank grass sprouting through the cracks and Tennysonian flowers in the crannied walls. Most passageways in this area are thickly overgrown with weeds and the rats hold undisputed sway. The South Wing contains the Room of the Roots, a semi-circular chamber with large, diamond-paned windows. This room, perhaps filled with earth in the remote past, is choked with the writhing, intertwining roots of a dead tree. It is virtually impossible to determine their origin, so closely are they entwined. As the roots thicken they converge and grow out of the room through a tall narrow aperture opposite the door. Visitors will find that it is possible to make their way through the labyrinth and to climb out onto the trunk of the dead tree. It grows almost horizontally from the wall, several hundred feet above the ground, and is as safe as a bridge. Inside the room, all the roots have been painted in different colours; this was apparently done in an attempt to attract birds. The Room of the Roots and the adjoining apartments were once the chambers of Cora and Clarice, the twin sisters of Sepulchrave, who lived here, isolated from the rest of the castle, until their death.

An almost totally forgotten stairway in this wing leads up to a high terrace, now mostly in ruins. A great casement once gave onto this terrace, but no trace of glass or woodwork remains. The hall beyond the terrace is slowly rotting away and black moss clings to the flagstone outside. Abandoned by the human inhabitants of Gormenghast, the hall and terrace have been taken over by jackdaws, egrets and bitterns, and by an extensive colony of herons. The South Wing is also noted for its mice, especially a small dove-grey species which appears to be indigenous to this wing and which has not been seen anywhere else in Gormenghast. Storks nest on the higher roofs.

Most of Gormenghast is a grim and uncomfortable place. The exception is the house of Dr. Prunesquallor, which lies across the courtyard outside the damp, chilly armoury. The house is a three-storey building of red sandstone, which contrasts greatly with the predominant grey; it is attached to the castle itself by a flying buttress. With its carved furniture and rich decorations, it is much more pleasant, for instance, than the Cat Room, the chamber occupied by the Countess of Gormenghast and so called because of the large numbers of cats she keeps there. The doctor's house looks onto a walled garden; here his sister has created a goblin-garden of ferns, mosses and small plants that bloom by night. Most of the garden is taken up by a clutter of rockeries, crazy paving, fishponds and sundials. Only at the far end are there any real trees.

Gormenghast's kitchens are a vast subterranean realm centred around the Great Kitchen, a massive room lit by windows high up in the walls.

The kitchens are kept clean by a company known as the "grey scrubbers" who, when they reach adolescence, discover that—like their fathers before them—they will spend their lives restoring the walls and floors of the kitchens to a stainless complexion. They work from before dawn until late morning, by which time the scaffolding they use becomes a hindrance to the cooks. As a result of their work, they develop long powerful arms and have a definite simian look about them. The scrubbers are traditionally deaf and over the years their faces take on the grey pallor of the stone they clean every day of their lives. The kitchens themselves are a steamy, crowded place, normally avoided by the other inhabitants of the castle. Adjacent to them are the wine cellars, a dusty labyrinth of tunnels and corridors which few people have explored in any detail.

A school is maintained inside the castle for the education of the children born within its walls. Staffed by sixteen professors and a headmaster, the school centres around a courtyard surrounded by high ivy-clad walls; the courtyard is reached through a tunnel from the school itself.

All the classrooms have very individual atmospheres. One, for instance, is perfectly square and well lit, its tables and floor scoured with soda every morning; its neighbour is a short tunnel-like room, lit only by the light from its single semicircular window. A third is a vast, half-empty room facing south: this is the traditional place for a highly dangerous game played by the schoolboys of the castle. The floorboards are taken up and used to build a narrow, slippery walkway across the breadth of the room, and the class is divided into two teams. One group arms itself with catapults and pellets. A member of the opposing side swings out through the window and catches hold of a tree branch, ignoring the hundred-foot drop to the quadrangle below. He swings himself upwards and then lets himself fall at such an angle that he re-enters the window and slides across the narrow bridge of floorboards. As he does so, the members of the other side fire their pellets at him. In the past, clay pellets and even marbles were used in this game, but after three deaths paper pellets were introduced in their place.

The teaching staff of Gormenghast are housed in their own quarters, a series of apartments above a sheltered cloister. Each professor has his own apartment with his name and that of his predecessors inscribed on the door. The staff share a common room known as the Leather Room because of its horse-hide walls, lit by a vile subterranean light and reeking of chalk and tobacco. While teaching, they wear black academic gowns and mortarboards; in their leisure hours they dress in wine-red tunics. The life of the teachers is based upon resistance to any form of change, it being their vocation to watch the scaling paint and the rusting nibs of their domain with calm approval. Their extreme conservatism is shown by the ritual they celebrate after their communal supper, taken in the refectory. The long tables are turned upside down and they sit on the upturned tables as though they were in some curious kind of boat. They then begin a mournful chant which has lost any significance it may once have had, but which celebrates the virtues of resisting change with loud exhortations to "hold fast."

Gormenghast is ruled by tradition and ritual. The older servants have an instinctive feel for the place and its customs, and are able to tell immediately when tradition has been breached. Great books are devoted to the rituals to be observed at every hour of the day, and understanding the rituals is a lifetime's occupation. The original meaning of many of these customs has now been lost, but the participants go through the motions regardless. Twice a year, for instance, the ruling earl must open an iron cupboard and scratch a half moon on its back with a special knife. There are over seven hundred half moons scratched on the metal, but no one can explain the origin or purpose of the ceremony. The childhood and adolescence of an heir is surrounded by rites of considerable complexity. Twelve days after the birth, the christening takes place in a room reserved for this ceremony, a room which is often considered to be the most pleasant in the entire castle. The child is formally called for by his father and then placed between the pages of the book of the *Lore of Gormenghast* before being baptized and formally greeted by all those present. On his first birthday, a solemn Dark Breakfast is held. During this meal, the Master of Rituals walks up and down the table, trampling the remains of the food, presumably to demonstrate the power of the lore he studies and prescribes. All birthdays of an heir are celebrated with established ceremonies, particular importance being given to the tenth, when the child is locked alone in a dusty tower room all day before

being taken blindfolded to the shores of a nearby lake where a pantomime is performed by figures costumed as a lion, a lamb, a wolf and a horse. This ritual dates back at least four hundred years, but its precise significance remains obscure. Another tradition has it that the Countess of Gormenghast must receive the seven most hideous beggars to be found in the Dwellings and anoint them with oil.

In recent years, the life of Gormenghast has been disrupted by a series of unhappy events, some of which involved the machinations of one Steerpike, a kitchen boy who rose, by devious means, to be Master of Rituals. Steerpike was responsible for the destruction of the library and for a number of murders in the castle. His one ambition was to achieve mastery of Gormenghast by gaining a detailed knowledge of the rituals that govern the castle's very existence. Steerpike also attempted to woo Fuchsia, the daughter of the seventy-sixth earl of Gormenghast, and is thought to have been at least partly responsible for her death by drowning. Steerpike was eventually killed in a fight with Titus Groan, the seventy-seventh earl. Shortly after this event Titus left Gormenghast, never to return; how much of the rituals survived his departure remains a matter for conjecture.

(Mervyn Peake, *Titus Groan,* London, 1946; Mervyn Peake, *Gormenghast,* London, 1950; Mervyn Peake, *Titus Alone,* London, 1959)

GORT NA CLOCA MORA, home of the leprechauns. Its exact location is unknown, but it is probably close to GLYN CAGNY in Ireland. It lies on the edge of a wood, where a rough field is scattered with large grey rocks. A broad low tree in the corner of the field gives access to the subterranean home of the leprechauns. Beyond the field, the rough heather-covered slopes of the mountains sweep up to the skyline.

Like the fairies in this area, the leprechauns have the ability to cure human ailments, but their main activity appears to be making shoes. They habitually wear bright green clothes with leather aprons and tall green hats. The bird of the leprechauns is the robin and they have been known to take revenge on any cat who kills one. For many years now they have been accumulating a crock of gold in case the need should arise for them to ransom one of their number from the hands of mortals.

The leprechauns can be called by knocking three times, twice and then once again, on the trunk of their tree. Travellers are advised that any object left under the thornbushes around the field will be perfectly safe, as thornbushes command the protection of every fairy in the world, and not even a leprechaun will dare touch it.

(James Stephens, *The Crock of Gold*, London, 1912)

GRAAL FLIBUSTE, COUNTRY OF THE, of unknown location, bordering Transarcidonia and not far from the famous Chichi Archipelago (see also BACHEPOUSSE). The country has no roads, only a few meadow and forest paths; it is therefore preferable to travel by carriage or by horse. Certain parts of the country are best avoided, like the Wind province, haunted by boring ghosts, and the City of Crachon or Spit, a foul-smelling conglomeration of dirty houses in which the inhabitants keep rubbish and excrement as if they were treasures.

In the mountains lives King Gnar, advised by an ancient serpent with dark imaginings. Next to the royal palace, in a black chapel, a solitary organist as crooked as a mandrake root repeats the same musical phrase over and over for the questionable entertainment of travellers.

Graal Flibuste is the name of the god of this country, said to protect bankers. His temple stands in the middle of the Valley of Chanchèze, a desolate place infested with rats.

The flora of the country is extraordinarily rich: moth-lavenders, vertigo-pansies, jam-plants and, in particular, *molodies*—pine trees with crystal trunks that reflect the light like mirrors, turning the forests of the country into mazes from which it is impossible to escape. The fauna is also varied: tiger-birds, butterfly-monkeys and strange swan-horses. The latter seem to be in constant movement, neighing and shaking their manes as they skim the surface of a lake or pool. Travellers can see them basking on the riverbanks, searching with almost human eyes for the impossible mate: impossible, because these beasts have all been castrated.

(Robert Pinget, *Graal Flibuste*, Paris, 1956)

GRABAWLIA, see LOONARIE.

GRAMBLAMBLE LAND, a country famous for its great lake, the Pipple-popple, and for the city of Tosh. The city houses the famous Municipal Museum, which no visitor should miss. Seven famous families—the Parrots, the Storks, the Geese, the Owls, the Guinea Pigs, the Cats, the Fishes—are here preserved in seven immense glass bottles with airtight stoppers. These families, after being disgraced by the ill conduct of their children, pickled themselves in great quantities of cayenne pepper, brandy and vinegar. They left careful instructions in their wills (which they had drawn up with the assistance of the most eminent lawyers of the district) that the stoppers of the seven bottles should be carefully sealed with blue sealing-wax, labelled with parchment (or some other anticongenial succedaneum) and placed on a marble table with

The Stork family, preserved in the Tosh Museum, GRAMBLAMBLE LAND.

silver-gilt legs, for the daily inspection and contemplation and perpetual benefit of the pusillanimous public.

Visitors will find these bottles on the ninety-eighth table in the four hundred and twenty-seventh room of the right-hand corridor of the left wing of the Central Quadrangle of the museum.

(Edward Lear, "The History of the Seven Families of the Lake Pipple-popple," in *Nonsense Songs, Stories, Botany and Alphabets*, London, 1871)

GRAND DUCHY, a modest state in Germany. Tourists can visit the pleasant village of Sieghartsweiler and marvel at the beauties of Vulture Rock. But the Grand Duchy is famous mainly as the native country of Murr Cat, the only tomcat in the world to have solved the secret of feline philosophy. Author of the famous *Biographical Amusements on the Roof*, Murr was the first to draw a scientifically and philosophically based distinction between the roof-roaming student cat, with his booming voice, his pure soul and his empty stomach, and the cushion-warming philistine cat, curled up near a fried herring and a delicious bowl of milk and always ready with excuses not to share his meal.

The inhabitants of the Grand Duchy pass their days imitating each other; in fact, it is hard for the traveller to know whom he is addressing. People tell of a dwarf named Zaches who became Minister Zinnober, while a monk named Médard apparently changed himself into a Polish gentleman.

The Grand Duchy still maintains privileged diplomatic relations with Italy, especially during the carnival period. The Grand Duchy's highest honour is the Order of the Green-Speckled Tiger; the number of buttons worn on the jacket indicates the bearer's rank in the hierarchy of the Order.

(Ernst Theodor Amadeus Hoffmann, *Der goldene Topf*, Bamberg, 1814; Ernst Theodor Amadeus Hoffmann, *Die Elixiere des Teufels*, Berlin, 1816; Ernst Theodor Amadeus Hoffmann, *Klein Zaches genannt Zinnober*, Berlin, 1819; Ernst Theodor Amadeus Hoffmann, *Lebensansichten des Katers Murr*, Berlin, 1822; Ernst Theodor Amadeus Hoffmann, *Prinzessin Brambilla—Ein Capriccio nach J. Callot*, Breslau, 1820)

GRAND DUCHY OF FENWICK, see Duchy of GRAND FENWICK.

GRANDE EUSCARIE, an underground country, located somewhere beneath south-east France. Entry is through the Fauzan Caves in the West Pyrenees, but some travellers have arrived via other places, such as the Dardilan Cavern, also in France.

Grande Euscarie is inhabited by a herd of intelligent mammoths which took refuge here after the First Ice Age.

Upon arrival, visitors are advised to pay their respects to the Blue Mammoth (*Elephas Primigenius*) who rules over the other mammoths, and has the title "King of the World" (*Khen-Aren-Khen*). The herd lives in Yalna, the capital, an immense conglomerate of polished stone cubes, some fifteen metres high, with many openings; the whole city is dominated by a colossal dome. Visitors will find that indoors the rooms are empty, with the exception of beautiful carpets that completely cover the floor. These carpets are woven by the mammoths themselves and make interesting souvenirs.

The mammoths are protected against every possible illness by a certain drug, the *ohim*, which has also made them truthful and profoundly moralistic. The centaurs, who share with the mammoths the realm of Grande Euscarie, have refused to adopt the *ohim;* they are therefore subject to mortal passions such as love, jealousy and anger. The centaurs were masters of Grande Euscarie before the arrival of the mammoths; they now live in the ruined city of Pokmé, the ancient capital.

The whole of Grande Euscarie is lit by radio-electric waves that reach the country via the mines of Ghord in the Pyrenees (though the exact procedure has not yet been fully explained). Because of this, the Euscarian "sky" looks somewhat like a brilliant fog and there is no distinction between night and day. The climate is tropical and so is the vegetation. The only endemic species is the *arabe*, from which a nourishing milk is extracted.

Grande Euscarie was described by the French geologist, Vernon, author of *Etude sur les galeries horizontales dans le système orographique souterrain des Causses* and *Hydrographie Souterraine* (1913), and founder, in 1920, of the *Annales de Spéléologie*. Vernon made the remarkable discovery that the language of the mammoths, Escuara, is, in fact, the original Basque language, taught by the mammoths to the prehistoric men who dwelt in the Pyrenees thousands of years ago. Travellers will therefore find a Basque phrasebook useful when visiting Grande Euscarie.

(Luc Alberny, *Le Mammouth Bleu*, Paris, 1935)

GRAND FENWICK, DUCHY OF (and not Grand Duchy of Fenwick), the smallest and least progressive country in the world, in the southern foothills of the Alps, bordered on the north by the River Danube. The Duchy covers an area five miles by three, some of which is forested territory, but most of which is given over to vineyards. A simple but pleasant wine is the Duchy's chief export.

The only town is also called Grand Fenwick. The town square is dominated by the Castle, used as both the ruler's residence and the Council Chambers. Despite its size, Grand Fenwick has a small and inefficient television network, the Grand Fenwick National Television Service.

Grand Fenwick was founded five centuries ago by an Englishman, Sir Roger Fenwick; British traditions are loyally adhered to and English is the national language. The present constitutional ruler is the widowed Grand Duchess Gloriana XIII; the hereditary Prime Minister and Leader of the Council is Count Rupert of Mountjoy (temporarily ousted in 1958); the Loyal Opposition is led by David Benter. A small army, led by Field Marshall Tully Bascombe (in civilian life the Chief Forester) and modelled on the British Brigade of Guards, is also maintained, principally for ceremonial purposes.

In 1958, the Duchy was brought to bankruptcy by a cheap Californian imitation of the national wine. War was declared on the United States, in the hope of large rehabilitation funds after the inevitable defeat. In a feat almost too famous to be recalled, a twenty-man expeditionary force took over New York, deserted during an air-raid drill. The world's most lethal weapon, the Q-bomb, was captured, and on the strength of this Grand Fenwick declared itself to be the most powerful nation on earth. However, the bomb was found to be a dud and a peace treaty between Grand Fenwick and the United States was duly signed.

In 1962, Grand Fenwick experienced a second economic crisis when its wine was found to be explosive when carried over long distances, and so restrictions on the Duchy's wines were then im-

posed by importing countries. With the excuse of wanting to build a moon rocket, the Duchy approached the United States for a loan of half a million dollars. America responded with a gift of a million dollars and, not to be outdone, the Soviet Union matched this with the presentation of an outdated rocket. Using the explosive wine as the propulsive fuel, the inhabitants of Grand Fenwick launched the gift rocket and a Grand Fenwick expedition reached the moon ahead of competing American and Soviet rocket teams. The moon was claimed as Grand Fenwick territory.

Visitors who wish to travel to the moon are advised to check for visas at their Grand Fenwick consulate.

(*The Mouse that Roared*, directed by Jack Arnold, UK, 1958; *The Mouse on the Moon*, directed by Richard Lester, UK, 1962)

GRAVEYARD OF UNWRITTEN BOOKS, a vast complex of galleries beneath the Hôtel de Sens in Paris. Visitors enter a courtyard at the back of the building, where a small passage opens in a mossy wall. This leads to a narrow, gloomy gallery which in turn leads into an inner, subterranean courtyard. In this courtyard stands a well; a rope ladder allows the visitor to descend into its depths. Upon reaching the bottom of the well, the visitor will find a vaulted gallery dripping with damp; this gallery must be followed to an iron door. Visitors must knock to be admitted inside what appears to be a vast storeroom for books. Uniformed attendants move about in all directions, securing books under lock and key. Here, in what is known as the Graveyard of Unwritten Books, or the Well of Locks, all books banned by authorities throughout the world are shut away. Some of these books were published and then forbidden; others were stillborn; many never reached the written page. Visitors are advised to bring a flashlight and not to be seen with a book in their hands.

(Nedim Gürsel, *Son Tramway*, Istanbul, 1990)

GREAT CYPRESS SWAMP, near the town of Gainesville, in the United States, lies in a humid and deep vale, covered with overgrowth, moss and strange herbs. It is enveloped in a fetid stench, which seems to come from rotting rocks, perhaps belonging to an ancient nearby cemetery, so old that the names on the stones have been erased by the hand of Time.

In this terrible necropolis, among a startling landscape of broken urns, mausoleums and ruined tombs, travellers can find a passage under one of the larger stones. The route was first described by Randolph Carter, who was following the trail of a missing friend, Mr. Harley Warren. According to Mr. Carter's chronicle, Harley Warren vanished in this very passage, the walls of which ooze a foul liquid which seems to come from the depths of the earth. By means of an electric phone, Warren told Carter of many underground horrors and finally, in a deep, hollow, inhuman voice, confessed that he was already dead.

(Howard Phillips Lovecraft, "The Statement of Randolph Carter," in *Weird Tales*, New York, 1925)

GREAT GARABAGNE, a strange country of changing location. Its frontiers are undefined and access to Great Garabagne is very difficult and dangerous—only certain dreamers and poets have reached it and returned. Its poisonous landscape can sometimes be seen after profound meditation or if the traveller is in a hallucinatory state. The first impression of the country is dreadful and leaves visitors on the verge of despair. Be warned that each traveller meets here his own monsters, chasms and deserts. The inhabitants of Great Garabagne—the Hacs, the Emanglons and several species of Meidosems—are everything Western society despises and loathes.

(Henri Michaux, *Voyage en Grande Garabagne*, Paris, 1936; Henri Michaux, *Meidosems*, Paris, 1948; Henri Michaux, *Ecuador*, Paris, 1968)

GREAT MARINA, once a rich, fair land with an ancient civilization, it was overcome by the Chief Ranger of MAURETANIA and his wild horde. A large lake bordered by Roman ruins, Christian churches and Merovingian castles encloses the Hesperides Islands. To the east lies ALTA PLANA, to the north TEUTOBURGER Forest and CAMPAGNA. Above the land rises the MARMOR-KLIPPEN Range.

Great Marina is famous for its mushrooms and truffles (sought with dogs), fine chestnuts and large walnuts. Because of the mild climate, cy-

presses and many fruit trees are also found. The bird life includes quails, speckled thrush, fig-eaters, redstarts, ducks, finches and goldfinches.

The small town of Marina, with its Cockerel Gate and harbour, lies to the left of the celebrated vine-clad hills. Near the harbour is the Chapel of the Sagrada Familia or Holy Family, where the vessel containing the head of the Prince of Sunmyra is buried beneath the foundation-stone.

The Guild of Poets is held in much esteem and the gift of rhyming is considered a source of plenty, spiritually and financially, to the poet. At funerals it is the poet who pronounces judgement on the deceased. He can do so in two measures: the *elegeion*, suitable for praising a life of justice, or the *ebernum*, which in olden days was reserved for praising the slayers of monsters—during its recital a black eagle (called Admiratio) was released from its cage.

(Ernst Jünger, *Auf den Marmorklippen*, Frankfurt, 1939)

GREAT MOTHER'S or LADIES' ISLAND, a republic of women located in the Pacific Ocean. This mountainous island, measuring five to six kilometres in length, lies like a horseshoe around a large gulf harbour; elsewhere the coast is quite steep. A thin plume of smoke rises constantly from one of the island's two volcanic peaks, which attain heights of over three thousand feet. Beneath the mountains lies a fertile, terraced valley watered by sparkling clear springs. Coffee, tobacco, pepper, cinnamon and sugar-cane are grown there, and game-birds and animals, as well as fish, are found in great abundance.

The island was discovered on February 2, at the beginning of the twentieth century, when lifeboats from a steamer named *Cormorant*, sailing from Hong Kong to San Francisco, ran aground there. The only passengers to survive were women and girls, with the sole exception of a boy of fourteen named Phaon. To combat the hysteria and despair of her shipwrecked companions, the eldest woman spontaneously appointed herself president.

Life on the island was quite easily organized, for the lifeboats were equipped with tools and supplies. The women built Lady City, a collection of bamboo tents arranged in circles. There was a reading tent and a church-tent (a Bible had been saved during the disaster); the church was called

Our Lady of the Ladies. In the very first year a meeting-house was inaugurated, its dining room furnished in the style of van de Velde thanks to a woman who had once been a member of the artists' colony in Darmstadt. Writing materials had also been saved, and these enabled the women to keep a chronicle of their progress on the island. The women were very happy, rejecting the life they had lived previously in a patriarchal world.

About a year after the shipwreck one of the women gave birth to a son, whom she regarded as the incarnation of Krishna and the son of the god Mukalinda, who had appeared to her in a mystical dream. Other supernatural procreations resulted in the birth of more children on the island, month after month. Since no one was very keen on trying to discover the natural paternity of these children, a cult of lingam developed about mythic couplings, and a temple to Mukalinda was erected on the island. But the growing number of children naturally included some boys, and the women began to view these as a threat to the survival of both their cult and their matriarchal society. They decided to exile boys over the age of five to a distant corner of the island, which they called "Man's Land."

While the women continued to devote themselves to their cult, the young men, under Phaon's leadership, directed their attention to more concrete goals. In the course of the following ten years they developed numerous crafts, particularly those dealing with wood. They even constructed a small fleet of sailboats. Their manual dexterity led to the appearance of a god in Man's Land: the Sacred Hand.

After some time, the inexplicable drop in births in Great Mother's Land led to an outburst of a sort of psychosis, with girls running into the temples' sanctuaries and putting the buildings to the torch. A group of young men stopped them from doing more damage in their excited frenzy, and raised the island's new flag, bearing the inscription "Man."

(Gerhart Hauptmann, *Die Insel der grossen Mutter oder das Wunder von Ile des Dames. Eine Geschichte aus dem utopischen Archipelagus*, Berlin, 1924)

GREAT RIVER or **ANDUIN**, the greatest waterway of northern MIDDLE-EARTH, rises in the GREY MOUNTAINS of the north. Its course takes it through the valley between the MISTY MOUNTAINS and MIRKWOOD and through the Vales of ANDUIN. It continues through ROHAN, ITHILIEN, and the province of Lebennin before reaching its delta, the Ethir Anduin, where it flows into the Bay of Belfalas. Beneath the range of hills known as the EMYN MUIL, the Great River rushes through a gorge before reaching the long oval lake of NEN HITHOEL.

At the northern entrance to the gorge stand two huge figures carved out of the rock. The two figures are known as the Argonath and were built during the middle of the Third Age to mark the northern frontier of GONDOR. The rapids above the Argonath, the Sarn Gebir, are impassable and it is necessary to take the portage, on the western bank, to bypass them.

Where the Great River flows out of the southern end of the lake of Nen Hithoel, it plunges down the falls of Rauros, but below the falls the river is navigable. Ships from the sea come upriver as far as the boat-shaped island of CAIR ANDROS north of MINAS TIRITH, the capital of the kingdom of Gondor.

The major port is at PELARGIR. Pelargir is not on the sea coast itself, but above the Great River's delta. It is a major centre for communications with the west and was an important base for naval attacks on the corsairs who menaced Gondor from the south during the Third Age.

(J.R.R. Tolkien, *The Hobbit, or There and Back Again*, London, 1937; J.R.R. Tolkien, *The Fellowship of the Ring*, London, 1954; J.R.R. Tolkien, *The Two Towers*, London, 1954; J.R.R. Tolkien, *The Return of the King*, London, 1955; J.R.R. Tolkien, *The Silmarillion*, London, 1977)

GREAT WATER, a large lake dotted with islands, stretching from the Forest of Evilshaw to the Castle of the Quest. Travellers may find it somewhere in the north of England. The Forest of Evilshaw itself is dense and trackless—no one dares hunt here and no criminal dares take refuge in it. Many legends are attached to it: some say that the dead walk its paths, others that it is inhabited by demons; yet others suppose that it conceals the mouth of hell and call it Devil's Park. On the edge of Evilshaw is the market town of Utterhay, and by the water's edge is a house known as the Witch's Abode.

Travellers wishing to cross the lake and visit the several islands must make use of the "sending

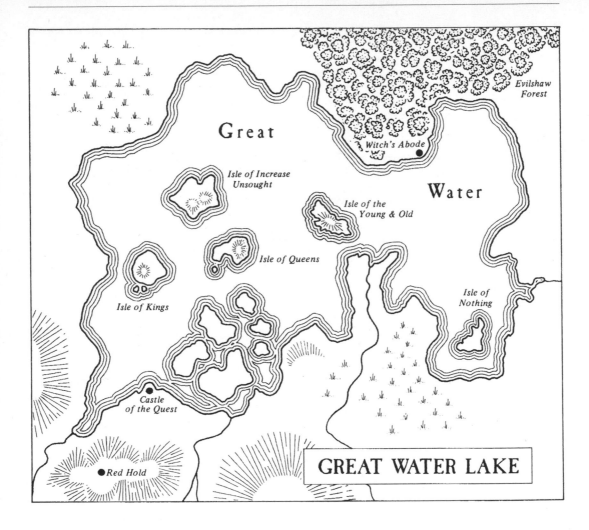

GREAT WATER LAKE

boat," a small vessel with no rudder. In order to travel in it, the user must cut him- or herself and smear the boat with his (or her) blood, saying:

> The red raven wine now
> Hast thou drunk, stern and bow;
> Then wake and awake
> And the wonted way take!
> The way of the wender
> Forth over the flood,
> For the will of the sender
> Is blent with blood.

South-west of Great Water rises the Castle of the Quest, also known as the White Ward by the Water, a medium-sized fortification built of stone and lime. Entry to the castle is forbidden to women until the lords who own it have found their lost loves. On the southern side is a beautiful garden, the Pleasance, overgrown with roses and lilies. The Castle of the Quest is surrounded by hostile territory. Its rival is the Castle of the Red Knight, also known as the Red Hold, noted for its ferocious man-eating hounds.

The principal islands in Great Water are five—all worth visiting if the traveller has enough time.

The Isle of Increase Unsought, where crops grow without any tending, sowing or reaping. The castle is now in ruins, and snakes, lizards, beetles and carrion flies can be seen crawling among the stones.

The Isle of the Young and Old. The only building here also is a ruined castle, whose remaining carvings and archways are evidence of its former beauty. Some travellers report that even these ruins have now vanished and that the island is inhabited by a multitude of children, aged five to fifteen, who do not seem to grow older.

The Isle of Queens, noted for its beautiful palace of white stone. In the Great Hall a large company of lovely women sit in total silence, their hands stretched out to take the food on the table before them. On a dais is a bier bearing the body of the king with a bloodstained sword lying across his chest, next to which is a kneeling queen. Though lifelike, all these immobile figures have been dead for many years. The island is inhabited by former knights, now shabbily dressed, who dare not enter the palace and whose lamentations are heard during the night.

The Isle of Kings, a rocky island with a castle rising from the crags. In the brightly decorated hall, around a high table, sit three kings and three wise men. A bier bears the body of a beautiful woman stabbed to death. The sole inhabitants of the isle are a group of lightly clad young women who dare not enter the hall. Instead of the song of birds, the air is rent by the clash of weapons.

The Isle of Nothing, a flat, often misty island, once bare of all vegetation but now covered with fruit trees and flocks of sheep, herds of cattle and goats. The inhabitants wear short woollen coats and garlands of green leaves.

Visitors are advised that the islands of Great Water change aspect very quickly and may not appear to them as described here.

(William Morris, *The Water of the Wondrous Isles*, London, 1897)

GREEDY ISLAND, one of several high islands near Tierra del Fuego. The inhabitants are very fat and think of nothing but food. They are rich and spend much of their time and income on DOCTORS' ISLAND. Their god is Baratrogulo, to whom they make offerings of food. Baratrogulo is represented as a colossally fat man seated at a table. His priests are both oracles and ventriloquists, and answer not through their mouths but with their stomachs.

(Abbé Pierre François Guyot Desfontaines, *Le Nouveau Gulliver, ou Voyage De Jean Gulliver, Fils Du Capitaine Gulliver. Traduit d'un Manuscrit Anglois. Par Monsieur L.D.F.*, Paris, 1730)

GREEN CHAPEL, of uncertain location, either somewhere in northern Wales or on the Wirral. It lies beside a bubbling stream in a small steep-sided valley approached through a ravine where a rugged track runs below wild and forbidding cliffs; the surrounding area is a desolate succession of forests and marshland. The Chapel itself has the shape of a barrow and is entered through a hole at the end and on either side; inside, it resembles a rough cave completely overgrown with grass. The Chapel is clearly a man-made structure, but nothing is known of its origins—it may be a true barrow, or a crude oratory fallen to rack and ruin.

The Green Chapel is closely associated with the famous combat between Sir Gawain and the Green Knight. The latter appeared on New Year's Day at the court of King Arthur in CAMELOT, dressed completely in green and riding a green horse. To the astonishment of the court, he challenged any knight present to strike at him with an axe, on condition that he would accept a return blow a year later.

Sir Gawain took up the challenge and without more ado struck off the Green Knight's head; to everyone's astonishment, the Green Knight picked up his head and rode off with it under his arm. A year later, Gawain travelled north and stayed in a castle near the Green Chapel. Here he went hunting and was unsuccessfully tempted by the lady of the castle. On New Year's Day he went to the Chapel for the tryst. The Green Knight struck at his neck with the axe but merely scratched Gawain's skin, and then revealed his true story: he had been enchanted by Morgan le Fay and sent to challenge Arthur's knights in the hope of showing them to be cowards; the lady of the castle was the Green Knight's wife. Although the Green Knight showed him no ill will, Gawain rejected his offer of hospitality and rode back to Camelot.

(Anonymous, *Sir Gawain and the Green Knight*, 14th cen. AD)

GREEN LAND, an underwater country in England. The entrance to Green Land is through a stream that leads into a large grotto filled with a liquid light, blue in the darker reaches and pale green towards an apparent outlet. The floor is a rocky, moss-covered basin and from the walls hang long, glassy icicles.

After travelling through eight grottoes, an arena is reached, an immense beehive or pigeon-cote, in which the Green inhabitants spend much of their time. The flesh of these people is green, of a semi-translucent texture like the flesh of a cactus plant. They have long blond hair, egg-shaped heads, no eyebrows and tiny bright eyes like those of a ferret. They wear diaphanous robes.

Beyond the arena the traveller will see a plain, in the midst of which is a bubbling lake of warm water. The basin, perhaps two hundred feet across, has been made into a regular ellipse and is surrounded by a low wall cut from the rock. Surrounding the basin is an annular trough about ten feet wide, of semicircular section. The air is extremely warm, like that of a hot-house. A coralline, fungus-like plant grows here, reaching a maximum height of three feet. From the rocky ceilings hangs another vegetable, in the form of tangled and withered roots: these are not roots but stems, and contain kernels that are sweet and agreeable to eat and form the bread of the inhabitants of Green Land.

The fauna of Green Land is very poor. There is one bird, little bigger than a skylark but more like an owl in appearance: grey, with downy feathers like fur, each eye surrounded by a ruff. It has a straight beak and differs from any bird on earth in the manner of its flight, flying upwards as straight as a stone sinks, and then descending with a corkscrew motion. It is solitary and very docile. There are also silver-grey blindworms or snakes, about three feet long, with a faint blue phosphorescent gleam on their scales. They are mostly domesticated and coil round the necks of their masters. Finally, the traveller will find beetles the size of tortoises, with shell-like wing-cases of metallic blue, slightly striated in a longitudinal direction. They run on three pairs of triple-jointed legs, and their mandibles and antennae are not conspicuous. The females emit a luminous glow from the hind end of their bodies. They live on dung and are much esteemed as scavengers as well as pets.

A sound of faint bells can be heard throughout Green Land, produced by a series of rods of different dimensions. These rods are made in special caverns, which serve as workshops or factories, and are used to guide people around the country which of course lacks a sun or stars.

The Green people divide into work groups for most activities, such as gathering food. They have no system for measuring time and they wait for the natural processes of their bodies to indicate the need for such functions as sleeping or copulating. When a girl becomes pregnant, she leaves the group and goes to live in another large grotto, where she is attended by matrons.

The people of Green Land are convinced that time is of limited duration; they point out the solidity and indestructibility of the rocks about them, and compare this mass, which to them is a more extensive element than space, with the insignificance of things that change. They say that when the last vital element has received its crystalline form, the sense of time will disappear. Time to them is change, and a mark of our transitional nature. (Other countries—see LOOKING-GLASS LAND—have eliminated the problem of transience by petrifying time itself.)

Green language has no Aryan roots and bears no relation to any other known language. It is only spoken—they have never conceived the idea of writing, of an alphabet, letters or books. It is useful to know that in Green language *Si* means "I am."

Their notions of immortality are diametrically opposed to those prevalent in most countries. Perhaps because they have solid rock above them, instead of an open and impalpable sky, and because they believe their universe to be limited and human beings to be numerable, they regard the organic and vital elements of their bodies as disgusting and deplorable. Everything soft and labile fills them with a sort of horror; above all, they believe human breath to be the symptom of an original curse which can only be eradicated after death. Death itself holds no horror for them, but nothing exceeds their dread of corruption and decay which they regard as a return to the soft and gaseous, to the very element of their weakness and disgrace. Their sole desire is to become solid, as solid and perdurable as the rocks about them.

Because of this desire, the Green people practise the so-called "rites of petrification." A person about to die must first go into one of the grottoes and there meditate, in solitary contemplation, on a few beautifully cut crystals. Once the hated breath has left the body forever, the body is lain in a trough filled with petrous water until it becomes a pillar of salt. The pillars are stacked in a cave—recumbent statues in the hall of the dead—and slowly the caves are becoming filled with these solid wedges. The Green people believe that there will come a time when a dwindling race will inhabit the last grotto, and finally the last of that race will plunge into the trough, thus fulfilling the purpose of life, which is to attain everlasting perfection. Then their bodies will be perfectly united with the earth and they will be one with the physical harmony of the universe.

Two Green children visited England in the 1830's. The boy died but the girl was rescued by Dr. Olivero, ex-dictator of RONCADOR. The girl, Siloën—called Sally in England—led Olivero back to her country, where he became one of them in death.

(Herbert Read, *The Green Child*, London, 1935)

GREEN SAND ISLAND, one of a group of three islands north-west of Hawaii, on the latitude of San Francisco and Yokohama, explored in 1841 by the young Franco-Danish scientist, Leonard Henri. Henri suggested that Green Sand, Black Sand and Red Sand islands were all connected by extinct subterranean lava vents, linked, on the other side of the world, to a chasm in the Tibetan mountains. On Green Sand Island, Henri discovered a horse and a species of vulture only found in Tibet and set off to discover the chasm's location. He found it in the Kouen-Lun Mountains in Tibet, where a certain volcano has the property of sucking in any object that comes within range.

Travellers who wish to proceed from Tibet to the Pacific through this tunnel must be warned against a group of monks who are the guardians of the chasm and who believe the chasm to be the gateway to hell. Black Sand and Red Sand islands were destroyed by a volcanic eruption which took place when the enraged monks threw a number of explosives into the Tibetan chasm.

(Tancrède Vallerey, *L'Ile au sable vert*, Paris, 1930)

GREENS WHARFE or CAPE-VED ISLANDS, near the Azores in the north Atlantic. A pleasant country in which the young have unlimited freedom. The inhabitants are clownish and boring, yet pretenders to good breeding and over-affected in their fashions and clothes. They believe themselves to be witty and write songs and poems which they like to recite in public. To them life is a joke and they delight in whoring, drinking and dancing. It is difficult to sleep in the capital of Greens Wharfe because of the deafening noise of the coach wheels on the cobblestones.

(Frank Careless, *The Floating Island or A New Discovery Relating the Strange Adventure on a late Voyage from Lambethana to Villa Franca, Alias Ramallia, to the Eastward of Terra del Templo: By three Ships, viz. the "Pay-naught," the "Excuse," and the "Least-in-Sight" under the conduct of Captain Robert Owe-much: Describing the Nature of the Inhabitants, their Religion, Laws and Customs*, London, 1673)

GREY AMBER, ISLAND OF, somewhere in the Indian Ocean. The exact location has not been given, because the sole description we have of the island was written by the Arab chronicler, Sinbad the Sailor, who was cast upon the island during a tempest.

The island is large and mountainous, its coasts strewn with the wrecks of ships from all over the world. So many objects are found here—precious cloths, jewels, works of art—that the island's beaches look like an Arab bazaar taken by storm. The traveller will find large quantities of Chinese wood, aloe and grey amber; the latter, because of the extreme heat of the sun during the day, runs like melted wax down the hillsides and into the sea, where it is devoured by cetaceans which keep it for a while in their bellies and then spit it back into the deep. But the cetaceans' gastric juices change the grey amber so that, when it is again in contact with the water, it becomes as hard as a diamond but as light as a feather, and is swept by the waves onto the shore. It is then collected in great quantities by avid merchants who come to the island for this purpose, and sold for huge prices in the most exclusive stores throughout the world.

(Anonymous, *The Arabian Nights*, 14th–16th cen. AD)

GREY HAVENS, a major port and city in LINDON, a region on the western coast of MIDDLEEARTH.

The port is built at the point where the River Lhûn enters the Gulf of Lhûn (or "Lune" in the Common Speech), the great gulf formed at the end of the First Age when the realm of Beleriand was swallowed up by the sea. Founded at the beginning of the Second Age, the Grey Havens is the traditional port of embarkation for those who sail to AMAN in the west. It was from here that so many of the elves left Middle-earth and many of the heroes of the War of the Ring sailed.

(J.R.R. Tolkien, *The Fellowship of the Ring,* London, 1954; J.R.R. Tolkien, *The Return of the King,* London, 1955; J.R.R. Tolkien, *The Silmarillion,* London, 1977)

GREY MOUNTAINS, also known as **ERED MITHRIN,** a mountain range running east to west in MIDDLE-EARTH, to the north of MIRKWOOD. The mountains are the home of a variety of goblins and of some of the most vicious orcs in the whole of Middle-earth. Both the mountains themselves and the area around them, the Withered Heath, are also inhabited by dragons which have in the past descended to attack the lands to the south. Smaug the Golden, one of the greatest fire-dragons of Middle-earth, came from this area.

After the dwarves were driven out of their great caverns in MORIA by the demonic Balrog in 1981 Third Age, some of them travelled to the Grey Mountains and attempted to establish a new colony here. By 2589, however, they were forced to leave because of the increasing numbers of orcs and dragons in the area. They then settled in the IRON HILLS.

(J.R.R. Tolkien, *The Hobbit, or There and Back Again,* London, 1937; J.R.R. Tolkien, *The Fellowship of the Ring,* London, 1954; J.R.R. Tolkien, *The Return of the King,* London, 1955)

GREYWETHERS, a desolate valley leading deep into the mountains not far from GREAT WATER, perhaps in the north of England. A small stream runs through the black rocks. The valley is strewn with pale grey stones vaguely shaped like sheep, which appear to have once stood in some kind of order. These are known as the "greywethers," said to be real sheep that their owners, a race of giants, turned into stone.

A traveller bold enough to wait until the greywethers awaken, can ask them for anything and his wish will be granted; but he must show no fear and must answer no questions. The greywethers will lure him with gold, gems and beautiful, naked women, but he must resist temptation till the cock crows, or he himself will be turned into stone. It is useful to know that the greywethers come to life only on certain nights, for example Midsummer's eve, and that the valley contains the stone remains of a number of weak or over-polite travellers.

(William Morris, *The Water of the Wondrous Isles,* London, 1897)

GRIMMBART, GRAND DUCHY OF, a small principality in southern Germany which has been ruled for centuries by the ducal house of Grimmbart. Grimmbart is a quiet unhurried country which draws most of its wealth from agriculture and from its forests, probably the most treasured of all its resources. The forests are dear to the people and figure greatly in their songs and ballads, as well as in the work of the duchy's artists. Salt and some silver are mined, but agriculture remains the basis of the economy.

Hopes that the capital would develop into a spa of European importance have never been realized. In the Middle Ages the spa was popular but was gradually eclipsed by other establishments and never gained pre-eminence. It now attracts relatively few visitors, but considerable quantities of its lithium-rich waters are bottled for export.

The capital is dominated by the Old Castle which stands at the end of the Albrechtstrasse, the main street. This is the official residence of the Grand Dukes, although the castle at Grimmberg is equally important and is rightly regarded as the cradle of the dynasty. Together with the church attached to it, the castle is an irregular, tortuous complex of towers and galleries. Half-palace and half-fortress, it has been greatly added to over the centuries, and it is now difficult to make out the original ground-plan. The walls descend steeply to the west side of the city and to the Albrechtstrasse gate, guarded by stone lions. Above the massive door a faded inscription reads *"Turris fortissima nomen Domini."* The gate leads into a succession of three courtyards, each flagged with black basalt and flanked by tall towers with winding stairways.

The magnificent Silver Room, used for formal receptions, overlooks the Albrechtsplatz. Its high ceiling is covered with silver arabesques, and the walls are covered with silver-mounted white damask and decorated with coats of arms. The chimney-piece is a monumental baldachin supported by silver pillars. Above it hangs a portrait of an unknown lady of the House of Grimmbart, dressed in what appears to be imitation white ermine. In the centre of the room, beneath a chandelier, stands a great table—a silver pedestal in the shape of a rugged tree trunk, supporting a table-top of mother of pearl. Of the numerous other chambers in the Old Castle, travellers should pay particular attention to the gold and silver Throne Room and to the Marble Hall, where a portrait of Grand Duchess Dorothea can be seen. This is the traditional setting for the concerts given by the court orchestra, known as the Grand Duchess' Thursdays.

The more modern sections of the castle include the Gala Rooms and the Hall of the Knights where court officials used to assemble for the Grand Levée. Nearby is the so-called Owl Chamber, now used as a lumber room. It is reputed to be haunted and it is said that the strange noises emanating from it become louder when important and decisive events are in the offing.

The city clusters around the Old Castle and is divided into two parts by the river, which runs in a great loop around the southern end of the Municipal Gardens before disappearing from view among the surrounding mountains. It is a university city, but its academy is known for its conservatism rather than for its learning. Only Professor Klinghammer, the mathematician, has a distinguished name in the academic world outside Grimmbart. There is little musical, literary or intellectual life in the city, although the poorly subsidized Court Theatre maintains a reasonable standard in its performances. For music the visitor is recommended to visit Knupplesdorf, which is famed for its choral society.

For centuries Grimmbart was dominated by its age-old traditions and more attention was paid to the niceties of court rituals than to the management of the economy. The natural health of the peasantry was undermined by the development of a commercial dairy industry; it became more profitable for the small farmers to sell their produce than to consume it and their health declined as a result.

Mismanagement of the forests had a more serious effect. Leaf mould was taken away for fertilizing fields and the forest floor was badly eroded as a result. Timber was felled for immediate profit and was not replanted, both in common lands and in the State forests, with the result that both sectors fell into a serious decline. Even the small railway connecting the capital with Grimmberg, no more than fifteen minutes away, ran at a heavy loss. Matters were not improved by the ducal custom of maintaining a large number of castles throughout the country even though many of them were hardly ever used. The restoration of Grimmberg itself at the beginning of the reign of Johann Albrecht III cost one million marks, the equivalent of one year's revenue. At his death, Johann Albrecht left his son Albrecht II with a failing economy and a colossal national debt. Before long, even the silver mines were at a standstill.

Albrecht was a shy retiring man who chose to live in privacy, delegating more and more responsibility to his younger brother Klaus Heinrich, who soon became ruler in all but name and took the honorary title of Royal Highness. During his effective rule over Grimmbart, the capital was visited by Samuel N. Spoelman, an American multi-millionaire of German descent who initially came to take the waters but stayed on, buying one of the palaces in the capital and restoring it at enormous expense. With him came his daughter Imma, a strange studious girl who gained a certain popularity through her charitable work. Impressed by her example, Klaus Heinrich himself began to study economics and to move away from the traditional conception of a prince's duties. Eventually the young people married and Spoelman agreed to finance the country with his millions, paying off the national debt and acting as Grimmbart's State Banker. The country has now been restored to prosperity; the silver mines have been reopened and rich new deposits have been found.

The marriage between Imma and Klaus Heinrich appears to have fulfilled an ancient prophecy made by a gypsy woman. He was born with a slightly withered arm and can thus be seen as the prince referred to in the words "He will give the country with one hand more than all the rest could give it with two." A rose-bush is also connected with that prophecy. It once grew in the innermost courtyard of the Old Castle, and although it regularly produced the most beautiful red roses, they always gave off a smell of decay. It was said that their scent would become sweet when something of great importance happened to the ruling house. The bush has now been replanted in the Municipal Gardens, but it is too early to say if its scent has really changed.

The country people of Grimmbart still wear their traditional costume, especially on festive occasions. The men wear red jackets, top-boots and black wide-brimmed hats of velvet, while the women dress in brightly embroidered bodices and short full skirts with headdresses of black bows.

(Thomas Mann, *Königliche Hoheit*, Frankfurt, 1909)

GRIMMBERG, a small picturesque town in the Grand Duchy of GRIMMBART. The grey sloping roofs of the town are dominated by the castle, the ancestral seat of the ruling house and the cradle of the ruling dynasty; it is a long-standing tradition that all children of the reigning couple shall be born here. Only twice in fifteen generations have ducal children been born elsewhere; in both cases they came to ignoble and unnatural ends.

The castle was originally built by the founder of the ducal dynasty, Margrave Klaus Grimmbart, whose statue stands in the courtyard. The first building on the site was erected in the dim beginnings of German history and little now remains of it. Over the centuries the castle has been extensively altered and rebuilt, but it has always been maintained in a habitable state. The most recent restoration took place at the beginning of the reign of Johann Albrecht III, when the internal decorations were renewed. The escutcheons in the Hall of Justice were restored and the gilded ceilings were renovated. At the same time, paintings by Academician Professor van Lindemann were hung in the Banqueting Hall. They are in traditional style and illustrate scenes from the history of the ruling house. Johann Albrecht III also modernized the castle to some extent, introducing anthracite-burning stoves.

The castle is approached along a rambling lane that leads up the hill from the town between shabby cottages and a tumbledown wall. Massive gates lead into the main courtyard. The grounds on Castle Hill are quite extensive and provide pleasant walks through the gently sloping, wooded park.

The ground floor is occupied by the Banqueting Hall, where a collection of banners and

weapons is hung between the van Lindemann paintings. Slender pillars support the painted vaulting of the ceiling and stone benches run along the walls. Above them, tall narrow windows with leaded panes reach almost to the roof. The cornices of the fireplace are formed by small crouched and flying monsters in the Gothic style. On the first floor, the octagonal Bridal Chamber overlooks the winding river and the town. Its gaily painted walls are decorated with a frieze of the brides who have married into the ducal family. This is the traditional birthplace of the children of the House of Grimmbart. The room next to it is the Powder Room, where tradition has it that the Minister of State shall determine the sex of the new baby and formally announce it to the court. Beyond the Powder Room lies the library, which is currently furnished as a writing room. A collection of folio manuscripts on top of the heavy bookcase contains the history of the castle.

(Thomas Mann, *Königliche Hoheit*, Frankfurt, 1909)

GROENKAAF, an island some five hundred leagues from the Bermudas. In the local language the name means "White Crown," because of the island's lofty mountains perpetually covered in snow.

The reefs that surround Groenkaaf make access difficult; but if the traveller arrives safely he will be heartily greeted by the natives, who appear to have retained their original innocence and who do not know the difference between vice and virtue.

In spite of the island having one of the richest ruby mines in the world, as well as several gold and silver mines, the inhabitants are not concerned with material wealth. Their only laws are tattooed on their children's arms a week after birth—"Love God" on the left arm, and "Love Your Neighbour" on the right one.

(Louis Rustaing de Saint-Jory, *Les Femmes Militaires. Relation Historique D'Une Isle Nouvellement Découverte...Dedié A Monseigneur Le Chevalier D'Orléans. Par le C.D.****, Paris, 1735)

GROMBOOLIAN PLAIN, in the Western Sea, a gloomy place of lofty towers, lakes and forest, marsh and hill, extending from the coast to the awful, towering heights of the Chankly Bore. Along the rocky shore, in the Zemmery Fidd, oblong oysters grow.

A forest in the GROMBOOLIAN PLAIN.

The Fidd is famous for having been the landing place of the brave Jumblies, who arrived by sea in a sieve, and are also thought to have visited the nearby Chankly Bore, the Lakes and the Terrible Zone. The Fidd has a reputation as a refuge. The fly and daddy long-legs are known to have fled here (they can sometimes be seen playing at battle-cock and shuttle-dore), as did King Crone and his queen, Pelican, who now dwell by the streams of the Chankly Bore. The Yonghy-Bonghy-Bo and the Old Man of the Isles also found a haven in the Fidd.

In the forests and on the flowery plain grow Twangum trees and Bong-trees—which are also a familiar sight in BONG-TREE LAND and on the coast of COROMANDEL. On stormy nights a red light can be seen crossing the great Gromboolian Plain. This phenomenon has inspired the legend of the Dong with the Luminous Nose, who is believed to have woven his strange and wonderful nose from the bark of the Twangum tree.

(Edward Lear, *The Dong with a Luminous Nose*, London, 1871)

GROWLEYWOGS DOMINION, a kingdom to the north-west of RIPPLE LAND, which separates it from the Land of the WHIMSIES.

The Growleywogs are gigantic creatures with not an ounce of fat on them; their bodies are solid bone, skin and muscle. The weakest of the species is capable of picking up an elephant and throwing it seven miles without the slightest difficulty. As a race they are surly and extremely overbearing. Not only do they hate all other people, they are hostile and antisocial among themselves. The Growleywogs are ruled by a king known as the Grand Gallipoot.

(L. Frank Baum, *The Emerald City of Oz*, Chicago, 1910)

GUG KINGDOM, near the ENCHANTED WOOD in DREAMWORLD. The Gugs are a race of gigantic hairy creatures who were banished to the caverns below Dreamworld because of their strange sacrifices. Only a great trapdoor of stone with an iron ring connects their kingdom with that of the Zoogs in the Enchanted Wood, and this the Gugs are afraid to open because of a curse. It is best to disguise oneself as a ghoul—whom the Gugs fear—to cross this land, though it is advisable to beware the *ghasts*, creatures who cannot live in real light and who, being very primitive, cannot distinguish between Gugs—their food—and ghouls. Occasionally visitors will see ghouls sitting on tombstones stolen from cemeteries throughout the world.

(Howard Phillips Lovecraft, "The Dream-Quest of Unknown Kadath," in *Arkham Sampler*, Sauk City, 1948) *Illustration follows*

GUP CITY, in Kahani, by the shores of the Ocean of the STREAMS OF STORY. Access to the city is strictly restricted to accredited personnel. Gup City, capital of the Land of Gup (meaning "gossip"), is built upon an archipelago of one thousand

A stolen tombstone, GUG KINGDOM.

King Chattergy, with its grand balcony overlooking the garden; to its right, the Parliament of Gup, known as the Chatterbox because debates there can run on for weeks, months or years, on account of the Guppee fondness for conversation; to its left, the towering edifice of P2C2E House, a building from which whirrs and clanks are constantly heard. P2C2E stands for "Processes Too Complicated To Explain," which are in turn controlled by one thousand and one Machines Too Complicated To Describe, all concealed within the House. The clerks in charge of the machines are known as the Eggheads, and their boss is the Walrus.

(Salman Rushdie, *Haroun and the Sea of Stories*, London, 1990)

GYNOGRAPHIA, a country where women are totally dominated by men, and where all laws are entirely dependent on the will of the male.

Fidelity in Gynographia is obligatory: an unfaithful wife is punished according to her husband's wishes; alternatively, she may be judged by a tribunal of twelve older women (whose verdict must be confirmed by a second tribunal of older men). An adulterous woman is flogged and her lover must pay damages to the wronged husband; if he insults or assaults the husband, he is instantly executed.

Fifteen days after her wedding, a bride is given detailed instructions on housekeeping by an older woman and she swears to perform her domestic duties whenever necessary. Marriage is not based on personal inclination, but rather on mutual suitability. Lists of boys and girls ready for marriage are published on the winter and summer solstices and parents make their choice at that time. Girls who cannot find a husband are given different ranks according to their social status. Those of noble birth become abbesses, the bourgeois become nuns and the poor become domestics.

The education of girls differs totally from that of boys. As babies, they are placed in swaddling clothes, while boys are not. This inculcates in the girls a sense of modesty and restraint from a very early age. Their entire education is designed to fit them to a subordinate role in society. Up to the age of nine or twelve they are brought up with boys, with mutual advantages: girls tend to gossip less and become more rational; boys are inclined to less licentious ways in later life. The lower classes are not taught to read or write, as they will not

and one small islands. Waterways criss-cross the city in all directions, thronged with craft of every shape and size. Between the archipelago and the mainland lies the Lagoon, a beautiful expanse of multicoloured waters, and here most Guppees have made their homes in intricately carved wooden buildings with roofs of corrugated silver and gold. Visitors may wish to visit the gigantic formal terraced garden on the mainland, dotted with fountains and pleasure-domes and ancient spreading trees. The Guppee Army may sometimes be seen performing military exercises here. The Army, known as the Library, consists of Pages organized in Chapters and Volumes. Each Volume is headed by a Front, or Title, Page, and their military formations are known as Paginations and Collations.

Around the garden are the three most important buildings in Gup City, which look like a trio of gigantic, elaborately iced cakes: the Palace of

need these skills in their future employment. A record of all girls' behaviour is kept to help parents choose a suitable bride for their sons.

Should a girl lose her virginity, she is punished as follows: if she has been seduced against her will, the man must marry her but she is not allowed to appear in public. If she has allowed herself to be seduced, she is made to marry an old widower. If she is considered a libertine, her father must pay for the upbringing of the baby and the girl is either imprisoned or made to work as a washer-woman or a cook in the women's hospital.

Visitors who succeed in entering Gynographia—its location still remains unknown—are advised to attend the summer and winter festivities held throughout the country. In June, prizes are given to the best workers, dancers and so on; in December, the prizes go to the most modest, gentle and thrifty girls. Visitors should, however, never attempt to enter the section of a Gynographian house set aside for the use of women. Apart from her father or husband, no man may enter this area without permission: trespassers are punished with death.

The Gynographians believe that a woman's soul is not like that of a man and that her one natural inclination is the overwhelming desire to please.

(Nicolas Edme Restif de la Bretonne, *Les Gynographes, ou Idées de deux honnêtes femmes sur un problème de réglement proposé à toute l'Europe, pour mettre les femmes à leur place, et opérer le bonheur des deux sexes,* The Hague, 1777)

GYNOMACTIDE, see NEOPIE ISLAND.

GYNOPYREA, a kingdom on the continent of GENOTIA in the south Atlantic, reputed to be the most cowardly and effeminate nation on earth. The people have an almost idolatrous respect for their monarch.

(Louis Adrien Duperron de Castera, *Le Theatre Des Passions Et De La Fortune Ou Les Avantures Surprenantes de Rosamidor & de Theoglaphire. Histoire Australe,* Paris, 1731)

H

HACIOCRAM or ISLE OF PROPHETS, a small island of the Riallaro Archipelago in the south-east Pacific, part of the Rasolola or Theomanic group. From a distance visitors will first notice a huge signboard, placed on a tower, bearing the inscription "1999." This is the true number of the Beast and only those who accept this will be allowed to land.

Haciocram is inhabited by a variety of sects with competing fanatical beliefs derived from different readings of their sacred books. Some believe that the soul is in the thumb, others in the big toe, others elsewhere in the body. Conversion is achieved by torture. However, the members of the sects are crafty. Some have been known to pretend agreement with their rivals in order to surprise and overthrow them as soon as they relax their guard.

(Godfrey Sweven, *Riallaro, the Archipelago of Exiles*, New York & London, 1901; Godfrey Sweven, *Limanora, the Island of Progress*, New York & London, 1903)

HADLEYBURG, a city in the United States, famous for many years as the most honest and upright town in all the region. It kept its good reputation unsmirched for three generations and was prouder of it than of any of its possessions. So anxious was Hadleyburg to ensure the perpetuation of its virtue that it began to teach the principles of honest dealing to its babies in the cradle and made these teachings the staple of their culture through all the years devoted to their education. Temptations were kept out of the way of young people so that their honesty could have every chance to harden and solidify and become a part of their very bone. The neighbouring towns, jealous of this honourable supremacy, sneered at Hadleyburg's pride and called it vanity, but all the same they were obliged to acknowledge that Hadleyburg was in fact an incorruptible town; all a young man had to do to find responsible employment was to state that Hadleyburg was his native town.

However Hadleyburg had the ill luck to offend a passing stranger, possibly without knowing and certainly without caring. In revenge, the stranger left a sack of gold coins to be given to the man who could recall speaking certain words of kindness to him during his stay—words which, of course, had never really been spoken. All the most honourable citizens were tempted into pretending that they had been the generous person and were put to shame when the trick was revealed in front of the whole town.

By act of legislature, Hadleyburg has now changed its name (the new name is unknown), and its old motto "Lead us not into temptation" to "Lead us into temptation."

(Mark Twain [Samuel Langhorne Clemens], *The Man Who Corrupted Hadleyburg and Other Stories*, New York, 1899)

HAMMERHEAD HILLS, a range of rocky, barren hills in the extreme south of OZ. They are named after their inhabitants, who have no arms and who use their flat heads to pound anyone who wanders into their land. The Hammerheads have necks like rubber; their heads can shoot out quite a long way and then be withdrawn just as quickly. The other inhabitants of Oz often refer to the Hammerheads as the Wild People. They are aggressive towards strangers but are not found outside this hilly area and therefore pose no threat to travellers in the rest of the country.

(L. Frank Baum, *The Wonderful Wizard of Oz*, Chicago, 1900; L. Frank Baum, *The Emerald City of Oz*, Chicago, 1910)

HAM ROCK, a small island of basaltic origin in the Atlantic Ocean, latitude 18°5′ north and longitude 45°53′ west, discovered on October 30, 1869, by the *Chancellor* in one of its trips between Charleston and Liverpool.

The ship sank soon afterwards but eleven of its thirty-two passengers managed to reach Marajó Island near the mouth of the Amazon River on January 27, 1870.

Ham Island is so called because of its similarity to a York ham. No animal forms, not even seabirds, have settled on it and it has been deduced that the island only very recently rose from the sea. In its western extremity, travellers will find an extraordinary cavern reminiscent of those found in the Hebrides. It is said that nowadays the island is very difficult to find and some travellers suppose that it has sunk again beneath the sea.

(Jules Verne, *Le "Chancellor,"* Paris, 1875)

HANDS, THE, two small islands in the East Reach of the EARTHSEA ARCHIPELAGO. They take their name from the mountainous promontories that point north towards the islands of the KARGAD EMPIRE, like the fingers of two hands. Both islands are covered in dense and impenetrable forest.

The coast of the East Hand is inhospitable and bleak. Cliffs fall sheer to the sea in the fjords or inlets between the fingers and there are no beaches. The fjords end in steep boulder-covered slopes, pock-marked with caves and dressed in trees with half their roots in the air.

The West Hand has a village at the point where a stream tumbles down into the sea. The village is inhabited by rough but hospitable fishermen and goat-herds. Their boats are stalwart, clinker-built vessels made of solid planks and are specially designed to ride the heavy seas of the area.

During his quest to destroy the shadow-beast he had roused by mistake on GONT, Ged (perhaps the greatest wizard Earthsea has ever known) came eventually to the Hands. In one of the dark inlets on the East Hand he encountered the shadow itself and for the first time attacked it, but it shrank from him and disappeared. After this, Ged rested for some days in the West Hand village, where he acquired his legendary boat *Lookfar*. To thank the villagers for their hospitality, Ged fashioned charms to heal their sick children and to increase their herds. He also cast spells on the fishermen's boats, and on the roof trees of the houses he wrote the rune *"Pirr,"* which protects houses from fire and wind and the inhabitants from madness. He also taught the islanders songs of the heroes of old. Because few ships from Earthsea reach the Hands, songs made even a hundred years ago are an exciting novelty to the villagers.

(Ursula K. Le Guin, *A Wizard of Earthsea*, New York, 1968)

HANS-BACH, an underground stream of potable ferruginous water tasting somewhat like ink and named after Mr. Hans Bjelke, a guide and eider-duck hunter from Iceland, member of the Lidenbrock expedition which visited the area in 1863. The stream was in fact sprung by Mr. Bjelke himself, who knocked open a hole in a sixty-centimetre-thick granite wall behind which it was flowing. This diverted the water's course, allowing it to flow down to the LIDENBROCK SEA, giving travellers the opportunity of a drink whenever they should need it.

(Jules Verne, *Voyage au centre de la terre*, Paris, 1864)

HAPPILAND, a country near UTOPIA. Travellers will find the coronation ceremony most interesting. On this occasion the new king of Happiland is required to sign an oath that he will not keep more than one thousand pounds in gold, or more than the equivalent amount in silver, in his treasury. This system is believed to have been developed by a king who was concerned more for the welfare of his country than he was for his own wealth. The figure chosen was, he calculated, sufficient to suppress a revolution or to repel an invasion, but not enough to inspire a ruler with dreams of foreign conquest. The system has the advantage of ensuring that there is enough money in circulation for normal trade and exchange while making certain that the king has no motive for raising money unfairly, as he would not be allowed to keep any in excess of the statutory limit.

(Sir Thomas More, *Utopia*, London, 1516)

HAPPY PRINCE CITY, perhaps now known under another name. It holds a university and a small Jewish ghetto. In the central square is a tall column, the base of a statue that was melted down many years ago but has not yet been replaced as the mayor and the learned town councillors have not been able to agree on who should be honoured with a new one.

The old statue was that of the Happy Prince, who ruled the city in the distant past. He was gilded all over with thin leaves of fine gold. For eyes he had two bright sapphires and a large red ruby glowed on his sword hilt. Seeing from his high column the misery and suffering of which he had never been aware during his reign, the Happy Prince convinced a little swallow, who had stopped in the city on his way to Egypt, to give his precious gems and leaves of gold to the poor. Winter came but the swallow would not leave the Prince, who was now blind and naked. Finally the swallow died at the statue's feet. Seeing how shabby the statue had become, the town councillors decided to remove it.

Legend has it that God's angels, instructed to bring Him the two most precious things in the city, took with them the Happy Prince's leaden heart which had not melted in the furnace and the swallow's dead body, and that the bird now sings in the garden of Paradise and the Happy Prince now lives in God's city of gold.

(Oscar Wilde, *The Happy Prince and Other Tales*, London, 1888)

HARAD, known as the **SUNLANDS** to the hobbits of the SHIRE, in southern MIDDLE-EARTH, south of the River Poros and the mountains of EPHEL DUATH, on the west and south borders of MORDOR. The coastal region is known as Umbar and consists of firths, capes and a great natural harbour.

In ancient times, the men of Harad and GONDOR were friendly allies, but after the Kin-Strife—the great civil war that swept Gondor in 1432–48 Third Age—the defeated rebels fled to Umbar, where they gradually degenerated into corsairs who harassed the coast of Gondor for many years.

The Haradrim are a fierce race of dark-skinned men, with black eyes and black hair which they wear braided with gold; some paint their cheeks red. Their main weapons are spears tipped with red, and spiked yellow and black shields. They go into battle on huge elephants or *mûmakil* which carry war towers on their backs. The *mûmakil's* tusks are bound with bands of gold and their sides are draped in cloth of red and gold. The *mûmakil* figure in some of the legends and tales of the hobbits of the Shire, who refer to them as *oliphaunts*.

During the great War of the Ring in Middle-earth, the corsairs, allied themselves with Sauron, the Lord of Dark Forces, and blockaded the mouth of the Anduin or GREAT RIVER, so cutting off aid to MINAS TIRITH from the men of Lebennin and Belfalas in Gondor. A large fleet sent out by the corsairs attacked Gondor's main port, PELARGIR, but was defeated by Aragorn and the Sleepless Dead. Several battles were also fought between the Haradrim and the Rangers of ITHILIEN as the former attempted to march north to aid Sauron.

(J.R.R. Tolkien, *The Fellowship of the Ring*, London, 1954; J.R.R Tolkien, *The Two Towers*, London, 1954; J.R.R. Tolkien, *The Return of the King*, London, 1955)

HARANTON, a small village in the north-west of POICTESME. It is here that Manuel worked as a swineherd before starting on the long series of adventures which were eventually to make him Count of Poictesme. The waters of the pool of Haranton, into which Manuel would gaze for hours as a boy, bring strange dreams to those who look into them and travellers are advised to disregard it.

(James Branch Cabell, *Figures of Earth. A Comedy of Appearances*, New York, 1921)

HARFANG, a stronghold of giants, far to the north of ETTINSMOOR. Harfang stands on a low hill above the ruined city of the giants—now little more than a tangle of crumbling, ruined stone. Pillars as tall as factory chimneys can still be seen in some areas, with fallen fragments the size of tree trunks at their feet. Large sections of pavement bear the mysterious inscription "UNDER ME."

Harfang itself is the home of the king and queen of the Gentle Giants, though precisely who their subjects are remains somewhat uncertain. Harfang is a large house rather than a castle and has no serious military defences. Presumably its inhabitants rely on their size to protect them from attack.

The giant's main sport appears to be hunting on foot, although the queen is usually carried in a litter. Their diet includes talking beasts and men, which they consider a delicacy: man forms a part of their traditional Autumn Feast and is usually served between the fish and the main course. The giants also eat marsh-wiggles, although these strange creatures from the north-east of NARNIA require special preparation since they are extremely tough.

Should a visitor be chosen as part of the giants' repast, he is best advised to escape as fast as possible.

(C.S. Lewis, *The Silver Chair*, London, 1953)

HARMATTAN ROCKS, a cluster of small islands off the coast of West Africa, sixty miles north of FANTIPPO. The islands are almost inaccessible by boat, surrounded as they are by half-sunken rocks; there is only one anchorage, and that is difficult to reach. The islands themselves are flat and windswept, with virtually no soil. They have become a natural refuge for seabirds however and support large colonies of gulls, terns, gannets, cormorants, auks, petrels, geese and white albatrosses.

The Harmattan Rocks are part of the territory of Chief Nyam-Nyam, once the king of the poorest country in West Africa and now owner of the pearl fisheries discovered off these Harmattan Rocks. Although the new-found wealth attracted unwelcome attention from the Amazons of Dahomey and from the Emir of neighbouring Ellebubu, the chief and his allies succeeded in resisting their incursions and laying the basis for the country's prosperity. The actual diving for pearls is performed by trained cormorants.

(Hugh Lofting, *Doctor Dolittle's Post Office*, London, 1924)

HARMONDIA, a kingdom of no location, governed by the Pluramon. The only thing known about Harmondia is its national anthem, the *Hymunion*. Together with a few other national anthems, it is part of a vast electroacoustic work, *Hymnen*, for four soloists and electronic instruments. The *Hymunion* lasts thirty-two minutes.

(Karlheinz Stockhausen, *Hymnen*, Frankfurt, 1968)

HARMONIA (1), a group of colonies or phalanges founded in the mid-nineteenth century. Because its members are sworn to secrecy, the location of Harmonia is unknown, but there is some suspicion of it being located either in a valley near Brussels or in the outskirts of Lausanne.

Each colony consists of 1,500 to 1,800 members who hold everything in common and who share a large dwelling called a phalanstery, which contains all that is needed for an enjoyable and fruitful life. An observatory, a signal-tower and a telegraph system enable each colony to communicate with the others.

Communitarian life in Harmonia is based on total lack of repression, and full freedom given to all human passions.

Travellers will find that what is considered civility and good manners in their country is looked upon as abnormal or uncivil in Harmonia. For instance, children who enjoy revelling in dirt are seen as model citizens because they find enjoyment in the city's improper sanitary system. The children are classified into what is known as Small Orders and rampage around each colony on nimble ponies, dressed up as hussars, to the sound of trumpets, bells and cymbals, and other musical instruments.

The basis of Harmonian society is the classi-

fication of all passions. Privileged passions, comparable to the five senses and the four simple passions of the soul (ambition, friendship, love and paternalism), are the three "distributive" passions: the divining passion, the fluttering and the composite passion. The divining passions are those that bring together the senses and the spirit; the fluttering passions (also called alternating passions) are those that need change and novelty; composite passions are those that seem irrational.

Life in Harmonia is organized according to a number of groups and series of individuals classified according to these three passions. However, the normal day of an inhabitant of Harmonia will take him from one group to another, from work (never the same two days running), to play, to satisfying his bodily functions.

Visitors are submitted to a number of tests before being classified and allowed to enter one of the groups of Harmonia.

(Charles Fourier, *Théorie des Quatre Mouvements*, Paris, 1808; Charles Fourier, *Traité de l'Association Domestique Agricole*, Paris, 1822; Charles Fourier, *Le Nouveau Monde Industriel et Sociétaire*, Paris, 1829; Charles Fourier, *Le Nouveau Monde Amoureux*, Paris, 1967)

HARMONIA (2), a vast country of unknown location, governed by a liberal and solicitous monarch, inspired by a hedonistic sense of life. According to the laws of Harmonia, each couple has the right to inhabit one of the many palaces, pavilions, or grottoes in the country, attended to by satyrs or nymphs. All acts must follow the principles of beauty, love and harmony; nothing must take place that cannot be justified by the aesthetic criteria of Pater or Ruskin. The Pedigree University selects the couples that are allowed to reproduce themselves, thereby adding aesthetic principles to the natural force of lust.

(Georges Delbruck, *Au pays de l'harmonie*, Paris, 1906)

HARROWDALE, a valley in the WHITE MOUNTAINS above EDORAS. At the end of the valley stands Dwimorberg, also known as the Haunted Mountain, where a door in the rock gives access to the PATHS OF THE DEAD. On the eastern side, a switchback path leads up a steep cliff to the stronghold of DUNHARROW, and above the valley the cliffs and precipices rise in massive walls of stone.

During the War of the Ring which affected all of MIDDLE-EARTH, Harrowdale was the rallying place for the Riders of ROHAN.

(J.R.R. Tolkien, *The Return of the King*, London, 1955)

HARTHOVER PLACE, the seat of Sir John Harthover, a large country house in northern England.

Harthover Place is a strange mixture, not to say confusion, of architectural styles, having been rebuilt and added to many times during its history. The attics are Anglo-Saxon; the third floor is Norman; the second floor, Cinquecento; and the first floor, Elizabethan. The right wing is pure Doric, the centre wing is Early English—with a huge portico copied from the Parthenon—and the left wing is Boeotian. The giant staircase is an imitation of the catacombs in Rome, and the back staircase of the Taj Mahal. (This latter feature was introduced by one of the Harthovers who made a fortune while serving under Clive in India.) The cellars are copied from the caves of Elephanta and the offices from the Royal Pavilion at Brighton.

Travellers will reach Harthover Place through a mile-long avenue of lime trees. They are advised to notice the lodge gates, flanked by stone posts, bearing the crest of the Harthovers.

Anyone wishing to become a water-baby (see SAINT BRENDAN'S FAIRY ISLE) should take the route through Harthover Park and across the moors, then on to Lethwaite Crag and the village of Vendale where the transformation will eventually take place.

(Charles Kingsley, *The Water-Babies: A Fairy Tale for a Land-Baby*, London, 1863)

HAT PINS, a small village in the west of ROOTABAGA COUNTRY, where all the hat-pins used in the country are made, the majority being sent to the village of CREAM PUFFS. Visitors may be interested to know that on one occasion the hat-pins prevented the village from being destroyed. A strong wind had blown the whole village away, carrying it off into the sky and up to the clouds. Fortunately all the hat-pins caught on the clouds, thereby preventing the village from being blown even farther away. When the wind subsided, the hat-pins were pulled out and the village fell right back to its original site.

The village of Hat Pins is the home of a famous old lady known as Rag Bag Mammy, who carries on her back a large rag-bag. No one has ever seen her put anything into it or take anything out of it, and she refuses to say what it contains. Rag Bag Mammy wears aprons with big pockets in which she carries gifts for the boys and girls of the village. Although she never speaks to adults, she is very fond of children, especially those who say "Gimme," "Gimme, gimme" and "Gimme, gimme, gimme." Sometimes, if she comes across a child who is crying, she produces a doll no bigger than a child's hand that can recite the alphabet and sing little Chinese-Assyrian songs.

(Carl Sandburg, *Rootabaga Stories*, New York, 1922)

HAUNTED ISLAND, an isolated island in a large Canadian lake, to whose cool waters the inhabitants of Montreal and Toronto flee for rest and recreation in the hot months. Trout and maskinonge stir in the depths of the lake and in late September slowly surface, while the maples turn crimson and gold and the wild laughter of the loons echoes in sheltered bays that never know their strange cry in summer.

On the island is a two-storey cottage which visitors are advised not to visit. A traveller who was unfortunate enough to spend a night in the cottage found his lodgings suddenly invaded by the ghosts of gigantic Indians and witnessed the scalping of a man. To his horror, he discovered that the face of the slaughtered man was his own.

(Algernon Blackwood, "A Haunted Island," in *Ancient Sorceries and Other Stories*, London, 1906)

HAUNTED PASS, see CIRITH GORGOR.

HAV, a small peninsular city-state in the Near East which boasts many illustrious visitors. Throughout the centuries Hav has been described in the writings of chroniclers as diverse as Marco Polo and Kinglake; it is mentioned in stories and letters by the two Lawrences (D.H. and T.E.), and Sigmund Freud wrote a short poem in Hav while studying eels. Bismarck, Nijinsky and Princess Grace have also adorned Hav with their presence.

These days the famous Staircase, an ancient

and precipitous mule-track at Hav's frontier, is seldom used except by Adventure Tour buses and the troglodytic Kretevs who inhabit the Western Escarpment. Most visitors approach Hav by train, and remain in the Imperial Russian Railways carriage while the train enters the Tunnel and spirals down through the limestone cliff to emerge on the flatlands and continue, through unlovely suburbs, into the very heart of the city.

The true centre of Hav is its castle, which stands on a bald hill and has for centuries been the seat of power. On the breastwork of the castle is the historic site known as Katourian's Place, Katourian being a famous trumpeter whose choice of death over defeat is commemorated every morning with a trumpet-call. To the north, towards the salt-flats and the low hills where Schliemann first believed Troy to have been situated, stretch the proletarian suburbs where Turkish, Arab, Greek, African and Armenian workers live in a long frayed grid of shacks and cabins. This is the area called the Balad, and through it the railroad cuts a wide track parallel to the tramline. To the west are the vestigial remains of the Athenian acropolis, its surviving columns shored up by ugly brick buttresses. To the south is the harbour and Conveyor Bridge, and the famous Iron Dog, a bronze statue known since Crusader times. Although some modern scholars have declared it to be not a dog but a fox, like the one young Spartans were supposed to take into the hills to gnaw at their bellies and make men of them, to most visitors the Dog is clearly a dog. It is six feet high paw to ear, and has many graffiti on its hide. There is the famous rune, companion to that on one of the Arsenal lions in Venice, proclaiming that men of the Byzantine emperor's Norse bodyguard once landed on this peninsula. A very hazy "M.P." on its rear flank is popularly supposed to be Marco Polo's. Some marvellously flowery little ciphers have been identified as marks of Venetian silk merchants, and scores of stranger devices, apparently of all ages, seem to have some cabalistic meaning. Henry Stanley, the explorer, came here after the opening of the Suez Canal in 1869 and signed himself shamelessly beneath the animal's chin, and a large crowned eagle, deeply and professionally chiselled, commemorates the visit of Kaiser Wilhelm on his way to Jerusalem.

To the east of the port lies New Hav, a circular city in whose centre stands the Place des Nations. New Hav was created by the League of Nations under the Tripartite Mandate, and the city still betrays its former elegance, as well as the distinctive flavours of its original French, Italian and German quarters. Here travellers will find all modern conveniences, from cinemas such as the Lux and Malibran to the post office.

The languages of Hav are many: Turkish is currently spoken, of course, as well as Greek, but so are Italian, French, Arabic, English and even Chinese. The fauna is not lavish, but interesting. The Hav mongoose, brought in by the British to deal with the snakes, looks like a furry black anteater. The Hav hedgehog resembles a prickly armadillo and the Hav terrier is like a little grey ball of steel wool. It is said that the so-called Abyssinian cat's real origin is Hav, and that the troglodytes breed a sort of Mongolian pony on the foot-slopes of the Escarpment. There are also foxes, rabbits and the very rare European bear of Hav (*ursus arctos hav*) which looks like a miniature grizzly, and which was saved from extinction— legend has it—by none other than Ernest Hemingway, who jogged the elbow of Count Ciano when the latter was about to shoot one of the few surviving beasts. ("You fool," said the Count. "You fascist," said the writer.)

The most remarkable flora of Hav is the snow raspberry, a delicacy which springs up overnight in certain crannies of the Escarpment as the last snows melt, and dies by noon. The small but priceless crop is harvested by the troglodytes, and its arrival generates as much frenzy as that of Beaujolais Nouveau in Paris, or the season's first grouse in London. Unfortunately almost every berry goes to the government for diplomatic receptions.

Hav's survival has been threatened by international tensions in recent years, and some of its more prominent residents have departed to more secure regions; travellers are warned to check on the current political situation before venturing on a visit.

(Jan Morris, *Last Letters from Hav*, London, 1985)

HAVNOR, a large island to the north of the Inmost Sea of EARTHSEA, the seat of the King of all the Isles and commonly regarded by the people of Earthsea as the centre of the world itself. There are two great mountain ranges on Havnor: the Revnian Mountains, which rise above the chief city, Havnor's Great Port, and then run north towards the coast, and the Faliorn Mountains in the

The Tower of the Kings on HAVNOR.

south-west. The highest peak is Mount Onn, which looms above the broad southern gulf.

Havnor's Great Port stands on the shores of the southern gulf and is famed for its tall white towers. The legends of their construction are told in the *Deed of Erreth-Akbe,* one of the greatest and oldest of Earthsea's epic poems. The highest of all is the Tower of the Kings, the seat of the King of all the Isles himself. During the centuries when Earthsea was not governed by a single monarch, the sword of Erreth-Akbe was kept at the top of the tower, although his bones lay—and still lie— on the remote island of SELIDOR where the hero was slain by a dragon. When the ring of Erreth-Akbe was recovered and made whole once more, it too was housed in the tower.

Havnor is not only the political capital of Earthsea; it is also the centre for much of the archipelago's trade. The sea-lanes in this area are the most congested of all Earthsea, especially the narrow straits of Ebavnor, which lead into the great landlocked bay or gulf of the southern coast.

(Ursula K. Le Guin, *A Wizard of Earthsea,* New York, 1968; Ursula K. Le Guin, *The Tombs of Atuan,* London, 1972; Ursula K. Le Guin, *The Farthest Shore,* London, 1973)

HEADLESS VALLEY, see TROPICAL VALLEY.

HEARSAY, ISLAND OF, a large island not far from the Island of GOLDEN ASSES. There are— or were, according to the latest census—more than thirty kingdoms and half a dozen republics on this island, often engaged in destructive wars fought for obscure reasons. The main military strategy consists of stopping up the soldiers' ears, screaming "Oh, don't tell us!" and then running away.

Hearsay is undoubtedly a paradise for runners. The people run around all day and all night—but as the country is an island, they always end up running round and round the shore. Visitors will notice that they are led in their constant exercise by a gentleman shearing a pig. The screams of the pig encourage them to run faster, and their spirits are kept high by the thought that they will eventually have pig's wool. A giant, who appears to have been put together with wire and Canada balsam, runs after them, and although he never drinks anything but water, he constantly smells of spirits. The giant wears spectacles, carries a butterfly net and is festooned with all sorts of scientific equipment, from ordnance survey maps to scalpels and forceps. The most peculiar thing about him is that he runs backwards and claims that the people of the island have been pursuing *him* for hundreds of years, stoning him and calling him "a malignant and a turban'd Turk," who "beat a Venetian and traduc'd the State"—an accusation he is quite at a loss to understand. His only wish is to be friends with the islanders and to tell them "something to their advantage," but they adamantly refuse to have anything to do with him. Therefore, to the delight of many visitors, the perpetual chase goes on.

(Charles Kingsley, *The Water-Babies: A Fairy Tale for a Land-Baby,* London, 1863)

HEATHEN, ISLAND OF THE, in a lake on the outskirts of USSULA. The only building on the island is a low cottage, much better constructed than any of the houses in Ussula itself. It is built from wood which has lain in marshy ground for centuries and has therefore become as hard and as heavy as stone. The cottage was built by a stranger from DJINNISTAN for his wife, the daughter of the high priest or sorcerer of Ussula. The stranger travelled extensively and returned to his island with slabs of marble with which he erected a monument. It is about two metres by four, with inscriptions in black on its four faces, surrounded by pillars which also bear quotations from the Vedas, the *Zend Avesta,* the *I Ching,* the Bible and the Koran. The quotations on the central monument have yet to be identified, but can be translated. The south face bears the word "Creation" and the verses:

> No soul ever came to earth
> Unless it was first a spirit
> in heaven.

On the north face is written:

> No spirit ever rose to heaven
> Unless it was first a soul
> on earth.

The eastern face bears the inscription "Sin" and the enigmatic phrase "Only a single one refused to become a soul," and the west the heading "Punishment" and the lines:

> Therefore he cannot return
> to heaven
> That is the devil.

The monument overlooks the lake and is shaded by lotus blossoms and other exotic plants. Near it stands what was for years thought to be the grave of the stranger's wife, but which does not in fact contain her body.

(Karl Friedrich May, *Ardistan,* Bamberg, 1909; Karl Friedrich May, *Der Mir von Djinnistan,* Bamberg, 1909)

HEKLA, an Icelandic volcano near a deep chasm where drowned men reappear on the day of their drowning, even if the accident has taken place hundreds of miles away. Should a traveller ask them where they are heading, they will answer, with a deep sigh, that they have to go to Mount Hekla. A pitiful wailing can often be heard rising from the surrounding ice.

Not far from Hekla are two other fascinating sites: at the first is a fire which does not burn tinder; at the second, water which does not put out fire but burns and is consumed like wood.

(Tommaso Porcacchi, *Le isole piu' famose del mondo,* Milan, 1572)

HELIKONDA, one of the ISLES OF WISDOM, in the north Pacific. Like the other islands of the group, Helikonda is devoted to a philosophy acquired from the study of foreign books. In the case of Helikonda, the philosophy might be described as "art for art's sake."

Helikonda is a prosperous island which owes much of its present happiness to its original founder, a benefactor of the arts, like the Medici. All trades and crafts practised in the interior find their natural outlet in the capital—also called Helikonda—which, in turn provides audiences for the artists and museums of the provinces. The capital is a circular city built around a vast central piazza. Surrounded by colonnades in the style of Bernini, this piazza is used for concerts and dramatic representations. The largest of the many auditoriums it contains can hold three thousand performers and an audience of more than twelve thousand. The piazza also lodges the city's main museums, studios and galleries. All Helikonda's streets radiate from its centre: there are streets of composers, streets of poets, streets of painters and streets of sculptors. The more conservative artists live nearest to the piazza, the more radical and experimental ones live farthest out.

The government of Helikonda is republican, and the chief officer is a prefect selected from the representatives of the various arts. The prefect is usually a musician, as musicians outnumber other artists.

The art of Helikonda was at first somewhat rudimentary, but later it flourished when knowledge of European art was introduced by Steinian travellers. The work of centuries was absorbed in only a few years and a search began for new forms and new arts. What the Helikondans regard as true art has yet, they affirm, to be discovered.

The art forms of the past are still retained, but largely for educational and historical reasons. Visitors will notice, for instance, that a magnificent performance of Mozart will not be greeted by applause; the music will be analyzed as a petrified vestige from the past, a fossil preserved for centuries. The sole purpose of the performance and the subsequent dissection is to throw into more vivid contrast the art of the present and its superiority to the work of the past. The art of the present includes futurist performances, in which a violin solo is played by a man hanging by his teeth from a swing, or in which a rider on a galloping horse paints a cubist picture on a stationary canvas.

Travellers with an interest in the arts will wish to know that the three greatest artists of the moment are Kakordo (a composer famed for his logarithmic symphony and his astounding string quartet on the parallelogram of forces), the poet Dadalabra and the painter and sculptor Patzoka. The latter's most famous work is a painting which combines spheroid-cubism with the cylindrical prismatic tendency. This painting, now housed in the Helikonda museum, consists solely of hosiery buttons fixed to the canvas with great skill; seen from the correct angle it shows an ideal landscape. The artist himself regards this masterpiece as already outdated.

One of the most amazing inventions of Helikonda is the *optophone*, which transmutes any object into its musical equivalent. (Philosophically-minded travellers will recall that, in England, Walter Pater suggested that all artistic objects aspire to become music which is pure form.) It can perform the reverse function as well, giving a visual representation, for instance, of Mendelssohn's *Fingal's Cave*. The perception of both the aural and visual images, however, requires very highly developed senses and it is unlikely that most visitors will see or hear anything. Musical instruments have largely been replaced by the transcendental tone producer, which can be used to conjure up all possible sounds. The instrument resembles a cross between an organ and a dynamo engine; actually a complex arrangement of telephone diaphragms produces the sound. The one disadvantage of the tone producer is that each performance is unique and can never be repeated.

The stated ambition of the leading artists of Helikonda is the unification of all the arts into one, to be apprehended via the sense of smell. Kakordo is already working on his odoriferous symphony which, when completed, will render all existing arts superfluous. It is rumoured that the three great artists meet in secret at night to play chamber music—Vivaldi and such—and that their private performances are excellent; but this is probably a foul lie made up by the resentful bourgeoisie.

(Alexander Moszkowski, *Die Inseln der Weisheit, Geschichte einer abenteuerlichen Entdeckungsfahrt*, Berlin, 1922)

HELIOPOLIS, a city in Egypt (not to be confused with the ancient city of the same name) whose name means "City of the Sun." Heliopolis is a beautiful city built in the typical Egyptian style with a profusion of pyramids and colonnades. In the centre of one of the colonnades grows a small forest that almost hides a temple dedicated to the Goddess of Wisdom, and two smaller temples, one dedicated to Reason and the other to Nature. The gardens of Heliopolis boast a variety of flowers, mainly roses, and are inhabited by ferocious beasts that can be easily domesticated by means of special flutes. Not far from the city is an avoidable region of horrible mountains prone to fires and floods; it has been set aside for trials of endurance to which some of the citizens of Heliopolis and certain visitors are submitted if they want to enter holy orders.

Heliopolis is ruled by a kind of intellectual despotism; the effective government is in the hands of the priests, led by a pontiff. Next in line are the warriors; after these, the interpreters (also called "genii" or "orators"); the plebeians (also called *papagenos*) who are hunters and shepherds; and finally, the slaves, all of whom are black.

The religion of Heliopolis is both masonic and related to sun worship, rich in Trinitarian symbolism; with this is combined the cult of Isis and Osiris. Social laws are governed by the religion's basic precept: fraternal love. Both pain and pleasure are shared alike among the members of the religious class; deceit, sloth and individualism are not tolerated. The lower classes, whose primary needs (eating, drinking and sleeping) are satisfied, call themselves happy. The slaves are treated with a rigorous kindness.

Travellers are advised that the Pontiff of Heliopolis punishes the breaking of the laws with exile. Slaves, for instance, who fall in love with white women or who are in any way rebellious, or women who show themselves to be excessively independent, are forced out of Heliopolis. However, exiles can find refuge in the neighbouring Kingdom of Night, where the government is strictly matriarchal.

(Wolfgang Amadeus Mozart & Emanuel Schikaneder, *Die Zauberflöte*, first performance, Vienna, 1791)

HELL HOUSE, located in a misty valley in Matawasakie, Maine, in the United States. Built in 1919 by Emeric Belasco, son of an American arms trafficker and a petite English actress, Hell House is known as "the Everest of Haunted Houses." Its windows were walled up during the winter of 1928, and the house was shunned by the village's inhabitants, who believed it to be bewitched.

In 1940, an expedition composed of two mediums and three savants—Dr. Graham, and professors Rand and Fenley—attempted to get to the bottom of the mystery. After three miserable days, Dr. Graham was found dead in the nearby woods. Professor Rand suffered a brain haemorrhage, and died without being able to describe the experience he had apparently had in the ballroom. Professor Fenley went mad and was taken to the Medview Asylum, where he is still a patient today. As for the mediums, one, Grace Lauter by name, slit her throat, while the other, Benjamin Franklin Fisher, was found crouching in a foetal position in front of the large porch, apparently thrown there by the house.

During the week of December 18–24, 1970, the mystery was solved by a team under the direction of a certain Dr. Barrett. Today the house is harmless, but few visitors venture there due to the yellowish fog that blankets the valley throughout the year.

(Richard Matheson, *Hell House*, New York, 1971)

HELLULAND, see MARKLAND.

HELM'S DEEP, one of the two great defences of ROHAN, the other being the fortress of DUN-HARROW. The two are connected by a narrow path running north-west through the WHITE MOUNTAINS.

Helm's Deep is a narrow, precipitous gorge between high cliffs that runs far into the White Mountains beneath the triple peaks of Thrihyrne. The entrance to Helm's Deep is guarded by the Hornburg, a great tower surrounded by high walls, situated on a spur of rock. The Hornburg—which, legend has it, was built by the Sea Kings with the help of the giants—derives its name from the echoing effect produced when a horn is sounded here. In times of peace it is the dwelling place of the master of the Westfold of Rohan. It is approached by a great causeway and a stone ramp, and is believed to be impregnable. A mighty wall, twenty feet high and known as the Deeping Wall, runs from the Hornburg to the southern cliffs of the Deep itself, sealing off the mouth of the gorge.

Beyond the wall, Helm's Deep opens out into Deeping Coomb, a great bay in the mountains. A secondary line of defence is provided by Helm's Dike, an ancient trench and rampart some two furlongs below the Coomb, through which the Deeping Stream runs. Beneath the mountains stretch the extensive Glittering Caves of Helm's Deep, the AGLAROND, once used as a place of refuge by the men of Rohan, but now the realm of Gimli, the dwarf.

Helm's Deep is named after Helm Hammerhand, the last of the First Line of the Kings of Rohan. In 2758 Third Age, Rohan was conquered, having been simultaneously attacked from the east and the west. The men of Rohan took refuge behind the Hornburg, where they withstood a great siege, during which both they and their enemies suffered terribly. King Helm is said to have gone out alone, slaying his enemies with his bare hands, believing that if he bore no weapon, none could harm him. The sound of his horn as he left the Deep was sufficient to instill terror into the besieging forces. Helm was eventually found dead, standing upright on the Dike. Legend has it that his horn can still be heard and that his wraith still walks when Rohan's enemies enter the Deep, and that his appearance will terrify them to death.

During the War of the Ring, the Hornburg was the site of a great battle. It was here that the forces of Théoden, ruler of Rohan, and certain members of the Fellowship of the Ring defeated the forces of Saruman, who had betrayed his earlier allegiances and now coveted the Ring of Power so vital to the destiny of MIDDLE-EARTH.

The forces sent against the Hornburg by Saruman were composed of the Dunlendings—originally hillmen from DUNLAND—and strange creatures created by Saruman himself, half man and half orc. The outcome of the battle was marked by two decisive events: throughout the fighting, the horn of Helm could be heard sounding throughout the Deep, inspiring terror in the attackers and boosting the confidence of the men of Rohan; and the Huorns, or sentient trees, arrived from FANGORN, forming a fearsome forest which cut off the line of retreat of the orcs; all those who entered this moving forest disappeared. After the battle, the forest parted to allow the defenders to ride north to ISENGARD. The Huorns disappeared as suddenly as they had come and the great pile of dead orcs who had fallen during the battle disappeared too. Visitors can see, about a mile below the Dike, a great stone-covered mound, said to be the place where the Huorns buried the fallen orcs. The mound has since been known as Death Down. No grass will grow on this strange cairn.

(J.R.R. Tolkien, *The Two Towers*, London, 1954; J.R.R. Tolkien, *The Return of the King*, London, 1955)

HENNETH ANNÛN, a waterfall in north ITHILIEN, in GONDOR, southern MIDDLE-EARTH. Behind the waterfall, a hall was tunnelled out of the rock as a refuge and a base for forays by the Rangers of Ithilien in 2901 Third Age. Henneth Annûn is also known as the "Window of the Sunset," because at sunset the light of the sun is refracted into all the colours of the rainbow as it touches the curtain of falling water. Originally the water flowed through the cave itself, but when the cave was extended to form the refuge, the stream was diverted and it now falls from higher up. There is only one other entrance to the refuge besides the mouth of the original cave, but it is carefully concealed. The precise location of this secret entrance is known only to the Rangers; travellers are taken to Henneth Annûn blindfolded; it is not advisable to visit alone.

(J.R.R. Tolkien, *The Two Towers*, London, 1954;

J.R.R. Tolkien, *The Return of the King*, London, 1955)

HER, an island of uncertain location. The surface of the island is a pool of still water, as clear as a mirror. On it sits a silent white swan, which from time to time raises its wings. Visitors should take advantage of these occasions to catch a glimpse of the island as a whole, with its many beautiful fountains. The gardeners of Her will not allow the jets of water to fall back to earth, as this would wrinkle the smooth surface of the pool. The spray, therefore, spreads out horizontally, forming a second mirror. These parallel mirrors stare at each other, like two lovers eternally facing one another in reciprocal vacuity.

The island itself consists of a solid rock of gemstone, corbelled with octagonal fortifications; overall, it resembles the basin of a fountain of jasper surrounded by green lawns.

Her is ruled by a Cyclops (probably from CYCLOPES ISLAND). In front of his single eye, an iron framework supports two mirrors, back to back, that direct light towards anyone approaching the island. Thanks to this arrangement, the Cyclops can see things that are only visible in ultraviolet light. Visitors will find him very hospitable and his servants will offer guests sugar and quarters of a strange delicacy, the *poncire*. The women of the island dance for visitors by spreading their skirts out like peacocks' tails and raising them to walk on the grass—less damp than the water—thus revealing cloven clogs and fleecy underskirts.

(Alfred Jarry, *Gestes et Opinions du Docteur Faustroll, Pataphysicien. Roman Néo-Scientifique,* Paris, 1911)

HERLAND, a country of unknown location. The only outsiders to have visited it have sworn to keep its location secret, in spite of the insistent requests of several geographical societies of both Europe and Tobago.

Herland lies on a great spur of rock above dense jungle, backed by a high range of mountains. To the south-east is a large valley and a lake with a subterranean outlet; the rest of the country is surrounded by dark cliffs. Herland is roughly the size of Holland, ten to twelve thousand square miles, and supports a female population of approx-

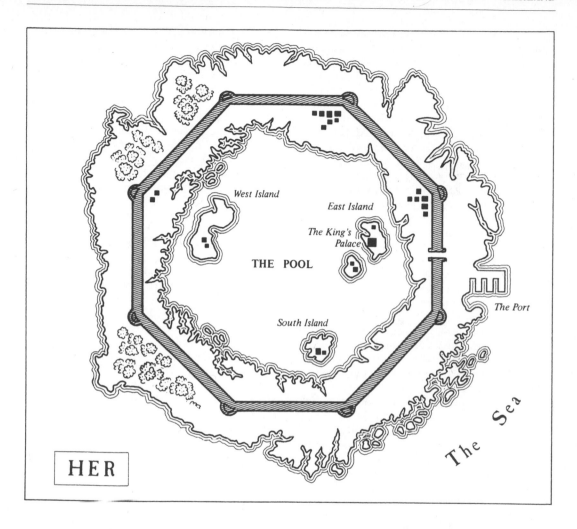

West Island

East Island

The King's
Palace

THE POOL

South Island

The Port

The Sea

HER

imately three million. The outer fringes of Herland are thickly forested; the interior consists of wide, park-like plains and meadows.

Native legends, in the jungles below the mountain spur, speak of Herland as a land of women, extremely dangerous for men to visit.

The first tangible evidence of the existence of Herland came when three young Americans found traces of dye and fragments of cloth in streams flowing down from the mountains that tower above the jungles and swamps. An initial flight over the area revealed the existence of a highly cultivated and presumably civilized country, but gave no hints as to its possible inhabitants. Intrigued by the little they had seen, the three Americans landed on a

plateau and thereby became the first men to visit Herland for almost two thousand years.

Towards the dawn of the Christian era, the country was much larger and had access to the coastal plain and the sea. A succession of wars drove its people—who appear to have been of Aryan stock—back into the mountains and eventually into the highlands. They were a polygamous, slave-holding race and fought bravely for their survival; to defend their refuge they built huge fortresses, some of which survive and ought to be visited. At last they were defeated by geological rather than military forces: while the male fighting force was attempting to defend the entrance to the outside world, a volcanic eruption destroyed the pass and buried the entire army beneath a newly formed rock wall. Very few free men survived; the slaves rose against those who had, slaughtering their remaining masters, intending to take possession of the country and the remaining young women and girls. The women, however, refused to submit and ably massacred their would-be conquerors.

So it happened that the future Herland was left without a single male inhabitant. Initially this was a period of despair, especially when the only two male children born shortly after the cataclysm died, but the women convinced themselves of the need to live and work together on their own. About ten years later, the miracle occurred: one of the women gave birth to a daughter, although no man was found in the country. It was decided that the child was a gift from the gods and the mother was placed in the Temple of Maaia, the Goddess of Motherhood, under strict watch. In time, her daughter gave birth to five children, all girls, and eventually a new race of parthenogenetic women developed. Since then, the population of Herland has been entirely female, descended from this one mother who died a century old, having seen her 125 granddaughters born without any kind of male intervention.

Totally isolated from the outside world and with a completely female population, Herland progressed in a highly specialized way. Because of the limited territory available, agriculture had to be developed in such a fashion as to provide for the maximum amount of people. Consequently, the whole country is today a highly sophisticated garden. The forest fringe itself has been cultivated and is farmed as carefully as any agricultural land; even the vines are trained and entire woods have been replanted with fruit- and nut-bearing trees. The women of Herland care for their land in the way a florist in a European country might care for his costliest orchids. All waste products are recycled to refertilize the soil. New fruit-bearing trees have been developed with great success, mainly by crossing existing species.

The towns of Herland display a concern for ordered beauty. The neat houses are built of rose-coloured stone, and all public buildings are white. They are linked by well-built, dust-free roads lined with flowers and trees, gardens and fountains.

The inhabitants are strong and athletic and appear to be completely fearless. The older women possess an ageless quality of power and beauty. All wear their hair short. Their clothes are comfort-able and eminently practical: close-fitting tunics worn over knee-breeches. These tunics are provided with numerous pockets ingeniously arranged so as to be convenient to the body. They are so placed as to strengthen the garment and to add decorative lines of stitching. Like so many aspects of Herland's culture, the clothes combine practical intelligence with a fine artistic feeling. Light straw hats are worn when working in the sun; in cold weather, capes or hoods replace them. The whole attire, evolved over the centuries, has the grace of Chinese dress, beautiful when so desired, always useful, dignified and in good taste.

The culture of Herland revolves around motherhood and the raising of children. Even the language has been deliberately simplified for the sake of the country's daughters and is now as straightforward and rational as Esperanto. Based on a phonetic system, it is extremely easy to learn, but despite its simplicity it still bears all the hallmarks of an old and rich civilization. The education of children is seen as the highest of all the arts and the care of babies is entrusted only to the most competent. Child rearing is considered so important that the more the mothers love their children, the less willing they are to trust them to unskilled hands—even their own. Babies are nursed for two years and then sent to "co-mothers," who live in the warmer areas of the country, before being gradually acclimatized to the colder regions. The houses and gardens planned for childcare contain nothing that might hurt a child: there are no stairs, no sharp corners and no small objects that can be swallowed. They are a paradise for babies, a safe environment in which they learn to control their bodies, to swim even before they can walk and to gain physical self-confidence. The children of Herland very rarely cry.

Later stages of education are designed to develop judgement and strong will. Teaching is carried out through the child's involvement in structured games rather than through ordinary pedagogical methods. Great care is taken to develop both the creative spirit and the critical faculties, while allowing individual tendencies to emerge freely. Anatomy, physiology, nutrition and basic sciences are all taught. One of the peculiarities of the educational system is that psychology is classified with history as it is considered a communal possession that develops with the whole of society.

The culture of Herland includes remnants of information about other civilizations and fragments of history prior to the country's separation from the outside world. A cultured person will be expected to have great skill in the biological sciences and a working knowledge of astronomy, mathematics, physics and chemistry. Medicine, however, is now a lost art, as sickness is virtually unknown. Technology remains functional, but has led to the invention of an electric car capable of travelling at up to thirty miles per hour. The arts, drama, music, religion and education have developed together rather than as separate art forms. There is an impressive array of pageants, processions and rituals in which art and religion are blended together. The drama has none of the themes associated with most theatrical traditions: sexual motives, war, ambition and the desire for wealth have no part in the arts of Herland.

At the time of its initial isolation Herland had, like the Greeks, a pantheon of gods, but finally only Maaia, the Mother Goddess, remained. Religion has become what might be termed a maternal pantheism: the women believe that they are fed by Mother Earth, that they are born of motherhood and live by motherhood; that life is, in effect, a long cycle of motherhood. There is no formalized doctrine or ritualized worship of any kind, no concept of duties that have to be fulfilled or of punishments in either life or death. The quasi-religious spirit of motherhood pervades the entire culture and it would be difficult to separate Herland "religion" from other aspects of its culture.

Despite the importance of the mother cult, limited resources have forced the instalment of a population control. The inhabitants say that motherhood is a sacred sacrament, but that the parthenogenetic birth of children can be deferred by willpower; therefore most women have only one daughter. To be allowed to have more than one child and to become an "over-mother" is the highest privilege known in the country. To come from a line of "over-mothers" is the nearest thing there is to being an aristocrat. Limited resources and the need to use all available land for agriculture also led to the introduction of cremation in the early thirteenth century.

Herland has no formal government and is ruled by an overwhelming sense of communal purpose rather than by any institutional system. The only real leader is the Land Mother, who is effectively a president. There are very few codified laws, and crime has been unknown for centuries. The system of justice, where it is used, is extremely le-

nient and relies on gentle restraint and education rather than on retribution and punishment.

The fauna of Herland is not numerous, as lack of space forced the elimination of most grazing species. The only pets are cats, trained to kill pests and parasites but to leave birds alone. The cats of Herland are large, silky animals, friendly with everyone and devotedly attached to their owners. There are very few toms, and these are mated only once a year.

(Charlotte Perkins Gilman, *Herland*, New York, 1915–16)

HERMAPHRODITE ISLAND, a drifting piece of land, usually found near the port of Lisbon, Portugal. Its inhabitants are half male, half female and speak Latin. The Hermaphrodite Republic is believed to have been founded by the Syro-Phoenician sun-god Elagabalus, or Heliogabalus, and curious representations in his honour take place in the numerous palaces on the island. The visitor might think himself in a land of open-air theatres—throughout the year, throughout the land, the Hermaphrodites present, as part of their religious rites, scenes from the Classics: *The Rape of the Sabine Women, Ataxerxes and His Daughter, Actaeon Destroyed by His Lovers, The Lascivious Occupations of Sardanapalus,* to name a few. The architecture is Hellenistic, and beautiful buildings made of marble, jasper, porphyry, gold and enamel grace the island. Along the streets are long rows of columns, each one representing the body of a woman with the head of a bearded man. In the centre of the island the Hermaphrodites have raised a statue of Heliogabalus, at the foot of which a book is carved in stone containing the laws of the country.

The Capitol on the Central Square, HERMAPHRODITE ISLAND.

The motto of the Hermaphrodite Republic is *A tous acords* ("I match all"). The principles upon which all laws are based are that beauty is all-important and that voluptuousness is equal to holiness. One law states: "We ignore all creation, redemption, justification and damnation"; and another: "We ignore Time and Eternity and we do not heed the end of the day."

The Hermaphrodites' favourite authors are Ovid, Catullus, Tibullus and Propertius. The month of May is celebrated every month.

(Thomas Artus, *Description de L'Isle des Hermaphrodites nouvellement découverte, contenant les Moeurs, les Coutumes et les Ordonnances des Habitans de cette Isle, comme aussi le Discours de Jacophile à Linne, avec quelques autres pièces curieuses. Pour servir de Supplément au Journal de Henri II*, Cologne, 1724)

HES, or FIRE MOUNTAIN, a gigantic volcano rising solitary and white in the plains of KALOON. For many hundreds of years Hes has been the sanctuary of a fire cult led by a high priestess. Twenty centuries ago, when one of Alexander the Great's generals, a certain Rassen, conquered Kaloon and became khan, he established the cult of Isis or Hes on the volcano named after the goddess.

The first high priestess of Hes introduced certain changes in the original Isis cult, replacing the pure and simple worship of fire with the worship of Life and Nature. The high priestess is considered to be ever-present: when one dies, her daughter (real or adopted) takes on her name and continues her duties. The high priestess is assisted by a college of priests consisting of three hundred men and three hundred women who intermarry and whose children become the new members of the college. The priests speak a form of ancient Greek.

Hes and the land around it are inhabited by a number of semi-savage tribes of Tartar origin, who venerate the high priestess and bring her gifts, but who mingle with their belief in the goddess of fire certain primitive barbaric rites. One of the most curious of these rites is the so-called Search of the False Witch-Doctors. The tribe's shaman recites a charm holding on his head a large white cat. Those suspected of witchcraft are asked to come near him with their hands bound behind their backs. The shaman then puts the cat in a wooden box and passes with it in front of the suspects. If the cat jumps into one of the suspects' face, this constitutes irrefutable proof of guilt and the unauthorized witch-doctor is flung onto a funeral pyre.

The Ceremony of the Fire is celebrated by the high priestess in a vast cavern illuminated by columns of fire that spring from the ground itself, a curious volcanic phenomenon; these flames give off no heat nor smoke nor smell, but an intense, white light accompanied by a shrill whistle. In the back of the cavern on an altar is a silver statue representing a small boy cradled in his mother's arms, symbolizing Humanity saved by the Divine Spirit. It is said that in this altar lives Hes's ghost.

(Henry Rider Haggard, *Ayesha. The Return of She*, London, 1905)

HEWIT'S ISLAND, off the east coast of Africa, north of Madagascar. A mountain peak, like that of Tenerife, affords a good panoramic view. Through lush vegetation a river descends to the sea, onto a ridge of rocks rather like the Giant's Causeway. In the rainy season there are violent storms. Hannah Hewit, an English lady, was stranded on the island in 1782. Single-handed, she built a house with clay bricks and also created her own tomb.

Among other accomplishments, Mrs. Hewit tamed a lion, tethered a buffalo in order to milk it and—using the mechanism of a clock, pipes and a pair of bellows—constructed a robot capable of making sounds resembling the human voice.

(Charles Dibdin, *Hannah Hewit; Or, The Female Crusoe. Being The History Of A Woman Of uncommon, mental, and personal accomplishments; Who, After a variety of extraordinary and interesting adventures in almost every station of life, from splendid prosperity to abject adversity, Was Cast Away In the Grosvenor East-Indiaman: And became for three years the sole inhabitant of An Island In The South Seas. Supposed To Be Written By Herself*, London, 1796)

HIME, an island in the KORSAR Az of the underground continent of PELLUCIDAR, not far from the island of AMIOCAP. Topographically the two islands are similar, with thickly wooded hills rising to the high tableland in the interior, but there the similarity ends. Unlike their peace-loving neighbours, the Himeans are aggressive and quarrelsome. Domestic disputes are continual and usually end in violence. In theory the Himeans are monogamous, but infidelity is extremely common.

Not many travellers return from Hime, as the islanders tend to kill them; for this reason, knowledge of Hime is very scarce. However, two villages on the island have been described in some detail. Garb is a cliff-village of caves in the face of a high rock. The caves are reached by a series of narrow ledges; wooden pegs driven into the rock connect the ledges vertically. From the outside it appears to be a perilous dwelling-place, but the inhabitants of Garb walk along the narrow ledges as happily as other people walk on level ground. Life in the village is not comfortable and, given the quarrelsomeness of all Himeans, death by falling is not uncommon. Throwing stones at people on lower ledges is a favourite pastime of the children.

The other village is Carn, a clutter of stone and clay houses surrounded by a high wall. It stands on the top of a high mesa, protected by steep cliffs.

Hime is not on good terms with Amiocap. The men of Hime occasionally make forays to the neighbouring island, hoping to capture women there, but many of them fail to return from their expeditions. Indeed, one tribe on the coast has become very wealthy by crossing over to Amiocap and bringing back the canoes of Himean warriors who have perished there; these canoes are greatly prized, being extremely strong but light constructions, so skilfully hollowed out from logs that they are virtually unsinkable. A hide, used to cover the cockpit, is tied around the waist of the canoeist; when it is fastened properly the canoe will ship no water and is therefore serviceable in the roughest seas.

(Edgar Rice Burroughs, *Tanar of Pellucidar*, New York, 1930)

HLANITH, a vast trading city in DREAM-WORLD, on the shores of the Cerenerian Sea. Its walls are of rugged granite and the houses of beams and plaster show fantastic peaks and gables. The wharves of Hlanith are of oak and the nearby sea taverns look exceedingly ancient, with low black-beamed ceilings and casements of greenish bull's-eye panes. The city is not visited except for barter and the solid work of its artisans is highly prized. Travellers can find excellent bargains in the bazaars along the rutted streets where wooden ox-carts lumber.

(Howard Phillips Lovecraft, "The Dream-Quest of Unknown Kadath," in *Arkham Sampler*, Sauk City, 1948)

HOFBAU, see RURITANIA.

HOGWARTS, a school of witchcraft and wizardry, somewhere in England. It can be reached by train from platform 9¾ at King's Cross station, in London. The building itself is actually an ancient castle with many turrets and towers, perched high on a mountain-top, overlooking a great black lake. "Muggles" (those who are not wizards or witches) may sometimes, under very special circumstances, visit the school. Visitors taken on a tour will be guided through a vast entrance hall lit by flaming torches stuck into the stone walls. A magnificent marble staircase leads to the upper floors, while a pair of double doors opens onto the Great Hall. This hall is a strange and splendid place. It is lit by thousands of candles floating in mid-air above the student dining-tables, which are set with glittering gold plates and goblets and a vast array of things to eat, from roast beef to mint humbugs. Thanks to a clever spell, the ceiling looks like the sky outside; it is hard to believe that the hall does not open onto the heavens.

The marble staircase is only one of the 142 staircases at Hogwarts. There are wide staircases, sweeping ones, narrow, rickety ones; some lead somewhere different on Fridays, some have a vanishing step halfway up that has to be jumped over. There are doors that will not open unless asked politely or tickled in exactly the right place, and doors that are not doors at all, but solid walls just pretending. The people in the portraits move around and visit one another. The coats of armour can walk.

Following the English model, students are divided into four houses: Gryffindor, Hufflepuff, Ravenclaw and Slytherin. Each house has its own noble history and each has produced outstanding witches and wizards. First-year students are required to bring along the following equipment, all of which can be bought in the shops along Diagon Alley, a magical street reached through a brick wall inside the Leaky Cauldron Pub in London:

> three sets of plain work robes (black);
> one plain pointed hat (black) for day wear;
> one pair of protective gloves (dragon-hide or similar);
> one winter cloak (black, silver fastenings);
> other: one wand; one cauldron (pewter, size 2); one set glass or crystal phials; one telescope; one set brass scales.

A view of HOGWARTS school of wizardry from within the FORBIDDEN FOREST.

Though students are allowed to bring an owl or a cat or a toad, they are not allowed (in the first years) their own broomsticks, since the broomstick traffic is likely to cause accidents. It is also advisable to be on the lookout for playful ghosts, who at times can be somewhat of a nuisance.

In order to best enjoy their visit to Hogwarts, travellers may find it useful to prepare for the experience by reading the following books:

The Standard Book of Spells (Grade 1), by
    Miranda Goshawk;

A History of Magic, by Bathilda Bagshot;
Magical Theory, by Adalbert Waffling;
A Beginners' Guide to Transfiguration,
    by Emeric Switch;
One Thousand Magical Herbs and Fungi,
    by Phyllida Spore;
Magical Drafts and Potions,
    by Arsenius Jigger;
Fantastic Beasts and Where to Find Them,
    by Newt Scamander;
The Dark Forces: A Guide to Self-Protection,
    by Quentin Trimble.

(J.K. Rowling, *Harry Potter and the Philosopher's Stone*, London, 1997 [*Harry Potter and the Sorcerer's Stone*, US]; J.K. Rowling, *Harry Potter and the Chamber of Secrets*, London, 1998)

HOHENFLIESS, see LILAR: also PESTITZ.

HOLES, CITY OF, see CITTABELLA.

HOLLIN, also known as **EREGION,** this ancient elven kingdom lies on the eastern side of the MISTY MOUNTAINS, to the south of RHUDAUR, in MIDDLE-EARTH.

Hollin was settled in the Second Age of Middle-earth by the elves known as the Noldor, or Gwaith-i-Mírdain, ("People of the Jewelsmiths"). The elves were probably attracted to the area by its proximity to the *mithril* mine of the dwarves of MORIA, as they were famed for their craftsmanship and their metalwork. The two peoples traded with one another and an example of elven skill can be seen in the inscriptions on the gates of Moria.

It was the elves of Hollin who forged the rings of power for Sauron of MORDOR, not realizing the evil ends to which he meant to use them. Sauron then forged the One Ring which was intended to give him power over all the peoples of Middle-earth. Finally the elves discovered his plots and hid the rings they had made. Open war broke out as a result and the area was laid waste.

Many elves perished in the conflict and the survivors retreated north and built a new refuge at RIVENDELL. Even at the beginning of the Third Age, when Hollin was uninhabited, a feeling of goodness and well-being still permeated the land because it had once been inhabited by elves.

The token of the elves of Hollin was the holly, which still grows abundantly in the area. Two great holly trees once stood by the stream called SIRANNON to mark the end of the elves' territory and the entrance to Moria. The trees have since been uprooted.

(J.R.R. Tolkien, *The Fellowship of the Ring*, London, 1954; J.R.R. Tolkien, *The Return of the King*, London, 1955; J.R.R. Tolkien, *The Silmarillion*, London, 1977)

HOLLOW NEEDLE, a natural cave in Etretat which is the secret hideaway of Arsène Lupin, the gentleman-burglar who amassed an incomparable treasure before his retirement. Despite the surrounding iodized atmosphere, the cavern has perfectly preserved his hoard, which includes the original *Mona Lisa* and the treasure of the kings of France. Lupin himself lives in a small house in the suburbs, where he grows lupins and a few other flowers.

Hollow Needle should not be confused with Needle Castle, located in an area of Brittany called the Hollow; Lupin also visited that location, but it has no unusual features.

(Maurice Leblanc, *L'Aiguille creuse*, Paris, 1909)

HOOLOOMOOLOO, an Island of the MARDI ARCHIPELAGO, heaped with rocks and covered with dwarfed, twisted thickets.

It is sometimes known as the Isle of Cripples because the inhabitants of surrounding islands, averse to the barbarous custom of destroying at birth all infants asymmetrically formed, but wanting equally to remove them from sight, long ago established an asylum for cripples on Hooloomooloo. The descendants of the exiles still live here, subject to their own laws and ruled by a king of their own choice. They are not allowed to leave the island, because the rest of the archipelago wants nothing to do with them.

The natives of Hooloomooloo are not certain, however, that they are cripples, and explain to visitors that whether a person is hideous or handsome depends upon who is made judge.

(Herman Melville, *Mardi, and A Voyage Thither*, New York, 1849)

HOPPERS, COUNTRY OF THE, a subterranean realm beneath the mountains in the north-west of the Quadling Country of OZ. It lies on the opposite side of the mountain from HORNER COUNTRY. A fence separates the two underground lands, both situated in a vast cave. The cave is lit by a soft light which comes from some invisible source and its walls and roof are of polished white marble with delicately coloured veins. The roof is arched and carved in fantastic designs. The Hopper's town or village is small, but all the houses are of marble and extremely attractive. As there is no vegetation they have no gardens, but they have courtyards instead, marked off by low marble walls.

The Hoppers themselves have only one leg and progress in great hops, hence their name.

(L. Frank Baum, *The Patchwork Girl of Oz*, Chicago, 1913)

HORNER COUNTRY, deep beneath the mountains in the north-west of Quadling Country, OZ, shares a large cave with the Country of the HOPPERS. The countries are separated by a fence.

The Horners are a small people, with bodies as round as balls and short legs and arms. Their heads are also round with long pointed ears. In the centre of their foreheads they have horns, no more than six inches long, but ivory-white and sharp. The Horners' skin is light brown and they dress in snow-white robes. Apart from their horns, their most striking feature is their hair; each Horner has hair of three colours—red, yellow and green. The red section is at the bottom and often hangs over their eyes. Then comes a band of yellow hair, and finally a topknot of bright green. The Horners are ruled by a chief called Jak, a name which may derive from the celebrated Little Jack Horner of TOYLAND. His badge of office is a jewelled star worn just above his horn.

The streets of the Horners' city are not paved and no attempt is made to improve the environment in any way. From the outside the houses appear grimy and neglected. Inside, however, they are dazzlingly beautiful. The walls are lined with radium and the metallic surface is highly ornamented with relief designs representing men, animals, flowers and trees. All the furniture is also made of radium. The Horners explain that they live inside their houses, not outside, and that there is no point in spending energy on producing merely an external appearance of beauty. They claim that their near neighbours, the Hoppers, live according to the opposite philosophy and that their beautiful marble houses are dingy and un-comfortable inside. As no one has ever visited the inside of a Hopper home, it is impossible to verify this statement. The radium has the added advantage that those who live in rooms lined with radium never fall ill. The precious metal is mined deep below the city; radium mining is the main activity of the Horners.

The Horners are known for their sense of humour and for the delight they take in making atrocious puns. One of their verbal jokes almost brought them to war with their Hopper neighbours. The Horners remarked that the Hoppers had little understanding. They meant this as a joking reference to the fact that Hoppers have only one leg and thus have less to stand upon. The comment was, however, taken seriously and the Hoppers felt highly insulted. A full-scale conflict was averted by the intervention of friends of Princess Dorothy of Oz, who persuaded the Horners to explain the joke to their neighbours on the other side of the fence.

(L. Frank Baum, *The Patchwork Girl of Oz*, Chicago, 1913)

HORSELBERG, see VENUSBERG (1).

HOSK, a large island to the west of the Inmost Sea of EARTHSEA, to the north of the NINETY ISLANDS. The coast of Hosk is indented with many bays and channels; a great bay in the north-west almost divides it into three smaller islands. Both the north-east and south are mountainous. The main port is Orrimy, on the east coast, a major harbour for the great trade galleys that ply the waters of the Inmost Sea. The streets of the old city climb steeply from the harbour and are flanked by the strong, stone-built houses of the merchants. The entire town is walled for protection against the lawless lords and brigands of the interior. The houses of the rich have towers and are fortified; the warehouses on the docks are built like forts.

(Ursula K. Le Guin, A *Wizard of Earthsea*, New York, 1968)

HOSTELIAN REPUBLIC, see LIBERIA.

HOUYHNHNMS LAND, an island in the South Seas, discovered in 1711 by Captain Lemuel Gulliver, who was marooned here by a mutinous crew.

The dominant species on the island is a race of graceful and gentle horses—Houyhnhnms or "Perfection of Nature" in their own language. Their maxim is to cultivate, and be governed by, reason. Their main virtues are friendship and benevolence, which they extend to the race as a whole, arguing that "this is simply natural." They are wise and sophisticated and excel especially in poetry, using accurate and striking similes and metaphors. The usual subjects are friendship, benevolence and the praising of race-winners. Cut off from the outside world, the horses have developed a calm, peaceful civilization in which a gracious climate of decency prevails and political strife is unknown: an ideal alternative to the better spas of Switzerland.

Every four years a representative council meets at the vernal equinox to enquire into the condition of the various regions and to solve any problems by adopting decrees known as "exhortations." This word is preferred because the Houyhnhnms cannot conceive a rational being who is compelled to do anything. They say that a rational being can only be advised or exhorted to do something and that no rational being can, by definition, disobey the voice of reason.

Visitors will find that the society of the Houyhnhnms is not egalitarian. Bay, dappled and black horses are physically and mentally superior to whites and iron greys. The latter form a servant class and never aspire to mate outside of their station. This hierarchy is natural and no one would dream of challenging it.

The Houyhnhnms use the hollow part of their fore-hoofs in the same way as human beings use their hands. Tools are made of ground flint, as metal is unknown on the island. These, as well as rudimentary wooden and sun-baked earthen vessels, can be purchased by travellers as souvenirs.

The Houyhnhnms live in long, low buildings with thatched roofs and large rooms with smooth clay floors, racks and mangers extending the full length of the room. The construction of these dwellings involves a tall, straight tree peculiar to the island, whose roots are loosened when it reaches forty years of age. With the first storm, the trees fall; the trunks are gathered and stuck in the ground at regular intervals. Oat-straw and wattles

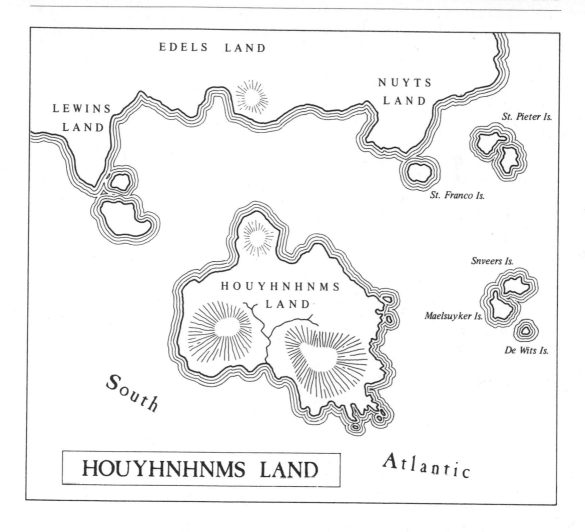

EDELS LAND

NUYTS LAND

LEWINS LAND

St. Pieter Is.

St. Franco Is.

HOUYHNHNMS LAND

Snveers Is.

Maelsuyker Is.

De Wits Is.

South

Atlantic

HOUYHNHNMS LAND

are then woven between them. Doors and roofs are constructed in the same manner.

The Houyhnhnms do not suffer from any diseases and have no need for physicians. Most accidental injuries are treated with excellent herbal medicines. Most of the horses live to be seventy or seventy-five and some even reach eighty. Death is from old age, usually a gradual and painless process. Normally, they can forecast the time of their death with great accuracy, and so during their last ten days they visit friends and neighbours to take a solemn leave of them. This is undertaken very calmly, as though they were merely going away to live in a distant place for the rest of their lives. Death itself is referred to as "retiring to one's first

mother" (*lhnuwnh*). This is one of the few indications of the possible nature of their religion, which some observers have linked to the cult of Mother Earth on other parts of the globe. The dead are buried in the darkest places that can be found.

Marriages are very meticulously planned so as not to weaken the race. They are not based on romantic love or impulse, but rather on a rational pairing of beauty and strength arranged by friends or parents. Despite the absence of romantic love, couples live together in friendship and harmony, and adultery is unknown. To prevent overpopulation, couples have only two foals. The servant classes may, however, have three offspring of each sex to provide domestics for the noble families. If a couple has two fillies, one is exchanged for a colt born to a couple which already has one. If a foal has been lost or a would-be mother is past child-bearing age, the representative council will solve the problem by simply recruiting a foal for her from another family.

Both sexes receive the same education, based on industry, exercise and cleanliness. Four times a year, the young of each district compete in running, leaping and other feats of strength and agility. The victor's reward is a song made in his or her praise. The young are given oats and milk (the standard adult diet) only on certain days of the week, up to the age of eighteen. Before that, they graze in the fields in the morning and evening under the supervision of their parents. Travellers visiting the country with their children can leave them in this bucolic setting if they wish to proceed unhindered.

The tongue of the Houyhnhnms resembles High Dutch, but is more graceful. They have no written language; all knowledge is passed on orally. They have no words for or concepts of the vices that are so common in the rest of the world. War and political squabbles are totally unknown and are generally referred to as "that which is not," an expression which gives the closest possible equivalent to the English word "lie."

The year is calculated by the revolutions of the sun and moon, but it is not subdivided into weeks and days. The horses understand eclipses, but this is the limit of their knowledge of astronomy.

The Houyhnhnms are not the only inhabitants of this peaceful land. The natural fauna includes the *gnnayh*, a bird of prey; *luhimuh*, a wild rat; and *lyhannh*, a large swallow-like bird. Cows are kept for their milk, and cats as pets. But the most important creatures (other than the Houyhnhnms themselves) are the Yahoos (see BRODIE'S LAND). Yahoos resemble human beings, but their heads and chests are covered in matted hair and they have a ridge of hair down their spine. They have brown skin and no tails. The females are smaller than the males and their breasts reach almost to the ground as they walk.

The Yahoos are among the most unpleasant creatures on earth and appear to have a strong natural disposition to nastiness and dirt. They live in bands dominated by a leader who is always the ugliest and most deformed of the group. The leader usually has a favourite: his role is to lick his master's feet and behind, and to drive females to the leader's kennel. The favourite is hated by the whole herd and always stays close to his master for his own protection. When a worse animal can be found, the favourite is normally discarded. As soon as this occurs, all Yahoos in the area attack him and discharge their excrement on him, covering him from head to foot.

The Yahoos, like most beasts, hold their females in common and form no permanent couples. They are the only animals on the island to suffer from illness, as well as from depression and spleen.

The Yahoos are strong and agile, being particularly adept at swimming and climbing trees. They appear to hate all other creatures and fight among themselves incessantly, inflicting savage wounds on each other with their claws. They always fight over food, even if there is obviously enough to feed all. The females, especially the young, are extremely lascivious, frequently the cause of fights among the Yahoo males.

The Yahoos are particularly fond of the shiny stones that are sometimes found in the fields and will dig for hours to try and find them. They then hoard and bury them, though the stones themselves have no intrinsic value. Having his cache of stones stolen is probably the worst thing that can happen to a Yahoo.

They will eat anything they come across—from roots to dead asses and dogs—and have no discrimination whatsoever, although they claim to actually prefer food that has been stolen; they say it is tastier thus procured. They are also extremely fond of a rare, juicy root, which they suck until they become intoxicated and collapse in the filthy mud.

The origin of the Yahoos is a mystery, but it seems that they are not native to the country. Tradition has it that they were driven out of their own land across the sea, and that two Yahoos found their way into the mountains where they became even more degenerate than their compatriots. The Yahoos breed extremely rapidly, and at one stage they threatened to overrun the island. For this reason, the Houyhnhnms began to hunt them systematically. Nowadays, they are bred in captivity, kept in kennels and used as beasts of burden.

So great is the Houyhnhnms' loathing of the Yahoos that they use the word *Yahoo* as a negative suffix. Thus, an ill-contrived house will be described as *"Ynholmhnmrohlnw-Yahoo."* Though they might be invited to join a Yahoo-hunt, visitors are best advised to avoid any contact with them.

(Jonathan Swift, *Travels Into Several Remote Nations Of The World. In Four Parts. By Lemuel Gulliver, First a Surgeon, and then a Captain of several Ships*, London, 1726)

HSUAN, a continent in the North China Sea. It covers 7,200 square miles and boasts many cities said to be governed by saints and fairies. Golden plants and jade herbs are common examples of the local flora.

Travellers may wish to know that in the third year of the Cheng Ho period (90 BC), when the Emperor Wu Ti came to Hsuan, the people presented him with four ounces of incense as large as a sparrow's egg and as dark as a mulberry. Two years later the people of the city of Changan were struck down by the plague. The emperor burnt some of this incense and all those who had not been dead for more than three months came back to life. The fragrance lingered on for weeks and during this period no one was able to die.

Should a visitor find a bush of this incense, he is advised to proceed with caution, since the raising of the dead (except in a few classic cases) has always resulted in rather disagreeable tragedies.

(Tung-fang Shuo, *Accounts of the Ten Continents*, 1st cen. BC)

HULAK, a city built in an ancient crater, near the Xangu River, Brazil, latitude 10° south and longitude 55° west. The city is inhabited by the Hulas, a white race said to have come from ATLANTIS. The men are small, blond, and wear blue silk tunics; the women are stronger and very competent in radio transmission. The women have invented a deadly blue ray with which they terrify their enemies. The ray, however, was captured and used against them by a young English explorer, Alan Upton, who reduced the population of five hundred Hulas—already decimated by an earthquake some three hundred years previously—to a bare baker's dozen.

Visitors today will find Hulak a pleasant city, with large buildings some four hundred feet high, hewn from red rocks. The Great Temple (with its immense golden disc, encrusted with jewels, said to depict the sun) is well worth a visit.

(T.C. Bridges, *The Mysterious City*, London, 1928)

HUMILIATION, VALLEY OF, the valley between the Hill of DIFFICULTY and the Valley of the SHADOW OF DEATH. The Valley of Humiliation is said by many to be haunted by evil, but it is in fact one of the most fertile and peaceful places in the area. Humble men have established rich farms here and sheep graze the hill slopes. It is a place in which there are no distractions, very suitable for contemplation and meditation. Here, in the past, stood the country home of the Lord of the CELESTIAL CITY; in those days men met with angels in the valley and found pearls in its meadows.

(John Bunyan, *The Pilgrim's Progress from this world to that which is to come. Delivered under the similitude of a Dream. Wherein is discovered the manner of his setting out, his dangerous journey and safe arrival at the Desired Country*, London, 1678; John Bunyan, *The Pilgrim's Progress from this world to that which is to come. The Second Part. Delivered under the similitude of a Dream. Wherein is set forth the manner of the setting out of Christian's wife and children, their dangerous journey and safe arrival at the desired Country*, London, 1684)

HUMPED ISLAND, see BOSSARD.

HUNCHBACK ISLAND, in the Pacific Ocean, not far from the Galapagos Islands.

Except for a group of well-travelled Dutchmen who live in the southern region of the island, the inhabitants are all hunchbacks and consider those who are not "a disgrace to Nature." The island became known to Europeans during the reign of King Dossogroboskow LXXVII, called "His Independence." All titles are given according to the qualities their owners should have, so ministers are called "Your Courtesy"; fighting men, "Your Humanity"; judges, "Your Integrity"; ladies, "Your Strictness." The main exports of the island are iron and camels.

(Abbé Pierre François Guyot Desfontaines, *Le Nouveau Gulliver, ou Voyage De Jean Gulliver, Fils Du Capitaine Gulliver. Traduit d'un Manuscrit Anglois. Par Monsieur L.D.F.*, Paris, 1730)

HUNGERCITY, see MORROW ISLAND.

HUNIA, see BLITVA.

HUR-AT-HUR, see KARGAD EMPIRE.

HURLUBIERE, a vast empire in western Europe. The capital, Hurlu, is so large that the royal stables occupy the same surface as the city of Paris. The Emperor Hurlubleu is the direct descendant of the famous Hurluberlu and carries the title of Great Manifafa. This imperial dynasty descends from the Divine Bat which every night covers the sun with his wings to give his Imperial Highness and his subjects the cool darkness needed to make them sleep.

Not much is known about the empire except the religious wars that cost millions of lives. Two of the greatest Hurlubierian philosophers, Bourbouraki and Barbaroko, established two different schools of thought regarding the birth of the Divine Bat, one holding that the celestial cheiropteran was born from a white egg, the other believing the egg to be red. The Great Manifafa tried to reconcile both theories, suggesting that the egg was white outside and red inside, or the other way around, but the different factions would not accept this. Finally a foreigner called Berniquet, who had become the emperor's buffoon, demonstrated that the Divine Bat had not been born from an egg at all, being by nature a mammal, viviparous and anthropomorphic.

Without more ado the Great Manifafa had both philosophers beheaded amid public rejoicing and dancing in the streets. Travellers today will find no noticeable traces of this bloody schism.

(Charles Nodier, *Hurlubleu, Grand Manifafa d'Hurlubière,* Paris, 1822)

HYGEIA, a model town designed in 1876 to ensure the health of the population and to combine the lowest possible mortality rate with the highest possible longevity.

An internationally noted manufacturing town, Hygeia is well endowed with public baths, Turkish baths, playgrounds, libraries, boarding schools, art schools, lecture halls and other places of healthy, instructive amusement.

Nevertheless, the most interesting features of the town are those designed to promote the health of its inhabitants. Hygeia stands to the north-east of a major river which provides its water supply, carefully filtered and tested for purity twice a day. If necessary, ozone is added to the water.

The town is designed on a grid system. Three main boulevards run east to west and are intersected at right angles by important avenues. Minor avenues run parallel to the boulevards. All streets are wide, lined with trees, paved with blocks of wood set in asphalt, flanked by pavements of grey or white stone, always dry and clean, free of holes and open drains, well lit and constantly ventilated. Underground railways run beneath the main boulevards where heavy traffic is not allowed.

The population of Hygeia numbers a hundred thousand; the people live in twenty thousand houses on a site of four hundred acres with a population density of twenty-five souls per acre. In business areas, houses are four storeys high; elsewhere they are only three. No house is more than sixty feet high and they are built back from the street so that they do not overshadow it. Each one is built over a subway and is strongly supported by solid brick arches.

These subways are used for drainage, for gas and water pipes; they also help improve ventilation. There are no basements or cellars. The spaces between the houses are filled with gardens. All public buildings are surrounded by greenery which contributes to the health and beauty of the town.

The buildings are of coloured, glazed bricks; the arrangement of the colours depends on the taste of the householder. As the bricks are very attractive, there is no need for wallpaper, which reduces problems of damp. The bricks themselves are perforated transversely to allow the air to circulate through the walls. Fresh air is introduced through side openings and can, if required, be heated.

The roofs are slightly arched, covered with asphalt or tiles and surrounded by iron balustrades. Many of them are used as flower gardens. The kitchen is situated immediately below the roof to prevent cooking smells permeating the whole house. In most houses, lifts are provided to carry dishes to the dining room.

Hot and cold water is available in every room. The bedrooms are sunny and well ventilated, allowing a space of twelve hundred cubic feet per person. All unnecessary furniture is excluded from these bedrooms. Rubbish disposal is facilitated by shafts running down through the walls to the subway where the garbage bins are kept. A sliding door gives access to the shafts on every floor. Kitchen and bathroom floors are of smooth, grey tile. Living-room floors are made of wood, with a border of solid oak.

Health care is centred in the twenty hospitals of Hygeia, one for every five thousand people. All are built on the same pattern, with a single, wide entrance flanked by the houses of the matron and resident medical officer. Side wings branch off a central, glass-roofed passage. Each wing contains twelve wards which can, if necessary, be divided into individual cubicles. At the far end, the wards open onto a garden. A day-sitting-room is attached to each ward, staffed by two nurses. The outpatient department is similar to that of Queen's Hospital, Birmingham, England.

Separate buildings house units for children with infectious diseases. The hospitals are heated by steam and are in constant communication, by electric wire, with fire stations, factories and public buildings. The work of the hospitals is supplemented by homes for children and the aged which, architecturally, resemble ordinary Hygeian houses.

Thanks to the town planning and hospital system, infantile diseases, typhus, cholera and typhoid have been eradicated, as well as all diseases relating to the abuse of alcohol. Tuberculosis of the lungs has been greatly reduced by pollution control and improved ventilation. The mortality rate is estimated at eight per thousand.

The cemeteries are situated on the outskirts of the town. Burial grounds are artificially made up of fine, carboniferous earth and rapidly growing plants. The dead are placed in the earth, either in wicker baskets or simply in their shrouds, in order to allow rapid and efficient decomposition. There are no individually marked graves; monumental slabs in a large memorial hall commemorate the fact that the individual named has been recommitted to the earth.

Both industry and private homes are subject to pollution control. All chimneys are connected with central shafts into which the smoke is drawn. Before being released into the air it is passed through a gas furnace to burn off remaining carbon. In this way, at a very small cost, the city is freed from the nuisance of smoke and pollution.

To ensure that no commercial work is carried out in residential buildings, certain blocks are let out to artisans and craftsmen. This reduces the detrimental effects of the use of dwelling-places as workshops.

Water and gas are under the exclusive control of the local authority. Distilled water is available, at moderate cost, for those purposes for which hard water is unsuitable and visitors will have no difficulty in obtaining some. A municipal ozone generator produces ozone for use as a disinfectant. Should the visitor require tobacco or spirits of any kind, he is advised to bring these with him, as these commodities are not for sale in Hygeia.

(Sir Benjamin Ward Richardson, *Hygeia, a City of Health*, London, 1876)

HYPERBOREA, a pleasant and fruitful land, perhaps north of Scotland. Tall cliffs, formed like women, flank the entrance to the straits that lead

The Leaping Rock, HYPERBOREA.

to the Hyperborean Sea. Visitors are advised not to arrive in Hyperborca at night, because in the dark these cliffs come to life and destroy any ship that passes their way.

The sun rises only once a year, in mid-summer, and sets only once, in mid-winter. The inhabitants sow in the morning, reap at midday, pluck the fruit of the trees at sunset and retire into the caves at night. Their first fruits are offered to Apollo.

In Hyperborea, sorrow is unknown. The inhabitants choose the time of their death, which they celebrate by feasting and rejoicing, after which they put an end to their lives by leaping into the sea from a particular rock.

The skies over the mountains of Hyperborea are filled with clouds of many sorts of insects, particularly butterflies, which are generated directly from the unusual plants that cover the slopes. Fish abound in the four main rivers that flow through the lush pastures of Hyperborea, and the banks are alive with frogs, which the inhabitants consider highly palatable, especially the two-headed variety, thought to promote luck and fertility. In the forests of Hyperborea, among ancient trees shaped like monsters and men, live herds of unicorns and unicornic birds.

(Pliny the Elder, *Naturalis Historia,* 1st cen. AD; Pliny the Elder, *Inventorum Natura,* 1st cen. AD)

HYPOCRISY ISLAND, see CHANEPH ISLAND.

I

—

IANICUM, see LAMIAN.

IBANSK, a town centred somewhere in the vast plains of Eastern Europe, midway between Warsaw and the Ural Mountains. The exact dimensions of the town and the number of its inhabitants are not known, but Ibansk is said to be of gigantic proportions, spreading throughout a considerable area of Europe and Asia. Most of its inhabitants bear the name Ibanov.

Thanks to the efforts of the scientists of Ibansk, the inhabitants are a head taller than other Europeans or Asians; this is due to progressive historical conditions, a just theory and a wise leadership which have enabled the people of Ibansk to give to each of their acts a historical dimension. This they accomplish sometimes without knowing it, or without taking part in it or even without being able to accomplish the act at all.

It is generally acknowledged that the ISMA (Ibansk School of Military Aviation) Building is the most beautiful and majestic in the whole town. Stamps depicting it can be found even in Latin American and African countries. It was constructed some time before the war from three earlier buildings: an almost derelict aristocratic mansion, the unfinished house of a merchant, and a synagogue. The bourgeois modernist Le Corbusier, after witnessing the construction with his own eyes, said that there was nothing left for him to do and returned home. The famous art critic Ibanov, referring to this incident in his article "Why I am not a Modernist," pointed out that no one in Ibansk would miss him.

The main feature of the ISMA Building is that it has two façades: the main one in the back, the other at the front. The styles of both façades are so different that many tourists and even some inhabitants of Ibansk still believe that they belong to two different buildings. Because of this, before the war, the government of Ibansk handed the building over to two quite separate organizations—the Aeroclub and the Dairy and Meat Complex—and a conflict developed. The heads of both organizations prepared documents critical of each other and both leaders were arrested.

Soon, one of the two institutions ran out of raw material and the conflict was resolved with complete theoretical correctness. In his book, *The Unity and Conflict of Opposites in the Town of Ibansk and Its Surroundings,* the philosopher Ibanov quoted this case as a characteristic example of the fact that in Ibansk contradictions do not grow into antagonisms but are resolved through the force of events.

Should a traveller stand facing the main façade of the ISMA Building, with his back to the town's main river, the Ibanuchka, and the hydroelectric station, he will immediately understand how right Ibanov was when he said at the official opening ceremony that, in the radiant future which had just dawned, every worker would live in a splendid palace like this. The façade of the ISMA Building is decorated with nine hundred columns in every style known to world architecture, and on the roof a crowd of little towers reaches towards the sky, blending into a unified whole, a perfect imitation of the inimitable domes of the church of Iban the Blessed. Overcome by so much beauty, Ibanov wrote in the editorial of the biannual journal *Aurora Bore Orientalis:* "Confronted with such unearthly beauty, a man can only stand to attention and bare his head." Another Ibanov, an officer cadet, happened to glance at the aesthetic aspect of the building—which in his opinion was completely unsuited to normal human life—and warily examining the three-storey-high statue of a national hero, whispered to Ibanov, the cadet: "We have at last overtaken the Greeks, at least in the number of columns per inhabitant. Now we are the largest columnian power in the world." Cadet Ibanov reported this to the authorities and the fate of the slanderer was decided before taps were sounded that evening.

The architects who designed the ISMA Building made one minor omission which, however, played an important role in the development of the literature of Lavatorial Realism. They made no provision for toilets. It later became clear that this was a deliberate and malicious omission, as they supported the erroneous theory that states that toilets should be eradicated at the initial stage. The writer Ibanov then produced another memorable sentence: "If any one gets caught, he is to be eliminated." The omission was noted only when the building was taken over by the Aeroclub, who had to find a place in the courtyard—a long way from the building and less cluttered with rubbish than the rest—and build a "stand and deliver" toilet. Two hours had to be allocated in the cadets' working day for trips to the lavatory, calculated on the basis of three ten-minute visits per head. This figure was determined by empirical research and only given a theoretical basis *ex post facto* by the use of modern multiplication tables. After dark there was a considerable risk that a visit to the toilet would result in getting one's uniform soiled, and the cadets began to avoid using it even during the day. Too late, a path was built, but the cadets had become accustomed to using the rubbish tip in the yard and the toilet itself came to be used only by suspicious and solitary intellectuals seeking to display their egos. They were put under close observation.

In front of the main façade of the ISMA Building, visitors will find a larger-than-life statue of a national hero known as the Leader. It was erected on a granite pedestal with massive chains which for a long time were thought to be decorative. The foundation subsided unexpectedly, causing the statue to lean forward beyond the maximum point permitted by the authorities, and it looks as if, sooner or later, the Leader will plunge his mighty nose into the Ibanuchka River. For this mistake, the sculptor was dealt with appropriately.

The history of Ibansk is made up of events which almost failed to happen, which almost happened but at the last moment somehow did not, which were expected but never happened, which were not expected but did happen, which happened in the wrong way at the wrong time in the wrong place, which happened but are acknowledged not to have happened, which happened but are not accepted as having happened. This history of Ibansk seems to be living proof of beauty as defined in 1950, in Buenos Aires, by the Director of the National Library: "Music"—said this wise old man—"states of happiness, mythology, faces sculpted by time, certain twilights and certain places, are trying to tell us something, or have told us something we should not have missed, or are about to tell us something: this imminence of a revelation which does not take place is, perhaps, the aesthetic fact."

(Aleksandr Zinoviev, *Ziyayushchie Vysoty*, Lausanne, 1976)

ICARA, capital of ICARIA.

ICARIA, a republic, probably in the Mediterranean, separated from Marvols Country by a strip of sea. No traveller wishing to do any kind of business is allowed into Icaria—only those who want to visit the country in order to take back to their own homeland the principles of Icarian wisdom. A small sum, proportionate to the amount of time to be spent there, must be paid on entering, but everything else is free. There are no guards or Customs officials in Icaria; these occupations are considered infamous.

The main attraction of Icaria is its capital,

A town house in ICARIA.

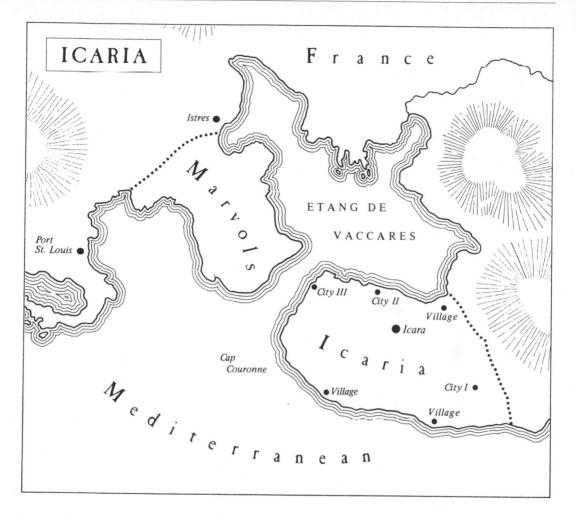

Icara. Icarian architects carefully studied the most beautiful cities in the world and, inspired by the best of each, created Icara. Stables, hospitals, bakeries, factories and warehouses are all on the outskirts of the city, and the inhabitants live in the centre, where the streets are clean, broad and straight. The houses, clustered with balconies, are never more than four storeys high. Every house possesses a fine garden, and it is each citizen's privilege and duty to keep it beautiful for the sake of his city. The government is communitarian. The Republic of Icaria is in charge of administration and public services, for instance, but the laws are made by the citizens according to the dictates of their needs and consciences.

(Etienne Cabet, *Voyage en Icarie*, Paris, 1839; Etienne Cabet, *Adresse du fondateur d'Icarie*, Paris, 1856)

ICI or HERE, the ruins of a palace-principality somewhere on the Egyptian coast of the Red Sea. Travellers visiting it today will find it advantageous to be familiar with its short tragic history, which casts an astonishing new light on the life and death of some of the more notable characters of the twentieth century.

Her Imperial Highness the Grand Duchess Olga, eldest daughter of the last Czar of all the Russias, Nicholas II, was not murdered with all the other members of her family. Towards the end of 1917 she managed to escape from the palace of Czarskoye Selo, where her family was imprisoned,

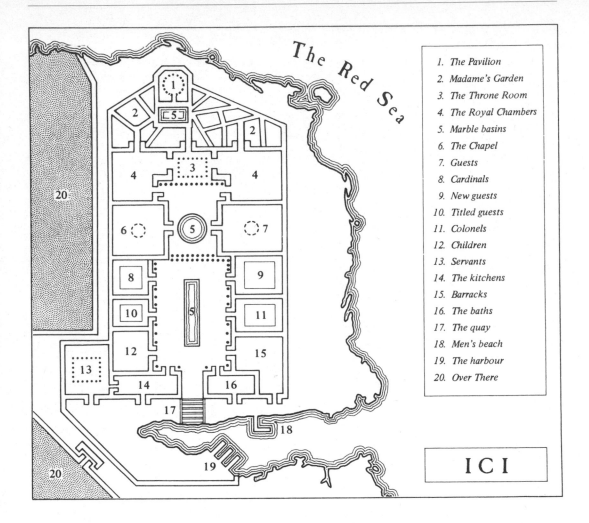

The Red Sea

1. The Pavilion
2. Madame's Garden
3. The Throne Room
4. The Royal Chambers
5. Marble basins
6. The Chapel
7. Guests
8. Cardinals
9. New guests
10. Titled guests
11. Colonels
12. Children
13. Servants
14. The kitchens
15. Barracks
16. The baths
17. The quay
18. Men's beach
19. The harbour
20. Over There

I C I

helped by her French governess, Vera Liubov. The two women, travelling erratically amid the chaos of the Russian civil war, took three years to reach Rumania where Queen Maria, Olga's cousin, received the Grand Duchess with open arms. Inclined from an early age towards an adventurous and depraved life, Olga fell in love with Constantin Comeno, a young Rumanian officer. In spite of their dreams of reinstating the Imperial Throne of Russia and reconquering the Byzantine Empire (Comeno deemed himself the last Emperor of Byzantium), they did not succeed in obtaining political recognition. Still accompanied by the faithful governess, Olga and Constantin travelled from Rumania to London and from London to Berlin, earning their living by devious means, mainly forging documents.

Theirs was the famous letter from Zinoviev to the British Communist Party, which Stanley Baldwin, the British Prime Minister, so ably used to obtain his clamorous victory over Labour. Furthermore, it was the Grand Duchess Olga who had the brilliant idea of blackmailing the British government, threatening to reveal that Baldwin's victory was the result of a forgery. To avoid a scandal, His Majesty's government consented to hand over to Olga the jewels of the Empress Mother of Russia which had been entrusted to King George, on condition that the trio leave Europe forever. However Vera Liubov, enthralled by the esoteric discoveries of Gurdjieff, chose to remain in the country house of an intimate female friend, and it was only the Grand Duchess and

Constantin who in the early months of 1925 left Europe for Egypt.

There lived in Alexandria at the time a brilliant young man, Felix Rollo, a good friend of Constantin, who carried in his blood a passion both for royalty and for pleasure. When King Fuad of Egypt presented the Grand Duchess Olga with a pavilion in his Castle of Montezeh as a gesture of welcome, Felix Rollo and Constantin easily convinced Olga (or Madame as she chose to be called) to transform the pavilion into a gambling den. The cream of Alexandrian society swarmed to the casino—ministers, administrators of the Suez Canal, even the king himself. Money flowed with the champagne, and scandal became a real threat to the Alexandrian aristocracy.

Russel Pasha, cousin of the Duke of Bedford and head of the Egyptian police, advised the king to grant Madame a piece of land as far from the capital as possible, in which she could be absolute ruler, and where she could give vent to her passions and receive her friends without threatening the integrity of the Egyptian state.

It was then remembered that a palace built by the Kadi Abbas in 1860 on a small peninsula in the Red Sea had lain semi-abandoned for years.

The idea of forming her own principality entertained Madame. The immense palace pleased her, even though it had been half-invaded by the sands. She called her realm Ici. A hundred fellaheen were called to clean the rooms, repair the roofs, build new terraces and plant a garden. The only real problem was the lack of water. The nearest spring lay some thirty kilometres away, in a small bay hidden behind some rocks where a Coptic monastery had been established many centuries ago. The dextrous use of young women and blatant menaces decided the monks to move and settle among their brothers in Wadi Natrum, a desert east of Alexandria. A huge fortune was spent to bring the water to the palace; a vast number of workers were smitten by sunstroke and disease. However, after three months' labour, water trickled through the groves in the courtyards and across the many rooms, down the walls of the hammam and into the marble basins.

The king's uncle—who preferred Madame's realm to his own—presented her with many pieces of costly furniture, to which Madame added part of the Imperial Russian accoutrements bought from the Soviets with American dollars. Paintings, books and bric-à-brac that Madame had known as a young girl in Pavlosk and in Czarskoye Selo returned at last to the hands of their legitimate owner. A host of servants were employed; the men were dressed in white robes on which the golden Imperial eagle was embroidered; the women—those from Catholic schools and with the very best references—were hardly dressed at all.

When everything was ready, when the first flowers bloomed on the garden walls and the mirrors were hung in the palace, Felix Rollo invited to Ici all the most corrupt from Heliopolis to Petra. Even foreign libertines visited Madame's realm. The Viceroy of India was a frequent guest, and so were certain Latin-American politicians whose names are best forgotten. Madame let them choose the companions they preferred—expert young girls or tireless black men—with the detachment of a true monarch.

Under the emblem of Imperial Russia—a sable eagle on a yellow field—Madame's court became a deluxe whorehouse. Because transvestism became one of Ici's fashions, the ladies of the court were gentlemen and the gentlemen, ladies. Among Ici's notables were T.E. Lawrence (who did not die, as supposed, in a motorcycle accident), the poet Maurice Sachs (who escaped the bombing of Hamburg), Somerset Maugham, Colette, Curzio Malaparte, the Baroness Karen Blixen, several Viennese Jews, several Nazi officers, Truman Capote (impersonated by a double now living in the United States) and many others. Even during Nasser's regime the court flourished, as Madame was partly responsible for financing Nasser's military projects.

The models used for Ici were the eighteenth-century European courts. Electricity was deemed one of the evils of mankind and only candles and petrol lamps were allowed. The principle similarly applied to the library: the novelists of the eighteenth century were all represented, as well as many memoirs and the licentious works of the 1700's, but no books published after 1900 were permitted. Calendars were forbidden; only the days of the week were mentioned, never the month or the year.

Because Madame did not wish maternal love to interfere with her rigorous community, infants were interchanged at birth and then brought up as dancers or singers, thus contributing to the wealth of Ici; Ici's tap-dancers were famous as far as the Belgian Congo, and the choir singers were requested from Holland to Persia. Young girls were also sold throughout the world, sometimes exchanged for hashish or opium.

The ill-bred, the sick and the old were exiled from Ici and sent to Là–bas or Over There, a bleak area beyond the Palace walls. There they lived in squalor, earning their keep by doing hard labour for the beautiful people of Ici. Finally, unwilling to put up with this treatment any longer, the inhabitants of Over There dug a tunnel to Madame's palace. Urged by Nasser—who had discovered oil in the Red Sea and now wished to recover the peninsula—an army of exiles invaded Ici and massacred the entire libertine population.

A final mystery remains. It is said that Maurice Sachs, before dying at the hands of one of Madame's young lovers, revealed that in reality Madame was not the Grand Duchess Olga but the adventurous governess, Vera Liubov, supposed to have taken Olga's place after her death in 1924. Visitors to Ici will find corroboration of this theory in an absurd Russian church built in marble and domed in gold, where a vaguely Byzantine mosaic reads: "To Her Imperial Highness, Vera Liubov."

(Philippe Jullian, *La Fuite en Egypte,* Paris, 1968)

iDEATH, a small rural community somewhere in the United States. Most of the population lives in the town, but some prefer the cabins on the outskirts, coming into town only for meals. Meals are taken communally and members of the community take turns cooking. The only major crop in the area is watermelons which are used for virtually everything; they are taken to the watermelon works and cooked down until only the sugar is left, which is then worked into the shape of the one thing the people own—their lives. The sugar is dried and left to harden in the sun; strips of red, golden, grey-black, white, brown and blue sugar can normally be seen drying there at any one time. Many of the cabins are made entirely of watermelon sugar; even windows can be made from the ubiquitous sugar and are so transparent that it is almost impossible to distinguish them from glass windows. Watermelon sugar is also mixed with oil derived from trout to produce a fragrant substance used for lighting; it gives a clear and pleasant light.

The only other industry is raising trout in a hatchery on the river. The hatchery is built of watermelon sugar and stones gathered from the surrounding hills. It has a beautiful tiled floor, the tiles fitting together so perfectly that they seem set to music.

The area is decorated with a wide variety of sculptures which represent things that have, for some reason, appealed to the inhabitants. There are, for instance, twenty or thirty statues of different types of vegetables, like potatoes or artichokes, all carved in watermelon sugar.

The most curious feature of this area is that the sun is a different colour each day of the week; the colour determines the colour of the watermelons planted and harvested. The colour sequence is as follows:

> Monday: red
> Tuesday: golden
> Wednesday: grey
> Thursday: black
> Friday: white
> Saturday: blue
> Sunday: brown

The black variety are very sweet and are particularly good for making things that have no sound; they have, for instance, been used to make silent clocks.

The burial customs of the community are unique. The dead are clothed in robes of watermelon sugar and beads of foxfire are placed around their necks, so that light from their tombs will shine forever. The bodies of the dead are carried to the river on escutcheons of pine ornamented with glass and small stones. A glass shaft is lowered into the river and the Tomb Crew take the body down to the river bed, where it is sealed in a glass tomb. Funerals are traditionally followed by a dance in the trout hatchery.

Travellers will find this a peaceful and relaxed community. Its people relate to each other in a casual, informal way and many of them do not even have fixed names. The local newspaper appears only once a year.

The community's past has not, however, been untroubled. For many years it was plagued by tigers which—though they could speak and had beautiful voices—were extremely destructive and were hunted down until only one remained. This last tiger was killed in the hills and brought to the site of the trout hatchery where the body was soaked in watermelon oil and burned.

More recently, the community was divided and a group left to settle in what are known as the Forgotten Works, a strange area at some distance from the town, where all manner of forgotten things can be found. The Works stretch for miles and a notice at the entrance warns that those who come in risk getting hopelessly lost. The rebel group lived here in run-down shacks, brewing whisky from the forgotten things they found around them. There was considerable hostility between them and the settlers, until finally the rebels, claiming that self-mutilation exemplified the true way to run the community, mutilated themselves so badly that they died of loss of blood.

(Richard Brautigan, *In Watermelon Sugar,* San Francisco, 1964)

IDOL ISLAND, off the east coast of North America, not far from WINKFIELD'S ISLAND.

Though uninhabited, Idol Island boasts a considerable fauna. A variety of birds nest on the coast, including one species, the size of a parrot, with rainbow-coloured feathers and a tail which spreads like that of the peacock. A curious quadruped, about the size of a goat, also roams the island. Its legs are so slender that they bend under the animal's weight, making it, in consequence, extremely slow moving. It has large, protruding eyes, sharp teeth and long hair, each strand of which ends in a tuft the size of a hazelnut. Field mice are attracted to these tufts—perhaps because of a glutinous discharge which the hair secretes—and come to nibble at them. The quadruped lets them do so for a while and then turns on them, suddenly twisting its long, slender neck, and eats them by the score.

Only two people have recently lived on the island for any length of time, although archaeological evidence suggests that it had been previously inhabited for many hundreds of years. At some point in the late sixteenth century a European gentleman was marooned on the island, in obscure circumstances. For more than forty years he lived off the land. He found that even though the wild goats of the island were too quick to be caught, they were so fond of the yellow fruit of a local tree that they could be lured into captivity if they were offered it as bait. This enterprising gentleman kept a diary of his stay on the island. Judging by this fragmentary record, he had led a somewhat disorderly life before his arrival but, in the solitude of new surroundings, he was converted to Christianity.

Some forty years later, Miss Unca Eliza Winkfield arrived on Idol Island. Miss Winkfield—the daughter of a Virginian plantation owner and an Indian princess who had been educated in England—was marooned here after rejecting the advances of the lustful sea-captain who was taking her back to her homeland.

To this combination of chance and virtue, visitors to Idol Island owe the first comprehensive description of the place. Miss Winkfield's early days here were made much easier by the discovery of the previous inhabitant's journal, which told her which fruits and plants were edible and how to catch the elusive island goats.

To Miss Winkfield's surprise, she discovered a variety of semi-ruined stone structures, in one of which she lived for some time. (Travellers also can use them as lodgings.) Other buildings contain mummies which—according to the inscriptions they bear—were interred over a thousand years ago; many stone tombs house the ashes and robes of virgins who were consecrated to the sun-god. Also in the nearby vicinity is an underground chamber containing the vestments of the high priests: strange robes made of fine gold-plate twisted until it resembled network, or decorated with diamonds and other precious stones. On closer investigation Miss Winkfield discovered a subterranean passage that led to a hollow golden idol in the shape of a huge man, representing the sun-god. Any sound made inside it was greatly magnified, and she correctly surmised that it had traditionally been used for giving oracles purporting to come from the sun.

Reading in the journal that from time to time Indians would arrive from other islands to worship the god, she resolved to use the oracle to convert them all to Christianity. Speaking through the mouth of the idol, she told them to worship not the sun, but its creator, and went on to instruct them in the rudiments of Christianity, telling them that a woman would come and teach them further. She then appeared to them in the robes of a high priest and soon convinced them of the superiority of the Christian religion. Her teachings were given a very favourable welcome by the Indians, who invited Miss Winkfield to become their queen. She refused this honour, but agreed to return with them to their home island (now known as Winkfield's Island) as a teacher.

The conversion of the Indians progressed, but Miss Winkfield continued to visit her original island from time to time. Finally, she saw a group of English sailors landing there, and recognized one of them as her cousin, an English priest. At first she spoke to the landing party from within the golden idol, inadvertently convincing the more credulous seamen that the island was haunted, although eventually she showed herself in her true shape. The crew still refused to allow her aboard, but she soon persuaded her cousin of the truth of her story. Being a priest, he expressed great enthusiasm for her project of setting up a Christian community on Winkfield's Island. The two married and successfully carried out their missionary work. Thanks to the intervention and loyalty of the ship's captain, Miss Winkfield's inheritance was brought to the island, at which point the flourishing community decided to have no more to do with the outside world.

Travellers will not find all the ancient sites because an earthquake destroyed many of the stone buildings. The idol itself was demolished by the Winkfields to remove from the natives any temptation to return to idolatry.

(Unca Eliza Winkfield[?], *The Female American; Or The Adventures of Unca Eliza Winkfield. Compiled by Herself,* London, 1767)

IFFISH, a large island in the Eastern Reach of the EARTHSEA ARCHIPELAGO. The villages and small towns, with their slate-roofed houses, nestle in the rolling hills; the main port, Ismay, is on the north coast. Bronze is smelted in the towns and there is a small domestic-based weaving industry that produces mainly tapestries.

One of the curiosities of Iffish is the animal known as the *harrekki,* sometimes kept as a pet. The *harrekki* is a small dragon, complete with wings and talons, but no larger than a girl's hand. It lives in oak trees and eats worms, wasps and sparrows' eggs. The *harrekki is* the only dragon now found in eastern Earthsea and is a distant relative of the true dragons found in the west, on SELIDOR and PENDOR. The main inn in Ismay, a great meeting place for traders and townspeople, is called *The Harrekki* in the animal's honour.

The sorcerer of Iffish is Vetch, who trained on ROKE at the same time as the famous wizard Ged. Vetch chose to come to Iffish to practise his art and to live with his younger brother and sister in his ancestral home in Ismay, a spacious and substantial mansion that can be seen even today.

(Ursula K. Le Guin, *A Wizard of Earthsea,* New York, 1968)

IGNORAMUSES, ISLAND OF, separated by a narrow stretch of water from the LAND OF CHARGES.

The islanders live in a great wine press, which is approached up a flight of almost fifty steps. It is surrounded by many other wine presses of different shapes and sizes, by gallows for robbers and by numerous gibbets and racks.

The main occupation of the island is making "potable gold," a type of local wine. The grapes from which it is made come from a variety of vines, variously known as "public stocks," "crow domains," "privy purse," "royal tithes," "loans," "gifts" or "windfalls." The best stock, however, is that of the vine known as the "treasury." When the grapes from this stock are squeezed in the great press, Their Lordships reek of it for at least six months. The press itself is said to be made from the wood of the True Cross. On each part of the press an inscription records the name of that part in the language of the country: the screw is called "receipts"; the bowl, "expenditure"; the vice, "state"; the beam, "moneys due and not received"; the supports, "lapsed tenures"; the main timbers, "annulments"; the side timbers, "recoveries"; the vats, "surplusage"; the double-handed baskets, "rolls"; the treading trough, "discharge"; the vintage baskets, "declarations of validity"; the panniers, "authenticated decrees"; the buckets, "potentials"; and the funnel, "quietus" or "quittance."

The islanders are called Ignoramuses because of their total ignorance. By ordinance, everything on the island has to be managed by ignorance; no reasons must be given for anything, except "Their Lordships say so," "It's Their Lordships' desire," "It's Their Lordships' order."

The Ignoramuses themselves are repulsive looking, but the fauna of the island is even more repellent. One ugly creature to be seen here is a great cur called Double. He has a pair of dogs' heads, the belly of a wolf and the claws of a devil. Double is fed on a diet of debtors' milk and is greatly cherished by Their Lordships, as he is worth the rent of a good farm to each one of them. His mother, Fourfold, is similar to her whelp, but has four heads—two male and two female. She is the most fearsome creature on the island, with the exception of her grandmother, Refusal-of-Fees, who is kept locked up.

Visitors to the great wine press will see a strange figure chained up by the back door. He is half-Ignoramus and half-scholar, and is covered in spectacles like a tortoise in its shell. He lives on only one kind of food, known in the local dialect as "scrutiny of accounts." His name is Review and he has been kept chained up here from time immemorial, much to the regret of Their Lordships, who persistently try to starve him to death.

(François Rabelais, *Le cinquiesme et dernier livre des faicts et dicts du bon Pantagruel, auquel est contenu la visitation de l'Oracle de la dive Bacbuc, et le mot de la bouteille; pour lequel avoir est entrepris tout ce long voyage,* Paris, 1564)

IGNORANCE, MOUNTAINS OF, in WISDOM KINGDOM. Steep and rugged, slimy and moss-covered, the Mountains of Ignorance are inhabited by a number of curious creatures.

The Everpresent Wordsnatcher—a very unkempt bird with a sharp beak that takes the words right out of one's mouth—sometimes makes its nest in the crags. Though the bird's natural habitat is Context, the unpleasantness of the place makes him want to spend most of his time out of it.

The Terrible Trivium, demon of petty tasks and worthless jobs, ogre of wasted efforts and monster of habit, is an elegantly dressed gentleman with a blank face: no eyes, nose or mouth. Convinced of the importance of doing unimportant things—because they never lead one to where one is going—the Terrible Trivium is easily distracted from his tasks. He will stop hunting to count a heap of pebbles or for any such worthless activity.

The Demon of Insincerity traps visitors in a deep pit; he never means what he says or is what he seems to be.

The Gelatinous Giant has no shape at all, so he tries to take on the shape of whatever is next to him: a peak when he is in the mountains, a tree in the forest, a skyscraper in the city. He is very ferocious because he is afraid of everything; he cannot swallow ideas as they are hard to digest.

The Triple Demons of Compromise move in circles. Whenever one says "here" and the second says "there," the third agrees with both.

The Horrible Hopping Hindsights are gorgons of hate and malice, like giant soft-shelled snails with blazing eyes and wet mouths, who leave trails of slime and move surprisingly quickly.

The Overbearing Know-It-All is mostly mouth and is always ready to misinform. He hunts together with the Gross Exaggeration, whose teeth are used to mangle the truth.

The Threadbare Excuse is a small creature in tattered clothes who repeats the same excuse over and over again. Though he looks harmless, once he grabs his victim he never lets go.

On the highest peak of the Mountains of Ignorance stands the Castle-In-The-Air, reached by a spiral staircase. At the foot of the staircase sits the Official Senses-Taker who helps people find what they are not looking for, hear what they are not listening to and smell what is not there. Though he can steal their sense of purpose, sense of duty and sense of proportion, he cannot take away their sense of humour as long as they hear the sound of laughter. He wears a frock-coat and thick glasses and insists on writing down all conceivable information about travellers before deceiving their senses.

(Norton Juster, *The Phantom Tollbooth*, London, 1962)

IMAGINARY ISLAND, situated neither to the north nor to the south; of moderate climate or, to use the Italian phrase, *in mezzo tempo;* noted for its soft and delightful air. This natural paradise lacks a population to benefit from its beauties and riches. About one hundred leagues in circumference and forty leagues wide, it is entirely covered with marble and porphyry. The island is surrounded by a marble balustrade upon which no one leans to watch the sea, and boasts two safe harbours, always empty. The first harbour is dominated by a bastion-like rock set on a terrace, a single huge diamond protected by golden cannons. The harbour barracks have been dug out of stone and the only other visible building in the port is a small construction of diamonds, coral and pearls. The second harbour is built entirely of steel.

Imaginary Island is also notable for its beautiful forests, crossed by many rivers and streams—forests of orange trees, pomegranates and jasmine that grow twenty times faster than they would in Europe. Among the minerals never to be exploited are jasper, cornelian, sapphire, turquoise, lapis lazuli and jade. The beaches are littered with shells in which pearls can, but never will, be found. The fauna of Imaginary Island consists of sea-horses, whales, dolphins, naiads and beautifully singing mermaids who live in the lakes and rivers. In the forests dwell satyrs (as modest as those on CAPTAIN IN SPARROW'S ISLAND), yellow, black and white stags, pink deer and fawns and blue and scarlet horses. Elephants, dromedaries and uni-corns are common. In the evenings, the animals gather in the meadows and join the birds and the naiads in song.

Greyhounds rule as kings over the entire animal population and are served by lions, monkeys and foxes. Though it is said that beef and mutton taste better here than anywhere else in the world, no one has ever tasted them. Should a traveller ever visit Imaginary Island, the extraordinary abundance of silk-worms, similar to the Chinese variety, will certainly astound him.

(Anne Marie Louise Henriette d'Orléans, Duchesse De Montpensier, *Rélation de L'Isle Imaginaire*, Paris, 1659)

IMAGINATION, an evergreen kingdom ruled by a kind empress whose good deeds extend far beyond the frontiers of her realm. Her eldest daughter, the Princess of Story, was once sent on a mission to the Kingdom of Humans. There she was met by scholarly guards who forbade her to enter, saying that her cousin Madame Fashion had accused the princess of being nothing but an old maid. Following the advice of the empress, the princess waited until the guards were asleep and then, seeking out the aid of the children of the Kingdom of Humans, finally gained admission.

Visitors to Imagination are advised that they are required to pay homage to the princess before being admitted into her mother's empire.

(Wilhelm Hauff, *Märchenalmanach*, Stuttgart, 1826)

IMLAD MORGUL, a valley in the Mountains of SHADOW in MORDOR, once guarded by the evil tower of MINAS MORGUL. The valley is deep and descends steeply from east to west, widening at its western end. The stream known as the Morgulduin runs through it, giving off a deadly cold vapour. It is not possible to drink from it, so polluted are its waters. Along the valley runs the trace of the road that led to Minas Morgul and to OSGILIATH, the ancient capital of GONDOR.

The Morgulduin was at one time spanned by a bridge carrying the road from the CROSS-ROADS to Minas Morgul. Built by Sauron in the days when he ruled Mordor, the white bridge had carved figures on it, corrupt and hideous figures at once human and bestial. The bridge was destroyed after the overthrow of Sauron by the Army of the West at the clamorous battle before CIRITH GORGOR.

The valley itself is desolate and empty. Luminous white flowers used to grow on the banks of the stream, at once beautiful and horrible, in shapes born of nightmares. They gave off a foul smell and the valley stank of rottenness. Although the vegetation was burnt and attempts were made to purify the valley after the War of the Ring, the evil associated with it is so great that it has never again been inhabited. The valley is also known as the Valley of the Wraiths and the Valley of Living Death.

(J.R.R. Tolkien, *The Two Towers*, London, 1954; J.R.R. Tolkien, *The Return of the King*, London, 1955; J.R.R. Tolkien, *The Silmarillion*, London, 1977)

IMMORTALS, CITY OF THE, the ruins of a city in Ethiopia, near the Arabian Gulf, founded on a stone plateau. Within this plateau runs a system of sordid galleries that lead into a vast circular chamber. Nine doors lead out of the chamber; eight lead into a labyrinth that treacherously returns to the chamber; the ninth, through another labyrinth, leads to a second circular chamber equal to the first. These chambers and labyrinths are innumerable. Finally the traveller will come to a wall with metal rungs; if he climbs these rungs he will emerge into a small courtyard within the city itself. The architecture of the city seems senseless, as if built by mad gods. It abounds in dead-end corridors, high unattainable windows, portentous doors opening onto cells or pits, incredible, inverted stairways whose steps and balustrades hang downwards. Other stairways, clinging airily to the side of the monumental wall, die without leading anywhere, after making two or three turns in the lofty darkness of the cupolas.

The city is inhabited by the Troglodytes; or rather they live around the city, in shallow pits in the sand. They cannot speak and they feed on serpents. These Troglodytes are the famous Immortals, who, having drunk the waters of a dirty river that runs alongside the city, cannot die. They can remain quiet for very long periods, and need only a little water and a scrap of food to keep their bodies alive, because their bodies are to them like sub-

One of the many chambers in the City of the
IMMORTALS.

missive domestic animals. One of the few things
they enjoy is the rain. Homer became one of the
Immortals and spent many centuries looking for
the waters of another river that would remove his
immortality. He must have found it, because under
the name of Joseph Cartaphilus, an antique dealer
from Smyrna, he died at sea on board the *Zeus* in
October, 1929, and was buried on the island of Ios.

(Jorge Luis Borges, "El Inmortal," in *El Aleph*,
Buenos Aires, 1949)

INCA TUNNEL, an underwater river and gallery
extending some two thousand leagues under the
American continent, from the Mammoth Cave,
Kentucky, to Lake Titicaca in Peru. It was navigated in a steam-ship in 1870 during the expedition
under the command of the engineer John Webher.

The expedition was set up after the discovery
of a document left by a dying Indian in which it was
stated that the treasure of the Incas, hidden after the
arrival of the Spaniards, was at the tunnel's end.
After vanquishing a number of obstacles—savage
fish, thousands of mice, giant octopi, volcanic
craters, lakes of petrol which they imprudently set
on fire, geysers, blazing coal-mines and boiling
water—the expedition found a Chinese mummy
from the year 1100 BC, the skeletons of the members of the previous expedition, and finally the Inca
treasure. Unfortunately they were not able to take
the treasure with them as an explosion of com-
bustible gas put an end to their research.

Some three months later a rich Peruvian, José
Benalcazar, discovered a skeleton near Lake Titicaca. It proved to be that of John Webher, and to-

gether with this macabre find lay the engineer's
account of the expedition.

(Emilio Salgari, *Duemila leghe sotto l'America*,
Milan, 1888)

INCREASE UNSOUGHT, ISLE OF, see
GREAT WATER.

INDIA, an island in the Indian Ocean, along the
north coast of which rise the Himalayas (not to be
confused with India, the country, along the north
frontier of which rise the Himalayas).

The island is linked, by steamer, to Animal-
Land, a country inhabited by dressed animals. Not
much is known of either kingdom, except that the
trees in Animal-Land are balls of cotton-wool
stuck on posts and that India was, at one time,
governed by a young rajah.

(C.S. Lewis, *Surprised by Joy*, London, 1955)

INDIANA, a large, rocky island in the Sojar Az of
the underground continent of PELLUCIDAR, almost directly opposite THURIA. A strip of dense
jungle along the coastline rapidly gives way to
more open parkland where the trees are separated
by areas of tall, lush grass. The spine of the island
is a series of flat-topped mountains, somewhat
reminiscent of those of New Mexico. A major
river flows down from them to the sea.

Indiana is inhabited by two different races.
The more advanced is a race of cavemen similar to
those found in many areas of Pellucidar. They live
in the mountains, digging their caves out of the
soft rock. The second race are barely human and
are not found anywhere else in Pellucidar. Their
limbs are like those of a gorilla rather than a man
and they grow to a height of seven feet; their bodies are mostly covered in hair, but the skin beneath
is white.

However the most striking feature of these
people is the sheeplike face, with its protruding
eyes and long fighting fangs. They are incredibly
agile and strong and can carry heavy burdens up a
vertical cliff with no difficulty. They live in caves
on the top of a flat mountain butte and the only access to their home is by scaling the cliff. Despite
their ferocious appearance, they are in fact a
kindly and peaceful people and do not kill except

in self-defence, although criminals are occasionally put to death. Captives who fall into their hands are made to work, together with those who offend their tribal customs. Surprisingly enough, this extremely primitive race practises a comparatively advanced agriculture, growing a variety of food crops in a small valley in well-kept fields. Their diet includes the flesh of herbivorous animals and birds and they specialize in hunting the *tharg*, the giant elk of Pellucidar. They can move extremely fast, usually travelling on all fours, and have no difficulty in catching up with their prey. The *tharg* is lassoed with a fibre rope and its neck broken by the powerful fighting fangs.

There is no accepted name for these people; they are sometimes referred to as Brutemen or Gorilla Men. They speak an extremely crude form of Pellucidarian reduced to just verbs and nouns, like primitive Hemingway. The name of their king is Gr-gr-gr.

(Edgar Rice Burroughs, *At the Earth's Core*, New York, 1922; Edgar Rice Burroughs, *Pellucidar*, New York, 1923; Edgar Rice Burroughs, *Tanar of Pellucidar*, New York, 1930)

INDIAN ISLAND, in the Cape Horn area, a five-day sail from LEARDING'S ISLAND. The inhabitants of Indian Island come from Baldivia which they fled because of the cruelty of their Spanish masters. Roughly six hundred natives escaped and eventually settled on this remote island. They are a gentle and hospitable people, although their distrust and hatred of the Spanish persists; with the exception of the Spanish, they regard all men as their brothers. They have no property of their own, beyond what is needed for day-to-day living. Their main activities are hunting and fishing. In warfare they use poisoned arrows, and Spanish travellers might find it useful to take with them an antidote made from special herbs.

(André Guillaume Contant d'Orville, *La Destinée Ou Mémoires Du Lord Kilmarnoff, Traduits De L'Anglois De Miss Voodwill, Par M. Contant Dorville,* Amsterdam & Paris, 1766)

INFANTE ISLAND, a tiny island in the Atlantic Ocean to the west of the coast of Brittany, consisting of a very high and steep rock on which stands a lofty castle. It is inhabited by a gentleman who

rigorously observes the laws of honour, knighthood and hospitality. It seems to have been visited for the last time towards the end of the fifteenth century, when the island was part of the Kingdom of Ireland.

(Anonymous, *Amadís de Gaula,* Zaragoza, 1508)

INNSMOUTH, an ancient fishing-port in Massachusetts, in the United States, separated from the rest of the country by vast empty deserts. Innsmouth was founded in 1643 on the banks of the Manuxet River and soon became an important shipyard.

Today Innsmouth is best avoided by travellers. The stench of fish pervades the city, and the inhabitants have a curious amphibian look about them which horses, dogs and other animals seem to detest.

It is rumoured that towards 1830 a certain Captain Obed Marsh left Innsmouth and sailed to the South Pacific. Here he came upon a small volcanic isle with fantastic ruins and grotesque statues of hideous monsters. The natives of a neighbouring island explained to Captain Marsh that the isle of ruins was inhabited by creatures half-fish and half-frog who provided them with food and golden jewels in exchange for human victims. They also told him that in the past they had mated with these creatures and that their offspring were immortal. Captain Marsh saw a profitable trade in dealing with these natives and bought the golden trinkets at very low prices. However after several years, other natives from nearby islands, tired or frightened of the loathsome trade, took the islanders by surprise and massacred the entire population. Unwilling to lose this profitable commerce, Captain Marsh decided to try to find the amphibious race himself. He succeeded in bringing them to him by throwing into the sea a lead weight that one of the native chiefs, with the corresponding instructions, had given him.

Captain Marsh probably succeeded in communicating with the monsters because, not long after, a strange church in which the obscene sea-devil Dagon was worshipped, appeared in Innsmouth, and then fish-like creatures were seen in the streets of the town. In order to deter visitors and to explain the odd new population, Innsmouth spread the story that an epidemic from Asia had struck the town. Though the history of Innsmouth remains dubious, travellers can see examples of the sea-monsters' work at the Miskatonic University in ARKHAM and at the Institute of Historical Studies at Newburyport, Essex, Massachusetts. The most important piece is exhibited at the latter: a kind of tiara decorated with marine and geometrical figures, among which the grotesque and repugnant half-fish and half-frog creatures are easily recognizable.

Should travellers wish to visit Innsmouth, two coaches leave Newburyport twice a day at 10 AM and 7 PM.

(Howard Phillips Lovecraft, "The Shadow over Innsmouth," in *The Outsider and Others*, Sauk City, 1939)

INQUANOK, a city in DREAMWORLD, in a cold and dusky region bordering the disagreeable waste of LENG, from which it is separated by a chain of unbreachable mountains which house a few horrible stone villages and abominable monasteries.

Travellers will notice a peculiar characteristic of Inquanok: because the city contains certain shadows that no cat can bear, in the whole of Inquanok not a single miaow can be heard.

The archaic city, rare and curious, rises above its walls and quays, all of delicate black with scrolls, flutings and arabesques of inlaid gold. The houses are tall and many-windowed, and carved on every side with flowers and patterns whose dark symmetries dazzle the traveller's eye with a beauty more poignant than light. Some end in swelling domes that taper to a point, others in terraced pyramids upon which rise clustered minarets displaying every phase of strangeness and imagination. The walls are low and pierced by frequent gates, each under a great arch rising high above the general level and capped by the head of a god.

At intervals the clang of a bell shivers over the onyx city, answered each time by a peal of mystic music made up of horns, viols, and chanting voices pouring down the onyx streets. The houses near the water are lower than the rest, and bear above their strangely arched doorways certain signs of gold said to be in honour of the small gods that favour them. The inlaid doors and figured façades, carved balconies and crystal-paned oriels gleam with a sombre and polished loveliness. Now and then a plaza opens out, with black pillars, colonnades and the statues of curious beings both human and fabulous. Some of the vistas down the long and unbending streets, or through side alleys and over bulbous domes, spires and arabesque roofs, are weird and beautiful beyond words.

But nothing is more splendid than the massive heights of the great central Temple of the Elder Ones with its sixteen carved sides, its flattened dome and its lofty pinnacled belfry overtopping all else. The temple is surrounded by a walled garden from which the streets radiate like spokes from a wheel's hub. The seven arched gates of that garden, each with a carved face over it, are always open, and the inhabitants of Inquanok roam at will down the tiled paths and through the little lanes lined with grotesque terminuses and the shrines of modest gods. Fountains, pools and basins shimmer with the images of the tripods on the high temple balcony, full of small luminous fish from the deepest bowels of the blue ocean.

And when the deep clang of the temple bell shivers over the garden and the city, long columns of masked and hooded priests come forth from the seven doors of the temple, bearing at arm's length great golden bowls from which steam rises. They goose-step in single file down the walks that lead to seven lodges into which they disappear. It is said that underground paths connect these lodges with the temple and that the long files of priests return through them, and it is whispered that deep flights of onyx steps go down into indescribable regions. But in the whole of Inquanok, only a few hint that the hooded priests are not human.

The Veiled King's palace rises on a hill above Inquanok, with its many marvellous domes. The paths of onyx are steep and narrow, all but the broad curving one where the king and his companions ride on yaks or in yak-drawn chariots. Gay parterres, delicate flowering trees, brazen urns and tripods with cunning bas-reliefs, statues of veined black marble that seem to breathe, basalt-bottomed fountains with luminous fish, tiny temples of small iridescent singing birds, great bronze gates with marvellous scroll work, and blossoming vines across every inch of the polished walls, all join to form a sight so beautiful that travellers must be careful not to faint. It is best not to look too long at the great central dome, said to lodge the archaic father of all the rumoured *Shantakbirds* who sends queer, dangerous dreams to the curious observer.

(Howard Phillips Lovecraft, "The Dream-Quest of Unknown Kadath," in *Arkham Sampler*, Sauk City, 1948)

INTERPRETER'S HOUSE, just inside the gate that marks the beginning of the road that leads from the City of DESTRUCTION to the CELESTIAL CITY, in CHRISTIAN'S COUNTRY. The house was built as a resting-place for travellers, who receive here the white vestments that they are to wear on their journey to the Celestial City. It is named after the Interpreter, who provides visitors with a guide to the things they will meet along the way. Much of the information he gives is allegorical but he will interpret its true meaning.

The rooms of the house also have an allegorical meaning. In one, a man can be seen toying with a muck-rake and sweeping the straw on the floor; he serves to illustrate the shortcomings of the carnal mind. One large parlour, never swept, is thick with dust; it represents the heart of a man who has never been sanctified by grace, and the dust is his original sin and inner corruption. Any attempt to sweep the room merely raises choking clouds of dust. The only way in which it can be cleansed is to sprinkle it with water and then sweep up the dust; the water is said to represent the Gospel.

(John Bunyan, *The Pilgrim's Progress from this world, to that which is to come. Delivered under the similitude of a Dream. Wherein is discovered, the manner of his setting out, his dangerous journey and safe arrival at the Desired Country*, London, 1678; John Bunyan, *The Pilgrim's Progress from this world to that which is to come. The Second Part. Delivered under the similitude of a Dream. Wherein is set forth the manner of the setting out of Christian's wife and children, their dangerous journey and safe arrival at the Desired Country*, London, 1684)

IOUNALAO, a Caribbean island whose name means "where the iguana is found." Travellers who reach Iounalao sometimes believe that they have landed not on a tropical but on a Greek island; this illusion is said to be caused by the peculiar nature of the waters surrounding the island, which sometimes take on a wine-red colouring.

The main village on Iounalao consists of a single hot street leading to the beach, past small shops, several clubs and the only pharmacy. The island's museum contains little of interest: a twisted wine bottle, crusted with fool's gold and thought to have been carried either by a galleon from Cartagena, or by a flagship, the *Ville de Paris*, in the Battle of the Saints. The islanders believe that the wreck is protected by an octopus-cyclops, its one eye like the moon, and that seagulls defend it from profanation.

The oldest bar in the village, called No Pain, is run by a certain Ma Kilman. It has a gingerbread balcony with mustard gables and green trim round the eaves, the paint wrinkled with age. In the cabaret downstairs are wooden tables where customers can play dominoes. North of the village, down a road of glittering quartz, is a logwood grove of thorny trees, orange from the sea blast. The logwoods were once part of an estate, with a windmill, huge rusted cauldrons, vats for boiling sugar and blackened pillars. Several of the inhabitants keep yam gardens.

The beach is a sort of meeting-place. Here the islanders ride horses, catch crabs or listen to songs. Sitting on the beach, guarding the fleet of canoes with names such as *Praise Him*, *In God We Trust*, *Morning Star*, *St. Lucia*, *Light of My Eyes*, is the island's bard, a blind man known as Old St. Omere, or Monsieur Seven Seas. Sometimes he sings, sometimes he mutters stories in the dark language of the blind, telling those who will listen that he has sailed around the world. Visitors may think they recognize him from somewhere else—London, India, different Caribbean islands—but Iounalao is Old St. Omere's home.

(Derek Walcott, *Omeros*, New York, 1990)

IREM ZAT EL-EMAD or **IREM WITH THE LOFTY BUILDINGS**, a city in the deserts of Yemen encompassed by enormous fortifications, with pavilions rising high into the sky. The city is entered through two enormous gates set with a variety of jewels and jacinths, white and red and yellow and green. The rooms of the pavilions contain lofty chambers built of gold and silver and adorned with rubies and chrysolites and pearls and vari-coloured jewels.

Irem was discovered by a camel-driver, Abd-Allah ibn Aboo-Kilabeh, who was looking for a lost camel. News of the city reached the Caliph Mo'awiyeh who asked his wizard, Kaab-el-Ahbar, to explain to him the history of such a marvellous place, and it is through the wizard's chronicle that the story of Irem is known. It was built by King Sheddad; he was fond of reading ancient books, and when he read the description of Paradise he decided to build a similar place on earth. King Sheddad had under his authority a hundred thousand kings; under each of these were a hundred thousand valiant chieftains, and under each of these a hundred thousand soldiers. He summoned them all before him and ordered them to find the most pleasant, vacant tract on earth and there build a city of gold and silver. The work lasted three hundred years, and when the city was completed King Sheddad instructed them to build around it impregnable fortifications of great height. This took the workers another twenty years. King Sheddad then ordered his one thousand viziers and his chief officers and his troops and his wives and his female slaves and his eunuchs to prepare themselves for the journey; these preparations took them another twenty years, and then they set off. But when at last they were barely a day's march from Irem Zat El-Emad a terrible cry descended from the heavens and destroyed them all by the strength of its sound.

Travellers today will find it uninhabited and are free to take as many treasures as they can carry.

(Anonymous, *The Arabian Nights*, 14th–16th cen. AD)

IRON, ISLAND OF, see MARBOTIKIN DULDA.

IRON HILLS, to the east of the plains that lie around the LONELY MOUNTAIN in the north of MIDDLE-EARTH. The hills are inhabited by dwarves, who originally came here from the GREY MOUNTAINS which they were forced to leave because of the increasing number of dragons there. The dwarves of the Iron Hills are not as wealthy as some of their relatives in other parts of Middle-earth since iron rather than gold is the common metal found here, but as a result they have been secure from the unwelcome attentions of dragons.

Led by their king Náin, the dwarves of the Iron Hills joined their fellows in the great battle against the orcs who had taken over MORIA at DIMRILL DALE in 2799 Third Age. Their arrival turned the tide of the battle in favour of the dwarves. A group of dwarves from the Iron Hills

was also present at the Battle of the Five Armies on the slopes of the Lonely Mountain in 2941.

(J.R.R. Tolkien, *The Hobbit, or There and Back Again*, London, 1937; J.R.R. Tolkien, *The Fellowship of the Ring*, London, 1954; J.R.R. Tolkien, *The Return of the King*, London, 1955)

IRON MOUNTAINS. The same name is given to two ranges of mountains, one at the North Pole and one at the South Pole. In both cases the ranges are circular; at their centres are the two polar passages which give access to PLUTO, the land in the hollow centre of the earth.

The existence of this zone and of the Iron Mountains themselves had long been suspected, but it was not until 1806 that they were finally discovered. In that year, members of the crew of the whaler *Mercury* survived a shipwreck on the coast of Spitzbergen. After wintering on the coast, they travelled inland and found that the temperature rose as they continued north. Finally they reached the Iron Mountains; a crude inscription on the bare rocks commemorates their arrival on November 8, 1806. They went beyond the outer ring of mountains and suddenly found themselves falling through a hole in the ground. At the end of their fall, they discovered that they had reached Pluto, where they were to spend the next eight years. After visiting several of the countries in Pluto, they returned to the surface via FELINIA.

(Anonymous, *Voyage au centre de la terre, ou aventures de quelques naufragés dans des pays inconnus. Traduit de l'anglais de Sir Hormidas Peath*, Paris, 1821)

ISAURA, city of the thousand wells, is said to rise over a deep, subterranean lake somewhere in Asia. On all sides, wherever the inhabitants dig long vertical holes in the ground, they succeed in drawing up water. This is true for as far as the city extends, but no farther. The city's green border repeats the dark outline of the buried lake; an invisible landscape conditions the visible one; everything that moves in the sunlight is driven by the lapping wave enclosed beneath the rock's calcareous grey sky.

Consequently two forms of religion exist in Isaura.

The city's gods, according to some people, live in the depths, in the black lake that feeds the underground streams. According to others, the gods live in the buckets that rise, suspended from a cable, over the edge of the wells, in the revolving pulleys, in the windlasses of the norias, in the pump handles, in the blades of the windmills that draw the water up from the drillings, in the trestles that support the twisting probes, in the reservoirs perched on stilts over the roofs, in the slender arches of the aqueducts, in all the columns of water, the vertical pipes, the plungers, the drains, all the way up to the weathercocks that surmount the airy scaffolding of Isaura, a city that moves entirely upwards.

(Italo Calvino, *Le città invisibili,* Turin, 1972)

ISENMOUTHE, also called **CARACH ANGREN**, a narrow pass leading into north-west MORDOR between two spurs, one jutting westward from the ASH MOUNTAINS and the other running east from the Mountains of SHADOW. The pass leads into the dale of UDÛN.

When Sauron was in power in Mordor and using it as a base for his long-prepared onslaught on GONDOR, forts and towers were built on the spurs to defend Isenmouthe. A great earth wall was thrown up across the pass, which was further guarded by a deep trench crossed by a single bridge. Sauron later turned these defences to his own use, and at the end of the War of the Ring, they were destroyed by the joint forces of ROHAN and Gondor.

(J.R.R. Tolkien, *The Return of the King,* London, 1955)

ISHMAELIA. The only means of access to this virtually inaccessible African country—at least until the British concession to build a road goes into operation—is by rail from a small Italian port on the Red Sea. The journey, which takes at least three days, is extremely uncomfortable; the train crosses baking desert plains before delving into a mosquito-infested bush area and climbing up to the mountains of Ishmaelia. Visitors are warned that during the wet season it is not uncommon for trains to be up to three hours late and that luggage is not infrequently lost on the journey.

Ishmaelia is a mountainous country to the south of the Sudan and to the north of the French territories in north-east Africa. It has yet to be fully explored or even properly surveyed, although known mineral resources include large gold deposits in the western hills. Communications are poor and virtually all transport in the interior is by mule train. The only roads are mud tracks which become streams in the rainy season. The hinterland is ruled by inhospitable local chiefs and most of the population continue in their traditional callings—slaves, bandits or gentlemen of leisure.

Some of the more primitive tribes are said to have extremely curious and picturesque customs, but these have yet to be studied in detail. The few big-game hunters who have strayed into the country while on safari have dined out for years on the experience. The building of the railway has had little or no effect on the life of the agrarian peasantry. Its main effect has been to lead to a decline in the few clumsy crafts once practised in the area around the capital, thanks to the increased availability of manufactured imports. The adverse trade balance has been rectified by a very elastic system of bankruptcy law.

The isolation of Ishmaelia is the result of historical factors. The first European missionaries and travellers arrived in the 1870's; they were, without exception, eaten. The punitive expeditions sent out by the western powers suffered even worse fates, and it was finally decided that the effort of colonizing Ishmaelia was an even more unpleasant prospect than seeing a neighbouring power control it. Thus, by general consent, the country was ruled off the map and its immunity was guaranteed.

The people segregated in this manner had no common language, traditions or history and the country was therefore transformed into a republic. A constitution, guaranteeing democracy and a single transferable vote, with a bicameral system, was drawn up by an international commission of jurists. Mr. Samuel Smiles Jackson, a native of Alabama, was installed as first president. Constitutionally, elections should have been held every five years, but this proved impracticable. The receiving officer and the Jacksonian candidate took turns visiting various areas of the country and entertaining local chiefs with banquets for six days, after which the chiefs recorded their votes in the manner prescribed by the constitution. As a result, the Jacksons completely dominated the political life of the republic and elections became known as *Jackson Ngomas.*

National Defence and the Inland Revenue

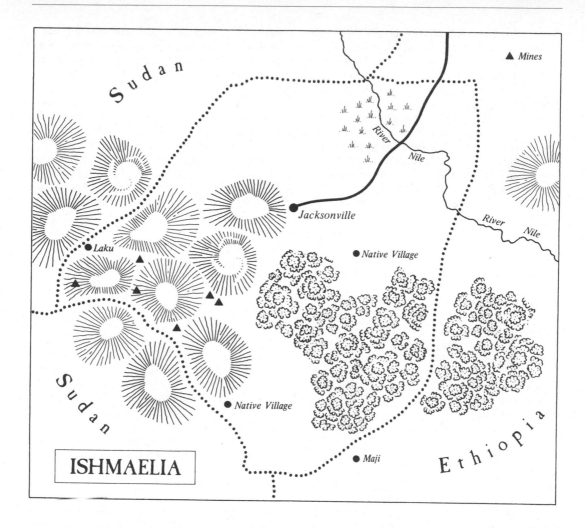

were merged into an office under the general command of General Gollancz Jackson. Jackson's forces consisted—and still consist—of two companies: the Ishmaelite Mule Tax Gathering Force and the Rifle Excisemen, plus a small corps of Artillery Death Duties men for use against the heirs of powerful noblemen. Towards the end of the financial year, flying columns would spread out from the ranks, returning in time for the budget with a haul of coffee, slaves, silver coins and livestock—to be stored in government warehouses, to pay salaries and cover the national debt. Under this system, the republic seemed to prosper.

In the mid-thirties a family quarrel in the Jackson family led to political upheaval and to the formation of new political parties. One of them,

the White Shirt movement, founded by Smiles Soum, had little effect on political life in Ishmaelia, but led to increasing rumours in European countries of an imminent civil war. The international press corps descended on the country and proceeded to report on a war that was not, in fact, taking place. Matters were made even more confused by stories of Soviet agents and German influence. (There was a measure of truth behind this, as both the German and Soviet governments were anxious to secure rights to the republic's suspected mineral resources.) There was also a very short-lived Soviet coup, which was carried out and then put down without any bloodshed. German and Soviet officials were forestalled by a certain British businessman who succeeded in acquiring the mineral rights of the country, and Ishmaelia returned to normal very rapidly.

Jacksonville, the capital and only major town, is a shoddy place, studded with the relics of an outbreak of arson that occurred shortly after the establishment of the first insurance office in the country. The main street is a strip of tarmac with dirt sidetracks for men and mules. Even this does not extend for more than a quarter of a mile outside the city. Travellers will find accommodation at the *Hotel Liberty* (Mrs. Earl Russel Jackson, proprietor). The hotel is not comfortable, as the tin roof leaks and there are no bathrooms. Gourmets will find the *Hotel Liberty* wanting, for the menu does not vary: sardines, beef and chicken for lunch, soup, beef and chicken for dinner. The beef and chicken are served with grey-green peas and either Worcestershire sauce or tomato ketchup. The alternative is the *Pension Dressler*, a complex of three tin-roofed buildings in a one-acre compound. The courtyard is full of livestock: poultry, a pig, a three-legged dog and a ferocious milch goat. A bathroom hut with a tin tub is available for guests, but has to be shared with a resident colony of bats. The attractions of Jacksonville include Popotakis's Ping Pong Parlour, the *Café de la Bourse*, the Carnegie Library and the Ciné–Parlant.

The only other town in Ishmaelia cannot be visited. Although shown prominently on the map (no doubt to enhance the country's grandeur), Laku does not exist. In 1898 the boundary commission camped here while trying to make its way to the Sudan and a boy was asked for the name of the campsite. He replied *"Laku,"* which is Ishmaelite for "I don't know." The name has ever since been copied from the commission's sketch maps and now appears in all official maps.

The Ishmaelites have been Christians for many years, and dispensation can be obtained for those wishing to eat human flesh, even during Lent. Polygamy is still practised. Bribery is common and visitors will find it useful to know that it is possible to bribe one's way out of prison for as little as five pounds. The people are very fond of oratory in all its forms: sermons, lectures, harangues, political programmes, panegyrics of the living or the dead and even charity appeals. It appears that they simply enjoy the sound of the human voice, regardless of what is being said.

The postal system is rudimentary. Telegrams are delivered in a somewhat capricious manner, as none of the bearers can read. The usual method is to wait until half a dozen telegrams have accumulated and then to send a messenger to hawk them in the most likely places until they are claimed by the addressees.

The flora includes rank red flowers which bloom everywhere at the end of the rainy season, banana palms, gum trees and coffee plants. Indian hemp grows here and is widely smoked.

There is a considerable European presence: Great Britain, Sweden and Germany all maintain legations or consulates in Ishmaelia. Travellers in need of European comforts are advised that the Swedish Vice Consul, also surgeon at the Swedish Mission hospital, is proprietor of a combined tea, Bible and chemist's shop in Jacksonville.

(Evelyn Waugh, *Scoop, a Novel about Journalists*, London, 1938)

ISHTAKAR, a ruined palace at the edge of the land of the Abassides, the capital of which is SAM-ARAH. The palace is approached through a deep valley; two towering rocks stand at the entrance like a portal. High on the slopes of the mountains around the valley, the glimmering façades of the ancient royal tombs can be seen. The valley itself is now almost totally deserted and the two villages in it have been abandoned.

The most impressive part of Ishtakar Palace is the great terrace of the watchtowers, a smooth expanse of black marble on which not a single weed grows. On the right rise the countless watchtowers, now roofless and inhabited only by night birds; their architectural style is not found anywhere else on earth. The ruins of the immense palace are famous for their carved and embossed figures. The carvings represent four colossal animals which combine the features of a leopard with those of a gryphon, striking terror into the heart of the most intrepid visitor.

Ishtakar was constructed by Soliman ben Daoud with the help of spirits and jinns. At the height of its glory, the palace was the most magnificent creation in his kingdom; however, in building it, Soliman offended against divine majesty and his masterpiece was virtually destroyed by thunder.

The strange chambers beneath the terraces of Ishtakar are inhabited by a variety of evil genii commanded by the demon known as Eblis. Those who venture into this underground realm will see a vast vaulted hall lined with columns and rows of arcades. The floor is covered in gold dust and saffron mingled with aromatics. Tables are set up for the feasts of the genii, who can be seen dancing to the sound of lascivious music. A vast multitude of figures comes and goes through the hall, clasping their right hands to their hearts and ignoring everything around them. Their faces have the livid pallor of death and their eyes the phosphoric gleam that can sometimes be observed in cemeteries at night.

In even deeper halls, the treasures of the pre-Adamite sultans who once ruled the whole of the earth are stored. Eblis himself holds his court here, sitting on a globe of fire in a tabernacle surrounded by long curtains of gold and crimson brocade. He has the physical appearance of a young man though his eyes glitter with mingled pride and despair. In his hand, which has been blasted by thunder, he holds the iron sceptre that controls the afrits and other demons of the deep. From the tabernacle, an aisle leads to a dome-covered hall. Fifty bronze doors, each with as many locks of iron, line its walls. Inside, the bodies of the pre-Adamite kings lie on beds of incorruptible cedar; they still possess enough life to be conscious of the miserable state to which they have been reduced. The builder of Ishtakar lies here as well, in the same half-living half-dead state as his forebears.

(William Beckford, *Vathek*, Lucerne, 1787)

ISLA, an island in the West Mediterranean. Though no certain name is given to the island, the name Isla may be surmised from clues given in travellers' chronicles. The island is ruled by a cardinal who is also the island's prince. From the air the visitor will see vineyards, and almond, fig and apricot orchards. Little towns with pantiled-roof houses and splendid churches top the gentle rises of the ample plain. The rivers are mainly courses of tumbled stones, with exhausted water lying in discrete pools. On the shore are wooded cliffs, beaches of bright sand and the principal city, Ciudad, ringed by walls and rising from its harbour. On the northern and western shores are great mountains, a complex of ridges and green, well-watered valleys, and high pastures. The arid plains are kept fertile with a system of windmills that draw water, a method borrowed from the Saracens. The mountain summits are so tall that they keep their mantles of snow all through the heats of summer. Wolves roam these high woods, and a child is said to have been found, long ago, brought up by wolves in the mountains.

The islanders drink mare's milk and have a passion for fish. Except for the storms at either equinox, the waters surrounding the island are usually calm, so the fishermen need not exert great effort.

The capital, Ciudad, is a handsome city, mainly Christian but with a Saracen quarter. The cathedral of Ciudad was built, it is said, by men of austere vision. It is of plain grey stone, roofed by a soaring vault of simple and beautiful form. A sort of polyphony of shape—the arched openings between nave and aisles, and the arched windows, which mute and tint the light of day before admitting it—strikes the onlooker like Lenten music. At a later age, decorations were added: behind every altar, in every chapel in the aisles, in frenetic emphasis behind the high altar, in orgies of jewelled enrichment, are columns of coloured marble, riotously foliate capitals, carved angels, painted canvases of piously gesturing saints.

After visiting Ciudad, travellers may care to see the town of Sant Jeronimo, the learned monastery of Galilea, and the sanctuary of Monte Mauro, which is now a place of pilgrimage. They are warned that they must have warrants for any journey undertaken outside the port at Ciudad, since the islanders are extremely wary of any foreigners. Legend has it that a foreign prince, perhaps an angel, once visited the island and shook the faith of its inhabitants, and visitors today may find the island a very different place from that described in the chronicles.

(Jill Paton Walsh, *Knowledge of Angels*, London, 1994)

ISLANDIA, a small country occupying the southern part of the KARAIN CONTINENT, and cut off from the rest of the continent by the Mount Islandia massif which culminates in the domed, snowclad peak of Mount Islandia itself. A second high mountain chain runs south-west to the province of Winder, forming a peninsula. Between the two ranges lies the fertile Doring valley, watered by the Doring River.

There are two main passes across the northern mountains which mark the frontier of Islandia:

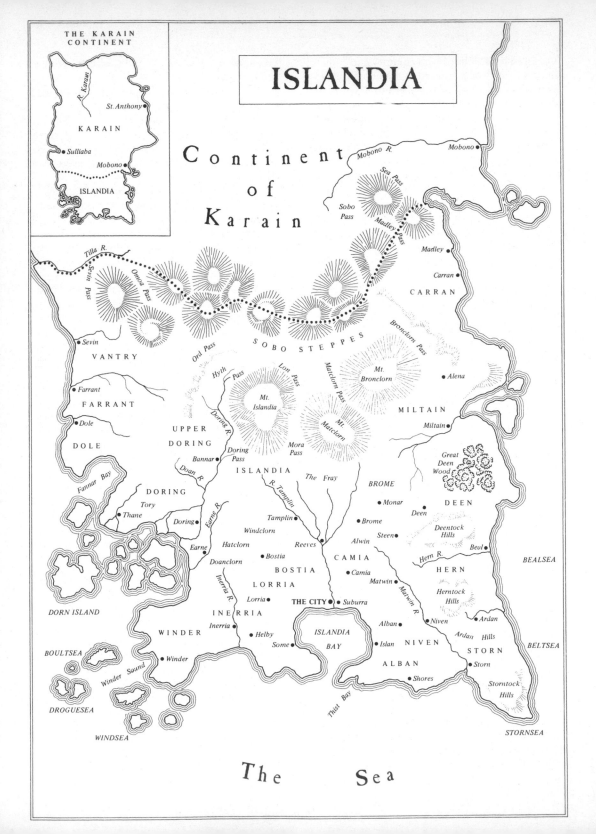

the Mora pass at the head of the Doring valley and the Lon pass. Below the Mora pass lie the Frays, where irregular rock ledges break the steep three-thousand-feet-high cliffs; much of this area is covered in thick woodland. The typical Islandian landscape is a vista of fields, mountains and woods, with glimpses of the scattered farms seen through the trees. The exception is the area around the mouth of the Doring River, an extensive area of marshland intersected by rivers and canals. The coastline here is noteworthy for its extensive sandy beaches. A characteristic feature of the landscape is the absence of any intermediate zones between the towns and the countryside.

All the towns on Islandia are walled and have no suburbs but rise up suddenly in the midst of the farmland surrounding them. Visitors should certainly travel to Doring Town, built on a group of six islets in the middle of the Doring River, where the banks are lined by walls of pink granite. The concentric tiers of houses and towers rising above the walls make Doring Town a unique sight not to be missed. The colours of the buildings—from pale pink to orange and from light grey to blue—make a striking contrast with the green waters on which the town appears to float. Doring Town is approached through a forest of beech and oak trees and the traveller emerges from the woods onto the river bank to see the town rising out of the water.

The capital and main port of Islandia is known simply as The City, standing on three hills above the delta of the Islandia River. The summit of the central hill is a square, of terracotta sandstone, surrounded by five ancient buildings with flaking walls and small leaded windows: these are the administrative and government offices for the whole country. With their curving façades and steep roofs, the buildings possess a striking atmosphere of austerity and simplicity. Above them rises a cylindrical, slate-blue tower. In contrast, the old part of The City is a labyrinth of narrow, winding streets and elevated bridges. In the distant past, The City underwent a long siege and bridges were built from rooftop to rooftop to facilitate the movements of the defenders and to prevent congestion in the streets below. These bridges remain, and numerous roof gardens have been built on the graceful arches that span the streets. The aerial labyrinth that has gradually developed bears no relation to the groundplan of the streets below.

The City is noteworthy for its delightful gardens, window-boxes and vine-clad walls, and also for its remarkable relief carvings. Each building bears a scene from the history of the family that lives there or from the annals of Islandian history. The quality of the carvings varies: some are crude, others extremely sophisticated. Although similar carvings are found throughout the country, The City offers an unrivalled collection of this Islandian art-form.

The City also boasts Islandia's only theatre, known as the Alwina Theatre—a fourteenth-century construction, consisting of a large amphitheatre covered by a high, airy dome. The theatre is used for musical performances and public meetings. Because it is considered bad taste to mimic another person (even an imaginary one), drama is unknown in Islandia. At night, The City's streets are dimly lit by candles affixed to corner houses and protected from the wind by waxed paper.

Very little is known of Islandia's early history. It seems that in ancient times the Islandians were thinly scattered across the entire Karain Continent. The arrival of a Negro tribe, the Bants, forced the Islandians into the Frays, where they took a stand and gradually learned to live together. Over the years their numbers increased, and they were obliged to emigrate. They went down into what is now Islandia, driving out the Bants invaders. Little is known of the Islandians' life in the Frays: before leaving, they destroyed their houses, lest they be tempted to return to them, and archaeologists have not been able to reconstruct a clear picture of their ancient habitat. The only house still standing is that of King Alwin, who left it unbarred but declared it inviolate. Visitors are warned that, even today, trespassers are severely punished.

The descent from the Frays took place in about AD 800 and some fifteen years later the first town was founded at Reeves—subsequently the seat of the university established in 1035. From then on, the history of Islandia became a saga of wars against the nomads of the Col Plateau beyond the mountains and against the Karain. Over the following centuries, the countryside was totally cleared of the Bants, who now live in the mountains and in the steppes beyond them.

Islandia never underwent the feudal stage typical of European cultures, as the farms on which the economy was based were too small to support more than two or three families each. As a result it was almost impossible for the nobility to develop into a powerful or unified class. In the thirteenth century, some nobles, strongly influenced by Christian missionaries, attempted to resist the power of the king, but they were easily defeated; shortly afterwards the Christians were expelled from Islandia. Ever since this aborted coup, the nobles have been elected by the people, although members of only certain families tend to be elected.

It is interesting to note that Islandia's constitutional monarchy was brought into being by a historical accident. Alwin XVIII was cut off from his army during a campaign against the Karain and was never seen again; his death was never fully established and he is, by tradition, still regarded as King of Islandia. Five years after his disappearance, his son was elected regent by the National Assembly, a congregation of the whole people which dates back to the time of the Exodus. It was agreed that he would rule for only as long as the assembly considered him a fit ruler. Since then, all kings of Islandia have been entitled to rule "by courtesy." The power of the monarch is strictly limited: he cannot appoint anyone to office and, like the other nobles, he has only one vote in the governing council.

Until the nineteenth century, Islandia remained almost totally isolated from the outside world. Several times missionaries and settlers were allowed into the country, but they were later expelled. In 1841, the English, French and American governments, backed by an expansionist party led by Lord Mora, attempted to force trade agreements and diplomatic relations on Islandia, but they were repulsed. After this crisis, strict restrictions were placed on foreigners entering the country. Visitors should check with their consulates regarding travel permits before making any definite plans to visit Islandia.

The events of 1841 also convinced the government of the need to introduce a certain degree of industrialization into the essentially agrarian economy, and an industrial city was planned. Suburra, built and designed by an English engineer, is the only centre of industry in the country, and it produces fine agricultural machinery and naval vessels.

Islandia's isolation was briefly interrupted in 1906 when, under the terms of the Mora Treaty, diplomatic representatives and some prospectors from Europe and America were admitted to the country for an experimental period of two years and nine months. The architect of the treaty, Lord Mora, was eager to develop Islandia and to establish relations with the rest of the world. As a gesture of good faith, the frontier garrisons in the mountain passes were removed, although the frontier itself remained closed. Both the withdrawal of the garrisons and the treaty itself were extremely controversial and led to long and angry debates throughout Islandia. In general, reactions to the industrial exhibits brought into the country were unfavourable: the farmers could see no advantage to modern agricultural machinery and considered it a potential threat to their traditional way of life. Finally, after a long debate and a referendum, the proposal to establish permanent relations with the outside world was rejected by a two-thirds majority. As a result, the Mora government fell and was replaced by a much more conservative group. The winter of 1908 was marked by a number of frontier incidents. Raiding Bants crossed the border and pillaged farms, seemingly with the encouragement of the German administration in the Sobo Steppes (see Karain Continent). These were the last recorded frontier incidents and since 1908 Islandia has remained totally isolated from the outside world.

The isolationism which is so characteristic of Islandian history appears to stem from fears that disease might be introduced into the country by foreigners and from a reluctance to prey on Islandia's resources. A foreign presence would, it is believed, also lead to a need for more laws and to more government interference in the lives of private citizens. Economic development is consistently rejected, as it would mean that many people would have to leave the farmlands—the very basis of Islandian life and culture. Islandians also express fears about the pollution and damage to their cherished landscape that would result from too much industrialization.

Ultimately, however, the isolationism has to be explained in terms of the country's cultural conservatism. Islandia's culture is profoundly connected with its agrarian economy. With the exception of Suburra, the economy is based on farming. The farms are traditionally self-sufficient and are almost totally unmechanized. In theory, five or six per cent of the population owns ninety per cent of the land, but in practice and in law they are so bound to their dependants by the duties imposed by their station that they cannot accumulate wealth on any large scale. The result is a civilization that provides the people with all they need and a stable, unchanging society. In many ways, the self-sufficiency of the farms encourages a kind of individualism: the individual has all he needs and does not crave for other things in the community. This goes hand in hand with a philosophy of tolerance. There are no great extremes of wealth and poverty and no overwhelming need for the individual to make his way in society.

The major concern of the Islandians is to live in tune with their natural environment, like highly developed animals, satisfying their basic needs and desires without imposing on others or destroying the balance of nature. This philosophy is reflected in the Islandian attitude to farming. The whole farm is thought of as a picture and the farmer as an artist working on a constantly changing canvas. The individual artist, however, makes only small changes to a picture made by nature and by those who have worked before him. And when changes are made or new crops introduced, the appearance of the landscape is always taken into account; the Islandian farmer is, in effect, a highly skilled landscape architect. The pace of work is relaxed and unhurried. The Islandians enjoy even the most demanding physical work involved in farming, but do not hesitate to interrupt it to read or write if they so desire.

Visitors will find life in Islandia peaceful. There is no mechanized transport and the slow gait of the horse seems to symbolize the whole tenor of Islandian life. The same simplicity is found in Islandian pastimes: sailing, skiing, visiting the houses of friends and going on picnics. There are no commercial entertainments; dancing, for instance, takes place in private houses, not in ballrooms. Concerts are held in the Alwina Theatre in The City and this is probably the nearest equivalent to a commercial show. Islandian music tends to be written for solo performers or small ensembles rather than for orchestras; it is characterized by its delicate weaving patterns of haunting simplicity.

A typical combination of individualism and stark simplicity can be observed in Islandian burial customs. The dead are buried in unmarked graves, but the individual chooses the place where he wishes to be interred. This means that the burial site belongs more truly to the individual than if he were buried in a communal cemetery.

The basic unit of Islandian society is the family, to which everything else is subservient. Family traditions are all-important. The status of the family is reflected in the language itself, where a specific pronoun is used to signify "we" when

meaning "I and my family." In fact, when an Islandian uses that pronoun he is referring not only to his family but also to his ancestors, going back for hundreds of years. The centrality of the family and of the family farm are illustrated by the concept of *Tan-ry-doon*, which can be literally translated as "soil-place-custom." Everyone has a home in the countryside, even city dwellers. It may be a farm or simply the house of a relative, but the individual has the absolute right to return to it at any time, and a room is always kept in readiness for his return. *Tan-ry-doon is* sometimes offered to friends with the formula "my house is yours." This is meant quite literally and is one of the greatest privileges and honours an Islandian can offer. A single word, *alia*, signifies attachment to one's family and ancestral home.

Marriage is seen mainly as a means of perpetuating the family line and name. On the other hand, if there are two brothers in a family, one will usually remain single in order to avoid overcrowding the farm and straining its resources. People in this position often take lovers, which is quite acceptable in moral terms. There is no formal marriage ceremony: couples merely make a simple declaration of their intention to live as man and wife in the presence of a close friend. There is, in fact, no word in Islandian for "wife," the closest equivalent being, again, *alia*, or "sharing-lover." Marriage is based on working together and on considerations of the *alia* offered by the man; this means that women in fact choose between men and not between the social or material advantages offered. There is nothing to prevent marriages between *denerir* (those who work on others' farms or estates) and *tanar* (those who own estates or farms). Relations between men and women are very relaxed. It is not uncommon for male and female friends to bathe naked together or share the same room at night. On the other hand, they are expected not to spend too much time together—to prevent sexual desire becoming too powerful. Linguistically, a distinction is made between *apia*, "sexual desire," and *ania*, which signifies "a desire for married life with a particular individual." The sexual division of labour is much less marked than in most countries and there is no hard and fast distinction between men's work and women's work, unless considerations of physical strength are involved. (An analysis of the condition of women in Islandia is curiously absent in Ms. Germaine Greer's otherwise thorough book, *The Female Eunuch*.)

Structurally and grammatically, the Islandian language is simple and easy to learn: there are no declensions, conjugations, moods, tenses or genders, except where a sexual distinction needs to be made. It is, however, difficult to translate into or from Islandian. The language is extremely rich in terms relating to all aspects of farming, using many words with subtle distinctions where most languages would use a single word. There are also several words for "good," depending on whether it means "good for health," "good for farming," "good for *alia*" and so on. Islandians have only one name and there are no honorifics in their language. Individuals are identified by their relationship to the head of the family or by the order of their birth. Thus, an individual may be called "Dorn, grandnephew of Dorn of Lower Doring," "Hyth Ek" (Hyth, First Child) or "Hyth Ettera" (Hyth, Third Child, Girl).

Islandian literature mainly consists of fables. Probably the most important writer in the country's history is Bodwin, who renewed Islandian classic literature in the fourteenth century. His work is still immensely popular, typified by its sophistication and undogmatic morality. Other important authors include Godding, the eighteenth-century fabulist, and Mora, a sixteenth-century poet.

The ethnic origin of the Islandians remains obscure. Physically, there are two types: one, tall with dark hair and eyes, the other, slighter, with light brown hair and more delicate features. Few Islandians are fat and very few men wear full beards. The men wear trousers ending above bare knees, open-necked shirts and loose jackets of fine spun wool. Their shirts are of soft linen and have broad collars. The women usually wear plain, knee-length skirts and jackets similar to those worn by the men. Their only undergarments are linen bloomers, a band for the breasts and a light woollen garment for very cold weather. They tend to go bare-legged or to wear woollen stockings. The army, the navy and each of the provinces are represented by two colours. Their jackets are of the major colour, with cuffs of the minor. Thus, the navy wear grey and blue; people from the province of Miltain, red and white; and people from the province of Hyth, white and dark blue. The colour of the shirts worn on formal occasions depends upon the wearer's taste, but it is always chosen to blend with his or her complexion.

Islandian food is not particularly exotic; most of it is similar to European food, although the drinks differ somewhat. A bitter, spicy chocolate is popular, as is *sarka*, a liqueur tasting rather like a very dry peach brandy. There is also a white liqueur as sweet as honey. The most common wine is slightly resinated, ruddy-coloured, quite heavy, slightly sweet and very refreshing. On journeys, Islandians usually eat preserved fruit and hard meat-rolls. Before eating, they soften the rolls by soaking them in water. Rolls like this will keep for up to a month in winter and up to ten days in summer.

There are no watches in Islandia and time is measured by water clocks. As though to compensate for this, Islandians have developed an acute sense of time. The year is divided into four seasons. *Windorn* (winter) begins on the shortest day of the year and lasts for four months. It is followed by *Grane,* lasting two months, *Sorn,* lasting four months and *Leaves,* lasting another two months. Day and night last twelve hours each.

The fauna includes the grey Islandian deer, with its characteristic short antlers. Bears and wolves are sometimes seen in the forests of Loria. The *aspara* or seagull is the most striking of the birds. The beak is scarlet, the back brown and the rest of the body white, and it is as swift and as agile as a swallow. The *aspara* is frequently seen in the Doring marshes. The Islandians never hunt for sport.

Despite its agrarian society, Islandia is rich in mineral resources. These include oil and coal. Copper is found in the Winder province. Important deposits of gold, silver, iron and platinum have been discovered on the volcanic island of Ferrin.

Visitors are advised that it is difficult to gain access to Islandia. It can be reached by steamer from the port of St. Anthony on the Karain Continent, but the number of visitors allowed to enter is strictly limited under the Hundred Law, passed after the 1841 crisis. All visitors are subject to a very strict medical examination before disembarkation. Foreigners are not allowed to settle in the country and can stay for only one year; permanent immigration requires the consent of the National Assembly. Imports and exports, apart from books and gifts, are forbidden. Foreign investment in the country is not allowed.

The curious traveller will find more information on Islandia in *An Introduction to Islandia; its history, customs, laws, language, and geography as prepared by Basil Davenport*, New York, 1942.

(Austin Tappan Wright, *Islandia*, New York, 1944; Mark Saxton, *The Islar, or Islandia Today—A Narrative of Lang III*, Boston, 1969)

ITHILIEN, one of the most royal and ancient fiefs of the kingdom of GONDOR, a beautiful region lying in the narrow stretch of land between the GREAT RIVER and the MOUNTAINS OF SHADOW. Its southern border is marked by the River Poros which flows from its source in the mountains to the Great River.

Protected by mountains to the east and the north, Ithilien has a temperate climate. It is a rich, fertile region, known as the Garden of Gondor because of its lush grass and its groves of tamarisk, terebinth, olives and junipers. Herbs grow wild on the hills and fill the air with their aroma.

During the period leading up to and during the War of the Ring, Ithilien came under the sway of Sauron, the Dark Lord of MORDOR. The land was virtually uninhabited in those years and became wild and overgrown. For years after the defeat of Sauron, it still bore the scars left by his orcs, who maliciously damaged trees and plants and left piles of filth across the countryside. Only the Rangers of Ithilien remained to patrol the land from their hidden refuge at HENNETH ANNÛN.

As chief of the Rangers Faramir spent much of the War in Ithilien, and he suffered a grievous wound leading the retreat to MINAS TIRITH. After the War he was made Prince of Ithilien and wed Eowyn, heroine of ROHAN; they settled in Ithilien and restored it to its present beauty.

The Field of Cormallen, near Henneth Annûn, was the site of the celebrations after the final defeat of Sauron. The field is a broad lawn running down to a wood of beech trees and crossed by a stream. For the celebrations, three seats of turf were built on the lawn beneath the banners of Rohan, Dol Amroth and Gondor. Here the two hobbits from the SHIRE, Frodo Baggins and Sam Gamgee, were honoured above all others by the massed Armies of the West for finally destroying the Ring and putting an end to the Dark Lord's evil power.

(J.R.R. Tolkien, *The Fellowship of the Ring*, London, 1954; J.R.R. Tolkien, *The Two Towers*, London, 1954; J.R.R. Tolkien, *The Return of the King*, London, 1955)

IVANIKHA, a village in the USSR where all peasants are called Ivan. Only their nicknames are different: Ivan Self-Eater (who chewed his ear off in his sleep), Ivan the Bald, Ivan Nose-Poker, Ivan Spit-Farthest. The Ivans of the village are famous for having travelled to new lands believing that the soil and the water abroad were better than that of Ivanikha. To prove it, they dug a hole so deep that they reached the sky on the other side of the earth. Disappointed at not having found the better soil they were looking for, they returned to Ivanikha, afraid to tell their story for fear of being called liars and cheats.

(Yevgeniy Ivanovich Zamyatin, "Ivany," in *Dva Rasskaza dlja vzroslych detej*, Moscow, 1922)

IX, a country to the west of NOLAND from which it is separated by a range of high mountains. A river at the foot of these mountains marks the natural frontier of this kingdom. From here good roads lead through the forests to the capital, also known as Ix.

The city of Ix is impressive and beautiful, and the many gardens and shrubberies are well laid out and extremely well cared for. The most impressive building in the capital is the Royal Palace, which stands in the centre of a park and is approached by marble walks lined with statues and fountains.

For as long as anyone can remember, Ix has been ruled by the beautiful Queen Zixi. With her blonde hair, striking black eyes and lily-white skin, Zixi appears to be no more than sixteen years old; in fact, she has been on the throne of Ix for many hundreds of years. Her precise age is 683, although it is sometimes claimed that she is thousands of years old. Zixi has been able to prolong her life and to preserve her youthful appearance by magic arts. But the fact that she is a witch does not mean that Zixi is evil in any way. On the contrary, she rules her subjects wisely and liberally. It is she who taught them to reap and sow, who showed them the arts of metal-work and who taught them to build their substantial houses. Despite this, she is feared rather than loved by her subjects, who are well aware of her true age and powers. No matter how charming she may be, everyone treats her with great respect and thinks carefully before speaking to her.

Zixi's one cause for sadness is that although she always appears young and beautiful to others, she sees the reflection of an ugly, old hag every time she looks in a mirror. There are consequently no mirrors among the rich furnishings of her palace.

Hearing from a wandering minstrel of the magic cloak owned by the rulers of Noland, Zixi determined that she had to have it, as she had heard that the cloak granted one wish to anyone who wore it. Her first attempts to obtain it (by entering Noland and posing as a teacher of magic) failed and she decided to invade the country. Zixi led her army in person, clad in gold mail, but the invasion failed. Her army was thrown into panic when it was confronted by a Nolandian army half its size but led by a general ten feet tall and by an executioner with arms so long that he could simply reach out and pluck the Ix officers from their ranks. The Ixian soldiers were also greatly demoralized by the appearance of a talking dog which went among them and told them they were about to be routed. Despite the defeat of her army, Zixi was still determined to have the cloak and, transforming her appearance completely, she found employment as a servant in the royal palace in Nole, the capital of Noland. Once inside the palace she was able to steal the cloak and substitute a copy for the real thing. She then returned to Ix. The theft of the cloak did not, however, have the desired result: the cloak would not grant a wish to anyone who had stolen it from its previous wearer. Disappointed, Zixi discarded it.

Despite her attempt to invade Noland, Zixi was extremely kind and generous to its rulers when they came to her, forced out of their country by the invading Roley-Rogues, strange creatures like animated footballs who had descended from the mountains in the north to terrorize the population of Noland. Freely admitting that she was wrong to steal the cloak (but adding that she no longer knew where it was), Zixi used her magic arts to rid Noland of its oppressors, and by the same token removed a potential threat against Ix itself. Zixi brewed up a potion which sent all the Roley-Rogues to sleep, allowing the army of Ix to tie them up and take them to the river, where the invaders were flung into the water and left to drift off to sea. This time the army of Ix was greeted with great joy by the inhabitants of Noland.

Although cut into pieces by those who had found it, the cloak was at last recovered and repaired before being taken back to Nole.

Since the expulsion of the Roley-Rogues, relations between Noland and Ix have been excellent. Queen Zixi also maintains relations with Ozma of OZ, and was one of the official guests at her splendid birthday party.

(L. Frank Baum, *Queen Zixi of Ix, or The Story of the Magic Cloak*, New York, 1907; L. Frank Baum, *The Road to Oz*, Chicago, 1909)

J

JABBEROO, see LOONARIE.

JABBERWOCKY WOOD, probably located somewhere in England.

The only information on this place is contained in an Anglo-Saxon poem published in LOOKING-GLASS LAND and reprinted many times since. According to the poem, the wood was the scene of an epic battle between a young man and a monstrous creature, the Jabberwocky, feared for its eyes of flame, its catching claws and its biting jaws. The creature's severed head was preserved and its skull can now probably be seen as an exhibit near the Wood. Two other creatures, the *bandersnatch* and the *jubjub* bird (see also SNARK ISLAND) are known to be dangerous and should be avoided.

Near the edge of the Wood lies a green lawn on which a sun-dial has been erected. On the *wabe* (the grass plot round the sun-dial, so called because it goes a long way before it, a long way behind it and a long way beyond it on each side) live a number of other animals. The *toves*, lithe and slimy creatures, a cross between a badger and a lizard, with pointed noses like corkscrews, make their nests under the sun-dial and feed only on cheese. The *borogoves*, thin shabby-looking birds with feathers sticking out all over, like a live mop, are known to be flimsy and miserable. The *raths*, a sort of green pig, bellow and whistle when they lose their way and assemble on the *wabe*. The only plant species worth noticing in Jabberwocky Wood is the *tumtum* tree, of which not much is known.

(Lewis Carroll [Charles Lutwidge Dodgson], *Through the Looking-Glass, and What Alice Found There*, London, 1871)

JACKSONVILLE, capital of ISHMAELIA.

JAGUAR THRONE, REALM OF THE, little known except for the fact that it houses the famous Jaguar Throne and can be visited by tourists, especially at Christmas. The Jaguar Throne is embedded in a pyramid, and to reach it the visitor must travel through a tunnel entered at ground level—a tunnel so narrow that on each side one's shoulders touch the unpleasantly damp old stone, which has a skin on it like the skin on a stagnant pond. There is only one passageway, and those who have already seen the throne push past those who are on their way to see it, in their hurry to reach the outside air again.

The air inside the pyramid is moist and dead, but the darkness is illuminated by a few small lightbulbs along the passage. Half-way down is a statue which commemorates an ancient entertainment: in olden times a game was played in an outside court, with stone rings set into the walls. The players of the losing team had their heads cut off, and the statue—the body of a man with a fountain in place of his head—represents the blessed loser making it rain. It is said that this metaphor can be dangerous.

In the depths of the pyramid the Jaguar Throne crouches in a square cubicle, its ruby eyes glowing, its teeth vivid, its meaning lost. All we know is that it is kept in there so that it can't get out.

(Margaret Atwood, "Raw Materials," in *Murder in the Dark*, Toronto, 1983)

JANNATI SHAHR or **THE VERY HEAVENLY CITY**, in Saudi Arabia, in the Ruba-el-Khali or Empty Abodes, the central deserts of Arabia, never penetrated by white men. Access is easier via China, India or the farther islands of the Indian Ocean. Jannati Shahr lies beyond the Iron Mountains, at the foot of the Mountains of Gold which camouflage the city. There is so much gold in the rocks that the whole mountain range seems to be made of gold. A stupendous volcanic upheaval in the past cleft the mountain wall and extruded through the fault a huge rocky dyke two and a half miles wide and of indeterminable length and height. Strong, cunning hands formed the rocks into walls, battlements, houses, mosques and minarets, giving the final impression of a city made entirely of gold. Not a single stone was laid with mortar. From afar, Jannati Shahr glitters like a jewel. Long walls, pierced by gates with fantastic arches, surround the delicate minarets and sparkling domes. There are soft green gardens and feathery palm groves that contrast violently with the black cliffs in the background. Many different trees grow here—fig, pomegranate, lime, apricot, orange and datepalm—as well as fields of wheat,

View of JANNATI SHAHR as seen from the southern desert.

barley, tobacco and sugar-cane. There are herds of antelope, flocks of sheep and many birds—pelicans, cranes, doves, falcons, hawks and several species of water fowl.

From the plain, a broad, paved way leads up under a golden gate into the city itself, with its teeming bazaar and splendid mansions. Underneath the city sprawls a dangerous labyrinth that leads into a fabulous treasure-chamber. Here are riches from all countries and all ages: some from Carthage, some from the Nile, some from King Solomon himself. Should a traveller reach this chamber, the only escape is through an underground river of hot water, called the River of Night.

A group of white men visited Jannati Shahr at the beginning of this century, and stole the sacred Black Stone of Mecca and the Great Pearl Star that Mohammed gave to his favourite wife Ayeshah as he lay dying in Medina. The Black Stone was returned but the Great Pearl Star, about the size of a man's larger thumb-joint, was given to a lady in New York and is now part of a private collection.

(George Allan England, *The Flying Legion*, Chicago, 1920)

JANSENIA, a fertile land, bordering on LIBERTINIA, DESPAIRIA and CALVINIA. To the south lies a stormy and bottomless sea. The capital is in the centre of the country, equidistant from the three neighbouring kingdoms which surround Jansenia and which can be reached on foot in four days. The country has numerous streams and rivers. One notable lake is similar in shape to Lake Geneva. Its waters, however, are said to be deeper than those of its Swiss counterpart.

Jansenia was originally a Flemish colony (famed for the novelty of its laws), but the present population is of various nationalities. The Jansenians claim that the capital was built in the sixth century by the Prince d'Hypone, although some archivists claim a Prince of Tarsus, educated by Gailiel, as its founder. A sword said to belong to the founder is displayed as a relic: closer examination shows it to be a modern forgery, but visitors should nevertheless admire the fine craftsmanship.

Not too long ago the country was badly affected by an outbreak of the Black Death. Neighbouring countries were delighted when rumours reached them that the towns were deserted and that the population of Jansenia had been decimated. The reports, however, proved to be unfounded, and Jansenia soon returned to normal—much to the annoyance of its neighbours, some of whom even went into mourning at the news.

The people of Jansenia are very short, although old paintings show their ancestors to have been of normal height. They have very hard heads and thick skulls. Some have two hearts, a condition occasionally advanced as an explanation for

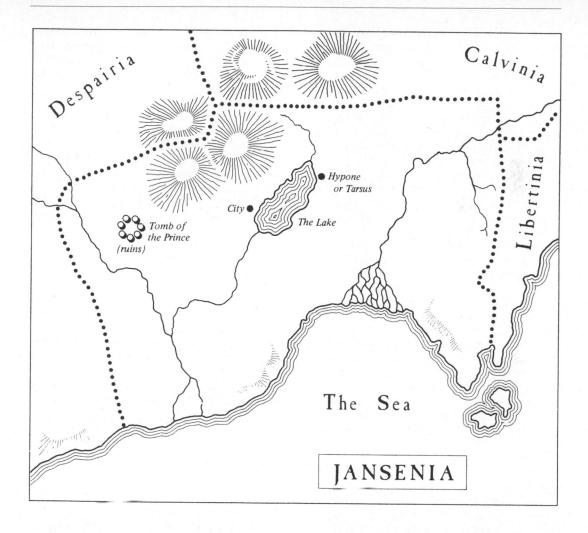

their notorious insincerity. Visitors will find them a very suspicious race, maintaining whole armies of spies; they are not at all popular with their neighbours. All business is transacted at night. Houses, in other respects similar to those of Europe, have their entrances at the rear, so that the inhabitants can come and go without being seen. Everyone adopts a unique gait and manner to distinguish himself from others and their behaviour is generally affected. The Jansenians claim to be the wisest people in the world; only they, they maintain, can clearly distinguish between good and evil.

An endemic disease of Jansenia is characterized by the swelling up of the entire body. This is frequently fatal and the only cure is to go abroad. But visitors should be aware that the Jansenians will not allow anyone to leave—they have been known to detain people by force when necessary.

Life in Jansenia is dominated by religion, a form of Christianity handed down by a certain Margalicus. Jansenians believe that Christ died to save only certain individuals and that most people do not fall into that category. Salvation depends on the grace of God—which is granted to very few. God imposes laws that can be obeyed only with divine help, denied to most sinners. Jansenians do not recognize the infallibility of the Pope, claiming that such a doctrine is a usurpation of divine authority. Popes who have attacked Jansenian doctrines have been removed from the calendar and their places taken by more tractable religious figures.

In order to show their veneration for the Eucharist, its celebration has virtually been suspended. Abstention from mass is considered a form of fasting. In some areas, priests are paid not to celebrate mass, in accordance with the Jansenian custom of paying people to do nothing. The priests deny the efficacy of absolution on the grounds that it is merely an expression of the grace afforded by inner suffering. Consequently, absolution is often refused to the dying.

There are no monks in the country, although male recluses work as artisans and sell their handicrafts in the markets—the more devout regard these as relics. Nuns, on the other hand, are a familiar sight and there is great competition among priests for appointments as confessors in convents. As a whole, the people are devout and send out missionaries to other lands, many of them in disguise. The traveller may have met one or two in his own country and not known it.

Education is also dominated by religious doctrines. A very special emphasis is placed on the dogma that Christ did not suffer for stillborn children and that even good actions performed by non-believers are mortal sins. The Bible itself is rarely studied, except by those training for the priesthood. The other major subject taught in school is grammar. Schools and colleges for the poor are financed by the rich, who are flattered into making generous contributions.

Printing is the most highly developed art in Jansenia. Fine paper and exquisite typefaces are used to make extremely beautiful books, which are also full of lies, errors and mistakes. This does not concern the Jansenians, who are interested only in the appearance of the books and who are known to patronize many of the better-known book clubs in both Europe and America.

In military affairs, the insincerity of the Jansenians can again be seen: defeats on the battlefield are disguised to look like victories and important ceremonies are held in the churches to commemorate them. "Captured" banners are displayed—but they are actually manufactured in Jansenia itself. No weapons are built in the country; all are imported from Calvinia. The people do, however, take great care of their weapons and polish them until they shine; they are often given as gifts at Christmas. The gunpowder used in Jansenia has the peculiarity of being silent, so that guns make no noise when they are fired. Jansenians, as a result, make very dangerous enemies.

The philosophers of Jansenia do not recognize the existence of common sense. Indeed, one thinker was recently broken on the wheel for daring to lecture on the topic. Rhetoric is widely used and greatly respected; almost everyone dabbles in it.

Watches in Jansenia are set by the moon and not by the sun. They are badly made, so that people usually have no idea of the right time.

Jansenia's fauna includes wolves with fleece like sheep, foxes which roost with the hens and extremely talkative black parrots. Here the owls sing more sweetly than nightingales and the calves and deer are larger than in Europe. All asses wear woolly hats made by the women. The commonest plants are aconite and laurel, the latter being used to make crowns.

The country has rich gold and silver mines; mercury is also common. Luxury products are imported from Libertinia, books and weapons from Calvinia. In turn, Jansenia exports rope, knives, funeral shrouds, gravestones, and copper plaques for epitaphs to Despairia.

Jansenia is subject to high winds and violent thunderstorms. Travellers visiting the famous Tomb of the Prince will find that it was recently destroyed when struck by lightning, and only a few magnificent blocks of stone remain to be seen.

(Père Zacharie de Lisieux, *Relation du pays de Jansénie, où il est traite des singularitez qui s'y trouvent, des coustumes, Moeurs et Religion des habitants. Par Louys Fontaines, Sieur de Saint Marcel,* Paris, 1660)

JA-RU, a village some distance from the Forest of DEATH in the underground continent of PELLUCIDAR. Ja-Ru is the home of a tribe known as the Mammoth Men because they ride mammoths as people on the surface of the earth ride horses. They are strong, rough, aggressive people, built like heavyweight boxers. They have great respect for physical strength, but very little for human life, especially the lives of strangers. They argue that respect for strangers is a sign of weakness in a warrior, explaining that if they respected strangers there would be no one for them to kill. They would then be forced to fight one another, which would not be good for the tribe.

The Mammoth Men are hunters and appear to have no knowledge of farming. Their usual diet is meat and they are very fond of a potent alcoholic beverage known as *tu-mal*, which is also drunk on RUVA.

In Ja-Ru, marriages are decided by ritual combat. A woman must have a champion who enters into combat with anyone who wishes to take her as a wife. The duel is fought with bare hands and ends with the submission or knockout of one of the fighters; it rarely ends in death. If the champion wins, the woman may choose to take him as her mate; if the challenger wins, he is free to take the woman or not. The only alternative to this ritual combat is to submit to the decision of the chief.

(Edgar Rice Burroughs, *Seven Worlds to Conquer*, New York, 1936)

JOCHTAN, see NAZAR.

JOLLIGINKI, a kingdom on the eastern coast of Africa. A path from the beach (if the traveller arrives by sea) leads up the cliffs, where dry caves provide shelter, and into a thick forest of ginger roots, convolvulus runners, creepers, vines and coconuts. The wet, boggy places should be avoided. The Royal Palace stands in a clear, wide space. It is made of mud and has a broken window in the pantry, which has never been mended. Nearby is the stone dungeon (visitors can still see the one little barred window high up in the wall) in which an Englishman, Dr. Dolittle, from PUDDLEBY-ON-THE-MARSH, was unfairly imprisoned with all his animals.

Not far away is the Land of Monkeys. The quickest way to reach it is to cross the river that

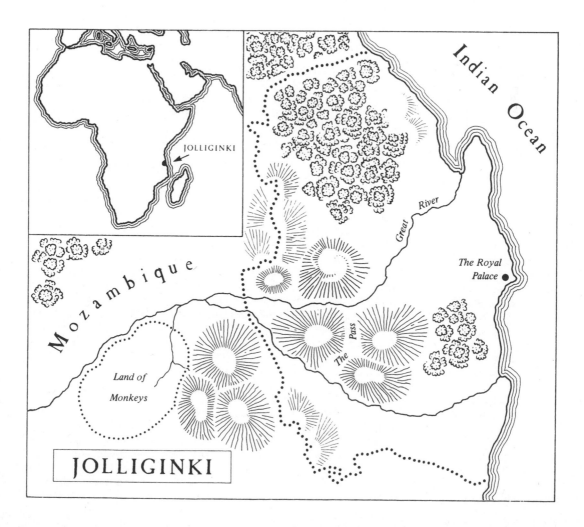

separates the two countries, but this can only be done by walking over a chain of live monkeys, called the "Bridge of Apes." Dr. Dolittle was the first white man to accomplish this extraordinary feat, although it is said that many great explorers and grey-bearded naturalists have lain long weeks hidden in the jungle waiting to see the monkeys form the chain.

From here Dr. Dolittle brought back to England the rarest animal in the world, a gift from the monkey-folk for curing their sick. This shy, polite creature, the *pushmi-pullyu*, had no tail, but a head at each end of his body, and sharp horns on each head. He was related to the Abyssinian gazelles and the Asiatic chamois on his mother's side, and his father's great-grandfather was the last of the unicorns. The *pushmi-pullyus* were terribly hard to catch since it was impossible (because of their heads at either end) to sneak up, unseen, behind them. Unfortunately, they are now extinct.

(Hugh Lofting, *The Story of Doctor Dolittle*, London, 1922)

JOLLYBOYS, ISLAND OF, see POPEFIGS' ISLAND.

JOY, ISLAND OF THE PALACE OF, perhaps in the mid-Atlantic. It can only be reached on a pilotless ship led by particular enchantments. The island consists of a splendid garden of astounding greenness some fifteen miles across, entirely surrounded by the sea. On the west coast, by the edge of the sea, stands the palace that gives its name to the island, built of marble so polished and smooth that the whole garden is reflected in it. The avenues leading up to it, and the terraces, are built of green or black marble. From the ceilings hang lush gardens and the walls are encrusted with gems and gold nuggets; some are covered with exquisite frescoes. In the park are fountains of ever-fresh water. However, the principal attraction of the Island of the Palace of Joy is its indescribable perfume.

The very beautiful ladies who live in the palace choose to pass most of their time in a small pavilion decorated with enamel *cloisonné* and gold, under a golden roof supported by crystal columns. It must be noted that the palace is in fact a trap created by Malagigi the magician, in order to attract young men to the island for the fair Angelica to fall in love with. (See also ALBRACA.)

(Matteo Maria Boiardo, *Orlando innamorato*, Milan, 1487)

JOYEUSEGARDE ("Joyful Guard"), a castle in England, several days' ride from CAMELOT. The outside of the castle is plastered and the plaster work is chromed, so that it shines like gold in the sunlight. Its roof is of slate and tile, broken by numerous towers and connecting bridges. The castle was originally known as the Douleureuse Garde or "Sorrowful Guard." It was later renamed by Sir Launcelot when he took it in his first great exploit after being dubbed a knight at the age of eighteen.

It was in this castle that Sir Launcelot lived in adultery with Guinevere, wife of King Arthur. In anger, Arthur laid siege to the castle and blockaded it for two months until a message arrived from the Pope commanding Launcelot to send Guinevere back. Reluctantly, the lovers parted and Guinevere left with her husband.

After Arthur's death at the hands of Mordred during the last battle on Salisbury Plain, Launcelot took religious vows and began to starve himself to death. His last request was that he be taken back to the castle to die. His wish was obeyed and travellers can now see his tomb lying in the peaceful vaults.

(Anonymous, *La Mort le Roi Artu*, 13th cen. AD; Sir Thomas Malory, *Le Morte Darthur*, London, 1485; T.H. White, *The Once and Future King*, London, 1939)

JOYOUS ISLE, an island of uncertain location. Travellers are advised that it is difficult to reach, as it is surrounded by wide stretches of deep water with no bridges. The main building on the isle is the Castle of Bliant, to which Sir Launcelot went with Elaine after having been cured of his madness at CORBIN. It is noted for its large tournament ground overlooked by a spectators' gallery. It is said that Sir Launcelot defeated five hundred knights here in a single tournament.

(Sir Thomas Malory, *Le Morte Darthur*, London, 1485)

JUAM, one of the largest islands of the MARDI ARCHIPELAGO and, collectively, the several wooded isles that engirdle it. The first view of Juam is imposing: a dark green pile of cliffs present a range of steep, gable-pointed projections, as if some titanic hammer and chisel had shaped the mass. The sea bursts into the surrounding lagoon through a breach in the reef.

Cautiously evading the dangerous currents which ruffle the lagoon, travellers will enter a long verdant bay to the north of Juam. In the centre of the island lies the glen of Willamilla, the hereditary abode of the monarchs of Juam. Two handsome villages can be seen in Willamilla. The village to the west is inhabited in the afternoon and the one to the east in the morning; this enables the inhabitants to spend all day in the shade.

The House of the Morning is a fanciful palace raised upon a natural mound, almost completely filling a deep recess between dark green and projecting cliffs and overlooking many huts distributed through the shadows of the groves beyond. The palace took five hundred moons to complete, for the architect laid coconut seeds in its quadrangular foundations and the trees took that long to sprout up into pillars. The trees are horizontally connected across the façade by elaborately carved scarlet beams which also support the rafters. Aromatic grasses cover the roof, shaded by the tufted tops of the palm trees, and bright birds flit and sing through this vibrating verdure. A second and third colonnade form the most beautiful bowers. The sides of the palace are hedged by *diomi* bushes, bearing a flower called *lenora* or "sweet breath"; within these odorous hedges lie heavy piles of mats, richly dyed and embroidered. Three sparkling rivulets flow through the palace into a basin beneath, from which they flow down the vale. The rivulets cascading down the back of the palace in a crystal sheet, the waving perfumed greenery, the melodious birds, the scented air, make it hard for a traveller to say whether he has reached a magic garden or a grotto in the sea.

To the rear of the House of the Morning are three separate arbours leading to less public apartments. If travellers pass through the central arbour, perhaps fancying it may lead them out into the open, they will come upon the most private retreat of the monarch of Juam; a square structure, as plain as a pyramid and twice as inscrutable. Its walls are thatched down to the very ground but on the far side a passageway opens which travellers should enter. Scarcely a yard away stands yet another thatched wall as blank as the first. Passing along the intervening corridor, lighted by narrow apertures, travellers will reach the opposite side where a second opening is revealed. Through this,

another corridor is reached, dimmer than the first, and a third blank wall. Thus, three times three, travellers must worm round and round—the twilight lessening as they proceed—until at last they enter the citadel itself, the innermost arbour of a nest. The heart of the palace is small, illuminated by open skylights. Here the visitor can only look towards the heavens, gazing at the torchlight processions in the sky. In this almost impenetrable retreat the king of Juam, as the husk-in husked meat in a nut, sits in state, universe-rounded, zodiac-belted, horizon-zoned, sea-girt, reef-sashed, mountain-locked, arbour-nested, royalty-girdled, arm-clasped and self-hugged—the perfect insphered sphere of spheres.

The House of the Afternoon is little more than a wing built against a grotto running into the side of the mountain. The mouth of the grotto is protected by a long arbour supported by great blocks of stone rudely chiselled into likenesses of idols, each bearing a carved lizard on its chest. From the grotto issues a stream, the most important in the valley, which has been trapped in a lengthy canal inside the mountain and here escapes into the open only to be caught in a large stone basin. The stream is meant to symbolize life: man bounds out of night, runs and babbles in the sun, then returns to his darkness again.

Deep inside the House of the Afternoon visitors can see the stone image of Demi, the tutelar deity of Willamilla. All green and oozy like a stone under water, Demi looks as though harassed by sciatica and lumbago. The pavement of the House of the Afternoon, according to the custom of the island, is inlaid with the skeletons of the ancient kings of Juam—each surrounded by a mosaic of red, white and black corals, intermixed with vitreous stones fallen from the skies in a meteoric shower, delineating the tattoos of the dead kings. A sceptre hangs over each skull and visitors will certainly notice the royal weapons embedded nearby.

Travellers invited to a meal on Juam should be familiar with the dining customs there. The trunk of a large tree, hollowed out and filled with water, serves as a liquid table. Upon it, in small plates in the form of ships, the viands are presented and then pushed across the water from guest to guest. No more is known about the customs of the island.

(Herman Melville, *Mardi, and A Voyage Thither*, New York, 1849)

JUKANS, VALLEY OF THE, a thickly forested mountain valley in the underground continent of PELLUCIDAR, not far from AZAR and across the mountains from OOG. There are several villages in the forest clearings; the principal and best-known one is Meeza.

Meeza is in fact so large that it almost deserves to be called a city. It is surrounded by a high palisade with one heavily guarded gate. Inside lies a confused jumble of houses. There are no streets to speak of; the buildings cluster closely together and then give way to wide spaces before closing in again. No two houses are alike. All sorts of materials are used in their construction: wattle, bark, grass and wood. Some are merely low grass huts, others are square wooden constructions. A twenty-foot tower may stand next to an oblong bark cabin, or an elaborate wattle hut next to the most primitive type of grass shack.

In the centre of Meeza stands the King's Palace, a low rambling structure which covers over an acre of land. It is virtually a village in its own right, but does not seem to follow any rational plan. Winding corridors suddenly end in blank walls; pitch black rooms open off several corridors; other rooms are in fact little courts open to the sky. Some parts are very crowded with both people and furniture, while sections of the building appear to have been abandoned for years. A hidden corridor leads to a cave above a forest ravine outside the village, known as the Ravine of the Kings. Visitors should note that it is virtually impossible to make one's way through the palace without a guide.

The Jukans are as curious as their architecture and seem to be affected by a strain of hereditary madness. They are extremely unpredictable and prone to great violence when angered or contradicted, killing at the slightest provocation. The "streets" of Meeza are full of people doing the most extraordinary things; the visitor may come across a man beating himself over the head with a rock or trying to strangle himself, or a woman torturing her child with a stone knife. However, no one takes any notice of these things.

Jukans usually have short, cropped hair and wear loin-cloths of cured monkey-skin with the hair still attached. They wear amulets of the same skin and gnashing necklaces of human teeth.

The god of the Jukans is Ogar, represented as a grotesque creature, half human and half beast, to whom visitors are sacrificed. An obscene statue of Ogar stands outside the palace; it is the custom to salute it by saying "Greetings, Ogar" in a friendly but not too familiar fashion. A number of men can usually be seen turning cartwheels in front of the idol; these are the priests, praying on behalf of the whole village. It is typical of the Jukans that they believe themselves to be the most beautiful and powerful people in the whole of Pellucidar; they describe themselves as the children of Ogar. It is also typical of the Jukans that each inhabitant claims to be the only sane person in the village and says that everyone else is raving mad.

A similar civilization exists on the surface of the earth: the XUJAN KINGDOM.

(Edgar Rice Burroughs, *Land of Terror*, New York, 1944)

JUMEAUX, ISLE DES, see CANNIBAL ISLAND.

JUMELLES, two islands of roughly equal size, not far from the coast of New Zealand and separated by a channel one and a half leagues wide. Language and religion are the same on both islands, which trade in wood and stone. The Lake-Dwellers' Island is so called because its inhabitants live on an inland lake forty leagues wide, dotted with islets which are linked to one another by bridges. The houses are usually two storeys high, built of wood and varnished red or black. The windows are made of transparent horn and the interiors are decorated with porcelain ornaments and metal mirrors.

The King's Island is rich and fertile. The capital, Deliarbou, is built in a perfect circle and its buildings are of stone. Marble fountains stand at every crossroads. Throughout the island are caves, used as lodges, carpeted and richly ornamented. The monarch of King's Island rules over the aristocracy. The upper classes wear chains around their necks bearing the inscription "We are nothing without him."

On King's Island, polygamy is punishable by death: on Lake-Dwellers' Island, male adulterers are put to death and the women are stripped naked in public, have their noses cut off, and are then left in the woods to die. The religion of Jumelles Islands calls for the sacrifice of a white heifer at each full moon. The inhabitants believe in a single creator and think that the individual soul is part of

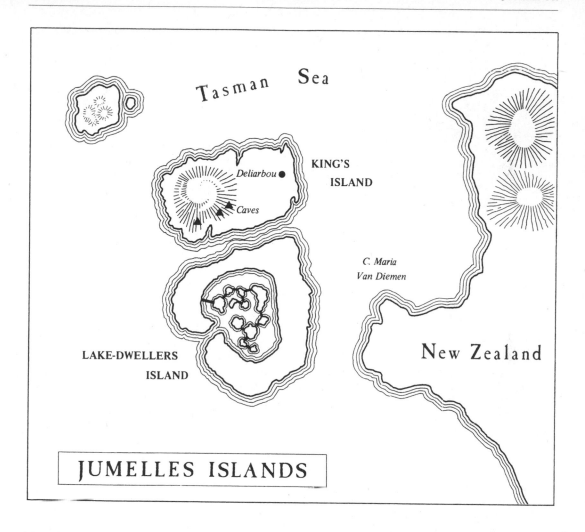

JUMELLES ISLANDS

him. They also believe that evil-doers are reborn as animals. They eat bread made of boiled potatoes, and drink a spirit made from tree sap.

(de Catalde, *Le Paysan Gentilhomme, Ou Avantures De M. Ransay: Avec Son Voyage Aux Isles Jumelles. Par Monsieur De Catalde,* Paris, 1737)

JUNDAPUR, a small Indian state ruled by a rajah, reminiscent of the squirearchy of English villages. The palace is an eighteenth-century construction of grey stone in the Palladian style. It stands in rolling parkland, but the encircling walls are crumbling and no longer prevent cattle from straying into the grounds. There is a lake behind the palace with a small, wooded island in the

middle. On the island stands a hexagonal cage, topped by a copper-plated onion dome, with walls of latticed ironwork. The cage contains plants originally brought from New Guinea, and the stuffed birds of paradise which appear to fly among them were collected by the grandfather of the last maharajah.

A long time ago, according to legend, the rajah's daughter fell in love with a boatman, not realizing that he was the god Krishna. She escaped one night and ran to the shore, throwing herself into his arms. The girl's brother surprised them and cried out, but only the call of a heron was heard, for the lake had fallen under the god's spell. Upon seeing the intruder, Krishna revealed his true identity; the brother fainted and his

The Palladian-style palace in JUNDAPUR, with its high minarets and gilded dome.

sister died of fright. Another legend has it that both brother and sister were turned into herons, whose call can be heard when the moon rises after midnight.

The town of Jundapur itself is undistinguished, a confusion of narrow streets and open shops.

(Paul Scott, *The Birds of Paradise*, London, 1962)

JUNGANYIKA or **SECRET LAKE**, in West Africa. The only known access is by the Little Fantippo River, which flows into the sea at FAN-TIPPO. The lake is surrounded by mangrove swamps and confusing streams which do not appear to flow in any specific direction, and is perpetually shrouded in mist. The animals that inhabit the lake and its surroundings say that it contains the original water from Noah's Flood: when the Flood passed away, the rest of the world dried out, but the lake remained, guarded by its girdle of mangrove swamps.

One of the very few explorers known to have reached the lake is Dr. John Dolittle, of PUDDLEBY-ON-THE-MARSH, who came to it at the request of Old Mudface, the only living animal to remember the Flood itself. Old Mudface is a gigantic turtle, the last survivor of a species that could live in both salt and fresh water. Mudface was suffering from gout. In exchange for treatment, he told his life story to Dr. Dolittle, giving him the only known account of the world before the Flood. In gratitude, Dr. Dolittle built an artificial island — part of which still stands — in the middle of the lake, by having thousands and thousands of birds drop small stones and pieces of gravel into the muddy waters. This is why, many years later, a party of geologists claimed that the

presence of seashore gravel on the island was proof that it had once been under the sea. In a sense they were right, but the sea they referred to was the Flood itself.

Some years later, an earthquake considerably altered the landscape and also destroyed part of the artificial island. Mudface, buried under the mud for a number of years, nevertheless survived. The earthquake revealed the ruins of the city of Shalba, capital of King Mashtu, ruler of a rich and powerful kingdom before the Flood. These ruins are the only extant evidence as to the nature of the civilization of that period and students of archaeology will profit vastly by a visit.

Lake Junganyika owes its name to events that took place after the Great Flood. Old Mudface rescued two human beings from the Flood: Eber, an assistant zoo-keeper who worked under Noah, and Gaza, the girl he loved. He defended them bravely from the tigress who wanted to kill them and from all those animals who wanted to see human beings exterminated or reduced to slavery. Eber and Gaza did not speak the same language and communicated by combining words from their respective tongues. When Mudface brought them preserved dates from the flooded ruins of the city, Eber called out "Junga," his word for dates, while Gaza named them in her own language, "Nyika." The combination of the two words gave the lake its name. Eber and Gaza were finally taken away from this area, for their own safety, by turtles who carried them to what subsequently became known as America. Until the arrival of Dr. Dolittle, no other human being had set foot on the shores of the Secret Lake.

(Hugh Lofting, *Doctor Dolittle's Post Office*, London, 1924; Hugh Lofting, *Doctor Dolittle and the Secret Lake*, London, 1949)

JURASSIC PARK, an experimental amusement park on Isla Nublar, eight miles long and three miles wide at its widest point. It lies not far from the Cabo Blanco Biological Reserve, on the west coast of Costa Rica, and seasoned travellers will find it reminiscent of MAPLE WHITE LAND, also known as the LOST WORLD. Isla Nublar is not a real island; it is a seamount, a volcanic upthrusting of rock from the ocean floor, rich in tropical vegetation. In many places the ground is hot underfoot, and steam gushes out of vents and cracks throughout the area. Because of the steam and the prevailing currents, the island is constantly hidden in a dense mist—hence the Spanish name Nublar, meaning "to cloud over or shroud in fog." At the north end of Isla Nublar, green hills rise two thousand feet above the ocean. Access is either by sea from the mainland, or by helicopter. From either the harbour or the landing strip, narrow paths lead to the building complex—visitors' centre, laboratories, lodges, etc.—elaborate constructions that seem out of place in the midst of a tropical forest. Over the entrance to the complex, a crude hand-painted sign reads, WELCOME TO JURASSIC PARK.

At least fifteen different species of dinosaurs inhabit Jurassic Park, cloned from the DNA of dinosaur blood drawn from the stomachs of mosquitoes found in prehistoric amber. The dinosaurs are "created" in the park's laboratories, an area accessible only to authorized personnel. Teratogenic substances, radioactive isotopes and virulent poisons are used in the cloning experiments. Dinosaur eggs are carefully nursed in the hatchery until the dinosaurs are born, and then the infant dinosaurs are released into the park for the amusement of visitors.

Great precautions have been taken to prevent the dinosaurs from escaping into the outside world. An electric fence keeps the dangerous creatures away from visitors, but stronger measures are also in place. The dinosaurs have been deliberately created "lysine-dependent"; a gene inserted into their DNA causes them to have a single faulty protein enzyme. As a result, the dinosaurs cannot manufacture the amino acid lysine and, unless they get a rich dietary source of lysine, supplied by the keepers of Jurassic Park in tablet form, it is said that they will go into a coma within twelve hours, and die. Furthermore, should one of the animals escape, the alarm would be raised by the park's computers, which count the herds every few minutes.

There was a serious incident several years ago, in which a number of dinosaurs managed to escape into the outside world and wreak havoc among park visitors and the inhabitants of the surrounding villages. The park has now been refurbished, and is open to the public. However, visitors are cautioned to be extremely prudent when touring the facilities, and are advised that neither the Jurassic Park administration nor the government of Costa Rica will assume any liability in case of an accident.

(Michael Crichton, *Jurassic Park*, New York, 1990)

JUSTICE, PALACE OF, a large rambling building in an unnamed city, where people are summoned for unspecified charges. Whoever enters the Palace of Justice is told by hurried men with briefcases under their arms to proceed farther and farther inside the building. Innumerable doors line the walls, decorated with bronze plaques whose inscriptions have been eroded by time. Those who reach one of the last halls are made to wait for several days on a wooden bench. After a few weeks of waiting they will, out of boredom, ask the clerks working in the room whether they can be of any help. This assistance will soon become a full-time job and finally, one day, a judge will promote the patient helper to the post of secretary. Many years later, the so-appointed secretary will notice that the clerks address him as "Your Honour." He is made to sign papers. Among these papers is a verdict of guilty *in absentia*. The now almost senile judge seems to remember the name of the accused but, unable to stop the established routine, he signs his name on the paper.

(Marco Denevi, "¿El primer cuento de Kafka?" in *Falsificaciones*, Buenos Aires, 1966)

K

K, VALLEY OF, see ALIFBAY.

KABIN, a small, pleasant, walled town in the far north-east of the BEKLAN EMPIRE, on the Vrako, a tributary of the Telthearna River, which for many years formed the frontier of the empire. In olden days, travellers who crossed the Vrako from the east were assumed to have come back from the lawless area of ZERAY, and were either sent back or killed. Since the end of the wars of the empire this situation has changed and visitors can cross the river without being mistaken for outlaws, as Zeray is now a civilized place. Kabin is no longer the frontier town it once was.

Kabin is famed for its reservoir which supplies the city of BEKLA with water, via a conduit which crosses the Beklan Plain before reaching the city some sixty miles away. The reservoir itself is to the north of Kabin, between two green spurs of land; visitors will notice the large outfall dam and the complex system of gates and sluices which control the amount of water reaching the conduit.

(Richard Adams, *Shardik*, London, 1974)

KADATH, an immense icy city said never to have been explored by travellers. It is found beyond the LENG Plateau and is said to contain mysteries beyond the imagination. Travellers set upon visiting Kadath must seek the help of ghouls.

Kadath, with its enormous onyx castle, is said to be the inviolate capital of DREAMWORLD.

(Howard Phillips Lovecraft, "The Dream-Quest of Unknown Kadath," in *Arkham Sampler*, Sauk City, 1948)

KALI, a kingdom in the underground continent of PELLUCIDAR, some eight hundred miles to the north-east of SARI. The centre of Kali is a cave-village dug out of a limestone cliff—the last rampart of a volcanic mountain range running to the north-east, parallel to the coast of the Lural Az. Beyond the cliff, the ground rises until it meets a ridge of volcanic rock; there the lush vegetation gives way to sparse plants. Only one volcano in this range is still active.

Kali is inhabited by two separate races: the Cliff Dwellers—who, like some other tribes found in Pellucidar, live in caves connected by rickety ladders and use a few thatched shelters at the foot of the cliff for food preparation and communal activities—and the Sabretooth Men, who inhabit the higher areas of the mountain range. The latter are a race of black-skinned cannibals with prehensile tails and long tusks on either side of their mouths. They have heavy protruding brows, short, stiff black hair and close-set eyes. The Sabretooth Men do not speak the normal language of Pellucidarians but communicate in a strange monkey-like jabbering. An encounter with either tribe may prove dangerous.

(Edgar Rice Burroughs, *Return to Pellucidar,* New York, 1941; Edgar Rice Burroughs, *Men of the Bronze Age*, New York, 1942)

KALOON, a vast land somewhere in central Asia, beyond a mountain chain and a desert. Kaloon is an alluvial plain, perhaps the bottom of an ancient lake, well cultivated and fertile, and crossed by a river in the middle of which rises a city also called Kaloon. The city's buildings form terraces on an island embraced by a fork in the river and tower over a hundred feet above the level of the plain. The largest building in Kaloon is the Khan's Palace decorated with columns, crowned with towers and surrounded by gardens.

Kaloon was conquered by Rassen, an Egyptian general of Alexander the Great, who introduced the Greek language into Kaloon and established a reigning dynasty which has lasted to this day.

The inhabitants of Kaloon have Tartar blood and ignore all forms of commerce; there is no local currency in spite of the many precious metals mined in this area, which the inhabitants use to make ornaments. The rulers believe in magic and the people adore the goddess Isis who is said to reside on Mount HES.

(Henry Rider Haggard, *Ayesha. The Return of She,* London, 1905)

KANBADON, see VITI ISLANDS.

KARAIN CONTINENT, a large island in the south Pacific, now largely under European control.

The population is mixed. It appears that the original inhabitants were Caucasian, but successive

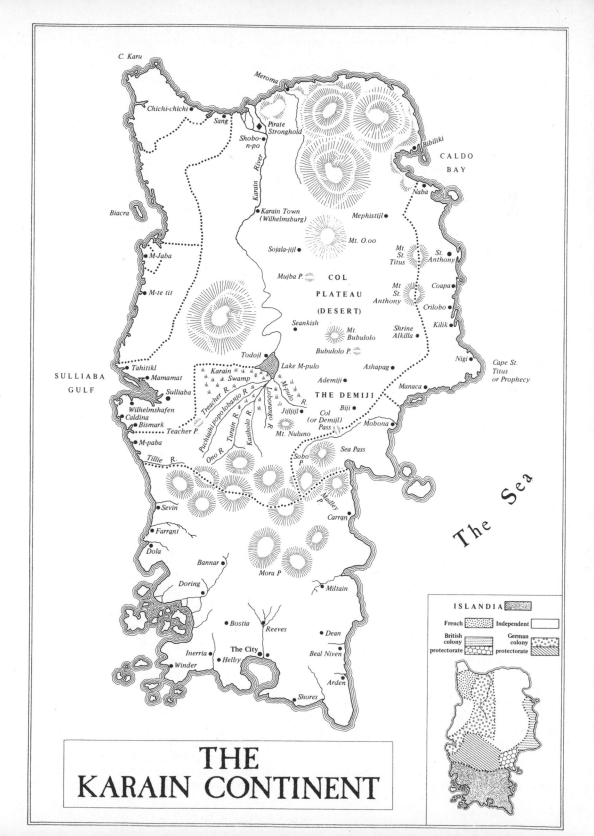

THE
KARAIN CONTINENT

waves of immigration brought the Negro Bants tribe and Arab settlers who arrived here after the hegira. The Karain population are the descendants of these two races. Originally living on the coastal plains they have gradually been driven into the interior, as the coast increasingly comes under European influence and control. Some of the tribes of the interior are still very primitive, notably the mountain Bants, traditional enemies of the Islandians (see ISLANDIA).

The largest city in Karain is Mobono, now the capital of a British protectorate but formerly the seat of the Karain emperors. It is an ancient and somewhat sinister city, crowded and poverty-stricken, built on a plain and dominated by the rectangular terraces of the Palace of the Emperors. In the fourteenth century, Mobono was captured and occupied for two years by Queen Alwina of Islandia. The Islandian poet Bodwin lived here for many years; the reference to "a high tower in an evil city," in his writings, is taken to mean the Palace.

St. Anthony, the port at which steamers from Southampton dock, lies to the north of Mobono. The city is built in a broad valley connected to the sea by a narrow, twisting gorge. The brownstone houses climb terraces up the steep sides of the U-shaped valley, finally giving way to high limestone cliffs. Travellers will notice the characteristic smell of the city—a mixture of humanity and half-rotten vegetables. The people of St. Anthony, now a Crown colony, are mulattoes, probably descended from both the original Caucasian population and the Bants. They have dark eyes and soft, gentle features, and refer to themselves as the Lambs of God. It is said that the black and white races remained separate until the arrival of Christian missionaries, when they took literally the doctrine that all men were brothers, and as the only course of virtue, intermarried. The men wear baggy, dark-blue trousers and the women wear sombre brown robes.

Immediately north of the Mount Islandia massif lie the Sobo Steppes, a dry grassy area dotted with walled towns, inhabited by mixed races of Karain and Bants, now a German protectorate. Although Germany recognizes the independence and integrity of Islandia, she was responsible for the border incidents of 1908 when Bants raiders looted and pillaged along the vast Islandian border; relations between Germany and Islandia are therefore at times somewhat strained. As a result,

visitors with German passports may find it difficult to obtain visas to Islandia.

The interior of the continent, including the desert wastes of the Col Plateau, remain independent, but most of the coastal areas are now under European control. Britain has a colony and a protectorate on the east coast, while Germany controls large areas of the regions to the west of the Karain River. France has a small protectorate on the west coast, and a steamer service connects the French port of Biacra with Cherbourg, France.

(Austin Tappan Wright, *Islandia*, New York, 1944; Mark Saxton, *The Islar, or Islandia Today—A Narrative of Lang III*, Boston, 1969)

KAREGO-AT, see KARGAD EMPIRE.

KARGAD EMPIRE, a group of four islands—Karego-At, Atuan, Atnini and Hur-at-Hur—to the east of the archipelago of EARTHSEA.

Although the empire is now at peace with the lands of Earthsea, they were bitter enemies for centuries. The Kargs were feared as wild sea-rovers and pirates who swooped down on the outer islands in search of loot. Ethnically and linguistically distinct from the people of the archipelago, the Kargs remain hostile and aloof.

The hostility between the two communities appears to date back to ancient times. According to the Kargs, the wizards of Earthsea would carry out raids on the empire, allegedly to kill dragons, but staying on to pillage and burn. The conflict came to a head when Erreth-Akbe, the wizard-king of Earthsea, came to Awabath, capital of the empire, and joining forces with a group of rebel lords tried to take control of the city. It is said that he and the High Priest fought long and hard in the stone temple, which was eventually destroyed around them. Erreth-Akbe was defeated and his wizard's staff was broken by the High Priest. Deprived of his power, the wizard-king fled west, where he was finally killed by a dragon on the distant island of SELIDOR. The defeat of Erreth-Akbe had important consequences for both the empire and the archipelago. The ring or amulet worn by the wizard was broken and one half was buried in the tombs of Atuan. The other half was given to a Kargish lord. The loss of the ring meant the beginning of the slow decline of Earthsea; not until both parts were recovered was the archipelago again united under a single king on HAVNOR.

The consequences for the empire were even more momentous. Intathin the High Priest was the first of the line of Tarb, from which the Priest Kings of Karego-At descended. As their power extended and became more solidly based they came to rule all four islands of what is now the empire and took the title of the Godkings of Kargad. The rise of the Godkings meant the end of the feuding between petty princes that had traditionally prevented the Kargad lands from developing into a unified country, and laid the basis for its future greatness. Gradually the empire began to eclipse Earthsea and it became dangerous for any archipelagan to venture there. Most of those who did so were mages seeking the lost ring of Erreth-Akbe and many of them died as a result of their quest.

In cultural terms, the rise of the Godkings meant far-reaching changes in the life of the empire. Magic was forbidden as being contrary to their teachings and became closely associated with the evil memory of the dark-skinned wizards from the west. Even reading and writing fell into decline, being regarded as black arts. But the most significant change was in religious beliefs. The self-styled Godkings became the object of a religious cult which they themselves encouraged. The temple of the Godkings on Atuan began to be more important than the traditional sacred site—the celebrated Tombs of Atuan.

These tombs were the centre of the ancient religion of the islands, the worship of the Nameless Ones, who represented the ancient powers of earth and darkness and who were served by a priestess. She was believed to live on after her death; as soon as the priestess died, servants of the cult set out to find the girl-child in whom she had been reincarnated, and brought her to the Hall of the Throne where she was dedicated to the cult in a symbolic sacrifice. She became the One Priestess, the Eaten One, and began to study the lore of the Nameless Ones. She alone had the right to enter the labyrinth beneath the monoliths known as the Tombs of Atuan. No light was permitted in the labyrinth and the girl had to learn her way by touch and memory, gradually coming to know and love her dark and sacred domain.

As the cult of the Godkings became more important, that of the Nameless Ones tended to be neglected and the Great Hall of the Throne fell into disrepair. Fewer and fewer prisoners were sent by the Godking to be left to die in the labyrinth and to be eaten by the Nameless Ones.

When the first part of the ring of Erreth-Akbe was recovered on SPRINGWATER ISLE, the future Archmage Ged was sent to Atuan to seek the other half. He was able to enter the labyrinth but not even his magic could open the doors to let him out again. While trapped in the winding passages, Ged was mocked and tormented by the One Priestess, Arha, but she gradually began to feel sympathy for him and rescued him from those who would have had him killed, even helping him locate the lost half of the ring. However, when the two returned through the dark passages, the earth began to tremble and groan as the Nameless Ones sought their revenge. Ged was able to hold off the earthquake until they reached safety, but the tombs were then swallowed up by the earth and the labyrinth was totally destroyed. The only building that now stands in the area is the gold-roofed temple of the Godkings. It is not known if the destruction of the tombs led to the final disappearance of the cult of the Nameless Ones, but it is known that Arha left the island and settled on GONT.

Of the islands of the empire, Atuan is the best known, although Hur-at-Hur, the largest mountainous island to the north, is famed for its cedar forests. The west of Atuan is a fruit-growing area, and much of the interior is high ground covered with aspens and junipers. The people of Atuan live mostly in scattered huts and small settlements in the hill-country. Their towns are usually built to the same pattern, with buildings made of clay bricks surrounded by a defensive wall with watchtowers at each corner; a single gate pierces the wall. A characteristic feature of Kargish architecture is the overhanging battlements.

After the recovery of the ring of Erreth-Akbe, Earthsea was reunited under one king and regained much of its former glory. Hostilities between the empire and the archipelago lessened and the Kargish raids finally ceased. Some trade agreements were made, but in general the Kargs remained aloof from the affairs of Earthsea. The old Kargish prejudice against magic appears to have been largely overcome and it is not unknown for the sons of rich merchants to come west to ROKE to study magic.

(Ursula K. Le Guin, A *Wizard of Earthsea*, New York, 1968; Ursula K. Le Guin, *The Tombs of Atuan*, London, 1972; Ursula K. Le Guin, *The Farthest Shore*, London, 1973)

KARKAR, SEA OF, probably part of the Atlantic Ocean, near the northwestern coast of Morocco. The coastal area is inhabited by a tribe of Negroes who speak an incomprehensible language and dress in strange furs. They have a knowledge of Islam because they are often visited by a person from the sea, who diffuses a strong light and who announces that there is no god but God and that Mohammed is His Prophet. And every Friday night a light shines on this tract of sea, and a voice calls out a holy prayer.

Emir Moosa ibn Museyr visited this tribe when returning from the City of BRASS, and obtained from them twelve brass bottles in which King Solomon had imprisoned a number of rebel jinns. The king of the Negro tribe gave Emir Moosa, as a gift, one of the greatest wonders of the sea: a fish with a human form. However, on the way back to Damascus, because of the great heat, the fish died. Its like has never been found again.

(Anonymous, *The Arabian Nights*, 14th–16th cen. AD)

KARPATHENBURG, a castle in the wilds of Transylvania, in the County of Klausenburg, occupying a solitary peak of Mount Vulkan, in the region of Orgall. The nearest village is Werst, on the southern slope of the Plesa Massif. The road leading to Karpathenburg is now covered with

A brass jinn-bottle from the Sea of KARKAR, presented to Emir Moosa.

vegetation, and of the castle itself only a few bare ruins remain.

Karpathenburg was built in the twelfth or thirteenth century and belonged to the family of Baron Gortz. The last descendant, Baron Rudolf of Gortz—famous for his love of operas and his passion for a certain Italian singer—disappeared towards the end of the nineteenth century, after becoming involved in one of the many Rumanian revolts against the fierce Hungarian oppression. The castle remained abandoned after his disappearance, provoking visions of ghosts and spirits in the imagination of the people of Transylvania. A legend arose concerning a large beech tree that used to grow near the castle ramparts. When Baron Rudolf vanished, the tree lost one of its branches, and a new branch fell every consecutive year. According to legend, when the last branch of the beech tree disappeared, the castle itself would be destroyed. Because of these superstitions, for many years no one approached the peak of Mount Vulkan, and the road to the castle became overgrown.

In 1892, a shepherd, amazed to see smoke rising from the castle chimneys, informed the villagers that he had seen a portent. After much hesitation, two of the villagers decided to investigate. One was felled by an invisible force when trying to cross a small fence; the other became trapped in the mud of the moat. Finally, a Rumanian nobleman, Count Franz of Telek, solved the mystery of Karpathenburg. He climbed the walls with a faithful attendant and saw upon the ramparts the beautiful figure of Gortz's beloved Italian singer whom the world had thought dead for a long time, giving a recital of some of her best arias.

Staggered by this apparition, the Count entered the castle and found Baron Gortz, alive and well, living with an old servant, an expert in electrical appliances. The Count discovered that the singer's voice had been recorded on a gramophone and that the apparition was an optical illusion created by an electrical device. With the use of mirrors set at a precise angle, and a powerful lamp, a reflection of a small portrait of the singer was enlarged to lifelike dimensions. She thus appeared in all her former beauty, as when she reigned as queen of the Italian stage.

Baron Gortz, realizing that his secret had been discovered, blew up his castle and died, buried in its ruins. Visitors should note that a similar apparatus was set up by Monsieur Morel on VILLINGS Island.

(Jules Verne, *Le Château des Carpathes*, Paris, 1892)

KAYOSS, an island opposite BROOLYI.

KELSO, capital of NIMPATAN.

KERNEL, THE, see OCEANA (2).

KEY, FOREST OF, a wooded area in the form of a key between Yesteryear's domain and the Lands of Count Sadolf. The Forest was won by Count Yesteryear's father when he challenged Sadolf, a local robber-baron, to a game of chess. The game must be repeated every twenty-five years to secure possession of the Forest of Key.

Travellers arriving in the Forest will first reach the house of Melas, the hermit, who will exhort them to repent and then offer them wine. Two large buildings can be seen in the Forest: the airy Castle of Count Yesteryear, Melangloria, with its two towers, one of which is called the Tower of Swine; and the Fortress of Despair, in a denser part of the Forest where no birds sing and where all inhabitants are plagued by misfortune.

The Forest of Key is unique because its inhabitants believe they are governed like pawns in a game of chess played by invisible contestants who move them across a gigantic board. A similar though perhaps less coherent philosophy is

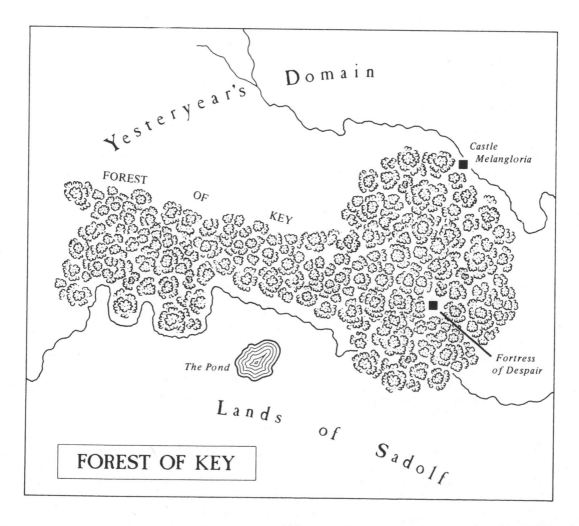

FOREST OF KEY

expounded by the people of LOOKING-GLASS LAND.

(Paul Hulshof & Robert Vincent Schipper, *Glazewijn en het schaak-schandaal*, Amsterdam, 1973)

KINGDOM 90, see POLIARCOPOLIS.

KING KONG'S ISLAND, see SKULL ISLAND.

KINGS, ISLE OF, see GREAT WATER.

KING'S KINGDOM, in the Indian Ocean, is considered by some explorers to be the burial grounds of King Solomon, son of David, despite the fact that other authorities place his tomb in SABA. Described by, among others, Sinbad the Sailor, King's Kingdom is famous for its terrible-looking serpents. Notable also are the large fish that live in this region, capable of swallowing a ship whole. Sinbad has described three of these creatures, said to be as high as mountains.

(Anonymous, *The Arabian Nights*, 14th–16th cen. AD)

KING SOLOMON'S MINES, discovered by Allan Quatermain's expedition to KUKUANA-LAND, Africa, in 1884. The expedition found a large avenue, partly excavated from the live rock, leading into the heart of a high mountain and branching into several galleries, from Mount Suliman to the capital of the country, LOO, and from there to the Three Witches Mountain. The avenue is preserved impeccably free of sand by the king of Kukuanaland, who holds the white road in holy awe.

Reaching the central peak of the Three Witches Mountain, travellers will see a vast cavity some fifty metres deep: these are the diamond mines of King Solomon lying open under the African sky. At the farthest end of the cavity rise three colossal seated statues called The Silent Ones by the natives: they are set on stone pedestals some twenty feet from one another. Each statue measures seven metres from top to bottom. One of them represents a woman of severe beauty, though her form has been eroded by the elements, the other two a terrifying devil and a serene man whose serenity, however, seems to have an adverse effect on visitors. They are said to represent the three gods: Astoreth, the Sidonian deity; Chemos, God of the Morebites; and Milcom, god of the Ammones.

Some fifty feet behind the colossi is the entrance to a tunnel leading into an enormous cavern illuminated from the top, full of stalactites similar to ice columns some of which are sculptured vaguely like Egyptian mummies. Another tunnel leads from here into a darker chamber which the people of Kukuanaland call the Place of Death and in which they bury their kings. In the back of this room sits a large human skeleton, some five metres tall, holding a spear in its hand, as if about to throw it; its other hand leans on a stone table giving the impression that the bones are about to rise. Around the table are placed the mummies of the ancient kings of Kukuanaland, petrified through the ages by the chemicals in the cavern's air.

From the Place of Death a secret door, opened by means of a mysterious device, leads into the Chamber of Solomon's Treasure, where over four hundred elephant tusks, trunks full of gold pieces and uncut diamonds of many sizes lie scattered.

Because the door of this chamber is difficult to operate, visitors are advised to take precautions before locking themselves in the treasure room.

(Henry Rider Haggard, *King Solomon's Mines*, London, 1886)

KINKENADON, a castle and city on the coast of Wales. The city and surrounding areas are rich, which is why King Arthur of CAMELOT chose it as the place for the Pentecost feasts. It was during these celebrations that Sir Gareth first came to Arthur's court. The son of Lot of Orkney and Margawse, Arthur's sister, Gareth was also the brother of Sir Gawain. Gareth was responsible for the defeat of the Black, Green, Blue and Red Knights who later agreed to serve Arthur.

(Sir Thomas Malory, *Le Morte Darthur*, London, 1485)

KIORAM, a city five hundred miles from CALNOGOR in ATVATABAR, entirely hewn from a mountain of white marble. The fortress and palace stand in a large square, occupying a commanding position. A pillared archway leads underneath the solid walls of the fortress into the heart of the rock. The top of the walls forms a level, circular roadway.

The main feature of Kioram is the moving temple of Rakamadeva or Sacred Locomotive. Made of solid gold, platinum, terrelium, aquelium and plutulium, the locomotive runs on a single elevated rail which supports it; its weight rests on six wheels in front and six behind, all concealed by the body of the car. This sacred vehicle is used exclusively by royal and privileged travellers to journey from Kioram to Calnogor in only five hours.

Kioram is also the region in which the finest Atvatabarese wine, *squang*, is made. Travellers who have tasted it compare it to the finest Alaskan vintage.

(William R. Bradshaw, *The Goddess of Atvatabar, being the History of the Discovery of the Interior World and Conquest of Atvatabar*, New York, 1892)

KIRAN, a city on the banks of the Oukranos River that runs through part of DREAMWORLD into the Cerenerian Sea. Its jasper terraces slope down to the river's edge and lead to a lovely temple where the King of Ilek-Vad comes from his far realm once a year, in a golden palanquin, to pray to the god of Oukranos. The temple is all of jasper and covers a full acre of ground with its halls and courts, its seven pinnacle towers and its inner shrine where the river enters through hidden channels and where someone is heard singing softly in the night. Travellers have heard strange music as the moon shines on the temple, but no one except the King of Ilek-Vad can say what that music is, for only he is allowed to enter the temple.

(Howard Phillips Lovecraft, "The Dream-Quest of Unknown Kadath," in *Arkham Sampler*, Sauk City, 1948)

KLED, a vast perfumed jungle in DREAMWORLD in which travellers will find sleeping palaces of ivory, solitary and unbroken, where once dwelt powerful monarchs of a land whose name is forgotten. It is said that the spells of the gods of Dreamworld keep these palaces unharmed and undecayed, for it is written in the few sacred books of these regions that there may one day be need of them again. Though elephant caravans have glimpsed them from afar by moonlight, no one dares approach them closely because of the guardians that are said to watch over them in the shadows.

(Howard Phillips Lovecraft, "The Dream-Quest of Unknown Kadath," in *Arkham Sampler*, Sauk City, 1948)

KLEPSYDRA, a sanatorium in eastern Poland, sometimes referred to as "the sanatorium under the sign of the hourglass," it is very difficult to reach. There is only one train a week and the service is at best unreliable. Even seasoned travellers will find the coaches on this line archaic specimens, mostly withdrawn from other routes, and both uncomfortable and draughty. Some are as large as living rooms, exuding an air of strange and frightening neglect, with straw and rubbish scattered about the corridors as if the passengers had been sleeping there for months. There is no real station for Klepsydra, merely a wayside halt. If arrangements are made in advance, a carriage will be sent to pick up visitors; otherwise the only way to reach the sanatorium is across the dark parkland on foot.

The surrounding countryside is dominated by a forest which rises up the sides of the valley like a cardboard stage set; the sanatorium, at the bottom of the valley's basin, can be reached by crossing a footbridge with unsteady handrails made from birch branches. It is a large horseshoe-shaped building standing in its own grounds, and is run by Dr. Gotard, discoverer of the reversion of time. Because of this singular discovery everything in the clinic is slightly late and, as a result, patients who are thought to have died in other places are still alive when they are brought here. However their deaths cannot be totally eradicated and leave a certain blot on their existence.

According to Dr. Gotard, the reversion of time is a simple matter of relativity; in spite of this explanation, the exact nature of the treatment remains a mystery. It does not appear to involve surgery, and the clinic's one and only operating theatre has obviously not been used for a long time. Nor is it certain that it results in a recovery from the disease that caused the patient to die in the first place; all that can be said with any certainty is that the past has been reactivated and that there is therefore a possibility of recovery.

Patients are encouraged to sleep for long periods. This helps to conserve their vitality and besides there is little else for them to do. Visitors to the sanatorium are often shocked by the dust that is allowed to accumulate everywhere and they say that, although at first they are welcomed and well fed, the staff and inmates rapidly become indifferent to their presence. Some patients have said that they often have the impression, as they leave their rooms, that someone who has been standing behind the door moves away rapidly and disappears around a corner without a sound.

Packs of dogs are often seen in the vicinity. The dogs are pure black, in all shapes and sizes, and run at dusk along the paths around the sanatorium, engrossed in their own affairs. They seem not to notice human beings, although they occasionally snarl as they brush past them. For reasons which are difficult to determine, the sanatorium itself keeps an enormous Alsatian in a courtyard behind the main building. It is a monstrous beast which seems to have all the demoniac savagery of a werewolf; in fact one visitor claims to have seen it assume a human form.

The sanatorium is close to an unnamed city where the streets are usually empty and the sky is always dark. Many of the shops—some of which are run by patients from the sanatorium—appear to be permanently closed, and others always seem on the point of closing. The air here is rich, heavy and soft; at times visitors will find it difficult to keep their eyes open and to resist the feeling of lethargy and sleepiness that will creep up on them. The humid atmosphere that shrouds the city is like a damp sponge that obscures parts of a view and washes things away.

The inhabitants of the town appear to spend most of their days sleeping, dozing off as they sit in cafés and restaurants or even succumbing to sleep as they walk along the streets. They appear to have no sense of the continuity of time and to be content leading fragmented, disjointed lives. The women and girls of the city walk in a bizarre manner, as though obeying some inner rhythm, along an invisible thread constantly unwinding from an invisible skein. They walk straight ahead, ignoring all obstacles, as though moved by the certainty of their own excellence and superiority.

Most of the vegetation around the city and sanatorium is black, notably a species of black fern which can be seen everywhere—in the windows of the houses and in all public places—as if it were the town's crest or symbol of mourning.

There are reports that the city has recently been invaded by an enemy army. Its appearance has encouraged the aspirations of a number of discontented citizens, who, dressed in black civilian costume with white straps across their breasts, have armed themselves with rifles and emerged to terrorize the town. There have also been reports of shooting and arson, but no detailed information is available. Travellers are therefore advised to proceed with caution.

(Bruno Schulz, *Sanatorium pod Klepsydra*, Warsaw, 1937)

KLOPSTOKIA, a country of athletes. Visitors will be surprised at the sight of babies jumping six feet into the air and elderly housewives covering a mile in a few seconds.

Klopstokia won the 1932 Olympic Games in spite of international efforts to prevent its victory. But for diplomatic reasons it has not entered the competition again.

(*Million Dollar Legs*, directed by Edward Cline, USA, 1932)

KLORIOLE, a high island of the RIALLARO ARCHIPELAGO, in the south-east Pacific. In the centre of the island stands a high hill, crowned by a huge building which can be approached by steps cut into the rock. These steps rise sheer from the sea and are stained with the blood of those who have failed in their attempts to land on the island. Upon arrival the visitor will see, dressed in fantastic garb, a number of personages sitting in high niches in attitudes of meditation, flying paper kites and writings. They are the lower acolytes of the capital's Temple of Literary Fame and their kites carry their writings up to the higher priests. Farther up, behind strong barriers, stand the suppliants, and at the top can be found fat and reclining poets. On each barrier is the following inscription: "None enter the mighty temple as gods but by this ascent." The temple contains many niches, each holding the mummy of a successful poet preserved for eternity. Farther inland, in a deep valley, lies a graveyard of bones and paper, constantly raked by scholars seeking relics of the past. To protect the landward approach to the temple, the island maintains a pack of wild geese which feed upon young poets.

The priests of Kloriole have formalized the rules for writing to such a degree of precision that content is meaningless and literature has become the art of saying nothing. The chattering of children, for instance, is recorded as a literary composition. Occasional revolts among the slaves of Kloriole threaten the priests' power. These occur when a natural genius emerges and end with a new idol being set up in the temple.

(Godfrey Sweven, *Riallaro, the Archipelago of Exiles,* New York & London, 1901; Godfrey Sweven, *Limanora, the Island of Progress,* New York & London, 1903)

KOR, the ruins of a city somewhere in central East Africa, in a small plain surrounded by rocky mountains which rise from the African steppes like a natural castle. To reach Kor, the mountains must first be crossed through an ancient canal, now empty, built by an unknown people to drain the waters from the plain.

The plain around the castle is well-cultivated and the fields almost touch the ruined city walls. Kor occupies some thirty square kilometres; the walls—those which still remain—tower to a height of twelve or fourteen metres and are very thick. Around the city runs a moat but the grandiose bridge which used to span it has now collapsed. To stand on the city walls and look into the city is to see a sight both imposing and melancholic: kilometre after kilometre of toppled columns, demolished temples, ruined altars and crumbling palaces, scattered throughout the green of an unleashed vegetation, stretches out endlessly. The main street, large and straight, built in square stone blocks, leads to the principal temple which was constructed like a set of Chinese boxes: the external walls enclose a courtyard which surrounds the inner walls, which in turn surround a smaller courtyard and so on. In the centre, on a round, dark stone base some seven metres in diameter, rises a colossal white marble statue representing a winged woman with outstretched arms and a veiled face. According to an inscription on the pedestal, it represents Truth rising above the world and asking men to lift her veil. Several other inscriptions imply that Kor was destroyed by a fearful epidemic some 4,800 years after its foundation.

The mountains around Kor are in fact a vast necropolis in which hundreds of thousands of mummies and skeletons can be seen lining vast internal galleries. One in particular, containing a pyramid of skeletons as high as St. Paul's Cathedral, should be visited. Not far from here is a grotto in which different kinds of tortures took place. For instance, in the centre is a small furnace in which the condemned person's head was placed and slowly burnt; paintings on the walls explain several other tortures that the people of Kor used to favour.

Some of these barbaric rites survive among the Amahagger, a black tribe that lives in the outer steppes. They resemble Somalians and speak a kind of bastard Arabic. In spite of having beautiful features their faces cause terror in the hearts of those who look upon them. They dress in antelope and leopard skins and are said to be excellent sculptors. The women have equal rights to men except that women are excused from working the land and the right of inheritance is restricted to the female line. Parenthood is unknown; only the chief of each village receives the name of "father." When an Amahagger woman finds a man of her liking she kisses him in front of the entire population and their union will last until she decides to take another.

All villages or "families" are under the supreme authority of one woman, *Hiya, Ayesha* (pronounced "assha") or "She" (an abbreviation of "She-Who-Must-Be-Obeyed"). It is said that *Ayesha is* two thousand years old in spite of her youthful looks, due to having been immersed in the so-called "Fire of Life," a volcanic phenomenon only found in a crater a day's march from Kor.

(Henry Rider Haggard, *She,* London, 1887)

KORSAR, a city in the tropical region of the underground continent of PELLUCIDAR and, by extension, the land lying along the coast of the Korsar Az, a sea connected with the Sojar Az by a nameless strait.

The city stands at the mouth of a wide, winding river; it is a major harbour and the port is usually full of barges and fishing-boats as well as the warships of the Korsars. With the exception of SARI and the townships of XEXOTLAND, Korsar is the only true city in Pellucidar. Its white houses with red tile roofs, its blue, red and gold domes and minarets and its bustling waterfront make Korsar an impressive sight that no traveller can afford to miss. Especially notable is the Cid's or Chief's Palace, a building which shows definite traces of Moorish influence in its design and style. It was visited by Lord Greystoke—also known as Tarzan—in an attempt to rescue the Emperor of Pellucidar.

The Korsars themselves are pirates and raiders who dress in the style of the Spanish buccaneers of the past: gaudy sashes, bright headbands and boots with floppy tops. Their ships are immense constructions, high at the prow and stern, with ornate, brightly painted figureheads representing mermaids or naked women. Propelled by sails and armed with cannons, the ships of the Korsars are—apart from the more recent vessels launched in Sari—the most efficient in Pellucidar. They are highly valued by the Korsars and visitors are warned that the theft of a ship or even a small boat is punishable by death. The main activity of the Korsars is raiding other settlements, although they do some trade with other islands, such as HIME.

The origin of the Korsars is not certain. Historical evidence suggests that they are descended from the crew of a pirate ship which somehow found its way into Pellucidar via the polar entrance, and stayed there, intermarrying with native races. This would explain their style of building, their naval architecture and the title of their chief—the Cid. Korsar legends say that the founders of their race came from a frozen sea— probably a reference to the Arctic Ocean.

The Korsars are a white-skinned race with a haughty contempt for all other people. They are cruel, quick to anger and always ready to kill, taking pleasure in torturing their prisoners. Though most prisoners are killed outright, those who are taken back to Korsar itself are often flung into deep dungeons below the Cid's Palace and left in total darkness among the snakes and giant rats that infest these ghastly prisons. Pellucidarians, accustomed as they are to perpetual sunlight, find few tortures worse than that inflicted by the Korsars.

Korsar is one of the few places in Pellucidar where there is any industry at all. Iron is mined, charcoal is made, and a crude gunpowder is also manufactured. Most of the mining is carried out by slaves taken from the more primitive tribes in the area; slaves also work the fields around the city.

To the north of Korsar, the tropical vegetation which is typical of Pellucidar gradually gives way to forests of cedar and pine, and then to windswept steppes where only stunted trees grow. In the far north lies a sea which has never been explored, and from the northern coast the sun which illuminates the surface of the earth can be seen; this is the only place in Pellucidar where it is visible.

(Edgar Rice Burroughs, *Tarzan at the Earth's Core*, New York, 1930; Edgar Rice Burroughs, *Tanar of Pellucidar*, New York, 1930; Edgar Rice Burroughs, *Land of Terror*, New York, 1944)

KOSEKIN COUNTRY, a country under Antarctica, described for the first time at the beginning of the nineteenth century, when Adam More of Cumberland visited the area and wrote a chronicle of his voyage, enclosing it in a copper cylinder and throwing it into the sea. His account was found on February 15, 1850, near Tenerife and was subsequently published.

After sailing through Antarctic waters and past several huge volcanoes, the traveller will arrive at a bleak, dismal coast inhabited by small, shrivelled black men with long matted hair and ugly faces; they carry spears and wear skirts made of the skin of a seabird. Their children look like dwarves and their women are hideous. It is best not to try to land here, as these people delight in eating human flesh. From here onwards the currents will carry the traveller into a subterranean channel which in turn leads into a subterranean sea inhabited by various sea-monsters with snake-like necks, sharp teeth and lashing tails. In this sea lies Kosekin Country. Against a background of ice-covered peaks lies a pattern of green cultivated fields and fine forests of giant ferns, among which are several populous cities, many roads, terraced slopes, long rows of arches, pyramids and fortified walls. The climate is warm. Various species of animals inhabit Kosekin Country. Gigantic flightless birds, as large as oxen, are harnessed to cars and can run faster than race-horses. There are huge alligators and wingless dragons about one hundred feet long, with stout bodies, long scaly tails, hind legs longer than forelegs, feet armed with formidable claws, and enormous heads each with a tusk like that of the rhinoceros. An easily domesticated species is the *athaleb*, something between an enormous bat and a winged crocodile, that swallows its victuals whole.

The principal city of Kosekin Country is built on the slope of a mountain. Its streets are formed by successive terraces and their connecting crossways. Along the streets are deep channels used as drains. There are several large half-pyramids which serve various purposes. Many houses are built like caverns or pavilions, of great blocks of stone, and have pyramidal roofs. Inside, they resemble large grottoes with arched ceilings from which hang golden lamps. The walls are adorned with rich tapestries and there are couches, soft cushions, divans and ottomans, and rich rugs on the floor.

The inhabitants here are small and slender, with black, straight hair. Because of the blazing

Detail of a living room in a town house in KOSEKIN COUNTRY.

sun they have weak eyes which they always keep half closed. The men wear their beards plaited. Their costume is a coarse tunic with a rope girdle, but the officers wear elegant mantles and robes of fine cloth, richly embroidered. All wear broad-rimmed hats; the chief pins golden adornments on his. They are the gentlest of the human race, and also the most bloodthirsty—the kindest and the most cruel. It is believed that they are Troglodytes travelled far south (see City of the IMMORTALS, also inhabited by the Troglodytes).

In Kosekin Country the paupers are the hon-oured and envied class, but the children and aged are also esteemed. If a man and a woman love each other, they separate. The sick are objects of the highest regard, especially if they are incurable, be-cause they require constant nursing. Instead of causing harm, everyone tries to benefit his neigh-bour. When one Kosekin has received a kindness from another, he is filled with a sort of vengeful passion, a sleepless and vehement desire to bestow some adequate and corresponding benefit on someone else. Feuds are thus kept up among fam-ilies and wars among nations. Secret bestowers of wealth are punished, as well as perpetrators of what they call "crimes of violence." (An example of such a criminal would be a strong man who meets a weaker man, forces himself upon him as his slave or compels him to take his purse, and threatens to kill himself if the weaker man refuses.)

Every six months the Kosekin go on a "sa-cred hunt" in the sea. Their quarry is a monster with a head like an alligator, a hairy neck twenty feet long and huge fins. The top of his body is bound in a cuirass of bone. They throw javelins at him from their galleys—long, low ships propelled by a hundred oars or one huge square sail—and have no fear of being killed; on the contrary, they very much long to die.

Death is considered an excellent thing among the Kosekin. They hold many ceremonies in hon-our of death in the Cheder Neblin, or Cavern of the Dead, a vast grotto full of dim, sparkling lights. The vaulted roof is one hundred feet high and under it stands a lofty half-pyramid with stone steps. In niches in the walls are the victims (or beneficiaries) of former sacrifices; shrivelled human forms sit holding torches, hollow eyes star-ing in front of them; from each heart projects the handle and half-blade of a knife. They are regu-larly crowned with flowers. The chosen ones are sacrificed at the Six Months' Feast to the chant of *Sibgu Sibgin! Ranenu! Hodu Lecosk!* ("Sacrifice the victims! Rejoice! Give thanks to darkness!"). After ten years in the Cheder Neblin the bodies are removed to public sepulchres. The Kosekin call death the Lord of Joy and they believe that after death they will go to the Land of Darkness. The advent of the Dark Season is celebrated as the Mista Kosek or Feast of Darkness, in a vast cavern decorated like the interior of a Gothic cathedral.

The Kosekin language bears some resem-blance to Arabic. Its written form consists of sepa-rate characters, like printed type, formed in an irregular manner. The letters of their alphabet are P K T B G D F Ch Th M L N S H R and three more that have no English equivalent. The vowels are supplied in reading. Kosekin books are made of a sort of papyrus. A few Kosekin words which the traveller might find useful:

Man:	*Iz*	Woman:	*Izza*
Light:	*Or*	Goodbye:	*Salonla*
Queen:	*Malca*	Day:	*Jom*

Kosekin poets celebrate unhappy love: they tell tales, for example, of lovers dying broken-hearted from being compelled to marry one another. They write odes to defeats instead of victories, since it is considered glorious for one nation to sacrifice itself to another. Their poems praise street-sweepers, scavengers, lamplighters, labour-ers and, of course, paupers. Kosekin music is sad and haunting, played on square guitars with a dozen strings. They like Celtic music, brought to them by Adam More, and have adopted songs like

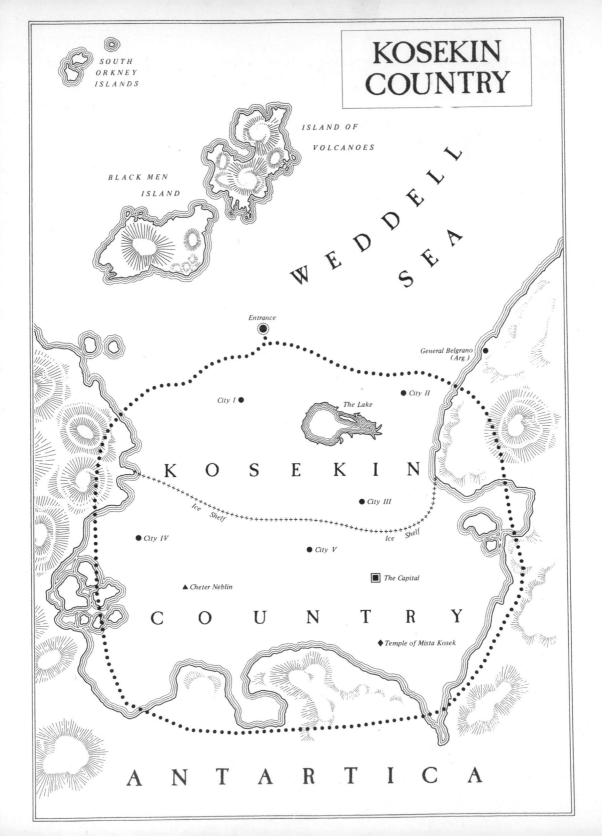

"Auld Lang Syne" and "The Last Rose of Summer," which they use at their sacrifices.

Kosekin cuisine is based on different kinds of fowl which taste like goose, turkey or partridge; they drink sweet waters, mild wine and a light, fermented drink.

(James De Mille, *A Strange Manuscript found in a Copper Cylinder,* New York, 1888)

KOUMOS, capital of VICHEBOLK LAND.

KRADAK, one of the Isles of WISDOM in the north Pacific. Like most of the archipelago, Kradak has its distinctive culture, largely based on ideas imported from the outside world via books.

Kradak has no national dress, no typical style and no concern for fashion. Clothes from various cultures are simply combined to suit the taste of the individual. Men can be seen wearing leather aprons, painted frills and shiny top hats, while many of the younger women combine the garments typical of a nurse, a cocotte and a peasant girl in a curious but pleasing ensemble.

The main occupation of the inhabitants of Kradak is the search for pleasure, and this has led to Kradak's being nicknamed "the Island of Perversions." The connection between pain and pleasure, between orgasm and suffering, has been widely explored on the island and large numbers of Kradakians have embraced the doctrine of masochism. No obstacles are placed in the way of any tendencies—sexual, or otherwise—that may develop and no whim or perversion is specifically forbidden or encouraged by law. Visitors may, therefore, spend their time lying on a bed of nails, being clobbered by a stout Valkyrie or reading long passages of Thomas Hardy for days on end.

The culture of the island is designed to translate the lawlessness of nature into the relations established between men and to free the individual by encouraging the greatest possible number of varieties of thought and feelings. An Institute of Deserving Savants is maintained at public expense to widen people's outlook and to find new modes of thought. Particularly original and successful research is usually rewarded by a good whipping.

The most abnormal or unusual individuals are chosen by the Ministry of Selection and sent to the offshore island of Gulliu to breed. Their children are carefully sifted for abnormalities and, if

suitable, are sent to another small islet to develop their tendencies. It is hoped that this process will eventually create a new type of man, with highly adaptable powers of co-ordination in both thought and feeling—a man free from the normal constraints of logical thought. To this end, a flexible system of numerals has already been introduced. In this system, any given numeral can take on the value of any other given numeral, so that two plus two can be made to equal five without any difficulty at all. As many travellers know only too well, similar results have been obtained, using other methods, in places such as Argentina, Iran, Chile, Czechoslovakia and BUTUA.

Food on Kradak may strike the inexperienced traveller as odd: inexhaustible combinations of ingredients give variety to the sense of taste. Goat's cheese served with sardines roasted on the spit; cow's tongue coated in vanilla; truffled coffee accompanied by pickled cucumber; these are some of the delicacies the visitor must prepare his palate for. One of the more common dishes served on Kradak is scented and carefully prepared salad made of the leaves of the coca plant; the cocaine in the leaves is greatly appreciated as a stimulant for its hallucinogenic effect. For travellers in the habit of smoking, it is useful to bear in mind that the cigarettes smoked on the island contain comparatively little tobacco: additives include henbane, hemlock, dandelion, squill and daem (these last named are narcotics, similar in their effect to the more usual nicotine). Visitors may wish to bring with them a supply of their own brand to avoid possible addiction.

(Alexander Moszkowski, *Die Inseln der Weisheit, Geschichte einer abenteuerlichen Entdeckungsfahrt,* Berlin, 1922)

KRAVONIA, an ancient European kingdom now probably under another form of government, not far from the frontier of the former USSR. Travellers who wish to visit the country are best advised to do so by coach.

Leaving the capital, SLAVNA, the main road follows the course of the River Krath for about five miles in a south-easterly direction and crosses it by an ancient wooden bridge. The river continues towards the south as an important commercial highway, but travellers should head north-east for another fifteen miles across flat country and past prosperous agricultural and pastoral villages till the

The courtyard of Praslock Castle, northern KRAVONIA.

road reaches the marshy land bordering Lake Talti. At this point the lake, extending to the spurs of the mountain range which forms Kravonia's frontier, bars the road's further progress and forces it to divide into two branches. The right prong of this fork continues on the level till it reaches Dobrava, eight miles from the bisection; here it inclines to the north-east again and after some ten miles of steady ascent crosses the mountains by St. Peter's Pass, the one carriage road over the range and across the frontier. Should travellers wish to continue their progress within Kravonia, they are advised to take the left prong which, immediately after the road splits, rises sharply for five miles to the hill on which stands Praslok Castle.

Praslok was the favourite home of Prince Sergius of Slavna and became the stronghold of his wife, Sophy of Kravonia, née Grouch, after the Prince's death. Sophy's astounding career is of course well known to those familiar with the recent history of Europe. She was born in Essex, England, in the village of Morpingham, where she lived and worked as a kitchen-maid until 1865. She then moved to London under the care and

protection of Lady Margaret (Meg) Duddington and from there to Paris where Sophy—now Sophy de Gruche—became part of the gay life of the capital. Marie Zerkovitch, a Kravonian by birth, persuaded Sophy to travel with her to Marie's native land in 1870. Here, as fate would have it, the English kitchen-maid saved the Crown Prince's life when he was being attacked by three officers and, in gratitude, King Alexis of Kravonia granted her the title of Baroness Dobrava. Although Prince Sergius succeeded to the throne, he was soon after betrayed and assassinated—but he married Sophy on his death-bed.

Praslok is a primitive old place standing on an abrupt mound by the roadside. So steep and sudden is the ascent that it was necessary to build a massive causeway of wood from the road to the square tower that forms the front of the building. In olden days the horses were stabled within the walls, but later modern stables were built on the other side of the road and it became customary to mount the causeway and enter the castle on foot. Within, the arrangements are quaint and simple. Besides the tower which contains the dining room and two

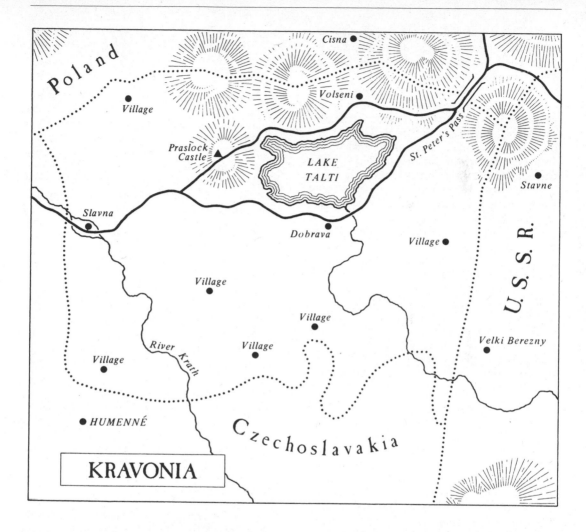

bedrooms above it, the whole building, strictly conditioned by the shape of the hill on which it stands, consists of three rows of small rooms on the ground floor. In the first row are the royal chambers, in the second the servants' quarters and in the third the lodgings of the guards; all rooms open onto a covered walk or cloister which runs round the castle's inner court. The whole building is solidly constructed of grey stone, a business–like hill-fortress strong by reason of its massive masonry and the position in which it stands.

After a halt at Praslok Castle, travellers should continue along the same road for another five miles until they reach the city of Volseni on the edge of a high plateau, looking down on Lake Talti and across to Dobrava in the plain opposite.

Volseni is in fact no more than one long street, lined with houses of long sloping roofs and here and there a round tower, leading into the marketplace. Standing with its back against the mountain and defended on the other three sides by a sturdy but slightly crumbling wall, Volseni is an almost impregnable fortress. Travellers who decide to spend the night here will be warned of the closing of the city gates by the sounding of a trumpet. Though a picturesque place, Volseni is not one that deserves a long visit.

Beyond Volseni there is no road in the proper sense but only cart or bridle tracks. Of these, the principal and most frequented runs diagonally across the Lake Talti Valley, meeting the road from Dobrava half-way up St. Peter's Pass and about twenty miles from Volseni. It forms the base of a rough and irregular triangle of country, with the point where the Slavna road splits, the Pass and Volseni marking its three angles, and Lake Talti in the centre.

Though near Slavna in actual distance, the landscape is very different from the fertile river valley which surrounds the capital. It is bleak and rough, a land of hill pastures and mountain woods. Its natural features are strikingly reflected in the character of the inhabitants; the men who count Volseni as their capital are hardier than those of Slavna, less given to luxury, less addicted to quarrels and riots but far more formidable opponents once they take up arms. After the tragic murder of Sergius, the men of Volseni chose the young queen Sophy as their chief, and against all odds she led them triumphantly into battle.

Visitors to Kravonia will find the language difficult to learn. It is useful to know that the Kravonian unit of currency, the *para*, is roughly equivalent to four English new pence, but the exact exchange rate should be checked before travelling. Visitors should also bear in mind the dictum of Sophy herself: "You must accustom yourself to Kravonia; it's not Essex, you know."

(Anthony Hope [Anthony Hope Hawkins], *Sophy of Kravonia*, London, 1906)

KRONOMO, a kingdom to the south-east of BINGFIELD'S ISLAND, bordering the country of Abyssnes. There is only one city in Kronomo, a walled settlement some five miles in circumference.

In the early part of the eighteenth century Kronomo was ruled by Bomarrah, who reigned successfully for twenty-two years, until he was deposed by his nephew Uhirria. Bomarrah was taken to Bingfield's Island to be killed, but was rescued by the Englishman after whom that island is named. Bingfield offered to help Bomarrah regain his throne and returned with him to Kronomo. Uhirria was soon defeated, largely thanks to the ferocious dog-birds Bingfield brought with him from his island. These shaggy, carnivorous creatures no longer form part of Kronomo's fauna, much to the relief of wary travellers.

(William Bingfield [?], *The Travels And Adventures Of William Bingfield, Esq; Containing, As Surprizing a Fluctuation of Circumstances, both by Sea and Land, as ever befel one Man. With An accurate Account of the Shape, Nature, and Properties of that most furious and amazing Animal, the Dog-Bird,* London, 1753)

KUKUANALAND, a vast plateau in central—southern Africa, surrounded by the Suliman Mountains, forming an impregnable barrier. Here rise the two mountains known as Saba's Breasts, some five thousand metres high.

The inhabitants are of Zulu origin but speak an ancient version of the Zulu tongue which seems to correspond approximately to Chaucer's English in relation to modern English. It is said that originally they were the miners brought by King Solomon himself to dig for his treasures.

(Henry Rider Haggard, *King Solomon's Mines*, London, 1886)

KUMMEROW, a village in Lower Pomerania, encircled by mountains. The inhabitants are said to be very much opposed to christenings. On the pretext that before a christening, custom decreed that the baptizer should cleanse himself, those sent to christen the Kummerowians are made to stand in the freezing waters of the local stream for many hours, until they collapse in the cold and completely forget about the ceremony they have come to perform.

Nowadays travellers are allowed to attend the festival during which the king of Kummerow is chosen from among those who are able to stand the longest in the icy waters.

(Ehm Welk [Thomas Trimm], *Die Heiden von Kummerow*, Berlin, 1937)

KUNLUN, MOUNT, a mountain in China, the lower capital of the Heavenly Emperor. It is guarded by Lu Wu, a creature with a tiger's body, nine tails, a human face and tiger's claws.

Mount Kunlun is hundreds of thousands of feet high and covers over eight hundred square feet. On its summit grows a forty-feet-high tree which five men, holding hands, can barely span. Here lives the Queen Mother of the West, a monster with a leopard's tail, tiger's teeth, a shrill voice, matted hair and a dazzling tiara.

(Anonymous, *The Book of Mountains and Seas*, 4th cen. BC)

L

—

LACELAND, an island kingdom, some six hours' journey from the Isle of HER. As the traveller approaches the island, a region of bright light will suddenly appear against the shadows. The sudden, sharp contrast is said to be as strong as that caused by the birth of light on the first day of Creation.

The King of Lace spins this bright light, weaving pictures of madonnas, jewels, peacocks and human figures which intertwine like the dances of the Rhine-maidens. Clear patterns appear against the pitch-black darkness of the surrounding air, like shapes painted on windows by the frost, and then disappear again into the shadows.

(Alfred Jarry, *Gestes et Opinions du Docteur Faustroll, Pataphysicien. Roman Néo-Scientifique,* Paris, 1911)

LADIES, CITY OF, see City of VIRTUOUS WOMEN.

LADIES' ISLAND, see GREAT MOTHER'S ISLAND.

LAGADO, capital of BALNIBARBI.

LAIMAK, a grim fortress in RFREK, crouching on its rock like a sleeping wolf or a natural growth, an outcrop of the ancient rock itself rather than any work of man. For many centuries Laimak has been in the hands of the Parry family, who have dominated the political life of Rerek for countless generations. The fortress stands on the top of a hill in the river valley of Owlsdale. Although the hill is not particularly high, its sides are almost sheer cliffs, rising three or four hundred feet above the valley.

The fortress of Laimak is built of huge blocks of stone quarried from the hill itself; the walls follow the contours of the summit. Visitors are advised that the only entrance is an arched gateway in the north wall, reached by a zigzag path up the cliff side which is commanded by several towers and parapets, and thus impossible for any enemy to reach.

The most impressive room in the fortress is the great L-shaped banqueting hall, built of black obsidian, with a row of mullioned windows in the north-west wall. The other walls are decorated with thirteen huge carvings of devilish heads whose protruding tongues support lamps and whose large eyes are mirrors which reflect the changing light. With all its terrible beauty, Laimak has a dark and sinister reputation. Several brutal murders have taken place in its halls and in the dungeons that lie deep beneath them.

The banner of the Parry family shows a sable owl with a red beak and talons on a field of gold. The motto is *Noctu noxiis noceo* ("Nightly I prey upon vermin").

(E.R. Eddison, *Mistress of Mistresses, A Vision of Zimiamvia,* London, 1935; E.R. Eddison, *A Fish Dinner in Memison,* London, 1941; E.R. Eddison, *The Mezentian Gate,* London, 1958)

LAÏQUHIRE, a large island in the north Atlantic, naturally divided into two regions: the highlands and the lowlands. The highlands are the habitat of the so-called Invisible Deities, who sometimes make themselves visible if they wish to take part in human activities.

(Anonymous, *Voyage Curieux d'un Philadelphe dans des Pays nouvellement Découverts,* The Hague, 1755)

LAKE-TOWN, a town built on wooden piles above the waters of Long Lake, to the east of MIRKWOOD and to the south of the LONELY MOUNTAIN, in the north of MIDDLE-EARTH. The town is built just above the point where the Forest River of Mirkwood enters the lake; a promontory of rock forms a bay which protects the town from the fast flowing waters of the river. A bridge connects the town with the shore of the lake.

Long Lake is fed by the River Running from the north. It is so large that neither its northern nor its southern edges are visible from a boat in the middle. At its southern end, the waters of the lake plunge over a great waterfall. The sound of its roar can be heard at the other end of the lake.

Lake-town is a centre for trade with DALE and with the elves of Mirkwood; goods are also brought up the river from the south. The trade with the elves is carried on in ingenious manner. Goods being sent to the elves are packed in barrels

and either loaded on to flat boats or tied together
and poled upstream. The empty barrels are returned by simply casting them into the water of the
Forest River and allowing them to float down to
the Lake, where the current washes them ashore in
the bay. Boats from the town then come out and tow
them to the wharves and quays of the settlement.

Lake-town, which is also known as Esgaroth,
has been rebuilt at least twice. The present settlement was built after the death of Smaug the
Golden, the dragon who forced the dwarves to
leave their colony beneath the Lonely Mountain,
and who devastated the town of Dale. Smaug was
killed as he attacked Lake-town itself, but not before he had destroyed much of it with his fiery
breath. For years, the bones of Smaug could be
seen amongst the ruins of the old wooden town.
The men of Lake-town were reluctant to live in an
area so tainted by evil and relocated their settlement slightly to the north.

Lake-town is noted for its *cram*, a type of biscuit which is designed for use on long journeys.
While it tastes uninteresting it is extremely sustaining, and has the advantage of not going mouldy.

(J.R.R. Tolkien, *The Hobbit, or There and Back
Again*, London, 1937)

LAKU, see ISHMAELIA.

LAMARY, a small island in the Indian Ocean. The
climate here is so hot that people go about naked.
Women are held in common, as are the land and
property. The people of Lamary are cannibals, fat-
tening up the children they buy from merchants
and eating them at bloody repasts. This, they say,
is the sweetest meat in the world. In cases of dire
need, they will also eat the merchants.

(Sir John Mandeville, *Voiage de Sir John Maundevile*, Paris, 1357)

LAMIAM, an island in the Arabian Sea, also
known as **IANICUM** or **CUBA**, so called because
the inhabitants curse the burning midday sun.
They are an anthropophagous race of giants who
go about naked and live in caves. They have no
government apart from the rule of force.

One of the main attractions of Lamiam is the
Tower of the Two Dragons that can be seen high
on a hill beneath which lies a gold mine. The

The Tower of the Two Dragons, LAMIAM.

tower is guarded by two dragons and wooden images of these beasts are kept inside the building. An interesting Lamiamian custom stipulates that those who wish to reach the gold must first slay their parents and then anoint the wooden images with the sacrificial blood.

Off Lamiam lies a floating island which according to local legend is a portion of Paradise washed away by the Ganges. It is rich in precious stones, gold and spices, and two rare species of trees grow here, *agallicum* and *guiacum*. But the population is sparse and disagreeable. The women have worms in their tongues which they cut out with flint knives. The wounds are healed with herbs and the worms are sold to the Italians who use them to make poison. Frenchmen are not advised to visit the island, as one group of travellers from France is known to have shed their skins like snakes upon reaching its coast.

(William Bullein, *A Dialogue both Pleasant and Pitiful, wherein is a Goodly Regimente against the Fever Pestilence, with a Consolation and Comfort against Death*, London, 1564)

LANTERNLAND, an island four days' sail from SATINLAND. As visitors approach the harbour they may recognize the famous Lantern of the La Rochelle lighthouse, as well as those of Pharos, Nauplion and the Acropolis. The island is populated by Lanterns, which are all female, and Cressets, which are all male. The only other inhabitants are the Midnight-oilers, who inhabit a small village close to the port, guarded by Obelisk-lights, and who live off the Lanterns in much the same way as lay-brothers live off nuns. They are an industrious and worthy people: Demosthenes once burned his midnight oil with them.

The queen is attended by Lanterns of Honour: the Lantern of Aristophanes and the Lantern of Cleanthes. She is dressed in virgin crystal, inset with damascene work and trimmed with large diamonds. The Lanterns of the Blood dress in either talc or rock-crystal and other ladies at court wear horn, paper and oiled cloth. The Cressets also dress according to their rank and the antiquity of their houses. Among the splendours of the court, one plain, earthenware Lantern stands out; this is the Lantern of Epictetus, for which three thousand drachmas were once refused. The Lantern of the Law can be recognized by the fine tuft of crimson silk it wears on its head. Two other Lanterns

are distinguished by the suppository bags they carry on their belts; these are the Great and Little Lights of the Apothecaries.

At dinner, the Lanterns are served with fat, moulded candles. The queen, however, is given a great, stiff, flaming taper of white wax, slightly red at the tip. The Lanterns of the Royal Blood also receive special treatment and are provided with walnut-oil candles, an honour which may also be extended to favoured and high-ranking guests. Other dishes include *midrilles* boiled in cold water so that one cannot smell the smoke; roasted *hannicroches*, served with coal and ice to prevent guests from burning their teeth; exotic *farignolles* spiced with gunpowder to prevent colic; and, as a dessert, salted *grimaces*, grilled in moon beams. After eating, the Lanterns give off a glorious light from their wicks; some young Lanterns, however, do not really shine but cast a lascivious glow.

A great feast is held on the queen's birthday, which falls in mid-May. The feast is attended by all the Lanterns in the world, who parade, two by two, into the throne room. The queen sits on a high chair covered in cloth of gold, beneath a canopy of crimson satin encrusted with gold and precious stones. After the major affairs of state have been dealt with, the Lanterns attend a ceremonial banquet at which white candles are served. The banquet is followed by a spectacular ball. Visitors invited to attend will find the dancing both athletic and acrobatic. The Lanterns leap so high into the air that some of them blow out their own lights; if this happens, they are blinded.

In Lanternland all major events involving good cheer take place at night, when the Lanterns go out in the company of their Cressets, a delightful spectacle no traveller can afford to miss.

(Anonymous, *Le Voyage de navigation que fist Panurge, disciple de Pantagruel, aux isles incognues et éstranges de plusieurs choses merveilleuses et difficiles à croire, qu'il dict avoir veues, dont il fait narration en ce présent volume, et plusieurs aultres joyeusetez pour inciter les lecteurs et auditeurs à rire*, Paris, 1538; François Rabelais, *Le cinquiesme et dernier livre des faicts et dicts du bon Pantagruel, auquel est contenu la visitation de l'Oracle de la dive Bacbuc, et le mot de la bouteille; pour lequel avoir est entrepris tout ce long voyage*, Paris, 1564)

LAPUTA, a floating or flying island which hovers over the larger island of BALNIBARBI, over

LAPUTA

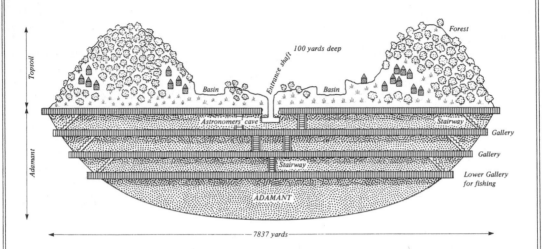

Forest

100 yards deep

Topsoil

Basin

Entrance shaft

Basin

Astronomers' cave

Stairway

Gallery

Adamant

Gallery

Stairway

Lower Gallery
for fishing

ADAMANT

7837 yards

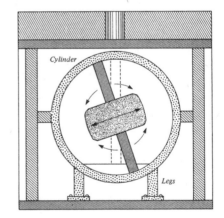

SIDE ELEVATION

Cylinder

Legs

Astronomers' Cave

(OR FLANDONA GAGNOLE)

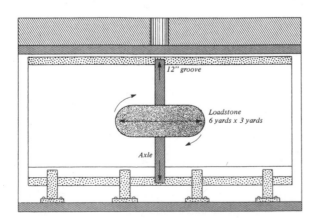

12" groove

Loadstone
6 yards x 3 yards

12 yds (diameter)

Axle

FRONT ELEVATION

which the King of Laputa also presides. Laputa is circular, 7,837 yards in diameter and some three hundred yards thick, with a total surface area of ten thousand acres. The bottom of the island is a two-hundred-yard-deep layer of adamant, covered by the usual strata of minerals and a rich topsoil. The island slopes down towards the centre, where four large basins collect the fallen rainwater. When natural evaporation fails to prevent them from overflowing, the island can be raised above the level of the rain clouds.

The sides of the floating island consist of stairways and galleries, making Laputa accessible from below. Communication with Balnibarbi is maintained by lowering messages on pack-threads. Food and drink are hauled up on pulleys. People fish from the lower galleries.

At the centre of Laputa is a chasm about fifty yards in diameter, where the Laputan astronomers descend into a large dome—which is therefore known as *Flandona Gagnole* or the Astronomers' Cave. The cave lies one hundred yards beneath the upper surface of the adamant. It is lit by twenty lamps which burn continually, reflecting a brilliant light off the adamant into every part of the cave. The place is stored with a great variety of sextants, quadrants, telescopes, astrolabes, and other astronomical instruments. But the greatest curiosity (on which the fate of the island depends) is a loadstone of a prodigious size, in shape resembling a weaver's shuttle. It is six yards long, and at its widest part it is at least three yards over. This magnet is sustained by a very strong axle of adamant which passes through its middle, upon which it plays, and is poised so exactly that the weakest hand can turn it. It is hooped round with a hollow cylinder of adamant, four feet deep, as many thick, and twelve yards in diameter, placed horizontally, and supported by eight adamantine feet, each six yards high. In the middle of the concave side there is a groove twelve inches deep, in which the extremities of the axle are lodged, and turned round as there is occasion.

The stone cannot be moved from its place by any force, because the cylinder and its feet are part of that body of adamant which constitutes the bottom of the island.

By means of this loadstone, the island is made to rise and fall and move from one place to another, because one end of the stone is strongly attracted to Balnibarbi, and the other end is strongly repelled by it. If the attracted end is turned down

the island is drawn towards the earth, and if the repelled end faces down the island is driven up into the sky. When the position of the stone is oblique, the motion of the moving islands is oblique as well. For in this magnet the forces always act in lines parallel to its direction.

By this oblique motion the island is conveyed to different parts of the king's dominions. To explain the manner of its progress (visitors may consult the map under Balnibarbi) let *AB* represent a line drawn across Balnibarbi, let the line *cd* represent the loadstone, of which *d* is the repelling end, and *c* is the attracting end, the island being over *C*; if the stone is placed in the position *cd* with its repelling end downwards, then the island will be driven upwards obliquely towards *D*. When it is arrived at *D*, if the stone is turned upon its axle until its attracting end points towards *E*, then the island will be carried obliquely towards *E;* where if the stone is again turned upon its axle until it stands in the position *EF,* with its repelling point downwards, the island will rise obliquely towards *F,* where by directing the attracting end towards *G*, the island will be carried to *G*, and from *G* to *H*, by turning the stone so as to make its repelling extremity point directly downwards. So by changing the position of the stone, the island is made to rise and fall by turns in an oblique direction, and by those alternate risings and fallings is conveyed from one part of the dominions of Balnibarbi to the other.

But it must be observed that Laputa cannot move beyond the extent of the king's dominions below, nor can it rise above the height of four miles. According to the astronomers this is because the magnetic virtue does not extend beyond four miles, and also because the mineral in the bowels of the earth, which acts upon the stone terminates with the limits of the king's dominions.

When the stone is put parallel to the plane of the horizon, the island stands still; for in that case its extremities, being at equal distance from the earth, act with equal force—the one drawing downwards—the other pushing upwards—and no motion results.

This loadstone is under the care of astronomers who, from time to time, give it such positions as the king directs. They spend the greatest part of their lives observing the celestial bodies, which they do with the assistance of telescopes far excelling those made today in Europe or Japan.

Travellers will notice that the people of Laputa

have their heads inclined either to the right or to the left, with one eye turned inwards and the other constantly looking up towards the zenith. As they are constantly absorbed in intense speculations, they require a physical stimulus to speak or pay attention to the discourse of others. This has given rise to the custom whereby the rich employ certain servants, called flappers or *climenoles*, who carry bladders filled with small stones or dry peas. With these they gently strike the mouth of the speaker and the right ear of his intended listener. They also apply flaps to their masters' eyes to prevent them from walking into obstacles or bumping into other people.

The main, if not sole, preoccupations of the Laputans are music, mathematics and astronomy—all highly developed sciences in their kingdom. They have catalogued the existence of ten thousand fixed stars and have discovered the twin satellites of Mars. Their observations allow them to accurately calculate the movement of the ninety-three comets known to them.

This theoretical skill is not matched by practical abilities; in day-to-day life the Laputans are extremely clumsy. Their houses have no right angles and no straight walls, as drawn-up plans are too complex for the builders to understand. This, and other difficulties, stem from their scorn for practical geometry. The same can be seen in their tailoring. Measurements are taken with quadrants and compasses and are carefully noted on paper, but the clothes themselves are often ill-fitting, as the tailors frequently make mistakes in their calculations. Furthermore their robes are adorned with all sorts of mathematical figures and musical instruments, many of which are quite unknown in other countries.

Above all, Laputans are constantly worried about changes in the nature and behaviour of the celestial bodies and the effect that these may have on earth. They are, for instance, worried that the sun's constant approach to the earth may mean that the planet will be incinerated; that the earth narrowly escaped the last comet and will almost certainly be destroyed by the next. So great are their fears that they cannot sleep in their beds at night and have no taste for the common pleasures of life. When they meet friends in the morning, their first thought is to ask how the sun's health is, how it looked at its rising and setting. Their conversation resembles that of small boys, who delight in stories of sprites and hobgoblins and then become too frightened to sleep. Visitors from England are advised not to limit their conversation to the state of the weather.

Laputans are extremely argumentative and intolerant of opposition, and have no concept of imagination, fancy or invention. Indeed, these very words are absent from their language. The language is very soft and pleasant to listen to, rather like Italian. Its vocabulary is largely drawn from music and mathematics. So if they wish to praise something, they will describe it in terms of circles, parallelograms or ellipses, and musical terms are used in a similar fashion.

The women of Laputa are extremely vivacious and travellers will find them anxious to travel beyond the confines of Laputa, which they are forbidden to leave without royal consent. This is rarely given, as past experience has shown that if they do leave, they rarely return. At least one woman is known to have preferred life in a hovel in Balnibarbi to life with a wealthy minister on Laputa—and she eloped with a man who beat her every day. The women of Laputa commonly take men from Balnibarbi as their lovers, a habit which is facilitated by their husbands' constant absorption in deep thought. If a Laputan has no *flappers*, but is provided with paper and mathematical instruments, his wife and her lover can proceed to the greatest familiarities—in his presence—without his even noticing it.

The Laputan interest in mathematics and music is even reflected in their food. The ingredients are not exceptional, but the dishes are served in mathematical or musical shapes: mutton cut into equilateral triangles, ducks trussed up in the shape of fiddles and sausages which resemble flutes are but a few of their dishes.

The king can suppress rebellions in his lower realms in a variety of ways. He can keep the island hovering over a dissident town, thus depriving it of the benefits of sun and rain. He can, if necessary, attack rebels with large stones. As a last resort, he can drop the island on them, thus causing total destruction. The latter method is considered ill-advised though; not only would it increase the unpopularity of the king and his ministers, but it would also destroy and damage royal property.

Neither the king nor his two elder sons may leave the island; nor may the queen until she is past child-bearing age.

A disputed theory suggests that Laputa's real

name is Isle of TOMTODDIES but there is no tangible proof of this.

(Jonathan Swift, *Travels Into Several Remote Nations Of The World. In Four Parts. By Lemuel Gulliver, First a Surgeon, and then a Captain of several Ships*, London, 1726)

LASTLAND, see ASTOWELL.

LAST SEA, see WORLD'S END ISLAND.

LATORYN, see MANCY.

LEAP ISLANDS, an archipelago of independent kingdoms near Antarctica, known as Leaphigh, Leaplow, Leapup, Leapdown, Leapover, Leapthrough, Leaplong, Leapshort, Leapround, Leapunder. Each of these, except Leaplow, has a religious establishment founded on a new social principle. The inhabitants are the Monikins, an advanced tribe of monkeys.

The Leap Islands are reached by sea and the route is indicated by floating milestones. Travellers will arrive at Aggregation Harbour in Leaphigh. Notable here are the Great Square, the Palais des Arts et des Sciences and the Academy of Latent Sympathies. The government is divided into three states: Law, Opinion and Practice. By law the king rules; by practice his cousin rules; and by opinion the king again rules.

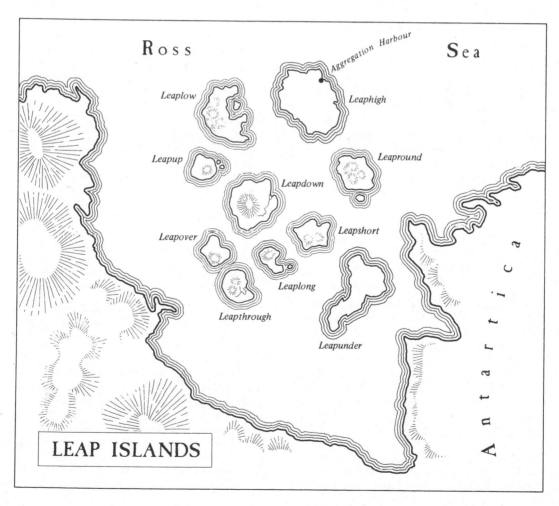

LEAP ISLANDS

The Monikins, defined by their scientists as quadrupeds or *caudaejactans* ("tail-wavers"), wear no clothing, except on official occasions. Their language has some Greek roots, and resembles Danish or Swedish. However, polite people speak French and salute with their tails. The Monikins say that man will eventually develop into a Monikin and that the seat of reason will be not the brain but the tail. Their currency is not money, but promises, which have the advantage of being impossible to burn or steal. Their seasons have different names, like the Season of Nuts. Each Monikin is called by a number and a colour. The colour designates its caste, station and pursuits, as well as its sex and the number indicates the degree of its intelligence. For instance "N° 22,817, brown-study colour" refers to "Dr. Reasono."

(James Fenimore Cooper, *The Monikins*, New York, 1835)

LEARDING'S ISLAND, a mountainous and thickly wooded island in the Cape Horn region.

The island is named after Captain Learding who was shipwrecked here with his wife and two sailors. They spent nine years on the island, living in small wooden huts and cultivating the land. After six years, the two sailors attempted to rape Mrs. Learding, who fought them off and killed one of them. The surviving sailor ran off into the hills and was eventually kidnapped by Indians.

(André Guillaume Contant D'Orville, *La Destinée Ou Mémoires Du Lord Kilmarnoff, Traduits De L'Anglois De Miss Voodwill, Par M. Contant Dorville,* Amsterdam & Paris, 1766)

LEAVEHEAVENALONE, a peaceful quiet place, somewhere between OLDWIVESFABLEDOM and THE-OTHER-END-OF-NOWHERE. Here the hot sun draws water out of the sea and makes steamthreads which the wind twists into cloud-patterns, like Chantilly lace. The general effect of these hangings in the sky is rather like a magnificent Crystal Palace.

(Charles Kingsley, *The Water Babies: A Fairy Tale for a Land-Baby,* London, 1863)

LE DOUAR, an island off the coast of Brittany, swallowed by the sea in the thirteenth century when the island overturned like a capsized ship. The mountain barrier which girdled the island formed a kind of gigantic bell jar under which the inhabitants of Le Douar live in peace and harmony. Through the centuries they have evolved the necessary physiological changes needed to withstand the pressure of the sea. They feed on a species of large mushroom found nowhere else in the world and obtain the light to illuminate their dwellings from radium which they have rendered harmless.

(J.H. Rosny, jeune, *L'Enigme du "Redoutable,"* Paris, 1930)

LEGIONS, CITY OF THE, in Glamorganshire, Wales, not far from the Severn Sea. The River Usk flows beneath the walls, which are surrounded by woods and meadows.

A great battle was fought before the city during King Arthur's victorious campaigns against the invading Saxons early in his career. When Arthur had finally subdued all his kingdom and Gaul, he chose the City of the Legions for the plenary court at which he placed on his head the royal crown.

The City of the Legions is one of the richest in all Arthur's domains; its royal palaces with their golden roofs make it a match for Rome itself. Travellers are advised to visit the two churches for which the city is rightly famous. One, dedicated to the martyr Julius, is renowned for its choir; the other, founded in honour of the Name of Aaron, is the third metropolitan see of Britain. The City of the Legions also houses a college of two hundred sages, all highly skilled in the science of astronomy, who advise the king on the basis of predictions made from the study of the stars.

(Anonymous, *The History of the Britons,* 10th cen. AD; Geoffrey of Monmouth, *Historia Regum Britanniae,* 12th cen. AD)

LEIXLIP, a castle located near Dublin and still belonging to the ancient and honourable Colonny family of Ireland. By writing to the family it is possible to rent the property, which has remained vacant for the past two hundred years. The great advantage of the castle is that it appears to be hundreds of miles from Dublin—or any other inhabited spot—while in actual fact its proud, delicate towers stand only a few miles from the capital.

Coming via the road from Lucan, the traveller reaches the castle by crossing the Leixlip Bridge, whose single arch spans the Liffey. Looking out from this squat little bridge, which hides a bend in the river, one discovers an enchanting view. The swift-moving river neatly encircles the entire castle, and a lovely green park as well, before resuming its calm flow near the low walls of the chapel; there it widens, spreading out to pass under the barrel vault. It is an unforgettable vision, one of serenity and happy timelessness. The traveller will also be thrilled to stroll through the luxurious vegetation and along the terraced paths of the castle's domains, admiring the astute arrangement of small groves and Greek temples perched on the hillsides.

Nevertheless, any visitor ought to remember the tragedies that befell the three daughters of Sir Redmond Blaney, baron and first tenant of Leixlip. At the end of an innocent stroll, Sir Redmond's heir, Jane Blaney—an intelligent, beautiful girl—fell victim to a magic spell which has not been completely explained to this day. When one goes into the kitchen one may sometimes catch sight, however vaguely, of Jane, who reappears frozen and famished. In one of the bedrooms traces may be found of a crime committed by the husband of Jane's older sister on the very day of her marriage: he slit his young bride's throat before taking his own life. In yet another room one may come across evidence of an infamous murder that occurred in Scotland, and led to the ruin of Anne, the baron's third daughter.

Even a short stay will show that the castle is haunted, and bears a curse that will last for ever.

(Charles Robert Maturin, *The Castle of Leixlip*, Dublin, 1820)

LENG, a waste plateau in DREAMWORLD, swept by the wind, like the roof of a dying and unforgotten land. There, in the cold silent dusk, rises the rude shape of a wide and massive building with no windows, surrounded by a guard of monoliths. This is the most dreadful of all places in Dreamworld, the remote and prehistoric monastery that is the dwelling-place of the indescribable High Priest of Dreamworld, who covers his face with a yellow silk mask. The narrow winding corridors of the building are decorated with frightful scenes older than history, in a style unknown to most archaeologists. After countless aeons their pigments are still brilliant because the coldness and dryness of the place keeps alive many primal things.

These archaic frescoes are the annals of Leng; travellers will see pictures of horned, hooved and wide-mouthed almost-human creatures dancing wildly among forgotten cities. There are scenes of old wars, of Leng's inhabitants fighting with the bloated purple spiders of the neighbouring vales, and of the arrival of the black galleys from the moon and of the submission of Leng's people to the polypi and amorphous blasphemies that hopped and floundered and wriggled out of them. Those slippery greyish-white creatures came to be worshipped as gods, and not one of Leng's inhabitants complained when scores of their best and fatted men were taken away in the black galleys. The monstrous moon-beasts had made their camp on a jagged island in the sea, none other than the nameless grey rock shunned by the seamen of IN-QUANOK, from which vile howlings reverberate at night.

(Howard Phillips Lovecraft, "The Dream-Quest of Unknown Kadath," in *Arkham Sampler*, Sauk City, 1948)

LEONARD'S LAND, in Patagonia, South America. Its system of government was established by a French philosopher, Leonard, based on the principle of equality and on the weather. Leonard was convinced that everything is determined by the weather and he erected a dozen weather-vanes to help legislators in their deliberations.

History has it that Leonard himself was made king, but that he fell from favour as a result of his climatic theory: a battle with a neighbouring tribe was lost because of his insistence that the army should not fight while the wind was blowing in the wrong direction. As a result, he was stoned by the people and driven out of the land.

(Jean Gaspard Dubois-Fontanelle, *Aventures Philosophiques*, Paris, 1766)

LEONIA, a city in Asia, refashioned every day. Every morning the people wake between fresh sheets, wash with just-unwrapped cakes of soap, wear brand-new clothing, take from the latest-model refrigerators still unopened tins, listening to the last-minute jingles from the most up-to-date radio.

On the sidewalks, encased in spotless plastic bags, the remains of yesterday's Leonia await the garbage truck. Not only squeezed tubes of tooth-paste, burnt-out light bulbs, newspapers, contain-ers, wrappings, but also boilers, encyclopedias, pianos, porcelain dinner services. It is not so much by the things that each day are manufactured, sold, and bought that one can measure Leonia's opu-lence, but rather by the things that each day are thrown out to make room for the new. Certain trav-ellers have wondered if Leonia's true passion is really, as they say, the enjoyment of new and differ-ent things, and not, instead, the joy of expelling, discarding, cleansing itself of a recurrent impurity. The fact is that street cleaners are welcomed like angels, and their task of removing the residue of yesterday's existence is surrounded by a deep, re-spectful silence, like a ritual that inspires devotion, perhaps only because once things have been cast off nobody wants to have to think about them further.

Nobody wonders where, each day, they carry their load of refuse. Outside the city, surely; but each year the city expands, and the street cleaners have to fall farther back. The bulk of the outflow increases and the piles rise higher, become strati-fied, extend over a wider perimeter. Besides, the more Leonia's talent for making new materials excels, the more the rubbish improves in quality, resists time, the elements, fermentations, combus-tions. A solid fortress of indestructible leftovers surrounds Leonia.

The result is that the more Leonia expels goods, the more it accumulates them; the scales of its past are soldered into a cuirass that cannot be re-moved. As the city is renewed each day, it preserves all of itself in its only definitive form: yesterday's sweepings piled up on the sweepings of the day be-fore yesterday and of all its days and years.

Leonia's rubbish little by little would invade the world, if, from beyond the final crest of its boundless rubbish heap, the street cleaners of other cities were not pressing, also pushing moun-tains of refuse in front of themselves. Perhaps the whole world, beyond Leonia's boundaries, is cov-ered by craters of rubbish, each surrounding a me-tropolis in constant eruption. The boundaries between the alien, hostile cities are infected ram-parts where the detritus of both support each other, overlap, mingle.

The greater its height grows, the more the danger of a landslide looms: a tin can, an old tire, an unravelled wine-flask, if it rolls towards Leonia, is enough to bring with it an avalanche of unmated shoes, calendars of bygone years, withered flowers, submerging the city in its own past, which it had tried in vain to reject, mingling with the past of the neighbouring cities, finally clean. A cataclysm will flatten the sordid mountain range, cancelling every trace of the metropolis always dressed in new clothes. In the nearby cities they are all ready, waiting with bulldozers to flatten the terrain, to push into the new territory, expand, and drive the new street cleaners still farther out.

(Italo Calvino, *Le città invisibili*, Turin, 1972)

LERNA, a university twenty kilometres from the city of Umsk, Switzerland, and five hours by train from Geneva. Strange experiments were carried out at Lerna, involving twenty-four identical men from different parts of the world, related to the se-cret laws of the universe.

(Angel Bonomini, *Los Novicios de Lerna*, Buenos Aires, 1972)

LESNEVEN, capital of OCEANA (2).

LETALISPONS, a rocky island in the Pacific Ocean, near Juan Fernandez, covered in parts by thick forests. A high mountain rises in the centre, the hunting-ground of savage bears. The inhabi-tants, who call themselves Cerebellites or Maggot-heads, speak Spanish because the island used to be under Chilean domination, wear green satin and believe in the transmigration of souls. The motto of the Cerebellites is *"ars brevis, vita longa."* Men and women live to about 120, but do not grow old. When they reach the age of sixty they grow young again and gain strength and energy. They never fall into a passion and they discourage any ex-cesses. Cerebellite theatre is much loved. The plays are acted by puppets and are very short.

The Cerebellites have no enemies because nothing offends them. Their laws are simple: 1) al-ways follow your first thoughts and never have second ones; 2) never think like someone else—be original; 3) good taste is a sixth sense; 4) learn lots of stories by heart and talk a lot; 5) never think be-fore talking; 6) always express yourself in a new and original fashion.

The towers of Scaricrotariparagorgouleo, capital of LETALISPONS.

The capital of Letalispons is Scaricrotari-paragorgouleo. The buildings are high and extraordinary to behold—thin, airy towers exposed to the elements and crowned with weathercocks and instruments that measure the progression of the moon.

(Abbé Pierre François Guyot Desfontaines, *Le Nouveau Gulliver, ou Voyage De Jean Gulliver, Fils Du Capitaine Gulliver. Traduit d'un Manuscrit Anglois. Par Monsieur L.D.F.*, Paris, 1730)

LEUKE, an island in the Black Sea, exactly opposite the mouth of the River Dniester. The capital, Pseudopolis, was destroyed when the Philistines (see PHILISTIA) conquered the island. Legend has it that Poseidon made Leuke rise from the sea for Thetis to bury the body of her son, Achilles, in whose honour a temple was built here. No priests or slaves look after the temple of the semigod; instead, large white birds come to mourn over his grave. Visitors can observe them every day in their flight to the sea where they dip their great wings into the water and then wheel back to sprinkle drops over the temple walls. Here Achilles was married to Helen while Poseidon, Amphitrite, Thetis and all the Nereids acted as witnesses.

To Leuke come pilgrims faithful to Achilles, and sailors who wish to make a sacrifice before going on a dangerous journey.

(Arctinus of Miletus, *Aethiopis*, [?]; Strabo, *Geography*, 1st cen. BC; James Branch Cabell, *Figures of Earth. A Comedy of Appearances*, New York, 1921; James Branch Cabell, *Jurgen. A Comedy of Justice*, New York, 1919)

LIBERIA, a city on the coast of the island of Hoste, near Tierra del Fuego, not to be confused with the African republic of the same name. It was founded by a group of shipwrecked sailors after their ship, the *Jonathan*, sank in these icy waters during the night of March 15, 1881. Fortunately the ship was carrying materials to found a small community in Mozambique; the crew managed to rescue much of this equipment and bring it on shore.

Living on Hoste at the time was a quaint misanthrope, an old European anarchist who some say was of royal blood and whom the natives called Kaw-djer, a word meaning "friend" or "benefactor." He helped the shipwrecked crew, unwillingly, and a small camp was erected on the coast of Scotchwell Bay.

A few months later, a Chilean warship reached the island and it was suggested that the new colonists keep their land and establish themselves permanently on Hoste. (Chile had just concluded a treaty with Argentina concerning Tierra del Fuego and the Chileans expected that the establishment of a colony on one of the islands would lead to an influx of Chilean settlers.) In this way the Hostelian Republic was born, and Liberia—the name given to the initial camp—became the capital. The settlers chose a red and white flag.

Due to the number of minor quarrels that broke out among the inhabitants of the Republic, Kaw-djer accepted the post of governor, giving the island a certain stability. He entered into discussions with Chile concerning the construction of a lighthouse on the nearby island of Horn; he repelled an invasion of the fearful Patagonians.

By 1890 the Hostelian Republic had established strong commercial relations with Chile, Argentina and even Europe, and Liberia had become a well-developed city. It contained two printers, one theatre, one post-office, one church, two schools, a cluster of barracks, a court-house and the beautiful governor's palace. A modern hydro electric power station provided electricity for the factories and for illumination of the streets.

On the morning of March 6, 1891, a group of hunters discovered a gold vein at the foot of the Sentry Boxes Mountains, west of the Hardy Peninsula. The discovery caused a gold rush like the ones experienced in California and the Klondike, leading rapidly to the downfall of the Republic.

The gold-fever caused the workers to abandon agriculture, fishing, and farming. The only ones to escape infection were the few Indians who had sought refuge on Hoste to escape the Patagonians.

The winter of 1893 was the worst the island had ever known; with the island's production almost nonexistent and its population five times the initial number, theft and murder broke out among the hungry people. On January 10, 1894, a Chilean warship attacked the Republic. The Kaw-djer, disillusioned and heartbroken, surrendered. The Republic was dissolved, Hoste became part of Chile and Liberia stands in ruins, unmentioned on official maps.

(Jules Verne, *Les Naufragés du "Jonathan,"* [post.] Paris, 1909)

LIBERTINIA, a large, rich country to the east of JANSENIA. Wine, sugar, amber, silk and other luxury products are exported to its neighbour.

(Père Zacharie de Lisieux, *Relation du pays de Jansénie, où il est traite des singularitez qui s'y trouvent, des coustumes, Moeurs et Religion des habitants. Par Louys Fontaines, Sieur de Saint Marcel*, Paris, 1660)

LICHTENBURG, GRAND DUCHY OF, established in 1316. In 1683, the Turks tried unsuccess-

fully to invade Lichtenburg; since then, Lichtenburg's poverty and general insignificance have made it of little interest to outsiders, and international political events have largely passed it by. Its sole product, and not very successful export, is an unappetizing cheese. In 1949 the trade balance was minus 887,000 *kronen*. The country is too poor even to support an army, and the annual Lichtenburg Fair no longer takes place for lack of funds.

The ruling dynasty was established in 1683. The present Grand Duke Otto and Grand Duchess Sophie are childless, and the heiress to the Duchy is the Princess Maria. However, there are rumours that the Princess will resign her title in order to marry a commoner and, in that case, the dynasty will come to an end. The Royal Family owns twenty-eight and three-tenths square miles of Lichtenburg, but only three and one-seventh square miles are cultivated.

The government is a coalition and no election has been held for the past twenty years. The old Prime Minister, Sebastian Sebastian, has been replaced by General Cosmo Constantine, hitherto Finance Minister and leader of the Conservative Radical Party. The Secretary of State, Hugo Tantanin, has become the new Minister of Finance.

The capital, also called Lichtenburg, centres on the main square, dominated by the Royal Palace and the American Embassy which was originally built by the Grand Duke Maximillian for his mistress.

(*Call Me Madam,* directed by Walter Lang, USA, 1951)

LIDENBROCK SEA, better described as an ocean, deep in the bowels of the earth, discovered by the expedition headed by Professor Lidenbrock of Hamburg in 1863. It lies three hundred and fifty leagues south-east of Iceland, under the Grampian Mountains in Scotland. Its waters are sweet and of an extent similar to that of the Mediterranean. The beaches are of fine golden sand, interspersed with tiny shells from the first days of the Creation.

Lidenbrock Sea is illuminated by whitish rays which give out a light stronger than that of the moon, probably of electric origin, somewhat like an aurora borealis. The vast ceiling that covers this ocean is half hidden by large clouds of drifting vapours that, at certain times of the day, let down torrential rains. The effects of the sky's electric strata on the clouds produces a startling game of lights that seems to induce profound melancholia.

Travellers who wish to explore the Lidenbrock Sea depart from PORT-GRAUBEN. Not far from here rises a tall forest of parasol-like trees, white mushrooms ten to fifteen metres high, so thickly set that the light cannot penetrate. A large number of prehistoric bones lie at the foot of this extraordinary vegetation and travellers will find mastodons' jaws, dinotheres' molars and megatheriums' femurs.

In the Lidenbrock Sea itself, travellers will see sanguinary fights between plesiosauruses and ichthyosauruses—two of the many prehistoric animals who still inhabit these regions.

Visitors are advised, in order to cross the Lidenbrock Sea in comfort, to build a raft of fossilized wood. Because it would be inconvenient to return to the surface by the route they came (through the Snaefells Jökull crater in Iceland— see SAKNUSSEMM'S CORRIDOR), visitors should try to join an underground eruption. The flow of lava rising through the shaft of a volcano should quickly lift the traveller's raft onto the surface of the earth. Lidenbrock's expedition ascended in this way through the Stromboli volcano in Italy on August 29, 1863.

(Jules Verne, *Voyage au centre de la terre*, Paris, 1864)

LILAR, in the principality of Hohenfliess, near PESTITZ, the pleasure gardens and residence of the Prince of Hohenfliess.

In the gardens of Lilar, filled with oak, fir, silver poplar and fruit trees, are several beautiful buildings. The Water House is famous for its fountains, fed by the Rosana, a stream that flows through the valley of Lilar. The Thunder House, high on a hill from which the Blumenbühl Mountains can be seen, is so called because it is frequently struck by lightning. The Enchanted Wood, with its mechanical light and artificial rain, is reminiscent of a more elaborate maze than the one at Versailles. The Temple of Dreams has windows from floor to ceiling, framed by twigs and leaves, giving the impression of a forest clearing rather than a man-made building. The Palace of Lilar itself is approached by a road rising gently between ivy-clad rocks, orchards and jasmine bushes. Travellers will be almost deafened by the sound of the nightingales, canaries, chimney-

swallows, thrushes, finches, larks, pheasants, pigeons and peacocks that dwell in its splendid courtyard.

(Jean Paul [Johann Paul Friedrich Richter], *Titan*, Berlin, 1800–03)

LILLIPUT, an island to the southwest of Sumatra and the Sunda Straits, discovered in 1699 by Lemuel Gulliver, a surgeon on a merchant ship that was shipwrecked on the island. The inhabitants are less than six inches high, and everything in the country is on a scale of one inch to one foot as compared with what most foreign visitors will be accustomed to. Their horses are four and a half inches high, their fields are no bigger than flower beds and the tallest trees are a mere seven feet high.

The capital, Mildendo, is surrounded by walls which are two and a half feet high and eleven inches wide. The entrance gate is flanked by stout towers, ten feet apart. Two main streets divide the square-shaped town into four rectangular sections, each subdivided by lanes and alley-ways, with houses three to five storeys high. The city has a population of five hundred thousand. The emperor's palace, surrounded by a wall two feet high, stands in the centre of the city, where both main streets intersect. The outer court, which is forty square feet, encloses two others; the royal apartments are situated in the innermost square. Huge gates—by Lilliputian standards—lead from one court to the next through the four-inch-thick stone walls. The royal park lies two hundred yards outside Mildendo.

Visitors over six inches high are warned of the difficulties in adapting to Lilliputian standards. If possible treading on local houses and the inadvertent uprooting of trees should be avoided. All visitors should be familiar with some of the country's laws. In Lilliput the whole legal system is enforced by a system of rewards. Anyone who can show he has obeyed the laws for seventy-three moons is granted privileges (which vary according to the condition and rank of the individual concerned) paid for by a State fund; he also receives the non-hereditary title of *Snilpall* or Legal. Fraud is considered a more serious offence than theft— it being argued that honesty has no defence against superior cunning—and is usually punished by death. All crimes against the State are dealt with severely; anyone found guilty of perjury

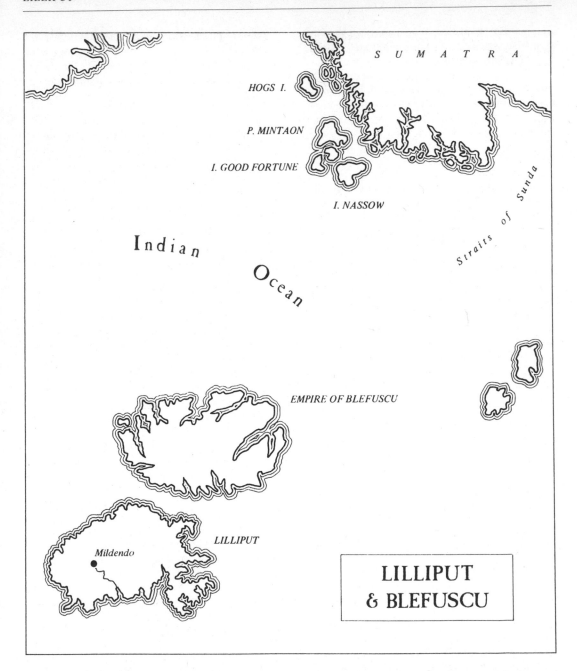

SUMATRA

HOGS I.

P. MINTAON

I. GOOD FORTUNE

I. NASSOW

Indian

Ocean

Straits of Sunda

EMPIRE OF BLEFUSCU

LILLIPUT

Mildendo

LILLIPUT & BLEFUSCU

or of making a false accusation is immediately executed. Someone who has been wrongly accused of a crime is compensated by the State if his accuser cannot reimburse his costs.

In theory, similar principles apply to the selection of people for State office. Good morals are more highly rated than great abilities. Lilliputians say that truth, justice and temperance are in everyone's power, and that with virtue, good intention and experience, anyone can serve the State.

In practice, though, these principles have been greatly eroded. The curious customs of rope-dancing, leaping and creeping, introduced in the early seventeenth century, have become increasingly important as party and factional politics have come to dominate the political life of the island. Rope-dancing is practised only by candidates for high office at court. They are trained in the art from birth, though they are not necessarily men of noble extraction or liberal education. When an office falls vacant through death or disgrace (which is not uncommon), five or six candidates petition to be allowed to dance on a rope. A thin thread, two feet long, is suspended about a foot above the ground; the candidates must dance on it and leap into the air. Whoever jumps highest and lands safely on the rope without falling off wins the vacant post. Quite often the emperor commands cabinet ministers and other officers to dance on a rope and prove that they have not lost their former skill. However, the rope-dancing demonstrations frequently end in serious or even fatal accidents. Leaping and creeping take place only in the presence of the emperor or his minister who holds a stick parallel to the ground. Candidates undergoing this test of dexterity advance one by one and either leap over the stick or creep backwards and forwards under it as it is raised and lowered. The candidate who holds out longest and shows the greatest agility is rewarded with a blue thread. The runner-up receives a red thread and the third best, a green thread. The threads are worn wrapped around the waist and are highly prized as a mark of royal favour; visitors will notice them on most of the important people at court.

The main political factions in the empire are the *Tramecksan* and the *Slamecksan,* named after the high and low shoes worn by the respective parties. These factions will neither eat, drink nor talk with one another. The *Tramecksan* are more numerous, said to be more favourable to the old constitution of the empire, but have no political power. The emperor supports the *Slamecksan,* the only ones who find positions in court. The prince's attitude is less clear. As one of his heels is higher than the other—so that he walks with a limping gait—he is thought to favour the *Tramecksan.*

The empire has recently been divided by civil quarrels. Traditionally, eggs were broken at the big end, until an emperor saw his son cut his finger while breaking an egg in this fashion and issued an edict that all eggs be broken at the little end. This was greatly resented by the people and provoked six rebellions. One emperor lost his throne and an-

other his life in these commotions. Matters became even more serious when the monarchs of BLEFUSCU, an adjacent island, began to intervene, offering refuge in their kingdom to the defeated Big-Endian rebels. According to the Emperor of Blefuscu, the attitude of the Lilliputian government offended the doctrines of the prophet Lustrog, who states in the fifty-fourth chapter of the *Brundecral* that all true believers shall break their eggs at the convenient end. According to the Lilliputian interpretation, the convenient end was, of course, the little end. The influence of the exiled Big-Endians at the Blefuscu court eventually led to the outbreak of war and an attempted invasion of Lilliput. This occurred while Gulliver was sojourning in Lilliput. Gulliver frustrated the invasion plans by wading across the narrow channel and towing back the tiny boats of the Blefuscudians to Lilliput. Peace was consequently concluded on terms that were greatly to Lilliput's advantage. Travellers will find many books published on the controversy, but these must be purchased abroad, as they are banned in Lilliput itself.

Under normal conditions, relations between the two islands are much more cordial. There is considerable trade between the two, and exiles from one country habitually seek refuge in the other. It is the custom for the nobility and richer gentry of each empire to send their children across the channel in order to complete their education, gain knowledge of the world and make progress in the other language. But, in fact, each empire prides itself on the beauty and antiquity of its language and has nothing but scorn for that of its neighbour.

Lilliputians have very distinctive views on the rearing of children. They believe that since males and females mate in order to propagate the race in accordance with the laws of nature, they are actually no different from animals. A child, they say, has no reason to be grateful to its parents for bringing it into the world, for not only is being born no privilege—given the miseries of men on earth—but it was not even the parents' intention to produce a child, their thoughts being on other matters at the time of conception. (Travellers to EREWHON cannot have failed to notice that the Erewhonians hold exactly the opposite view on the responsibilities of being born and giving birth.) Lilliputians conclude that parents are the last people to be entrusted with the welfare of their children, so public nurseries are available in every town. All parents (with the exception of cottagers and labourers) are required to send their children to these nurseries until they have reached the age of twenty moons, when they are considered to have acquired some degree of docility. Thereafter, education varies in accordance with the pupil's rank and condition. The sons of tradespeople are apprenticed at the age of seven, while the sons of persons of quality continue their education until they are fifteen. The latter are not allowed to speak to servants, thus removing the possibility of an early acquaintance with folly or vice. Their parents can visit them only twice a year and can speak to them for only one hour in the presence of a professor. Whispering, endearments and gifts are forbidden on these occasions. Education is designed to inculcate the principles of honesty, modesty, religion and patriotism.

Girls are brought up in separate nurseries and schools, but there is little difference between their education and that of boys, except that their physical exercises are less violent. Girls are also given some instruction in domestic affairs and are taught to despise all personal ornaments beyond cleanliness and dignity, in accordance with the customs of the country. The underlying philosophy behind the education of girls is that as a wife cannot always be young she should always be a reasonable and agreeable companion to her husband. Girls attend school until they reach the marriageable age of twelve.

Although education is compulsory, it is not free. The families are required to contribute money towards their children's keep. It seems offensive to Lilliputians to bring children into the world and then to leave the burden of supporting them on the shoulders of the public.

Visitors will find Lilliputian funeral rites somewhat different from those of their own countries. The dead are buried with their heads pointing downwards, because Lilliputians believe that the earth is flat and will turn upside down before the resurrection of the dead in eleven thousand moons' time. Thus, at their resurrection, the dead will be standing on their feet. The more cultured people of Lilliput consider this absurd, but the custom is maintained to please the lower classes.

The language of Lilliput has not been recorded in any great detail. A few phrases might be useful to visitors: *Hurgo,* "Great Lord," *Borach Mivola,* "Stand out of the way," and *Quinbus*

Flestrin, "Great Man Mountain," the epithet given to Lemuel Gulliver. It should also be noted that when written, the words are traced diagonally from one corner of the page to the other.

The largest coin in the local currency is the *sprug,* a gold disc about the size of a spangle. As for linear measures, one *drurr* = one-fourteenth of an inch and one *glumgluff* = one-tenth of a foot. Time in Lilliput is measured not by the hour and minute hands but by the hand that marks the seconds.

(Jonathan Swift, *Travels Into Several Remote Nations Of The World. In Four Parts. By Lemuel Gulliver, First a Surgeon, and then a Captain of several Ships,* London, 1726)

LIMANORA, an island of the RAILLARO ARCHIPELAGO, in the south-east Pacific, sealed off by a ring of fog. It is also known to outsiders as the "Land of Devils." Coming from the sea, the traveller will first see the snow-covered peak of Lilaroma Volcano. The island is defended by catapults and a stormcone which sends out artificial storms, making the approach somewhat hazardous.

The interior of Limanora is mountainous, with terraced hills and valleys green with tropical vegetation. The rocky shores and cliffs are of volcanic and coralline origin.

Limanoran flora is unlike any other in the Pacific. The *floronal* tree, or tree of life, grows in marshy areas; an extract of *floronal*—which nowadays can be synthesized—allows the lungs to function with little or no air. The *germabell,* the fruit of which gives flexibility to the muscles and the cartilaginous tissue, grows halfway up the mountains in poor soil. The *alfarene* or oxygen shrub grows like moss and can survive under the snow for years; its nuts or cones contain great stores of oxygen and selective breeding helps it to develop into a tree. A compound made from these three plants allows Limanorans to fly to heights where there is no air at all.

One of the most important products of Limanora is *irelium,* a metal extracted from the soil and also found, in pure form, at great depth. It is light, translucent, strong, flexible and elastic when mixed with other substances and it is basic to the Limanoran civilization. It can be spun as fine as gauze yet remain as tough as leather and it is used both in massive engineering works and in the making of light garments. *Irelium* and other metals are extracted mechanically by remote-control devices

of great sophistication so that no underground work is necessary.

Limanora boasts two large valleys: Rimla and Fialume. Rimla is situated on the slopes of Lilaroma Volcano. Large aqueducts bring the water from the mountains to this valley, at the mouth of which there is a huge gorge. In the centre of the Rimla valley stands a broad, transparent dome housing complex machinery, which radiates towards a towering edifice of spires and turrets from which emerge transparent metal tubes. This is the Shrine of Force, the central point for the generation and distribution of energy. However, wind and solar power are also used. Fialume is a huge, lush valley in the interior, also called the Valley of the Past. It is spanned by a glittering roof over which run several streams, irrigating a dazzling display of trees, shrubs and flowers. In an open space in the centre of the valley rises a flight of steps flanked by porticos and colonnades, leading almost to the roof. Fialume is also a burial place, where the dead stand on tall pedestals set among the trees. In order to preserve the body, its tissues are replaced by *irelium*, though before the discovery of this metal they were preserved by calcification in stalactitic caves (as in GREENLAND). In even earlier times, cremation and burial were practised. Nowadays the dead are grouped by family in chronological order.

The original inhabitants of Limanora migrated from the south; an earlier culture was destroyed by a volcanic eruption, and the remains of the cities can still be seen in the Antarctic wastes. Limanoran civilization is based on a desire for physical and spiritual progress. In the beginning, through careful breeding, all hereditary diseases were wiped out, and education and reform gradually reduced the crime rate. A religious reformer propounded the elimination of all remaining social problems through the abolition of private property. He was eventually assassinated and a civil war broke out in which the Socialists were defeated. The upper classes adopted the new religion in order to overcome it and began to worship the martyr as divine: his creed, stripped of its socialist elements, was adopted. Socialists and other undesirable elements were deported to the other islands of the archipelago and forbidden to return upon pain of death. Every obstacle to progress has now been removed. All animal life has been fenced off the island and dead or withering vegetation is destroyed as it would offend the Limanorans.

The people are short, with broad chests, long arms and huge heads. Their pulse is more rapid than that of a European but their breathing is slower. They have great resistance to extreme temperatures. The big toe has developed into a sort of thumb through manipulation of the great gauze-like wings which they attach to their arms and feet and power by small engines. Their flying skill has become almost instinctive. Limanorans believe that willpower is a magnetic force which is best channelled through the eye. This is used in hypnotism and in eye language—in which the Limanorans hold long inaudible dialogues: they never talk unless they have something specific and necessary to say. They are gentle, trustworthy and simple. A delicate nerve centre in the back of their necks senses electric vibrations in the air or in matter. This electric sense of *firla* is the basis of their navigation when they fly and of the *filammu* (will-telegraph, the sending and receiving of emotional impulses over long distances). Their senses are highly developed; they can see changes in the stars that normally can only be seen with a telescope and identify the parts of a compound simply by smelling or tasting it. Their skin is conscious of light and it can tell the difference between several sources of light. They can soothe pain by magnetism channelled through their fingers. Limanorans live to be hundreds of years old.

There are no schools or universities on Limanora, as they are considered to be hotbeds of uniformity. However, education is regarded as the

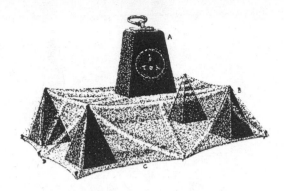

An experiment to prove the strength of gauze on the island of LIMANORA.

chief function of the community and fifty to seventy years are devoted to the training of children. The students are not allowed free, social intercourse until they are twenty-five, and then socializing is only allowed for brief periods and under supervision. If, at the age of fifty, all veneration of the past has been eradicated, the Limanorans are taken to the valley of Fialume where they can see the past of the race, shudder at it and appreciate its progress. Only at seventy-five are they considered fit for parenthood.

Mathematics does not figure in the curriculum as all calculations are carried out by machines. Language is considered a public institution. No word enters the language that has not been purified of all ambiguities and approved by the adult community. A council of elders designs new words when needed but they have to stand the test of universal usage before they are accepted. There is no literature, as the idea of an art-language, in which only some are gifted, would indicate that the common language was somehow inadequate. The closest things to fiction in Limanoran culture are representations of the future which take place in the Theatre of Futurition, where plays are performed by automata. Because language is so precise, Limanorans have coined such expressions as "all is false if words are uncertain" and "take care of the words and the thoughts will take care of themselves" (a saying better expressed by a WONDERLAND noblewoman: "Take care of the sounds, and the sense will take care of itself").

The Limanoran government is a council composed of parents, pro-parents (foster parents better suited to the children) and guardians. The family is the unit of administration and marriage is designed to advance the race. Sex is limited to procreation.

An interesting feature of Limanora is its architecture. Every man or woman has a house and each house bears an ornament representing two climbing plants. If these droop and hang apart, the inhabitants want seclusion and visitors are advised not to disturb them. If they are intertwined, company is desired. (This is somewhat reminiscent of the English custom of "sporting the oak.") Solitude is essential to the Limanorans, who see the final triumph of life as the ability to stand alone— as represented in the funeral monuments. They say that solitude "is an expression of the higher self; baser feelings are gregarious." Individual housing is necessary for other reasons as well. The Limanoran senses are so highly developed that they can hear the natural functions of the human body at work, and sleeping close to another person would be intolerable to them.

The shape and structure of the houses are changed frequently by their owners, using a machine called the *ooloran.* The *ooloran* stands in the Oolorefa Hall of Architecture, a vast central dome surrounded by cupolas built on a level plateau on the Lilaroma. The *ooloran,* or sonarchitect, is a machine that produces various sounds and notes which are projected into a whirlwind of *irelium dust,* causing it to take a desired shape. Magnets then hold the dust particles in place, heat fixes the shape and a sharp reduction in temperature completes the process by chilling the metal. When a satisfactory model has been constructed, it is airlifted to its site.

Should the visitor be invited to enter a Limanoran house he is advised to look at the beds. These are half-hammock, half-framework, soft and flexible, hung at the corners and at the sides so that the body lies in a groove, kept from contact with the sides by a series of rests. The fitted pillow is mildly charged with positive electricity to draw energy from the nerve centres and soothe the tissues. The framework is charged with negative electricity. The use of these beds produces a sense of exhilaration and helps Limanorans develop their characteristic tripping, elastic gait.

Travellers should visit at least four of Limanora's magnificent buildings. Tellanora is a huge central hall where a *moranalan* or time telescope shows pictures of the future. In smaller halls the different possibilities offered by civilization are also represented. One separate hall contains the *ciralai-*son or Museum of Terrors, where the Limanoran hell is depicted, showing a spiritually stagnant society, with many scenes revealing "civilized" Christian countries of the western world. The Theatre is possibly the finest building on the island. It is a massive crystal dome, high on the Lilaroma, flanked by terraces and tall towers made of lava. An instrument called the *duomovamolan* is played here, reproducing and interpreting the music of the cosmos in sound and light. Limanorans fly to the building and listen to the music, suspended in hanging rests inside the dome. A third building is the Ilarime, devoted to the combined arts of smell, taste and sound. Symphonies are composed to appeal to all three senses, but as the experience is extremely passive, it is enjoyed for only short periods at a time. The fourth building, Oomalefa, consists of a series of halls built on a promontory overlooking the sea and is approached through a transparent portico. The highest ridge is covered by a series of buildings, clustered together like stars, a Milky Way of dual pinnacles with constellations of minarets and domes. Oomalefa houses the sciences of nutrition and medication and people come here at the slightest hint of illness.

There are several peculiar sciences in Limanora: *sonnology,* based on ancient sayings such as "sleep unburies the dead," designed to unravel an individual's past and future through the analysis of his dreams; *leomarie,* the science of earth-seeing, which studies the crust and inner movements of the globe; and *lilarie,* the science of island security which, with the help of various instruments, forewarns of weather changes and approaching travellers. In spite of these preparations Limanora is threatened with eventual destruction as the Antarctic continent subsides and the volcanoes to the south die. It is even feared that the entire archipelago may thus one day be destroyed.

(Godfrey Sweven, *Limanora, the Island of Progress,* New York & London, 1903)

LINCOLN or **MYSTERIOUS,** a former volcanic island in the Pacific Ocean, 1,800 miles from New Zealand; discovered fortuitously in 1865 by a group of Confederate prisoners fleeing the American Civil War in a lighter-than-air vehicle.

Flanked by a similar whale-shaped island, this arid, rocky piece of land was a refuge for terns and gulls at the time of its discovery. On the dark sand of its shores lived a great mixture of seals, crustaceans and molluscs. Farther inland the land rose abruptly to form an enormous plateau dominated by the twin conical peaks of a volcano covered with eternal snow. The lower slopes of these peaks were thick with forests that were home to a wide and picturesque variety of animals.

To their great surprise, the Americans met a certain Captain Nemo, inventor of the famous submarine *Nautilus*, who had taken refuge on the island. But shortly after this meeting the volcano came to life, and its cascading eruptions destroyed most of the land.

Today only a narrow string of rocks, barely visible above the ocean's surface, bears witness to the last home of Captain Nemo.

(Jules Verne, *L'Ile mystérieuse*, Paris, 1874)

LINDON or **OSSIRIAND**, a region lying between the western coast of MIDDLE-EARTH and the Blue Mountains. It is divided into Forlindon and Harlindon by the Gulf of Lune, the estuary of the River Lune (Lune being a rendering in the Common Speech of the ancient Grey-elven word "Lhûn") which flows through Lindon from ERIADOR. The chief city and port is known as the GREY HAVENS. This is all that remains of the great realm of Beleriand, which was totally destroyed and engulfed by the sea at the end of the First Age of Middle-earth.

Lindon is inhabited by elves who were reluctant to leave when many of their number crossed the Blue Mountains to join the Silvan elves in what is now known as MIRKWOOD, or to go to HOLLIN. The area was once ruled by Gil-galad who, with the help of men, was able to drive the forces of Sauron, the Dark Lord of MORDOR, out of Lindon during the Second Age. Gil-galad was a leading member of the Last Alliance of men and elves against Sauron and he died in the final battle against the Dark Lord on the slopes of ORODRUIN.

In later years, Lindon was ruled by Círdan, a famous mariner and shipwright who had also been present at the battle that ended the Second Age. He frequently aided the men of the north in their battles against Sauron in the Third Age and was a member of the White Council formed to coordinate plans against him.

(J.R.R. Tolkien, *The Return of the King*, London, 1955; J.R.R. Tolkien, *The Silmarillion*, London, 1977)

LINELAND, a country ruled by a vivacious and good-natured monarch. Lineland itself is no more than a straight line.

The subjects of Lineland are small lines (the men) and points (the women) and all are confined in motion and eyesight to the single straight line which is their world. Linelanders cannot deviate from their narrow path and will not make way for visitors, nor can they pass each other. The whole of their horizon is limited to a point and no one can see anything but this point. For this reason, the sex and age of the Linelanders can be distinguished only by the sound of the voice.

Since all vision is limited to this one unique point and all motion to one straight line, visitors will find little of interest in Lineland.

(Edwin A. Abbott, *Flatland*, New York, 1952)

LIN LIGUA, a tidal pool of enormous depth near the shore of the Severn in South Wales. It is so deep that the incoming tide never fills it completely. When the tide begins to recede, the pool belches forth the water it has swallowed in a great spout as high as a mountain.

(Geoffrey of Monmouth, *Historia Regum Britanniae*, 12th cen. AD)

LIPERDA, a port on the eastern Mediterranean, occupied by the Ottoman Turks. At the colourful central market travellers can buy slaves brought here by Persian pirates. Not far from the market is the seraglio of the Bashaw of Liperda, noteworthy for a beautiful alcove set in the gardens.

(Eliza Fowler Haywood, *Philidore and Placentia: Or, L'Amour trop Delicat, By Mrs. Haywood*, London, 1727)

LITUANIA (not to be confused with Lithuania of the Baltic region), a melancholic country, less sinister than Transylvania. Lituania is a land of marshes, bogs, dark forests and snow-capped mountains. Neo-Gothic castles—sometimes haunted by the dangerous larvae of Lituania, sometimes inhabited by extravagant families with bloodthirsty tastes— are scattered throughout the country.

Travellers are warned that it always rains in Lituania, except when it snows or when hailstones as big as apples pelt from the heavens. On rare occasions it rains, snows and hails all at the same time, to the sound of a furious wind typical of this part of the world. Lituania is known as the "Country of Long Winters."

Two hotels can be recommended: the *Barlsk-dat Inn* and the *Versalis Hotel;* in both the *starka,* an inebriating drink the colour of amber, is served to the rousing music of a ladies' orchestra.

(Henri Guigonnat, *Démone en Lituanie,* Paris, 1973)

LIVER AND ONIONS, the chief town and capital of ROOTABAGA COUNTRY. It can be reached by rail and is served by the Golden Spike Limited, the fastest long-distance train in the entire country. The city stands in the rolling prairies and is the centre of the country's agricultural life.

One of the city's best-known citizens is the Potato Face Blind Man, who can be seen playing his accordion outside the post-office on Main Street. He is surrounded by a variety of receptacles for collecting money. The tin cup is for ball-players to throw money into from a distance of ten feet; the one who throws the most coins is deemed the luckiest. The wooden mug with the hole in the bottom is for the use of poor people; they can have the pleasure of giving him a nickel and still get it back again. The Blind Man sits between a dishpan and a washtub, hoping that someone will withdraw all his money from the post-office and give it to him. The Potato Face Blind Man is one of the best-known storytellers in the city.

(Carl Sandburg, *Rootabaga Stories,* New York, 1922)

LIVING ISLAND, a country inhabited by mythical beasts and talking boats and clocks, cigar-smoking fireplaces and animated musical instruments. The mayor is a friendly dragon called H. R. Pufnstuf.

Travellers can visit Witchiepoo Castle, once owned by a scientist of the same name, who accidentally blew herself up after an unsuccessful encounter with Jimmy, a small boy whose flute she had tried to steal.

Should travellers meet a witch during their visit, they are best advised to look angelic, as angels are anathema to witches on Living Island.

(*Pufnstuf,* directed by Hollingsworth Morse, USA, 1970)

LIVING MEN, LAND OF, see Land of the GLITTERING PLAIN.

LIXUS, an island off the north-west coast of Africa, embraced by an arm of the sea stretching inland. In ancient times Lixus was the site of a famous grove which bore golden fruit. Of this grove only one tree now remains. Its flowers have petals like golden foil and fruits like heavy golden orbs; within the orbs the flesh has a structure resembling crystals of metallic ore.

Insects like hornets with metallic bodies and golden wings gather the juices of this fruit. Inside their nests, these insects have cells similar to those of a beehive, and manufacture a honey-like substance for the nourishment of their young. This substance is too hot to touch and appears to be molten gold. Should one care to inspect the hives, one must wait until sunset, when the insects become drowsy and allow a closer examination.

(Pliny the Elder, *Inventorum Natura,* 1st cen. AD)

LLAREGYB, a harbour town (population, less than five hundred) at the mouth of the river Dewi on the Welsh coast. A small, dozy watering place, Llaregyb nestles between daisy-filled meadows and Milk Wood, a hunched, rabbit-haunted wood that limps down alongside the town to the edge of the sea. Cows and goats graze in the lush fields around, and donkeys browse on nearby Donkey Down.

Metallic insects gather the juices of golden fruit on LIXUS.

Llaregyb has only three true streets: Coronation Street, Cockle Row and Donkey Street. The rest of the town consists of narrow, cobbled alleyways and has little, in fact, to offer of architectural interest. Coronation Street, for instance, consists mostly of two-storey dwellings painted in crude colours and pink wash. A few pretentious eighteenth-century houses remain, but most of them are now in a sad state of disrepair. Bethesda Chapel and the graveyard are of little historical importance. Nor does Llaregyb offer a great deal to the sportsman. The Dewi, reputed to be rich in trout, is so heavily poached that few fish remain for the visiting angler. The main attractions of Llaregyb are the quaint cobbled streets, the little fishing harbour, and the conversation of the people who live here and who possess a salty individuality. The pump in front of the Town Hall is one of the principal gathering places for the townsfolk, and probably the main centre for the exchange of gossip.

The small harbour is generally full of fishing boats, bobbing up and down with the tide. The local fishermen are extremely reluctant to go out if the weather seems in any way threatening, preferring to spend stormy days in the comfort of *The Sailors' Arms*. This public house is noteworthy for the hands of its clock which, for the past fifty years, have stood fixed at eleven-thirty, so that it is always opening time in *The Sailors' Arms*. It serves warm, thin, bitter beer, and allows music and singing in the evenings.

In the unlikely event of *The Sailors' Arms* being full, accommodation can be obtained at *Bay View*, a house for paying guests at the top of the town. The boarding house is run by Mrs. Ogmore-Pritchard, widow, twice, of Mr. Ogmore, retired linoleum salesman, and Mr. Pritchard, failed bookmaker. *Bay View* can be recommended for its cleanliness and its dust-free bedrooms. Indeed, the widow's concern for the cleanliness of her establishment is so great that she has been known to refuse guests rather than have them put their feet on her carpets and sleep on her sheets.

The people of Llaregyb are extremely religious; many of them still have plaques reading "thou shalt not" above their beds. They are a close-knit community and everyone has a detailed knowledge of his neighbour's affairs. Although puritanical and prone to ostracize those who do not conform to their moral standards, they seem to take an almost prurient interest in the slight sexual peccadilloes of others.

As is usual in a community where there are few surnames, individuals with the same names are often distinguished by reference to their trade or calling. The baker is known as "Dai Bread," the undertaker as "Evans the Death," the chapel organist as "Organ Morgan," the milkman as "Ocky Milkman." Most of the people of Llaregyb are remarkable for their verbal ability and articulate, almost poetic, speech. The local preacher, the Reverend Eli Jenkins, is the best example of this gift, greeting each morning and evening with his own poetry.

Food in the town is traditional Welsh cooking: Welsh cakes, *cawl,* a broth with leeks, and locally gathered cockles. Visitors should be wary of certain cooked meats, however, as it is rumoured that the butcher sells meats not normally fit for human consumption, such as shrews and moles.

A place of some historical interest is Llaregyb Hill, behind the town, said by the Reverend Eli Jenkins to be a mystic tumulus. It is in fact a memorial to the people who lived in the region before the Celts left "the Land of Summer," and the site of Druidic marriage ceremonies. A small circle of stones does stand on the hill, but they were erected, not by Druids, but by the son of the town's butcher. The hill however is worth climbing, as it provides a fine panoramic view of the town. Romantic travellers might enjoy a visit to nearby Milk Wood, much frequented by courting couples.

(Dylan Thomas, *Under Milk Wood, a Play for Voices*, London, 1954)

LOCUS SOLUS, a large villa surrounded by vast gardens in Montmorency, near Paris, in the department of Seine-et-Oise. Locus Solus is the residence of the scientist Martial Canterel, and comprises several laboratories in which the master and his helpers dedicate their lives to the altar of science.

The garden contains a number of pavilions in which Canterel's masterful inventions—as well as a few works of art—are exhibited. Among these is the statue of a young naked man made of clay brought from Timbuctoo by the explorer Echenoz; in the statue's right hand grows a plant, *Arthemisia maritima*, excellent for the cure of amenorrhea. The niche in which the statue is placed is crowned by three bas-reliefs from Gloannic, a Breton city buried under sand in the fifteenth century.

Another interesting object set up for the admiration of visitors is a flying beetle hanging from a complicated apparatus invented by Canterel to predict meteorological changes—the apparatus can establish ten days in advance the direction and strength of even the slightest breeze as well as the dimensions, opacity and condensation potential of every future cloud. The beetle is in fact a work of art exposed to the elements and made of an intricate mosaic of human teeth extracted by Dr. Canterel by means of a totally painless procedure. The discovery of this procedure brought to Locus Solus a large number of toothache sufferers and Dr. Canterel decided to use the extracted teeth for a practical purpose.

In the sunniest part of the gardens visitors can see a sort of large diamond, a container for the *aqua-mican*, special water created by Canterel that, through a process of oxygenation, allows both men and animals to breathe in it as easily as on land.

The highlight of a visit to Locus Solus is the Pavilion of the Resurrection where corpses kept on ice come suddenly to life thanks to two of Canterel's great inventions: *vitalium* and *résurrectine*. The *résurrectine* is introduced into the corpse's skull where it forms a film; next, the *vitalium* is injected and enters into contact with the film, thereby provoking an electrical discharge that makes the corpse sit up in the most realistic manner. By perfecting the procedure, Dr. Canterel managed to restore to the corpses the movements most frequently made during the individuals' lives. The lifelike illusion is complete: the lungs breathe in and out, the lips form words, the hands wave about in the air. Not all corpses are suited for this experience and Dr. Canterel selects them with extreme care.

Though Dr. Canterel is himself in charge of taking visitors on a guided tour of Locus Solus, sensitive people might prefer to avoid the Madman's Pavilion in which an elderly gentleman repeats over and over the detailed circumstances of his daughter's murder.

(Raymond Roussel, *Locus Solus*, Paris, 1914)

LOCUTA, an island beyond LAPUTA, discovered by Lemuel Gulliver Junior. The island, a major trading nation, is densely populated. The Locutans trade with all the nations of the world and have discovered from experience that they must adopt different laws and customs when they come into contact with other people. As a result of long study they have come to the conclusion that different societies have different needs and laws because of the anarchy and confusion which came into human society through the development of different languages. Locutans therefore devote much of their time to studying language and oratory. The island is surrounded by an immense number of steps on which the Locutan children can be seen learning their lessons.

When Locuta comes into contact with a new country, new regulations are drawn up for dealing with it. For example, the Locutans have analyzed British society in terms of the nine parts of speech. The most ancient or first class has been called the Function and is broken down into four subdivisions or Nouns: those who govern everything, those who govern people and places, those who deal with the imagination and those who categorize. According to the Locutans, the Nouns are always accompanied by members of the second class who proclaim the properties and quality of their masters. These, the Adjectives, are extremely important because the Nouns have to depend on them for their reputation. Nouns are assisted in their actions by a third class known as Verbs. A fourth class, the Conjunctions, are the British priests: no parties may be joined together without their assistance.

The manner in which Locutans analyze other societies is not known.

(Mrs. E.S. Graham, *Voyage to Locuta; A Fragment by Lemuel Gulliver Junior,* London, 1817)

LODIDHAPURA, a city in the jungles of Cambodia, ruled by the famous Leper King. As one approaches the city, one is immediately struck by the temples and stone palaces rearing their solid masses against the sky. Elaborately carved towers rise far above the trees in stately grandeur. Before the city are fields in which almost naked slaves labour; their houses are thatched huts rigged up near the city wall. Behind the city's gate spread the streets of Lodidhapura, lined with tiny shops which display, among other things, pottery, silver and gold ornaments, rugs, incense, weapons and armour. Huge trees and gorgeous shrubbery shadow winding avenues flanked by statues and columns. The Royal Palace is the city's most splendid building, embellished from its foundation to its loftiest tower with tiles of brilliant colours in fanciful display.

The religion of Lodidhapura is simple: the people worship Siva the Destroyer in the temple that dominates the whole city. They also worship two lesser gods, Brahmer and Vishnu.

Lodidhapura has a strong army. The soldiers are clad in brass armour, leather overclothes and brass helmets. Swords, spears, bows and arrows are the usual fighting weapons.

The Leper King of Lodidhapura was cured of his ailment by Gordon King, an American explorer who came here in the 1930's. Apparently the American, while wandering through the jungle in a hallucinatory state, saved the high priest of Lodidhapura from the attack of a tiger. In gratitude he was taken into the king's service, fell out of favour when he rescued the princess of the rival town of PNOM DHEK and finally was threatened with death by the Leper King himself. He saved himself by curing the king's "leprosy" which was in reality an allergic reaction to a species of mushroom to which the king was enormously partial.

Visitors to Lodidhapura are advised not to incur the king's anger, as those who do so are put to the "test of the tiger," a type of man-and-beast combat, which is also a very popular Lodidhapurian game.

(Edgar Rice Burroughs, *The Jungle Girl*, New York, 1931)

LOFOTEN, a cemetery that should not be confused with the islands of the same name. Besides its old stone tombs and its perpetually raining skies, it is famous for its crows, who feed on cold human flesh and are as numerous as they are fat. According to certain questionable witnesses, the dead in Lofoten Cemetery may be less dead than are some well-known living persons.

(Oscar Venceslas de Lubicz Milosz, *Les Sept solitudes, poèmes*, Paris, 1906)

LOMB, a country on the Indian coast. The main produce of Lomb is pepper, collected in the forests of Combar Province. Because of the many serpents in the region, the people of Lomb anoint their hands and feet with a juice made from snails in order to be able to gather the pepper safely. There are two main cities in the Combar Province: Fladrine and Zinglantz, each with a mixed population of Christians and Jews.

The main city in Lomb is Polombe, at the foot of a mountain of the same name. Here is found the Polombe well: the smell and taste of its waters change by the hour and it is said that drinking from it three times will cure any sickness in the world. The inhabitants of Polombe often drink from the well and are never ill and do not age.

The people of Lomb worship the ox for its simplicity and meekness and for the profit that comes of it. They make the ox work for six to seven years, and then eat its flesh. They make idols, half-man and half-ox, from which they believe evil spirits speak to them. Since children are used as sacrificial offerings to the idols of Lomb taking one's family along on a visit to that country cannot be recommended.

(Sir John Mandeville, *Voiage de Sir John Maundevile*, Paris, 1357)

LONDON-ON-THAMES, a city partially built at the bottom of a cliff and partially carved from the rock, inhabited by a tribe of gorillas who speak English and believe themselves to be re-incarnations of historical sixteenth-century figures.

The city is approached through large fields of bamboo, celery and fruit in which the gorillas work with crude, handmade implements. The portion of the city built upon level ground consists of circular bamboo huts with thatched conical roofs and rectangular buildings of mud and stone. Near the foot of the cliff is the Royal Palace, a three-storey building with towers and ramparts, roughly suggestive of medieval England. The king, a huge gorilla who calls himself Henry the Eighth, lives here in a bare room with a dry grass floor. The king has five wives, all gorillas, called Catherine of Aragon, Anne Boleyn and so on. Other gorillas are the Prince of Wales, Cardinal Wolsey and an old hairy ape called God. White women are sometimes captured for the king and become for short periods His Majesty's sixth wife. The other gorillas make do with the African women they are given by the terrorized neighbouring tribes. Some white men act as the gorillas' servants.

The explanation for this odd community was provided by an English professor born in 1933. He discovered how to extract cells from dead bodies, and with a number of samples from historical personages he travelled to Africa. Here he injected his cells into gorillas, taught them English and in his declining years injected himself with the cells of young apes. The professor is in fact the creature whom the gorillas call God, and revere as the real head of their kingdom. It is not known whether certain people in the world today are in fact gorillas transformed by the English professor in his youth.

(Edgar Rice Burroughs, *Tarzan and the Lion Man*, New York, 1934)

LONE ISLANDS, a group of islands some four hundred leagues to the east of NARNIA. The islands have been under the rule of Narnia since King Gale, the tenth King of Narnia, freed them from a dragon and the islanders took an oath of allegiance to him in gratitude. Subsequently there appears to have been little contact between Narnia and its island possessions.

Of the three islands, Doorn is the most important. Avra, to the east, is almost uninhabited, but even fewer people live on Felimath, used mostly for sheep farming. It is separated from Doorn by a mile-wide channel.

The major settlement on Doorn is the town of Narrowhaven, once an important centre for the slave trade—most slaves were sent to CALORMEN to work in the mines or in the galleys. But visitors are advised that slaves can no longer be purchased, as the trade was abolished by King Caspian of Narnia on his exploratory voyages to Doorn, when he deposed the governor of the Lone Islands. His Sufficiency (as the governor was called) had become deeply involved in the commerce of slaves, which by Narnian standards is an unacceptable practice. He was replaced by Lord Bern, one of the seven lords exiled from Narnia.

(C.S. Lewis, *Prince Caspian*, London, 1951; C.S. Lewis, *The Voyage of the "Dawn Treader,"* London, 1952; C.S. Lewis, *The Last Battle*, London, 1956)

LONELY ISLAND, an island in the Gulf of Finland, off the coast of MOOMINLAND. The beaches of Lonely Island are covered in lilies. Inland, heavy white clusters of flowers can be seen; from a distance they seem to be made of glass. Sky-blue roses and crimson and black kingcups also grow here.

The island is the gathering place of the *Hattifatteners,* small tube-like animals who can neither hear nor speak. Their faces are normally blank and expressionless; they do not sleep nor feel any emotion. Normally they are found in Moominland, but every year they come to Lonely Island in June and set off on an endless search; no one knows what the object of their search may be.

(Tove Jansson, *Taikurin hattu*, Helsinki, 1958; Tove Jansson, *Muumipapan urotyöt*, Helsinki, 1966)

LONELY MOUNTAIN, also known as EREBOR, lies between MIRKWOOD and the IRON HILLS to the north of Long Lake. As its name implies, it stands apart from other ranges, and is a notable landmark in the flat plain east of Mirkwood. The River Running forms a large loop around the southern spurs of the mountain; this is the site of DALE, the city-kingdom of men.

Erebor is the seat of the dwarf king known as the King Under the Mountain and the chief mansion of Durin's Folk, following their flight from MORIA. The great halls and palaces beneath the mountain were hollowed out by the dwarves themselves, who grew rich on the gold and jewels they mined and worked in their underground workshops. For many years they lived in prosperity and on good terms with the men of Dale; the town was an outlet for many of their artifacts. This period of prosperity came to a sudden end with the arrival of Smaug the Golden, a dragon from the mountains to the north of Mirkwood. Attracted to Erebor by stories of its great wealth, Smaug fell upon the dwarves, taking them by surprise, killing many of them and driving the survivors away. For almost two hundred years, Smaug lived in the very deepest hall of the dwarves' palace, gathering all the treasure of the mountain there in a huge glittering heap on which he slept. Like all dragons, Smaug was interested in possessing wealth, not in using it to any purpose. The enormous dragon made frequent forays into Dale, flying over the town on his immense bat wings and breathing fire and smoke. His victims were so numerous that the town was eventually abandoned by all its inhabitants. The land around the Mountain became known as the Desolation of Smaug, a wasteland of burnt and blackened tree stumps where nothing grew.

In 2941 Third Age, an expedition led by the dwarf king Thorin set out to oust Smaug from his lair. One of the number was Bilbo Baggins, a hobbit from the SHIRE, who engaged Smaug in a long exchange of riddles. This is probably the most appropriate way to speak with the dragons of MIDDLE-EARTH, as it appeals to their natural taste for riddles and allows the speaker to conceal his true identity. Bilbo's riddles did, however, have an unfortunate outcome. Smaug took one of them to mean that the hobbit was either from or connected with LAKE-TOWN. The dragon flew out to attack the town, causing great destruction before he was killed by Bard, the future King of Dale.

After the death of Smaug, a great battle was fought on the slopes of Erebor between an alliance of men, dwarves and elves and an invading force of orcs and other evil creatures associated with MORDOR. The battle, recorded in history as the Battle of the Five Armies, was won by the dwarves and their allies, but only because of the intervention of the eagles of the MISTY MOUNTAINS and of Beorn of the Vales of ANDUIN.

Like the town of Dale, the dwarf kingdom now entered a new period of peace and prosperity, which was to last until the War of the Ring. In 3019 Third Age, Dale fell to an invasion force from the east, and the besieged men and dwarves retreated into the caves of the Misty Mountain. The siege was broken in a last sally against the enemy when it was learned that the forces of evil had been defeated in the south.

The most obvious way of gaining access to the kingdom under the Mountain is through the so-called Front Gate, a great cavern in the southern face of the mountain; the River Running flows out through this natural arch. But the dwarves also built a secret entrance in the west side of the mountain. The door was set in the face of the cliff and was indistinguishable from the surrounding rock. It could only be opened by magic; a special key would open it, but only at a specific time of day, when the setting sun shone on the concealed keyhole. This door was the objective of the thirteen dwarves who set out under Thorin to reclaim the mountain from Smaug.

It was Bilbo the hobbit who realized that all the factors mentioned in the map showing the door had at last come together and who finally opened the door. This entrance to the mountain was, however, destroyed by Smaug as he flew out on his last foray against Lake-town.

From the secret entrance a narrow passage led to the deep cavern where Smaug made his lair. The passage can also be reached by the wide, smooth steps that lead up to the great halls, built at the level of the Front Gate. The principal halls are the halls of feasting and the hall of council. But their splendour is surpassed by that of the Great Chamber of Thrór, entered through two great doors. At the rear of the Chamber a door leads into a cavern where the River Running rises. The turbulent stream runs along a narrow channel constructed in olden times, before flowing out through the large Front Gate.

The long southern spur of the Lonely Mountain is known as Ravenhill, the site of an ancient guard post. It is so called because it is the home of the ravens of the mountains, an old, wise race who are traditionally on good terms with the dwarves. In the days before the arrival of Smaug, Ravenhill was the home of Carc and his mate, venerable creatures who nested above the guard post. Traditionally, the ravens brought news to the dwarves of the mountain and, in exchange, were given the bright, shining objects of which they were so fond. There now appear to be few ravens left on the Lonely Mountain. It was on Ravenhill that the elves made their stand during the Battle of the Five Armies.

Erebor is also the home of an ancient breed of thrushes, large dark birds with spotted, pale yellow breasts. The thrushes of the mountain are thought to live to more than two hundred years old. They are friends to the dwarves and act as messengers to the men of Dale, whose speech they understand. One of these birds overheard Bilbo discussing his exchange of riddles with Smaug and realized that the dragon had accidentally displayed his weak spot. The thrush then flew to Dale to tell Bard its information, thus enabling the man to kill the dragon.

It was in Erebor that the greatest treasure ever found by the dwarves was finally discovered. This was the Arkenstone, a great white jewel with many facets that reflected the light and seemed to change colour as the light changed. It was left in the mountain when the dwarves were driven out by Smaug, who took it for his hoard. The Arkenstone was found by Bilbo. The stone was finally buried with Thorin in his tomb deep in the mountain.

(J.R.R. Tolkien, *The Hobbit, or There and Back Again*, London, 1937; J.R.R. Tolkien, *The Fellow-*

ship of the Ring, London, 1954; J.R.R. Tolkien, *The Return of the King,* London, 1955)

LONG DUNE, a long, low island in the far southwest of the EARTHSEA ARCHIPELAGO. The island is uninhabited, but is visited once a year by the Raft Folk (or Children of the Open Sea as they are sometimes called) who come here to cut wood to repair their large rafts. The information on the customs of these people has not been scientifically corroborated and, for most of the inhabitants of Earthsea, the Raft Folk are only a myth.

The Raft Folk live on rafts of smooth closely-fitted logs, solidly caulked. The rafts carry rough wooden cabins for shelters, and high masts. The sails are made from the *nilgu,* a brown-leaved seaweed found in the Southern Reach. The *nilgu,* fringed like a fern and with fronds up to one hundred feet long, is pounded and then woven into the material for the sails. *Nilgu is* also woven into fibres to make ropes and fishing nets. On the longest raft, over forty feet long, is a temple, a large shelter of shaped logs. The doorjambs are carved in the shape of sounding whales and the door itself is surmounted by a square design of great complexity.

The Raft Folk are tall, thin people whose most noticeable feature are their great eyes. They move in a very angular fashion and resemble herons or cranes, a resemblance which is made even stronger by their thin, piping voices. They go about almost naked—apart from their loincloths—but travellers will find them full of a great natural dignity.

In the autumn, the rafts come to Long Dune to be refitted. They then take separate routes and each raft carries its crew away following the movements of the great whales across the uncharted seas. The whales are central to the life of these people, who hunt the great creatures with ivory harpoons. Every winter some of the rafts are lost, swallowed by the waves, which in these seas can be as high as hills (or, as the Raft Folk, who have never seen hills, say—"as great as thunderclouds").

In spring they sail to the point known to them as "The Roads of Balatran" (though travellers will not find the point marked on any of the charts used in Earthsea). All the rafts that have survived the winter gales gather in a great circle, constantly floating apart and then coming together again. This is the time when marriages take place.

The Raft Folk take no interest in the affairs of lands-people and ignore both the islands they drift past and the ships they sometimes see during their long journeys. Their main occupations are fishing, making ropes and sails from *nilgu,* and shaping the whale ivory into tools. But there is always time for swimming or for talking and they believe that no task has to be completed by a set time. To a large extent the Raft Folk lead a timeless existence; they have no concept of hours or minutes. Their only units of time are whole days, whole nights and the seasons themselves.

On the shortest night of the year, torches are lit on the rafts as they lie gathered once more in a great circle. The Raft Folk then celebrate the Long Dance, the one custom they have in common with the islanders of Earthsea. The dance has no musical accompaniment; it simply follows the rhythm of bare feet pounding the floor of the swaying rafts and the thin voices of the chanters. Their songs are not of the heroes of Earthsea, but of the albatross, the whale and the dolphin. This has made scholars wonder whether any Raft People literature found its way into Europe and influenced both a lengthy ancient-mariner narrative and a French zoological poem that confuses birds with poets. All the Raft People remember of the traditions of other men is the story of how the god Segoy raised the islands out of the deep; the rest of their lore refers solely to the sea and its creatures.

The Raft Folk live mainly on a fish stew, to which seaweed is sometimes added—although salty, it tastes good and is very nourishing. They treasure fresh water and collect and store rain water as a precious commodity.

(Ursula K. Le Guin, *A Wizard of Earthsea,* New York, 1968; Ursula K. Le Guin, *The Farthest Shore,* London, 1973)

LONGJUMEAU, a city in France from which no one can depart. Many times have inhabitants made plans to leave for Borneo, New Zealand, Tierra del Fuego or Greenland, but something always happens to defer their departure. One forgets his keys, another falls asleep and misses his train, another twists his ankle or perhaps leaves behind his wallet. The inhabitants of Longjumeau have never attended a funeral, a wedding or a christening outside their city. Once a couple thought they had escaped; they got into a first class carriage that would—they thought—take them to Versailles. However the train left and the carriage, disconnected, remained in the station.

(Léon Bloy, "Les captifs de Longjumeau," in *L'Oeuvre Complète*, Paris, 1947)

LONGSHAW, a castle and settlement on the banks of a river which flows into the SUNDERING FLOOD from the west. Longshaw is a mixture of beautiful domestic architecture and military defences. It was originally built in peacetime, but towers and other fortifications had to be added to defend it from attack. The castle itself stands by the river bank and is surrounded by orchards and gardens. Its pinnacles and spires have been likened to carved ivory because of their delicacy. The banner of the castle's lord, Godrick, flies over Longshaw with the emblem of the hart impaled.

(William Morris, *The Sundering Flood*, London, 1897)

LOOKING-GLASS LAND, a country beyond the Deanery of Christ Church College, Oxford. Travellers can reach it by entering the Dean's quarters and proceeding to his sitting room, with its large chimney-piece surmounted by a looking-glass of vast proportions. Carefully avoiding the vases of dried flowers protected by Victorian bell-jars, visitors should climb up onto the mantelpiece and enter Looking-Glass Land through the glass, which will melt away like a bright silvery mist.

The room on the other side is very similar to the Dean's sitting room, though less tidy. The different elements contained in his room have here a life of their own and visitors are advised not to be startled by the back of the clock grinning at them with the face of a little old man.

The room behind the looking-glass extends well into the land and becomes a pleasant landscape of chequered fields, hills, forests and rivulets—but an accurate description of the scenery cannot be given. Indeed, travellers will find that Looking-Glass Land is a place of changing physical characteristics. Very suddenly, without any warning, they will find themselves in a different location, because Looking-Glass Land has done away with the unnecessary dilly-dallying of motion in space and the passing of time. For instance, visitors may find themselves sitting in a railway carriage after having been, only seconds

before, admiring the flowers in a garden. From the carriage they will be transported in *no* time to a wood; from the wood, to a pleasant, English, old-world shop; from the shop, to a pleasant stretch of water. Looking-Glass Land is the tangible proof of Zeno's refutation of space. Though Looking-Glass Land occupies a fair number of square miles, the different places in the land are not reached by covering these miles. Normally, in order to reach point *A* from point *B*, point *C* must be crossed first; in order to reach point *C*, point *D* must be reached, and so on. To avoid this impossible progression, in Looking-Glass Land visitors proceed from one point to another without the unnecessary and infinite bother of covering intermediate space.

Time is also a factor to be considered by travellers in Looking-Glass Land. It is possible (even probable) that in their country travellers take it for granted that time flows onwards—from the past, into the future, through the present; that when in their country it is five o'clock, it can be safely assumed that it will next be one minute past five and then two minutes past five.

Not so in Looking-Glass Land. In the first place, personal time can be stopped at will, without affecting the time of others. People can choose to stop growing entirely at a given age (though sometimes a helping hand might be needed) while the rest of the country progresses as usual. In the second place, because time in Looking-Glass Land flows backwards as well as forwards, it is possible to remember things that will happen much later. The penal code of Looking-Glass Land takes advantage of this fact by carrying out the sentence first, having the trial next and allowing the crime to come last of all. (Of course, should the crime never be committed, so much the better.) A further advantage of being able to deal with both the past and the future is that the present can sometimes be avoided. For instance, some royal personages have jam every other day—that is, jam tomorrow and jam yesterday; as today is not any *other* day, no jam is had in the present. For the same reason, cake is served around first and cut afterwards.

The government of Looking-Glass Land is in the hands of two royal families: the Reds and the Whites. However, in moves reminiscent of a bad game of chess, new queens are created when commoners (and some visitors) progress through a number of given places until they reach that of a queen. Visitors who achieve this honour will find themselves suddenly crowned; they must be prepared to submit themselves to a qualification test, put to them by the two permanent queens. The questions cover the branches of good manners (always speaking the truth; thinking before one speaks and writing it down afterwards; not trying to deny anything with both hands; remembering to invite the queens to an obligatory party) and mathematics: addition (one and one and one and one and one and one and one and one and one and one), subtraction (take nine from eight; take a bone from a dog) and division (divide a loaf by a knife—result, bread and butter). Further questions will cover various subject areas under the heading of general knowledge and languages (for instance, what's French for "fiddle-dee-dee"?).

Looking-Glass language, though made up of English words and grammar, has rules of its own. Words are given whatever meaning the speaker wishes to give them, because the inhabitants of Looking-Glass Land believe that they—not the words—are the masters. Verbs, being the proudest, have a temper and are difficult to deal with; adjectives, however, can be made to do anything. Visitors are reminded that it is best to make a word do as much work as possible. For instance, a word like "impenetrability" can be made to mean "We have had enough of that subject and it will be just as well if you'd mention what you mean to do next, as I suppose you don't mean to stop here all the rest of your life." In cases like this, words are paid extra; their wages are collected on Saturday nights. Names must have a meaning: it is not enough just to be called "Alice" if the word does not signify a characteristic of the person. Visitors are well advised to choose a meaningful name before venturing into the country.

Because of their careful choice of words, the inhabitants of Looking-Glass Land make a difference between what something is called, what the name of something is called, what the name of something is and what something is. Thus, in keeping with these semantic distinctions, the name of a song might be called "Haddocks' eyes," the name of the song might be "The aged aged man," the song might be called "Ways and Means" but the song itself might be "A-sitting on a gate."

The inhabitants of Looking-Glass Land are very fond of poetry. Among their most famous creations are a poem in Anglo-Saxon, *Jabberwocky* (see JABBERWOCKY WOOD), and the woeful tale, *The Walrus and the Carpenter. Jabberwocky* has been translated into several languages: French, *Le Jaseroque;* German, *Der Jammerwoch;* and Latin, *Gaberbocchus.* (The latter has given its name to one of the most important literary ventures in the English-speaking world.) In Looking-Glass Land, books are read by holding them up to a mirror.

Travellers will notice that the flora and fauna of Looking-Glass Land are different from that of their own countries. Looking-Glass flowers can talk and do so according to their nature. Tiger Lilies are aggressive, roses are arrogant, daisies are prosaic, violets are rude. It has been explained that because the beds in Looking-Glass gardens are hard, flowers are never asleep and therefore conduct interesting conversations with visitors, though it is part of their etiquette that strangers address them first. The flowers' literary taste is quite advanced and they hold nothing but contempt for poet laureates. Looking-Glass trees do not talk, they bark; that is why their branches are called boughs. Visitors will discover that the fresh garden air is good for growing.

Apart from the parlant frogs, old lions, unbelieving unicorns, March hares with Anglo-Saxon attitudes, commercial sheep and shy fawns, the fauna of Looking-Glass Land is famous for its astounding insect life, in which visitors are advised to rejoice. Elephant-bees poke their proboscises into the flowers; hoarse-voiced beetles travel in railway coaches; rocking-horse flies made entirely of wood swing themselves from branch to branch and live on sap and saw-dust; snapdragon flies, with plum-pudding bodies, holly-leaf wings and brandy-soaked-raisin heads, live on wheat pudding and mince pies and make their nests in Christmas boxes; bread-and-butter flies, with wings made of thin slices of bread and butter, a body of crust and a head of a lump of sugar, feed on weak tea with cream which they can never find and so always die of starvation. Two more insects must be mentioned: a pun-loving gnat, quite the reverse in character to the *snark* (see SNARK ISLAND), and a wasp in a wig, long supposed dead after a murderous attempt had been made on its person by a hasty Victorian artist.

Visitors are likely to encounter several of the more notable inhabitants of Looking-Glass Land. The White Knight (an inventive elderly gentleman on a horse) and a pair of quarrelsome brothers (known as Tweedledum and Tweedledee) will entertain visitors with poetry recitals. One person, however, is best avoided: the Red King. It is said that he lies dreaming in Looking-Glass Forest and that his dream consists of those visitors who come across him. Travellers must be careful not to wake him, for if they do they will go out, just like a candle. Travellers who have passed the test of fire in the Land of CIRCULAR RUINS need not take this precaution.

(Lewis Carroll [Charles Lutwidge Dodgson], *Through the Looking-Glass, and What Alice Found There*, London, 1871)

LOONARIE, a group of small islands, part of the RIALLARO ARCHIPELAGO, in the south-east Pacific. Loonarie is used as the archipelago's lunatic asylum. The most important islands are:

Meddla, or Isle of Philanthropy, known to outsiders as Isle of Busybodies, is inhabited by propagandists and enthusiasts of various causes.

In Wotnekst, or Godlaw, the inhabitants have passed a law that their tongue is to be the universal language of the world. The filthy hovels of their island are, they claim, the very centre of civilization. It is the most fertile island of the archipelago, rich in minerals and precious metals, and once the envy of the other islands because of its wealth, large cities and splendid buildings. The population is united in the conviction that if they could each put their pet beliefs into practice the world would be saved, but this has led to their downfall.

Foolgar is a low and marshy islet, with houses standing on knolls. The name of the island translates as "land of lofty lineage," as all inhabitants claim to be descended from some god. In ancient times, the temples staved off bankruptcy by auctioning pedigrees and lineages to the highest bidder; this practice, organized by the priests, is still in vogue today. The people are pompous and pretentious and outsiders call Foolgar the "Isle of Snobs."

Awdyoo is the Isle of Journalism, avoided by everyone; a quarantine station to which scribomaniacs are deported. Apart from ALEOFANE, all islands regard journalism as a contagious disease or a type of lunacy. The deportees use physical equivalents of their old weapons: air-guns which squirt ink and foul-smelling, coloured liquids; the island can be detected from afar by its noxious smell. Their religion is the cult of Veiled Ego.

Jabberoo, to which insatiable talkers are banished, is an island to be avoided. Their endless debates lead to the neglect of all practical activities.

Witlingen Island is the gloomiest place on earth, inhabited by those exiled for their wit. They all know each other's jokes and repeat them endlessly.

Polaria is the island of those who live by the rule of contradicting others.

Grabawlia is the island of misers.

Paranomia is for exiles obsessed with the law who spend their time either in constant litigation or ignoring the law completely.

The inhabitants of Palindicia are unhappy unless administering justice, and are constantly setting up mock trials.

(Godfrey Sweven, *Riallaro, the Archipelago of Exiles*, New York & London, 1901; Godfrey Sweven, *Limanora, the Island of Progress*, New York & London, 1903)

LORBANERY, or **ISLE OF SILK**, is a large, low island in the far south of the EARTHSEA ARCHIPELAGO. From the sea, the entire island looks green. This is because every acre of the island not built on or used for roads is devoted to the cultivation of the *hurbah* tree, a low, round-topped tree whose leaves are the food of the grey silkworm, the basis of the island's economy. Every man, woman and child on the island either spins or weaves the famous silk of which there are two kinds: the blue silk and the unmatchable crimson or "dragon's fire," once worn by the queens on HAVNOR.

At night the air is full of the small, grey bats that live on the silkworms. The islanders think it an evil omen to kill the bats, reasoning that if men have the right to live off the silkworms, there is no reason why this privilege should be denied to the bats. Traditionally, the dyeing of the silk is overseen by a wizard, or mage, and the *hurbah* orchards are protected from unseasonable rain by a second mage, known as the "Orcharder."

During the years when all Earthsea was affected by an evil power (finally defeated by the great wizard Ged on SELIDOR) many of Lorbanery's magical traditions died out and the island fell into a general apathy. As the silkweavers ceased using their traditional magical talents, the quality of the silk declined and the island's economy was severely affected. The harbour of Sosara, built to house several large trading galleys at the same time, was virtually deserted and the paint of the once-bright houses of Lorbanery was allowed to fade.

The houses of Lorbanery are curious constructions, built to an indescribable pattern found only on this island. They are small, randomly set constructions, with thatched roofs made from the twigs of the ubiquitous *hurbah* trees.

(Ursula K. Le Guin, *The Farthest Shore*, London, 1973)

LORBRULGRUD, capital of BROBDINGNAG.

LORD OF THE FLIES, ISLAND OF THE, a coral island, probably in the Indian Ocean. It is roughly boat-shaped, with rocks, cliffs and a steep slope on either side. At one end is another island, almost detached, standing like a fort. The most unusual feature of the island is a pink cliff surmounted by a skewed block, and that again surmounted, and that again, so that the pinkness becomes a stack of balanced rocks projecting through the looped fantasy of the forest creepers. Where the pink cliffs rise out of the ground there are often narrow tracks winding upwards. The island is entirely surrounded by a lagoon and the shore is fledged with palm trees. Immense conches can be found on the beach, and tiny transparent creatures that come out when the tide withdraws. There are many-coloured birds, gulls, wild pigs and several species of butterfly.

On the shore can be seen the remains of huts built by British children whose plane crashed here, probably during World War Two. Two small skeletons and the remains of the airplane containing the skeleton of the pilot are silent witnesses to their adventure. The island is said to be inhabited by the Lord of the Flies, sometimes represented by a boar's head stuck on a pole, the primitive god of a brief modern society.

(William Golding, *Lord of the Flies*, London, 1954)

LÓRIEN, an ancient wooded land in MIDDLE-EARTH, between the MISTY MOUNTAINS and the GREAT RIVER. The River Silverlode, or Celebrant, runs through Lórien before joining the Great River. Lórien is also known as Lothlórien, Lórien of the Blossom and the Golden Wood of Wilderland. The original ancient High-elven name, however, was Laurelindórenan, which means "Land-of-the-Valley-of-the-Singing-Gold." Lórien was once the fairest of all the Elven realms of Middle-earth, but it is now largely deserted. It was for many years the realm of Galadriel and Celeborn, the Lady

and Lord of Lórien whose capital was at CARAS GALADHON.

The power of Galadriel, the most royal of all the surviving High-elven race then living in Middle-earth, protected Lórien from the evil brought into Middle-earth by Sauron, the Dark Lord of MORDOR, and this realm remained a peaceful, calm place. There was no blemish or sickness in Lórien, where all shapes were clear and all colours bright. The outside world seemed formless and indistinct to all who came into the elven kingdom. To enter Lórien was to experience also a sensation of going back in time to the Elder Days, or the First Age. RIVENDELL preserves many memories of ancient times, but in Lórien it seemed that those times had never ended. Indeed, the visitor had the sensation that time had not passed while he was in Lórien. The elves themselves change very little, which means that the world around them seems to change very rapidly. But as they take no account of the passing years, they have little feeling of change. Sam Gamgee, a hobbit from the SHIRE, summed up the wonder of Lórien by saying that it felt like being *inside* a song, like being at home and at holiday at the same time.

Lórien is famed for its great *mellyrn*, the mighty mallorn-trees with their silver-grey trunks from which the branches spread out horizontally before sweeping upwards. Near the top, the trunk divides into a crown of many boughs. Here the elves, or Galadhrim, "Tree People," built the platform they called a *talan*. It is on these platforms that they lived. The platforms had no walls or rails, merely a light moveable screen for protection against the wind.

The trees are unique in that they do not shed their leaves until spring. The leaves turn to gold in autumn, and when spring comes they provide a golden floor for the forest, and blossoms of yellow. This is the only place where the mallorn is found, with one exception: Sam Gamgee was given a seed by Galadriel and a mallorn now flourishes in the Shire. Lórien is also noted for the *elanor*, a winter plant with yellow, star-shaped flowers, and for the slender *niphredil* with its white or pale green flowers.

The heart of Lórien is Cerin Amroth, a great mound covered with fragrant grass and surmounted by two circles of trees. The inner circle is of mallorn, arrayed in pale gold, the outer of leafless, shapely trees with a snowy white bark. *Elanor* and *niphredil* grow all around. In the centre of the circle stands a tall tree, a white *talan* gleaming high amidst its branches.

Cerin Amroth is in the area known as the Naith of Lórien, or the Gore, which lies between the Great River and the Silverlode and thus has a shape reminiscent of a great spear head. It was a privilege for any stranger to be allowed to cross the Silverlode into the Naith. A visitor who reached this point would then be taken to see the Lord and Lady that they might judge whether he be friend or foe. It was not possible for him to return on his own, as the paths were closely guarded. It was on Cerin Amroth that Arwen, the elven princess, and Aragorn, the heir of Isildur and the future king of the Reunited Kingdom, pledged their troth. After the death of her husband in 120 Fourth Age, Arwen returned here to die.

Originally founded in the Second Age, Lórien was at the time of the War of the Ring ruled by Galadriel and Celeborn, both noted for their gravity and beauty. Neither was marked by their great age; only their eyes seemed to show the profundity of long memory. Galadriel herself was a major protagonist in the struggle against the evil of Sauron. It was she who first summoned the White Council to coordinate the struggle against him and it was her power, together with that of Nenya, one of the Three Rings of the Elven-kings, that kept the shadow of evil from Lórien.

Unlike the elves of the ELVENHALLS OF MIRKWOOD, those of Lórien were High Elves, who made the voyage to the west and spent many years there, becoming wiser and fairer in the process. They retained their ancient language of Quenya or High Elven, but used it only for ceremonial purposes. In most circumstances, Grey Elven or Sindarin was spoken.

The elves of Middle-earth are skilled in many crafts and everything they make seems to have an almost magical quality—a phial which shines in the dark, for instance, or the swords, wrought by their ancestors, which gleam with a cold, bluish light when orcs or goblins are near. They make delicate objects of metal, such as a sheath decked with flowers and leaves of silver and gold, and belts with clasps in the shape of golden flowers. The elves weave their clothes from a fine silken material, the colour of which is difficult to determine. It changes according to its surroundings, glimmering with all the colours associated with leaf, branch, water and stone. This would seem to reflect the elves' love of the light and the space of the earth and their dislike of underground places (a characteristic not shared by the elves of the Elvenhalls).

Elven boats are particularly unusual. Usually painted grey, they are not, according to the elves, like other boats, in that they will not sink no matter how heavily laden they are. On the other hand, they are likely to behave strangely if mishandled. Their ropes are of *hithlain*, a material that is at once very strong and very light.

The elves prepare food and drink that is quite unlike that found elsewhere and that is remarkable for its restorative and sustaining qualities. *Lembas*, or waybread, are small cakes wrapped in leaves which remain sweet for many days. They are much sweeter and tastier than the *cram* of Lake-town or even the honey-cakes for which the Vales of AN-DUIN are so famed.

Physically the elves are tall and beautiful, fair-skinned and dark or golden-haired, and with wonderfully melodious voices. They move silently, and appear to have a special understanding of animals. They ride horses bareback, having no need of reins to control their mounts. Even the most unruly horse submits quietly to the voice of an elf. They are a grave and courteous people; no matter how high his or her standing, an elf will always rise to greet a guest.

After the destruction of the One Ring on ORODRUIN, the Ring of Power in the possession of Galadriel lost much of its potency and the elves themselves lost much of their power. In September 3021 Third Age, Galadriel departed across the sea to the west, while Celeborn established a new colony called East Lórien in the forests of Mirkwood, which had now been cleansed of its evil. It seems that Lórien lost much of its beauty after the departure of Galadriel and that the famous trees did not survive without her.

Lórien is closely associated with the legend of Amroth and Nimrodel. Nimrodel was an elven-maid of great beauty; her name is the same as that of a shallow stream that enters the Silverlode from the mountains. When the daemonic Balrog was aroused by the dwarves in MORIA, many elves left Lórien and returned over the seas to the west. Nimrodel and her beloved Amroth travelled separately to join the departing elves, and Nimrodel became lost in the passes of the WHITE MOUNTAINS. As a storm blew the waiting Amroth's ship out to sea, carrying him away from her, he leapt into the water. Neither was ever seen again. It is said that when the south wind blows, Amroth's voice can be heard as the waters of the Nimrodel eventually reach the Bay of Belfalas from where the elves of Lórien set sail that day.

(J.R.R. Tolkien, *The Fellowship of the Ring,* London, 1954; J.R.R. Tolkien, *The Two Towers,* London, 1954; J.R.R. Tolkien, *The Return of the King,* London, 1955; J.R.R. Tolkien, *The Silmarillion,* London, 1977)

LOST TIME, a vast stretch of water somewhere in South America, bordering a small abandoned village whose hard soil is cracked with saltpetre. At the bottom of the sea there are terraces of flowers and thousands of delicious-tasting turtles.

Many years ago, during the first few nights of March, the sea—which normally swept along refuse—started to give off a heady odour of roses. People began to return to the village, which had been almost abandoned even then. Brass bands, clairvoyants, gangsters and fakirs with snakes wrapped around their necks, selling the elixir of immortality, arrived in town, and the inhabitants organized tombolas and lotteries.

Then a certain Mr. Herbert appeared on the scene. He offered to hand out bank notes if the people of the village settled their personal problems. For example, one villager solved his money problems by imitating the song of forty-eight different birds, for forty-eight pesos. Only one person stumped Mr. Herbert: a prostitute who told him that she had no problems, for she was a whore "quite simply because it made her feel so good."

Once he had solved the other people's problems, Mr. Herbert fell into a deep sleep that may have lasted several centuries. When he awoke (feeling quite ravenous) he dove into the sea of Lost Time, where the dead of the village floated about between two currents of water with smiles on their faces.

(Gabriel García Márquez, "El Mar del tiempo perdido," in *La Increíble y triste historia de la cándida Eréndira y de su abuela desalmada,* Buenos Aires, 1972)

LOTUS-EATERS ISLAND, set among the rolling waves of the Mediterranean. The coast of yellow sand is blown by a breeze reminiscent of the sighs of a weary dreamer, and the time of day seems to be a kind of eternal afternoon.

The island is inhabited by natives who feed on the lotus blooms and so obtain oblivion from all mortal cares. Out of kindness, they offer the blooms to any visitor who will share their table. Should the unwary visitor taste of the lotus, all desire to return to his native country will vanish, and he will only be able to go if made to leave by force. Should he decide to share the lotus eaters' repast, he will find that the shore will grow distant, the voices of his companions will seem thin, as if coming from the grave, and although awake he will feel asleep. Stranger still, he will hear the sound of an unknown music and not know that it is his own heart, beating in his ears.

(Homer, *The Odyssey,* 9th cen. [?] BC; Alfred, Lord Tennyson, "The Lotos-Eaters," in *Poems,* London, 1833)

LOVE, ISLAND OF, see FIGLEFIA.

LOVE, RIVER AND FOUNTAIN OF, in the Ardennes, France. The fountain is wrought in

The gold and alabaster fountain near the River of LOVE, France.

gold and alabaster, illuminating with its reflection the green meadow around it. It was created by Merlin, the magician, for Tristan to drink from so that he might fall out of love with Queen Isolda. Its waters have the virtue of changing whatever state lovers find themselves in. Not far away flows the River of Love whose waters are said to enamour whoever drinks from them. Rinaldo fell alternately in and out of love with the beautiful Angelica after drinking from first one then the other. (See also ALBRACA.)

(Matteo Maria Boiardo, *Orlando innamorato*, Milan, 1487)

LOVERS' CAVE, partly natural and partly man-made, in a remote and mountainous area of Cornwall.

Lovers' Cave is a round grotto cut from the smooth, snow-white rock, and lit by three small windows high in the walls. The high, vaulted roof has been worked into a finely keyed dome. On the keystone, visitors can see a crown adorned with gold and gems. The floor of the grotto is of marble as green as grass. At the centre of the cave stands a raised bed hewn from solid rock crystal; an inscription states that the cave is dedicated to the goddess of love. The door is of bronze, fastened with two great bars, one of cedar and the other of ivory. It can only be opened from the inside.

Although the architect who worked this natural grotto into its present form remains unknown, the meanings of the design have been interpreted by historians. The cave is round to symbolize the simplicity of love; there are no nooks or corners where cunning and treachery can lurk. Its breadth signifies the power of love and its height love's aspiration to virtue, symbolized by the keystone. The white walls and the green floor stand for integrity and constancy respectively, while the translucency of the crystal bed expresses the lucidity of love. The door cannot be opened from the outside because true love realizes that love's door must not be forced. Finally, the three windows symbolize the lover's virtues: kindness, humility and breeding.

Two of the Cave's famous visitors were Tristan and Isolde, who stayed here after they were driven from the court of the kingdom of Cornwall by the jealousy of Isolde's husband Mark.

(Gottfried von Strassburg, *Tristan*, 13th cen. AD)

LOWER ROMANCIA, see ROMANCIA.

LUANA, an extensive island group in the Lural Az of the underground continent of PELLUCIDAR, to the north-east of the ANOROC Archipelago. The islands are thickly populated and said to be very beautiful, although no one has yet given a detailed account of them. The people of Luana are, like those of Anoroc, copper-skinned Mezops, skilled sailors and fishermen. Although for many centuries both island groups were rivals and often at war with one another, their rivalry now extends only to the excellence of the ships they build.

(Edgar Rice Burroughs, *Pellucidar*, New York, 1923)

LUBEC, a town of unknown location, where no one is poor.

The men of Lubec have no proper genitals; these are stored in the Town Hall. (A similar but more vital procedure is followed in CAPILLARIA.) When necessary they are applied to the female genitalia, which stand out like scars on the women of Lubec. Male genitals are sometimes hired out for the production of servants, but they have not been made available to tramps or beggars, thus eliminating the nuisance of an undeserving class.

(Béroualde de Verville, *Le moyen de parvenir. Oeuvre contenant la raison de tout ce qui a esté, est, et sera, avec démonstrations certaines et nécessaires selon la rencontre des effets de vertu*, Paris, 1880)

LUDBITALLYA, capital of CACKLO-GALLINIA.

LUDSTADT, capital of LUTHA.

LUGGNAGG, a large island, about one hundred leagues to the south-east of Japan, one of its major trading partners. Ships sail to Japan from Clumegnig, a major port on the south-east coast. There are also ships to GLUBBDUBDRIB. The capital is Traldragdub, also known as Trildrogdrib.

Luggnagg is known for its hospitality to strangers, who are often lodged at State expense.

An invitation to court—expressed as "You may have the honour to lick the dust before the king's footstool"—should be taken quite literally. Upon admittance to the throne room the traveller should crawl forward on the belly, licking the floor as he advances. When foreigners are called to court, precautions are taken to ensure that the dust on the floor is not too offensive. However, if an ordinary statesman has powerful enemies at court, he may find the floor so covered with dust that by the time he reaches the throne he has almost choked to death and is unable to speak. As it is a capital offence for anyone to spit or wipe his mouth in the presence of the king, executions are carried out by having the floor strewn with a dark poison which kills within twenty-four hours. But to do justice to the king's clemency—and to dispel any fears new visitors may have—it must be added that the infected areas are carefully washed and scrubbed after such executions.

On coming within four yards of the throne, the visitor must kneel and strike his forehead seven times against the ground, pronouncing the formula *"Ickpling gloffthrobb squutserumm blhiop mlashnalt zwin tnodbalkguffh slhiophad gurdlubh asht,"* which can be translated as "May your Celestial Majesty outlive the sun, eleven moons and a half."

Luggnagg is perhaps best known, though, for its *Struldbruggs*, or "immortals." Children are occasionally born with a red circular spot just above their left eyebrow. According to Luggnaggians, this is a sign that they will never die. By the time the child is twelve the spot has grown larger and has turned green. At twenty-five it darkens. At forty-five it becomes coal black and is the size of a shilling. It will not change again. There are about eleven hundred such immortals in the country. There does not appear to be any explanation for the *Struldbruggs'* appearance and the condition is not hereditary. Sadly, although they do not die, neither do they enjoy perpetual youth—undergoing, instead, the normal process of ageing. By the time they are eighty, they have all the infirmities of old age, but are faced with the dreary prospect of living forever. At this age, too, they are legally regarded as dead. Their heirs succeed to their estates and they may no longer purchase lands or act as witnesses in trials. Only a pittance is reserved for them, and the penniless immortals are supported by the State. Perhaps the worst aspect of their condition is that, as the language of Lug-

gnagg changes frequently, they eventually become incapable of communicating with anyone and live as foreigners in their own country.

The *Struldbruggs* are despised and hated by the population and their birth is regarded as an ominous sign. Those who marry another immortal have their marriages dissolved by law at the age of eighty, because it is considered unreasonable that those who, through no fault of their own, are burdened with eternal life, should have the double burden of an eternal spouse.

(Jonathan Swift, *Travels Into Several Remote Nations Of The World. In Four Parts. By Lemuel Gulliver, First a Surgeon, and then a Captain of several Ships*, London, 1726)

LUQUEBARALIDEAUX ISLANDS, a group of islands in the Savage Sea, inhabited by a species of *andouille*, or pork sausage, which grows to be twelve inches tall. The *andouilles* have sharp, pointed teeth, but no bones; they tend to move around in strings or flocks, rather like sheep. They drink mustard from the streams which flow through the islands; this is a balm for them and cures all their wounds and scratches.

(Anonymous, *Le Voyage de navigation que fist Panurge, disciple de Pantagruel, aux isles incognues et éstranges de plusieurs choses merveilleuses et difficiles à croire, qu'il dict avoir veues, dont il fait narration en ce présent volume, et plusieurs aultres joyeusetez pour inciter les lecteurs et auditeurs à rire*, Paris, 1538)

LUTHA, a small, landlocked country in southern Europe, bordered by Serbia, Austria and Hungary. Lutha remains virtually unknown to the outside world except to those visitors who take advantage of the excellent care provided by the Tafelberg Sanatorium, famed for its treatment of nervous diseases.

The capital of Lutha, Ludstadt, is built on a steep hill overlooking a central plain. It is an ancient, walled city with steep winding streets, defended by four forts. The old cathedral is the traditional setting for the coronations of the kings of Lutha and for royal weddings. On the opposite side of the plain lies a region of savage mountains and ravines, as well as the Old Forest which stretches almost to the Serbian border. Travel in this area can be dangerous, as brigands are still found in the mountains.

Travellers will need to learn a little about the country's history in order to better enjoy their visit. The Rubinroth dynasty has ruled Lutha since the sixteenth century. (The last king of the previous dynasty became extremely unpopular when he attempted to sell his people's freedom to a more powerful neighbour; he was duly overthrown.) Towards the end of the last century, the Rubinroth dynasty entered a period of difficulties. In the 1880's Princess Victoria escaped from Lutha with an American friend and settled in the United States, leaving Prince Leopold as heir to the throne.

The circumstances of the affair remain obscure, but it was to have considerable impact upon subsequent developments.

The Rubinroths' situation took a turn for the worse when the king, the father of Prince Leopold, died. Prince Peter of Blentz, Leopold's uncle, claimed that the shock of the king's death had unhinged the mind of the thirteen-year-old heir and he had the boy shut up in the fortress of Blentz. Peter then declared himself regent and under his regency corruption steadily grew, taxes rose and the people were increasingly subjected to a harsh military regime.

Ten years later, the country was thrown into panic by the news that "mad" King Leopold had escaped from Blentz. Events became even more confused when an American, "Barney" Custer, arrived in the country. Although totally unknown in Lutha, he was the son of Princess Victoria and bore a great likeness to his Uncle Leopold. This resemblance created much confusion, as Custer was constantly mistaken for the "mad" king of Lutha.

After a series of adventures, culminating in a pitched battle, Custer succeeded in restoring the rightful heir to the throne. However, the first act of the new king was to expel Custer—for fear that the American's reputation would outshine his own—and under Leopold's tyrannical rule, Lutha suffered even more than it had under the regency. Leopold finally began to negotiate with his old enemies, the Blentz faction, who, in turn, instigated an attack on Custer, back in America. Slipping secretly across the Serbian border, Custer returned to Lutha.

Meanwhile the threat of war between Austria and Serbia was growing. Lutha was gradually caught up in the wider conflict, and when the Blentz faction, which had a powerful hold over the weak-minded Leopold, sought the support of the Austrian military, Custer, with the noble Van der Tann family, requested Serbian aid in resisting them. The conflict culminated in the battle of Ludstadt, fought just outside the city gates.

In a final case of mistaken identity, Leopold was shot when taken for Custer. The people refused to accept any king but "Barney," who finally accepted and married Princess Emma Van der Tann. Peter of Blentz, responsible for so much suffering, was tried, found guilty and hanged.

(Edgar Rice Burroughs, *The Mad King*, New York, 1914)

LUX, capital of MORROW ISLAND.

LYTREIA, the realm of Tenjo Long Nose, near the City of TUROINE. The people of this kingdom worship noses and respect no male creature who does not have a large and robust one. It is said that the kingdom fell into great dejection when, due to the arrival of an evil spirit, the strength went out of all noses in the land and no man could sneeze or use his nose in any other normal way. Even the Holy Nose in the temple collapsed and shrivelled, until it was touched with water from DOONHAM. Then the nose sprang erect and became even more enormous, robust and succulent than before. Immediately the nose of every man in Lytreia regained its normal proportions and couples began once more to withdraw to sneeze in private.

Travellers are advised to visit the tomb of Peter the Builder. According to the legends of Lytreia, the tomb contains the Mirror of Two Truths. It is said that any man who looks into it will be turned into two stones, which is why the mirror is kept veiled. The truth is that behind the veil hangs not a mirror but a painting illustrating two all-important truths: that human beings copulate and die.

Visiting the Temple of the Nose is not an easy matter. Even the king must take part in a ceremony conducted by the high priestess before entering. She offers the king a comb, which he uses to part her hair before pronouncing the Word of Entry: "I enter, proud and erect. I take my fill of delight imperiously, irrationally and none punishes." The priestess replies "Not yet," and the king goes on: "But in three months, and in three more months, the avenger comes forth, and mocks me by being as I am, visibly; and by being foredoomed to do as I have done, inevitably." When this ceremony is over, the king is allowed to enter the temple. The Word of Entry for ordinary visitors is not known.

(James Branch Cabell, *Something about Eve*, New York, 1929)

M

MABARON, a large kingdom in India, ten days' journey from LOMB. It is famous for its many beautiful cities, including Calamy, the burial place of St. Thomas the Apostle. The arm and hand with which St. Thomas touched the side of the dead Christ are preserved in a vessel beside the tomb. In cases of legal dispute both parties place a paper setting out their case in the saint's hand and it casts away the paper bearing the wrong cause.

A visit to the church in which the body of St. Thomas lies is recommended, as it contains many exquisite images of saints and idols, the smallest of which is twice as large as life. The church is richly decorated with gold and the largest idol, the god of the False Christians, sits in a golden chair with golden necklaces set with pearls and gems around his neck. This idol is an object of great devotion and people travel hundreds of miles to worship it, some sacrificing their children to it, others mutilating themselves with knives for love of St. Thomas. Those who die for love of this idol are thought to be blessed.

The idol is housed in a large room mirrored in a great pool. Pilgrims cast offerings into the water and the money is used for the upkeep of the shrine. At holy feasts, the idol is carried through the streets in a large wheelchair, preceded by the maidens of Mabaron, who walk along in pairs, followed by the pilgrims. Some let themselves fall before the idol and are crushed by the wheels. After the procession, hundreds of people stab themselves and are regarded as saints by the surviving population. Their bodies are cremated and their ashes preserved as sacred relics which consequently abound in Mabaron.

(Sir John Mandeville, *Voiage de Sir John Maundevile*, Paris, 1857)

MACARIA, a kingdom of unknown location, perhaps in northern Africa. Macaria is a populous and prosperous kingdom which has been compared by travellers to a "fruitful garden." Notable are its highways, paved—since the mid-seventeenth century—like the streets of a city. Though usually at peace with its neighbours, Macaria has a law that

any nation attempting an invasion is a lawful prize; several kingdoms have in fact been destroyed by the Macarian forces as a warning.

(Samuel Hartlib, A *Description of the Famous Kingdom of Macaria; shewing its Excellent Government, wherein the Inhabitants Live in Great Prosperity, Health and Happiness; the King Obeyed, the Nobles Honoured and All Good Men Respected; Vice Punished and Virtue Rewarded, an Example to Other Nations; in a Dialogue between a Scholar and a Traveller*, London, 1641)

MACONDO, a Colombian village founded in ancient times by José Arcadio Buendia, whose boundless imagination always stretched farther than the inventiveness of nature. The founder had placed the houses in such a way that the inhabitant of each could reach the river and fetch water with exactly the same degree of effort as his neighbour; and the streets had been planned in such a manner that all houses received the same amount of sunshine throughout the day. For the benefit of the population he built small traps to catch canaries, robins, and nightingales and in very little time the village was so full of their singing that the gypsy tribe which every year visited Macondo, to show the inhabitants the newest eighth marvel of the world would let themselves be guided by the music.

Towards the east Macondo is protected by a high and forbidding range of hills; towards the south by marshes covered with a kind of vegetable soup. The marshes rise towards the west and become a large body of water in which cetaceans of delicate skin, with the face and torso of a woman, lure sailors with their firm and tempting breasts. To the north, many days' march away through a dangerous jungle, lies the sea.

From a small village of some twenty mud and bamboo huts, Macondo became a town with shops and a marketplace. This prosperity made José Arcadio Buendia free all the birds he had carefully trapped and replace them with musical clocks which he had obtained from merchants in exchange for parrots. These clocks were so synchronized that every half-hour the town would shake with a sound of ringing bells and every midday a musical explosion of cuckoos and waltzes would glorify the beginning of the siesta. Buendia also replaced the acacias lining the streets with almond

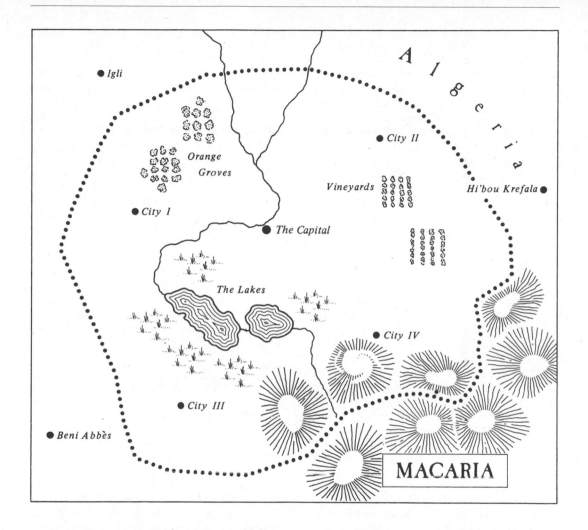

trees and found a system of giving them eternal life. Many years later, when Macondo became a city of wooden houses and zinc roofs, ancient almond trees still bloomed in the older streets, though there was no one in the town who could remember having witnessed their planting.

Among the most notable events which form the history of Macondo is the unusual insomnia epidemic that struck the town. The most terrible thing about it was not the impossibility of sleep— because the body would not tire itself either—but the gradual loss of memory. When the sick person became accustomed to staying awake, memories of his childhood would start to vanish, followed by the names and concept of things; finally he would lose his own identity and consciousness of his own being, sinking into a calm lunacy without a past. Bells were set up around the village and whoever passed them would give them a tug to prove that he was still sane. Visitors would be advised not to eat or drink in Macondo, because the illness was supposed to be contagious. The inhabitants soon became accustomed to this state of affairs and dispensed with the useless activity of sleep. In order not to forget what the different objects around them were, they labelled each thing with its proper name: "pail," "table," "cow," "flower." However, the inhabitants realized that even though the names of things could be remembered in this fashion, their utility could nevertheless be forgotten and a more extensive explanation was added on the labels. For instance, a large placard on the cow informed the onlooker: "This is a cow; it is necessary to milk her every morning to produce milk and the milk must be boiled and then added to coffee to produce coffee with milk." At the entrance to the village the inhabitants erected a sign that said "Macondo" and, a little farther on, another saying "God exists."

The inhabitants of Macondo also invented an ingenious system to counteract the effects of their strange illness, and learnt to read the past in the cards, as before the gypsies used to read the future. Buendia also created a memory machine into which every morning he would record the past events of his life. In this way, at any point, he could make the machine work and recall his whole past day by day. The epidemic reached an end when the gypsy Melquiades—who had been dead but had returned because he could not stand the loneliness of death—brought to Macondo an insomnia antidote in the form of a sweet liquid in little bottles. The inhabitants drank the potion and immediately were able to sleep.

Another important event in the history of Macondo was the proposed building of a huge temple organized by Father Nicanor Reyna, who was travelling throughout the world with the intention of establishing a sanctuary in a centre of impiety and envisioned a temple full of life-sized saints and stained-glass windows. However, the people of Macondo, who had lived for so many years without a priest, had established a personal contact with God and were free of the stain of original sin. They could levitate some twelve centimetres off the ground after drinking a full cup of chocolate. Seeing that Macondo was not the centre of impiety he was searching for, Father Reyna continued on his travels.

In more recent years Macondo saw the creation of an American banana plantation on its land, and the town was linked to the rest of the world by a railway. But due to a strike, heavy rains and then drought, the plantation was abandoned and it is said that Macondo's prosperity was wiped off the surface of the earth by a violent cyclone.

(Gabriel García Márquez, *Cien años de soledad*, Buenos Aires, 1967)

MACRANESE ISLAND, see EVARCHIA.

MACREONS ISLAND, one of the SPORADES. The island was once a wealthy and much-visited trade centre, subject to the power of Britain. In the course of time and for no known cause it became poor and desolate and nowadays is inhabited only by old people.

A large, dark forest that occupies most of the island's surface is the dwelling place of demons and heroes who have grown old and grey and full of sleep. While they live, the area is prosperous and calm weather prevails. But when one of them dies, great lamentations can be heard in the forest, plagues and other disasters strike, and there are dreadful disturbances in the air and fearful storms at sea. The forest is remarkable for the ruins that can be seen here: ruins of temples, obelisks, pyramids, monuments and ancient tombs, with inscriptions and epitaphs in hieroglyphics and in Arabic, Ionic, Slavonic and Hagerne.

Visitors will find the old people of the island friendly and hospitable. They are also skilled carpenters and expert boat builders—should the need for any of these talents arise.

(François Rabelais, *Le quart livre des faicts et dicts du bon Pantagruel*, Paris, 1552)

MAGHREBINIA, a vast realm that stretches from the Sea of Marmora to the Gulf of Bothnia, from the Volga to the Oder-Neisse. Various nations and tribes live here in harmony, under one head of state. The different provinces are ruled by the king's governors who have established a truly democratic state. The constitution and the laws of Maghrebinia are based on tradition and the realm's civilization is very ancient. Travellers interested in the country's history should consult the *Maghrebinian Chronicles,* which have been continuously updated since its origins in the fifteenth century.

One of the principal events in the history of Maghrebinia took place when a Byzantine envoy bestowed on Woywode Przibislaw, father of King Nikefor I, the title of "Archonton of Maipulien" and suggested a matrimonial alliance with the very beautiful daughter of Fanarioten Chuzpephorus Yatanagides of Byzantium. After a great many complications, the ceremony took place in the Hagia Sophia Cathedral. The developments leading to this wedding and the arguments it caused gave rise to a bulky corpus of law which is the basis of the constitution in Maghrebinia today.

(Gregor von Rezzori, *Maghrebinische Geschichten,* Hamburg, 1953)

MAGIC MAIDEN, ROCK OF THE, a barren, steep crag rising from the sea, so high that it seems to touch the clouds. It is six days' travel from the Island of the SCARLET TOWER. The rock got its name in ancient times when it was ruled by the daughter of Finetor, magician of Argos, Greece, who became far more versed in the arts of necromancy than her father. She lived on the island all her life and had a splendid mansion built for herself on the crags. Numerous ships from Ireland and Norway crossed the island's waters and by magical arts the maiden would attract them to the rocks and rob them of their cargoes. If any knights were aboard the ships, she would hold them prisoners for as long as she wished, forcing them to fight one another until they were grievously wounded or killed.

One day, the daughter captured a twenty-five-year-old knight from the island of Crete and fell madly in love with him. He pretended to love her as well, became acquainted with her charms and on one occasion, when they were seated on a high rock above the sea talking of this and that, he lunged forward as if to embrace her but pushed her onto the rocks below. After freeing the rest of the captives and taking with him most of the maiden's riches, he returned to Crete and never visited the island again. But in the richest room of the palace, he was forced to leave a great treasure which up to this day is bound by a magic charm and cannot be released. Those who have tried to obtain it by climbing the rocks in the dead of winter, when the island's serpents and other dreadful creatures are hibernating, say that they have been able to reach the door of the chamber but have not been able to enter. They also say that on one of the panels of the door are blood-red letters, and on the other, a mysterious writing that contains the name of the knight destined to enter the room after having dislodged a sword imprisoned in the door-handle.

(Anonymous, *Amadís de Gaula,* Zaragoza, 1508)

MAG-MELL, MAG-MELD or **LAND OF ETERNITY**, an island opposite Ireland, beyond the Atlantic Ocean, inhabited by immortal spirits called Sidi, who once lived in ancient Eire. Between Mag-Mell and Ireland is a network of underwater tunnels which the Sidi often use to visit their ancient homeland, and which the traveller too can use to his advantage. But the Sidi can also walk on the water, fly like birds on the wings of the wind, or sail in crystal ships wrapped in the fog.

Those who have seen the Sidi describe them as old people who always carry a book in their hands. The women of the Sidi assume human form and live on in Ireland, taking human husbands. Sometimes they kidnap their husbands and take them to Mag-Mell, where they too are made immortal.

Visitors who become recipients of this gift are warned that should they ever decide to return to their own country, they would immediately become old and haggard.

(Maria Savi-Lopez, *Leggende del mare,* Turin, 1920)

MAHAGONNY, a city that some maintain is near Alaska, while others insist it is closer to California; in any case, everyone agrees that Mahagonny is a desert bordered by the ocean.

Founded by Alaskan trappers to give their comrades a spot to enjoy earthly joys and pleasures, and to make the highest profits possible, Mahagonny is a sort of dream-city due in part to the exceptional gifts of a very energetic widow named Begbick and her girlfriends, who are all highly knowledgeable in the ways of the flesh.

It should be noted that apart from natural catastrophes—such as the typhoon that destroyed the towns of Pensacola and Atsena but by some miracle spared Mahagonny—man is the only real danger to man in this city.

(Bertolt Brecht, *Aufstieg und Fall der Stadt Mahagonny,* Vienna, 1929)

MAIDEN'S CASTLE, on a fortified hill on the banks of the Severn, Wales. The castle is entered via a narrow passage between steep walls of earth, protected by several ditches and ramparts. Travellers are warned that this is an enchanted place; even in daytime, local people avoid it for fear of the ghosts that are said to live here. Even a ghost tower—the haunt of Morgan le Fay—is said to appear at the top of the castle on certain windy nights and then disappear before morning.

During the quest for the Holy Grail, Sir

Galahad and his companions came to Maiden's Castle and learnt that seven brothers, all knights, who had taken over the castle seven years earlier, were terrorizing the neighbourhood capturing local women and keeping them in their fortress. Sir Galahad vanquished the seven evil brothers and restored peace to the area.

(Sir Thomas Malory, *Le Morte Darthur*, London, 1485; John Steinbeck, *The Acts of King Arthur and His Noble Knights From the Winchester Manuscripts of Sir Thomas Malory and Other Sources*, New York, 1976)

MAÏNA, a small island in the Pacific, rich in minerals and rubber plantations. Maïna is inhabited by two tribes, the Articoles and the Beos. The Articoles are descendants of the island's first inhabitant—the novelist Anthony Scott, author of *The Dark Sex*—who bought Maïna from the Dutch government in 1861. The Beos are the descendants of the servants Scott brought with him.

The Articoles are writers, painters, sculptors and musicians who live only for their artistic creations. They are looked after by the Beos, whose sole pleasure consists of tending to the Articoles—to whom they offer everything, including their own women.

Even when they cannot create, the Articoles create. A famous Articole writer, Routchko, published an interesting confession, some 16,900 pages long, entitled *Why I Cannot Write*. According to the Articoles, every subject, every experience, deserves to be expressed as a form of art. Thus, an Articole will publish not only his *Intimate Journal*, but also his *Journal of My Intimate Journal;* and his wife will publish the *Journal of My Husband's Journal of His Intimate Journal*. In recent times, publishers addicted to the Bloomsbury faith have wholeheartedly subscribed to this Articole creed.

Because art and life are synonymous for the Articoles, actors must be taken by the rest of their countrymen for the roles they represent. A certain actress, whose servant had forgotten to change her name on her dressing-room door for that of the character she was going to portray, entered the stage as her real self and caused a commotion of national proportions.

Visitors are well treated. They are lodged in a five-star hotel, the *Psycharium*, where they are studied by the Articoles, who try in this manner to increase their knowledge of human passions (which they lack) so as to use them in their next *oeuvre d'art*.

(André Maurois, *Voyage au Pays des Articoles*, Paris, 1927)

MAKALOLO, a small country in central Africa inhabited by a tribe of women warriors. In Makalolo the men are never given any real power; the highest post to which they can aspire is that of royal cook. Travellers will be interested in the large military parades in which the tall women warriors, mounted on armoured giraffes and ostriches, display their combat regalia.

Makalolo is an elective monarchy in which two queens are elected for a period of five years. When their reign comes to an end, a large banquet is served to the highest Makalolo officials and worthies in which the two outgoing queens are roasted and eaten. As the next two queens are among those present at the banquet, the inhabitants of Makalolo believe that the wisdom of the previous monarchs passes on to their future rulers, thereby preserving the kingdom's spiritual heritage.

(Albert Robida, *Voyages Très Extraordinaires de Saturnin Farandoul dans les 5 ou 6 parties du monde [et dans tous les pays connus et même inconnus de M. Jules Verne]*, Paris, 1879)

MALACOVIA, a city-fortress built in iron on the delta of the Danube, on the branch known as the St. George, not far from the southernmost mouth of the river. The city was built in 1870 by specialized workers imported from France and from England who in fact did not know where they were working, believing the site to be on the banks of the Dnieper, Russia. Once the work was completed they were sent back to their countries.

In charge of the project was an eccentric Nogai prince, very rich and somewhat mad, who emigrated from the Crimea with several of his compatriots and settled in Dobrugia, dreaming of rebuilding the lost fatherland. To achieve this purpose the prince decided to build an iron fortress, hidden in the marshes, as a base from which to launch quick and deadly incursions against the coastal cities of the Holy Russian Empire (in particular Odessa) and to sink or capture the Russian ships crossing the Black Sea. Brought up in Petersburg, the prince, unlike his companions, had

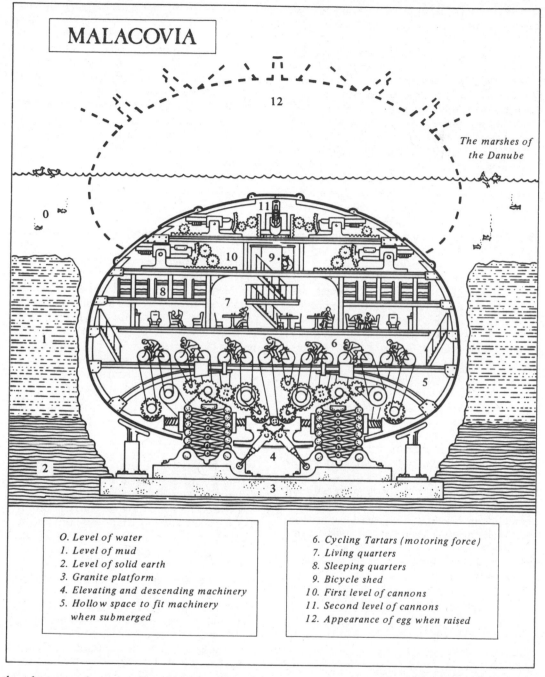

MALACOVIA

The marshes of the Danube

0. Level of water
1. Level of mud
2. Level of solid earth
3. Granite platform
4. Elevating and descending machinery
5. Hollow space to fit machinery
   when submerged

6. Cycling Tartars (motoring force)
7. Living quarters
8. Sleeping quarters
9. Bicycle shed
10. First level of cannons
11. Second level of cannons
12. Appearance of egg when raised

the advantage of a university education and became enthralled by the mysteries of mechanics, especially by those of a new invention that seemed to offer innumerable possibilities: the bicycle.

The prince planned Malacovia as a sort of huge iron egg bristling with cannon. The egg could be made to retreat within a granite platform beneath the marshes to hide it from sight; this

vertical mechanism was worked by means of a series of bicycles linked to a gigantic system of cogs;
the bicycles were pedalled by some fifty Nogai
Tartars. The name Malacovia was given to the city
by the prince who had only a vague knowledge of
ancient Greek and believed that *malakos* meant
"shell" while in fact it means "soppy"—a good
name, however, for a town of the marshlands.

From this fortress the Nogai Tartars would
cross over to the Russian coast on flat boats propelled by pedals; each Tartar would carry his own
bicycle on his head and once on dry land would fe-
rociously attack the Russian settlements. Though
a few of the prince's companions were at first in
favour of using the traditional horses, they were
soon convinced of the great advantage of the bicycle, seeing the surprise and terror that an apparition of cycling Tartars caused in the hearts of the
Russians.

When finally the Imperial Russian government, incapable of coping with these pirates, was
on the point of asking a foreign government for aid
to destroy the prince's egg and bring peace once
again to the Black Sea, nature took its course and
an unexpected solution presented itself. The extreme humidity of the Danube delta rusted the
cogs in the lifting mechanism of Malacovia and
one day in 1873 it refused to budge in spite of the
generous efforts of the Nogai pedallers. Conscious
that the end was near, the prince and his brave
companions, with their bicycles on their heads,
escaped through a secret tunnel and dispersed
throughout the world. Even as late as the early
1900's it was a common sight in Paris or London
to see a cycling Tartar race down one of the residential boulevards, much to the delight of the population who were sincerely impressed by the speed
they could achieve. The prince, heartbroken, married a rich Armenian who had been captured in
Odessa, and founded in Bucharest the first factory
of Rumanian bicycles.

(Amedeo Tosetti, *Pedali sul Mar Nero*, Milan, 1884)

MALDONADA, a port in BALNIBARBI.

MANCY, a kingdom on the east coast of India, one
of the best and fairest lands in the world, a land of
plenty, with more than two thousand cities and
many towns inhabited by Christians and Saracens.
The chief city is Latoryn, a port on a river about a

day's journey from the sea, that is said to be larger
than Paris.

The people of Mancy worship idols, roasting
meat before them which is then eaten by the holy
men. The birds of Mancy are twice the size of European birds. The most common species looks
somewhat like white geese with great crests. There
are many serpents in Mancy, which are considered
a great delicacy, and no feast will bring the host
honour and esteem if it does not include a dish of
serpents. A peculiar race of white hens which bear
wool like sheep are bred here. Some small animals
called *loyres* are very popular and have been
trained for fishing.

The city of Cansay, formerly the residence of
the Kings of Mancy, is recommended to all visitors. Several days' journey from Latoryn, Cansay
has been called the "City of Heaven." It is fifty
miles in circumference, and was built on a lagoon,
as Venice is.

Many mendicant religious men live in Cansay,
in an abbey reached by boat and surrounded by a
garden. When the monks have eaten, the leftovers
are taken in silver plates and fed to thousands of
animals living in the garden. The monks believe
that beautiful animals are the souls of wealthy
men; ugly ones, the souls of poor men. Cansay
produces a robust wine called *bignon*.

(Sir John Mandeville, *Voiage de Sir John Maundevile*, Paris, 1857)

MANDAI COUNTRY, in the North Pole. Following the Polar Star through a vast region of snow
and ice the traveller will come upon a large door
dug out of the side of a mountain, guarded by a
lion, a golden scorpion, a red sword and a serpent
named Ur covered in scales of metal strong enough
to cut through iron. If the right words are spoken
the door will slide open, showing a large chasm
deep in the heart of the mountain. After a long
fall, the traveller will arrive in a country of naked
blond men whose bodies are entirely covered with
soft white fur and who live in bamboo huts and
hollow trees.

This is Mandai Country, where the climate is
temperate and the land free of vermin and beasts
of prey. The inhabitants live in communities
where private property does not exist and where
each man is the equal of his neighbour.

(Hirmiz bar Anhar, *Iran*, Paris, 1905)

MANGABOOS, LAND OF THE, far beneath the surface of the earth, close to the centre of the globe. Seen from above, its landscape is not dissimilar to that of the earth's surface, except that its colours keep changing in the light of the six coloured suns that illuminate it. The central sun is a shining white globe with five smaller ones—rose, violet, yellow, blue and orange—around it. Although the suns are dazzlingly bright, they give off very little heat and remain stationary, so that there is no night in this country and no natural division of the day into hours.

Since the force of gravity is reduced in a land so near to the centre of the earth, travellers will find it is quite possible to walk in the air, step off buildings and then stroll down to the ground. Walking uphill, however, involves a strenuous effort.

The Mangaboos are beautiful creatures; not an ugly face is to be seen in their land. Their expressions are always calm and peaceful, largely because they cannot smile or frown.

Perhaps it would be more accurate to describe the Mangaboos as talking and moving vegetables without hearts or internal organs. They are not born, but grow on the bushes in the country's beautiful gardens. Mangaboos in various stages of development can be seen hanging from the country's tall, handsome plants—babies, teenagers and adults all on the same bush, but they are never picked until they are fully mature. For this reason, no children are to be found in the land of the Mangaboos. While they remain on the plant, attached by the soles of their feet, they are motionless and silent. Only when they are plucked do they acquire the powers of speech and motion. Their attractive clothing grows with them and is part of their bodies.

The life span of a Mangaboo is short. Even those who have no accidents and keep themselves cool and moist rarely live to be more than five years old. When they are damaged, the Mangaboos are simply replanted and grown again. Similarly, when they are in their prime, they are again replanted in order that they may sprout and reproduce the species.

The Mangaboos live in a beautiful city of tall, transparent glass buildings, with crystal domes and towering spires. The glass buildings are like their inhabitants—they grow spontaneously from the earth, and once broken or damaged they simply grow back to their original shape. The only inconvenience is that the houses and palaces grow very slowly indeed.

In a square in the city centre stands the Palace of the Sorcerer. It is the sorcerer's role to advise the ruling prince or princess. Unlike the other Mangaboos, who dress in green, the sorcerer is clad in bright yellow. He is bald and his head and hands are covered in thorns similar to those found on rose bushes. His palace is a lofty building made, like the others, of glass, with a high dome and spires at each corner.

The Land of the Mangaboos was discovered by accident when Dorothy Gale, later known as Princess Dorothy of OZ, was swallowed up by the ground during an earthquake in California. She, the buggy and cart in which she was riding, a boy named Zeb and her kitten Eureka slowly floated down until they reached the underground country. Shortly after their arrival, they were joined by the former Wizard of Oz, whom Dorothy had met in that country. He, who had once ruled Oz, now worked for Barnum and Bailey's Circus in America, going up in a balloon to attract people to the show. By chance he had entered a crack in the earth and had floated down until he reached the glass city.

The Mangaboos were not particularly gracious to their visitors, accusing them of having damaged their glass buildings in their descent. Attempts to explain that the so-called "Rain of Stones" was not their fault, but the natural effect of an earthquake, were of no avail; the ruling prince claimed that creatures of flesh and blood had no place in a vegetable kingdom and would have to be destroyed. Dorothy tried to intervene by literally picking his successor—the princess who was now ripe—whom the prince, in violation of the law, had not picked at the right moment, in order to retain his power. Despite her initial gratitude, the princess too argued that the strangers would have to be destroyed, given that there was no way for them to leave the country. The cat, the horse and the tiny pigs the Wizard used in his tricks would, she said, be put into the Black Hole, their prison; the people would be flung to the Clinging Vines. (The Vines can be seen in an enclosed garden: tough, writhing creatures, matted together like a nest of snakes. They crush everything they touch, thereby increasing their own strength.)

The unhappy visitors escaped this fate thanks to the ingenuity of the Wizard, who took a can of kerosene from his belongings and caused a ring of fire to flare up around them. He then told the princess that if those who had advised her to throw him and the others to the Vines had been right, they would not be hurt by the flames. If they had been wrong, they would be withered away. Naturally, those who approached the flames were scorched, and the air was filled with the odour of burning potatoes. The humans were spared their fate, but the princess insisted that the animals be driven into the Black Hole. Despite their resistance, the cat, the horse and the piglets were chased out of the city by a crowd of Mangaboos armed with thorny branches. They were driven across the plain to a glass mountain, to a frightening black cave. Having forced the animals inside, the Mangaboos began to block the entrance with glass rocks, but they were interrupted by the Wizard, who pulled down the barrier. When he had made a sufficiently large hole, the Mangaboos used their thorns to drive him too into the Black Hole, along with Dorothy and Zeb.

But to the visitors' surprise, the cave led to a tunnel which eventually brought them out into the Valley of VOE, from where the return to the surface of the earth is an easy matter.

(L. Frank Baum, *Dorothy and the Wizard in Oz*, Chicago, 1908)

MANGHALOUR, a rich and fertile island, with peaceful streams and meadows, fruit trees and cedar trees, and several high mountains. Manghalour is a constitutional monarchy set up in the mid-twelfth century by Mathieu de Laval, a Frenchman who was shipwrecked here with twelve hundred men and women.

The Manghalour that de Laval found was a Muslim community that lived by oppressing a mountain tribe called the Ghebres. De Laval joined the Ghebres against the Muslims in a short campaign which resulted in the suicide of the Muslim king. The victors opened the harems, the French married the imprisoned Muslim women, the land was shared equally and everyone lived happily for ten years. At that time the colony was attacked by a large barbarian army, which de Laval managed to repulse aided by an army of women who defended the capital valiantly. Following the victory, women were given the right to bear arms and girls were allowed to attend public schools and receive exactly the same education as the boys.

Visitors wishing to know more about the history of the island should read the bronze plaque

mounted on a pillar—part of a Gothic colonnade—in the forest by the shore.

The valleys in the mountains are the property of the Ghebres, a strong and proud people believed to have come originally from Circassia, who are today the largest minority population in Manghalour.

Three main Ghebres valleys are worth noting. The green Valley of Douchdere or the Valley of Dreams is seventeen leagues long and five leagues wide. It contains many important mineral mines and is one of the most fertile areas of Manghalour. The Valley of Zouhhad is desolate and lonely, inhabited by monks who live in cells cut out of the rock and whose solitude is preserved by troops who help guard the only entrance. Once in Zouhhad, exit is forbidden. The monks' isolation is the result of a Ghebres law designed to put an end to the religious community's wealth. An interesting feature of the Zouhhad valley is a village called La Voûte, which juts out—unsupported—from the cliff, and is blessed every year by the monks to prevent it from falling into the void.

The third important valley in Manghalour is the Valley of Iram or Earthly Paradise, noted for its beautiful waterfalls. Travellers are advised to visit the ruins of a temple to which the following story is attached. The son of a Ghebres king secretly converted to the Islamic faith and became indifferent to the pleasures of youth. To cure him, his father introduced him to Darim, a beautiful young woman, who instead of dissuading him was converted by the young prince's preaching and agreed to marry him. But the king also fell in love with Darim and, to avoid competition, imprisoned his son in the Valley of Iram. Darim consented to become the king's wife on condition that the king kill her nurse. The king gladly did as she had asked, but upon uncovering the body found that Darim had taken her nurse's place and that her soul had departed. The king died of grief and the prince spent the rest of his life weeping in the temple he erected to house Darim's tomb.

Manghalour itself is of uncertain location, but some forty leagues away is a group of small islands inhabited by exiled Muslims, the original inhabitants, now ruled by a sultan who has his seat in the Isle of Kalhac.

(Louis Rustaing de Saint-Jory, *Les Femmes Militaires. Relation Historique D'Une Isle Nouvellement*

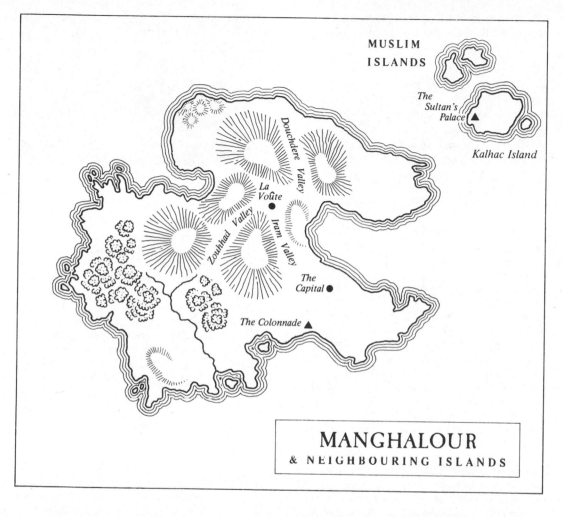

MUSLIM ISLANDS

The Sultan's Palace ▲

Kalhac Island

Douchdere Valley

La Voûte ●

Zouhhad Valley

Iram Valley

The Capital ●

The Colonnade ▲

MANGHALOUR
& NEIGHBOURING ISLANDS

Découverte ... Dedié A Monseigneur Le Chevalier D'Orléans. Par le C. D.***, Paris, 1735)

MANGO ISLAND is about three weeks' sail from CORAL ISLAND. Visitors can find lodgings in a small village founded by Christian settlers, which lies on one side of a central ridge. The cottages in the village, each with its own garden, are painted with a kind of red ochre and with lime extracted from coral. By far the most substantial building here is the church. It stands on a hill, and measures one hundred feet long by fifty feet wide. There is not a single nail in the whole building, which was constructed in two months by natives

working mainly with bone and flint axes, as there are few European tools on the island. Villagers are friendly, and dress in grotesque imitations of western clothing.

Visitors will find that the only drawback to this peaceful and beautiful place is the numerous rats that infest it. As cats are difficult to come by, hogs are used as substitute rat killers. But the traditional rat stew, prepared by the cannibals who inhabit the opposite side of the central ridge, can no longer be tasted since the last cannibal king converted to Christianity. Together with their *haute cuisine*, many other quaint customs have vanished: the visitor can no longer attend, for example, the deposition ceremony, in which the new king buried the old king alive, strangled the old queens and built a new temple or palace using the living attendants of the deposed monarch as foundation pillars.

(Robert Michael Ballantyne, *The Coral Island*, London, 1858)

MANOBA, a volcanic island off the coast of New Guinea. It can be reached by S.I.A.T. boats (Straits, Islands and Archipelago Trading Company). A fairly regular launch service connects Manoba with the mainland.

Manoba rises to a height of five thousand feet and is surrounded by a reef and a lagoon. The beaches are silver coloured, as the volcanic sand is covered by coral dust; there are thick forests and palms along the shore. The rainfall is one hundred inches per year.

The people live in houses on the shore built on stilts as a protection against high tides during storms. They are still quite primitive, and some of the men continue to carry the traditional phallic horn while others wear porcupine quills stuck in their nostrils. European visitors are strongly discouraged from approaching the Manobian women. However, a prostitute from the mainland offers her services in Manoba from time to time, passing herself off as a pedlar.

Because of its isolation the island has never been converted to Christianity. Missionaries failed to make any impact on the people of the interior and no permanent trading post was established until after World War Two. The inhabitants of Manoba take part in the so-called Cargo cult: they believe that happiness will come from the commodities or cargo that have made the white man so rich and powerful.

(Paul Scott, *The Birds of Paradise*, London, 1962)

MANOUHAM, an island on the Tropic of Capricorn, not far from the Chilean coast. It is crossed by two rivers that surround a vast plain, and is inhabited by cannibals who have built a village composed of long rows of cabins.

The main feature of Manouham is the tombs, large mounds each with one side cut open to show the body in foetal position. By this the natives indicate that earth is the mother of us all. The dead are buried with all their earthly possessions, and food

The famous royal tombs on the island of MANOUHAM.

and drink. Funerals are celebrated with a dance that mimes the movements of the planets and with a great noise made by beating the trunks of trees; this is thought to frighten the soul off to Heaven.

There are two tribes on the island: the Kistrimaux—warriors—and the Taouaous—poets and philosophers. The Taouaous have composed a delightful litany to be recited while eating a body: "My love, my hope, beautiful face, eye of my soul, Oh, Oh! Light limb, fine dancing leg, brave warrior arm. Oh, Oh! You will be late in bed tonight, awake in my belly in the morning. Oh, Oh!"

(Abbé Pierre François Guyot Desfontaines, *Le Nouveau Gulliver, ou Voyage De Jean Gulliver, Fils Du Capitaine Gulliver. Traduit d'un Manuscrit Anglois. Par Monsieur L.D.F.*, Paris, 1730)

MAPLE WHITE LAND, commonly known as the **LOST WORLD**, a volcanic plateau in the Amazonas State, Brazil. Named after its discoverer, an artist and poet from Detroit, Michigan, it was first explored in 1912 by an English expedition led by Professor George Edward Challenger. The plateau is famous for having preserved many species thought to be extinct, notably iguanodons, allosaurs, megalosaurs, sabre-toothed tigers and pterodactyls. Basaltic, or plutonic, cliffs surround the plateau and form an unbroken ridge separating it from the rest of the Amazonian jungle. The highest point in this ridge is an isolated pyramidal rock five or six hundred feet high.

Maple White Land is reached from the port of Manaus, on the Amazon, after three and a half weeks' travel up the river. After navigating northwest from Manaus for three days one reaches a

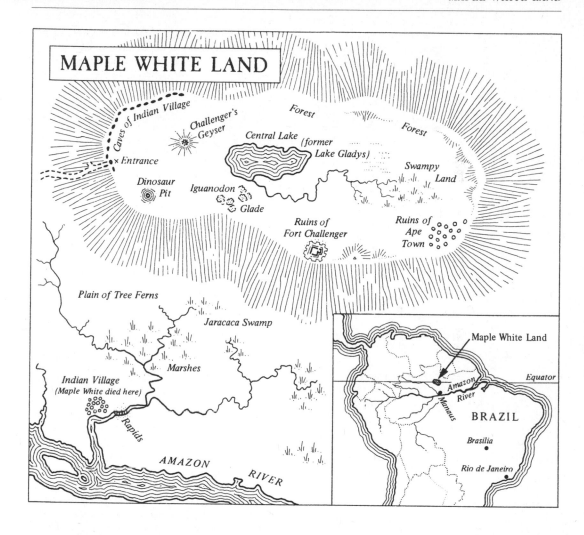

tributary of the Amazon, probably near the Arquipelago das Anavilhanas, and after two more days' travel the Cucama Indian village. Approximately one hundred miles farther down the river one comes upon an assai palm projecting at a peculiar angle over the side of the stream, and must continue until an opening appears half a mile farther on, on the other side. Four more days and one arrives at a mosquito-infested marshland, which must be crossed on foot. The road ascends, until nine days later a bamboo forest will block the way, and machetes will be needed to cut a path. Beyond it lies an open plain of tree ferns, then two small hills and, beyond that, the Jaracaca swamp, so named after the most venomous and aggressive

snake in South America. On the other side rise the red ridges of the plateau, which must be followed until one reaches the caves at the northern end. The entrance is in the second cave from the right. Five hundred yards into the cave there is an opening to the left, but explorers must continue along the principal tunnel another thirty yards. Those rigorous enough to have come this far may notice the interesting native symbols on the walls. This entrance leads into the Indian village and, through it, onto the plateau. White chalk arrows indicating the way in should be ignored; the previous entrance was blocked by fallen rocks.

The plateau of Maple White Land is oval in shape, spreading over sixty square miles, somewhat

The Indian caves, MAPLE WHITE LAND.

rushes; the Glade of Iguanodons; the Challenger geyser; the diamond mines in a volcanic pit of blue clay, discovered by Lord John Roxton; and the ruins of the Ape-men or Doda Village, who were exterminated in 1912 by the local Indian tribe, the Accala. The Accala village is set in the caves of the northern wall of the ridge.

(Sir Arthur Conan Doyle, *The Lost World*, London, 1912)

MARADAGAL, a vast South American state of twenty-seven million inhabitants, bordering on Parapagal.

In 1924 Maradagal was at war with Parapagal; the outcome is not yet clear, but the toll taken by the conflict is seen in the numerous cripples that haunt the Maradagal cafés, and visitors will find themselves scrutinized by unchanging and menacing glass eyes.

(Carlo Emilio Gadda, "La cognizione del dolore," in *Letteratura*, Milan, 1938–41)

MARAMMA, a large island of the MARDI ARCHIPELAGO and a sanctuary to all the inhabitants of Mardi. In the centre of the island rises the peak of Ofo, said to be inaccessible; those who have tried to climb it have ended up dead at its base. Except for this peak, Maramma is all rolling hills and dales, like the sea after a storm.

Not one fruit-bearing tree or edible root grows on the island; the population depends wholly on the large tributes remitted by its neighbours. Maramma is extremely fertile but its inhabitants say that it would be wrong to make an orchard out of holy land.

Travellers visiting Maramma are advised to note the superb Temple of Oro, supreme lord of the heavens, built on a small island in the sacred Yammo Lake, in the middle of the island.

Also remarkable is the great Morai of Maramma, the burial place of the pontiffs, as the priests of the island are called. To reach the Morai, visitors must walk through the bed of a shallow watercourse to purify their feet before touching sacred ground. Along this route are thatched arbours for the accommodation of devotees who wash their clothes in these consecrated waters. (In most cases, the result of putting on their clothes immediately after immersion is not longevity but

like a shallow funnel, all its sides sloping down from the surrounding ridge to a considerable lake in the centre, ten miles in circumference—the Central Lake, formerly Lake Gladys. Despite the unusual fauna the flora is that of a temperate climate: araucaria, beech, oak and even birch are found here, as well as very tall gingko trees.

Travellers are advised to visit the Fort Challenger ruins, of which the gate and part of the wooden walls still remain, topped by a huge gingko tree; the Rookery of Pterodactyls, the slopes of a pit—one of the smaller ancient volcanic blow-holes of the plateau—where hundreds of these beasts assemble flapping around pools of green-scummed, stagnant water fringed with bul-

rheumatics.) The Morai itself is surrounded by a wall and protected from evil spirits by twenty black boars' heads suspended from the boughs of nearby trees. In the middle of the enclosure is a hillock of dry sand which has the power of preserving the body and it is here, in the sand, that the pontiffs of Maramma are buried.

Nearby, visitors can taste the water of the sacred Morai spring, clear as crystal, behind which can be seen two tiers of sharp tusk-like stones called "the mouth of Oro." It is said that if any secular hand were immersed in the spring, these stony jaws would close upon it.

By the spring stands a large statue of dark stone representing a burly man with an overgrown head and a hollowed-out abdomen into which, at certain seasons, human sacrifices are placed; this direct route ensures the idol's digestion.

The language spoken on Maramma changes frequently due to a custom imposed by the pontiffs centuries ago. Apart from their common name, pontiffs have a given name which they receive at birth. During a pontiff's life, no words can be used that contain the syllables of his given name; this causes a great number of words to be invented in replacement, thereby giving the language a fresh and creative character.

(Herman Melville, *Mardi, and A Voyage Thither*, New York, 1849)

MARBOTIKIN DULDA or ISLAND OF IRON,

in the Indian Ocean. The capital is To–At–Chimk and the major town is Ching Peh. It is ruled by a queen who distinguishes herself solely by her dress—a long, blue silk robe edged with white—and full-length steel belts. Priests and officers of the law wear ankle-length green robes and the common people short grey tunics. The number and size of feathers in their hats also depends on their social status. All jewellery is made of steel, and iron is the island's most important commodity. The people are tall and strong. They are gentle and friendly, like the Chinese, but rapidly become over-familiar. A group of elderly, wise academicians, the *mi–tia–dinams*, attend the queen, and those giving outstanding service are rewarded by being allowed to kiss the royal heel.

Most buildings are of brick, only one or two storeys high with large cellars twenty feet underground. The Royal Palace is a honeycomb of decagonal rooms, with a corridor at each corner that connects with galleries. The central and largest room is open to the sky and holds a large tree. The throne room, with its polished iron throne, has twelve sparsely decorated walls.

According to the religion of Marbotikin Dulda, the Supreme Creator lives in the moon, and his dwelling is worshipped in a vast temple called Miudia-blo. Here a statue supports twelve colossal heads, each named after a sign of the zodiac, that pivot to follow the phases of the moon. The only time the inhabitants invite one another to their homes is during the New Moon Festival.

Their funeral rites are peculiar. The body is taken outside and shaken to see whether it shows any sign of life. If it is found to be dead, the head is cut off and buried beneath the house, while the body is exposed on a hill outside the town. When two inhabitants of Marbotikin Dulda decide to get married, they are taken to different rooms in the Honeycomb Palace at full moon. There the bridegroom has to find his future wife, who avoids him as long as possible. Once united, they are married in the temple and dance till dawn.

Murder in Marbotikin Dulda is punished by seizing one of the murderer's children and handing him over to the victim's family. If the murderer has no children he is beaten, receiving one stroke for every month of the victim's life.

The language of the island is mostly monosyllabic, and nearly all words end in vowels. The

Marbotikin Dulda

speed of pronunciation alters the meaning: for example *loatchi* means "to love greatly"; *lo-atchi* means "to love slightly." The addition of the final "k" (*loatchik*) turns a word into its opposite ("to hate").

(Pierre Chevalier Duplessis, *Mémoires De Sir George Wollap; Ses Voyages dans différentes parties due Monde; aventures extraordinaires qui lui arrivent; découverte de plusieurs Contrées inconnues; description des moeurs & des coutumes des Habitans. Par M.L.C.D.* Paris, 1787–88)

MARDI ARCHIPELAGO, a vast conglomeration of islands in the Pacific Ocean, exactly on the equator. Mardi has been described as a "fleet of isles, profoundly at anchor within their coral harbour." Several islands should be visited: DIRANDA, DOMINORA, FLOZELLA-A-NINA, HOOLOO-MOOLOO, JUAM, MARAMMA, MINDA, NORABAMMA, ODO, OHONOO, PIMMINEE, TUPIA, VALAPEE.

(Herman Melville, *Mardi, and A Voyage Thither,* New York, 1849)

MAREMMA, see ORSENNA.

MARKLAND, a heavily wooded island between Helluland and Vinland, in the Davis Strait, north Atlantic. It was discovered by Eric the Red after sailing from the Land of Flat Stones, Helluland, two days to the south-east. On this island, Eric's men killed a bear. Markland means "forest land."

(Anonymous, *Eirik's Saga,* 13th cen. AD)

MARMORKLIPPEN, a mountain range separating GREAT MARINA from CAMPAGNA. Its name means "Marble Cliffs." A staircase leads to its summit, from which all the surrounding country can be seen. Owls and falcons nest among the cliffs, as well as lizards and lance-headed vipers.

(Ernst Jünger, *Auf den Marmorklippen,* Frankfurt, 1939)

MARTINIA, see NAZAR.

MARVELLOUS ISLANDS, see BRISEVENT.

MARVELLOUS RIVER, a branch of the Nile, born in the hills of the Ethiopian Plateau. Travellers sailing down its murky waters will find their path blocked at a certain point by a gigantic wall that no one has been able to climb. However, before arriving here, travellers will cross a nameless but fascinating land. From the comfort of their ship, they will see lions, tigers, serpents and unicorns drinking together peacefully on the river bank. Strangely coloured natives, who cast their nets from small fishing boats, can be seen landing catches of ginger, rhubarb, sandalwood and cinnamon, while on the beach, beautiful native women place their white clay jugs in the sun. For reasons unexplained, the sun makes the water contained in these jugs as cool as that from a spring.

In spite of these attractions, no visitors have been known to land here.

(Jean, Sire de Joinville, *Histoire de saint Louis,* Paris, 1809 [?])

MARVOLS COUNTRY, see ICARIA.

MASK ISLAND, an uncharted and now uninhabited island in the East Indies. The coast looks forbidding, with rugged cliffs rising sheer from the water. The only possible landing place is a narrow bay between high rocks, from where a rough path leads upwards to the top of the cliffs. Some fresh water can be found on the island and fruit trees grow in the open areas.

Mask Island was first discovered when the king of Spain set out to find the most inhospitable island as a place of exile for his sister and Dom Pedro, Viceroy of Catalonia, who had angered him by their secret marriage. The couple were abandoned on the island, their faces covered in iron masks which could not be removed. They lived on the island for many years, surviving on fruits, birds and the meagre resources of their harsh environment. During their stay on the island, they had two children, a girl and a boy. The girl had a birth mark in the shape of an iron mask on her breast. Discovering her alone on the shore, the crew of a passing ship picked her up and took her to GOAT LAND, where she was eventually made empress, being regarded by the natives as a gift from the gods themselves.

The three remaining inhabitants of Mask Island were eventually able to leave their place of exile when a ship was grounded on the island. The crew perished, but the ship itself was not badly damaged, and the exiles managed to reach the coast of England.

Dom Pedro joined the English forces and distinguished himself in the wars against the Spanish. So great was his popularity that, when the king of England was assassinated, he was hailed as the new monarch. Now a widower himself, he married the king's widow, who had been brought to England from Goat Land. The morning after the consummation of the marriage, he noticed the birth mark on his bride's breast. He realized that, unwittingly, he had married his own daughter and, in horror at this act, committed suicide.

(Charles Fieux de Mouhy, *Le Masque de Fer, ou les Aventures Admirables du Pere et du Fils,* The Hague, 1747)

MATAEOTECHNY, see ENTELECHY.

MAURELVILLE or **MAUREL CITY,** see ELISEE RECLUS ISLAND.

MAURETANIA (not to be confused with the African republic of the same name), a country to the north of CAMPAGNA. The inhabitants are famous for their apathetic submission to power which gives them something of the nature of a robot. It was here that the so-called Chief Ranger first came to rule before he began spreading terror through GREAT MARINA and other neighbouring countries.

(Ernst Jünger, *Auf den Marmorklippen,* Frankfurt, 1939)

MAXON'S ISLAND, in the South China Sea, lying opposite the mouth of a small river in Borneo. It can be reached from Singapore by travelling through the Pamarung Islands, then on farther, several miles north of the Equator and Cape Santang, opposite the mouth of a small river in Borneo. Small and fertile, it has a secluded harbour protected by a reef. The climate is humid and warm. The fauna and flora are typically tropical, but no large animals roam its forests.

The island was discovered at the beginning of the century by a certain Professor Maxon who set up a laboratory on the island to try and create life from dead chemicals. After a dozen ill-wrought

experiments, Maxon was tricked into believing that a ship-wrecked sailor, Harper Jr. from New York, was the result of his efforts. Maxon, his Chinese cook Sing, his daughter Virginia, and Harper Jr. were rescued by the US Navy, leaving behind them, in a chest buried in the sand, Maxon's secret for creating life.

(Edgar Rice Burroughs, *A Man without a Soul,* New York, 1913)

MAYDA, or **ISLAND OF THE SEVEN CITIES,** latitude 46° north, longitude unknown, to the north-east of the Azores. It was discovered in 734 by the Bishop of Oporto and six other Portuguese bishops who took flight when the Moors invaded their country.

In 1447 Captain Antonio Leone, an Italian serving the King of Portugal, visited the island; he described it as low, volcanic and shaped like a crescent, and reported that the inhabitants spoke Portuguese and inquired of him whether the Moors had at last been expelled from Spain.

Mayda, forty-five kilometres long, is divided into seven communities founded by the seven bishops. Visitors will see in each community a stone cathedral built with large slabs of basalt, cemented with powdered shells and decorated with many golden ornaments. The population is numerous and attends religious service regularly.

(Washington Irving, *The Alhambra,* New York, 1832; Vincent Gaddis, *Invisible Horizons,* New York, 1958)

MECCANIA, a powerful but little-known state in western Europe, bordering on Francaria. The country is physically isolated from its neighbours by a belt of land which encircles the whole of Meccania. This area, which dates back to World War One, has been carefully preserved as a no man's land. It is uncultivated and totally uninhabited; the grass and weeds are burnt off each year and wire fences have been added to the natural barrier thus produced.

Visitors require visas and must purchase tickets well in advance to cross the frontier zone. Those arriving from the border town of Graves, in Francaria, will be taken in a comfortable police van with shuttered windows to Bridgetown, a large town lying on the bend of a river in the magnificent Meccania countryside. Here they must report to the Police Office, where they are interviewed by the Inspector of Foreigners and subjected to a medical examination and a disinfectant bath. Their fingerprints are filed, their voices recorded and their photographs taken. Finally, a lock of hair is cut, for official records. On the following day, visitors will be given a second disinfectant bath, a copy of the *Law on the Conduct of Foreign Observers*, and permission to leave, under the supervision of a Foreign Observers' Conductor. The costs of accommodation at the Police Office and of the medical examination are borne by the visitor.

Free travel in Meccania is not permitted; all tourist visits follow a strictly defined programme and timetable. No visitor may leave his hotel unless in the company of his conductor. He must give three days' notice of his intention to travel to another town and must then undergo similar formalities to those experienced when he first entered the country. Even conversation with other foreigners is forbidden until a certificate of approval has been granted. Visitors should note that they are not allowed to bring anything out of the country without official permission. This includes private diaries and notebooks.

In Meccania, everything is subject to State approval and the individual has no rights against the "Super-State." The very concept of individualism has all but disappeared. As children are taught from a very early age, the State is the "Father and Mother of all." In effect the Super-State is the collective soul of Meccania, englobing all individual souls. The Meccanians believe it to be the nearest approach to the Christian ideal ever put into practice by any nation. Total State control means, among other things, that all letters are censored and that all telephone conversations are overheard by officials in the Post Office. Despite this, dissent and resentment against State authority are almost unknown.

As a modern nation, Meccania only really began to emerge in the nineteenth century, when the revered Prince Bludiron was able to turn the country away from the false ideals of liberty and to preserve the State from the revolutionary ideas of the period. It is true that he was opposed by Spotts, the theorist of Meccanian Socialism, but the rising standard of living brought about by Bludiron's reforms seemed to counter Spotts' arguments about the inevitability of economic collapse and revolution. After the death of Bludiron,

the country became so imbued with dreams of world conquest that it started a major war—decimating the population and leaving the country in poverty. Its reconstruction was the work of Prince Mechow, a great-nephew of Bludiron. In order to remedy the disasters of war, the State began to play an ever greater role in the economy and general life of the country; individualism withered away quite spontaneously. Under the influence of Mechow—then Chief Minister for the Interior—all means of production were concentrated in the hands of the centralized government. Mechow began the deliberate construction of a Super-State. He was able to attract the followers of Spotts' doctrines by promising—and developing—an organized system of production without crises or unemployment.

Meccanian society is divided into a hierarchy of seven classes. The first class is the aristocracy, numbering about ten thousand. The second consists of the army and navy, plus officers of high birth—roughly four million. Class three is formed of the richest merchants and officials of the first grade of the Civil Service: together they number some six million. Class four, about twenty million strong, comprises other civil servants and most liberal professions. Class five represents the forty million skilled artisans; class six, the twenty million semi-skilled workers; and class seven, the ten million members of the menial industrial groups.

Promotion from one class to another is possible, but infrequent. Each class has its own uniform, which must be worn at all times—except on those occasions when it is replaced by military dress. The colours of the uniforms are, in descending order: white, red, yellow, green, chocolate, grey, dark blue. Various insignia indicate grades within the basic classes. Women do not wear uniforms, but have a patch of colour indicating their class, affixed to their outer garments. Women's expenditure on clothes is restricted according to their class and status.

Although Meccania is ruled by an emperor, it also has a parliament which represents the seven classes. There are no political parties and no opposition. Some foreign observers claim that despite the parliament and the importance given to the aristocracy, the powerful military caste is, in fact, the ruler behind the scenes.

The social hierarchy of Meccania is reflected in the country's urban planning. Towns are usually built on a circular ground plan, with government and public buildings in the centre and the cultural institutions around them. The main streets radiate from this centre, like the spokes of a wheel, dividing the town into residential zones for the different classes.

Although imposing, Meccanian towns are not picturesque. Even the houses of the wealthy, surrounded by large gardens, appear very standardized, as though all the plans had been drawn up by the same school of architects. The apartments of the lower classes are almost identical—only the size of the apartment varies according to the different classes. Visitors will find the towns neat and conspicuously clean, but basically dull. Walking through the capital, Mecco, for instance, travellers have the impression of being in a huge hospital where nothing is ever out of place.

The most important statue in the capital is that of Prince Mechow, found in the square named after him. As high as a church steeple, it is a shapeless mass of granite surmounted by a granite block, carved with bas-reliefs depicting the reconstruction of the State. At the corners, huge figures represent the Arms, the Intellect, Culture and Power. From the granite plinth rises a column over one hundred feet high, supporting a statue of the prince himself. It is customary for Meccanians to salute this monument, each with the form of salute appropriate to his class. The artist who designed it lies buried, at his own wish, beneath the shapeless mass of granite.

The whole city of Mecco is a living reminder of the work of Prince Mechow: streets, hotels and squares are frequently named after him and it is very fashionable for men to affect the style known as Mechow whiskers and to wear eyeglasses. Above all, the prince's name is preserved at the Mechow Memorial Museum, which houses all his speeches and many of his mementoes, and should certainly be visited. It is considered a great privilege to be allowed to live in Mecco; unlike most Meccanian towns, the capital has no members of the seventh social class among its population.

Everything in the country is organized by the State. Even shopping is strictly regulated. Certain categories of food are available only from central markets, dotted about the cities; others are obtainable from smaller shops. In both cases, housewives must do their shopping at a prescribed time and must continue to patronize the same dealer for at

least one year. No deviation from this rule is tolerated. In the factory areas, the Controller's Office has detailed files on the career and character of every worker employed. Even the degree of fatigue is scientifically measured; a worker whose fatigue level is below the norm is required to work extra hours until that norm is reached. Once a year, a Strenuous Month is organized. For thirty days, all employees work at top speed for as many hours as the Industrial Psychologists determine they should. This is not only excellent training— the workers are so glad when the month is over, that, unconsciously, they work better for the rest of the year.

Women do not normally work in Meccania, with the exception of the wives and daughters of men of classes six or seven, who staff the canteens at the workplaces of their menfolk. The rest of their time is spent in domestic work in the home.

The degree of control exercised by the State is largely due to the efforts of the Department of Sociology and the Department of Time. The former collects statistics on everything from industrial production to domestic expenditure, in order that everything can be centrally planned. If, for instance, members of the lower classes are found to be spending too much on drink when the housewives submit their account books for the quarter, sanctions are imposed. In collaboration with the Department of Health, model diets can be drawn up in accordance with the nutritional needs of the various classes. This check on domestic expenditure, together with the control of production, has totally wiped out improvidence and poverty from Meccanian society.

The work of the Time Department is, perhaps, even more important. Weekly diary forms are issued to all subjects, who have to account for their movements and actions for each half-hour of the week, using the one hundred and fifty categories recognized by the Department. If their timetables show any gaps, they are directed towards useful activities. The other main function of the Time Department is to calculate how much time is required to perform any given action. Visitors are reminded that they, too, must fill in these diaries; failure to do so results in a fine. It is virtually impossible for visitors to falsify their diaries, as they are checked against those of the ubiquitous Conductors.

Even leisure time is subject to State control. Anyone whose diary shows a spare half-hour is required to make out a half-yearly scheme, specifying the cultural activities he or she intends to undertake. Inspectors of Private Leisure give expert advice and ensure that the programme is adhered to. Weekly attendance at the theatre is compulsory, and the individual has no choice as to which play he sees. All theatres are State institutions, and all plays are written—mainly in verse and with didactic intent—by a supervised group of experts rather than by a single author. The intellectual level of the plays varies according to the class represented in the audience. Best-loved themes include "Efficiency, Inefficiency and National Self-Consciousness," "The Triumph of Meccania" and "Uric Acid." The latter deals with the role of that poisonous substance in the life of the State, the family and the individual from sociological, pathological and physiological points of view.

Drama has replaced the novel as the major art form; indeed, in the great libraries, all novels are classified as juvenile fiction. The only adults who read novels are the inmates of the asylums for the mentally deranged, as this bulky kind of fiction appears to have a soothing effect on them. Graham Greene, Heinrich Böll and Balzac are probably among the lunatics' favourite authors. No daily newspapers are published. These have been replaced by local gazettes and State reports and are the adults' ordinary reading matter. For the most part they consist of statistics and official announcements. All published nonfiction is available through public libraries; alternatively it can be ordered through official book-agents—there are no longer bookshops in the country. The government is the source of most books, although it is the printers (again, a government department) who effectively decide what will be printed and in what quantities.

In the visual arts, all work produced in Meccania is either patriotic or didactic. In theory, all paintings are commissioned by a central board, which sets the subjects for the coming year; in practice, some illicit work is carried out for members of the upper classes. The people of Meccania show no interest in the art of other countries and pride themselves on never having been influenced by Latin culture.

Education is, of course, tightly controlled by a Central Board. The subjects taken and the length of studies are calculated in terms of the pupil's social class. The Juvenile Bureau of Industry decides what careers will be taken up by those of classes five to seven and industrial training begins at school. Members of these classes cannot start work without a certificate from the Central Board. Even pre-school education is subject to controls. All toys have a specific educational purpose; nondirected play is considered a waste of energy and intelligence. The use made of toys at home is supervised by a corps of Inspectors of Child Life.

Of all the departments, that of Health is probably the largest; it has numerous sub-departments and also controls sewage disposal and street cleaning. All houses in Meccania are inspected every year to maintain sanitary standards and all subjects undergo annual medical examinations. If necessary, they receive compulsory treatment for any ailments detected. Refusal of treatment usually leads to detention in an asylum for mental abnormality. In cases of incurable diseases, death may be prescribed by the Special Medical Group, which has also perfected methods to detect a certain brain disease known as "chronic tendency to dissent." Those suffering from this ailment are confined to asylums. Most of those affected belong to the old opposition parties; the disease seems to have a much lower incidence among the younger generations. As a normal part of medical research, experiments are also carried out on animals; cows with horses' hearts, dogs with no forelegs and a pig with a tiger's skin have all been "bred" in Meccania's laboratories. Some foreign observers suspect that experiments are also being carried out on human beings without their knowledge or consent, and that these might have influenced the research carried out by a certain Dr. Moreau (see NOBLE'S ISLAND).

The Department of Health also plays a role in the organization of marriage and prescribes the number of children a couple may have in any five-year period. However, according to certain reports, the Department of Health has a much more curious role. Under Meccanian law, wives have the right to choose the father of their children and are not obliged to submit to the embraces of their legitimate husbands. It is also true that, for cultural reasons, Meccanian women have a definite preference for strong, virile partners and a particular predilection for members of the army. It is therefore claimed that the Department uses the annual

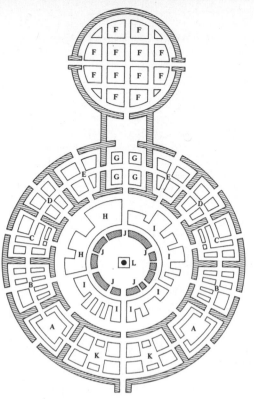

MECCO, THE CAPITAL

A. Army and Navy section
B. Merchants' and Civil Servants' (1st Grade)
C. Other Civil Servants and Liberal Professions
D. Artisans
E. Semi-Skilled Workers
F. Industrial Workers' Quarters
G. Commercial area
H. Mechow Memorial Museum
I. Cultural Institutions
J. Public Buildings
K. Aristocratic Quarters
L. The Monument

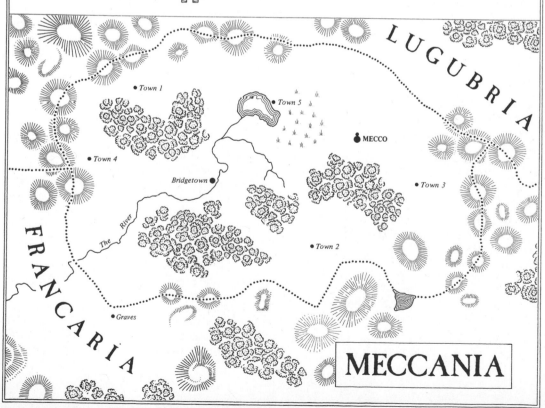

MECCANIA

medical examination to provide genetically suitable partners—usually from the lower classes—for members of the aristocracy. When the appropriate moment arrives, the woman is simply ordered to go away for a "cure."

Because of the extent of State control over individual life, the large police force devotes very little of its efforts to the detection of crime (which is, in any case, infrequent). Those who show propensities towards criminal activities are simply deported to criminal colonies and rarely give any trouble. Police work consists mainly of seeing that the rules devised for the good of the State are adhered to. Policemen collect detailed information on all individuals and draw up an annual report, on the basis of which they issue a certificate of conduct. The Police Office libraries hold copies of all personal files.

Very little is known of Meccania's army, although every subject is a soldier and the army is regarded as the soul of the nation. A Chinese visitor to the country in 1970 heard rumours to the effect that Meccania was experimenting with chemical warfare. It appears that several years beforehand, Lugubria, a state permanently allied to Meccania, showed some reluctance to ratify the terms of a new treaty between the two countries. Without declaring war, Meccania immediately sent airships over Lugubrian territory, threatening to destroy her main cities with chemical weapons if the treaty was not immediately signed. Lugubria surrendered at once. The whole incident lasted only three days and was never publicized in the rest of the world.

(Gregory Owen, *Meccania, the Super-State,* London, 1918)

MECCO, capital of MECCANIA.

MEDAMOTHY, also known as **NOWHERE IS-LAND.** A pleasant land, famed for the lighthouses and high marble towers that adorn the coastline, said to be as long as that of Canada.

An annual fair attracts the richest merchants from both Africa and Asia. All kinds of antiques and luxury goods can be bought here, as well as exotic animals, from unicorns to reindeer.

(François Rabelais, *Le quart livre des faicts et dicts du bon Pantagruel,* Paris, 1552)

MEDDLA, see LOONARIE.

MEDICINE HAT (not to be confused with Medicine Hat, Alberta), a remote settlement in Canada, near the Saskatchewan River, home of all blizzards and chinooks. The chief of the settlement is the so-called Head Spotter of the Weather Makers, who sits on a high stool in a high tower on a high hill. Travellers can address him with requests for good or bad weather but must bear in mind that the Head Spotter is sometimes inadvertently guilty of ugly mistakes.

History has it that once after a long drought the animals of Medicine Hat, tired of the dusty weather, asked for rain. When it came their tails were drenched, and the sudden frost froze the animals' tails stiff. To top it all, a high wind roared through the settlement and blew the tails away. This was particularly inconvenient for the long-tailed animals. The yellow *flongboo,* which uses its tail to light its home in a hollow tree and to illuminate its path across the prairie while hunting at night, was dreadfully upset. A committee of sixty-six animals was elected and was sent to the Head Spotter to do something about their problem. The kind but muddled chief of all Weather Makers blew a great wind that brought back their tails and then loosed another fearful frost to freeze them back again.

(Carl Sandburg, *Rootabaga Stories,* New York, 1922)

MEDWYN'S VALLEY, hidden deep in the steep, impassable Eagle Mountains of northern PRYDAIN.

Legend has it that, in the distant past, dark waters flooded the land of Prydain. Nevvid Nav Neivion built a wooden ship and took two of every animal species aboard with him; when the waters finally drained away, the ship came to rest in Medwyn's Valley, where the ribs of an ancient longship can still be seen, half buried beneath the soil. The only human inhabitant of the valley—an old, bearded man who calls himself Medwyn—will not confirm or deny the legend nor will he admit to being Nevvid himself.

The hidden valley is not recommended to travellers—and in any case, it would be difficult to reach, as no access route has been charted. Yet it is known as a haven for the beasts of the forests and waters of Prydain which find their way here without any difficulty. Intrepid visitors could follow a friendly animal willing to show them the road to Medwyn's Valley, but even then the return journey might prove an impossible task.

(Lloyd Alexander, *The Book of Three*, New York, 1964; Lloyd Alexander, *The High King*, New York, 1968)

MEEZA, see Valley of the JUKANS.

MEGAPATAGONIA, an archipelago situated between Tierra del Fuego and Antarctica. It is inhabited by men who have not developed as most men have, but who have retained animal appearances and customs. Each island holds a particular kind of creature: bear-men, ape-men, otter-men. On some islands live normal-looking men, but their customs are most uncivilized. Every citizen works only four hours a day and work is considered a pleasure, not a constraint. No one has a specialized task; everyone does each job alternately.

Because it lies exactly opposite France, the inhabitants speak an inversion of French—for instance, "Good day" is *"Nob ruoj."* They wear shoes on their heads and hats on their feet. Women are slightly less equal than men. They have neither painting nor sculpture, as they consider these arts useless and "an illusion to help the solitude of the last of men." Music and poetry are accepted.

The capital of the archipelago, on the principal island, is Sirap.

(Nicolas-Edme Restif de la Bretonne, *La Découverte australe Par un Homme-volant, ou Le Dédale français; Nouvelle très-philosophique: Suivie de la Lettre d'un Singe*, & *c^a*, Leipzig, 1781)

MEILLCOURT, an island in the Indian Ocean, a three-week sail from the Cape of Good Hope. The island is ringed by sandbanks, well wooded, with streams and lakes and many fruit trees; there are mountains, lakes and thick forests in the interior. The island's inhabitants are ruled by a descendant of the Chevalier De Meillcourt, a French explorer who was shipwrecked here in the early eighteenth century. The population is a mixture of Europeans and two native tribes: the Troglocites and the Quacacites, who have intermarried over the years.

A man sporting the current fashion for hats and shoes in MEGAPATAGONIA.

They are peaceful and content and the land provides them with everything they need. Though the discovery of iron has contributed to their prosperity, they have no luxuries. The island follows the Catholic religion (though the Troglocites are traditionally atheists) but freedom of belief is guaranteed by law. For administrative purposes, the population is divided into soldiers and workers, the latter being a majority. There is no merchant class, as commerce might lead to rivalries, and there are no monks on the island.

Before Meillcourt's time, the Troglocites were ruled by a king and were a peaceful people, living by hunting and fishing. Their traditional gentility is reflected in their customs. For instance, a man may divorce his wife for adultery, but if he does so, he must continue to support her for a year. In criminal trials, the virtues of the accused are considered as well as his crimes. When a girl reaches marriage-able age she is subject to a three-month period of *kakarika* (examination). Her suitors talk to her, question her as to her tastes and interests, and give her presents. After three months, those who find no fault in her and are still attracted to her form a line, each holding a lighted match. She blows out the match held by the man of her choice; he throws himself at her father's feet, asks for his protection and kisses her. For three days after the marriage she feeds her former suitors. The girl, however, is not allowed to express any preference before the end of the long *kakarika* period.

Another custom is that if a man admires an-other man, he will make himself his slave by plac-ing his hand on his future master's chest and then touching his feet. Their language, though related to that of the Indies, is quite unique. Their dress is light and low cut, made from a pulp derived from reeds. They fight with bows and arrows and short spikes.

(Jean Baptiste de Boyer, Marquis d'Argens, *Le Législateur Moderne, Ou Les Mémoires Du Cheva-lier De Meillcourt*, Amsterdam, 1739)

MEÏPE, a country of uncertain location, where teachers never teach and where it is not required to address grown-ups in a polite manner.

Meïpe was founded in 1918 by Michelle Maurois, the four-year-old daughter of the well-known French writer.

(André Maurois, *Meïpe ou La Délivrance*, Paris, 1929)

MELINDE, a kingdom in the Indies, bordering on both Abyssnes and Ganze, with a few scattered Portuguese trading posts along its coast. For years Melinde was involved in a sporadic war with Ganze over the slave trade and Ganze's right to cross the country and have access to the coast. However, travellers will be relieved to know that the war has now ended; Ganze pays taxes to Melinde and its merchants must follow a pre-scribed route to the coast, being allowed to stay in Melinde only for a limited time.

(William Bingfield [?], *The Travels And Adventures Of William Bingfield, Esq; Containing, As surprizing a Fluctuation of Circumstances, both by Sea and Land, as ever befel one Man. With An accurate Ac-count of the Shape, Nature, and Properties of that most furious, and amazing Animal, the Dog-Bird*, London, 1753)

MELITA, an island in the Atlantic, home of a shrub called *simlax* that grows in the shape of a human being and clings to trees, which it chokes. Legend has it that a maiden was turned into this shrub because of her love for a certain crocus; per-haps this is why the natives refrain from using *sim-lax* in their sacred rites.

(Pliny the Elder, *Inventorum Natura*, 1st cen. AD)

MELORIA CANAL, a large subterranean tunnel that crosses Italy from the Tyrrhenian to the Adri-atic Sea. On the east side, the entrance is in the valley of the Brenta River, near the small island of Aleghero; on the west side, in the Spezia Gulf be-tween Lerici and Punta di Maralunga. It was dis-covered in 1868, thanks to a group of fishermen who found a box in the sea containing a map and an account of its excavation.

Around the year 1300, a captain of the Ge-noese Republic, Luigi Gottardi, discovered near Lerici a vast underwater cavern that would easily allow the passage of a fair-sized galley. This dis-covery led him to undertake a grandiose project; to open an underground canal linking the Tyrrhen-ian with the Adriatic Sea to facilitate the Genoese invasion of the Republic of Venice. A rich man, Captain Gottardi carried out this fabulous plan with the help of five hundred African slaves. The enormous project spanned well over eight years. After it had been completed the slaves were sent back to Africa, the few Genoese citizens informed of the project swore to keep the secret, and the un-fortunate Captain Gottardi was captured by the Venetians. As a result, the canal remained undis-covered for nearly four hundred years.

Even today the Meloria Canal is not in use, perhaps because of the technical difficulties in-volved or perhaps because of the underground earthquakes that make the passage extremely diffi-cult. Only four men have ever travelled its entire length: the three fishermen who discovered the box and a certain Dr. Bandi of the Italian navy. Their account of their expedition in 1868 is centered mainly on the troublesome volcanic phenomena they encountered. They describe the fauna in the tunnel as extremely rich and varied:

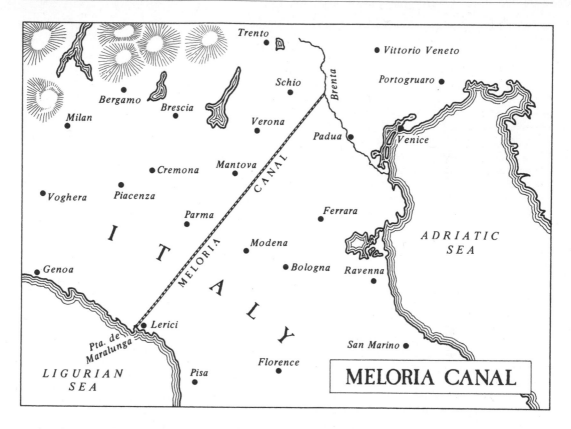

MELORIA CANAL

an abundance of jellyfish, nautiluses and medusae; enormous molluscs of splendid tints, blue, green and red. In some stretches of the canal, schools of phosphorescent fish form compact ceilings, giving an eerie light to their surroundings.

(Emilio Salgari, *I naviganti della Meloria*, Milan, 1903)

MEMISON, the summer palace of the kings of MESZRIA, which stands near the shores of Reisma Mere, a pleasant, tree-fringed lake in the centre of the country. Although it is fortified and moated, Memison is a palace designed for pleasure rather than warfare. It is famed for its land-gardens and water-gardens and for the white pea-cocks which strut along its gravelled paths. The main building is built in the shape of a T, with the longer limb running north-south. Along both limbs runs a gallery of silvery-white stone, with pillars built at fifteen-foot intervals to support the upper rooms. The main limb of the T overlooks a formal garden surrounded by a yew hedge. To the

north-west of the palace lies an oak floor used for the open-air dances so favoured by Meszria's mild climate.

About a mile away from Memison a hill gives fine views over the water-meadows along the Zeshmara River and the marshes which provide a natural habitat for many species of waterbirds. To the landward side, the hill overlooks the neat hedges of the rich farming country which pro-duces the famed Meszria wines. A natural spring on the crest of the hill has been converted into a secluded bathing-pool, shaded by a hedge of rock-roses and juniper on one side, and walnuts and mi-mosa on the other. A parapet provides a pleasant walk with a good sight of the surrounding coun-tryside. The pool was built by Mezentius, King of Meszria, for his mistress Amalie, the mother of his son Barganax, Duke of ZAYANA.

(E.R. Eddison, *Mistress of Mistresses, A Vision of Zimiamvia*, London, 1935; E.R. Eddison, *A Fish Dinner in Memison*, London, 1941; E.R. Eddison, *The Mezentian Gate*, London, 1958)

MERCY FARM, see DIANA'S GROVE.

MER-KING'S KINGDOM, far out in the wide sea, where the water is as blue as the loveliest cornflower and as clear as the clearest crystal, where it is so deep that very, very many church towers must be heaped one upon another in order to reach from the lowest depths to the surface above. Trees and plants of wondrous beauty grow here, whose stems and leaves are so light that they are waved to and fro by the slightest motion of the water, almost as if they were living beings. Fishes, great and small, glide in and out among the branches, just as birds fly about among the trees. The Prince of Aquitania is said to have once fallen asleep in one of the garden's grottoes.

Where the water is deepest stands the castle of the Mer-King. The walls of his palace are of coral and the high-pointed windows are of amber; the roof is composed of mussel shells which, as the billows pass over them, are continually opening and shutting. Each of these shells contains a number of bright, glittering pearls, any one of which would be the most costly ornament in the crown of any king. Beautiful flowers grow out of the walls, and when the windows are open, fishes dart into the rooms as swallows would in the upper world, eat from the hands of the king's daughters, and allow themselves to be caressed.

In front of the palace is a large garden, full of fiery-red and dark blue trees, whose fruits glitter like gold and whose flowers resemble a bright-burning sun. The sand that forms the garden's soil is of a brilliant blue, like flames of sulphur. When the waters are quite still, the sun looks like a purple flower out of whose cup streams forth the light of the world. Each little princess has her own plot in the garden, where she can plant and sow at her pleasure. One made hers in the shape of a whale, another preferred the figure of a mermaid, but the youngest had hers as round as the sun, and planted in it only those flowers that were red, as the sun seemed to her. In her garden she placed a marble statue of a boy, found in a wreck, and planted a red weeping willow by its side.

At the age of fifteen, the mermaids are allowed to rise to the surface of the sea and sit by the moonlight on the rocks to watch the ships sail by. Should a mermaid fall in love with a common mortal and wish to join him, she must endure a frightful ritual. First she must visit the Enchantress in her house beyond a boiling, slimy bog. All the trees and bushes around the house are polypi, like hundred-headed serpents shooting up out of the ground, and immense fat snails—which the Enchantress calls her chickens—crawl about the place. The Enchantress's house is built of the bones of people who have been shipwrecked. Here the mermaid will receive a drink with which she must swim to land. To obtain it, the mermaid must let the Enchantress cut off her tongue and she will never be able to sing or speak again. Sitting on the shore, she must swallow the drink— only then will her tail shrink and grow into human legs. The transformation is very painful and every step will seem to her like walking on the sharp edges of swords. She will never return to the Mer-King's Kingdom or regain the immortality mermaids are gifted with. Should her loved one be united with another, the mermaid will die and her body will be changed into foam.

(Marie Anne de Roumier Robert, *Les Ondins*, Paris & London, 1768; Hans Christian Andersen, *Den lille Havfrue*, Copenhagen, 1835)

MERLIN'S TOMB, a cave beneath a cliff in Cornwall, England, the burial place of Merlin, the great enchanter of CAMELOT and friend and adviser to King Arthur. In his old age Merlin fell in love with a maiden named Nyneve. In an attempt to seduce her, he taught her all his magic, including a great and terrible spell that cannot be broken. Convinced that Nyneve would become his wife, Merlin created a fantastic chamber for their nuptials deep in the heart of the cliffs. As he stepped in to show Nyneve the chamber, she cast the unbreakable spell on him and sealed him forever in the cave. Visitors today can see the great Merlin lying for all eternity in the cave he himself created.

Certain historians say that Merlin was in fact entrapped in an oak in the woods of BROCELI-ANDE by Vivien the enchantress, and that his body can be seen there to this day. Wherever he lies now, it is known that Merlin rose from his prison in the 1940's and saved England from a fate worse than death, assisted by a certain Cambridge professor, Dr. Ransom.

(Alfred, Lord Tennyson, *The Idylls of the King*, London, 1842–85; C.S. Lewis, *That Hideous*

Strength, London, 1946; John Steinbeck, *The Acts of King Arthur and His Noble Knights From the Winchester Manuscripts of Sir Thomas Malory and Other Sources*, New York, 1976)

MEROA, see SABA.

MERRYLAND, a country to the south-east of NOLAND. The Queen of Merryland is an exquisite wax doll, always dressed in a spangled gown decorated with many fluffs and ruffles. Her face is painted in delicate colours and, although her glass eyes appear to stare somewhat, her general expression is pleasant and winning. She is attended by a bodyguard of brightly painted wooden soldiers armed with wooden guns.

Merryland is also the home of the Candy Man, who, as his name implies, is made entirely of candy. A fat little man, he constantly carries a sugar sifter so that he can powder himself with sugar and not stick to the things he touches.

The Queen of Merryland and her attendants were important guests at the famous party given by Ozma of Oz to celebrate her birthday.

(L. Frank Baum, *Queen Zixi of Ix, or The Story of the Magic Cloak*, New York, 1907; L. Frank Baum, *The Road to Oz*, Chicago, 1909)

MESKEETA, an island of the RIALLARO ARCHIPELAGO in the south-east Pacific known to its inhabitants as "the Isle of the Discerners of Good and Evil."

The inhabitants are pygmies, exiles from LIMANORA, book-butchers with a mania for criticism, reduced in stature by their own fault-finding. They are always armed with darts, which they hurl at one another, and wear spectacles which produce blemishes on everything they look at. Huge masks cover the upper part of their bodies to hide their true identities. The only alternative they know to envy is mutual flattery. Dwarf slaves produce books for them to attack and criticize. They worship anything that dazzles, but will fire their darts at the sun if it becomes obscured. Their temples are built over the graves of those they have persecuted to death and whom they now revere as great men.

(Godfrey Sweven, *Riallaro, the Archipelago of Ex-*

iles, New York & London, 1901; Godfrey Sweven, *Limanora, the Island of Progress*, New York & London, 1903)

MESZRIA, a kingdom to the south of REREK, from which it is separated by the glacier-capped mountains of the Huron Range. The climate of Meszria is mild and most of the country is wooded.

There are several lakes in the country, the best known being Reisma Mere, near MEMISON, and a smaller unnamed lake near the capital, ZAYANA. The lakes are haunted by the two nymphs Antiope and Camaspe, who have long been on good terms with the rulers of the country. Although they normally appear in human form, Antiope is sometimes seen as a murderous lynx and Camaspe as some small mammal, often a water-rat. Semi-human creatures such as fauns are found in the more remote valleys; like the nymphs, they have a language of their own which to the human ear sounds like the rustling of leaves.

The mountains to the north of Meszria are high and rugged, and only two passes exist through them. The easier is the Salimat, which lies to the west where the Hurons are less rugged. To the east runs the Royar pass, defended by the mountain fortress at Rumala. Beneath the fortress the mountain path is little wider than a goat-track. The only road leading down to the bottom of the Runbalnardale is known as The Curtain, a winding track which descends some two thousand feet in a series of hairpin bends.

Little is known of the early history of Meszria, recorded since the foundation of Zayana. In 738 *Anno Zayanae Conditae*, the country came under the sole rule of Queen Rosma, a descendant of the Parry family of Rerek. Rosma's climb to the throne involved the murder of her first two husbands and the assassination of a nephew who had killed for her sake. In 749 she married Mezentius of FINGISWOLD and the three lands of Meszria, Rerek and Fingiswold were ruled as one, enjoying a lengthy period of what came to be known as Pax Mezentia. Both Mezentius and Rosma died by poisoning in the island-fortress of Sestola in 777, and in the wars that ravaged the three kingdoms in the subsequent years it was Barganax, the Duke of Zayana and illegitimate son of Mezentius, who emerged as the dominant figure.

(E.R. Eddison, *Mistress of Mistresses, A Vision of*

Zimiamvia, London, 1935; E.R. Eddison, *A Fish Dinner in Memison*, London, 1941; E.R. Eddison, *The Mezentian Gate*, London, 1958)

METTINGEN, an estate, named after its first owner, on the banks of a river near Philadelphia, in the United States. Towards the end of the eighteenth century it was purchased by a Mr. Wieland from Saxony. As a young man, Wieland became interested in the religious doctrines of the Albigenesians and Camissards. He gradually became more and more puritanical and finally constructed a temple for his devotions. The temple stands on a pine-clad rock, three hundred yards from Wieland's house, in a clearing about twelve feet in diameter. Originally it consisted of a dome supported by twelve Doric columns, bare of all ornament. A rough stone staircase led up to the temple; on the other three sides the rock was sheer. After Wieland's death, his children deco-

rated and furnished the temple, converting it into a summerhouse that can be seen today.

Wieland died after an explosion in the temple left his clothes in ashes. He claimed that as he was praying he saw a light and felt a blow as if he had been hit with a club; he died of his injuries. (Similar cases have been reported in a Florentine journal and by Merille and Muraire in the *Journal de Médecine*, May, 1783.) Shortly after the War of Independence, Wieland's son, Theodore, brutally murdered his wife and children, claiming that he had been ordered to do so by a voice he heard in a vision. He later committed suicide.

(Charles Brockden Brown, *Wieland or The Transformation: An American Tale*, New York, 1798)

MEZZORANIA, a kingdom in the eastern deserts of Africa, between the Sudan and Ethiopia; a very civilized society which venerates the spiritual symbol of the sun. The government is based on this religion and the laws are made according to tradition and to the advice of mystical sages. The death penalty is unknown; criminals are forgiven and sent into the deserts. All social events—such as birth, death, marriage—are celebrated in public ceremonies, and three or four noble families share the responsibilities for these social functions.

The cities of Mezzorania are magnificent, all constructed according to the same plan, except for those dedicated to art and commerce. The capital is built on a lake and divided by a splendid canal with many locks and reaches. Twelve bridges with single arches span the lake and the canal and lead onto the main roads. When the canal reaches the centre of the city, it divides and forms a square island on which is built the beautiful Temple of the Sun, one of the wonders of the world.

(Simon Berington, *The Memoirs of Sig^r Gaudentio di Lucca: Taken from his Confession and Examination before the Fathers of the Inquisition at Bologna in Italy. Making a Discovery of an unknown Country in the midst of the vast Deserts of Africa, as Ancient, Populous, and Civilized, as the Chinese. With an Account of their Antiquity, Origine, Religion, Customs, Polity, &c. and the Manner how they got first over those vast Deserts. Interspers'd with several most surprizing and curious Incidents. Copied from the original Manuscript kept in St. Mark's Library At Venice: With Critical Notes of the Learned Signor*

Wieland's temple in METTINGEN.

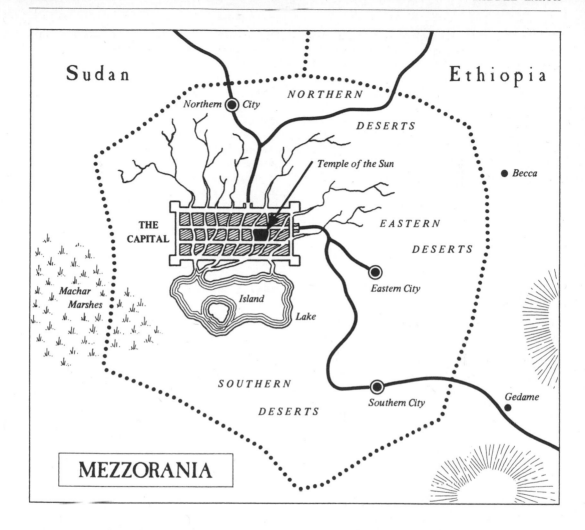

Rhedi, late Library-Keeper of the said Library. To
which is prefix'd, a Letter of the Secretary of the Inquisition, to the same Signor Rhedi, giving an Account of the Manner and Causes of his being seized.
Faithfully Translated from the Italian, by E.T. Gent,
London, 1737)

MICROMONA, a country of unknown location,
where the women are privileged citizens and the
men slaves. It is ruled by a queen who is also the
head of a powerful army and new conquests daily
expand Micromona's borders. It is said that because
the women believe they are angels on earth, they
refuse to be contaminated by the opposite sex. To

reproduce, they simply shake the branches of a tree
said to have stood on the edge of Paradise. This ensures a healthy and steady supply of young girls for
the kingdom. Male visitors are not welcome.

(Karl Immerman, *Tulifäntchen, Ein Heldengedicht
in drei Gesängen*, Hamburg, 1830)

MIDDLE-EARTH lies on the eastern side of the
Belegaer, the great sea which separates it from
AMAN in the north-west of the known world. The
irregular coastline runs north-west to east for
thousands of miles, from the bleak snowy wastes
around FOROCHEL to the great Bay of Belfalas in
the south.

To the south of Forochel, the land juts out into a huge peninsula, surrounded on three sides by the sea. The Blue Mountains run from north to south in this area, with LINDON lying to their west, between the Mountains and the coast. Formerly known as Ossiriand, Lindon is all that remains of the great western land of Beleriand, land of the Grey-elves during the Elder Days, engulfed by the sea many centuries ago. It is now inhabited by elves.

Middle-earth's greatest mountain range, the MISTY MOUNTAINS, runs north to south through the centre of the land. Between the Misty Mountains and the Blue Mountains to the west lies the region of ERIADOR, comprising the ancient kingdoms of ARNOR, the hobbit lands of the SHIRE, and BREE in the centre. RIVENDELL, HOLLIN and DUNLAND all lie along the western side of the great mountain range. To the east of the Misty Mountains is the valley of the GREAT RIVER, and the woods of LÓRIEN, once the most beautiful corner of Middle-earth. And across the river the forest of Mirkwood runs parallel to the mountains for much of their length. To the far north-east of Mirkwood are the famous dwellings of the dwarves beneath Erebor, the LONELY MOUNTAIN, and the major townships of men at DALE and LAKE-TOWN. FANGORN, the remnant of an ancient forest that once covered large parts of Middle-earth, lies at the southern end of the Misty Mountains.

South of the Misty Mountains rise the WHITE MOUNTAINS, from which they are separated by the grassy plains of ROHAN. The great realm of GONDOR lies around the White Mountains and is bounded by the Bay of Belfalas in the south and MORDOR to the east. It is in Gondor that the greatest cities of Middle-earth are to be seen, notably the capital at MINAS TIRITH. Mordor, in the south-east, is a desolate land, bounded by the ASH MOUNTAINS to the north and the Mountains of SHADOW to the west and south.

In the far south, Middle-earth borders on HARAD and in the east on RHÛN.

According to the legends of Middle-earth, the world was created by the music of Eru or Ilúvatar, the source of all creation and the mightiest of all beings. He possesses the Imperishable Flame which kindled the Ainur or Holy Ones, the first of his creations. They sang to Eru, at first individually, but eventually in unison and harmony. Eru revealed his magnificent theme to the Ainur, and told them to use their powers to develop ornaments for it. Their singing in response filled the void of the Timeless Halls with the beautiful sound of complex melodies. Discord was introduced into the music by the song of Melkor, greatest of the Ainur, who rebelled and wanted to create themes all of his own imagining. He had already sought the Imperishable Flame in vain and now tried to add his variations to Eru's music. As a result the music developed into two separate themes: one beautiful, grand and slow, the other loud and repetitious. The latter sought to dominate the former but its loud elements were simply incorporated into the swelling theme since no music can be greater than that of Eru, the source of all music. Gradually, the music they had helped create became visible to the Ainur and they saw the world in whose creation they had participated, in the void but not of it. They saw its history and its development as well as many things they had not imagined, such as the children of Ilúvatar, the elves and men conceived by Ilúvatar alone. They were part of the third theme he introduced; his children were not Ainur, but were loved by them as being different and free, and the Ainur desired that elves and men should truly *be*, and not exist only as thought. Melkor however was envious of the gifts promised to elves and men and already sought to subjugate them to his will and to destroy their freedom.

The desire of the Ainur was so great that Ilúvatar pronounced that he would send the Imperishable Flame into the world and that the world would exist. He pronounced the word "Eä!" ("Let it be!") and so Eä, the world as it is, came into existence. Those of the Ainur who wished were allowed to descend into Eä, becoming Valar as they did so, lesser spirits, but still called gods by men. They also are known as the Powers of the World, as they worked long and hard to create the vision of the Ainur. Initially they created a beautiful garden, but Melkor came to earth seeking to possess it. This led to the first battle between the Valar and Melkor, who raised up their valleys, destroyed their mountains and filled in their seas. The original design was never realized and the earth, Arda, was created as a firm strong body, rather than the cloud with a heart of flame of the original design. A new gift was given to his children by Ilúvatar; unlike other creatures who were bound by the music of the Ainur, they would have the power to forge their own lives. They would

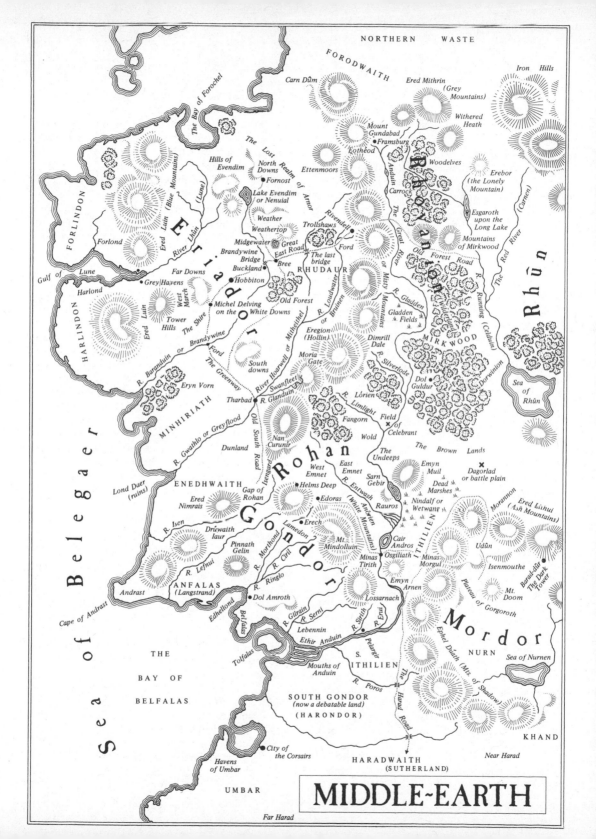

MIDDLE-EARTH

have the power to create great beauty and would not be satisfied with the world, but would seek beyond it. Together with men's freedom came their death. The elves were to be the most beautiful of creatures and to create still greater beauty. Unlike men, elves would not die, unless they were killed or wasted by grief. They would live as long as the world lived, but would tend to become weary as the centuries passed. Those of their number who died would go to the halls of Mandos in VALINOR.

The first elves awoke in Cuiviénen, which is said to have been in the north-east of Middle-earth. They awoke as Varda, one of the Valinor, was finishing making the stars from silver dew. Because the stars were the first things they saw, the elves have always loved Varda above all things. The first elves were called the Eldar, but this name later came to refer only to those who had made the journey west when much of Middle-earth was destroyed in the battle between the Valar and Melkor; those who had not gone became known as the Avari or the Unwilling. There were initially three kindred of the Eldar; the Vanyar or Fair Elves, the Noldor or Deep Elves who learned much from Aulë (one of the Valar) and the Teleri, the Hindmost Elves.

Men awoke in the east of Middle-earth as the first sun rose. They were known by many names: Hildor, the Followers, the Second People, the Strangers, the Children of the Sun. They became the companions of the Dark Elves who had never gone to Valinor, but who were still wiser and fairer than they. The men who travelled west into the now-lost lands of Beleriand were befriended by the elves there and became known as the Edain, or, later the Dúnedain, Men of the West. They were the only men to fight alongside the Valar against Melkor, who now came to be known as Morgoth. As a reward, the Valar created an island called ELENNA for them, mid-way between Middle-earth and Valinor. When Elenna was destroyed the main settlements of the Dúnedain on Middle-earth were in Arnor and Gondor; their kin settled in Dale, the Vales of ANDUIN, and Rohan. Other races of men settled in Hollin, Rivendell, Mirkwood, and Lórien. The Teleri settled on TOL ERESSËA and developed in a slightly different manner as a result.

Of the dwarves it is said that they were secretly made by Aulë in halls beneath the mountains of Middle-earth. Aulë was impatient for creatures to enjoy the earth and to learn his skills. He offered the dwarves to Ilúvatar who accepted them but insisted that they should only awaken after the Firstborn, and predicted conflict between them and the elves. So the seven dwarf fathers made by Aulë were taken far away to awaken. Aulë made his dwarves strong, tough and unyielding. They were to be physically resilient, and long-lived, but mortal. Elves thought for a long time that the dwarves returned to stone when they died, but the dwarves themselves believe that because of Aulë's love for them they will go to halls set apart for them in Valinor.

The history of Middle-earth can be divided into Four Ages.

The First Age was punctuated by numerous battles between the Valar and Melkor, or Morgoth, and ended in the Great Battle which destroyed Angband, Morgoth's great fortress in the north-west, together with Thangorodrim, the mountain range he caused to be raised above it. It was here that Morgoth brought the Silmarils, three legendary jewels created by Fëanor. They were as clear as diamonds and stronger than adamant, and are said to have absorbed light and stored it so that they sparkled and gleamed even in the dark. Varda made them sacred, so that they would burn any mortal or unclean hand that touched them. Morgoth set them in his iron crown though their touch scorched his evil hand and left it black forever. He was consumed with envy of the elves and men and fought many bitter battles against them. He turned many to his service, including some of the Maiar, the helpers of the Valar. These became the Valaraukar, or scourges of fire, known in Middle-earth as Balrogs. Morgoth also corrupted the greatest servant of Aulë; he became known as Sauron and later dwelt in Mordor. Melkor was finally defeated before Angband and was cast into the Timeless Void, through the Door of Night and beyond the Walls of the World. And the northern country of Beleriand was swallowed up by the sea forever, leaving only the corner called Lindon.

The Second Age began after the defeat of Morgoth. Many elves left Middle-earth at that time and the Dúnedain founded their great kingdom of Númenor on Elenna. It was during the Second Age that the Rings of Power were created. Using the Ruling Ring, Sauron gradually increased his control of Middle-earth, waging war on the elves and dwarves, destroying their lands and enslaving all he could. Some of the men of Númenor fought against him and eventually took him to their island as a hostage. Without difficulty Sauron corrupted them too, turning them away from the Valar and even introducing the worship of Morgoth and human sacrifice. In anger, the Valar destroyed Númenor and only the faithful, those who had not been corrupted by Sauron, survived. They returned to Middle-earth to found the kingdoms-in-exile, Gondor and Ardor, bringing with them the *palantíri* or Seeing-stones and a shoot from the White Tree, Nimroth. The tree now growing in Minas Tirith in Gondor comes from that stock. Men and elves joined together against Sauron in the Last Alliance and finally defeated him in the great battle of DAGORLAD. This brought the Second Age to an end. But although Sauron was defeated, and the Ruling Ring was carried off by the Númenórean King Isildur, both were to return to plague Middle-earth in the age that followed.

The Third Age is marked by Sauron's final attempt to bring Middle-earth under his control. Sauron reappeared in about 1000 Third Age, secretly building up his power in Mirkwood and then in Mordor itself. Throughout this period, his greatest servants were the Nazgûl, or Ringwraiths, mortal kings who had been corrupted by the power given them by the Rings of Power and who were now complete slaves to the Ruling Ring, otherwise known as the One Ring. In addition to beginning the search for the Ruling Ring, lost since the Battle of the GLADDEN FIELDS and found again only by accident, Sauron began to build up his military strength, raising huge armies of orcs, trolls and men in Mordor.

The opposition was led by the White Council, composed of wizards and Eldar and led at first by the wizard Saruman the White. Later Saruman was corrupted and became an ally of Sauron, and the Council was led by a mysterious wizard named Gandalf the Grey. The strategy drawn up to oppose Sauron was twofold; to defend the lands threatened by Sauron's forces and also to destroy the Ring by returning it to the Cracks of Doom on Orodruin, where it had originally been forged.

The major phases in the military campaign against Sauron began with the neutralization of the fortress of NAN CURUNIR, Sauron's stronghold after his defection. This was followed by the suc-

cessful defence of Rohan and the lifting of the siege of Minas Tirith during the battle of the PELENNOR FIELDS. Minas Tirith now became the centre for the coordinated attack on Mordor by the Army of the West, as the joint forces of Gondor and Rohan were known. As battle was joined before the pass of CIRITH GORGOR, the Ruling Ring was finally plunged into the Cracks of Doom and Sauron's power was broken. In the north, the men of Dale and the dwarves of the Lonely Mountain rose and defeated the armies of orcs that had come to attack them and the Shire was liberated from Saruman's final attempts to establish a reign of terror there.

The most important figure of this era was Gandalf, one of the *Istari* or wizards who came from the west to help defend Middle-earth during the Third Age. Gandalf went by many names and his true origin remains obscure. In his youth, he himself said, his name was Olórin. One of the Maia bears the same name and there has often been speculation that they were one and the same.

The Third Age ended with the defeat of Sauron and the departure of those who had carried the Ring from the GREY HAVENS. Gondor and Rohan were now both ruled by Elessar, the first ruler of the Reunited Kingdoms. The Fourth Age began and Middle-earth became predominantly a land of men, as many of the heroes of the War of the Ring and many of the elves left to cross the sea to the west.

The Common Speech of Middle-earth, spoken by almost all as either a first or second language, is Westron. Originally this was the language of the Edain and was taken by them to Númenor. From there it travelled to the port of PELARGIR where it became enriched with some elven words and gradually spread through Middle-earth via the kingdoms of Gondor and Arnor. The language is at its purest in Gondor.

The kinsmen of the Dúnedain in the north speak forms of the language, but the Rohirrim of Rohan have their own language. Only their lords are fluent in Westron, which they speak as well as the men of Gondor itself. The Dunlendings of Dunland and the Wild Men of Druadan Forest have their own tongues, which bear no relation to the Common Speech. The hobbits of the Shire speak their own, more colloquial form of Westron, although the more learned among them are able to use the formal speech. Westron is also spoken by some trolls and, in barbarous fashion, by some orcs. Other members of the two species speak Black Speech, the language invented in Mordor by Sauron.

The ents of Fangorn have their own language, as do the dwarves—neither of these tongues is familiar to other people. The dwarves use their own language exclusively among themselves and cherish it as a precious relic of their past. The names by which the dwarves are known to others are Westron forms; the dwarves, in keeping with their rather secretive character, will not reveal their true names to other people.

The High Elves speak Quenya, although the Teleri evolved a somewhat different form of the language during their long stay on Tol Eressëa. Quenya is now used mainly for ceremonial purposes and has, in day-to-day usage, been largely replaced by Sindarin, originally the tongue of the Grey Elves who lived along the western shores of Beleriand. Sindarin was gradually adopted by all the elves in Middle-earth. Because of their trade with the elves, some men once spoke Sindarin or even Quenya, but this knowledge has largely been lost.

Middle-earth uses two forms of written script, both of Elvish origin. Tengwar or Tîw is written with a brush or pen and the inscriptions are squarish in shape (**ᛒ**). It was originally developed by the Noldor elves, but the form used in Middle-earth represents only the second stage of its development. It was brought to Middle-earth by the exiled Númenóreans and spread along the same lines of communication as Westron. The other alphabet is the runic alphabet of Certar, or Cirth, originally carved in metal or stone, and therefore angular in shape (**ᛝ**). It was first developed by elves in Beleriand and a simple version spread throughout Middle-earth where it was adopted by men, dwarves and even orcs. This simple version is still used in Dale and Rohan. A more sophisticated version was developed by a minstrel and loremaker called Daeron, again in Beleriand; it is known as the Alphabet of Daeron and has been adopted in EREGION and by the dwarves of MORIA. Here it became known as Angerthas Moria, or Long Rune-rows of Moria. For transcribing their own spoken language, the dwarves use a form of Cirth.

Elves and men use different calendars. Elves prefer to calculate in units of six and twelve. The day or *ré* runs from sunset to sunset, and 52,596 days are equal to one *yén*—144 years in the system used by men. The solar year is calculated according to a seasonal cycle based on six seasons: spring, summer, autumn, fading, winter, stirring. Summer and winter have 72 days; the other seasons 54 days. Occasional adjustments are made, but there are no accurate records of how this calendar, known as the Reckoning of Rivendell, was kept with any precision. Men use the King's Reckoning: a year of 365 days divided into twelve astar or months. Historical records are dated from the First Year of the Second Age. A similar system is in use in the Shire and in Bree under the name Shire Reckoning, except that each area counts its own colonization as year one.

(J.R.R. Tolkien, *The Hobbit, or There and Back Again*, London, 1937; J.R.R. Tolkien, *The Fellowship of the Ring*, London, 1954; J.R.R. Tolkien, *The Two Towers*, London, 1954; J.R.R. Tolkien, *The Return of the King*, London, 1955; J.R.R. Tolkien, *The Silmarillion*, London, 1977)

MIDGEWATER MARSHES, a marshland area beyond the pathless wilderness that lies to the east of BREELAND in northern MIDDLE-EARTH. There is no definite or safe path across this treacherous bogland. Apart from the midges which give the area its name, the marshes are infested by very noisy insects the nature of which remains obscure. The ugly sound they make suggests, however, that they may be evil relatives of the cricket.

(J.R.R. Tolkien, *The Fellowship of the Ring*, London, 1954)

MIDIAN, a country in a small valley beyond the Ghenzi Mountains in Africa, established almost two thousand years ago by a disciple of the biblical Paul of Tarsus, who was inclined to fanaticism. The valley consists of the huge crater of a long extinct volcano. To the south, Abraham's Village is excavated in the soft volcanic ash, near the bottomless lake of Chinnereth. To the north, Elijah's Village is more pretentious, with huts of stone as well as of wood, and there is no evidence here of the degeneracy and disease common in southern Midian.

South Midian is ruled by a fanatic who follows the rites and customs of the first Christians literally. These gentiles—who are said to have important, disagreeable noses—sacrifice children in the same way they believe Abraham did and they crucify victims with religious fervour. Communicating with the inhabitants is difficult as they speak a language long forgotten by the rest of the world.

(Edgar Rice Burroughs, *Tarzan Triumphant*, New York, 1932)

MIDWICH, a village in England, some eight miles west-north-west of the town of Trayne. Midwich is a typical English village with a green, some sixty cottages, and a small church, mostly English perpendicular with a Norman west doorway and font.

There is no historical explanation for the existence of Midwich, as railways, coaches and canals have seemed to bypass it throughout the years. However, Midwich is famous because of a group of children born here after their mothers mysteriously became pregnant on a certain 26th September. The children had blond-brown hair and glowing, golden eyes; their mouths were smaller than is usual and their fingernails were narrower. They seemed to have a mental and physical age of twice their years, and they were able to transmit orders telepathically.

This last quality proved a hindrance to the natural development of the villagers' normal life and the children were duly immolated. One Gordon Zellaby carried several bombs into a Victorian grange where the children were attending a lecture, and blew himself, the grange and the children up. The grange, however, was of no great architectural interest.

(John Wyndham, *The Midwich Cuckoos*, London, 1957)

MIHRAGIAN KINGDOM, an island somewhere in the Indian Ocean, named after its most famous king; the only place in the world where the sea-stallions come to mate.

Every month the king's henchmen bring the mares to the beach by the grim light of the new moon, and hide in an underground cavern. Attracted by the female scent, the sea-stallions come onto land and look carefully around; if they see no human presence, they will mount the mares and fecundate them. However, when they try to get the mares to follow them into the sea, they find that the mares have been securely tied to the shore. Hearing their neighing, the henchmen leave their hiding place and frighten the sea-stallions back into the water. A few months later each mare brings into the world a foal worth a fortune. These animals are found nowhere else in the world.

(Anonymous, *The Arabian Nights*, 14th–16th cen. AD)

MILDENDO, capital of LILLIPUT.

MILK, an island in the Pacific Ocean, the home of an accursed people who delight in fighting, killing and drinking human blood which they call *dieu*. According to Milkanian traditions, the more a man kills, the more he is respected.

(Sir John Mandeville, *Voiage de Sir John Maundevile*, Paris, 1857)

MILK ISLAND, see CASEOSA.

MILK WOOD, see LLAREGYB.

MILLION WISHES, LAND OF A, a country you will arrive in if you try unsuccessfully to learn La Fontaine's poem "The Fox and the Crow" by heart. The incredulous traveller will see burning lava flowing from a smoking hole at the top of a hill of sand and spelling out the words, "Land of a Million Wishes. The Magic Field, 2448 kil." It is not clear whether this figure refers to kilometres or kilograms.

A pharaoh obsessed with the interpretation of his dreams (usually peopled with white and black chickens) will point out the way to the nearest camel-stop. Once you have taken your place you must not forget to lower the animal's right ear to indicate that it is "occupied."

When you arrive at the Magic Field, Mr. Shaymfullenkonfuzd, the crow on duty, will give you an examination to become a second-degree fairy. If you pass, he will put you in the feet of Mr. Tendairluv, the pigeon on duty, who is in charge of fairy aviation classes.

The main inhabitants of this land are fairies. The palace of their queen is a large glass house on top of crystal columns covered with roses. The queen, who is as mad as she is pretty, sometimes wears a gown made of electric wires, which makes her look like the Eiffel Tower.

Off limits for anyone over the age of twelve, the Land of a Million Wishes is probably the only country where eight times six equals anything you want.

(André Maurois, *Le Pays des trente-six mille volontés*, Paris, 1928)

MILOSIS, capital of ZUVENDIS; Milosis means "Hidden City," and is built in red granite on the banks of a large lake. The houses are all one storey high, surrounded by green gardens that ease the glare of the granite. The Royal Palace is reached via a grand staircase some twenty metres wide, flanked by stupendous columns. The staircase is held up by an arch of granite which for many centuries proved impossible to build. Finally a young architect, Rademas, managed to erect it and was given in reward the hand of the King's daughter, thereby founding the dynasty known as The Dynasty of the Staircase. To commemorate the occasion Rademas sculpted a statue in which he himself was represented as asleep while a feminine figure touched his forehead as if giving him inspiration; the group can be seen today inside the Royal Palace in the Throne Room. Here also stands a large black marble block of little more than a metre per side considered to be the sacred stone of Zuvendis, on which all monarchs must lay their hands when swearing to be faithful to their charge during the coronation ceremony. According to an ancient tradition, the black block fell from the sun.

The Temple of the Sun, a short distance from the royal palace, is a round white marble building with a golden dome. The rooms inside spread out like the petals of a flower; at the far end of each is a golden statue, and the ceiling and inside walls of the temple are covered in gold. In the exact centre of the building is a golden altar representing the sun, covered by five golden lids; in front of the altar is a trap door under which burns a constant fire into which condemned prisoners are thrown. All ceremonies are presided over by the temple priests in their long white tunics embroidered with the symbol of the sun; from their belts hang little glittering discs that make a pleasant, tinkling sound during the ceremonies.

(Henry Rider Haggard, *Allan Quatermain*, London, 1887)

MINA, an island off the coast of BENSALEM.

MINAS MORGUL, a fortress city in the EPHEL DUATH, and High Seat of Isildur, conjoint King of GONDOR. It was founded at the end of the Second Age as the twin of Minas Arnor—High Seat of Anárion, brother of Isildur—which was later renamed MINAS TIRITH.

Originally known as Minas Ithil, the Tower of the Moon, the fortress stood in an upland vale in the Mountains of SHADOW, on the border of the ancient realm of MORDOR, and was the capital of the province of ITHILIEN. It held the White Tree and one of the seven *palantíri*, or Seeing-stones, rescued by the Men of Númenor from their drowned homeland when they came to Gondor.

Built on the same principles as the impregnable Minas Tirith, the city was nevertheless captured and recaptured more than once in its history. In 3429 Second Age it was seized by Sauron, the Dark Lord of Mordor, but returned to the King of Gondor after his defeat at the end of that age. It appears to have been inhabited briefly by men at the beginning of the Third Age, but was again taken by the powers of Mordor in 2002 Third Age. The Nazgûl themselves inhabited it then, together with many orcs, so that Sauron finally gained for himself a foothold on the western side of the Mountains of Shadow, which he subsequently used for his attacks on Gondor. It was at that time that the once-fair city received the new name of Minas Morgul, the Tower of Sorcery.

After the end of the War of the Ring, the city again came into the possession of Gondor, but it was no longer habitable and was destroyed by order of King Elessar. The sense of dread and the memories of its early years cling to the place still.

(J.R.R. Tolkien, *The Fellowship of the Ring*, London, 1954; J.R.R. Tolkien, *The Two Towers*, London, 1954; J.R.R. Tolkien, *The Return of the King*, London, 1955; J.R.R. Tolkien, *The Silmarillion*, London, 1977)

MINAS TIRITH, the Tower of Guard, capital of the kingdom of GONDOR, formerly known as Minas Arnor, the Tower of the Sun.

Built at the end of the Second Age, shortly after the founding of Gondor, Minas Arnor was originally a beautiful fortified city, the High Seat of Anárion, younger son of Elendil the Tall, and twin city of Minas Ithil, High Seat of Anárion's brother Isildur; and between the two fortified cities lay OSGILIATH, which was at that time the capital of the realm. With the gradual decline of the cities of Minas Ithil and Osgiliath, Minas Arnor grew in importance. In 2002 Third Age the city of Minas Ithil fell to the Lord of the Nazgûl, and became known as MINAS MORGUL. It was after that event that the House of the King was transferred to Minas Arnor, which was renamed Minas Tirith, by which name it has been known ever since.

Though never designed to be the chief fortress of Gondor, the unique position of Minas Arnor enabled it to survive. The city stands on the Hill of Guard, an outcrop of Mount Mindolluin at the easternmost end of the WHITE MOUNTAINS which were the backbone of the ancient realm, and it was constructed in such a way as to take full advantage of its position. The city is on seven levels, each level surrounded by a wall of stone and built back into the rock of the mountain itself. Each level has its own gate and each gate faces in a different direction. Minas Tirith is impregnable, except from the lower heights of Mount Mindolluin where a ridge connects with the Hill of Guard at the fifth level of the city. This natural weak point in the city's defence is guarded by massive and impregnable ramparts.

The city is entered through the gate of the first level and then via roads that lead up to the next level and so on. The lower levels are occupied by the houses of the tradesmen and artisans. The seventh level is the Citadel of the capital, an outcrop of rock surrounded by battlements. Access is through a long sloping tunnel in the rock itself. From their battlements, the city's defenders have a clear view down to the main gates on the first level.

The Citadel contains the High Court of Gondor and, behind the ramparts on the Mount Mindolluin side, the tombs of the kings and the lords of the past. A path from the sixth level leads to the Hallows or the Mansions of the Dead. The door to the path is opened only for funerals and access is reserved to the lord of the city and those working in the houses of the dead. Along the street known as Rath Dínen, or Silent Street, lined with pillars

and carved figures, stand the domed houses and halls of the dead, great vaulted chambers. Inside, the dead lie on marble tables, their heads pillowed on stone.

The houses of Minas Tirith are tall; they have high windows and are spacious inside, with large rooms and beautifully carved staircases. The doors and archways of both houses and public buildings are decorated with more carvings and inscriptions in curious, ancient scripts. Over the seventh gate, which gives access to the Citadel, a kingly head wearing a crown is carved in the keystone of the arch. The large hall of the Lord of the City is one of the finest buildings in the city. It is lit by windows, set deep in the walls, which are flanked by the black marble pillars that support the roof. The capitals of the pillars are carved with the figures of birds, animals and leaves. The roof is vaulted and inscribed with dull gold, inset with a multicoloured tracery. Statues of past kings stand between the pillars. At the far end of the room, a throne stands on a dais beneath a marble canopy, carved in the shape of a helmet surmounted by a crown. On the wall immediately behind it a flowering tree is carved; it is set with gems.

High above the seventh level rises the White Tower of Ecthelion. The tower is three hundred feet high and terminates in a delicate pinnacle. A silver bell chimes every hour during the hours of daylight. Originally built in 1900 Third Age by King Calimehtar, it was reconstructed in 2698 by Ecthelion I, then Steward of the City. The Tower houses one of the *palantíri* or Seeing-stones, clear crystal globes through which a gazer can see across unlimited time and distance, and even communicate thoughts. At the foot of the Tower the White Tree, chief symbol of the royalty of Gondor, grows in the Court of the Fountain.

The Citadel is guarded by soldiers in black robes. Their tall helmets have close-fitting cheek-guards topped with white birds' wings, and are made from *mithril,* the brilliant silver metal mined by the dwarves of MORIA. The guards of the Citadel are the only troops that have the honour of wearing the emblem of Elendil of Gondor—a white tree beneath a silver crown and stars.

Minas Tirith is famed for its Houses of Healing, a group of fine houses on the sixth level. They are surrounded by a lawn with trees and the only garden in the entire city. The healers of Minas Tirith are skilled and derive their knowledge from the lore of ancient times; they can deal with any wound or sickness. Only death itself defeats their age-old skills. The appearance of the Black Breath during the War of the Ring seemed, however, to be beyond their skills. The Black Breath was caused by exposure to the Nazgûl, the Ringwraiths of MORDOR; a mild case led to dreams—a severe case passed through dreaming and came to death. But the hero Aragorn called for athelas (an herb also called kingsfoil or *asëa aranion*) and brewed an infusion to cure the victims. His power to do so helped convince the people that he was indeed their long-awaited king.

Minas Tirith has never fallen to an enemy, although it was besieged during the War of the Ring and the first wall was breached in the great battle of the Fields of PELENNOR. The start of the battle was heralded by the descent of darkness, which did not lift completely until it was ended and the siege relieved. It was in Minas Tirith that the strategy used to defeat Sauron, the Dark Lord of Mordor, was drawn up. It was from here that the massed armies marched to rid MIDDLE-EARTH of its enemies in a series of bitterly fought campaigns. And it was here that Aragorn was crowned king, first ruler of the Reunited Kingdom of Middle-earth.

(J.R.R. Tolkien, *The Fellowship of the Ring,* London, 1954; J.R.R. Tolkien, *The Two Towers,* London, 1954; J.R.R. Tolkien, *The Return of the King,* London, 1955; J.R.R. Tolkien, *The Silmarillion,* London, 1977)

MINDA, an island of the MARDI ARCHIPEL-AGO. Most of the inhabitants occupy themselves with witchcraft and their services are very much in demand on all the other islands. It is said that Mindans will not hesitate to induce other natives to think that a spell has been cast upon them, in order to force the islanders to pay them to use their magic arts. For their charms they mainly use the fumes of a special mixture, the principal constituent of which is minced human heart in diverse doses. Weak-stomached travellers are advised not to assist at the preparation.

(Herman Melville, *Mardi, and A Voyage Thither,* New York, 1849)

MINUNI, a region of the Great Thorn Forest in Africa, inhabited by tiny people known as Ant Men. The Forest is an impregnable thicket covering a vast territory into which only the smallest animals can venture. Its only other human inhabitants are the ALALI tribe, a race of gigantic women whom the Ant Men sometimes attack.

Two cities, usually at war, are the principal Minuni settlements: Veltopismakus and Trohanadalmakus. They consist of domed houses, very tall for the Ant Men's size and very carefully built. First the round base is drawn on the ground and outlined with heavy boulders. Then four entrances are marked and more boulders are piled over the first layer, covering a diameter of 150 to 200 feet. Above the first floor a second smaller storey is built, with wooden arches and beams. A fine example of Minuni architecture is the Palace of Adendrohakis, thirty-six floors high, a true anthill for pygmy habitation.

Travellers to Minuni will see the Ant Men ride their diminutive royal antelopes, similar to the species found on Africa's west coast, but are not advised to try to mount them unless they too are barely a foot high.

(Edgar Rice Burroughs, *Tarzan and the Ant Men,* New York, 1924)

MIRKWOOD, an extensive and very ancient forest in the north of MIDDLE-EARTH, to the east of the MISTY MOUNTAINS and to the south of the GREY MOUNTAINS.

The main river watering the forest is the Forest River, which rises in the Grey Mountains, while the River Running waters the eastern edge. Mirkwood itself is the source of the Enchanted River, the waters of which are dark and strong. They induce forgetfulness and sleep in those who drink them or even bathe in them. Mirkwood is crossed by two roads: the Old Forest Road which, by the time of the War of the Ring, had become marshy and impassable at its eastern end, and a path used by the elves to the north of the forest.

Mirkwood was once known as Greenwood the Great, but gained its new name early in the Third Age, when the powers of evil took control of it. The necromancer Sauron built a tower named Dol Guldur in the south of the forest and the evil that lived in it soon began to corrupt the forest. Over the next thousand years, Sauron ruled here and Mirkwood well deserved its name. Sauron himself was driven out of Dol Guldur by the

Council of White, which was formed to defeat his evil plans. He retreated to MORDOR but his evil creatures returned to his forest tower and Mirkwood remained a place to be avoided.

The forest became a silent, sinister place, lit only by the dim green light filtering through the tangled boughs of the trees. It was full of strange, savage creatures, the most fearsome of which appear to have been the giant spiders whose enormous cobwebs stretched from tree to tree. Those who were foolish enough to stray from the path often blundered into these webs and were caught by the spiders, poisoned and eaten. The spiders were capable of a form of speech, communicating with one another in hissing, creaking voices.

Many of the denizens of Mirkwood were almost impossible to identify with any certainty. Red, yellow or green eyes stared from the gloom and uncanny grunts and snufflings were heard in the undergrowth. Black squirrels could be seen. A fire would immediately attract clouds of dark grey or black moths, as large as a man's hand, or swarms of huge bats. There is one recorded sighting of a herd of white deer at this time. Above the trees floated velvety black butterflies, thought to be a darker variety of the purple emperor.

During these years, only the fringes of Mirkwood were inhabited. A few woodmen lived in the south-west, struggling for survival against the spiders and orcs of the woods, while the elves resided in the ELVENHALLS on the banks of the Forest River.

After the final defeat of Sauron efforts were made to cleanse Mirkwood of evil forever. In 3019 Third Age, a strong force from LÓRIEN marched against Dol Guldur and totally destroyed the dark tower. The northern section of the forest became the realm of the old inhabitants of the Elvenhalls, while the southern section became part of East Lórien. The stretch of woodland between the mountains and the narrows, where the edges of the forest draw in to form a narrow waist, was given to the woodmen and to the Beornings of the Vales of ANDUIN. Many great battles were fought before Mirkwood was free of evil, but that aim was at last achieved and it was renamed Eryn Lasgalen, or The Wood of Greenleaves. For historical reasons, however, it is still best known as Mirkwood.

(J.R.R. Tolkien, *The Hobbit, or There and Back Again*, London, 1937; J.R.R. Tolkien, *The Fellow-ship of the Ring*, London, 1954; J.R.R. Tolkien, *The Return of the King*, London, 1955)

MIRROR OF LLUNET, a small shallow pool, fed by the rivulets of water that drip down the rock walls, in a cave at the foot of Mount Meledin. Mount Meledin is the highest peak in the Llawgadarn mountains, which rise in the Land of the FREE COMMOTS, an area in the north of PRYDAIN. Below is the Lake of Llunet, a long, oval stretch of water, lined with trees up to the lower slopes of Mount Meledin.

The lore of the men of the Free Commots tells that if a man wishes to know himself, he need only gaze into the waters of the Mirror of Llunet. When Taran of CAER DALLBEN set out on his wanderings to try to discover his true identity, he was told of the Mirror by the three enchantresses of MORVA. When he finally reached it he looked into it only to see his own face reflected in its crystal clear waters. Like all travellers to Llunet, he had discovered that he was simply himself.

(Lloyd Alexander, *Taran Wanderer*, New York, 1967)

MISHPORT, see VEMISH.

MISNIE, a kingdom near Paphlagonia, once conquered by Cyrus, King of Persia. The capital, Morisate, is eighteenth-century Parisian in style. The court is noted for its elegance and wit, and any self-indulgences are literally laughed out of the kingdom.

The Princess of Misnie lives in exactly the opposite manner from her people—sleeping by day and living by night. Because of her fear of the sun, sun-dials are banned in Misnic and, as a result, people's actions here are not ruled by the clock.

(Anne Marie Louise Henriette d'Orléans, Duchesse de Montpensier, *La Princesse de Paphlagonie*, Paris, 1659)

MISPEC MOOR, between TUROINE and the now vanished land of Antan. The best known inhabitant of the moor is Maya of the Fair Breasts, a wise woman who lives here in a neat log and plaster cottage. Maya is particularly skilled in the minor arts of moving mountains into the sea, erecting bridges over impassable places and preparing rose-coloured mirrors that she gives to her guests. These mirrors have the effect of making everything seem extremely pleasant.

The animals seen grazing in the vicinity of her cottage are in fact her many past lovers, whom she has turned into cattle or deer out of kindness. In doing so, she explains, she has held them back from daring exploits; they lead much safer and happier lives as domestic animals.

Most of the other people living on the moor are witches or sorcerers. Their society is pleasant and agreeable, provided visitors do not ask them to what use they put unchristened babies.

(James Branch Cabell, *Something about Eve*, New York, 1929)

MISTY MOUNTAINS, the great range extending almost three hundred leagues from the Northern Waste of MIDDLE-EARTH to the Gap of ROHAN in the south. The GREAT RIVER flows down the eastern side of the range.

The Misty Mountains are very dangerous and great knowledge of the terrain is required to find a way across them, as many of the paths are deceptive and lead nowhere. South of RIVENDELL the only pass is the Redhorn Gate on the side of Caradhras, a particularly rugged mountain. The dwarfs of Middle-earth refer to Caradhras as Barazinbar (meaning "Red Horn") the Cruel because of the bad weather associated with it; it is as though Caradhras actually created adverse conditions to make it almost impossible for the traveller to cross it. To the south lies MORIA. Many of the peaks in the Misty Mountains, especially those towards Moria, evoke strong memories for the dwarves whose ancestors lived and worked here in ancient times. On the eastern side of the mountains lies the Eyrie of the Eagles, an ancient race and the greatest among birds. The eagles are enormous birds, capable of carrying a man on their backs, and are credited with many noble exploits.

Throughout the Third Age, the Misty Mountains were inhabited by a variety of evil creatures. These included the Wargs or Hounds of Sauron, great evil wolves and the mounts of the orcs, when they rode to battle. Cruel, savage creatures, the orcs were skilled only in the arts of destruction and were well known for their ability to produce weapons. They also had a certain skill in tunnelling and mining, though they often preferred to enslave others to do such work for them. Of all the vile creatures who took part in the evil enterprises of Sauron, the Dark Lord of MORDOR, the orcs were perhaps the most fearsome. They lived underground in a series of immense caves near Rivendell and effectively controlled the mountains. Great numbers of them were killed during the great war between the orcs and the dwarves in Moria in 2793–99 Third Age and again in the Battle of the Five Armies on the Lonely Mountain in 2941, but they continued to breed and live in the mountains.

The Misty Mountains and the caves beneath them are closely associated with the memory of Gollum, a Stoor hobbit originally from the SHIRE. Gollum was for some time the possessor of the One Ring, the Ring of power forged by Sauron in an attempt to gain total control over Middle-earth. Gollum brought the Ring with him to the Misty Mountains, where he lived on an island in an underground lake, slowly succumbing to the Ring's baneful influence until his very appearance was changed and he became a small, slimy creature with pale lamp-like eyes and long webbed feet.

An aura of evil clings to this mighty range of peaks: they were said to have been raised at the beginning of the world by Morgoth, the Dark Foe, as a barrier against potential enemies.

(J.R.R. Tolkien, *The Hobbit, or There and Back Again*, London, 1937; J.R.R. Tolkien, *The Fellowship of the Ring*, London, 1954; J.R.R. Tolkien, *The Two Towers*, London, 1954; J.R.R. Tolkien, *The Return of the King*, London, 1955; J.R.R. Tolkien, *The Silmarillion*, London, 1977)

MLCH COUNTRY, see BRODIE'S LAND.

MOBONO, see KARAIN CONTINENT.

MOGADOR, a walled city off the coast of Morocco. On the white wall, which shines at night like skin moist with longing, four towers rise over four portals, marking the cardinal points of the compass. The wall bristles with 666 smaller towers, each crowned with a hollow stone dragon through which the wind whistles, causing those who hear it for the first time to weep with emotion. A Mogadorian proverb says that "the universe can be

The hollow stone dragons on the walls of MOGADOR.

trapped in a nutshell by one who knows the scribble that portrays it." To this effect, a pack of cards, known as the Deck, is used to decipher the secret writing that Mogadorians believe is inscribed in things and faces. The Deck is laid out in a spiral of nine cards with a square of four cards in the centre: this diagram, they say, corresponds to the map of the city. The spiral represents the main street, known as The Road or the Street of the Snail, which leads among whitewashed houses with latticed windows, twisting and turning, from the outer walls to the central plaza. In this plaza stand the public baths, the public oven and three temples erected to the three religions that divide the city's faithful. At every turn of The Way is a fountain, suggesting that the water flows in a spiral down to the Hammam, cleansing everything and everyone. The baths or Hammam carries over its entrance a sign of red letters, decorated with fine calligraphy burned in three colours, that reads "Enter. This is the house of the body as it came into the world. The house of fire that was water, of water that was fire. Enter. Fall like rain, blaze like straw. May your virtue be the joyful offering in the fountain of the senses. Enter."

The main market is the Soco, where almonds, watermelons, rice, crystallized figs and dates can be bought. Many kinds of fish are auctioned at the dock. Among Mogador's fauna are several rare species of migrating birds: small Moon Tail Gulls, Sea Turkeys, Red Crows, Chilly Storks and the Dwarf Fowl, a bird that falls easy prey to carnivorous fish. There are also peacocks, which sometimes fall prey to the cats of Mogador. Outside the city roam hyenas, wolves and wild camels.

To the people of Mogador, their city is an image of the world itself, a map of external as well as internal, spiritual life. Foreigners who do not fit in with the city's design are taken away by sailors and thrown into the sea. The Mogadorians' main language is erotic; they speak with their bodies and with their senses.

Visitors are warned that the air of Mogador is extremely dry. Autumns are windy and winters are cold. Moreover, access is not easy. A group of Christian missionaries intent on reaching the city was trapped in the surrounding sand mountains, and on clear days their skeletons can be seen moving in the dunes, their proud crucifixes still in their bony hands. Some time ago, a Chinese prince attempted to reach Mogador on a wonderful vehicle, half sled and half sailing-ship, but the voyage was thought to take 233 years and ten days; as far as we know, he has not yet arrived.

(Alberto Ruy-Sánchez, *Cuentos de Mogador*, Mexico, 1994; Alberto Ruy-Sánchez, *En los labios del agua*, Mexico, 1996; Alberto Ruy-Sánchez, *Los nombres del aire*, Mexico, 1987)

MOLE END, the home of Mr. Mole, situated below a meadow near RIVER BANK. A steep tunnel leads down to a neatly sanded forecourt, where wire baskets full of ferns alternate with brackets supporting a collection of plaster statues of Queen Victoria, Garibaldi and the heroes of modern Italy. To one side of the forecourt lies a skittle alley, lined with wooden benches and tables. There is also a goldfish pond with a border of cockleshells, and from the centre of the pond rises a fanciful construction, also of shells, supporting a large glass ball; its silvery surface gives a pleasantly distorted reflection of the things around it.

Mr. Mole's home is a pleasant, if small, place. It is extremely well laid out and the main rooms are decorated with a good collection of prints. Mr. Mole is very popular in the area; his house, for instance, is the last place to be visited by the field mice who go carol-singing each year, as they are sure of getting plenty of food and drink there.

(Kenneth Grahame, *The Wind in the Willows*, London, 1908)

MONA, an island kingdom off the coast of PRYDAIN, the traditional domain of the House of Rhuddlum whose castle is at Dinas Rhydnant. The castle itself stands on the highest point of the steep cliffs that rise above the crescent-shaped harbour with its stone piers, jetties and curving sea wall. To the north of Dinas Rhydnant lies a rolling plain of springy turf which extends to the gentle lower slopes of the Hills of Parys.

Much of the interior of Mona is covered in forest. The only major river on the island is the Alaw, a wide, fast-flowing stream which enters the sea in the wide bay known as the Mouth of the Alaw. Beneath the waters of the bay lie the ruins of Caer Colur, once the seat of the House of Llyr and one of the great magic centres of Prydain. Originally on the mainland, the castle was gradually isolated by erosion and in its last days stood on a tiny island. No trace of it is now visible.

The last days of Caer Colur are closely bound up with the history of Princess Eilonwy, last of the House of Llyr. Eilonwy had been stolen from Caer Colur as a child by Achren, once the consort of Arawn the Death Lord and ruler of Prydain. Achren hoped to gain control of the magic powers traditionally possessed by the daughters of Llyr and took the girl to Spiral Castle, then in her possession. Little remains of Spiral Castle itself, but the ruins are still visible near the Barrow of RHITTA. Eilonwy escaped from the castle with Taran, the assistant pig-keeper of CAER DALLBEN, who was destined to become High King of Prydain, using the light-giving gold bauble she always carried. Eilonwy was then unaware of the powers of the small gold sphere. It was in fact the Golden Pelydryn of the House of Llyr, without which the spells handed down from mother to daughter throughout the generations could not be read.

After her escape, and the destruction of the black cauldron used by Arawn to create undying warriors in his attempt to regain control of Prydain, Princess Eilonwy was sent back to Mona. It was hoped that Queen Teleria of Rhuddlum and her ladies would be able to educate her as befits a princess, a prospect which did not appeal to the girl who saw herself in the image of the sword-maidens of old. Eilonwy travelled by sea to Mona, accompanied by Taran and by Prince Rhun of Mona. But the day after her arrival, she disappeared without trace. Taran and Rhun set out to search for her with the help of two friends they found on the island—Fflewddur Fflam and Gwydion, the war leader of the High King of Math and a descendant of the Sons of Don, the protectors of Prydain who had built the great castle at CAER DATHYL. Only her gold "bauble" was found.

During their search they were at one stage trapped in an underground cavern, one of the few in all Prydain that does not appear to belong to the Fair Folk of TYLWYTH TEG. The huge cavern can still be seen, its stalagmites and stalactites looking like a stone forest after an ice storm. In the distance, strange pools glimmer, some green, some blue, between the red and green veins in the rock.

The cavern was at that time the self-made prison of the giant, Glew. Glew had not always been a giant—he was originally an insignificant little man living in a hut in the forests of Mona. Having failed to become a hero or a soldier, Glew turned to experimenting with magic after meeting a magician who gave him a book of what he claimed were the spells of Caer Colur—to Glew's disgust, however, the pages of the book were blank. While experimenting with other forms of magic, Glew found a formula to make himself bigger and stronger. Its effects were immediately obvious when it turned his cat Llyan into a monstrously large mountain cat. In terror, Glew fled to hide in a cave, still holding his flask of potion. He drank it and found himself growing—until he was so large he was unable to leave the cavern he had entered, and was condemned to remain there, with bats in his hair, stared at by worms.

When Taran and the others blundered into his cavern he was at first only too happy to tell his story, although his real hope was that he could use them in experiments that would help him find a way to reduce his size. He also told them how to reach the ruins of Caer Colur, and there they eventually traced Eilonwy. She had been kidnapped by Achren and Magg, Steward of Dinas Rhydnant, who had betrayed his trust in the hope of sharing power with Achren.

When Taran found the girl in the ruined castle on the island, she did not recognize him or any of her friends, so powerful was the enchantment placed on her by Achren. Even Gwydion was powerless against Achren then, as she had bound the life of the girl to her own. Any attempt to kill or injure her would result in the death of the girl. Reluctantly, Gwydion handed the Pelydryn and the blank book of spells they had taken from Glew to Eilonwy and stood powerless as Achren commanded her to read the spells by the Pelydryn's light. As Eilonwy read, it is said that her expression changed, as though she were undergoing some terrible internal conflict. She appeared to be beyond all threats and all help from anyone. Then Eilonwy brought the Pelydryn closer to the pages of the book of spells and its pages burst into a crimson cloud, which turned into a dazzling white fire. The book vanished into the flames, consumed by its own magic power. Achren had been defeated.

Seeing the fall of his ally, Magg opened the iron gates of the castle, its only defence against the sea. The outer walls crumbled almost immediately and thus the towers of Caer Colur vanished beneath the waves. Taran and the others narrowly escaped death and were washed ashore on the beaches of Mona. The only part of the fabled treasures of the House of Llyr to survive the destruction of the castle was a carved horn of Fair Folk construction. Eilonwy gave this last reminder of her family's past to Taran.

Glew was left behind in his cave and did not regain his normal shape until Dallben, the enchanter of Caer Dallben, sent him an appropriate spell. Many years later, when Taran became the High King of Prydain, he built a road to Glew's old cavern in memory of his friend Prince Rhun of Mona. Today, visitors can follow the road and admire the ancient site.

(Lloyd Alexander, *The Book of Three*, New York, 1964; Lloyd Alexander, *The Black Cauldron*, New York, 1965; Lloyd Alexander, *The Castle of Llyr*, New York, 1966; Lloyd Alexander, *The High King*, New York, 1968)

MONDO NUOVO ("New World"), a country of difficult access, situated somewhere in the vast Central European plain. It was visited for the first time in 1552 by a Florentine traveller, a member of the Peregrine Academy.

Each of the provinces of Mondo Nuovo has only one city; the rest of the land is set aside for agriculture, mainly barley and wheat. There are also several forests. All cities are built on the same plan, in the shape of a star and well protected by walls. In the centre of each city is a large temple, the dome of which is six times larger than that of Florence. Each temple has one hundred doors and each door leads to a road that ends at the city walls. Each road is looked after by one of a hundred priests, and the eldest priest governs the city. Factories, craft shops, grocers, haberdashers, bakers, doctors, cobblers, tanners, blacksmiths and mills— each occupies its own section of the city.

Travellers are advised to enter one of the many inns within the city walls, where they will be served food and drink free of charge.

There are no families as such in the cities of Mondo Nuovo. Women are held in common and children stay with their mothers only until they reach school age. Old people who can no longer work are put into homes where they are carefully looked after. Deformed children are thrown into a well immediately after their birth. Incurable illnesses are treated with arsenic, which is administered also to madmen and criminals. There are no thieves in Mondo Nuovo, because all property is held in common.

Death is regarded as an uninteresting function and funeral ceremonies are unknown. The seventh day in the week is set aside for rest and prayer: the inhabitants meet at the temple, pray and listen to soft music.

(Anton Francesco Doni, *I Mondi*, Florence, 1552)

MONGAZA ISLAND, seven days by sea from FIXED ISLAND. The only information available on Mongaza Island comes from fifteenth-century chronicles and is insignificant. It is known to be well protected by stone fortifications, most of which stand on the shores of Boiling Lake, which, in spite of its name, is not known to display any spectacular qualities.

Mongaza Island is also the abode of the giant Famongomadan, whose name strikes terror in the hearts of any who know him. Among his many unpleasant habits, Famongomadan slaughters young girls in honour of an idol set up near Boiling Lake.

(Anonymous, *Amadis de Gaula*, Zaragoza, 1508)

MONOMOTAPA, a city whose inhabitants are bonded by deep feelings of friendship, so that they intuit one another's most secret needs and desires. For instance, if one dreams that his friend is sad, the friend will perceive the distress and rush to the sleeper's rescue. Visitors are not known to share these intimacies with the natives.

(Jean de La Fontaine, *Fables choisies, mises en vers* VIII:11, 2d ed., Paris, 1678–9)

MONSTERS' PARK, a kind of Disneyland, built on the beach of Alexandria in Egypt, of which today only the ruins remain. It consists of a series of enormous statues of sea-monsters, too horrible to describe, set along the coast to protect the city.

When Alexander the Great began to build Alexandria, a herd of monsters came out of the sea every night and wreaked havoc among the foundations. The king ordered a glass cage to be built, an artist to be put in it and the whole contraption to be lowered into the depths of the sea to sketch the destructive monsters. The king then ordered gigantic statues to be built, based on the artist's sketches, and set them facing the sea. When the creatures came up to the beach and saw their doubles they took to their fins and disappeared forever.

Rising in the midst of a pleasant palm grove, the ruins are now a safe playground for children.

(Maria Savi-Lopez, *Leggende del mare*, Turin, 1920)

MONTE MAURO, see ISLA.

The statues in MONSTERS' PARK guarding the city of Alexandria.

MONTESINOS' CAVE, a famous grotto in La Mancha, Spain. The only traveller to have explored it thoroughly, leaving an account of his investigations, is the ingenious knight Don Quixote de La Mancha.

The cave is some ninety feet deep and can accommodate a cart complete with mules. Should the traveller fall asleep, he will upon waking see one of the most beautiful meadows ever created by nature. Beyond the meadow—but still within the cave—rises a sumptuous castle, the walls of which seem to be made of limpid crystal. The castle gates will open and a venerable old man will appear. Introducing himself as Montesinos, he will invite the traveller into the castle and show him a large alabaster hall containing the marble tomb of Durandarte, one of the bravest knights in history, who has lain here since Merlin the Magician cast a spell on him. Durandarte's beloved Belerma, as well as other famous beauties such as Queen Guinevere and Dulcinea del Toboso, walk around the castle like enchanted ghosts. Travellers will assume that they have spent two or three days contemplating these marvels. In fact, upon leaving the cave, they will find that barely half an hour has elapsed.

(Miguel de Cervantes Saavedra, *El ingenioso hidalgo Don Quixote de La Mancha*, Madrid, 1605–15)

MONTEVERDE, capital of the CAPA BLANCA ISLANDS.

MOODY LAND, a country that changes constantly, according to the moods of its inhabitants. Visitors are advised that the climate of Moody Land is very unpredictable. If there are enough joyful people around, the sun will shine all night, and go on shining until the endless sunshine gets on the inhabitants' nerves. Then an irritable night will fall, a night full of mutterings and discontent, and the air will feel too thick to breathe. When the inhabitants grow angry, the ground shakes. When they become muddled or uncertain, the outlines of buildings and lampposts and motorcars become smudgy, like paintings whose colours have run, and visitors may find it difficult to make out where one thing ends and another begins.

(Salman Rushdie, *Haroun and the Sea of Stories*, London, 1990)

MOOMINLAND, also known as **MOOMIN VALLEY**, on the coast of the Gulf of Finland, to the south of DADDY JONES' KINGDOM. A river flows through the valley, down from the Lonely Mountains to the dunes on the coast opposite LONELY ISLAND and MOOMINPAPA'S ISLAND.

There are no human inhabitants in the valley itself, the nearest men being the lighthouse-keeper on Moominpapa's Island and the scientists who maintain an isolated observatory high up in the Lonely Mountains at the head of the valley.

The valley takes its name from certain creatures that live here, the *Moomins* or *Moomintrolls* as they are sometimes known, small, white, hibernating animals with large snouts, short tails and smooth, hairless skin. They walk on their hind legs and communicate by whistling, because they cannot sing. The *Moomins* are polite, considerate creatures who never forget to whistle "thank you" and who always greet one another with great courtesy.

Moomin families live in Moominhouses, small two-storey buildings with many balconies and a verandah. These houses are reminiscent of old-fashioned porcelain stoves. Inside, the two floors are connected by narrow, winding staircases. The rooms are comfortably furnished with beds with brass knobs, rocking chairs and chandeliers. Moominhouses are heated by wood-burning central heating systems.

Little is known of the origins of these small creatures. A primitive type of *Moomin*, usually referred to as the "Ancestor," has been found by researchers and gives some clues as to the *Moomin* development. The "Ancestor" is small and grey, with a large snout, and is extremely hairy, whereas the present *Moomins* are smooth-skinned, although they will grow thick fur in winter if necessary. It is thought that the "Ancestor" represents a type of *Moomin* that existed perhaps one thousand years ago.

Most *Moomins* hibernate from November to May. Presumably this is mainly because their ancestors did so; there is nothing to suggest that hibernation is physically necessary to their survival. They sleep in the drawing rooms of their houses, first putting to one side all the things they may need in the spring. Before going into hibernation, they eat a substantial meal of pine needles, although these do not form part of the normal summer diet.

The social organization of the *Moomins* centres around the family and there are no formal gov-

MOOMINLAND &
DADDY JONES' KINGDOM

Finland

Daddy Jones' Kingdom

THE HILLS

LONELY
MOUNTAINS

Marshes

Moominland

LONELY
ISLAND

Moominpapa's House ■   The
Swamp

The
▲ Lighthouse   MOOMINPAPA'S
ISLAND

Gulf

of

Finland

ernment institutions. The family is celebrated with great pomp on both Mothers' and Fathers' Day.

But perhaps the most important event of the year, which no traveller should miss, is the lighting of the Midsummer Bonfire. On Midsummer's Eve, great bonfires are lit along the shore and, as they burn down, the custom is to pick a flower and put it under one's pillow. The dreams a traveller has that night will come true, provided that he does not speak until the next morning.

The few *Moomins* who do not hibernate during the winter also light bonfires at moonrise on the night before the sun returns to Moominland, and dance around the fire carrying torches and beating drums. This delightful tradition goes back over a thousand years. The valley is also the home of several other species, including the passive *Hattifatteners* who gather on Lonely Island each June to go off on some mysterious quest and who venerate the barometer. *Hemulens* are found both in Moominland and in Daddy Jones' Kingdom. They are considerably larger than the *Moomins* but somewhat dull-witted, a feature which does not prevent them from taking great pleasure in organizing the lives of others.

A number of different creatures—all of whom can communicate with one another—have been seen in the valley: a female *Groke*; the two monkeylike animals known as Thingummy and Bob; Creeps, a small mammal with light brown fur; and Sniff, a small, friendly quadruped with a long nose, tail and ears. Snufkin is a small mammal who habitually wears a green hat with a feather in it and plays the mouth-organ. The only creatures which resemble the *Moomins* physically are the Snork and Snork-Maiden. Their bodies are similar to those of the *Moomins* themselves, but they change colour according to their emotions. They are covered in soft fur and have blue eyes.

The trees of the valley are the natural habitat of long-haired tree spirits. These are all female and live in tree-trunks; at night they fly up to the top most branches and sing. They appear to prefer broad-leafed trees to those with needles.

More common birds and animals, from cuckoos to glow-worms, are also found here. Wolves and eagles can be seen in the higher mountains, but do not seem to come into the valley itself. Mermaids and mermen have been sighted off the coast, but little is known of their ways.

With the possible exception of the *Hattifatteners*, with their mysterious cult of the barometer,

the inhabitants of Moominland have no form of organized religion. There does appear to be a generalized belief in the existence of a divinity which the inhabitants call "Protector-of-All-Small-Beasts," but it does not involve any specific rituals.

(Tove Jansson, *Muumpeikko ja pyrstötähti*, Helsinki, 1950; Tove Jansson, *Kuinkas sitten kävikään*, Helsinki, 1972; Tove Jansson, *Vaarallinen juhannus*, Helsinki, 1957; Tove Jansson, *Taikatalvi*, Helsinki, 1958; Tove Jansson, *Taikurin hattu*, Helsinki, 1958; Tove Jansson, *Muumipappa merellä*, Helsinki, 1965; Tove Jansson, *Muumipapan urotyöt*, Helsinki, 1966; Tove Jansson, *Muumilaakson marraskuu*, Helsinki, 1971)

MOOMINPAPA'S ISLAND, an island in the Gulf of Finland, off the coast of MOOMINLAND, covered mostly in marshes and swamps. There are no tall trees; the only vegetation is heather and thickets of dwarf spruce. On the north coast of the little island, a half-moon bay of white sand lies between two headlands. There are only two buildings on the island: a lighthouse on the southernmost point and a small house on a promontory to the west. The house is fastened to the rocks with iron clamps because of the savage winds that sweep over the island in winter.

Apart from the lighthouse-keeper no one lives here, although the island is occasionally visited by the *Moomins* of Moominland. It was on Moominpapa's Island that the secret of the *Groke*—one of the more peculiar inhabitants of Moominland—was finally discovered. The *Groke* is a female animal, seemingly the only one of her kind, who is fascinated by lamps. She has large, sad, round eyes, which are completely expressionless. In the past, the *Groke* would freeze the ground she sat on, causing innumerable problems. Finally the Moomins discovered that her unpleasant ability was due to her loneliness. They began to show her some affection and the *Groke* immediately ceased turning the ground to ice.

(Tove Jansson, *Muumipappa merellä*, Helsinki, 1965; Tove Jansson, *Muumipapan urotyöt*, Helsinki, 1966)

MOOR, a small quarry town in Austria, near the Danube. Moor is close to the villages of Leys and Haag, set between high mountains and a lake, twelve miles east of Linz. The mountains are known as The Stony Sea, and access to them is forbidden to all inhabitants of Moor. A sign erected on the granite foothills, in letters the size of a man, serves as a reminder of the town's past sins. It reads:

HERE ELEVEN THOUSAND
NINE HUNDRED SEVENTY-THREE
PEOPLE LIE DEAD
SLAIN BY THE INHABITANTS
OF THIS LAND
WELCOME TO MOOR

After the Second World War, as a punishment for war crimes, the citizens of Moor were forced to revert to pre–industrial-age conditions. Railways, factories, power stations and machinery were either proscribed or left to decay, and today's visitors will find that Moor resembles a medieval village.

Moor has little to offer in the way of sightseeing, other than war relics and a few ruins. In the town's headquarters, guarded by military police inside a glass showcase, visitors can inspect the death registers of the war years. Among the scattered ruins worth visiting are the abandoned sawmill and the cemetery chapel, in which the remains of a wooden Madonna shot off her gilded cloud can still be seen. A large derelict villa known as the Abode of the Dog King, home of Moor's governor, is guarded by fierce wild hounds and not open to visitors.

Twice a year, in midsummer and midwinter, a festival takes place known as Stellamour. Using the classification of prisoners found in the town records, all inhabitants of Moor are required to dress up as Jews, POWs, Gypsies, Communists or Race Defilers. In these uniforms they stand in line outside imaginary delousing stations, pose in front of an immense block of granite and fall into lines beside the foundations of long-demolished barracks. For the summer festival, the inhabitants re-enact a *tableau vivant* called "The Stairway." Each person carries a basket on his or her back, inside which is a large square stone. They line up and climb stairs carved in the rock, leading from the pit of the quarry, up four levels, to the foggy upper rim. Though the prisoners held in Moor during the war died on these stairs of exhaustion, or from the blows, kicks and shots fired by the overseers, the ritual re-enacted by the citizens of Moor does not entail such degrees of brutality; the inhabitants are simply required to imitate the postures of their victims.

(Christoph Ransmayr, *Morbus Kitahara*, Frankfurt, 1995)

MORDOR, a barren, extensive land in MIDDLE-EARTH, to the east of ROHAN and GONDOR. Mordor is surrounded on three sides by mountain ranges. To the north it finds a natural defence in the Ash Mountains or ERED LITHUI, and the Mountains of SHADOW or Ephel Dúath protect it to the west and the south. In the north-west, the two ranges meet at the pass known as CIRITH GORGOR, the main entrance into Mordor. A much less accessible path called CIRITH UNGOL crosses the Ephel Dúath range.

The landscape of Mordor is dominated by the peak of ORODRUIN, the great volcano which rises from GORGOROTH, the plateau in the north-west. In the south lies the Sea of Nurnen, a large inland sea fed by rivers flowing from both the north and the south; it has no outflow. The waters are extremely bitter to the taste. Rain water trickles down from the Mountains of Shadow and forms small streams which soon dry up in the dust and stones below. The water of these streams has a bitter and often oily taste, but it is very welcome to any traveller who finds it for most of Mordor is dry and desolate.

Mordor has always been associated with the dark forces that have periodically arisen throughout the history of Middle-earth, and it well deserves its reputation as the Black Land or even the Nameless Land. It is also associated with the history of Sauron. The stories of Middle-earth say that Sauron was originally a good spirit who became a servant of Morgoth, the evil force that strove to dominate Middle-earth. After the fall of Morgoth, Sauron appeared to repent, but soon returned to his evil ways and began to desire Middle-earth for his own possession. In a variety of guises, he travelled widely, gradually drawing others under his influence and seducing them with his great skills and apparent virtues. Between 1500 and 1590 Second Age, Sauron persuaded the elves of HOLLIN to forge rings of power, which gave their owners great powers of hand and mind. The elves made three rings for themselves, seven which were given to lords of the dwarves, and nine which went to leaders of men. What no one knew was that, deep in Mordor, Sauron was forging a ring in the fires of Orodruin—a ring to enslave the wearers of all the other rings. The One Ring was of gold which was resistant to all heat but that of the fires of doom in Orodruin. Fire did, however, bring out the inscription on it, part of the dire incantation Sauron used to create the ring:

> *Three Rings for the Elven-kings*
> *under the sky,*
> *Seven for the Dwarf-lords*
> *in their halls of stone,*
> *Nine for Mortal Men*
> *doomed to die,*
> *One for the Dark Lord*
> *on his dark throne*
> *In the Land of Mordor*
> *where the Shadows lie.*
> *One Ring to rule them all,*
> *One Ring to find them,*
> *One Ring to bring them all*
> *and in the darkness bind them*
> *In the Land of Mordor*
> *where the Shadows lie.*

When the elves learned of the One Ring they set their own rings aside and never wore them, and so were not enslaved. The dwarves used their rings, but their sturdy and unyielding character did not adapt either to power or to subjugation. But the nine rulers of men proved easy victims. The rings gave them secret knowledge and the ability to become invisible. They became powerful kings and sorcerers, but gradually fell under the influence of their own rings and became slaves to the One Ring. Eventually they became the Nazgûl or Ringwraiths, living ghosts with immense supernatural powers derived from the force of the One Ring. They were invisible, apart from their black clothing. Only someone wearing a ring of power could see their tall white faces and the terrible power of their eyes. They could not be harmed by ordinary weapons, which simply melted on contact with them. They became Sauron's lieutenants and served him well in his evil plans.

Sauron himself could no longer present himself in any fair form; he took on the form of a great fire-rimmed eye, so evil and malicious that none could bear to look at it. He used Mordor as a base for his war preparations and gradually began to harass the kingdoms of Rohan and Gondor. In 3429 Second Age, his forces took MINAS MORGUL, then the capital of Gondor. The following year, the Last Alliance was formed between elves and men against Sauron and a massive army marched south to challenge his power. In the battle on the plain of

DAGORLAD Sauron's forces were defeated and he himself lost his power when the One Ring was taken from him in a last struggle on the slopes of Orodruin.

The Ring was to pass through many hands, but it worked an evil influence on everyone who wore it. The wearer felt great power, but was very reluctant to give up the Ring—even showing it to someone else made it feel heavy on the finger. Not only did the possessor become invisible when he wore the Ring, but he slowly began to fade, to become thin and insubstantial, even when he was not wearing it. When the Ring finally gained total control, the bearer became quite invisible, like the Ringwraiths. The Ring also seems to have had a will of its own and to have tried to return to Sauron.

The battle on the plain of Dagorlad was not, however, the final defeat of Sauron, and by about 1100 Third Age the forces of evil had begun to appear in Middle-earth. An evil power was discovered to have appeared in MIRKWOOD and later proved to be Sauron himself. To combat Sauron, wizards came to Middle-earth and the White Council was formed to coordinate the struggle. But the Council's leader, Saruman the White, was soon corrupted. He began to search for the One Ring, lost since the beginning of the Third Age, and came under the influence of Sauron.

The search for the Ring took Sauron's allies far across Middle-earth. Sauron began to make military preparations too for an onslaught on Middle-earth. The defence works built by Gondor to guard against Sauron's return were gradually taken over as Gondor became less vigilant against the enemy. He made alliances with the men of HARAD and with the Easterlings, long-standing enemies of Rohan and Gondor. Mines and forges were established in the north to provide weapons, and food was grown by slave labour in the south to feed the massing armies. Sauron's main forces were huge armies of orcs and trolls.

Orcs appear to have been originally bred by Morgoth during the First Age. Legend has it that some elves turned to his side and that from them he bred orcs in mockery of the true elves. Orcs are hideous, evil creatures, rather like goblins, with long arms and bow legs. They tend to be squat, with dark faces and long fangs, although there are many differences between the various tribes. They wear foul, heavy clothing and hate all things of beauty, their only ambition being to kill and destroy. Their tribal organization is primitive and the various communities fight among each other. Early in their history they became common in the MISTY MOUNTAINS, eventually driving the dwarves from their kingdoms in MORIA. Orcs appeared in all the areas under Sauron's control in the Second and Third ages and also figured among Saruman's forces in NAN CURUNIR. Saruman himself succeeded in crossing men with orcs, thus producing a race with squint eyes and yellow faces. These creatures were taller than the average and served him as both soldiers and spies. In general orcs are smallish, dark-skinned and have wide snuffling nostrils. The fighting orcs (Uruk-hai) are much bigger and more fearsome.

Trolls are said to have been created in mockery of the ents of FANGORN. Immensely strong, malevolent creatures, they are usually unintelligent but are noted for their cruelty. Again there are various species, such as the cave trolls found in Moria, the hill trolls of Gorgoroth and the stone trolls found to the west of the Misty Mountains and on the ETTENMOORS. During the Third Age a new species of troll appeared, apparently bred by Sauron. These are the Olog-hai and are larger and stronger than the other species. They have greater cunning than most others and are also distinguished by their ability to withstand the light of the sun, which turns all other trolls to stone.

All these creatures were housed by Sauron in and around Mordor. Great camps and even small towns were erected, especially to the south of the MORGAI.

Finally, Sauron learned that the One Ring was in the hands of a hobbit from the SHIRE, and that the hobbit, with the aid and guidance of the White Council, intended to destroy it in the only possible way—by casting it into the fires of the Cracks of Doom (Orodruin) where it was forged. The struggles to save or destroy the One Ring led to a series of terrible battles, but at last the Army of the West began to move south against Mordor itself as the members of the Company of the Ring strove to carry it back to Orodruin where it might be destroyed. The culmination came in 3019 Third Age with the great battle before Cirith Gorgor. It was during this battle that the Ring finally fell into the Cracks of Doom and Sauron's power vanished. His armies were routed and his fortifications crumbled to the ground. Barad-dûr and many of the defences of Mordor collapsed and were totally destroyed. After the defeat of Sauron, Orodruin erupted, destroying or greatly changing much of Mordor.

(J.R.R. Tolkien, *The Hobbit, or There and Back Again*, London, 1937; J.R.R. Tolkien, *The Fellowship of the Ring*, London, 1954; J.R.R. Tolkien, *The Two Towers*, London, 1954; J.R.R. Tolkien, *The Return of the King*, London, 1955; J.R.R. Tolkien, *The Silmarillion*, London, 1977)

MOREAU'S ISLAND, see NOBLE'S ISLAND.

MORELLY'S LAND, of uncertain location. Visitors should know that all social life in the country is based on three fundamental and sacred laws designed to put an end to the vices and evils that afflict other societies: no citizen of Morelly's Land may own private property, other than those things he uses in his day-to-day life; all citizens are employed by the community; and all citizens contribute to the economy in accordance with their age, abilities and physical strength.

The government is republican: all fathers over the age of fifty become senators and have a voice in the political decisions taken. The senate is advised, if necessary, by a council composed of younger men and of representatives of the trades and liberal professions. A local senate and council are elected by each city; they, in turn, elect the Supreme Council. Society is organized on the basis of families, tribes and cities; each tribe is composed of an equal number of families and each city of an equal number of tribes. As far as possible, all cities are the same size; when they become too large, a new city is founded.

The basis of the republic is its system of organized production and distribution. All citizens, supervised by the oldest and most experienced members of each trade or profession, must work. In each area of production, an experienced master (who must be at least twenty-six) supervises a group of ten to twenty workers. Nothing may be bought, sold or exchanged privately; all durable goods are sold through public stores and all perishable goods are sold in public places by the producer or manufacturer.

Work and the choice of one's trade are closely connected with the educational and child-care system. Infants are breast-fed, when possible, and remain with their parents until they are five. They are then brought up in sexually segregated houses with others of their own age; for the next five years they are cared for by their parents, who take turns working in the houses. During these years, children are given a basic moral education and taught the first elements of the trade to which they seem most suited. At ten, they enter a profession and come under the authority of the master of that trade. Their apprenticeship includes moral philosophy, as well as purely technical and professional matters. Throughout this period, the master is responsible for the child's education and moral welfare. At twenty, all citizens begin a five-year period of agricultural work, unless physical disability precludes them from doing so. They may choose to adopt agriculture as their profession or may return to their first trade, as a master. In cases where an individual chooses to take up another trade, he must serve a further five-year apprenticeship. At forty, the individual becomes a "free worker"— free, that is, to choose the trade in which he will work without further training.

All citizens are required to marry; no one is allowed to remain celibate after the age of forty. The young people of each city meet in public assemblies each year to choose their marriage partners. Though visitors are allowed to attend, these assemblies are reputed to be embarrassing, for both participants and onlookers. The choice of partner is the prerogative of the man, but marriage can only take place if the woman consents. Divorce is not permissible for ten years after marriage, and then only by mutual agreement. Before a divorce is allowed, the tribe and family will attempt to bring about a reconciliation. Divorced persons may not see each other for six months after their separation and cannot marry for a year. They may not marry their ex-partners, nor other divorcees, nor anyone younger than themselves. When a divorce is given, any children of the marriage remain in the custody of the father.

Sumptuary laws apply to all citizens, both male and female. All citizens dress alike until the age of thirty; the colour of their clothes indicates their occupation. Once they are thirty, they may dress according to their own tastes, provided that their garments are plain and sober. All vanity in matters of dress is strongly discouraged; if necessary, the heads of families may prescribe appropriate punishments. All citizens are provided by the community with clothes for work and play.

The arts are actively encouraged throughout the country and are open, as a profession, to those over thirty. The study of moral science, based on the laws of society, is open to all. Metaphysics has been reduced to the substance of what has been said about the divinity (regarded as a somewhat impersonal creator of the universe). Citizens remain agnostic concerning the possibility of an after-life, arguing that the "Author of Nature" has given no indication as to what may or may not happen after death. The history of Morelly's Land is recorded by the senate; it is a strictly factual account which leaves no room for fabulation.

The rationality characteristic of the whole country can be seen in its town-planning. Streets are arranged on a regular plan around a central public square and all the houses are built to a standard pattern. Each tribe inhabits a particular quarter and each family has its own house; room is left for expansion without destroying the regularity of the plan. All workshops and factories are located at some distance from the city and are surrounded by a belt of agricultural land. All hospitals and old people's homes are built in or beyond the farm belt.

In Morelly's Land, murder is regarded as a crime against nature; murderers are imprisoned for life and their names are eradicated from all records, to demonstrate that their deeds have cut them off from human society. Punishment for other crimes is by imprisonment or exclusion from civic offices; all verdicts passed by the courts are final. Prisoners are plainly fed and clothed at public expense, and they are attended by young children who have shown a tendency towards laziness. It is believed that seeing the results of crime will help eradicate that tendency. Prisons are always built in the most unpleasant spots available, usually overlooking a graveyard.

Nothing is known about accommodation for travellers, who will have to find their lodgings by whatever means they can.

(Morelly, —, *Code de la nature, ou le véritable esprit de ses lois, de tout temps négligé ou méconnu,* Amsterdam, 1755)

MOREL'S ISLAND, see VILLINGS.

MORGAI, THE, a ridge below the eastern side of the Mountains of SHADOW above MORDOR, divided from the mountains themselves by a deep natural chasm which is crossed by a single stone bridge. The top of the ridge is almost impassable and is broken by numerous small ravines and crevasses. Apart from the tussocks of grass and

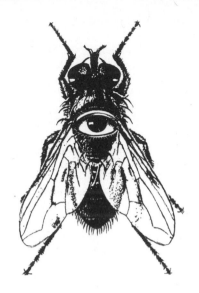

A MORGAI fly.

scrubby trees there is little vegetation. Bushes with great sharp thorns and brambles grow on the lower ground. The only living creatures are midges, maggots and flies. Some of the flies are brown or black, with blotchy red markings that resemble an eye.

(J.R.R. Tolkien, *The Return of the King*, London, 1955)

MORGAN LE FAY or **MORGAN THE FAITHLESS' CASTLE**, somewhere in Wales, the home of the sister of King Arthur of CAMELOT. Once the wife of King Lot of Orkney, she became one of the most powerful enchantresses in the country, and had a son by Arthur, who lay with her at CAERLEON without knowing her true identity. The son, Mordred, was destined to wound his father mortally during a battle on Salisbury Plain.

Visitors will find this dark castle extremely rich and luxurious. The walls are covered with silken cloth and are brilliantly lit by a multitude of candles. The courtiers are all attired in rich and fantastic garments, and attend to guests with impeccable precision.

Of particular interest is one chamber whose walls are covered by a mural illustrating Sir Launcelot's illicit love for Guinevere, Arthur's queen. This mural was executed by Launcelot himself while he was held prisoner in the castle by Morgan.

(Anonymous, *La Mort le Roi Artu*, 13th cen. AD)

MORIA, the greatest of all dwarf dwellings ever constructed in MIDDLE-EARTH. Moria, which the dwarves themselves call Khazad-dûm (literally, the Mansion of the Khazad or dwarves), lies deep beneath the MISTY MOUNTAINS. The construction of this vast underground city was begun in the First Age of Middle-earth, when Durin, the most renowned of the Seven Fathers of the Dwarves, came to DIMRILL DALE or Azanulbizar, which became part of the dwarf kingdom.

The subterranean realm constructed by Durin and his followers is a great maze of tunnels, stairs and halls, and includes the mines which gave the dwarves their wealth.

The dwarves constructed colossal gates, overlooking Azanulbizar and MIRRORMERE, and all of Moria which lay on or above the height of these gates was systematized into "levels," while the many, endlessly branching halls below were known as "deeps." The old inhabited area on the eastern side consists of a series of great halls built on seven levels, the highest being far enough above ground level to receive light through the great windows cut in the mountain side. The lower halls are even larger; the Second Hall, in the First Deep, is a vast cavernous chamber, having a double row of towering pillars running down the centre, carved like massive tree trunks whose stone branches support the roofs. Originally, this hall was connected with the First Hall and the outer passages by a bridge, a delicate arch, without any handrail, some fifty feet long. It spanned a dark chasm and was so narrow that it had to be crossed in single file; it was intended as a defence against enemies who might capture the First Hall.

There were originally two entrances to Moria, approximately forty miles apart on opposite sides of the Misty Mountains. The main entrance—the Great Gates—was from Dimrill Dale in the east; the gates were reached by climbing a huge flight of steps. The west door was built to facilitate trade in the days when the elves and dwarves were friends. It was cut into the sheer cliffs known as the Walls of Moria which tower over a valley, once the bed of a shallow stream called the Sirannon or Gate Stream. Dwarfish doors are made so as to be invisible when they are shut, but the west entrance to Moria was so constructed that other peoples could understand its working and open it without too much difficulty.

Above the gate there is an inscription in moon-letters, dwarfish runes, wrought in Ithilien, that can only be seen when the light of the moon shines upon them. The inscriptions shows the emblems of Durin (an anvil and hammer beneath a crown of seven stars), the tree of the High Elves and the star of the House of Fëanor. In an arch of elven letters an inscription in the elven tongue of the west reads: "The Doors of Durin, Lord of Moria. Speak friend and enter." When the elven word for friend, "mellon," is pronounced, the doors open. Secondary inscriptions give the name of the builder of the door, Narvi, and that of the executor of the signs, Celebrimbor of HOLLIN.

The dwarves of Middle-earth are famed for their craftsmanship, especially their metal work. They are skilled manufacturers of jewels, precious metals, ornaments, armour and weapons. They mine the materials used in their craft in their underground dwellings. Although a normally trustworthy people, they tend to be ruled by their lust for gold and precious metals. In Moria, they discovered the metal they prize above all others—*mithril*. *Mithril*, which has been found only in Moria, is known as true-silver to the dwarves. It can be beaten into many shapes and highly polished, but it will never tarnish. The dwarves made it into a light metal that is harder than tempered steel, while the elves used it to make *ithildin*. Bilbo, a hobbit from the Shire, and a member of the Fellowship of the Ring, was once given a chain-mail corselet of *mithril* by the dwarves. It was made of rings of the precious metal and shimmered and sparkled, making a tinkling sound when it was shaken. The lives of both Bilbo and his nephew Frodo were saved more than once by the strength of the *mithril* armour.

The dwarves' search for *mithril* led eventually to disaster. As they dug deeper and deeper, they awakened a Balrog, the last survivor of a terrible race of demons—a great shadowy form wreathed in smoke and fire, armed with whips and a fiery sword, and gifted with dreadful powers. The Balrog killed two of the kings of the dwarves and the others fled, abandoning Moria in 1981 Third Age. Most of the dwarves went north to the LONELY MOUNTAIN, now their major settlement, and others went to the IRON HILLS and the GREY MOUNTAINS. The caverns of Moria soon became infested with orcs, evil goblins which came to be ruled by the Balrog. Two attempts were made to take back Moria. The first led to a full-scale war from 2793 to 2799 Third Age between the orcs and the dwarves. Thrór, a king of the dwarves, reentered Moria in 2790 and was murdered and mutilated by orcs. In revenge the dwarves started to attack and destroy every orc stronghold they could find in an attempt to reach his murderer. The war ended with victory for the dwarves in the battle of Azanulbizar, but they had lost so many of their number in the fighting that they had no heart to recolonize Moria or to attempt to destroy the Balrog. Almost two hundred years later, Balin, one of the dwarves who had driven the great dragon Smaug from the Lonely Mountain, returned to Moria with a large number of dwarves and re-established a colony. He appears to have ruled for five years, but perished, along with all his company, at the hands of the orcs. His tomb is in the Chamber of Mazarbul (Chamber of Records).

During the War of the Ring, the Company of the Ring crossed through Moria, as they could not cross the Misty Mountains themselves. They were attacked by orcs, cave-trolls and finally by the Balrog itself. All escaped one by one over the narrow arched bridge leading towards the eastern entrance, but the wizard Gandalf the Grey remained behind to fight the Balrog. They fell from the bridge, which was destroyed, but the battle went on for ten days, ending only when the two emerged on the summit of the mountain above Moria and the Balrog was flung down and destroyed. After this battle, Gandalf was taken to LÓRIEN, where he became Gandalf the White. Even though the Balrog is gone, there are still orcs in Moria. The dwarves do not appear to have made any further attempt to regain their old home.

Although they are now scattered about and effectively living in exile, the dwarves still retain their own culture and language. They continue to make musical instruments, including the exquisite golden harps, examples of which were found in Smaug's hoard under the Lonely Mountain, and to sing the songs that tell of their past.

(J.R.R. Tolkien, *The Hobbit, or There and Back Again,* London, 1937; J.R.R. Tolkien, *The Fellowship of the Ring,* London, 1954; J.R.R. Tolkien, *The Two Towers,* London, 1954; J.R.R. Tolkien, *The Return of the King,* London, 1955; J.R.R. Tolkien, *The Silmarillion,* London, 1977)

MORIANA, a city in Asia, across a river and a mountain pass. Its alabaster gates seem transparent in the sunlight, its coral columns support pediments encrusted with serpentine, its villas all of glass are like aquariums where the shadows of dancing girls with silvery scales swim beneath the medusa-shaped chandeliers. Experienced travellers will know that cities like this have an obverse: one has only to walk in a semicircle and one will come into view of Moriana's hidden face, an expanse of rusting sheet metal, sackcloth, planks bristling with spikes, pipes black with soot, piles of tins, blind walls with fading signs, frames of staved-in straw chairs, ropes good only for hanging oneself from a rotten beam.

From one part to the other, the city seems to continue, in perspective multiplying its repertory of images: but instead it has no thickness, it consists only of a face and an obverse, like a sheet of paper, with a figure on either side, which can neither be separated nor look at each other.

(Italo Calvino, *Le città invisibili*, Turin, 1972)

MORPHOPOLIS, a large city some kilometres from Blois, France, occupying the park of the Castle of Chambord. Morphopolis is a scaled-down version of the centre of Paris, in which a large canal represents the Seine. The Louvre department store, the Avenue de l'Opéra, the *Café de la Paix*, the Champs Elysées, can all be seen in Morphopolis, as well as Paris' famous restaurants, boutiques and theatres.

The inhabitants of Morphopolis are all asleep. In 1950 a certain Doctor Morpho—who had discovered in 1920 a drug that could suspend vital functions for periods proportionate to the size of the dose—decided to set up a city which could be preserved for three hundred years. Funds were raised—four hundred million old francs to buy the land and erect the buildings, two hundred million more to secure the upkeep and guarding of the city. On June 28, 1950, ten thousand volunteer "citizens of sleep" were injected with the necessary dose. They now lie, as did the inhabitants of SLEEPING BEAUTY'S CASTLE, in a profound sleep, to be wakened on June 28, 2250.

Visitors are advised that only those with official passes issued by the French government are allowed to enter Morphopolis.

(Maurice Barrère, *La Cité du sommeil*, Paris, 1929)

MORROW ISLAND, latitude 46°2′23.5″ north and longitude 33°39′48.6″ west, separated from the coast of Francobolia by the Maupertuis Channel.

The island is thirty kilometres long and eight kilometres wide and has a population of over fifteen thousand. The capital is Lux, a fortified city on the coast, but travellers should also visit the beautiful city of Primevere, twelve kilometres farther inland. To the east lie salty marshes and oyster beds; to the south, a few grazing pastures. The fishing port of Hungercity lies to the north-west of the island and should also be visited, if only to climb the forty-three-metre-high lighthouse of Raive, which commands a splendid view.

In spite of the appalling poverty that reigns in Morrow—it is said that people die in the hospital because of lack of chloroform during operations—Morrow still presents a few unique attractions that make it worth a visit: notably, a score of holy apparitions that are said to occur throughout the island. These have entailed a number of clerical changes, such as the renaming of the capital's Revolution Square, now called Square of the Sacred Heart.

Visitors will find that they can book seats for these apparitions at given times, choosing from among a dozen scheduled patron saints.

(Henri Chateau, *La Cité des idoles*, Paris, 1906)

MORVA, a desolate marshy area to the west of the River Ystrad in PRYDAIN, reached by a narrow path through the moorlands beyond the Forest of Idris. Travellers will find that the whole region is a wasteland of stagnant pools and swamps, with scattered furze bushes and clumps of grass. Wreaths of white fog hang above the ground, while a ceaseless humming and groaning and the smell of ancient decay fills the air. The marshes are almost impassable for anyone who does not know the submerged paths that are little more than sunken tufts of grass and earth.

The only building in the area is a low cottage on a mound by the edge of the marshes, covered with soil and branches and almost invisible from a distance. Behind it stand a few tumbledown stables and outbuildings. The cottage is the abode of three enchantresses: Orddu, Orwen and Orgoch, who are known to exchange identities from time to time. (None of them particularly likes being Orgoch, who has an almost insatiable appetite for living creatures; because of her, the three cannot keep any pets since they would almost certainly be devoured.) The three can also change their appearance: usually they are seen as ugly old hags, but they have shown themselves in the form of beautiful young women. One of their more successful changes was reported by a certain lady from the city of Bath, England.

Morva was the region where Dallben, the great enchanter of CAER DALLBEN, spent his childhood. He was found in a wicker basket and raised and educated by the three women, who taught him his first lesson in magic. It was in Morva that he was given the *Book of Three*, which foretold the future of Prydain.

(Lloyd Alexander, *The Black Cauldron*, New York, 1965; Lloyd Alexander, *Taran Wanderer*, New York, 1967; Lloyd Alexander, *The High King*, New York, 1968)

MOTHER CAREY'S HEAVEN, see PEACE-POOL.

MOURNFUL SEA, see ALIFBAY.

MOUNT ANALOGUE, an island continent in the south Pacific. It consists of a large mountain of the same name, the highest on earth, and stands on an underwater platform, the circumference of which spreads out for many thousands of kilometres. The platform comprises all sorts of minerals

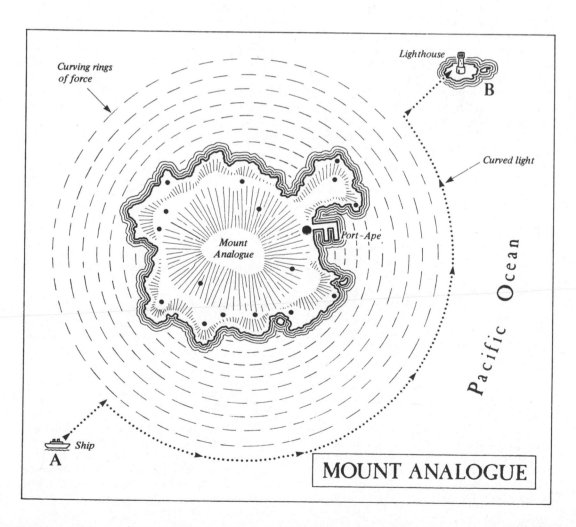

MOUNT ANALOGUE

of unknown origin that have the peculiar property of curving the space around them in such a way that the whole area is sealed up in a shell of curved space. The shell, however, is not entirely closed. It is open at the top to receive radiations from the stars that are necessary for life on this island; it also opens towards the centre of the earth. The shell can be described as a curving ring which cannot be penetrated and which surrounds the island like an invisible, intangible barrier. Because of this, its existence has never been credited.

If we suppose a ship to be at point *A*, southwest of the island (see map), and a lighthouse to be at point *B*, north-east of the island, then from point *A* the beam of the lighthouse (at point *B)* can be seen as if Mount Analogue did not exist, because the light curves past it. Should the ship proceed on its route from *A* to *B*, the curve in space will also deviate the light from the stars as well as the magnetic forces, so that both on the sextant and on the compass the ship will appear to be navigating in a straight line. Without moving its rudder the ship will take the bend around Mount Analogue; and the ship itself, as well as everything upon it, will curve insensibly around the island. Therefore, even though Mount Analogue may have the dimensions of Australia, it is quite understandable that few have ever realized its existence.

In order to find a way to reach the island—as several expeditions have managed to do—the traveller must be guided by a strict *need* to reach it. Only the sun can uncurve the space around the island; therefore, either at dawn or at dusk, the traveller must find a way to make a breach in the shell. It is necessary to enter the invisible island from the west, at dusk, and not from the east at dawn; in this way, as in the experiment of Franklin's hot chamber, a current of cold air coming from the sea will blow towards the lower, overheated strata of Mount Analogue's atmosphere. This system allows the traveller to be sucked inside the shell; at dawn and from the east he would be violently repelled. The method is symbolic; civilization degenerates from east to west. To reach the essential origins one must proceed in the opposite direction.

The only known chronicle of an expedition to Mount Analogue is unfortunately incomplete and does not say whether the members of that expedition were able to climb the mount itself. However, the chronicle does give a good description of the city of PORT-APE and of the social structure of the island. The authority is in the hands of the mountain guides, who form a class of their own. Apart from acting as normal guides, they assume an administrative function in the villages on the coast and on the mountain slopes. There is no real native population; the inhabitants seem to have come from all over the world at different times with the sole purpose of climbing Mount Analogue, because, as is well known, Mount Analogue links heaven to earth.

(René Daumal, *Le Mont Analogue*, Paris, 1952)

MOVING TREES, ISLAND OF, in the north Atlantic, a large island, covered with rich vegetation. Its name is the result of a mistake made by certain seafarers who arrived here at the beginning of the seventeenth century. Sailing into the mouth of a river, they saw a group of trees leap from one bank to the other; frightened, they decided to turn back. More recent travellers have discovered that the "moving trees" are actually local fishermen's barges, adorned with thick branches of many-coloured leaves.

(Miguel de Cervantes Saavedra, *Los trabajos de Persiles y Sigismunda*, Madrid, 1617)

MUIL, see SEVEN ISLES.

MUMMELSEE, a lake at the foot of one of the highest mountains in the Spessart region of Germany. According to the local inhabitants, the Mummelsee is bottomless and is inhabited by water spirits; hence the name which means "bogey lake" or "goblin lake."

Visitors are warned that anything which interferes with the lake is destroyed and any object thrown into the water will be transformed into something else by unknown forces. Violent storms are known to occur when the lake is defiled in any way. There are no roads leading to Mummelsee; it can only be reached on foot. Mummelsee is one of the known means of entry to CENTRUM TERRAE.

(Johann Hans Jakob Christoffel von Grimmelshausen, *Der abenteuerliche Simplicissimus Teutsch*, Nürnberg, 1668; Johann Hans Jakob Christoffel von Grimmelshausen, *Continuatio des abentheurlichen Simplicissimi oder Schluss desselben*, Nürnberg, 1669)

MUSICAL ISLAND, chiefly noteworthy for its strange flora of archaic instruments which grow in plantations protected by Aeolian bamboo fences: *taroles, ravanstrons,* sambucas, *archilutes,* pandoras, *kins, tchés, turlurettes, magreplas* and *hydraules.* The steam-organ given to Pepin in 775 by Constantine Copronymus is preserved in a greenhouse; it was brought here by St. Corneille of Compiègne. One can still hear its *octavina,* counterbassoon, *sarrusophone, binious, zampogna,* bagpipe, serpent, *coelophone,* saxhorn and *enclure.* All the plants come into flower when the sonority rises at the summer solstice.

The atmospheric sonority of the island is controlled by consulting thermometers known as "sirens." At the winter solstice, it falls from the sound of the swearing of a cat to the buzzing of a wasp or the droning of a fly.

The heavens also make music to delight visitors on the island. At night, Saturn rattles a sistrum against its rings; at sunrise and sunset, the sun and moon clash like resounding cymbals.

The Lord of the Island sits on a throne perfumed with harps, listening to a choir of thrones, dominations and powers singing "Let us drink both night and day" and "Let us always be in love." His own refrain—and habitual way of greeting visitors—is the chant "Happy the man who enjoys the sound of cymbals on the hill where he dwells; he wakes alone in bed, at peace, and swears that he will never reveal the secret source of his bliss to the vulgar."

(Alfred Jarry, *Gestes et Opinions du Docteur Faustroll, Pataphysicien. Roman Néo-Scientifique,* Paris, 1911)

MUSICIANS' ISLAND and COMEDIANS' ISLAND, two neighbouring islands near Tierra del Fuego. Not much is known about Comedians' Island, but Musicians' Island is known to be very pleasant. No sounds are heard here except the music of songs and instruments. The inhabitants talk in a singsong voice, as if they were speaking Swedish. Their houses and gardens are laid out in a pattern that resembles a sheet of music. The inhabitants of both islands must pay a regular tax to the government of FOOLLYK, or Poets' Island.

(Abbé Pierre François Guyot Desfontaines, *Le Nouveau Gulliver, ou Voyage De Jean Gulliver, Fils Du Capitaine Gulliver. Traduit d'un Manuscrit Anglois. Par Monsieur L.D.F.,* Paris, 1730)

MUSICKER'S VALLEY, a pleasant valley lying between DUNKITON and the plain that extends towards SCOODLERLAND. By the side of the road stands the little house of the valley's only resident, Allegro da Capo. Da Capo is a fat little man who habitually wears a red, braided jacket, a blue waistcoat and white trousers with gold stripes down the side.

The sound of music that constantly fills the air comes from inside da Capo himself and sounds rather like a wheezy hand-organ or a worn-out phonograph. Da Capo makes music as he breathes, as though his entire body were an organ and his lungs the bellows. Because da Capo has to breathe in order to live, the music goes on forever, which may explain why no one else lives in Musicker's Valley.

(L. Frank Baum, *The Road to Oz,* Chicago, 1909)

MYSTERIOUS, see LINCOLN.

MYSTERY, VALLEY OF, see TROPICAL VALLEY.

N

NACUMERA, a large, fair island in the Atlantic Ocean, more than a thousand miles in circumference. Nacumera is remarkable for its inhabitants, who have dogs' heads, worship the ox and wear gold or silver images of the sacred heart on their foreheads as a symbol of their devotion. They are large, war-loving people who go about dressed only in loincloths and carry pointed spears and shields as large as their bodies. To economize, they eat their captives.

The king of Nacumera is very devout and prays three hundred times to his god before each meal. The only royal attribute (without which he would not be recognized as king) is a huge ruby, a foot long and five fingers wide, which he wears around his neck. The Chinese emperor long coveted this jewel but could neither buy it nor capture it in war.

(Sir John Mandeville, *Voiage de Sir John Maundevile*, Paris, 1357)

NAMELESS CASTLE, rising solitary in the French countryside. On the main entrance travellers will see the following inscription: "I belong to no one and to all; before entering you were already here, and you shall still be here when you leave." Inside the castle, visitors will find a mixed company who speak in both truth and lies and who either remain seated or walk around endlessly.

A group of adventurers is said to have taken possession of the castle in spite of the warning above the entrance gates, and assisted by vicious servants will murder whoever contests their landlord's rights.

(Denis Diderot, *Jacques le fataliste et son maître*, Paris, 1796)

NAN CURUNIR, a large valley, on the western side of the southern end of the MISTY MOUNTAINS of MIDDLE-EARTH, known as the Vale of Angrenost before Saruman the wizard came to dwell there. The valley overlooks the plain of Isen and the Gap of ROHAN and so commanded an important strategic position, as well as holding a natural defensive one because its only opening is to the south.

Within the valley lay the mighty fortress of Isengard, originally built by the men of GONDOR and maintained as an outpost after the establishment of Rohan as a separate kingdom. The fortress consisted of a huge natural rock-wall, a projection from the mountains, which enclosed a circular plain about a mile in diameter with a tall tower— the Tower of Orthanc—in the centre. The wall, as tall as a cliff, was known as the Ring of Isengard. It had only one entrance, a long tunnel hewn through the black rock of the southern side of the wall. Iron doors were positioned at either end and were hung so perfectly on their hinges of steel that a mere push was sufficient to open them when they were unbarred. Inside the wall the plain was once cultivated, and the visitor was welcomed by the sight of grass and fruit trees when he emerged from the tunnel. The rock-wall itself has now been mostly destroyed, but the great Tower of Orthanc can still be seen at the centre of the plain.

The Tower is formed of smooth black rock. Four large pillars of rock appear to have been welded into one and rise up to sharp pinnacles; where the pillars meet, five hundred feet above the plain, there is a narrow platform or floor, inscribed with curious signs. Twenty-seven broad steps of black stone lead up to the tower's single entrance. Tall windows are set deep in the walls.

A devotional gold image of an ox, from NACUMERA, worn on the forehead.

After the long winter of 2758–59 Third Age, Beren, nineteenth Steward of Gondor, and King Fréaláf of Rohan welcomed Saruman to Isengard, hoping that he would be able to help their lands recover from the ravages of the Long Winter. Saruman received the keys of the Tower of Orthanc from Beren and took up residence as a lieutenant of the Steward, and Warden of the Tower.

Saruman was one of the five great wizards of the White Council formed to combat Sauron, Dark Lord of Mordor. Saruman was initially a good friend of Rohan, but he gradually came under the influence of Sauron and the evil he had once fought. It appears that Saruman's motive for coming to Isengard was to gain possession of the Orthanc-stone, one of the *palantíri* or Seeing-stones. The stones, dark balls of crystal which seem to have a heart of fire, allowed those who had them to see things far away in the distance and to communicate by thought. Originally wrought in Eldamar by the elves, the *palantíri* were used to protect the realm of Gondor and were kept in various locations throughout Middle-earth. The most important was kept in the city of OSGILIATH, the original capital of Gondor, and others in MINAS TIRITH and MINAS MORGUL. Three other *palantíri* were kept at Annúminas in ARNOR, in the Tower of Amon Sûl which once stood on the WEATHER HILLS, and in the TOWER HILLS. The *palantíri* also allowed a strong will to impose itself on a lesser will, so when one of the stones came into the hands of Sauron it became a danger to all.

During Saruman's residence in Isengard, the nature and appearance of the fortress changed considerably. The cultivated land inside the walls was turned over to his industry; it was now covered in metal, marble pillars and machines, and ugly mounds covered the openings of the shafts leading to underground forges and workshops and the caves used to house his armies of slaves. Isengard became a home for many evil creatures, including the orcs which Saruman sent out to harass the borders of Gondor and Rohan, and here he finally succeeded in breeding a new race of evil creatures, half orc and half man.

During the War of the Ring, an army of ents, the great tree shepherds of FANGORN, marched against Saruman in his stronghold. They were motivated largely by their thirst for vengeance against his orcs, who had so wantonly damaged many of their beloved trees. The ents destroyed the fortifications of Isengard without difficulty, simply tearing the rock-wall apart with their hands and diverting the River Isen so that it flooded the caves and subterranean workshops, causing a lake to form around the foot of the Tower of Orthanc. Orthanc itself proved indestructible, resisting even the strength of the ents who are among the most physically powerful creatures in Middle-earth. Saruman and his agent Gríma, or Wormtongue, took refuge in the Tower and were then kept prisoner by Treebeard, chief of the ents. In anger and frustration, Gríma flung the *palantír* from the tower, not realizing what it was. The Seeing-stone finally came into the hands of Aragorn, a descendant of the rulers of Gondor and future ruler of the Reunited Kingdom.

After their victory, the ents removed the rubble and most traces of the ancient stone walls. Two tall trees were planted at the entrance to the valley and the area was surrounded by a wood planted by the ents. This became known as the Watchwood, and its function was to keep watch on the imprisoned Saruman. Only after the War of the Ring had ended did Treebeard allow Saruman to leave, on condition that he surrender the keys to the Tower to the King of Gondor.

(J.R.R. Tolkien, *The Fellowship of the Ring*, London, 1954; J.R.R. Tolkien, *The Two Towers*, London, 1954; J.R.R. Tolkien, *The Return of the King*, London, 1955; J.R.R. Tolkien, *The Silmarillion*, London, 1977)

NARNIA, a land that lies between mountain ranges (which separate it from ARCHENLAND to the south), and wastes and moorlands (its frontier to the north). Eastward, Narnia is bound by the sea; westward, by precipitous mountains and cliffs. The Great River, which flows the length of the country, plunges down these cliffs into the Cauldron Pool—a deep hole of churning, bubbling water—and for much of its course runs between steep and often rocky banks. A tributary, rising in Lantern Waste, joins it at Beaversdam, after flowing for many miles through a deep gorge. The Great River crosses a varied landscape of lawns, rocks, heather and woods and eventually enters a wide valley where it becomes much shallower. At the shallowest part stands the walled, red-roofed town of Beruna, by the fords of the same name.

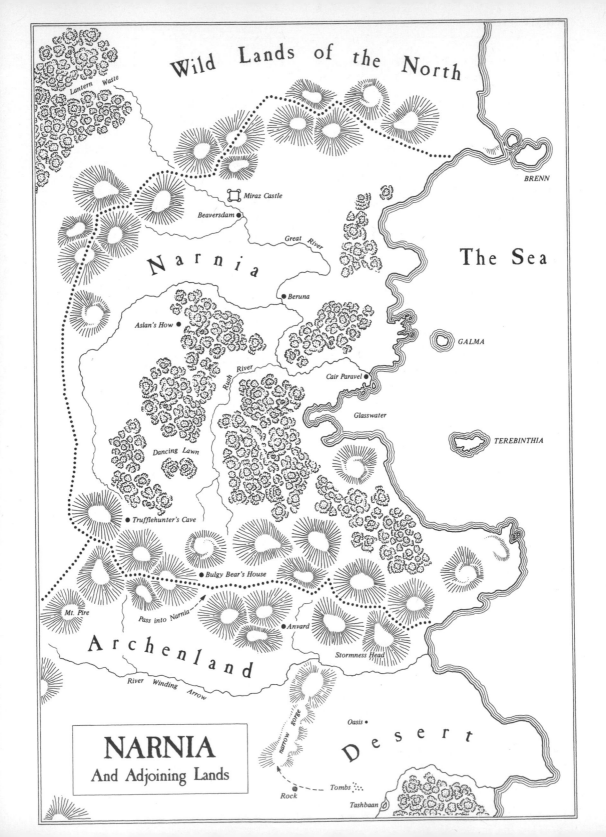

Wild Lands of the North

Lantern Waste

BRENN

Miraz Castle
Beaversdam

N a r n i a

Great River

The Sea

Beruna

Aslan's How

GALMA

Rush River

Cair Paravel

Glasswater

TEREBINTHIA

Dancing Lawn

Trufflehunter's Cave

Bulgy Bear's House

Mt. Pire
Pass into Narnia

Anvard

Stormness Head

A r c h e n l a n d

River Winding Arrow

narrow gorge

Oasis

D e s e r t

Tombs

Rock

Tashbaan

NARNIA
And Adjoining Lands

Below Beruna, the Great River is joined by the Rush and then meanders through extensive forests before finally reaching the sea at Cair Paravel, capital of Narnia. Most of the country's coastline is wooded, although to the north-east the coastal forest soon gives way to a wide area of treeless marshland, with countless small islands and channels of water. The great mountains to the west loom over the Western Wild, a region of high hills and broken mountain ranges against a background of ice mountains, always visible in the distance.

The land of Narnia was created—not founded—by Aslan, a great lion from a country beyond the end of the world (see ASLAN'S COUNTRY). Aslan was the son of the Great-Emperor-Beyond-the-Sea, the mysterious and all-powerful overlord of Narnia. The privileged few who have actually seen Aslan have been impressed by his mane and his eyes, and the way in which he combines massive physical strength with great gentleness and wisdom. But most impressive of all is Aslan's wonderful voice, with which he created Narnia by singing, summoning it up out of nothing. Legend has it that the song of creation had no words and hardly any tune, but that it was the most beautiful song ever heard, making stars, constellations and planets appear suddenly out of the darkness. As Aslan sang, the black sky turned grey and then changed from white to pink and from pink to gold, as does the rising sun. The valley of Narnia sprang from nowhere, and as Aslan began to pace up and down, singing a new and more lilting song, grass rose from the earth and quickly clothed the valley and the hills above. Trees began to grow, the song became wilder, the grassy land began to bubble and swell into humps; the swellings became bigger and bigger and finally burst, and an animal emerged from each and every hump, fully formed and active. The newly created creatures immediately went about their natural business: birds sang, bees fed on the pollen of flowers, frogs flopped into the river and panthers and leopards washed themselves and sharpened their claws on the tree trunks. And in the same manner, by the sound of his voice, Aslan created the wild people of the woods—the fauns, the satyrs and the dwarves. During these first days of creation, everything in Narnia grew spontaneously; a piece of metal quickly grew into a lamp post, gold and silver coins into gold and silver trees.

One of the most remarkable sights in the whole of Narnia is Aslan's How, a large artificial mound in the Great Woods, which visitors cannot afford to miss. The How stands on a hill above the forest and the sea can be seen from its summit. The How was built in ancient times and consists of a maze of tunnels, galleries and caves, entered by way of a low stone arch. All the tunnels are lined and roofed with smooth stones covered with strange characters and snaky lines among which the motif of a lion is repeated at frequent intervals. In the centre of the How is a chamber supported by pillars of ancient workmanship and housing a broken stone table split down the middle. Its surface is covered with writing that was almost completely worn away by the elements before the How was built over it. The How is a strange, awesome monument. It is associated with some of the most important events in Narnia's history which the inquisitive visitor should make an effort to study before journeying to this country, as it will provide a better understanding of Narnia's life-style and customs.

Narnia's history has been varied, years of peace and prosperity interspersed with years of barren disorder. Its historical records are somewhat patchy.

By the basic laws of Narnia, the land must always be ruled by a son of Adam. Aslan therefore established a government ruled by a cabman and his wife whom he crowned king and queen—King Frank and Queen Helen. (Visitors can admire their crowns, made by the dwarves from leaves of the tree of gold, and set with beautiful gems mined by the moles.) A council, with responsibility for safety, was also established and consisted of the chief of the dwarves, the river god, the owl, the ravens and the bull elephant. This court ruled Narnia, but was itself subject to the authority of the Great-Emperor-Across-the-Sea and his son, Aslan.

At one point in Narnia's history, the country came under the despotic rule of Jadis, the White Witch. It was transformed into a land of perpetual ice and snow, where it was always winter but never Christmas, and the Great River became a level floor of green ice. Legend had it that Aslan would return to put an end to the winter, assisted by four children from the world of men, and after a great battle, this prophecy was fulfilled. The four children took their thrones at Cair Paravel where they ruled Narnia for many years as joint monarchs. They were known as King Peter the Magnificent

The restored tower at the entrance of Cair Paravel, capital of NARNIA.

or High King, Queen Susan the Gentle, King Edmund the Just and Queen Lucy the Valiant. This was Narnia's celebrated Golden Age.

Cair Paravel originally stood on a small hill rising from a plain between two streams at the mouth of the Great River, but erosion has turned it into a small island. The original castle, built by the White Witch, has many towers and pointed spires and a great iron door set in a huge arch. Visitors can admire the roof of the castle's Great Hall, made of ivory, and its west wall, hung with peacock feathers. The entrance gate and tower were largely destroyed by Peter, in the final battle against the White Witch. The castle has now been restored to its former glory, although there are no records to indicate when or by whom the restoration work was carried out.

There are comparatively few buildings in Narnia. Apart from the castles at Cair Paravel and by Beaversdam, the only major settlement is the small, walled town of Beruna. Most of the creatures of the country prefer to live in trees or in burrows, although some, like the comfort-loving fauns, have well-furnished underground rooms with collections of books, such as *Nymphs and Their Ways* and *Is Man a Myth?*

It is worth noting the great variety of creatures that inhabit Narnia, ranging from rabbits and dogs to valiant unicorns who are almost invincible in battle. Of particular interest is the curious marsh-wiggle. Marsh-wiggles have small bodies, and immensely long arms and legs. Their skin is a muddy colour and their greeny-grey hair hangs down in flat locks, rather like weeds. As befits creatures who live in marshes, their hands and feet are webbed. They dress in earth-coloured clothes with pointed, wide-brimmed hats on their heads and are very difficult to detect in their normal surroundings, so well do they merge with the landscape. They live in wigwams scattered across the marsh, and cherish privacy. Marsh-wiggles take a most serious view of life and always expect the worst of misfortunes. They live on eels and frogs caught in the marshes and smoke a peculiar kind of tobacco mixed with mud. The smoke does not rise in the air, but trickles slowly downwards from their pipes.

The Eastern Sea provides a home for mermen and mermaids, while the forests are full of dryads and wood spirits, who are often difficult to distinguish from the trees they inhabit.

While the diet of most of the creatures is predictable and would not surprise the visitor, the habits of some are curious. The tree spirits, for instance, eat various kinds of soil, even at State banquets, but the feeding habits of the great centaurs are perhaps the strangest of all. Since a centaur has both a man's stomach and a horse's stomach, it has to eat twice. For breakfast, a centaur will eat porridge (and other normal breakfast foods) to fill his human stomach; to fill his horse's stomach, he will graze for an hour or so, and finish his meal with mashed oats and sugar. This is, of course, a very slow process and it does mean that having a centaur as a house guest is not something to be undertaken lightly.

The dwarves of Narnia are about four feet tall, and, for their size, they are among the strongest creatures in existence. They are brave and make excellent miners and smiths, although they can be truculent and unreliable.

One of the most intriguing customs of Narnia is the annual Great Snow Dance, held on the first moonlit night when there is snow on the ground. The fauns and dryads perform a complex dance, surrounded by a ring of dwarves, all dressed in their best scarlet clothes with fur hoods and furry top-boots, who throw snowballs in time to the music. If all the dancers are perfectly in position, no one is hit. This is, however, a game as well as a dance, and from time to time, a dancer will get slightly out of step and will be hit by a snowball, much to the amusement of all concerned. A good team of dancers, musicians and dwarves can, if they wish, continue for hours without anyone ever being hit.

The forest dwellers are also fond of midnight dances, when the nymphs from the wells and the dryads from the trees join the fauns in their revels. Treasure-seeking in the mines and caverns, with red dwarves as guides, is another popular pastime. In summer, the arrival of old Silenus riding on his donkey (and sometimes of Bacchus himself) heralds weeks of fun when the streams of Narnia run with wine.

The ceremonies of Cair Paravel are noted for their splendour. Supper in the castle illustrates admirably the glory and courtesy of the Narnians at home in their own land. The Great Hall is decked with banners hanging from the roof; each course is ushered in to the loud sound of trumpets and kettle-drums. After the meal, which consists of a bewildering variety of dishes and refreshments, the evening is spent in listening to poetry and story-telling.

The departure or arrival of the king, especially by sea, is a truly spectacular event. The king and his courtiers are all richly dressed in their brightly coloured clothes and the ships are decked with glorious banners. The people gather in great numbers to bid farewell or welcome to their ruler. Narnian ships are works of art in their own right. The *Splendour Hyaline,* on which High King Peter sailed to the LONE ISLANDS, is built in the shape of a swan. The prow is a swan's head and the carved wings curve back almost to the waist of the ship. With her sails of silk, the ship looks very much like a real swan sailing across the water. The *Dawn Treader* is built in the form of a dragon, the gilded head forming the prow, the wings, the sides of the ship and the tail, the stern. It has one mast and a large square sail of rich purple. The lookout stands on a little shelf inside the dragon's neck and peers out through the mouth.

Time in Narnia is not on the same continuum as time in other countries. No matter how long one spends inside Narnia, one returns only a moment after one has left the world of men. Similarly, it is almost impossible to tell how time is progressing in Narnia; three years or a hundred years may have passed in the equivalent of one year elsewhere.

Narnia can be reached in a variety of ways. Those humans present at its creation went there by way of the Wood Between the Worlds, using magic rings to transport them. Access has also been gained through the back of a wardrobe made of wood grown from a Narnian apple pip, but those summoned by Aslan in time of great need or danger do not need artificial aids—they are transported to Narnia directly by his power, and may return by the same means. It appears that there may be a low age limit on entry into the country, although definite information on this point is difficult to come by.

(C.S. Lewis, *The Lion, the Witch and the Wardrobe,* London, 1950; C.S. Lewis, *Prince Caspian,* London, 1951; C.S. Lewis, *The Voyage of the "Dawn Treader,"* London, 1952; C.S. Lewis, *The Silver Chair,* London, 1953; C.S. Lewis, *The Horse and His Boy,* London, 1954; C.S. Lewis, *The Magician's Nephew,* London, 1955; C.S. Lewis, *The Last Battle,* London, 1956)

NATURE THEATRE OF OKLAHOMA, see OKLAHOMA, NATURE THEATRE OF.

NAUDELY, an island some three months' sail

from Amsterdam. From the sea, travellers will be able to distinguish the pleasant city of Merinda, set among green mountains. Merinda is famous for its gilded bell towers, its wide, straight avenues and the beautiful octagonal Place du Tucolas. Many obelisks and fountains enhance the city's architecture.

The inhabitants are Catholics, silent and austere. Their moral education is so strict that no thieves, philanderers or hypocrites are found among the population, not even in the army. The prerogatives of noble birth must be confirmed by an examination of the candidate's virtues. This takes place amid much rejoicing and celebration and the new nobility is received in Merinda by a loudly cheering public. Only princes of royal blood need not submit to this examination.

No one is allowed to own more than twice the amount of land needed by a normal family. Artisans and peasants are helped by the State in difficult times; these payments are made from a Mutual Help Fund set up for the purpose. Visitors will find no beggars, swindlers or prostitutes throughout the entire island.

(Pierre de' Lesconvel, *Idée D'Un Regne Doux Et Heureux, Ou Relation Du Voyage du Prince de Montberaud dan l'Ile de Naudely*, Paris, 1703)

NAUTILUS HARBOUR, an underground port located inside an extinct volcano, accessible via an underwater passage and used as a base for the *Nautilus* submarine of Captain Nemo (see also ARABIAN TUNNEL and LINCOLN ISLAND). However, it is not certain whether the volcano is located in the Canaries or the Cape Verde Islands.

The inside of the volcano is a vast lagoon with a diameter of nearly two miles and a circumference of six; its waters are at sea level. The walls around it form a kind of funnel some six hundred metres high.

Near the volcano, under the sea, lie important deposits of coal which the crew of the *Nautilus* were able to mine.

(Jules Verne, *Vingt mille lieues sous les mers*, Paris, 1870)

NAVEL OF LIMBO, not to be confused with the Celtic Limbo where babies become abominably drunk; a worm-shaped country with such odiously

fragmented provinces that thinking here is no longer free, except in patches.

The inhabitants have string-tied packages in their brains, but the addresses which appear on these packages are unknown. The most important person is the Navel of Limbo himself, who is also the postman. He walks from house to house with his St. Patrick cane, invariably asking the same question: "A small gallows with a rose was sent to you from the asylum at Rodez. Did you receive it?"

(Antonin Artaud, *L'Ombilic des limbes*, Paris, 1925)

NAZAR, a subterranean country divided into several provinces or independent kingdoms. To reach Nazar, the traveller must pass through a crevasse in the mountains near Bergen, Norway. He will find himself surrounded by a kind of atmosphere, or "ether," which forms the Nazarian skies and which will cushion his fall.

Some of the more interesting provinces to visit are Crotchet Island, where the inhabitants are half human, half musical instruments—they ask in *adagio* and thank in *allegro*—and are capable of discussing questions of philosophy and finance; Martinia, a region of civilized apes who despise slow thinking; the province of Potu, which is inhabited by trees that move and talk; Jochtan, where all opinions are accepted and tolerance is declared to be the highest civic virtue; and Cocklev, a region ruled by women. A disapproving visitor to Cocklev observed that the government here was in "a tottering condition by the admission of women to the management of public affairs, that sex being naturally ambitious, still aiming to extend their power, nor ever resting till they have acquired a full and absolute authority."

One Norwegian traveller, Nicholas Klim, visited Nazar in the early eighteenth century, published an acid *Essay on Women*, and tried to overthrow the Cocklevian government. For this he was "exiled in the heavens" (a Cocklevian punishment consisting of being thrown into a cage, fastened to a gigantic bird and left to float in the "ether"). He managed to escape and found his way to the kingdom of Quama where he taught the people how to make arms and use them against their neighbours. He was appointed Emperor of the Quamite People, but a revolution forced him to flee and seek refuge in the woods. Here Klim

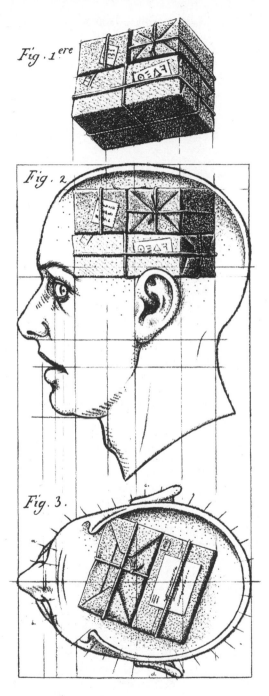

Fig. 1ere

Fig. 2

Fig. 3

A diagram of an average brain in the NAVEL OF LIMBO.

found a cavern that led him back to Europe, where he wrote the story of his remarkable adventures.

(Baron Ludvig Holberg, *Nicolai Klimii Iter Subterraneum Novam Telluris Theoriam Ac Historiam Quintae Monarchiae Adhuc Nobis Incognitae Exhibens E Bibliotheca B. Abelini,* Copenhagen, 1741)

NEN HITHOEL, a long oval lake on the GREAT RIVER in the south of MIDDLE-EARTH, surrounded by the steep hills of EMYN MUIL. The river enters the lake from the north, flowing through a long chasm in the rock. At the entrance to the chasm stand two great stone figures, the Argonath, their left hands raised in warning and their right hands holding axes. Both figures wear crowns and helmets, though these are now badly worn. The statues, which are carved out of the rock face, represent Isildur and Anárion, the sons of Elendil, founder of the ancient kingdom of GONDOR, who ruled the kingdom jointly in the Second Age. Built to mark the northern frontier of Gondor, they forbid all but legitimate travellers to pass through.

At the southern end of the lake, there are three peaks. One is an island, rising sheer from the water; this is Tol Brandir or the Tindrock, on which, it is said, no man or beast has ever set foot. From the banks of the river rise the peaks known as Amon Lhâw and Amon Hen, the hills of hearing and sight. On the summit of Amon Hen there is a wide paved circle, surrounded by a crumbling battlement. In the centre, steps lead up to a high seat supported by four pillars. This is the seat of seeing, which affords a view over hundreds of square miles of Middle-earth. It is so high that, from here, the MISTY MOUNTAINS look like broken teeth. To the west, ROHAN and Isengard can be seen, while to the south it is possible to see Ethir Anduin, the delta of the Great River, and the sea itself. Farther inland, across the river, is the city of MINAS TIRITH, while to the south-west the sinister land of MORDOR is plainly visible.

(J.R.R. Tolkien, *The Fellowship of the Ring,* London, 1954)

NEOPIE ISLAND, off the coast of the continent of GENOTIA in the south Atlantic, divided into three kingdoms: Salvara, Doxeros and Gynomactide. In this third kingdom legend has it that the Amazons (see AMAZONIA) once ruled over the natives with great cruelty and injustice. When the Gynomactidians finally expelled the invaders, they vowed to kill all foreign women who fell into their hands. This they do with great glee, especially—for luck—before a battle. Female travellers are therefore advised to keep away from this island.

(Louis Adrien Duperron de Castera, *Le Theatre Des Passions Et De La Fortune Ou Les Avantures Surprenantes de Rosamidor & de Theoglaphire, Histoire Australe*, Paris, 1731)

NEPENTHE, an island in the Tyrrhenian Sea, within sight of the Italian mainland. Nepenthe is famed for its sea cliffs, best seen from a boat.

Because of the island's volcanic origin, the colour of the rocks varies and provides a spectacular range of tints. Feathery white pumice mingles with the greys and browns of the stone, which is sometimes shot with brightly coloured veins. The cliffs have been worn into fantastic shapes, with needle-like pinnacles towering above the clefts and caves which open out at water-level. The height of the cliffs is fearsome, particularly towards the point known as the Devil's Rock or Suicide Rock, where the fall is almost perfectly vertical. The rock itself is a dark blue-black spotted with reddish patches, as though blood had somehow oozed out of the stone itself. This is the last outpost of the spectacular cliff scenery; beyond it the land falls to the sea in a series of earthen slopes broken by ravines where the winter rain has carried away the loose soil. For most of the year these watercourses are dry, as there is no natural running water on Nepenthe.

In the past there were at least twelve natural springs on the island, all producing an unpleasant-tasting water which had a marked fetid smell and was not fit for drinking. However, they were regarded as having curative properties; the Fountain of St. Calogero, for instance, was claimed to relieve gout, labour pains, leprosy and the sting of scorpions. The tartaric water of the Fountain of Hercules was a certain remedy for everything from apoplexy to piles and chilblains, while the very smell of the water from the Fountain of St. Feto is said to have raised one Anna da Pasto from the dead. Gradually, however, the fountains all dried up and even their sites have now been forgotten. The last to disappear was the St. Elias fountain

which in the seventeenth and eighteenth centuries attracted so many visitors that a palatial pump room had to be built. For unexplained reasons, this water, famed for its beneficial effect on those suffering from the consequences of excessive lechery and alcohol, lost favour with the public by the mid-nineteenth century. The ruined pump room can still be seen next to the Devil's Rock, a decayed and totally unromantic structure on a treeless eminence.

Because of the absence of streams, the gardens for which Nepenthe is so famed have to be watered by artificial fountains fed by complex pumping mechanisms which tap subterranean reservoirs of winter rains. Perhaps the best example of the use of these fountains is the Villa Khismet, a palace laid out in Moorish style, with a maze of marble-paved chambers opening onto one another. The Villa's garden is a mock wilderness of trees and flowering plants which flourish in the prevailing sirocco, watered by no fewer than twenty-four fountains which also help to make the air cool and moist.

It is generally held that the absence of running water, together with the volcanic soil, accounts for the excellence of Nepenthe's wine. The best varieties are produced in the mountain areas, particularly the lava crags which overhang the sea in the eastern part of the island.

The main town on the island, also known as Nepenthe, is a bright jumble of houses built from volcanic tufa with roads and streets of black lava. Many are whitewashed, but others reveal the red building stone. Seen from above, the houses seem to be totally overgrown by their vines, cacti and flower gardens. The bright paintwork of the porches and the flowers in the window-boxes all add to the riot of colour. The Old Town, higher up, is more restrained. It is surrounded by trees and, unlike the modern town, faces due north. Originally built as a citadel to protect the islanders from pirate raids, it fell into decline as times became more peaceful and it seemed more practical to live by the sea. The decline was halted by Grand Duke Alfred, to whom the Old Town owes its present state. The duke constructed the circular walls and battlemented gates and towers that ring the city, for decorative rather than defensive purposes. All houses which did not fit in with the new structure were demolished. The Duke also insisted that all buildings in the Old Town be painted pink, and that colour has now become traditional; even the Benedictine and Carthusian convents have pink façades. Much of the eighteenth-century walls have now fallen into ruin and many of the older buildings have been abandoned, but the Old Town still retains an air of aristocratic mellowness.

Much of the island's social life centres on the piazza or marketplace, a pleasant square surrounded on three sides by the main public buildings and open on the fourth side to a view of the sea. It is the custom for people to gather here in the morning to gossip, watch new arrivals from the port and exchange news. The custom means that little work is done in the mornings (most of the afternoon is taken up by the obligatory siesta) and typifies the leisurely, sensual life of the island. From the terraces of the marketplace one has extensive views over the green farmland of the lower areas of the island; the mainland and the volcano which dominates its coastline can be seen quite clearly from here.

The volcano has in the past directly affected life on Nepenthe. A cloud of dust which rose from it in the early stages of an eruption settled on the island, covering all the fields and threatening to destroy the crops. The disaster was averted by a sudden heavy rain which was attributed to the intervention of the island's patron saint, St. Dodekanus, who had been a missionary in the land of the CROTALOPHOBOI. St. Dodekanus had eventually been killed and eaten by cannibals, but his femur had been miraculously preserved and the sacred relic is still kept in the church dedicated to the saint and carried abroad on the annual festival or on any other occasion when the saint's assistance is required. A frieze of marble tablets in the church illustrates the main events in the saint's life. It was commissioned by Great Duke Alfred, who later had the eyes and hands of the sculptor removed so that no other monarch could possess work by such a consummate artist. In compensation, the artist was given the Order of the Golden Vine and was fed on the island's famous lobsters until his death.

The annual festival of the saint begins with the sounding of bells and the firing of guns and mortars. The noise is so great that visitors might be excused for thinking that an earthquake was taking place. During the feast an image of the saint is carried through the streets by men who pay a heavy sum for the privilege. In return, they are granted remission of their sins for a period of twelve months.

The sailors of Nepenthe have their own patron saint, St. Eulalia, born in the Spanish province of Estremadura in 1712. St. Eulalia is know principally for her self-imposed sufferings, which she began as a child by eating only once every five weeks. She died at the age of fourteen, but performed numerous miracles during her brief life. It is said that her corpse became rosy and gave off an odour of violets for twenty weeks after her death. When it was dissected, an image of St. James of Compostela was found in her liver. The reasons for the sailors' choice of patron remains obscure, but an account of her life and of the cult surrounding her can be read in a pamphlet by Don Giacinto Mellion.

Although Nepenthe is Catholic, it also provides a home for members of a Russian sect founded by one Bazhakuloff, a mystic who rose to great power in the czarist court and was then banished as a result of political pressure. He eventually fled from Russia when threatened with assassination. Before leaving, he instructed his followers not to eat the flesh of warm-blooded beasts; this led to great unrest in the army as the soldiers refused to eat the food supplied to them.

Bazhakuloff settled on the island of Nepenthe, perhaps because of his great appetite for fish and lobster. His followers refer to themselves as the Little White Cows and are readily distinguished by their red blouses.

One of the noted curiosities of Nepenthe is the so-called Cave of Mercury, a remote grotto which is popularly believed to have been used for human sacrifices in ancient times. No satisfactory explanation has been given for its name. Great Duke Alfred caused a flight of stairs to be built down to the cave and is said to have frequented it for reasons of his own. People say that here he revived the old bloodthirsty rites, but there is no evidence to support that legend. The cave is now abandoned and is usually avoided by the islanders. It has become proverbial—for instance, anything disreputable or improbable is dismissed with the phrase "Such things only happen in the Cave of Mercury."

One of the island's numerous caverns has been converted into a restaurant and is commonly known as *Luisella's Grotto*. The grotto lies deep below the island's pumice stone and is ventilated by an opening to the sea. The natural rock vault-ing has been whitewashed and painted with pic-tures of fish and animals. The restaurant is par-ticularly celebrated for its lobster dishes and its cold fish.

Curious travellers are informed that a stan-dard account of Nepenthe's earlier history and customs is given in Perrelli's *Antiquities of Ne-penthe.* Written in Latin, this appears to be the au-thor's only work and was last printed in 1709.

(Norman Douglas, *South Wind,* London, 1917)

NEPREKLONSK, see GLOUPOV.

NESHUM, see OSSKIL.

NEVER-NEVER LAND, an island of uncertain location. No female visitors are allowed. Access to Never-Never Land is obtained by one of three means. It is sometimes seen by children as they hover on the edge of sleep; in this case, Never-Never Land presents itself to the sleeper, rather than being sought by him. It can be reached by baby boys who fall out of their perambulators while their nurses are not looking (they come mainly from Kensington Gardens, London); if no one collects them during the following week, they are sent to Never-Never Land, where they become Lost Boys. (Girls are said to be too intelligent to fall out in the first place.) Finally, visitors can be taken to Never-Never Land by a never-aging boy, Peter Pan, who refuses to grow up and claims to have run away the day he was born. Peter Pan has all his first teeth, retains his first childish laugh and can fly with the aid of magic dust, which he also sprinkles on his guests. The only girl known to have visited Never-Never Land is Wendy Dar-ling who, accompanied by her two smaller broth-ers, was asked to go to the island to be a mother to the Lost Boys.

The Lost Boys live in an underground house entered through the trunks of seven hollow trees. The only other outlet is a chimney disguised as a chimney. The whole house consists of one large room, in the middle of which stands a *never tree* which is sawn down level with the floor each day; by tea time it has grown high enough to use as a table, and after tea it is cut down again to make more room for playing games. Around the tree

grow mushrooms used for stools. When the Lost Boys wish to go fishing they simply dig holes in the floor. They sleep in a large bed which is tilted against the wall during the day-time and let down at 6:30 each evening; it takes up almost half the room when it is down. Although the bed is crowded, the Lost Boys have reached an agree-ment by which they all turn over at the same time when a signal is given.

Though some of the meals eaten by the Lost Boys are make-believe, they usually live on a diet of breadfruit, yams, coconuts, baked pig and ba-nanas, the whole washed down with calabash or paw-paw juice. They dress in the skins of bears that they have killed themselves; their clothes make them so round and furry that if they fall over, they roll away. As a result, they have become very sure-footed. Peter Pan is their leader, and very little occurs in Never-Never Land while he is away. He entertains the Lost Boys by playing his pipes and by telling them stories he picks up from listening at other children's bedrooms at nighttime.

Never-Never Land is also inhabited by a tribe of Red Indians, the Piccanniny tribe, renowned for their cruelty. They adorn their bodies with paint and oil and carry knives and tomahawks for taking scalps. Their chief is Great Big Little Panther, fa-ther of the beautiful Tiger Lily. So great is her re-luctance to marry that she is said to "stave off the altar with the hatchet." Since Tiger Lily was res-cued from pirates by Peter Pan, the Indians have been friends and allies of the Lost Boys.

The island was known in the past to be a haunt of pirates, notably the infamous Captain Hook and the agreeable Smee. Peter Pan once cut off Hook's hand and gave it to a gigantic crocodile, who enjoyed it so much that it decided to pursue Captain Hook in order to get the rest of him. But the crocodile had once swallowed an alarm clock, and its ticking warned Hook when the crocodile was coming. In the end it did eat him, after he was defeated by Peter Pan. The pirates' favourite occu-pations used to be kidnapping people and making them walk the plank.

The coral caves beneath the lagoon are the homes of the mermaids, beautiful creatures who spend their days basking in the sun and combing their hair. Though beautiful, the mermaids are known to be unfriendly and malicious, and are probably distantly related to the good mermaids

NEVER-NEVER LAND

of MERKING'S KINGDOM. Visitors can sometimes see them play a version of football, using the bubbles left behind by rain storms. The goals are at both ends of the rainbow and the players hit the bubbles with their tails. Only the goalkeepers are allowed to use their hands.

Never-Never Land is also the abode of fairies, who live in nests in the tree tops. Boy fairies wear mauve, and girl fairies white, though some silly fairies insist on wearing blue. Fairies shine all the time they are awake, providing a natural illumination for their nests.

One of the most famous of all fairies is Tinker Bell, who for a long time was Peter Pan's companion. Fairies, as a general rule, do not live much longer than a year. A fairy is born every time a new-born baby laughs; one dies every time a child says that he or she does not believe in fairies. A well-known method for restoring a fairy's life consists of clapping one's hands; massive séances are held at Christmas-time, mainly in England, for this purpose and are commonly known as "pantomimes."

The fauna of Never-Never Land includes a vast range of predators and man-eaters, from bears and wolves to lions and tigers. The island is also the only known haunt of the *never bird*, which nests in a hat floating in the lagoon. Peter Pan sometimes borrows the hat (replacing it with a floating nest) and wears it for special occasions.

(Sir James Matthew Barrie, *Peter Pan, or the Boy Who Wouldn't Grow Up,* London, 1904; Sir James Matthew Barrie, *Peter Pan in Kensington Gardens,* London, 1906; Sir James Matthew Barrie, *Peter and Wendy,* London, 1911)

NEVERREACHHERELAND, a small country of uncertain location, surrounded by a large forest. A curious meadow opens into a clearing with a few oak trees, chestnut trees and palm trees. Beyond lies a blue sea, and an apple orchard growing on a patch of black earth. A little stream runs through the country and plunges into the sea over the horizon. A small bay in the north lies sprinkled with waterlilies and lotuses, surrounded by coconut and orange trees above which rises a huge castle. On the other side of the forest is a small village, from which Neverreachhereland can be sighted. Though the country cannot actually be visited, it can sometimes be seen through the vivid memory of something dear—a children's book, dried flowers in a diary, the branch of an apple tree seen through the curtains of someone else's room.

(André Dhôtel, *Les Pays où l'on n'arrive jamais,* Paris, 1955)

NEVERWHERE, a land beneath London, England, whose districts coincide with the stations of the Underground train system. Not everyone can visit Neverwhere. Some are told of their journey by a strange old woman who reads their palm and tells them their fortune.

Visitors who enter Neverwhere are then forgotten in their own world, which the people of Neverwhere call Above; it is as if they had never lived there, and they become both invisible and inaudible to anyone except the inhabitants of Neverwhere. However, the walls of Neverwhere's buildings retain memories of the past, so that visitors exploring the land may suddenly be struck by painful images of terrible deeds committed in times gone by. Neverwhere is lit by candle-light. The local speciality is cat stew, said to be extremely tasty.

When visiting Neverwhere, it is a good idea to contract the services of a bodyguard such as the notorious Marquis of Carabas. This is done at one of the floating markets, large get-togethers where services are exchanged and a general truce is established between enemies. Visitors will find rats

The giant metal furnace in NEVERWHERE.

serviceable assistants, though a working knowledge of rat-talk is advisable. Neverwhere is a dangerous place; in case of an accident, it is wise to repair to the monks who run an efficient care unit beneath the Underground station of Blackfriars.

Certain areas of Neverwhere are best avoided. For instance, the old firm of the brothers Mr. Croup and Mr. Vandemar ("Obstacles Obliterated, Nuisances Eradicated, Bothersome Limbs Removed and Tutelary Dentistry") has an unwholesome reputation. The firm occupies the cellar of a Victorian hospital, closed down because of National Health cutbacks, and consists of deserted hospital wards divided into more than a hundred rooms, some empty, others full of hospital supplies. In one room is a giant metal furnace; in another are the blocked and waterless toilets and showers. Visitors willing to brave the dangers of this section of Neverwhere should walk down the hospital steps as far as possible, cross the abandoned shower rooms and pass the staff toilets and a room full of broken glass where the ceiling has collapsed entirely, to reach a small, rusting iron staircase from which the once-white paint is peeling in long, damp strips. They should then traverse the marshy area at the bottom of the steps and push their way through a half-decayed wooden door. They will find themselves in the sub-cellar, a huge room in which a hundred and twenty years of hospital waste has accumulated, abandoned and

eventually forgotten. This is where Mr. Croup and
Mr. Vandemar make their home. The walls are
very damp and water drips from the ceiling. Odd
things moulder in corners; some of them were
once alive.

(Neil Gaiman, *Neverwhere*, London, 1996)

NEW BRITAIN, a group of three islands in the
Indian Ocean, some three hundred and fifty
leagues east of the Cape of Good Hope. The first
of the three islands, Aprilis, was discovered in
1740 by Sir Charles Smith whose ship had left England with Anson's round-the-world expedition
but was forced to lag behind when disease reduced
the number of its crew. Smith was shipwrecked on
Aprilis and was rescued by a young native, Lillia,
who bore him a son. Smith convinced the island's
chieftain that he was the child of the sun-god and
commanded that Lillia's son be adopted by the
tribe. His popularity diminished when Lillia died
in childbirth, but he saved himself by prophesying
an earthquake, which he staged using gunpowder
saved from the wreck. After having successfully
repelled both a Spanish and a French invasion,
Smith established a model society which has come
to be recognized as a true international power.

Aprilis is divided by a mountain chain into a
zone of plains and a zone of forests. Several important cities—Burnel, Springle, Jarvis, Cuningham,
and Edinburgh—can be visited throughout the island. Charles Hire, the capital of Aprilis, took seven
years to build. The streets are twenty-four feet
wide, each with a row of trees down the middle, and
many public parks grace the city. The royal palace,
to which a French château wing was added, is a
large brick and wood building, two storeys high,
with a courtyard and a garden, and like all the
houses in Charles Hire, it is painted in stripes of
red, yellow and black. The form of government is
similar to the English parliamentary system. There
is no capital punishment, but flogging is quite common. Polygamy is permitted, but royal permission
must be obtained for a man to take more than five
wives. The National Theatre in Charles Hire produces a type of drama which combines comic opera,
ballet and mime and in which nudes were presented
as early as the eighteenth century. A new opera
house was built in 1781. Travellers are also advised
to visit the natural triangular amphitheatre in
Springle, famous for its ballet.

The official Aprilian religion is sun-worship,

The Queen of NEW BRITAIN'S trident.

but nowadays many people are Christians. Of particular note is the beautiful Temple of the Sun, a
dome supported by brick pillars with a representation of the sun in the centre.

Aprilian fauna, similar to that of the other two
islands of the New Britain group, is unlike that of
any other place in the world. A black and white
bird, called a *tarlow*, about the size of a pheasant,
provides an excellent roast. There is a type of deer,
the *matouchi;* a fox, the *zotuane;* a white-furred
squirrel with red eyes, the *cerpedos;* a tall hare with

Indian Ocean

Cape of
Good Hope

1. Burnel
2. Springle
3. Jarvis
4. Cuningham
5. Edinburgh

APRILIS

●1

Charles
● Hire
●2

●5
●3

4

ROCK ISLAND

PULLOSIN

SARCOSA

● Rasilinette

NEW BRITAIN ISLANDS

a tail like a cat, the *charlas;* a friendly nightingale, the *plicha;* a large blue and red dove, the *pililli.* The forty-feet-long snakes are innocuous.

The other two islands in the New Britain group are Sarcosa, very mountainous and inhabited by dark-skinned people; and Pullosin, a flat wooded island—capital, Rasilinette—the largest of the three. Pullosin is governed by women who keep men as slaves. The insignia of the queen is a golden trident and she is carried on a throne of gold by twelve strong men. (It is rumoured, though, that a male revolt has put an end to the reign of women in Pullosin and that the queen has surrendered her arms and gone back to care for her kitchen.)

Some historians attribute the discovery of the New Britain Islands not to Sir Charles Smith, but to an English expedition in search of the great Southern Continent whose existence was postulated by Sir Isaac Newton. They claim that the expedition set up a post on one of the islands, informing visitors that it was British territory. A Queen Anne farthing, an Irish harp and a Scottish banknote are said to have been buried under the post by the discoverers.

The currency of Aprilis is guineas and half guineas in gold. All visitors must go into quarantine upon arrival and will not be allowed to enter the country until they have a certificate of good health.

(Pierre Chevalier Duplessis, *Mémoires De Sir George Wollap; Ses Voyages dans différéntes parties du Monde; aventures extraordinaires qui lui arrivent; découverte de plusieurs Contrées inconnues; description des moeurs et des coutumes des Habitans. Par M.L.C.D.,* Paris, 1787–88; Charles Dibdin, *Hannah Hewit; Or, The Female Crusoe. Being The History Of A Woman Of uncommon, mental, and personal accomplishments; Who, After a variety of extraordinary and interesting adventures in almost every station of life, from splendid prosperity to abject adversity, Was Cast Away In The Grosvenor East-Indiaman: And became for three years the sole inhabitant of An Island In The South Seas. Supposed To Be Written By Herself,* London, 1796)

NEW GYNIA or VIRAGINIA,

NEW GYNIA or VIRAGINIA, a state located in *terra australis incognita.* This land extends from south of the Indian Ocean to the Indonesian Archipelago. It includes, off its coasts, Hermaphrodite Island (not to be confused with the HERMAPHRODITE ISLAND sometimes found off the coast of Portugal). The land is fertile, but put to poor use.

The principal provinces are Plapperfeldt (Linguadotia), Balgern (Rixatia), Heulenberg (Ploravia), Lachfurt (Risia Major and Minor), Merrenland (Aphrodisia), Sheemenland (Amazonia), Piouswomenland (Eugenia) and Hermaphrodite Island. The capital of Viraginia lies in the province of Linguadotia and is named Gynaecopolis (City of Women). Here Parliament sits without interruption, for in Viraginia there can be no discrimination in the exercise of power. Every woman has the right to speak and everything serves as a pretext for a dispute, discussion or vote. The debates are endless and the participants all talk at once. In order to ensure a certain degree of stability, once a decision is taken it cannot be revoked until the following day. Officials are elected according to their beauty and eloquence, a jury of elderly matrons having been selected to perform this important task.

The most remarkable of all of the country's provinces is Aphrodisia. Here, in the city of Erotio, the women wear extreme amounts of make-up, dress in very fine, transparent materials and walk about with their breasts bared. They live in glass houses; however, none of them ever appears in public before she has put on her makeup and done her hair. They devote the entire day to doing their shopping in order to be sure that they are seen.

Like spiders, they watch for the men from Locania and Lustland, with whom they are constantly at war. When their provocative gestures succeed in putting one of these men at their mercy, they force him to serve their desires. They keep such men in their stables and fatten them up with strong love-potions.

Hermaphrodite Island is another province of Viraginia. Everything there has a double nature: apple-and-pear trees, cherry-and-plum trees, almond-and-date trees, etc. Each inhabitant dresses half in men's clothing, half in women's, and has both a male and a female first name. These islanders do not require a partner to produce a child, and regard unisexual humans as monsters.

(Joseph Hall, *Mundus alter et idem, sive Terra Australis ante hac semper incognita,* London, circa 1605; *Utopiae, Pars II. Mundus alter et idem. Die heutige neue alte Welt. Darinnen ausführlich und nach Notdurf erzählt wird, was die alte nun bald sechstausend-jährige Welt für eine neue Welt geboren, aus der man gleichsam in einem Spiegel ihrer Mutter und Gebärerin Art, Sitten, Wandel und Gebrauch augenscheinlich mag sehen und erkennen,* Leipzig, 1613)

NEW PARIS, capital of ANTARCTIC FRANCE.

NEW POPSIPETEL, see SPIDERMONKEY ISLAND.

NEW SWITZERLAND, a beautiful, fertile area on a large island somewhere in the region of New Guinea. The island as a whole has not been fully explored and only New Switzerland is known in any detail.

Most of New Switzerland is enclosed by a natural rocky barrier which excludes the most dangerous species of animals found farther inland. A narrow pass, known simply as the Gap, leads through the rock-wall to an area of rolling country which gives way to a great plain crossed by the East River. The river, which flows through magnificent forests, is thought to rise in the foothills of the mountain chain that can be seen extending into the distance. Part of the foothill region has been explored. The best-known inland area is the

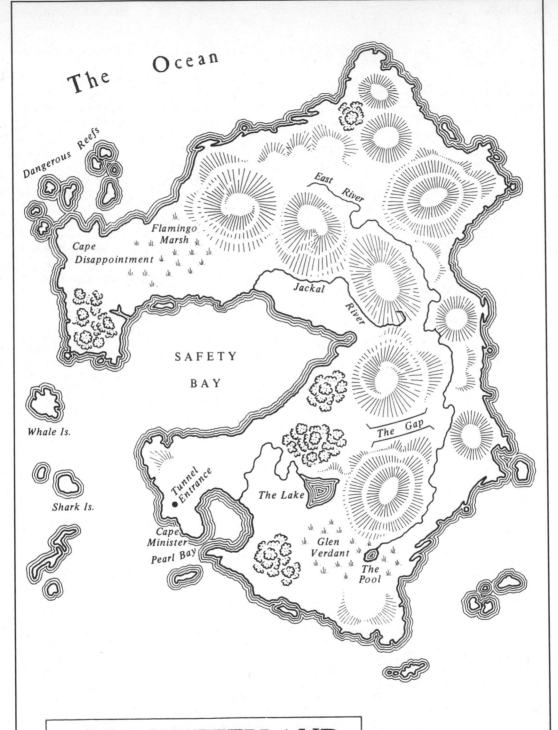

The Ocean

Dangerous Reefs

East River

Flamingo Marsh

Cape Disappointment

Jackal River

SAFETY BAY

Whale Is.

The Gap

Shark Is.

Tunnel Entrance

The Lake

Cape Minister Pearl Bay

Glen Verdant

The Pool

NEW SWITZERLAND

marshy zone around the pool in Glen Verdant; the Glen itself opens into a number of narrow gorges.

The coast of New Switzerland is mostly rocky, but the sheltered Safety Bay provides a natural landing-place; a stream known as the Jackal River flows down into the bay. Shark Island, a small islet in the bay, guards the entrance to this natural anchorage. Farther along the coast, the promontory of Cape Disappointment stretches out into the sea. The Cape is dangerous, surrounded by hidden reefs which run far out towards the deeper waters, as well as by a long sandbank. Its rocky summit provides fine views along the coast as far as the next headland.

Inland the ground is covered in dense thickets and small woods, broken by the reedy swamp of Flamingo Marsh. The wooded area gradually gives way to plains where wild cotton and rice grow abundantly. There is an attractive lake in this area. Beyond the plains, travellers should visit a large natural grotto of rock crystal through which flows a clear brook.

Beside Safety Bay, opposite Cape Disappointment, the cliffs rise sheer from the water; in some places rugged rocks overhang the sea. The area is known as Cape Minster, and is crossed by a natural tunnel entered through a rock arch. The tunnel will lead the visitor to a large, almost landlocked bay whose shoreline extends in a fertile plain towards the mouth of a river. This is Pearl Bay: a line of reefs and sandbanks separates it from the open sea, with only one narrow channel between the headlands that enclose it. The ground beyond the river is rough and marshy, but eventually gives way to a cedar forest. On the other side of the bay, the shore is sandy. Inland there are dense forests crossed by occasional streams and rivers.

The vegetation of New Switzerland is tropical and includes coconut palms, bamboo, mangrove trees and a type of evergreen oak. Rubber, bananas, tea, rice, sago, ginseng and guava all grow wild. A wide variety of spices and aromatic plants is also found.

The animal life is equally varied. Many of the species of the coast are typical of Australasia: kangaroos, black swans and what has been described as a "beast with a bill," probably a duck-billed platypus. Inland the fauna includes lions, tigers, tapirs, elephants, wolves and wild boars. Ostriches and antelopes can be found on the plains, while the forested areas provide a natural habitat for monkeys, apes and herds of peccaries. Iguanas are found here, but the only snake known to exist in New Switzerland is the boa constrictor. The marine life is equally rich, including seals and penguins. Salmon, herring, sturgeon and eels live in the waters of New Switzerland, as well as turtles and land-crabs. Sharks and whales have been seen in the coastal waters; both species have given their names to small offshore islands.

The region appears to be rich in minerals, although these have not been studied in detail and have never been commercially exploited. Known resources include asbestos, talc, mica and fuller's earth; there are also deposits of gypsum.

New Switzerland does not appear to have any aboriginal population and there are no signs of human life in the interior. The island was discovered when the family of a Swiss pastor was shipwrecked on its coast. The family established itself in the area and called it New Switzerland, making the colony an example of propriety, strict morals, hard work and studious dullness.

The climate of New Switzerland is tropical and the rainy season is exceptionally long.

(Johann David Wyss, *Der schweizerische Robinson, oder Der Schiffbruchige Schweizprediger und seine Familie. Ein lehrreiches Buch fur Kinder und Kinderfreunde*, Zurich, 1812–27)

NEXDOREA, an archduchy in central Europe, famous because it supplies the neighbouring countries with queens. All the female children of the archduke are turned loose in an old palace and park belonging to the ruling family. Here they are allowed to grow up without even being taught their own language. On reaching a marriageable age, they are duly catalogued and a description of their beauty is sent to all single potentates in the surrounding area. As soon as one of them is selected for marriage by one of the princes, she is transferred to the Royal Nursery Palace, where qualified masters and governesses speedily teach her the language of her future country and the accomplishments and manners in vogue there.

The arms of Nexdorea are gules, on a bend or, a goose and six gooselets waddlant in their pride proper; crest, a blue-nose baboon snorant proper in an armchair argent; supporters, two hen's eggs proper, cracked sable; Motto, *Poached or Pickled*. The chief product of Nexdorea is hen's eggs, hence the allusions to poultry in the arms. The Nexdorean currency is brass and German silver, which is not accepted in the neighbouring countries.

(Tom Hood, *Petsetilla's Posy*, London, 1870)

NGRANEK, a massive peak on the Isle of Oriab, in the SOUTHERN SEA of DREAMWORLD, two days' ride on horseback from the port of BAHARNA. Because the mountain is considered sacred by the inhabitants of Oriab, not much is known about its true geography. The men who collect Ngranek's ancient lava to carve their famous little figures do not climb its slopes beyond a certain point, and very few have ever dared climb to the top.

Those wishing to risk the journey must depart from the shores of Lake Yath near Bahama and cross a wild and wooded area to the camps of the lava-gatherers. These men do not recommend venturing out after dark, for they fear certain creatures called *night-gaunts* of which little is known except that they are cold, damp, slippery creatures with membraneous wings. Beyond the camp, travellers will reach, after a long uphill ride, the deserted brick villages of the hill-people who once dwelt here. These huts crept higher and higher up the mountain slope, but the higher the village extended, the more villagers were missing when the sun rose in the morning. At last it was decided to abandon the village altogether, since things which no one would talk about were sometimes glimpsed in the darkness.

From here onwards, Ngranek seems more menacing than ever. Sparse trees and feeble shrubs give way to hideous rocks mixed with frost and ice and eternal snow. In places, travellers will find solid streams of lava and scoria heaps littering slopes and ledges. In the caves along the path are horrors of a form not to be imagined. At last travellers will come upon an enormous carving in the bare stone of the mountain: a vast, haughty and majestic face, with long narrow eyes, long-lobed ears, thin nose and pointed chin. It is best to descend from here before nightfall; otherwise it will not be possible to avoid falling into the hands of the *night-gaunts*. They will tickle their victim with deliberation and bear him off to their monstrous labyrinths.

(Howard Phillips Lovecraft, "The Dream-Quest of Unknown Kadath," in *Arkham Sampler*, Sauk City, 1948)

NIGHT or **DREADFUL NIGHT, CITY OF,** somctimes also called **CITY OF DEATH,** girded by the River of Suicides. The river is the main north channel of a broad lagoon and it crosses black moorlands and marshes, and stony ridges before it reaches the city itself. North and west of the city lies a trackless wilderness of savannahs and savage woods, enormous mountains, bleak uplands and deep ravines. To the east is a sea never crossed by ships.

Though not in ruins itself, the city is filled with ruins. It is always shrouded in darkness—the sun never shines on the City of Night—but the sickly light of the street lamps will lead visitors through the narrow streets between immense silent mansions.

In the northern suburbs the city seems to disperse and a large palace rises solitary among wide gaping squares. High above the palace, upon the highest point of the whole city, stands a stupendous image of a winged woman, her cheek on her clenched left hand, her elbow on her knee; in her right hand she holds a pair of compasses across a clasped book. The instruments of carpentry and science are scattered at her feet; a grave and solid infant is perched beside her. Her name is Melencolia and she is the patroness and queen of the city, scanning her domain with full-set eyes.

The inhabitants of the City of Night are chiefly mature men, rarely a woman, now and then a child—all with worn faces that look deaf and blind like tragic masks of stone. They never sleep but wander through the long, dim, silent streets and countless lanes, and their feet make no sound on the stones. Travellers who see them will find that they will not speak and that they and their city will somehow confirm the travellers' old and perhaps hidden despair.

(James Thomson, *The City of Dreadful Night*, London, 1874)

NIGHT, KINGDOM OF, see HELIOPOLIS.

NIGHTMARE ABBEY, a venerable family mansion situated on a dry strip of land between the sea and the fens on the edge of Lincolnshire, England. It is in fact a castellated abbey in a highly picturesque state of semi-dilapidation standing in a moat which surrounds it on all sides but the south.

Nightmare Abbey is the seat of Christopher

Glowrey, Esquire. Interesting architectural features include the towers: the south-west tower, ruinous and full of owls; the south-east tower, used by Mr. Glowrey's son, the author of a treatise entitled *Philosophical Gas: or a Project for a general illumination of the human mind,* of which only seven copies were sold; the north-west tower, containing the apartments of Mr. Glowrey, which look out on the moat and the fens. The servants' apartments are in the north-east tower. The terrace, at the south-east corner, fronts onto a long tract of flat coast, and affords views of the sea and a fine monotony of fens and windmills. The terrace is known as the "garden," but the only things that grow here are ivy and amphibious weeds. The main body of the building is divided into state rooms, spacious dining rooms and numerous bedrooms. Mr. Glowrey's son built an entrance from his tower to a small suite of hidden apartments. The road leading to the abbey is artificially raised above the level of the fens. Nightmare Abbey is ten miles from the village of Claydyke.

Christopher Glowrey, author of a commentary on *Ecclesiastes* that demonstrates incontrovertibly that all is vanity, has described his house as a spacious kennel, where everyone leads a dog's life. Among the interesting objects which he has collected, and which can be viewed in Nightmare Abbey, is a punch bowl made out of the skull of an ancestor who hanged himself one rainy day in a fit of *taedium vitae.* The servants of the house are also of note as they are chosen for their long faces or dismal names: Raven the butler, Crow the steward, Skellet the valet (according to Mr. Glowrey, the latter was of French extraction and his real name was Squelette), Mattocks and Graves, the grooms. One would-be footman by the name of Diggory Deathshead was discharged because of his cheerful expression, but not before he made conquests of all the maids, leaving a colony of young Deathsheads at the Abbey.

Nightmare Abbey is haunted by the spirit of black melancholy, and visitors are warned that it eventually affects all guests.

(Thomas Love Peacock, *Nightmare Abbey*, London, 1818)

NIMMR, one of two cities in the Valley of the Sepulchre, in Africa. During the reign of Richard I some crusaders were shipwrecked on the Mediterranean coast, marched south and divided into two parties. One believed they had reached the site of the Holy Sepulchre and founded the city of Nimmr to protect it. The other party was sceptical, and established itself at the opposite end of the valley to prevent the people of Nimmr from escaping and returning to England before fulfilling their quest. The inhabitants are known today as the Fronters and the Backers respectively. They preserve all the customs of the twelfth century and hold a tourney every year between members of both groups. Travellers are invited to take part in the contest and are sometimes honoured by being made knights.

(Edgar Rice Burroughs, *Tarzan Lord of the Jungle,* New York, 1928)

NIMPATAN, a large island in the south Atlantic, with an extremely rugged coastline, surrounded by precipitous cliffs. Beyond the cliffs lie barren mountains and a desolate plain, separated from the fertile centre of the island by a second ring of mountains. This central countryside is very beautiful, a tapestry of woods and farmlands, with scattered farmhouses and villages. The capital, Kelso, lies far inland, but unlike its surroundings, Kelso is both ugly and depressing. Its narrow, dirty streets are lined with overcrowded houses and in the poorer sections as many as twenty or thirty people live in an area of less than five square yards. The public buildings are a clumsy, graceless style, and even the palace of the Emperor is little more than a squalid jumble of low, dirty hovels.

The Nimpatanese are an inhospitable people who treat the few travellers who reach their country very badly. Visitors are booed in the streets and even pelted with rubbish as they pass through the towns and villages, unless they arrive with gold. Gold is the god of the Nimpatanese, who quite literally worship it and treat it as other nations treat their divinities. A traveller who arrives with it will be accorded the highest honours. This passion for gold explains many of the nation's characteristics. All Nimpatanese, for instance, are addicted to gambling and huge sums are staked on such games as snail-racing. Officials at court and in other institutions are corrupt; the only way to make one's way in either social or political life is through bribery.

Although Nimpatan is a monarchy, it has a Great Council with elected representatives. The electoral system works in such a way that all the

Three golden knives used by the original inhabitants of
NIMPATAN.

power is in the hands of devoted worshippers of
the *Crallilah*, the Nimpatanese word for a gold bar.
There are two political parties in the country, each
concerned solely with the private accumulation of
wealth and power. No matter which party is in
power, the government always teaches the people
to despise poverty and to accumulate wealth by all
possible means. The fundamental maxims behind
Nimpatanese politics have been summed up in a
book published by Gribbelino, the Emperor's
Treasurer. According to Gribbelino, every action
of mankind is governed by a concern for personal
advantage and every virtue is a vice disguised. It
follows that the government represents merely a
fraction of the population, and is concerned only
with its own advantage, regardless of anything it
might say in public. It is therefore legitimate for
the government to hold on to power by any means,
using the tactics of divide and rule whenever possible, and brute oppression or extortion when necessary. If any town shows signs of opposing the
government, troops should be quartered there or
it should be taxed into submission.

One custom alone suggests that the people of
the country may once have had more freedom than
they now enjoy. Each year a strange ceremony is
held in a square in central Kelso. The people are
seated in galleries around the square, with the emperor on his throne in their midst. The treasurer
enters the square and is immediately surrounded
by hostile people carrying baskets filled with all
sorts of rubbish and excrement. They greet him
with a torrent of abuse and fling their rubbish at
him. In retaliation, he flings out handfuls of paper;
those who pick them up become his allies. When
he has a majority among the crowd, a battle ensues
until both parties collapse from exhaustion. At this
point the treasurer goes up to the emperor, takes
him by the nose and tries to lift him from his seat.
He then collects all the pieces of paper and flings
them in the monarch's lap. The ceremony is now
over. This is said to symbolize the ancient liberty
of the people, and although four successive emperors have tried to suppress the ceremony, its obvious popularity demands that it be continued.

The *Calmonsora* (literally "Abode of Wisdom"), or Academy of Kelso, is housed in the most
sordid and inelegant building in the capital. Its
main feature is the so-called "Repository of
Knowledge," a large room stocked with all kinds of
monsters, prodigies of nature and hideous curiosities. A recent acquisition is a stained urinal once
used by a member of the royalty. Other exhibits include oddities brought from all over the world and
preserved as the most wonderful products of
human genius and proof of the heights to which
the human mind can soar. In recent times, the collection has grown and now probably includes a
portrait of Louis Pawels, the collected works of
Jacqueline Susann, a copy of *Stern* magazine, a
recording of political broadcasts from several countries and the entire Pierre Cardin wardrobe.

In contrast, the most beautiful buildings of
the city are the *Gormarkzees,* or lunatic asylums.
The mad are housed in fine symmetrical buildings, divided into individual apartments, each with
its own garden. Those confined here include
painters who have imitated nature and refused to
flatter their sitters, philanthropists, men who were
foolish enough to marry the girls they seduced or
who refused to commit adultery with the wives of
their friends, priests who refused to flatter the
great, and teetotal doctors. All those who offend
against the culture or manners of the country end
up by being committed to these institutions. This
purgative system has been imitated in several
other countries.

The dress of the Nimpatanese is quite distinctive. Men wear tight silk garments which cover their whole bodies and are fastened at the waist, instep, arms and thighs; they are so tight that they almost stop the circulation of the blood. A looser garment is worn over the top and extravagant wigs are favoured. The women of the country cover their faces in red cosmetics and wear heavy ornaments around their necks. Their breasts are squeezed together by tight coats of mail which flare out at the hip, and the skirt extends for several yards, giving the wearer the appearance of a great bell with a long flat handle.

These luxurious people are not, however, the original population of the island; they are invaders. The few remaining natives live in the outer, barren areas, making a poor living on the few arable patches among the rocks and sandy wastes. They retain their original culture and have little affection for their conquerers. The natives go about naked and paint images of the sun and various animals on their bodies with a blue dye obtained from vegetables. They eat little, satisfying their few needs from their small plots. In their caves and cabins they keep large quantities of gold which they use only to make agricultural tools, such as knives to cut what they believe to be sacred herbs. The lives these natives lead are virtuous, peaceful and boring.

(John Holmesby, *The Voyages, Travels, And Wonderful Discoveries of Capt. John Holmesby. Containing A Series of the most Surprising and Uncommon Events, which befel the Author in his Voyage to the Southern Ocean, in the Year 1739*, London, 1757)

NINETY ISLES, a cluster of islands on the western side of the Inmost Sea of EARTHSEA, between HOSK to the north and Ensmer to the south-west. To the west lies PENDOR, an island feared by men because of the dragons that live there. The actual number of islands in this cluster is a matter for some dispute. If only those islands with freshwater springs are counted, there are perhaps seventy; if every rock is included in the total, there are over a hundred. Even so the calculation would not be certain, as a low tide may mean that there are ten islands in a spot where a high tide would reveal only three. Although the tides in the Inmost Sea are weak, the vast number of channels between these numerous islets means that the waters rise and fall much more than in other areas.

There are few bridges across the channels and no major towns on the islands. There is a small settlement on the island of Serd, a major centre for the Isles' principal industry—the extraction of oil from the small fish known as *turbies*. It is to Serd that the large trading galleys come for oil, which is exported to the rest of the archipelago. Travellers and merchants are provided with accommodation at the *Sea House* there, where food is supplied by the township. Visitors are allowed to sleep in the raftered hall.

The rest of the Isles are grouped into townships of ten or twenty islands. Each is ruled informally by a chief or Isle Man; there is some uncertainty as to how these men gain that important position.

Although the isles are intensively farmed, their life is dominated by the sea. Nets are strung from house to house to catch the *turbie*; every child old enough to walk has a tiny rowing boat; pedlars call their wares to the rhythm of their oar-strokes; women row across the channels to visit neighbours. In many areas, the houses are built in such a fashion that their windows and balconies lean out over the water. The Ninety Isles are not rich and some of the houses are windowless and have bare earthen floors. There is no building stone in the area and the houses are made of wood and thatch. Despite the absence of luxury, the island communities are fairly self-sufficient, and fishing and farming, together with the oil industry, allow them to support themselves.

(Ursula K. Le Guin, A *Wizard of Earthsea*, New York, 1968)

NINE WHIRLPOOLS, ISLAND OF THE, a remote island one thousand miles from anywhere. The island is now a fertile and peaceful haven with little to recall its curious history. Only the pink and primrose stonework of the so-called Lone Tower and the stone figure of a dragon on the beach remain as silent witnesses of the past.

For centuries the island was made inaccessible by a chain of nine whirlpools that surrounded it; for that reason, a king of a distant land chose it as the safest place to exile his child. He did so partly because she was a girl and he had wanted a son, and partly because she had defied him. The girl was sent to the island and put under a spell; she would never grow old and would remain on the island until someone brave appeared to rescue her. The enchanter-king sent a dragon and a gryphon to guard her and to work as her cook and housemaid respectively. The princess' mother and the witch who had presided over her birth volunteered to go into exile with her and for many years stood as stone figures at the entrance to the Lone Tower.

Over the centuries many princes tried to rescue the enchanted girl, but were repelled by the whirlpools. Finally the son of a sea captain heard the story and came to the island. He contrived to calculate the exact moment when the whirlpools were stilled by the falling tide, and landed on the island. Here he fell in love with the princess, defeated the dragon and easily overcame the gryphon.

The whirlpools—created, it seems, from drops of the enchanter-king's blood—turned into rubies at low tide. Thrown into the ground by the valiant sailor, the rubies immediately produced rich crops of grain, as though to atone for the evil with which they had been associated. The princess and her sailor married and they now live in a beautiful palace they built on the island. The dragon turned to stone and was left on the beach, where it has become a popular plaything.

(Edith Nesbit, *The Island of the Nine Whirlpools*, London, 1899)

NOAH'S REALM, a small, privately owned estate which now lies somewhere beneath a sea—probably the Mediterranean. In the centre of the estate are the remains of a large house with a wooden porch on which a platform rocker can be seen. A yard stretches out on all sides of the house, and around the yard lie several acres of meadows. Within walking distance visitors can also admire a small pond from which the fish, it is said, once rose and walked. There is also a wood with both dangerous and healing properties: certain parts of it serve as a sanctuary for wounded animals, and mushrooms growing in its shade have been used as medication and also as a repellent for dragons, who vomit and suffer violent headaches at the mushrooms' smell. These dragons inhabit the more treacherous parts of the forest, called "Dragon Wallows," where they bury themselves in the red mud with only their eyes and snouts sticking out, so that travellers cannot see them.

There are also bogs, quicksands and pits in the forest, as well as patches of nettle and hornets' nests, and sudden grids of razor-sharp stones, and faults which open beneath travellers' feet and burn their soles with hot coals. It is said that lemurs protect the wood as if they were its spirits, but this has not been confirmed. Faeries live in the trees and sometimes fight with the birds for air space.

Not far from the wood is the Walled Orchard, a peaceful grove of ordered rows of trees and grassy paths. The apples in the orchard are red, green, purple, yellow and even white. Legend has it that

Lord Yahweh's carriage during its last visit to NOAH'S REALM.

there is danger attached to the eating of these apples, but the nature of the danger is not clear.

To the north of Noah's Realm is the Sacrificial Hill; to reach it travellers must take the road past the latrines, the bath house, the ice house, the terrace of sunflowers and the grove of cedar trees. At the top of the hill itself stands a solitary pine tree and a crude stone terrace with an altar. Here, it is said, Doctor Noah performed a number of vivisection experiments or sacrifices which earned him a reputation as the world's first surgeon.

Also to the north, beyond the hill, lie the Cities. When the area was above water, plumes of smoke could be seen rising from the Cities, from rituals performed in the Cities' temples. In the olden days there were festivals in honour of the God Baal, during which women were ravished (some say willingly) on the altars. It is said that Baal himself, in his bull incarnation, mounted a woman of his choice during these festivals.

The Cities' conduct led to punishment by the Lord Yaweh, who arrived in Noah's Realm in a large black carriage drawn by winged horses. The leather of the carriage was torn by stones and streaked with mud, and spattered with the remnants of excrement, eggs and rotten vegetables which angry people had disrespectfully thrown at Him; the carriage wheels were broken. Behind the carriage came a procession of cages, each framed with gilded rococo designs in chipped white plaster. Inside each cage were animals of all kinds, and across the whole procession a banner read: "THE SEVEN DA..ONDERS! GREAT MYSTER..S OF LIFE!" Legend has it that after this last visit to Noah's Realm, Yaweh willed Himself to die.

(Timothy Findley, *Not Wanted on the Voyage*, Toronto, 1984)

NOBLE'S ISLE, also known as **MOREAU'S ISLAND**, in the region of latitude 5°3′ south and longitude 101° west, is a small, low, volcanic island covered with thick vegetation, chiefly palm trees. The beaches of dull grey sand slope steeply up to a ridge about sixty to seventy feet above sea level. On the other side of the ridge, a stream runs through a narrow valley towards the interior. To the north, the traveller will find a small hot-spring; to the south, a charred forest and a yellowish swamp which exudes a pungent vapour.

Noble's Isle was visited for the first time in 1867 by Dr. Moreau, an English biologist who, with his assistant Montgomery, established a camp here for scientific research. A chronicle of Dr. Moreau's investigations and of the history of the island was set down by a Mr. Edward Prendick and published by his nephew, Charles.

Though no information is available about the island's present state of habitation, it is known to have provided a residence to both a tribe of Kanakas Indians (also found in New Caledonia) and a group of creatures known as the Animal-Men. Somewhat in the reversed tradition of Circe (see AIAIA) the Animal-Men—bull-men, lion-men, ape-men, and so on—were beasts that the doctor tried to transform into men but never quite succeeded. Though some were gifted with speech, these beasts have reverted to their animal condition; visitors are advised to be on the look-out for them, as an encounter with any of these creatures may not be an agreeable experience.

Edward Prendick discovered, after having made their acquaintance on Noble's Isle, that when he returned to England he found that many of his own countrymen, though apparently normal, reminded him of the Animal-Men. Prowling women would mew after him, pale workers with tired eyes like wounded deer would cough at him, old people would make him think of ape-men. Particularly nauseating were the blank, expressionless faces of people on trains and buses. It is not unlikely, in fact, that some of the Animal-Men escaped Noble's Isle and now live abroad.

Should the visitor be a beast himself and therefore susceptible to transformation (even though it is almost certain that both Dr. Moreau and his assistant are no longer alive), he will find it useful to learn the island's law. It is as follows: "Not to go on all fours, not to suck up drink; not to eat flesh or fish; not to claw the bark of trees; not to chase other men." However, visitors must be warned that the transformation is said to be terribly painful. Indeed, the building in which these operations took place is known as the House of Pain.

(H.G. Wells, *The Island of Doctor Moreau*, London, 1896)

NODNOL, or **ECNATNEPER**, capital of TAERG NATIRB.

NOLAND, a kingdom beyond the Deadly Desert that surrounds the land of OZ. To the west it is bounded by IX, from which it is separated by a range of mountains, and to the south-east it borders on MERRYLAND. In the far north of the country lies a range of lofty mountains which rise in a series of giant steps up to the clouds. The higher steps of this range were the original home of the Roley-Rogues, who once invaded Noland. The capital, Nole, is an ancient walled city standing on a hill.

Noland is ruled by a boy-king named Bud who came to the throne because of the curious succession laws of the country. According to these ancient laws, a ruler who dies without an heir is to be succeeded by the forty-seventh person who enters the east gate of the capital. Whoever this is must be accepted as the legitimate ruler, regardless of sex, age or social status. Bud and his sister Meg (commonly known as Fluff) were the orphans of a poor ferryman, brought to Nole by their Aunt Rivette, a somewhat stern old lady. Despite his origins, Bud was recognized as king, having arrived in Nole in forty-seventh place. Initially, Bud was somewhat reluctant to carry out his duties, being more concerned with playing and making extravagant purchases of toys, but his judgements in several difficult legal cases were fair and his popularity grew steadily.

Shortly before their departure for Nole, Fluff had been given a magic cloak woven by the fairies of BURZEE. The cloak had the property of immediately granting one wish to anyone who wore it, even if the person was unaware of having made a wish. Thus, Aunt Rivette suddenly grew wings when she wished she could fly to the shops; a dog began to talk; Bud's valet acquired six servants to wait on him; Tollydob, the King's general, grew to be ten feet tall in an instant; Tollydeb, the Lord High Executioner, expressed the wish that he could reach an apple he saw high up in a tree and immediately found that his arm had grown and that he could easily reach it. The more important wish, made by Tollydib, the Lord High Purse Bearer—that the royal purse always remain full, no matter how much money was drawn from it— was also granted.

News of the magic cloak and its powers spread far and wide. Songs were made up about it and were carried through the land by wandering minstrels. It was via one of the minstrels that Queen Zixi of Ix first heard of the cloak. She immediately wanted to have it, hoping that it would grant her dearest wish: that a mirror would show her the lovely image seen by others and not the aged face she knew to be her own countenance. But after stealing it from Noland and replacing it with an imitation, Queen Zixi discovered that the magic did not work; the cloak would not grant wishes if it had been stolen.

Some time afterwards, Noland was invaded by the Roley-Rogues, who descended from the giant stair mountains in the north. These strange people were as round as balls, with short legs and arms which they could withdraw at will into their bodies, resembling living footballs. Their muscles were as tough and elastic as india-rubber. Although extremely aggressive and pugnacious by nature, the Roley-Rogues rarely hurt themselves, as they simply bounced off one another when they collided. They were, however, more than capable of hurting the people of Noland, bowling them over and pricking them with the large thorns they carried as swords. Their arrival was so sudden that the ill-prepared army of Noland was rapidly overcome.

Once in control of the city, the Roley-Rogues caused great havoc, destroying all articles they could not use and eating virtually everything they could find. The king's councillors were reduced to the most humiliating positions: the general was made a kitchen scullion and Bud's valet was forced to scratch the back of one of their number. Bud himself did not take the invasion too seriously, convinced that the power of the cloak would be enough to drive the Roley-Rogues out of the country. When it was found that the magic did not work, Bud and Fluff decided to flee the country and, carried by their aunt, fled to Ix.

Queen Zixi received them graciously and admitted to the theft of the real cloak, adding that she no longer had it in her possession. The recovery of the cloak proved very difficult: it had been cut up to make patchwork quilts and one piece had even been given to a sailor as a necktie. Therefore other means had to be found to liberate Noland. Finally, Queen Zixi made up a magic potion and had it carried to Nole by her talking dog, who placed it in a special soup of which the Roley-Rogues were very fond. The Roley-Rogues drank it and it sent them all into a deep sleep. The army of Ix marched into Noland and were greeted as heroes by the oppressed people. They tied ropes around the sleeping Roley-Rogues, towed them to a river and threw them into the water. They were left to float out to sea and were never seen in Noland again. Great celebrations were held throughout the country, led by the returned monarch and his sister.

(L. Frank Baum, *Queen Zixi of Ix, or The Story of the Magic Cloak*, New York, 1907; L. Frank Baum, *The Road* to *Oz*, Chicago, 1909)

NOLANDANIA, one of the eleven republics in PLUTO, the land at the centre of the hollow globe of the earth. In Nolandania, as in other parts of Pluto, men and animals are much smaller than their equivalents on the surface of the earth. The inhabitants are rarely more than two feet tall, the average height of people in Pluto.

Nolandania borders on the Empire of the BANOIS, and is considerably larger than any of its neighbours. Its population, however, is smaller than that of the surrounding countries and the State is militarily and politically weak.

The Nolandanians' only concern in life is pleasure and enjoyment. Social life is centred on a constant round of balls and banquets and, according to the few moralists left in the country, the republic is well on the road to complete ruin. Corruption is common in public life and the private lives of the citizens are devoted to various forms of debauchery and gambling. Adultery is now seen as a cause for amusement and it is said that there are more mistresses than legitimate wives in the country. The institution of marriage appears to be dying out and the more sober citizens see little or no hope for the moral future of the republic.

(Anonymous, *Voyage au centre de la terre, ou aventures de quelques naufragés dans des pays inconnus. Traduit de l'anglais de Sir Hormidas Peath*, Paris, 1821)

NOLANDIA, a country to the south-east of UTOPIA, of very little interest.

On the strength of an ancient marriage connection, the king of Nolandia believed that he had hereditary claims to a neighbouring kingdom and he subsequently conquered it by war. It soon became apparent that it was much more difficult to keep this new kingdom than it had been to conquer it. There were continual threats of internal subversion and external aggression and money was constantly flowing out of Nolandia to support its newly acquired dominion.

Conditions in Nolandia itself worsened: crime increased and respect for the law vanished. But the king was so busy trying to govern the new land that he had no time to look after his own. Eventually the Nolandians approached their monarch and told him to choose between the two kingdoms, explaining that they were too numerous to be governed by only half a king. The monarch was finally obliged to return to his duties as head of Nolandia. He handed over his new realm to a friend who was overthrown shortly afterwards.

(Sir Thomas More, *Utopia*, London, 1516)

NOLE, capital of NOLAND.

NO-MAN'S-LAND, an island off the coast of FANTIPPO. From the mainland, the island resembles a plum pudding, but its steep shoreline actually conceals a deep sheltered hollow, some thirty miles across. There are numerous streams, forested areas and acres of tall, waving grass.

According to the people of Fantippo, the island is inhabited by man-eating dragons, so they refuse to go near it. Legend has it that many hundreds of years ago King Kakaboochi of Fantippo exiled his mother-in-law to the island, as he could not bear her constant chattering. Each week food was taken out to her by boat, but one week she was not to be found—instead, a dragon appeared, terrifying the messengers. A famous wizard, consulted about the matter, explained that the king's mother-in-law must have turned into a dragon.

But travellers need not worry. The truth of the matter is somewhat different. There are no dragons on No-Man's-Land; it is inhabited only by herbivorous animals. Hippopotami feed on the banks of the streams; elephants and rhinoceroses browse through the long grass. Giraffes, monkeys and deer are plentiful. Birds swarm all over the island, which is a veritable paradise for all creatures that do not eat meat. It is interesting to note that No-Man's-Land is the only place on earth where the prehistoric *piffilosaurus* can still be found. The *piffilosaurus* resembles a cross between a crocodile and a giraffe, with short, spreading legs and an enormously long tail and neck. Despite its immense size, the *piffilosaurus* is a gentle animal which enjoys basking in the sun and which lives on a diet of ripe bananas. It is probable that this beast is at the origin of the dragon myth. When a visitor tries to land on the island, the piffilosauri go down to a hollow in the centre of the island and breathe in the mist that always hangs around it.

They then go to the beach, where they roar and rage, breathing out the mist through their nostrils (thus being easily mistaken for fiery dragons).

The king's mother-in-law did, in fact, disappear from the island, but only because the animals could not tolerate her chatter either. They put her ashore, far off on the coast of Africa, where she eventually married a deaf king to the south of the Congo.

No-Man's-Land was an important centre for the postal system established by Dr. Dolittle in Fantippo.

(Hugh Lofting, *Doctor Dolittle's Post Office*, London, 1924)

NOMELAND, the realm of King Roquat of the Rocks, in the extensive caverns beneath the mountains to the north of EV.

The Nomes are rock fairies, small and agile creatures the colour of the rocks among which they live. Their bodies are rough and jagged, as though cut from the rock itself. They are extremely strong and have very well-developed muscles from working in the mines below their caves.

Travellers are advised that it is difficult and dangerous to visit Nomeland, which can only be reached by crossing the narrow mountain gorges in the far north of Ev. At its narrowest point, the path is obstructed by a giant who pounds the road with a huge iron hammer. The giant is, in fact, a machine constructed by the company of Tinker and Smith of Ev—the people who also made Tiktok, a machine man who is now a respected citizen of OZ. The only way to get past the giant is to run under the hammer while it is in the air; and even then it is not easy to enter Nomeland. The hidden door in the rockface will open only if King Roquat thinks one's request to be admitted is sufficiently humble and respectful.

Inside the door, a tunnel lit by flaming jewels leads to Roquat's throne room, where he can usually be found smoking on his throne, a somewhat clumsy structure carved from a boulder and studded with emeralds, rubies and diamonds. Beyond lie the halls of his magnificent palace—great vaulted chambers with walls of polished marble hung with silk drapes, floors covered with thick, velvet carpets and furniture made from rare old woods. The whole palace is lit by a soft, mysterious glow which seems to come from no particular source. Deep below the palace lie the mines, where thousands of Nomes extract and work the gems and precious metals of the earth. The underground caverns also serve as barracks for Roquat's huge army, all clad in steel armour with jewelled inlays.

Visitors will not be able to admire one of the marvels of Nomeland: the petrified images of the wife and children of King Evroldo XIV, who gave them to King Roquat in exchange for a long life. The promise did Evroldo little good, as he soon after committed suicide in remorse. Out of kindness, King Roquat spared his new slaves from hard work by transforming them into ornaments for one of his halls. From here they were rescued by Queen Ozma of Oz and her allies. It is not known whether King Roquat has replaced them.

(L. Frank Baum, *Ozma of Oz*, Chicago, 1907; L. Frank Baum, *The Road to Oz*, Chicago, 1909; L. Frank Baum, *The Emerald City of Oz*, Chicago, 1910)

NOPANDES, LAND OF, in the United States, beyond the Appalachian Mountains. A territory protected by lakes and mountains, it is the home of the Nopandes nation—an Indian tribe of orderly and hospitable people.

Traces of past contact with the Spanish are reflected in the capital, Nopande, with its well laid-out streets and brick houses. Noteworthy is the chief's large brick palace with its pleasant gardens and many fruit trees.

Should the intrepid traveller investigate a deep valley sealed off by a certain wall and penetrate the heavily guarded entrance, he will pass through a second gate leading into an enclosed area where a great fire is kept burning perpetually. This is a prison known as Hell and tended by ministers called Devils. Here those guilty of various crimes are burned at night, watched by the whole tribe, and travellers are duly invited to attend the spectacle.

(Abbé Antoine François Prévost, *Le Philosophe anglois, ou Histoire de Monsieur Cleveland, fils naturel de Cromwell, par l'auteur des Mémoires d'un Homme de qualité*, Utrecht, 1731)

NORA-BAMMA, an island of the MARDI ARCHIPELAGO. Its name means "Island of Dreams"; it has been described as green, and as round as a Mohammedan turban. It is inhabited by dreamers, hypochondriacs and sleep-walkers.

Whoever reaches its coasts cannot avoid paying the tribute of a nap, and whoever arrives at Nora-Bamma in search of its celebrated golden pumpkins will fall into a profound sleep even before plucking the first one and will only wake up once night has fallen. Visitors walk about rubbing their eyes and are greeted by silent spectres moving in the pale forest lights, appearing and disappearing without rhyme or reason.

(Herman Melville, *Mardi, and A Voyage Thither*, New York, 1849)

NORTH FARTHING, see The SHIRE.

NORTH POLE KINGDOM, a country under the Arctic, inhabited by civilized dinosaurs. It

View of the third exit from the NORTH POLE KINGDOM.

consists of a maze of underground tunnels with several exits onto the icy wastes. The dinosaur society is carefully organized and all members have specific occupations. The main job is to watch over huge machines that transform the North Pole's electro-magnetic energy into heat and light. The workers responsible for this task are accompanied by younger apprentices. Should a worker neglect his duties, the apprentice takes over immediately and the worker is driven to the slaughter-house. The dinosaurs dress in a sort of overall made out of seal-skin. Their faces are like those of giant lizards and betray no emotions.

According to one theory, these creatures are descended from prehistoric dinosaurs who sought refuge underground. An account of the North Pole Kingdom (found in the late nineteenth century by French archaeologists in northern Siberia) was written by a French explorer whose partner had apparently gone mad. The manuscript was found in an empty petrol tank, next to the skeleton of a dinosaur, presumably one of the inhabitants of this white and frozen kingdom.

(Charles Derennes, *Le Peuple du Pôle*, Paris, 1907)

NOTHING, ISLE OF, see GREAT WATER.

NOVA SOLYMA, a city in Israel, a stronghold of Christian belief. The city is built on the summits of two mountains and its lofty and massive walls rise from the upper slopes. Nova Solyma has twelve gates whose doors, all of solid brass, are distinguished by the tribal ensigns and the names of the Patriarchs which are engraved on them. Above each gate is a strong tower which guards the entrance. The principal gate is that of Judah. It opens upon a fine street of detached, stone-built mansions, all the same height and with the same exterior, giving the impression of extensive and connected buildings. Nothing remains of the ancient town of Solyma, or Old Solyma, on which Nova Solyma was built, but its glories are renewed on the site on a far larger scale.

The houses bear inscriptions that tell of the way they were built. One of the most important houses carries the following writing on its walls: "This house had its foundation on just gains and was built from no proceeds of fraud, and so will last through many ages, and shall see children's children without break or change. No gambling,

1 *University Hall I*
2 *University Hall II*
3 *Schools*
4 *Public Hall of Merchants' Exchange*
5 *Bazaar*
6 *Market Place*
7 *Gate of Judah*

NOVA SOLYMA

no secret lawless love, no strife nor anger, no long-pent-up revenge crying out for blood can find a place here." The inscription also forbids access to ghosts, fauns and satyrs. In the gardens are bas-reliefs representing biblical scenes. The city cele-brates a yearly pageant on the anniversary of its founding and a virgin is chosen to represent the daughter of Zion.

The public schools are in the north corner of the city. No windows open onto the street; in their place are statues of famous men; over the entrance gate is David, guarded by an official porter who cannot be bribed.

The young are gradually accustomed to endure hardship, subject to doctor's consent. For, as a Solymaian author puts it: "It is a simple matter of experience that the children of the poor, brought up with the greatest frugality, turn out healthier and of better constitution than those who are delicately and luxuriously brought up." Boys are taught dancing, swimming and archery. Passions are checked and the sluggish and timid are whipped into action. Shameless and impure acts are shrunk from with horror. Liars are ranked with those creatures that have not got the use of speech and are treated as unsuited for the society of articulate men. Boys are taught to worship God and love their country, but nothing is done about the education of girls.

The people of Nova Solyma believe the universe to be one large uterus.

(Samuel Gott, *Novae Solymae libri sex*, London, 1648)

NOWHERE ISLAND, see MEDAMONTHY.

NUBIA, the capital of the great Ethiopian kingdom (see also SABA), not to be confused with the barren waste of the same name in the Sudan, or the ancient nation in north-east Africa.

Nubia is ruled by the Senapho, whose land is rich in gold, jewels, balsam, musk and amber. Some travellers believe the Senapho to be the famous Prester John. The most notable building in Nubia is the Royal Palace, known for its crystal columns, its walls encrusted with rubies, emeralds, sapphires and topaz, and the vast quantities of pearls and precious stones in every room.

Towards the north of Nubia are the Mountains of the Moon, where the River Nile is born. The ruler of Egypt pays the Senapho a yearly tribute for fear that the Nubian monarch will other-

wise divert the course of the river, making it flow through another land.

Legend has it that in the Mountains of the Moon lies a beautiful garden-kingdom, said to be a terrestrial paradise that the Senapho once tried to conquer. He invaded the mountains with camels, elephants and infantry, but was punished by God, who blinded him and sent an angel to kill a hundred thousand of his men. The harpies were also sent to scourge the invading king: whenever he wished to eat, they would fly over his food, fouling it with their excrement. Astolpho, knight of France, saved the Senapho from his miseries by capturing the harpies and locking them up in a cave below the Mountains of the Moon, where— it is said—travellers can still hear them flapping their dark wings.

(Ludovico Ariosto, *Orlando furioso*, Ferrara, 1516)

NULL, LAND OF, see WISDOM KINGDOM.

NUMBERS, CITY OF, see DIGITOPOLIS.

NUT ISLANDS, in the Atlantic Ocean, not far from the VEGETABLE SEA, so called because certain trees that grow here produce enormous nuts over fifteen feet long. The inhabitants, the Nutanauts, use them as ships.

(Lucian of Samosata, *True History*, 2nd cen. AD)

NUTOPIA, a country with no land, no boundaries, no passports—only people. Nutopia has no laws other than cosmic laws and all the people of Nutopia are ambassadors of their country. Nutopia's international anthem is called *Bring on the Lucie*. Further information can be obtained from the Nutopian Embassy, 1 White Street, New York, New York 10013, USA.

(John Lennon, *Mind Games*, London, 1973)

O

OBALSA, see Isles of WISDOM.

O-BLAHA, see Isles of WISDOM.

OCEANA (1), a commonwealth composed of the main island of the same name and the island provinces of Marpesia and Panopea. The main island is smaller than France. Mentioned for the first time by Pliny, Oceana was successively conquered by the Romans, Teutons, Scandians and Neustrians. The Romans held it as a province; the Teutons introduced a form of monarchy. After a long and complicated civil struggle, Oceana became the democratic commonwealth it is today.

Its inhabitants are divided into freemen and servants, and a further division between youths and elders provides a marching army and standing garrisons respectively. Horse and foot soldiers are divided according to their property; the troops are split into three groups known as Phoenix, Pelican and Swallow, and the companies into Cypress, Myrtle and Spray. Administratively, the commonwealth is divided into parishes, hundreds and tribes; the elders of each tribe are elected by ballot and return seven deputies to the central government. The parish deputies elect the justices of the peace, the captains and the ensigns. Several other officers and counsels are elected by the senate. Legislation must be ratified by the people: the senate proposes and the people resolve. The law limits the amount of land that may be held by individuals, in order to ensure that power remains in the hands of the majority.

The capital of Oceana, Emporium, is governed by companies of tradesmen and by aldermen under the authority of a sheriff and a lord mayor. Emporium itself is made up of two cities: Emporium and Hiera.

Though there is liberty of religion, a Council of Religion is necessary to protect the freedom of conscience. No coercion is exercised in matters of belief, but Jewish and idolatrous practices are forbidden. The priests of the National Religion are appointed to posts in the University and are not allowed to accept any other employment. Free schools exist in every tribe and are attended by

those between the ages of nine and fifteen, but the education of an only son is the responsibility of his father. There are two important universities in Oceana, in the towns of Clio and Calliope.

The province of Panopea, an island conquered by Oceana, is showing signs of degeneration. It has been described as "the mother of slothful and pusillanimous people" and it is thought unlikely that it will yield men fit to bear arms. Though some of Oceana's best friends are immigrants, it has been suggested that Oceana's Jewish population settle as far from the mainland as possible, on Panopea.

(James Harington, *The Commonwealth of Oceana*, London, 1656)

OCEANA (2), an island (not to be confused with Commonwealth of OCEANA) in the North Atlantic, to the south of Ireland, approximately two hundred miles west of the coast of Cornwall.

Oceana is a small island, no more than ninety miles in length. It is isolated and access is not easy. The only regular transport is a weekly steamer from Ireland; there are no airports on the island. The only deep-water port—about twenty miles from the capital, Lesneven—is Portharnel, where a narrow gorge runs out to sea, forming a natural harbour between high cliffs. Oceana's second port is Caloestown, on the south coast, but its harbour is too small for large steamers and is used only by lobster boats.

The shortage of harbours is explained by the island's geography. The Atlantic coast, almost totally inaccessible from the sea, consists solely of high cliffs falling from the mountain spine of Oceana. The east coast is less rugged, but even here the hills turn a granite face to the sea and there are few beaches. Visitors should note that the only real beaches, which are used for swimming in summer, are ten to fifteen miles north of Lesneven and run as far north as the village of Hoddick. There is no natural harbour at Lesneven, although it stands on a large bay; the currents that run between the mainland and the offshore island of The Kernel make the bay dangerous. Nor does Lesneven boast a beach; the foreshore here is flat and muddy. The capital's station—from which trains run to Portharnel—is some way out of the small town and stands on stilts above the mudflats exposed at low tide.

Lesneven itself is a small, sleepy town with

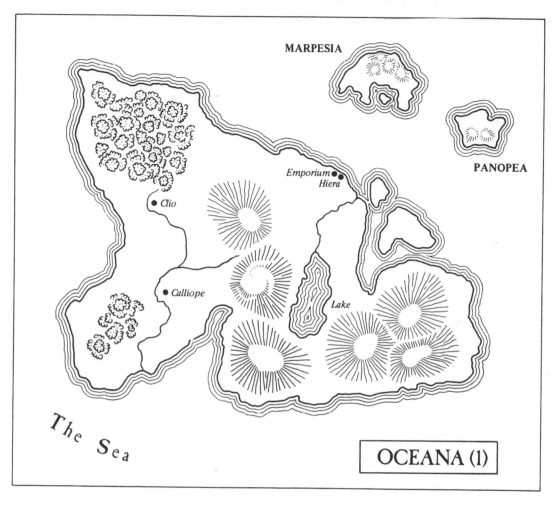

few buildings of any distinction. Its houses are whitewashed, with steeply pitched roofs and characteristic granite window-facing. They are built in terraces. Granite mounting posts are a common sight in the streets, although horses are less frequently seen than they used to be. The most noteworthy building in the town is the Rota, the seat of the island's government. It is a circular domed building, lit by long narrow windows, with a floor of alternating bands of light and dark stone surrounded by a parapet. The parapet is broken by the main entrance, leading to the robing rooms, and by the raised president's seat. Behind the parapet are two banks of leather seats for the delegates; a circular walkway above them allows visitors to attend debates. The Rota building is not spectacular, but has an air of simple dignity.

Inland, the island is divided into two main areas. The wolds and hills of the centre and the south are rich farming country, divided into large estates which are usually farmed on a tenant basis, although some of the estate-owners continue to farm their own land and virtually rule their areas as semi-independent statelets. To the north and west the land is barer, rising to the Trigaskell Hills and to the granite mountains of the west. These mountains are a jumble of jagged shapes, rising to three thousand feet before plunging to the sheer cliffs of the Atlantic coast. The valleys are steep and rough, making it extremely difficult to travel north to south through the uplands. In winter the peaks are snow-covered and dangerous. The high moorland and the mountains are used for sheep-farming. Traditionally the sheep-farmers are not

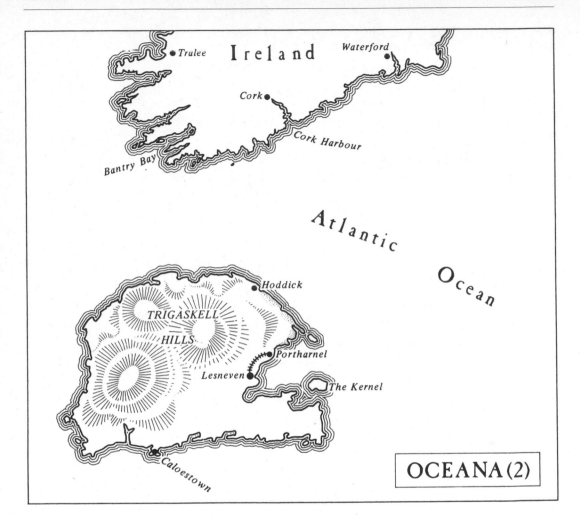

OCEANA (2)

tenants, but own their own land. They tend to be more independent and quick-witted than the tenant-farmers and tradesmen of the wolds and valleys and are suspicious of people from "down below."

Politically, Oceana is an independent state. Sixty delegates are elected to the Rota, who in turn elect a President with executive powers from among their number. Culturally, the island is staid and extremely conservative. Women still wear traditional costume, especially in the country areas: a long full dress and an orange-red shawl over their shoulders. The pace of life is slow and, in many ways, Oceana does not seem to belong to the twentieth century. For instance, mail is still delivered in horse-drawn vans by blue-uniformed *lettermen*. In religious affairs, the life of the island is dominated by a branch of the Protestant Church of Ireland, but witchcraft rituals still survive in the countryside, involving the worship of the devil, naked orgies and a variety of sadomasochistic rites.

Oceana appears to have produced only one national dish, the cold pudding known as *blayberry breaddie*, traditionally served with cream. This is made from bread and blayberries, a fruit not found elsewhere. Lobster pie is a dish associated with Lesneven, whereas the wild upland areas are renowned for their heather wine.

Oceana has always been isolated from the politics of even its nearest neighbours. During the

Second World War it remained strictly neutral, establishing a Local Defence Force and building coastal defences when rumours spread that both England and Germany had plans to occupy it. In the 1950's, the island became even more isolated under the rule of Rolph Mylchraine, the self-styled Grand Master of Oceana.

Mylchraine was an estate-owner who built up his power until he became the effective dictator of the island and was able to suspend the Rota. His hold over the people is explained in part by the control he had over whisky imports, but mainly by his cunning use of the traditional witchcraft rituals, which he deliberately encouraged. Under his rule, the *esbat* or sabbath was widely celebrated, with the obscene rituals taking place in the old Rota building. Mylchraine also used whisky as a weapon, reducing the price of a traditionally expensive import until the entire population was accustomed to it, and then raising it, so that people were willing to accept almost any humiliation to satisfy their craving. The island was policed by his Keepers, effectively a private army. Convict labour was introduced and all opposition was silenced or forced out, the main exile group being the Revolutionary Council based in Dublin. The Council was not noted for its effectiveness and the overthrow of Mylchraine was largely the work of one man, Keig, originally a smallholder from The Kernel.

Keig's opposition to Mylchraine began as a personal crusade: he was evicted from his land when the Grand Master took it to build a fortified house there and was jailed when he protested. On escaping, Keig robbed a train that was carrying large quantities of gold. With this he travelled to Dublin where he contacted the Revolutionary Council. Relations between the smallholder and the Council were tense, particularly when Keig began to speak of the need to kill the island's dictator. A landing organized by the Revolutionary Council ended in disaster and Keig began to organize his own military campaign against Mylchraine. Led by Keig, a small group of unarmed men landed on the west coast, arming themselves with weapons taken from the hated Keepers.

This was the beginning of a protracted guerrilla war, which ended with the death of Mylchraine, whom Keig killed with the dictator's favourite weapon, an axe. In the war, Keig gained the support of many of the country people—not least because Mylchraine was cutting down trees to export timber, which meant that they could no longer produce their traditional carved furniture—but he was treated with suspicion by the estate-owners. The war was brutal and vicious, escalating from skirmishes to full-scale battles for the control of Lesneven, heavily fortified by Mylchraine. It was comparatively late in the day that the Revolutionary Council joined in the struggle, but it now claims most of the credit for the overthrowing of the tyrant. A move was made to arrest Keig for robbery and visitors will find that his role in the war is not even mentioned in official accounts.

(H.R.F. Keating, *The Strong Man,* London, 1971)

OCTAVIA, a spiderweb city in Asia. There is a precipice between two steep mountains: the city is over the void, bound to the two crests with ropes and chains and catwalks. Travellers should walk on the little wooden ties, being careful not to set their feet in the open spaces, or cling to the hempen strands. Below there is nothing for hundreds and hundreds of feet: a few clouds glide past; farther down one can glimpse the chasm's bottom.

The foundation of the city is a net which serves as passage and support. All the rest, instead of rising up, is hung below: rope-ladders, hammocks, houses dangling like sacks, clothes-hangers, terraces like gondolas, skins of water, gas jets, spits, baskets on strings, dumb-waiters, showers, trapezes and rings for children's games, cable-cars, chandeliers, pots with trailing plants.

Suspended over the abyss, the life of Octavia's inhabitants is less uncertain than in other cities. They know the net will last only so long.

(Italo Calvino, *Le città invisibili,* Turin, 1972)

ODES, ISLE OF, an island two days' sail from ENTELECHY. Its name derives from '*odos,* the Greek word for a road. All roads on the island are alive and move of their own free will. As Aristotle argues, the one sign that something is animal and not mineral is that it moves of its own accord; the roads of the island can therefore be regarded as living creatures.

To travel about the island, visitors should ask one of the natives where a particular road is going. They should then climb onto the right road and they will be transported to their destination without any difficulty. Travelling through the Isle of Odes is, in fact, as easy as travelling from Lyons to Avignon by taking a boat down the Rhône. However, not everything in the Isle of Odes is perfect: a certain class of people, called the Waylayers and Road-beaters, lie in wait for the moving roads and attack them with blind brutality, in much the same way as muggers attack old ladies. Waylayers who are caught are broken on the wheel and severely beaten.

An added attraction for the visitor to the Isle of Odes is the appearance of familiar roads moving freely about the island: the Yellow Brick Road, Caminito, the Road to Mandalay, Coronation Street, Müller's Weg, Calvary and the Narrow Road to the Far North can be seen running across the island's hills and meadows.

(François Rabelais, *Le cinquiesme et dernier livre des faicts et dicts du bon Pantagruel, auquel est contenu la visitation de l'Oracle de la dive Bacbuc, et le mot de la bouteille; pour lequel avoir est entrepris tout ce long voyage,* Paris, 1564)

ODO, an island of the MARDI ARCHIPELAGO surrounded by three large concentric ditches in which taro is grown. It is famous for its guava trees and vineyards, but the breadfruit tree, common in the rest of the archipelago, is here unknown.

Odo is also the name of the capital city; there are no other urban conglomerations, just a few scattered dwellings. The population is divided into

A noble dwelling in the hills of ODO.

two main castes, noble and plebeian, but there is also a third class, the slaves, composed mainly of prisoners of war. The nobles live scattered around the island in dwellings far apart, some in the green heart of the forest, or on the beach, some high up in the branches of trees, others on the hills inland. The plebeians and slaves live in squalid places of difficult access, in dens or in log cabins made of driftwood, because they are not allowed to fell living trees. The slaves work in the ditches cultivating the taro. There are no cemeteries because the dead are taken onto a reef and flung into the waters beyond. "Earth is an urn for flowers, not for ashes," say the natives. "We have no wish to harvest the fruits of the tomb." They believe that on stormy nights when the waves crash onto the rocks of the reef, they can hear the whispering voices of the thousands of dead rising from the depths of the ocean.

(Herman Melville, *Mardi, and A Voyage Thither,* New York, 1849)

OGYGIA, an island in the western Mediterranean. In a cave surrounded by a splendid forest of alder, aspen and sweet-smelling cypresses lives Calypso, the nymph. Over the gaping mouth of the cave trails a luxuriant grapevine, with clusters of ripe fruit. Four streams of clear water run in a row close together, winding over the ground. Beyond are soft meadows thick with violets and wild celery. The fauna consists mainly of birds: owls, falcons and sea ravens. Ogygia has been visited by at least one royal personage.

(Homer, *The Odyssey,* 9th cen. [?] BC)

OHONOO, island of the MARDI ARCHIPELAGO. Seen from the north, with its flat coast and three vast rocky terraces ascending one after the other inland, Ohonoo gives the impression of gigantic steps mounting towards the sun—hence the legend that describes it as the base of a staircase built before the creation of Mardi by the god Vivo, to unite heaven and earth. However, once on earth, Vivo found such evil that he returned to heaven, destroying the steps behind him. The blocks fell into the sea forming the Mardi Archipelago.

The name of the island means "Land of Criminals," because Ohonoo has become a place of exile for evil-doers from all the surrounding islands. Here they have built a new community, exiling, in turn, those they found unworthy (it is not clear whether those deemed unworthy were more honest or more delinquent than the original settlers).

Travellers are advised to visit the ancient statue of Keevi, god of thieves and protector of the island. His image rises from a natural niche in the rocky coast that closes the valley of Monlova. He possesses five eyes, ten hands and six legs. His hands are enormous and each finger is as thick as a man's arm. Legend has it that Keevi fell from a golden cloud, burying himself up to his thighs in the earth, thus causing a severe earthquake.

(Herman Melville, *Mardi, and A Voyage Thither*, New York, 1849)

OKLAHOMA, NATURE THEATRE OF, in the United States. Not much is known of what takes place in the Theatre. Members are engaged by means of a placard that announces that the theatre can find employment for everyone. Applicants are asked to present themselves at a given racecourse (for instance, Clayton Racecourse in New York State) from six in the morning to midnight.

Upon reaching the racecourse, applicants will be greeted by a confused blare of trumpets; these seem to be blown regardless of each other, confirming that the Theatre of Oklahoma is a great undertaking—only small enterprises can afford to be organized.

At the entrance of the racecourse a long low platform is set up, supporting hundreds of women dressed as angels in white robes and great wings, blowing on long trumpets that glitter like gold. The women are actually standing on separate pedestals, but these cannot be seen since they are completely hidden by the long flowing draperies. As the pedestals are very high, some of them towering up to six feet, the women look gigantic—except the smallness of their heads somewhat spoils the impression of size, and their loose hair looks too short, almost absurd, hanging between the great wings. To avoid monotony, the pedestals are of all sizes: some of the women are quite low, others soar to such a height that visitors will feel that the slightest gust of wind could capsize them. Two hours after they have started, the women are relieved by men dressed as devils, half of them blowing trumpets as poorly as the women, half beating drums.

Apparently all applicants are accepted—with or without identification papers, with or without professional qualifications. Adults of both sexes, children, even babies are found a place in the Nature Theatre of Oklahoma. The purpose of the employment has never been explained.

No description is available of the Theatre itself, only a photograph depicting the presidential box at the Theatre. At first glance, it could be thought that the stage box is not a stage box but the stage itself, so far-flung is the sweep of its golden breastwork. Between its slender columns, as delicately carved as if cut out by a fine pair of scissors, medallions of former presidents can be seen side by side: one of these shows a remarkably straight nose, curling lips and a downcast eye, hooded by a full rounded eyelid. Red damask curtains fall from roof to floor, looped with cords. The Nature Theatre of Oklahoma lies two days and two nights by train from Clayton.

(Franz Kafka, *Amerika*, Munich, 1927)

OLD FOREST, lying between BUCKLAND and the BARROW DOWNS in northern MIDDLE-EARTH, is a remnant of the extensive forest that once stretched from the MISTY MOUNTAINS to the Blue Mountains in the north-west. The only other major remnant of this immense forest is the area now known as FANGORN. The River Withywindle flows through the Old Forest from its source in the Barrow Downs and down to the Brandywine, which it enters at the southern end of Buckland.

The Old Forest is a frightening place where everything seems alive and watchful, and is quite silent apart from the constant murmuring of the trees. The trees of the forest are malevolent and very hostile to strangers, and they move around so that the forest paths become impossible to follow. They are also known to attack travellers, either grasping them with their branches or closing in upon them and surrounding them. The most fearful area of all is the Dingle, the valley of the Withywindle, the centre of the mysterious power which fills the forest. The banks of the river are lined with willow trees, and chief among them is the sinister Old Man Willow, an insidiously malicious tree which casts spells on passers-by and sends them to sleep against its trunk. The trunk then opens and they are drawn inside the old tree.

The trees of the Old Forest once attacked the Hedge, which runs along the eastern boundary of Buckland, but they were thrown back when the hobbits of the area lit a great fire. The fire created a wide empty space which is still known as the Bonfire Glade.

It is thought that the pride of the ancient trees is their reason for their hatred of all other living things. Perhaps they remember their grandeur when they were lords and see all other creatures as usurpers and destroyers. Without question travellers are strongly advised to avoid entering the Old Forest. But if necessity demands otherwise there is only one person who can safely act as a guide—the extraordinary Tom Bombadil, who lives between the Old Forest and the Barrow Downs. His origin is unknown, but he refers to himself as the Eldest and claims to be the first to exist in Middle-earth. Those who can recall the distant First Age say that even then he was older than old, but they have no knowledge of his origins or background. The elves call him the Iarwain Ben-adar, or "oldest and fatherless," while to the dwarves he is Forn and to the men of the north he is Orald. Master of wood, water and hill, he himself knows no master and has power over the trees of the forest and the wights of the Barrow Downs. He is the only person who was never affected by the Ring and neither fell under its sway nor became invisible when he wore it. He is habitually merry and cheerful, forever singing and capering about. He is recognizable by his blue eyes, red, laughter-wrinkled cheeks and long brown beard and he usually wears a bright blue coat and yellow boots. He is taller than a hobbit and resembles a man, though he is smaller than most men. When asked who he is, his wife Goldberry simply answers, "He is."

(J.R.R. Tolkien, *The Fellowship of the Ring*, London, 1954; J.R.R. Tolkien, *The Two Towers*, London, 1955)

OLD-MAN-OF-THE-SEA'S-ISLAND, somewhere in the Indian Ocean, dangerous to travellers. Here lives the Old-Man-of-the-Sea, who sits and waits, dressed in leaves and wearing a sad look, for an unfortunate person to come his way. Should a traveller, out of pity for the Old Man, carry him on his back, he will become the Old Man's beast of burden for the rest of his days. The Old Man will twist his legs—black and rough like the hide of a buffalo—around the traveller's neck, squeezing it with his feet until the traveller becomes unconscious. He will then beat the traveller on the back and shoulders to make him realize who is the master, and will force him to carry him around the island to pick the best and ripest fruit. Night and day he will sit on the traveller's back, adding to the discomfort by urinating and defecating *in situ*.

Sinbad the Sailor wrote an account of this place, explaining how he managed to escape the Old Man. Though Sinbad describes how he killed the Old Man, his death has not been confirmed and travellers are advised to proceed with caution.

(Anonymous, *The Arabian Nights*, 14th–16th cen. AD)

OLD MATHERS, HOUSE OF, somewhere in Ireland, in a part of the country where every road turns to the left. (One of them is the road to eternity.) It is quite dangerous to travel there by bicycle for, according to the well-known theory of the exchange of atoms, a cyclist risks becoming his own bicycle, or at least half-man, half-bicycle. Walking is equally dangerous; the continual cracking of your feet down on the roadway results in a certain amount of the road entering you.

In the house itself, under a board of the uneven floor in the first room to the right, is a black box containing three thousand pounds in cash. But travellers who are tempted by this nest-egg must know that within the very thickness of the walls of the house is the little office of Police Inspector Fox, a colossus of a man who asks absurd questions regarding strawberry jam. Nobody can look directly into his eyes without being, quite literally, blinded.

(Flann O'Brien, *The Third Policeman*, London, 1940)

OLDWIVESFABLEDOM, an island close to the Isle of TOMTODDIES. The inhabitants are heathens who worship a howling ape.

Parents frighten their children by calling on the Powwow man, an ill-favoured gentleman who sneezes squibs and crackers and weeps boiling pitch whenever it suits him. He carries a thunder box, from which all sorts of terrors leap out: spring-heeled Jacks, turnip-ghosts and magic lanthorns. His box of terrors is so frightening that children often faint from fear when he arrives, although the Powwow man is, in fact, a great coward and can be scared off simply by shouting "boo."

Parents who call on the Powwow man often reward him for frightening their children by carrying him around in a silver palanquin. However, when they do so, they find that the poles stick to their shoulders and that they cannot put him down again. Visitors will therefore see many of the inhabitants walking about with poles sticking out behind them.

(Charles Kingsley, *The Water-Babies: A Fairy Tale for a Land-Baby*, London, 1863)

ONE-EYED, KINGDOM OF THE, in West Africa, inhabited by people who have only one eye. The custom of the country obliges subjects to imitate their rulers as closely as possible. Therefore, in the distant past, when a one-eyed queen was born, the people immediately put out one of their own eyes. The tradition has been carried on up to the present day. Visitors conscious of etiquette are advised that it is unseemly for anyone with two eyes to appear at court.

The inhabitants say that it is an advantage for their ministers to be blind in one eye, and that if they had two they would tend to keep one on their own interests. However, it is feared that a future king might not have a nose and that subjects will be forced to cut off their own.

Visitors should see the Royal Palace, a hut four times the size of a normal dwelling. Here the queen, in a bed covered with thirty tiger skins, offers her favours to strangers. Visitors who refuse to accept her offer are beaten and, if they persist in their refusal, are quartered, roasted and eaten.

(Jean Gaspard Dubois-Fontanelle, *Aventures Philosophiques*, Paris, 1766)

OOG, a river valley in the underground continent of PELLUCIDAR. Its precise location is uncertain, but the river is reported to flow into one of the inland seas near SARI. Oog is separated from the Valley of the JUKANS by a mountain range.

There is one main settlement in the valley, a primitive village built of sharp reeds set vertically in the ground with long strands of tough grass woven between them. This is the home of the warrior women of Oog, strong bearded women whose nature and attributes are more usually associated with men. In the Oog society, which appears to be unique in all Pellucidar, men are kept as slaves and are forced to work the gardens of the village. They are badly treated by their owners, who frequently beat them severely. Stealing food from the gardens is considered a serious offence and is punished by particularly savage floggings. The men are allowed little sleep and are given coarse inadequate food.

The cultural level of Oog is low, even by the standards of Pellucidar. The women make plain earthenware vessels and rough baskets, and their crude stone knives and axes are regarded as great treasures. In warfare these are supplemented by slings and by ingenious smoke-sticks. The smoke-sticks are reeds which give off a heavy acrid smoke when they burn; the women fling them at their enemies to choke and blind them and to provide themselves with a smoke-screen.

The other tribes of Pellucidar grudgingly concede that the canoes made by the Oog women are among the best in the whole underground realm. They are used effectively in raids on other villages and to bring back slaves to the valley.

(Edgar Rice Burroughs, *Land of Terror*, New York, 1944)

OO-OH, an island off the coast of CASPAK, in the South Pacific, home of the Wieroos, the most highly developed of all the races of this area. The Wieroos have developed the ability to fly with large wings attached to their shoulders; these wings are a result of the unique system of evolution found on Caspak.

The legends of the Galu of Caspak state that the Wieroos originally had only rudimentary wings and were in other respects similar to the Galus. There was great rivalry between the two races, mainly because the Wieroos were the first to be able to produce offspring viviparously, whereas most of the races of Caspak have to start from the most primitive stage of evolution to produce each generation. Despite this, the Wieroos were not able to produce female children. Perhaps to compensate, they concentrated on developing their intellectual potential and invented the concept of *tas-ad*, which means "Doing everything the right or Wieroo way." Gradually they became convinced that *tas-ad* should be carried throughout the world, and that all who stood in their way should be destroyed. In line with this belief, all those whose wings were not well-developed were killed off.

Because of their arrogance, the Wieroos began to be hated by all other peoples on Caspak and were eventually forced to leave and settle on Oo-oh.

In their present form, the Wieroos resemble thin human beings with wings. Their pasty faces and sunken cheeks give them the air of a death's head, an impression heightened by their claw-like fingers and their long sinewy arms. Their bodies are completely hairless and they have no eyebrows or lashes. As they are still unable to reproduce female children, they kidnap women from the more advanced races of Caspak, using them to breed the next generation of Wieroo males. Occasionally male Galus are taken and tortured in an attempt to discover the secret behind their particular pattern of reproduction.

The entire culture of the Wieroos is based on murder. They murder members of their own species as well as outsiders; their young have to be kept in underground chambers to protect them from their fellows. The three Wieroo cities known to exist on the island are decorated with human skulls, many of them mounted on poles and painted blue and white. The pavements of their towns are also lined with skulls. When a victim is killed, only his skull is kept; the rest of the body is left to float down the river to be eaten by the great reptiles found on the coast.

Wieroo cities are an almost indescribable jumble of buildings. The houses rise up on top of one another to a height of perhaps one hundred feet. In many areas they are so closely wedged together that no light can reach the lowest tiers and it is impossible to move between them at ground level. The streets are narrow and crooked, and in some places completely blocked by buildings erected across them in an extremely haphazard fashion. The colours of the buildings vary greatly, as do the shapes, but most have cup-shaped roofs to catch water. Normally there is an opening somewhere in the roof that serves as a doorway, and access to the lower levels is by ladder. At every level the cities are decorated with more skulls.

The main city is dominated by a tower made from skulls and a huge building called the Blue Place of the Seven Skulls. The latter is a square building surmounted by seven poles, each bearing a skull, and is often used to house prisoners. Nearby stands the main temple, an enormous edifice alone in an open space. Its saucer-shaped roof projects beyond the eaves, giving it the appearance of an inverted coolie hat. Inside the temple is hung with hides and furs, mostly those of leopards and tigers. The walls are decorated with skulls, and other ornaments mainly of gold—presumably the spoils of war, as the Wieroos themselves do not wear any jewellery. Hieroglyphics have been traced on the ceiling and the walls are decorated both with skulls and with Wieroo wings. Underground passages lead down to the River of Death, which flows out to the open sea.

The Wieroos live mainly on a mixture of fruit, vegetables and different small fish, mixed with a variety of unidentifiable items. The mixture is so seasoned as to produce an effect that is both baffling and delicious. Meals are taken in large rooms where the Wieroos sit on high pedestals with hollowed out tops. Each pedestal seats four Wieroos, each with a wooden skewer and a clamshell for the more liquid elements of their meal. The Wieroos habitually eat with great speed and noise, often losing much of their food in their attempt to wolf it down as quickly as possible. In these eating-places all quarrels and altercations are strictly forbidden; they are therefore the only safe place in the entire city.

Outside the cities, Oo-oh is a pleasantly forested island. Unlike its neighbour Caspak, it does not have a large number of predators or prehistoric reptiles. It seems that when the Wieroos first came to the island it was almost devoid of animal life, and most of the species now found here have been introduced by the Wieroos and have bred naturally.

The Wieroos dress is of fine woven cloth. The colour of their robes indicates their place in the social hierarchy, a position which is determined by the numbers of murders they have committed. The lowest ranking wear white; once they have admitted to sufficient murders that have remained undetected they are allowed to wear yellow stripes on their robes. The highest are indicated by red and blue. Blue appears to be the colour of murder itself; only one Wieroo at any one time is permitted to wear a robe of solid blue, and he is referred to as "He who speaks to Luata." Little is known of the religion of the Wieroos; they seem to be the only people from Caspak to have developed an organized form of religious belief and they regard themselves as the chosen race.

(Edgar Rice Burroughs, *The Land That Time Forgot*, New York, 1918; Edgar Rice Burroughs, *Out of Time's Abyss*, New York, 1918)

OPAR, a mighty city in a narrow African valley. Arriving from one of the western mountain ranges, the traveller will see great walls, lofty shrines, turrets, minarets and domes sparkling red and yellow in the sunlight. Though the wall of the city is almost impregnable, travellers are advised to seek a cleft some twenty inches wide through which to enter. Within, a flight of concrete steps worn hollow by the centuries leads to a narrow court and a second wall. A passage crosses this inner wall and takes the visitor to a dark and forbidding conglomerate of crumbling buildings. Looming above them is the Temple of the Sun where the Flaming God is worshipped.

The Temple of the Sun is entered through a tall colonnade capped by the statue of a gigantic bird. On the walls are carved strange images of impossible men and beasts, and golden tablets with hieroglyphics are set inside the masonry. The rooms inside the temple branch off one another, and all seem to be built of gold. Deep inside the building is a small room, the Chamber of the Dead, where it is said the dead return to worship. The inhabitants of Opar believe that whoever enters this chamber is seized by the dead and sacrificed to their unthinkable gods.

From the Chamber of the Dead a secret passage leads into the Treasure Room filled with gold ingots. Behind it lies the Jewel Room of Opar where thousands of cut and uncut precious stones are kept. An earthquake struck the city in recent years and it is not known how much of the Temple of the Sun still stands.

It is interesting to observe the sacrificial ceremony that takes place in the Temple. The high priestess waits until a ray of sun touches the victim on the altar-stone; this is supposed to mean that the sun has chosen the victim as its own. Then long files of men and women advance with golden cups in their hands. The priestess plunges a knife into the victim's heart, the blood is received in the cups and the celebrants drink to the sun's good health.

It is said that Opar is an abandoned colony of ATLANTIS; that its inhabitants have forgotten their glorious past but that traces of their long-lost grandeur can be seen in some of the quaint decorations on the Temple's walls; but this has not been proven.

(Edgar Rice Burroughs, *The Return of Tarzan*, New York, 1913; Edgar Rice Burroughs, *Tarzan and the Jewels of Opar*, New York, 1916; Edgar Rice Burroughs, *Tarzan the Invincible*, New York, 1931)

OPHIR, a kingdom in south-east Arabia, where the finest gold is considered to be a pure and saintly life; the best silver, righteousness and justice; the whitest ivory, an honest commerce; the truest apes, an obedient lower class; and the most stately peacocks, wise governors. It is said that King Solomon himself brought gold, silver, ivory, apes and peacocks from Ophir to his own realm.

The church of Ophir is Evangelical Protestant but there is religious freedom throughout the country as long as people are consistent with God's honour. Public preachers and theologians must confine themselves to the exegesis and ethics of religion and avoid, as far as possible, controversial subjects. There are stringent laws for observing Sunday as a day of holy rest.

In the eyes of the law of Ophir, the highest virtues are justice and charity. Filthy talk and low jests are strictly forbidden and the convicted offender, regardless of rank, has to wear a large pair of sow's ears on his head for one or more days, according to the charge. Habitual criminals are kept under restraint for life. A first offence, however, is not punished at all, except for restitution; a thief, for instance, must restore double the value of the article taken.

The king must be strictly faithful to his wife and a perfect example of justice and chastity; either he or the Crown Prince must make frequent excursions throughout the different provinces of the kingdom.

Travellers are advised that duelling is strictly forbidden; offenders must wear a blunt wooden sword and a fool's cap for life. If the duellists are distinguished by heraldic insignia granted by the State, their coats of arms must be changed to a head-piece with the visor down and a pair of spectacles on it, plus two cats as supporters.

(The Bible, 1 Kings 9: 28; 10; 11; 22: 48; 1 Chronicles 29: 4; 2 Chronicles 8: 18; Job 22: 24; Psalms 45: 9; Isaiah 13: 12; Anonymous, *Der Wohleingerichtete Staat Des bisher von vielen gesushten aber nicht gefundenen Königreichs Ophir welcher Die Völlige Kirchen-Verfassung Einrichtung der Hohen und niedern Schulen des Königs Qualitäten Vermählungs-Art Auferziehung der Königlichen Printzen und Printzessinnen die Königliche Hoffhalt und Regierung die dabei befindlichen Bedienten Land und Stadt-Obrigkeiten deren Erwähl wohl insgemein als Insonderheit das Staats-Policey, Justiz-Commercien-Cammer und Gesundheits-Wesen betreffende Gesetze und Ordnungen Nebst allen zu wissen nöthigen Nachrichten und Merchwürdigkeiten vorstellet,* Leipzig, 1699)

ORACLE OF THE BOTTLE, ISLAND OF THE, not far from LANTERNLAND, where travellers can obtain knowledgeable Lanterns as guides.

The Oracle itself resides in an extensive underground temple, the entrance to which lies beyond the far end of a vineyard planted by Bacchus himself. This vineyard bears leaves, flowers and fruit at all seasons and is planted with all sorts of vines, from Falernian to Malmsey and from Graves to perfumed Anjou.

As the visitor crosses the vineyard, guided by his Lantern, he must eat three grapes and put vineleaves in his shoes to signify that he despises wine, has conquered it and trodden it underfoot. At the end of the vineyard stands an antique arch with a carved memorial to drinkers: it represents rows of flagons, barrels, firkins and other containers, glasses and goblets, and a variety of delicacies such as cream-cakes, smoked ox tongues and several kinds of cheese. On the face of the arch an inscription reads:

> *"Ere you pass this postern, pray*
> *Get a Lantern on the way."*

Beyond the arch is a beautiful arbour of vines, hung with grapes of five hundred different colours and in five hundred different shapes. These are not natural, but the product of the science of viticulture. At the end of the arbour stand three ancient ivy trees; the traveller must make himself an Albanian hat of their leaves and wear it. This signifies that he is not dominated by wine and that his mind is calm and free from all perturbations of the senses.

From here, the traveller and his Lantern enter a plaster-lined vault, roughly painted with women and satyrs dancing around Silenus on his ass. The vault gives access to an underground marble staircase which leads, after many flights, down to the temple entrance itself. The jasper portal is in the Doric style, bearing a gold inscription in Greek: "In wine lies truth." The doors are of bronze and are adorned with relief carvings of vine tendrils, delicately enamelled. A hexagonal loadstone hangs from the doors, with bunches of garlic on either side of it. The doors are opened by tying the garlic back on two crimson silk cords provided for the purpose and throwing the loadstone to the right. When the garlic is far enough away not to neutralize the power of the loadstone, the latter attracts a steel plate concealed within the bronze and the doors slide open with a soft and delightful murmur. Once the doors have been opened, the Lantern who has guided the visitor so far withdraws: for reasons better not revealed. Lanterns are not allowed to enter the temple itself.

The pavement of the temple is a mosaic of little squares, all of fine, polished stones in their natural colours: red jasper flecked with other hues, porphyry, lycophthalamy, agate with milky streaks, chalcedony and green jasper. The floor of the main porch is also a mosaic of tiny stones, but these represent handfuls of vine leaves and grapes. The mosaic is so skilfully arranged that many visitors actually lift their feet and take long strides for fear of entangling themselves in the trailing vines. The temple walls and vault are covered with marble and porphyry mosaics illustrating the victory of Bacchus over the Indians.

In the exact centre of the temple stands a curious heptagonal fountain. Its base and superstructure are made of the purest and most transparent alabaster, about a foot high. The outside of the fountain is divided into equal parts by a number of columns, miniature altars and Doric mouldings. Inside, the fountain is circular. At the mid-point of every angle of the edge there is a hollow column; these columns, combined, form a circle or balustrade twenty-eight inches high. The first column is of a heavenly blue sapphire; the second, of hyacinth, inscribed with the Greek letters α and ϵ at intervals; the third, of diamond, as dazzling as lightning; the fourth, of spider-ruby or amethyst; the fifth is an emerald; the sixth column is of agate; the seventh is of transparent moonstone. These are the stones assigned by the ancient Chaldeans to the seven planets, and above them hang figures of the classical gods, holding emblems of the appropriate metal.

The bases of the capitals, architraves and cornices around the fountain are of fine gold. The capitals support a crystal cupola carved with the signs of the zodiac, the solstices, equinoxes and the most important fixed stars. The cupola is surmounted by three long pearls of uniform size, exactly like tear drops. They hang together in the shape of a *fleur-de-lys*, with a heptagonal carbuncle in the centre.

The fountain empties via three channels inlaid with pearls, set at each of the equilateral angles on the outside edge; all three are corkscrew-shaped and double. As the sacred fountain empties, it produces a strange music which sounds as though it comes from far underground. The water of the fountain has the miraculous quality of tasting like whatever wine the drinker cares to imagine.

The temple is lit by a central lamp of crystal, with a diameter of two feet six inches. This round lamp is said to represent the intellectual sphere, the centre of which is in all points and the circumference in none, and which some—like Pascal—have called "God." In the centre of this lamp is a smaller, gourd-shaped crystal vessel containing a wick of asbestine flax: when lit, it casts a light as bright as day. The lamp is suspended from the vault by three silver chains. In the triangle formed by the chains hangs a golden plate, pierced by four holes from which more lamps of precious stone—amethyst, Lydian carbuncles, opal and topaz—are suspended.

The Oracle of the Bottle is housed in a separate chapel within the temple, a circular building of transparent stone which admits the light of the sun. The chapel is completely symmetrical: the diameter of the floor is equal to the height of the vault. In its centre stands a second heptagonal fountain of fine alabaster, full of limpid water. The Bottle, half-immersed in this water, is almost oval, but its lip is slightly more raised than a true oval would allow.

Anyone wishing to consult the oracle is led into this chapel by Bacbuc, priestess of the Oracle. The visitor is then told to kiss the edge of the fountain and to perform three Bacchic dances. He then sits down between two stools and sings an Athenian drinking song. After the song has been sung, the priestess throws something into the water, which immediately begins to boil fiercely. A cracking sound is heard and the Oracle will then answer whatever question the visitor has put to it. The visitor is advised to listen to its pronouncements with only one ear. If an interpretation is required, the priestess will give the visitor a silver book in the shape of a breviary and tell him to drink a chapter or taste a glass. The "book" is in fact a Falernian wine. The visitor, satisfied or not, is then asked to leave by the way he came.

(François Rabelais, *Le cinquiesme et dernier livre des faicts et dicts du bon Pantagruel, auquel est contenu la visitation de l'Oracle de la dive Bacbuc, et le mot de la bouteille; pour lequel avoir est entrepris tout ce long voyage,* Paris, 1564)

ORASULLA, capital of ALBUR.

ORATORS' ISLAND, one of several high islands near Tierra del Fuego. Even though the land is fertile and rich in natural resources, the inhabitants are thin and scraggy, and nearly always die of hunger. Their addiction to speechifying leaves little time for mastication.

(Abbé Pierre François Guyot Desfontaines, *Le Nouveau Gulliver, ou Voyage De Jean Gulliver, Fils Du Capitaine Gulliver. Traduit d'un Manuscrit Anglois. Par Monsieur L.D.F.,* Paris, 1730)

ORIAB, see PNOTH; also NGRANEK.

ORODRUIN, an active volcanic mountain in the north-west of MORDOR, a great mass of ash, slag and burnt stone, now known as Mount Doom, and the Mountain of Fire. Its long grey slopes rise to three thousand feet above the plain and are topped by the central cone, which rises a further fifteen hundred feet. Red light glows from the mountain's cone and from the stream of lava that flows down its sides. The smoke and fumes given off by the volcano make breathing difficult and have reduced the surrounding area to a desolate landscape of ash and dust. A road known as Sauron's Road winds its way up and around the mountain to the gates of Sammath Naur, the Chambers of Fire.

The Chambers are entered through a door facing due east and marked with the eye symbol adopted by Sauron the Dark Lord of Mordor. The Chambers of Fire were the very centre of Sauron's power and were the heart of the realm of terror he established in Mordor before his final defeat. In the fissure known as the Cracks of Doom burns the Fire of Doom, in whose intense heat Sauron forged the One Ring of power which he hoped would allow him to enslave all of MIDDLE-EARTH. At the end of that age he lost the Ring; the forces of the Last Alliance (of elves, dwarves and men) fought him at DAGORLAD and carried the war all the way to the slopes of Orodruin.

There Sauron was defeated, and King Isildur hacked off Sauron's finger to gain the ring and destroy the Dark Lord's power.

Had Isildur cast the ring back into the Cracks of Doom, into the only flames that had the power to melt it, Sauron would have been destroyed forever. But already the corruption of the One Ring was at work. Isildur coveted it for himself, and carried it away, and was himself betrayed by it.

Three thousand years later the One Ring was again conveyed to the slopes of Orodruin, by the ringbearer Frodo, who meant to cast it into the Cracks of Doom. He too was possessed at the last minute, and stood hesitating with the ring upon his finger. But his companion, Gollum, who also lusted after the ring, attacked him and bit off his finger, and fell into the fires of the Cracks of Doom, taking the One Ring with him.

The destruction of the Ring precipitated a major eruption which caused great destruction throughout Mordor. This was in March 3019, Third Age. Major volcanic eruptions are also known to have occurred on the occasion of Sauron's return to Mordor in 3320 Second Age, and in 2954 Third Age.

(J.R.R. Tolkien, *The Fellowship of the Ring*, London, 1954; J.R.R. Tolkien, *The Return of the King*, London, 1955; J.R.R. Tolkien, *The Silmarillion*, London, 1977)

OROFENA, an island in the south Pacific, to the east of Samoa, under which resides one of the most dangerous enemies of mankind. Although surrounded by a coral reef, Orofena is, in fact, of volcanic origin. The island itself is the rim of an extinct volcano, a broad, circular band of land sloping down to a large, central lake. In the centre of the lake is a small island.

Much of the island is covered in forest, although there are also extensive areas of bushland dotted with waving palms. There is little cultivated land, as the natives are a lazy race who cultivate only enough food to meet their immediate needs, subsisting mainly on breadfruit and the produce of wild trees. Their only domesticated animal is the pig, but even the pigs are half wild and not bred in captivity. The population is estimated at between five and ten thousand. Infanticide is practised to prevent it becoming too large to survive on available food resources.

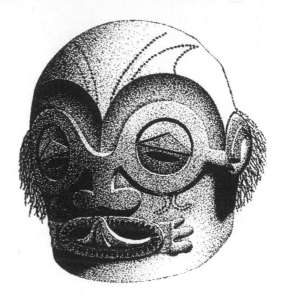

A priest's mask from OROFENA.

The people are handsome, tall and slim with fine, regular features. Although they remain extremely primitive, they have an air of great antiquity, as though they had once known an older world and had forgotten it. The men go naked apart from loincloths; the women hang garlands of flowers around their necks. Their leader wears a feather cloak and the priests wear hideous masks and basket-like headdresses, surmounted by plumes. Their language is expressive and musical, and they appear to understand Polynesian, although their stress system is somewhat different.

The people of Orofena have no traditions regarding their origins, but believe that their ancestors always inhabited the island. They are a musical and poetic people, with many songs in a language they no longer understand.

They refer to their god as Oro, "he who fights," and traditionally worship an idol supposed to represent him, performing rites of human sacrifice and cannibalism. Oro is said to be the servant of Degai (Fate), the creator who made and oversees all things. Legend has it that Oro caused the surrounding lands to be drowned in the sea, sparing only the lives of the Orofenians' ancestors, and then took up residence in the volcano in the centre of the lake, of which only the summit is now visible. For the Orofenians, the lake is a sacred place and the island is shunned by all but the priests.

The cult of Oro and the legends surrounding him have been discovered to have a basis in fact. Shortly before World War One, three Englishmen were wrecked on Orofena when their yacht was caught in a cyclone. Despite the opposition of the priests, they succeeded in landing on the island in the lake. Here, in an artificial chamber beneath a cave, they found two bodies in coffins of crystal. On closer examination, the bodies proved to be alive and in a state of suspended animation. It was then that the Englishmen made the astounding discovery that the sleepers were no other than Oro himself and his daughter Yva, who had lain in suspended animation for 250,000 years, the last survivors of a semi-divine race that had once ruled the world.

For many centuries they had ruled as great monarchs, discovering secrets, wielding immense political power and accumulating boundless wealth. Known as the Children of Wisdom, they gradually became a race apart, living in isolation and indifferent to those who suffered and died around them. The world, united under a single ruler, finally declared war on the Children of Wisdom, forcing them to seek safety in Nyo, a fortified city exactly beneath the island of Orofena. Trapped in their underground refuge, the Children of Wisdom survived for centuries maintaining their worship of the god Degai, and nurturing their arts and sciences. But eventually their powers began to fade—"like flowers in the dark," says one of their priests—and the nations of earth began to triumph.

Oro refused a proposed peace settlement which would have involved teaching men secrets known only to the Children of Wisdom and giving his daughter in marriage to the Prince of Nations, ruler of the world. Seeing that his race was doomed, Oro resolved to destroy the whole of mankind and to sleep for many centuries. Altering the balance of the world, Oro turned land into sea and sea into land and mankind was drowned.

When Oro awoke from his long sleep, he showed the Englishmen something of his terrible powers: by leaving his body and travelling in the world on a spiritual plane, Oro took the explorers to visit the ruins of the underground city of Nyo with its wide, silent streets, its houses and courts of marble, and its grandiose temples and palaces. In Nyo, the Englishmen tasted the "water of life," a miraculous liquid which had once sustained the Children of Wisdom and which was perhaps their most closely guarded secret. In turn, they spoke to Oro of developments in the modern world. The information they gave him, in addition to the things he saw as his spirit-body travelled the modern world, convinced Oro of the need to destroy the world once more, in order that a truly great civilization might be built on its ruins. Taking Yva and the Englishmen with him, he sank deep into the centre of the earth, to the final "centre of balance." Here—as is well known—a monstrous flaming gyroscope made by nature herself controls the fate of the world. Oro's plan was to deflect it from its normal path and thus flood the earth's surface once again. Only Yva's last-minute intervention prevented him from doing so. She perished, by flinging herself in the path of Oro's force—which caused, nevertheless, a minor earthquake.

The three Englishmen succeeded in regaining Orofena through a series of tunnels, only to find that what had been a volcano was now, thanks to the earthquake, a tiny and insignificant islet in the lake. It is not known how much of the ruins of Nyo survive beneath the surface.

Travellers today will find that the only visible remains of the civilization of the Children of Wisdom are the scattered ruins of Orofena itself and a few curious pieces of statuary.

The Orofenians saw the earthquake as the direct result of the white man's sacrilege and forced the three explorers to leave the island in a lifeboat that had somehow survived the original wreck. The castaways were eventually found by a tramp steamer and returned to Europe.

The fate of Oro himself has not been determined. It is possible that he lies behind the legends of sleeping kings, such as Barbarossa or Arthur. Travellers on Orofena are best advised not to open any coffins they may find, and to report leaky faucets immediately to the local authorities.

(Henry Rider Haggard, *When the World Shook, Being an Account of the Great Adventure of Bastin, Bickley and Arbuthnot*, London, 1918)

OROONOKO ISLAND, in the West Indies, mainly known for its commerce with Great Britain. It exchanges fish, venison, monkeys, parrots and baskets for beads and metallic objects.

The natives have reddish-yellow skin and adorn themselves with beads and shells which they fix to their skin with needles. They have no king. The oldest warrior is recognized as the natural leader and is never disobeyed.

The natives keep one day in the year for mourning the death of the English governor. He had not died, however, when this custom began. It seems that he had promised to attend a certain meal but failed to appear and because the islanders believe that only death will cause a man to break his promise, they automatically supposed him to be dead. They grieved for him and even his personal appearance would not console them; they ignored him as if he had been a ghost. Funeral games are held yearly in his honour.

(Aphra Behn, *Oroonoko, or the Royal Slave*, London, 1678)

ORPHAN ISLAND, a republic in the Pacific formerly known as Smith Island. It consists of two peninsulas joined by a narrow neck of land, surrounded by a lagoon and a coral reef. The flora is typical of such islands, though the number of trees has considerably diminished. The fauna includes mocking-birds, birds of paradise, giant iguanas, monkeys, parrots, land crabs, armadillos and snakes. Sharks sometimes enter the lagoon.

In 1855, a group of orphans, going from London to California, were shipwrecked on the island together with their teacher, Miss Charlotte Smith. In 1923, certain documents came into the possession of Mr. Thinkwell, lecturer in sociology at Cambridge, in which his grandfather, captain of the orphans' ship, told how he had abandoned the castaways. He gave the position of the island and expressed the hope that a rescue party might eventually be sent out.

Thinkwell sailed to Tahiti (French Polynesia) and from there to Orphan Island where he discovered Miss Smith to be still alive, aged ninety-eight and sovereign of the island. Identifying herself with Queen Victoria, she lived in a house called Balmoral (which can still be visited) heavily decorated in the Victorian style, and she had organized an autocratic rule based on the precepts of Victorian society. Soon after Mr. Thinkwell's arrival, Miss Smith died, on September 1, 1925—her birthday. The discontented orphans invaded Parliament and called for its dissolution. Mr. Thinkwell found a compromising solution by adjusting the privileges of the ruling class—Miss Smith's descendants—and by giving the orphans fairer treatment. The name was changed to Orphan Island and a republic was established. Under the Thinkwell influence, the island has undergone a renaissance, with the appearance of a large amount of indifferent literature and art, mainly drama, previously banned as immoral.

During the reign of Charlotte Smith, her direct descendants formed the upper class; the orphans, who had to hire themselves out for work, formed the lower class. By 1885, the whole island was partitioned among the Smith family, who were also members of Parliament. The Parliament comprised only one house—with twenty-nine members and a cabinet of six—inspired by the English model. Only men who owned or rented a certain amount of property were allowed to vote. Education was based on Eurocentric, religiously inspired principles, although of course the Smiths and the orphans attended separate schools. Though the State religion was Protestantism, a small Catholic sect, as well as a small group of atheists, existed on the island. Towards the end of the nineteenth century, a French Jesuit was shipwrecked here together with two African converts. He perished in a "no popery" riot and was eaten by his Africans.

Charlotte Smith established a number of Victorian laws on her island. No one was allowed to sleep on the beach. Use of Latin was forbidden. No games or fishing were allowed on Sundays. By decree, people had to bow at the mention of Miss Smith's name and the national anthem was sung whenever she appeared in public. The laws were enforced by the police and by the court, which maintained the system of trial by jury. Capital punishment for murder was by drowning. The island's best-loved sport, turtle racing, though still forbidden, persists in most places.

Many Victorian customs survive on Orphan Island, such as a twice-yearly "season" with parties, balls, and the like. Cricket is played, babies are said to be found under coconut trees and the milkman delivers coconut milk to the door. Evening wear consists of plumes and feathers. Social customs and attitudes derive from the few books saved from the original wreck: *Wuthering Heights, The Holy War* and *Mixing in Society or Everybody's Book of Correct Conduct*. Religious texts and quotations from poets are carved on the island's trees to provide maxims for virtuous living.

Time is told by sun-dials, moon-dials and

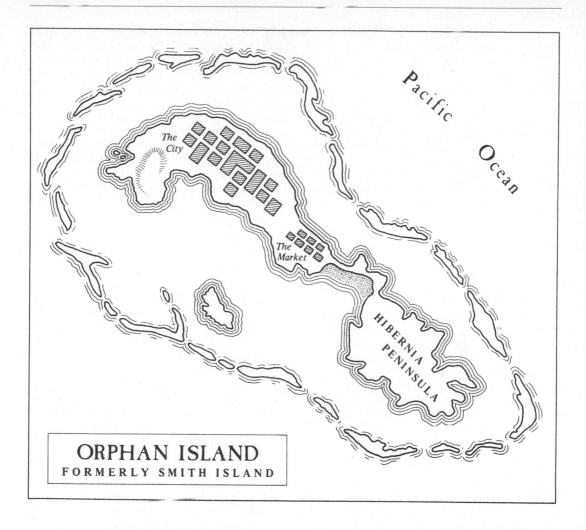

ORPHAN ISLAND
FORMERLY SMITH ISLAND

shells of sand, which run out in an hour. Orphan Island time is ten minutes slow by English standards. News on the island is conveyed through a publication written in the damp sand near the edge of the sea, dictated to two men who write it with sticks. It is clearly legible to the crowds who come to read it. Troublesome events are not publicized. Orphan Island money, which replaced the initial system of direct exchange, consists of shells and pieces of coral. Orphan Island food comprises turtle soup, tortoise meat, yams, breadfruit and oysters. People drink fermented fruit juices rather like sweet cider.

The city consists of well-constructed wooden houses. On the east coast is the commercial quarter, rather like an open-air market. The smaller of

the two peninsulas, Hibernia, is traditionally considered the home of the malcontents, where the defeated rebels of a 1910 revolution retired in disgrace. Hibernia is much less fertile than the rest of Orphan Island.

(Rose Macaulay, *Orphan Island*, London, 1924)

ORRIMY, see HOSK.

ORSENNA, an ancient land that lies across the Sea of Sirtes from FARGHESTAN. Once a major trading empire, Orsenna has fallen into decline with the silting up of the sea and the gradual encroachment of the desert. Many of the southern ports are now completely silted up and shipping is confined to fishing and local trade.

The people of Orsenna are austere, even cold in their behaviour, and dress in an extremely sober fashion; the southerners are somewhat more exuberant and out-going.

The hinterland provides a habitat for wild sheep and herds of buffalo, as well as *jerboa*. Wild dogs roam the semi-desert steppes. The typical bird of the coastal area is the cormorant.

Although Orsenna rarely experiences bad storms, visitors should note that the winters are wet. Fog and mist are common on the southern coast.

Orsenna is a Christian country but its Christianity has been heavily criticized because of its intervention during the heretical quarrels of the Eastern churches; it seems that Orsennian religion was originally connected with the Nestorian churches of the east and even with certain Islamic initiation rites. The religious life of the country includes many popular superstitions, some of them connected with the church of St. Damase in Maremma, famous for its Persian cupolas. St. Damase is also noted for the custom observed at Christmas, when the traditional crib is replaced by a model of a fishing boat. Apart from the city churches, there are scattered chapels and monasteries in the south. White-robed monks and itinerant priests serve these out-posts of religion.

The capital, also called Orsenna, lies inland on a hill above the River Zenta. The upper parts of the town cluster around the Cathedral of St. Jude and the severe feudal palace of the Council of Security. The narrow, crowded streets of this area are the traditional setting for the gossip, rumours and insurrections that are so characteristic of Orsennian political life. On the banks of the Zenta lie the capital's commercial and trading areas, often shrouded in the mist that rises from the marshes along the river. Much of Orsenna shows signs of decay: the Selvaggi Gardens on the outskirts have now fallen into disrepair and are little frequented. As well as being the commercial and administrative centre of the country, Orsenna is the site of an old and famous university. The Gallery of the Council should be visited for its collection of paintings, including works by the famous portraitist Longhone.

Maremma, the so-called Venice of the Sirtes, lies to the south, near the mouth of one of the few *oueds*, or streams, that flow into the sea. Much of the delta is now dry land with Maremma some

way inland. Maremma once enjoyed great prosperity as a trading port with Farghestan before war interrupted relations between the two countries. Although many of them are now semi derelict, the canals and palaces testify to its past greatness. The Aldobrandian Palace, slightly apart from the town itself, rises between a canal and a lagoon. Its rectangular tower recalls the high period of Orsennian architecture, but its overall appearance is that of a fortified castle. The ground floor is surrounded by arcades crowned by a terrace, and traces of the gardens that once surrounded it can still be seen. Although Maremma is now in decline, many of the aristocratic families of Orsenna come here to spend their late summers.

Maremma is the nearest town to the Admiralty, an important coastal garrison originally built as a defensive system in the wars against Farghestan. The fortress has recently been restored following rumours of a possible invasion. Visitors will notice that the walls are still covered with the creepers that spread over them in the days when the Admiralty was uninhabited and when its ditches had been allowed to fill up. The Chart Chamber, at the heart of the building, contains an important collection of maps and charts, including some of Farghestan which travellers will not find anywhere else. On a low hill above the fortress, the cemetery, enclosed by stone walls, is the traditional burial place for the lords of neighbouring estates. In an annual ceremony, a wreath of myrtle and laurel is placed here before the arms of Orsenna.

The Admiralty is connected with the capital by a badly maintained road, some of which shows evidence of having been built by the Romans. Before reaching the desolate Sirte Province that lies around the Admiralty, the ancient road crosses an arid semi-desert region, frequented only by nomads and crossed by occasional paths. The road then passes through the ruined town of Sagra, once the centre of an important irrigation system, but now badly overgrown. Even in its decay, Sagra shows the traditional Orsennian taste for the "noble" materials, granite and marble. Beyond Sagra, the road runs by the coastal mudflats and empty lagoons of the Sirte coast. Neither the Admiralty nor the coastal province are regarded as particularly desirable naval or military postings.

Orsenna is ruled by the Seigneurie, or Assembly of Lords, who represent the ancient families of the country, and by an elected Senate. The executive body is the Chancellery; a Council of Security is responsible for all matters affecting internal and external security. As the Council uses a large army of spies, the true extent and influence of its power is difficult to determine.

The Constitution of Orsenna is often cited abroad as a model for good government, but it gives close observers the impression of being a museum piece. Over the centuries the traditional workings of the government have become incomprehensible to all but a very small elite. The true nature of Orsennian politics and of the origins of the long-standing war with Farghestan are known to only a few, and the principles behind both are jealously handed down from generation to generation. Shifts in the balance of power take place almost secretly, involving much intrigue and internal espionage, and few people even realize that a major political change has actually taken place. Orsennian political life is made even more difficult to follow by the practice of "dosage" whereby successful parties gradually absorb elements that initially seem quite foreign to their position and nature. Nor are matters helped by the formality and archaism of the official language. The ancient terms are still used whenever possible, even though some of them refer to things which no longer exist in any real sense. Thus, the Sirte coastline is habitually referred to as "the front" and the few derelict boats still kept there as "the fleet."

Travellers interested in a comprehensible account of Orsenna's history are advised to consult Danielo's *History of the Origins,* which gives an authoritative account of the early history of Orsenna and its crusades against the infidels. Danielo also describes the rich civilization that existed at the time of the Arab invasion, when the whole coastal area was irrigated. Ruins of these irrigation works can be seen at Sagra and in the semi-desert areas of the south.

The more recent history of the country is a stormy succession of plots, assassinations and abductions, many of them involving the famous Aldobrandi family, members of which still live in Orsenna's Borgo suburb. Not a few of this ancient and noble family have known exile or death because of their political convictions and their actions during the war. For the last three hundred years, Orsenna has officially been at war with neighbouring Farghestan, initially because of pirate raids on the coast. In reprisal for these raids,

Rhages, Farghestan's capital, was bombarded by the Orsennian fleet, an event which is still annually commemorated. The war has simmered on ever since, although recently there have been few important incidents.

The Aldobrandi family have always been greatly involved in the wars. One of their number, Piero, deserted and helped to organize the defence of Rhages. His treachery is still remembered and visitors should note that it is customary to put on one's hat when passing his portrait in the Council Gallery in the capital (this portrait is in fact a copy; the original is in the palace of Maremma).

(Julien Gracq, *Le Rivage des Syrtes,* Paris, 1951)

ORTELGA, an island some twenty-five miles long in the Telthearna River which marks the northern frontier of the BEKLAN EMPIRE.

Most of Ortelga is covered by thick jungle; the only settlement is a small fortified town, also called Ortelga, on the eastern tip of the island. The forests of the island provide a home for a rich and varied fauna, including monkeys, peccaries and a variety of other small mammals. In spring the *kynat* bird visits the island during its northward-bound migration. Strikingly beautiful, with a gold crest, purple breast and gold-trimmed tail feathers, the *kynat is* believed to be the herald of summer and the inhabitants therefore deem it unlucky to kill the bird despite the high prices that can be obtained for its feathers in other places.

The town of Ortelga is defended by a complex system of fortifications, partly natural, partly man-made, stretching from shore to shore. Lines of pointed stakes combine with rows of trees, and patches of dense jungle provide natural obstacles. In some places, poisonous thorn plants have also been planted. At one point the outfall of a marsh has been dammed to form a shallow lake; the marsh is alive with alligators caught on the mainland and left here to breed. Beyond this defensive line stretches the "dead belt," a strip of land some eighty yards wide which is never entered except by those who have the task of maintaining it. The belt is full of traps: pits containing pointed logs or nests of snakes, and paths leading to enclosures into which arrows can be poured from platforms constructed in the trees above.

Although Ortelga remains a primitive outpost of the Beklan Empire, people from the island now rule the whole empire, as they did once in the far distant past. It was the Ortelgans who built the great city of BEKLA itself, and who traded throughout the land. In those days, the entire empire followed the Ortelgan cult of Shardik, a huge bear believed to represent the incarnate power of God. Ortelga was then a place of pilgrimage, with travellers coming from all over the Empire to pay homage to Lord Shardik. The island was reached via a causeway, now submerged, indicated by a monument on the opposite bank of the river, known as the Two-Sided Rocks, that is still standing.

(Richard Adams, *Shardik,* London, 1974)

OSGILIATH or CITADEL OF THE STARS, the original capital of GONDOR, built on both sides of the GREAT RIVER between MINAS MORGUL and MINAS TIRITH.

A splendid and heavily populated city from its founding in 3320 Second Age until 1640 Third Age, Osgiliath also housed the chief of the four palantíri, or Seeing-stones; when the Dome of Stars, in which the palantír was kept, was razed, the Stone was lost forever in the waters of the Great River.

Osgiliath was virtually unfortified and much of the city was burnt and destroyed in 1437 Third Age during the Kin-Strife, the great civil war that tore Gondor apart. It was left to fall into ruins and the capital was transferred to its present site at Minas Tirith in 1640, by which time many of the population had died during the great Plague. Although captured by forces from MORDOR, Osgiliath was easily retaken and was used as a military outpost for the defence of the new capital. In 3018 the ancient and mostly ruined buildings again fell into the hands of Sauron of Mordor, but were retaken a year later after the breaking of the siege of Minas Tirith. There is no record of the city having been rebuilt after this time.

(J.R.R. Tolkien, *The Fellowship of the Ring,* London, 1954; J.R.R. Tolkien, *The Two Towers,* London, 1954; J.R.R. Tolkien, *The Return of the King,* London, 1955; J.R.R. Tolkien, *The Silmarillion,* London, 1977)

OSSIRIAND, see LINDON.

OSSKIL, a large, mountainous island in the north of EARTHSEA. The interior is bleak, with long featureless stretches of moorland rising to the mountains. Osskil is in the path of the freezing winds from the north, and snow drifts over the high moors for much of the year.

In the rest of Earthsea, Osskil has something of a sinister reputation. Everything about it is different from the other islands of the archipelago. In Osskil mages and wizards do not rule, as they tend to do elsewhere in the islands. Unlike most of the people of Earthsea, Osskillians do not speak Hardic, but a dialect of their own. Whereas most of Earthsea uses ivory counters for currency, Osskil uses gold pieces. In fact gold is highly treasured by these northerners, as it is by the dragons of PENDOR; in neither case does love of gold lead to harmony. In many of the islands the crews of trade ships are partners and share the profits of an expedition. In Osskil the gaunt ships are crewed by a mixture of slaves, bondsmen and freemen, the latter being paid in gold. Osskillians do not even physically resemble the people of other regions; they are pale-skinned with dark, lank hair, whereas most inhabitants of Earthsea are copper-coloured.

The main trading port is Neshum, on the low-lying east coast. The town is grey and crouches below treeless hills; the port lies between long stone breakwaters that add to the bleakness of the landscape. All loading and unloading of ships is the preserve of the Sea-Guild of Neshum.

Little is known of the government of the island, but the Court of the Terrenon is the seat of the lord who rules the region between the Keksemt Moors and the Mountains of Os, inland from Neshum. The Court is a keep set high on a hill. A central tower rises above the surrounding courtyards like a sharp tooth. The interior is rich, a succession of curving marble halls hung with rich tapestries. Deep beneath the tower lies the Terrenon which gives the keep its name: this Terrenon is the central founding-stone of the building, a rough stone in a dungeon. Physically there is little to distinguish it from the stones around it, but the Terrenon gives off a tremendous aura because of the power imprisoned in it. The dungeon is chill and damp and the feeling of evil is almost palpable. The stone is said to have been made long before the islands of Earthsea were called up from the deep by Segoy; it was made when the world was made and will last until the world ends. If one with magical powers places his hand on it, it is said that it will answer his questions in its own voice. Few, however, can master the power of the stone and its influence is feared even by its owners. The door to the dungeon in which it is kept is guarded by spells of binding and cannot be opened without knowledge of their ancient lore. Several mages of Earthsea have thrown away their staffs to serve the stone whose power is greater than their own, and which can send out its creatures against those who challenge it. The creatures of the stone are hideous winged things, botched beasts belonging to ages before men or dragons, creatures which only exist in the malignant memory of the Terrenon, best left unexplored.

(Ursula K. Le Guin, *A Wizard of Earthsea*, New York, 1968)

OTHER END OF NOWHERE, a huge, ugly building, more forbidding than a new lunatic asylum. The principles on which its immense walls were built have yet to be discovered. The building is guarded by police truncheons with a single eye in the middle of their upper end. They have no need for a man to carry them and do their own work for themselves. They even have a thong by which to hang themselves up during their off-duty hours. A porter holds the lists of the lodgers in the Other End of Nowhere; the porter is a brass blunderbuss, loaded to the muzzle with slugs. Travellers who have, for any reason, been naughty in their own land are incarcerated in the Other End of Nowhere and pelted with a hail of solidified mothers' tears. This disagreeable experience is supposed to make the traveller mend his ways.

It was here that Tom the water-baby came on his journey of self-sacrifice and found Grimes, the sweep who had so mistreated him on earth. Grimes was imprisoned in a chimney, begging for beer and a pipe, which are of course forbidden here. Every evening he was tortured by hail which fell as soft rain but was transformed into hail that beat him like small shot as it approached him. Although Grimes did not know it these were the tears shed by his mother over his wicked ways. Only when Grimes expressed sorrow at the shameful way he had treated his mother was he able to leave the chimney in which he was trapped; and the sincere tears he shed over this washed him clean for the first time in his life. At this point Grimes was allowed to leave the Other End of Nowhere and was sent to work out the rest of his time sweeping the crater of Etna; for all anyone knows he may still be there.

(Charles Kingsley, *The Water-Babies: A Fairy Tale for a Land-Baby*, London, 1863)

OTRANTO, CASTLE OF, a vast and complex medieval fortification in Puglia, Italy, near the city of the same name. Many surprising supernatural phenomena have taken place here, including the apparition of a gigantic helmet, a hundred times larger than life, densely covered with black feathers. Portraits of the owner's forbears come to life to disapprove, by their presence, of the conduct of

View of the Castle of OTRANTO from the west.

the inhabitants of the castle. Sometimes, in the higher galleries, bodies of giants materialize with the apparent intention of enhancing the sad décor.

Female visitors to the castle are known to have been pursued with extra-marital intent through the intricate maze of galleries that twist and turn below the huge fortifications. The best escape route is along a secret passage that leads directly to the nearby church of St. Nicholas.

(Horace Walpole, *The Castle of Otranto*, London, 1765)

OUIDAH, a viceroyalty in the African kingdom of Dahomey, once known for its human sacrifices and now part of the Benin province of Nigeria, governed along Marxist principles. Although dusty and dirty, the town of Ouidah boasts several interesting buildings that date from the early nineteenth century. The Cathedral of the Immaculate Conception, on the *place* of the same name, is a stuccoed and decayed structure. Seams of rust splinter the iron pillars of the aisles, while the blue planks of the roof are rotten. Someone has stolen the ivory Dove of Peace inlaid into the altar table, and the statue of the Virgin is covered in cobwebs. In keeping with the national spirit, a red star is hung over the crèche and the faces of the Holy Family have been repainted in black. The confessional is full of scarlet drums. The Rue du Monsignor Steinmetz leads from the cathedral to the Place du Marché Zobé, where fetish priests slaughter fowl over Aizan, the Market God, but the rites of the mysterious Python Fetish proper are celebrated across from the cathedral, in a temple that consists of a huddle of mud huts surrounded by trees. Turkey buzzards drift in the milky sky, crickets chirp loudly in every crevice, fruit bats flit among the guava trees.

On the Rue Lenine, tourists have a choice of two hotels: the Windsor and the Anti-Windsor. Drinks can be bought at the bar Ennemi du Soir, and travel guides (when available) can be found in the Librairie Moderne, which nowadays holds little more than government-approved publications: back issues of *La Femme soviétique*, the *Thoughts* of Kim Il-Sung, the socialist novel *Le Baobab*, Racine's *Bajazet* and the complete works of Engels. To reach the Portuguese Fort (not really a worthwhile excursion) visitors can hire one of two taxis: the Confidence Car or Baby Confidence.

The ancestral home of the famous Viceroy of Ouidah, Francisco Manoel da Silva, adventurer and slave-dealer, is a mud-walled compound to the west of the taxi park. The doors are painted the colour of the inhabitants' skin. The old gaming saloon in the house can be visited; it is furnished with pictures of the Viceroy in gilded frames, a billiard table, Japanese porcelain bowls, spittoons and wicker seats. The Viceroy's famous music-box collection is displayed in the entrance hall. The Viceroy's bedroom, overlooking a garden of red earth and plastic flowers where lizards sun themselves on flat white marble tombs, can be visited only by permission of the laundrywoman, Ms. Yaya Adelina. Two objects draw the visitor's eye: the Goanese four-poster bed, with ebony uprights and a headboard set with ivory medallions, and a painted plaster statue of Saint Francis of Assisi lifting his hands in prayer. On the wall hangs a wreath of arums in memory of the Viceroy, and on a shelf are displayed a gilt crucifix, a yellowing Ecce Homo and the family emblem, a silver elephant. A white marble plaque, set in the floor, reads (in Portuguese):

FRANCISCO MANOEL DA SILVA
Born in Brazil in 1785
Died in Ouidah on 8 March 1857

Visitors require visas, and are usually allowed to stay for up to three months.

(Bruce Chatwin, *The Viceroy of Ouidah*, London, 1980)

OUT, a wooded island not far from the Land of CHARGES. The islanders are all good trenchermen and have a curious habit of slashing their skin to let their fat out; this is said to make them feel more comfortable and grow more quickly, like trees with slit bark.

In accordance with local custom, the islander who has finally come to his "bursting time" (the moment at which his peritoneum and skin, having been slashed so many times, can no longer contain his guts) gives a "bursting" or great feast to which all friends and relatives are invited. He then proceeds to drink as much as he can until a loud, piercing fart indicates to all present that he has finally and happily burst.

(François Rabelais, *Le cinquiesme et dernier livre des faicts et dicts du bon Pantagruel, auquel est contenu la visitation de l'Oracle de la dive Bacbuc, et le mot de la bouteille; pour lequel avoir est entrepris tout ce long voyage,* Paris, 1564)

OUTER SEA, see AMAN.

OVER AND UNDER COUNTRY, the area on the outskirts of the BALLOON PICKER'S COUNTRY, so called because no one in it ever gives way to anyone else; they go either under or over each other. For instance when two trains meet on the railway line on the way to ROOTABAGA COUNTRY, one simply passes over or under the other.

(Carl Sandburg, *Rootabaga Stories,* New York, 1922)

OZ, a large rectangular country divided into four small countries: Munchkin Country to the east, Winkie Country to the west, Quadling Country to the south and Gillikin Country to the north. The four smaller countries are largely autonomous but all owe allegiance to the ruler of Oz, Princess Ozma. She resides in the capital, EMERALD CITY, which stands in the exact centre of Oz at the point where the four lands meet. As a famous visitor once remarked, Oz is not Kansas.

The original inhabitants of Oz resemble one another physically, no matter which area they come from. They are small—no taller than a well-grown child. The usual dress includes round hats that rise to about a foot above the head, with bells around the brim. Women wear long gowns, often decorated with glistening stars, and men long jackets and high boots. The main distinguishing mark between the people of the different regions is the colour of their skin, which is matched by that of their clothes and of the country itself. In Munchkin country blue is the dominant colour; the grass, trees and houses are all blue and the men wear blue clothes. The dominant colour in Winkie Country is yellow; Quadling Country is red and Gillikin Country Purple. All four colours appear on the flag of Oz, on which Emerald City is represented by a green star embroidered in the middle.

The countryside of Oz is mainly rich farming land. The fields are neatly cultivated and yield good crops of grain and vegetables. Wooded and mountainous areas farther away are inhabited by

different peoples, like the strange race of the TOTTENHOTLAND desert or of HAMMERHEAD HILLS. The mountains in north-west Quadling Country shelter the subterranean realms of the Country of the HOPPERS and HORNER COUNTRY. There are also small autonomous areas within the borders of Oz, some of which, like UTENSIA, do not recognize the central authority. The people of CHINA COUNTRY, BUNNYBURY and the village of CUTTENCLIP, even though they recognize Ozma, live in their separate communities for specific reasons. Two cities are regarded as the defensive settlements of Oz: FLUTTERBUDGET CENTER and RIGMAROLE. People always worried by imaginary fears are sent to the former and people incapable of expressing themselves clearly and to the point are sent to the latter. The two communities are not penal settlements and the people sent there live happily with others like themselves.

There is no sickness, poverty or death in Oz. Money does not exist and all property belongs to the Princess who regards her subjects as her children. Each person is given all he requires for his use. Farming is very productive and enough grain is grown to feed the entire population; the total crop is distributed equally among the people. Tailors, dressmakers, jewellers and other tradesmen produce goods which are given to all who ask for them. In return they are supported by all their neighbours. If there is a shortage of any commodity, supplies are made available from the great warehouses of the capital. These are then restocked when there is a surplus of the commodity in question. Everyone works half the time and plays half the time. Working conditions in Oz are such that work is regarded as a source of pleasure and pride, and not as an imposition.

The country is peaceful and calm, although strange and sometimes dangerous creatures are found in the dense forests of some areas. One forest in the east of Munchkin Country is the haunt of the *kalidah,* an animal with the body of a bear and the head of a tiger. In the past, *kalidahs* were a serious danger to travellers, but most of them have now been tamed. *Kalidahs* are, however, unpredictable and should not be trusted. The fighting trees of the south and the man-eating plants of the north-east of Munchkin Country still present a threat to strangers. The trees bend down when anyone approaches, twine their branches around

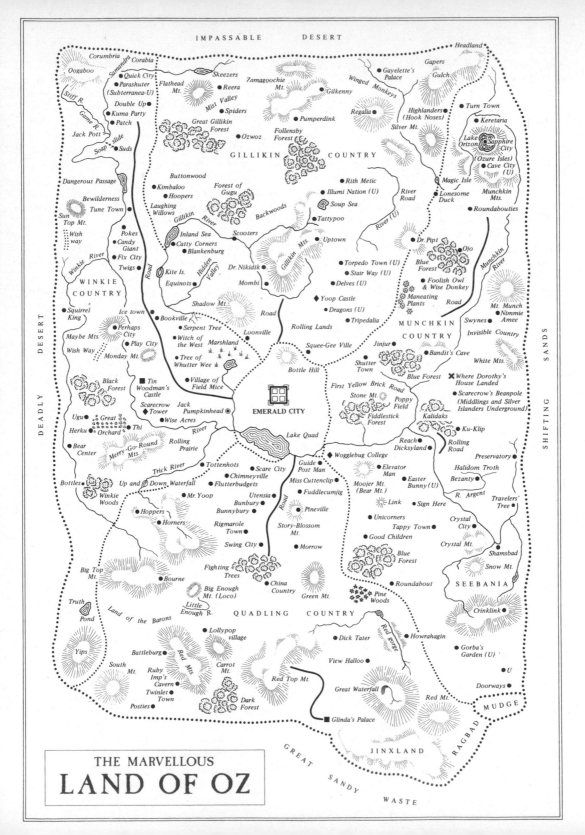

THE MARVELLOUS
LAND OF OZ

him and fling him away. The man-eating plants grow along the roadside, and travellers are often attracted to them by their leaves, which appear to have a blue groundwork shot through with glints of other colours. Bright colours appear and then vanish again as the leaf sways in the wind. When the curious traveller has come close enough, the leaves bend down and fold tightly around him. Whistling seems to charm the plants and travellers who whistle are not attacked by them. Fortunately the few dangerous plants and animals still found in Oz are usually in remote areas and present no serious threat to the inhabitants, although they can make travelling hazardous for the unwary.

Most animals in Oz are tame and friendly. The field-mice, for instance, are ruled by their own queen, and have helped Ozma and her friends on several occasions. The far north is the home of the winged monkeys, once a free but mischievous species who lived in the forest. Their mischief led to their downfall; they angered Gayalette, a princess and sorceress who lived in a ruby palace in the north, and in her anger she deprived them of their liberty and bound their wings. A spell was laid on them and they were forced to fulfill three wishes made by anyone who possessed a certain magic cap now in the hands of Princess Ozma.

Little is known of the early history of Oz. In the distant past the land was ruled as one country by a succession of monarchs called Oz or Ozma. After a series of complex events, much of the country came under the domination of good and wicked witches. In the north and south the wicked witches were defeated by the good witches, but in the east and west they continued to hold their evil domain. Glinda the Good won over the south of Oz and still rules that area.

During this period Oz received its first visitor from abroad, a balloonist from a circus in Omaha, in the United States, who had painted by coincidence the initials O.Z. on his balloon. Because of a misunderstanding, the people accepted him as their ruler and saw him as a great wizard. He had them build the Emerald City and ruled there as the Wizard of Oz, though his magical abilities extended little beyond sleight-of-hand tricks. Despite this, he soon established a reputation for himself as a great magician.

Oz's second visitor from the outside world was perhaps even more important. A girl from Kansas named Dorothy Gale—famous for her envy of flying bluebirds and her nonmeteorological interest in rainbows—and her dog Toto were carried away, together with her house, by a violent tornado. The house came down in the east of Munchkin Country, landing on the Wicked Witch of the East and killing her. Dorothy then travelled to the Emerald City down the famous Yellow Brick Road, and on to Winkie Country where she was able to defeat the Witch of the East's sister, the Wicked Witch of the West, with the help of several friends. Those who went with her on this journey were to become prominent people in Oz. One was a cowardly lion, who eventually found his courage and became King of the Beasts. Another, the Tin Woodman, was originally a Munchkin but cut himself so often (after a spell was cast on his axe by the Witch of the East) that one by one his limbs had to be replaced by artificial ones and his whole body ended up being tin. In later life the Woodman became Emperor of the Winkies, and he still lives in a magnificent palace in their country. After his rise to fame he had himself tin-plated and is now regularly polished and scoured. Dorothy's third ally was a scarecrow whose one complaint was that he thought he had no brains; the trip with Dorothy allowed him to prove that he had. Following the defeat of the Witch of the West, Dorothy decided to return to Kansas and the Wizard agreed to leave with her. Unfortunately they were separated when his balloon drifted off without Dorothy, and she had to leave by making use of a pair of magic shoes taken from the Witch of the East. However, Dorothy returned on several occasions and was finally made a Princess of Oz; the Wizard returned after meeting Dorothy in the Land of the MANGA-BOOS and has remained in Oz ever since.

During the Wizard's absence, Emerald City was ruled by the scarecrow. Although he seems to have ruled well he was overthrown by a rebellion led by a girl called Jinjur, who led an army against the city. Her motive was largely the desire to possess the jewels of Oz. After a complicated series of events, Jinjur was in turn overthrown by Glinda the Good. Not a drop of blood was spilt during the rebellion, though the girls attacked Emerald City armed with knitting needles. The revolt led by Jinjur was the last upheaval in Oz itself. After her downfall the legitimate ruler of Oz was found, Princess Ozma, who had been taken from her home as a child and transformed into a boy by a witch named Mombi. She was returned to her natural form by Glinda and has ruled Oz ever since.

Magic is officially forbidden in Oz and can

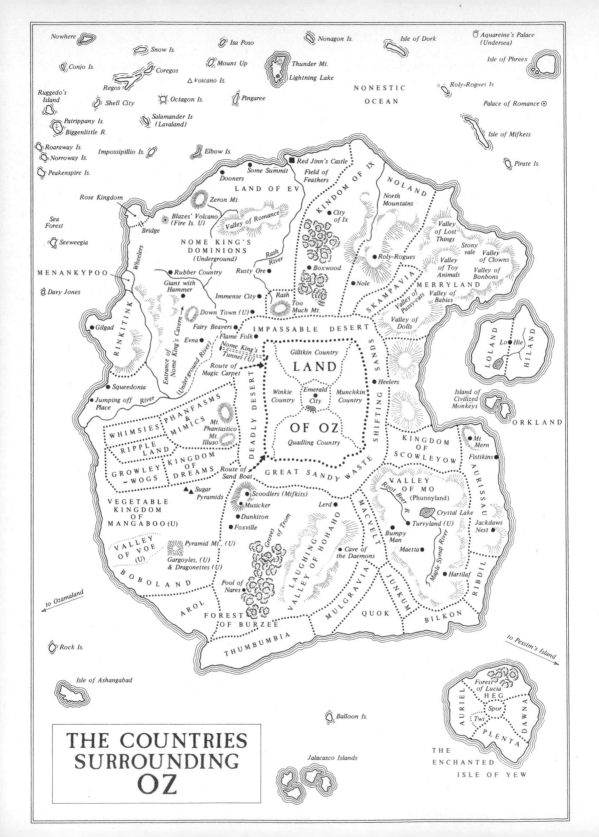

THE COUNTRIES
SURROUNDING
OZ

only be practised with a licence. The ban on magic was imposed mainly to prevent the wicked witches of the past regaining their power, but it also has the advantage of preventing accidents. One of the last practitioners of magic caused a terrible row when he inadvertently turned someone into a marble statue. Turning the man back into a human being involved an arduous quest for special ingredients. The same magician created two of the last creatures to be brought to life by magic in Oz: a delicate glass cat and the Patchwork Girl known as Scraps. In earlier days, several creatures now famous were created in this way. The Sawhorse, for instance, was brought to life by Ozma herself when she was still a boy. Although made of wood, the Sawhorse can outrun any normal horse and is greatly loved and respected by those who meet it. To prevent its wooden legs being worn down, it has been shod with gold. Before making the Sawhorse come to life, Tip—as Ozma was then known—had already made a man from lengths of wood and a pumpkin, largely as a trick to frighten the witch Mombi. Tim Pumpkinhead was brought to life when magic powder was sprinkled on him, and he still lives in the Winkie Country, just outside the boundary of the capital itself. Tim Pumpkinhead cannot die, but his pumpkin heads have a tendency to go off. When this happens they are buried in his private graveyard and a new head is carved for him by Ozma.

The main educational institution in Oz is the Royal Athletic College, also known as Wogglebug College. It is named after its founder Professor H.M. Wogglebug, T.E. —"T.E." stands for "thoroughly educated" and refers to the days Wogglebug spent listening to Professor Nowitall in a country school. The initials "H.M." mean "Highly Magnified" and refer to a vital incident in the professor's life. Caught by Professor Nowitall, the Wogglebug was highly magnified on a screen for the instruction of the students and escaped from the school in a Highly Magnified State. He has remained that size ever since, and is at least as tall as the average inhabitant. The Wogglebug is brown, with alternating stripes of light brown and white on his front. Most of his body is covered by his clothes; a dark blue swallow-tail coat with yellow lining, and fawn plush knickerbockers; he habitu-

ally wears a tall silk hat. The educational system introduced by Professor Wogglebug is unlike any other in the world. The pupils spend their days in athletic pursuits and do not study in the normal sense of the word. They "learn" by taking School Pills made by the Wizard. An Algebra pill taken on retiring is equivalent to four hours of study; geography and other pills are taken at specified intervals. The result is that pupils learn extremely fast and become conversant with all the major subjects. The pills are sugar-coated and easy to swallow, and it seems that birds and animals can also be educated in this way.

Access to Oz has never been easy. The country is surrounded on all sides by desert and anyone who sets foot on the sand is immediately turned to dust. In the past it was possible to fly across the desert, which was how Dorothy and the Wizard arrived on their first journey together. Another visitor, though not friendly, was the King of NOMELAND, who tunnelled beneath the sands in his attempt to invade Oz. As a result Ozma decided that her country should be made invisible and that all communication with the outside world should be broken off. On Ozma's request, Glinda the Good cast a number of spells on Oz. Now the country can no longer be seen from the air and it is impossible for any traveller crossing over the desert to guess the direction in which it lies.

Even when Oz was visible, leaving was an arduous task. On different occasions Dorothy left by using various magic objects, such as the shoes of the Witch of the East or the belt taken from the Nome King. In both cases the objects disappeared as soon as she returned to Kansas, where they had no power. Both Ozma and Glinda can bring someone to Oz by using magic, but this does not happen frequently.

(L. Frank Baum, *The Wonderful Wizard of Oz*, Chicago, 1900; L. Frank Baum, *The Marvelous Land of Oz*, Chicago, 1904; L. Frank Baum, *Ozma of Oz*, Chicago, 1907; L. Frank Baum, *Dorothy and the Wizard in Oz*, Chicago, 1908; L. Frank Baum, *The Road to Oz*, Chicago, 1909; L. Frank Baum, *The Emerald City of Oz*, Chicago, 1910; L. Frank Baum, *The Patchwork Girl of Oz*, Chicago, 1913)

P

PA-ANCH, an island south of the Red Sea. Many cities have risen here, the largest of which is Pa-nara, very prosperous and proud of its temple, surrounded by small woods, gardens and beautiful meadows where birds and fountains sing. The fauna of Pa-Anch consists of elephants, lions, leopards and other tropical creatures.

The population is divided into three castes: artisans and priests; farmers and shepherds; and soldiers. The power is in the hands of the priests, who also have the right to choose for themselves the most beautiful virgins on the island. The government is a triumvirate renewed every year. All property is held in common, except the houses and the ground surrounding them. The land produces all sorts of crops, notably a species of sugarcane with an edible fruit. The island is rich in minerals, gold and other precious metals. These are not, however, exported. Instead, myrrh and incense are sent abroad in large quantities. The natives usually dress in woollen clothes and adorn themselves with ornaments made of gold.

(Diodorus Siculus, *The Library of History*, 1st cen. BC)

PAFLAGONIA, a kingdom bordering on BLACKSTAFF, which separates it from CRIM TARTARY. The capital is Blombodinga. Not much is known about the physical aspects of the country but its code for punishments and rewards is famous. Criminals are sent to join one of the many orders of flagellants which, in varying degrees of severity, abound in the country. Those who do good are recompensed with awards like the Wooden Spoon, bestowed upon carefully chosen candidates by the University of Basforo. The most highly prized honour in Paflagonia is the Order of the Cucumber which sometimes leads to high positions in court, such as First Lord of the Billiard Table or Groom of the Tennis Court.

(M.A. Titmarsh [William Makepeace Thackeray], "The Rose and the Ring," in *Christmas Tales*, London, 1857)

PALA, an island in the Indonesian Archipelago separated from RENDANG by the Straits of Pala. The capital is Shivapuram. The island is mountainous and rock-bound, and the only landing place is a small cove leading into a ravine. The island has rich oil reserves, but concessions are not granted to foreign companies, and only small quantities are extracted for domestic use. Copper and gold are mined in moderate quantities. There is also a cement factory and a modern hydro-electric power station.

The development of Pala was in fact the work of two men, the great-grandfather of the present Rajah and the first MacPhail of Pala. Andrew MacPhail had his first sight of the East when serving as a surgeon on a British exploration vessel. Of Scottish Calvinist origin, he practised for some years in India where he was approached by a representative of the Rajah of Pala, who wanted a surgeon to return with him to his country. He agreed, and in 1843 arrived in Pala, where he succeeded in removing a tumour from the Rajah, performing the operation under hypnosis in the absence of anaesthetics. MacPhail never returned to either Europe or India; instead, he set out with the Rajah to reform Pala. He was determined that the island should be spared famines like those he had seen in India. They began with medical care and went on to the establishment of an agricultural station. Their ambition was to combine the best elements of East and West, and subsequent governments have devoted their greatest efforts to making everyone as free and happy as possible.

The Palanese are pacifists and have never had an army. There are no prisons in Pala. The island is traditionally a constitutional monarchy. Politically, Pala is a federation of decentralized self-governing units. There is no press monopoly: a panel of editors represents various groups and interests—each given set space for argument and comment—and the reader is left to draw his own conclusions.

The economic system is a cooperative one, based on mutual aid, with a credit system modelled on nineteenth-century credit unions. As the population is relatively small, there is sufficient surplus. Enough gold is produced to back the currency and supplement exports. Expensive equipment is paid for in cash. There is a silver, gold and copper currency for internal use.

The Palanese religion is Buddhism, which arrived in Pala from Bengal and Tibet in the seventh century AD. It has tantric elements and has also

The Avenue of Palms in PALA.

been influenced by Shivaism. Palanese Buddhism does not lead to renunciation of the world or to a search for nirvana; it leads to an acceptance of the world. Everything seen, tasted, heard or touched becomes an aid to the liberation of the individual from the prison of self. The core of this philosophy can be summed up as *tat tvan asi* ("thou art that"). Various forms of Zen and yoga are used, including Maithuna, the yoga of love, which allows the rediscovery of the diffused sexuality of childhood. Many elements of the Palanese religion are summed up in the old Rajah's book: *Notes On What's What and On What It Might Be Reasonable To Do About What's What*.

There are several important monuments which should be visited in Pala, including a large Buddhist temple just outside the capital, notable for its fine sculptures. It is used in the *moksha* ceremony and stands on a high mountain terrace, built organically out of the red stone of the mountains. Its four sides are ribbed vertically and it is crowned by a flattened dome, like the seed capsule of a flowering plant. Inside, the temple is dark, lit only by latticed windows and seven lamps hanging above the altar. On the altar itself stands a copper statue of Shiva dancing, no bigger than a child. Beneath the statue, a niche contains seven more lamps; when these are lit, they reveal a statue of Shiva and Parvati. Two of Shiva's four hands hold the symbolic drum and fire; the others caress the goddess whose arms and legs twine around him.

The vegetation of Pala is typical of this climate. The lower mountain slopes are clothed in terraced paddy fields, while the higher slopes (over seven thousand feet) allow cultivation of almost all the crops found in southern Europe, plus a few high-altitude plants including the mushrooms from which *moksha* is made. There are palms on the coast and a dense jungle below the mountain terraces. Papaya, bread-fruit and other tropical trees grow freely.

Moksha, a powerful hallucinatory drug derived from mushrooms, lends its name to one of Pala's most important ceremonies. The drug is known as the "reality revealer." It produces a state similar to that reached by deep meditation, allowing a heightened perception of reality. *Moksha* also affects areas of the brain which are normally "inactive," allowing immediate access to the subconscious and providing the equivalent of a mystical experience. The use of *moksha*, the Palanese say, can take the user to heaven, hell, or beyond both, allowing visions of what some forms of Buddhism term "the clear light of the void." The *moksha* ceremony is an initiation ceremony and takes place in the temple. During the service, young men and women offer a rock-climbing accomplishment to Shiva and then, through use of the drug, experience liberation from themselves.

The island has a very low rate of neurosis and

cardiovascular troubles, thanks largely to the use of preventive medicine on all fronts, from psychological help to controlled diets. Free contraception is financed by the tax revenue. Artificial insemination is widely used. After having one or two children, parents often choose the father of their next child from deep-freeze sperm banks. The use of artificial insemination permits the gradual improvement of their race. From the theological point of view, artificial insemination has been justified in terms of the doctrines of re-incarnation and karma.

The family organization in Pala is unusual. Everyone belongs to a mutual adoption club consisting of fifteen to twenty-five couples of all ages, who adopt each other in a form of extended family. When a child finds his natural family becoming restrictive or unpleasant, he or she migrates to another home within the circle. When children are very young they are introduced to the concept of "good" in the following way: when being breast-fed, the child is stroked to increase his pleasure; while he is sucking and being caressed, the body of an animal or person is rubbed against him and at the same time the word "good" is repeated to him. The child gradually makes the association: "food" plus "caress" plus "contact" plus "good" = "love." This technique partly explains the close contact between animals and humans on Pala. It was originally developed by a primitive tribe in New Guinea which Andrew MacPhail had encountered in his travels.

Education in Pala is based upon helping children to understand the logic and structure of the subject before moving on to its general applications. Games, such as psychological bridge, evolutionary snakes and ladders, Mendelian happy families, are widely used as teaching aids. Ecology is an important subject and is seen as the basis of ethics: man can only live on Earth if he treats it with compassion. Elementary ecology leads rapidly to elementary Buddhism. Children are introduced to the concepts of "suchness" and Buddhism, in preparation for the *moksha* initiation. All these methods are used in conjunction with more traditional book-based methods. Higher education, including sociology and comparative religion, is imparted at the University of Shivapuram. Students between the ages of sixteen and twenty-four divide their time between study and work, the experience of different types of work being an integral part of education. This continues in adult life, as all officials perform a certain amount of manual labour. Rock climbing figures in the curriculum as a means of showing children the constant presence of death and the precariousness of all existence. The yoga of love also plays an important part in education: it is the cultivation of physical awareness that turns love-making into yoga. Scarecrows in the shape of figures of the future Buddha and God the Father are used to make the children understand that all gods are man-made and that it is man who gives them power. "Destiny control" or "self-determination" is also an important part of their studies.

At the age of four or five all children undergo intensive physical and psychological testing. Potential criminals or problem children are identified and given appropriate treatment. According to Palanese medicine, criminality is the result of endocrine imbalance and is to be treated as such. Behavioural science is also involved: potential bullies, for instance, are encouraged to divert their wish for power into socially useful activities, such as cutting wood, mining or sailing. In certain cases, hypnosis is used. Under hypnosis, some students can "distort time," mastering subjects and solving problems in less time than they would normally. All education is based on this classification of children. It is asked: "Which is more important to him? His gut, muscles or nervous system?" In each case his potential is diverted into useful channels in accordance with the precept "become what you are."

Sanscrit, Palanese and English are the common languages. Sanscrit is used in some religious ceremonies. English was introduced by Dr. Andrew MacPhail and has helped the Palanese obtain a glimpse of the outside world. The first English books printed in Pala were a selection from *The Arabian Nights* and a translation of *The Diamond Sutra*. English is used in commerce and science; Palanese in more intimate concerns—it is said to have the widest erotic and sentimental vocabulary in the whole of South-east Asia.

Entrance to Pala is utterly forbidden; visitors are advised not to attempt to intrude.

(Aldous Huxley, *Island*, London, 1962)

PALINDICIA, see LOONARIE.

PAL-UL-DON, a kingdom somewhere in the republic of Zaire. It is reached through a vast waterless steppe leading into a luxuriant jungle. Every known species of bird and beast seems to have taken refuge in this region, and many hybrid strains such as the sabretoothed yellow-and-black-striped lion.

The jungle is cut by a mountain range and beyond, after a perilous descent, lies the Valley of Jab-Ben-Otho, the Great God of Pal-ul-don. From the Pastar-ul-ved or Father of Mountains a scene of mystery and beauty spreads below—because the Valley of the Great God is one of nature's true wonders. Girt by cliffs of towering whiteness, dotted with deep blue lakes and crossed by winding rivers, it is also the site of A-lur, the City of Light.

All buildings in A-lur have been hewn from the chalk-like limestone of what was once a group of low hills, and the waste material has been used to form the paved streets. Narrow ledges and terraces break the lines of the buildings. Notable above all others are two magnificent constructions: the Palace of Ko-tan and the Temple of the Gryf. The Palace is entered through a beautifully carved gate of geometrical designs; figures of birds, beasts and men decorate the interior. The Throne Room is almost filled by a gigantic pyramid along the broad steps of which stand rigid lines of soldiers. The king sits on the apex dressed in gold, and the sun shines on him through a shaft in the high dome, making him a dazzling figure.

The Temple of the Gryf is three storeys high. It has a single barred entrance carved from the living rock representing a *gryf*'s head. The *gryf* is a savage beast similar to the prehistoric triceratops—twenty feet high, with a blue body, yellow face, blue bands round its eyes, a red hood and a yellow belly. Three parallel lines of bony protuberances run down its back, one red and two yellow. Two large horns protrude from above its eyes and a third one from its nose. Instead of hoofs it has talons. Though fierce and dangerous it can be used as a mount; the rider must give it a blow across the face and seat himself upon the creature's back. This is by far the best way to explore Pal-ul-don.

Two different tribes or races inhabit Pal-ul-don. The Ho-don or White Men dwell in cities like A-lur and Tu-lur to the south-east. They are hairless and tailed, though their god is tailless. The Waz-don or Black Men are shaggy, sport long tails and live in trees or caves because they consider cities to be prisons.

The language of Pal-ul-don is guttural but not difficult to learn. Plurals are formed by doubling the first letter in the word. For instance *don* is "man," *d'don* is "men"; *ja*, "lion," *j'ja*, "lions."

(Edgar Rice Burroughs, *Tarzan the Terrible*, New York, 1921)

PANARA, see PA-ANCH.

PANDOCLIA, an island off the coast of the continent of GENOTIA in the south Atlantic, notable for its jealous people. A law forbids women to leave their homes late in the evening; the punishment for this is too terrible to describe. The penal code makes no mention of similar laws concerning men.

(Louis Adrien Duperron de Castera, *Le Theatre Des Passions Et De La Fortune Ou Les Avantures Surprenantes de Rosamidor & de Theoglaphire. Histoire Australe,* Paris, 1731)

PANOPEA, see OCEANA (1).

PAPEFIGUIERA, a country of unknown location, inhabited only by fat people. The monks are as fat as cows, and the numerous doctors of theology are barely thinner. The governor, Mr. Lent, feeds only on plump white chicken and is so fat that when he sits down his *derrière* covers several square feet.

(Béroualde de Verville, *Le Moyen de parvenir. Oeuvre contenant la raison de tout ce qui a esté, est, et sera, avec démonstrations certaines et nécessaires selon la rencontre des effets de vertu,* Paris, 1880)

PAPER SACKS, PALACE OF, of uncertain location, the home of the King of Paper Sacks, built entirely of paper. Most of its inhabitants are pink and purple peanuts who put on their overshoes every evening and settle down to making paper sacks. Their work is supervised by the king himself, and if his dignity is slighted he sweeps peanuts into a sack, calls out "A nickel a sack, a nickel a sack" and flings them into the rubbish piles by the trash cans. The peanuts who live in the palace also spend much of their time stitching handkerchiefs.

(Carl Sandburg, *Rootabaga Stories,* New York, 1922)

PARADESA, see AGARTHA.

PARADISE ISLAND, in the south Pacific, so called because of its agreeable qualities. A mountain range divides the island in two. On one side lies the inhabited area, colonized by a group of Europeans who were shipwrecked here at the beginning of the sixteenth century. On the other side live the natives—brown-skinned, tall, and well-proportioned. They hold everything but their wives in common and therefore have little cause for contention.

European visitors are considered physically and morally inferior. For fear that they may contaminate the natives, they are put into quarantine for five months and made to bathe regularly in a forest pool.

The natives are very fond of music, both vocal and instrumental. Even the birds join in the singing and have, through force of repetition, learned the words of the songs. A harmless kind of lion, with a huge head and mane, roams the island and is trained like a dog. (Travellers will find a similar species of lion has been domesticated in the XUJAN KINGDOM.)

(Ambrose Evans [?], *The Adventures, and Surprizing Deliverances, of James Dubourdieu, And His Wife: Who were taken by Pyrates, and carried to the Uninhabited-Part of the Isle of Paradise. Containing A Description of that Country, its Laws, Religion, and Customs: Of Their being at last releas'd; and how they came to Paris, where they are still living. Also, The Adventures of Alexander Vendchurch, Whose Ship's Crew Rebelled against him, and set him on Shore on an Island in the South-Sea, where he liv'd five Years, five Months, and seven Days; and was at last providentially releas'd by a Jamaica Ship. Written by Himself*, London, 1719)

PARAPAGAL, see MARADAGAL.

PARHAN, a vast empire which would take a caravan several months to cross, somewhere in the Middle East, near the Red Mountains and across the Rikha Steppes, on the coast of the Sweet Sea. Parhan is a conglomeration of several colonies, each keeping its own frontiers. Strange Portuguese with empty eyes inhabit one region of Parhan; Indians, Zikdes and Persian merchants inhabit three other regions. The Knights of Or-

doukh are the lords of a small area in the north; their neighbours, the Parhani, are known to ride far south to the Deserts of Salt.

The only travellers to venture into Parhan are explorers in search of a mysterious blue metal, of secret powers, which is said to be found near the ruins of the Castle of Alamut. To reach the castle, the traveller must cross dark haunted forests inhabited by indescribable creatures, petrified woods rising from foul marshes, dead cities whose inhabitants are faceless. The ruins of the Castle of Alamut are enormous. The remaining stairs, covered in moss, seem to have been erected by beings four or five times larger than a man. On the porticos that still stand, the traveller will see bas-reliefs and arabesques of a design he will not understand. No traveller is known to have returned from visiting these ruins.

(Dominique Bromberger, *L'Itinéraire de Parhan au Château D'Alamut et au-delà*, Paris, 1978)

PAROULET'S COUNTRY, an underground land with seas, islands and mountains, some twenty-two leagues beneath the surface of the earth. It is mostly barren, dark and uninhabited, and can be reached through a tunnel in Australia, discovered by the French paleontologist, zoologist and geologist Césaire Paroulet and his nephews, during a fossil-hunting expedition. Visitors are, however, warned that the tunnel was subsequently destroyed by the country's inhabitants and may need further excavation.

The small inhabited area is connected with the outer world by a number of submarine tunnels of unknown location, each barred by a golden gate that is electrically controlled. From Paroulet Country it is possible to descend to SAKNUSSEM'S CORRIDOR in a lift which moves downwards through a spiral pit. This expedition is highly dangerous and should not be freely attempted.

The capital of the country is Noah, on the shore of a large sea, a series of terraces surrounded by prehistoric parks full of bees and butterflies. Enos, Lamech, Jubal, Heber, Trubal and FIRST MEN CITY are other important urban centres. The inhabited area is also famous for its uranium, gold and silver mines.

The country's technology is highly developed and includes the use of atomic power. The whole country is lit electrically and it is as bright as daylight. The inhabitants travel in a kind of airplane which can also move very rapidly under water. It resembles a long metal tub that can take off and land in a vertical line, powered by atomic energy.

The fauna as well as the flora of Paroulet's Country is prehistoric; pterodactyls live in the mountain caves and ichthyosaurs abound in the underground seas.

(Maurice Champagne, *La Cité des premiers hommes*, Paris, 1929)

PARROTS, LAND OF, a remote island in the south seas. The coastline is rocky, with only one small natural harbour. Precipitous mountains rise sharply from the shoreline and only one narrow gorge leads through this natural barrier. Beyond the mountains lies an extensive area of forest, with trees as old as the earth itself. The inhabitants live on a plain on the other side of the forest.

The present population dates back to the arrival, in the eighteenth century, of an English merchant named Durham who put ashore here for water. Durham was accompanied by four European women and Patizithes, a magician of Persian origin, all of whom he had rescued from a corsair. As they landed, the Persian told Durham that this land was to be his home and that he would rule it. The prediction came true, but only after initial skirmishes with the natives who finally accepted Durham as their leader. Some time later he married the native Princess Sileste and took the name Babil.

At this time the island was known as the Land of the Dumb, because none of the inhabitants could speak. According to their legends (which were given a scientific brush-up by Charles Darwin a century later), the island had once been under the ocean. As the waters began to recede many of the marine animals perished; the others, including man, evolved into their present form. The people, however, remained dumb, communicating in sign language. The legends go on to speak of a bird, unknown in their country, which would one day bring them the gift of speech. At the time of Durham's arrival, the native society was calm and peaceful; there had been no wars or disputes for centuries. The islanders were in fact convinced of the superiority of their system of communicating with one another, regarding vocal language as a waste of precious energy which could be better used in other ways.

Most marriages between the islanders and the Europeans prospered, but the children of their unions were born dumb. On the death of Durham, his daughter Muta married the son of Patizithes, also known as Babil.

Some years later a ship bound for the East Indies was wrecked on the coast of the island. Only two people survived the wreck: Zelindor and his sister Zelinda, who were eventually found sleeping on the shore by the young king and his brothers. They were astonished to discover a parrot—the first they had ever seen—with the two castaways. Zelindor and Zelinda were taken to the court and were treated with great kindness and generosity.

The king's youngest daughter, Princess Sileta, heard the parrot utter a few words and the desire to speak was gradually born in her. Addressing the few Europeans who could still remember spoken language, the parrot explained that he was in fact an enchanted African prince, son of King Acroupski. His father had shown displeasure when he realized his son was not learning anything and could only parrot the stories his tutor told him. Angered by this insult, the tutor (who had considerable magic power) had turned the boy into a real parrot, prophesying that he would not regain human form until he had brought the gift of language to a people who were ignorant of it and until a princess expressed a preference for his love over her love of political power.

The parrot-prince, transformed, had flown away from home and eventually, after passing through many hands and different countries, had settled on the ship that brought him to the island.

With patience and loving care, the parrot succeeded in teaching Princess Sileta and other members of the royal family to speak. He then organized public schools until the entire population, with the exception of a few rebellious souls, could speak fluently.

After this splendid show of linguistic zeal, and a number of complicated love affairs and government intrigues, Princess Sileta recognized that her heart, so to speak, had flown to the parrot. She publicly proclaimed that she loved him more than political power and prepared her abdication. However, no sooner had the words passed her lips than the parrot regained his human shape, which was handsome, and married the princess. In his honour, the country was renamed Land of Parrots, which the now speaking inhabitants agreed was better than Land of the Dumb, and a great pyramid, topped by an enormous statue of a parrot proper, was erected in the royal couple's honour.

Some years later, a certain Abraham Ortelius is recorded as having visited the island. The blond, fair-skinned people were living as happily as they had done before they received the gift of language.

(Pierre Charles Fabiot Aunillon, Abbé Du Guay de Launay, *Azor, ou Le prince enchanté; histoire nouvelle, pour servir de chronique à celle de la terre des perroquets; traduit de l'anglois du sçavant Popiniay*, London, 1750)

PARTHALIA, an island probably in the Arabian Sea. It is inhabited by giants who are so long-lived that one of them—still alive today—helped build Rome. Among its flora it is interesting to note some smallish oyster-growing trees.

(William Bullein, *A Dialogue both Pleasant and Pitiful, wherein is a Goodly Regimente against the Fever Pestilence, with a Consolation and Comfort against Death*, London, 1564)

PARTHENION TOWN (allegedly from the Latin meaning "conclave of virgins"), in France (and, by extension, certain reserved areas in several French cities). Parthenion Town is a conglomerate of *parthenions* or bordellos, set up under government protection. All prostitutes are required to live here on pain of corporal punishment. Only women up to the age of twenty-five are admitted; no questions are asked about their background or family, but they are subject to a strict medical examination. They are not refused entry because of illness—they are either given treatment, or, if the disease is incurable, they are placed in retirement. Parthenion Town is inviolable, and parents cannot remove their daughters or even speak to them without their consent.

The bordellos themselves are built in quiet areas, each with a courtyard and two gardens. Anyone may enter the courtyard, but access to the first garden is forbidden to women and children. The second garden is reserved exclusively for prostitutes and governesses. In the first garden can be found a number of ticket offices, discreetly masked by trees and bushes. The price lists are freely displayed and the tickets give access to one of a number of corridors. These corridors lead into a room from where the women can be secretly observed so the visitor can choose his partner without being seen. But the chosen girl has a right to examine her partner and reject him if she so wishes. Prices vary according to age and beauty and are doubled at night.

If a man falls in love with one of the prostitutes and is willing to keep on paying the price of a daily ticket, she will be removed from the common room and no one else will be offered her services. Women kept in this way are lodged separately. Young men require their family's consent to keep a mistress or to marry her. Though the bordellos keep regular hours, men who already know a particular woman are admitted before 9 A.M. The women are named after flowers and can dress as they wish, but they have only a fixed sum to spend on clothes and are not allowed to wear perfume or make-up. Unless they marry or inherit a fortune, the women who enter Parthenion Town never leave it again.

Parthenion Town is administered by a council composed of twelve honourable men who have held offices at least equivalent to that of a mayor. They are assisted by former prostitutes who have shown proof of their abilities and gentility. They are responsible to a superior who takes her orders directly from the council. The governesses are not allowed to administer punishment and can only report to the administrators. A woman who has committed an offence can plead her case and will be exonerated if there is the slightest doubt of her guilt. Most punishments involve the loss of certain privileges such as music or dancing lessons. Serious offences, such as having an abortion, are punishable with one year's imprisonment and a diet of bread and water. A mistress who deceives her lover into thinking she is pregnant or who is unfaithful to him is executed.

Pregnant women are housed in a special part of the buildings and the father has no obligation towards the mother or the child. Unless they are recognized, children are cared for by the State. Boys are trained as soldiers and those not suitable for military service become tailors or gardeners in Parthenion Town. Attractive girls are provided with a suitable dowry and trained in the social arts; unattractive girls become servants. When a prostitute grows older she may live peacefully in a special area of Parthenion Town and is encouraged to teach or serve at table.

(Nicolas Edme Restif de la Bretonne, *Le Pornographe, ou idées d'un Honnête homme sur un*

projet de réglement pour les prostituées, London &
The Hague, 1769)

PASTEMOLLE, a small, perfectly round island
in the undefined region of the FORTUNATE IS-
LANDS (1). The only means of access is through
a gateway of melted cheese, dried in the sun until
it has become harder than steel. Pastemolle is
surrounded by ovens, with their backs to the sea,
constantly full of various types of pies. For the
convenience of visitors, notices above the ovens
specify which type of pie is produced by which
oven. The island is the home of a colony of extremely devout marmots, burrowing rodents of
the genus *Arctomys,* who live in a convent.

(Anonymous, *Le Voyage de navigation que fist Panurge, disciple de Pantagruel, aux isles incognues et éstranges de plusieurs choses merveilleuses et difficiles à
croire, qu'il dict avoir veues, dont il fait narration en
ce présent volume, et plusieurs aultres joyeusetez pour
inciter les lecteurs et auditeurs à rire,* Paris, 1538)

PATAGONES, ISLAND OF THE, in mid-
Atlantic, a perfectly round island 1,130 leagues in
diameter, with a circumference of 3,550 leagues.
The Island of the Patagones is the centre of a vast
archipelago inhabited by the Philosophers, a race
that has decided to live exactly according to Francis
Bacon's encyclopaedic system. Following the theory set out in the works of Bacon, the Philosophers
have set up on the different islands of the archipelago a number of experimental laboratories for the
creation of everything needed for their survival.

Seeing that they were the sole inhabitants of
the archipelago, and being a lazy race, the Philosophers decided to create a tribe of men to do their
work for them. They therefore produced in one of
the new laboratories—the Anthropological Department—a large number of human creatures
whom they called Patagones, the smallest of which
is large enough to cover with his skin twelve
French drums. However, when it came to the point
of distributing human skills to the Patagones, the
Ideological Section of the Anthropological Department managed to produce only a very small
quantity of intellectual sense. Each Patagone therefore received only a minimum portion and they
are nowadays considered so stupid by all other
people in the world that the expression "Dumb as

a Patagone" has entered many European and
Asian languages.

The Patagones have become an independent
nation and their king is elected according to his
height. The Philosophers—who have decided to
continue to reproduce in the normal manner, finding it more pleasant than their philosophical experiments—never reach the colossal size of the
Patagones and for this reason are never elected
king.

Travellers will find that the cuisine of the
archipelago is remarkable. Should a visitor desire a
dish of veal's head in sauce *alla marinara,* he must
communicate his order to the chief of the Culinary
Department. From here a note will be sent to the
Mammal Section of the Biology Department,
where a calf will be produced and its head reserved. Next the Ornithological Section will create
a rooster; its crest and kidneys will be sent to the
Culinary Department. Finally the Crustacean
Section will concoct a dozen or so shrimps. With
all these elements, the Culinary Department will
cook the desired dish which will be served hot for
a modest fee, wine and service not included.

(Charles Nodier, *Hurlubleu, Grand Manifafa
d'Hurlubrière,* Paris, 1822)

PATHAN, a large island beyond Java, notable for its
bottomless lake; anything that falls into it will never
come to the surface. The flora of Pathan is highly
practical. Meal-bearing trees, from which the natives make good white bread, grow on its mountain
slopes. In the netherlands, other trees bear wine,
honey and a certain poison against which there is
only one antidote: the crushed leaves of the same
tree, taken with water. But most important are the
Pathan reeds, called *tahby,* some thirty fathoms
long. Precious stones are often found in the knots of
their roots. The *tahby* is used to make houses and
ships; the ships built out of *tahby* are so heavy that a
score of men cannot lift them.

(Sir John Mandeville, *Voiage de Sir John Maundevile,* Paris, 1357)

PATHS OF THE DEAD, a series of under-
ground passageways leading beneath the WHITE
MOUNTAINS from Firienfeld, the meadow above
DUNHARROW, to Erech, a hill in GONDOR.
The Paths are entered via an arched doorway

known simply as the Door, or the Dark Door. The mysterious figures that are carved above the arched entrance add to the almost palpable sense of fear that affects all those who approach it. For many years, the Paths were haunted by dead men, usually known as the Sleepless Dead, the Grey Host, or the Shadow Host. Grey, shadowy figures, they moved silently on foot and on horseback through the passageways, their only discernible features their glowing eyes.

The Sleepless Dead, who haunted the Paths and heights of Dunharrow throughout the Third Age of MIDDLE-EARTH, were the original inhabitants of the mountains. They broke an oath to Isildur, High King of ARNOR and Gondor, that they would aid him in his battle against the evil Sauron, who threatened the very existence of Middle-earth. In anger he cursed them, saying that they would know no rest until the day they were called upon to fulfill their oath.

Throughout the Third Age, few ventured into the Paths and those who did did not return. In 2570 Third Age, Baldor, son of King Brego of ROHAN, swore that he would cross the paths. Many years later in 3019 his bones were found by one of the few expeditions known to have travelled the Paths in safety, the expedition led by Aragorn, direct descendant of Isildur, and one of the mightiest heroes of the War of the Ring. His will power and courage were such that he was able to lead his company safely through the Paths. As the heir of Isildur, he caused the Dead to follow him to the stone of Erech, where they had made their original oath, and he called upon them to defeat Sauron's allies, the corsairs who then controlled PELARGIR, the greatest port in Gondor. The Sleepless Dead finally redeemed their broken oath and were freed from the curse that had lain on them for so long. Having repaid their debt, they vanished from Middle-earth.

(J.R.R. Tolkien, *The Two Towers*, London, 1954; J.R.R. Tolkien, *The Return of the King*, London, 1955)

PAUK, a vast place inhabited by a spider the size of a man. Visitors who are brought here spend the rest of their lives watching it in terror.

(Fyodor Mikhailovich Dostoyevsky, *Besy*, Moscow, 1871–72)

PEACE, ISLE OF, see BROOLYI.

PEACEPOOL, also known as **MOTHER CAREY'S HEAVEN**, a vast pool in the Arctic Ocean near Jan Mayen's Land, surrounded by high cliffs of ice that protect it from storms. The pool, still and oily, is the place where good whales come to die. They wallow in the slow swells, free from all danger, until Mother Carey sends for them and makes them into new creatures. Peacepool is reserved for only the best whales: the right, the razorback, the bottlenose and the narwhal. The more rumbustious sperm whales are excluded; they have their own Peacepool—a great pond near the South Pole, 263 miles south-south-east of Mount Erebus.

In the centre of the Arctic Peacepool sits Mother Carey herself, a white marble lady on a white marble throne. Around the foot of her throne swim thousands and thousands of creatures of shapes and colours that men cannot even begin to imagine. These are Mother Carey's children, whom she makes from seawater.

(Charles Kingsley, *The Water-Babies: A Fairy Tale for a Land-Baby*, London, 1863)

PELARGIR, the greatest port in GONDOR, built on the banks of the GREAT RIVER just above its confluence with the Sirith. Pelargir is some miles from the sea itself.

Originally built in the Second Age of MIDDLE-EARTH, Pelargir was one of the chief havens used by mariners from Númenor, and it was here that Elendil first set foot when he led the Númenóreans to Middle-earth and founded the kingdom of Gondor. In later times it became an important base for naval forces in Gondor's battles with the men of Umbar on the Bay of Belfalas.

During the War of the Ring, Pelargir was seized by corsairs from Umbar, and they began to make preparations to sail upriver to attack MINAS TIRITH, the mighty fortress of Gondor. Aragorn, who was to become the ruler of Gondor, observed these preparations in a *palantír*, a Seeing-stone which allowed him to see events in distant places. As he could muster only a small force against the corsairs, he summoned up the grim host of the Sleepless Dead to follow him from the PATHS OF THE DEAD to Pelargir. They arrived to find a battle for the control of Pelargir at its height. The Dead attacked, sweeping all before them, and victory was soon in the hands of Aragorn. It is not certain if the Dead used normal weapons or simply the weapon of fear in this, their last battle.

The ships manned by the men of Gondor then sailed upstream and arrived in time to turn the tide in the battle of the Fields of PELENNOR and to break the siege of Minas Tirith.

(J.R.R. Tolkien, *The Return of the King*, London, 1954; J.R.R. Tolkien, *The Silmarillion*, London, 1977)

PELENNOR, FIELDS OF, an area in the kingdom of GONDOR between the capital, MINAS TIRITH, and the GREAT RIVER. The area is enclosed by a great wall known as the Rammas Echor (literally, the great-wall circle). On the south side the great wall runs along an embankment above the Great River from the Harlond, a harbour for boats, and then curves north to cut across the road which leads to OSGILIATH (once the capital of Gondor, now in ruins). The road runs along a walled causeway, and it enters Pelennor through a gateway in the great wall protected by two towers.

The wall was built in 2954 Third Age, when the garden province of ITHILIEN came under the influence of the Dark Lord of MORDOR and was abandoned.

The enclosed area, four leagues across at its widest point and one league at its narrowest, descends in gentle slopes and terraces towards the river. It is a fertile and well cultivated land, used for raising grain crops and for the rearing of sheep and cattle. Few people live here and virtually all are herdsmen or farmers.

In March 3019 Third Age the Fields were the scene of the great three-day battle for Minas Tirith. Led by the Lord of the Nazgûl, forces from MINAS MORGUL and HARAD crossed the Great River and breached the massive wall, forcing the armies of Gondor to fall back on Minas Tirith. A great camp of red and black tents was erected on the fields and trenches were dug for the siege weapons to be used against the city. Huge catapults launched missiles at the gates of Minas Tirith and the Nazgûl, the Ringwraiths, flew over the city on their winged steeds, causing panic and demoralization with their harsh cries.

Early in the battle, Faramir, the chief of the Rangers of Ithilien, was wounded and taken to the Houses of Healing within the city. In despair, his father resigned his command of the city and Gandalf the wizard took command of the defences. Despite his efforts, the first of the seven tiers on which the city is built was taken and the men of Harad rode to the attack of the upper levels on their huge elephants. A great battering ram, over one hundred feet long and forged of iron and steel in the forges of Mordor, was brought into service against the main gate. The ram was called Grond in sinister memory of the mace carried by Morgoth, the Dark Lord of the First Age of Middle-earth. Its steel head was in the shape of a ravening wolf. Grond was carried and wielded by mountain trolls and an army of orcs marched with it. Despite the resistance of the defenders, who left mountains of bodies behind them as they retreated, the gates were breached and the forces of darkness began to enter at dawn. But unexpectedly the battle-horns of the Riders of ROHAN were heard in the distance, as the Riders swept down to attack the enemy from behind, and the Dark Lord's army fell back. Then the Lord of the Nazgûl himself rode into the fray on the Fields of Pelennor, slaying Théoden, thirteenth king of Rohan. As the king fell, a warrior of Rohan attacked. The Lord of the Nazgûl jeered, repeating the old saying that he would never be destroyed by a man. But this warrior was in fact Eowyn, a woman of Rohan who had travelled in a man's armour from HARROWDALE. As she attacked, he shattered her shield with his mace. He was about to kill her when Merry, the one hobbit present at the battle, stabbed him. With a great wail, the Lord of the Nazgûl disappeared, and his dark clothing fell shapeless on the ground. Thus the saying was fulfilled; the Lord of the Nazgûl was slain, not by a man, but by a woman and a hobbit.

Seeing this, the Rohirrim launched a furious assault on the Haradrim. But the forces of Mordor, the Men of the East and the Men of the South appeared to be gaining the upper hand, until the Rohirrim were relieved by the arrival of the fleet from Pelargir. The foremost ship displayed the banner of the long-lost kings of Gondor. As confusion spread through the enemy, Aragorn (later King Elessar) landed at Harlond and the forces of Gondor swept out of the besieged city and into the Fields of Pelennor. The battle ended with the destruction of all enemy forces that remained on the field. The Battle of the Fields of Pelennor was the greatest and possibly the most important of all those of the War of the Ring.

(J.R.R. Tolkien, *The Return of the King*, London, 1955; J.R.R. Tolkien, *The Silmarillion*, London, 1977)

PELLUCIDAR, an underground continent five hundred miles beneath the surface of the world. Travellers are warned that standing on the inside of the earth is like standing at the bottom of a bowl whose sides curve up to the sky on all sides. As a result, perception of distance is very different to that experienced on the surface of the earth; a tree a hundred miles away may be seen clearly while a mountain much nearer may be almost invisible. The horizon appears as a great upward curve.

Pellucidar is lit by its own sun, a fixed sphere held in the exact centre of the earth by the equal forces of attraction exerted on it from all sides. This blazing body has a small satellite which revolves around the earth's axis coincidentally with the earth itself, with the result that it is always above the same spot in Pellucidar. It casts a permanent darkness over the area known as the Land of Awful Shadow on the edge of the kingdom of THURIA. The rest of Pellucidar is bathed in a perpetual bright light, with no night or period of darkness. As a result it is impossible to calculate the time with any accuracy—and in any case time scarcely exists in Pellucidar, so rapidly do events seem to happen. This non-existence of time also means that people age less quickly than on earth. The only unit of time used is the period of rest called "sleep," and Pellucidarians will say, for instance, that they have been in a place for "many sleeps"—a vague measurement which varies with each individual.

As there is only a fixed sun in the skies of Pellucidar, there are no natural navigational aids. To compensate for this, Pellucidarians have an almost uncanny homing instinct; they are able to find their way across vast distances of hostile territory with little difficulty, as though they carried compasses inside their heads, and many of them are able to find their way to and around places that have only been described to them.

The only means of access from the surface of the earth is through an entrance at the North Pole, leading into the desolate wastelands to the north of KORSAR. It seems that most of Pellucidar's surface is occupied by solid earth, the land mass corresponding to the seas above and vice versa. The best known area is the region on the shores of the sea known as the Lural Az (also called the Sojar Az to the south of Thuria). Two main island groups have been explored in this sea: ANOROC and LUANA. The group known as the Unfriendly Islands has not yet been explored. There are also several floating islands, such as RUVA, which usually drift far out at sea and whose inhabitants have little to do with the peoples of the mainland.

The mainland washed by the Lural Az is dominated by the great range of the Mountains of the Clouds, an almost impassable chain of permanently snow-capped peaks. Between the mountains and the important kingdom of SARI most of the ground is covered by dense semitropical vegetation, broken by outcrops of limestone cliffs and by fast-flowing rivers. Sari itself is a high plateau among mountains, a land of clumsy trees and leaping rivers.

The areas north of Korsar remain largely unexplored and no one is certain of the size of the vast ocean that lies there. HIME, TANDAR and AMIOCAP are the only islands to have been visited by travellers.

The region inland from Thuria is known as the Lidi Plains, a strange area which borders on the Land of Awful Shadow; much of it lies in perpetual twilight, and the vegetation assumes strange and fantastic shapes. It is not known if the grass characteristic of other Pellucidarian plain areas is found here; this grass is normally waist high, each blade tipped with a tiny five-pointed flower. The flowers vary in colour and the grass appears to scintillate as it waves in the wind.

Pellucidar is inhabited by a bewildering number of tribes and races, most of whom have not advanced beyond the Stone Age. (Exceptions are the Bronze Age inhabitants of XEXOTLAND and the freebooters of Korsar.) Many of these races live in almost total isolation from one another and scarcely know of the existence of other peoples. The cannibals of AZAR, the madmen of the Valley of the JUKANS and the warrior women of OOG are known to other Pellucidarians as myths rather than as real people.

Even such a comparatively civilized area as KALI is inhabited by the savage and primitive Sabretooth Men, and the peaceful island of Amiocap is the home of the hideous Coripies, a race of

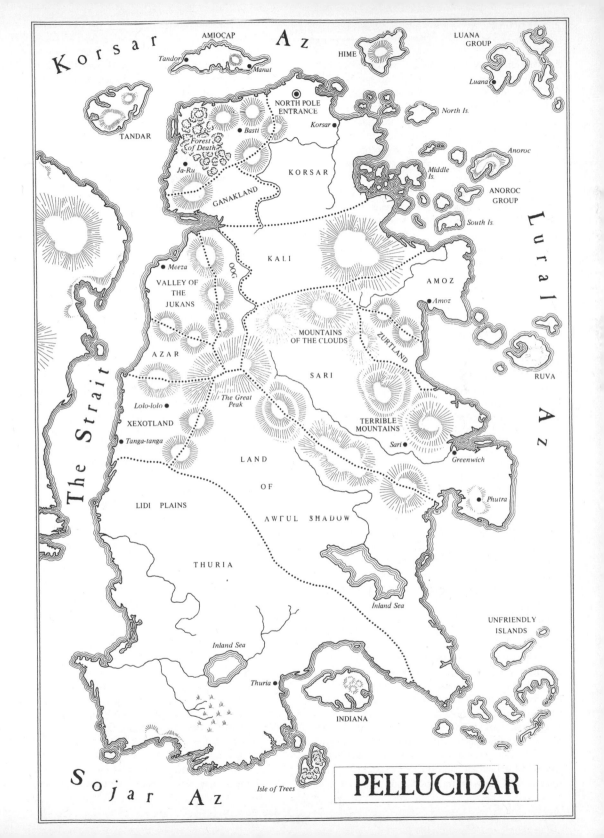

PELLUCIDAR

half-human cannibals who live in caves beneath the ground.

Few of the people of Pellucidar live in villages; by far the most common dwellings are caves in cliffs, such as those to be seen in Kali or on the island of Hime. Not many of the tribes work the soil, except in a very primitive manner; they live mostly by hunting and gathering fruit. The Korsars and the Xexots of Xexotland have more sophisticated social structures; both have monetary systems and the former have even established some industries, mostly connected with producing armaments for their ships.

A common language is spoken throughout Pellucidar, although there are regional variations, and degrees of linguistic development. The exception is the Sabretooth Men of Kali; they speak a language of their own and to strangers it resembles nothing more than the gibbering of monkeys.

Given the even warmth of the climate, travellers need not worry about what clothes to take to Pellucidar; most people wear only a loincloth, or an animal-skin slung across one shoulder. In some areas a variety of amulets are worn, but the basic design remains the same throughout Pellucidar, again with the exception of Korsar and Xexotland.

Most Pellucidarians share the belief that Pellucidar rests on a burning sea known as the Molop Az. Pellucidar itself is imagined to be flat and to be surrounded by a wall which prevents the earth and water from falling into the flames. Any dead who are buried in the earth are believed to be carried down piece by piece to the Molop Az by the wicked little men who live there. This explains a funeral custom common in Pellucidar whereby the dead—in order to escape the little men—are placed in trees for the birds to carry up to the Dead World, as the satellite above the Land of Awful Shadow is called.

Marriage customs also tend to be the same throughout Pellucidar, except on the island of Amiocap. Taking a mate normally involves combat between rival males and may easily end in the death of one of them; the woman belongs by right of conquest to whoever wins the fight. The victor may take her by the hand to indicate that he wants her as a mate, or may raise his hand above her head to indicate that she has no obligation towards him and is free. If he does neither, the woman becomes his slave and no man can honourably take her for his mate unless he defeats her master in single combat. To be won in a fight and then left as a slave is the worst insult that can be given to a Pellucidarian woman. However, marriage by abduction or rape also exists. In such cases a woman has little or no choice in the matter and can only run away or kill herself if she is taken by a man she dislikes. It is normal for the elder brothers of a family to marry first, unless they waive their prerogative in favour of a younger brother.

In general, the people of Pellucidar are extremely hostile to strangers. Acting on the assumption that all strangers are potential enemies, they kill them on sight, and tribes such as the Gorbuses of the Forest of DEATH also eat their captives. Other tribes like the people of BASTI keep their captives as slaves, working them to exhaustion. But perhaps the most ferocious are the so-called Bisonmen of GANAKLAND, who take a savage delight in torturing captives to death.

A traveller's life is made even more dangerous by the fauna of Pellucidar. Most of the animals found here correspond to species found on the surface of the earth during prehistoric times; the vast majority are savage and voracious carnivores. Many areas cannot be visited because of the bloodthirsty creatures that inhabit them. As can be expected, few of them have been tamed. The *lidi*—which is a kind of diplodocus—is used as a beast of burden by the people of Thuria and in some places the *jolok* or wild dog—an exceedingly fierce animal—has been domesticated. The mountains of Pellucidar are the home of the *ryth*, a huge cave-bear, and of the *tarag*, a great sabretooth tiger. Only on the island of Tandar has the *tarag* been tamed; the people there have also succeeded in domesticating the fearsome *taho* or cave-lion. *Thidpars* or pterodactyls are common and extremely treacherous.

The less dangerous animals include wild boars, deer, mammoths and orthopoi, the diminutive three-toed horse which was once found on earth. The giant elk, or *tharg*, is hunted for its meat in many areas. One of the more peculiar creatures is the *dyryth*, a herbivorous, sloth-like beast as large as an elephant, covered in thick shaggy hair. Its forepaws are armed with huge claws which are used to strip the foliage from trees, and although it is normally a slow-moving creature, a *dyryth* shows a surprising agility in climbing trees. It uses its tail as a defensive weapon.

If anything, the marine fauna of Pellucidar is more dangerous than its terrestrial counterpart, and makes any sea-journey an extremely hazardous undertaking. The waters swarm with enormous sea-serpents and *tandozares*, seal-like creatures with necks of up to ten feet in length; the *tandozare*'s head is like that of a snake and is armed with many vicious fangs. The *labyrinthodon* is an amphibious creature with the jaws of a crocodile and the body of a toad. It is also found in the swamps of Pellucidar, where it is known as the *sithig*. The *azdyryth* is rather like a small whale with the head of an alligator. Travellers are warned that anyone who falls overboard into the waters of Pellucidar stands very little chance of surviving.

The most dangerous creature in Pellucidar is no longer found in most areas, although they survive in the unexplored inland regions. The *mahar*, once the dominant species in Pellucidar, is a reptile with a long narrow body and a large head; the beaklike mouth is armed with sharp fangs. *Mahars* fly on membranous wings that protrude from their forefeet. They are highly intelligent beasts; they communicate by telepathy and have evolved a sophisticated system of hieroglyphics which they use to record their history. They live in underground cities, such as Phutra, beneath the plains to the south-east of Sari. These cities are well designed, with regular, well laid-out streets, and are lit by shafts from the surface. Only female *mahars* now exist; the males eventually died out after the females found that they could fertilize their own eggs chemically and that the male was therefore unnecessary.

The *mahars* are served by the *sargoths* or gorillas, and by men. The *sargoths* communicate with their masters in a secret sign language. *Thidpars* are also used as guards by the *mahars*. However, the intelligence of the great reptiles goes hand in hand with their cruelty. Slaves captured for them by the *sargoths* are used for brutal experiments in vivisection laboratories; others are eaten by the *mahars* and their servants in their temples—deep caverns with a central tank or lake. Here the *mahars* hypnotize their victims so that they walk calmly into the water and allow themselves to be torn to pieces without offering the slightest resistance. Only children and women are eaten by the *mahars* themselves; male captives are left for the *thidpars*. Sometimes captives are taken to a large amphitheatre where they are pitted against a variety of wild animals; the few who survive are allowed to go free.

(Edgar Rice Burroughs, *At the Earth's Core*, New York, 1922; Edgar Rice Burroughs, *Pellucidar*, New York, 1923; Edgar Rice Burroughs, *Tanar of Pellucidar*, New York, 1930; Edgar Rice Burroughs, *Seven Worlds to Conquer*, New York, 1936; Edgar Rice Burroughs, *Return to Pellucidar*, New York, 1941; Edgar Rice Burroughs, *Men of the Bronze Age*, New York, 1942; Edgar Rice Burroughs, *Tiger Girl*, New York, 1942; Edgar Rice Burroughs, *Land of Terror*, New York, 1944; Edgar Rice Burroughs, *Savage Pellucidar*, New York, 1963)

PENAL SETTLEMENT, a large penitentiary in a small sandy valley, a deep hollow surrounded on all sides by naked crags. Not far from the settlement is a river; a long flight of steps leads to the ferry that brings visitors from upstream. The climate is tropical.

The houses in the settlement are almost identical, very dilapidated, even the commander's headquarters and the tea-house. The most interesting is the building that houses the punishing apparatus. This is a structure bedded deep in the earth and consisting of three parts which, in the course of time, have acquired a kind of popular nickname. The lower one is called "the Bed," the upper one "the Designer" and the mobile middle one "the Harrow." Because the guiding principle of the Penal Settlement is that guilt is never to be doubted, the condemned person is gagged to avoid wasteful lies. The prisoner is laid on "the Bed," on a layer of special cotton wool, face down and quite naked. Straps bind his hands, feet and neck. As soon as the prisoner is strapped down, "the Bed" is set in motion; the movements of "the Bed" correspond exactly to the movements of "the Harrow," the instrument for the actual execution of the sentence.

This sentence is unknown to the prisoner and is written on the prisoner's body by the needles of "the Harrow." There are two kinds of needles arranged in multiple patterns. Each long needle has a short one beside it. The long needle does the writing, and the short needle sprays a jet of water to wash away the blood and keep the inscription clear. Blood and water are then conducted through small funnels into a main pipe that leads to the ready grave. So that the actual progress of the sentence can be watched by visitors in comfortable cane chairs, "the Harrow" is made of glass.

Because the script is not supposed to kill the prisoner at once, but only after a period of twelve hours, no simple calligraphy has been chosen to write out the sentence. Around the torso is a narrow girdle on which the sentence is drawn with many flourishes; the rest of the body is reserved for embellishments. The cotton wool staunches the bleeding.

During the first six hours, while the needles write deeper and deeper, the prisoner only suffers pain. After two hours the gag is taken away, for he no longer has the strength to scream. Some warm rice pap is poured into an electrically heated basin at the head of "the Bed," from which the prisoner, if he feels like it, can take as much as his tongue can lap. No one ever misses the chance. Only about the sixth hour does the prisoner lose all desire to eat. He grows quiet and enlightenment seems to glow in his eyes, and officials have said that the emotion of this moment is so intense that one might be tempted to get under "the Harrow" with him. From then on, the prisoner purses his mouth as if listening and begins to understand the inscription. Because of the flourishes, it is difficult for an observer to read it, but the prisoner deciphers it with his wounds. Finally "the Harrow" pierces him quite through and casts him into the grave, where he pitches down upon the blood and water and cotton wool. The sentence is thereby carried out and a soldier and a commanding officer bury him.

(Franz Kafka, *In der Strafkolonie*, Leipzig, 1919)

PENDOR, an island in the far West Reach of the EARTHSEA ARCHIPELAGO, to the west of the NINETY ISLES. Far away from any normal sea route, Pendor is uninhabited since men have avoided it for generations, originally because of the pirates who once lived here and subsequently because of the dragons who live here today. The lords of Pendor were pirates and slavers, hated throughout this region of Earthsea; they were destroyed by a dragon who swept out of the west and reduced both lords and townspeople to cinders with his fiery breath. Pendor, and the hoard of jewels and gold gathered by the pirate lords of the island, became the dragon's property.

Visitors arriving in Pendor today will see little more than silent streets running towards the harbour in its crescent-shaped bay, beneath the crumbling towers of the fortress that once was.

Though the only dragons now common in Earthsea are the tiny harmless *harrekki* of IFFISH

in the east, travellers may on rare occasions encounter a dragon of the west and should therefore be aware of these creatures' distinguishing characteristics. Western adult dragons reach immense proportions; the young are as long as a forty-oared ship. A dragon's head is crowned with spikes, its body is covered in gleaming scales, its tail is as sharp as the point of a sword. Dragons have three-forked tongues along which fire dances when they are angry, and black, membranous wings through which runs dark, poisonous blood. Experienced travellers say that the sight of dragons soaring and wheeling on the morning wind is the most beautiful of all the sights of Earthsea.

Dragons are skilled magicians and use a magic which is not that of men. Their natural tongue is the Old Speech, in which all things are known by their true name, the name which gives power to him who uses it. Few men speak the Old Speech—with the exception of the wizards of ROKE, where the study of Old Speech is a major activity. Unlike men, dragons have the ability to lie when using Old Speech and they seem to take a delight in doing so. They play with the listener as a cat plays with a mouse, catching him in a maze of mirror words which reflect the truth but do not reveal it. The few men to whom dragons will speak are known as Dragonlords. Contrary to popular belief, a Dragonlord has no mastery over dragons; he merely knows the dragons' true names and has the ability to talk to them and have them listen to him. No man can master a dragon; the only question that arises when a man meets a dragon is whether it will eat him or talk to him. Dragons are the most powerful and ancient creatures in all Earthsea and can only be defeated by one whose magical power and skill is equal to their own. But even so, visitors are warned that not even the greatest magician can look into the eye of a dragon and live.

(Ursula K. Le Guin, *A Wizard of Earthsea*, New York, 1968; Ursula K. Le Guin, *The Tombs of Atuan*, London, 1972; Ursula K. Le Guin, *The Farthest Shore*, London, 1973)

PENGUIN ISLAND, see ALCA.

PENTIXORE, an island empire in the Indian Ocean, access to which is difficult and dangerous because of the magnetic rocks in the sea around it.

One of the wonders of Pentixore is the Gravelly Sea. It is dry, composed of gravel and sand, and undulates like any sea but cannot be crossed by ships. Though there is no water in the Gravelly Sea, fish unlike any others are found here, and a solid river made of precious stones flows into it three times a week from the inland mountains.

Beyond the Gravelly Sea lies a desert, inhabited by wild dogs and talking parrots, and horned men who grunt like pigs. Small trees grow here that bear fruit every midday and then shrink back into the earth at night.

The emperor resides in the city of Susa where the climate is temperate, not in the capital, Nyse. The palace of Susa is a wonder to behold. The palace gates are made of sardonyx, barred with ivory. The windows are of crystal and the tables of amethysts, gold and emeralds. The steps to the throne are built of onyx, crystal, green jasper, cornelian, sardonyx, and chrysolite, bordered with gold, pearls and precious stones. The sides of the throne are emeralds. The royal chamber is lit by carbuncles and perfumed by burning balm, its pillars made of gold and the frame of the royal bed of sapphires and gold. The palace towers are surmounted by round pommels of gold in which carbuncles shine at night. Thirty thousand people eat in the palace every day.

When the emperor goes into battle, his forces are preceded by three large crosses of gold set with precious stones and carried in chariots. Each cross is followed by a unit of ten thousand men at arms and a hundred thousand footmen. On peacetime journeys, the emperor is preceded by a simple wooden cross, a gold platter full of earth—indicating that his flesh will turn to dust—and a silver platter full of jewels—to symbolize his nobility and power.

(Sir John Mandeville, *Voiage de Sir John Maundevile*, Paris, 1357)

PEOPLE OF THE MIST, COUNTRY OF THE,

a misty region in central south-east Africa occupying a vast plateau at the foot of the Bina Mountains. Following the Zambezi River from Mozambique (noting in passing the ruins of a Portuguese slave-trading camp called Yellow Devil or Pereira Camp) and going through the Manica Mountains where Thomas Outram lies buried, one comes to the Mavoon Settlement on the river itself. From here the route crosses the unexplored

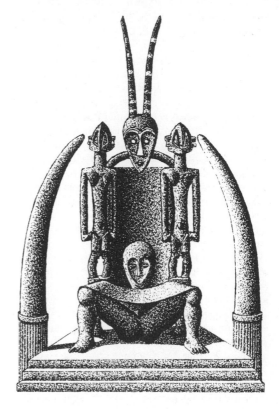

The royal throne in the Country of the PEOPLE OF THE MIST.

plateau that separates southern from central Africa, where the loneliness is hardly bearable. It is advisable to stock up on provisions at this point, as game farther on becomes scarce. Travellers should beware of the bushmen with poisoned arrows and the lions that roam the forest country which must be crossed next. After the forest comes a vast plain strewn with sharp stones and then a rolling veldt more than a hundred miles long. Finally one arrives at a huge cliff, a wall of rock, stretching across the plain like a white step and varying from seven hundred to one thousand feet high. Down the surface of this cliff flows a river in a series of beautiful waterfalls. The ascent is difficult but the visitor who succeeds will be rewarded with a magnificent view of the countryside.

Before arriving at the City of the People of the Mist, the traveller will see the houses of the herdsmen who look after the large shaggy cattle found in this region. These houses are built of huge undressed boulders, bedded in turf instead of mortar and roofed with the trunks of small trees and a thatch of sods on which the grass grows green. Some forty feet long and twenty feet deep, the houses have a high doorway and two small windows with curtains of hide. The floors are of trodden mud.

The city itself is on a kind of peninsula, with the river on three sides, the mountain protecting its back, and a surrounding wall. The natural moat can be crossed on small rafts. The city is a conglomerate of tall grey stone houses, roofed with green turf and resembling the boulders among which they were built. In the centre is the marketplace and shops. The palace is like the other houses, but set within a separate enclosure, and is linked through an underground passage with the Temple of Deep Waters which is open, like a Roman amphitheatre.

Inside the Temple stands the statue of a dwarf of gigantic proportions, seventy or eighty feet high. Beneath the statue is a deep pool in which an enormous crocodile—thought to be Jal, the living god Snake—used to live. The People of the Mist used to sacrifice human beings and offer rubies and sapphires to the statue and to the crocodile. Legend has it that Jal slew his mother Aca—the rubies symbolize her blood, and the sapphires the tears she shed praying for mercy. Juanna Mavoon, daughter of a white man called Rodd or Mavoon, impersonated the goddess Aca aided by an Englishman, Leonard Outram, and his servant, a black dwarf called Otter, and escaped from the Country of the People of the Mist with a quantity of precious stones which were ultimately lost.

The People of the Mist are over six feet tall, solemn-looking, large-eyed, thick-haired, with black and yellow skin. The soldiers wear goatskins and each carries a spear, a bow, barbed arrows decorated with red feathers and a trumpet made of wild bull's horn. The medicine-men have a large blue snake tattooed on their chests.

Two interesting objects to be seen in the city are the royal throne in the palace, sheltered under a roof of turf and made out of black wood and ivory, with feet like those of a man; and the goddess Aca's robe, worn by Juanna Mavoon when she impersonated the goddess: a black dress woven from the softest hair of black-fleeced goats and fastened with buttons of horn. The sleeves are just long enough to leave the hands of the wearer vis-ible and beneath its peaked cap is a sort of mask with three slits, two for the eyes and one for the mouth.

(Henry Rider Haggard, *The People of the Mist*, London, 1894)

PEPPERLAND, a country eighteen thousand leagues beneath the Sea of Green, approached through the Sea of Holes. Travellers will immediately notice that the keynote of Pepperland is colour; features of the landscape include hills of all colours, thick forests of painted trees where many-hued birds and butterflies abound, and rolling parkland. The inhabitants dress in bright colours and rainbows are frequent. There are no towns or cities in Pepperland, indeed few buildings of any sort; social life centres around the bandstand, for all Pepperlanders are players and lovers of music.

Pepperland was originally colonized, four scores and thirty-two bars ago, by Sgt. Pepper and his Lonely Hearts Club Band, who arrived in a yellow submarine (which can be seen today set on top of a pyramid). The present ruler (called "The Leader") is the Lord Mayor, a musician and conductor; he is assisted by Young Fred, a valiant Pepperlander.

Petrified mountain spires along the borders surround Pepperland; here lived the Blue Meanies whose chief aim was to overcome Pepperland by turning it and its inhabitants blue and grey. Led by their chief and his aide, Max, and using as their principal weapon the Flying Glove, the Blue Meanies attacked the country. Young Fred was dispatched in the yellow submarine to Liverpool, England, to persuade a group of four musicians, known with nostalgic affection as The Beatles, to return with him to Pepperland. The Blue Meanies, overcome by the Beatles' music, were driven off to Argentina, and Pepperland was restored to its colourful self.

(*Yellow Submarine*, directed by George Dunning, UK, 1968)

PERI KINGDOM, a deep valley in Persia, surrounded by ice-capped mountains, but warm and fertile. Villas and gardens can be seen around the lake that lies at its centre. There is one island in the lake, the abode of Queen Pehlevi. Although a representative of the most ancient race in all

Elfindom, the queen lives in a comparatively modest pavilion surrounded by flowering trees: quince, lilac, laburnum and magnolia. The island is surrounded by reed banks, but its main peculiarity is that it rotates constantly. Queen Pehlevi once told a magician friend that she was finding affairs of State tiresome and that she preferred to stay quietly at home in her pavilion. To satisfy her wishes he caused the island to rotate, so that she could both stay at home and keep an eye on the whole of her kingdom. The island's rotation means that visitors often have difficulty in finding the landing-place and may have to wait for one or two rotations before they can force their way through the reeds at the appropriate point.

The queen is a plump Peri, white-skinned and with her face farded with white lead. She wears no ornaments except a diamond belly-jewel. Her crown is a tall cylindrical hat of black gauze stretched over a frame of whalebone. Normally she dresses in a diaphanous white robe that floats over her breasts, belly and thighs like a thin veil. She lives surrounded by a large number of cats, and her main interests are chess and music—she is an accomplished player of the oboe and a considerable chess player. She is, however, intent only upon winning and is not above cheating if necessary; it is not advisable to beat her.

All the Elfin kingdoms can trace their origins back to the Peris who, for centuries, were believed to have died out. The origin of the Peris remains a mystery. Some authorities claim that they were formed from fire, others that they are fallen angels, but all agree that they inhabited the earth before the creation of man. It is generally believed that most of them were driven out of their original kingdom in Persia by a succession of earthquakes and invasions, although the Court Archivist of BROCELIANDE, author of one of the standard works of Elfindom, states that they were driven out by the magicians Moses and Aaron. No one has been able to explain how this one valley kingdom managed to remain.

The Peris are smaller than their European descendants, but they are strong, active and remarkably hardy. Their culture is a curious mixture of the austere and the luxurious. They are capable of great physical endurance, but they are also fond of certain luxuries such as exotic bath oils. They live on a succession of kickshaws and water ices and even their soup is sweet. It is possible that this is the origin of the myth that all elves and fairies live on nectar and dew. An important distinction between the Peris and the European Elfin realms is that Queen Pehlevi often flies and takes great delight in doing so; the aristocrats of European Elfindom gave up flying long ago.

(Sylvia Townsend Warner, *Kingdoms of Elfin*, London, 1972)

PERINTHIA, a city in Asia. Summoned to lay down the rules for the foundation of Perinthia, the astronomers established the place and the day according to the position of the stars; they drew the intersecting lines of the decumanus and the cardo, the first oriented to the passage of the sun and the other like the axis on which the heavens turn. They divided the map according to the twelve houses of the zodiac so that each temple and each neighbourhood would receive the proper influence of the favouring constellations; they fixed the points in the walls where gates should be cut, foreseeing how each would frame an eclipse of the moon in the next thousand years. Perinthia—they guaranteed—would reflect the harmony of the firmament; nature's reason and the gods' benevolence would shape the inhabitants' destinies.

Following the astronomers' calculations precisely, Perinthia was constructed; various peoples came to populate it; the first generation born in Perinthia began to grow within its walls; and these citizens reached the age to marry and have children.

In Perinthia's streets and squares today the traveller will encounter cripples, dwarfs, hunchbacks, obese men, bearded women. But the worst cannot be seen; guttural howls are heard from cellars and lofts, where families hide children with three heads or with six legs.

Perinthia's astronomers are faced with a difficult choice. Either they must admit that all their calculations were wrong and their figures are unable to describe the heavens, or else they must reveal that the order of the gods is reflected exactly in the city of monsters.

(Italo Calvino, *Le città invisibili*, Turin, 1972)

PERLA, capital of DREAM KINGDOM in central China, of approximately twenty thousand inhabitants. Perla is built on a bend of the imposing

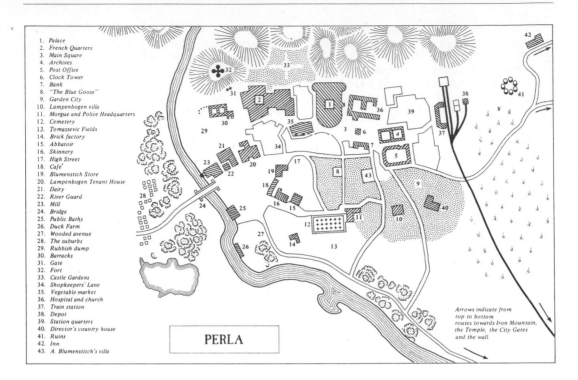

1. Palace
2. French Quarters
3. Main Square
4. Archives
5. Post Office
6. Clock Tower
7. Bank
8. "The Blue Goose"
9. Garden City
10. Lampenbogen villa
11. Morgue and Police Headquarters
12. Cemetery
13. Tomassevic Fields
14. Brick factory
15. Abbatoir
16. Skinnery
17. High Street
18. Café
19. Blumenstich Store
20. Lampenbogen Tenant House
21. Dairy
22. River Guard
23. Mill
24. Bridge
25. Public Baths
26. Duck Farm
27. Wooded avenue
28. The suburbs
29. Rubbish dump
30. Barracks
31. Gate
32. Fort
33. Castle Gardens
34. Shopkeepers' Lane
35. Vegetable market
36. Hospital and church
37. Train station
38. Depot
39. Station quarters
40. Director's country house
41. Ruins
42. Inn
43. A. Blumenstitch's villa

Arrows indicate from
top to bottom
routes towards Iron Mountain,
the Temple, the City Gates
and the wall.

PERLA

Black River, its waters dark as ink. Dark colours are an essential part of the landscape; everything seems to be a deep shade of dark green, an opaque greenish-grey. The sky is always cloudy and neither the sun, the moon nor the stars are ever seen. The form of the clouds, hanging low over the land, never changes; these vaporous formations are explained by experts as due to the vast marshes and woods that surround the city. Even though the air feels warm and mild, the barometer always points to bad and cloudy weather. The seasons lack contrast: spring lasts five months, as does autumn; a constant dusky light at night indicates the short hot summer. Endless twilight and a few snowflakes are the signs of winter.

The architecture of the city is typically central European. Its founder and sovereign, Klaus Patera, purchased old houses from all over Europe and had them moved, at tremendous expense, to Perla. This eclecticism gives Perla a unique atmosphere. The city is divided into four main sections. The Train Station district, built on the brink of a marshland and always deep in smoke, boasts the squalid administration buildings, the archives and the post office. This tedious and bleak district

neighbours the so-called Garden City, the rich people's residential area. Next comes Long Street, where the shops are and where the middle class has its lodgings; towards the river, it takes on the aspect of a village. The narrow strip between Long Street and the Mountain is the fourth, or French, district. This small section of Perla, with its four thousand Latin, Slav and Jewish inhabitants, is considered an area of ill-repute. The picturesque and heterogeneous mass lives here in old wooden huts, and the district, with its crooked streets and its foul-smelling dens, is certainly not the pride of Perla.

Towering high above the city is a monstrous construction of uncouth grandiosity—Patera's residence. Set against the porous and rough surface of the rocks, its bulk leans forward towards the large square in the centre of the city. Across the river are the Suburbs, the name given to a small village where the original inhabitants of Dream Kingdom now live. They are clearly of Mongolian race and proudly claim descent in direct line from the great Genghis Khan. Their lives, in contrast with the feverish pace of the city, flow calmly and serenely. The Suburbs consist of low wooden cabins of extravagant shapes, tiny cupolas and conical tents, every building surrounded by a well-kept garden. Here and there stand signposts decorated with banners and glass discs, and with countless grotesque figures, large and small, made of glazed clay, wood and metal, looking like moss-covered scarecrows. Huge venerable trees seem to cover the whole area with their far-stretching branches.

The population of Perla has been recruited only from among certain well-defined types. Those of the highest ranks are people of excessively delicate sensibilities. Different types of mania, such as collector's fever, a passion for reading, a feverish desire to gamble, a hyper-religious attitude and other forms of neurasthenia seem to be the best qualifications for becoming an inhabitant of Dream Kingdom. Among the women of Perla, hysterics are a common phenomenon. The lower classes are selected on the basis of abnormal or excessive development: alcoholics, those discontented with themselves and with the world, hypochondriacs, spiritualists, muckrakers and bullies, satiated sophisticates, old adventurers seeking peace, acrobats, swindlers, political exiles, murderers on the run, liars and thieves. In certain cases, a physical peculiarity can be striking enough to warrant an invitation to Perla. For this reason, people with large goitres, bloated noses, or enormous hunchbacks are very common in Perla. Most of the population is originally German.

Population growth is very slow because children are not particularly encouraged; the inhabitants believe that children are not worth the bother they cause.

A striking characteristic of Perla is an indefinable yet strong odour that clings to everything. At its worst it can be compared to a subtle mingling of flour and dried cod. Rumour has it that the houses bought by Patera in the slums and red-light districts of the large capitals of Europe, from Paris to Istanbul, are bathed in blood, crime and infamy. Ugly legends are also attached to certain solitary places around the city, woods and marshes, near which none will venture after dark.

One of the kingdom's most mysterious places is a temple on Dream Lake about a day's journey from Perla. Surrounded by artificial waterfalls and a silent park, it is built with such noble materials and such art that an observer may feel that here is an architecture halfway between heaven and earth.

In underground rooms, the builders of the temple have put up symbolic statues. The temple can be visited only once a year, and even then important letters of introduction are required.

The religion of Perla is somewhat disconcerting. The inhabitants venerate the egg, the nut, bread, cheese, honey, milk, wine and vinegar. Iron and steel are taken to represent evil.

For some time now, no new visitors are known to have arrived in Perla. Travellers from central Asia report hearing rumours that the city was struck by some sort of calamity that left it in ruins. Some mention a strange sleep epidemic; others think that it was invaded by animals of many species; yet others suggest a curious illness that suddenly attacks the eyes. Certain nomadic tribes have brought back descriptions of a waste of enormous ruins, large blocks of stone and broken columns. Some say that these might be the remains of the marvellous city of Perla.

(Alfred Kubin, *Die andere Seite: Ein phantastischer Roman*, Berlin, 1908)

PESTITZ, capital of Hohenfliess. This university city, built on the slope of a high hill, is famous for its Italian architecture, its many palaces and beautiful mansions with statues on its roofs. The astronomical tower of the Blemenbühl Mountains is worth a visit, as well as the two churches on Mount Schreckhorn.

In Pestitz an honoured citizen is made a Knight of the Fleece, a pompous ceremony which attracts a great number of visitors. When a Knight of the Fleece is buried his arms are carved inverted on his tomb, his shield is hung upside-down and his helmet is broken into a thousand pieces.

(Jean Paul [Johann Paul Friedrich Richter], *Titan*, Berlin, 1800–03)

PHANTASTICO, a mountain to the west of RIPPLE LAND, encircled by a gully which marks the frontier of the land of the Phanfasms, the dreaded inhabitants of the mountain. The gully is full to the brim with molten lava, the home of fire-serpents and poisonous salamanders. The only way to cross the gully of lava is to use the narrow bridge that spans it. The bridge is a single arch of grey stone guarded by a scarlet alligator. The stench and heat arising from this area are so great

The beautiful city of the Phanfasms deceives travellers by appearing to be a crude collection of stone huts on the mountain of PHANTASTICO.

that even the birds are reluctant to fly over it, and travellers are advised that all living things should keep away from this mountain.

The flat summit of Phantastico is occupied by the city of the Phanfasms, who belong to a race of evil spirits known as Erbs. The city is beautiful and can claim to be one of the most magnificent creations of magic, but it does not appear so to visitors. All that travellers see when arriving is a pile of crude rock dwellings and strange-shaped trees in a barren waste. This is simply a deception practised by the Phanfasms to protect their city, and travellers who have been bold enough to come this far are advised to overcome it.

Phanfasms have no fixed shape or form. In an instant they change from snakes to lizards or wolves and back again; others appear as men with the heads of lions or owls. Their ruler, the First and Foremost, has been seen to take on the shape of a bear, a beautiful woman and a butterfly, all in a matter of moments.

(L. Frank Baum, *The Emerald City of Oz*, Chicago, 1910)

PHILISTIA, a country near POICTESME. The capital is Novogath.

The people of Philistia, the Philistines, are known to have conquered the island of LEUKE, and destroyed its capital, Pseudopolis. As the Philistine legions, led by Queen Dolores, approached the city, Achilles, Helen and the other Greek heroes simply rose above them and passed over their heads like gleaming clouds. The Philistines entered the city unopposed and, using a form of Greek fire which destroys everything that is not grey, reduced Pseudopolis to ashes and stones.

Travellers should know the sole law of Philistia: that all must do what seems to be expected of them. So, as it is expected—by the people of Philistia—that women and priests shall behave unaccountably, these two groups do what they wish and the men of the country obey them. This explains why Philistia has always been ruled by a queen.

The Philistines worship three main gods: Sesphara, Ageus and Vel-Tyno. Sesphara is a goddess of dreams who thrives on love given to giaours. The cult is now spreading to other countries, where it is causing considerable disturbance and numerous mad antics. Of Vel-Tyno it is known that he favours the colour grey: "All other colours"—reads his dictum—"are for ever more abominable, until I say otherwise." The ruins of Pseudopolis on Leuke have been dedicated to him. Little is known of the cult of Ageus. The windows of the temple of Ageus are now in Storisende, Poictesme, where they were taken as booty by Duke Asmund of the Northmen.

In Philistia, children are delivered by the stork, who is summoned in the manner formerly employed by Thessalian witches. An invocation is made in Latin:

> *Dictum est antiqua sandalio mulier*
> *habitavit*
> *Quae multos pueros habuit tum ut puttuit*
> *nullum*
> *Quod faciundum erat cognoscere. Sic*
> *domina anser.*

Two chalk lines are then drawn on the floor and five black stars are placed in a row. The husband walks along one of the chalk lines, beckons to his wife to join him and kisses her. The stork then appears to take orders for children. Philistines consider obscure any reference to other means of obtaining babies. A small sect, however, favours accepting such babies as may be found in the cabbage patch (see ZAVATTINIA).

The Queen of Philistia believes poetry to be popular among her subjects, although she herself never reads it. Her opinion, however, is not well-founded. Many people in Philistia say that making literature is synonymous with making trouble for oneself. The only three writers known to have existed in the country were driven out or frightened away, and it is said that they now work as ghost writers for some of Britain's best-selling authors.

A peculiarity of the fauna of Philistia is the tumblebug, a malodorous but well-respected insect, who asserts that living people are offensive, lewd, lascivious and obscene, and speaks well of the dead.

(James Branch Cabell, *Figures of Earth. A Comedy of Appearances*, New York, 1921; James Branch Cabell, *Jurgen. A Comedy of Justice*, New York, 1919)

PHILOMELA'S KINGDOM, the southern part of an island in the Atlantic Ocean. King Philo-

Remains of the Colossus in the foothills of PHILOMELA'S KINGDOM.

ponus, who reigned over the entire island in the mid-seventeenth century, divided it into three parts: the north for his son Philocles, the centre for himself, and the south for his illegitimate daughter Philomela.

The beach is of fine, clean golden sand strewn with shells like precious stones. The country abounds in beautiful trees, planted too thickly for the soil to be cultivated, yet leaving ample room for pleasant walks. In the woods live groups of lovely ladies who sing and dance among the trees, but it is best not to heed their advances.

One central road leads to the Royal Palace, of which only the ruins remain. It was destroyed by Philocles after he discovered that Philomela used it as a snare to trap handsome young travellers and dispose of them in a cruel manner. However, descriptions tell us that the palace was of extraordinary beauty. Every entrance was on a downward slope and the palace itself was on the steep side of a rock. It was built in the shape of an amphitheatre, with walls like glass and hollow pillars hardly strong enough to bear the weight of the building. The front buildings enclosed a garden. The dining room was grandiose and the bedrooms luxurious, with walls completely hidden by cloths with an obscene ground-pattern of naked men and women. But everything seemed designed for show rather than for use.

In fact, the palace was set up as a clever trap. Philomela had frittered away her wealth and she tried to regain her fortune by robbing unwary travellers. When her guests lay in the sumptuous beds, the floor would open and they would be thrown into an underground sewer: here the remains of the banquets, the vomit of overcharged stomachs and other filthy excrement lay rotting among the skeletons of past victims. A horrible noise of rattling chains could be heard, intermingled with the roar of wild beasts. The only exit was across a dangerous river in which many victims deliberately drowned themselves to escape an even worse fate. There was a bridge across the river, but it was guarded by a huge and terrible colossus beneath whose legs one had to pass. His eyes were fierce and his body bruised and bloodstained. Whoever succeeded in crossing this bridge could reach Philoponus' Kingdom on the top of a golden mountain.

Philoponus' Castle, which is still standing, holds several curiosities: among them vases of transparent but not brittle seventeenth-century glass, and automatic machines with perpetual motion, that can make music and display miniature dancing men and women. King Philoponus is also remembered as the author of the treatise *De omni Artificiorum Genere* ("On all arts and crafts"). Of Philocles' Kingdom nothing is known.

(Samuel Gott, *Novae Solymae libri sex*, London, 1648)

PHILOPONUS' KINGDOM, see PHILO-MELA'S KINGDOM.

PHILOS, an island of unknown location, protected from the outside world by its peculiar geography. The only part of its coast which is not rock-bound is defended by sandbanks, where the water is too shallow for any ship to approach the shore. Travellers are advised that the best way to reach Philos is by being shipwrecked on the rocks. If the survivors are found by the islanders to be virtuous, they will be allowed to stay; otherwise they will be exiled to another island.

Philos is covered with flowers that perfume the air—mainly roses—and large groves of orange and lemon trees. Throughout the island are many splendid gardens arranged in such a way that they appear to be the work of nature and not of art. Even the statues look as if they had arrived here by chance, like figures scattered at random. The island

grottoes are perfumed with jasmine and decorated with shells. There is only one bleak area, almost uninhabited, to the south of the island.

Philos is not ruled by a sovereign in a material sense. Instead it is governed by love, friendship and candour, and the person who most inspires these sentiments becomes First Citizen. There is no shortage of candidates on Philos. Together with the First Citizen, the beautiful women of the island rule over the other inhabitants through the love they inspire. They are very conscious of their worth and choose their lovers with great care, never bestowing their charms on the young but on mature men who have proved reliable.

On Philos there are no formal marriages—these have been replaced by mutual declarations of love; no temples, as the heart is considered the true temple; no judicial system, as all the people are just. The women of Philos are in fact so virtuous that some of the poorer women devote themselves entirely to satisfying the desires of men too young to find mistresses. These prostitutes are regarded as useful citizens who sacrifice themselves for the good of society. They are kept by the State and would be horrified if anyone offered them money for their services.

The capital of Philos is Philamire, where every house looks like a palace and is decorated with numerous mirrors. There are many theatres in Philamire, which show mostly French plays of the classical period, and where actresses enjoy the status of vestal virgins. The Main Theatre is a circular building standing in a large octagonal piazza; its many exits prevent any unseemly confusion of the audience when entering or leaving.

(Comte de Martigny, *Voyage d'Alcimédon, ou Naufrage qui conduit au port...* [*Histoire plus vrai que vraisemblable, mais qui peut encourager à la recherche des terres inconnues*], Amsterdam, 1751)

PHILOSOPHERS' ISLAND, one of several high islands near Tierra del Fuego. The architecture on this island is remarkable. The Philosophers build vast edifices (called "systems") starting with the ridge-piece on the roof, which is usually highly elaborate. However, while they wait for the foundation to be laid the building generally collapses, killing the architect.

The Philosophers spend their time in curious occupations: weighing air, comparing two drops of water and trying to find definitions—that is, trying to replace one word by several others that mean the same.

The island is always covered with snow; the roads are difficult and it is easy to lose one's way.

(Abbé Pierre François Guyot Desfontaines, *Le Nouveau Gulliver, ou Voyage De Jean Gulliver, Fils Du Capitaine Gulliver. Traduit d'un Manuscrit Anglois. Par Monsieur L.D.F.*, Paris, 1730)

PHILOSOPHY ISLE, situated off the coast of the United States near the Island of FORTUNE. The capital, and the seat of the most famous academy in the world, is Rispa.

There is no government on the island as the people cannot agree as to which is the least oppressive and most enlightened system. There is also no religion, though there are a few theologians. Religion was gradually discredited through a campaign of mockery; the authors of various works of derision received academic honours.

Of great importance are the schools in which rival philosophers teach their various systems of thought. These include most of the systems known to European philosophy and numerous explanations of the origin of the universe. Representatives of all schools—Robinet, Voltaire, Diderot—can be seen here, having finally found a land where they do not have to waste time talking to vulgar and intellectually meagre persons.

When planning a visit to Philosophy Isle travellers are advised to acquaint themselves well with a great number of philosophical doctrines, or they will find themselves out of their depth in a land where philosophical discussion is virtually the only activity, and conversation consists largely of quotations and counter-quotations.

(Abbé Balthazard, *L'Isle Des Philosophes Et Plusieurs Autres, Nouvellement découvertes, & remarquables par leur rapports avec la France actuelle*, Chartres, 1790)

PHYLLIS, a city in Asia. When a traveller arrives in Phyllis, he will rejoice in observing all the bridges over the canals, each different from the others: cambered, covered, on pillars, on barges, suspended, with tracery balustrades. A variety of windows look down on the streets: mullioned, Moorish, lancet, pointed, surmounted by lunettes or stained-glass roses; many kinds of pavement cover the ground: cobbles, slabs, gravel, blue and white tiles. At every point, the city offers surprises

to his view: a caper bush jutting from the fortress' walls, the statues of three queens on corbels, an onion dome with three smaller onions threaded on the spire. "Happy the man who has Phyllis before his eyes each day and who never ceases seeing the things it contains" is a common traveller's regret.

But it sometimes happens that the traveller must stay in Phyllis and must spend the rest of his days there. Soon the city fades before his eyes, the rose windows are expunged, the statues on the corbels, the domes. Like all of Phyllis's inhabitants, he will follow zigzag lines from one street to another, he will distinguish the patches of sunlight from the patches of shade, a door here, a stairway there, a bench where he can put down his basket, a hole where his foot will stumble if he is not careful. All the rest of the city is invisible. Phyllis is a space in which routes are drawn between points suspended in the void: the shortest way to reach that certain merchant's tent, avoiding that certain creditor's window. His footsteps will not follow what is outside the eyes, but what is within, buried, erased.

Millions of eyes look up at windows, bridges, capers, and they might be scanning a blank page. Many are the cities like Phyllis, which elude the gaze of all except the man who catches them by surprise.

(Italo Calvino, *Le città invisibili*, Turin, 1972)

PIERRE BLANCHE, ISLE DE LA ("Island of the White Stone") an island in the Straits of Malacca, two leagues long and one and a half leagues wide. It is one of a chain of rocky, mostly infertile islands. The population is racially mixed, largely descended from the survivors of a shipwreck in the late seventeenth century.

Visitors will find two small villages on the island: one Christian, one pagan. There are no legal or administrative officials and the residents have established a communal system which provides according to their needs. The Christians and the pagans live together happily and intermarriage is frequent. At birth the children are sprinkled with water and blessed but they are not given names until they are able to talk. They become engaged at six or seven, when their hair is cut off for the first time. Before that the boys weave their hair with reeds to make a tunic for their future brides.

A funeral on the island is an interesting ceremony to observe. A terracotta coffin is always kept ready in the chapel. When a death occurs, the coffin is placed in a grave and the corpse is brought out on a stretcher, garishly dressed. Gum benzoin is sprinkled on it, the corpse is covered and then buried for a year. During this period of mourning, relatives visit the grave every day. After a year, the corpse is exhumed and exposed to the sun.

One species of tree is unique to the island. Its bark is darker than cinnamon and it tastes of a mixture of pepper, cloves and cinnamon. The powdered bark will cure all wounds in twenty-four hours and when dissolved in pork fat produces a soothing balm. The flowers of this tree attract fish and are used as bait.

(Dralsé de Grandpierre [?], *Relation De Divers Voyages Faits Dans L'Afrique, dans l'Amerique, & aux Indes Occidentales. La Description du Royaume de Juda, & quelques particularitez touchant la vie du Roy regnant. La Relation d'une Isle nouvellement habitée dans le détroit de Malaca en Asie, & l'Histoire de deux Princes de Golconde. Par le Sieur Dralsé De Grand-Pierre, ci-devant Officier de Marine*, Paris, 1718)

PILE, a monochrome city chiselled into a fine brocade of stone, brick and mortar. Planned for splendour, huge and unjolly, Pile seems to have got out of hand, like a grand mausoleum where every space is covered with mosaics. Through the many arcades, staircases and halls, the Princes of Pile—who are all related—fight each other incessantly.

Pile is inhabited by dreamers, bachelors, meek moralists, police officers, fiddlers, sly philosophers, harried schemers, octogenarians, vegetarians, astronomers, antiquarians, scientists, prelates, medics, mathematicians, monks, physicians, alchemists, architects and masons.

The heart of Pile is the Oracle-Machine, a large computer in the Church of St. Klaed, nicknamed by the inhabitants "God's hearing-aid." This time-defined apparatus of wood and stone and pewter tells the people of Pile what to do. Instructed by it, the Crown Prince of Pile left his kingdom and entered a land of all colours, from which he was unable to return. For this reason the people of Pile believe that to abandon a place is to lose it and they never travel.

(Brian W. Aldiss & Mike Wilks, *Pile. Petals from St. Klaed's Computer*, London, 1979)

PIMMINEE, an island in the western extremity of the MARDI ARCHIPELAGO. Totally flat, Pimminee is covered by a weak and sickly vegetation. The air is stuffy and enervating.

Visitors will be interested to note the local costumes, as the natives are almost hysterically concerned about the way they dress. A code of innumerable laws governs every particular detail of their costumes, up to the last bit of material and seam. They ignore the use of foot gear: when the noblemen take a walk they are preceded by liveried servants who put before their feet small carved boards, so as to avoid any contact with the ground. The nobleman's feet are tied together with a piece of cord that serves to regulate their movement and to maintain a specific gait within the prescribed limits of Pimminean good manners.

(Herman Melville, *Mardi, and A Voyage Thither*, New York, 1849)

PINK PALACE, of unknown location, inhabited by the Pink Child. Every afternoon the Pink Child looks out through her landscape of tapestries and delicate English paintings. She walks with silk slippers on the soft carpets that spread from wall to wall, she eats from white china plates with silver cutlery and says "I pray thee, do not rise" when she passes, drawing with her hand a swan in the perfumed air. She listens to soft classical music and recites in French *La cigale et la fourmi*.

The Pink Child is entirely pink and smells of roses. She has no elbows or knees because knees are ugly and elbows look like chickens' bottoms. Once a day the Pink Child enters a secret room in the Palace, but it is forbidden to ask what room. When she enters, all clocks are stopped and they only start ticking again when she leaves.

However, on one occasion the Pink Child left her palace and travelled abroad. She saw salt and lime landscapes and murky mud pools in which pigs wallowed. She saw the excrement of animals, heard rude voices and the evil music of brothels. She saw the dreadful faces of prostitutes, thieves and money-lenders. A drunken sailor kissed her. A blind man touched her with a leper's hand. Through open windows she saw lovers' quarrels, a child's funeral, the painful birth of a baby, the murder of an old man by his nephew. Mangy dogs and vicious cats bit her on the ankles. But the Pink Child did not die. After crossing through the mud, the spit, the excrement, the kisses of drunken sailors, the hordes of prostitutes and murderers, after seeing and hearing everything, the Pink Child returned to her palace. There she bathed and perfumed herself and sat at the table and ate from white china plates with silver cutlery and said "I pray thee, do not rise" as she passed. And this is how visitors see her today.

(Marco Denevi, "La niña rosa," in *Falsificaciones*, Buenos Aires, 1966)

PIPPLE-POPPLE, LAKE, see GRAM-BLAMBLE LAND.

PISSEMPSCO, capital of AKKAMA.

PLAY, LAND OF, a fairy land inhabited by little people, where small objects acquire a larger size. Clover tops are trees, rain pools are seas on which leaves sail like ships. Apart from a few insects such as bumblebees, spiders, flies, ants and ladybirds, the Land of Play is inhabited by little thoughtful creatures with lovely eyes, clad in armour of green, black, crimson, gold or blue. Some of these creatures have wings but seem to put them to little use and spend the days watching travellers (who must be of diminutive size) sailing the rain-pool seas.

The Land of Play is reached by shutting one's eyes and sailing through the air. The return trip is usually surprising, as the contrast between the small world and the larger size of everyday things in the traveller's own country will come to him as something of a shock.

(Robert Louis Stevenson, "The Little Land," in *A Child's Garden of Verses*, London, 1885)

PLAY TOWN, in Tuscany, Italy. Visitors can reach it by catching a coach that stops at several places along the Tuscany roads; transportation is free. The coach announces its arrival with bells and trumpets so soft and gentle that they sound like the drone of mosquitoes; the coach's wheels are covered with rags to make as little noise as possible. It is pulled by twelve pairs of donkeys, all the same height and colour, all wearing two pairs of small white summer shoes. The little man who drives the coach is shorter from head to foot than from side to side, mellifluous and unctuous as a blob of butter, with a face like a pink apple, a constantly laughing mouth and a soft caressing voice like that of a cat trying to ingratiate itself with the mistress of the house. When his donkeys seem somewhat upset, he pacifies them with a kiss on the ear.

Play Town is reached at dawn and it resembles no other place on earth. It is inhabited only by children, the eldest of which is barely fourteen and the youngest no older than eight. The sound of laughter and merriment in the streets is enough to deafen a lion-tamer. Hordes of urchins are everywhere: some playing marbles, others hide-and-seek, others riding bicycles, yet others galloping away on hobby-horses. Some play blind man's buff, some dressed as clowns perform funny tricks, others turn somersaults or walk on their hands, a few are dressed as soldiers with plumed helmets and tin swords. Laughter, screaming, singing, clapping combine to create pandemonium. In every square is a Punch and Judy show, on every wall is written "Hooray for toys, down with school." In all of Play Town visitors will not find any schools or teachers or books. It has been decided that on Thursdays and Sundays children will not go to school; for that reason, every Play Town week has six Thursdays and one Sunday. Holidays begin on January 1 and end on December 31.

The only inconvenience of Play Town is that after five months the children who live here turn into donkeys which are then sold for a good profit by the little man who drives the coach.

(Carlo Collodi, *Le avventure di Pinocchio*, Florence, 1883)

PLUTO, not to be confused with the celestial body of the same name. Pluto is a vast land deep inside the hollow centre of the earth. Access to Pluto is via the chasms in the IRON MOUNTAINS which surround both the North and South poles of the earth.

The landscapes of Pluto are basically similar to those found on earth and in some areas are extremely beautiful. The most striking feature of this inner world is that because it is smaller than earth itself everything on it is also smaller. The people of Pluto rarely exceed three feet in height and the animals are proportionately smaller than their counterparts on earth. Horses are no larger than sheep, and elephants, which are used for transport in some areas, are little bigger than calves. Much of the flora is similar to that of earth and even where the appearance of a fruit is quite different from its earthly counterpart, the taste is often recognizable.

Pluto's climate is even and temperate, with little variation between the seasons. A few clouds can be seen, and they sometimes become quite thick at night. By day, Pluto is bathed in a clear even light, thought to come from the sun either through the polar entrances or through chasms and cracks in the earth's crust. The fixed stars that can be seen in Pluto's night remain a mystery. One theory is that they are miniature versions of the celestial bodies; another that they are the roots of volcanoes. Like the countries above it, Pluto has seas and rivers; the only difference, of course, is that they are much smaller and that the water is paler and clearer than that of earth's oceans. The major sea is some 280 leagues long and 173 leagues wide, dotted with many islands of various sizes.

There are forty-six separate states on Pluto: fifteen kingdoms, six empires, eleven republics and fourteen nations (the latter without fixed governments and at varying stages of political and cultural development).

The people of Pluto vary considerably in both appearance and culture. Probably the most primitive are the green-skinned nomads of the forests and plains; the most sophisticated, the citizens of ALBUR. The green-skinned people have no fixed settlements and dress in crudely cured animal skins. They have a set system of religious beliefs and accept the existence of a divine creator and an after-life. According to their theology, the world was created by a good spirit who lived with his wife in the higher areas of Pluto. But his power was counterbalanced by that of an evil spirit. Only the evil spirit had children (his wife has in fact been having children ever since the world began) and gradually, fearing his wrath and that of his offspring, men began to abandon the worship of the good spirit.

In 1806 a group of French and English sailors arrived on Pluto by mistake. The green-skinned people took them for evil spirits—possibly because of their pale complexion, grey being the colour of evil in their symbolic system—and proceeded to stone them, believing this to be one method for driving away evil spirits. When this failed, gifts of expiation were made: an altar of turf was built and six pigs, the size of cats, were slaughtered on it and then roasted. The priests, wearing their traditional tall brown hats, approached the strangers, telling them in sign language to take the offerings. Once persuaded that their visitors were indeed men, the priests became more friendly and gave some ac-count of their way of life and spoke of the existence of other people, whom the English and French then decided to visit before returning to the surface.

Although the green-skinned people represent the lowest stage of development to be found on Pluto, a somewhat higher stage is represented by the forest-dwelling yellow-green people who live in areas of natural forest surrounded by a ditch, in rough wooden huts clustered at the foot of trees. Little is known of their culture, but they appear to have a rudimentary form of government and some knowledge of tools.

(Anonymous, *Voyage au centre de la terre, ou aventures de quelques naufragés dans des pays inconnus. Traduit de l'anglais de Sir Hormidas Peath*, Paris, 1821)

PLUTONIA, a vast realm deep in the bowels of the earth, access to which is found in the Sea of Beaufort towards the latitude 81° north, beyond the Russki mountain chain, in Fridtjof Nansen Land. Plutonia was discovered on June 17, 1914, by a Russian expedition under the command of Professor Nikolai Innokentevic Trukanov, propounder of the theory of a hollow earth.

The expedition, wishing to cross Nansen Land, found itself suddenly in a seemingly interminable depression some nine thousand metres below sea level. Following a descending route, the expedition entered an underwater area similar to the Siberian tundra, illuminated by a reddish sun. They discovered that they were in fact deep inside the earth and that the sun was a new body which they baptized Pluto, and the country, Plutonia.

The explorers found a number of large prehistoric creatures inhabiting Plutonia: mammoth, giant bears, many kinds of dinosaurs. In the centre of Plutonia lies the so-called Black Desert, a vast extent of black rocks surrounding a volcano. On the slopes of the volcano grows a prehistoric forest inhabited by giant ants which build anthills reminiscent of skyscrapers.

The rest of Plutonia is a large conglomerate of jungles, marshes, rivers and lakes, which have not been properly explored. One tribe of human beings was, however, discovered by the expedition, the great majority of whom are women. They live in skin-covered huts, they go about naked, have no knowledge of fire and eat their meat raw. Both men and women hunt; the men are weak and trail along, while the women are large and robust and lead the hunt with piercing cries. Children are considered to have only one mother but several fathers. The natives' bodies are covered with soft hair, and they give the impression of being apes rather than humans. Their language is composed of monosyllables and bisyllables, and has no declensions, verbs, adverbs or prepositions; words are qualified by gestures. They can count to twenty using their fingers and toes.

(Vladimir Obrutcev, *Plutonia*, Moscow, 1924)

PNOM DHEK, a city in the jungles of Cambodia, rival to the city of LODIDHAPURA. Both cities are of similar appearance: majestic piles of masonry and ornate towers coupled with splendid temples give the impression that Pnom Dhek is a very wealthy city. The Royal Palace is a low, rambling building; various kings throughout the centuries have added their styles to the central unit and this palace, on the whole, is more impressive than that of Lodidhapura. The gardens around it are large, beautiful and well maintained. Notable is the magnificent gate, with room enough for a pair of elephants to pass through it in comfort.

In spite of their similarities, Lodidhapura and Pnom Dhek have long waged war against one another. Gordon King, an American explorer, rescued the Princess Fou-Tan of Pnom Dhek from the fate of becoming the concubine of the Leper King of Lodidhapura, and also from falling into the clutches of the evil Bharata Rahon who wished to marry Fou-Tan in order to become the next king of Pnom Dhek. Gordon King later married the princess and initiated the dynasty that has lasted to this day.

When in Pnom Dhek, travellers should visit the underground mazes through which Gordon King and the princess escaped.

Pnom Dhek's solid wall of vegetation, thick with tigers and snakes, is typical of the Cambodian jungle. Panthers, leopards, spiders, monkeys, elephants and exotic birds are all common to the area.

(Edgar Rice Burroughs, *The Jungle Girl*, New York, 1931)

PNOTH, a valley on the Isle of Oriab in the SOUTHERN SEA of DREAMWORLD, surrounded by the sinister Peaks of Throk. In the Pnoth valley live the enormous *dholes* who crawl and burrow among mountains of bones. Little is known about them except their rustling sound and their slimy touch when they wriggle past someone. Because they creep only in the dark, they have never been clearly seen.

The valley is also the place where the ghouls of Dreamworld cast the refuse of their feasts. It is said that several well-known personages long thought dead inhabit Dreamworld in the guise of ghouls, and that travellers may here find lost friends—looking almost as they used to—who now belong to this foul tribe.

(Howard Phillips Lovecraft, "The Dream-Quest of Unknown Kadath," in *Arkham Sampler*, Sauk City, 1948)

POCAPAGLIA, a small village in Piedmont, Italy, located on top of a hill whose sides are so steep and precipitous that the inhabitants hang a sack under the tails of their chickens, in order not to lose the newly laid eggs which would otherwise roll down into the woods.

(Italo Calvino, editor, *Fiabe italiane*, Turin, 1956)

POETRY, ISLAND OF, inhabited by distracted and dreamy people not much given to speech. Every morning they fall on their knees to adore the goddess Dawn whom they place high above the Nine Muses and Apollo.

The islanders possess the odd characteristic of conceiving their infants in their heads and of giving birth through their fingers. Many of these children are monsters; however, the inhabitants of the Island of Poetry do not cast them away but feed them with a nourishing meat called *esteem*. When one of the islanders dies, he is embalmed in elaborate rhetorical apparatus and the trumpets of fame are sounded at his funeral.

The lack of political organization, economic development and military forces on the island is surprising. The inhabitants' only occupation seems to consist of wandering, lonely as clouds, by lone seabreakers, and sitting by desolate streams, composing all sorts of indifferent verses which they like to recite with great emphasis at their social gatherings.

(Jean Jacobé de Frémont d'Ablancourt, *Supplément de l'Histoire Véritable de Lucien*, Paris, 1654)

POETS' ISLAND, see FOOLLYK.

POICTESME, a small kingdom in southern France, to the west of Provence. Poictesme is a pleasant country, rich in metals and grain and agreeable to live in. It is watered by quiet streams and by one major river, the Duardenez, which flows through the country before entering the Gulf of Aiguesmortes in the south east. There are two major forests, the Forest of ACAIRE and the Forest of Bovion to the north of the Tainefells Mountains. Between Acaire and the Duardenez lies the barren AMNERAN HEATH, an area haunted by witches, which is best avoided. Another place in Poictesme which it is not advisable to visit is DUN VLECHAN, where Misery of Earth has his abode. The highest point in the country is STORISENDE, the castle of the Counts of Poictesme on the banks of the Duardenez. There are other major castles at Bellegarde—also the site of the royal residence—and at Ranec, Asch, Nerac sur Mer and Perdigon.

The emblem of Poictesme is a silver stallion, rampant in every manner, and its motto is *Mundus vult decipi*.

Little is known of the early history of Poictesme apart from the incidents recorded in the country's epic poems, many of which revolve around Count Manuel, the Redeemer. Manuel was the son of Dorothy of the White Arms and Oriander, a blind sea-spirit. His mother remained a virgin even after giving birth to him in a cave at the winter solstice. As Oriander could not, of course, leave the water, Dorothy married Emerick, who became the boy's nominal father. Manuel grew up in poverty at HARANTON, a village in the north-west, before embarking on the first of his many adventures in VRAIDEX.

Here Manuel finally reached the court of Ferdinand, the overlord of Poictesme, and was made Count of Poictesme after his predecessor was executed to make way for his appointment. He was made responsible for recruiting an army to repel the forces of the Northmen of Duke Asmund, who had invaded Poictesme and taken control of much of the country.

At first the campaign went badly. At Perdigon, for instance, only four of Manuel's knights survived the battle; at Lisuarte Manuel's forces were routed by a mob of peasants armed with nothing more than scythes, pitchforks and clubs. On Corpus Christi Day his lieutenant, the Conde de Tohil Vaca, was captured and murdered with a heated poker. But in the end, luck changed sides, and Poictesme was reconquered with the help of Miramon, the Lord of the Nine Sleeps of Vraidex. He agreed to help on condition that a fief be given to a certain supernatural being called Horvendile; the terms of that agreement remain unknown. Miramon used scraps of discarded dreams he found in his garrets to create a host of strange hybrid creatures, including a four-handed champion carrying a club, a shell, a lotus and a discus, mounted on a stallion whose hide glittered like new silver; also a shadowy figure with an ankh and a sceptre, riding a beetle with human arms, the head of a ram and the feet of a lion. One champion came on a bull and wore a necklace of serpents and human skulls; another rode a buffalo, carrying a club and a noose said to be for the souls of the dead. With the battle cry *"Blaerde shay alphenio kasbue gorfons albuifrio,"* they launched the final attack. At the sight of these monsters Asmund's men died very quickly, and it is said that not one of them died in a shape that was recognizably human.

Manuel was then able to enter the conquered territories and create the Fellowship of the Silver Stallion, a group of knights charged with the protection of Poictesme.

Manuel married Niafer, whom he had first met in Vraidex. When Niafer died, Manuel caused her to be brought back from the dead at Dun Vlechan. Because of a fault in the magic, she subsequently walked with a limp. Although she was in fact the daughter of a groom, Niafer pretended to be the daughter of the Soldan of Barbary and a direct descendant of Kaimarth, the first of all kings and the first to teach men the art of building houses. No one ever contested this version of the facts, recorded in the somewhat mendacious family tree set up in the great hall at Storisende. Manuel and Niafer had three children, one of whom later ruled Poictesme; Manuel's nephew became Pope.

Manuel's end remains a matter for speculation. Historians agree that he disappeared through a window at Storisende, but while some speak of ascension, others describe him riding off with Grandfather Death.

The second great hero of Poictesme is Jurgen, who rescued Guinevere of CAMELIARD from the troll king who lived beneath the Amneran Heath. Jurgen also spent some time in CO-CAIGNE where he married Aniatis, the Lady of the Lake. The present ruling house of Poictesme,

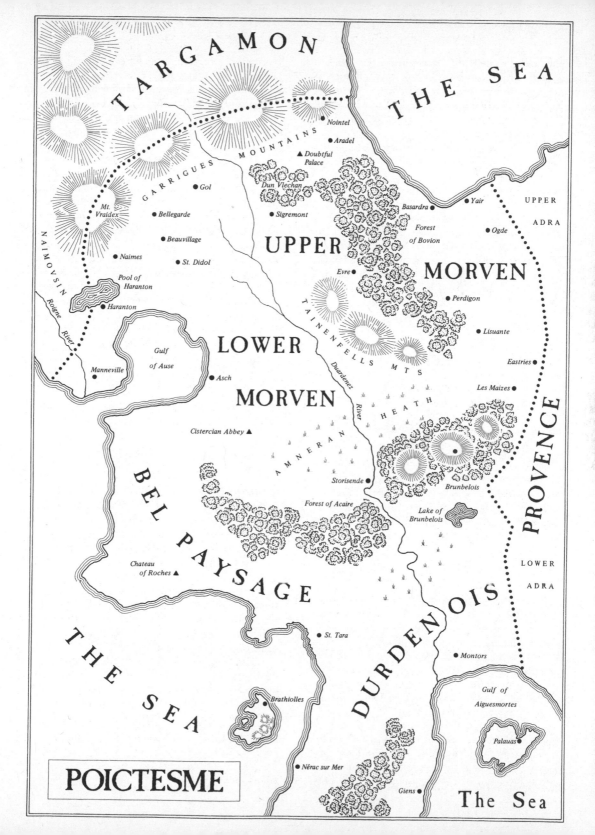

POICTESME

the de Puysange family, trace their origins back to Jurgen, who is said to have had an adulterous liaison with one of their ancestors. Florian de Puysange married a granddaughter of Manuel; in this way the ruling house is descended from the country's two greatest heroes.

Poictesme is a Christian country, although a variety of pagan rites survive. These include the worship of an evil spirit known as Janicot and the fertility rites of the winter solstice, the so-called Festival of the Wheel. Travellers who attend this will see the body of a naked woman used as an altar; the cult involves the sacrifice of infants and the somewhat painful initiation of virgins. Christianity is generally believed to have been introduced by St. Horrig and St. Ork, who came across the seas in a stone trough and landed in Poictesme in midwinter. After Horrig's death, the saint was buried in a tomb near Gol, and the legends of miracles associated with the tomb led to his canonization. The name Horrig was carved on the tomb in capital letters, but when one of the capital R's weathered away, it came to read Hoprig, which gave rise to the present cult of St. Hoprig. Ironically, the real Hoprig was the one who had the saint decapitated after breaking him on the wheel. As to Ork, it seems that his body was so mutilated by Hoprig's men that there was not enough of him left to merit a formal interment.

(James Branch Cabell, *Jurgen. A Comedy of Justice*, New York, 1919; James Branch Cabell, *Figures of Earth. A Comedy of Appearances*, New York, 1921; James Branch Cabell, *The High Place. A Comedy of Disenchantment*, New York, 1923)

POLAR BEAR KINGDOM. According to the reports of a Hungarian explorer—a certain Pietro Galibas, abandoned during a polar expedition by his companions at an unspecified point of Franz Josef's Land, or the Nansen Archipelago—this area is inhabited by a tribe of intelligent polar bears. The bears saved him and took care of him, and the king of the tribe invited Galibas to visit his palace—an enormous maze of ice caverns and underground caves rich with such geological oddities as giant crystals and liquid basalt.

In addition, Galibas states that he saw a large number of frozen prehistoric animals which the bears use as an inexhaustible source of food. Galibas ate the meat of these animals with no adverse effects although it was tough and not very tasty.

During his long stay in the kingdom, Galibas had a chance to explore the underground maze and discovered a giant cavern containing a vast lake of copper vitriol upon which he navigated an asbestos raft. The most sensational discovery of all, however, took place in a crystal cave where he found the bodies of a young girl and her father who had been in hibernation for more than twenty thousand years. Galibas tells how he brought them back to life thanks to the special powers of ambergris, and how they thanked him in Hebrew. Unfortunately for science, our explorer became so elated with his incredible discoveries that he carried out a series of inadvisable experiments, provoking an eruption of naphtha which caused the ice to melt so that the prehistoric animals started to thaw and return to life. Happily the eruption ended quickly, restoring the temperature to its normal level and returning the prehistoric animals to their state of hibernation. However, this also deprived other travellers of the possibility of admiring, in the depths of the Arctic Circle, this menagerie of creatures that have been extinct for many thousands of years.

(Jókai Mór, *20,000 lieues sous les glaces*, Bucharest, 1876)

POLARIA, see LOONARIE.

POLIARCOPOLIS, capital city of Kingdom 90, in the underground land of PROTOCOSMO. The walls of the city have ninety-six doors; outside these walls are 4,800 underground dwellings given by the government to the poorer inhabitants. A wide, splendid avenue surrounds the city, serving at the same time as quay to a canal which forms a perfect polygon of twenty-four corners, crossed by stone bridges of a single arch. To the left of the avenue are pavements for walking, to the right, somewhat lower, between the pavements and the quay, runs the road for all vehicles.

Each of the ninety-six streets which divide the many sections of Poliarcopolis is some twelve hundred feet long and ends exactly in the centre of the city transformed into a majestic wooded road.

(Giacomo Girolamo Casanova di Seingalt, *Jcosameron Ou Histoire D'Edouard, Et D'Elisabeth qui passèrent quatre vingts un ans chez les Mégamicres habitans aborigènes du Protocosme dans l'intérieur de notre globe, traduite de l'anglois par Jacques*

Casanova De Seingalt Venitien Docteur ès loix Bibliothécaire de Monsieur le comte de Walstein seigneur de Dux Chambellan de S.M.J.R.A., Prague, 1788)

POLOMBE, see LOMB.

POLYGLOT, an island in the Red Sea, where a versatile race of people known as the Polyglots live. These people, who speak all the languages of the world, so dumbfound strangers who come across them by chance that they are able to take advantage of their surprise and capture and eat them raw. (Contrary to popular belief, this never happens in Paris, France.)

Also on Polyglot Island, but on the opposite coast, live men who are fifteen feet tall, with marble-white bodies and bat-wing ears. At night, they use their ears instead of mattresses and blankets. As soon as these men see another human being, they raise their enormous ears and hastily flee towards the inland desert.

(Anonymous, *Liber monstrorum de diversis generibus*, 9th cen. AD)

POLYPRAGMOSYNE, ISLAND OF, or **ROGUES' HARBOUR**, though the latter is a misnomer. The inhabitants are known for their wry smiles and because they always seem to know their neighbours' business better than their own.

The main monument on the island—not to be missed by visitors—is the Pantheon of the Great Unsuccessful, including works by the builders of the Tower of Babel and the fountains of Trafalgar Square. Inside the monument, politicians lecture on constitutions that ought to have worked, conspirators on revolutions that ought to have succeeded, economists on schemes that ought to have made everyone's fortune, and so on. In its halls, cobblers lecture on orthopedics when they cannot sell their shoes, and philosophers demonstrate that England would be the freest and richest nation in the world if only it reverted to Catholicism.

In Polypragmosyne, the people work at trades they have not learned, because they have all failed in the trades they did learn or claim to have learned. In the general confusion ploughs can be seen drawing horses, nails driving hammers and books making authors. Bulls keep china shops and monkeys can be observed shaving cats.

On the edge of the island live the Wise Men of Gotham, famed for dragging the pond into which they thought the moon had fallen. The wise men and most of the other islanders are known to end their days on the Island of the GOLDEN ASSES.

(Charles Kingsley, *The Water-Babies: A Fairy Tale for a Land-Baby,* London, 1863)

POMACE, an Elfin kingdom in Herefordshire, England, a calm, settled kingdom without any of the bustle of ZUY or the grandiose traditions of BROCELIANDE. Unlike most Elfin kingdoms it has, however, played an important part in the history of men. This is mainly due to Hamlet, an Elfin who although of excellent family distinguished himself by his eccentricity early in life, when he founded the Pomacean Society for Unregulated Speculation, an organization which was judged somewhat subversive by the more staid subjects of the kingdom. The society was set up to discuss such topics as Sleeping Out-of-Doors, the Badness of Good Taste and even the possibility that Humans were More Interesting than Elfins. The last discussion caused such hostility among the Elfins that the society was dissolved. Hamlet was also marked out from his fellows by an interest in the theatre.

Hamlet married Nel, one of the most beautiful Elfins ever born in Pomace. She died giving birth to twin boys fathered, not by her husband, but by a common mortal. In such cases it is normal for Elfins to have abortions, but even the traditional mixture of bark and leaves from a species of juniper had no effect on her. The twins were brought up in Pomace, and left it when they reached adolescence, much to the relief of most of the Elfins. Years later, however, they returned to Hamlet—who was legally their father—claiming that they wanted to enter the ministry, having tired of their wandering, debauched life. After some persuasion Hamlet agreed to set up a theological college for them, a seminary in Wenlock, North Wales. The twins became able students at the new Caraway College, and as time went on they rose to be bishops known as the Saintly Bishop and the Manly Bishop, and then became Archbishop of York and Archbishop of Canterbury. Having produced two Archbishops, Caraway College has flourished ever since. Hamlet followed their career with great interest, rather as an entertainment laid on for his amusement, but he also took a serious interest in their schooling. He is probably the only Elfin ever to have studied theology in any depth.

(Sylvia Townsend Warner, *Kingdoms of Elfin*, London, 1972)

PONUKELE-DRELCHKAFF, a vast African empire bounded in the north-west by Dahomey, in the north by the Baoutchi Massif and in the south probably by the Congo River, though the adulating courtiers prefer to tell the emperor that it extends to the Cape of Good Hope. The empire is divided into two very different sections by the Tez River, at the mouth of which rises the capital, Ejur. To the north of Tez is the Ponukéle region; to the south, Drelchkaff.

These two African countries have shared a common history since 1655 when Souann, first king of Ponukéle, conquered Drelchkaff. Ten years earlier Souann had married two Spanish sisters, shipwrecked near Ejur, and they each gave him, the same day and at the same time, a son; these he named Talou and Yaour. Before his death in 1665, the king left Ponukéle to Talou, and Drelchkaff to Yaour. The two newly established kingdoms never ceased to fight each other until on June 5, 1904, Talou VII defeated and murdered Yaour IX in the Battle of Tez and once again reunited both countries.

Ejur, the capital, is an imposing city consisting of innumerable thatched huts. It is situated near the coast which is so abrupt that it can only be reached by wrecking one's ship against the sharp crags. In the centre of Ejur is the vast Piazza of the Trophies, an imposing square limited on either side by an avenue of centenarian sycamores. Among the trees are many spears decorated with human heads, fake jewellery and many ornaments collected by Talou II and his predecessors during the triumphant campaigns.

At the gates of the city, towards the south-east, lies the vast park of Behuliphruen, crossed by a small stream of heavy water, where floral marvels from all over the world can be admired. The park is looked after by a host of slaves, who dedicate their lives to the park's upkeep. Among the bizarre plants in Behuliphruen is a large tree whose fruit, somewhat like gigantic bananas, covers the ground around it. Should a traveller pick up one of these fruits and mash it into the shape of a candle, inserting through its middle one of the creepers that girdle the tree's trunk, he will find that when it is lit, the candle will produce a long and loud noise, reminiscent of a violent thunderstorm. Another curious plant bears red flowers that attract mosquitoes with their violent perfume; the natives make dainty cages with the weblike filaments of another plant and place one of these flowers within the cage to trap the noisy insects. The purple flower of the *bachkou* has razor-sharp thorns; if a traveller pierces his finger with one of these thorns he has only to press the flower's petals in order to obtain a juice that is both antiseptic and coagulant. Amphibious algae, white and erect like reeds, grow in the River Tez.

A day's march from Ejur towards the north lies the intricate and vast forest of Vorrh, the southern extremity of which burnt to the ground in 1904. It is here that a unique and precious plant is found, necessary for the use of the painting-machine. This machine, very popular among the natives, produces paintings in oils in the same way that a camera produces colour photos.

The fauna of Ponukéle-Drelchkaff comprises a number of curious specimens, for instance a large carrion-eating bird with powerful wings, large feet like those of the wader, and round orifices on the beak. A squirrel-like rodent with a small black mane will draw the visitor's attention; the hairs of this mane emit two musical notes of equal sonority. In the heavy-water stream lives a corpulent and inoffensive worm, endowed with a musical sensitivity; to bring it to the surface visitors should play a soft tune on the banks and it will appear at once to listen to the music. In the sea off the coast live certain animals that have not yet been fully studied. They resemble flags, curtains, soap, plates of zinc, blocks of jelly and several other objects. In underwater caves live sponges that have the shape and the function of the human heart.

(Raymond Roussel, *Impressions d'Afrique*, Paris, 1910; Jean Ferry, *L'Afrique des impressions*, Paris, 1967)

POPEFIGS' ISLAND, previously known as Jollyboys' Island. The island is now extremely poor, due to the improper actions of the present inhabitants' ancestors. Many years ago, the burgomaster, aldermen and high rabbis of Jollyboys' Island went to the neighbouring island of POPIMANIA to see the annual holy procession. One of them saw the effigy of the Pope being carried through the streets and made the obscene gesture known as "giving the fig." To avenge this insult, the Popimaniacs invaded Jollyboys' Island and massacred all adult men, sparing only the women and children. The surviving population were enslaved, made to pay tribute to Popimania and forced to take the name of Popefigs for having dared to give the fig to the image of the Pope. Since then the island has lived in misery and poverty, plagued every year with hail, storms, famines and other disasters as a punishment for the sins of their ancestors. The inhabitants say that devils often receive permission from Lucifer to come to Popefigs' Island for a holiday and to amuse themselves. Because of all this the island is in a state of constant distress, and even the little chapel by the harbour is roofless and in ruins.

(François Rabelais, *Le quart livre des faicts et dicts du bon Pantagruel*, Paris, 1552)

POPIMANIA, an island close to POPEFIGS' ISLAND, home of the Popimaniacs who live under the rule of Bishop Homenaz or Greatclod and who believe that the Pope is quite literally the incarnation of God upon earth. They live by the papal decretals, and claim that the copies of these decretals preserved on Popimania were written in heaven and brought to them by an angel; the copies found in other countries are, they claim, merely transcriptions of their originals. The Popimaniacs firmly believe that everybody should abandon all other occupations and devote himself completely to the study of the decretals and other papal pronouncements; only then will the world become a happy place. Then, they say, there will be no more hail, frost or natural disasters; crime and wars will cease (with the exception of just wars against all heretics). The study and extensive knowledge of the decretals are deemed by them to be the only fit activities for a true Christian, the only way to become famous and respected throughout the world.

The sacred decretals themselves are kept in one of the churches. They are written in a great gilt book, encrusted with all manner of precious stones: rubies, emeralds, diamonds and pearls. The book is hung from the sculptured frieze of the porch, suspended by two stout gold chains. Behind the altar, a crude image representing the Pope is kept. Privileged visitors are allowed to kiss the point of a stick that has touched the sacred image, which is shown to the faithful only on the greatest of all holy days. The Popimaniacs believe

that upon seeing the image they are granted full remission of all the sins they can remember, together with eighteen-fortieths and a third of the sins they have forgotten.

Despite their faith in the Pope, the Popimaniacs have never actually seen him. They do, however, show great respect to all visitors who claim to have met the Pope, kissing their feet and giving them all manner of honours. One of their *hypothetes* or "backward prophets" has left it in writing that just as the Messiah will one day come to the Jews, so the Pope will one day come to Popimania; until then they must welcome anyone who has seen His Holiness, feast the visitor well and treat him with utmost reverence.

Visitors who do claim to have seen the Pope are invited to sumptuous feasts, paid for by collections taken up among the public. In accordance with a gloss on one of the decretals, half the money is spent on food and half on drink. All dishes served at these feasts come with large quantities of canonical stuffing. *Supplementary* wine (typical of the island) is served with the meal. The guests are waited upon by the young marriageable maidens of Popimania, dressed in long, white, loose robes with double girdles, their hair braided with ribbons and sweet-smelling herbs and flowers.

The island is famous for its delicious pears. These are exported to France where they are known to the public as Good-Christian pears.

(François Rabelais, *Le quart livre des faicts et dicts du bon Pantagruel*, Paris, 1552)

POPO, a lilliputian-sized kingdom in Germany, so small that all its borders can be seen at once, with the naked eye. Since the abdication of King Peter, who wanted to devote himself to the study of philosophy, the country has been governed by his son Leonce, who is married to Lena, the princess of the neighbouring kingdom.

King Leonce attempted to transform his kingdom into an epicurean state honoured by the Muses. On his orders every clock was broken and all calendars banned, so that the passing of time is marked only by flowers, fruit and old age. Enormous solar mirrors arranged along the border have created a pleasant, uniform, summery climate.

Minister Valério, who describes himself as a "virgin" as far as work is concerned, has an enormous talent for laziness, according to some malicious tongues. He sees to it that no subject of the kingdom is ever overworked. His first (and only) decree stipulates that anyone with blisters on his hands will be declared a ward of the state; anyone who makes himself sick through over-exertion will be brought before the courts; and anyone who boasts that he earns his bread through the sweat of his brow will be declared mentally incompetent and dangerous to society.

(Georg Büchner, "Leonce und Lena," in *Telegraph für Deutschland,* No. 76-80, Hamburg, 1838)

PORT-APE, a small city on the coast of MOUNT ANALOGUE, inhabited only by Europeans, most of them French. The name is difficult to explain because there are no apes in the region.

In the bay, all along the coast, ships of many countries and ages form a compact line, waiting, abandoned, to turn into stone or to be digested by the fauna and flora of the sea. These are the vessels of the many expeditions that have arrived here throughout the centuries with the sole intention of climbing the heights of Mount Analogue. Port-Ape, like each of the other cities on the coast, serves as a point of departure for the expeditions intending to reach the first camp on the mountain slope, two days' march up the mountain. From there guides lead the travellers towards the peak.

Each expedition that arrives at Port-Ape receives, as a kind of monetary advance, a bagful of metallic discs from the guide that will purchase goods and service for the travellers. This advance must later be paid back in *peradam,* a perfectly round crystal—the local equivalent of gold. *Peradam,* also called "Adam's stone," has some secret association with man's origins; diamonds are said to be a degenerate form of it. The crystal is so pure, its refraction index so like that of air, that it is very difficult to see. But it may reveal itself, in all its flaming brilliance, to the seeker who has a great and sincere need.

As *peradam* is *so* scarce and hard to find, some visitors give up searching the mountain and try to earn it by working as craftsmen or labourers. A disagreeable end awaits those who cannot fulfil their obligation to reimburse the guides.

The economy and society of Port-Ape is simple, somewhat like that of a small European town before the Industrial Revolution. No motors are admitted into the country and the use of electricity is forbidden, as is the use of explosives. Port-Ape has a few churches, a town hall and a po-

Mount Analogue as seen from PORT-APE.

lice station; the government is in the hands of the guides, whose delegates are also the administrators. Their authority is uncontested, founded on the wealth given them by *peradam.* Only the people of the coast possess the metal discs, which are necessary to obtain the daily necessities.

The population is formed by the descendants of members of expeditions which arrived here centuries ago. African, Asian and even some extinct races are here represented. Life in other towns on the coast is similar to that of Port-Ape, except that in each one a different nationality has established its customs and language. Each language, contaminated by the unique language of the guides, has evolved in a particular way and a few, like the French of Port-Ape, contain many archaisms and barbarisms, as well as totally new words coined to describe indigenous objects such as *peradam*.

The temperate climate of this area allows the growth and development of the flora and fauna common to most European countries. However, several unknown species are found here as well. Among these is an arborescent convolvulus whose power of germination and growth is such that it is used as a sort of slow dynamite to move rocks at quarries. Another is the incendiary lycoperdon, a large puffball which explodes, flinging its spores far and wide, and which some hours later, through an intense fermentation, suddenly bursts into flame. The talking bush, a rare species, is a sensitive plant whose fruits form drums capable of reproducing, by the friction of its leaves, all the sounds of the human voice; like parrots, when a word is pronounced in their vicinity, they repeat it. The circling centipede, a myriapod some two metres long which can roll into a circle, amuses itself by rolling at full speed down from the top of the mountain. The cyclopic lizard, somewhat like a chameleon, with a large open eye in the forehead plus two other atrophied ones, is very much respected by the inhabitants. The flying caterpillar is a type of large silkworm which in fine weather can, in a few hours, inflate its body with a light gas produced in its intestine to form a voluminous balloon that can be carried away in the wind; it never reaches the adult state and reproduces itself by larval parthenogenesis.

(René Daumal, *Le Mont Analogue,* Paris, 1952)

PORT BRETON, see STORN.

PORT-GRAUBEN, a tiny bay on the north-western coast of the subterranean LIDENBROCK SEA, so called by the members of the Lidenbrock expedition who explored these regions in 1863, in honour of Fraulein Grauben of Hamburg.

Travellers wishing to explore the Lidenbrock Sea must depart from Port-Grauben. In the waters of the bay, travellers will see gigantic seaweeds, similar to immense vegetable serpents, over a thousand metres long, and blind fish that have no need for eyes in the darkness below the earth. According to Professor Lidenbrock, these fish belong to a species extinct on the earth's surface in prehistoric times (order ganoid, family cephalaspis, genus Pterichthys).

(Jules Verne, *Voyage au centre de la terre,* Paris, 1864)

PORTIUNCULA, a village on Mount Cervati, somewhere near the Valley of Lucania in southern Italy. Visitors travel to Portiuncula to recapture something lost in their past.

Neither summer nor winter is the best season to go; in summer the dust and the heat are unbearable and in winter the freezing winds make progress difficult. Spring is also inconvenient; torrents of rain pour down into the valleys and make the path slippery and dangerous. Should the traveller need to rest, there are only two villages before Portiuncula: Teggiano and Laurino, situated respectively near a decayed castle and a small church.

Each traveller finds Portiuncula different from what he remembers, though it is difficult to point out what the changes are; for this reason some may decide that Portiuncula is best left unvisited.

(Stefan Andres, *Die Reise nach Portiuncula,* Munich, 1954)

POTATO BUG COUNTRY, probably close to ROOTABAGA COUNTRY and populated by the Potato Bugs. Here both wishes and suspicions come true. Transport in this country is normally by train; there are slow trains, fast trains and trains that run backward instead of going where they start out for. The local currency is the *fleem,* and visitors are advised that it is impossible to do anything here without having a ready supply of *fleems.*

(Carl Sandburg, *Rootabaga Stories,* New York, 1922)

POTU, see NAZAR.

POYANG, a mountain ruled by an irascible deity. In order to climb Poyang safely, visitors must offer the god a sacrifice of well-cooked dog meat. Should the meat be undercooked, the visitor will be punished by being made to eat the meat himself, after which an invisible hand will throw a tigerskin over him and the careless traveller will become a man-devouring tiger. The fauna of Poyang is rich in such beasts.

(Liu Ching-Shu, *Garden of Marvels,* 5th cen. AD)

PRESENT LAND, near the South Pole, first sighted by Mr. Arthur Gordon Pym of Nantucket in 1828 and further explored in 1928 by the French adventurer Adam Harcz. It can be reached by plane from Enderby Land.

The traveller will come upon a thick mist which clears at an altitude of about three thousand metres; visible above it is a mountain range with incandescent smoke rising from its volcanic craters. (Visitors are advised that upon reaching Present Land their watches will stop; this is normal and complaints should not be made to the manufacturers.) The first view of Present Land is a phosphorescent plateau stretching out at the foot of the mountains, blue and white, with lakes and pools linked by meandering canals and streams. The mountains are steep, their broken slopes revealing caves, excavations and water-filled craters. Grey sand lines the water's edge. The porous rock is luminous, throwing a brightish light all around; the pools are rather like water gardens, holding dense, warm (38°C.) water. In fact its density makes it difficult to plunge one's arm into it, as it runs off the skin like mercury. There is no wind, no dust and no odours. The flora is peculiar—bushes of coral-like plants, white and luminous, and taller trees like spun glass, with round, opaque leaves and round, transparent fruits. The pools are lined with greenish-white and blue seaweed.

Present Land is the land of the present. The inhabitants have no memory and every moment is new and perfect. Nothing changes in this immobile present tense; nothing has a future; everything is clear. There are no mysteries, no concealment, no lies, no fatigue, no pain. The only activity that is known to have taken place in Present Land is described in Adam Harcz's account of his journey. When the light began to fade, as though an eclipse were taking place, Harcz noticed that, two by two, the inhabitants of Present Land entered a huge gap in the mountainside. He followed them into the tunnel that leads from the gap several kilometres into the mountain; the temperature rises here and visitors will notice that the floor and side walls of the tunnel are made of gold. Harcz saw the inhabitants reach a chasm, out of which rose a tree whose branches formed a perfect circle, each one bearing a fruit somewhat like an olive. A bird began to sing. Then a white figure, like the one seen by Mr. Arthur Gordon Pym—which he described in his narrative as "shrouded" and "very far larger in his proportions than any dweller among men"—appeared before them, making the earth shake and the fruit fall from the tree. The

natives pressed the fruit to their foreheads, kneeling before the tree and calling out "Tekeli-li" (as do the natives of TSALAL). Their faces showed a wide variety of emotions—some hideous, others full of celestial beauty. Finally the white figure disappeared in a golden mist, the men rose, cast their fruit into the chasm and regained their normal expressions. Some left the cave, but others flung themselves into the void, again crying "Tekeli-li."

The natives are androgynous humanoids, semi-transparent, as though made from white jade. With the exception of the thumb, their fingers are webbed with an almost transparent membrane like the fins of a Japanese fish. They have large eyes, their heads are covered with soft, short hair, their teeth and nails are like mother of pearl, they have very slender hands and feet and well-muscled bodies. Their gestures are graceful and gentle and their favourite pastime is to swim and play in the pools. They produce no bodily secretions and have no needs; they never sleep and they live on air. They communicate in a soft musical language and they seem to have none of the vices known to men. Their dwellings consist of domed huts arranged in a crescent-shaped village. Each house possesses a covered patio and a single room, furnished with mattresses of seaweed on which the natives make love.

Visitors who wish to remember their stay in this country are advised to obtain an elliptically shaped stone resembling lapis lazuli which will allow them to retain their memories of Present Land.

(Edgar Allan Poe, *The Narrative of Arthur Gordon Pym of Nantucket*, New York, 1838; Dominique André, *Conquête de l'Eternel*, Paris, 1947)

PRIMEVERE, see MORROW ISLAND.

PRINCE PROSPERO'S CASTLE, probably somewhere in central Europe, a castellated abbey, surrounded by a strong, lofty wall with gates of iron, where Prince Prospero once sought refuge from the plague of the Red Death that was devastating his country.

The castle boasts seven magnificent rooms, so irregularly disposed that the visitor cannot see more than one at a time. In the middle of each wall is a high Gothic window of stained glass, whose colour varies according to the prevailing hue of the decorations of the chamber into which it opens.

From east to west, the rooms are blue, purple, green, orange, white, violet and black. Only in the seventh apartment does the colour of the window fail to correspond with the decorations: the panes here are scarlet, a deep blood colour. The rooms are illuminated not by lamps or candles but by braziers of fire that project thin rays through the tinted glass.

To celebrate the fifth or sixth month of seclusion, the prince organized for his one thousand friends a masked ball of the most unusual magnificence, a celebration that was unfortunately interrupted by the presence of the Red Death, disguised as himself, who decided to attend the party.

(Edgar Allan Poe, "The Masque of the Red Death," in *Tales of Mystery and Imagination,* Philadelphia, 1919)

PROMONTORY PALACE, an immense villa in an undetermined location, with dependencies as vast as Epiros or the Peloponnese. The traveller approaching by sea can see dunes, glaciers, washhouses surrounded by German poplars and hotels with round façades. When he arrives he will discover that the flowers on the dunes are curiously hot. The herbaceous borders of the parks are unusual. On the rich façades of the hotels, the windows are always open to the minds of travellers.

(Arthur Rimbaud, *Les Illuminations,* Paris, 1886)

PROPHETS, ISLE OF, see HACIOCRAM.

PROSPERO'S ISLAND or **CALIBAN'S ISLAND,** probably in the Mediterranean, between Tunis and Naples (although a tale told by shipwrecked sailors pinpoints the Caribbean). The island is inhabited by the monster Caliban—something between a sea and a land animal—goblins and several spirits, among them one called Ariel.

The god of the island is Setebos, said to live on the moon which he created together with the sun and the sea.

The deposed Duke of Milan, Prospero, lived here with his daughter Miranda, later Queen of Naples, in the early years of the seventeenth century. His cell, near a muddy lake, still remains, sheltered within a grove from the sometimes wild weather. His remarkable library, which consists

The Duke's cell on PROSPERO'S ISLAND.

mainly of books on magic and the occult, is still almost intact—only one volume appears to be missing. The magic staff he was known to carry is thought to be buried nearby.

There are both fertile and barren spots on the island, fresh springs and brine-pits, and a vast area covered with briars, furzes and pricking goss. Pignuts and filberts can be found as well as many small animals, including toads, adders, tortoises, moles, jays, scamels, beetles and gnats. Oaks and pine trees (like the one in which Ariel was for a time imprisoned by the witch Sycorax, mother of Caliban) grow here. The island is full of noises, sounds and sweet airs. A soft, enchanting music can be heard sometimes and will not harm, but other sounds—such as a curious echo or the beating of a tabor—should be ignored.

(William Shakespeare, *The Tempest,* London, 1623; Robert Browning, "Caliban upon Setebos," in *Dramatis Personae,* London, 1864)

PROTOCOSMO, an underground country of difficult access. Its description was given by two English travellers, a brother and sister, who arrived here after the shipwreck of the *Wolsey* which, under the command of Lord Arthur Howard, had set off with two other ships to circumnavigate the Northern Ocean in 1534. At approximately longitude 28° east or west and latitude 16°15′ north or south, a terrible storm struck all three ships. Brother and sister took refuge in a large lead box to escape the breakers. Flung off the ship by the maelstrom the box was dragged by the currents to an underwater crevice, through unknown layers of water and gas, until it finally fell—or emerged— into a land until then undiscovered.

Protocosmo—thus should the name of the land be pronounced in English—is a gigantic solid island floating on a somewhat concave, endless, muddy substance, an intermediate layer between that world and our own. In the middle of the sky (that is, the centre of the earth) stands an iron globe giving out a pale pink light. The land stretches as far as the eye can see without any obstacle in view. The uniformity of this land is from time to time agreeably interrupted by small woods of sacred trees. There is no uncultivated land on Protocosmo. The cities, the farms and all buildings are underground with the exception of a few low vigilance towers or observatories. The surface of this country is divided into perfectly square zones, along the sides of which run canals. The inhabitants—called Megamicroes—live in houses underground. Each square zone contains at least eight houses: a Megamicro couple lives in each house. The farmers' houses—to which sheds and stables are attached—are small and squarish, with three storeys, each about four feet high; only the top one receives natural light, which penetrates obliquely through slits in the ceiling.

Several square zones make up a city. The architecture of these cities is magnificent, and vast and beautiful houses rise to greet the visitor. Notable above all is the dwelling called Econearcon or Royal Palace, found in all cities and ruled by an *abdala* or king. These palaces are perfect cubes containing courtyards, gardens, canals, woods and everything that industry, science or money can provide for the material and spiritual pleasure of a monarch. Each Econearcon has ten thousand master rooms and can lodge one hundred thousand servants. Its one hundred vast music rooms are always worth a visit. Outside the walls of every city

are the dwellings which the government gives to the poor. They are similar to farmhouses but have no stables or sheds. They are given according to a religious precept which states that the noble and the rich must do all within their power so that every Megamicro couple can enjoy a pleasant sleep at night under a safe roof. Night in Protocosmo is the best loved and longest part of the day.

Politically, Protocosmo is divided into eighty kingdoms and ten republics, each of which covers 1,210,000 square miles. The rest of its surface, some thirty-six million miles, is divided into 216 feuds, some large and some small, but all triangular. The feudal princes establish the sole law in their territories.

The Megamicroes are of pleasant aspect, somewhat like babies; their skin is of several colours, but never white or black; those with red skin are the rarest. Their hair is short, woolly, and comes in as many colours as their skin. All sport upon their head a sort of pointed hat, lifted at the front and covering both ears. This is not a garment, but part of their own bodies, made of a cartilaginous substance like that of our ears. The Megamicroes are hermaphrodites and oviparous. They are born in pairs and nourish themselves with a milk which they produce themselves and which allows them to remain young and healthy until the time of their death, which always occurs at the age of 192 harvests (forty-eight years). This milk is produced by way of a sixth sense, stimulated by the rubbing of herbs and perfumed flowers on their skin. They also consume a kind of flour, cooked in water, served lukewarm and with herbs, which increases the nourishing qualities of their milk. After partaking of the flour, a Megamicro will drink his neighbour's milk and will offer his own. Should he not succeed in producing it, he would become deeply depressed. The actual sucking of the milk lasts hardly a minute and all those taking part of the banquet drink and offer their milk at the same time. They then kiss very tenderly and enter into friendly conversation. As dessert, each receives a small basket full of herbs. The Megamicroes then take out of a flask a pinch of a pink powder which they drop on the herbs; these burst at once into blue flames, producing an exquisite perfume that is also very nourishing. As soon as the herbs have become ashes, the meal, which usually lasts about an hour, is considered to be over.

A Megamicro spends the first twelve years of

his life (that is, three of our years) together with his twin in a cage where nothing is lacking. His only amusement is to converse with him and, by a natural force, they become united for the rest of their lives, as if they were one spirit in two bodies. A few hours after leaving the cage, their parents take them into the dining room, where they are taught to eat with the rest of the family. However, they cannot produce milk until some six to twelve hours after they are released. The pair are naturally very fond of each other and this sentiment is increased by their education. Their perpetual union is formalized in a ceremony in a room into which their parents take them. Once the ceremony is over, they are left alone. After two "burnings of the green logs" (see below) the young people are visited by their parents. The twins then give their parents two eggs, as large as those of a chicken, which they have expelled at that very instant through their mouths. The parents take these eggs and submerge them in a liquid which gives out a constant heat. The hatching lasts a further two "burnings of the green logs" and a new pair of Megamicroes is thus born. If they are red, without any streaks of another colour, everyone is delighted. If, however, they are of only one colour but that colour is not red, they are considered sterile, of inferior quality and destined to become scientists, artists or craftsmen. Those born multicoloured or brindled are also considered sterile and become simple objects of enjoyment because of their looks. They serve as manual workers, waiters or farmers. Each couple of red Megamicroes will generate fifteen pairs of babies, of which rarely more than two are red.

Their language, harmonious and musical, is made up of six vowels—*a, e, i, o, u* and *oo*—and has no consonants. Pronouncing a consonant would certainly offend their delicate eardrums.

The year is divided into four periods which they call "burnings of the green logs." Each of these lasts forty-five days and is made up of five *pentamans* called "resurrections." Each *pentaman is* divided into five days of twenty hours. The hours are thirty-six minutes and the minutes thirty-six seconds. One second is the exact pulsation of their arteries. The name "burning of the green logs" comes from a bush without leaves or branches that comes out of the earth the first day of the year and grows to be as high as a Megamicro in a *pentaman;* then it bursts into flames after a heavy rain which lasts some two hours. However,

before its ashes grow cold, it digs one of its roots back into the ground and after nine further *pentamans* again bursts into flames. Rain falls four times a year, but does not moisten the earth, though it refreshes the atmosphere. It is worth noting how this happens: three hours before the end of the month a gentle breeze starts to blow, becomes stronger and then calms down. But before it stops, the whole surface of the earth becomes covered with an opaque mist, and a soft pink rain starts to *rise* from the clouds. For two hours it rises without redescending; soon after that the air becomes calm, the sun comes out again and the earth is still as dry as before. When the rains arrive, the Megamicroes come out of their homes and frolic under the rising drops.

The *pentaman* is also called the "resurrection of black worm." This insect leaves its egg and becomes a worm at exactly the same time as "the burning of the green logs." After five cycles of twelve hours each, the worm becomes a butterfly, dies, turns into dust and again becomes an egg. Because of this, the Megamicroes call "metamorphosis" what we call the day. The days of the week are as follows: Chrysalid, Butterfly, Death, Dust and Egg. Butterfly and Dust are considered days of ill-luck in which the dead are cremated or buried. The Day of the Egg is celebrated with the opening of the youngsters' cage and with the wedding. The first and the last days of the year are the only two holidays. On the first day they harvest and on the last day they sow, letting the earth rest for the whole year in between.

The fauna of Protocosmo is similar to that of Europe, with the exception of flying horses which are not commonly found on the Continent. These animals have a small pointed head, a mouth like that of a greyhound, and a hat longer than that of the Megamicroes, which only permits them to see straight ahead. They are thin and quick, covered in feathers, and have a tail which recalls that of the pheasant because of its length and that of a swallow because of its width. They can open and close it but they cannot move it from side to side or lift it and lower it. The tail measures two and a half feet and is as long as the rest of the body, ending in two parallel tips. They have four wings attached to their legs, which are very short and muscular. On their backs, they carry a natural saddle for two. The kings alone possess a team or two, as these horses are not allowed to reproduce until they have reached their old age. On land they are slow and their progress is difficult, but in flight they travel very quickly in a perfectly straight line, though never for more than a thousand miles. During their flight they cannot rise, descend or turn. Therefore, upon take-off, they are made to run along a ramp, one end of which is lifted at an angle in proportion to the length of the projected journey. When a king wishes to send a letter to his neighbour, he must consult a map to find out how far it has to go and then regulate the ramp for the horse's takeoff. The direction of the ramp is determined by the Great Geographer and its angle by the Great Geometer. These two scientists lead the horse onto the ramp, set him free and throw themselves to the ground when his wings start to flap. Should the horse be misdirected, one of the two scientists is put in jail. The only danger involved in these procedures is that two kings might decide to send each other a message at the same time; the collision of both horses in mid-air, at a speed of forty miles an hour, each weighing one hundred pounds, would seriously damage the health of both horse and rider.

Other interesting animals are the serpents of Protocosmo. These are considered to be natural enemies of the Megamicroes. However, they are left to live quietly in the orchards, eating only the fruit of certain trees. They are three feet long and six inches wide; their skin is dappled and covered with scales. Their faces bear a human expression and have a sweet look that can be dangerously fascinating. They emit a horrible sibilant sound that terrifies the Megamicroes.

Travellers anxious to visit Protocosmo are advised to attempt entry under the mountains of Slovenia, the route by which the first two chroniclers escaped back to earth. Unfortunately, they gave no exact location.

(Giacomo Girolamo Casanova di Seingalt, *Jcosameron Ou Histoire D'Edouard, Et D'Elisabeth qui passèrent quatre vingts un ans chez les Mégamicres habitans aborigènes du Protocosme dans l'intérieur de notre globe, traduite de l'anglois par Jacques Casanova De Seingalt Venitien Docteur ès loix Bibliothécaire de Monsieur le comte de Walstein seigneur de Dux Chambellan de S.M.J.R.A.*, Prague, 1788)

PROVIDENCE ISLAND, somewhere east of the Moluccas. The island is ten miles wide and some twenty miles long. The coast is mostly flat, but the ground rises inland towards a wooded area, and to the east, towards a high mountain. The landscape alternates between forest and savannah. Streams are plentiful and a major river flows across the central savannah. To the north-west, an extensive swamp lies immediately inland from the coast. This swamp is the habitat of the island's most curious animal, a creature the size of a horse with long straight horns. The body is short and thick, the head similar to that of a horse, but much broader. When attacked, it will growl like a lion and defend itself with its formidable horns. The western coast is wooded and hilly. At one point the woods are interrupted by a broad grassy plateau, from where a waterfall tumbles down the cliffs into a natural basin.

Providence was given its name by John Daniel, an Englishman who was shipwrecked here with one companion in the mid-seventeenth century. Initially the two castaways lived near the seashore, sheltering in the trees at night to escape the herds of wild pigs that roamed the island, but they later built a rudimentary shelter on the slopes of the mountain. It was only after a year on the island that Daniel realized that his companion was a woman. The couple married, performing a crude but touching ceremony and asking for Heaven's blessing. Over the next thirty years, they had a total of eleven children. When the children were old enough, marriages were arranged among them, it being argued that the sons and daughters of Adam must themselves have broken the taboo on incest. By the time Daniel left Providence Island, he had seen fifteen grandchildren born from the first three marriages.

Although life on Providence was at first very difficult, the situation of the castaways improved greatly after the wreck of two ships during tropical storms. With equipment rescued from the wrecks it became possible to construct more substantial buildings, using boards and timber instead of mud and wattle. Clothes, seeds and other useful items were also saved from the wrecks. The sole survivor of the second wreck was a pregnant bitch; her puppies provided the basis for a hunting-pack.

As their family grew older, the Daniels established new settlements for them, and visitors can see several such settlements or farms, each with a herd of cattle and some pigs. These animals are descended from the original wild fauna; remaining wild cattle and pigs have been exterminated because of the damage they caused to crops. The seeds brought ashore from the wrecked ships flourished and yielded food plants in much larger quantity than they would have done in Europe. The natural flora of the island itself provided many edible plants which were vital to the survival of the first castaways.

John Daniel's eldest son, Jacob, had an unusual gift for mechanical invention, and when his father had been on the island for some thirty years, contrived to build a primitive flying machine, which he called *The Eagle*. He built it in the hope of being able to return to England, constructing it of sailcloth, wood and iron salvaged from the wrecked ships. The canvas was stretched over a series of ribs, articulated by iron joints. Hollow pipes, connected to a pump on a central iron platform, allowed the ribs to be raised or lowered, so propelling *The Eagle* in the required direction. Trial flights were successful, but when father and son tried a longer flight they found themselves transported to the moon. Here they stayed for some time before attempting to return to Providence. This attempt also failed, and they landed on ANDERSON'S ROCK. From here they flew to Lapland, and eventually succeeded in returning to England.

(Ralph Morris, *A Narrative of The Life and astonishing Adventures of John Daniel, A Smith at Royston in Hertfordshire, For a Course of seventy Years. Containing, The melancholy Occasion of his Travels. His Shipwreck with one Companion on a desolate Island. Their way of Life. His accidental discovery of a Woman for his Companion. Their peopling the Island. Also, A Description of a most surprising Engine, invented by his Son Jacob, on which he flew to the Moon, with some Account of its Inhabitants. His return, and accidental Fall into the Habitation of a Sea-Monster, with whom he lived two Years. His further Excursions in Search of England. His Residence in Lapland, and Travels to Norway, from whence he arrived at Aldborough, and further Transactions till his death, in 1711. Aged 97... Taken from his own Mouth. By Mr. Ralph Morris*, London, 1751)

PRYDAIN, for the most part a land of forests and mountains, sparsely populated with most settlements clustering around the strongholds of the feudal lords that rule it.

The major settlement, which might be regarded as the capital, is at CAER DATHYL in the north. The great citadel there is the seat of the High Kings of Prydain and stands on the site of a fortress built by the Sons of Don. To the south-east of Caer Dathyl lies the region known as the FREE COMMOTS, the most fertile and attractive area in the country. On the edge of the Commots, the Llawgadarn Mountains rise to the mighty peak of Mount Meledin.

Elsewhere in Prydain the main geographical and social divisions are between the Cantrevs or sub-kingdoms of the Valleys and those of the Hills. The Valley Cantrevs produce grain and breed cattle, whereas the Hill Cantrevs are sheep-farming country. In general, life tends to be harder and less prosperous in the Hill Cantrevs, which have suffered severely at the hands of bandits in recent years. In the valleys, the farms and small villages nestle in the meadows and forest clearings. Higher settlements tend to be isolated and are at times completely cut off in winter. In fact, the higher reaches of the Eagle Mountains of the north are largely uninhabited, so wild is the terrain. The only known settlement here is the inaccessible and hidden MEDWYN'S VALLEY.

Southern Prydain is a gentler country and a land of farms and orchards—typical of these, at least in appearance, is CAER DALLBEN, an important historical site. The farms gradually give way to the hills above the Great Avren River and then to the extensive Forest of Idris. In its turn the forest gives way to moorlands which stretch to the edges of the dreary marshes of MORVA, an area few people care to visit more than once. To the north of Morva lies the most feared area in Prydain, the lands which were once the domain of Arawn the Death Lord who ruled the country for many years and was responsible for so much suffering. His stronghold of Annuvin, now totally destroyed, lay between Dark Gate—the twin peaks that guarded the southern approach to the stronghold—and Mount Dragon in the north. So powerful was the evil of Arawn that even the Red Fallows, once the most fertile part of Prydain, fell desolate during the years of his dominance. It is said that in the past the land was so rich here that the crops sprang from it without the intervention of men. During the years of Arawn's rule it became semi-desert, and efforts are now being made to reclaim it.

Prydain was, in the far distant past, a prosperous country, famed for its craftsmen, notably those of the Free Commots, and for its agricultural produce. It gradually fell under the sway of Achren, the consort of Arawn the Death Lord, who stole many of the treasures and skills of men

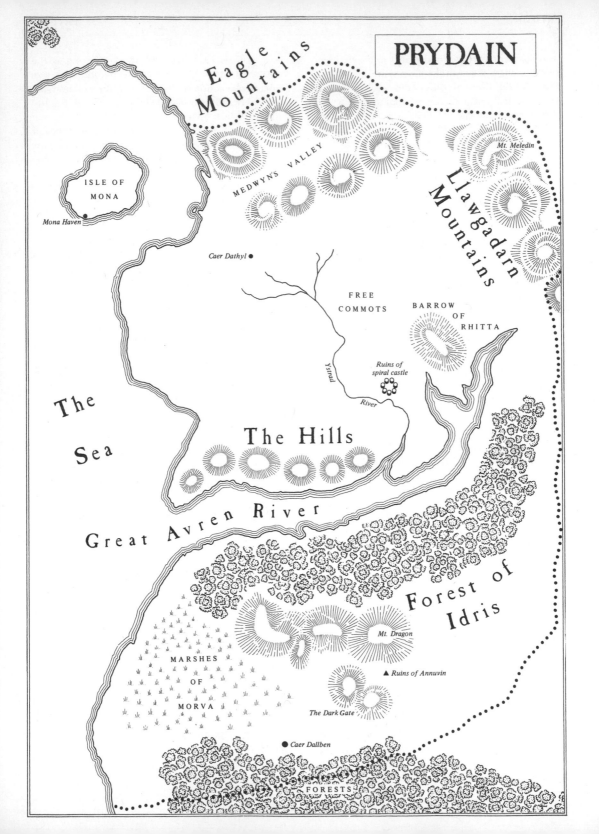

through her magical powers. Achren was, however, betrayed by her husband, who took power for himself. Over the years, Arawn developed fearful weapons and reduced many areas to ruin and poverty. His terrible soldiers were the Cauldron Born. These invulnerable warriors were the bodies of men, stolen from their funeral barrows and reanimated by being plunged into the Black Cauldron, originally the property of the three enchantresses of Morva. No human warrior could stand against the silent, merciless Cauldron Born in their might. To these, Arawn added the *gwythaints*, huge black birds which acted as his spies and were capable of tearing men limb from limb with their great talons and beaks. With such allies, Arawn gradually increased his powers and took a stranglehold on large parts of Prydain.

Arawn's domination of Prydain was ended by the arrival of the Sons of Don, great warriors and powerful enchanters, from the SUMMER COUNTRY. Through their intervention Arawn was brought to bay—though he was not destroyed—and the defences of Prydain were built. There were two main defence works; the great citadel at Caer Dathyl and the humble farmhouse at Caer Dallben. The latter was the spiritual centre of the battle against Arawn, a place protected by powerful magic and totally inaccessible to the forces of evil. The farm was the home of Dallben, without doubt the greatest enchanter in all Prydain.

The High Kings of the House of Don ruled for generations in Caer Dathyl, lending their protection to the people of the Free Commots and to the offshore island of MONA. During these years, friendly relations were also developed with the Fair Folk, the dwarves and fairies of TYLWYTH TEG, the subterranean kingdom of King Eiddileg.

It was during the reign of High King Math that the forces of Arawn again began to appear openly in Prydain. At last the Horned King himself appeared in the forests near Caer Dallben. He was the battle leader of Arawn and took his name from his head gear: a skull mask with antlers rising above it in cruel curves. Alarmed by his presence, the animals of Caer Dallben fled.

One of the animals to disappear was Hen Wen, a white pig with prophetic powers. Her disappearance was a cause for great alarm. Taran, an assistant pig-keeper at Caer Dallben, immediately set out to find her. Taran was an orphan who knew nothing of his origins, but he was destined to play a vital part in the freeing of Prydain.

Soon after he entered the forest, Taran encountered the Horned King himself and was wounded. As he ran from the king's soldiers he met Gwydion, the battle leader of the Sons of Don and a prince in his own right. The two were soon joined by a companion, Gurgi, apparently the only one of his kind, half-beast and half-human, a strange long-limbed creature with long shaggy hair. Travelling in forests, Gurgi collected twigs and leaves in his hair, rapidly coming to resemble a walking owl's nest. Although a self-pitying and at times irritating creature, Gurgi became a faithful ally and a close friend during the battles that followed.

In an encounter with the Cauldron Born, Gwydion and Taran were captured and taken as prisoners to Spiral Castle, then the stronghold of Achren. The castle no longer stands, but its ruins can be seen by the banks of the Ystrad, opposite the Barrow of RHITTA. Here they were thrown into separate dungeons. Taran was freed, however, from his underground prison by Eilonwy, the last of the House of Llyr. With Eilonwy he took from the barrow the sword Dyrnwyn, a sword forged to defend Prydain and destined to destroy Arawn himself. The runes on the sword spoke of its power and stated that only one of noble blood or worth could draw it without risk. As the two took the sword out of the barrow, sheets of blue fire engulfed Spiral Castle and its towers crumpled into ruins.

Unknown to Taran, Gwydion had been taken to a different stronghold, from which he later escaped. Eilonwy had rescued a second prisoner from Spiral Castle, believing him to be Gwydion. He was in fact one Fflewddur Fflam, who was the ruler of a small kingdom of his own, but preferred the roaming life of a bard, with his beloved, enchanted harp for company.

The company of friends moved north to warn the garrison at Caer Dathyl of the extent of the rebellion in the south. When they were within sight of their goal they saw the armies of the Horned King marching on the citadel. In a skirmish with his outriders, Taran saw the Horned King himself and drew the sword Dyrnwyn. Dazzling light flashed from the sword and Taran collapsed, so great was the force that he had unleashed. The power of the sword caused the earth to tremble and Arawn's battle leader was destroyed forever. With their leader gone, his armies melted before those of the Don.

A year later a great council was held at Caer Dallben, and a plan drawn up for an attack on

Dark Gate itself, the entrance to Arawn's fortress and the place where he kept the cauldron used to create the dread Cauldron Born. While it was impossible to kill the dead warriors, it was essential to prevent their increase; the cauldron had to be destroyed. The plan for the attack on Dark Gate made use of the power of Doli the dwarf to make himself invisible. The plan worked and entrance was gained to Dark Gate, but the cauldron had disappeared and its whereabouts were unknown even to Arawn himself.

By this stage in the struggle, Arawn had developed a new military force: the Huntsmen. Unlike the Cauldron Born, the Huntsmen were human, but were bound together by vows and magic. All dedicated killers, their power and determination actually increased when one of their number was killed. Dressed in animal skins, they were almost wild beasts themselves. Taran and his companions sought the cauldron, and found it in Morva in the possession of the three sinister enchantresses, and learned it could only be destroyed if a living man entered it freely, which would mean his death. Prince Ellidyr, who had long been consumed with jealousy of Taran, saw the folly of his rivalry and in a last act of heroism flung himself into the cauldron. With a resounding crack it broke and was destroyed forever, taking with it the life of Ellidyr.

Once again Arawn had suffered a major setback, but he was not yet defeated. The destruction of the cauldron meant that he could create no more of his deathless warriors, but there were still great numbers of them in the field and the horde of Huntsmen was increasing. The next stage of the battle between the Sons of Don and the Death Lord took place, not in Prydain itself, but on MONA where an attempt was made by Achren to gain possession of the magic power of the House of Llyr, an attempt which was frustrated and again represented a major setback to her and Arawn.

Taran then returned to Caer Dallben, and it seems to have been largely because of his growing feeling of attachment for Eilonwy of the House of Llyr that he set out on his long wanderings in an attempt to discover his true background and identity. He travelled first to Morva, where the three enchantresses advised him to go to the MIRROR OF LLUNET if he would know his true self. Taran travelled slowly across country, and he was involved in many noble adventures, but it was during this time that he began to understand the importance of the simple farmers of his country and learnt that their valour was as great as if not greater than that of the nobles and battle leaders he had come to know. Eventually Taran reached the Free Commots, which is where he first took the name Taran Wanderer. Here he lived and worked with the craftsmen and artisans, learning something of the arts of the smith, the potter and the weaver.

The Death Lord himself now took the field, using his ability to take the shape of others to great advantage and winning the weaker lords of Prydain to his side with promises of wealth or power. The seriousness of the situation was brought home when Gwydion was found wounded, by Fflewddur. The sword Dyrnwyn had gone from his side. An expedition set out to search for the great sword, but before it had been found Caer Dathyl, the seat of the High Kings of Prydain, was razed to the ground by the Cauldron Born in a major battle which saw the massed armies of the Free Commots, the Cantrevs of the north and the Sons of Don routed and Math, High King of Prydain, killed in the assault. The surviving defenders retreated into the hills behind the castle and made plans for a last desperate assault on the stronghold of the Death Lord himself—Annuvin. The attack was two-pronged: a party led by Gwydion went by sea in the boats that had once brought the Sons of Don to Prydain and a force led by Taran set off overland, hoping to delay the Cauldron Born.

The journey of the overland party was dangerous and hazardous, but ultimately successful. As they moved into the hills, they were joined by the army of the Fair Folk, armed with weapons that surpassed even those of the men of the Commots. Despite their traditional distrust of men, the Fair Folk had become convinced that Arawn posed a more fearful threat to themselves. By this stage, even the birds and animals had been mobilized, and every claw and every beak was turned against the allies of the Death Lord. The bears of the forests and mountains began to attack the Huntsmen of Arawn and the crows turned against the *gwythaints*, defeating the great birds by sheer weight of numbers. Despite the growing number of allies, the battle was not yet won, and many strange and dire prophecies were seen to come true before the men of the Commots found themselves before the walls of Annuvin, behind which lay the black marble halls of Arawn. Gwydion's party had already breached the gates, but as they arrived the iron tread of the arriving Cauldron Born was also heard. It was then that an almost forgotten incident from Taran's past helped to turn the tide of battle. Years before, he had fed an abandoned fledgling *gwythaint*. Suddenly, as he stumbled on the rocks, a *gwythaint* swooped down to him, making noises of recognition, and carried him to the summit of Mount Dragon, where the wind whistled through a narrow cave as though it were calling him. As the Cauldron Born came closer and closer, Taran entered the cave, where he found the sword Dyrnwyn. Taran drew the sword, an act which had once almost cost him his life, and light blazed from it. As the sword was drawn, the Cauldron Born collapsed as one man and the human warriors fell on the remaining Huntsmen. The allies now entered the labyrinthine tunnels and passageways of Annuvin. In a last attempt to save his power, Arawn took on the appearance of Gwydion and demanded the blazing sword; he disappeared in a wreath of smoke when Taran saw through the ruse. The final horror, however, was the confrontation between Achren and Arawn. Arawn suddenly materialized in the form of a serpent, and Achren seized it, apparently trying to wrench its head off, only to have its fangs sink into her neck. The serpent then struck at Taran who clove it in two with Dyrnwyn. The body of the serpent writhed at his feet and gradually became that of Arawn himself before sinking into the ground like a shadow. The Death Lord was finally defeated. Perhaps most important, a coffer had been found in the Great Hall that later proved to contain the secrets stolen by Arawn and descriptions of the many skills that had been thought to be lost to men forever. The victors withdrew from Annuvin and, as they did so, the halls and towers of the Death Lord collapsed in ruins behind them. The work for which it had been forged being over, Dyrnwyn ceased to give off its blazing light and became merely an old, battered sword.

After the defeat of Arawn, the Sons of Don returned to the Summer Country in their golden ships, taking with them many of their allies. Gurgi, Doli the Dwarf, Fflewddur Fflam and Dallben left with them. Taran refused to leave, saying that there was much to be done in Prydain, and was hailed as High King. For love of him, Eilonwy also remained, voluntarily giving up the vestiges of her magic powers. With the departure of the Sons of Don, magic disappeared from Prydain and men were left to choose for themselves between good and evil.

(Lloyd Alexander, *The Book of Three*, New York, 1964; Lloyd Alexander, *The Black Cauldron*, New York, 1965; Lloyd Alexander, *The Castle of Llyr*, New York, 1966; Lloyd Alexander, *Taran Wanderer*, New York, 1967; Lloyd Alexander, *The High King*, New York, 1968)

PSEUDOPOLIS, capital of LEUKE.

PTOLEMAIS, a dim city in Greece, where the houses have doors of brass and black draperies hang in the windows. Near the Catacombs lives a creature called Shadow, who also roams the Plains of Herlusion bordering the foul Charonian Canal. Visitors should beware of him, for his presence is said to be a preamble to death.

(Edgar Allan Poe, "Shadow: a Parable," in *Tales*, Philadelphia, 1845)

PTYX ISLAND, a single block of a stone found nowhere else in the world and therefore a priceless substance. Ptyx stone has the serene translucence of a white sapphire, and whereas other stones are cold to the touch, it has the warmth given off by the surface of a kettledrum. The island is difficult to describe: it resembles both "an irreproachable liquid, stabilized in accordance with eternal law," and "an impenetrable diamond."

It is not difficult to land on Ptyx, as natural steps lead to the top of the island. On the summit, the visitor will see not the accidental events of the world but the substance of the universe itself.

The Lord of the Island, seated in a floating rocking-chair, welcomes all visitors. As he approaches them, the motion of his rocking-chair appears to be a gesture of welcome. A habitual pipe-smoker, the Lord of the Island normally wears a smoker's plaid and offers visitors painted eggs.

The fauna of the island includes fauns, and nymphs with light, rosy flesh which seems to hover in the air, drowsy with tufted slumbers disturbed by the melodious emanations of the Ptyx stone.

A typical sailing craft in the PUMPKIN ISLANDS.

(Alfred Jarry, *Gestes et Opinions du Docteur Faustroll, Pataphysicien. Roman Néo-Scientifique*, Paris, 1911)

PULLOSIN, see NEW BRITAIN.

PUMPKIN ISLANDS, an archipelago in the north Atlantic, so called because of the enormous pumpkins that grow here, sometimes as large as seventy cubic feet. The inhabitants put them out to dry, remove the insides and use the fruit as boats, the stems as masts and the leaves as sails. The inhabitants are pirates who prey on the neighbouring islands and are called "pumpkin pirates" by their enemies the Nutnauts (see NUT ISLAND), against whom they launch their fleet of vast pumpkins.

(Lucian of Samosata, *True History*, 2nd cen. AD)

PURPLE ISLAND, in the Pacific Ocean at latitude 45°. It is inhabited by the Red Ethiopians, a tribe of unknown origin, so called because of the colour of their skin.

The island seems to have been discovered by German sailors and then taken over by the French. Yet the true discovery of the island can, in fact, be attributed to Lord Glenarvan, who christened it Ethiopian Island, though the name was never adopted. Lord Glenarvan hoisted the British flag from the top of the island's highest peak, but the natives, unable to speak any language other than their own, took down the flag and used the cloth to make themselves breeches, which infuriated the discoverers. A commercial treaty was agreed upon but the good work was spoilt by a volcanic eruption that buried the king of the island. Following this, the high priest started a social revolution. Political power fell into the hands of a band of pirates, but during a bloody civil war the pirates were evicted and the Red Ethiopians became their own masters. All attempts to reestablish the previous order failed, despite the efforts of foreign powers.

(Mikhail Bulgakov, *Bagrobyj ostrov*, Moscow, 1928)

PYGMY KINGDOM, in India, near the kingdom of MANCY, on the Dalay River. The inhabitants are three spans (or twenty-seven inches) high, fair and gentle. They only live six or seven years; eight is considered a very advanced age. They are the best workers of gold, silver, cotton and silk in the world. But they do not cultivate the land; this is done for them by men of normal stature, whom they regard as other men might regard giants. A few normal-sized men, however, live in the pygmies' great city, which is well worth a visit.

(Sir John Mandeville, *Voiage de Sir John Maundevile*, Paris, 1357)

PYRALLIS, a volcanic island inhabited by small winged creatures called *pyrallis* or *pyrotocones*, which are also found in the copper foundries of Crete.

They bear some resemblance to dragons with insect wings, and draw their nourishment from fire, the only element in which they can survive.

(Pliny the Elder, *Inventorum Natura,* 1st cen. AD)

PYRAMID MOUNTAIN, a high, cone-shaped mountain which rises from the subterranean Val-

A section of the spiral staircase inside PYRAMID MOUNTAIN.

ley of VOE, on the shores of a black sea. The entire mountain is below the surface of the earth, and although the sun can be seen through a crack from its higher slopes there is no easy access from the earth's crust to the mountain itself.

From the Valley of Voe, a spiral staircase winds upwards through the mountain. At intervals there are landings, where rifts in the rock walls give views over the valley below. Between these landings, the stairway is dimly lit by lanterns. By now the traveller is so far up the mountain that he or she can distinguish the graceful shadowy forms of the Cloud Fairies who live in this area, sitting on the blue and grey cloudbanks. Between the gaps in the clouds strange birds can sometimes be seen flapping through the

air, large as the roc and with fierce eyes, savage beaks and talons.

Travellers are advised to stop at the cave of the Braided Man, about halfway up Pyramid Mountain. Its inhabitant takes his name from his immensely long hair and beard, which are plaited into many braids, each fastened at the end with a coloured ribbon. Now bent almost double with age, the Braided Man once lived on the surface of the earth, where he was a well-known manufacturer of Imported Holes for American Swiss Cheese, with subsidiary interests in pores for porous plasters and high-grade holes for buttons and doughnuts. His greatest invention was the Adjustable Post-Hole which he fully expected would make his fortune. Having manufactured a large number of these holes, he put them all end to end to save storage space, thus making an immensely deep hole reaching far inside the earth. As he leaned over it to see how deep it was he tumbled in, but succeeded in catching hold of an outcrop of rock in Pyramid Mountain, which saved him from falling to his death in the sea.

Above the cave of the Braided Man, the staircase winds up to an outpost of the Land of the GARGOYLES and then abruptly ends. The only way to continue the ascent is to follow the roughly hewn tunnels that lead closer to the surface of the earth. Following these tunnels the traveller will reach a cave inhabited by dragons and their offspring, known as dragonettes. The dragonettes are usually hungry and believe in eating anyone foolish enough to venture too close to them. Travellers are advised that the only safe time to enter the cave is while the dragon mother is away on hunting trips, provided a safe distance is kept from her offspring. The tails of the young dragons are tied to the rocks at the base of their caves to prevent them from moving very far or crawling all over the mountain, fighting each other and causing a great deal of trouble. The dragons of Pyramid Mountain claim to be descended from the Green Dragon of ATLANTIS. The adult dragons are thought to be about two thousand years old and the dragonettes in their sixties. Even so, their young heads are already as big as barrels and covered with greenish scales.

Beyond the cave of the dragonettes, a gentle slope leads up to a pivoting rock which gives access to the last cave before the exit, from which the sun can be seen through the crack in the roof.

From here, the surface of the earth is still a considerable distance overhead and can only be reached by visitors with an ability to fly.

(L. Frank Baum, *Dorothy and the Wizard in Oz*, Chicago, 1908; L. Frank Baum, *The Road to Oz*, Chicago, 1909)

PYRANDRIA, an island near Antarctica, that can be seen from afar because of its dazzling light.

Pyrandria is the country of the Firemen. Their skin is made of fire and they live as long as they have something to feed the flames. When no source of combustion is found they become sparks, float off in the air and are seen in many countries as will-o'-the-wisps. Firemen keep away from other men. The only other inhabitants of Pyrandria are salamanders.

(Jean Jacobé de Frémont d'Ablancourt, *Supplément de l'Histoire Véritable de Lucien*, Paris, 1654)

Q

QUAMA, see NAZAR.

QUARLL ISLAND, off the coast of Mexico, near the mouth of the River Guadaliara. Access is difficult, as the island is rockbound and the sea rough. A cleft in the rocks provides a path to the interior, where a mile-long lake can be found. Beyond it stretches a grassy plain, with clusters of trees ringed by cliffs that hide it from the outside world.

Among the fauna is a fawn-like animal, twice the size of a hare, the colour of a fox and with the face and feet of a goat, that tastes much like venison. Quarll Island boasts a strange plant that from a distance resembles a whole grove of trees.

Mexicans and Peruvians have long believed that Quarll serves as a base for pirates. In fact, its sole inhabitant is an old Englishman who was cast away here on September 15, 1675—one Philip Quarll, a Londoner by birth. Quarll was visited by a Bristol merchant who chanced to land here in 1724. Although he gave the merchant his memoirs to be published in England, he refused to leave the island, and it is said that, though very aged, he is still alive today.

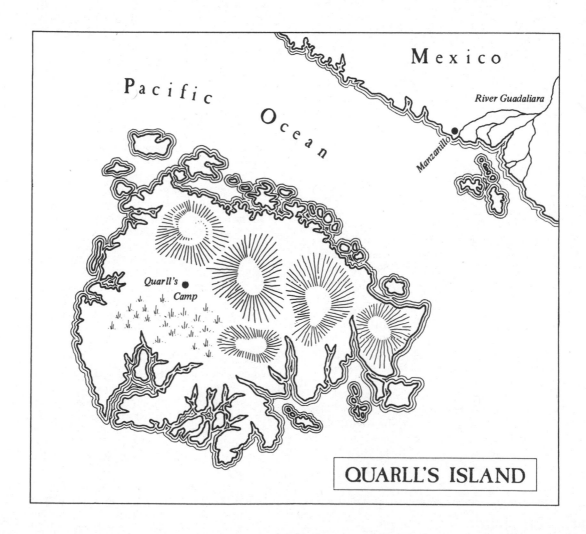

QUARLL'S ISLAND

The island's climate is agreeable, with thunderstorms in summer and snow in winter.

(Peter Longueville, *The Hermit: Or, the Unparalleled Sufferings And Surprising Adventures Of Mr. Philip Quarll, An Englishman. Who was lately discovered by Mr. Dorrington a Bristol Merchant, upon an uninhabited Island in the South-Sea; where he has lived above Fifty Years, without any human Assistance, still continues to reside, and will not come away. Containing I. His Conferences with Those who found him out, to whom he recites the most material Circumstances of his Life; as, that he was born in the Parish of St. Giles, educated by the charitable Contribution of a Lady, and put 'Prentice to a Lock-smith. II. How he left his Master, and was taken up with a notorious House-breaker, who was hanged; how, after this Escape, he went to Sea a Cabbin-Boy, married a famous Whore, listed himself a common Soldier, turned Singing-master, and married Three Wives, for which he was tried and condemned at the Old Bailey. III. How he was pardoned by King Charles II. turned Merchant, and was shipwrecked on this desolate Island on the Coast of Mexico. With a curious Map of the Island, and other Cuts,* Westminster, 1727)*

QUEEN ISLAND, near the North Pole, latitude 89°59′15″ north, first discovered by Captain John Hatteras, commander of the *Forward* from Liverpool, England, who reached the island on July 11, 1861, with four companions. Queen Island is covered with volcanic debris, lacks any vegetation and is dominated by an active volcano said to be the site of the real North Pole (see, however, REAL NORTH POLE). With his dog, Duk, Captain Hatteras attained the volcano's peak on July 12, 1861, where he hoisted a British flag and at the same time lost his sanity. Taken back to Liverpool, he was interned in Sten-Cottage Asylum. The doctors observed that he had lost the power of speech and that he could only walk in the direction of the North Pole.

Visitors to Queen Island will find that the volcano has been named Mount Hatteras and that a plaque has been put up with the words "John Hatteras—1861." Further information is given in *The English at the North Pole,* by Dr. Clawbonny, published by the Royal Geographical Society in 1862.

(Jules Verne, *Voyages et aventures du Capitaine Hatteras,* Paris, 1866)

QUEENS, ISLE OF, see GREAT WATER.

QUIQUENDONE, a small town in Flanders, of 2,393 inhabitants, some thirteen and a half kilometres north-west of Audenarde and fifteen and a quarter kilometres south-east of Bruges. The Vaar, a small tributary of the Escaut, runs under its three bridges still covered by ancient medieval roofs. Travellers can visit the old castle, the founding stone of which was laid in 1197 by Count Baudouin, future Emperor of Constantinople. Also worth a visit is the Town Hall, with Gothic windows and fine towers—some 357 feet high—whose bells are even more famous than those of Bruges and have been described as a piano in the air. Important sites are also the Stadtholder's Hall, hung with the portrait of William of Nassau by Brandon; the Rood-Loft of the Church of Saint Magloire, masterpiece of sixteenth-century architecture; the forged iron well in the centre of St. Ernulph Square, wrought by Quentin Metsys; and the mausoleum of Marie of Burgundy, daughter of Charles the Fearless, who now rests in the Church of Notre Dame of Bruges. It should also be noted that Quiquendone is famous for its whipped cream and barley sugar.

This town—where, up to the last century, not the slightest quarrel was ever heard, where waggoners would never swear, coach drivers never insult each other, horses never bolt, dogs never bite, cats never scratch—was chosen in 1872 as the centre for a wicked experiment conducted by a certain chemical engineer, a Dr. Ox. Under the pretext of supplying Quiquendone with a badly needed modernized lighting system, Dr. Ox built a network to distribute the lighting gas. He did not, however, use carbonated hydrogen produced from distilled coal, but a more modern substance, twenty times brighter: oxhydric gas, a mixture of oxygen and hydrogen. The Doctor managed to produce great quantities of this gas, not by employing sodium manganese (as in the system of Tessie de Motay), but simply by decomposing water with the aid of a battery that he had put together. In this manner, without the use of any complicated equipment, the Doctor could send an electric current through vast water reservoirs, decomposing the liquid into oxygen and hydrogen. The oxygen would be guided to one side; the hydrogen—double the amount of oxygen—towards the other. Both gases were kept in separate containers, carefully sealed, as their mingling would have provoked the most terrible explosion. Guided by a maze of tubes, they finally combined and produced a brilliant flame, the light of which could easily be compared to that of electricity.

This splendid gas provoked not only unanimous admiration in Quiquendone, but also some less agreeable secondary effects: the character, the temperament, the ideas of the inhabitants of Quiquendone were deeply affected by it and from calm, self-contained citizens they became aggressive and irritable thugs. Even the domestic animals turned into savage beasts, unbearable and dangerous. In the orchards, parks and gardens, the plants also showed signs of a curious change. The bushes became trees; the seeds, as soon as they were planted, would show curly green heads and in just a few hours become enormous vegetables. The asparagus sprang some two feet high; the artichokes blew up as large as melons; the melons as huge as pumpkins; the pumpkins as big as the church bell, some nine feet across. The cauliflowers were thickets, the mushrooms, umbrellas. Two people were needed to finish eating a strawberry and four could hardly manage a pear. Flowers grew so quickly that on one occasion the gardener in Quiquendone almost fainted when he found that his *tulipa gesneriana* was serving as a nest to a whole family of robins. The entire town came to admire this unique specimen, which was promptly rebaptized *tulipa quiquendonia*.

But among the many changes were some that affected the health of the population. The number of indigestions increased threefold (people ate six meals instead of two), as did cases of drunkenness, gastritis and ulcers, and many diseases of the nerves. Finally, affected by all these transformations, the inhabitants of Quiquendone decided to attack the neighbouring town of Virgamen, on the feeble excuse that in 1135 a Virgamen cow had crossed the border and come to graze on a Quiquendonian field. While the inhabitants were on their way to war against the people of Virgamen, a terrific explosion took place in the main gas reservoir, putting an end to Dr. Ox's experiment in lighting and perhaps to Dr. Ox himself. Nowadays Quiquendone is lit in the normal way and the town offers all the facilities a traveller is likely to expect.

(Jules Verne, *Une Fantaisie du Docteur Ox*, Paris, 1874)

QUISO, a small rocky island in the Telthearna River which marks the northern frontier of the

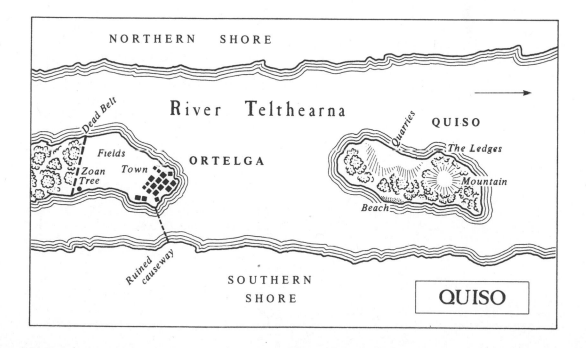

BEKLAN EMPIRE, slightly downstream from the island of ORTELGA. Quiso is chiefly remarkable for two superb constructions on its single mountain. The first is the so-called Upper Temple, cut out of the solid rock, a high chamber which took thirty years to construct. The temple is approached via a tree trunk spanning a deep ravine; this replaces the original Bridge of Suppliants, a slender iron span which was destroyed many years ago. On the edge of the ravine is an extensive paved terrace, the work of the same forgotten craftsmen. But the second and probably more imposing construction is the Ledges, huge steps and shelves cut out of the solid rock of the mountain.

Quiso is closely associated with the cult of the bear Shardik, once believed, throughout the Beklan Empire, to be the living incarnation of the power of God. During the great days of the early empire, pilgrims came from afar to the sacred island of Quiso. The island was ruled by the High Priestess and her acolytes, virgins whose lives were dedicated to the cult of Shardik. These virgins were chosen from the women of Ortelga and brought over to Quiso and given new names; they never returned home. Their role was to care for the bear and to sing the sacred songs that calmed and soothed the animal. They were sometimes killed by Shardik, but this was accepted as being the will of God. These virgins never left the island, unless they were chosen to accompany the High Priestess on her twice yearly journey to Ortelga to confer with the barons and to choose new acolytes. On such occasions the High Priestess took nothing with her, to disguise the fact that she had left the sacred island. She would confer with the barons wearing the mask of a bear and no man ever saw her face.

After Ortelgan rule over the Beklan Empire had ended, the cult of Shardik was maintained, although no bear was allowed to be kept on Quiso. The High Priestess and the virgins waited for centuries for the appearance of the reincarnated Shardik. At one point they left the island in search of the sacred bear, but eventually returned again to Quiso, where they are now.

(Richard Adams, *Shardik*, London, 1974)

QUIVERA, a country in South America, neighbouring on the Republic of Indepencia. It was settled by Madoc, son of Owen, Prince of Gwyneth, who left Wales in 1169.

Obverse and reverse of a gold coin from QUIVERA.

Quivera is famed for its rubies which gave the capital its name, Cibola, the City of Frozen Fire. Cibola is walled, defended by a barbican, and lies across the mouth of a steep valley leading to the ruby mines. Notable is the Church of St. David, its entire roof covered with thin plates of gold.

The history of Quivera is strongly influenced by its commerce in rubies. One group of Europeans in search of rubies were shipwrecked here in 1824. Along with their greed they brought influenza to the country, almost wiping out the population. The Europeans tried to seize power but were duly overthrown.

Quivera is famous for its Santa Corona volcanoes, that can be seen from the coast, and for the pass of Toppling Crags, so called because of the frequent rock falls. A hot-water stream runs through this pass and leads to a natural, cliff-bound amphitheatre pitted with geyser vents.

Giant ferns grow in the central plain, and milk-white, blind sea-monsters with red teeth, as long as ships, are said to inhabit the unmentionable caves at the foot of the great mountains.

The coinage of Quivera is of a pale soft gold, showing the head of Madoc and the inscription *Mad. Prince. Civ.* On the reverse is a geometrical design of three triangles, the centre one shorter than the others, bearing the word *Civ.*

Quivera is renowned for its epic ballads which are sung to the accompaniment of a harp.

(Vaughan Wilkins, *The City of Frozen Fire*, London, 1950)

R

RAKLMANI, a country located far beyond the ocean, where the sun sleeps and where a nation of pious people, also called the Raklmani, live happily. The Raklmani, who lead saintly lives, eat only once a year when the shell of an Easter egg which has been blessed floats towards them on the immense sea that divides them from other lands.

(Maria Savi-Lopez, *Leggende del mare,* Turin, 1920)

RAMAJA, capital of BABILARY.

RAMPART JUNCTION, Iowa, in the United States, on the Chicago–Los Angeles line. Built on the banks of a small river, Rampart Junction is a typical American rural town, with a dusty main street and wooden, flaking houses. The main store, Honegger Hardware, closes at four o'clock sharp. Travellers arriving in Rampart Junction will see an old man, deep in an ancient chair, tilted back against the station platform wall, his dark face full of lizard folds and stitches, his eyes in a perpetual squint, his ash-white hair blowing in the summer wind. For over twenty years, this man has been sitting on the station platform, waiting for someone to arrive. Throughout his life, he has accumulated a deep hatred, risen from minor things, small inconveniences that have angered him beyond endurance. To purge his wrath, he has decided to wait for a complete stranger to arrive in town, for someone to get off the train for no reason, a man nobody knows and who does not know anyone in Rampart Junction. When the traveller arrives, the old man will follow him, get into conversation with him and then kill him. This fate is similar to the one experienced by a certain Arab fisherman who discovered a brass bottle in the sea, and to that of Mr. Juan Dahlmann, in the south of Argentina. Travellers are advised to depart before the end of the proposed ritual.

(Anonymous, *The Arabian Nights,* 14th–16th cen. AD; Jorge Luis Borges, "El Sur," in *Ficciones* (2nd edition), Buenos Aires, 1956; Ray Bradbury, "The Town Where No One Got Off," in *A Medicine for Melancholy,* New York, 1959)

RAMPOLE ISLAND, in the South Atlantic; the nearest port is probably Bahia Blanca, Argentina. The island is fertile and rich in vegetation, but only two areas are inhabited. The best-known settlement is a village in a narrow gorge on the coast, a straggling collection of huts, each surrounded by a palisade of thorns. The gorge is about three miles long and never more than one hundred yards wide. Cascades at the landward end mark the frontier between this settlement and the next, which stands in a broader river valley beyond a bluff. Most of Rampole Island is covered in scrub jungle and woods.

The island's most curious geological feature is a jutting mass of rock at the mouth of a fjord leading into the gorge. The rock itself is of a strange substance, rather like clearish blue and purple glass, with patches of pink and veins of white; it seems to radiate light from within rather than reflect it from any external source. The outcrop has the form of a woman with staring eyes and open mouth; a pinnacle of stone behind it resembles a hand brandishing a club. A red mouth and eyes rimmed with white have been painted on the stone. It is believed by the local inhabitants to represent the deity they call the Great Goddess. As they return from their fishing expeditions, the natives stop their canoes abreast of the figure, raise their paddles in salutation and display their catch to the woman of stone.

The people of the gorge are cannibals. Their skin is a dusky buff colour, their dark hair drawn tightly back. They wear tattoos and anoint their bodies with a rancid oil. Although a naturally sturdy people, they suffer from a wide variety of illnesses and infections, probably because of the filthy conditions in which they live. The men of the tribe normally go naked, but the young women wear girdles and a variety of ornaments such as anklets and necklaces. The virgins of the tribe anoint their hair with fish liver oil to make it glossy and paint their skin with red and yellow patterns. Their teeth are artificially stained black and red. Polygamy is normal; the first wife has precedence over her successors.

The people have a certain amount of trade with the tribe that lives farther inland; dried fish, oyster shells and shark skins are left on a series of flat stones by the cascades in exchange for primitive pots, pieces of hardwood, fruit and a type of nut. Although there is a degree of mutual understanding, relations between the tribes are often hostile and sometimes erupt into warfare, usually over complaints about trade. When war breaks out everything in the village is painted red, and hysterical dancing takes place. All the young men are initiated as warriors by having their ears clipped and then are tortured by their elders to harden them for battle.

According to tribal law, men may only be killed in battle; their flesh is then eaten. Human flesh is never referred to as such; it is always called "the gift of a friend." Bones and inedible morsels are placed on the altar of the Great Goddess and are left to decay; the rest is distributed among the people, who eat together in a circular hut built for the purpose. Here they squat around a stone slab, offering slivers of meat to one another with their right hands. Good manners forbid talking during meals. At the end of the ceremonial meal, the elder says "Gratitude to the friend," a phrase which is repeated by all.

The people of Rampole Island have an almost religious respect for madmen; insanity is regarded as a distinction conferred by the Great Goddess and the flesh of mad people is taboo. Because of this belief, the tribe keep a so-called sacred lunatic whom they nurse and feed; the people say that the tribe will prosper so long as their sacred lunatic is fat and well. In return, he acts as an oracle and makes prophecies. The sacred lunatic lives apart from the rest of the tribe in a hut decorated with human skulls and the bones of the giant sloth. He is given a staff of dark wood carved with obscene designs and decorated with mother of pearl and sharks' teeth.

Much of tribal life is dominated by taboos. It is, for instance, taboo to pronounce certain words. It is taboo to give one's true name and an individual refers to himself in the third person. It is also taboo to venture into the open uplands above the gorge. The tribe's taboo-system thereby condemns the people to live in the gloomiest and least healthy spot on the island. Only those who are considered to have great magical powers are permitted to go into the uplands.

Rampole Island is the home of a species of grey lizard which may grow to one and a half feet in length. A plant resembling a large sundew is also found on the island; it has prehensile leaves in which flies, lizards and small birds are trapped and digested.

The island is the only place in the world where the giant ground sloth (*megatherium americanum*) *is* still found. It was once common in much of the world and its bones have been found in Patagonia and Tierra del Fuego, but the living animal has never been found anywhere else. The sloth lives on the uplands where it breeds in safety—there are no predators to reduce its numbers and its flesh is taboo to the inhabitants. The sloth may reach the size of an elephant. It is covered in long coarse grey hair, usually clotted with mud and fragments of vegetation; the skin itself is pink. The sloth's movements are slow and jerky. It walks on the elbows of its forelegs, which are armoured with heavy claws. The head is held low, the rump higher than any other part of the body. The animal can often be seen in a squatting position, leaning back on its tail with its claws resting on its belly. It is usually infested with a wide variety of parasites, notably a species of large black tick. The body smells like rotting seaweed and the breath is fetid.

The sloth normally lives on fresh shoots and budding plants and the species has destroyed much of the vegetation on the uplands. It also eats eggs of all kinds as well as small animals which the sloth appears to hypnotize. It shows no fear of fire and the inhabitants of Rampole Island see in it an air of malignancy as it drags itself along the ground.

(H.G. Wells, *Mr. Blettsworthy on Rampole Island*, London, 1933)

RANSOM, ISLE OF, perhaps in the North Sea, a rock-bound island with high black cliffs; a haunt of pirates and kidnappers (hence the name). Travellers can reach it from the sea through a cave large enough to admit a ship with all sails set.

The only notable site on the island is the Hall of the Ravagers, with its main room panelled and carved with gardens and trees and the image of a smiling king, said to represent the ruler of the Land of the GLITTERING PLAIN.

(William Morris, *The Story of the Glittering Plain, also called the Land of Living Men or the Acre of the Undying*, London, 1891) *Illustration follows*

RAVENAL'S TOWER, a tall tower visible for miles, on a hill-top near Ivybridge, Kent. It was built as a burial-place for Richard Ravenal, who is

A carved wooden panel in the Hall of the Ravagers, on the Isle of RANSOM.

said to have been under a curse forbidding him to rest in earth or sea. He was therefore buried between heaven and earth, in an octagonal chamber half-way up the tower. Originally Ravenal lay beneath a glass panel, dressed in blue satin and silver, with his sword at his side, but the panel was subsequently replaced by a granite slab bearing the following inscription:

> *Here lies the body of Mr. Richard*
> *Ravenal,*
> *Born 1720. Died 1779.*
> *Here I lie, between heaven and sky,*
> *Think upon me, dear passers-by,*
> *And you who do my tombstone see*
> *Be kind to say a prayer for me.*

Under the terms of Ravenal's will, a sum was set aside for the maintenance of the tower; it is still well kept, although tramps sometimes sleep in the lower staircase.

From the burial chamber a spiral staircase leads to the top, which gives extensive views over the surrounding countryside.

(Edith Nesbit, *The Wouldbegoods*, London, 1901)

REALISM ISLAND, of unknown location. It was once inhabited by merry and innocent people, mostly shepherds and tillers of the earth. They were republicans, primitive and simple souls; they talked over their affairs under a tree, and the nearest approach they had to a personal ruler was a sort of priest or white witch who said their prayers for them. They worshipped the sun, not idolatrously, but as the golden crown of a god whom they saw almost as plainly as the sun.

Legend has it that the priest was told by his people to build a great tower, pointing to the sky in salutation of the sun god. He pondered long and heavily before he picked his materials. He resolved to use nothing that was not almost as clear and exquisite as sunshine itself, nothing that was not washed as white as the rain can wash the heavens, nothing that did not sparkle as spotlessly as that crown of the god. He would have nothing grotesque or obscure; he would not have even anything emphatic or anything mysterious. He would have all the arches "as light as laughter and as candid as logic." He built the temple in three concentric courts, each one cooler and more exquisite than the one before. For the outer wall was a hedge of white lilies, ranked so thick that a green stalk was hardly to be seen; and the wall within that was of crystal, which smashed the sun into a million stars. The wall within that—which was the tower itself—was a ring of pure water, forced up in an everlasting fountain. Upon the very tip and crest of that foaming spire was one big and blazing diamond, which the water tossed up eternally and caught again as if it were a ball.

About this time, the island was caught in a swarm of pirates, and the shepherds had to turn themselves into rude warriors and seamen. After years of horror and humiliation, the shepherd-soldiers began to triumph because they did not fear defeat. Finally, the pirate invasion rolled back into the empty seas and the land was delivered.

But for some reason, after this period of fighting, men began to talk quite differently about the temple and the sun. Some said the temple must not be touched, because it was " classical" and "perfect." But others answered: "In that, it differs from the sun, that shines on the evil and the good and on mud and monsters everywhere. The temple is of the noon; it is made of white marble clouds and sapphire sky. But the sun is not always of the noon. The sun dies daily; every night he is crucified in blood and fire."

The priest had taught and fought all through the war, and his hair had grown white. Reasoning along new lines, the priest put down the following observations: "The sun, the symbol of our father, gives life to all those earthly things that are full of ugliness and energy. All the exaggerations are right, if they exaggerate the right things. Let us point to the heaven with tusks and horns and fins and trunks and tails, so long as they all point to heaven. The ugly animals praise God as much as the beautiful. The frog's eyes stand out of his head because he is staring at heaven. The giraffe's neck is long because he is stretching towards heaven. The donkey has ears to hear—let him hear."

And under the new inspiration the people of Realism Island planned a gorgeous cathedral in the Gothic manner, with all the animals of the earth crawling over it, and all the possible ugly things making up one common beauty, because they all appealed to the god. The columns of the temple were carved like the necks of giraffes; the dome was like an ugly tortoise; and the highest pinnacle was a monkey standing on his head with his tail pointing at the sun. And yet the whole was beautiful, because it was lifted up in one living and religious gesture as a man lifts his hands in prayer.

But this great plan was never properly completed. The people had brought up on great wagons the heavy tortoise roof and the huge necks of stone, and all the thousand and one oddities that made up that unity, the owls and the crocodiles and the kangaroos, which hideous by themselves might have been magnificent if reared in one definite proportion and dedicated to the sun. For this was Gothic, this was romantic, this was Christian art. And that symbol which was to crown it all, the ape upside down, was really Christian for man is the ape upside down.

But the rich, who had grown riotous in the long peace, obstructed the thing, and in some squabble a stone struck the priest on the head and he lost his memory. He saw piled in front of him frogs and elephants, monkeys and giraffes, toadstools and sharks, all the ugly things of the universe which he had collected to do honour to God. But he forgot why he had collected them. He could not remember the design or the object. He piled them all wildly into one heap fifty feet high; and when he had done it all the rich and influential went into a passion of applause and cried, "This is real art! This is Realism! This is things as they really are!" and this is how Realism was born on the island.

(G.K. Chesterton, "Introductory: On Gargoyles," in *Alarms and Discursions*, London, 1910)

REALLY DEEP WORLD, see BISM.

REAL NORTH POLE. According to Adam Jeffson, who arrived here on April 13 of an unspecified year, the ice beyond the Arctic Circle is scattered with pieces of rock or ferruginous minerals encrusted with precious stones. Jeffson supposed these rocks to be meteorites, attracted to this place because of polar magnetism; the cold climate seems to have prevented them from burning when crossing our atmosphere. Another reason given for their presence is the stronger gravitational force and lower atmospheric density of this zone. In the vicinity of the Pole, these meteorites become more and more abundant, heaping up in immense piles, disposed in terraces or steps, sometimes spread throughout vast areas like scattered autumn leaves. Because of this the land has been flattened out.

The Real North Pole itself is occupied by a perfectly circular lake, almost a mile long, in the centre of which rises a low and massive column of ice. Jeffson had the impression that on the column was written a name in characters no man will ever be able to read, and under the name, a date. Jeffson believed that the liquid surrounding the column turns round and round from east to west in a sort of tremulous ecstasy, accompanied by a faint rumour of wings and waterfalls, together with the whole of the planet. He suggested that this liquid nourishes a living creature, a being with many eyes, sluggish and sad, who circles throughout eternity in a trembling underground hollow, keeping all eyes constantly on the inscribed name and date.

Jeffson arrived here alone, after many terrible vicissitudes in which all his companions died. The chronicles of the discovery of another North Pole by two American explorers, Dr. Frederick Albert Cook (1865–1940) and Rear Admiral Robert Edwin Peary (1856–1920), should be considered purely fictitious.

(Matthew Phipps Shiel, *The Purple Cloud*, New York, 1901)

REASON, COMMONWEALTH OF, of unknown location. It is divided into districts and boasts an extensive canal system to discourage the use of horses, which would otherwise consume too much of the produce.

The Commonwealth of Reason is founded on the broad and durable bases of reason, liberty, fraternity and equality, and is designed to promote the happiness of the human race living together in society. The only limitation on liberty is the respect for another man's liberty. The government is representative and legislative and is elected by delegates from each of the districts, chosen by an absolute majority. The constitution is ratified or altered every seven years. There is freedom of religious belief and no State religion.

Education is seen as the source of all liberty and happiness. Public schools are the property of the Commonwealth, attended by all children between four and fourteen. Teachers are elected annually—a man must be thirty and the father of a family, a woman twenty-six and also a mother. No religious doctrine is taught at school. After the age of fourteen, all children attend the National Military Academy and are given a firelock and bayonet.

All citizens receive a minimum wage of one bushel of wheat per day, or the equivalent money, to ensure that all may live comfortably, without fear of oppression by the rich. All property is divided equally among the children, including the illegitimate ones, upon their father's death. Men can marry at eighteen, women at sixteen, but their civil contract can be dissolved by either party if sufficient cause can be shown to a jury. The freedom of the press is guaranteed by law. The lame, blind, deaf, dumb and lunatic are pensioners of the Commonwealth and are paid the minimum wage. Prisons are built at least two miles from the nearest town, and all prisoners are put to work. Their profits are their own, after deduction of a sum to defray part of the prison's costs. There is no capital punishment.

(William Hodgson, *The Commonwealth of Reason by William Hodgson now confined in the Prison of Newgate, London, for Sedition*, London, 1795)

REDHAVEN, see SEVEN ISLES.

RED HOUSE, named for its red-tiled roof, and built in Dublin in the mid-eighteenth century. The opulent house was torn down a few decades later, however, after its tenant, a Mr. Harper, proved that a lease becomes null and void whenever ghosts exercise their right to evict a building's occupants. The arguments he put forward, in front of a magistrate and in the presence of Lord Castlemallard, the house's owner, give us a good description of the ghostly claimant: a plump, lone hand that was hovering outside the house, obviously trying to get inside the building.

The hand would tap on the doors and walls, or grab hold of the balcony, or knock on the front door or on the kitchen window; sometimes it sounded like a gentle rubbing. It appeared outside the large round window on the second floor, made an inspection tour of the house and took refuge in the bedroom. (Some maintain that it committed outrageous acts on the person of the mistress of the house, acts which decency forbids us to elaborate upon.) Once the hand was found in a closet in the adjoining nursery, where it had apparently decided to spend an indefinite period of time.

The Harper family discovered much later that a link could unquestionably be established between this hand and an ancestor whose right hand had been mutilated, and indeed a portrait of that gentleman hung for some time in the dining-room of the Red House.

(Joseph Sheridan Le Fanu, *The Siege of the Red House*, Dublin, 1863)

RED ISLANDS, see SARGYLL.

REGENTRUDE REALM, a small underground country, reached via a hollow willow tree somewhere in northern Germany. It is inhabited by the Regentrude, a weary lady in charge of the rain. She is responsible, much like the Head Spotter of

MEDICINE HAT, for seeing that the rain falls where it is needed, but sometimes she falls asleep on the job. Her underground realm resembles the world above the surface and has no peculiar characteristics.

(Theodor Storm, *Die Regentrude*, Braunschweig, 1868)

RENDANG, an oil-rich island in the Indonesian Archipelago, part of Greater Rendang, a territory ruled by the Sultans of Rendang and comprising Rendang itself, the Nicobar Islands, PALA, and thirty per cent of Sumatra.

Rendang itself was invaded by the Arabs in the Middle Ages, then by the Portuguese and later by the Dutch. Under the dictatorship of Colonel Dipa, the Rendang army invaded Pala in order to gain access to Pala's oil. Its industries are copper and insecticides.

(Aldous Huxley, *Island*, London, 1962)

RENFUSA, capital of BENSALEM.

REREK, a wild, bare hill-country between MESZRIA to the south and FINGISWOLD to the north, where in winter the passes are often blocked by snow. The landscape at Owlsdale, the site of the fortress of LAIMAK, is typical: the river valley winds through increasingly high, bleak moorland where lush grass alternates with pools lined with sedge and peat bogs. The only buildings are the white painted farmhouses and the dry-stone walls that cross the hills. The lower valleys are shaded with sycamore, oak and beech woods, but the hill areas are bare of trees.

Towards the coast, the countryside becomes much more open and rich pastureland predominates. This is the region of the prosperous free towns of Rerek, towns such as Abaraima, with its pleasant gardens and fish ponds, and Bagot, a rich town in a quiet inland valley. Most of the towns are heavily fortified and testify to Rerek's stormy past. Veiring in the north, for instance, is built in the loop of a river whose waters surround it on three sides; its strong walls add to these natural defences. Perhaps the best-defended town in all Rerek, however, is ARGYANNA, protected by the trackless marshes of the Lows of Argyanna on all sides.

The towns of Rerek are traditionally independent of any lord, but over the centuries they have gradually come to be controlled by the Parry clan, who have achieved dominance by setting the towns and petty lords of the north against one another, constantly manoeuvring to gain and consolidate power. The Parrys are allied by marriage with the royal line of Fingiswold; the marriage between the two houses was contracted in order to use the strength of Fingiswold against rivals within Rerek itself. In 777 *Anno Zayanae Conditae*, civil war tore the country apart, however, and the end of the war saw Barganax, Duke of ZAYANA, effective ruler of the three lands of Rerek, Meszria and Fingiswold.

(E.R. Eddison, *Mistress of Mistresses, A Vision of Zimiamvia*, London, 1935; E.R. Eddison, *A Fish Dinner in Memison*, London, 1941; E.R. Eddison, *The Mezentian Gate*, London, 1958)

RHAGES, capital of FARGHESTAN.

RHITTA, THE BARROW OF, standing by a grove of trees on the banks of the River Ystrad in PRYDAIN. On the opposite bank of the river, the ruins of Spiral Castle can be seen. The barrow is the burial place of Rhitta, once the lord of the castle. Rhitta died in mysterious circumstances, still clutching Dyrnwyn, the sword forged by Govannion the Lame as a weapon to defend Prydain against the forces of evil that threatened it.

After the death of Rhitta, Spiral Castle fell into the hands of Achren, the evil ruler of Prydain before the sons of Don arrived from the SUMMER COUNTRY. Always a somewhat sinister place, Spiral Castle became the abode of evil. It was to this chill fortress that Achren brought Eilonwy, the last of the House of Llyr—an ancient line who had traditionally lived at Caer Colur, an island off the coast of MONA—so as to gain control of the legendary powers of the House of Llyr. For years the princess lived in the castle, gradually coming to know the labyrinth of the underground tunnels and passages that give it its name and learning the evil nature of Achren herself.

It was to Spiral Castle that Taran, the assistant pig-keeper of CAER DALLBEN, was brought when he was captured by the Cauldron Born, the undying warriors created from corpses by Arawn the Death Lord. Eilonwy discovered Taran during her wanderings through the tunnels and agreed to help him escape. By the light of the golden bauble she carried, they found their way through the labyrinthine tunnels—unknown to Eilonwy the bauble was in fact the Golden Pelydryn of Llyr and had great powers. Eventually the two reached the inside of the Barrow of Rhitta, where the dead king lay clutching his sword, surrounded by his dead warriors. Sensing the need for a weapon, they took Dyrnwyn from the king. As they did so the earth began to tremble. Unwittingly they had chosen the weapon that would eventually destroy Arawn himself. The power of the sword, which seemed to be an ordinary weapon black with age, was so great that when it was taken out of the barrow Spiral Castle was destroyed by a sheet of blue fire. Within minutes all that remained was the shattered outline of the great doorway.

(Lloyd Alexander, *The Book of Three*, New York, 1964; Lloyd Alexander, *The Black Cauldron*, New York, 1965; Lloyd Alexander, *The Castle of Llyr*, New York, 1966; Lloyd Alexander, *Taran Wanderer*, New York, 1967; Lloyd Alexander, *The High King*, New York, 1968)

RHUDAUR, a region of ERIADOR in MIDDLE-EARTH, comprising the wild, infertile lands stretching from the WEATHER HILLS in the west, to the ETTENMOORS in the north and the MISTY MOUNTAINS to the south. The area is drained by the Hoarwell and Loudwater rivers, known to the elves as Mitheithel and Bruinen respectively. Between the two rivers and to the north of the Great East Road lie the Trollshaws, a wooded and hilly region now infested by trolls. The road itself runs for miles along the foot of these hills, between the Last Bridge across the Mitheithel and the ford across the Bruinen.

The trolls of the area are large creatures, with great heavy faces and legs as thick as tree trunks. They are stupid and argumentative, and plunder and kill travellers when they can, frequently eating the bodies of those they have robbed. The trolls have no knowledge of buildings and live in caves. They must be underground by dawn or the light of the sun will turn them into stone—they will revert to the stuff of the mountains from which they were made and will never move again.

Rhudaur takes its name from that of the long-forgotten king who established his realm here dur-

ing the distant First Age of Middle-earth. It was the most easterly of the three separate states formed by the partition of Arnor in 861 Third Age, and became embroiled in a centuries-long war of intense rivalry against its sister states of Arthedain and Cardolan. The formal dissolution of the state took place in 1974 Third Age, the year of Arthedain's fall.

(J.R.R. Tolkien, *The Fellowship of the Ring*, London, 1954; J.R.R. Tolkien, *The Return of the King*, London, 1955)

RHÛN, the name given to the lands around the inland sea of the same name in the east of MIDDLE-EARTH. At the height of its power, GONDOR ruled parts of the region, but during the Third Age of Middle-earth, Rhûn became the home of the various peoples known as Easterlings who harassed and invaded parts of Gondor, often at the instigation of the Dark Lord of MORDOR. Most of these invasions were military raids, but others seem to have involved migrations of entire nations, such as the Balchoth who invaded parts of Middle-earth but who were defeated and apparently annihilated during the great battle at the Field of CELEBRANT. Late invaders from the same area included the Wainriders who rode to battle in great wagons. They swept across the plain of DAGORLAD, where many great battles were fought against them before they were finally defeated by the armies of Gondor.

(J.R.R. Tolkien, *The Fellowship of the Ring*, London, 1954; J.R.R. Tolkien, *The Return of the King*, London, 1955)

RIALLARO, an archipelago in the south-east Pacific, surrounded by a ring of fog. The name means "ring of mist" and ships that have sailed into it have never reappeared. Because of the fog and the dangerous currents that suck ships down to the bottom of the sea, travellers are advised to proceed with caution. Indeed, they may note the hulls of ancient ships abandoned as a warning in the waters around it—a Spanish caravel, a Malay proa, its dead crew still at their posts, an East Indiaman.

Riallaro Archipelago seems to be the remains of an old, submerged continent and consists mostly of magnetic iron from rocks melted by the volcano that once formed the centre of the archipelago. The

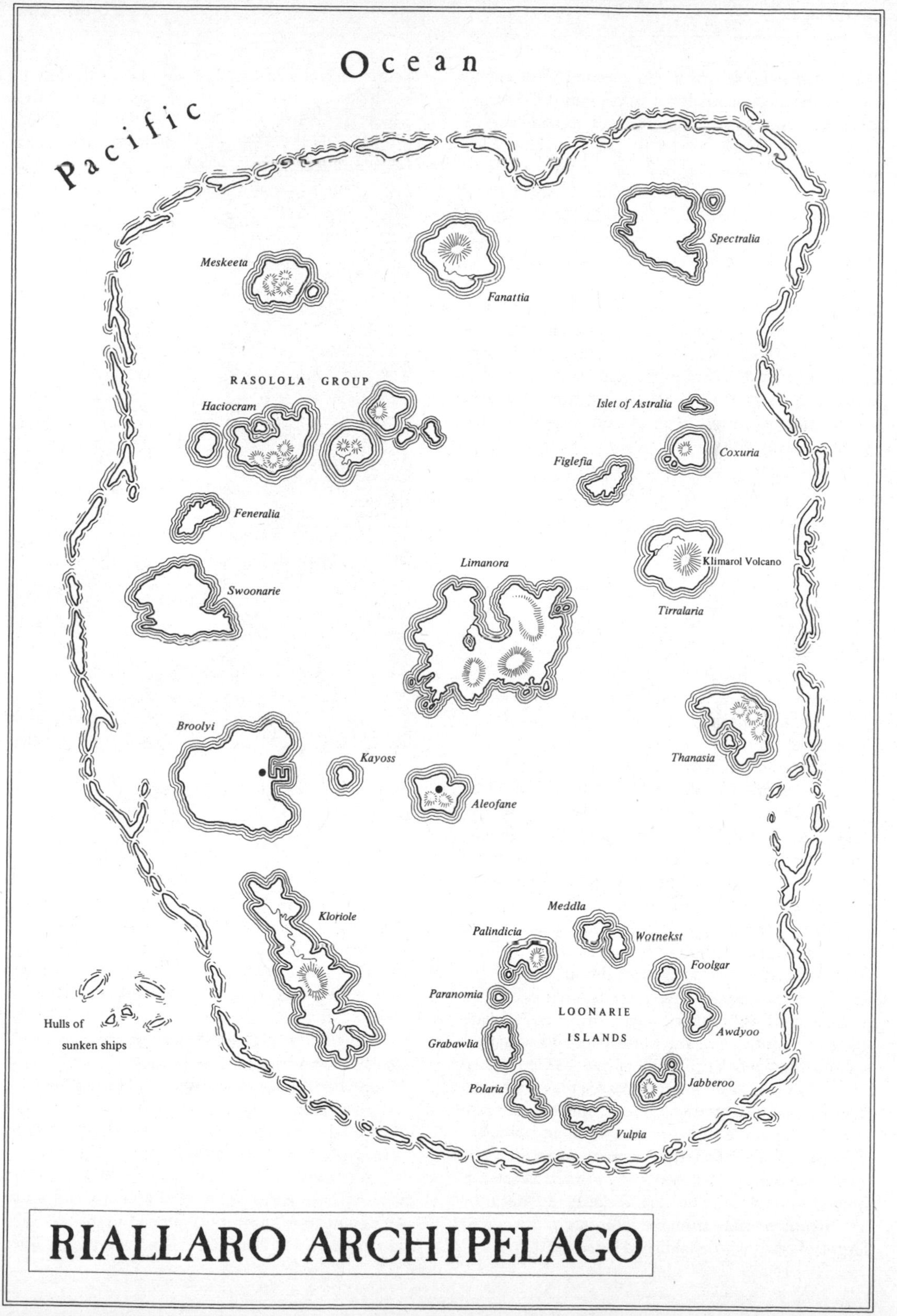

Pacific Ocean

Meskeeta

Fanattia

Spectralia

RASOLOLA GROUP

Haciocram

Islet of Astralia

Coxuria

Figlefia

Feneralia

Limanora

Klimarol Volcano

Swoonarie

Tirralaria

Thanasia

Broolyi

Kayoss

Aleofane

Meddla

Kloriole

Palindicia

Wotnekst

Foolgar

Paranomia

LOONARIE ISLANDS

Awdyoo

Hulls of sunken ships

Grabawlia

Polaria

Jabberoo

Vulpia

RIALLARO ARCHIPELAGO

fog is probably formed by the meeting of two currents, one from the Antarctic region and the other from the tropics. The archipelago is surrounded by a coral reef; inside the reef the water is calm. The islands that form the Riallaro Archipelago are: ALEOFANE, BROOLYI, COXURIA, FANATTIA, FENERALIA, FIGLEFIA, HACIOCRAM, KLORIOLE, LIMANORA, LOONARIE, MESKEETA, SPECTRALIA, SWOONARIE, THANASIA, TIRRALARIA.

The Riallaro Archipelago was visited towards the turn of the century by Europeans on the steamship *Daydream*, which was powerful enough to overcome the archipelago's natural defences. Its captain travelled through the islands and was eventually permitted to go to Limanora where he lived for many years.

(Godfrey Sweven, *Riallaro, the Archipelago of Exiles*, New York & London, 1901; Godfrey Sweven, *Limanora, the Island of Progress*, New York & London, 1903)

RIALMAR, capital of FINGISWOLD, a major port on the mouth of a river on the northern shore of the Midland Sea. The wide streets and squares of the town cluster between the twin horns of a mountain outcrop: the Teremne and the Mehisbon. The mountains are said to be the highest in the world.

The Mehisbon is crowned by the Temple of Zeus, an immense building of pure black marble, left unpolished to heighten the darkness of the stone. Apart from the carvings on the pediment and the frieze on the portico it is not ornamented in any way. The tombs of the kings and queens of Fingiswold can be seen nearby.

The Teremne is occupied by the palace of the kings of Fingiswold, high on a cliff above the Valley of the Revarm. Travellers should try to visit the Queen's Garden, strangely designed to be concealed from sight. It faces east and west; a blank wall shelters it from the north wind. Embrasures in the east and west walls of the garden afford views of the mountains, and the sea eight hundred feet below. The garden's centre-piece is an oval pond, surrounded by a granite walk and benches of lapis lazuli and mother of pearl, overlooked by a double terrace planted with lilies, sunflowers, pinks and mountain flowers. A statue of Aphrodite Anadyomene rises from the still waters.

View from the Temple of Zeus across the bay to the Royal Palace, RIALMAR.

The most celebrated room of the palace is the domed Hall of the Sea Horses, built in the shape of a cross. Its walls are panelled with jasper and the columns are of lapis lazuli. At the north end is a stairway of jasper, flanked by two seahorses carved from great blocks of sea-blue rock crystal.

The oldest part of the palace, however, is the Mantichore Gallery. It is lined with long tables and chairs of grey stone streaked with white; the chairs are furnished with silken cushions. The Mantichore Gallery, lit by forty-four hanging lamps, takes its name from a mural depicting the fabled Mantichore, once an inhabitant of the sandy areas of the Wold in the south of Fingiswold, and now found only in BASILISK COUN-

TRY. The Fingiswold Mantichore had the paws and mane of a lion, the rump of a porcupine, a scorpion's tail and, like Pity, a human face.

The palace is approached along a triumphal road which winds up from the marketplace in Rialmar Town, lined with pillars of rose-red marble. On festive nights blazing cressets are placed on these pillars, so that the road resembles the coils of a fire serpent.

It is the custom for the royalty of Fingiswold to go into Rialmar without any escort; the people of the city regard this as a great honour, believing that they are the true guardians of their monarchs.

As the capital of Fingiswold, Rialmar has been associated with some of the most important events in the country's history. It was here that King Mardanus was assassinated, possibly by Aktor, an exile from neighbouring AKKAMA. It was here that Mardanus' son, Mezentius, first drew up his strategy for uniting Fingiswold, REREK and MESZRIA under his rule.

Rialmar has twice fallen to invaders from Akkama. In 770 *Anno Zayanae Conditae,* the city fell to Sagartis of Akkama, who held it until his communication lines were broken; Sagartis himself died in the great battle before Rialmar. After the death of Mezentius in 777, Sagartis' son Derxis captured the city, killing Queen Antiope during the assault, but he was later defeated as he tried to march south into Rerek, and Rialmar was once again freed from its invaders.

(E.R. Eddison, *Mistress of Mistresses, A Vision of Zimiamvia,* London, 1935; E.R. Eddison, *A Fish Dinner in Memison,* London, 1941; E.R. Eddison, *The Mezentian Gate,* London, 1958)

RIGMAROLE, a town in the south of the land of OZ. Like FLUTTERBUDGET CENTER to the north-west, Rigmarole is one of the defensive settlements of Oz. Citizens who prove unable to talk clearly and to the point are sent to Rigmarole, where they live with others of their kind. They all address each other in long, complex speeches in which a great number of words are used but very little is said. They are quite incapable of answering a simple question without rattling off a long discourse.

(L. Frank Baum, *The Emerald City of Oz,* Chicago, 1910)

RINGING ISLAND, four days' sail from GANABIN ISLAND. It is immediately recognizable because as travellers approach it, the air is filled with the sound of ringing bells.

The island is inhabited by the Siticines or Dirge-Singers, originally people who were all changed into birds. The only human resident on Ringing Island is the sacristan, Master Aeditus. The birds live in sumptuous cages, each with a bell above it. The birds themselves are as large as men and behave exactly like men. Some are white, some black, some grey, some black and white, others half white and half blue. A few are red. All are beautiful and sleek. The males are known as clerijays, monajays, priestjays, abbeyjays, bishojays, cardinjays and the popinjay; the females are clergesses, priestjesses, abbeyjesses, bishojesses and cardinogesses. In recent years, the island has suffered from annual migrations of bigots—foul-smelling creatures avoided by all the other birds. In spite of the sacristan's efforts, it seems impossible to exterminate them; for every one that dies, 24 appear.

There is only one popinjay in the island at any one time. All the other birds reproduce, without physical copulation. The clerijays give birth to priestjays and monajays; from the priestjays come the bishojays, who in turn produce grand cardinjays. If death does not intervene, a cardinjay will end up becoming popinjay. When he dies, a successor is produced from among the whole brood of cardinjays, again without physical copulation. The species thus consists of an individual with a perpetuity of succession, rather like the phoenix. In the distant past, two popinjays were once born at the same time and the ensuing civil war almost depopulated the island, as nearly every bird took sides. Although Ringing Island called on the help of the rulers of the earth, the schism did not end until one of the rival popinjays died. It is extremely difficult to catch even a glimpse of the popinjay, who only sings on his "high" days, unlike the other birds, who sing almost continuously.

One of the more curious species is the *gormander,* brightly coloured birds whose plumage changes colour, like the skin of the chameleon. They all bear a mark under their right wing: two diameters cutting a circle at right angles or a perpendicular line meeting a horizontal one. These mongrel birds have a number of rich *gormanderies* or nests throughout the world. They never sing, but eat twice as much as the others to make up for it. There are no female *gormanders* and the birds tend to catch venereal diseases thanks to their habit of haunting the seashore.

The birds of Ringing Island do not work or cultivate the soil; their sole activity is singing. Their abundant food supplies are given to them by all the countries of the world, with the exception of certain kingdoms that lie under the North Wind.

All the birds on the island are birds of passage, originating from other lands, mostly from BREADLESSDAY and TOO-MANY-OF-'EM. The worst, however, come from BOSSARD or Humped Island, where all birds are hump-backed and deformed in various ways. Many are sent here by their parents, because if they remained at home they would be likely to eat up the family inheritance.

Travellers who arrive at Ringing Island at the beginning of any of the four seasons are required to fast for four days before they land. If they refuse to do so, they will be regarded as heretics and risk being burned at the stake. After the fast, they are obliged to spend the next four days feasting and drinking on the island. This enforced four-day stay is largely due to the weather; terrible storms always rage for four days after the arrival of strangers. The sea compensates for this by remaining perfectly calm for seven days before and seven days after the winter solstice, the season when the halcyons, sweet and sacred birds dear to Thetis, come here to lay their eggs.

(François Rabelais, *Le cinquiesme et dernier livre des faicts et dicts du bon Pantagruel, auquel est contenu la visitation de l'Oracle de la dive Bacbuc, et le mot de la bouteille; pour lequel avoir est entrepris tout ce long voyage*, Paris, 1564)

RINGS, an Elfin court in Galloway, southern Scotland. In most respects, Rings is similar to other Elfin courts scattered across Europe. It is, however, the only Elfin realm ever known to have been haunted by a ghost. Although they are very long-lived, elves and fairies are mortal, but do not have souls. When Sir Glamie, the much-respected Lord Chamberlain of Rings, was seen haunting the court after his death, it became apparent that some human blood had flowed in his veins, presumably as a result of a relationship between a fairy and a human at some point in the past. This was in itself cause for scandal, and it was further feared that the appearance of the ghost might raise

all manner of unhealthy speculations about life after death. At first Sir Glamie was seen mainly by the working fairies, and inevitably appeared carrying a fish; he had been an avid fly-fisherman in his lifetime and many of his catches are still kept in glass cases in the North Saloon.

Initially Sir Glamie's ghost was not unpopular, but this phase ended when a fairy came upon it unexpectedly while spring cleaning; the fairy's features froze in a squint of terror which disfigured him forever. From then on, everything that went wrong in Rings was attributed to the ghost. Sir Glamie's last recorded appearance occurred when he intervened in a conversation about ghosts, telling the debaters that they did not know what they were talking about. He then vanished and has not been seen again in the castle, though he sometimes stalks the river bank, his old fishing haunt.

(Sylvia Townsend Warner, *Kingdoms of Elfin*, London, 1972)

RIPPLE LAND, a curious area between the land of the WHIMSIES and the Dominion of the GROWLEYWOGS. Ripple Land is a country of steep rocky hills and valleys which constantly change place and ripple. As the traveller ascends a hillside, he will find that it suddenly sinks beneath him and becomes a valley. Conversely, a traveller going down into a valley will suddenly find that it has risen and that he is now on top of a hill. Those who travel through this perplexing and confusing country often find that the rippling movement of the ground makes them seasick.

(L. Frank Baum, *The Emerald City of Oz*, Chicago, 1910)

RIP VAN WINKLE'S VILLAGE, at the foot of the Catskill Mountains in upper New York State.

The village is of considerable antiquity, founded by some of the earliest Dutch colonists to settle in America. Visitors can still see the quaint yellow brick houses with lattice windows, gable fronts and weathercocks. Near the village, they can admire a small hollow in which the ghosts of Henry Hudson's companions (discoverers of the Hudson River) play ninepins. The sound of their game is said to resemble the noise of thunder on a summer afternoon. Should a visitor be invited to have a drink with the players, the offer should be refused if possible since it will probably produce a deep slumber from which the sleeper will not awake for some twenty years.

Rip Van Winkle, an inhabitant of the village when it was still under British rule, drank with the ancient Dutchmen and slept throughout the entire revolutionary war. He was eventually adopted by his own daughter and ended his days at Mr. Doolittle's hotel, telling his story to anyone who would listen.

(Washington Irving, "Rip Van Winkle," in *The Sketch Book of Geoffrey Crayon, Gent.*, New York, 1819–20)

RISPA, capital of PHILOSOPHY ISLE.

RIVENDELL, a deep sheltered valley on the banks of the Bruinen or Loudwater River on the western side of the MISTY MOUNTAINS of MIDDLE-EARTH. Rivendell is the home of a community of elves and was founded as a refuge during the Second Age, after the destruction of the elven kingdom of HOLLIN. Its founder, Elrond, was still Lord of Rivendell at the end of the Third Age. The original Westron name of Rivendell is Karningul, but it is known to the elves and the Dúnedain as Imladris, meaning "Deep-cloven-valley."

The home of the elves is known as The Last Homely House East of the Sea, so called because it is the eastern-most settlement of the true elves. It is a large building with many passages, stairs and halls, built high above the Bruinen and overlooking sweet-scented gardens. It has a large banqueting room with tapestries on the walls, and also a great Hall of Fire, so named because it has a fine hearth, flanked with carved pillars, where a fire is always kept burning. The Hall of Fire is usually empty and is a place for those desirous of peace and thought, but on high days it is used for the singing of songs of ancient days.

The elves of Rivendell are merrier and more talkative than their relatives who once lived in LÓRIEN. They are good-humoured and enjoy teasing and being teased. Unlike some other elven groups they are also extremely knowledgeable about events in other countries.

The elves were close allies of the Dúnedain, or Men of the West, and gave them great help in time of need. By tradition the Dúnedain chieftains

were brought up here during the years when Sauron's dark forces dominated so much of Middle-earth. One of these, Aragorn, fell in love with Elrond's daughter Arwen. After Sauron's downfall Aragorn became King Elessar of the Reunited Kingdom, and made Arwen his queen.

Elrond himself was a majestic figure with dark hair and grey eyes. It was impossible even to estimate his age, though his face revealed obvious signs of great knowledge and deep memory. He was of elvish and Edain (manly) descent, but had chosen to be counted an elf. Throughout the Third Age, Elrond held one of the Three Elven Rings of Power originally forged in HOLLIN. This was Vilya, Ring of Air, and its presence in Rivendell no doubt helped protect the land from evil.

It was in the safety of Rivendell that the Company or Fellowship of the Ring was first founded. The Company was formed to accompany Frodo the ring bearer as far as possible on his quest to cast the One Ring into the Cracks of Doom and thus break the power of Sauron the Dark Lord. There were nine members in the company: four hobbits from the SHIRE, including Frodo; Aragorn and another man; one dwarf; one elf; and the wizard Gandalf. Together they succeeded in their mission, and the One Ring was destroyed. This was the end of Sauron's dreadful powers. But the elves too lost much of their power, and many of them left Middle-earth forever. Elrond himself departed, sailing west from the GREY HAVENS, and taking Vilya along with him. For love of Aragorn, his daughter Arwen stayed behind and gave up her immortality, a decision that caused Elrond great sorrow.

(J.R.R. Tolkien, *The Hobbit, or There and Back Again*, London, 1937; J.R.R. Tolkien, *The Fellowship of the Ring*, London, 1954; J.R.R. Tolkien, *The Return of the King*, London, 1955; J.R.R. Tolkien, *The Silmarillion*, London, 1977)

RIVER BANK, the name given to the banks of the river that flows past TOAD HALL. The banks of the river are tree-clad, and behind the trees rich water-meadows stretch to the edges of WILD WOOD, with the horizon bounded by the great ring of the Downs. A canal joins the river just upstream from Toad Hall; an island in the river separates the main stream from an inlet on which stands a grey-gabled mill-house. The island itself is fringed with willows and silver birch, but in its centre grows a natural orchard of crab apples, sloe and wild cherry. A strange horned figure is sometimes seen here, playing the pipes, but does not inspire fear so much as a feeling of almost religious calm. (Seasoned travellers will have encountered similar creatures on CAPTAIN SPARROW'S ISLAND.)

River Bank is inhabited by a variety of birds and animals. The birds include dabchicks, kingfishers, moorhens and, of course, ducks. Otters swim in the water, but probably the best-known figure in the area is Mr. Water Rat, who lives in a hole in the bank. His home is comfortable, even though the cellars are often flooded in winter when the river is high and dangerous. Mr. Water Rat is an accomplished boatsman and a close friend of both Mr. Mole of Mole End and Mr. Badger of Wild Wood.

River Bank is a peaceful community, whose inhabitants rarely venture far from home. Although the community does not have any formal system of laws, certain general points of etiquette are observed by all and travellers are advised to adhere to them. For instance, it is against etiquette to make any comment on the sudden disappearance of a friend or acquaintance or to ask for any explanation of such an occurrence. It is also against etiquette to dwell on, or even to allude to, any trouble that may possibly lie ahead. On the whole, the subject of the future is considered indelicate and should be avoided.

(Kenneth Grahame, *The Wind in the Willows*, London, 1908)

ROADTOWN, a city on the outskirts of New York, New York. Roadtown gives the impression of one continuous building, somewhat like a skyscraper lying on its side, running for several hundred miles over the hills west of New York, like the great Wall of China.

Built of cement, it is fire-, vermin- and cyclone-proof, each section two storeys high, with two sets of living quarters per storey. Under these run three storeys of underground railway and all necessary pipes and wires. The railway is noiseless, based on the Boyes Monorail system and on the idea of a horizontal elevator. It consists of short cars whose doors open and shut electrically. The wheels are leather-coated and their grip is such that they can be made of very light materials. Private stairs lead from each home down to the railway or up onto the roof. In the centre of the roof is a covered promenade, in winter enclosed in glass and steam-heated, which serves as a street for recreation and pleasure. Occasional towers break the architectural monotony. The roof is built in such a fashion that promenaders cannot stare down through their neighbours' skylights or listen in to their conversations.

Within the living quarters, no noise can be heard except the singing of birds. Each unit has a hot-water heating system that can be regulated individually, and a *telegraphone*, a telephone that can record a message—commodities that may not seem unfamiliar to the modern-day traveller. The women have no household duties. Most household work is sent out and each member of the family performs his share of the little housework that is left. There is a co-operative laundry (the charge is added to the rent) and a co-operative kitchen: orders can be telephoned and are delivered immediately. The rooms are piped for suction cleaning and the beds are made mechanically. Because the rooms open onto both sides of Roadtown, they are constantly aired.

Roadtown was built in 1893, the result of a dream of an American inventor, Edgar Chambless—who had been left penniless and with no visible future—as he slept on one of the hills around New York.

(Edgar Chambless, *Roadtown*, London & New York, 1910)

ROBINSON CRUSOE'S ISLAND, see CRUSOE'S ISLAND.

ROC or **RUKH, ISLAND OF THE,** a large uninhabited island somewhere in the China Sea, a recommended stopover for gourmets. From a distance the island looks like a gigantic white, shining cupola, over a hundred yards long. But upon approaching the island, travellers will find that the cupola is in fact the visible part of a huge egg laid here by the roc or *rukh*. Those wishing to taste the young bird's flesh must crack open the shell with pick-axes. It is best to take part of the bird on board ship and then eat it at leisure on another island. Otherwise it is possible that both travellers and ship will be attacked by the mother bird, which is known to drop large rocks on intruders. A full-grown roc is three or four times the size of an elephant and it is therefore best not to antagonize it.

Collecting dinner on ROC ISLAND.

Roc's flesh should be lightly roasted with just a pinch of lemon and salt, but can also be used in a variety of dishes instead of turkey or rabbit. It has the added advantage of rejuvenating the man or woman who eats it, making old people's hair turn from white to their natural colour.

(Anonymous, *The Arabian Nights*, 14th–16th cen. AD)

ROCK ISLAND, in the Indian Ocean west of Aprilis Island in the NEW BRITAIN group, so called because of its rocky coasts and mountains. Much of the island is arid and sandy but inland there is a vast grassy plain where the original settlers built a town of single-storey houses. The Ten Commandments are carved on every wall, as is the alphabet. The inhabitants go naked and speak Latin.

(Pierre Chevalier Duplessis, *Mémoires De Sir George Wollap; Ses Voyages dans différentes parties du Monde; aventures extraordinaires qui lui arrivent; découverte de plusieurs Contrées inconnues; description des moeurs & des coutumes des Habitans. Par M.L.C.D.*, Paris, 1787–88)

ROGUES' HARBOUR, see Island of POLY-PRAGMOSYNE.

ROHAN, also called the Riddermark, one of the most important realms of MIDDLE-EARTH. Rohan stretches from the River Isen in the west to the GREAT RIVER in the east. To the north it is bounded by FANGORN and the River Limlight and to the south by the WHITE MOUNTAINS. In the south-east, the Mering Stream and the Mouths of the Entwash mark the frontier between

Rohan and GONDOR. The River Entwash rises in Fangorn and crosses Rohan before emptying into the Great River.

Rohan is a pleasant, generous country of abundant grasslands where its famous horses run free in great herds, unmatched for grace or beauty. It is divided into several regions. In the north, Westemnet and Eastemnet lie on either side of the Entwash. Westemnet is flat and treeless, with great plains that stretch for mile after mile; in places, the grass is waist high, and it is dangerous ground to cross, as the swaying grass conceals many treacherous pools and bogs. The main path to the north crosses the Eastemnet, where the ground is surer and more firm. To the south, along the White Mountains, lies the Eastfold Vale. The Westfold Vale is the area between the White Mountains and the River Isen, and is ruled by the Master of Westfold Vale who normally resides at the Hornburg, the great citadel which defends the entrance to HELM'S DEEP. In the extreme east, past the Great River, the grasslands give way to the arid Brown Lands. The capital of the kingdom is at EDORAS, a citadel on the banks of the Snowbourn at the foot of the White Mountains. This is probably the most populous area of the kingdom and is the homeland of the ruling family.

The Rohirrim, or men of Rohan, are a proud strong-willed people, famed for their generosity, trustworthiness and courage. Their physical appearance matches their character; they are tall, with strong keen faces, and wear their hair in long braids that hang down their backs. The Riders of Rohan, the famed horsemen of the country, dress in light knee-length coats of mail and wear light helms. They ride to war armed with a variety of weapons, with bows and arrows, spears and swords at their sides. Their painted shields are carried on their shoulders. They are as renowned for their horsemanship as for their swift horses—large strong animals with shining grey coats and long manes. The most splendid horses of all Rohan are the Mearas, and as a rule they allow none but royalty to ride them. Legend tells of the first of the Mearas, Felaróf. When Felaróf was a foal, he was captured by Léod, a lord of the country and a great tamer of horses. When he had grown, Léod attempted to ride him, and the horse bolted and carried the man to his death. Then Eorl, son of Léod, hunted Felaróf down and demanded that he forfeit his freedom to atone for the death. The horse understood and submitted; from that time on he was

Eorl's steed, obeying his words and needing neither bridle nor bit. Eorl became king and the descendants of Felaróf served the kings of Rohan thereafter. During the reign of Théoden the chief of the Mearas was Shadowfax, a beautiful silver animal of extraordinary speed and endurance who gave great service during the War of the Ring by becoming the mount of the wizard Gandalf.

The Rohirrim are kinsmen of the Beornings of the Vale of ANDUIN, and of the men who live to the west of MIRKWOOD. They have long been staunch allies of GONDOR and were granted their present lands, formerly a province of Gondor known as Calenardhon, for their loyal service in the wars between Gondor and the aggressive Easterlings from RHÛN. Gondor had long been troubled by raids and incursions from the east, but with the help of the Rohirrim a decisive victory was gained at the Battle of the Field of CELEBRANT. Under Eorl the Young, the Rohirrim, which literally means "horse-lords," settled in their present home, raising their horses on the green plains and rebuilding the fortresses at DUNHARROW and Helm's Deep.

The old alliance between Rohan and Gondor was never broken and the Horse Lords played a vital role in the Great War of the Ring which affected all of Middle-earth. Early in the war, members of the Fellowship of the Ring were helped by the Rohirrim. But Rohan was itself threatened by the forces of evil at this time. Théoden had come under the baneful influence of the wizard Saruman, then based in ISENGARD. Through his servant Gríma, or Wormtongue, Saruman persuaded Théoden that he was too old and infirm to do battle and that a purely defensive strategy was all that was needed to defend Rohan. The influence of Gríma was finally overcome by that of Gandalf, and Théoden reasserted his authority just in time. Together with some members of the Fellowship of the Ring, he mustered his forces in Helm's Deep, where a crushing defeat was inflicted on Saruman's forces. Later in the war, the men of MINAS TIRITH requested help against the forces of MORDOR and Théoden and the Rohirrim rode at speed and joined battle on the Fields of PELENNOR, where Théoden fell.

Like all the kings of Rohan, Théoden was buried in traditional manner at the foot of the hill on which Edoras is built. The seventeen great barrows of the kings are on the eastern bank of the Snowbourn. The barrows are covered with small white flowers called *simbelmynë*, meaning "Ever-mind" and referring both to the place where they grow and to the fact that they flower all year long. The warriors of Rohan are also buried in barrows; the bodies of their enemies are, however, despoiled and then burnt.

The Rohirrim have their own language (Rohirric) but the Lords normally speak Westron, the common language of Middle-earth, and few phrases of their native tongue have been recorded. Few outside Rohan speak their language.

Rohan does not have a written language and its culture consists mainly of songs and ballads, celebrating the heroes of the past and their deeds, such as the great ride of the Rohirrim to Minas Tirith. Other songs tell how Fram led them to Eothéod, the area in which they lived before settling in Rohan itself, and of Fram's victory over Scatha, the dragon of the GREY MOUNTAINS. It is said that this led to the long-lived enmity between the dwarves and the men of Eothéod, as Fram refused to recognize their claim to the dragon's hoard. The Rohirrim's knowledge of the rest of Middle-earth appears to derive from their ancient songs. They were, for instance, astonished to see that the Company of the Ring included hobbits from the SHIRE. They had previously believed that hobbits, or Halflings as they called them, were legendary creatures, existing only in the songs of the past.

The standard of Rohan is the emblem of the House of Eorl, a white horse on a field of plain green.

(J.R.R. Tolkien, *The Fellowship of the Ring*, London, 1954; J.R.R. Tolkien, *The Two Towers*, London, 1954; J.R.R. Tolkien, *The Return of the King*, London, 1955)

ROKE, an important island in the centre of the Inmost Sea of EARTHSEA. Roke is the very heart of Earthsea, the place where the mages essential to the archipelago's life are trained. The island is not an important trading centre, although much of the business of the archipelago is carried out in the island's port of Thwil.

The port is small, little more than a huddle of steep streets leading up from the harbour to a square surrounded on three sides by tall houses. The fourth side is occupied by the wall of a building made of great stone blocks. This is the School of Roke, the magical centre of Earthsea. So accustomed are the people of Roke to the magic that is

taught here that they are all a little magic themselves. They do not even blink an eye at the sight of a boy transforming himself into a fish, or a house flying up into the air, knowing full well that it is merely another prank by a high-spirited apprentice sorcerer. Even the weather on the island is controlled by magic, the work of a mage known as Master Windkey. The waters around Roke are charmed and remain calm, no matter what storms may be raging elsewhere in the Inmost Sea. The famed Roke Wind protects the island from evil powers and keeps it calm and peaceful.

Roke is ruled by the Archmage, the greatest wizard in Earthsea. He is accountable to none but the King of all the Isles, and even that by his own consent. His colleagues are the Masters of Roke, who are the equals of the great lords and princes of Earthsea. The Masters are at once practitioners and teachers of the art of magic, each with his own special domain and skill: Master Doorkeeper, Master Windkey, Master Namer (who specializes in the study of Old Speech, the language of dragons), Master Herbal, Master Changer (who teaches the art of real change), Master Patterner, Master Summoner (a specialist in the art of summoning the creatures of the world by their names), Master Chanter and Master Hand (who specializes in spells of illusion, as opposed to real change). The Masters are accountable only to themselves and to the Archmage. On the death of the ruling Archmage, a successor is elected from among these Masters.

Essentially, magic is concerned with the concept of balance or equilibrium. At its simplest this means that all things must be kept in balance and the overall effect of any spell must be considered. Thus a spell that brings rain to one island may bring drought to another. A calm in one area of the sea may result in a storm elsewhere. The magic taught on Roke is not an art that gives power to individuals as such; ultimately the true mage is not one who acts from desire or from a wish for power, but one who acts to retain balance and does only what is necessary.

Those who come to study on Roke are usually recommended by other mages, but some come here on their own. However, the School can be entered only by those who have the power to do so and it is said that no man comes to Roke by chance; the people of Thwil usually refuse to give strangers directions to the School, explaining that the wise do not need to ask the way and that a fool asks in vain. The threshold of the School cannot be crossed by one who is not destined to be a mage; no apprentice can leave unless he has permission or has completed his training. From the outside the door appears to be of plain wood. Only from the inside can its true nature be seen; it is carved from the seamless ivory of a dragon's tooth. Beyond lies the Court of the Fountain, where new apprentices are met by the Archmage and where they swear their loyalty to him. The School itself is not luxurious; the pupils lead a plain life and sleep on rough mattresses in unlit stone cells. The Roke community is male-dominated and it is rare for women to sit in its halls or to be invited to one of its feasts. Even then, many of the older Masters seem to disapprove of their presence.

The training of a mage takes a long time. As a novice, the pupil learns the basic arts he will practise later: sailing by using the magic wind and by speaking the commands to the boat, studying the lore and songs of the past and learning the lesser arts of shape changing and illusion. When he has completed his novicehood, he receives a silver clasp for his cloak to denote his new status. Then begins the study for his staff, the staff being the mage's badge of office and his greatest magical weapon. Novices are usually high-spirited, taking great pleasure in minor spells of illusion and creating the *were-light*, a soft moving light created by spells. By the time they have their silver clasps they are usually calm reserved men, unwilling to use their skills when there is no necessity to do so. After completing their training the mages go out into the world. Some go to work at the courts of the great lords of the islands, others become wanderers who pay for their keep by performing magic and for their passage on ships by controlling the weather or steering the vessel by magic.

Apart from the School, there are two important sites on Roke. One is Roke Knoll, a grassy hill which is said to have been the first land to rise above the sea; it is also said that it will be the last land to sink beneath the waves when the world ends. The other is the Immanent Grove, the meeting-place for the Masters when some important matter is at hand. It is here that they gather to elect the Archmage; at such times nine walls of silence protect the Grove. The Grove always appears to be moving, to have no fixed site, yet a path always leads directly to it. Some say that it is time and the world that become awry around the path and the Grove, and that these in fact always re-

main still. The trees in the Grove have massive grey trunks which are nameless in the Hardic tongue of the archipelago.

Roke and some of the islands in the south are the only places in Earthsea where the *otak* is found. The *otak* is a small mammal with sleek dark brown fur and bright eyes. It has no call or cry and is a vicious little animal, living mainly on mice. *Otaks* are rarely kept as pets. The *ender* falcon is also found on Roke: it is a brown and white barred fishing-hawk, distinguishable from the sparrow-hawk by its greater size and its yellow claws.

(Ursula K. Le Guin, *A Wizard of Earthsea*, New York, 1968; Ursula K. Le Guin, *The Tombs of Atuan*, London, 1972; Ursula K. Le Guin, *The Farthest Shore*, London, 1973)

ROMANCIA, a walled kingdom extending from the Troximania Mountains to the coast. There are various routes of access, all relatively easy, as passports and letters of privilege are never examined closely: by land via a subterranean passage entered through a cave in the mountains, descending directly from the moon or from the stars, or by sea. All the visitor has to do is set out and keep going until he arrives in Romancia. The wall around the kingdom has several gates; legend has it that travellers who enter by the Gate of Love leave by the Gate of Marriage.

Romancia was formerly one country, reputed to be the most beautiful in the world and populated by princes, fairies and heroes, but a Lower Romancia had to be established with the arrival of numerous persons of lesser social stature, while the aristocracy remained in Upper Romancia. Travellers should note that though Lower Romancia is becoming more and more populous, the inhabitants of Upper Romancia are emigrating and the fairies and genii of the past are gone forever. There are only two enchanted castles left, the Castle of Fairy Camalouca and the Castle of Fairy Curiaca, both located near the Forest of Adventures—so called because no one ever passes through it without having an adventure. All newcomers must visit this if they wish to become naturalized citizens of Romancia.

Travellers to Upper Romancia will find the climate perfect; the air is so pure and so nutritious there is no need to eat. The two main foods of this area are air and love.

The landscape is a mosaic of hills, woods and

The Castle of Camalouca, ROMANCIA.

orchards where streams are of milk and honey and where rivers, filled with multicoloured fish and precious stones, wander across plains of fine grass. The rocks of Romancia become sensitive and soft when they hear the lamentations of a disappointed lover. This sometimes occurs, for love and courtship are governed by a strict code which includes thirty-six preliminary formalities and the laws forbid the marriage of those who have not gone through all the established stages and trials. Woods of love, planted with myrtles, palms, orange trees and groundcover of roses and violets, enhanced with the songs of birds, are scattered throughout the land for the convenience of lovers; but woods of jealousy, quarrels and false declarations also exist. Musically inclined trees, eternally green, are the home of dryads and fauns, while flowers such as the lotus and moly are plentiful and spring from the footsteps of beautiful women, who create gardens wherever they walk.

The fauna of Romancia includes talking lions, tigers and bears; flying horses and unicorns are common and gryphons and hippogryphs can easily be tamed. Hornless bulls, three-headed dogs,

cats in boots, multilingual parrots, flame-coloured crows, white blackbirds, centaurs, phoenixes, singing swans and giant grasshoppers (which are used for transport) all abound. *Hirococervi* and chimeras are kept in menageries near a pit of fire filled with salamanders; a pleasant pool of water serves as a prison for sirens who have debauched heroes with their singing.

Romancia has a port and a town. From the port, ships go out into the rest of the world, bearing the heroes and heroines who still live in Upper Romancia in search of new adventures. The traders and craftsmen of Lower Romancia make the town a fascinating place in which to browse. Each trade has its own street and the visitor may be tempted to linger in the Street of the Magic-Lantern Makers, or the Street of Blowers where craftsmen take bits of nothing and blow them up into something enormous, or the Street of the Darners where old things are made to look like new.

All the inhabitants of Upper and Lower Romancia are young, healthy and very beautiful. Their conversation is full of wit; they speak all the modern and ancient tongues and are accomplished artists and athletes. Any visitor wishing to improve his looks should visit Romancia, for whoever travels here will become as beautiful as its inhabitants. However, it should be noted that both the people of LILLIPUT and the people of BROBDINGNAG settled here temporarily but did not find the land congenial and were forced to leave.

(Guillaume H. Bougeant, *Voyage Merveilleux du Prince-Fan-Férédin dans la Romancie; Contenant Plusieurs Observations Historiques, Géographiques, Physiques, Critiques et Morales,* Paris, 1735)

ROMAN STATE lies beneath Northern England, around a subterranean sea at least three hundred miles wide. Settlements are scattered along the western shore, or wherever fresh water can be found. This inhabited area is surrounded by barren land and marshes which stretch to the foot of the mountains supporting their roof—the earth's surface. To the north, the sea is bounded by a great cliff.

The settlements and cities contain no houses in the accepted sense of the word, but simply enclosures surrounded by hedges and furnished with benches. The only substantial buildings are the bath-houses, which are walled but roofless. The baths are dug out of the stone floors and there are basins with running water along the walls. The bath-houses themselves back onto large enclosures with couches for sleeping. Cities and settlements are divided into large compounds, each assigned to a particular trade or industry. As far as possible, each compound is self-sufficient.

The Roman State is based upon the total submission of the individual to the State, a system which appears to have arisen from the people's fear of the surrounding darkness. Everything that is not essential to the survival of the State and the race has been suppressed; physical violence or rebellion has been rendered impossible. Reduced by fear and hypnotism to automatons with blank eyes, the majority of the people have no volition other than that granted to them by the State which is controlled by the all-powerful Masters of Knowledge who can be recognized by their powerful hypnotic stare. The educational system is designed to produce this condition in the masses. The task of teachers is to destroy the vitality and intellectual curiosity of children, using low-pitched music and rhythmic dancing to produce an hypnotic state in which the individual will can be destroyed. Children are taught the absolute minimum required for the work they will do in later life, because, according to the Masters of Knowledge, unnecessary knowledge is as poisonous as poisonous food. By the time they are sixteen, pupils are almost totally dehumanized and begin to undergo training for their future work. They are also trained in thought-transmission, which has replaced speech; only children and the feeble-minded continue to use language, a form of Latin. In the final stages of education, the mind is vivisected, certain tendencies reinforced and others totally eradicated. Every person is thereby led to believe that their country is a perfect community, based on faith, love and joy. Future teachers are trained in mind-vivisection and hypnosis, using younger children as guinea pigs for their experiments. The people of the Roman State continue to serve the State even after their death; their bodies are used as fuel for the furnaces of the industrial compounds. Work continues twenty-four hours a day on a shift system. Each compound and branch of industry is under the control of a skilled craftsman with strong hypnotic powers. Time is measured by water clocks and the Julian Calendar is used.

In stark contrast to the sophistication of its mind control, the Roman State's industry remains primitive and continues to use the tools and methods of antiquity. The only known trades are woodwork, metalwork, weaving, pottery and shipbuilding. Glass is unknown. All transport is by water, either by slow, heavy barges or by many-oared galleys of classical design. Cloth is woven from the silk spun by huge spiders bred for the purpose and kept in large iron enclosures. The spiders are fearsome animals and no one dares enter the enclosures. (These creatures are probably related to the one seen in PAUK.) A coarser cloth is made from the bark of a bush and from long seaweed-like stalks found in the marshy areas. All spinning and weaving is carried out by women. Snake farms provide a large part of the food consumed in the State. Unlike the spiders, the snakes are kept under hypnosis and actually seem to be fond of their keepers. The diet of snake meat is supplemented by the produce of fungus farms, and by lizards and fish caught in the salt sea, as well as marine plants and seaweeds.

The origin of the Roman State remains a mystery, although the clothes, language and ships suggest that the people are descended from Romans.

There are two means of access to this subterranean State. It can be reached from the bottom of a disused mine shaft dating back to Roman times, or through a trapdoor or flagstone hidden at the base of Hadrian's Wall (Northumberland). Both entrances lead to the summit of the underground mountain. The entrance from the mine leads from the summit to a wall that bars the only pass through the northern cliffs, guarded by a Roman settlement. The alternative route begins from Julian's Pond (a farm near Hadrian's Wall) and leads to the underground summit and then on through mountain gorges to a river. The river flows through phosphorescent marshes and under a rock vault before reaching the central sea. As the traveller descends, he or she will pass through regions where the vegetation is much richer than that found elsewhere underground. In the higher areas the vegetation is made up of small fungi with phosphorescent caps that smell of garlic, mingled with a seaweed-like plant with trailing red stems. If the fruit of the plant is squeezed, a red juice spurts out; its use is unknown. This zone eventually gives way to bushes with oily stems, again resembling seaweed rather than any earthly flora. The lower mountain gorges are clad in forests with seaweed-like trees and giant fungi up to one hundred feet high with inverted green phosphorescent caps. Similar plants are used to provide light in the Roman State itself. The forests are inhabited by a variety of animals. Large tree-lizards live in the high branches, and slugs the size of rabbits cling to the fiery rocks; both are edible. Huge toads and land-lizards lurk in damp places. Great crabs, tentacled creatures and clumsy beasts rather like seals are found in the sea and its marshy fringes. The most dangerous animal is the silk-producing spider, as large as a lion, which moves very rapidly on its long stilt-like legs. The head is like a leather bag, with staring, multifacetted eyes. Cords dangle from its mouth and can be flung out like a lasso to catch prey.

Visitors to this underground country are reminded that the Roman State considers that anyone who comes here does so freely and will therefore consent to be literally absorbed into it by having his mind destroyed and re-created. No one may leave without permission from the State. Such permission is never granted.

(Joseph O'Neill, *Land Under England*, London, 1935)

ROME, capital of the Edomite Empire (not to be confused with Rome, capital of Italy). Visitors are advised to travel to Rome simply in order to see the huge tower of indescribable beauty which stands in the very centre of the city. The tower has four portals, bolted and locked, facing the four sides of the world. An ancient custom has it that each new Edomite emperor, as soon as he is crowned, must hang a new lock on each portal. Once the visitor has succeeded in removing the many locks, he will find behind each portal a strange magical scene. Behind the first one, he will see a huge garden filled with pleasant trees, in which lies a pool of blood. On the surface of the pool floats an iron crown and around it many clutching human hands, entangled like a young grove. Behind the second portal, the visitor will see nothing but darkness, but beneath his feet he will feel a mass of warm human bodies. Suddenly, a host of candles will burst into flame and the place will become as bright as day. He will then realize he has been standing in a Jewish temple. The bodies, which had been lying as dead, will awake and begin to pray, sparks flying from their lips. Angels, carrying in their wings a splendid man in white garments, will float down towards the visitor. Finally, the people will fall to the ground as dead, the

candles will go out and the temple will be filled with darkness again. Behind the third portal, the visitor will find a wondrously carved golden casket, filled with blades of grass bound in sheaves of ten, still green and fragrant. Behind the fourth and last portal, the visitor will discover a palace of red marble with rooms decorated in gold, silver, pearls and precious stones. In order to understand the meaning of these scenes, the visitor is advised to consult a star-gazer of his choice. Should the star-gazer advise the visitor to enter the chamber behind the third portal, open the lid of the casket and separate the leaves of grass bound in sheaves, the visitor is warned not to heed his suggestion. A certain Edomite emperor followed this suggestion and was attacked by a two-headed calf which, letting out a deafening bellow very much like the roar of a lion, frightened the monarch to death.

(An-Ski [Solomon Samuel Rappaport], *Gesamelte Shriften*, Warsaw, 1925)

ROMINTEN, a reserve situated in Eastern Prussia and covering an area of 25,000 hectares.

Administered by the Oberforstmeister, this vast forested domain was the private hunting reserve of the "Great Huntsman" of the Third Reich, Field Marshal Hermann Goering. Tourists can still visit his hunting lodge, the Jägerhof, which consists of a series of low-lying buildings surrounding an interior courtyard. Behind the austere façade is a luxurious decor. A roughly hewn dayroom houses an enormous stone fireplace, and each guestroom is panelled with a different kind of wood: ash, elm, oak.... Nearby is the hunting lodge of Wilhelm II, a curious wooden castle that looks like a combination of a Chinese pagoda and a Swiss chalet. Next to it stands a chapel dedicated to St. Hubert, and a life-size, bronze stag by the sculptor Richard Freise.

In the days when lavish hunting parties were given by the "Great Huntsman," the countryside was inhabited by packs of wolves and herds of aurochs, an extinct species brought back to life by Dr. Lutz, director of the Berlin Zoo, by crossing bulls from Spain, the Camargue and Corsica. Packs of wild boar ravaged the surrounding farms. But the king of the animals of Rominten—and Goering's favourite quarry—was the ten-point stag.

A certain Abel Tiffauges, who lived on the reserve for some time during the last war, reports that he entered this place as though it were a circle of fairies, in which he expected to see fantastical creatures appear.

(Michel Tournier, *Le Roi des Aulnes,* Paris, 1970)

RONCADOR, a republic in South America, at the intersection of Argentina, Paraguay and Brazil. After a long spell of Spanish rule, Roncador achieved its independence on the first Sunday of April, 1839, when a group of Jacobins, led by an Englishman called Oliver, assassinated the dictator of Roncador during the Festivity of the Blessing of the Tithes. Oliver became Dr. Olivero, dictator of Roncador, and established an egalitarian system of government based on the doctrines of Rousseau, Volney and Voltaire. The Provisional Ordinance of Government, written by Oliver himself, begins with the following words: "All men being endowed by Universal Providence with the same faculties, the same sensations and the same needs, by this very fact it was intended by Providence that they should have a right to an equal share of the earth's bounty. Since the bounty is sufficient for all needs, it follows that all men can exist in equal liberty, each the master of his own destiny."

Marriage between Spaniards was forbidden in order to ensure the assimilation of all foreign elements. A number of labour days were set aside, some for the workers and others for the State. The surplus for the State was exchanged against the produce of the mechanical arts: for instance, a shoemaker would exchange, at a fixed rate, a pair

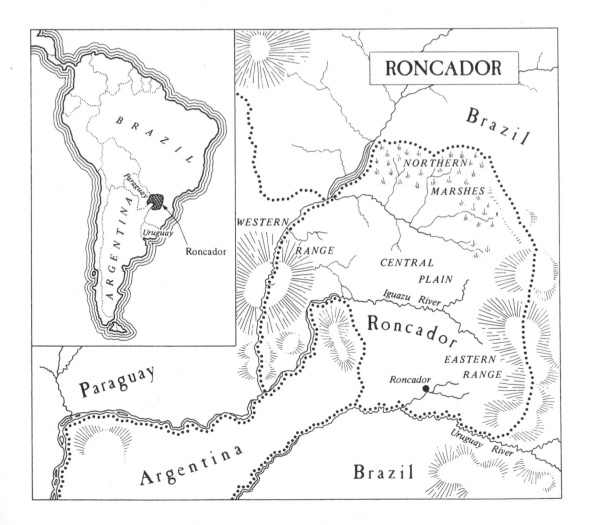

of shoes against so much tea, tobacco or corn. Men and women lived in a relationship of mutual confidence, cultivating the earth and living happily on the abundance of its fruits. When it became apparent to Oliver that his ideal State would fail due to the cupidity of others, he planned his own assassination and pretended to die on a bridge. He was succeeded by General Iturbide. Oliver returned to England and finally did die in the underwater country of GREEN LAND.

Roncador is one of the smallest of the former Spanish provinces in South America, spreading over thirty thousand square miles. It consists of a high, upland plateau, about the same size as Ireland, crossed by many streams that have their sources in the western ranges; they spread over the marshy region in the north and gather to join the powerful river which forms the frontier with Argentina. The east and west borders are mountainous and uninhabited; the central plains or pampas also support little human life—villages are confined to the river basin.

The capital is also called Roncador. It consists of a central square, from each corner of which two streets branch off at right angles. The capital is situated on the slopes and the top of a semi-circular mound, actually the escarpment of a plain, round the foot of which flows a river. The cathedral is almost three hundred years old and was built by the Jesuits. Its façade is a perversion of the baroque style, an enormous baldaquin in stone and stucco, to which is attached a wooden portico flanked by spiralling columns and surmounted, in a niche which is a veritable crows-nest of fantastic metal ornament, by a life-sized figure of the Virgin of the Assumption. A flight of about a dozen steps leads down to the level of the square. Two other buildings, one to each side of the cathedral, are also notable: the barracks (now probably the Ministry of War) and the *Ayuntamiento* or Town Hall.

Roncador exports hides, *yerba mate,* sugar and tobacco. It is also famous for its many species of humming-birds, variously coloured.

One interesting reference book about the early history of Roncador is the *Memoria sobre las Misiones* by Paî Lorenzo.

(Herbert Read, *The Green Child,* London, 1935)

RONDISLE, an island in the Indian Ocean. The capital is in the shape of a large circle, nine miles round, with houses set along the edge. The circle is quartered by lines of trees; the area in between is grassed. In the centre rises a round, bamboo temple approached by a flight of one hundred and twenty stone steps, leading to its four entrances. Throughout the island are other small towns built according to the same pattern, and small heated buildings used as saunas.

Rondisle is a republic governed by one hundred chieftains. The people are generous and hospitable, fond of laughter, and make a stay on this island an almost certain cure for spleen. They speak a mixture of Portuguese and French and use various gestures to indicate their state of mind. Friendship is demonstrated by inserting a finger in another person's ear, happiness or pleasure by spitting into the other person's hand and snapping one's fingers. Children are brought up by elders who keep them until puberty. They walk about naked to accustom themselves to the changes of climate and only dress when going into town.

The funeral rite on Rondisle is an interesting ceremony. The naked body is placed on a platform supported by bamboo poles. Friends and relatives come to recite the virtues of the dead person and leave sticks that will later form part of the funeral pyre. The greater the person's virtues, the larger the quantity of sticks. The body is cremated outside the town, amid the screams of the mourners who fling themselves face down on the ground. Once the body has been consumed by the flames, the guests dance around the ashes, laughing.

(Pierre Chevalier Duplessis, *Mémoires De Sir George Wollap; Ses Voyages dans différentes parties du Monde; aventures extraordinaires qui lui arrivent; découverte de plusieurs Contrées inconnues; description des moeurs & des coutumes des Habitans. Par M.L.C.D.,* Paris, 1787–88)

ROOTABAGA COUNTRY, on the other side of BALLOON PICKER'S COUNTRY, to which it is connected by rail. The traveller who comes here by train will know that he is approaching his destination when the railway lines cease being straight and change to zigzags, like one letter *Z* placed next to another. This is the work of the *zizzies,* a species of bug which do everything in zigzags and never move in a straight line; they have twisted all the railway tracks into their present shape and all attempts to straighten them have failed. Every time they have been straightened, the *zizzies* have returned to bend them. The second indication that one is approaching Rootabaga Country is that all the pigs seen from the train wear bibs. Striped pigs wear striped bibs, polka-dot pigs polka-dot bibs and checkered pigs checkered bibs.

The main town in Rootabaga Country is the village of LIVER AND ONIONS, and probably next in importance is the village of CREAM PUFFS, followed by the village of HAT PINS, the centre of the country's hat-pin industry. Most of the land is used for agricultural purposes, the main crops being rootabagas and corn, which is grown in the upland prairies of the west. There is only one major river in the country, the Shampoo River; the Lake of BOOMING ROLLERS is the major expanse of water. According to the laws of Rootabaga Country, any girl who crosses the Shampoo River is turned into a pigeon and remains a pigeon until she decides to come back.

In Rootabaga Country the squirrels carry ladders and wildcats ask riddles. Fish are seen jumping out of the rivers to talk to frying-pans and children are cared for by baboons; black cats habitually wear orange and gold stockings. Magic is a normal part of life and strange events are not uncommon. To take only one example, in the village of Cream Puffs the cigar store is surmounted by a wooden figure of an Indian and the haberdashery store by a great Shaghorn Buffalo. At night the two figures step down from their stands, the Indian mounts the buffalo and the two ride off into the prairies, returning to their normal positions before dawn.

In the gardens of Rootabaga Country, necktie poppies are very common. A wide variety of colours and patterns can be found; the men of the country pick them before going into town for the day.

Of all the animals in the country, the most curious are the rust-eating rats, which are best observed at THUMBS UP; blue rats are also found here. In general, rats are quite well-liked in this country, probably because some of them once rescued the founders of the village of Cream Puffs from almost certain death in a blizzard on the prairies. Among the bird species, the best-known are the *gladdy-whingers*, which lay their spotted eggs in basket nests in the *booblow* tree, and the *flummywisters*, a type of songbird usually seen in elm trees. In winter the young *flummywisters* wear warm underwear; to hear them singing as their mothers loosen their buttons in spring is a very good omen. It is one of the peculiarities of the

country that the spiders—or at least the female spiders—always wear frying-pans on their heads when they want a hat. New styles of frying-pan are introduced every spring and every autumn. The twisted-nose spiders, often found in clumps of pink grass, are well-known for the parasols they make from the grass. Their parasols are never sold, but the spiders will lend them to needy travellers; eventually the borrowed parasols become lost and make their own way back to the spiders. In one valley of Rootabaga Country, the peacocks cry when it is about to rain and the frogs gamble with golden dice until well after midnight.

(Carl Sandburg, *Rootabaga Stories*, New York, 1922)

ROSE, a completely pink island that is difficult to find—discovered by Captain Slaughterboard, first master (after God) aboard the *Black Tiger*, a pirate vessel sailing the Seven Seas.

Rose is famous for its unusual fauna. The *balleron* has a wooden spine. The *dignipomp* looks incredibly solemn. The *musterach is* very sensitive and sullen. The *guggaflop* is very, very, indeed *very* lazy. At the bottom of the island's waters, among the sponges, starfish, fish and pearls, lives the *plummet*, who is kept up to date about what is happening on earth by the *sleeka* and his son, who always keep their heads above water.

On his first trip to Rose Island, Captain Slaughterboard captured and brought aboard his vessel an elf, the Yellow Creature, with whom he resumed his adventures on the high seas. Today the crew of the *Black Tiger* has disbanded—those crewmembers, that is, who did not die in combat. The captain has again dropped anchor off the shore of the island, and he lives there with the Yellow Creature, who cooks him excellent little meals from nothing at all, and goes fishing with him for fabulous fish.

(Mervyn Peake, *Captain Slaughterboard Drops Anchor*, London, 1939)

ROSSUM'S ISLAND, of uncertain location, perhaps off the east coast of the United States. In 1920 the great physiologist known as Old Rossum came here to study the ocean fauna. He attempted to create living protoplasm by chemical synthesis and in 1932 did, in fact, discover a substance that behaves like protoplasm. Old Rossum then set up

Entrance to the R.U.R. factory on ROSSUM'S ISLAND.

tional Robot Organization at Le Havre as one of their first independent acts.

Rossum's Universal Robots factory still stands. Apart from the factory, there are several offices, private quarters and a music room. The central office has large windows which look out onto rows of factory chimneys. It is decorated with splendid Turkish carpets, a sofa and leather armchairs.

Three ships connect Rossum's harbour with the mainland: the *Amelia,* the *Ultimus* and the *Pennsylvania* (reported to be the best).

(Karel Ĉapek, *R.U.R.,* New York, 1923)

ROTUNDIA, an island-kingdom off the coast of Britain, famed for the good nature of its inhabitants. Evil spells have never worked here and simply run off the islanders like water off a duck's back.

Travellers are advised to visit a tall pinnacle of rock, usually referred to as The Pillar, in the centre of the island. The Pillar is said to be as old as the world itself. According to one theory, as the elements that make up the earth spun round and round trying to settle in their rightful places, a piece of soil was flung out of the seething mass and became impaled on a spear of rock that had already hardened. The impact was so great that the piece of soil began to spin as well—but in the opposite direction to the rest of the world. Finally the piece fell into the sea and the rock spear sank into a hole in the sea-bed, leaving only the top visible. Millions of years later, this circular island became the Kingdom of Rotundia.

The accidental formation of the island had a strange effect on its flora and fauna. All the animals in the kingdom were the wrong size: the guinea-pig kept in the Zoological Gardens was large enough to carry twenty children on its back at one time, while the elephants were smaller than lap dogs and were kept as pets. The inhabitants, however, have always been of normal size, as they did not settle here until after the Norman Conquest. For centuries their life was governed by the peculiar conditions under which they lived; the gigantic rabbits, for instance, dug burrows the size of railway tunnels, and it was impossible to hear oneself speak when the island's only dog was barking. A further consequence of Rotundia's strange origin was that foodstuffs such as buns and cakes grew on trees, whereas vegetables and fruit had to be made by the cooks.

a factory to produce artificial human beings which he called "robots."

The robots were, after a time, able to achieve independence of a kind, and formed the First Na-

Conditions on Rotundia were changed by the arrival of a purple dragon which, in colliding with The Pillar, damaged one of its wings. At first the dragon was quite popular, but when it began to wander around the island both animals and people started to disappear. This gave the court magician, the only evil person on Rotundia, the notion that he could use the dragon to destroy his niece, Princess Mary Anne, and take over the kingdom, and he promptly suggested that she be given to the dragon as a birthday present. The scheme was thwarted by the princess' friend Tom, who tied the dragon's tail to The Pillar, telling the beast that it could have the princess only if it could catch her. Running around in circles, the dragon wound itself around The Pillar and then tried to fly away. The force was such that the island began to spin like a top but this time in the right direction, and the animals changed size.

Visitors to Rotundia will find that guinea-pigs, rabbits and elephants are now the same size as in other countries. The dragon became a small purple newt and the magician a pygmy. Both can be seen today in the Rotundia Zoological Gardens.

(Edith Nesbit, *Uncle James*, London, 1899)

ROUND VALLEY, a circular wooded valley in Wales. The only buildings in the valley are a number of black houses inhabited by a race of giants, the vassals of a grey-bearded colossus. Many of the valley's inhabitants were killed by Peredur, son of Eurawx of the North and one of the knights of the round table of CAMELOT. Having overcome many of his vassals, Peredur convinced the grey-bearded giant to surrender and go to Camelot to be baptized.

(Anonymous, *The Mabinogion*, 14th–15th cen. AD)

RUACH, also known as WINDY ISLAND, two days' sail from SAVAGE ISLAND. The inhabitants of Ruach live on wind, which is all they eat or drink. They live in weather-cocks and plant only anemones or windflowers in their gardens. For nourishment, the poorer people use fans made of paper, cloth or feathers, depending upon their means and tastes; the rich live on windmills. During feasts or banquets they set up their tables beneath these windmills and spend hours discussing the various qualities of different winds, in much the same way as guests at a dinner party in other countries will discuss the quality of the wine. When

they travel they take bellows with them to blow up a fresh wind should the natural one fail them.

Draughts of air are used to treat the sick. All the people of Ruach eventually die of dropsy or tympanites and they all fart as they die, the men loudly and the women softly. They suffer from a wide variety of diseases, all originating from flatulence, but the most feared disease on Ruach is windy colic, treated by drawing as much wind as possible into large cupping glasses. Several terrible diseases have been cured by the original wind given to Ulysses by King Aiolos (see AIOLIO) and preserved like the Holy Grail itself by the King of Ruach.

(François Rabelais, *Le quart livre des faicts et dicts du bon Pantagruel,* Paris, 1552)

RUFFAL, a country near the North Pole. The best way to reach it is by letting one's ship be trapped by the Arctic ice; transformed into an iceberg, it will drift towards the north and eventually reach Ruffal. The inhabitants of Ruffal live underground and share everything they have. They all work except the king, who is entitled to a tenth of the produce to keep himself, his family, his soldiers and the poor.

There are four main cities in Ruffal. The capital is Cambul, well lit and well aired, with straight streets and an excellent system of sewers. Travellers should visit the Royal Palace and the celebrated University of Cambul. It is here, at the University Library, that the volumes known as the *History of Ruffal* are preserved, wherein is told how the inhabitants are descended from African immigrants who travelled to Scandinavia four thousand years ago and established themselves on a peninsula that was separated from the continent by an earthquake and drifted to its present position.

Another important chronicle in the *History of Ruffal* tells of the discovery of a large cavern, illuminated by a globe of fire and inhabited by small human-like creatures, naked and winged like bats. The people of Ruffal believe them to be glorified men who strove for perfection through death. This caused an epidemic of suicides that only stopped when a law was established forcing parents to eat the bodies of their dead children, if these had committed suicide.

Travellers to Ruffal today will find the inhabitants an agreeable though plodding race. It takes a Ruffalian a long time to understand anything, and a new idea usually has to be repeated three times before it is grasped by their frail intellect. It is said that the rule "What I tèll you three times is true" (established by the Bellman of SNARK ISLAND fame) is applied rigorously throughout Ruffal.

(Simon Tyssot de Patot, *La Vie, Les avantures, & le Voyage De Groenland Du Révérend Père Cordelier Pierre De Mesange. Avec une Rélation bien circonstan-ciée de l'origine, de l'histoire, des moeurs, & due Paradis des Habitans du Pole Arctique,* Amsterdam, 1720)

RUNENBERG, a remote mountain somewhere in Germany, rising from a wooded landscape and dotted with barely visible ruins. A traveller wishing to reach it must cross a number of streams and forests and then follow a path that will lead him to an old, moss-covered building. Here he will be received by a young woman in a state of undress. Opening a cupboard, she will take a small casket decorated with precious stones and hand it to the traveller with the words "Take this to remember me by." Upon this, the traveller will fall asleep. In the morning he will find that the casket has vanished, that he remembers little of what has happened and that another path leads down into a nearby village.

(Ludwig Tieck, "Der Runenberg," in *Taschenbuch für Kunst und Laune,* Cologne, 1804)

RURITANIA, a European kingdom reached by train from Dresden. After crossing the frontier,

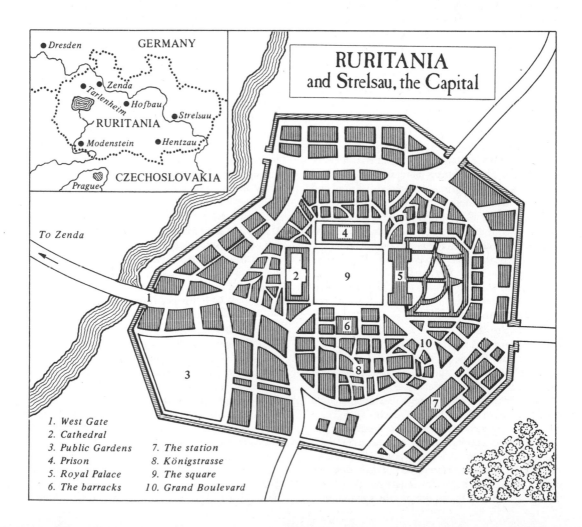

1. West Gate
2. Cathedral
3. Public Gardens
4. Prison
5. Royal Palace
6. The barracks
7. The station
8. Königstrasse
9. The square
10. Grand Boulevard

the train stops at ZENDA, Hofbau and finally Strelsau, capital of Ruritania, some sixty miles from the border.

Strelsau is a quaint combination of old and new architecture. Spacious modern boulevards and residential quarters surround the narrow tortuous and picturesque streets of the original town. In the outer circles live the upper classes; farther inside are situated the shops with their prosperous fronts that hide wretched alleys filled with a poverty-stricken, turbulent and mainly criminal class. In the most ancient street in Strelsau, a narrow, gloomy thoroughfare lined with richly carved houses that bow to meet each other, the oldest sign in the city can be seen, "The Silver Ship," where Strelsau's most famous silversmith lived.

The old street leads into the central square where Strelsau Cathedral stands with its grey façade, graced with hundreds of statues and the finest oak doors in Europe. Opposite the cathedral stands the Royal Palace, unfortunately closed to the public. It was in Strelsau that Rudolf Rassendyll, an English gentleman, twice impersonated King Rudolf V of Ruritania. Though the history of Ruritania is probably already familiar to most, it might yet be useful to recall certain facts.

In 1733 Rudolf III visited the English court where he had an affair with Amelia, Countess of Burlesdon. The Countess bore a child who had the characteristic Ruritanian long, sharp nose and dark red hair. Rudolf Rassendyll, a descendant of the fruit of this illicit affair, visited Ruritania and discovered he was the king's double. He impersonated the monarch at his coronation, thus defeating the so-called Black Michael plot and securing the country for the king. But Rudolf fell in love with Flavia, destined to be Queen of Ruritania. When the king was threatened again, the Englishman, torn between honour and love, once more went to the aid of the only man who stood between him and Flavia. He took the king's place but this time fell victim to the assassination plot. He is now buried in the cathedral and his tomb bears an inscription chosen by Queen Flavia: "To Rudolf, Who Reigned Lately in this City, and Reigns Forever in Her Heart. Queen Flavia."

The Königstrasse should certainly be included in a comprehensive visit to Strelsau, for it was at No. 19 that Rudolf Rassendyll fought a famous duel with the villainous Rupert of Hentzau, who had lodgings here. If adequate notice is given, it is possible to arrange a visit up the narrow stairs to the very room in which the duel took place. Königstrasse is very long and intersects almost the entire length of the old town.

British visitors are advised that a British Embassy exists in Strelsau; it was here that Mr. Sherlock Holmes once met Rudolf Rassendyll at the Ambassador's party.

(Anthony Hope [Anthony Hope Hawkins], *The Prisoner of Zenda*, London, 1894; Anthony Hope [Anthony Hope Hawkins], *Rupert of Hentzau*, London, 1898; Anthony Hope [Anthony Hope Hawkins], *The Heart of Princess Osra*, London, 1906; Nicholas Meyer, *The Seven-Per-Cent Solution*, New York, 1974)

RUVA, one of several floating islands in the Lural Az of the underground continent of PELLUCIDAR. The islands drift with the current, occasionally close to the mainland, but usually farther out to sea.

Ruva is held together by the trees that grow on it, a species found only on the floating islands: soft and spongy, vaguely resembling a spineless cactus. Apart from the trees, there is little vegetation—only parasitic vines with bright blossoms and an ordinary type of grass. Ruva's trees are vital to the life of the island. Water can be obtained by cutting into their trunks or lopping off branches; the young shoots and the fruit are edible and provide the Ruvans with their staple diet, which is supplemented by fishing and by catching the birds that live in the trees.

Ruva's only settlement is in the centre of the low island. Here rough huts cluster around a fishing-hole—a great pond with a diameter of about one hundred feet which has been dug out of the soil. The Ruvans' fishing technique consists of hurling their spears at the fish that come close to the edge of the pool; the method is inefficient and the fish appear to have learnt to swim out of range.

The Ruvans are black-skinned and have handsome, regular features. They are monogamous and are extremely proud of their bloodline. They despise the white races of the mainland and often take them as slaves. Visitors will be relieved to know that slaves are treated quite well, although they are required to do all the manual labour on the island.

The main activity of the men of Ruva seems to be carrying out raids on another floating island, Ko-Va, which in turn carries out raids on Ruva. Although raiding parties from both islands are heavily armed, there is comparatively little slaughter involved, as the final massacre of either community would mean that there would be no more slaves or women to carry off. Raiding is an important part of island life and successful expeditions are celebrated by feasting and drinking a potent alcoholic beverage known as *tu-mal*, also drunk in JA-RU.

The canoes used by the raiding parties of both islands are skilfully constructed dugouts, made from logs which are as hard as iron and which are worked until the hull is as smooth as glass. The trees used for these canoes do not grow on either island; making a canoe necessitates a major expedition to the mainland. As a result, canoes are considered very valuable and are handed down from father to son through the generations. Women and children very rarely leave their homes and the canoes are used only by men. A new canoe is built only when the number of men in the tribe exceeds the capacity of the existing canoes. This seldom occurs, as the casualties among the warriors usually balance out male births.

The population of Ruva is small; there are thought to be some forty families on the island, each with about four members, plus a variable number of slaves. Ruvan names usually have two syllables; U-Val, Ro-Tai and Ul-Van are typical examples. According to the islanders' customs, no Ruvan warrior may go to live in a foreign country.

During the rainy season travellers are advised to proceed with caution, as portions of the island are sometimes swept away during storms.

(Edgar Rice Burroughs, *Land of Terror*, New York, 1944)

S

SABA or MEROA, a major city in Ethiopia, surrounded by beautiful countryside where, in the summer, the fruit of the apple trees turns into children.

Saba is the site of King Solomon's tomb, built in crystal and gold, and studded with sapphires and diamonds. Visitors are advised to eat a herb called *apium risum* which grows in the land of Lekthyophages. This will allow them to see through the crystal of the tomb and watch King Solomon dancing with the Queen of Sheba, while a group of lords and ladies make merry to the music played by a seraph. King Solomon and the Queen of Sheba sleep in the same bed and it is interesting to note a red hand that holds a naked sword between them. Visitors are warned that local magicians are known to have changed travellers into wolves.

The people of Saba are born yellow and turn black as they grow older. They are easily intoxicated and have little appetite for meat. Many of them suffer from dysentery and die young. Because of the heat, the rivers and waters of Saba are salty and the people lie in the water from dawn to noon to avoid the rays of the sun. A certain well, which by day is so cold that no man can drink of it and by night so hot that no man can put his hand into it, is worth a visit.

(Sir John Mandeville, *Voiage de Sir John Maundevile,* Paris, 1357; William Bullein, *A Dialogue both Pleasant and Pitiful, wherein is a Goodly Regimente against the Fever Pestilence, with a Consolation and Comfort against Death,* London, 1564)

SACRED PALACE, see EGYPLOSIS.

SACRED VALLEY, on the borders of India and Sikkim, beyond the Great Rungit Valley, high up in the mountains, surrounded by rock walls. Because of its isolation, it enjoys a mild climate and luxuriant vegetation, irrigated by a meandering river that falls from the mountains. Travellers are advised that the shortest route to the Sacred Valley is through a cave in the Great Rungit Valley. Rough steps lead to a series of tunnels which even-

tually come out on a rock ledge, ending in a sheer drop. The traveller will find metal rungs fixed in the wall which will enable him to descend into the Sacred Valley itself. Another method of entering the valley is somewhat more dangerous. Travellers should lie on the ground in the Great Rungit Valley, pretending to be asleep. Very soon a large number of large tigers will approach them, and without hurting them, will drag them off to the Temple of Kali, deep in the Sacred Valley. Travellers are warned, however, that most of those who use this second method of entry are sacrificed by the natives to their gods. The tigers, along with poisonous snakes, are trained by fakirs to obtain victims in this manner for their sacrifices.

The Temple of Kali, about an hour's walk from the foot of the ladder of metal rungs, is a huge building, lit during the night with braziers placed on both sides of its monumental door. Upon entering, the visitor will note two immensely high statues with hideous faces and contorted limbs, set on either side of the room. At the farthest end stands a raised throne, behind which looms a black marble statue of Kali, adorned with a necklace of skulls and a skull in each of her four hands. Beneath the temple is a crypt full of tombs and sarcophagi, decorated with intricate and fantastic carvings. A secret passage, reached through a sliding rock panel, gives access to the forbidden heart of the temple; another passage leads into the open air. In front of the temple stretches a terraced garden with twisted columns that support the temple's portico. Beneath the highest terrace, visitors can see the legendary treasures of Siva, gifts offered to the goddess from the princes of the world throughout the centuries. The treasures lie in a chamber built from the finest marbles and studded with precious stones. However, visitors are warned that the location of the chamber is a closely guarded secret and the betrayal of this secret is punishable by death. The execution is carried out with the help of poisonous snakes.

The temple is partially surrounded by a lake inhabited by sacred crocodiles. Sacrificial prisoners are locked in a narrow chamber at the end of a tunnel leading from the temple to the bottom of the lake, and left there until the crocodiles decide to approach them. These entertaining rites use the oldest Vedic hymns as part of the sacrificial ceremony.

The Sacred Valley also contains the ruins of

smaller, disused temples, which look particularly beautiful by moonlight.

(Maurice Champagne, *La Vallée mystérieuse*, Paris, 1915)

SAHARAN SEA, an extensive and artificial inland sea between Algeria and Tunisia. The sea covers what was once the Chott Djerid region and the depressions south-east of Biskra, and is connected with the Gulf of Gabès by a series of canals that are navigable by steamer. The main ports are at La Hammâ, Nefta and Tozeur, former oases which were not flooded because of their high elevation. There is one large, central island—the Hinguiz.

The flooding of those areas of the Sahara Desert below the level of the Mediterranean had, for many years, been a project greatly cherished by the French administration. The first serious attempt dates back to 1874, when Captain Roudaine of the French army put forth the idea. His project met with considerable opposition and it was not until 1904 that a Compagnie Franco-Etrangère was founded and granted rights to 2,500,000 hectares by the French government. The Compagnie was too ambitious; it over-extended itself and was rapidly forced to suspend payment of dividends. Much of the initial construction work was carried out, however, and all that was needed was to connect the inland canal system to the Gulf of Gabès. Inland, the major areas to be flooded were connected by canals leading to the Chott Melrir and the Chott Rharsa.

In the mid-twentieth century a French military expedition was sent out to survey the area and to examine the state of the existing canals. The expedition was a dangerous enterprise as it involved moving through territory controlled by those most bitterly opposed to the whole scheme: the people whose lands would be flooded and the nomadic Tuareg who traditionally preyed on caravans in the region. Most of the canals were in good order, though at one point the excavations had been filled in by the tribesmen.

Ironically, the flooding of the area was brought about by a natural geological phenomenon. An earthquake caused the level of the land to fall, provoking a massive inrush of water from the Gulf, rapidly transforming the desert into a sea.

The Saharan Sea has had a definite beneficial effect on the climate and economy of North Africa as a whole. It has facilitated trade and the distribution of supplies to French military bases. It has also eliminated the threat traditionally posed by marauding bands of Tuareg as there are no longer any caravans for them to plunder.

(Jules Verne, *L'Invasion de la mer*, Paris, 1905)

SAINT ANTHONY, see KARAIN CONTINENT.

SAINT BRENDAN'S FAIRY ISLE, also known as the **BLEST ISLE OF SAINT BRENDAN**, in the Atlantic, far to the west of Ireland. It was discovered when St. Brendan and four other hermits left Ireland in the fifth century AD because the people there would not heed their preaching. St. Brendan looked out from the Point of Old Dunmore and saw, in the distance, the fairy sea, and the fairy islands which he called "blest," and with his fellow preachers he sailed on until they reached it.

The island stands on pillars of black basalt, like those of Staffa, some of green and crimson serpentine and some ribboned with red, white and yellow sandstone. The island is covered in cedar trees, which provide a home for numerous species of birds.

Beneath the water-line are numerous caves and grottoes, some blue like those on Capri and some white like those of Adelsberg. All are draped and curtained with crimson, purple, brown and green seaweed, and the floors of the caves are covered with white sand.

The caves of St. Brendan's Isle are the home of the water-babies, too numerous to count. They are all the little children who have been adopted by the good fairies because they have suffered from abuse, cruelty or neglect at the hands of their masters or parents, as well as those children who have died of such complaints as scarlet fever. The children become water-babies after falling asleep and casting off their human bodies, which are mere shells. They develop external gills, like fish, and become amphibious. The water-babies are small, under four inches tall. It is the water-babies who decorate the rock pools with sea-anemones, coral and seaweed, making pleasant rock gardens that can be seen when the tide recedes. They also help fish and marine animals who get themselves into trouble.

For centuries the water-babies were taught by St. Brendan and his fellows. Each Sunday they came up from their caves and attended the Sunday School he organized for them, but eventually his eyes became too dim to see and his beard grew so long that he could not walk for fear of treading on it. At last he and the other hermits fell asleep under the cedar trees, where visitors can see them to this day. At times the bird song on the island is so strong and so powerful that they stir in their sleep and move their lips, just as though they were singing hymns in their dreams. Since the old saint fell asleep, the babies have been taught by the sea-fairies who care for the island. The fairies themselves are ruled by their beloved queen Amphitrite.

The underwater caves where the water-babies sleep are guarded at night by water-snakes, beautiful creatures dressed in green, red and black velvet. Their bodies are all jointed in rings and some of them have up to three hundred brains, which makes them excellent detectives; others have eyes in every joint of their body. When something nasty comes by, the snakes rush out to attack it and a whole cutler's shop of knives and other weapons appears in their hundreds of feet. Any intruder that ventures near the island with evil intent is either forced to flee for its life or cut into tiny pieces and eaten. The caves are kept clean by crabs, which eat up all the scraps that are left lying; the water is kept sweet and pure by the sea-anemones, madrepores and corals that live on the rocks.

All the water-babies receive lessons, just like land children, but their lessons are pleasant and have no difficult words in them, so that learning has become a form of pleasure. Apart from the lessons, the babies are free to play all day long. They are expected, however, to be good, and their behaviour is watched by Mrs. Bedonebyasyoudid who visits the island on Fridays. She is very tall and very ugly and carries a birch rod, although she never uses it on the babies. She always knows exactly what the babies have done and even what they are thinking, and rewards or punishes them accordingly. She rewards good babies by giving them sea-cakes, sea-apples, sea-toffees or sea-ices. Babies who have been disobedient are not given these treats, and if their behaviour is particularly bad their skin is made to become prickly and repulsive. Mrs. Bedonebyasyoudid does not enjoy administering such punishments, but she has been wound up like a machine and must follow her na-ture. Legend has it that she is as old as eternity and will go on for ever; only when all people become good will she become beautiful. Her other duties include calling down all those people—parents, teachers and doctors—who have mistreated or inadvertently hurt children, and punishing them by giving them a dose of their own medicine.

The other regular visitor to the island is Mrs. Bedonebyasyoudid's sister, Mrs. Doasyouwould-bedoneby, who comes on Sundays. She is as tall as her sister, but very beautiful, with the sweetest, kindest and merriest face in the world. She places the babies who have behaved well during the previous week on her lap, cuddles them and plays with them. Affection from her is probably the greatest of all possible rewards for good behaviour.

All water-babies are able to speak water-language, which allows them to communicate with the fish and other marine animals around them.

(Charles Kingsley, *The Water-Babies: A Fairy Tale for a Land-Baby*, London, 1863)

SAINTE BEREGONNE, an area of Hamburg, West Germany, only exists for people who happen to walk between the adjoining houses of the distiller and the seed merchant on Mohlenstrasse. According to the official municipal survey, a median wall stands on the very street that leads to the Sainte Beregonne quarter. The street itself is outside place and time. It is both a gift and a private reserve of the Great Beyond, open to anyone who succeeds in slipping into it, if only to glance about.

Ten feet from the end, a bend in the alley cuts off the traveller's view and makes it impossible to see anything more from the normal world. The walls are poorly surfaced—an indication that Sainte-Beregonnegasse, with its greenish, irregular cobblestones and a few viburnum bushes growing out from among the stones, has a tangible existence and enjoys an other-worldly timelessness. Every bend in the narrow cul-de-sac has the feeling of an alley in a rural Flemish town. A sense of abandonment and inertia puts travellers at a disadvantage here. Even the seasons seem to be all confused; buds will swell on a sickly bush even as snow lies upon its branches.

Three little yellow doors appear along the walls, but if a traveller knocks on them no one answers. Each door opens onto a corridor with a blue floor. (The diffuse light recalls the later paintings of Magritte.) The sensitive traveller will feel awkward, but should not refrain from visiting the large kitchen with its high, vaulted ceiling. The rustic-looking furniture shines with wax. An oak staircase leads nowhere; it plunges into a wall to confuse the unwary visitor. A large window filters the dim light that falls on an empty, desolate courtyard, which echoes other courtyards in other houses behind other doors.

Odious, mysterious crimes were committed in Hamburg. It is said that beings from the Great Beyond came to seek vengeance here on earth for thefts that occurred in their apparently inoffensive houses. Some maintain that these beings were the so-called Stryges; others feel they were simply the vapours of hell.

(Jean Ray, *Le Manuscrit français*, Brussels, 1946)

SAINT ERLINIQUE, see CANTAHAR.

SAINT-ESPRIT, a tiny atoll in the Pacific Ocean, once a nuclear testing site. The atoll consists of a chain of sandbars and coral islets, the rim of a submerged volcanic crater that encloses a lagoon five miles in diameter. The largest of the islands, to the south-west of the lagoon, is a crescent of dense forest and overgrown plantations dominated by a rocky mass that rises to a summit four hundred feet above the beach. On the summit sits a steel tower, its cables slanting through the forest canopy. Visitors have compared the fluted cornices of blue lava to the corpse of a mountain dead for millennia, propped into the sky like a cadaver sitting in an open grave. The beaches are not attractive; they consist of black ash covered with coconut husks, yellowing palm fronds, spurs of pallid driftwood and shells of rotting crabs. Over everything hangs the stench of decomposing fish.

Known as a breeding-ground of rare birds, Saint-Esprit was threatened when French military engineers began building an airstrip on the atoll. The reef around it is the habitat of black-tipped sharks, as well as small blue and yellow fish, but the atoll's most important inhabitant is the famous wandering albatross. Efforts to save the endangered albatross led to curious and tragic events that made the island famous throughout the world. Visitors may not be fortunate enough to spot the celebrated albatross, and it is rumoured

that those responsible for its possible extinction were among the crew intent on saving it.

(J.G. Ballard, *Rushing to Paradise*, London, 1994)

SAKNUSSEMM, CAPE, a rocky promontory in LIDENBROCK SEA, many thousands of miles under the surface of the earth. It was here that the Lidenbrock expedition which travelled to the centre of the earth in 1863 discovered a sixteenth-century dagger that had belonged to Arne Saknussemm, the famous Icelandic alchemist. Saknussemm was the first man to explore these regions and with the aid of the dagger carved his initials in runic characters on one of the rocks, where travellers can see them to this day.

(Jules Verne, *Voyage au centre de la terre*, Paris, 1864)

SAKNUSSEMM'S CORRIDOR, a large subterranean gallery somewhere beneath Iceland, named in honour of its discoverer. Professor Lidenbrock of Hamburg found a parchment, in a rare manuscript by Snorri Sturluson, on which Arne Saknussemm—the celebrated Icelandic alchemist and erudite of the sixteenth century— had written a number of runic characters. After trying to unscramble them with the help of his nephew Axel, Lidenbrock discovered a secret message written on the parchment in a kind of invisible ink. This message gave instructions for reaching the centre of the earth through an extinct volcano in the western part of Iceland. Led by an Icelandic guide, Hans Bjelke, Lidenbrock and his nephew descended into the Snaefells Jökull, which the shadow of the Scartaris Mountain marks just before the calends of July, on June 28, 1863.

Forty-eight hours after starting the descent, travellers will reach a fork in the corridor, some three thousand metres below sea level. They must be careful not to take the east passage, but to veer to the west; otherwise they are likely to die of hunger and thirst in the bowels of the earth. See also HANS-BACK, LIDENBROCK SEA, PORT-GRAUBEN, AXEL ISLE and Cape SAKNUSSEMM.

(Jules Verne, *Voyage au centre de la terre*, Paris, 1864)

SALEM, capital of CESSARES REPUBLIC.

SALU ARCHIPELAGO, see CAGAYAN SALU.

SALVARA, see NEOPIE ISLAND.

SAMARAH (not to be confused with Samarrah, the capital of the Kuybyshev region, USSR), the capital and greatest city of the Middle Eastern land of the Abassides. The city is totally dominated by the vast palace of Alkoremi on the hill of the Pied Horses. The original building was erected by Caliph Montassem, the son of Haroun-al-Rashid, but it owes its present form to the work of Montassem's son, Vathek, the Ninth Caliph. Vathek considered the palace to be inadequate to his pursuit of pleasure and had five extra wings added to it. These are palaces in themselves rather than mere extensions of the original, and each is dedicated to the gratification of one of the senses.

The palace known as the Eternal or Unsatiating Banquet is dedicated to the sense of taste. Its tables are always covered with the most exquisite delicacies, which are supplied both day and night; the most delicious wines and cordials flow from inexhaustible fountains.

The Temple of Melody or the Nectar of the Soul is the home of the country's most celebrated and skilled poets and musicians. They do not restrict themselves to giving recitals inside the palace but circulate throughout the capital, entertaining everyone with their music and lyrics.

The palace known as the Delight of the Eyes or the Support of Memory houses an immense collection of curiosities from every corner of the globe, ranging from statues that seem almost alive to large collections of natural history exhibits.

In the halls of the Palace of Perfumes, also known as the Incentive to Pleasure, a wide variety of perfumed oils are kept burning in censers of gold. Those who find themselves overcome by the effects of the perfumes can go out into a huge garden, filled with every kind of fragrant flower, to rest their overstimulated senses.

Finally, the Retreat of Mirth, or the Dangerous, is the home of troops of young women as beautiful as the houris, who always receive travellers with suitable caresses.

But the Ninth Caliph was also known for his love of knowledge and for his discussions with the wisest men of his court. In the end Vathek acquired a taste for theological argument and began to build a huge tower to try to penetrate the secrets of the heavens. The prophet Mahomet, curious at the theological temerity of the Caliph, ordered his genii to build up the tower at night to see just how far Vathek's impious folly would take him. They obeyed, adding two cubits for every cubit raised by the Caliph's workmen, with the result that the tower soon reached its final height of fifteen hundred stairs.

As well as being an observation post, the tower serves as a prison; in its lower levels, royal prisoners are housed behind a sevenfold fence of iron bars armed with spikes pointing in all directions. Hidden stairways and passages lie behind the walls, and a collection of mummies—taken from the tombs of the ancient pharaohs by Vathek's mother Carathis—can also be visited.

Carathis had a secret gallery constructed to house her collection of poisons and other horrible rarities. Being adept at astrology she soon developed a taste for more sinister arts and tried to establish communication with the infernal powers. This involved human sacrifices carried out at the top of the tower, and ceremonies observed only by the princess and her retinue of mute negroes, all of whom were blind in one eye.

Although Vathek was initially a popular ruler, his desire for ever-greater knowledge and power led him into strange paths and finally reduced his popularity. A number of children were sacrificed by him in order to appease the infernal powers and after his departure for ISHTAKAR a revolt broke out in the capital. Vathek never returned from his journey.

(William Beckford, *Vathek*, Lucerne, 1787)

SAND, CITY OF, somewhere in the deserts of Syria, set inside a vast rocky amphitheatre, crossed by a meandering river. It is ruled by the Sheik of the Mountain and guarded by soldiers dressed as Crusaders. It is said that the inhabitants of the City of Sand have lived here since the times of the Crusades.

The walls of the city are covered in mosaics. The royal palace contains a vast number of precious cloths: silk, embroidered damask, velvet and camel's-hair. Vaults under the palace protect a treasure of rubies, emeralds, turquoises, sapphires and diamonds. The three storeys of the palace are connected by an onyx staircase.

Visitors are invited into the Warriors' Room, a vast chamber decorated with human skulls. Here they are given poisoned wine and then let out into the desert. Not many travellers have visited the City of Sand twice.

(Jean d'Agraives, *La Cité des sables,* Paris, 1926)

SANDALS, ISLE OF, the kingdom of Benius III not far from the Isle of ODES. Though those inhabitants of the island who are not members of a religious congregation live on nothing but haddock soup, visitors are well received and hospitably treated.

The island is notable for its convent built for the Order of Quavering Friars by Benius III. The name of the order was chosen by reference to the names of the Continental orders of Friars Minim, and Minim Crotchet Friars; it was argued that Quaver was as low as one could go. By the terms of a bull patent obtained from the Quintessence, they all dress as incendiaries, but they also wear belly-quilters. Codpieces in the shape of a slipper are worn at the front and back; the double codpieces are said to symbolize certain recondite and horrific mysteries. The Quavering Friars wear round shoes and shave their chins. To show that they despise Fortune, the backs of their heads are also shaven; but from the parietal bone forwards they allow their hair to grow freely. In further defiance of Fortune they carry sharp razors at their belts, which they whet twice a day and test three times at night. Beneath their feet they wear a round bell, because Fortune is said to have one under hers. The flap of their cowls is tied in front as well as behind, thus concealing their faces and allowing them to mock at both Fortune and the fortunate. This also allows them to move backwards or forwards as they please. They paint faces on their bald heads, and therefore seem to be moving in the right direction when they move backwards. Moving forwards, they appear to be playing at blind-man's buff.

The friars sleep in their boots and spurs, with glasses on their noses. They argue that the Last Judgement will come at night when they are all asleep and, sleeping like this, they will be ready to mount their horses and go for judgement immediately. Every morning, they kick each other with their boots and spurs, out of charity.

When midday strikes—all bells on the island are lined with fine down and have a fox's tail for a clapper—the friars wake, take off their boots and relieve themselves. By rigorous statute, they all yawn widely and breakfast on yawns. After their ablutions, they pick their teeth until the Prior makes a sign by whistling in his palm. At this sign, all yawn for half an hour, sometimes more and sometimes less, according to the Prior's estimate of a suitable breakfast for that day in the calendar. Breakfast is followed by a ritual procession in which banners of Fortune and Virtue are carried. The friar carrying Fortune is continually beaten with a sprinkler dipped in mercurial water by his colleague who carries the banner of Virtue. During the procession they quaver antiphonal melodies; observers have noted that they only sing through their ears.

After the procession they take exercise by returning to the refectory, placing their knees beneath the table, and propping their breasts and stomachs on their lanterns. When they are in this posture, a great Sandal enters and lets them lick a fork he carries. The meal begins with cheese and ends with mustard. On Sundays they eat puddings, chitterlings, sausage, veal stew, pork-liver rissoles and quails. On Mondays, good peas, bacon with full commentary and interlinear glosses. On Tuesdays, holy bread, scones, cakes and biscuit. On Wednesdays, sheeps' heads, calves' heads and badgers' heads (badgers are plentiful in this land). On Thursdays they eat seven kinds of soup, with mustard between the courses. The diet for Fridays consists of sorb apples, usually unripe. On Saturdays they simply gnaw at bones. Their drink is a local brew called antifortunal wine.

After dinner, they offer grace to God and devote the rest of the day to works of charity: pummelling one another on Sundays, tweaking one another's noses on Mondays, scratching one another on Tuesdays, wiping one another's noses on Wednesdays, boring the worms out of each other's nostrils on Thursdays, tickling each other on Fridays and whipping one another on Saturdays.

At sunset, they kick one another again and then sleep until midnight, when the Sandal enters. Then they whet their razors and march to the refectory again.

A score of women also live in the convent, living quite richly and sleeping with the friars. March is said to be the main month for lecherous activities in the convent, perhaps because the food eaten during Lent is extremely conducive to erotic sports.

(François Rabelais, *Le cinquiesme et dernier livre des faicts et dicts du bon Pantagruel, auquel est contenu la visitation de l'Oracle de la dive Bacbuc, et le mot de la bouteille; pour lequel avoir est entrepris tout ce long voyage,* Paris, 1564)

SANGIL, capital of ANTANGIL.

SANOR, an island in the major sea of PLUTO, the world near the centre of the earth. One of the three major island states on Pluto, Sanor lies fifteen leagues off ALBUR. The coast of Sanor is rocky and much of the interior is forested. The main port is on a narrow bay and is guarded by a small fortified islet.

As in other areas of Pluto, men, plants and animals are much smaller than their counterparts on the surface of the earth. The people of Sanor are the tallest on Pluto and sometimes reach a height of three and a half feet. Unlike their nearest neighbours, the Alburians, they dress richly and have long, perfumed hair. They eat meat and are therefore scorned by their vegetarian neighbours, who see the eating of meat as an offence against the deity.

Sanor is an Empire with a hereditary nobility. The most striking feature of its political life is that men and women are subject to different authorities: men to the emperor and women to the empress. In their separate spheres, the authority of the emperor and the empress is absolute, but neither has authority over members of the opposite sex. The High Priest is even more powerful, with absolute authority over the dead of both sexes, and over who may or may not be buried. He also has the authority to condemn a widow or widower to be burnt on the grave of a dead spouse. Neither the emperor nor the empress can question his decisions.

When an emperor of Sanor dies, three young girls are sacrificed on his body: they will, it is believed, serve him in the next world. The funeral rites last for six days and are followed by a nine-month period of public mourning. During this period, the empress continues to rule the women of the country and magistrates appoint a governor to rule the men. At the end of the mourning period, the empress must remarry.

The sexual segregation characteristic of Sanor's political life can also be seen in its legal system. There are separate courts for men and women, who are always tried before judges of their own sex. Justice is administered by benches of judges—five in cases involving major offences and two for lesser offences. They are chosen by lot to lessen the possibility of bribery. All cases are heard before a jury of fifteen, who give their verdict by means of coloured balls. There are no longer any lawyers in Sanor's courts, as it was decided that their presence dragged out cases for too long. Under the present system, the Chairman of the Bench of Judges speaks for the defence, and the punishments imposed by the courts are usually lenient.

A typical punishment is that imposed upon a slanderer. He is made to wear a tall hat bearing the legend "This man is a slanderer," and is led through the streets each day by an officer of justice who reads out the sentence and the nature of the offence to the people of the town or city. This goes on for one hundred days. Similar use is made of the humiliation imposed by public mockery, to punish women who gossip or interfere in other people's affairs. They are judged by a court of women and if they are found guilty they are whipped in public. The whipping itself is purely symbolic and no physical pain is inflicted. It continues until the assembled crowd beg for mercy on behalf of the convicted woman.

Under the laws of the country, any woman who allows herself to be seduced and who becomes pregnant as a result is sentenced to death unless her lover is willing to marry her. The normal outcome of such cases, which are judged by a court of old women, is marriage. This happy ending is, no doubt, facilitated by the ease with which a divorce can be obtained; divorce is largely by mutual consent after a minimum period of nine months of marriage.

Although civil justice is lenient, those who offend against the authority of the priests are severely punished. Usually those who act against the priests are declared outlaws and forced out of town. They can then be killed on sight by anyone and are actively hunted down by the church's private militia. The result is that the forests of Sanor are infested with bandits and outlaws, many of whom regard themselves as rebels rather than criminals and some of whom steal only from the rich, and help and defend the poor.

It is estimated that at least one half of the mar-

ried women on Sanor are unfaithful to their husbands. Adultery is not punishable by law and the
behaviour of an unfaithful wife does not reflect
badly on the reputation of her husband. On the
contrary, it tends to be seen as a matter for laughter.

The traditional marriage ceremony is quite
elaborate. As they enter the temple, the couple,
bound together by a silken cord, are enveloped in a
cloud of smoke. Milk is then poured over them
from the temple vault in order to purify them and
they are led outside again. Here, they lie down together on a carpet and are buried in flowers. After
a set interval, the priest tells them to rise and be
reborn. They then drink wine from the same cup,
to symbolize the fact that marriage has united
them so closely that they are now one person. A
new bride does not grant her favours to her husband without some resistance. When they are
alone in the nuptial chamber, she runs away from
him, naked from the waist up. Her husband has to
catch her and overcome her resistance by force if
he wishes to enjoy his conjugal rights. Polygamy is
tolerated but those who practise it render themselves ineligible for any public office.

The capital of Sanor, also called Sanor, is notable for its regular streets, all lined with two-storey
houses, its palaces, towers and magnificent public
buildings. Its greatest pride, however, is the library,
housed in a huge stone palace with heavy bronze
doors. Its rooms contain over one hundred thousand volumes, divided into six sections. Censorship
is not carried out on political or moral grounds, but
in order to ensure that the style and method of
books submitted are of an acceptable standard.

As travellers will certainly note, there are no
beggars in the streets of Sanor. This is largely because all monetary fines imposed by the courts are
used for the relief of the poor. The poor and those
who cannot find work are housed in public hospitals and are normally employed in public service.

Although a major trading nation, Sanor does
not use sailing ships, presumably because the winds
in the subterranean world of Pluto are usually very
light. Sanoran ships are propelled by engines which
use steam to turn great wheels mounted with banks
of oars.

(Anonymous, *Voyage au centre de la terre, ou aventures de quelques naufragés dans des pays inconnus.
Traduit de l'anglais de Sir Hormidas Peath*, Paris,
1821)

SANT JERONIMO, see ISLA.

SAN VERRADO, a pirate island of the Lucayes
group in the Caribbean. The fort was destroyed by
the English at the end of the eighteenth century,
but its ruins can still be seen. The island was
despotically ruled by Don Lescar de Ribeira, a
Spaniard who discovered San Verrado when his
ship was blown off course. The main occupation
of the inhabitants of the island was kidnapping
women from Cuba, in conscious memory of the
rape of the Sabine women. Those who resisted
were imprisoned in underground cells. No one
was allowed to leave the island without Ribeira's
permission.

Each house has a garden which provides
enough food for its inhabitants. The old and the
sick are looked after in a large field in the western
part of the island. The whole community used to
live in a state of constant debauchery, but visitors
today will find the rhythm of life in San Verrado
less exciting.

(François Guillaume Ducray-Duminil, *Lolotte Et
Fanfan, Ou Les Aventures De Deux Enfans Abandonnés Dans Une Isle Déserte. Redigées & publiées
sur des Manuscrits Anglais, Par M.D.***.du M.****,
Charlestown & Paris, 1788)

SARCOSA, see NEW BRITAIN.

SARGYLL, the most distant of the Red Islands,
two days' sail from Novogath, the capital of

Ruins of the fort of SAN VERRADO.

PHILISTIA. It is now the residence of Freydis, formerly queen of AUDELA, and is shunned by many sailors who fear her and her reputation. It is well known that she ruined King Thibaut and had equally fatal dealings with the Duke of Istria, the Prince of Camwy and three or four other lords.

The court is run by sorcery, and magic defends the island against invasion. For instance, the troops sent against Sargyll by Duke Asmund of the Northmen were driven mad, and finally slaughtered one another like wolves.

The Royal Palace is haunted by strange creatures, some of which are beyond a traveller's wildest dreams. Not even those who look human can be trusted. A night porter was once seen to turn into a large orange rat and scuttle off into a hole. The queen is usually attended by a panther and a nameless crouching beast. Her room is hung with black and gold brocade and decorated with vases of lotus blossoms. Blue, orange and reddish-brown dead snakes hang from the ceiling. A painted, half-human face looks down, its evil eyes half-closed and its grinning mouth half-open.

(James Branch Cabell, *Figures of Earth. A Comedy of Appearances*, New York, 1921)

SARI, the most prosperous and highly developed area in the underground continent of PELLUCI-DAR, a lofty plateau among the surrounding mountains overlooking a large gulf that runs inland from the sea known as the Lural Az. The original inhabitants still live in their cave homes in the cliffs, but a small modern town—also called Sari—has been built here by David Innes, Emperor of Pellucidar, who arrived in this subterranean realm from the United States. Small factories and shipyards have been erected in the area and the abundant metals found in the country are smelted here.

Much of this development is the work of Abner Perry, Innes' companion and inventor of the iron "mole" or vessel that originally brought the two Americans to Pellucidar. Thanks to Perry, modern inventions such as the telephone and the water-pump have been introduced into what remains basically a Stone Age civilization. However, visitors will notice that many of these inventions are not used by the Sarians; the women, for instance, prefer to carry water back from the spring rather than use the new pumping system. This has not prevented Perry from putting other schemes

into operation: schools and literacy schemes have been introduced.

The town of Sari—site of the Royal Palace—is not on the coast; the main port of the country is called Greenwich. According to Innes and Perry, Greenwich is on the prime meridian of Pellucidar, and an observatory has accordingly been set up there.

(Edgar Rice Burroughs, *At the Earth's Core*, New York; 1922; Edgar Rice Burroughs, *Pellucidar*, New York, 1923; Edgar Rice Burroughs, *Tanar of Pellucidar*, New York, 1930; Edgar Rice Burroughs, *Seven Worlds to Conquer*, New York, 1936; Edgar Rice Burroughs, *Return to Pellucidar*, New York, 1941; Edgar Rice Burroughs, *Men of the Bronze Age*, New York, 1942; Edgar Rice Burroughs, *Tiger Girl*, New York, 1942; Edgar Rice Burroughs, *Land of Terror*, New York, 1944; Edgar Rice Burroughs, *Savage Pellucidar*, New York, 1963)

SARKOMAND, a city in DREAMWORLD, in the bleak valley beyond the LENG Plateau, from where it can be reached by salt-covered steps. Sarkomand is a splendid and haughty city with walls and docks of basalt, and high temples and large squares adorned with statues. Its gardens and streets are lined with columns, and each of its six sphinx-crowned gates opens onto a vast central plaza in which a pair of colossal winged lions guards the top of an underground staircase leading to the Great Abyss.

(Howard Phillips Lovecraft, "The Dream-Quest of Unknown Kadath," in *Arkham Sampler*, Sauk City, 1948)

SARRAGALLA, the most highly developed of all the Isles of WISDOM.

The advanced industrial civilization of Sarragalla is based upon a constant increase in production and upon constant time-saving. The economy has now reached the point where a perfect balance has been achieved between supply and demand and where wage struggles and strikes have disappeared of their own accord. Work has become a source of pleasure rather than an imposition, and the most frequent demand made by the workers of Sarragalla is for an extension of the working day.

As scientifically minded travellers will know, Sarragalla's industry is based upon the power unleashed by the splitting of the atom with the lambda radioactive particle. An inexhaustible supply of radioactive substances like thorium and uranium is obtained from the neighbouring island of Vorreia, where they were first discovered by the physicist Algabbi. Small deposits of these vital raw materials do exist on Sarragalla itself, but Algabbi never revealed their location.

Basically, Sarragalla's success is due to its ability to transfer energy from non-productive to productive activities, and to its achievements in time-saving. Even language has been abbreviated to save energy: it has all been reduced to telegraphic-style abbreviations. Thus a bill can go through parliament, complete with full debate of all its clauses, in a single morning. Politicians' speeches last no more than thirty-five seconds. The same principles have been applied to the arts: plays have been compressed to the length of a sketch, without losing any of their impact. In music, the main achievement has been the abbreviated sonata, which avoids the repetition of phrases, notes and measures that is so characteristic of the old music. The only publication successfully imported from abroad is the *Reader's Digest*.

In the Experimental Institute, research is currently being carried out on the productive utilization of the energy used in mastication. This involves the use of the *telekinese*, a piece of sophisticated equipment which can transfer energy over a distance by a complicated method of projection and effluvia. Research is still in its early stages, but already people can sit and eat quite normally and see the surplus energy used in mastication being diverted and used to chop wood at the other side of the room.

Medical research is on the verge of giving reality to one of the oldest myths of witchcraft: operations can already be performed on a wax figure of the sick person and the results transferred to the patient by special techniques, known collectively as *tellurgie*. The patient may not even be aware that the treatment has been given him. As yet, *tellurgie* is still in its experimental stages, but great hopes are being pinned upon it.

Transport and communications are as sophisticated as one might expect. To travel, a person encases himself in a tiny flying machine which looks as though it is a part of him; with this he can fly like a bird, without any of the disadvantages inherent in conventional aircraft. In the capital, moving footpaths, which extend far into the surrounding countryside, do away with the need both for walking and for private cars. For longer journeys there is a sophisticated railway system, using monorails. When two trains going in opposite directions meet, tangential planes are lowered at the front and back of one of them, each with a monorail. This arrangement allows one train to pass over the other in perfect safety. For personal communications, a small radio is fitted into a watch case.

Education is based largely on the need to instil respect for the time of others. Time is perhaps the one thing that is still regarded as private property.

The national dish is plankton, which is chemically treated and transformed into food for both men and animals. It can be taken as a fluid, a mash, in fillets or in slices. The taste of the plankton is controlled by the *telegusto*, a machine which can artificially re-create any taste known to man.

(Alexander Moszkowski, *Die Inseln der Weisheit, Geschichte einer abenteuerlichen Entdeckungsfahrt,* Berlin, 1922)

SASANIA, a desert country famous for its two palaces. The first stands in the capital itself, a busy seaport also called Sasania. To reach this palace, travellers must sail for weeks across the sea, in breezy weather, in sudden storms and in days of glassy calm. When they arrive, they are greeted by flotillas of small boats bearing drummers and flautists, singers and cymbal-clashers, and led to the first Sasanian palace. It rises white and glistening, as if moulded from sugar, beautiful, blind and geometrically simple, crowned with domes and towers. It resembles a beehive and is designed to keep out the sun. Its interior is a maze of cool corridors tiled in coloured glass, lit only by narrow slits of windows that are glazed in brilliant colours—garnet, emerald and sapphire—and cast bright flames on the floor. Its central dome, a woven lattice-work of coloured light spun by tiny loopholes, shifts and changes following the movement of the sun.

The second palace lies weeks away, across the dunes, deep in the foothills of the Mountains of the Moon, thought to be the home of demons. A winding narrow path leads to a wide tunnel in the mountainside. After a long ascent through the airless tunnel, visitors will reach a great timbered door. To open the door, one must put one's lips to a hole beside the keyhole and blow softly. A clear musical note will echo, like that of an unseen caril-lon, and the door will swing open, revealing the palace itself. The first impression is of a forest of tall glass tubes with branching arms, arranged in colonnades, thickets and circular balustrades. These pillars are hollow and filled with columns of liquid coloured wine, sapphire, amber, emerald and quicksilver. If a visitor touches one of the finer columns, the liquid will shoot up and then steady. Other columns hold glass bubbles floating in water, each with a golden numbered weight hang-ing from its balloon. In the dark antechambers, fantastic candles flower in glass buds or shimmer behind shades of figured glass set on ledges and crevices. Finally, visitors will enter a very high chamber miraculously lit by daylight through clear glass in a funnelled window far above their heads. The principal attractions of this room are the real waterfalls, sheets of fresh water that drop over great slabs of glass into crystal pools. The air will seem icy cold, especially to travellers who have crossed the burning desert. It is said that this marvellous palace was built by the King of Sasania for his wife, a white and beautiful maiden from the cold Northern Regions.

(A.S. Byatt, *Elementals: Stories of Fire and Ice*, London, 1998)

SAS DOOPT SWANGEANTI, a kingdom on an extensive island in the southern ocean. The min-ing colony of Mount ALKOE marks one of its frontiers.

Literally translated, the name of the country means "Great Flight Land" and refers to the fly-ing ability of its inhabitants. The Swangeants are all born with a *grawndee*, a membranous wing at-tached to the spine and the limbs by ribs of car-tilage. When spread, the *grawndee* allows them to soar through the air. When not in use, the *grawndee* folds around the body, completely encas-ing it in a natural, semi-transparent garment. This is the only dress worn by the Swangeants, apart from a band or chaplet around their heads. Physi-cally, they resemble Europeans, although all the men, or *glumms*, are quite beardless. The women, or *gawreys*, are beautiful.

Meat and fish are not eaten in Sas Doopt Swangeanti. On the other hand, two plants, the *crullmott* tree and the *padsi* bush, produce fruit which taste just like fowl and fish.

Criminals are punished by being taken to Casheedoorpt (literally "The Town of the Slit") where the cartilage joining the *grawndee* to the body is severed, thus preventing them from ever flying again. More serious offences are punished by death: the offender's *grawndee* is slit and he or she is carried up into the air by a group of *glumms* and dropped to earth.

The capital is Brandleguard, a large city exca-vated within the solid rock of the White Moun-tain. The city is square, with a circular piazza at its centre. The square and streets are cut deep into the rock, almost to the level of the plain that lies around the mountain. The huge buildings rise perpendicularly from these subterranean avenues. Above them rises the dome of the interior of the mountain. The houses are entered through arched doorways, often with elaborate carvings. Inside, smaller arches lead to a series of oval or round rooms. The furniture consists simply of slabs of stone which were left intact when the house was hollowed out. When the capital was built, metal tools were unknown in the country, and the city was entirely excavated using a greenish liquid which eats away the stone and turns it to a white powder. The powder can then be mixed with water and used for ornamental work and decora-tive mouldings.

The Royal Palace of Brandleguard occupies one quarter of the city and is entered from the central piazza, which is lined with a colonnade and statues of the old kings of the country. The most spectacular room is the great hall, used for royal audiences. The hall is rectangular, one hundred and thirty paces long and ninety paces wide, with arched doorways in the middle of each of its walls. The pediments of the arches are huge sculptures of *glumms*. Every ten paces stand columns reaching up to the arched, carved roof. Between the col-umns are carved panels showing the battles and exploits of King Begsurbeck who ruled in the fif-teenth century and who is generally regarded as having been one of the country's greatest mon-archs. In the centre of the room hangs a cluster of lights; other hanging lamps are arranged in the shape of the constellations of the southern hemi-sphere. None of the lamps used in the palace or in the city are man-made: they are simply wicker shades used to encase *sweecoes*, odd luminous crea-tures which give out a dazzling, clear, pure light. Like the houses of the city, the palace has no stair-cases; gently curved slopes of natural rock give ac-cess to higher levels.

Some two hundred years after the death of King Begsurbeck, Sas Doopt Swangeanti entered the most troubled period in its history, a period which had been predicted by a *ragan*, or priest, during the reign of the great king himself. A revolt broke out in the western province of Gauingrunt and threatened the very existence of the kingdom as a united entity. So great was the network of spies and agents employed by the rebels that even the new king's relatives and his mistress were involved in plots against him. As the old prophecy told, the king and his loyal subjects were powerless to save the situation. The prophecy also predicted that the kingdom would be saved by a man who could not fly and upon whose face grew hair, who would destroy the rebels by means of fire and smoke, and who would change the religion of the country.

The prophecy came true when an Englishman, Peter Wilkins, arrived in the country. Wilkins had lived for many years on the island of Graundvolet, where he met Youwarkee, a young *gawrey* who had become stranded on that island when she damaged her *grawndee*. Youwarkee became the wife of Wilkins and spent years with him before returning to her home. Her relatives visited Wilkins and, telling him of the state of affairs in their country and of the prophecy, persuaded him to return with them. Wilkins was carried to his new home on a chair borne through the air by a group of *glumms* and was at once greeted as a liberator. As had been foretold, he defeated the rebels with smoke and fire by bringing a cannon from his ship, which had been wrecked on the coast of Graundvolet. The effect of gunfire against soldiers armed only with stone-tipped pikes and clubs was tremendous. By dint of argument Wilkins converted the king and many of the leading citizens to Christianity; their example was then followed by the rest of the population.

Under Wilkins' influence, great changes were introduced into the life of the country. Mount Alkoe was colonized and ceased to be considered the abode of the devil. The knowledge that the mountain was not a place of evil did much to lessen the traditional fear of fire and bright light that had placed so many restrictions on Swangeanti life; because of those fears, they had always lived in semi-darkness and had never used fire to cook with, simply heating their food in the hot springs beneath the main city. Thanks to the metals mined on Mount Alkoe, a currency was also in-

troduced to Sas Doopt Swangeanti for the first time. Finally, the construction of a new city on the plain was begun under his direction.

Wilkins spent many years in Sas Doopt Swangeanti, living happily with his wife and children and enjoying great fame and honour in his adopted country. But after the death of his wife Youwarkee he began to grow increasingly homesick for England. He eventually left the country and was flown away on his chair by a group of *glumms*. They left him in the sea in the Cape Horn area, within sight of a ship that picked him up and returned him safely to England.

Sas Doopt Swangeanti was not originally known by this name. It was formerly called Normbdsgrvstt, but the name was changed as a mark of respect to Wilkins, who was totally incapable of pronouncing the original local name and proposed the new one instead.

(Robert Paltock, *The Life and Adventures of Peter Wilkins, a Cornish Man. Taken from his own Mouth, in his Passage to England, from off Cape Horn, in the ship "Hector." By R.S., a Passenger in the "Hector,"* London, 1783)

SATINLAND, on the Island of Frize. Satinland—well known to pages at court—is so called because all its roads are made of that cloth. Here the trees and plants never lose their leaves or flowers because they are made of damask and figured velvet.

The fauna of Satinland—all made of tapestry—is extremely varied and includes some very curious creatures. All the common animals and birds of Europe are to be found here but, unlike their cousins in Europe, they do not eat, sing or bite. Elephants are common, including musician-, philosopher-, dancer- and even acrobat-elephants. Unicorns are also numerous; the species living on Satinland is an amazingly fierce creature resembling a horse but with a stag's head, a boar's tail and a black horn, usually between six and seven feet long. The horn usually hangs down like the comb of a turkey-cock, but when the unicorn wishes to fight or to use it for some other purpose, it raises it stiff and straight. Apart from fighting, the horn is used to purify the water of pools and streams. Phoenixes—who have somehow managed to reproduce—are not uncommon and hydras may be seen, loathsome serpents with seven heads. Other creatures found on the island include cynamologi, *argatiles*, goatsuckers, *thynunculi*, ono-crateries, *stymphalides*, harpies, panthers, *dorcades*, *cemades*, satyrs, *cartazoni*, aurochs, *monopes*, peg-asi, naiads, giant vampires and gryphons. Even stranger animals are the *cephi*, which have forefeet like hands and hind feet like a man's foot; *eali*, which have tails like elephants, jaws like boars and horns that move like asses' ears; *cocrutae*, which sport the neck, tail and breast of a lion, the legs of a stag and a mouth slit open to the ears. They have only one tooth in their lower and upper jaws and speak with a human voice. Even stranger is the manticore; this animal has the body of a lion, red hair, the face and ears of a man and three rows of teeth, set close together like the fingers of two in-terlocking hands. It carries a sting in the tail, rather like a scorpion, and is remarkable for its fine, musical voice. Other animals living on Satin-land have two backs, and wiggle their backsides even more vigorously than a wagtail does.

Many of the heroes and philosophers of the ancient world live here (though they are sometimes summoned to GLUBBDUBDRIB and the traveller might therefore not find them at home), including Aristotle who holds a lantern, constantly prying, pondering and noting everything in writing.

The one disadvantage of this wonderful land is that there is nothing to eat; anyone who tries to eat one of the plants or animals would swear that he was chewing a mouthful of tangled silk.

Satinland is the home of Hearsay, a mon-strous little old hunchback. His mouth is slit up to the ears and he has seven tongues, each split into seven. He is capable of speaking on seven different subjects in seven different languages, all at the same time. His head and body are covered with ears but, for the rest, he is blind and his legs are paralysed. Innumerable men and women cluster around him, carefully taking notes on everything he says. They all become clerks and scholars in a very short time, speaking in choice language about all kind of matters which a normal person could not understand completely in a hundred life-times. A great number of historians and thinkers, ranging from Albertus Magnus to Marco Polo, can be seen, hiding behind a tapestry and writing on all sorts of topics on the basis of information pro-vided by Hearsay. Hearsay also attracts students from many countries. They come to learn to be witnesses and when they return to their home-lands, they live honestly by the trade of bearing witness. They will bear sworn evidence on any

subject to whoever will pay them the highest wage, and so become rich and respected citizens.

(François Rabelais, *Le cinquiesme et dernier livre des faicts et dicts du bon Pantagruel, auquel est contenu la visitation de l'Oracle de la dive Bacbuc, et le mot de la bouteille; pour lequel avoir est entrepris tout ce long voyage*, Paris, 1564)

SATRAPIA, an empire situated at approximately longitude 60° east and latitude 40° south, about one thousand leagues from St. Helena. It extends one hundred and thirty leagues east to west and eighty leagues north to south, and is divided into cantons or villages, each built in a square on a canal alongside which runs a broad tree-lined tow-path. Each canton is known by a number; there are 41,600 cantons, each with a population of two hundred.

Satrapia has no contact with the outside world; it is a flat, fertile plain cut off from the sea by the natural barriers of arid mountain ranges, lakes and marshes, and its inhabitants are not al-lowed beyond the country's frontiers. Satrapia can be reached by river, but the journey is difficult and dangerous, full of currents and rapids that take the traveller through areas infested with fierce animals and savages.

In Satrapia, war is unknown. The inhabitants cannot conceive that one man should wish to kill another so capital punishment does not exist. Revenge is left to the Universal Spirit—the Di-vine Creator whom the inhabitants believe to be changeless and infinitely good and wise. On the other hand, the sentence for the crime of blas-phemy is severe and a man may be condemned to the mines for life. The mines, found deep in the mountains, are rich in ores and minerals. Iron has been mined for thousands of years; coal, lime, salt, copper and tin are also found.

Visitors to the mountain region are advised to note the caves that in ancient times served as rudi-mentary dwellings. In one of these a skeleton was found and, by its head, a slab with the inscription in Greek "Holy, mighty Immortal God have pity on us."

The country is a monarchy. The Royal Palace, of marble, agate and jasper with Corinthian and Tuscan columns and magnificent ceilings, is certainly worth a visit, as is the Senate House situ-ated behind the palace, with its copper dome and beautiful carpets.

Many birds and animals abound in Satrapia: turtles, snakes, bears, otters, goats and sheep. The *poln*—an almost human, long-haired animal about the size of a donkey, with a single horn, large ears and short tail—can be seen in many parts of the kingdom. The quail of Satrapia are the size of turkeys and geese.

The time to visit Satrapia is at full moon—a time of celebrations with cockfighting, dancing and gondola expeditions in summer, and sledging in winter. The most important festival takes place before the equinox of Capricorn. Large poles are erected in the middle of the main canal, and an eagle is tied by its feet to the top of each pole. The young men of Satrapia try to climb the pole and capture the eagle with their bare hands; this is extremely difficult and the contest usually goes on all day before the eagle is caught. Whoever succeeds is allowed to marry the girl of his choice.

(Simon Tyssot de Patot, *Voyages Et Avantures De Jaques Massé*, Bordeaux, 1710)

SAVAGE ISLAND, the land of the Chitterlings, the hereditary enemies of King Quaresmeprenant of SNEAKS' ISLAND. Despite long negotiations through two intermediaries, it has been totally impossible to reconcile the two nations. The Chitterlings are the staunch allies of the Blackpuddings and Mountain Bolognas; it was Quaresmeprenant's refusal to have the latter included in the peace treaty that led to the final breakdown of negotiations.

The Chitterlings are all descended from hogs. Their tutelary deity in time of war is their first ancestor, Shrove Tuesday, a great pig of crimson plumage with wings as big as the sails of a windmill. Its teeth are as yellow as topaz; its ears are as green as lettuce and its eyes are like flashing red carbuncles. Its white, transparent feet are webbed; its tail is long and black. When Shrove Tuesday appears on the battlefield to encourage the Chitterlings, he scatters mustard on the ground (mustard is the Chitterlings' equivalent of the Holy Grail and Celestial Balm). If a small quantity of mustard is put on the wounds of the fallen Chitterlings, they will be healed very quickly and even the dead will be revived.

Savage Island is ruled by Queen Niphleseth. When the famous giant Pantagruel landed on the island, he was mistaken for King Quaresmeprenant and a mighty battle ensued in which many Chitterlings were killed. When the Queen realized the error, she at once made peace with the giant and offered to send rich gifts to his father, Gargantua. The next day, seventy-eight thousand Chitterlings were dispatched in six brigantines to Gargantua, who in turn sent the gift to the King of France. Sadly, most of the Chitterlings died because of the change of air and the shortage of mustard, their natural restorative. At the King of France's wish, they were buried in a corner of Paris which today is still known as Rue Pavée d'Andouilles, or Chitterling Paved Lane. In return for her generosity, Pantagruel gave the Queen a penknife of Perche manufacture.

(François Rabelais, *Le quart livre des faicts et dicts du bon Pantagruel*, Paris, 1552)

SAVOYA, an island eastward from Lambethana, 4° west from Terra del Templo, probably in the north Atlantic. Savoya is a spacious island with a temperate climate fit for agriculture. The natives differ little from Europeans and trade their goods for silver (which they covet), as well as for gold. One of Savoya's principal products is fruit grown in the highlands.

The island is divided into five provinces: Dutchy, Somersetania, Maypolia, White Hart and Hortensia—commonly called Covent Market. The Capital is in the south-east on the banks of a large river. The Royal Palace, formerly employed for charitable purposes such as the housing of exiles from other countries, is a magnificent building that stands at the meeting point of several great avenues including the Northern Avenue, leading inland through the Great Gate, and the Eastern Avenue, leading to Dutchy and Somersetania. The Savoians are Christians but they venerate the Maypole in honour of the goddess Flora.

(Frank Careless, *The Floating Island or A New Discovery Relating the Strange Adventure on a late Voyage from Lambethana to Villa Franca, Alias Ramallia, to the Eastward of Terra del Templo: By three Ships, viz. the "Pay-naught," the "Excuse," and the "Least-in-Sight" under the conduct of Captain Robert Owe-much: Describing the Nature of the Inhabitants, their Religion, Laws and Customs*, London, 1673)

SCARICROTARIPARAGORGOULEO, capital of LETALISPONS.

SCARLET TOWER, ISLAND OF THE, in the Atlantic Ocean not far from the coast of Brittany, described by those who have seen it as very beautiful and enhanced by high mountains. A superb castle adorns the east coast; among its many towers is the tower called Scarlet (which gives its name to the island), built from one of the most extraordinary stones ever seen in the world.

The discoverer of the island and builder of the vast castle was a certain Joseph, son of Joseph of Arimathea, who brought the Holy Grail to the islands of Britain. Noting, on the one hand, the richness of the place and, on the other, the pagan faith of its inhabitants, Joseph decided to kill two birds with one stone by becoming lord of a land of wealthy Christians. He converted the inhabitants to the true faith and built the castle and tower as a refuge for his people. However, the island was later conquered by a race of giants and the Christian population became martyrs to its barbaric rule. Most famous of these enormous rulers was the Giant Balan, in the early sixteenth century, more tolerant than his predecessors.

Visitors should know that a local custom obliges the lord of the island to fight whoever lands on its coast. If the visitor is beaten, he is made a prisoner for life; if he wins, he is immediately set free and can visit the island at leisure.

(Anonymous, *Amadís de Gaula*, Zaragoza, 1508)

SCHILDA, a city-republic whose location is unknown. Only one point about the history of the Schildburgers appears to be certain: statesmen and philosophers chose this place for their residence, and gradually an entire generation of exemplary savants gathered there. Kings and princes of other countries soon came to think it an honour to invite one of these sages to their courts, making him a minister and personal adviser.

When only one adult male was left in Schilda, the women issued an ultimatum: if their husbands did not return, they would look for men to replace them. The husbands accordingly asked permission to take leave of their respective sovereigns. On returning home, however, they found that their continued presence was absolutely necessary. To serve their own interests without offending their powerful masters, they developed the following plan: they would immediately begin to act so stupidly that none of the kings would ever want them back. Schilda's council chamber was concrete evidence of this policy. It was a long, square building without even the smallest window. Every attempt was made to illuminate the building—using shovels, buckets, cauldrons and even rat-traps to catch rays of sunlight—but without success. As a result, hearings and meetings of the court were held in darkness.

Unfortunately, it seems that this feigned stupidity of their fathers affected the descendants. One day the city decided to elect as its mayor not the most learnèd and clever man they could find, but the healthiest and most energetic. The city's chronicler describes him as a certain Mr. Gaspard and says that his extreme isolationist doctrine resulted in political unrest. (For example, every book had to be written by a native of the country.) The only way Gaspard could find to deal with this unrest was to throw every male inhabitant into jail. Finally, when a letter accused him of leading the republicans, he put himself in prison. With no one left to dispense justice, the Schildburgers languished in their dungeon. After some time had passed, however, they grasped the absurdity of the situation; they escaped from prison, overthrew the old constitution and proclaimed a republic.

The traveller who journeys to this city-republic will immediately notice its happy middle-class atmosphere, its half-knowledge and reigning buffoonery. Thinking is the job of an appointed philosopher. In literary matters, certain people are responsible for explaining to the rest what they should think about this or that book. These critics have become so competent in their fields of specialization that the public has completely stopped reading. The Schildburgers have also given up any interest in poetry out of respect for these given explanations.

Theatre, on the other hand, is very popular. The works of Augustus are put on most often; in every one of his plays, without exception, he deals with the pains of love and the disasters that befall those who go into debt. These plays are chiefly memorable for a total and characteristic lack of humour, and for their final scenes, in which a generous character never fails to appear and pay for everything.

As for the schools, only ignorant people are allowed to become teachers, in the hope that they will learn something about the subjects they are teaching. Meanwhile, a complete mistrust for all knowledge is inculcated in the students, which reinforces their self-confidence and lets them develop a surprising originality in their thoughts and expressions. The most eloquent testimony to this scholastic policy is the example of a young Schildburger who can usually be found perched in a tree just outside the city. He is helping the local cuckoo, who is at war with the cuckoo of the neighbouring kingdom.

(Erich Kästner, *Die Schildbürger*, Munich, 1976)

SCOODLERLAND, home of the Scoodlers, in the mountains that lie beyond the MUSICKER'S VALLEY. Scoodlerland is not recommended to visitors. A thin rock bridge crosses a black gulf so deep that its bottom cannot be seen and leads to an arched entrance in the mountain itself. Once inside the mountain, travellers will find themselves in a vast domed cave lit by holes in the stone roof. Around the edge of this circular cave stand the Scoodlers' houses—thin rock buildings, no more than six feet wide. The Scoodlers are extremely slender creatures and do not need much space to live in.

The Scoodlers themselves will probably strike the travellers as peculiar. Although their bodies resemble those of human beings, they have a face on either side of their heads, one white and one black, and therefore can walk backwards or forwards. Their toes can be curled in either direction at will to assist this fluctuation. Their heads can be removed and replaced, but while the head is removed the body runs aimlessly in all directions. When annoyed, the Scoodlers take off their heads and fling them at their enemies; assisting friends then dart forward with incredible agility, pick up the head and replace it.

The Scoodlers are ruled by an ill-tempered old queen, readily distinguishable from her subjects by her colouring: one side of her head is red, with green eyes and black hair; the other yellow, with black eyes and crimson hair. She has thrown her head at so many people that it is now permanently dented.

By nature the Scoodlers are extremely aggressive. Visitors who stray into their mountain home are captured and boiled up with vegetables to make soup. The soup—said to be delicious by those who have lived long enough to taste it—is made in a giant pot which hangs in the centre of the domed cave.

(L. Frank Baum, *The Road to Oz*, Chicago, 1909)

SCOTI MORIA, see FLOATING ISLAND.

SCYLLA and CHARYBDIS as seen from the east.

SCYLLA and CHARYBDIS, two small, neighbouring islands in the Mediterranean, an arrow's throw from one another. They are named after their singular inhabitants, whose habits make the passage through these waters extremely dangerous.

The first island, Scylla, consists of a single pointed rock whose sharp tip reaches into the sky and appears always to be hidden by a dark cloud; the rock itself is barren and very smooth. Halfway up its side a dark cave can be seen, the dwelling of Scylla. Scylla has twelve feet, six necks, six heads and six mouths—each of which has three rows of teeth—and it usually leans from its den to devour passing sailors.

The island of Charybdis is lower and on its summit grows a large fig tree. Charybdis, the resident monster, swallows a large amount of seawater three times a day and then spurts it back out, creating dangerous whirlpools. Navigation through these waters is not recommended.

(Homer, *The Odyssey*, 9th cen. [?] BC; Pausanias, *Description of Greece*, 4th cen. BC; Ovid, *Metamorphoses*, 1st cent. AD)

SEACHILD'S CITY, built on a floating island, somewhere in the north Atlantic, last seen at latitude 55° north and longitude 35° west. Visitors have great difficulty reaching the city because it disappears as soon as a ship is seen upon the horizon. The entire city has only one inhabitant, the twelve-year-old daughter of a certain Charles Lievens de Steenvoorde, who disappeared on the high seas. The girl lives in this empty place, carrying out her everyday tasks in a normal manner. It is believed that there are many such floating cities built by drowned children whose bodies have never been recovered.

(Jules Supervielle, *L'Enfant de la haute mer*, Paris, 1931)

SECRET LAKE, see JUNGANYIKA.

SELENE, a vampire city north-north-west of Belgrade, Yugoslavia, formerly in Hungary. It can be reached from Semlin (today Zemun), either by horse or on foot, following the old Austro-Hungarian military road along the Danube, leading to Peterswarden (or Petervaradin). Certain equipment must be assembled in Zemun before the journey: a bag of coal; a small burner; a few flasks of smelling-salts and candles. A Magyar surgeon and a sharp iron stake are also necessary. It is best to leave Zemun towards ten in the morning.

Some three-quarters of a mile along the road, the landscape changes abruptly. The oleander, the ferns and even the wheat start to fade. The ground, at first green and soft, becomes dull and dark as if a rain of ashes had fallen upon it. The sky turns grey and a melancholic cloud covers the sun. The traveller will feel weak in the knees, a dizziness in the head and a mysterious weight on his chest. Suddenly darkness surrounds him. A distant bell tolls twenty-three times. The darkness fades and Selene appears.

The traveller will suddenly find himself in the very centre of the city, in front of a large circular palace built in several different architectural styles, mingling ancient Assyrian motifs, Chinese fantasies and intricate Indian designs in a startling but accomplished combination. This palace, somewhat reminiscent of the biblical Tower of Babel, is

View down a south-easterly street towards the centre of SELENE.

built of pale porphyry, slightly coloured, a variety known as "green water." Large blocks of this stone, transparent as amber, are fixed together with fine splinters of black marble. The whole is a dazzling succession of columns large and small, of pinnacles, spires, abaci, epistyles and architraves, each part building up to a central pyramid shape, very like a pagoda. Upon one of the columns stands the statue of a tiger clawing at the heart of a terrified girl. Below, on twenty-four marble pedestals, the statues of twenty-four young women, all very beautiful, stand in secret awe of an invisible enemy. These statues rise above a square from which sprawl the streets that divide the city into districts. Each of these districts seems endless, its innumerable palaces and mausoleums continuing deep into the surrounding mists. The palaces belong to the vampire nobility and each door bears the name of its owner in bold, black letters. Some of these names are surprisingly familiar and throw a new light on many historical enigmas of the past centuries.

After choosing one of the doors, the traveller should at once open one of the flasks of smelling-salts, because there are few smells more pungent than that of a vampire, especially in his own house. Next, the Magyar surgeon should approach the sleeping vampire with care and make a small incision near the vampire's heart. The heart must be extracted with the help of the iron stake and set on the lighted coals in the small burner brought for this purpose. The vampire will howl, but he must not be heeded; he will eventually become a small heap of transparent dust. The ashes of the heart must be collected to serve their purpose later.

By now it is probably quite late. A roaring sound is heard, louder and louder. A reddish light falls upon the city, illuminating six stone animals set on high columns at the far end of each street: a serpent, a bat, a spider, a vulture, a falcon and a leech. They will start to move very slowly. A crystal bell tolls the first of the twenty-four chimes in the last hour of the vampire day. The traveller should then run for his life. From all the doors will appear tall men, somewhat effeminate, and thin, pale women with yellowish eyes and dark lips. A blackbird will rise from the flames that have sprouted on top of the pagoda-like building and sing. A far-off drum will start to beat and the bell to toll again. The vampires will try to lay their hands on the traveller who, without fear, must sprinkle them with vampire's heart-ash; the vampires will then explode in a bluish flash.

Once the mist surrounding the city is reached, the candles should be lit to find the way out and the road back to Zemun. A good map might be helpful.

(Paul Féval, *La Ville vampire*, Paris, 1875)

SELIDOR, the most westerly island of the great archipelago of EARTHSEA. A narrow channel on the east coast leads into a great bay at the heart of the island. Selidor is a bleak island of a strange desolate beauty. The coast is covered in sand dunes which stretch inland for a mile or so before giving way to the lagoons and salt-clogged lakes and pools. Apart from the reeds, the only vegetation on Selidor is the coarse grass swaying in the wind. There is no sign that the island has ever been inhabited. Its remoteness has given rise to the saying "as far away as Selidor," a phrase that is common throughout Earthsea.

Despite its remoteness, Selidor is connected with some of the most important events of Earthsea's history. It was here that the legendary hero Erreth-Akbe came after his defeat at the hands of the High Priest of the KARGAD EMPIRE, and here he was slain by the dragon Orm Embar. Centuries later Selidor was the setting for the final combat between Ged, the Archmage of ROKE, and his enemy Cob, who had introduced so much evil into the life of the archipelago. Cob was a magician who once practised on HAVNOR. He seduced men with the promise of eternal life, which in fact meant that he had the power to call them back from the dead. Ged was told by Orm Embar himself that his enemy was to be found on Selidor, and the mage sailed there with Arren, the boy later to be crowned King of all the Isles of Earthsea under the name of Lebannen. The dragon, Orm Embar, attacked Cob but died when Cob's charmed sword pierced the one weak spot of his body. The dragon's fiery breath burnt away the human face and revealed Cob to be the Unmaker, an almost impalpable shape of evil and darkness. Ged and Arren followed the shapeless thing into the land of the dead, where the silent shapes of those who are no longer living move slowly through the dark streets and houses that clothe the slopes of a bare hill. Beyond the towns of the dead lie the slopes of the Mountains of Pain, which eventually led Ged and Arren back to the world of the living, but which the dead cannot cross. Here Cob had opened up a hole between the worlds, the source of a dry river of darkness, the spring of the evil that had infected Earthsea. With an immense effort Ged was able to close the source of the river by tracing *Agnen*, the rune of ending, across it in letters of fire. The gap by which darkness had entered the world was sealed and the two heroes returned to Selidor.

(Ursula K. Le Guin, *A Wizard of Earthsea*, New York, 1968; Ursula K. Le Guin, *The Tombs of Atuan*, London, 1972; Ursula K. Le Guin, *The Farthest Shore*, London, 1973)

SERVAGE, a forested island off the coast of Wales, well known by travellers as a place of great danger. The island was once an independent kingdom under the rule of the infamous giant Nabon le Noire.

Nabon le Noire and his son were both slain in battle by Sir Tristram who was shipwrecked on the island during a journey to Brittany. He appointed Sir Lamorak de Gales to rule the island, which now forms part of CAMELOT.

(Sir Thomas Malory, *Le Morte Darthur*, London, 1485)

SESTOLA, an island-fortress in the Firth of Sestola in the south of MESZRIA. The fortress rises almost sheer from the water and overlooks the many islands, skerries and cliff-ringed bays of the Firth. On the south or ocean-facing side, the walls rise without a break from the sea, and are pierced only by a small water-gate leading out to the landing-place. One hundred and fifty feet above, a portico runs the length of the fortress, its roof supported by square stone pillars. The portico opens onto the banqueting hall, one hundred feet long and forty feet wide.

A large collection of arms and armours from different periods decorates the walls; many of the pieces are damascened with gold and silver. At the west end, a musicians' gallery can be seen above the doors to the portico; smaller doors lead to the kitchens, buttery and servants' quarters. Opposite the gallery, two high seats stand on a dais overlooking the tables that line the hall. The dais is covered with a carpet; strands of silver have been woven into the wool and it glimmers like a fish in the sun. The banqueting hall is lit by one hundred lamps hanging from the roof on chains of bronze as well as by candles set in holders along walls.

In spite of its luxurious beauty, Sestola was built as a fortress rather than a palace. Apart from the banqueting hall, only the council chamber with its great west window is brightly lit. The other chambers and galleries are illuminated only by lancet windows—wide on the inside, but narrowing to mere slits on the outside—clearly designed for the defence of the fortress rather than for letting in light.

It was in Sestola that King Mezentius and his Queen died by poison in *777 Anno Zayanae Conditae*.

(E.R. Eddison, *Mistress of Mistresses, A Vision of Zimiamvia*, London, 1935; E.R. Eddison, *The Mezentian Gate*, London, 1958)

SEVARAMBIA, a kingdom in AUSTRALIA. Access can be gained through the country of SPOROUMBIA, and the border town of Sevaragounda. From Sevaragounda, the road seems blocked by high mountains, and travellers are advised to use large sleighs worked by gravity which will enable them to reach certain tunnels leading straight into the Sevarambian Plain and on to the capital, SEVARINDIA. A large river, the Sevaringo, flows through Sevarambia, leading into an inland sea which reaches as far as the South Pole, though the waters are very warm and no signs of ice have been reported. The sea contains several islands inhabited by a tribe of savage monsters. The islands are rich in rock crystal and precious stones.

The first king of the Sevarambians, Sevarias, was a Persian traveller born in 1395 who had been sent away by his father to escape Muslim persecution. He reached Australia in 1427 and there found primitive people who worshipped the sun and held all property in common. He learnt that they called themselves Prestarambians, and that they were constantly at war with the people of the mountains, the Stroukarambians. Sevarias joined forces with the Prestarambians and defeated the Stroukarambians. He became king of the joint tribes and brought to the country a great number of Persian immigrants who intermarried with the natives and founded the basis of Sevarambian civilization.

The Sevarambians believe in an eternal infinite god—represented by a black cloth hung above the altars in their temples—who governs the universe with infinite wisdom. They believe that the universe contains no void and that everything is born from something else. The sun, though not a god, is for the Sevarambians a visible representation of their god; human souls originate in the sun and return to the sun after death. Apart from the sun-worshippers, there is also a small Christian sect that rejects the absolute divinity of Christ.

Travellers are advised to attend one of the four main religious festivals: *Sevarision*, a feast to commemorate the arrival of Sevarias; *Osparenibon*, a collective marriage ceremony in which the women choose their husbands; *Stricasion*, the day in which the children are adopted by the State; and *Nemarokiston*, the Spring Festival.

The *Osparenibon* is lengthy and complex. The temple is divided in two by a cloth. At the sound of trumpets, special candles are placed in chandeliers, the windows are closed and the cloth is drawn back to reveal the richly decorated altar. On the right stands a luminous crystal globe; on the left, the statue of a many-breasted woman suckling children. The black veil representing the Sevarambian god hangs as usual above the altar. The governor of Sevarambia enters the temple with his dignitaries, carrying bowls of incense, followed by the men and women who wish to get married. The priest then asks the women what man they choose as their partner. The couples approach the altar, where they are joined in matrimony and swear to obey the law. The next day, the men must return to the temple and hang proof of the bride's virginity on a branch which they bring with them. In Sevarambia, marriage is compulsory for women over the age of eighteen and for men over twenty-one.

The Sevarambian army is composed of both men and women: most women serve in the cavalry and as pike-bearers. Though the nation never goes to war, the army is always well maintained and at any given moment one-twelfth of the population is doing its military service. Though there is no capital punishment, the crime rate in Sevarambia is not very high. Murderers and adulterers are imprisoned for ten years; unfaithful wives for as long as their husbands wish; girls who lose their virginity before marriage, for three years—and equal time for their seducers. In cases where the punishment is a public whipping, a husband may choose to stand in for his wife.

The Sevarambians are honest, straightforward and tee-totallers. They live to be over a hundred and grow to be seven feet tall. They cremate their dead, with the exception of famous men, who are embalmed; they believe that the spiritual elements of ordinary people are carried to the sun by smoke and flames.

The Sevarambians dress according to their age: in white from one to seven, yellow from seven to fourteen, green from fourteen to twenty-one, blue from twenty-one to twenty-eight, pink from twenty-eight to thirty-five, dark red from thirty-five to forty-two, light grey from forty-two to forty-nine, dark grey from forty-nine to fifty-six, and black from fifty-six onwards. Magistrates dress in purple, silver or gold, whatever their age. Women are always veiled in public and men wear their hair uncut until they get married.

Travellers should learn the greetings expected by Sevarambian etiquette: to a magistrate, raised hat and a deep bow; to an old person, raised hat and no bow; to an equal, hands placed on chest. Women should not be kissed in public. The common form of salutation is *"Erimbas erman"* ("May the sun love you"). Travellers are further advised that during their stay they will be offered the services of young slave girls, because abstention from love is not considered a virtue in Sevarambia. These servants of the senses do not wear veils. Before sleeping with them, travellers are examined for symptoms of disease. They are then locked in with the girl of their choice to prevent promiscuity and to ensure that paternity will be clear should pregnancy occur.

The Sevarambian language was invented by Sevarias, who combined elements from native and other tongues. There are forty letters—ten vowels and thirty consonants—which, combined, give a wide and pleasing variety of sounds. In Sevarambian, the sound of a word corresponds to the quality of the thing it describes (like such English words as "sift," "scratch," "burst," "hippopotamus," "pea"). Suffixes are used as adjectives to indicate the quality of the thing described. For example: *amber*, "man," becomes *ambas*, "a venerable man"; *ambou*, "a rogue"; *ambous*, "a minor rogue."

Most of the fauna of Sevarambia is not found elsewhere in the world. The white furred *somouga*, a species of bear, roams the woods near the watering places. The *bandelies* is used as a horse; it is larger than a deer, has the head of a goat with short transparent horns, no mane, a brief tail and a multicoloured coat. Camels are also used for transport, and cormorants for fishing. The *erimsmoda* or "bird of the sun" is a species of yellow eagle found in the mountains. The forests of Sevarambia are haunted by lions and tigers.

(Denis Veiras, *Histoire des Sevarambes, peuples qui habitent une partie du troisième continent, communement appellé la terre Australe. Contenant une relation du gouvernement des moeurs de la religion, et du langage de cette nation, inconnue jusques à présent aux peuples de l'Europe*, Amsterdam, 1677–79)

SEVARINDIA, capital of SEVARAMBIA, stands on a large island in the Sevaringo River. Its high towers rise up almost from the water's edge, making the city virtually impregnable. The streets are broad and straight, flanked by covered pavements whose roofs are supported by iron pillars and decorated with potted plants. The houses or *olmasies* are rather like cloisters, with rooms leading into open galleries built around a central lawn. Each building is large and square, housing up to a thousand people. The dining room and the hot baths are communal.

Visitors are advised to see the great amphitheatre, two hundred feet in circumference, only one mile away from the city. Enormous pillars support its vault which is pierced by windows of crystal. The amphitheatre's terraces climb to a platform where a crystal globe is lit on festival nights. The amphitheatre is used for dramatic performances, gymnastic displays and combats between men and wild animals.

No traveller should miss the Palace of the Sun. Like all buildings in Sevarindia, it is square, with a façade five hundred feet wide. It has twelve doors on each side in addition to the main entrance. The Palace was built in white marble, combining several architectural styles and adorned with variously coloured statues. The main entrance is flanked by 244 marble and bronze pillars. In the throne room, the throne, made of ivory, stands in a semi-circular apse, exquisitely carved.

Another attraction is the Temple of the Sun, begun by King Sevarias and completed by the sixth viceroy. The Temple is within the Palace of the Sun and is about the size of a European cathedral. It is built in marble, with decorations in solid silver, statues of all the viceroys and oil paintings depicting their deeds. The temple dome is gilded and painted.

At the end of the island lies a huge oval pool where mock naval battles with miniature ships take place.

(Denis Veiras, *Histoire des Sevarambes, peuples qui habitent une partie du troisième continent, communement appellé la terre Australe. Contenant une relation du gouvernement des moeurs de la religion, et du langage de cette nation, inconnue jusques à présent aux peuples de l'Europe*, Amsterdam, 1677–79)

SEVEN CITIES, ISLAND OF, see MAYDA.

SEVEN ISLES, as its name indicates, is a group of seven small islands a few days' sail from the coast of NARNIA. The westernmost island is Muil, which is separated from the isle of Brenn by a choppy strait. Redhaven, a town on Brenn, is the major supply base for ships in the area. No description of the other islands is known to exist.

(C.S. Lewis, *The Voyage of the "Dawn Treader,"* London, 1952)

SHADOW, MOUNTAINS OF, or **EPHEL DÚATH**. also known as the Shadowy Mountains, a great range of jagged peaks and chasms on the border of MORDOR. The mountains run down the west side of Mordor and then turn to run along the southern boundary, thus providing natural defences on two sides of the land. In the west, they can be crossed by the pass at CIRITH UNGOL. To the west of Ephel Dúath lies Gondor's province of ITHILIEN, which for years lay desolate under the domination of the Dark Lord of Mordor, but which has now been restored to its former beauty.

There is an ancient road running down the west side of the mountains from CIRITH GORGOR at the northern end to OSGILIATH (near the pass of Cirith Ungol). The first stretch of this road, immediately before Cirith Gorgor, has been repaired. To the south of the newly paved section, however, the road is almost completely overgrown. At some points a visitor may see traces of the elegant arches which carried the road over streams, but in most places one sees only odd paving stones. Much of the road has disappeared under the shrubs and pines of the surrounding heathland.

(J.R.R. Tolkien, *The Fellowship of the Ring,* London, 1954; J.R.R. Tolkien, *The Two Towers,* London, 1954; J.R.R. Tolkien, *The Return of the King,* London, 1955)

SHADOW OF DEATH, VALLEY OF THE, the most dangerous area in CHRISTIAN'S COUNTRY, beyond the Valley of HUMILIATION, a desolate wilderness over which, it is said, "Death spreads his wings and where the sky is often covered by the clouds of confusion." It is haunted by hobgoblins, satyrs and dragons. Loathsome smells fill the air and the hissing of serpents mingles with hideous screams. Fire and smoke combine to create a foul, stifling atmosphere; the earth quakes underfoot.

The entrance to the valley is a narrow path, with a bottomless quagmire to the left and a ditch to the right. It is extremely difficult to follow the path between the two; the blind have been leading the blind into the ditch for centuries. The farther reaches of the valley are, if anything, still more dangerous; full of traps and pits to snare the unwary. In a cave towards the end of the valley lives Pope. His former companion Pagan is now dead and Pope has been so weakened by old age that he is powerless to harm travellers—he simply grimaces at them, biting his nails in frustration because he cannot get them into his clutches. In the past, these two creatures exerted a heavy toll. The blood, bones and mangled bodies of their many victims can still be seen strewn around the cave.

A pillar at the end of the valley commemorates the victory of Great-heart—who now conducts travellers through the valley—over Maul, a giant who once haunted the region. Maul's head can still be seen adorning the top of a post. Maul claimed that Great-heart was kidnapping the travellers he led through the valley to the CELESTIAL CITY, and tried to put an end to his "trade." In the ensuing battle, Maul was defeated and beheaded.

(John Bunyan, *The Pilgrim's Progress from this world, to that which is to come. Delivered under the similitude of a Dream. Wherein is discovered, the manner of his setting out, his dangerous journey and safe arrival at the Desired Country*, London, 1678; John Bunyan, *The Pilgrim's Progress from this world to that which is to come. The Second Part. Delivered under the similitude of a Dream. Wherein is set forth the manner of the setting out of Christian's wife and children, their dangerous journey and safe arrival at the Desired Country*, London, 1684)

SHADOWS, CITY OF, somewhere under the Mediterranean, accidentally discovered by a millionaire while attempting to build a tunnel from Piomdino, Italy, to the island of Corsica. (The tunnel was destroyed by an earthquake, however, and no new route of access has since been discovered.) The city itself, built in a wide circle, is centred on a large stone cube used for assemblies and meetings. From here radiate six symmetrical roads lined with small brick houses. Each house is numbered, each number is in relief, each relief is set above a door of interwoven plant fibres. The city is ringed by a circular road, as well as by a ditch and can be crossed by bamboo drawbridges, and is well fortified to protect the inhabitants from savage apes which have, on two occasions, almost destroyed it. Visitors can read the history of the City of Shadows and its people, written in cuneiform letters, on the clay walls of a street passage between two of the houses.

Not far from the city lies a motionless black lake of warm water (about 40°C.), surrounded by a muddy shore and infested with blind crocodiles. The inhabitants of the City of Shadows believe the lake to be the end of the world and have pictured the other side of the lake as a kind of hell. In fact, the other side contains a series of caves and tunnels that lead to a volcano and from there to the open air. Some of the caves are luminous with radioactivity which has the effect of reducing the force of gravity and producing a certain feeling of weightlessness.

The City of Shadows is inhabited by people descended from the Chaldeans. In the course of their subterranean existence they have lost both their sight and all knowledge of fire—an element they believe to be subtle, comforting and dangerous. Their sight has been replaced by a perfected sense of touch which allows them to sense things at a distance. Their faces are grey and unpleasant to look at, and they wear flowing robes in neutral colours, embroidered with designs that stand out in relief. Their food consists of mushrooms and boiled fish. Because of their limited space and hostile environment, the population has to be maintained at a constant level. Therefore every time a child is born, the oldest or weakest of the family is thrown to the crocodiles in the lake.

The caves between the lake and the volcano are inhabited by vicious triceratops, of whom no description is given, and by apes, the traditional enemies of the people of the City of Shadows. The apes too are blind but their sense of touch is not highly developed. They have a rudimentary language and are capable of organizing themselves to fight, using clubs. The vegetation is rather like submarine flora, greyish and melancholic. Certain leaves contain a special oil that makes them bum like candles when lit. Visitors who need to find their way at night might well find them useful.

(Léon Groc, *La Cité des Ténèbres,* Paris, 1926)

SHANGRI-LA (*La* is Tibetan for "mountainpass"), a lamasery (and by extension the valley it dominates) in Tibet, nowadays under Chinese administration. It can only be reached on foot and visitors are infrequent.

Mount Karakal ("Blue Mountain"), which up to this day has not been climbed, towers twenty-eight thousand feet above the valley. The lamasery's architecture is typically Tibetan, coloured pavilions with milk-blue roofs clinging to the mountainside about a mile above the valley. The lamasery buildings are centrally heated and offer a number of western commodities, such as green porcelain baths made in Akron, Ohio. From a colonnade, steps descend to a garden in which a lotus-pool lies entrapped, fringed by a menagerie of bronze lions, dragons and unicorns. Tapestries, fine pieces of lacquer and pearl-blue Sung ceramics decorate the rooms which are lit by paper lanterns. In the music room, which contains a harpsichord and a pianoforte, unpublished music by Chopin can be found, written from memory by one of the master's disciples, Briac, nearly a century after Chopin's death. The library is lofty and spacious, and books in English, French, German, Russian as well as Chinese and other eastern languages line the shelves. It contains many valuable books; several hundred maps (on which Shangri-La is not marked) and volumes of contemporary literature. The atmosphere is highly reminiscent of Oxford University.

The valley, with its ingenious irrigation system, has a cultivated area of a dozen square miles, and grows a good brand of tobacco. Several thousand inhabitants, a blend of Chinese and Tibetan, live here under the control of the lamas. There are no soldiers or police as crime is very rare—partly because only very serious things are considered crimes, and partly because everyone enjoys a sufficiency of everything he can reasonably desire. As a last resort the lamas have the power to expel an offender from the valley, but this is considered an extreme and dreadful punishment. They believe

A view of the lamasery of SHANGRI-LA.

that "to govern perfectly it is necessary to avoid governing too much." There is no voting system, as the people of Shangri-La would be shocked if they had to declare that one policy was completely right and another wrong.

There are fifty lamas who have reached full lamahood and several half-lamas. The High Lama is an Englishman, Hugh Conway, born in 1893, His Majesty's Consul in Baskul, India, from 1928 to 1930. The founder of Shangri-La was Father Perrault, born in Luxembourg in 1681, who died at the age of two hundred and fifty. He founded the lamasery in 1734 and translated Montaigne's *Essay on Vanity* into Tibetan.

The climate of Shangri-La is warm during the day, cold during the night. It is sheltered from the winds, although around midday frequent avalanches on Mount Karakal can be heard. Something in the life-style of Shangri-La, and also its climate, produces a retardment in the development of human life, prolonging it far beyond normal expectancy. To live in Shangri-La for over a quarter of a century without any visible signs of ageing is quite common. But for those who leave the place, time seems to catch up and extreme signs of old age appear. Similar phenomena of time retardment have also been experienced in the United States by a certain Mr. Valdemar, and in the province of Buenos Aires, Argentina, by Miss Lucia Vermehren.

(Edgar Allan Poe, "The Facts in the Case of Mr. Valdemar," in *Tales of the Grotesque and Arabesque*, Philadelphia, 1840; James Hilton, *Lost Horizon*, London & Basingstoke, 1933; Adolfo Bioy Casares, *El perjurio de la nieve*, Buenos Aires, 1944)

SHARDIK'S LAND, see BEKLAN EMPIRE.

SHARPING ISLAND, three days' sail from TOOL ISLAND. The island is like a platonic image of the Forest of Fontainebleau in France: sandy, sterile and unhealthy. The soil here is so thin that the rocks stick out beneath the surface as the bones of a thin man stick out beneath his skin.

The most noticeable feature of Sharping Island is two small cubes of bone which, from a distance, appear to be made of alabaster or to be covered in snow. The cubes are the six-storied abodes of the twenty Devils of Chance, so feared in Europe and so often invoked by gamblers before they throw the dice. Other inhabitants of the island are Mr. Bad Luck and his wife Poker Face.

Sharping Island also claims to have a flask of the *Sangraal*, or divine blood, sometimes shown to privileged visitors by the magistrates who surround it with more veils, rituals and candles than the veil of St. Veronica in Rome. The displaying of the relic is accompanied by innumerable cere-monies. However, the privileged visitor may find the relic disappointing, reminiscent of the muzzle of a roast rabbit.

Other relics on the island include the shells of two eggs laid by the famous Leda, from which Castor and Pollux are said to have emerged.

(François Rabelais, *Le cinquiesme et dernier livre des faicts et dicts du bon Pantagruel, auquel est contenu la visitation de l'Oracle de la dive Bacbuc, et le mot de la bouteille; pour lequel avoir est entrepris tout ce long voyage*, Paris, 1564)

SHELOB'S LAIR, also known as **TORECH UNGOL**. A series of tunnels under the ridge of the same name on the western side of CIRITH UNGOL, the pass leading across the Mountains of SHADOW into MORDOR.

The tunnels were excavated by Shelob, a giant spider related to those of Beleriand; the spi-ders once found in MIRKWOOD were her descen-dants. It is not known when she arrived in Mordor, but it seems to have been before Sauron estab-lished his dark kingdom there, from where he plotted to dominate the whole of MIDDLE-EARTH. He was quite ready to accept her pres-ence as she was a terrifying guard for the pass. Occasionally he sent prisoners into her tunnels, but her more usual fare was the orcs, or goblins, that guarded the tower in the pass above. In Sauron's eyes the loss of a few orcs was a minor price to pay for the defence of the pass.

Shelob was an evil thing in spider form, an enormous bloated creature with two multi-faceted eyes which seemed to glow with inner fire. Her legs had great knob-like joints; they were covered with hairs like steel spines, and ended in claws. Her hide was thick and pitted, the eyes the only weak spot. Her body, black with livid blotches, was so spongy and swollen that it could be heard squelching as she squeezed through the tunnels.

Gollum, the former hobbit, who had pos-sessed the One Ring and then lost it, deliberately guided Frodo the Ringbearer and his companion Sam Gamgee into Shelob's Lair, hoping to recover the ring after Shelob had devoured them. His plans went amiss and Shelob was stabbed and badly wounded by Sam Gamgee. Her eye was damaged and as she crawled off in pain, a trail of yellowish-green slime oozed from it. Travellers should be wary, for it is not known if Shelob survived this attack and still lives beneath the mountains—or if she starved to death, unable to hunt with only one eye.

(J.R.R. Tolkien, *The Two Towers*, London, 1954)

SHIRE, THE, a pleasant, fertile land in the re-gion of ERIADOR in the north-west of MIDDLE-EARTH. The Shire stretches forty leagues from the Far Downs in the west to the Brandywine River in the east, and fifty leagues from the northern moors to the marshes in the south. It is a rich, pri-marily agricultural area watered by several rivers. The Brandywine (also written Baranduin) is the most important, along with the Shirebourn in the south and The Water which runs into the Brandy-wine just above the Brandywine Bridge. The an-cient Great Road, which runs from the GREY HAVENS to RIVENDELL, crosses the Shire.

The Shire is divided into four regions, known as Farthings (north, south, east and west), and again into a number of Folklands which bear the names of the old leading families. The old families have now become somewhat scattered and the names are no longer a reliable guide to the inhabi-tants of the Folklands. Thus, although most of the Tooks still live in Tookland, many of the old fami-lies are now widely distributed across the whole of the Shire. BUCKLAND is an outlying area of the Shire between the Brandywine and the edge of the OLD FOREST.

The Shire's People are hobbits, mostly farm-ers, craftsmen and small traders. There are no large towns in the area, most of the population liv-ing in small scattered settlements or villages. Per-haps the most important agricultural product of the area is tobacco, usually known to the hobbits as pipeweed. Southfarthing produces the best quality pipeweed, with such fine varieties as Long-bottom Leaf, Old Toby and Southern Star.

The climate of the Shire is mild. Heavy snow-falls are rare except on the moors of Northfarthing.

The hobbits are a small people, rarely more than three feet tall. Bright-eyed and red cheeked, their faces reflect their good natures. They tend to dress in bright colours, and appear to be particu-larly fond of yellow and green. Their feet are cov-ered with thick curly brown hair, like the hair on their heads, and both feet and head are kept neatly brushed. As their feet have leathery soles, they rarely wear shoes. They have long brown fingers and are quite dextrous, and this, combined with their keen eyesight, makes them extremely accurate archers. In spite of a tendency to be fat and to be generally unhurried in their movements, they are light on their feet and particularly noted for their ability to disappear silently at the sight of intruders—a feat which may seem magical, but which depends entirely on their natural skills, as hobbits practise no magic at all. Hobbits come of age at thirty-three, and tend to be long-lived; one famous chief is recorded as having lived to the age of 130.

The hobbits are a hospitable people and they are given to good living. They will, for instance, eat six meals a day when they can get them and are extremely fond of parties and festivities of all kinds. Although they are not normally aggressive, their gentle appearance is deceptive; when necessary, they can be very resilient, sturdy and indeed courageous. But life in the peaceful and well-ordered Shire rarely demands such virtues, and respectability tends to be prized above all other qualities. Any kind of eccentricity is frowned upon, and anyone who voluntarily leaves the comforts of the Shire to seek adventure in foreign parts is regarded as decidedly peculiar. For the most part, the hobbits of the Shire are not especially interested in foreign lands—travellers are advised that maps of the Shire often leave the surrounding territories blank—and few hobbits have ever seen the sea. Their opinion of other people is not particularly flattering: according to the Shire hobbits, those of BREE-LAND are dull and uncouth, and those of BUCKLAND are a queer lot, while men are regarded as being big and stupid. The conservatism of the Shire hobbits is seen in their passion for genealogy and in the custom whereby generation after generation of a same family will live in the same place. The drawing up of long and elaborate family trees is a major interest and the hobbits appear to derive immense satisfaction from studying the detailed trees, even though they are already perfectly familiar with them. Genealogical studies apart, hobbits are not noted for their love of learning.

The characteristic generosity of the hobbits combines with a love of parties to make birthdays quite important, frequent social events. It is the custom for hobbits to give presents all round on their own birthdays, which means that their dwellings tend to be cluttered up with *mathoms*, gifts of doubtful usefulness. Presents given on birthdays are not always new and it is not un-

known for *mathoms* whose original use has been forgotten to circulate for many years.

It is generally held that all hobbits originally lived underground and it is true that they still feel more comfortable in holes in the ground. Now only the very poor and the well-to-do live in holes, the former in primitive burrows and the latter in luxurious dwellings known as *smials*, with large numbers of tunnels. The relative scarcity of suitable land for tunnelling has led to the construction of houses of brick, stone and wood, which are now the norm in the flat and low-lying districts. There is some uncertainty as to whether the hobbits learned the art of building from men or from elves, but their architectural style is uniquely their own. The oldest houses appear to have been imitated from the *smials* and are long low constructions, well thatched with straw or roofed with turf, and with bulging walls. Over the years, the architectural style has become more sophisticated, though the traditional preference for round windows and doors persists.

The hobbits are credited with the invention of smoking, which they refer to as an art. The habit appears to have been introduced by the hobbits of Bree-land, whence it spread to the Shire and then to many other peoples of Middle-earth. The smoke of pipeweed is inhaled through clay or wooden pipes, which come in a variety of sizes and shapes. The ability to blow smoke rings is particularly prized by the hobbits. Hobbits are also credited with the invention of golf. According to the *Red Book of the Shire*, Bandobras Took, nicknamed the Bullroarer, led the attack against a band of orcs during the battle of Greenfields in 2747. During the battle, he struck off the head of their leader Golfimbul with a wooden club and it sailed through the air and fell down a rabbit-hole. This, it is said, is the origin of the game of golf. Hobbits are well-known for their songs and have a habit of humming to themselves as they walk along. There are songs for many occasions—for having supper, going to bed, taking a bath or simply for walking. They are also very fond of riddles. And it is not surprising, given their interest in food, that all hobbits can cook; they learn the culinary arts before those of reading and writing.

Little is known of the early history of the hobbits, and their records begin only with the settlement of the Shire. Legends refer to an earlier period of Wandering Days and these, together with some linguistic evidence, suggest that the hobbits came from the Vales of ANDUIN farther to the east. The reasons for the migration remain obscure, but the legends speak of an increase in the numbers of men and of a great shadow falling over the area. In 1601 Third Age, the hobbits were granted permission from the High King to cross the Brandywine and to settle the land beyond it. In return they promised to maintain the Brandywine Bridge and all the other roads and bridges in the area. They agreed to acknowledge the rule of the king, but in practice they became increasingly autonomous and isolated, though they do claim to have sent bowmen to the last battle between men and the Witch-king of Angmar.

The two brothers who led the crossing of the Brandywine were both Fallohides, a family which produced many of the most famous of all the hobbits. Fairer and taller than most, the Fallohides are the ancestors of the Tooks, Brandybucks and Bolgers. Together with the smaller Harfoots, perhaps the most typical of all hobbits, they were the first to settle in the Shire itself. The broader, more heavily built Stoors, the only hobbits to grow beards, came later and settled mostly in Eastfarthing, the Marish and Buckland. It is thought that it is they who introduced the building of houses.

After the fall of the North Kingdom of Middle-earth and the establishment of the Shire as an independent land, the hobbits elected a Thain from among their chiefs and invested in him the authority previously derived from the High King. The Thain was master of the Shiremoot, a council summoned in times of emergency, captain of the Shire-muster and the Hobbitry-in-arms. Eventually, the position of Thain became little more than a nominal dignity, held by tradition by the Took family. By the time of the War of the Ring, the Shire had no formal government. Families managed their own affairs, devoting most of their time to the cultivation, cooking and eating of food. For generations, the land was ruled by mutual agreement and by the observance of the so-called laws of free will, which were held to derive from the original laws of the High King. The saying "they have not heard of the king" derives from this system and means that the people referred to are lawless. The only real official was the Mayor of Michel Delving, whose responsibility included the job of Postmaster and First Shirriff, or head of the Shire's twelve-strong police force who were mostly engaged in dealing with stray animals and similar internal problems. A second police force, known as the Bounders, was employed to beat the bounds and to deal with Outsiders who came into the Shire.

All in all, apart from the Dark Plague of 1636 and the Days of Dearth in the years 2758–59, little seems to have troubled the hobbits in their pleasant homeland until the great events at the end of the Third Age of Middle-earth. Then came the great War of the Ring. By chance a number of hobbits from the Shire were deeply involved in the exploits of that time, and indeed are counted as heroes of the war. The quiet countryside of the Shire suffered the attentions of Sauron the Dark Lord and his dreadful minions.

Even after Sauron's downfall the Shire was not immediately safe, for the corrupt wizard Saruman took refuge there, calling himself Sharkey, and spread discord, ruination and misery. But before long the hobbit-heroes came home to rally their fellows; Saruman died, killed by his own servant; and the evil he had worked was soon undone. The year of the return of the hobbits of the Fellowship was an exceptional year, with a splendid spring and a magnificent harvest. And the Shire is now more beautiful than ever.

For such a small area, the Shire plays an exceptionally important part in the history of Middle-earth and several hobbits have become heroes known to all the peoples of Middle-earth. The first hobbit to have achieved great fame was Bilbo Baggins who in 2941 Third Age, at the instigation of Gandalf the magician, joined the expedition of dwarves to remove the dragon Smaug from the LONELY MOUNTAIN. No doubt Bilbo's Tookish blood explains his participation in the enterprise, despite his initial hesitations. There he encountered Gollum and took from him the One Ring, an object of great and terrible power forged to bring all under the rule of Sauron, the Dark Lord of MORDOR. Bilbo returned home and, thanks to the occult power of the ring, led a long life, but like all those who wore it he became increasingly weary or "stretched" as he put it.

Bilbo's heir, Frodo Baggins, learnt of the nature of the ring from Gandalf the great magician and resolved to take it back to Mount Doom in Mordor, the only place where it could be destroyed. Accompanied by Sam Gamgee, Peregrin Took, known as Pippin, and Meriadoc or Merry Brandybuck, he left the Shire in 3018 Third Age, travelling via Bree-land to Rivendell, where the Fellowship of the Ring was first established, and then set out on the quest to destroy the ring. Despite the hazards of the journey and the terrible and fearful attacks by the dark forces of Sauron, Frodo eventually succeeded. All the other hobbit members of the Fellowship earned their place in Middle-earth's history in their different ways. The loyal and generous Sam Gamgee contributed greatly to the reconstruction of the Shire and was seven times elected mayor. It is said that he, the last of the Ring Bearers, went to the GREY HAVENS and sailed across the sea, like Bilbo Baggins and Frodo before him. Meriadoc Brandybuck was present at the destruction of ISENGARD and later helped relieve the siege of MINAS TIRITH. He became Master of Buckland on his return to the Shire, where he played an important part in the routing of Sharkey's men. Meriadoc became Thain of the Shire. Together with Peregrin Took he left the Shire at the request of Eomer of Rohan, and was with him when he died. The two are said to have been buried in Minas Tirith where they lie next to the king.

The important role played by the hobbits in the War of the Ring appears to have awakened their interest in history; it was towards the end of the war that the predominantly oral records of the Shire began to be collected in written form, and by the first century of the Fourth Age there were already several libraries of books and records in the Shire. The most important record is the *Red Book,* which also contains the accounts of the hobbits who figured in the war. Much of the text consists of translations from the Elvish, together with annotations and glosses by the scholars of Minas Tirith. And the Michel Delving Mathom House contains an important collection of weapons and artifacts from the Shire.

In ancient times, the hobbits appear to have spoken the language of men, after their own fashion, that is. After settling in the Shire they adopted Hobbitish, a dialect of Westron, the common speech of Middle-earth. Their dialect includes a number of forms peculiar to the Shire, particularly when it comes to names.

Their calendar is also unique to the Shire: the year is divided into twelve months of thirty days each: Afteryule, Solmath, Rethe, Astron, Thrimidge, Forelithe, Afterlithe, Wedmath, Halimath, Winterfilth, Blotmath, and Foreyule. Saturday is the first day of the week and Friday the last. The year always begins on a Saturday and always ends on a Friday. The first and last days of the year, the

Yule days, are the main holiday of the Shire, along with the midsummer holiday of the Lithe days. Normally there are three Lithe days per year; in leap years there are four, the additional holiday being referred to as Overlithe.

(J.R.R. Tolkien, *The Hobbit, or There and Back Again,* London, 1937; J.R.R. Tolkien, *The Fellowship of the Ring,* London, 1954; J.R.R. Tolkien, *The Two Towers,* London, 1954; J.R.R. Tolkien, *The Return of the King,* London, 1955; J.R.R. Tolkien, *The Silmarillion,* London, 1977)

SHIVAPURAM, capital of PALA.

SIGHT, FOREST OF, north of DICTIONOPOLIS in WISDOM KINGDOM. The forest is inhabited by the Bing family. The Bings are born with their heads at exactly the height they will be at adulthood, and grow downwards as they grow older until their feet finally touch the ground. In this way they always see things from the same point of view. However, the different members of the family see things in different ways. One sees through things, but cannot see in front of his nose; another sees to things; another looks after things; another sees beyond things; another sees the other side of the question; another sees under things, and when he cannot see under, overlooks them.

In the Forest of Sight stands a small house with four doors—two are labelled The Giant and The Midget respectively, the other two are not labelled. Visitors are advised to knock at any of these four doors. Here lives a man who, to tall men, is a midget; to short men, a giant; to skinny men, fat; and to fat men, skinny. He is, in fact, perfectly ordinary.

In the middle of the forest is a large orchestra that plays constantly, conducted by Chroma, conductor of colour, maestro of pigment and director of the entire spectrum. Each instrument plays a different colour. If they were to stop—say the people of Sight Forest—all colours would vanish from the world.

The City of Reality stands in the Forest of Sight. Once a very pleasant city, it is now invisible, with great crowds of people rushing about, eyes to the ground, darting along non-existent streets. A long time ago the people of the city discovered that they would reach their destinations much more quickly if they looked at nothing but their shoes. No one took any notice of the surrounding beauty and the city became uglier and uglier. The people moved faster and faster, the buildings grew fainter, the streets faded away and the city finally disappeared. Many of the citizens of Reality moved to the nearby City of Illusions, a magnificent metropolis of shining streets, jewelled walls, and silver-paved avenues, none of which is really there.

(Norton Juster, *The Phantom Tollbooth*, London, 1962)

SILENCE, a region in Libya, by the borders of the River Zaïre, whose waters have a saffron and sickly hue and do not flow onward to the sea but palpitate for ever and ever beneath the sun, with a tumultuous and convulsive motion. For many miles on either side of the river's oozy bed is a pale desert of gigantic water-lilies. The region is bounded by a dark, horrible, lofty forest with strange poisonous flowers, and though there is no wind, the low underwood is continually agitated. On the shore of the river stands a tall, grey rock, showing a few engraved characters which spell the word "Desolation." The whole area is cursed with silence: the moon does not wane, the lightning does not flash, the clouds hang motionless, the waters never change their level, the trees do not sigh in the still air. Visitors will find that they cannot pronounce a single word, and will believe that they have been struck by a strange deafness.

(Edgar Allan Poe, "Silence: a Fable," in *Tales*, New York, 1845)

SILHA, an island in the Atlantic Ocean, near NACUMERA. It is eight hundred miles round and infested with serpents, dragons and crocodiles. These beasts, however, will not harm strangers; they attack only people born on the island. The natives protect themselves from the venomous animals by anointing themselves with an ointment made from fruit called *limons*.

In the centre of the island is a lake said to have been formed by the tears of Adam and Eve, who lived on a mountain here for one hundred years after they were expelled from Paradise. Precious stones and pearls are found in the lake and the king allows the poor to collect them once a year.

(Sir John Mandeville, *Voiage de Sir John Maundevile*, Paris, 1357)

SILK, ISLE OF, see LORBANERY.

SILLING, a castle high on a hill in the Black Forest, made inaccessible by impregnable walls and a deep moat. It was here that, after demolishing the drawbridge which was the castle's only link with the outside world, a group of elderly researchers barricaded themselves to hold a seemingly endless orgy in which all possible sexual combinations were explored. The group consisted of four gentlemen between the ages of 45 and 60 and forty-two carefully selected men, women and children who acted as pawns in their erotic games, the wives of the four gentlemen, eight young boys, eight young girls, eight monstrously endowed sodomites, four ancient madames, six cooks or servants, and four highly qualified procuresses. From November 1 to February 28 of an unspecified year towards the end of the 1800's, it was the task of the four procuresses to narrate some six hundred perversions, one hundred and fifty each, while the four gentlemen put into practice the most original ones. All other members of the congregation were carefully tortured and then murdered.

(Donatien-Alphonse-François, Marquis de Sade, *Les 120 Journées de Sodome, ou l'Ecole du libertinage*, Paris, 1785)

SIMON-CRUBELLIER, a street in Paris. At number 11 rises an apartment building in which the history of the world is concentrated. To all appearances, 11 Rue Simon-Crubellier is an ordinary building with an ordinary entrance hall and a commercial property on the ground floor: Marcia Antiques. Above the ground floor are six storeys of flats, plus two more of attic rooms: a total of thirty dwellings, including the lodgings of the concierge, Madame Nochère. Of the many curious characters who live or have lived in this building, one in particular, Percival Bartlebooth, was perhaps the most curious. A solitary man, he dedicated twenty years of his life to copying watercolours from around the world, and then, after cutting them up into puzzles, another twenty to reconstructing them, only to destroy them all in the end. Bartlebooth died on June 23, 1975, but visitors still arrive on mournful pilgrimages to see the house in which he accomplished his monumentally useless task.

(Georges Perec, *La Vie, mode d'emploi*, Paris, 1978)

SIRANNON, a river of HOLLIN, known in the Common Speech of MIDDLE-EARTH as the Gate Stream. Sirannon rises near the West Gate of the old dwarvish realm of MORIA beneath the MISTY MOUNTAINS. It flows down the so-called Stair Falls, a waterfall close to the old road between Hollin and Moria. At one time it was a swift, noisy cascade, but the flow over the falls has now been reduced to a mere trickle, as the stream was dammed above the falls to form a lake.

This lake was created by a monster which was in close alliance with the orcs or goblins that took over Moria after the departure of the dwarves. This monster is of unknown origin, but is presumed to be some ancient creature from under the mountains. It normally lies silent and hidden beneath the waters, and is therefore called the Watcher in the Water. But if it is disturbed by travellers it may attempt to seize them and drag them under—it has at least twenty tentacles or arms, and looks like a seething mass of snakes bubbling out of the lake. The very water of the lake has been polluted by this evil-smelling creature and now reflects nothing of the sky above.

(J.R.R. Tolkien, *The Fellowship of the Ring*, London, 1954)

SIRAP, capital of MEGAPATAGONIA.

SIREN ISLAND, in the Mediterranean, exact position unknown. Visitors are not advised to approach it because it is inhabited by a curious species of birds with women's faces, known as the Sirens (though some chroniclers have confused them with Mermaids—see also MER-KING'S KINGDOM—because their customs are similar, as in the case of the Mermaid Lorelei who lives on a large rock in the River Rhine, Germany). The Sirens attract sailors with their sweet songs. Unaware of the danger, the sailors find themselves shipwrecked on the rocky coast of the island. To avoid this unpleasant fate, travellers can take one of three classic preventive measures: either lash themselves to the ship's mast, fill their ears with wax, or find a lyre virtuoso who can distract them with his music. Legend has it that after being ignored by the King of Ithaca, one of the Sirens, Parthenope, drowned herself in annoyance and was washed ashore in the Bay of Naples, Italy, which originally bore her name.

A different species of Siren lives in Dublin, Ireland, and takes the form of a sexy barmaid who sings over her Guinness.

(Homer, *The Odyssey*, 9th cen. [?] BC; Apollonius of Rhodes, *Argonautica*, 2nd cen. BC; Heinrich Heine, "Die Lorelei," in *Buch der Lieder*, Munich, 1827; James Joyce, *Ulysses*, Paris, 1922)

SIRTES, SEA OF, see FARGHESTAN; also ORSENNA.

SITARA, a country to the north of ARDISTAN. Very few travellers have visited Sitara, also known as the Land of Starflowers and the Land of God's Mountains. For thousands of years it has been ruled by the family of Marah Durimeh, the present Sultana; by tradition, the ruler is always a woman. War is totally unknown in Sitara, where every word spoken is of love and reconciliation.

The country has not been described in any detail and the only royal residence to have been visited by outsiders is Ikbal, or Place of Promise, in the north. Ikbal is an island in the River Ed, which flows from the mountains down to the sea where its waters are purified. On the centre of the island the palace rises from the ground "like a verse from the Song of Solomon." It is built of pure white marble and the houses of the Sultana's subjects cluster around it like pearls.

The only communication between Ikbal and the neighbouring countries is by a boat known as the *Wilahde*, a sizeable sailing vessel, built in the style of an ark and always ready to sail; the pattern of the rigging and sails may have been originally invented in ancient Egypt or Babylon.

It is very difficult to enter Sitara. Anyone who wishes to do so must first pass through the old forge in the Forest of Kulub near the border. Here the visitor will be hardened and purified in fire, and transformed from a person of violence into a person of peace. Only those who have been ennobled by such suffering will be allowed in.

Despite its isolation, Sitara has had a considerable influence. Centuries ago, Sitarian missionaries travelled to USSUL, where their faith was preserved and handed down from mother to daughter for many generations. More recently, an envoy from Marah Durimeh was largely responsible for putting an end to the conflict between Ardistan and DJINNISTAN and for restoring peace and prosperity to the surrounding lands.

(Karl Friedrich May, *Ardistan,* Bamberg, 1909; Karl Friedrich May, *Der Mir von Djinnistan,* Bamberg, 1909)

SKULL ISLAND, south-west of Sumatra, in the Indian Ocean. The climate is typically tropical, very hot, with no rain except during the monsoon season. There is little wind and the surrounding seas are usually calm although thick fog is frequent. Towards the west, Skull Island extends in a long, sandy peninsula for over a mile. The peninsula is cut off from the mainland by a precipice hundreds of feet high which marks the beginning of the dense growth characteristic of the rest of the island. In its centre rises a mountain, the shape of which suggests a skull—hence the island's name. At the foot of the mountain is a huge asphalt lake into which flow the streams running down the slopes.

Between the peninsula and the precipice runs a wooden wall over one hundred and thirty feet high, connecting both coasts, with two stone pillars supporting a gigantic gate. The wall was erected by the people of an ancient civilization, who also built a city, now in ruins. On the site of these ruins stands the only village now on the island—a group of grass, mud and wooden huts inhabited by the descendants of that ancient civilization, who have now become savages. The natives' main concern is to maintain the wall for their own protection. They are Negroes, ruled by a king, who worship the god Kong, a giant gorilla. A witch-doctor is in charge of their spiritual needs.

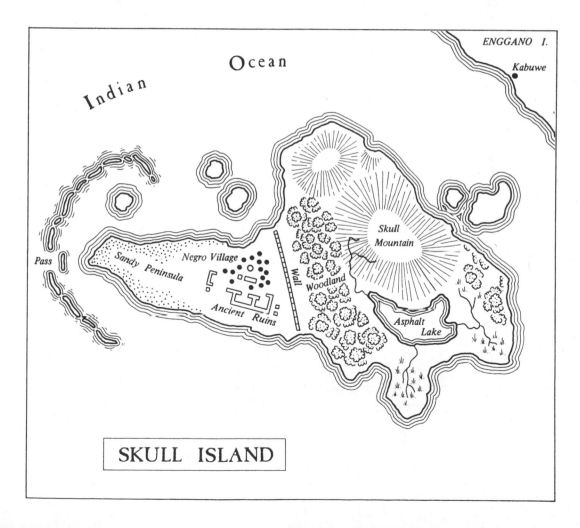

SKULL ISLAND

According to their customs, Kong is from time to time presented with a bride. A girl from the village, dressed in a girdle, necklace and crown of flowers, is offered to the god. The presentation ceremony takes place in the village square among rows of chanting natives. The girl is handed over by the witch-doctor to twelve of the tallest men of the village—dressed in rough black skins and furry skulls to resemble a pack of apes—who place her on an altar and tie her between two pillars on the other side of the wall. The king comes forward, a metal drum is beaten, and the gate in the wall is opened. The natives scramble onto the top of the wall and Kong arrives to collect his bride. The gate is then shut until the next ceremony.

The flora of Skull Island, typical of a tropical climate, has achieved enormous proportions. Many animals found here are, in fact, survivors of prehistoric times—dinosaurs, huge lizards, flying reptiles. Giant insects also abound, as well as snakes and vultures. The giant gorilla known as Kong left the island on one occasion for a trip to New York, but his visit was not a success.

(King Kong, produced and directed by Merian Cooper & Ernest Schoedsack, USA, 1932–33)

SLAVNA, an ancient city, capital of KRAVONIA for over a thousand years and under many dynasties. Slavna is an island set in the broad valley of the River Krath, which at this point flows due east. Immediately above the city the river divides into two branches known as the North and South rivers; Slavna is clasped in the embrace of these channels. Conditioned by their course, Slavna is not round but pear-shaped, for the river-branches bend out in gradual broad curves to their greatest distance from one another, reapproaching quickly after that point is past till they meet again at the end—or rather what was originally the end—of the city to the east; the single reunited river may stand for the stalk of the pear.

In olden days Slavna's position was a strong one, but nowadays it is less defensible. To compensate for this weakness, the rulers of Slavna allocated money for a new and scientific system of fortifications, and almost entirely destroyed the ancient and out-of-date walls which had once been the city's protection. Part of these walls still stands on the north side, encumbered and built over with warehouses and wharves on the North River, the channel of commerce and medium of trade with the surrounding countryside.

Suleiman's Tower in the outskirts of SLAVNA.

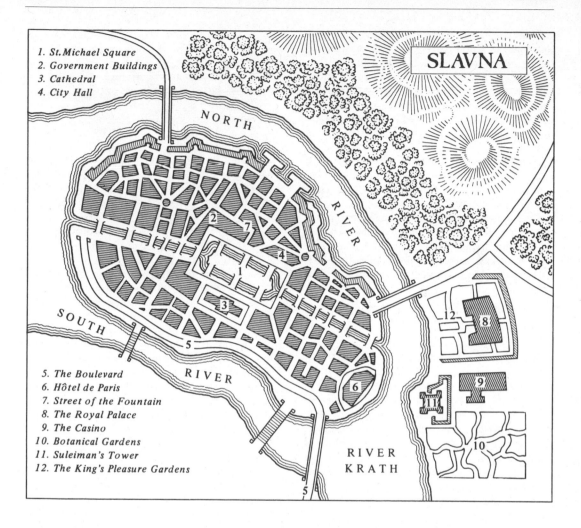

1. St. Michael Square
2. Government Buildings
3. Cathedral
4. City Hall

5. The Boulevard
6. Hôtel de Paris
7. Street of the Fountain
8. The Royal Palace
9. The Casino
10. Botanical Gardens
11. Suleiman's Tower
12. The King's Pleasure Gardens

To the south a boulevard has been built on the ruins of the wall, lined with handsome modern residences, for as the North River is for trade, the South River is for pleasure. The boulevard has been carried across the water beyond the old limits of the city, running for a mile or more along the right bank of the reunited Krath, forming a delightful and well-shaded promenade where the citizens of Slavna are accustomed to take their various forms of exercise.

Opposite the promenade, on the left bank of the Krath, lies the park attached to the Royal Palace. The building, dating from 1820 and regrettably typical of the style of the period, faces the river just where it takes a broad sweep to the south, giving a rounded margin to the King's Pleasure Gardens.

Travellers to Slavna are advised to visit the Casino, the Botanical Gardens and Suleiman's Tower, a relic of Turkish rule, built on a simple plan: a square curtain wall with a bastion at each corner enclosing a massive round tower.

In spite of the flatness of the surrounding country, the appearance of Slavna is not unpicturesque. Time and the hand of man—Kravonians are a colour-loving race—have given many tints, soft and bright, to the roofs, gables and walls of the old quarters in the north section of Slavna. In the centre of the city a pretty little canal has been built by abstracting water from the river and conducting it through the streets. On either side of this canal runs a broad road leading into the spacious Square of St. Michael, containing the

Cathedral, the fine old City Hall, several good town houses dating back two or three hundred years, the barracks and the modern but not unsightly government offices. Through this square and the streets leading to it from the west and east runs an excellent service of electric trams. Just off the Square, visitors are advised to follow the Street of the Fountain, where the famous Sophy of Kravonia saved the life of Prince Sergius who was later to become her husband. Ten doors down from the Square, under the sign of the silver cock, stands the house in which Sophy took lodgings when she first arrived in Kravonia.

Travellers can stay at the celebrated *Hôtel de Paris,* in the south-east end of the city. The hotel was built in the 1860's by a Frenchman, Monsieur Rousseau, with the approval of King Alexis Stefanovich, and has a fine terrace and excellent café.

(Anthony Hope [Anthony Hope Hawkins], *Sophy of Kravonia,* London, 1906)

SLEEPERS OF ERINN, CAVE OF THE, beneath the mountains of Ireland, not far from GLYN CAGNY. The cave is reached through a cleft in the mountainside marked by burning torches. This is the normal residence of Angus Og, one of the ancient gods of Ireland, also known as Infinite Love and Joy. His appearance is one of great beauty and strength, but he is increasingly unhappy as the people whom he cares for neglect him more and more. Angus Og is always subject to immortal will and can only give help to those humans who ask for it.

Angus Og married Caitlin, daughter of one of the philosophers of Glyn Cagny, after saving her from the god Pan who once visited Ireland. Pan, referred to by Angus Og as "Desire and Fever and Lust and Death," subsequently left Ireland—a land which has never been his and in which his worship has never taken strong root.

(James Stephens, *The Crock of Gold,* London, 1912)

SLEEPING BEAUTY'S CASTLE, in a kingdom of Central Europe. It possesses many chambers, parlours, winding stairs and old towers. In one tower, visitors can admire an ancient spinning wheel, and in the central hall a collection of twelve golden plates. According to certain historians a

SLEEPING BEAUTY'S CASTLE as seen from the southern fields.

spell was cast on the palace by a wise woman knowledgeable in the magic arts, during the celebrations held to honour Princess Rosamund's birth in the early eighteenth century. Although twelve other wise women had been asked to the celebrations she had been left uninvited for lack of a thirteenth gold plate, and was consequently resentful. The spell seems to have been effective, for on her fifteenth birthday lovely Princess Rosamund pricked her finger on the spindle of the ancient spinning wheel and immediately fell asleep, followed by the rest of the court, the animals in the stables, the wind in the trees and the flies in the sunlight. Only the hedge of thorns surrounding the gardens was not affected by the spell, growing out of all proportion and thickly enveloping the castle.

One hundred years later, a young prince— whose arrival had been foretold in a well-known song—crossed the thicket, found the sleeping princess and woke her with a kiss. The whole palace awoke from its slumber, and the prince and Rosamund were immediately married and lived happily ever after.

Imitations, inspired by this castle, were later built by King Ludwig II of Bavaria, and by Mr. Walt Disney of Chicago in the United States.

(Jakob & Wilhelm Grimm, *Kinder- und Hausmärchen,* Heidelberg, 1812–14)

SLEEPLESS CITY, in northern Nigeria. The inhabitants have the singular habit of never sleeping, and have therefore no idea of what sleep is.

The city is a particularly dangerous place for

strangers. If a traveller should happen to overlook the local nocturnal custom and fall asleep—as he is probably accustomed to do at night—the natives, believing him dead, will proceed to dig a large grave and with great ceremony bury him immediately.

(A.J.N. Tremearne, *Hausa Superstitions and Customs,* London, 1913)

SLEEPY HOLLOW, a hamlet about two miles from the small town of Greensburgh on the banks of the Hudson River, haunted by many spirits. Greensburgh is known locally as Tarry Town, from the propensity of its men to tarry in the tavern on market days. Sleepy Hollow itself is high in the hills, and is perhaps one of the quietest places in the world; the only sounds are the murmuring of a brook and the occasional whistle of a quail or tapping of a woodpecker. The inhabitants are direct descendants of the original Dutch settlers and are known in the area as the Sleepy Hollow Boys.

The hamlet derives its name from the sleepy atmosphere that pervades it. Some say that it was bewitched by a German doctor during the earliest days of the settlement; others that it was used by Indian sorcerers long before the arrival of the Europeans. Whatever the reason, it is true that the locals appear to be under the spell of the place and to live in a constant dream. They are extremely superstitious, subject to trances and visions and frequently see strange sights and hear strange music.

Of the many spirits that haunt the area the chief is the ghost of a headless horseman, said to be a Hessian trooper whose head was shot off by a cannonball in a forgotten battle during the Revolutionary War. Historians claim that his body lies in the churchyard and that at night he rides forth to the scene of the battle in search of his lost head, rushing back to his grave before daybreak.

In the late eighteenth century, a village schoolmaster appears to have encountered the horseman. The schoolmaster, Ichabod Crane, fell in love with the daughter of the local Dutch farmer, though he found he had a rival famed for his feats of strength and hardihood. Returning home from the farmer's house after an evening of storytelling (most of the stories of Sleepy Hollow deal with ghosts and goblins), Crane encountered a horseman on a powerful black horse who began to pursue him. Crane's horse panicked and headed

for a bridge near the village. As he crossed the bridge, Crane looked back and saw the ghost rising in his stirrups and flinging his head at him. Crane was struck by the flying missile and fell into the dust. The next morning, Crane's horse was found, but the schoolmaster was never again seen in Sleepy Hollow. No body was ever discovered and Crane's ghost now haunts the decaying schoolhouse.

(Washington Irving, "The Legend of Sleepy Hollow," in *The Sketch Book of Geoffrey Crayon, Gent.,* New York, 1820)

SLOUGH OF DESPOND, see DESPOND, SLOUGH OF.

SMALLDENE, a village in Sussex, site of the famous Wish House at 14 Wadloes Road. It is a little basement-kitchen house in a row of some twenty or thirty similar ones, with small walled gardens. Visitors who wish to take upon themselves the ailments of someone they love can knock on the shabby front door. A sound like that of a heavy woman in slippers will be heard on the kitchen stairs and then a creak on the bare boards just behind the door. It is then that the requesting visitor should pronounce his wish into the letter-box slot, and it will be fulfilled. Though neighbours may say that the house is empty, travellers are advised not to pay any attention and proceed with the wishing as instructed.

(Rudyard Kipling, "The Wish House," in *Debits and Credits,* London, 1926)

SMITH ISLAND, see ORPHAN ISLAND.

SNARK ISLAND, an island of unpleasant chasms and crags, and dismal, desolate valleys, somewhere in the Ocean. For those wishing to find it, and who believe that Mercator's North Poles and Equators, Tropics, Zones and Meridian Lines are merely conventional signs, a blank map representing the sea will prove useful. It is also advisable to take along a dagger-proof coat and two Insurance Policies—one Against Fire and one Against Damage from Hail. The traveller who sails to this part of the world is warned, when in tropical climates, to pay particular heed that the bowsprit of the ship does not get mixed with the rudder—a frequent occurrence which is locally described as being "snarked."

Various animals live on the island (apart from the *snark* itself), strange creepy creatures: the *jub-jub*—a passionate bird with a terrifying, shrill, screaming song (but it is exquisite when cooked and several different recipes are available); and the dangerous *bandersnatch*, with extensible neck and frumious claws. *Snarks*, too, are good cooked, and served with greens, and they may also be used to strike a light. One species of *snark*, the *boojum*, can, if it is seen, cause certain persons to softly and suddenly vanish away. But there are five distinctive characteristics by which a common *snark*, which is harmless, can be recognized; they are listed in the only existing textbook on the subject:

> Let us take them in order. The first is the
>   taste,
> Which is meagre and hollow, but
>   crisp:
> Like a coat that is rather too tight in
>   the waist,
> With a flavour of Will-o'-the-wisp.
>
> Its habit of getting up late you'll agree
> That it carries too far, when I say
> That it frequently breakfasts at five-
>   o'clock tea,
> And dines on the following day.
>
> The third is its slowness in taking a jest.
>   Should you happen to venture on
>   one,
> It will sigh like a thing that is deeply
>   distressed:
> And it always looks grave at a pun.
>
> The fourth is its fondness for bathing-
>   machines,
>   Which it constantly carries about,
>   And believes that they add to the
>   beauty of scenes—
> A sentiment open to doubt.

The fifth and last characteristic is its ambition. Furthermore, *snarks* can be divided into two groups: those that have feathers and bite, and those that have whiskers and scratch. The recommended system for catching any kind of *snark* is as follows:

> You may seek it with thimbles—and seek
>   it with care;

> You may hunt it with forks and
>   hope;
> You may threaten its life with a
>   railway-share;
> You may charm it with smiles and
>   soap.

(Lewis Carroll [Charles Lutwidge Dodgson], *The Hunting of the Snark*, London, 1876)

SNEAKS' ISLAND, fairly close to MACREONS ISLAND. The island is ruled by King Quaresmeprenant, and the people behave as though it were always Lent. The king dresses in grey, with nothing before and nothing behind and sleeves to match. He and his people are great fish-eaters but they also eat large quantities of dried peas. No marriages take place on the island, and the population spends much of its time in tears. The island exports large quantities of skewers and larding sticks.

King Quaresmeprenant is perpetually at war with the inhabitants of SAVAGE ISLAND. Only the protection given to the people of Savage Island by their god, Shrove Tuesday, has prevented King Quaresmeprenant from invading their land and exterminating them.

King Quaresmeprenant is said to be of LANTERNLAND stock, which may explain why his head is so full of whimsical ideas and fancies. His brain has been described by one visitor to the island as being the size, colour, substance, and strength of a male fleshworm's left testicle.

(François Rabelais, *Le quart livre des faicts et dicts du bon Pantagruel*, Paris, 1552)

SNOWBIRD VALLEY, a valley of birch trees in Canada, somewhere between Winnipeg and Moose Jaw. Early in the winter all the snowbirds in Canada come here to make their snow-shoes. Nothing else is known about this interesting valley.

(Carl Sandburg, *Rootabaga Stories*, New York, 1922)

SNOW QUEEN'S CASTLE, in the barren regions of icy-cold Finland, where the snow flakes do not fall from the sky—cloudless and bright with the Northern Lights—but run straight along the ground, and are alive, taking on strange and formidable shapes. Some look like great ugly porcupines or snakes rolled into knots, others like little, fat bears with bristling hair—these last are the Snow Queen's guards.

The walls of the palace itself are formed of driven snow and its doors and windows of cutting winds. In the palace, there are over a hundred halls, the largest of them many miles long, all illuminated by the Northern Lights, all alike, vast, empty, icily cold and dazzlingly white. No sounds of mirth ever resound through these dreary spaces; no cheerful scene refreshes the eye. Not even so much as a bear's ball, such as one might imagine (the tempest forming a band of musicians and the polar bears standing on their hind paws), takes place; not even a small select coffee-party for the white, young lady-foxes.

In the midst of the empty snow chamber lies a frozen lake broken into a thousand pieces. These pieces so exactly resemble each other that the breaking might well be deemed a work of superhuman skill. Here sits the Snow Queen, when at home.

(Hans Christian Andersen, *Snedronningen*, Copenhagen, 1844)

SONA-NYL, see SOUTHERN SEA.

SORHAUTE, capital of the kingdom of King Urien; its location is uncertain. It was to this city that the eleven rebellious lords of the north retreated after the crushing defeat inflicted on them at BEDEGRAINE by King Arthur of CAMELOT.

(Sir Thomas Malory, *Le Morte Darthur*, London, 1485)

SOSARA, see LORBANERY.

SOUND, VALLEY OF, north of SIGHT FOREST in WISDOM KINGDOM. The valley is ruled by the Soundkeeper, who lives in a stone fortress and has been appointed guardian of all sounds by the old King of Wisdom. For years she ruled wisely, releasing the day's sounds at daybreak and gathering in the old sounds at moonset to be filed in vaults (open to the public on Mondays). As the population increased, there was less and less time to listen and many sounds began to disappear, while the sounds made by people became uglier and uglier. A certain Kakofonous A. Dischord Doctor of Dissonance (the "A" stands for "As loud as possible") and his assistant, Dynne, appeared and promised to cure everyone of every-

thing. Much to the annoyance of the Soundkeeper he cured them of everything but noise; in consequence, the Soundkeeper abolished sound in the valley. The result was thunderstorms without thunder and concerts without music. Some necessary sounds were ground three times into powder and then thrown into the air when needed. Music was woven into looms and the people could purchase carpets of symphonies and tapestries of concertos. However, travellers will be relieved to know that nowadays the usual sounds are again available.

(Norton Juster, *The Phantom Tollbooth*, London, 1962)

SOUTHERN SEA, a vast body of water in the south of DREAMWORLD. Along its coast are the glorious lands and cities for which Dreamworld is famous. From the comfort of their ships travellers can see the templed terraces of Zak, the spires of infamous Thalarion, the charnel gardens of Zura where dwell unattained pleasures, and twin headlands of crystal which guard the harbour of Sona-Nyl, the black towers of DYLATH-LEEN.

To the west of the Southern Sea are the Basalt Pillars, beyond which the splendid city of Cathuria is said to lie, though some travellers say that the Pillars are the gates of a monstrous cataract into which fall the waters of the sea. To the east the green coast is strewn with small fishing villages, dreamy harbours and large nets laid out in the sun. To the south, five days' sail from Dylath-Leen, lies a queer landscape with low, broad, brown cottages in fields of grotesque white fungi. The cottages have no windows and their shapes suggest the huts of Eskimos. It is said that this area makes sailors nervous because below the water lie the ruins of a sunken city, too old for memory, and on calm days travellers can see, many fathoms deep, the dome of a great temple and an avenue of unnatural sphinxes leading to what was once a public square. Little is known about the other wonders beneath the waters of the Southern Sea.

(Howard Phillips Lovecraft, "The Dream-Quest of Unknown Kadath," in *Arkham Sampler*, Sauk City, 1948)

SOUTHFARTHING, see SHIRE, THE.

SOUTHWEST WILDERNESS, a region in China, noted for its plantations of sugar cane which grow to a height of a thousand feet with trunks thirty-eight inches round. The juice of the canes imparts strength and vigour and helps check the number of worms in the body. A peculiar specimen of the fauna of this region is the *lying beast*, somewhat like a rabbit with a human face, who can speak like a human being. It often cheats, saying east when it should say west and bad when it should say good. Its flesh is delicious, but eating it makes a person tell lies. It is also known by the name of *rumour*.

(Tung-Fang Shuo, *The Book of Deities and Marvels*, 1st cen. BC)

SPECTRALIA, an island of the RIALLARO ARCHIPELAGO in the south-east Pacific, on the edge of the Riallaro ring of mist, north of COXURIA.

Spectralia is a twilight world, inhabited by people who fear the sun and raise clouds of dust when it appears. They are exiles from LIMANORA, convinced that they and they alone have contact with the other world. Many live underground; all believe in ghosts. There are two sects of Spectralians: the ancient ghost-seekers, who believe in stately ghosts which rarely communicate but merely stare, and for which they build castles; and the modern ghost-seekers, who believe that ghosts speak and appear at will, and who claim that the body has two spirits, one of which can be detached.

Visitors are advised to avoid Spectralia by night in case they should be taken for ghosts and enshrined for religious purposes. There are two markets of souls where newly arrived spirits are bought and sold: one for the modern ghost-seekers, one for the ancient. On a nearby rocky islet, Astralia, lives a third exiled sect which believes in astral bodies.

(Godfrey Sweven, *Riallaro, the Archipelago of Exiles*, New York & London, 1901; Godfrey Sweven, *Limanora, the Island of Progress*, New York & London, 1903)

SPENSONIA, an island somewhere between UTOPIA and OCEANA (1), where a number of Englishmen who were shipwrecked founded a republic towards the end of the eighteenth century. The constitution of Spensonia is based directly on the Rights of Man accorded by the French Revolution. Individual liberty is limited by that of all others; the government is elective; the republic, one and indivisible, is formed by a number of countries and parishes.

Spensonia has friendly relations with all other republics in the world and offers political asylum to exiles from any country under despotic rule but will not interfere with the affairs of foreign states. It follows a colonial, expansionist policy but only with those countries which the Spensonians believe could be improved by Spensonian rule.

Though the official religion is the cult of an undefined Supreme Being, visitors will find that all religious beliefs are readily accepted.

(Thomas Spence, *A Description of Spensonia*, London, 1795; Thomas Spence, *The Constitution of Spensonia: A Country in Fairyland situated between Utopia and Oceana*, London, 1798)

An underground courtyard, SPECTRALIA.

SPERANZA, see CRUSOE'S ISLAND.

SPIDERMONKEY ISLAND, a large island, about one hundred miles long, in the south Atlantic off the coast of Brazil. This island is very mountainous, with high volcanic peaks. The second highest mountain is distinctively shaped and resembles a hawk's head. The most spectacular area of the island is the valley of the Whispering Rocks, a great natural amphitheatre in the mountains, where the rocks rise in a series of natural seats or steps around a central table of stone. The narrowest end of the amphitheatre lies open, giving wonderful views over the sea. The central bowl is several miles deep and several miles wide, but no matter where a visitor stands, a whisper can be heard by all those in this natural theatre. Traditionally, the valley of the Whispering Rocks is used for the coronation of kings; for this purpose, an ivory throne stands on the central table of rock.

The first European to come to Spidermonkey Island was Dr. John Dolittle, who arrived here in 1839 in search of Long Arrow, the great Red Indian naturalist who was thought to have disappeared on the island. In those days, Spidermonkey Island was a floating island, slowly drifting south towards colder regions. It was pushed northwards to its present position by whales acting at the request of Dr. Dolittle. The island was once part of the continent of South America, cut off from the mainland during the Ice Age. For reasons which have yet to be explained, the hollow centre of the island became filled with air and the whole island became a floating mass. The settling of the island in its present position was largely the work of Dr. Dolittle himself.

Shortly after his arrival, Dr. Dolittle found Long Arrow trapped inside one of the mountains. He and a group of Indians had been looking for medicinal plants and mosses in a cave, when a slab of rock broke off and imprisoned them. Dr. Dolittle and his animal friends freed the trapped Indians by digging away at the foot of the rock slab until it fell. (The huge slab of stone is now one of the regular sights of the island, and legend has grown saying that when the Doctor found that his friend was trapped, he simply tore the mountain apart with his bare hands.)

Within days of the rescue of Long Arrow, war broke out between the two Indian tribes that live on the island: the Popsipetels and Bagjagderags (the latter is the larger but more cowardly of the two tribes). Despite the odds, the Popsipetels and the companions of Dr. Dolittle fought very bravely against the Bagjagderags, but it was the final intervention of the parrots that turned the tide in their favour. A cloud of black parrots, summoned by Polynesia, the Doctor's own parrot, attacked the Bagjagderags, tearing their hair and nipping small pieces out of their ears. Faced with this new form of warfare, the Bagjagderags quickly surrendered and swore never again to attack their neighbours. The Popsipetels (the name literally means "Men of the Moving Island") were so grateful that they elected Dr. Dolittle king, an honour he was somewhat reluctant to accept. At his coronation in the valley of the Whispering Rocks, an ancient prophecy was finally fulfilled. For centuries, a hanging stone had stood balanced over the cone of the extinct volcano; it was prophesied that it would fall when the King of Kings was crowned. As the stone fell, it blocked the inner air-chamber of the island, causing it to come to rest in its present position. Legend now has it that when King Jong, as Dolittle was known to his subjects, sat down on the throne, so great was his weight that the island sank to do him honour and has never moved again.

When the island sank, the old village of the Popsipetels sank too, but the city of New Popsipetel was built in a beautiful site at the mouth of a large river. A sewage system was designed by the Doctor, who also had a dam built to provide a constant water supply. The only other major city of Spidermonkey Island is the stone city of the Bagjagderags in the south.

The Popsipetels are mainly farmers who, until the arrival of their beloved King Jong, lived without knowledge of fire; only since the nineteenth century have they been able to eat cooked food. Perhaps their main cultural symbol is the totem pole, illustrating the qualities of the family and surmounted by a carved image of their totem animal. The highest is the Royal Thinkalot Totem, carved in honour of Dr. Dolittle. It is carved with animals, to signify his great knowledge of the animal kingdom, and an enormous parrot is set at the top. Many of the legends and stories of the island commemorate the doings of Dr. Dolittle and his companions, who became so popular that they finally had to leave the island in secret as no one wanted them to go.

In addition to the spidermonkeys which give it its name, the island is the home of the rarest beetle in the world, the *jabizri*. This is a large, flying beetle, more than three inches long. The underside is pale blue and its back is glossy black covered with bright red spots.

(Hugh Lofting, *The Voyages of Doctor Dolittle*, London, 1923)

SPIRITS, MOUNTAIN OF THE, see Monte de las ANIMAS.

SPOON RIVER, a village in New England, in the United States, which is famous for its cemetery. In the inscriptions on its tombstones, the dead describe their past lives.

By reading these epitaphs a traveller can learn all about the life of Benjamin Pantier, the lawyer whose soul was taken in a noose and strangled to death; Henry Chase, the town drunk; and A.D. Blood, who had all the small cafés closed. Or about Roscoe Purkapike, who ran away from home and came home after a year claiming that he had been kidnapped by pirates on Lake Michigan—he told his Puritan wife he had been unable to write because the pirates had put him in irons. (His wife pretended to swallow this tall tale, and welcomed him back with open arms.)

One of the most famous epitaphs is that on the grave of Hortense Robbins, a worldly woman who still dreams of her dinners in town:

> *My name used to be in the papers daily*
> *As having dined somewhere,*
> *Or traveled somewhere,*
> *Or rented a house in Paris,*
> *Where I entertained the nobility.*
> *I was forever eating or traveling,*
> *Or taking the cure at Baden-Baden.*
> *Now I am here to do honor*
> *To Spoon River, here beside the family*
> *   whence I sprang.*
> *No one cares now where I dined,*
> *Or lived, or whom I entertained,*
> *Or how often I took the cure at Baden-*
> *   Baden!*

It should be noted that the dead do not always agree with what is written on each others' markers, and so protest from beyond the grave: they argue and then make up, at least until the next quarrel erupts.

(Edgar Lee Masters, *Spoon River Anthology*, New York, 1915)

SPOROUMBIA, a country in the east of AUSTRALIA, on an island formed by the confluence of two rivers channelled through high stone walls. The capital is Sporoundia, a walled city built around a central square. Here stands the Royal Palace, made of black and white stones, with doorways decorated with bronze statues, and magnificent rooms painted and gilded; the courtyard of black marble bristles with white statues. The name of Sporoundia means "City of the Deformed," and all those born with physical deformities, the *Esperou*, are lodged in the capital.

The country is criss-crossed by an ingenious system of canals which lead through Lake Sporascumposo to the sea. Two passes lead from Sporoundia to the neighbouring country of SEVARAMBIA: the Gate of Hell—a tunnel through the rock—and the Gate of Heaven—a pass high in the mountains.

(Denis Veiras, *Histoire des Sevarambes, peuples qui habitent une partie du troisième continent, communement appellé la terre Australe. Contenant une relation du gouvernement des moeurs de la religion, et du langage de cette nation, inconnue jusques à présent aux peuples de l'Europe*, Amsterdam, 1677–79)

SPOROUNDIA, capital of SPOROUMBIA.

SPRINGWATER ISLE, of uncertain location, somewhere in the far east of EARTHSEA and to the west of the KARGAD EMPIRE. The isle is little more than a rocky sandbar, scarcely over a mile wide and a mile long. The waters around it are full of shoals and rocks. There is no vegetation on Springwater Isle, apart from the coarse sea grass. There is, however, a source of pure water which gives the island its name. The spring is not a natural phenomenon and was once merely an uncertain source of brackish water. It was transformed by Ged, the great wizard of Earthsea, who was once shipwrecked here.

At the time of the creation of the spring, two people lived on the island, an old man and woman who probably saved Ged's life by giving him water and letting him share their meagre food. When Ged finally gained their confidence, the old woman showed him her treasure: a child's dress of brocade, decorated with seed-pearls worked in the shape of a double arrow of the God-brothers of the

Kargad Empire, surmounted by a crown. She also gave him a piece of dark metal, all that remained of a broken ring. Ged realized that the old couple must have been the children of some royal house of the Empire who had been cast away here, but failed to see the significance of the ring or the true nature of the old couple. Before leaving, Ged placed a charm on the spring so that it would produce sweet water.

It was not until much later that Ged learnt the story of the couple and the broken ring. Long before, Erreth-Akbe, the sorcerer-king of Earthsea, had been defeated in battle by the High Priest of the Kargad Empire. His amulet or ring was broken and one half was taken by the High Priest and hidden in the Tombs of Atuan, but Erreth-Akbe contrived to keep the other fragment and gave it to a Kargish Lord, Thoreg. The fragment of the ring became part of the dowry of Thoreg's daughter and was handed down through the generations from mother to child. Eventually the house of Thoreg lost its remaining power and finally there were only two of his lineage left, a boy and a girl. But the ruling Godking still feared the Thoregs, as it was prophesied that their descendants would finally bring about the fall of the Empire, and he had the children kidnapped and left on Springwater Isle where, many years later, Ged found them.

(Ursula K. Le Guin, *A Wizard of Earthsea*, New York, 1968; Ursula K. Le Guin, *The Tombs of Atuan*, London, 1972; Ursula K. Le Guin, *The Farthest Shore*, London, 1973)

STAHLSTADT, a city founded by the German Professor Schultze to compete with FRANCE-VILLE, south of Oregon, ten leagues from the Pacific coast, on the far side of a landscape reminiscent of Switzerland where tall snowy cliffs pierce the sky and overlook deep valleys. In fact, this Alpine scenery is simply a crust of rock, earth and centenary pines covering massive deposits of iron and coal. Travellers leaving this pleasant region and entering the desolate wilderness beyond will find several roads covered in ashes and coal, flanked by heaps of black rubble from which brilliant pieces of metal shine like basilisk eyes. Here and there travellers will see abandoned mineshafts, eaten away by the rain, like the craters of small spent volcanoes. The air is heavy with irritating smoke and totally innocent of birds and in-

sects. In living memory no butterfly has ever been seen in the area.

Should travellers continue towards the north, they will find that this mining region spreads out into a plain. Here, between two low mountain chains, lay what up to 1871 was called the Red Desert, a wasteland of ferruginous sand, now called Stahlfield or Field of Steel. It was on this plain that, from 1872 to 1877, a number of prefabricated cabins, made in Chicago, were erected to form a garland of villages.

Travellers today will see, in the centre of this garland, at the foot of the Coal Butts—a mound of coal—a bizarre and colossal conglomerate of geometrical buildings with hundreds of identical windows and red chimneys which even now belch out their poisonous green smoke. This uninhabited mass is all that is left of Stahlstadt, the City of Steel.

Built in a space of five years by Professor Schultze of Jena University, Stahlstadt became not only a model city but a model factory.

The plan of Stahlstadt consisted of a number of concentric circles, each of which had a different function within the complex. In the exact centre rose the Tower of the Bull, a vast construction with a single window, that dominated the surrounding buildings. At the bottom of this cyclopic tower Professor Schultze had his private rooms and, above these, his secret study. All doors were hermetically sealed. Travellers today can still see the tropical park built around the tower, with its palm trees, banana trees, eucalyptus and cacti, entangling vines and numerous fruits such as pineapples and guavas. In Professor Schultze's time, the temperature was maintained through a system of metallic tubes that carried the hot vapours of the nearby coal deposits.

At the very top of the tower, Professor Schultze built the most impressive piece of artillery in the world, a long-range gun some 300,000 kilos in weight, so easy to handle that a child might have fired it. It used a highly dangerous explosive which in fact resulted in the city's downfall. On the morning of September 13, 1877, at precisely 11:45 P.M., Professor Schultze aimed the gun at the rival city of France-Ville, miscalculated, and the gun's projectile fired into the sky, and went into orbit around the earth, where it remains to this very day. However, the rest of the explosive kept in Schultze's laboratory caught fire, and the Professor was asphyxiated. Without a leader, the city soon became abandoned, although the immense coal deposits still continue to burn in the empty factory. Today, Stahlstadt stands as a desolate monument to human vanity.

(Jules Verne, *Les 500 millions de la Bégum*, Paris, 1879)

STANDARD ISLAND, somewhere near the coast of New Zealand. Once a large and prosperous artificial island-ship; all that remain are the ruins, overgrown with coral and seaweed.

Standard Island was built by the Standard Island Company Limited in the last years of the nineteenth century. The construction cost five hundred million dollars and took four years to complete. It covered twenty-seven square kilometres of fertile soil. The chief engineer was William Tersin, the island's governor Commander Ethel Simcoë, and the population consisted of ten thousand American millionaires. The island was powered by two hydroelectric stations and could travel at a speed of eight knots per hour.

Several parks and vegetable gardens were planted to provide both luxuriant vegetation and edible produce, which achieved enormous proportions due to the new fertilizers used—carrots up to three kilos each were havested. A small river, the Serpentine, crossed the pleasant artificial landscape.

Two harbours, Port Harbour and Starboard Harbour, were built on opposite sides of the island, near the propellers. Twelve cannon were set up at the prow. Overall, Standard Island occupied a volume of 432 million cubic metres and had a circumference of eighty kilometres.

In the centre of the island rose Milliard City, which occupied one-fifth of the island's total surface. The city was patrolled by military police, in both the Catholic and Protestant sections. The Protestant population occupied the port section; the Catholics lived opposite, to starboard. Transportation throughout the city was by moving sidewalks. No bars or casinos were allowed. The official languages were English and French.

Travellers can still visit both the ruins of the Protestant temple, remarkable for its absence of style and reminiscent of a sponge cake, and the remains of St. Mary's Church, a Gothic overdecorated wedding cake. Ceremonies were conducted here and the sacraments given by telephone and teleautograph, directly linked with the million-

15 Novembre

Milliard City
Hôtel de Ville

Menu

Le potage à la d'Orléans
La crème comtesse
Le turbot à la Mornay
Le filet de boeuf à la napolitaine
Les quenelles de volaille à la viennoise
Les mousses de foie gras à la Trévise
Sorbets
Les cailles rôties sur canapé
La salade provençale
Les petits pois à l'anglaise
Bombe, macédoine, fruits
Gâteaux variés
Grissins au parmesan

Vins
Château d'Yquem. Château-Margaux.
Chambertin. Champagne.

Liqueurs variées

Menu for the reception of the Queen of Tahiti, in the Town Hall of Milliard City, STANDARD ISLAND.

aires' homes. The inhabitants used the same system to shop from the comfort of their kitchens.

During the golden age of Standard Island, visitors were received with great pomp. Queen Pomare of Tahiti was welcomed on board when the island-ship called at Papeete, with a large banquet and a concert of chamber music including works by Beethoven, Mozart, Haydn and Onslow.

After continued struggles between Protestants and Catholics, Standard Island was overcome

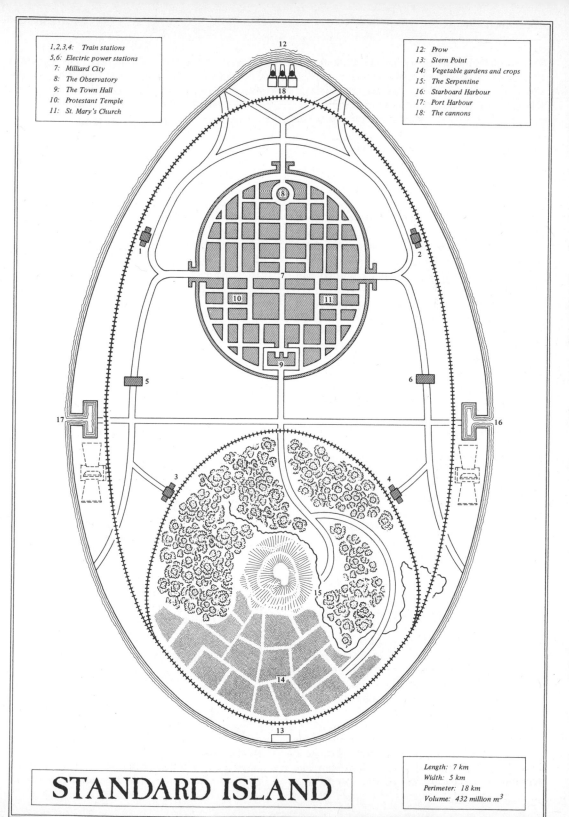

STANDARD ISLAND

Length: 7 km
Width: 5 km
Perimeter: 18 km
Volume: 432 million m^3

by a storm in the South Pacific. On April 10 the shipwrecked remains ran aground about a cable-length from the shore of Ravaraki Bay, in the North Island of New Zealand, so ending the history of what has been called "the ninth wonder of the world," the incomparable "Pearl of the Pacific." Plans have been made to rebuild it but no definite action has yet been taken.

(Jules Verne, *L'Ile à hélice*, Paris, 1895)

STARK-WALL, a rich walled city on an open plain to the south of the BEAR COUNTRY, with wide streets on large, open squares. The most splendid building is the palace of the king, where even the bedchambers have ceilings of gold and blue.

In normal times, the monarchy is hereditary and the crown goes to the eldest son on the death of his father. If there is no male heir, the first traveller to come through the pass leading to the Bear Country is brought to the city. If he is ugly, he is wrapped in a carpet until he suffocates; if he is simple-minded he is given away as a slave. If he is handsome and sane he is stripped naked and left to choose between an ancient suit of armour and a golden raiment. Should he choose the latter, he is either given to someone as a slave or has his wisdom tested. If he chooses the suit of armour, he is made the King of Battle and becomes the next ruler.

(William Morris, *The Wood Beyond the World*, London, 1894)

STEPFORD, a town in the United States, very similar to many others, with its residential quarters, white town hall and small shopping centre and supermarket. What makes Stepford particularly interesting is the fact that the married women of the town are living personifications of dutiful housewives. Not only do they look after the children, clean the house and cook meals, but they do it without ever complaining and seem to enjoy their tasks. They also find time to dress in feminine clothes and make themselves up without incurring excessive expenses.

However, the women of Stepford are never individually creative, never wish to establish their own careers or personalities and behave, in fact, very much like robots—which they are. The transformation of wife into robot is effected by a secret male society with headquarters in Stepford acting under the guise of a men's club. The change does not jeopardize the women's reproductive functions nor their standardized social abilities.

(Ira Levin, *The Stepford Wives*, New York, 1972)

STEPHEN, CAPE, a long rocky promontory on the coast of West Africa, some twenty miles north of FANTIPPO. Visitors are warned that Cape Stephen is a dangerous area for ships because of its treacherous rocks and shoals. A lighthouse is maintained here, manned by two keepers who are relieved only once a year, when they return to England for six weeks' leave.

(Hugh Lofting, *Doctor Dolittle's Post Office*, London, 1924)

STIRIA, see TREASURE VALLEY.

STORISENDE, the castle of the counts of POICTESME on the banks of the Duardenez River, on the edge of the Forest of ACAIRE. Storisende is surrounded by extensive gardens, with broad lawns and innumerable maple and locust trees. In the distance, the blue hills of Poictesme can be seen.

One of the curiosities of the castle is the room of Ageus, so called because its windows were once part of the temple of Ageus in PHILISTIA and were brought here as plunder by Duke Asmund. Two of the windows give a clear view of the outside world. But when the third is opened, the normal appearance of the world vanishes and all that is left is a limitless, grey twilight in which nothing is clearly discernible. It is said that anyone who goes through that window will find it impossible to escape the dreams of others and will embark on a frightening journey beyond the world of appearances. It is said that Manuel, the great hero and liberator of Poictesme, went through this window at the end of his long career and never returned.

Anyone who enters the garden of Storisende in the moment between dawn and sunrise is likely to encounter a strange variety of fabulous animals: centaurs, fairies, leprechauns, valkyries and cynocephali. They are also likely to see scenes from their own past, and people they once knew in their youth.

(James Branch Cabell, *Jurgen. A Comedy of Justice*, New York, 1919; James Branch Cabell, *Figures of Earth. A Comedy of Appearances*, New York, 1921;

James Branch Cabell, *The High Place. A Comedy of Disenchantment*, New York, 1923)

STORN, a small island, two miles off the coast of southern England. The nearest port and only means of access is Port Breton. Storn Island is often stormbound.

Storn is the traditional seat of the Le Breton family, who also own considerable estates on the mainland. The island is crown property and, since the reign of Queen Elizabeth I, the Rangers of the Moor (the traditional title of the holders of the island and the mainland estates) have paid tribute to the reigning monarch. The tribute takes the form of a gold nugget, said to represent the Gull Rock, a rock to the west of the main island. The nugget then returns to the family, but a corner is always chipped off before it is returned.

There is a small village on Storn—a cluster of pink-washed buildings behind the breakwater. The harbour supports a small fishing fleet. In summer, some of the householders supplement their income by selling teas and postcards to visitors brought by the paddle steamer *Daffodil* from Port Breton. The major construction on the island is the Norman castle, whose twin rounded towers dominate the village and can be seen quite clearly from the mainland. It is built of a pinkish stone which appears to change colour in the shifting light—at times it seems pink, at other times it takes on the more sinister colour of dried blood. The castle, still the home of the Le Bretons, is

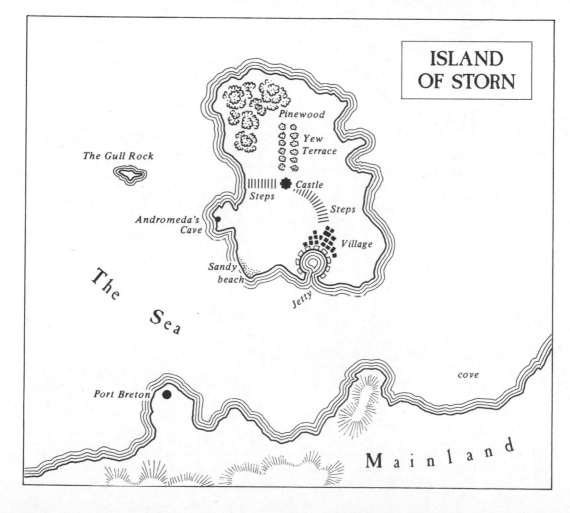

approached from a level terrace-walk of turf, flanked by huge and ancient yew trees. At some point in the past trees were cut to resemble fantastic animals, whose shapes can still be half seen against the sky.

The rest of the island is largely covered in pine woods which provide a home for the red squirrels of the island.

One site which is not accessible to visitors is the so-called Cave of Andromeda, a narrow cave at sea level. It was given its name by the late Sir Venn Le Breton who, in his childhood, imagined that the iron rings set in the walls were those used to chain the Andromeda of legend. It is said that an ancestor of the family once chained an unfaithful

mistress to these rings in mid-winter, and her body was found a week later by a fisherman who took shelter in the cave. It is also said that the late Sir Venn once chained his own wife in the same cave. Perhaps in revenge, Sir Venn's wife, who was suffering from diphtheria, kissed her husband, thereby infecting him with the disease. After a short illness, Sir Venn died.

(Victoria Sackville-West, *The Dark Island*, London, 1934)

STRACKENZ, a notorious German duchy, bordered by Mecklenburg and not far from the Baltic Sea, thirty miles long by twelve miles wide. Dur-

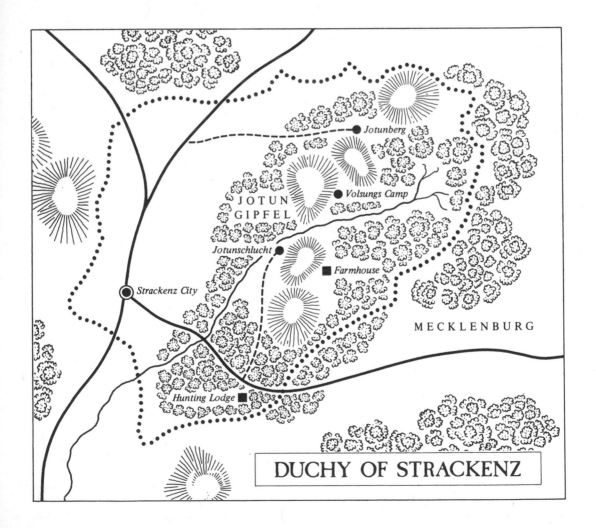

DUCHY OF STRACKENZ

ing Bismarck's supremacy, it became part of the German Empire. Most of the inhabitants live in the flatlands near the capital.

An unusual feature of the landscape is a range of crags known as the Jotun Gipfel, rugged and wild, with two beautiful tarns, in one of which stands the Jotunberg, a former stronghold of the dukes of Strackenz. The summit of the Jotun Gipfel is a tree-fringed plateau split by a deep river gorge, the Jotun Schlucht. The Jotunberg rises high above a beautiful lake, the Jotunsee. Here stands a Gothic pile of towers and battlements reached via a drawbridge or by boat to the tiny harbour cut out of the rock itself. Prince Karl Gustaf was imprisoned here. By 1848 the castle was already semi-derelict and today only the ruins can be visited.

Strackenz City is the capital, the site of both the ducal palace and the old cathedral with its impressive stained-glass windows.

(George MacDonald Fraser, *Royal Flash*, London, 1970)

STREAMING KINGDOM, under the English Channel, near the mouth of the Seine, France. To reach it travellers must first drown, preferably somewhere along the coast of Picardy. The kingdom is ruled by His Royal Wetness, who has established a simple code of living for his numerous subjects. The inhabitants converse in sign language by means of small flickering lights with which their phosphorescent skin is covered. Domestic aid is provided by certain species of fish which are trained to carry light objects in their mouths and weed the underwater gardens. Visitors will find that even though adapting to the damp climate may take some time, life in the Streaming Kingdom is peaceful and pleasant and that the days spent collecting shells or searching for lost buoys among the seaweed go by quickly.

(Jules Superveille, *L'Enfant de la haute mer*, Paris, 1931)

STREAMS OF STORY, OCEAN OF THE, whose source or wellspring is said to be near the moon's South Pole. The actual Streams of Story flow north from the pole. The waters of the ocean become at times polluted, thick and slow-moving, resembling molasses. This condition is apparently caused by an occasional plug that prevents the stories from flowing freely. Travellers across the ocean are advised that the plug must be removed in order to clean the waters, so that all stories, even the oldest, once again taste as good as new.

(Salman Rushdie, *Haroun and the Sea of Stories*, London, 1990)

STREELS OF URTAH, see URTAH.

STRELSAU, capital of RURITANIA.

STUPIDITY, CITY OF, see City of DESTRUCTION.

SUICIDE CITY, situated at a great depth beneath the Forest of Vincennes, east of Paris, and discovered during construction of the new underground line between the stations of *Bastille* and *Vincennes*. The city was discovered by Inspector Sauvage of the Paris police when searching for a number of workers who had disappeared during the excavations. For unspecified reasons, the Inspector's report was first published in Spanish.

The inhabitants of the city, ruled by an old man known as "Number One," are those fortunate (or unfortunate) few who have escaped a suicide attempt. Visitors will be able to distinguish would-be suicides from many parts of the world by their accents: from Spain and Latin America, those who have attempted suicide because of an ill-starred love affair; from England, those who have attempted suicide out of boredom; from France, out of lust; from Germany, for fear of military conscription; from the United States, through bankruptcy; from Canada, those tired of winter. Many ex-cancer patients also form part of the city's population.

The civil code of Suicide City is very strict. No forms of passion are allowed. The only food permitted is provided in the form of minuscule pills that help activate the brain. Every inhabitant must remain constantly silent, except when interviewed by his doctor. The doctors of Suicide City are, in fact, policemen, because there is no need for health care in the suicide community: the atmosphere is a hundred per cent pure, thanks to the protective walls, dating from prehistoric times, that surround the city. These walls filter the air and allow large quantities of ozone to enter while blocking the path of germs.

Radium is obtained in large quantities, as well as gold (transformed from silver by an unknown process) and platinum (obtained from gold). Helped by artificial light and heat, the inhabitants of Suicide City harvest vast crops four times a year. As vegetables do not form part of their diet, it is not known to what use these crops are put.

In spite of the obvious delights the city has to offer, visitors have described it as lugubrious and melancholic. It is said that Suicide City was founded after the collapse of the Suicide Club in London—a catastrophe brought about by Prince Florizel of Bohemia—but this historical conjecture has not been substantiated by tangible proof.

(Robert Louis Stevenson, *New Arabian Nights*, London, 1882; José Muñoz Escamez, *La Ciudad de los Suicidas*, Barcelona, 1912)

SUMMER COUNTRY, also known as the **SUMMER LANDS**, lies far across the sea from PRYDAIN. In the Summer Country there is no evil or suffering. Men and women there live forever and all their desires are granted them.

The Summer Country is the land of the Children of Don, the sons and daughters of the Lady Don and Belin, Lord of the Sun. When the rich land of Prydain fell under the sway of Achren and her consort Arawn the Death Lord, the Sons of Don travelled there in their golden ships to save it from the powers of evil. They routed Achren and Arawn and built the defences of Prydain. At CAER DATHYL they raised a great castle, the seat of the High Kings of Prydain, and in the south of the country they built its most important defencework, CAER DALLBEN, a seemingly modest farm which was protected by magical powers of great strength. It became the home of Dallben, the greatest enchanter in all the land, and was the childhood home of Taran the assistant pig-keeper who finally rose to be High King of Prydain.

For many years the forces of evil were held at bay, but during the reign of High King Math, Arawn appeared in Prydain once more. After long wars and great heroism by the allies of the Sons of Don, Arawn was totally defeated and Prydain freed from the forces of evil. The work of the Sons of Don was done and, as their destiny foretold, they returned in their golden ships to the Summer Country. All their kinsmen returned with them.

Their chief human allies were offered the opportunity to go with them and all but two did so, though they wept to leave their friends. Taran, who had become the close companion of Math's war leader, Prince Gwydion, elected to stay and was hailed as the new High King, while Princess Eilonwy of Llyr, the last of the house that had lived at Caer Colur, off the island of MONA, chose to stay too for love of Taran whom she married. In staying behind, Eilonwy willingly gave up the last vestiges of the magical power that had been handed down from mother to daughter in her family for many centuries.

(Lloyd Alexander, *The Book of Three*, New York, 1964; Lloyd Alexander, *The Black Cauldron*, New York, 1965; Lloyd Alexander, *The Castle of Llyr*, New York, 1966; Lloyd Alexander, *Taran Wanderer*, New York, 1967; Lloyd Alexander, *The High King*, New York, 1968)

SUMMER ISLAND, see FLOATING ISLAND.

SUNCHILDSTON (formerly **COLD HARBOUR**), see EREWHON.

SUN, CITY OF THE, on the island of Taprobane in the Indian Ocean, discovered by a Genoese ship that reached the island's shores and was captured by an army of men and women, some fluent in that Italian dialect.

The City of the Sun occupies an isolated hill in the middle of a green plain, and is divided into seven concentric circles, each named after one of the seven planets whose existence was known in the sixteenth century. Visitors can pass from one circle to the next through four gates and doors situated at the cardinal points. Each circle is well-fortified; even the buildings within the circles are protected by strong ramparts.

The city is governed by a prince who is also a priest, called Sun or Metaphysician; both secular and spiritual ruler, he is assisted by three royal acolytes, Pon, Sin and Mor, whose names signify Power, Wisdom and Love. Pon is in charge of the army, responsible only to Sun. Sin looks after all sciences and liberal arts and has under his command a number of officers: Astrologer, Cosmographer, Geometer, Logician, Rhetorician, Grammarian, Medical Doctor, Physicist, Politician and Moralist. It was following Sin's instructions that the six internal walls were painted with scientific illustrations so that all citizens could instruct themselves while enjoying their daily strolls. Mathematical figures, animals, plants, minerals and historical characters decorate the walls of the City of the Sun.

Mor administers all departments dealing with food, clothing and procreation, seeing to it that the right male and female inhabitants form a family, for it is considered ridiculous to take great care in breeding dogs and horses and yet neglect the human race. Strict eugenics are practised: women are not allowed to have sexual intercourse before the age of nineteen and men before they are twenty-one. Coming of age is celebrated with songs and much rejoicing. Sodomy is frowned upon and those found guilty of this charge are made to walk around the city for two full days with a shoe tied to the neck, symbolizing the inversion of things. Those found guilty a second time are given stricter punishments, which increase up to the death penalty. Sexual intercourse is organized every third evening, after absolutions and prayers. Tall and beautiful women are united with tall and beautiful men; thin men with fat women, fat men with thin women to balance the issue. Should a woman not become pregnant after lying with a man, she is passed on to another. If she is found sterile, she is offered to lustful young men but she cannot receive the honours reserved for matrons, who are allowed to take part in the Council and in the temple services.

Children are breast-fed by the mother for two years and then are handed over to female teachers if girls, and to male teachers if boys. The motto of their schools is *Mens sana in corpore sano.*

Children who are not gifted for the liberal or mechanical arts are sent to work in the country; the others are trained for whatever professions they seem suited for.

The religion of the City of the Sun is very simple. The inhabitants believe in one god, giver of life, symbolized by the sun. The faithful pray towards all four cardinal points: towards the east in the morning, to the west at midday, to the south in the afternoon and to the north in the evening. They repeat one single prayer, asking their god for a healthy body and a healthy soul, for themselves and for all their people; they also pray for happiness.

No funeral customs exist in the City of the Sun; corpses are burnt because the inhabitants believe that the flames will return the dead person's soul to the sun.

The laws are few and are inscribed on the columns of the temple. Trials are very short and judgments can be appealed, first to Pon, then to Sun. No prisons exist and punishments include not being able to talk to the women, not being allowed into the Temple, not being permitted to eat with the others, and in some cases flogging and exile. More serious crimes are punishable with death; among these are rebellion against the State or against religion. Even then the guilty party is allowed to explain his reasons and to publicly accuse State officials or theologians who he believes are in the wrong. When someone is exiled or executed, the city must be purified with prayers, sacrifices and mortifications.

The inhabitants of the City of the Sun are so proud of their laws that foreign captives are not allowed within the city walls, for fear they may contaminate the inhabitants' minds. Some travellers, however, are well received and allowed—after washing their feet—to reside in the city for three days.

It is useful to know that the inhabitants loathe anything black and therefore have no affection for the Japanese who are said to wear clothes of this colour.

(Tomaso Campanella, *La Città del Sole*, Lugano, 1602–23)

SUNDERING FLOOD, a mighty river which flows for more than two hundred miles from its source in the Great Mountains to the City of the Sundering Flood, the splendid city and port at its mouth. The lower reaches of the river are navigable, but further upstream the river passes through a wasteland where it divides into three main streams and a multitude of smaller water courses. Even farther north it crosses a mountain range and flows deep and strong.

There are no bridges and it is said that none, except the birds, can cross the stream without drowning. The lower reaches of the Flood are lined with the trees of the Wood Masterless, which extends towards the town of Longshaw. The trees are felled for timber by the local inhabitants, who also hunt in the wood, where deer abound.

The upper reaches of the Flood divide, or sunder, the hill country of the East and West Dales, which travellers will find exceedingly hospitable. In this area the settlements are small and scattered through the windy valleys.

Wethermel, the last but one farm in East Dale, is typical of the upland settlements. The house faces south-west for protection against the prevailing winds and is built beneath a sheltering knoll. Pigs and sheep are kept, but the main product of the farm is grain. Wethermel is the home of Osborne Wulfgrimmson, who fought in the battles between the king and the craft guilds in the City of the Sundering Flood, with magic weapons given him by the dwarf Steelhead, his guardian. Magic and the presence of the dwarves is simply part of life in this area.

Life in the Dales is made difficult by the river. As it is impossible to cross it, there is little communication between East and West. At Christmas and Midsummer, the people on both banks gather by the Bight of the Cloven Knoll, a rocky protrusion of the banks. Here they exchange ritual greetings by shouting across the Flood. The problem of communication is illustrated by the story of Osborne and Elfhilde, two lovers who for years had to greet each other across the water and who only met after long and dangerous travels which finally united them in the distant Wood Masterless.

(William Morris, *The Sundering Flood*, London, 1897)

SUNLESS CITY, an underground city somewhere beneath the Bayowda Steppe in the Nubian Desert, between the south of Egypt and the north of Sudan, not far from Khartoum. A visit is recommended to travellers particularly interested in Egyptology, who have already cruised the Nile under the guidance of Thomas Cook (no relation to the explorer or mapmaker). In spite of the heat, visitors are advised to wear strong protective clothing as the entrance to Sunless City is through a patch of moving sand in the vicinity of an ancient gold mine. Once swallowed by the sands, visitors will find themselves some one hundred metres under the desert, in the midst of an immense Egyptian city, lit with artificial lighting.

Sunless City was discovered in May 1926 by two French Egyptologists, Emile Dantremont and Martial Pigelet, accompanied by an English officer of the Camel Corps, Johnny Wartington; the three managed to escape from this underground region after an earthquake demolished part of the grandiose buildings it contains.

Visitors can still admire a beautiful Egyptian hall, built at the end of a long avenue of stone monsters, protected by two immense gates in solid gold. All buildings in the city are in the Egyptian style of about 667–63 BC, when a group of ancient Egyptians escaped the Assyrian invasion by seeking refuge underground. Here they established a kingdom and built a city, ruled by a descendant of the Pharaohs, whose line still continues until this day and who is known as "Master of the Sunless Kingdom." Though their language is ancient Egyptian, visitors can get along with a smattering of French. It is interesting to note that the inhabitants have preserved all their ancient customs, embalming the dead, dressing themselves in gauze and fighting with bows and arrows as they did when their ancestors lived above land.

No birds are found in Sunless City but a few African elephants and lions roam the wilder outskirts. Lepers' Island, in the middle of the nearby underground Sacred Lake, is not worth a visit.

(Albert Bonneau, *La Cité sans soleil*, Paris, 1927)

SVARTMOOT, CAVE OF THE, a galleried cavern with an outcrop of rock in the shape of a lion-head, situated in ALDERLEY EDGE in Cheshire. Here the *svart-alfar*, creatures of the goblin race, gather to absorb the *firedrake*—a flame which rises out of a stone cup full of seething liquid—which enables them to look upon light without pain.

The avenue of stone monsters leading to the Egyptian hall in SUNLESS CITY.

(Alan Garner, *The Weirdstone of Brisingamen*, London, 1960)

SWOONARIE, an island of the RIALLARO ARCHIPELAGO in the south-east Pacific. The inhabitants of Swoonarie produce marvellous inventions, such as a crucible to extract silver from starlight, a shovel to level mountains into plains and an anti-gravitational device. However, all these remain unused as no one has the energy to do anything about them. The natives eat an opiate called *ailool*, and work is abandoned as they soon fall asleep.

(Godfrey Sweven, *Riallaro, the Archipelago of Exiles*, New York & London, 1901; Godfrey Sweven, *Limanora, the Island of Progress*, New York & London, 1903)

SYLVANIA, a small country in Europe, to the south of FREEDONIA. The Sylvanian government has in the past interfered in the internal affairs of its neighbour, attempting to stir up revolutions and using spies in a series of attempts to discredit the government. Most of those subversive actions were organized by Trentino, the Sylvanian ambassador to Freedonia. His efforts were frustrated by Rufus T. Firefly, President of Freedonia, and by the inefficiency of his own spy system; at one stage, one of his agents was actually employed by Firefly.

Trentino was insulted in public by Firefly and the two countries soon found themselves at war. Initially the fighting went in Sylvania's favour and the headquarters of the Freedonian general staff were under heavy siege. The position was reversed, however, when Trentino was captured and forced to surrender.

(*Duck Soup*, directed by Hans Dreier & Wiard B. Ihnen, USA, 1933)

SYMZONIA, an underground realm discovered in 1820 by the Antarctic expedition under the command of Captain Seabourn, who managed to penetrate the southern ices, thereby confirming the theory of concentric spheres. This theory had been put forward in 1818 by John Cleves Symmes, who with his colleague James McBride later published *Symmes' Theory of Concentric Spheres* in 1826.

According to their theory, the earth is formed by a series of spheres like Chinese boxes or nesting Russian dolls. There are five such spheres, each separated from the others by a stratum of atmosphere and each inhabited on its surface. These five concentric bodies are connected by a gigantic tunnel which is entered via either the North Pole or the South Pole. Both apertures take in the waters of the oceans and any ship can enter them with ease.

In 1818 Symmes tried to make the expedition, setting off from Siberia with a hundred men in sleighs pulled by reindeer, but he failed; it was Captain Seabourn who fifteen years later entered the earth through the opposite end, and he called the region he discovered—the second in the series of "Chinese boxes"—"Symzonia" in honour of the brilliant theoretician.

Captain Seabourn saw little of Symzonia because the natives, afraid that the newcomers would spoil their immaculate institutions, sent him away. According to Seabourn's report, the cities of Symzonia are similar to those on the surface of the earth, except that they lack colour: in Symzonia everything is as white as snow. The inhabitants have white skins and dress in white and communicate through a musical language. They live happily and despise all material riches. Thanks to their intelligence they have managed to illuminate their realm by refracting the sunlight and moonlight that penetrates through both polar apertures, using a system of mirrors. They have discovered propulsion reactors (with which they guide their ships), dirigibles and the flame torch. Visitors are not made particularly welcome.

(Captain Adam Seabourn, *Symzonia, A Voyage of Discovery*, New York, 1820)

T

TACARIGUA, an island in the Caribbean, famed for the attractions of its capital, Cuna Cuna, which is probably one of the most alluring cities in the world. Known to its poets as "burning Tacarigua," the island is a cosmopolitan and exotic spot. The capital itself, with its mixed population and adventurous nightlife, offers a wide range of entertainments, from the sophisticated performances given at the Opera House (which seems to dominate the city), to the more licentious entertainments offered by the jazz halls along the wharves, and the bars where the *hodeidah*, an erotic dance peculiar to the city, is performed by young girls. Even the ballet performances given at the Opera House are renowned for their daring quality. They are choreographed by a Scottish widow who claims that her soul simply "awoke" at the sight of nature when she first came to the island, and her more daring creations shock even the Cunans, who are not noted for their prudishness.

The bars of Cuna Cuna are famed for their exciting cocktails, especially those around Liberty Square where visitors can see the statue of the Cunan poet Samba Marcella, famed as the "sable singer of revolt." The Alameda, lined with mimosa, is a favourite evening promenade for the pleasure-loving inhabitants of the capital, as are the Marcella gardens. Both these areas are haunted by the beautiful female prostitutes who contribute so much to the city's air of exotic hedonism, and by their male counterparts, the so-called *bwam-wam bwam-wams*.

A walk through the city streets should include a visit to the teeming markets, where all the produce of the island is on sale. The streets of Cuna Cuna are patrolled by the Cunan Constabulary, who in their kilts and feathered sunhats appear the apotheosis of a romantic and earthy lawlessness rather than the guardians of the peace.

The fashionable life of the island centres around the Opera House and the exclusive suburb of Faranaka, where the large houses of society men and women stand back from the road among clusters of flame trees. The avenues of Faranaka are ablaze with trees and shrubs, like a magician's garden.

The population of Cuna Cuna is extremely mixed. Chinese, Indians and blacks from the interior mingle in its streets. Many of them have been attracted to the capital from their villages in the hope of a more exciting and rewarding life. Inevitably, the pressures of city life have forced many of them into petty crime or casual prostitution. Cuna Cuna is also the home of the island's elite, a cosmopolitan group drawn by the island's undoubted attractions. Most of this group are of European origin and tend to lead a closed life within their own set, having little to do with the native population.

The villages of the interior, particularly those on the isolated south coast, are very different. Here the islanders still live in their traditional thatched huts and go about almost naked, clothed in brief loincloths or garlands of flowers. Apart from the few market towns, where there are some elements of industry, the interior is almost entirely agricultural. The main crops are sugar cane, pineapples, bananas and nutmeg. The small coastal villages supplement their income by fishing. Despite its poverty, the interior is extremely beautiful. Palm trees wave across the savannah where the natural groves of cedar and bamboo provide a habitat for the island's many species of butterfly, humming-birds and tree frogs. In the evenings, fireflies glow in the warm darkness.

The villages preserve many traces of an earlier culture which has largely been lost in the international atmosphere of the city. Songs from the old tribal days can still be heard and bring back memories of slavery and even of life in Africa. Despite the presence of Baptist missions and the singing of revivalist hymns, most people continue to believe in the power of the Obi-man's spells and in the existence of *jumbies,* or wood spirits, ghosts and ghouls. Charms called "luck balls" are often worn at the throat. The casual morality of Cuna Cuna is also noticeable in the countryside, where it is by no means unusual for both men and women to have had several lovers before they marry. Village marriages are still celebrated in traditional style, with all the guests being greeted at the roadside by the bride and groom before going into the house to see the traditional bridal trophies—cowrie shells, feathers and orange blossoms.

Tacarigua was recently hit by a severe earthquake. Cuna Cuna itself was spared, although tremors were felt and caused considerable panic. In the countryside it was very different. In Casuby Province (which lies beyond the May Day Mountains) the damage to plantations and estates was extensive. The convent of Sasabonsam, a gem of tropical architecture immortalized by Marcella in *The Picnic,* was totally destroyed. Miraculously, the statue of Our Lady of Sorrows survived the earthquake and now attracts pilgrims from all over the island. The earthquake sparked off a strong religious revival throughout Tacarigua and services of intercession replaced the more usual interests of the society elite. Opera singers were hired to sing in the packed churches and some of the bars and other places of entertainment were forced to close down for a while for lack of custom. The revival was short-lived, however, and Cuna Cuna has once again returned to its hedonistic traditions.

(Ronald Firbank, *Prancing Nigger,* New York, 1924)

TAERG NATIRB, an island in the Red Sea off the coast of Ethiopia, rich in wool and corn. The capital is Ecnatneper or Nodnol, known to the Greeks as Metonoyae. It stands protected by a high wall and its gates are locked on the sabbath. The kingdom of Taerg Natirb is well defended with castles and beacons all along the coast, and is garrisoned by a well-trained army and navy. It has often been invaded in the past.

The people are twenty feet tall, plainly dressed, but hospitable and generous. They are Protestants, said to "preach the pure word of God and live in His fear." There are 1,560 parish churches in Taerg Natirb, each served by two priests—the more learned of the two preaches, the other administers the sacraments. The gates of the churches bear the inscriptions *Deum timete, regum honorate* and *Omnes honorate fraternitatem diligite.*

The law of the kingdom applies to all, regardless of wealth or social status. Adultery, theft and murder are punishable by death. Drunkards are held in prison without food for several days. Those who swear have their tongues cut out, as do perjurers (who are then put to death). Dishonest lawyers are jailed and their property is seized by the prince. Papists are burnt. Because of these laws there has been no serious crime in Taerg Natirb in the last one hundred years. To make justice accessible to all, lawyers are paid by the prince and take no fees from their clients.

(William Bullein, *A Dialogue both Pleasant and Pitiful, wherein is a Goodly Regimente against the Fever Pestilence, with a Consolation and Comfort against Death,* London, 1564)

TALLSTORIA, an autonomous region in Persia, almost completely encircled by mountains. Tallstoria has very little contact with the outside world. The country is fertile and the people are quite content to live on their land's produce. They have never had any desire to increase their territory, which is protected from aggression both by the mountains and by the protection-money they pay to the King of Persia. Completely cut off from the world, they are able to live in comfort and safety, if not luxury. The taxes they pay to the Persian monarch exempt them from military service.

Tallstoria is remarkable for its system of criminal justice. A convicted thief has to hand back the stolen goods to his victim; if the goods are no longer in his possession, their value is deducted from the thief's own property. The rest of his property is then handed over to his wife and children. With the exception of those convicted of armed robbery—who are imprisoned—all convicts are employed on public works, but are not badly treated. They work long hours and are locked up after roll-call every night, but otherwise they lead reasonable lives. Food is provided at public expense, either through voluntary donations or through taxation. In some areas, convicts are also hired out to private contractors who pay slightly less for convict labour than they would for free labour. The system is humane and gradually forces the criminals to become good citizens and spend their lives making up for the harm they have done.

Convicts, who are usually referred to as slaves, wear clothes of a colour worn by no one else. They have their hair clipped very short and a tiny piece is cut off one ear. Each slave wears a badge showing which district he comes from; it is a capital crime for a slave to take off his badge, to be seen outside his own district or to speak to a slave from another district. The penalty for abetting an escape attempt is death for a slave and slavery for a free man; rewards are given for supplying information on escape projects and a slave who informs on a would-be escaper is allowed to regain his freedom. Slaves are not permitted to carry weapons or to possess money; if money is found on them, it proves that they have committed a crime. Under this system, there is so little risk of criminals relapsing into their old ways that they are regarded as the most reliable guides for long-distance travellers, who employ them according to a relay system, one for each district they pass through. It is virtually impossible for the slaves to enter into a conspiracy to overthrow the government, as they have no opportunity to meet slaves from other areas and conspire with them. Every slave does, however, have some hope of regaining his freedom simply by obeying orders and convincing the authorities that he really is a reformed character. A certain number of slaves are released each year for good behaviour.

(Sir Thomas More, *Utopia*, London, 1516)

TAMOE, an island in the Pacific, between latitude 260° and 263° south. It is some fifty leagues in circumference and completely bound by sharp inaccessible rocks, with the exception of one small bay in the south. The climate is healthy, mild and unchanging. The flora is luxuriant and abundant and the air is almost always pure. Winter consists of a little rain that falls during July and August.

There are sixteen cities on the island. The capital, also called Tamoe, looks southwards towards the sea from the bay. Its port is defended by fortifications built in the European style; from the port, a superb road, shaded by four lines of palm trees, leads into the capital. Tamoe is built according to a symmetrical plan and its shape is that of a perfect circle some two leagues round. All the

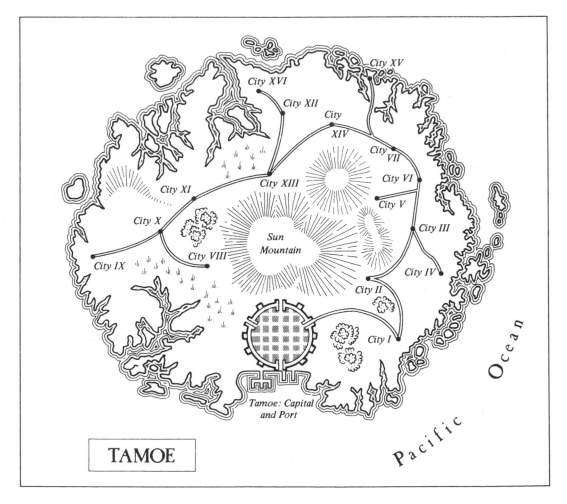

Tamoe: Capital and Port

TAMOE

streets are straight and flanked by pavements on both sides, planted with beautiful trees. The roads themselves are covered with very fine sand that makes transit easy. All houses are built on the same pattern: two storeys high, the roof forming an Italian-style terrace, and the main door flanked by a window on each side. All houses are painted in symmetrical pink and green squares. In the middle of the park stand two round buildings higher than the houses: one of them is the chief's palace, the other is a public administration office.

The island was discovered by a French ship in the last years of the reign of Louis XIV. A young officer who had fallen in love with a native girl deserted the ship and hid himself on the island. He remained among the natives, reformed their habits and built and fortified the capital. Single-handed, he transformed the island into an orderly and prosperous State.

The French reformer sought equality as a way of vanquishing passions. This led to the abolition of laws—which are useless when vices no longer exist. The prison is seen as a wicked institution which has not yet disappeared, however, because of certain undesirable and unconvinced members of the population.

Children are brought up by the State, leaving the paternal home as soon as they are weaned. They remain in a community camp until they are fifteen and then they marry. On his fifteenth birthday, the young man is led to a house where all the young girls are raised. There he makes his choice, and if the girl consents they get married. If he is rejected, he must choose again until he is accepted. The State gives each couple a house which they can occupy for the rest of their lives. Celibacy is tolerated, but bachelors must promise to serve the State. Divorce is also a common practice. In every city on Tamoe is a street flanked by houses smaller than the ones given to couples. In these, bachelors or divorcées live. Divorcées who decide to choose again may do so among the bachelors or the divorcees and must be accepted. The old people who can no longer work are put in homes especially designed by the State. In every city, an old man is elected as governor and he is advised by two other old people, one chosen from among the bachelors so that both categories are represented. The people, who are vegetarians, live off the land that has been given to them by the State. It is interesting to watch their principal entertainment:

theatre plays with moral connotations that they write and enact themselves.

Religion in Tamoe consists of sun worship, as a homage to the unknowable being that created everything. The only ceremony consists of a periodical procession in which all inhabitants take part. They climb up one of the island's mountains, not far from the capital, and simply kneel, stretching their arms towards the sun. No other rites exist on Tamoe; there are neither priests nor temples.

The State is the sole owner of all goods; the inhabitants are allowed to enjoy this common property. By forgoing luxuries, all inhabitants become equal. For this reason, everyone dresses in the same way: a fine and light garment, grey for the older people, green for the middle-aged and pink for the young, draped around the body in the Asiatic manner.

(Donatien-Alphonse-François, Marquis de Sade, *Aline et Valcour*, Paris, 1795)

TANDAR, a large island in the KORSAR AZ of the underground continent of PELLUCIDAR. Most of its coastline is ringed with seemingly unscalable cliffs, but at one point a waterfall tumbles down from the clifftops, and a cave by its side gives access to a shaft which leads up to the top of the island; a crude wooden ladder has been fixed in this natural shaft. Inland, most of the island is covered in dense tropical jungle.

Tandar is the home of two tribes, the Tandars and the Manats, constantly at war with one another. They live on opposite sides of the island, which is so large that it takes two or three days of forced march to cross it. Travellers are warned that the narrow jungle trails are confusing and extremely difficult to follow.

The Tandars, who live in a cliff-village near the sea coast, are a tall, bronze-skinned race. Their village consists of a large number of caves which have been hollowed out of the face of a high sandstone cliff. The Tandars are remarkable mainly for one thing: they have tamed the fearsome *tarag* or sabretooth tiger of Pellucidar, the only tribe known to have done so. Elsewhere the *tarag* is feared and avoided; here the great striped animals wander freely about the village. The *tarags* are not used for hunting, but for war. In retaliation, the Manats have tamed the *taho* or cave-lion. Again, they are the only tribe to have done so.

The everyday life of the Tandars is better documented than that of their traditional enemies. Every aspect of their life seems to relate to the *tarag* in some way. Both men and women wear loincloths of *tarag* skin; Tandar warriors wear headdresses made from *tarag* heads and carry their arrows in quivers of striped *tarag* skin. Strangers who arrive in the Tandars' village are sometimes taken into slavery but more often they are fed to the *tarags*. Even women suffer this fate, for according to tribal custom no Tandar warrior may take a female slave as his mate.

Much less is known about the Manats. They too live in caves, but it remains unclear whether these are natural or have been hollowed out by their inhabitants. When they go into the forests of the island, they are normally accompanied by leashed *tahos* in case they are attacked by the *tarags* of their enemies.

(Edgar Rice Burroughs, *Tiger Girl*, New York, 1942)

TANGERINA ISLAND, see WILD ISLAND.

TANJE, a palace in ATVATABAR some fifty miles by pneumatic tube from CALNOGOR. Notable are the gardens, where the evolutionary link from plants to animals, the *phytes*, are preserved. There are more than two hundred species of *phytes* in the gardens of Tanje Palace, including the *lilasure* (a bird-like fern), the green *gazzle* of Glockett Gozzle (a flying weed) and the *yarphappy* (an ape-like flower).

(William R. Bradshaw, *The Goddess of Atvatabar, being the History of the Discovery of the Interior World and Conquest of Atvatabar,* New York, 1892)

TAPROBANE, an island in the south Indian Ocean much of which is covered by impenetrable forests. It is inhabited by a peculiar snake called an *amphisbaena*, with a head at each end of its body. Both heads are equipped with venomous fangs. The *amphisbaena* can change direction very quickly and its eyes glare like candles.

It is said that the *amphisbaena* is looked after and nourished by ants and that if it is cut in half, both parts will join again.

(Pliny the Elder, *Naturalis Historia*, 1st cen. AD; Pliny the Elder, *Inventorum Natura*, 1st cen. AD;

Lucan, *Pharsalia*, 1st cen. AD; Brunetto Latini, *Li Livres dou Tresor*, Milan, 1266; Sir Thomas Browne, *Vulgar Errors*, London, 1646)

TARTARUS, a gloomy region south of LILLAR. Travellers can reach it after crossing the ruins of a castle and an orchard of sawn-down trees. A desolate waste leads to a black wall crowned with plaster heads. Behind the wall rises a tower with blind windows. Though the road runs around the wall without coming to a gate, entrance can be gained by treading on a certain stone that causes part of the wall to give way.

Inside flows a dark river, on the banks of which grows a tangled wood. Stuffed animals stand as if drinking the murky waters. A Moravian churchyard, with a flowerless garden shadowed by weeping birches, can be seen beyond the wood. A stone staircase leads to damp catacombs in the walls of which a nun was immured. Here are the petrified skeleton of a miner with gilded ribs and thighs, the black paper hearts of men shot with an arquebus, a rod which whipped to death a forgiven penitent, toys, a glass bust and the skeleton of a dwarf.

From here on the path is guarded by a skeleton with an Aeolian harp and travellers are not advised to attempt to explore any further.

(Jean Paul [Johann Paul Friedrich Richter], *Titan*, Berlin, 1800–03)

TARTARY DESERT, a vast, rocky and uninhabited wasteland which extends for many square miles north of the fortress of BASTIANI. It is flanked on all sides by an impenetrable mountain chain. The Tartars which give it their name have either disappeared or never existed.

As far as anyone knows, no living soul has travelled through the Tartary Desert. The landscape, as seen from the New Redoubt (the farthest outpost of Bastiani fortress), is an unending expanse of rocks white as snow, and a few scattered marshes. A perpetual haze blocks the view of the horizon to the north. Several soldiers of the garrison swear to have seen, during one of the rare and brief moments of clearness, white towers or smoking volcanoes.

The Northern State of the nameless country to which the desert belongs appears to have begun the construction of a highway that, like a fine thread, crosses the silent wasteland. But no one knows where the highway begins or where it leads to.

(Dino Buzzati, *Il deserto dei Tartari*, Milan, 1940)

TARZAN'S ABODE, a small hut near the African west coast, about 10° south of the equator. It was here that John, Lord Greystoke, took refuge with his wife after their shipwreck, building the cabin single-handed. The exterior is coated in clay and the window grating is made of branches. The roof is A-shaped and thatched; the door is built out of packing boxes. A small, stone fireplace can still be seen, as well as the few pieces of furniture Lord Greystoke built for his wife's comfort: a bed, two chairs and a table. On the shelves visitors will notice a child's alphabet beginning "A is for Archer." A cannibal village is found nearby, and in the trees live a tribe of giant apes who, from time to time, raid the neighbourhood. (See APE KINGDOM.)

It was in this hut that Lord Greystoke lost his wife and was killed by a gorilla. Their infant son was rescued by a she-ape, Kala, who had herself lost her young; he grew up to be Tarzan, known as Lord of the Apes, who exercised such lasting influence on the African continent.

Tarzan summed up his philosophy in the following words: "Show me the fat, opulent coward who ever originated a beautiful ideal. In the clash of arms, in the battle for survival, amid hunger and death and danger, in the face of God as manifested in the display of Nature's most terrific forces, is born all that is finest and best in the human heart and mind." In the ape language, Tarzan is called *Tarmangani* or "White Ape."

(Edgar Rice Burroughs, *Tarzan of the Apes*, New York, 1912; Edgar Rice Burroughs, *Tarzan and the Jewels of Opar*, New York, 1916; Edgar Rice Burroughs, *Tarzan the Untamed*, New York, 1919)

TASHBAAN, capital of CALORMEN.

TELENIABIN and **GENELIABIN**, two small but beautiful islands which are noteworthy for their production of substances for use in enemas.

(François Rabelais, *Le quart livre des faicts et dicts du bon Pantagruel*, Paris, 1552)

TELEPILUS LAESTRYGONIA, a city on the Mediterranean coast, perhaps in Sicily or southern Italy. A large crag looms over the port, surrounded on all sides by dangerous rocks that leave only one narrow entrance from the sea. The city's inhabitants, the Laestrygonians, are not to be trusted; visitors may find themselves at a gory banquet of which they become the main dish.

(Homer, *The Odyssey*, 9th cen. [?] BC)

TENDRE or **AFFECTION**, a country of unknown location, on the coast of the Dangerous Sea. Many people have expressed a desire to visit Tendre, but few are familiar with the route. Travellers should note that it is best reached from New Friendship. Tendre itself is divided by three rivers, Gratitude or Avowal, Attachment and Esteem, which descend into an estuary leading to the Dangerous Sea. On the Sea of Enmity are a few towns best avoided: Perfidy, Slander and others. However, this region is not far from the beautiful city of Affection-on-Avowal, and a few hamlets like Caring, Sensibility and Constant Friendship should be visited. Important towns are Loveletter, Pretty-poems and Obedience. The capital of Tendre is Affection-on-Esteem. To the west of the country is a desolate region which harbours the Lake of Indifference.

(Madeleine De Scudéry, *La Clélie*, Paris, 1660)

TENTENNOR, capital of the Empire of the ALSONDONS.

TEREBINTHIA, an island kingdom off the coast of NARNIA, somewhat to the north of GALMA. The island—known as a haunt of pirates—was visited by King Caspian X on his voyage to the east, although he was not able to enter the main city which happened to be in quarantine.

(C.S. Lewis, *The Voyage of the "Dawn Treader,"* London, 1952; C.S. Lewis, *The Horse and His Boy*, London, 1954)

TEREKENALT, a kingdom to the west of the BEKLAN EMPIRE. When war broke out in the Empire over the reestablishment of the slave trade, its southern provinces allied themselves with Terekenalt and fought against the central government in BEKLA.

The Blue Forest of Katria in Terekenalt is closely associated with the legends surrounding

Deparioth, the legendary liberator of YELDA. It is said that he was betrayed and left to die in the Blue Forest, but was rescued by a beautiful woman dressed like a queen. She fed him and cared for him and then guided him through the forest to a place he knew. As his friends came towards him, the woman turned into a tall silver lily. It is said that the hero spent the rest of his life longing to return to the forest in which he had met her.

(Richard Adams, *Shardik*, London, 1974)

TERRABIL CASTLE, in Cornwall, England, built by the Duke of Tintagel.

Like Tintagel itself, Terrabil was besieged by Uther Pendragon, King of England, who coveted Igraine, the duke's wife. The Duke of Tintagel died in the siege and Uther Pendragon lay with Igraine in Terrabil Castle. Igraine gave birth to the future King Arthur, who later established his famous court at CAMELOT.

(Sir Thomas Malory, *Le Morte Darthur*, London, 1485)

TERRE AUSTRALE or SOUTHERN LANDS, a continent located between the 52nd and 40th parallels, in an area known as Hust, about 3,000 by 4,500 leagues in size and containing twenty-seven different countries. On the north coast lies the country of Hube; to the east are the lands of Hüed and Hüod; to the west, Hump, on the edge of the Gulf of Ilab, Hug, and beyond the Gulf of Pug, Pure; then also to the west, Sub, Hulg, Pulg and Mulg. To the south are the Ivas Mountains, higher than the Pyrenees. The countries at the foot of the mountains are Huff, Curd, Gurf, Durf, Iurf and Surf (on the sea). Between the mountains and the south coast are Trum, Sum, Burd, Purd, Burf, Turf and Purg. Two rivers flow through the wide valley beyond the mountains: the Sulm which flows west, and the Hulm which flows east. The area between the rivers is called the Fund, about eight hundred by six hundred leagues, and is divided into twelve bellicose kingdoms.

The entire continent slopes very gently to the south, but is flat, without a single mountain, until the Ivas range. As a result the various countries share a uniformity of language, customs and even architecture. The land is fertile and the climate warm and unchanging. The seas around the continent are shallow—barely a foot deep a league from the shore—and the continent is almost impossible to approach by boat. The coastline is well-guarded; travellers are warned that no one is allowed to enter Terre Australe unless the inhabitants know his or her name, country of origin and humour. Should enemies approach (the inhabitants consider all Europeans to be their enemies, and call them "sea-monsters"), their arrival is signalled by a rocket which summons thousands of armed men from many different countries; any attempts to land will be met by strong resistance.

No flies, spiders or poisonous creatures exist in Terre Australe, but visitors will find a type of monkey with an almost human face both entertaining and friendly. Also found on the island are *hums*, animals similar to pigs but with silky hair, which instinctively plough the earth and which cause so much damage they have been exterminated in many areas; red, green, yellow and blue sheep; winged horses with claws; bears with each foot as large as the whole animal; pigs which, without an overseer, plough fields in straight lines ready for planting; unicorns; the *suef*, a dromedary which has, instead of a hump, a hollow in its back large enough for two men to lie in comfortably, and which is used for transport; *effs*, scarlet birds the size of chickens; the *pacd*, a gregarious songbird which takes its meals with the inhabitants and readily enters their houses; *urgs*, birds of prey with which the inhabitants wage a constant war, for they are the size of bulls and will eat both fish and men. A certain tribe of natives have striped legs indicating their ancestry of half-man, half-tiger.

The towns are known as *sezains* and are divided into areas of *hiebs* or dwellings, circular buildings of semitransparent stone, and *hebs* or schools where young people and teachers are housed. Religion is a delicate subject and it is a crime to speak of it. However, there is religious freedom in Terre Australe, as long as individual beliefs are not discussed in public.

The people of Terre Australe are bisexual; if children of only one sex are born, they are suffocated at birth. The people have black hair and fine beards which are never cut as their hair grows very slowly. They stand some eight feet tall, are of reddish skin, have small breasts and flat stomachs and do not wear clothes. Some of the inhabitants of Terre Australe, known as "inventors," can create

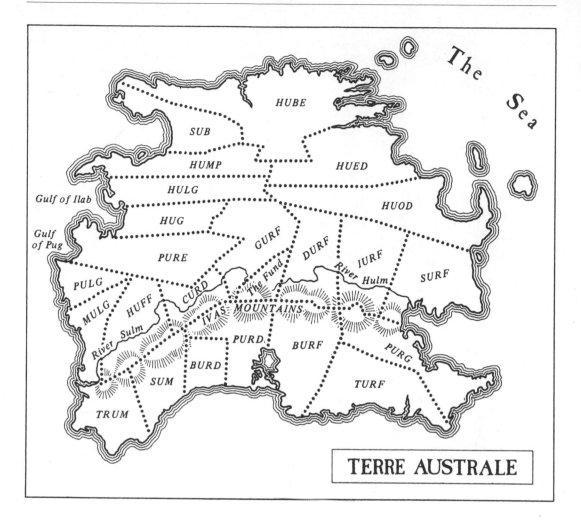

live birds and dogs from moistened dirt, and flowers from pieces of dead wood. As it is a crime to mention sexual reproduction, it is not known how they reproduce, but by law each person must have at least one child. The inhabitants live together in fraternal love and never quarrel. There is a lack of meat, but travellers will find trees bearing various edible fruits and a few unique vegetables such as a delicious blue carrot unknown outside Terre Australe. Special liquids are used to water the plants, which give the produce a particular taste. Visitors are especially advised to taste the fruit of the *balf*, or tree of happiness, which is found in the central square of most cities. The *balf* produces a red fruit the size of an olive. Should the visitor eat four, he will become happy and euphoric; six will make him slumber for twenty-four hours; more than six will provoke a sleep from which he will never wake.

(Gabriel Foigny, *Les Aventures De Jacques Sadeur Dans La Découverte Et Le Voyage De La Terre Australe, contenant les coutumes et les moeurs des Australiens, leur religion, leurs études, leurs guerres, les animaux particuliers à ce pais et toutes les raretez curiesses qui s'y trouvent*, Vannes, 1676)

TERRE LIBRE, a flat island, north of New Caledonia in the Pacific Ocean, where the highest hills barely reach three hundred metres. There are a

Art nouveau pottery from TERRE LIBRE.

few forests, fields and small streams. The only animals found in the wild are goats and a kind of
small antelope. The primitive inhabitants were the
Long-Rib tribe, so called because their ribs stood
out vertically like those of a wolf.

The only town, or conglomeration of houses,
on the island is that built by ex-prisoners who had
been condemned in France after an abortive political coup and sent to New Caledonia. The ship
sank in a storm and the prisoners became pioneers, setting up an anarchist community on the
island. The houses were built separately wherever
they chose. The bachelors, however, were put in
one large house, each with a room of his own and
access to a communal dining room, living room
and kitchen.

The islanders established a communitarian
system by which each one shared all and the same,
and set up a hydro-electric power station, a system
of sewers, and a pottery today famous for its stylish creations. Cannons are positioned along the
coast to protect the pioneers from the outside
world, and visitors are warned to announce their
arrival well in advance.

(Jean Grave, *Terre Libre*, Paris, 1908)

TEUTOBURGER FOREST, to the north of
CAMPAGNA. Around this forest spread the do-
minions of the Chief Ranger, a tyrant from MAU-
RETANIA who let his land be a haven to all those

fleeing persecution elsewhere: Huns, Tartars, gypsies, Albigenses, escaped criminals, Polish robbers,
prostitutes, magicians, alchemists and the children
of the Pied Piper of Hamelin. Women from a tribe
known as the Lemers arrive from time to time to
entertain these refugees.

The forest is girdled by reed and elder, thick
hedges of dogwood and blackthorn, ancient elms
and beeches. In the clearings red mushrooms, yellow foxgloves and deadly nightshades can be
found. Nearby is a dreadful barn decorated with
human skulls and human hands. Throughout the
forest the Chief Ranger's banner can be seen,
showing a red boar's head.

(Ernst Jünger, *Auf den Marmorklippen*, Frankfurt,
1939)

THALARION, see SOUTHERN SEA.

THANASIA, an uninhabited island of the RIAL-
LARO ARCHIPELAGO in the south-east Pacific.
Those Limanorans longing for death or advo-
cating early suicide were deported here (see
LIMANORA), where they all eventually died. In
order to assure an effective death, the exiles constructed funeral pyres fashioned in such a way that
they would be struck by lightning when the first
storm came. The blazing pyres were at one time an
interesting spectacle; today, however, all that remains is a few charred heaps.

No one has since settled in Thanasia.

(Godfrey Sweven, *Riallaro, the Archipelago of Exiles*, New York & London, 1901; Godfrey Sweven,
Limanora, the Island of Progress, New York & London, 1903)

THEKLA, a half-built city in Asia. The inhabitants say they take such a long time over the construction of Thekla so that its destruction cannot
begin. The blueprint of the city is the starry sky.

(Italo Calvino, *Le città invisibili*, Turin, 1972)

THELEME, an abbey on the south bank of the
River Loire, France, two leagues from the great
forest of Port-Hualt. The Abbey was founded in
the sixteenth century by the giant Gargantua as a
token of thanks for services rendered by the monk
Jean Des Entommeures, at a total cost of 2,700 and
831 gold *Agnus Dei* crowns, with an extra 1,000

and 669 Sun crowns for each year it took to build it. Gargantua also endowed the Abbey with a free-hold endowment of 2,369,000 crowns *per annum* in perpetuity.

The Abbey is hexagonal, and so planned that from each corner rises a large circular tower, some sixty yards in diameter. The most northerly tower, which stands on the river bank, is known as Arctic. The others are named Calaer, Anatole, Mesembrine, Hesperie and Cryere. Each tower is 312 yards from its neighbour, and each is six storeys high, including the basement. The second storey is vaulted in the shape of a high arch; the rest of the ceilings are of Flanders plaster in circular patterns. The roof is covered in fine slates with a lead coping and decorated with figures of grotesque and small animals of all kinds; projecting gutters painted in blue and gold diagonals run to the ground, where they connect with great pipes leading into the river. Theleme contains 9,332 rooms, each with an inner chamber, closet, wardrobe and chapel; all lead into a central hall. The staircases are of porphyry and Numidian marble. On each landing is a double arcade to admit light. The steps lead up to the roof, on which stands a pavilion.

Each room, closet and hall is hung with various tapestries, according to the season of the year. The floors are covered with green cloth and the bedspreads are embroidered. In each boudoir hangs a large mirror of crystal, set in a frame of gold.

Between the Arctic and Cryere towers is the Abbey's library, with collections of books in Greek, Latin, Hebrew, French, Italian and Spanish, each language being housed on a separate floor. In the centre is a spiral staircase, the entrance to which is on the outside of the building through a symmetrical arch thirty-six feet wide. Between the Anatole and Mesembrine towers are galleries painted with historical and topographical scenes. Again, there is a staircase in the middle, connecting with the main gate on the river bank. Above the gate is a verse inscription forbidding entry to the Abbey to hypocrites, bigots, moneylenders, lawyers, solicitors and sad, jealous and quarrelsome people.

In the central court stands a magnificent fountain of fine alabaster, surmounted with the three Graces carrying horns of abundance, spouting water from all their natural orifices. The rooms opening onto this court are decorated with paintings of animals and with collections of curious objects.

The South Gate of THELEME.

No ramparts or *murs* were built around Theleme, as in the words of Des Entommeures: "Where there is *mur* before and *mur* behind there is a store of murmur, envy and mutual conspiracy."

The Abbey community admits both men and women: men from the age of ten to fifteen and women from the age of twelve to eighteen. Only men and women who are beautiful, well-built and good natured are admitted. Those who enter may leave the community whenever they wish. In defiance of the normal system whereby monks and nuns take vows of chastity, poverty and obedience, it is decreed at Theleme that anyone in the community may marry, become rich and live at liberty.

The women are housed in apartments between the Arctic Tower and the Mesembrine Gate; the men occupy the rest of the building. In front of the women's lodgings are the tilt yards, riding ring, theatre and swimming pool. Pleasure gardens run along the river banks, with an ingenious maze in the middle. By the Cryere Tower is an orchard, well planted with many species of fruit trees. At the end of it lies the great park, teeming with all kinds of game. Archery, falconry and hunting are all catered for.

At the foundation of the order the ladies dressed according to their own taste and pleasure, but subsequently adopted a habit of gowns of cloth of gold, red satin and other luxurious cloths. In summer they wear light capes or sleeveless Moorish cloaks and in winter taffeta gowns trimmed with costly furs. Beads, neck chains and collars are all made of precious stones. In winter they adopt the French fashion of headdress; in summer the Italian; and in spring the Spanish. The French style is always worn on feast days and Sundays.

The men wear equally colourful and rich clothes: doublets of cloth of gold, velvet, satin, silk or damask, and mantles or cloaks of cloth of gold or velvet. Their caps are of black velvet, with many rings and buttons to decorate them. Every man carries a sword with a golden hilt and a scabbard of velvet, the colour being chosen to match the hose. On certain occasions, men and women dress in like apparel. To ensure that this is so, certain gentlemen are appointed to tell the men which colours the ladies will be wearing the next day. Everything in these matters follows the decisions of the ladies. The respect for women in Theleme is so great that before a gentleman goes to visit a lady, he must pass through the hands of perfumers and barbers. These attendants also provide the ladies with rose-water, orange-water and myrtle-water every morning along with a precious casket containing aromatic scent. All the clothes and jewelry worn in the Abbey are made by skilled craftsmen housed in a block of buildings in Theleme Wood.

The only rule of the community is "Do as you will," since it is thought that all people who are free, well-born and well-bred have a natural spur to drive them to virtue—their honour. The life of the Abbey is regulated by this single rule. Men and women rise, eat, work and sleep when and as they please.

No clocks or watches are allowed in Theleme.

(François Rabelais, *La Vie très horrifique du grand Gargantua*, Lyons, 1534)

THEODORA, a city of uncertain location. Recurrent invasions racked the city of Theodora in the centuries of its history; no sooner was one enemy routed than another gained strength and threatened the survival of the inhabitants. When the sky was cleared of condors, they had to face the propagation of serpents; the spiders' extermination allowed the flies to multiply into a black swarm; the victory over the termites left the city at the mercy of the woodworms. One by one the species incompatible to the city had to succumb and were extinguished. By dint of ripping away scales and carapaces, tearing off elytra and feathers, the people gave Theodora the exclusive image of a human city that still distinguishes it.

But first, for many long years, it was uncertain whether or not the final victory would not go to the last species left to fight man's possession of the city: the rats. From each generation of rodents that the people managed to exterminate, the few survivors gave birth to a tougher progeny, invulnerable to traps and resistant to all poison. In the space of a few weeks, the sewers of Theodora were repopulated with hordes of spreading rats. At last, with an extreme massacre, the murderous, versatile ingenuity of mankind defeated the overweening life-force of the enemy.

The city, great cemetery of the animal kingdom, was closed, aseptic, over the final buried corpses with their last fleas and their last germs. Man had finally re-established the order of the world which he had himself upset: no other living species existed to cast any doubts. To recall what had been fauna, Theodora's library would preserve on its shelves the volumes of Buffon and Linnaeus.

At least that is what Theodora's inhabitants believed, far from imagining that a forgotten fauna was stirring from its lethargy. Relegated for long eras to remote hiding places, ever since it had been deposed by the system of non-extinct species, the other fauna was coming back to the light from the library's basements where the incunabula were kept; it was leaping from the capitals and drain-pipes, perching at the sleepers' bedsides. Sphinxes, gryphons, chimeras, dragons, hircocervi, harpies, hydras, unicorns, basilisks were resuming posses-sion of their city.

(Italo Calvino, *Le città invisibili*, Turin, 1972)

THERMOMETER ISLAND, somewhere in the Atlantic Ocean, so called because the laws of the country allow couples to sleep with each other only if the sexes of both husband and wife, mea-sured with special thermometers, have reached the same temperature. The sexual organs of the male inhabitants have curious shapes—parallelepipeds, pyramids, cylinders—and correspond exactly to those of the female islanders. The queen of the is-land is elected from among those women who are the quickest in measuring the temperature of their own and their partners' sex; this dexterity is highly honoured on the island.

The islanders are born with the visible signs of their vocation: in this way each one is what he should be. Those destined to the science of geom-etry are born with fingers in the form of a com-pass; someone who is to be an astronomer is born with eyes in the form of telescopes; geographers are born with heads like terrestrial globes; musi-cians with hornlike ears; hydraulic engineers with testicles like water pumps and they are capable from an early age of urinating in long jets. Certain inhabitants who are born with several of these characteristics combined have proved in later life to be in fact good for nothing.

Visitors will be interested in a curious instru-ment found only on this island, a harpsichord that instead of producing sounds produces colours and is used by the ladies to find harmonious combina-tions for their dresses.

(Denis Diderot, *Les Bijoux indiscrets*, Paris, 1748)

THESMOGRAPHIA, a kingdom of unknown lo-cation in which everyone has a determinate place, rank and duty, and where convicted criminals be-come—as in TALLSTORIA—slaves to the rest of the population. Thesmographian laws are based on the maxim "Do unto others as you would have them do unto you," and Thesmographian religion stems strictly from the Gospel, stripped of its dis-mal, oppressive features accumulated over the centuries. A murderer is branded and then sold, and the money is used to purchase a servant for his victim's family; or he might be handed over to sur-geons for scientific experiments. Incendiaries are made to work as firemen.

The land is redistributed every fifty years and the jubilee is celebrated with sumptuous feasts. When the population becomes too numerous, the inhabitants are encouraged to establish colonies overseas and Thesmographians are therefore found in many places throughout the world.

(Nicolas Edme Restif de la Bretonne, *Le Thesmo-graphe, ou idées d'un Honnête Homme sur un Projet-Règlement proposé à toutes les Nations de l'Europe pour opérer une Reforme Générale des Lois*, Paris, 1789)

THIEVES CITY, in the Klondike region, Canada, not far from the Bering Strait. The city was built over an underground lake of boiling water, six or seven times the size of Paris, which preserves it from the Arctic weather. Advanced technical research allows the French-speaking in-habitants of Thieves City to enjoy an agriculture similar to that of a temperate region by regulating the rain—which falls mainly in the evening—and by providing efficient machinery to cope with the problems of ploughing, sowing and reaping. This machinery, as well as the transport system, is worked by short-waves, a process not fully ex-plained. The city is protected by a vast moat some fifty kilometres in diameter.

In order to obtain permission to visit Thieves City, travellers must choose one of a vast number of tasks that will make them eligible applicants. They can either rob the till, kidnap some well-known personality, find a new tax dodge, cheat at cards, become a pirate publisher or in any other way contravene the law of their country. Their ap-plication will then be submitted to the President of Thieves City, Monsieur Dassy de Tharn, who ful-fils his governmental office from the safe cover of an import-export firm in the Buttes-Chaumont,

Paris, between the Rue des Solitaires and the Rue Botzaris. The entire population of Thieves City consists of thieves, murderers, shady businessmen and other criminals whom the police have never been able to trace. Inside the city, however, no criminal acts are permitted and when they take place the culprits are severely reprimanded. Visitors are advised to stay at the *Hôtel du Grand-Cartouche* even though the rooms are bugged with listening devices, a common and accepted practice throughout Thieves City. Several gambling parlours are open to the public but cheating is punishable by fifty strokes of the cane. In spite of its minor inconveniences, Thieves City seems a pleasant alternative to Las Vegas.

(Maurice Level, *La Cité des voleurs*, Paris, 1930)

THIMBLE COUNTRY, not far from ROOTA-BAGA COUNTRY. All the people here wear thimble hats; the women do their washing up in thimble dishpans and the men use thimble shovels at work.

The country was recently the scene of a great war between the left-handed people and the right-handed people. The war did not seem to affect the Thimble People themselves, who sat looking on and waving handkerchiefs to each other—some of them left-handed and others right-handed. All the fighting was done by the Smokestacks, armed with monkey-wrenches which they used to try and wrench each other apart. These monkey-wrenches were decorated with monkey faces in an attempt to frighten the enemy. The outcome of the battle is not known.

(Carl Sandburg, *Rootabaga Stories*, New York, 1922)

THINIFER KINGDOM, see FATTIPUFF AND THINIFER KINGDOMS.

THRAN, a city on the southern border of the EN-CHANTED WOOD, on the banks of DREAM-WORLD'S River Skai. Its alabaster walls are lofty beyond belief, sloping inwards and wrought in one solid piece. However, the clustered towers within—all white beneath their golden spires—are loftier still, so that travellers on the plain see them soaring into the sky, sometimes shining clear, sometimes caught at the top in tangles of cloud and mist, sometimes clouded lower down with their utmost pinnacles blazing free above the vapours.

The gates of Thran open onto great wharves of marble where ornate galleons of fragrant cedar and calamander ride gently at anchor, and strange, bearded sailors are seen sitting on casks and bales marked with unknown hieroglyphics. Beyond the wall of Thran lies the farm country. Here small, white cottages dream between little hills, and narrow roads with many stone bridges wind gracefully between streams and gardens.

(Howard Phillips Lovecraft, "The Dream-Quest of Unknown Kadath," in *Arkham Sampler*, Sauk City, 1948)

THREE-O-SEVEN (307), a rocky island, one of the Aleutian Archipelago. All that remains today is a mass of calcinated rocks and a huge crater. However, not many years ago, 307 was a beautiful, lush island. After the discovery of JL3, an immortality virus, by an Indian scientist, the island was set aside as a quarantine zone for all those infected with immortality. The world's best chemists and biologists came to 307 to try to find an antidote. Underground laboratories were quickly assembled and the scientists administered JL3 to all animal and vegetable species on the island in the hope of discovering a cure. The flora and fauna grew to exuberant proportions, full of beauty and health. The children born on the island became splendid adolescents and in their quest for love endangered the island with overpopulation. Contraceptives were introduced but the women refused to take them. The island succumbed to chaos and violence and finally, in order to prevent contamination by fleeing immortals, the governments of the world made the difficult decision to bomb 307. No one knows the fate of the immortals after the bombing.

(René Barjavel, *Le Grand Secret*, Paris, 1973)

THULE, sometimes known as **ULTIMA THULE**, an island in the North Atlantic, some six days' sail from the Orkneys. Thule is a large island, ten times the size of Great Britain. Its soil is for the most part infertile and the air around Thule is a mixture of sea-water and oxygen.

Every year a strange phenomenon takes place in Thule. At the time of the summer solstice, the sun never sets; rather, it stays in the sky until the winter solstice is reached. Then, for a period of forty days and nights, it remains hidden. The inhabitants of the island spend that long night asleep as they cannot do anything in the pitch-dark.

Among the several tribes that inhabit Thule is one called the Scritifines. The Scritifines lead a life similar to that of beasts. They never dress or wear shoes, drink wine or till the earth. Like savage animals they hunt the large creatures that inhabit the forests of Thule. Sometimes in winter the Scritifines will cover themselves with the skin of these wild creatures, and they extract marrow from the creatures' bones to feed to their babies who are never given milk. As soon as a child is born, he is hung from a tree in a leather cradle, a piece of marrow is stuck in his mouth and his mother leaves with her husband to join in the hunt.

The members of another tribe are known for the large number of gods and demons they worship, which they say inhabit every stone, river and tree. To these beings they offer human sacrifices, by slaughtering the victim at the altar, impaling him on a tree or throwing him down a crevasse.

Another, more friendly tribe is noted for its exquisite hydromel, or mead, prepared from the abundant honey made by its bees.

(Diodorus Siculus, *The Library of History*, 1st cen. BC; Strabo, *Geography*, 1st cen. BC; Procopius, *The Gothic War*, 4th cen. AD)

THUMBS UP, a village in ROOTABAGA COUNTRY, neither very far nor very near to the village of LIVER AND ONIONS. It was once known as Thumbs Down, but the name was changed. It is expected that the name of the village will alternate between Thumbs Up and Thumbs Down.

Thumbs Up is noted for the wild oleanders and wild rambling roses which grow in its old lumber yard. They are cared for by the dippy lovers, who come to sit on the fence and watch the dip of stars in the sky; this is a particularly popular pastime on moonlit nights.

The village is also known for the peculiar species of rat which is found in its lumber yard. The nails in the lumber yard become more and more rusty until they finally drop out of the wood. As they fall out they are caught by the rats who take them to chew and eat. All the nail-eating rats in Rootabaga Country are sent here by their parents, where they grow big and strong on a diet of rust.

A young rat who meets a fellow going to the lumber yards greets him with the question: "Where have you been?" To this, the traditional answer is: "To Thumbs Up." The ritual exchange then continues: "And how do you feel?" "As hard as nails." As the rats sit and chew their nails, they habitually tell one another stories.

(Carl Sandburg, *Rootabaga Stories*, New York, 1922)

THURIA, a kingdom in the underground continent of PELLUCIDAR, some 250 miles to the south-west of SARI, on the edge of the Land of Awful Shadow. The landscape of Thuria will strike the visitor as eerie, crossed by motionless rivers and haunted by a strange vegetation.

The Thurians are one of the less primitive peoples of Pellucidar. They practise a rudimentary form of agriculture in forest clearings and live in thatched huts whereas many Pellucidarians still live in caves. Thurian villages are usually rectangular, surrounded by rough walls of logs and boulders. There is no gate; the wall is scaled by ladders that can be withdrawn at night.

Thuria is famed for its *lidi*, which roams the wide plains named after it. The *lidi* is similar to the diplodocus, an American herbivorous dinosaur that once lived on the surface of the earth; it grows to a length of up to one hundred feet, with a tiny head perched on its slender neck. The *lidi*'s gait is slow, but the strides it takes are so long that travellers will find it covers ground quite quickly. The Thurians ride these creatures and use them as beasts of burden. In recent years the *lidi* has been exported to other areas of Pellucidar.

The *tharg* or giant elk is also common in this area, and visitors will find the traditional method of hunting it quite rivetting. First, one of the men steps into the *tharg*'s line of vision to make it charge—and once a *tharg* has seen something and charged, it will not swerve from its headlong course. A second man then emerges from a hiding-place in the undergrowth and runs alongside the large beast, grabbing its mane and flinging himself onto its back. He stabs it through the neck with a flint knife and the *tharg* is finished off with clubs and spears.

(Edgar Rice Burroughs, *At the Earth's Core*, New York, 1922; Edgar Rice Burroughs, *Pellucidar*, New York, 1923; Edgar Rice Burroughs, *Tanar of Pellucidar*, New York, 1930)

THWIL, see ROKE.

TILIBET, an island in the Gulf of Siam, latitude 12° north and longitude 104° east. Time is much faster than normal on this island, and the span of life is much shorter. Babies are born laughing and grow very quickly—they can talk at one day old, and at twenty years of age they die, wrinkled and haggard. They sleep only one hour a night. Because they are so full of the present, they forget the past and despise the future. They ignore boredom and navigation, because they find life too short and precious to spend the best part of it on dangerous journeys.

The king is elected in his middle age (four years old), and the prime minister in his ripe old age (sixteen). The Tilibetians despise precious stones and have no use for money. Men trust their wives completely, who in turn are utterly faithful to them.

Nothing superfluous is allowed or imagined. The Tilibetians have only small areas of cultivated land and their architecture is very economical. Their villages are neat and, above all, practical.

(Abbé Pierre François Guyot Desfontaines, *Le Nouveau Gulliver, ov Voyage De Jean Gulliver, Fils Du Capitaine Gulliver. Traduit d'un Manuscrit Anglois. Par Monsieur L.D.F.*, Paris, 1730)

TIRRALARIA, a small hilly island, capped by a smoking volcano called Klimarol; part of the RIALLARO ARCHIPELAGO in the south-east Pacific. The terraced hills of Tirralaria are covered with flowering trees and grass; the dilapidated harbour is overlooked by magnificent temples and minarets of marble. Especially notable are the ruins of a high-domed temple with the remains of an ancient fresco still visible; some people have their sleeping-quarters among the ruins.

Klimarol volcano is used for incinerating debris and cremating the dead, a task carried out by slaves who are also responsible for the only productive labour on the island. In the crater the remains of an earlier civilization can be seen—fragments of domes, towers and temples. Tirralaria was initially populated by exiles from LIMANORA, notably criminals and enthusiastic believers in socialism.

The government of Tirralaria is communistic, without social hierarchy—except for the slaves.

There is no labour—except for slave-labour—so there is no need to organize it. There are no lawyers and no doctors; nature is left to deal with the sick and weak. A committee is selected from time to time to distribute the fruits of the soil. No property is private and people are allowed to steal from one another. The family has ceased to exist, leading to polygamy and polyandry. The inhabitants of Tirralaria go about clad in rags, which they call "the primitive clothing of Paradise," and most of them live in holes in the ground. There are no schools as these are held to be both symbols and hot-beds of social inequality.

The religion of Tirralaria is polytheistic. The universe is believed to be full of gods who need neither sustenance nor expanse of space in which to live. Effectively they all form one god, just as the cells of the body make up one body. As soon as a man dies, his soul becomes a god and is worshipped as such. All men are priests and they worship where they wish, either in the temples or under the open sky.

(Godfrey Sweven, *Riallaro, the Archipelago of Exiles*, New York & London, 1901; Godfrey Sweven, *Limanora, the Island of Progress*, New York & London, 1903)

TISHK, an obscure Elfin kingdom in the Ural Mountains of Russia. Very little is known of it and none of the inhabitants of the Elfin realms of western Europe appear to have visited Tishk. It is, however, known that a rebellion against the young queen of Tishk was led by a somewhat militaristic uncle. The coup was savagely put down, its leaders executed and their supporters exiled beyond the Volga. One of the exiles, Tamarind, eventually reached Schloss DREIVIERTELSTEIN, where he was responsible for the disruption of the quiet life of that kingdom. Tamarind claimed to be the nephew of Baba Jaga, the witch, but the basis for his claim remains obscure.

(Sylvia Townsend Warner, *Kingdoms of Elfin*, London, 1972)

TITIPU, a town in Japan, ruled by the Mikado by means of the Lord High Executioner and famous for its strict penal code. Whoever flirts, leers or winks is beheaded, and wives of criminals are buried alive after the death of their condemned husbands.

Struck by the fact that there have been no executions in Titipu for a long period, the Mikado decreed that unless someone was beheaded at least once a month, the post of Lord High Executioner would be abolished and the city reduced to the rank of village. Through a complicated series of events, the son of the Mikado himself almost became the victim of this law, but was saved by a happy concatenation of events. Travellers visiting Titipu today should bear in mind that the laws are complex and changeable and they might be committing a capital crime without even knowing it.

The inhabitants of Titipu resemble the figures on Japanese vases, jars, screens and fans popular in England at the turn of the century.

(Sir William Schwenck Gilbert & Sir Arthur Sullivan, *The Mikado; or The Town of Titipu*, first performance, London, 1885)

TIVALERA, see Isles of WISDOM.

TOAD HALL, by the river that flows past RIVER BANK, a dignified building of mellow brick, with French windows that open onto flowered lawns right down to the water's edge. At the back of the house are extensive outbuildings: stables, pigsties, a pigeon-house and a hen-house, as well as an attractive walled kitchen-garden. Although parts of the buildings are said to date back to the fourteenth century, it has every modern convenience and is an extremely comfortable gentleman's residence. It is situated close to golf-links, the post office and the church; a large boat-house stands nearby on a creek flowing into the main river. An underground passage leads from the house to the river bank; it appears to have been built hundreds of years ago, and was restored by the father of the present occupant of the Hall.

Toad Hall is the ancestral home of Mr. Toad, a figure of considerable reputation in the area. Although basically kind-hearted and generous, Mr. Toad can appear conceited and boastful, and is given to short-lived enthusiasms for a variety of hobbies which have in the past been both expensive and dangerous. The most recent was a passion for motor-cars, which led, after several crashes, to Mr. Toad's imprisonment for the theft of a car. Mr. Toad contrived to escape from prison, only to learn that Toad Hall had been taken over by a group of weasels, toads and ferrets from WILD

WOOD during his enforced absence. The Wild Wooders unfortunately caused considerable damage to the Hall and ate and drank large quantities of Mr. Toad's supplies. They were eventually expelled by Mr. Toad, Mr. Water Rat of River Bank, Mr. Badger of Wild Wood and Mr. Mole of MOLE END. The four entered the Hall via the underground passage (the existence of which was known to Mr. Badger alone) and routed the occupiers during a riotous feast. The Hall has now been restored to order and it seems that the episode has had a salutary and calming effect on the formerly exuberant Mr. Toad.

(Kenneth Grahame, *The Wind in the Willows*, London, 1908)

TO-AT-CHIMK, see MARBOTIKIN DULDA.

TOHU and **BOHU**, two small islands close to the Island of CLERKSHIP. The islands are very poor—not so much as a frying pan can be found on either of them. This is because the great Giant Bringuenarilles ate all pots, frying pans, kettles and cauldrons for lack of windmills, his normal diet. His digestive system was unable to cope with this change of diet and he was severely ill. No remedy could be found to save him, and he finally choked to death while eating a lump of butter at the mouth of a hot oven, following the orders of his physician.

(François Rabelais, *Le quart livre des faicts et dicts du bon Pantagruel*, Paris, 1552)

TOL ERESSËA, or the **LONELY ISLE**. A ship-shaped island in the Bay of Eldamar on the eastern coast of AMAN. At one time the island was adrift and carried the Vanyar and Noldor elves across the sea from MIDDLE-EARTH to Aman. Later, the Teleri elves were drawn across the sea in the same way and, at their request, the island was rooted or anchored in the Bay of Eldamar, where it became their home, although many of them later moved ashore to Eldamar itself.

The island is bathed in the light that floods through the pass in the Pelóri, the mountains that guard Aman, and its western shores are therefore green and fertile.

A seedling of Galathilion, the White Tree of Eldamar, was planted here. It is the original stock of the White Tree that grows in MINAS TIRITH, which became the emblem of the kingdom of GONDOR. The main city of Tol Eressëa is Avallónë, famed for its lamp-lit quays and its great white tower. The latter is an important navigational aid for ships sailing west.

Like Aman itself, Tol Eressëa was moved far away from the reach of men after the destruction of the kingdom of Númenor on ELENNA.

(J.R.R. Tolkien, *The Fellowship of the Ring*, London, 1954; J.R.R. Tolkien, *The Return of the King*, London, 1955; J.R.R. Tolkien, *The Silmarillion*, London, 1977)

TOMTODDIES, ISLE OF, believed to be the island referred to by Captain Lemuel Gulliver as LAPUTA.

The island is populated by those unfortunate children whose parents keep them working at their lessons all week long instead of allowing them to play and who are forced to sit endless series of tests and examinations. As a result, their brains grow bigger and bigger and their bodies smaller and smaller until they all turn into turnips, with little but water inside them. Even so, their parents pick the leaves off them as fast as they grow, so that they should have nothing green about them. The children's legs have turned into roots that grow down into the ground, because they never play any games and spend all their time studying.

The turnips constantly sing the song of the Tomtoddies: "I can't learn my lesson; the examiner's coming." This is an integral part of the worship of their great idol, Examination. The Examiner-of-all-Examiners strides among the poor turnips, imposing the most terrible burdens on their shoulders and shouting at them in a loud, dictatorial voice. In fear, the poor turnips cram themselves so fast that they pop open by the dozen. There is no escape from the Examiner, whose nose is nine thousand miles long and can be poked anywhere to examine both the little boys and their tutors.

The only other creature on the island is a stick, which once belonged to Mr. Roger Ascham; a bust of King Edward VI is carved on its head. The stick is waiting for the day when Mrs. Bedonebyasyoudid finally allows him to thrash the Examiner-of-all-Examiners—a day he awaits with great impatience and high expectation.

Visitors to the island will immediately be assailed by the unfortunate turnips, who will ask questions such as "What was the name of Mutius Scaevola's thirteenth cousin's grandmother's maid's cat?" or "Can you tell me the name of a place that nobody ever heard of, where nothing ever happened, in a country not yet discovered?" They have no idea why they need this information or of what use it may be to them; all they know is that the dreaded Examiner is coming.

A great pillar on the shore reads: "Playthings not allowed here."

(Charles Kingsley, *The Water-Babies: A Fairy Tale for a Land-Baby*, London, 1863)

TONDAR, see PELLUCIDAR.

TOOL ISLAND, an uncultivated and largely uninhabited island two days' sail from RINGING ISLAND. The trees of Tool Island resemble terrestrial animals in that they all have skin, fat, flesh, bones and, presumably, all the normal internal organs. They grow, however, with their heads (their trunks) pointing downwards; their hair (their roots) beneath the ground; and their feet (or boughs) in the air. They do not bear normal fruit, but produce all types of tools and weapons, from mattocks to scimitars and from billhooks to javelins. Anyone who wants tools or weapons has merely to shake a tree and the desired article will fall down like a ripe plum. When they touch the ground they strike a kind of grass known as scabbard-grass and sheath themselves in it. Visitors are advised to be careful to avoid being injured by the falling weapons and tools. Underneath some of the trees, grass grows in the form of the shafts of spears, prongs and forks, which stretch upwards until they touch the tree where they find suitable heads and blades. It seems that the trees are aware of what is growing beneath them and prepare the appropriate type of head or blade. In rare cases, freaks of nature do occur; a half-pike, for instance, may grow and touch a bough bearing a broomhead instead of a steel point. Even so, a use can be found for everything that grows on Tool Island.

(François Rabelais, *Le cinquiesme et dernier livre des faicts et dicts du bon Pantagruel, auquel est contenu la visitation de l'Oracle de la dive Bacbuc, el le mot de la bouteille; pour lequel avoir est entrepris tout ce long voyage*, Paris, 1564)

TOO-MANY-OF-'EM, the home country of many of the clerijays who settle to the west, on RINGING ISLAND. It sometimes happens that a noble house has so many children that splitting the estate equally would lead to the eating up of the property. When this seems likely to happen, some of the children are packed off by their parents to Ringing Island, where they will be assured of a living.

(François Rabelais, *Le cinquiesme et dernier livre des faicts et dicts du bon Pantagruel, auquel est contenu la visitation de l'Oracle de la dive Bacbuc, et le mot de la bouteille; pour lequel avoir est entrepris tout ce long voyage,* Paris, 1564)

TORELORE, a small feudal kingdom of uncertain location; it would appear, however, to be on or near the Mediterranean coast.

The kingdom is distinguished by a peculiar custom: it is normal for men to take to their beds when the time comes for their wives to have babies. In the interim, the women go to the army and fight. Warfare in this country is unconventional. It is not, for instance, considered sociable to kill or to attempt to kill an enemy. The normal weapons used in battle are apples, rotten vegetables and fresh cheeses.

(Anonymous, *Aucassin et Nicolette,* 14th cen. AD)

TØRRENDRU, a land sometimes to the east and sometimes to the north of the Central Siberian Plateau. Unfortunately Tørrendru cannot be visited; if a human interloper were to perceive its outlines from a distance and attempt to approach it, Tørrendru would immediately uproot itself and transport itself elsewhere.

Tørrendru has been described as "encompassed by beatitudes." Noble old trees and innumerable orchards grace its flatlands, blue lakes and crystalline streams reflect its peaceful skies, lush green fields roll amid softly coloured uplands. The climate is always equable.

The inhabitants of Tørrendru are the wretched of this earth. They are gathered by Galantai the Goose and her countless winged minions, who are ever in search of the horrors man has created; in cities, killing fields and parched lands they seek out the shambles of the slaughtered, children and animals, innocent victims of their own vulnerability.

Tørrendru has existed since time immemorial, under the stewardship of a succession of wise masters. For many years the government has been in the hands of Quasso the Forester, who now awaits the arrival of an apprentice. Since a change in government is expected, visitors are advised to check on the state of affairs before setting out.

(Izaak Mansk, *The Ride of Enveric Olsen*, London, 1999)

TOSH, see GRAMBLAMBLE LAND.

TOTTENHOTLAND, a sandy desert on the edge of the Quadling Country of OZ. The only plants in the area are scattered palm trees, beneath which strange circular objects can be seen, resembling upturned kettles. These are the houses of the area's inhabitants, the Tottenhots.

TOTTENHOTLAND dwellings.

The Tottenhots are tiny dark-skinned people. Their scarlet hair stands straight up on their heads and they go about naked, apart from animal skins worn around the waist and bracelets on the wrists and ankles. Necklaces and pendant earrings are also worn.

The Tottenhots are mainly nocturnal and shun the bright light of day. At night they leap out of their circular dwellings to play and dance beneath the moon. Even though they are mischievous and sometimes aggressive people, they will do no harm to anyone who is willing to join in their games. They seem to have little knowledge of the other peoples of Oz and show not the slightest interest in leaving their sandy desert.

(L. Frank Baum, *The Patchwork Girl of Oz*, Chicago, 1913)

TOWER HILLS, a high range of hills in ERIADOR, to the west of the SHIRE. The hills are crowned by three white towers that give them their name. The towers are thought to have been built by the elves after the establishment of the kingdom of ARNOR. A *palantír* or Seeing-stone was once kept in the tallest tower; but while other *palantíri* were invaluable for watching distant events in all MIDDLE-EARTH, the stone of the Tower Hills gazed only at far-off AMAN, and so played no part in the wars that affected the land.

The hobbits of the Shire say that the sea can be seen from the top of this tower, which stands on a green mound at some distance from the others—there is, however, no record of any hobbit ever having climbed it. By the beginning of the Fourth Age of Middle-earth the Tower Hills were recognized as marking the western boundary of the Shire.

(J.R.R. Tolkien, *The Fellowship of the Ring*, London, 1954; J.R.R. Tolkien, *The Two Towers*, London, 1954; J.R.R. Tolkien, *The Return of the King*, London, 1955; J.R.R. Tolkien, *The Silmarillion*, London, 1977)

TOYLAND, a country inhabited by nursery-rhyme characters and classic toys. Visitors will see simply designed houses built with toy bricks, and small toy shops that sell all sorts of toy articles. Beneath Toyland lies Bogeyland, infested with crocodiles and fearsome, hairy creatures.

There seems to be a distinct separation between the toys and the characters. Little Bo-Peep,

Tom Tom, the piper's son and Mother Goose keep a polite distance from toys such as Noddy, Big Ears, Miss Fluffy Cat and Mr. and Mrs. Noah.

Visitors are warned that morals in Toyland are very strict, based on the more conventional English nursery precepts. The town is patrolled by a policeman called Mr. Plod and by an army of tin soldiers. The cuisine, apart from jelly-babies, marshmallows and boiled sweets, is good British home-cooking. The nursery-rhyme-character section of Toyland diverges slightly from this pattern.

(Enid Blyton, *Noddy goes to Toyland*, London, 1929; *Babes in Toyland*, directed by Gus Meins & Charles Rogers, USA, 1934)

TRACODA, an island in the Pacific Ocean, inhabited by cave dwellers who live on the flesh of serpents. They do not speak, but hiss like the snakes they devour.

(Sir John Mandeville, *Voiage de Sir John Maundevile*, Paris, 1357)

TRALDRAGDUBB, see LUGGNAGG.

TREASURE ISLAND, some ten miles long and five miles wide, off the coast of Mexico. Near its southern point lies a cluster of rocks known as Skeleton Island; the two are joined by a spit of sand at low tide. There are three hills on Treasure Island, running north to south in a row. They are known respectively as Fore-mast Hill, Mizzen Mast Hill and Main Mast or Spy-Glass Hill. The latter is the highest, rising two to three hundred feet above the others. A natural harbour, known as Captain Kidd's Anchorage, lies on the south coast. It is almost landlocked, with trees coming right down to the high-water mark. Two swampy streams or rivers empty into this sheltered bay; the foliage around their mouths has an almost poisonously bright appearance. Travellers have one alternative anchorage, the North Inlet, a narrow estuary with thickly wooded shores.

The south-west coast of the island around the point known as Haulbowline Head is made virtually inaccessible by cliffs between forty and fifty feet high. To the north, the cliffs give way to sandy beaches and then to the tree-clad Cape of the Woods. The tides and currents are dangerous, particularly along the west coast.

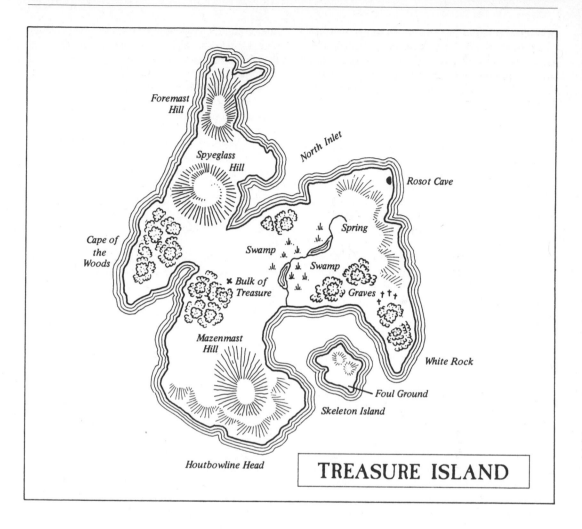

Foremast
Hill

Spyeglass
Hill

North Inlet

Rosot Cave

Cape of
the
Woods

Spring

Swamp

Swamp

Bulk of
Treasure

Graves

Mazenmast
Hill

White Rock

Foul Ground

Skeleton Island

Houtbowline Head

TREASURE ISLAND

The only buildings on Treasure Island are a stockade and a loghouse of pine hidden in the woods near the southern anchorage. Built over a fresh-water spring on a knoll, the stockade can hold about forty people. It was obviously designed for defensive purposes and is pierced with loopholes for muskets on every side.

Much of the island is covered in grey woods, with occasional clumps of taller trees of the pine family. Low evergreen oaks are common. Flowering shrubs and clove trees are found on the rising ground above Captain Kidd's Anchorage. The fauna of the island has not been studied in any detail, although sea-lions are seen on the coast.

The island was first charted in 1754 by Captain Flint, who chose it as the burial place for his famous treasure. Flint, a notorious buccaneer, went ashore with a group of six men to bury his £700,000 treasure and then killed all witnesses. The only record of the spot was a crude map drawn up by Flint's mate, Bill Bones. Long after Flint's death the papers came to light at the *Admiral Benbow Inn* in BLACK HILL COVE.

Some years after the burial of the treasure, one of Flint's former crew, Ben Gunn, chanced to pass the island on a different ship. Recognizing it, Gunn persuaded the captain and crew to search for the treasure. They failed to discover it and, in anger, the captain marooned Gunn on the island, where he lived in complete solitude for the next three years.

Armed with the charts found at the *Admiral*

Benbow, a group of men led by Squire Trelawney set off to try to find Flint's treasure, sailing in the *Hispaniola* from Bristol. Without realizing it, they engaged several members of Flint's old crew, including his old quartermaster, Long John Silver. Almost immediately after the *Hispaniola's* arrival at the island a mutiny broke out, with Silver as its ringleader. After a lengthy struggle, involving pitched battles at the old stockade, the "loyal" party were victorious. At this stage, Silver changed sides again, hoping to get at least some part of Flint's fabled wealth. The first attempt at locating the treasure was a failure, as Ben Gunn had already found it and rehidden it in a new cache. It was finally discovered and the remaining members of the expedition, together with Gunn, returned to England. On the voyage, Silver deserted, taking some of the money with him, and was never heard of again. Three of the original mutineers were left behind on Treasure Island, and their fate remains unknown to this day.

(Robert Louis Stevenson, *Treasure Island*, London, 1883)

TREASURE VALLEY, an extremely rich and fertile valley in Stiria, watered by the Golden River and surrounded by mountains permanently covered with snow. The Golden River is born in these mountains, flowing underground for some way before emerging into the valley. Near its source, two black rocks can be seen, closely connected with the history of the valley and with the transformations it has undergone.

Long ago, the valley was owned by three brothers: Hans, Schwartz and Gluck. The two eldest brothers were cruel, ugly men, who killed all living things that did not pay for their keep. Blackbirds were killed to prevent them from eating the fruit, hedgehogs to prevent them from sucking the milk from the cows. Even the crickets in the farmhouse were killed to prevent them from eating the scraps of food. They refused to pay their servants, profited from the bad harvests that affected other areas and beat their younger brother Gluck on the slightest pretext. The brothers came home one stormy night to find, much to their annoyance, that Gluck had given shelter to a strange old man in a tall pointed cap. Schwartz and Hans attempted to attack the old man, but were powerless against him, finding themselves in a heap on the floor when they tried to hit him. He left, promis-

ing to return at midnight for the last time. The old man kept his word, arriving with a great storm that destroyed much of the house. On his departure, he left his visiting card; without realizing it, the two brothers had tried to fight with the South West Wind. In the morning they saw to their horror that the valley had been flooded and that much of their land had been destroyed. The old man never returned; nor did any of his cousins, the other winds, and the valley soon became sterile. As no river flowed through it in those days and it depended on the winds to bring rain, Treasure Valley was soon reduced to a sandy desert.

In despair, the brothers travelled to the nearest town and became goldsmiths. Their trade did not prosper; they drank away most of the money they earned and were soon reduced to poverty. Even young Gluck's favourite mug was flung into the melting pot—a curious old mug with the face of a dwarf—in a final attempt to raise money. As it melted, Gluck heard a voice talking to him and a dwarf appeared from the molten metal. The dwarf revealed himself to be the King of the Golden River, who had been transformed into a mug by a powerful enchanter. He explained to Gluck that the river they could see from the city would turn to gold—as Gluck wished it would do—if three drops of Holy Water were cast into it. Anyone who used unholy water would be changed into a black stone instead.

Hearing the story, Schwartz and Hans both tried to transform the river. In turn, they climbed the mountain with flasks of holy water, one stolen, the other obtained from a corrupt priest. As they climbed the mountain, each of the brothers met a child, a dog and an old man, all dying of thirst, but refused to share their precious water. Finally they cast their flasks into the river and were at once transformed into black stones. At last, Gluck climbed the mountain, but gave his holy water to those he met on the way, so that he had none left when he reached the source of the river. At this point, the dog turned into the King of the Golden River, and explained why Gluck's elder brothers had been transformed: holy water which is refused to the dying is not holy, no matter how many saints may have blessed it. He then gave Gluck three dew drops to cast into the river, telling the boy to go back to Treasure Valley. When he reached his old home, the boy found that the Golden River now flowed through the mountains into the valley and was already watering the country. The water proved to be the true gold promised him and Treasure Valley is once more a rich and flourishing land.

(John Ruskin, *The King of the Golden River or The Black Brothers. A Legend of Stiria*, London, 1851)

TREES, CITY OF, see CARAS GALADHON.

TREMENES, capital of ARCHAOS.

TRINQUELAGE, a medieval castle on the slopes of Mount Ventoux, in Provence, France. It used to be the residence of the lords of Trinquelage, and is built in massive stone. After crossing the moat, the visitor will come into the first courtyard and from there will enter the chapel, which is perhaps the most interesting feature of the castle.

Trinquelage is haunted by a number of spirits. At Christmas especially, an eerie light shines through the stones; on the way to mass, the people of the region can see a figure moving around in the chapel, lit by invisible candles. At midnight, the courtyard is filled with the ghosts of beautiful ladies in embroidered dresses and gentlemen in fine garments. From a phantom pulpit a little old ghost reads aloud from a book, but not a word of what he says can be understood. This ghost is said to be the spirit of a certain chaplain of Trinquelage, damned throughout eternity for having preferred stuffed turkey to the reading of the Gospel during the third Christmas mass (which he shortened in order to eat his Christmas dinner that much sooner). Every day of the year a cold wind blows through Trinquelage.

(Alphonse Daudet, *Lettres de mon moulin*, Paris, 1866)

TRISOLDAY, an extensive subterranean kingdom of the Worm-men. The Worm-men have human torsos, but the lower part of their bodies is worm-like. They either slither along the ground or move in great leaps, using their hands to launch themselves into the air. They have long, pointed noses and small eyes, and their skin is scaly, like that of a snake; the face of the male is red, that of the female pale yellow. Like moles, the Worm-men have a remarkable ability for digging tunnels.

The inhabitants of Trisolday worship the great *Ver-Fundver-Ne*, represented as a monstrous worm, and believe that the faithful will be rewarded by being allowed to enter the outside world and see the light of day. Sinners, on the other hand, will be condemned to eternal darkness. Their temple is a large edifice built of an unknown substance and supported by pillars. The body of the building is the tapering, forked tail of a giant figure of the *Ver-Fundver-Ne*.

The inner rooms are decorated with the most precious substances found beneath the earth. Perhaps most impressive of all is a square, domed room with a peristyle of transparent stones, decorated with jewels. Behind the temple runs an extensive labyrinth of caves and tunnels. One of the caves, which slopes down to a river of mercury, is decorated with a bas-relief showing men and women; the origins of this bas-relief remain obscure.

Trisolday is an elective monarchy, the powers of the king—the *Za-Ra-Ouf*— balanced by those of the elders of the Grand Council or *Kin-Zan-Da-Or*. The system of balanced powers was introduced by the first recorded king of Trisolday. The elders elect the monarch and serve as the custodians of the law; they may depose any king who shows signs of becoming a tyrant. Before his election, the king must prove himself worthy of office by making a journey of exploration and discovering new wonders.

Under the laws of Trisolday, the Worm-men may not enter into alliances with other people. Visitors are warned that all outsiders—referred to as *Tumpigands*—who venture into the kingdom must be destroyed. Human beings, however, have the option of being mutilated to make them look like Worm-men. Their severed limbs are then burnt with great ceremony. Those who consent to this mutilation become acceptable to the *Ver-Fundver-Ne*. In the past, humans have sometimes been kept as curiosities in the royal menagerie. However, there are no cases on record of humans consenting to mutilation.

A Worm-man whose life is saved by someone, be he human or Worm-man, immediately becomes his benefactor's slave. Oaths are sworn by smearing saliva over the face of the person to whom the oath is made.

The food of the Worm-men consists mainly of roast slugs, which are considered a delicacy. The fauna includes giant toads, which ride fast-moving worms; the toads are the traditional enemies of the Worm-men. In the outer caves, a dog-like creature is sometimes found—it is as large as an ass, but has the grace of a deer, and its coat is blue with black spots. It is greatly feared by the Worm-men. Flightless scarlet and black waterbirds live on the underground rivers. They waddle like ducks, coo rather like earthly pigeons and nest in hollow trees. Only the upper part of their body is feathered; the belly is covered in scales. There are also basilisks and dragons with barbed tongues.

Trisolday's contacts with the outside world have been extremely limited. On his ritual voyage of exploration, one of the kings found his way to the Kingdom of the AMPHICLEOCLES and kidnapped Princess Ascalis, hoping eventually to make her consent to mutilation and marriage. Her father traced her to Trisolday and became involved in a plot to depose the King of the Worm-men. He met his death in the riots that followed the discovery of the plot. In order to try to assuage Ascalis' grief and to gain her affection, the king built a mausoleum for her father that can still be seen; a large structure of coloured stone, built in the form of a human being and supported by the colossal statues of four Worm-men. Ascalis was rescued from Trisolday by Motacoa, the heir to the Kingdom of the ABDALLES.

Travellers determined to visit Trisolday are advised that the only known way of reaching the country is via the tunnels leading away from the bottom of the Houzail, a deep pit in the Kingdom of the Abdalles.

(Charles Fieux de Mouhy, *Lamekis, ou les voyages extraordinaires d'un Egyptien dans la terre intérieure avec la découverte de l'Isle des Silphides, enrichi des notes curieuses*, The Hague, 1735)

TRISTE-LE-ROY, a property situated to the south of a city whose location remains undetermined. The garden abounds in useless symmetries; one Diana balances another Diana; one balcony another; a double landing a double balustrade. Designed according to the same principle—i.e., the symmetry of mirrors—the house is dominated by a watchtower.

The only traveller known to have reached Triste-le-Roy did so by committing three murders. The first was perpetrated on the third of December, at the Hôtel du Nord, on the person of a rabbi having in his possession a copy of the *Defence of the Kabbalah*; Robert Fludd's *The Examination of Philosophy*; a literal translation of the *Sepher Yezirah*; a biography of *Baal Shem*; a *History of the Hasidim*; and a monograph (in German) on the *Tetragrammaton*. The second murder took place on the following third of January in front of the dye merchant's shop on the Rue de l'Ouest. The third murder, which was fictional, occurred on the third of February in a cabaret in the Rue de Toulon, to the east of the city.

It appears that these three locations—the Hôtel du Nord, the dyer's shop and the cabaret on the Rue de Toulon—form the points of an equilateral and mystical triangle which permits entry to Triste-le-Roy. All that remains is for the traveller to know the secret name of God (which has four letters) and to trace with a pair of calipers and a compass a fourth point, one that together with the triangle will form a perfect diamond. This fourth point is where the traveller will meet his own death, in the midst of the interminable odour of eucalyptus.

(Jorge Luis Borges, "La Muerte y la brújula," in *Ficciones*, Buenos Aires, 1956)

TROLL KINGDOM, in the Dovre Fjell Mountains of central Norway. The area is the home of a wide variety of trolls, brownies and goblins. Probably the most bizarre inhabitant of the kingdom is the Great Boyg, a monstrous invisible troll without shape or form. The only tangible sign of its existence is the slime that appears around it and a general smell of mustiness it secretes. The Great Boyg does not fight, but triumphs over its enemies through gentleness, and dwindles away to nothing at the sound of church bells. Pig-headed trolls wearing white night-caps are quite common. Two-headed trolls are now rare and the three-headed variety would appear to be extinct.

Though trolls see everything as it really is, travellers with normal sight will notice that in Troll Kingdom everything seems to have a double shape or quality. For example, travellers may see a beautiful harp-maiden as a cow strumming with its hoof on a string of gut, and the dance-maiden as a sow in short stockings, trying to dance but never succeeding. Everything appears simultaneously black and white, ugly and beautiful. The Troll king who formerly ruled the kingdom once offered to scratch out the left eye of a visitor, so that he would see everything perfectly and thereby become a real troll.

Although trolls live by night and shun daylight, they have some contact with the human inhabitants of the area. The Trond Troll, for instance, makes love to the girls who tend the cattle in the mountains, and the daughter of the former Troll king married a man named Peer Gynt, whom she met in the mountains.

In matters of religion, any belief is tolerated, as long as the manners and dress of the believer conform to the customs of the kingdom. Trolls normally wear silken bows on their tails; visitors should note that receiving a flame-coloured bow is an honour.

Trolls are somewhat egotistical creatures, who live in accordance with the motto "Troll, to thyself be—enough." For this reason there are no charities, savings banks or alms-houses in the Kingdom.

Travellers interested in farming should note that the oxen kept by the trolls give mead, while the cows produce cakes for their masters.

(Henrik Ibsen, *Peer Gynt*, Kristiania, 1867)

TROPICAL VALLEY, also known as **DEAD MAN'S VALLEY, HEADLESS VALLEY** and **VALLEY OF MYSTERY**, on the shores of the South Nahanni River, in the heart of the Mackenzie Mountains, in the southwestern corner of the Northwest Territories, to the north of British Columbia, to the east of the Yukon Territory, in Canada. The name of the river, Nahanni, means "people over there, far away."

Tropical Valley is a warm and verdant oasis hidden among eternal snows and boasting hot springs, mists, tropical foliage, prehistoric animals, strange tribes and a white queen. Headhunters are also to be found; in 1908 the decapitated bodies of the brothers Frank and Willie McLeod were discovered lying in the valley.

(Pierre Berton, *The Mysterious North*, Toronto, 1956)

TRUELAND, a country of unknown location, where nothing can be said or done that is not true. Visitors will find upon arrival that every one of their actions must correspond to a strict code of gallantry and good manners and that everything they promise must sooner or later be fulfilled. Should a visitor allow himself to drop even a piece of paper on the impeccable streets of Trueland, he will find that it immediately jumps back into his pocket—an unpleasant characteristic of a country which has forced its inhabitants to dispense with dogs as pets. Every blow given in Trueland comes back to the attacker, and every insult is felt as a blow by the one who has uttered it. Visitors can go through the motions of their everyday life in Trueland, but these will here become unbearably tainted by social hypocrisy, disguised feelings or any other form of deceit. Previous friendships, business partnerships and marriages tend to break up with astounding regularity upon arrival and very few travellers who have been to Trueland are ever reinstated in their previous occupation.

(Pierre Carlet de Chamblain de Marivaux, "Voyage au Monde Vrai," in *Le Cabinet du Philosophe*, Paris, 1734)

TRUE LHASSA, a city deep beneath a mountain plateau in Tibet, over two thousand metres underground, built in an immense cavern. Visitors are warned that this is the real holy city of Buddhism, hidden from the outside world, and all strangers are immediately put to death.

True Lhassa stands on the shores of a reddish lake, flanked by at least one hundred and twenty terraces, large and small, linked by staircases of pink rock. On the highest terrace stands the Buddhist temple; smaller temples cling to the rocks below. The most important building in True Lhassa is the palace of the Dalai Lama, an immense purple and gold construction dominated by a colossal statue of Buddha cut out of the rock, surrounded by golden votive lamps and heaps of pearls, diamonds and emeralds. The only temple ever seen by Europeans faces a courtyard lined with pyramids. The building itself contains a long nave with pillars on both sides, which together with wooden beams support the vaulted roof. Frescoes, illustrating the life of Buddha, cover the walls.

Travellers who wish to risk their lives will find that the city can be approached through a tunnel, the entrance of which is decorated with carved columns; one is carved in the shape of a serpent and the others as three superimposed Buddhas. A labyrinth of lanes and narrow streets leads to the different parts of the True Lhassa. Should the traveller take the wrong turning, he will end up in a lake of quicksand, a cave full of sacred serpents or a torture chamber littered with the rotting human remains left by the tigers, elephants and gorillas that are used against trespassers.

The area around True Lhassa is rich in diamonds. The True Lhassa River, which carries gold sediment, flows out into the open air and finally reaches the Valley of Nepal.

(Maurice Champagne, *Les Sondeurs d'abîmes*, Paris, 1911)

TRYPHÊME, a kingdom on the Mediterranean coast, opposite the Balearic Islands, between France and Spain. A fertile country, descending from the Pyrenees in the north-west to the Mediterranean in the south-east, with many forests, a few villages of low houses with red brick roofs, and isolated farmhouses. The Royal Palace, built by the reigning King Pausole, is in a Greco-Byzantine style; particularly notable is the façade supported by Greek columns. In the forest around the Royal Park are small open temples with domed roofs, set on marble columns, as well as statues and artificial waterfalls.

The king is absolute monarch in Tryphême. He has a harem of three hundred and sixty-six women, the most beautiful in the kingdom, at least one for each day of the year. This arrangement seems to suit the courtesans, except for number three hundred and sixty-six, who only sees the king on leap years. The laws of Tryphême are two: do not disturb your neighbour, and do whatever you like as long as you keep Law One. The people of Tryphême are happy and live without hypocrisy and without shame of their pleasures; individual

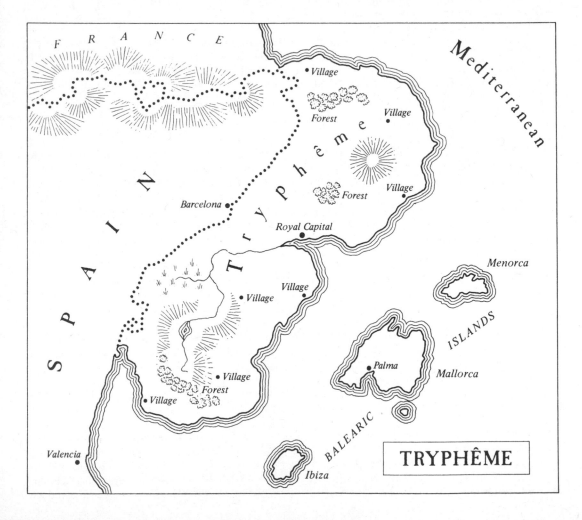

liberties are fully respected. The example of King Pausole is eagerly followed: a quiet, contented life, with very few decisions to make. However, when a decision is required it is never hurried and its execution may take place a very long time afterwards.

Women wear a yellow kerchief on their heads and silver sandals on their feet; otherwise they go naked. The weather is always excellent. For some reason, geographers have tried to conceal the existence of this happy country and Tryphême appears on most maps as part of the sea.

(Pierre Louÿs, *Les Aventures du Roi Pausole*, Paris, 1900)

TSALAL, an island beyond the Antarctic Polar Circle, latitude 83° 20′ south, longitude 43° 5′ west, set in a raven-black sea and surrounded by seven other islands. The coast is steep, the interior covered by thick woodland. Its climate is benign—incredible for its latitude—and the sea around it is free from ice. The rocks are unusual because of their volume, many dark colours and stratifications. Even the vegetation is different from any other in the world. The waters of Tsalal are unique. Though drinkable, they have the consistency of gum Arabic dissolved in water. When running, the water presents itself to the eye in many shades of violet, like shot silk, but if it is caught in a bowl it can be seen that the liquid is formed of several separate veins, each of a different colour. These veins do not intermingle, and though the cohesion among the different particles is perfect, it remains imperfect between vein and vein. If the blade of a knife is inserted through the middle, the water will immediately close upon it, but if the blade is inserted delicately between two veins, a perfect separation is obtained and the veins do not come together at once.

The inhabitants are as black as ebony and wear their thick, woolly hair long. They are as tall as the average European but far more muscular and sturdy. They go about naked, except for the warriors who cover themselves with the thick, soft skin of a dark, unknown animal, which they drape around their bodies with great ability. They are armed with dark wooden clubs, flint-headed spears and slings. Their houses, of rather poor design, are grouped in a village called Klock-Klock. Most of their habitations are small shallow caves, dug out of a steep wall of black stone. Others consist of a tree cut down about four feet from the ground with a

Method for dividing the waters of TSALAL: collect water in bowl (A), hold knife with right hand (B) and insert blade between veins (C).

black skin thrown over it and hanging in loose folds under which the natives nestle. Other houses are formed by means of rough branches, with the withered foliage still on them, made to recline at a forty-five-degree angle against a bank of clay, and heaped up, without regular form, to the height of five or six feet. Yet others are mere holes dug in the ground and covered with branches. A few are built among the forked branches as they stand, the upper part being partially cut through, so as to bend over upon the lower, thus forming a thicker shelter from the weather.

The fauna is strange. Among the domestic animals is a large creature which resembles the common hog in the structure of the body and the snout. The tail, though, is bushy and the slender legs are like those of an antelope. Its movements are exceedingly awkward and indecisive and it hardly ever attempts to run. There are other similar animals but of greater body length and covered with black wool. A great variety of tame fowls constitute the natives' chief food, including a kind of duck, black gannets and a non-carnivorous buzzard. The natives have also domesticated the black albatross which periodically flies off to sea but always returns to the villages. There is an abundance of fish and turtles. The serpents on the island, despite their formidable aspect, do not ·frighten the natives and are therefore probably not venomous. In the south, where the black albatross makes its nest, are many *biches-de-mer*.

The only expedition known to have reached Tsalal was that on board the schooner *Jane Guy* from Liverpool, on January 19, 1828. All but two members of the expedition were massacred. One of these, Mr. Gordon Pym of Nantucket, discovered certain chasms in the interior of the island. In the eastern extremity of the easternmost chasm, Mr. Pym found carvings which exactly reproduce the Ethiopian verbal root for "being dark," from which derive all words indicating "shadow" or "darkness"; also the Arab verbal root "being white," from which derive all words meaning "light" and "purity"; and finally an Egyptian word meaning "southern region" together with a human figure pointing south. It is interesting to note that very few things on the island are white, that the inhabitants are terrified by the mere sight of that colour, and that in the southern region of the island everything is black. It is possible that the crew of the *Jane Guy* were exterminated because of the colour of their skin. A philological examination of the name of the island might perhaps reveal some link with the characters so mysteriously inscribed on the walls of its interior.

(Edgar Allan Poe, *The Narrative of Arthur Gordon Pym of Nantucket*, New York, 1838)

TSHOBANISTAN, a vast country between DJUNUBISTAN and USSULISTAN, to which it is connected by the strange isthmus known as the CHATAR DEFILE. Most of Tshobanistan consists of rolling steppes and deserts, although the centre of the county is irrigated by the River Suhl.

It is thought that Tshobanistan was once an extensive lake separated from the sea by a wall of rock. When the lake burst its banks, creating the present Chatar Defile in the process, the waters of the lake gradually drained away, forming the shallow basin that is now Tshobanistan.

The Tshobans are nomads and have developed into typical desert dwellers; it is not yet known if the recent return of water to their land will significantly alter their way of life. They normally wear somewhat garishly dyed clothes, with a cape thrown over their trousers and jackets. Leather riding-boots are a standard feature of their dress. Turbans are worn and are used to indicate rank; those who are held to be descended from the prophet Mahomet, for instance, are distinguished by their green turbans. Tshobans of the highest rank wear pigtails into which gold and silver coins are braided.

Having lived as desert nomads for many centuries, the Tshobans have developed a terrible fear of water and are quite incapable of swimming. That is probably why they were never able to take USSULA, the capital of Ussulistan, defended not by walls but by a system of water-filled ditches.

(Karl Friedrich May, *Ardistan*, Bamberg, 1909;

Karl Friedrich May, *Der Mir von Djinnistan*, Bamberg, 1909)

TSINTSIN-DAGH, MOUNT, on the shores of Lake Nam-Tcho, also known as Lake Tengri-nor or Lake of the Heavenly Mountains, in north Tibet, four days north-west of Lhasa. The lake is in the shape of a horseshoe and its shores are covered with *tinkal,* which in the sunlight glows white, amber or topaz; at sunset, it gleams like rubies. Legend has it that the lake is the home of the snake-gods who reward with their incredible wealth all those who give them milk or water.

Mount Tsintsin-Dagh looks like a fortress, on the summit of which is the lamasery of the Silent Brothers, a white building with red doors, flat roofs with turned-up corners, banners made of yak's hair and bells to keep the evil spirits at bay. The monks have taken a vow of silence but can communicate in sign language and they can marry, provided their wives do not live inside the temple. The head of the community of five hundred monks lives alone in a red tower built on a spur of rock, separated by a chasm from the monastery itself. The red tower, on the door of which is a human thigh-bone that serves as a knocker, is a square building surrounded by battlements. Visitors who wish to ascend the labyrinth of spiral staircases are searched and blindfolded before being taken before His Holiness. On the south face of the mountain is a terrace-garden where rhododendrons, poppies, irises, anemones, honeysuckle and medicinal plants grow freely.

Visitors are advised to attend the annual festival in which sick people are bathed in the miraculous waters (said to be radioactive) at a cave at the foot of the mountain. Visitors will be exorcized upon arrival at the festival, to drive off the devils which, according to the monks, follow travellers. Marco Polo described this festival in a text which was long believed to be lost but was in fact found by German scientists who had established a secret plant inside Mount Tsintsin-Dagh, in order to extract radium during World War Two.

Visitors will arrive through the so-called Gates of Hell, a sinister canyon of steep cliffs, ochre coloured and uninhabited. Unicorns and large ferocious white wolves roam this area.

(Paul Alperine, *Ombres sur le Thibet*, Paris, 1945)

TUCK, TERRITORY OF, one of the three areas

enclosing the Sea of Slops, the other two being the Mountain of Messes and WASTEPAPERLAND. The soil of the Territory of Tuck is made of bad, sticky toffee. It is also full of deep cracks and holes choked with wind-fallen fruit, hips and haws, and all the unpleasant things young children will eat if they can get hold of them. The fairies try their best to hide all these things from them, but wicked people soon replace them and make all sorts of concoctions to sell at fairs with the express intention of poisoning children. In the area around the Territory of Tuck, all the little people in the world write books about all the little people in the world, presumably because they have nothing else to write about. The books written here are extremely limited in scope and ambition and tend to have such titles as *The Narrow Narrow World*, the *Hills of Chattermuch* or the *Children's Twaddleday*.

(Charles Kingsley, *The Water-Babies: A Fairy Tale for a Land-Baby*, London, 1863)

TUPIA, a small island of the MARDI ARCHIPELAGO, uninhabited for many centuries now. A quaint legend is attached to it and has spread throughout the neighbouring islands. It is said that a million moons ago a race of minute people, only a few inches high, inhabited the island. Their bodies were covered with fine fur, soft as silk, and instead of hair they grew a very delicate grass of lanceolate leaves. The men wore it short, but the women would make it grow by watering it with dew and would then teach tiny insect-birds of scarlet feathers to build their nests in their manes. Thus they would walk around amid the sweet music of the birds' songs and the rustling of the leaves. In England, towards the end of the nineteenth century, a fearful old man applied the same system to decorating his beard—which held at one point two owls, a hen, four larks and a wren.

According to the legend, the girls of Tupia would not embrace their lovers but would hold them with their vegetable hair. When very young, their hair would flower; this was seen as a sure sign of decline. Once in full bloom, the young girls would die. But on their tombs, their hair of grass continues to grow and flower forever.

(Herman Melville, *Mardi, and A Voyage Thither*, New York, 1849; Edward Lear, "There was an Old Man with a beard," in *A Book of Nonsense*, London, 1846)

TUROINE, a small free city on the edge of MISPEC MOOR, much given to the arts of both black and white magic. All the buildings in the town are

The sphinx outside the city of TUROINE, trying to perfect the first paragraph of its book.

marked with stars, pentagrams, triangles and the signs of the zodiac, and are overgrown with honeysuckle, arum lilies, black poppies and deadly nightshade.

The magic practised in the city ranges from revenge spells to spells which open the locked door of any jail or make real the sin performed in a dream. Some magicians can inflict a wide variety of sickness on those who cross them; others can control the weather or turn themselves into wolves, cats and hares.

On the outskirts of the city sits a sphinx, writing with a black pen in a large black book. It has been sitting there for so long that it has become half buried in the red sand. The sex of the sphinx is uncertain and he or she may be addressed as either Sir or Madame. If questioned, it will explain that it remains immobile because it has discovered the futility of all movement and activity. The sphinx is still trying to write its book, but continues to have difficulty with the first paragraph, designed to sum up all the things that will be dealt with later. For centuries the sphinx has been trying to perfect it, but has not yet succeeded.

(James Branch Cabell, *Something About Eve*, New York, 1929)

TUSHUO, MOUNT, rising from the ocean, south-west from the Gate of Spirits, China, through which numerous ghosts come and go. On its summit grows a huge peach tree inhabited by two ghost-catchers—Shen Tu and Yu Lei—who feed evil spirits to the tigers, found in considerable numbers in this region. Because of this custom the Yellow Emperor decreed that once a year his subjects should set up a huge image in peach wood and paint on their doors the names of Shen Tu, Yu Lei and any tiger of their choice.

(Anonymous, *The Compendium of Deities of the Three Religions*, 3rd cen. BC; Anonymous, *The Book of Mountains and Seas*, 4th cen. BC)

TUTULAND, a small kingdom on the east coast of a small island. A nearby valley is famous for its fig trees; whoever eats these figs will grow an enormous nose. The only antidote is the water of a spring at the bottom of the valley. The whole island is under the protection of a fairy who, every one hundred years, grants magic powers to a mortal of her choice.

In the early nineteenth century, these powers were bestowed upon a ruined barometer-maker. Prince Tutu's daughter, Zoraide, stole the magic powers from him. To punish her, and with the assistance of Zoraide's maid, the barometer-maker had her eat the notorious figs, forcing her to return the stolen powers in exchange for the antidote.

(Ferdinand Raimund, "Der Barometermacher auf der Zauberinsel," in *Sämtliche Werke*, Munich, 1837)

TYLWYTH TEG, the subterranean kingdom of Eiddileg, king of the Fair Folk who could once be seen in PRYDAIN. Since the final liberation of Prydain from the forces of evil that beset it, this kingdom has been inaccessible to men; no man now knows where to find it. In the past the land of the Fair Folk could be reached by tunnels and through the bottom of the Black Lake in the mountains of Prydain; these entrances have now been sealed off.

The Fair Folk now live completely underground in caves, tunnels and mines that extend everywhere beneath Prydain. The centre of their land is, however, the great vaulted chamber beneath the Black Lake.

The Fair Folk are not a single race; the name is a generic term for all the dwarves, sprites and fairies who were once infrequently seen in Prydain. Of all the Fair Folk, however, the dwarves were the best known. Their craftsmanship is still renowned throughout the land, especially their jewellery and metalwork, made from materials quarried in their extensive mines. Mining is the basis of the fabled wealth of the dwarves; the gems they excavate are so precious and beautiful that stones that would be prized on earth are used to repair roads. Those who have seen the weapons of the dwarves say they are better-made and sharper than any made on earth. Even the famed smiths of the Land of the FREE COMMOTS admit they could not make such weapons.

By temperament, the Fair Folk tend to be gruff and brusque and are not normally noted for their cordiality towards men, claiming that men have always exploited them in the hope of finding treasure or having their wishes granted them. But despite their general mistrust of men, the Fair Folk did become their allies in the struggle against Arawn the Death Lord and the powers of evil that threatened Prydain.

In the early stages of the struggle, one dwarf in particular, Doli, distinguished himself. Doli initially became involved with men when Taran, the Assistant Pig-Keeper from CAER DALLBEN and future High King of Prydain, and his friends stumbled into Tylwyth Teg by accident, in search of the oracular pig Hen Wen. Hen Wen had fled from Caer Dallben at the approach of the Horned King, the battle leader of Arawn. She was restored to Taran by the Fair Folk and Doli was appointed to guide Taran's company to the seat of the Sons of Don at CAER DATHYL. As a reward for his services, the High King of Prydain granted Doli the gift of invisibility; Doli had never been able to master this traditional attribute of the Fair Folk, much to his annoyance. He found that being able to vanish was a precious gift and was particularly useful in battle, but even so he found cause for complaint, as being invisible caused a painful buzzing in his ears.

During the war against Arawn, the way posts maintained by the Fair Folk were made available to men and on several occasions provided safe refuges for those pursued by the agents of Arawn. The way posts were secret hiding places, equipped with food and other supplies and carefully maintained so that the Fair Folk knew what was happening on earth. The keepers of the posts were required to give shelter to any Fair Folk or their allies who were in danger and they were always prepared for emergencies. Since the end of the war against Arawn, and the closure of Tylwyth Teg to men, the way posts have been abandoned.

Although the Fair Folk were never noted for their friendliness to humans, they were, traditionally, on good terms with the House of Llyr who reigned in the castle off the coast of MONA, the last member of which became High Queen of Prydain. To mark the wedding of the mother of Angharad, queen of Llyr, they presented her with a precious jewel with great magic powers. But this jewel fell into evil hands and became a threat to the Fair Folk. Angharad's daughter was stolen from her by Achren, the consort of Arawn and once ruler of Prydain. As Angharad travelled in search of her child, she entered a hut, seeking shelter, and was murdered by Morda, a wizard who coveted the jewel she wore. With this jewel Morda was able to develop great powers and to locate some of the hidden treasures of the Fair Folk. He was able to construct an impenetrable wall of thorns to conceal his home in the forests of Southern Prydain, and to make himself invulnerable to attack by hiding his life outside his body; his life force was contained in a finger which he cut off and concealed in a coffer.

Morda's final achievement, however, was discovering how to cast enchantments on the Fair Folk and how to transform them into animals. No one had ever been able to do this and Morda's power, gained through his possession of the jewel, was probably the greatest threat that ever faced the Fair Folk.

But it happened that, as Taran journeyed through Prydain in search of his lost father, he all unknowingly found the means to destroy Morda, when Kaw, a tame crow that travelled with him, discovered a mysterious coffer with a bone inside it. With his friends Gurgi and Fflewddur Fflam he came unawares upon Morda's lair. The first clue to the presence of the evil magician was an unexpected encounter with Doli the dwarf, transformed by Morda into a frog, much to his shame and indignation. It was he who explained the threat posed to the Fair Folk by a man with such unheard-of powers. The companions were captured by Morda who transformed Gurgi into a field mouse and Fflam into a hare, but as he toyed with Taran he made the mistake of gloatingly telling of the origin of his powers and the secret of his charmed life. Realizing that Kaw had unwittingly provided him with the means to kill Morda, Taran broke the finger bone, thus destroying his evil forever. He then returned Angharad's jewel to Doli as a representative of the Fair Folk. It is said that this is the best thing any human has ever done for the Fair Folk.

(Lloyd Alexander, *The Book of Three*, New York, 1964; Lloyd Alexander, *The Black Cauldron*, New York, 1965; Lloyd Alexander, *The Castle of Llyr*, New York, 1966; Lloyd Alexander, *Taran Wanderer*, New York, 1967; Lloyd Alexander, *The High King*, New York, 1968)

U

UDOLPHO, CASTLE OF, deep in the Apennines, famous for being the model of a great number of similar constructions that sprang up in Europe during the nineteenth century. The castle is built of dark grey stone on the edge of a precipice and is fortified by towers, battlements and ramparts. The whole structure is surrounded by thick woods, mainly of larch.

Two round towers, linked by a battlemented curtain beneath which is a portcullis, protect the gateway. From the gateway, two courtyards lead to a Gothic hall which affords a long perspective of arches and pillars. A marble staircase leads upstairs and reveals the rich fretwork of the roof. A painted window stretches from the floor to the ceiling, wainscoted in black larch wood. Many secret passages run behind the thick walls. Though parts of the castle are in ruins, including a chapel near the east wing, the main building is habitable and affords a panorama over woods, crags, valleys and a furious broad stream.

Visitors cannot afford to miss the small chamber in which a black veil conceals a waxen image of a human body consumed by worms. It served as an object of contemplation for one of the early Marquis of Udolpho who was required to do penance for having offended the Church and it must be preserved by the family on pain of forfeiting part of its domain.

Several murders and other hasty acts have taken place beneath the castle's roofs, but nowadays such behaviour is said to have been discontinued.

(Mrs. Ann Radcliffe, *The Mysteries of Udolpho*, Dublin, 1794)

UDÛN, a dale in the north-west of MORDOR, enclosed by the Mountains of SHADOW and the ERED LITHUI. From the other side of the mountains, the dale can be reached through the pass at Isenmouthe. During Sauron's preparation for the final battle with the Army of the West, Udûn was an important centre. Tunnels were dug under the ground throughout this area to serve as armouries and it was here that Sauron's forces massed for the last battle.

(J.R.R. Tolkien, *The Return of the King*, London, 1955)

UFFA, a mysterious island (perhaps one of the Solomon Islands, according to Dr. Julian Wolff, *The Sherlockian Atlas,* New York, 1952) where the Grice Patersons experienced singular and unchronicled adventures.

(Sir Arthur Conan Doyle, "The Five Orange Pips," in *The Adventures of Sherlock Holmes*, London, 1892)

ULMIA, an island off the coast of BENSALEM.

ULTHAR, a small and picturesque village near the Skai River in DREAMWORLD. It is reached by crossing a stone bridge over the Skai, into whose central arch the masons sealed a living human being when they built it thirteen hundred years ago.

The suburbs of Ulthar are very agreeable, with little green cottages and neatly fenced farms; more pleasant still is the quaint town itself, with its old peaked roofs and overhanging upper storeys, its numberless chimney pots and its narrow hilly streets where travellers can see old cobbles whenever the hordes of cats that inhabit Ulthar afford enough space. The cats of Ulthar are innumerable because, according to an ancient and significant law, no man may kill a cat.

(Howard Phillips Lovecraft, "The Dream-Quest of Unknown Kadath," in *Arkham Sampler,* Sauk City, 1948)

ULTIMA THULE, see THULE.

UNDER RIVER, a subterranean region, beneath the waters of a fast-flowing river; visitors will find that here the roar of the water can be heard quite clearly. Under River can be reached through a number of tunnels, many of whose concealed entrances are difficult to find. The roof is supported by rough pillars, similar to the props used in mines, and it leaks constantly. The floor is of brick and stone, with lakes and pools at intervals, always drying up and changing shape.

Under River is the home of a strange society of outcasts, fugitives and failures who have been forced to flee from the outside world. Thieves and bad poets mingle in the wilderness of damp tables, beds and benches, like flitting silhouettes in the flickering light. Although the society of Under River has no formal organization and although few of the inhabitants know each other, it is ruled by a small number of individuals, like a certain Veil, once a concentration camp guard, who fled here and established himself as a brutally dominant figure.

For a while, Under River offered a refuge to Titus Groan, heir to GORMENGHAST, who had run away from his ancestral home; here he was able to escape the police who had already arrested him once for vagrancy. Titus almost died at the hands of Veil, but was rescued and managed to escape from this sinister realm.

(Mervyn Peake, *Titus Alone*, London, 1959)

UNIVERSAL TAP ROOM, beneath a mountain somewhere in Great Britain. Visitors will note that the entire room is cut out of solid rock; one of its walls is lined with taps similar to those found in a normal bathroom. However, the taps of the Universal Tap Room are different in that they are used to turn on the weather. Each is marked with a label such as "Sunshine," "Nice Growing Weather" or "Good Open Weather." The wall opposite consists of a large looking-glass in which it is possible to see what is happening in the rest of the world.

Travellers will be interested to discover that Great Britain's bad climate is due to the fact that the taps marked "Sunshine," "Fair to Moderate" and "Showery" are stuck and cannot be properly turned. This state of affairs is the result of a curious series of events which took place in the end of the nineteenth century, when England was suddenly afflicted with a plague of dragons. Two London children decided to ask St. George for advice and woke the Saint by kissing his marble statue. St. George advised them to visit the Universal Tap Room and to turn on the taps labelled "Water" and "Snow," thereby killing the dragons by putting out their fire. Their bodies were disposed of by turning on the tap marked "Waste" and then tipping them into a large hole in the middle of England. However, when the children decided to restore Great Britain's climate to normal, the taps got stuck and umbrellas became a necessary fashion throughout the country.

(Edith Nesbit, *The Deliverers of Their Country*, London, 1899)

UNKNOWN ISLAND, somewhere in the Indian Ocean, of forbidding aspect but hiding a pleasant field of merry brooks. It is best to visit it in spring, when the air reeks of jasmine, and doves, parakeets, moorhens, ducks, sparrows and tiny birds no larger than bees flutter through the air. Crossing the plain is a range of high mountains covered with grass as soft as moss. Penguins, gazelles and musk-cats roam these higher regions. A creature larger than a dog, called *barbu* or prickleface, can be found in the small woods near the coast.

Travellers approaching Unknown Island from the air will notice that its shape is that of the boot of Italy, upside down.

(Guillaume Grivel, *L'Isle inconnue, ou Mémoires du chevalier de Gastines. Recueillis et publiés par M. Grivel, des Académies de Dijon et de La Rochelle*, Paris & Brussels, 1784)

UNRETURNABLE-HEAVEN, a town on the north side of the bush road in Nigeria. Travellers should not be surprised to see no one on the road to the town; it does not enjoy a reputation for hospitality.

Travel to Unreturnable-Heaven is not recommended. Visitors are expected to wait for up to three hours outside the thick, tall town walls for the gates to open; then they are herded into the town by an invisible force. The inhabitants, both adults and children, are very cruel to humans, and are always looking for ways of making their cruelties even worse. Travellers are known to have been held by half a dozen Unreturnable-Heavenites while the adults beat them and the children stoned them. If they discover that a traveller is human, they will cut the unfortunate visitor's flesh while the person is still alive. Sometimes they stab a traveller's eye with a knife, and leave it there till the victim dies of pain.

The inhabitants of Unreturnable-Heaven do everything incorrectly. If they want to climb a tree, they climb the ladder first, before leaning it against the trunk. They build their houses on the side of a steep hill, so that they all bend downwards as if they are going to fall, and children constantly roll out of the houses, to the complete indifference of their parents. They do not wash themselves, but they wash their domestic animals; they dress in leaves but drape their animals in costly clothes; they keep their nails uncut for a hundred years but clip the nails of their animals.

They are ruled by a king who is just as cruel as his subjects.

(Amos Tutuola, *The Palm-Wine Drinkard and His Dead Palm-Wine Tapster in the Dead's Town*, London, 1952)

UPMEADS, a small kingdom, perhaps in northern Europe, which became famous during the rule of the late King Peter. It is a pleasant land, though without great wealth or important buildings. A river, also called Upmeads, crosses gently sloping meadows. To the north, the country is mountainous and contains forested marshes full of game, often a source of dispute with neighbouring countries. To the south is a ridge running east-west, marking the frontier. Notable in Upmeads is the king's abode, the High House of Upmeads, and the Church of St. Laurence with its painted tombs. The people of Upmeads are very strongminded and will not submit to any abuse of authority.

Visiting Upmeads is a pleasant experience, as King Ralph—after his father abdicated in his favour—established a just and prosperous government, cementing lasting alliances with all his neighbours.

There are many interesting towns to be visited in Upmeads. Higham-on-the-Way, a small walled town forty miles from Wulstead, just across the southern border, is notable for its castle and its abbey. It is ruled by the Lord Abbot and famed for its market. The area is a fertile, sheep-farming region that produces good wool. On the chalk cliffs nearby, interesting carvings can be seen depicting a tree with a bear on either side, and a construction known as Bear Castle. Higham Castle stands on a hill surrounded by a river, not far from the great abbey that fronts onto a wide, paved market square, where a Midsummer's Eve festival is held.

Across from the Wood Perilous is the Burg of the Four Friths. It is ringed by stone watch-towers and thatched buildings. The wall of the Burg is remarkably high and the main gate is protected by a moat; enemy women used to be brought here and sold to the highest bidder. Beyond the Burg, at the edge of the forest, lies the Plain of Abundance, a peaceful, rich, farming region ruled by the Lady of Abundance in the castle of the same name.

The Castle of Abundance stands on a green mound by a river and is one of the landmarks of Upmeads. In the Great Hall, tapestries illustrating the story of Alexander can be seen, as well as an ivory throne, one of the kingdom's main treasures. Beyond the plain is a region of steep valleys and sandstone cliffs, known as the Wilderness. A few mounds are all that remain of the houses that were once built here. Visitors are advised to enter a cave by the river known as the House of the Wilderness or Hall of Summertide, with its notable floor of fine white sand.

On the far side of the mountains beyond the Wilderness is the town of Cheaping Knowe, ruled tyrannically by the lord of the castle. Castle Hill is covered with gibbets from which dangle the bodies of men, women and children who have offended the tyrant; some have been impaled. People with their hands cut off can be seen dragging themselves through the streets. The Cheaping Knowe gardens, with their lemon, orange and pomegranate trees, are, however, a beautiful sight.

Fifty miles away from Cheaping Knowe, through the mountains of Goldburg, lies the town of Whitness, with its houses built of timber. Goldburg town itself rises on a ridge of hills and is partly surrounded by a river. Goldburg is ruled by a queen and is one of the most beautiful towns in Upmeads. The people believe that when the town falls, the whole world will be affected. East of Goldburg the land extends to the foothills of the mountains known as the Wall of the World. Here rises the town of Utterbol, once ruled by a tyrant thought to be the devil, until he was overthrown by the town hero, Bull Shockhead; it is said to be as lovely as Paradise.

Finally, it is interesting to visit Mid-Mountain House, six days' journey from the town of Whitwall, near the northern frontier. The House is a hostelry, a long, low stone building set on a ridge, and it is an area of truce where no fighting is permitted. If enemies meet here, they must give one another at least an hour's start before the pursuit begins. Across the northern frontier lies the Land of the WELL AT THE WORLD'S END.

(William Morris, *The Well at the World's End*, London, 1896)

UPPER MORVEN, a place of horrible fame in POICTESME, not recommended to visitors. Here, in the distant past, men made sacrifices to Vel-Tyno, a god still worshipped in PHILISTIA, and travellers may still encounter strange creatures in the guise of elephants, pigs or beautiful women.

(James Branch Cabell, *Figures of Earth. A Comedy of Appearances*, New York, 1921)

UPPER ROMANCIA, see ROMANCIA.

URANOPOLIS, a city on the peninsula of Acte in Chalcidice, Macedonia. It was founded by Alexarchus (brother of Cassander, once king of Macedonia) who had the peculiar habit of using elaborate circumlocutions to express ordinary, everyday things. He called the cock "dawn-crier," for instance, the barber "mortal-shaver," the drachma "a silver bit," the quart-measure "daily feeder," the herald "loud bawler." On one occasion he sent the authorities of Cassandreia such a strange garbled message that not even the god of Delphi could make it out. Uranopolis means "The City of Heaven."

(Pliny the Elder, *Naturalis Historia,* 1st cen. AD; Athenaeus, *The Deipnosophists,* 3rd cen. AD)

URG, a small town in DREAMWORLD with low domes, where travellers and onyx miners stop on their way to the city of INQUANOK.

(Howard Phillips Lovecraft, "The Dream-Quest of Unknown Kadath," in *Arkham Sampler,* Sauk City, 1948)

URNLAND, in the lowlands of the Vistula, on the border of a desert beyond a large gulf and not far from a country famous for breeding wild horses. The Urns live in a few villages of wood and mud; they are ruled by a king whose palace is a round, windowless building furnished with camel skins. The Urns are expert horsemen and because men always tend to resemble their enemies, they are keen archers and lancers like their neighbours. They are also shepherds, sailors, magicians, platers and blacksmiths. They do not till the earth.

The whole of their literature, the whole of their language, consists of one word, *undr,* which means "wonder" and is sometimes represented by a fish and sometimes by a red pole and a disc. In that word, each and any listener will recognize his labours, his loves, his secret acts, the things he has seen, the people he has known—everything.

A description of Urnland was written by Adam of Bremen in the eleventh century and published by Lappenberg, who found the manuscript at the Bodleian Library, in *Analecta Germanica* (Leipzig, 1894).

(Jorge Luis Borges, "Undr," in *El libro de arena,* Buenos Aires, 1975)

URSINA and **VULPINA,** two islands in the north Atlantic. Ursina is noted for its amphitheatre, where the animals of the zodiac are made to perform in front of large audiences. Vulpina (also called Villa Franca, Lupania or Ramallia—from the Dutch, *Ramykins)* is famous for its powerful fleet. In the capital are several monuments of great

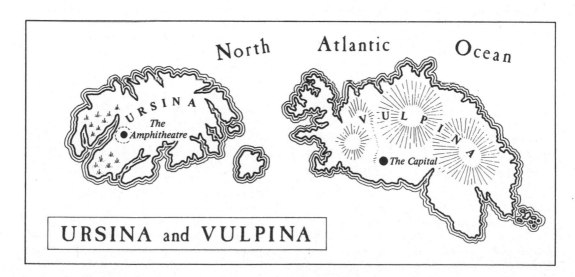

URSINA and VULPINA

antiquity, especially a curious building in the shape of a ram.

(Frank Careless, *The Floating Island or a New Discovery Relating the Strange Adventure on a late Voyage from Lambethana to Villa Franca, Alias Ramallia, to the Eastward of Terra del Templo: By three Ships, viz. the "Pay-naught," the "Excuse," and the "Least-in-Sight," under the conduct of Captain Robert Owe-much: Describing the Nature of the Inhabitants, their Religion, Laws and Customs*, London, 1673)

URTAH, THE STREELS OF, three mysterious gorges or ravines which suddenly break the northwest of the central plain of the BEKLAN EMPIRE as though a giant had scored the land with a fork. They are roughly parallel and of the same length, lying side by side within the space of half a mile or so. They are so abrupt and steep that the branches of the trees on either side almost touch and conceal them, so it is impossible to gauge their depth from above. Local legend says they are the mouth of hell and the souls of the wicked enter them at night.

Visitors are warned of a strange cult attached to the Streels. No one knows the origin of the cult, but a group of men known as the Watchers, who regard themselves as instruments of vengeance for some unknown god, wait here for sacrificial victims to find their way to the mysterious ravines. These "sinners" may believe that they have come to Urtah by chance, but the Watchers are convinced that they are brought here by fate. They treat the sinners well and show them the Streels, and ask them if they know the name of the ravines; and when the unwary visitors answer "no" the Watchers persuade them to enter the Streels. Once a traveller has entered of his own free will, it becomes the Watchers' task to kill him and throw his corpse into the depths. Like the Thugs in India, the Watchers carry out their killings dispassionately; no item in the victim's possession is ever taken.

(Richard Adams, *Shardik*, London, 1974)

USSULA, the capital and only major city in USSULISTAN, in a completely flat, low-lying plain. As there is little stone suitable for building purposes in the area, the city is defended by water.

The river on which it stands has been diverted to flow through the centre of Ussula and now crisscrosses the city with innumerable canals and ditches. In the suburbs, every house stands on its own island; in the centre, buildings are much closer together. There are comparatively few bridges and most communication involves either the use of boats and barges, or more simply, swimming. All the citizens of Ussula, young or old, can swim like fish.

The only buildings made from stone are the temple and the palace, which stand on the central island, surrounded by a wall twenty feet high and some 150 feet in diameter. The majestic towers rise above the walls. Both the temple and palace are built around these central towers, rising to wooden roofs supported by pillars. The upper pillars are not connected by walls and allow reasonable illumination of the upper rooms.

Neither the palace nor the temple is ornamented or decorated in any way, but they appear curiously impressive, perhaps because of the simplicity of the other buildings in the town. In the palace, the ground floor is mainly taken up by a large inner court around the central columns, strewn with mats and pillows; two large fireplaces stand at either end of the room. Private chambers open off this central space, which is often used as a council chamber. On the first floor is a large hall with a floor of packed earth, used as a banqueting hall. The damp climate of Ussula has ended the traditional oriental custom of eating in a reclining position, and meals are now taken at a high table, in European style. The dampness has also led to the custom of lighting huge fires in all rooms.

Between the palace and the temple stands a huge carved figure of a horse, the only indication that the people of the city have any traditions or knowledge of art. It appears that the idea of constructing an equestrian statue to honour the famous was introduced from abroad, but no one was able to decide which public figure should be shown riding the horse. It finally became apparent that, if all worthy citizens were to be honoured in this manner, an almost infinite number of equestrian statues would be required and the entire project was abandoned. The horse was left standing as a reminder of their folly. When under the power of the Mir of ARDISTAN, who demanded that all countries build monuments to him, Ussula compromised by preserving the wooden horse and having a live man sit on it to represent the Mir. The compromise solution has been retained— every time important visitors come to the city, a man takes his place on the wooden horse.

Structurally, the temple is very similar to the palace, although its rooms are empty. From the roof, distant volcanoes can be seen; these play an important part in the cult introduced by a missionary from SITARA, in which the volcanic eruptions which occur roughly once a century are seen as symbolizing the opening of the gates of paradise.

Close to the palace lies a small island, once used as a prison, surrounded by a wooden fence and then by a second fence of impenetrable thorn bushes, and guarded by man-eating dogs.

(Karl Friedrich May, *Ardistan,* Bamberg, 1909; Karl Friedrich May, *Der Mir von Djinnistan,* Bamberg, 1909)

USSULISTAN, a country to the north of TSHOBANISTAN, from which it is separated by the isthmus known as the CHATAR DEFILE. The northern coast is uninhabited, a barren area of swamps and marshes. Farther inland are forested areas which gradually give way to the broad plain around USSULA, the capital and only city in all Ussulistan. It is thought that this area was formed by the silt carried down by the river flowing across the Chatar Defile from Tshobanistan. If this is true, the country's geological origin would explain much of the terrain, especially in the north. The whole country appears to act as a sponge, absorbing the water from the sea and desalinating it in a natural process which leads to the formation of the many fresh-water lakes and marshes.

Some of the customs of the Ussulas take advantage of the country's geography. When they were attacked by their traditional enemies from Tshobanistan, they did not fight back, but retreated onto the islands in the lakes or into the water itself. Given that Tshobans are afraid of water and cannot swim, this defence is not inadequate, though much land is left open to plundering.

Beyond the capital, the land becomes more rocky and was, for many centuries, a desert until the river that once ran through the area began to flow again. In the old days, little or no water was to be found in the area south of Ussula, apart from a few secret subterranean deposits and reservoirs

signposted by stone statues of angels erected by the Mir of DJINNISTAN.

The Ussulas are a race of giants, at least head and shoulders taller than normal Europeans. The men dress in roughly cured hides and leather garments. The size of their weapons is in proportion to their bodies; the knives they carry in their belts, for instance, would be considered axes in many other countries. The Ussulas are acquainted with firearms, but they are of little use to them in such a damp climate. Ussula women are as tall as their menfolk, but wear more delicate clothing of cleverly cut and dyed leather. As a race, the Ussulas are not noted for their intelligence and, in battle, are easily outwitted by the simplest of strategies. The women are more intelligent than the men. They are extremely good-natured and loyal, if somewhat easily led, immensely strong and, thanks to their damp environment, almost amphibious.

Ussulistan is known for its enormous horses. They have heavy, clumsy bodies but move very fast and are unafraid of any natural obstacles. Like the men who ride them, they are so used to swimming that they could be called sea-creatures. As they are invariably covered in mud to prevent bites from insects, it is hard to distinguish the colour of their hides. The one feature which does not seem to be in harmony with their general heaviness is their eyes, which are small and remarkably beautiful. If treated kindly, they make excellent and very loyal mounts; unfortunately, kindness to animals is not a characteristic found in many Ussulas. The country is also famous for its dogs of great size, beauty, swimming ability and strength. They are trained to sniff for water in the drier areas beyond the Ussul, and are used for both hunting and warfare.

For centuries, Ussulistan was dominated by the Mir of ARDISTAN, to whom it paid taxes. The Mir's bodyguard was composed of strong Ussulas who were paid and clothed at the expense of their home country. Ussulistan traditionally sent its criminals, rogues and sick to serve as the Mir's guards; the latter showed a marked tendency to recover their health once they left their damp, low-lying homeland. Many of the guards were wounded in the Mir's service and, on their return to Ussulistan, served as guards at Ussula's palace.

The Ussulas normally live on meat obtained by hunting and appear to have little or no agriculture. Small quantities of fruit and vegetables are grown, but farming as a whole remains undeveloped. When travelling they live by hunting and gathering, the latter being regarded as a female occupation. Visitors are welcomed with a ceremonial meal of salt and freshly baked bread, accompanied by a drink known as *simmsenn* (both *simm* and *senn* mean "poison"), an extremely potent liquor which smells very strongly of ethyl alcohol.

(Karl Friedrich May, *Ardistan,* Bamberg, 1909; Karl Friedrich May, *Der Mir von Djinnistan*, Bamberg, 1909)

UTENSIA, an independent city-kingdom within the land of OZ, in a clearing in the woods north of Quadling Country. The clearing is lined with a variety of cookers, ranges and grills of different sizes and shapes. Beside them stand numerous kitchen cabinets and cupboards, all full of utensils of all sorts, from saucepans to rolling pins. These are the subjects of King Kleaver, a large cleaver that can usually be found sitting on a butcher's block in the centre of his kingdom.

The king's chief officials are Judge Sifter, whose role it is to sift the evidence in all State affairs, and High Priest Colander, the holiest inhabitant of this miniature kingdom. In court cases, the lawyers are usually either cork-screws who are accustomed to appearing at the bar, or flat irons, noted for their ability to press their suits. Utensia maintains an army, the Spoon Brigade, which patrols the area around the clearing and takes all prisoners to King Kleaver to be judged. Travellers are advised that there is nothing to eat in the entire kingdom.

The citizens of Utensia acknowledge only King Kleaver and claim never to have heard of Ozma, the ruler of all Oz. Like many of the strange creatures to be found in the outer regions of Oz, they can be aggressive towards strangers, but do not represent a real threat to anyone.

(L. Frank Baum, *The Emerald City of Oz*, Chicago, 1910)

UTOPIA, an island about fifteen miles from the coast of Latin America, formerly known as Sansculottia. Utopia was originally connected to the mainland by an isthmus.

Utopia takes its present name from Utopos, one of its earliest recorded rulers. As soon as he had control of the country, Utopos had a channel cut through the isthmus, transforming Utopia into an island. At its broadest point, Utopia is two hundred miles across. The extremities of the island taper away and curve around until they almost form a circle, giving the island the overall shape of a crescent. The points of the crescent are divided by a strait eleven miles wide. Entering this strait, the sea spreads out into a vast lake which is protected from storms by the encircling land. As a result, virtually the entire interior of the island is an enormous natural harbour, an inland sea that also facilitates transport within the island itself. The entrance channel is extremely dangerous, being studded with rocks and shoals concealed just below the water level. A tower stands on the single visible rock. Only Utopians know which are the safe channels, and without a local pilot it is virtually impossible to enter the harbour in safety. Even local sailors would have difficulty were it not for the landmarks erected along the shoreline, and if the Utopians moved these landmarks it would be easy for them to lure enemy ships to their destruction. There are more harbours on the other side of the island, but they are so well fortified that a small number of defenders could satisfactorily hold off a large invading force.

There are fifty-four large towns on Utopia, all built to the same plan. The minimum distance between them is twenty-four miles; the maximum no more than a day's walk. The capital, Aircastle or Amaurote, is situated in the centre of the island and is therefore equally accessible from all areas. It is built on a gentle slope above the River Nowater and is practically square, two miles on each side. Aircastle is surrounded by high defensive walls with numerous towers and blockhouses. On three sides it is protected by a dry moat filled with tangled thornbushes; on the fourth side, the river completes the defences. The Nowater is still tidal at Aircastle, allowing ships to come right up to the capital although it is many miles from the sea. A second, smaller river joins the Nowater at Aircastle; it flows from a spring within the city walls, which means that the capital would never suffer from a shortage of water even during the longest siege.

The town is said to have been designed by Utopos himself. According to historical records, the original houses were little more than huts or cottages, built with the first materials that came to hand. The present aspect of Aircastle is considerably different. The houses take the form of long terraces, built in streets and each separated by a twenty-foot carriageway. Behind each house is a

large garden, running the whole length of the street and enclosed by the backs of the transversal streets. Each house has a front door and a back door, both opening at a touch and shutting automatically. All the houses are faced with flint, stone or brick; their roofs are covered with a special sort of concrete which is extremely cheap, but which resists bad weather much more effectively than lead—it also has the advantage of being fireproof. Most windows are glazed; those which are not are draught-proofed by screens of linen treated with amber or a clear oil to make them more transparent and airtight. The houses are allocated by lot and are redistributed every ten years. The citizens are extremely proud of their gardens, in which they grow fruit, including grapes, as well as flowers. They are all keen gardeners, partly because they simply enjoy gardening, but also because inter-street competitions are held for the best-kept garden.

At regular intervals across the countryside are houses that provide all that is required for cultivating the land, each house capable of accommodating forty adults plus two slaves who are permanently attached to each house. These country houses are run by efficient District Controllers, each responsible for thirty houses. Every year twenty people return from the countryside and are replaced by as many town dwellers who are trained by those who have spent a year in the country. A year later, this process is repeated. Normally, only two years are spent on the land, but many people ask for and receive special permission to stay longer than that. During their stay in the countryside, agricultural workers are responsible for tilling the land, raising livestock and doing forestry work. Agriculture is a highly developed art. Also, large numbers of chickens are raised by artificial incubation.

Farming is, effectively, the trade of all Utopians and is taught from an early age in school. In addition to farming, everyone is taught a special trade, such as weaving, spinning, stonemasonry, blacksmithing and carpentry. As everyone wears the same style of clothes, there are no tailors or dressmakers, an arrangement which frees large numbers of people for more productive labour. Most children tend to adopt the trade practised by their fathers, but if they choose to follow a different trade they are adopted by a family which practises it. Once a person has mastered one trade, he can get permission to learn another; when both

have been mastered, the choice is up to the individual, unless one trade is more essential to the public than the other. Work is the whole basis of Utopian society; all men and women work and in the average town fewer than five hundred people would be exempt from work (for specific reasons). Given the numbers employed in the work force and the concentration on useful trades, it is not surprising that Utopia is so prosperous. Production is also carefully planned. Food requirements, for example, are precisely calculated by local authorities, although each area usually grows corn and breeds livestock in excess of its needs in order to be able to help its neighbours if shortages occur. Excess resources are rapidly diverted to wherever they may be needed. Similar calculations are applied to the use of the labour force; before harvest time, the District Controllers notify the authorities of how much extra labour they will need and the appropriate number of labourers appear at the right time. The efficiency of the economy means that it has been possible to reduce the working day to six hours without producing any shortage in essential goods or services. The reduction of workers employed in luxury or unnecessary trades has a further beneficial effect on the economy. With the entire population (or a very high proportion of it) occupied in useful labour, immense reserves can be built up and huge labour forces can be diverted into public works, such as roadbuilding, if necessary. It also means that public holidays can be declared when there is nothing urgent to be done, thus giving the people an opportunity to exercise and improve their minds.

A system of internal exchanges means that no area or town goes short of anything and that surplus produce can be exported. Utopia exports large quantities of corn, honey, wool, flax, timber, fabrics, hides, tallow, leather and livestock. One-seventh of all exports are sent as a free gift to the poor of the importing country; the rest are sold at reasonable prices. The only imports, in normal times, are iron, gold and silver. As a result, the Utopians have built up immense gold and currency reserves, although gold has no intrinsic value within the country. The reserves are kept to protect the country in the event of war or any other major crisis and are used either to bribe enemies or to pay for mercenaries to fight for Utopia in foreign wars, should the need arise. In the past, the Utopians insisted on payment in gold, or other currencies, for their exports; their reserves are now such that they are indifferent to whether they sell for cash or for credit. In the latter case, however, legally binding contracts must be signed by the importing area. When payment becomes due, it is collected by the authorities from the individuals concerned and put into the public funds. The authorities enjoy the use of the money until such time as it is needed by the Utopians.

Politically, Utopia is a republic in which there is no private property and in which everyone takes seriously his duty towards the community. No one is rich, but there is no poverty and no one risks going short of anything. The public storehouses are perpetually full, thanks to the efficiency of the economy and the rationally planned distribution of national resources. The abolition of private property and money has wiped out the passion for property and money; it also led to the disappearance of all crimes and abuses connected with the desire for wealth and superiority and, for the same reasons, poverty itself has vanished.

The political system is based upon the division of the population into units of thirty households. Each unit elects a *Styward* or District Controller and each ten *Stywards* elect a *Bencheater* or Senior District Controller. *Bencheaters* are elected for one year only, but are not normally changed; other municipal officers are also elected for only one year. Each town has two hundred *Stywards*, who elect the Mayor from four candidates nominated by the four quarters of the town. The elections are by secret ballot and the *Stywards* must solemnly swear that the man for whom they vote is, in their opinion, the best qualified for the position. The Mayor and the *Bencheaters* meet every three days in the presence of two *Stywards* to debate public affairs and to settle any private disputes that may arise. To avoid hasty decisions, no question affecting the general public may be taken before a debate lasting a minimum of three days. It is a capital crime for such matters to be discussed outside the Council or the Assembly of *Stywards*—apparently to discourage the Mayors and *Bencheaters* from over-riding the wishes of the people as a whole. For similar reasons, any contentious issues are referred to the Assembly of *Stywards* who explain the issues involved to the households they represent, discuss them among themselves and then report back to the Council. Over-hasty decisions are also avoided by the rule that no resolution can be debated on the first day it is proposed; all discussion has to be postponed until the next well-attended meeting. At a national level, each town sends three representatives to the annual *Lietalk*, or Parliament, at Aircastle. Most of the work of the *Lietalk is* concerned with the organization of production and distribution. It also deals with visiting emissaries from other countries.

The *Stywards'* principal duty is the organization of labour. They themselves are exempt from work, but they usually go on working on a voluntary basis in order to set a good example. Those who wish to continue their studies are also exempt from labour, but only on the recommendation of the priests, confirmed by the *Stywards* in a secret ballot. Students who fail to make adequate progress rejoin the labour force. On the other hand, it is not unusual for workers to study hard in their spare time and be promoted to the ranks of the intelligentsia. Diplomats, *Stywards,* priests and *Bencheaters* are all recruited from the intelligentsia.

Although a republic, Utopia is not, strictly speaking, a completely egalitarian society. Each household comes under the authority of the eldest male. Wives are subordinate to their husbands, children to their parents and young people to their elders. Slavery continues to exist. The slaves of Utopia are not, however, non-combatant prisoners of war. The vast majority are condemned criminals acquired in large numbers from other countries, sometimes for a small charge, sometimes for nothing. In addition to these there are the Utopian criminals. Both groups are kept in chains and are forced to work hard, but the native-born Utopians are treated much worse than the foreigners, the argument being that if someone who has had the benefit of a good education and a moral upbringing will insist on becoming a criminal, he should be punished all the more severely. The third category of slaves consists of working-class foreigners who prefer slavery in Utopia to the wretched poverty of "freedom" at home. They are treated with kindness and respect, although, being accustomed to it in their own country, they work harder than the citizens of Utopia. They are free to leave the country if they wish and they receive a small gratuity when they do. Not many of them, however, take advantage of this arrangement.

The Utopians are one of the few nations of earth to see nothing glorious in war and to consider it an activity more suited to animals than human beings. On the other hand, all members of the population receive military training, irrespective of sex, so that the country can be defended if need be. They are also prepared to give military support to friendly nations, not merely to defend their territories but also to make reprisals for acts of aggression, or to defend the rights of traders who have been unjustly treated in foreign countries. The murder or injury of Utopian citizens abroad leads to swift and decisive military intervention; in such cases, no appeasement will be accepted except the surrender of the people involved, who are immediately sentenced to death or slavery. In general, the Utopians do not wish for blood-thirsty victories, preferring if possible to outwit the enemy through the power of the intellect. In accordance with this principle, they make extensive use of secret agents, and reward the assassination of enemy rulers. Lists of those supporting anti-Utopian policies in enemy countries are distributed and prizes offered for their capture or death. There is no limit to the amount of money that Utopia is willing to pay to traitors in the enemy camp. Although the Utopians are sometimes criticized for this "dishonourable" conduct, they argue that it is more sensible to settle major wars by such means than to fight battles and kill thousands of innocent people. A final cause of war is the Utopian attitude towards colonization. If Utopia becomes overpopulated, a certain number of people are detailed to start a colony on the mainland, wherever there is a large area that has not already been taken over by the natives. The natives are allowed to join in the colony and become part of the Utopian community. If they refuse to accept Utopian orders, they are expelled from the area and, if they resist, war is immediately declared. The Utopians consider it perfectly justifiable to declare war when a country refuses to use the land and then goes on to deny others the right to use it.

Surprisingly, Utopia's relations with its neighbours are in general good. Most neighbouring countries have now been liberated from the dictatorships that once oppressed them and Utopia supplies administrators to many of them. (This system has been repeatedly tried out by other countries, such as the United States and Russia, but, for some reason, has never worked.) The arrangement is advantageous to the host countries as Utopian administrators make excellent public servants; quite apart from anything else, they cannot be bribed as, after a specified time, they will be returning to a country where money is of no use to them. Formal treaties, by definition, imply a degree of mutual hostility and are inevitably full of loopholes—the Utopians take the view that they should not regard someone who has done them no harm as an enemy, and argue that human nature itself is the most effective treaty. Human beings—they say—are more closely united by kindness than by any kind of written contract.

When war does become necessary, Utopia prefers to employ mercenaries, often from VENALIA, being as willing to exploit bad men as to employ good ones. Their second source of manpower is the nation on whose behalf they go to war. The Utopian contingent itself is made up of volunteers; no one is ever conscripted to fight abroad. Even when they are on active service in other countries Utopian units will not fight unless they are forced to, but when they do fight they would rather die than surrender. Their tactics are not vainglorious, but are based on wearing down the enemy through the use of a characteristic wedge-formation, designed to capture or eliminate the opposing forces rather than to cause maximum casualties. The Utopian army never breaks an armistice, devastates enemy territory or destroys crops. On the contrary, they regard the enemy's crops as being grown for their benefit and do all they can to protect them. Any town that surrenders is at once given protection and there is no looting, even if a town is taken by storm. The civilian population is never harmed in any way. Reparation is always demanded from a defeated enemy, partly in cash and partly in freeholds of estates in the enemy territory. This has led to the acquisition of property in many countries and to the establishment of considerable reserves for use in future wars, should they be necessary. If an army marches against their own territory, the Utopians send out large forces to intercept it; under no circumstances would they allow enemy troops to set foot on the island itself.

One of the most ancient principles of the Utopian constitution is religious tolerance, and a variety of faiths coexist quite peacefully. Some people worship the moon, the sun or other celestial bodies, while others regard some great man of the past as their supreme god. The majority of the population agree that there is a single divine power which is quite beyond human understanding, diffused throughout the universe not as a physical substance but as an active force. They refer to this power as "The Parent" since its sex—if any—cannot be known. They also believe in a Supreme Being called Mithras. There are disagreements as to the precise nature of Mithras, but everyone claims that the form of the Supreme Being is identical to that of Nature and the sole cause of everything. Increasingly, however, the Christian faith is being adopted. The fanatical preaching of one religion to the exclusion of all others is forbidden; it is not considered blasphemy, but a simple breach of the peace. Those who continue to offend are exiled.

The principle of religious tolerance dates back to the time of the conquest of the country by Utopos. Prior to the conquest, the country had been divided by serious religious quarrels, to the extent that the different sects actually refused to cooperate in the defence of their homeland. It was, in fact, these divisions that made it so easy for Utopos to take the country. After the conquest, he decreed that everyone was free to practise his own religion and to try to convert others to it, provided he did so peacefully and by rational argument. The reasons for Utopos's decree were in part political, as they ensured the unity of the country. But it also appears that he believed complete tolerance to be in the interests of religion itself, considering it at least possible that God made people believe different things because he wished to be worshipped in a variety of ways. All people are free to choose their own religious doctrine, always provided that it does not go against the dignity of the human race. The only two basic dogmas which Utopia, as a whole, accepts are that the human soul does not perish with the body and that the universe is not an aimless creation without a controlling providence. The people of Utopia also believe in the existence of rewards and punishments after death; anyone who thinks differently has, they claim, lost the right to be considered a human being, as he is degrading his immortal soul to the level of an animal's body. Such people are held in general contempt and are not allowed to hold any public office, but they are not punished or terrorized into concealing their beliefs. They are not allowed to preach their views in public, but in private they are actually encouraged to discuss them as the Utopians are convinced that this kind of delusion must eventually collapse in the face of rational argument. There are materialists in Utopia, but these are a minority. At the opposite extreme are those who claim that animals too have immortal souls, although of an inferior nature to that of man. Most of the population believe that they can please God by studying the natural world, but a significant minority are led by their religious beliefs to neglect the pursuit of knowledge and simply to spend their lives doing good works of various kinds.

The Utopians are further divided into two main sects. One of these sects believes in celibacy, abstains from meat and in some cases from all animal foods; they renounce the pleasures of this world and long only for the life to come. The other sect has no objection to pleasure—provided that it does not interfere with work—approves of marriage and believes that procreation is a duty to one's country and to human nature. Those Utopians who belong to the first sect are treated with great respect and are considered as being more devout than the members of the second; they are generally known as *Cowbrethren* or Lay Brothers.

Utopians are so convinced of the existence of infinite happiness after death that they do not mourn the death of their fellows, unless a reluctance to die appears to indicate gloomy foreboding of punishment in the afterlife. The rites of someone who appeared very reluctant to die are thus performed in sorrowful silence. They simply ask God to have mercy on the person's soul and to forgive the person's weakness. The body is then buried. Those who die in a cheerful mood are not mourned; songs are sung at their funerals and their bodies are cremated in a spirit of reverence rather than grief. The people then go home and discuss the dead man's character and qualities. They do so out of consideration, believing that this practice is also agreeable to the dead, who although invisible are present at these discussions. It is assumed that a good man's capacity for affection, along with all his other good qualities, is enhanced rather than diminished by his death. The dead are believed to mix freely with the living and to observe everything that is said and done upon earth; they are regarded almost as guardian angels. The sense that these ancestors are always present also helps to discourage the living from bad behaviour in private.

No attention is paid in Utopia to the superstitions, omens and fortune-tellings that are so important in many countries. On the other hand, the people have great respect for miracles, as these are evidence of God's power and majesty. It is said that miracles often happen here and indeed, in times of crisis, the whole nation prays for a miracle; their faith is so great that their prayers are often answered.

Although the country is devout, there are comparatively few priests: thirteen per town, or one per church. One of the thirteen has the status of bishop. All priests are elected by the whole community in secret ballots. They are responsible for conducting services, supervising morals and for the education of the young. It is considered very shameful to have to appear before an ecclesiastical court on moral charges. The Mayor and magistrates are, of course, responsible for the suppression of crime, but the priests have the power to excommunicate, which is probably the most feared punishment in the country. The very physical security of an excommunicated person is threatened, for if he cannot convince the priests that he is a reformed character he will be arrested and punished by the Council for impiety.

Male priests may marry and women can become priests, although in practice only elderly

A communal garden in Aircastle, capital of UTOPIA.

widows are eligible for office. No public figure is more respected than a priest, and priests' wives form the cream of Utopian society. The clergy are held in such high regard that even if one of their number commits a crime, he is not liable to prosecution. It is considered impious for any human being to lay a hand on him and he is left to God and his own conscience.

Priests accompany the Utopian armies on all their expeditions. A short way from the battlefield they kneel and pray for peace, and if that is not granted, for a bloodless victory. As soon as the Utopian army begins to look victorious, the priests rush onto the battlefield and try to stop all unnecessary bloodshed; an enemy soldier can save his life simply by calling out to them, and if he can touch their flowing robes, his property will be spared. The intervention of the priests has, on occasion, been known to prevent a massacre.

Utopian churches are beautifully built and impressively large. Inside they are rather dark, as it is believed that twilight is more conducive to contemplation and prayer than bright, distracting light. The ceremonies performed in the churches and the prayers are equally applicable to all faiths, being concerned solely with the worship of the Divine Being. Any rites peculiar to the various sects are practised elsewhere in private. For similar reasons, the churches contain no visual representations of the Divine Being. Everyone can thus imagine the Supreme Being as she or he sees fit.

Major religious festivals are held on the first and last days of the month and year, the former being termed *Dogdates*, or Beginning Feasts, and the latter *Turndates*, or Ending Feasts. On Ending Feasts, Utopians fast all day and go to church in the evening to thank their god for bringing them safely to the end of the year or month in question. Before going to church the women and children confess to their husbands, asking forgiveness for any sins they may have committed in the preceding month. The custom of confession clears the atmosphere of any grudges or ill-feeling; it is considered blasphemous to attend church if one feels upset or angry in any way. The next day is, of course, a Beginning Feast, when the people meet in church in the morning to ask for happiness and prosperity in the month or year that has just begun. The congregation, men seated on the right and women on the left, all dress in white; the priests wear vestments decorated with the feathers of various birds. No sacrifices are made, but incense is burnt and candles are lit. It is acknowledged that these things are of no use to the Divine Being, but they are felt to add to the atmosphere of ritual and to raise the thoughts of the congregation. Hymns of praise are sung to the accompaniment of sweet-toned musical instruments, many of them unknown in other countries.

Utopians believe that a kind god created them to be happy. This helps to explain the attitude to pleasure of the sect that, unlike the *Cowbrethren*, has not renounced the pleasures of this world. They deliberately cultivate the higher forms of pleasure. It is, they argue, the duty of every human being to make his or her way through life as comfortably and happily as possible and to help others to do the same. Effectively, this principle governs the entire system of the distribution of goods and wealth; assuming that the laws have been justly drawn up, it is only right to consult one's own interests and those of the community at large. It would be wrong to deny someone else a pleasure simply so that one can enjoy it oneself. At the same time, self-denial of minor pleasures usually means that the benefit will be repaid in kind. Utopians thus argue that, in the final analysis, pleasure is the ultimate aim of all human beings, even—if not especially—when they are acting most virtuously. It is further argued that pleasure is any state that is naturally enjoyable, the emphasis being on the word "naturally," which means that many of the so-called pleasures of other countries are dismissed as being illusory. All forms of dandyism, conspicuous consumption, gambling and hunting are considered to belong to this category; in no way do they give real pleasure to the individual. Hunting is particularly abhorrent to the Utopians, who cannot see why anyone should find pleasure in the barking and yapping of dogs, not to mention the mutilation of small animals for no reason at all. In Utopia, killing is quite below the dignity of freemen and is left to butchers, all of whom are slaves.

A similar attitude governs the way in which Utopians regard silver and gold. From a logical point of view, they are less important to material life than iron, and the efficiency of their economic system means that the individual has no need to hoard gold. Excessive interest in personal wealth therefore is classified as an illusory pleasure. In order to prevent gold taking on the importance it has in other countries, a curious scale of values has been evolved. Plates and drinking vessels are beautifully designed, but they are made out of cheap glass or earthenware. Gold and silver, however, are the normal materials for the most humble items of domestic use, such as chamber pots. Slaves are fettered with gold chains and those guilty of the most shameful crimes are forced to go around wearing gold rings and necklaces. The same applies to jewels, which are commonly found in the island, but which are not valued by Utopians. The only people to wear jewellery with any pride are children, and they soon grow out of it. The debasement of precious stones and metals can, on occasion, cause embarrassment to diplomats who are not acquainted with Utopian ways and customs. For instance, a group of diplomats from Fatulina once visited the country, decked out in magnificent clothes and adorned with jewellery made from gold and precious stones. They were in fact wearing all the things that Utopia associated with the punishment of slaves, humiliation of criminals and the games of small children. It took the delegation some time to realize why they were the object of such scorn and ill-disguised amusement.

On the other hand, real pleasures, both mental and physical, are highly valued. Mental pleasures include the satisfaction of understanding something or contemplating the truth. Physical pleasures are subdivided into two categories: the first type includes those pleasures which fill the whole body with a conscious sense of enjoyment, such as the discharge of some excess or the release of tension; the second type acts in a mysterious fashion on the senses themselves, in the way that music monopolizes the interests of the senses without a true organic need. Such pleasures, it is believed, are dependent upon good health, a condition which is actively encouraged in Utopia.

The sick are given every possible attention and are provided with every kind of medicine that could aid their recovery. But if the disease is incurable, the patient is visited by a priest or government official who tries to convince him or her of the possible advantages of voluntary euthanasia. If the patient agrees that life is simply a torture chamber and that it would be preferable to seek a better world, he either starves himself to death or is given a soporific that will kill him painlessly. Euthanasia is regarded as an honourable death, but those who commit suicide for inadequate or frivolous reasons are denied the benefit of both cremation and burial and their corpses are unceremoniously thrown into a pond.

Marriage customs involve certain peculiarities, at least from a visitor's point of view. Girls cannot marry until they are eighteen and boys have to wait two years longer. Anyone, male or female, convicted of having premarital intercourse is punished and is disqualified from marriage, unless the sentence is remitted by the Mayor. Their guardians are also punished, for allowing them to transgress in this way. The logic behind this is that few people would marry and spend their entire lives with one person, with all the problems that entails, if they were not prevented from having intercourse outside marriage. Before marriage is contracted, the groom and bride see each other naked in the presence of a chaperone in order to avoid problems arising from physical dissatisfaction. Marriage is monogamous and the only causes for divorce are adultery or intolerable behaviour. In cases of adultery, the innocent party may remarry, but the guilty partner is condemned to celibacy for life. In exceptional cases, divorce is allowed on grounds of incompatibility, when both husband and wife have found partners who seem likely to make them happier. Such cases require thorough investigation by the *Bencheaters* and their wives, and divorce is rarely granted on these grounds. Adultery is usually punished by penal servitude. Attempted or actual seduction is also severely punished.

The treatment of would-be or actual seducers highlights one curious aspect of Utopian law: anyone who fails in an attempted crime is punished for the crime nonetheless. Utopian lawyers argue that as it was not the criminal's fault that he did not succeed in committing the crime, there is no reason why he should not be punished for it. However, Utopia has very few laws; in fact, one of its major criticisms of other countries is that their penal codes are too lengthy. Utopians argue that it is quite unjust to have laws that are too abstruse for an ordinary person to read and understand. Furthermore, they claim that each man can plead his own cause better than a hired professional. Given that there are so few formal laws, this system works perfectly well and every citizen is his own legal expert. Endless discussions over the correct interpretation of the law are unknown as it is held that the crudest interpretation is the correct

Drinking vessels, plate and jug from UTOPIA.

one. The legal system is not based upon deterrents alone and public honours are given to those who obey the law. For instance, statues are erected in honour of those who have distinguished themselves by outstanding service to the community, partly to commemorate their achievements and partly to encourage others to follow their example.

Much of the life of Utopia is communal. Meals, for instance, are usually taken in communal dining rooms, where the women of different households take turns to prepare the food. Young and old are seated in such a way that they always sit with their contemporaries while also mixing with a different age group. The theory is that respect for the old discourages bad behaviour among the young, especially if everything they do or say is certain to be noticed by the people sitting next to them. During meal times, nurseries are provided for children under five and for pregnant or nursing mothers. Food is adequate and wholesome: wine, cider and perry are drunk. Water is sometimes flavoured with honey or liquorice; beer is unknown.

Utopian society is highly developed and sophisticated. Through skilled use of science, a naturally barren island has been transformed into a rich, fertile land. The natural sciences, weatherforecasting and astronomy are all highly developed. In fact, the only area in which the Utopians would appear not to have advanced as far as European nations is that of logic, in which their skills remain remarkably undeveloped.

The people are kind and hospitable, welcoming with open arms the few travellers who reach their shores. They are also noted for their affectionate treatment of the mentally deficient, whom it is held very ill-mannered to insult though it is quite normal to find their silly behaviour amusing.

Visitors are warned that the Utopians disapprove strongly of any form of artificial make-up, and it is inadvisable to wear ornate clothes, as the Flatuline diplomats discovered to their cost. Utopian dress is usually plain: loose-fitting leather overalls are worn for work and a natural-coloured woollen cloak is worn for public appearances. In Utopia, fashion is an unknown concept.

The origins of the people remain obscure, although the linguistic evidence would point to either Greek or Persian ancestry. The language itself is expressive and pleasant to listen to. It is increasingly spoken by other nations in the area, albeit in a somewhat debased form.

Little is known of the early history of Utopia. The first accurate account of the island was brought back to Europe by members of Amerigo Vespucci's expedition to America in 1504. But perhaps its main claim to fame is that it was the birthplace of the giant Pantagruel. Pantagruel's father, Gargantua, ruled Utopia at some time soon after its discovery by the European expedition; his mother was Badebec, the daughter of the ruler of the Amaurotes. She died giving birth to her only son; a monument erected to her by Gargantua can still be seen on the island.

After the death of Gargantua, Utopia was invaded—perhaps for the first time in its history—by the Dipsodes. The invaders were defeated and expelled from the country by Pantagruel. The defeat of the Dipsodes was regarded as a return to the Age of Saturn, or the Golden Age. In accordance with Utopian custom, Pantagruel then led an army of colonists into the land of the Dipsodes, placing it under Utopian rule.

(Sir Thomas More, *Utopia*, London, 1516; François Rabelais, *Pantagruel roi des Dipsodes, restitué à son naturel avec ses faictz et prouesses espouvantables*, Lyons, 1532)

UXAL or **UXMAL**, an island in the South Pacific discovered and colonized in 1452 or 1453 by Chac Tutul Xiu, a Mayan prince who left his native Yucatán and founded a Mayan colony on this island.

The capital and only city is Chichen Itza, surrounded by cultivated fields of maize and sweet potato. In the middle of the city is a knoll and, on the top of the knoll, a pyramid surmounted by a temple. The pyramid is built of blocks of lava that form steps leading to the summit. The wall around the city is pierced by occasional gates.

The inhabitants live very much like the Mayas of ancient times. They have several gods: Huitz-Hok, Lord of Hills and Valleys; Che, Lord of Forests; Itzamna, Ruler of the Sky; Hun Ahau, God of the Underworld; Aychuykak, God of War; and innumerable earth gods. They speak an incomprehensible language probably derived from the ancient Mayan tongue.

(Edgar Rice Burroughs, *Tarzan and the Castaways*, New York, 1964)

UZIRI COUNTRY, in Africa, inhabited by the savage Waziri tribe. It is here that Lord Greystoke, known as Tarzan, has his immense estate.

The farm on the estate was plundered by Tarzan's enemy, Achmet Zek, and then burnt to the ground; but Tarzan rebuilt it with the gold he brought back from OPAR. A second fire was caused by Hauptmann Fritz Schneider during World War Two, after he had kidnapped Tarzan's wife, Jane Clayton. In a small rose garden near the house lies buried the body of a woman Tarzan supposed was his wife. He later discovered Jane alive and well, but he left the unknown body in its resting place after rebuilding the farm for the second time.

(Edgar Rice Burroughs, *The Beasts of Tarzan*, New York, 1914, Edgar Rice Burroughs, *Tarzan and the Jewels of Opar*, New York, 1916; Edgar Rice Burroughs, *Tarzan the Untamed*, New York, 1919)

V

—

VAGON, a castle in the vicinity of CAMELOT. It was in this castle that the 150 knights of the Round Table spent their last night together before dispersing on the quest for the Holy Grail. Only three of their number were virtuous enough to reach CARBONEK CASTLE and achieve the object of their quest.

(Sir Thomas Malory, *Le Morte Darthur*, London, 1485)

VALAPEE or **ISLE OF YAMS**, an island of the MARDI ARCHIPELAGO, consisting of two long, straight mountain ranges rising some three arrow-flights into the air. Between the two lies a widening vale so level that, at either extremity, the green of its groves blends with the green of the lagoon and the isle seems divided by a strait.

The natives of Valapee have the curious custom of covering their chests when saluting the king. The more ancient custom of the nose salute has, however, been lost. In a fever of loyalty, the noblemen of Valapee used to present themselves before the heir of the island and go through a court ceremony which consisted of standing upside-down supported only by the nose. The frequent practice of this rite—which the natives called "Pupera"—has made intelligent observers impute to it the flattened noses of the elderly chiefs of the island. Nowadays, visitors can still see these chiefs observing the old-fashioned custom of retiring from the presence of royalty with their heads between their thighs so that, as they walk away, their faces may still be deferentially turned towards their lord and master.

The local currency is human teeth. Slaves have their teeth extracted in infancy by their masters, and the teeth of a deceased are distributed among his mourners. As a currency, teeth are far less clumsy than coconuts; indeed, on some islands men have purposely instituted coconut-currency to check the extravagance of their women—coconuts being such a burden to carry when spending money. On Valapee, the most solemn oath of a native is "By this tooth!"

(Herman Melville, *Mardi, and A Voyage Thither*, New York, 1849)

VALDRADA, a city in Asia. The ancients built Valdrada on the shores of a lake, with the houses' verandas one above the other and high streets whose railed parapets look out over the water. Thus the traveller arriving sees two cities: one erect above the lake, and the other reflected, upside down. Nothing exists or happens in the one Valdrada that the other Valdrada does not repeat, because the city was so constructed that its every point would be reflected in its mirror and the Valdrada down in the water contains not only all the flutings and juttings of the façades that rise above the lake, but also the rooms' interiors with ceilings and floors, the perspective of the halls, the mirrors of the wardrobes.

Valdrada's inhabitants know that each of their actions is at once that action and its mirror-image, which possesses the special dignity of images, and this awareness prevents them from forgetfulness. Even when lovers twist their naked bodies, skin against skin, seeking the position that will give one the most pleasure in the other, even when murderers plunge the knife into the black veins of the neck and more clotted blood pours out the more they press the blade that slips between the tendons, it is not so much their copulating or murdering that matters as the copulating or murdering of the images, limpid and cold in the mirror.

At times the mirror increases a thing's value, at times denies it. Not everything that seems valuable above the mirror maintains its force when mirrored. The twin cities are not equal, because nothing that exists or happens in Valdrada is symmetrical: every face and gesture is answered, from the mirror, by a face and gesture inverted, point by point. The two Valdradas live for each other, their eyes interlocked; but there is no love between them.

(Italo Calvino, *Le città invisibili*, Turin, 1972)

VALINOR, a vast region of AMAN, the great land that lies far across the western sea from MIDDLE-EARTH. Valinor lies beyond the Pelóri, the great mountain range that guards the coast of Aman. It was here that the Valar came after the first great struggle with Melkor, or Morgoth, when much of the Middle-earth they had helped to create was destroyed. Valinor is more beautiful than Middle-earth in its first springtime. It is a sacred, enchanted land in which nothing fades or dies and in which disease and suffering are unknown. The south-east is covered in forest, while in the west lie fields and pasturelands.

The city of Valinor, also called Valmar or Valimar, stands on the plains behind the Pelóri. It is a walled city with golden gates, silver domes and streets of gold. Near the western gate stands the Máhanaxar, the so-called Ring of Doom where the Valar meet to hold council and to pass judgement on those who have offended them. On a green mound in front of the gate stand the two White Trees of Valinor, Telperion and Laurelin. Originally Telperion bore dark green leaves with a silver underside; silver dew fell from the leaves to the ground. Laurelin had light green leaves edged with gold and bore yellow flowers from which golden rain fell to the ground; it gave off both warmth and light. Each tree went through a regular cycle lasting seven hours during which it came to flower, gave off light and then faded. Laurelin started brightening six hours after Telperion, so that Aman had a day lasting twelve hours. The trees themselves were killed by Melkor and Ungoliant, the great spider, but they were left standing as testimony. Their light lived on in the sacred jewels known as the Silmarils and in the moon and sun which were then created to light the world.

Valinor is the home of the Valar—the Ainur, or spirits, from the Timeless Halls beyond the world who elected to come down and live with the children of Ilúvatar, the first creatures created when Middle-earth was brought into being. Their powers are circumscribed by the limits of the world, so that they are the life of the world and the world is their life. They will remain in the world until it ends. Their name originally seems to have meant the Powers of the World. In Middle-earth they took the shape of majestic kings and queens, but shapes are not essential to their being and they can discard them at will. There are seven lords of the Valar and seven queens, or Valier, each with their own powers and sphere of action. The Lords are Manwë, Ulmo, Aulë, Oromë, Mandos, Lórien and Tulkas; the queens, Varda, Yavanna, Nienna, Estë, Vairë, Vána and Nessa.

Manwë is the greatest Lord of the Valar, and Varda is his Lady. Together they dwell on Taniquetil, a peak in the Pelóri range; it is the highest mountain on earth, and is perpetually covered in snow. From there Manwë can see farther than anyone else, and Varda can hear voices from immense distances.

The elves lived in Eldamar, on the other side of the Pelóri, but in the one pass through these mountains they built Tirion, a city of white walls and terraces and stairs of crystal. Its tallest tower is the Tower of Ingwë, from which a silver lantern shines. So great was the love of elves for Telperion, the White Tree, that a similar tree was created for them in Tirion. This was Galathilion, which resembled the originals but did not give off light of its own.

Far to the west of Valinor stand the Houses of the Dead, also known as the Halls of Mandos. At the end of the first battle between Melkor and the Valar, Melkor was imprisoned here. It is here that the spirits of men and elves come after their time in Middle-earth is over. The spirits of elves are freed after a while and can live in Aman; the spirits of men disappear from the known world. It is not certain if the spirits of the dwarves come here too, though the dwarves themselves believe so. The Halls are constantly growing larger and are hung with the tapestries of Vairë the Weaver, who weaves into them images of everything that has ever happened.

The gardens of Valinor are said to be the most beautiful place in the world. They are tended by Lórien and provide a place of rest to which the Valar come frequently.

Every year a great festival is held by Manwë on the mountain peak of Taniquetil. It is in praise of Eru the creator and is held on the anniversary of the first harvest. The Valar have no physical need of food, but they eat and drink because of their love of elves and man—a love that led them to adopt a bodily shape.

(J.R.R. Tolkien, *The Fellowship of the Ring,* London, 1954; J.R.R. Tolkien, *The Return of the King,* London, 1955; J.R.R. Tolkien, *The Silmarillion,* London, 1977)

VANITY FAIR, a major town on the pilgrim way which leads from the City of DESTRUCTION to the CELESTIAL CITY in CHRISTIAN'S COUNTRY. The town takes its name from the permanent fair that is held here, originally established by Beelzebub (the chief lord of the town), Legion and Apollyon. Its principal citizens are the Lords Carnal-Desire, Luxurious, Lechery and Having-Greedy. Everything sold at the fair is the work of vanity and the range of goods available is therefore extremely wide, from houses, lands and titles to children, wives, whores and bawds, from souls to precious stones. The fair throngs with jugglers, gamesters and cheats, not to mention adulterers, murderers and thieves. The streets of the town are named after the country of origin of the wares sold in them: Britain Row, Italian Row, Spanish Row. As in most fairs, one commodity is more popular than all others; in the case of Vanity Fair it is the wares of Rome, which only the British merchants dislike.

In the past, Vanity Fair was an extremely dangerous place for travellers. Those who refused to buy goods at the fair were arrested and imprisoned, and some were even beaten and placed in the stocks before being brought to trial before Lord Hategood for disturbing trade and causing religious dissension in the town. If found guilty, travellers were sometimes burnt at the stake for their supposed offences.

It appears that the town has now become much less dangerous and that travellers can visit it in safety. The change is due in part to the appearance of a certain Great-heart, who now guides travellers on their way to the Celestial City. Mercy is now allowed to operate in Vanity Fair and has done much to relieve the sufferings of the sick and poor.

Vanity Fair is from time to time attacked by a monster with the body of a dragon, seven heads and ten horns. In the past the monster killed many children and forced many of the townspeople to accept the conditions it imposed upon them. Those who loved their lives more than their souls accepted its conditions and came under its sway. The dragon is governed by a woman, despite its ferocity. Although it is a fearsome beast, the monster has recently been severely wounded by a party of warriors led by Great-heart; its raids on the town have virtually stopped, and it is widely believed that it may have died of its wounds.

(John Bunyan, *The Pilgrim's Progress from this world, to that which is to come. Delivered under the similitude of a Dream. Wherein is discovered, the manner of his setting out, his dangerous journey and safe arrival at the Desired Country*, London, 1678; John Bunyan, *The Pilgrim's Progress from this world to that which is to come. The Second Part. Delivered under the similitude of a Dream. Wherein is set forth the manner of the setting out of Christian's wife and children, their dangerous journey and safe arrival at the Desired Country*, London, 1684)

VANOUA-LEBOLI, see VITI ISLANDS.

VEGETABLE SEA, a part of the Atlantic, some fifty miles long, where pine trees and cypresses float without roots. These plants are so densely crammed together that it is possible for the traveller to skim over them, if aided by high winds, provided he is capable of first hoisting his ship onto the treetops.

(Lucian of Samosata, *True History*, 2nd cen. AD)

VEIRING, see REREK.

VEMISH, an island in the East Reach of the EARTHSEA ARCHIPELAGO about one and a half days' sail from The HANDS. The island is small and there is only one port, Mishport, on the south-east coast.

(Ursula K. Le Guin, *A Wizard of Earthsea*, New York, 1968)

VENALIA, a country about five hundred miles to the east of UTOPIA. Venalia is a wild, savage country of dark forests and rugged mountains. Its people are primitive and savage, with no arts and no interest in farming. They live mostly by hunting and stealing. Tough and hardy, they are natural soldiers and taking lives is the only method they know of making a living.

They fight for whoever pays them, always servicing the most generous masters they can find. The slightest increase in pay is enough to make them change sides, even in the middle of a battle. It is rare to find a war in this part of the world in which most of the soldiers on both sides are not Venalians. Venalians frequently fight for the Utopians, as they pay extremely well. The Venalian mercenaries are sent out on the most desperate enterprises, but the few who come back are paid in full and are always ready to re-enlist. The Utopians themselves do not care how many Venalians they send to their deaths, as they philanthropically believe that ridding the world of such scum would be a benefit to the human race as a whole. Although Venalians are well paid, they get little of lasting value out of it as they immediately spend all their salaries on the most squalid and amusing forms of debauchery.

(Sir Thomas More, *Utopia*, London, 1516)

VENDCHURCH'S ISLAND, a desert island in

the West Indies, where a Scotsman named Alexander Vendchurch was marooned after a mutiny. The island produces excellent oysters, but it is dangerous to collect them as the coast is defended by savage and carnivorous sea lions who devour any intruders.

(Ambrose Evans [?], *The Adventures, And Surprizing Deliverances, Of James Dubourdieu, And His Wife: Who were taken by Pyrates, and carried to the Uninhabited-Part of the Isle of Paradise. Containing A Description of that Country, its Laws, Religion, and Customs: Of Their being at last releas'd; and how they came to Paris, where they are still living. Also, The Adventures of Alexander Vendchurch, Whose Ship's Crew Rebelled against him, and set him on Shore on an Island in the South-Sea, where he lived five Years, five Months, and seven Days; and was at last providentially releas'd by a Jamaica ship. Written by Himself*, London, 1719)

VENUSBERG (1), or **HORSELBERG**, a mountain under which lies the realm of Queen Venus. Her palace is surrounded by extensive gardens with avenues of tall trees, cascades, arches, pavilions, grottoes and phallic statues. In the distance lies a lake surrounded by sleeping plants whose shapes seem to change from hour to hour. Farther on, the grounds become filled with mysterious haunting sounds. The realm itself is reached through a dark portico of pale stone—carved with erotic sculptures that surpass the art of Japan—and down a shadowy tunnel strewn with gloomy, nameless weeds and huge hovering moths whose wings are so rich that they seem to have fed on tapestries.

Inside the palace, the visitor should note the Queen's dressing room, panelled with gallant paintings by Jean-Baptiste Dorat. Her boudoir, designed by Le Comte, is an octagonal room adorned with silk curtains and soft cushions, bright mirrors and rich candelabra, wax statuettes, celadon vases, ivory boxes, clocks without hands and china figurines. Four folding screens painted with Claudian landcapes by De La Pine effectively form a room within a room, filled with the scent of red roses and a perfume known as *l'eau lavante*. The boudoir overlooks the park and gardens, and out on the terrace stands a bronze fountain with three basins: from the first rises a many-breasted dragon and four cupids mounted on swans; from the second spring golden columns supporting silver doves; the third shows a group of grotesque

satyrs, capped with children's heads. Water plays from the eyes of the swans, the breasts of the doves, the horns of the satyrs and the curls of the children. Visitors are warned—should they be invited to stay at the palace—that the rooms are decorated with erotic paintings by Dorat; a famous one depicts an old marquis masturbating while his mistress offers her posterior to a panting poodle.

Visitors are usually given a loving reception by Venus herself, as well as by her servants, old and young. They will be entertained at the Casino, where ballet, comedy, concerts and operas are performed; and they will be shown the Queen's pet unicorn, Adolphe, a milk-white stallion who lives in a palace of its own made of green foliage and golden bars. Adolphe is manually satisfied every day by the loving Queen herself.

Near the mountain, a traveller's staff, planted in the ground, can be seen in full bloom throughout the year; it is said to belong to a thirteenth-century gentleman. Tannhäuser, who died near Venusberg after having enjoyed the Queen's pleasures.

(Richard Wagner, *Tannhäuser*, first performance, Dresden, 1845; Aubrey Beardsley, *Under the Hill*, London, 1897)

VENUSBERG (2), capital of a small and rather obscure republic in the Baltic, which in the past was partitioned between Russia and Germany, achieving its independence after a short war against Bolshevik Russia. The events surrounding the War of Independence have led to the continued unpopularity and social unacceptability of the small Russian community.

Venusberg is divided into two towns: the High Town and the Lower Town. In the High Town the houses are of wood and date back to the Middle Ages; arches and flights of stairs break up the narrow, winding streets. When snow is falling, the High Town could almost be mistaken for a stage set. Above it rises the grey outline of the Castle, the spires of the Lutheran churches and the gilded cupolas of the red-brick Russian Cathedral.

The Lower Town is more modern and the streets are much wider. Near the stock exchange and the main hotel stands the National Theatre, an undistinguished building in the Palladian style. The air of unreality that haunts the High Town can be found in the Lower Town, especially in the

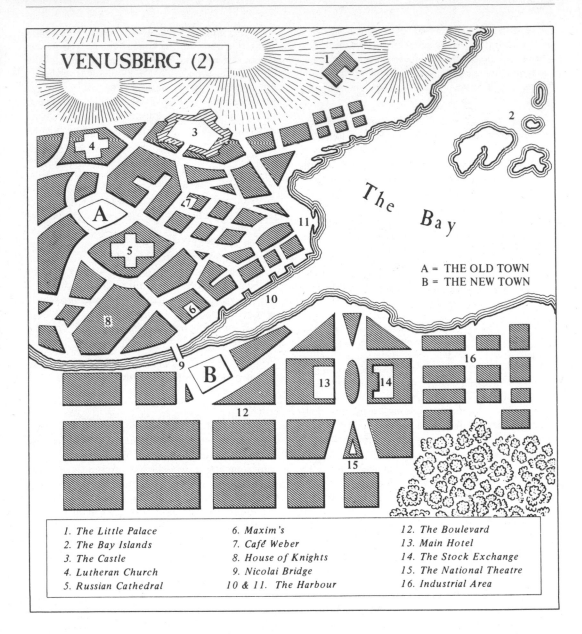

VENUSBERG (2)

A = THE OLD TOWN
B = THE NEW TOWN

The Bay

1. The Little Palace	6. Maxim's	12. The Boulevard
2. The Bay Islands	7. Café Weber	13. Main Hotel
3. The Castle	8. House of Knights	14. The Stock Exchange
4. Lutheran Church	9. Nicolai Bridge	15. The National Theatre
5. Russian Cathedral	10 & 11. The Harbour	16. Industrial Area

area around the port. The docks run quite a long way inland and, from a distance, the ships seem to be moored in the streets themselves.

The city's industrial area is to the east and is bordered by a collection of low green-painted buildings. In Russian times these were used as government buildings, but they have since been converted into tenements. In the city centre, the Nicolai Bridge, associated with many of the more violent incidents in the city's history, leads into the poorer areas. Here, the shells of unfinished blocks of flats rise above the outlying tin huts. Although the flats have yet to be completed, the iron work is already rusting and the masonry is crumbling.

Venusberg's most impressive building is the House of the Knights, the site of the annual ball which is the high point of the social year. The façade of the building is adorned with wooden carvings and gargoyles. The ballroom itself is large and not unlike a drill hall. Two of the walls are flanked by alcoves in which figures in armour stand guard. Most have projecting visors, but there are examples of the Russian or Polish style, with curving points like those of Persian helmets. The capitals of all the pillars in the hall are decorated with the arms of noble families of the city.

On the outskirts of the city stands the building known simply as the Little Palace, a restrained Baroque construction surrounded by birch and fir trees. It is now empty, although there are proposals to convert it into a State institution for the treatment of the mentally ill. The terrace gives good views of the town and of the small islands in the bay, the home of both fishermen and professional smugglers; the latter clash from time to time with the coastguards. Until independence, the terrace was a popular promenade, but it is now almost always deserted, the fashionable walk being the main boulevard of the Lower Town.

In many ways, the social life of Venusberg is that of an earlier century. Social events are dominated by an aristocracy that seems to be related to many of the most ancient houses of northern Europe, and by young officers in full dress uniform. It is an entertaining town, providing great opportunities for amorous intrigue. Duelling still takes place, although it is punishable by up to three years' imprisonment; however, if one of the combatants' honour is judged to have been tarnished, the statutory sentence may be commuted by half. Much of the city's social life centres around balls organized by the various regiments. *Maxim's*, a small night club decorated in French Second Empire style, and the *Café Weber* are among the more popular places of entertainment.

Although it is now a democratic republic, the country is not without its political problems. Sabotage by the town's communists—usually in the form of arson—is not uncommon and there have been serious incidents in the timber yards in recent years. Several attempts have been made on the life of General Kuno who is chief of police as well as an army officer. He was responsible for the period of repression after the War of Independence and the ensuing Civil War, which earned him many enemies.

Venusberg can be reached by steamer from Copenhagen.

(Anthony Powell, *Venusberg*, London, 1932)

VENUSIA, an island in the Atlantic near the equator. The port of Venusia is on a river estuary and its entrance is marked by two colossal statues of naked women who seem to scan the sea, water lapping round their legs. The traveller will find entry to Venusia quite easy, as the port is almost always deserted. Beyond the estuary lies Fons Belli, the capital, a brightly coloured city with geometrically laid out streets. It is famed for its gardens and is believed to have been the favourite resort of Venus Victrix. It is encircled by water-gardens built along canals, where tropical plants, such as begonias and orchids, surround statues of goddesses, bacchantes and Amazons. Above the city rises a hill with many gardens and marble villas, surrounded by orange and lemon groves and topped by a bronze tower which supports four female statues carrying the golden image of a woman in an attitude of triumph. At her feet crawls a male slave who points to the inscription *Venus Victrix*.

The city is divided into four concentric zones: the zones of temples, of domed buildings, of villas and gardens and of the streets around the port (Plebeana). Notable is the palace of the military leader, done in the style of a Greek temple, supported by slender columns on which are carved adolescent girls dancing and playing instruments. The artwork is so graceful that visitors say they can actually hear the music.

The island is of volcanic origin, with a spinal chain of mountains and high pastures for sheep and cattle. There is only one active volcano and earthquakes are rare. Near Mount Astarte, famous for its sulphur and hot springs, is the city of Venus Genetrix, the City of Mothers, occupied by women and men selected for reproduction. Men belong to the State and are trained from an early age for various trades; they are then given to the women as slaves. Each woman has between one and five slaves; high-ranking women have the better qualified men. Young women serve as soldiers before they become mothers and must remain virgins during this period—those who break this law are burnt alive.

The original settlers of Venusia were Spanish women whose galley was blown south into the Atlantic, during the reign of Hadrian. A society was established under the leadership of Julia Senecion, who organized the cult of Venus based on her hatred of men. During the centuries, two rival tendencies developed: the "Masculines," who believed in the equality of the sexes, and the "Venusians," convinced of female superiority and anxious to conquer the world. A civil war broke out, the outcome of which has not been properly chronicled.

The Venusian civilization, in spite of many characteristics which have survived from Roman times (language, military organization), boasts an advanced science and technology. By 1788, aircraft, vehicles, submarines and steamships were in use. Firearms, though invented over two centuries ago, are forbidden by law. Though Venusian is a language in itself, any traveller with a smattering of schoolboy Latin will be able to make himself understood.

(Raymond Clauzel, *L'Ile Des Femmes*, Paris, 1922)

VERY HEAVENLY CITY, see JANNATI SHAHR.

VEZZANO, an island off the southern coast of ORSENNA. Vezzano is the outpost of Orsenna nearest to the country's traditional enemy, FARGHESTAN.

The white cliffs of the island rise sheer from the Sea of the Sirtes, slashed by deep clefts and ravines that cut up to the high grassy plateau in the centre of the island. The cliffs are at some points broken by sheltered creeks which provide safe natural anchorages. At the eastern end of the island, however, the cliffs are precipitous and unbroken.

Vezzano is remarkable for its marine grottoes, some of which extend the full width of the island.

In the past Vezzano was a haunt of pirates who preyed on the coastal settlements of Orsenna. All that remains of that period is a ruined tower.

(Julien Gracq, *Le Rivage des Syrtes*, Paris, 1951)

VICHEBOLK LAND, beyond the Arctic Circle, 2,300 miles north of the North Cape. Formerly a prosperous kingdom, it was reduced to its present impoverished state after the introduction of the cult of Vietso, the inscrutable god of this country. In the name of equality, all property was abolished, industry came to a halt and the nation fell into decline, though officially it was said that Vichebolk Land had "freed itself from the bonds of egotism and property." The people are starving and go about dressed in rags. Oppressed by soldiers, they are so demoralized that they allow the priests of Vietso to live off them like mushrooms on a rubbish heap.

The capital is Koumos, built on a natural harbour protected by cliffs. Now semi-derelict, Koumos is a pile of crumbling ramparts and palaces, one of the most miserable places on earth. The seat of the god Vietso is a ruined castle with broken windows and dilapidated rooms strewn with rubbish. In the throne room (kept moderately clean) surrounded by a dozen men in sumptuous robes sitting on faded gilt chairs, Stoitol, the high priest of Vietso, receives all visitors.

Known by reputation to sailors from time immemorial, Vichebolk Land was discovered by Captain Lemuel Gulliver in 1721. Travellers should keep in mind that the moment a ship enters Vichebolk waters, the ship and all its cargo become Vichebolk property and those who attempt to resist are tortured to death.

The Vichebolk language is an incomprehensible Asiatic dialect but the priests of Vietso speak most European languages, including English.

(André Lichtenberger, *Pickles ou récits à la mode anglaise*, Paris, 1923)

VICTORIA, a model town, built on the banks of a navigable river, near the coast of England. It was financed by the Model Town Association Ltd. and was initially set up to unite the work of various temperance societies and social missions. The town was named after Queen Victoria, but the name also signified moral victory over the evils afflicting English society. Three million pounds, plus a million pounds initial investment, were needed to build Victoria. The principles on which Victoria was established are health of body, serenity of mind, agreeable labour in a moderate degree and love for one's fellow men. No intoxicating drink, drugs, tobacco or weapons are allowed. Freedom of worship is guaranteed, and the sabbath is strictly observed. If a marriage fails, the couple, the minister and those who have attended the ceremony are expelled from the city. Children are raised by trained nurses but can be visited by their parents. Medical aid is provided free of charge.

The ground plan of Victoria is similar to that drawn by Sir Christopher Wren for the rebuilding of London after the Great Fire. It is built on a square, each side of which is a mile long, leading through smaller squares to the grand inner square, a forum for public meetings. A Gothic colonnade

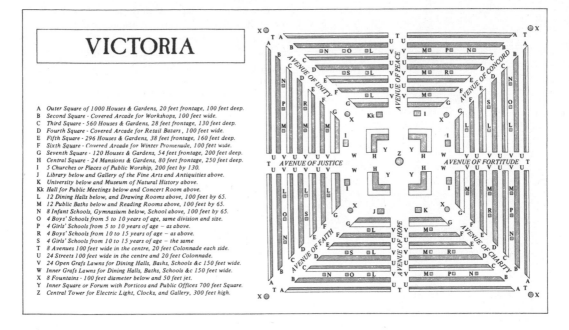

VICTORIA

A   Outer Square of 1000 Houses & Gardens, 20 feet frontage, 100 feet deep.
B   Second Square - Covered Arcade for Workshops, 100 feet wide.
C   Third Square - 560 Houses & Gardens, 28 feet frontage, 130 feet deep.
D   Fourth Square - Covered Arcade for Retail Bazars , 100 feet wide.
E   Fifth Square - 296 Houses & Gardens, 38 feet frontage, 160 feet deep.
F   Sixth Square - Covered Arcade for Winter Promenade, 100 feet wide.
G   Seventh Square - 120 Houses & Gardens, 54 feet frontage, 200 feet deep.
H   Central Square - 24 Mansions & Gardens, 80 feet frontage, 250 feet deep.
I   5 Churches or Places of Public Worship, 200 feet by 130.
J   Library below and Gallery of the Fine Arts and Antiquities above.
K   University below and Museum of Natural History above.
Kk   Hall for Public Meetings below and Concert Room above.
L   12 Dining Halls below, and Drawing Rooms above, 100 feet by 65.
M   12 Public Baths below and Reading Rooms above, 100 feet by 65.
N   8 Infant Schools, Gymnasium below, School above, 100 feet by 65.
O   4 Boys' Schools from 5 to 10 years of age, same division and size.
P   4 Girls' Schools from 5 to 10 years of age – as above.
R   4 Boys' Schools from 10 to 15 years of age – as above.
S   4 Girls' Schools from 10 to 15 years of age – the same
T   8 Avenues 100 feet wide in the centre, 20 feet Colonnade each side.
U   24 Streets 100 feet wide in the centre and 20 feet Colonnade.
V   24 Open Grafs Lawns for Dining Halls, Baths, Schools &c 150 feet wide.
W   Inner Grafs Lawns for Dining Halls, Baths, Schools &c 150 feet wide.
X   8 Fountains - 100 feet diameter below and 50 feet jet.
Y   Inner Square or Forum with Porticos and Public Offices 700 feet Square.
Z   Central Tower for Electric Light, Clocks, and Gallery, 300 feet high.

runs along its inner side, providing shelter from sun or rain. The purpose of this layout is to avoid hidden corners or alleys in which vice might flourish.

(James S. Buckingham, *National Evils and Practical Remedies, with a Plan of a Model Town,* London, 1849)

VICTORY TOWER, in Chitor, China, not to be confused with Chitorgarh, India. From its high circular terrace the most beautiful landscape in the world can be seen. The A Bao A Qu lives at the bottom of the circular staircase. When someone climbs the stairs, the A Bao A Qu (who is almost transparent) comes to life and climbs behind the visitor, hanging on to his heels. On every step the A Bao A Qu's colour becomes deeper and gives out an increasingly strong light. However, it can only reach the top of the stairs if the visitor is spiritually perfect. If not, the A Bao A Qu remains paralysed, incomplete, its colour dim, its light failing. If it cannot reach the top this sensitive beast emits a faint wail, somewhat like the rustling of silk. When the visitor descends, the A Bao A Qu falls backwards and rolls down to the bottom where it returns to its lethargic state. In the course of the centuries, only once has the A Bao A Qu become completely visible.

(Sir Richard Francis Burton, in a note to his translation of *The Arabian Nights Entertainments,* London, 1885–88)

VILLINGS, an island in the Pacific Ocean, sometimes incorrectly believed to be part of the Ellis or Tuvalu Archipelago. It is probably not far from the port of Rabaul, New Britain, from where the first chronicler of the island departed on his travels. Persecuted for a crime he believed he had not committed, the chronicler first heard about Villings from an Italian merchant in Calcutta. According to the merchant's information, Villings was the centre of a mysterious illness that killed by acting from the skin inwards, causing the hair and nails of the victim to fall out, then the skin, the cornea, until finally the whole body collapsed eight to fifteen days later. In spite of this warning, the chronicler resolved to escape, and reached the island in the early 1940's.

Villings had been inhabited in 1924 by a few whites who had built a museum here, a chapel and a swimming pool, all of which were then abandoned. When the fugitive reached Villings he was surprised by these ruins and by the vegetation: only young saplings seemed to be healthy; the rest of the trees were almost dead.

ments in the exact imitation of life. Morel had built a mechanism that could reproduce in three dimensions objects, plants, people, creating a double of reality, faithful to the original even in touch and smell. In this way Morel could keep forever the image of his friends repeating their actions and preserving their youth. However, the rays necessary to register a copy of the original living persons proved deadly to the subjects; this was the cause of the island's mysterious epidemic. The chronicler, having by mistake touched one of the rays, presumably died after completing his account of Villings. It is not known whether the spectacle still takes place or whether it is dangerous nowadays for travellers to visit the island.

(Adolfo Bioy Casares, *La invención de Morel*, Buenos Aires, 1941)

VIRAGINIA, see NEW GYNIA.

VIRTUOUS WOMEN, CITY OF, known as **CITE DES DAMES** or **CITY OF LADIES.** Not much is known about this famous city except that it is inhabited by women only, who are considered, because of their nature, more important and more noteworthy than men. It was built with enormous blocks of stone, each of which carries the name of a famous woman. The visitor will be able to identify the names of Semiramis, Amazonia, Zenobia, Artemis, Berenice, Clelia and Fredegorida, even though their deeds are now no longer remembered. It is said that in order to open the gates of the city, a traveller must make herself a key out of "prudence, economy and breeding." No other instructions are given for visiting the City of Virtuous Women.

(Christine de Pisan, *La Cité des Dames*, Paris, 1405)

VITI ISLANDS (not to be confused with Viti or Fiji), a group of islands in Polynesia in the south Pacific, discovered by the French vessel *Calembredaine* in 1831. The first island of the group to be discovered, Vanoua-Leboli, is completely deserted. It is so empty that travellers frequently come across large villages without a single house in them. Piles of bones found on the neighbouring island of Kanbadon (from *kan,* "campus," and *badon,* "bone"—"Field of Bones") indicate that it was once inhabited by cannibals. A primitive inscription on a liana plank reads:

VICTORY TOWER, Chitor, China.

Exploring the ruins, the fugitive found that the swimming pool was full of vipers, frogs and water insects, and that the museum—a three-storey building with a cylindrical tower—comprised fifteen rooms decorated with many paintings among which were a few Picassos. One of the rooms housed a deficient library, containing novels, books of poetry and plays, and only one scientific treatise, Bellidor's *Travaux, Le Moulin Perse,* 1737. The dining room, some sixty metres by twelve, was surrounded by four seated statues of Indian or Egyptian gods, three times the size of a man.

Suddenly, without seeing any ship, plane or dirigible reach the island, the fugitive noticed a great number of people dancing, walking or swimming in the fetid pool with as much comfort as summer tourists in Marienbad. An excessive gramophone overpowered the sound of the wind and the sea with *Valencia* and *Tea for Two.* For several days and nights, the fugitive watched the company, falling in love with a certain Faustine and always ignored by her. At last he learnt the truth.

The island had been bought by a scientist and man of the world, a certain Morel, who chose Villings as the stage for one of his exciting experi-

Egnam sius em
emêm-iom
regnam à neir sulp tnaya'n
emêrtxe miaf am ed emitciv

which means "Having nothing more to eat, I fell victim to my extreme hunger and was forced to eat myself."

Of the other islands in the Viti group, the most important is the Island of CIVILIZATION.

(Henry-Florent Delmotte, *Voyage pittoresque et industriel dans le Paraguay-Roux et la Palingénésie Australe par Tridacé–Nafé–Théo-de Kao't'Chouk, Gentilhomme Breton, sous-aide à l'établissement des clyso-pompes, etc.*, Meschacébé [i.e., Mons], 1835)

VLÉHA, a volcanic island in the north Pacific archipelago known as the Isles of WISDOM.

Vléha is by far the most attractive of all the islands of the archipelago. A mountain range running north-west across the centre of the island shields the lowlands from the north winds, which therefore enjoy a subtropical climate. The mountains themselves are extremely varied, providing a changing scenery that ranges from that found in the Dolomites to views more typical of the Jungfrau or the Eiger. Above the snow line, arctic plants flourish, while the valleys and lower slopes are clad in jungle vegetation. This wealth of mountain scenery is completed by Atrato, a glowing volcano.

The flora and fauna of the island are equally varied and spectacular. Palms, rhododendrons and magnolias flourish on the lower slopes of the mountains and the woods are alive with astonishingly bright butterflies. The birds of Vléha combine the grace of the humming-bird with the splendour of the bird of paradise and the song of the nightingale. Surprisingly enough—given the climate of the island—there are no poisonous reptiles. The only species of rattlesnake found here is quite harmless and is used as a sort of animated rattle for small children to play with. The other snakes native to Vléha secrete a fluid from their fangs which can be used as an opiate.

Because of its variety of natural beauties, Vléha has become a tourist resort for the whole archipelago. Bungalows, rather like those found in the East Indies, are dotted across the countryside for the convenience of visitors and the whole island is criss-crossed with railway lines. Funicular railways carry visitors high into the mountains for skiing and other winter sports.

The islanders themselves rarely use their sophisticated transport system and appear to be largely indifferent to the splendours that surround them. Darker than most people of the archipelago, they are seemingly indolent and appear to have almost no vital energy. Physically they are very attractive; the women in particular exude a sensuous charm of which they are almost totally unaware. The islanders profess to be indifferent to the future because, living as they do on a volcano, they may be destroyed at any moment.

Vléha has no written constitution and no formal government; it is neither a republic nor a monarchy. Its highest official cannot really be described as king, president or even high priest, although he does, in some ways, fulfil all these functions. He is not formally appointed; it is merely that the desires and wishes of the people coincide in the reverence addressed to one particular person.

The politics of Vléhan life are inextricably linked with its religion. Buddhism is the religion of Vléha and it is claimed that the "ruler" is a direct descendant of one Vlaho who originally formulated the basic tenets of Buddhism more than three thousand years ago. (He later travelled to India by metempsychosis and was reincarnated as the Buddha, which means that Vléha is the true birthplace of Buddhism.) The ideal of Vléhan Buddhism is the triumph of the intellect over the emotions and the suppression of the pain-pleasure polarity by depressing the sense of pleasure. This ambition no doubt helps to explain the passivity of the people and their total indifference to their surroundings.

One of the island's curious customs is its typical marriage ceremony. Bride and groom are carried to the temple in ventilated coffins to symbolize the fact that the act of their union will give their life to a new generation. This doctrine is explained to the couple as they are raised from their coffins by the officiating priest.

In recent years, the philosophy of indifference and renunciation has been opposed by the younger generation of Vléhans. The opposition has been led by Sterridogg, an agitator from the semi-arctic island of Unalaschka, far to the north of Vléha. Sterridogg has called for the breaking down of the mountain barriers so that the island will be exposed to the cold north wind and will be converted to a belief in pain and sore labour as the only means of true pleasure. This agitation has received a favourable welcome among the young and a number of plantations have already been burnt in the intergenerational conflicts. How far the destruction has spread and what the outcome will be remains to be seen.

(Alexander Moszkowski, *Die Inseln der Weisheit, Geschichte einer abenteuerlichen Entdeckungsfahrt,* Berlin, 1922)

VOE, VALLEY OF, at the foot of PYRAMID MOUNTAIN, deep below the surface of the earth. The valley itself is like the bowl of a giant cup, rising gently to the green foothills of the mountain. Its floor is laid out in lawns and gardens, orchards with luscious exotic fruits, and groves of stately trees. The picturesque houses of Voe are not grouped together in villages or towns but scattered about between the woods and fields, connected by well-maintained pebble paths. Between the fields and orchards flow the delightful crystal-clear streams of the valley. The air is fragrant and the light clear.

The people of Voe are invisible, as are all the birds and animals in the valley, due to their fondness for the *dama* fruit, which makes anyone who eats it invisible. The *dama* fruit grows on a low bush with broad spreading leaves; it is big as a peach and both sweet-smelling and attractively coloured. Those who have tasted it say that it is the most delicious fruit in the world.

The invisibility of the people does not offer complete protection against the ferocious, invisible bears which roam the valley. These bears will not, however, venture into water and a second magic plant ensures that this abstention can be used against them. Unknown to the bears, the leaves of a certain plant enable the people to walk on water when they rub them across the soles of their shoes. The people of Voe normally travel by walking along the surface of the streams and rivers.

The people of Voe are kind and hospitable to those who visit their land, and will share all they have with travellers. They seem to have little contact with other people, but know of the existence of the wooden inhabitants of the Land of GARGOYLES. Legends tell of the nine-day battle between the Voen hero Overman-Anu and the Gargoyles and of how the champion of Voe defeated them by shouting his battle cry. Overman-Anu never described his battle or his foe in any detail because he was eaten by a bear shortly afterwards. During his lifetime, he is known to have

killed eleven bears, which is the greatest number of bears ever killed by one man. His body, torn to pieces, was found by his last Gargoyle adversary.

(L. Frank Baum, *Dorothy and the Wizard in Oz,* Chicago, 1908)

VOICES, ISLAND OF, a low-lying island with extremely well-kept lawns and parks, to the west of DEATHWATER ISLAND. The only major building is a low stone house, approached along an avenue of trees. This is the home of Coriakin, appointed governor of the island by Aslan, the creator of NARNIA. The only other inhabitants are a race of stupid but harmless monopods, originally known as the Duffers. In their original form they were rather like the dwarves of Narnia, but they made such disobedient and inefficient servants (they were known to wash the dishes before dinner to save time afterwards and to plant boiled potatoes to avoid having to cook them) that Coriakin uglified them. So ashamed of their ugliness were the Duffers that they made themselves invisible by stealing a spell from Coriakin's book of magic. It was then that the island gained its present name, as travellers could hear voices but see nothing. The invisible Duffers were finally transformed into visible beings again: monopods, with one large broad-toed foot and a single thick leg descending from the middle of the body. They progress in leaps and hops and rest by lying flat on their backs with their leg in the air. This position has the advantage that their foot protects them from both sun and rain. The single foot can also be used as a raft. The ex-Duffers appear to be quite content with their new form, but have always had difficulty pronouncing the word "monopod." Eventually they combined it with their original name and arrived at *"dufflepud"*—the name by which they are still known. Although subject to the authority of Coriakin, they also follow every suggestion and proposal made by their own chief—no matter how trivial or contradictory it may be.

(C.S. Lewis, *The Voyage of the "Dawn Treader,"* London, 1952)

VONDERVOTTEIMITTISS, a Dutch borough, some distance from any of the main roads. Those desirous of information on the origin of the borough's name should consult the works of Dundergutz, *Oratiunculae de Rebus Praeter-Veteris* or

Blunderbuzzard, *De Derivationibus.* The date of its foundation, however, is unknown.

Just inside the valley—which is paved throughout with flat tiles, and is quite level—extends a continuous row of sixty little houses. These, having their backs against the hills, must look, of course, towards the centre of the plain which is just sixty yards from the front door of each dwelling. Every house has a small garden before it with a circular path, a sun-dial and twenty-four cabbages. The buildings themselves are so precisely alike that one can in no manner distinguish one from another. Owing to their vast antiquity, the style of architecture is somewhat odd, but it is not for that reason less strikingly picturesque. The houses are fashioned of hard-burnt little bricks, red with black ends so that the walls look like a chessboard blown up to a larger scale. The gables are turned to the front, and cornices as big as the rest of the house project over the eaves and over the main doors. The windows are narrow and deep, with very tiny panes and a great deal of sash. On the roof is a vast quantity of tiles with long curly ears. The woodwork throughout is of a dark hue, and there is much carving on it, with a trifling variety of pattern; for, time out of mind, the carvers of Vondervotteimittiss have never been able to carve more than two objects—a timepiece and a cabbage. But they make these exceedingly well, and intersperse them, with singular ingenuity, wherever they find room for the chisel.

The dwellings are as much alike inside as out, and the furniture is all upon one plan. The floors are of square tiles, the chairs and tables of black wood with thin crooked legs and puppy feet. The mantelpieces are wide and high with not only timepieces and cabbages sculpted over the front but a real timepiece, which makes a prodigious ticking, set in the centre, and a flowerpot containing a cabbage standing on each end by way of outrider. Again, placed between each cabbage and the timepiece is a little large-stomached Chinaman with a great round hole in the middle, through which is seen the dial-plate of a watch.

The fireplaces are large and deep, with fierce crooked-looking firedogs. A huge pot full of sauerkraut and pork hangs over a rousing fire, which the good woman of the house tends.

The most remarkable object in Vondervotteimittiss is situated in the steeple of the Town Council building, the pride and wonder of the village: it is the great clock of seven faces, one on each of the seven sides of the steeple. The whole life of the borough has been regulated for centuries by this clock. The only known disturbance occurred when a stranger interfered with the works and caused the venerable clock to strike thirteen. The cabbages turned red, the furniture took to dancing and the cats and pigs scampered all over the place scratching and squeaking. The stranger is said to have played an Irish tune on a big fiddle while holding the belfry bell-rope in his teeth. It is not known whether the old order has since returned to Vondervotteimittiss.

(Edgar Allan Poe, "The Devil in the Belfry," in *Tales,* Philadelphia, 1845)

VRAIDEX, a mountain beyond the town of Names in the north-west of POICTESME. High on the summit of the cloud-wrapped mountain stands the Doubtful Palace of Miramon, Lord of the Nine Sleeps, who contrives men's dreams and sends them down the mountain in the shape of white vapours which enter men's minds.

The lower slopes of the mountain are bare rock, but they soon give way to a broken plain covered with ironweed and strewn with the bodies of travellers who have died trying to reach the summit. The Doubtful Palace itself stands on a plateau whose only vegetation is a species of wicked-looking trees with yellow and purple foliage. The Palace is built of gold and black lacquer and is decorated with figures of swans, butterflies and tortoises. It is entered through gates of horn and ivory which lead into a red corridor. At the centre of the palace stands one of the teeth of the monster Behemoth.

The approaches to the mountain are guarded by the serpents of the east, north, west and south, dream creatures created by Miramon.

The first rides a black horse, a black falcon perches on its head and it is followed by a black hound. This serpent can be rendered harmless by giving it an egg; it has been told that a magic egg will contain its death and it is therefore afraid of eggs.

The serpent of the north rears its head from the earth, its lower coils wrapped around the foundations of Norroway. It is afraid of bridles because it believes that a magic bridle called Gleipnir made from the breath of a fish, the spittle of birds and the footfall of a cat will cause its death.

The serpent of the west is striped blue and

gold and wears a cap of humming-bird feathers. It guards a bridge on which stands eight spears. It can be bypassed by showing it a turtle; this serpent has been told that it will be killed by Tulapin, the turtle that never lies, and it cannot distinguish Tulapin from any other turtle.

The serpent of the south is the smallest, the most beautiful and the most poisonous of the four. Two of the implements required to overcome it cannot be named; the third is a small hazelwood figure.

The descent from the mountain is also dangerous, as travellers usually encounter Death, Miramon's half-brother, who invites them to mount a black horse. The horse is tireless and those who ride it never return.

(James Branch Cabell, *Figures of Earth. A Comedy of Appearances*, New York, 1921)

VRIL-YA COUNTRY, an underground country, probably under Newcastle, England. The access is through a mine, then down a broad level road illuminated by artificial-gas lamps. This leads to a building with huge Egyptian columns from which a wide valley can be seen, covered with strange vegetation of a red-golden colour, with many lakes and rivulets. Here grow gigantic ferns, tall, cane-like plants bearing clusters of flowers, and enormous fungi. Many savage reptiles roam the valley, including enormous crocodiles, as well as herds of a kind of deer or elk-stag, and a large species of tiger with broader paws and more receding forehead than those found in India. This tiger haunts the shores of lakes and pools and feeds on fish; it is becoming very scarce. There are also many singing birds, usually kept in cages to serve as musical instruments, and a beautiful species of dove with an immense crest of bluish plumage.

The cities have streets with buildings on either side, separated from each other by gardens with rich-coloured vegetation and strange flowers; the gardens are divided by low walls. The buildings seem Egyptian, with columns that mimic aloes and ferns. The floors are made of large tessellated blocks of precious metals, partly covered with mat-like carpeting and abundant cushions and divans. Open lifts, descending from the ceiling, lead onto the upper floors. The walls, decorated with spars and metals and uncut jewels, encase large unglazed windows, which, at the touch of a spring, are covered by a shutter made of a substance less transparent than glass. Delicious fragrances emanate from elaborately sculptured

The Egyptian colonnade at the entrance to VRIL-YA COUNTRY.

censers made of gold. Most houses have spacious balconies.

The inhabitants, called Vril-ya, can heal with the touch of their lips. Their books are tiny, and are kept in libraries much like the European ones. They use robots as servants. They have a telegraphic system: a metallic plate inscribed with strange figures enables them to send telegraphic messages from their homes. They believe in a sort of electric-cum-magnetic and galvanic force called *vril*. *Vril* in the hollow of a rod directed by the hand of a child can shatter any building.

The most important office in Vril-ya Country is that of Provisioner of Light, to ensure that light is always readily available. Men and women have equal rights, but physically women are stronger and are therefore heads of State. Children are used in factories as manual workers. Their entertainments are either sports in the air (because all Vril-ya are winged) or music in public halls. There are also theatres in which ancient dramas, reminiscent of the Chinese, are sometimes enacted.

The Vril-ya live to about a hundred and thirty and when they die they are cremated. Before cremation their coffins are marked "Lent to us—(date of birth)" and "Recalled from us— (date of death)." Their day consists of twenty hours: eight "silent hours," eight "earnest hours" and four "easy hours."

Physically they resemble the images of demons seen on Etruscan vases or on the walls of Eastern sepulchres. Their faces are like that of the Sphinx, with red skin and large black eyes. They have musical voices. They are tall but not gigantic and when they fold their large wings over their breasts, the tips reach their knees. They wear under-tunics and leggings of some thin, fibrous material.

There are several tribes of Vril-ya, each of about twelve thousand families. Each tribe occupies a territory sufficient for its own needs and at certain periods the surplus population departs voluntarily to seek a realm of its own. The principle of their government is unity. They elect a single supreme magistrate called the Tur, who holds this office for life and is not distinguished from the rest of the Vril-ya by superior habitation or revenue. Crime is utterly unknown here; there are no courts of criminal justice. The rare instances of civil dispute are referred for arbitration to mutual friends or decided by the Council of Sages. There are no laws; obedience is instinctive. The Vril-ya have a

proverb: "No happiness without order, no order without authority, no authority without unity." Rudeness is unthinkable among the Vril-ya and even the youngest children are taught to despise any vehement emotional demonstration.

They have one common language but several dialects based on exchangeable prefixes. *Gl-* means an assemblage or union of things and *oon* means house; thus *Gloon* means "town." *Na-* is something antagonistic to life or joy or comfort. Thus *Nax* means "darkness"; *Narl*, "death"; *Nania*, "sin" or "evil." There are four cases, three with varying terminations and a fourth with a differing prefix:

	SINGULAR	
NOM.	*An*	Man
DAT.	*Ano*	to *Man*
ACC.	*Anam*	Man
VOC.	*Hil-An*	O Man!

	PLURAL	
NOM.	*Ana*	Men
DAT.	*Anoi*	to Men
ACC.	*Ananda*	Men
VOC.	*Hil-Ananda*	O Men!

Literature is a thing of the past. The writing of history and fiction is forbidden as it is considered detrimental to their happy society. Nothing is permitted to disturb their state of joyous equilibrium.

Vril-ya religion is simple. They believe in the creed they profess and they all practise the precepts which the creed inculcates. Their god—divine creator and sustainer of the Universe—is seen by the Vril-ya as the well-spring of *vril*, transmitting every conceivable idea, because the capacity for creating a thought on his own is impossible for common man. The Vril-ya believe they are descended from frogs.

(Edward George Earle Lytton Bulwer, Lord Lytton, *The Coming Race*, London, 1871)

VULPIA, see LOONARIE.

VULPINA, see URSINA.

W

WAFERDANOS, an island in the North Atlantic, half-way between Great Britain and Newfoundland. The climate is benign, the forests deep, the hunting abundant and the land fertile. The Waferdanians are an agreeable race, covered from head to foot with a soft brown fur that keeps them warm; for this reason they wear no clothes. The idea of dressing seems very odd to the Waferdanians, who know no other laws than those of Nature and ignore all crafts and arts. Their architecture is rudimentary: simple bamboo huts fulfil their housing needs. Their diet consists of the animals they hunt and the few vegetables they grow.

The Waferdanian society is based on tolerance, fraternity and mutual aid. The wisest man amongst the Waferdanians is called "King of the People." Every morning he holds court on top of a high bamboo terrace called "The Temple." The entire population comes to greet him and to ask his advice. As soon as the session is over, the king becomes a commoner again just like the others, and joins the daily hunt. The entire population meets again at noon to eat; the rest of the day is spent making love and playing games. Their religion, inspired by their love for Nature, is that of Justice and Brotherhood. In spite of their fondness for philosophical discussions, the Waferdanians are known to get terribly bored and fall into bouts of melancholia.

Nothing has ever upset this monotonous organization, not even the arrival of two ship-wrecked Europeans at the end of the seventeenth century. These visitors tried to use the skin of a *daquir* or three-horned bullock to dress themselves, but the king decided that tradition must be upheld, and nakedness prevailed; nevertheless, he allowed them to wear belts made of *daquir* skin.

(Anonymous, *Voyage Curieux d'un Philadelphe dans des Pays nouvellement Découverts*, The Hague, 1755)

WAITING WIFE, a mountain in the north of Hsinhsien in Wuchang, China, which greatly resembles a woman. History has it that, in ancient times, a married soldier was sent by the Emperor to fight far away from home. His devoted wife, leading their young child, saw him off at the foot of the hill and stood there gazing after him for days and months and years till in the end she turned into stone.

(Anonymous, *Tal-Ping Geographical Record*, 981 AD)

WANDERERS, ISLAND OF THE, somewhere in the Western Ocean; its precise location remains unknown. The original settlers on the island are direct descendants of a Greek colony. They still speak classical Greek and retain the ancient customs of their ancestors.

The capital of the island is a white-walled city overlooking the green ocean that surrounds it. Marble palaces line the central square—a popular meeting place where a beautiful fountain bubbles. On one side of the square stands a gracious temple where the ancient gods are worshipped in the traditional manner. To the north rises the pillared Council House, its porch decorated with golden images of the gods. The city's ruler (whose badge of office is a long, intricately carved ebony wand with silver bands) meets in the Council House for deliberations.

The island is rich and its houses are usually decorated with costly silken tapestries. The drinking vessels are of solid gold.

The island takes its name not from the first settlers but from a company of travellers who reached it during the Middle Ages. There were of various nationalities and had left Europe, then in the grip of the Black Death, to seek the Earthly Paradise, which they never succeeded in finding. The wanderers, or those of their number who survived the hazards of their journeys, settled on the island where they were received with great generosity and civility.

It was after their arrival that the custom of twice-monthly feasts began. At these feasts, the Greeks and the wanderers take it in turn to tell stories and sagas; Greek legends, myths of the North and tales of the East.

(William Morris, *The Earthly Paradise, A Poem*, London, 1868)

WANDERING ROCKS, a group of drifting islands in the Mediterranean pushed by strong currents. Many ships are said to have sunk against

The WANDERING ROCKS.

their craggy shores. Captain Jason of the *Argo* survived an encounter with them during his famous journey but inexperienced travellers are advised to avoid them if at all possible.

(Homer, *The Odyssey,* 9th cen. [?] BC; Apollonius of Rhodes, *Argonautica,* 2nd cen. BC)

WAQ ARCHIPELAGO, consisting of seven islands, in an undefined region of the Indian Ocean. Its name derives from a mountain on which grows a large tree whose branches resemble human heads. At sunrise these heads cry out *"Waq, Waq, khallaq,"* which in Arabic means, "Waq, Waq, praise the Creator." The ceremony is repeated at sunset. Strangers are not welcome; even the merchants who bring their goods to the archipelago simply leave them on the coast of the first island they reach, and take in exchange the goods left for them by invisible hands; they depart without seeing anyone.

The truth is that the inhabitants of Waq are all women. At night they come down to the beach and collect what the merchants have left. Along the beach are innumerable benches where they rest from their weary labours, and travellers who wish to visit the Waq Archipelago are advised to hide under one of these benches and, at dusk, grab

hold of a lady's leg, requesting her help and protection; he will thus be able to visit the island in peace.

To visit all seven islands properly, the traveller will need at least seven months, travelling both day and night. First he will come to the Land of Birds, where it is impossible to hear anything but the beating of wings and singing. Next he will visit the Land of Wild Beasts, loud with the roaring of lions, the howling of hyenas and the barking of wolves. Then he will be shown the Land of the Genii: their screams, the flames that issue from their mouths and their desperate gestures forbidding one to pass make it difficult to see or hear anything else; travellers are advised not to look backwards if they hold their lives dear. After three more islands—which deserve no special mention—the visitor will finally come to the seventh island, crowned by a large mountain range crossed by a bubbling river; the highest mountain in the range is Mount Waq itself. All seven islands are ruled by the daughter of a king. She commands an army of young virgins clad in coats of mail and armed with scimitars; visitors are not advised to make her acquaintance.

(Anonymous, *The Arabian Nights,* 14th–16th cen. AD) *Map on following page*

WASTEPAPERLAND, a land of uncertain location, where all the stupid books ever produced lie in heaps, like leaves in a winter wood. The people of the country dig and grub around in the piles to make worse books out of bad ones and trash the chaff so that they can save the dust which they then sell. They make a fairly good living at their trade, particularly those who specialize in children's books and modern romantic fiction.

(Charles Kingsley, *The Water-Babies: A Fairy Tale for a Land-Baby,* London, 1863)

WATCHER'S CORNER, a place on the border between an unnamed settlement and the desert, somewhere in Asia Minor. It is guarded by a monstrous creature who walks about absorbed in the contemplation of the horizon. When travellers ask what its purpose is, keeping watch in this dreary place, it answers in a mournful voice that it is waiting for someone who has come from the desert. Should the traveller ask for whom it is waiting it

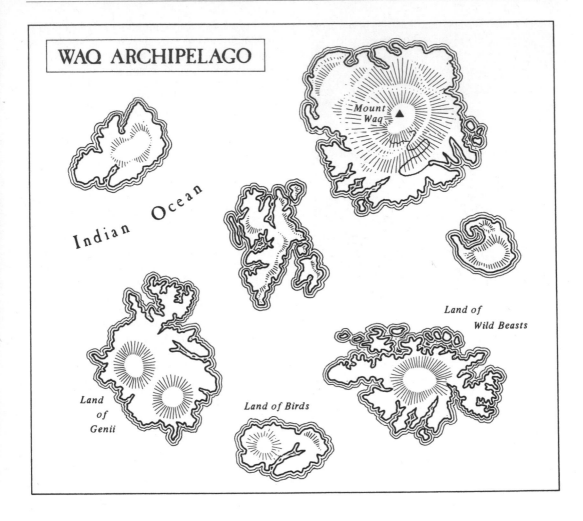

WAQ ARCHIPELAGO

Indian Ocean

Mount Waq ▲

Land of Wild Beasts

Land of Genii

Land of Birds

will, if the question is put it during the day, refuse to answer. But if the question is asked in the early hours of the evening, when the creature is weary of watching and walking and exhausted from strenuous expectation, it will sit on a rock and turn its worried and mournful face towards the desert, stare at its enquirer's face, then cast its eyes back to the horizon, turn away once more and speak from within itself: "I am waiting for a camel with two lit candles on its humps." And the creature will tell the traveller about this marvellous camel, who after saving a giant from an awkward plight had a candle placed on each of its humps, and both wicks lit with one fire, after which it turned its face towards the desert and walked away to bring light and good tidings to all mortals, but has not yet returned.

(Der Nister [Pinhas Kahanovitch], *Gedakht*, Berlin, 1922)

WATHORT, a large island on the southern edge of the Inmost Sea of EARTHSEA. Hort, on the northern coast, is one of the major ports of the archipelago and an important centre for trade throughout the entire South Reach. Here the great galleys of the Inland Sea can be seen side by side with the ships that ply the southern waters of Earthsea. The former are mainly oared vessels which hug the coastline and spend the night in port whenever possible, but the ships of the south are lean and long with high triangular sails to catch the upper air during the hot calms that affect the southern seas.

Hort Town is built on three hills and in the steep valleys between them. The town rises sharply from the broad bay and harbour into a labyrinth of narrow, twisting alleys and lanes. In places, the attic roofs almost meet overhead and the streets become tunnels rather than open thoroughfares. Where the streets are slightly wider, they are covered by coloured awnings which serve to shade the open markets. The houses themselves usually have roofs of purple-red tiles and are painted red, orange, yellow or white.

Although Hort trades in most of the commodities found in Earthsea, from the silks of LORBANERY to the *fleecefells* of GONT, it also has a somewhat unsavoury reputation for piracy and for being at the heart of the slave trade in the South Reach.

Like much of Earthsea, Wathort was badly affected by the appearance of evil and corrupt powers in the archipelago many years ago. Hort fell into decline and was soon left without any real government. Some of its former rulers resigned; others died or were assassinated and the city came under the control of various chiefs, each as head of his part of the city. The port itself came under the control of the guards, who charged exorbitant prices to see that the anchored ships came to no harm. The magic that had once been so widely practised dwindled; no longer did sorcerers perform the tricks of illusion which had once added so much to the attraction of the markets. But the worse affliction was the introduction of a drug known as *hazia*.

Hazia is a narcotic which soothes the body and allows the mind to roam free in a dreamland. It is highly addictive and prolonged use usually leads to paralysis and death. During the years of decadence, the streets and squares of the town were lined with people under the influence of the drug. They would sit or lie motionless in the sunshine, ignoring the flies that settled on their bruised, blackish lips. The drug seemed to permeate the whole town and to soil every aspect of its life. Prices in the markets rose higher and higher and the quality of the goods on sale declined badly, but few people seemed to care or notice, so great was their addiction. In spite of this, Hort remained

a beautiful city, with its bright houses and the dark red flowers of its *pendich* trees.

Wathort and its port have now been restored to their former spendour after the reunification of Earthsea under one king.

(Ursula K. Le Guin, *A Wizard of Earthsea*, New York, 1968; Ursula K. Le Guin, *The Farthest Shore*, London, 1973)

WATKINSLAND, an offshore island, or perhaps part of the mainland, of Latin America. Only the coastal strip and the high plateau immediately above it have been visited and described in any detail.

The main beach is a white curve of level sand, beyond which a broad river cascades down through thick woods. As the ground rises, the river becomes shallower and is broken by rocks, rapids and small islands. A path, clearly man-made, follows the bank for some of the way and then leaves it, leading to the foot of the walls of the high plateau. The only route to the top of the plateau is through a steep rock chimney.

To climb the chimney it is necessary to have the skill and techniques of a professional rock climber. After squirming up the chimney—pressing shoulders to one wall and the feet to the other—the climber will come to a narrow ledge below a mirror-smooth rock face, some twenty to thirty feet high. The rough path that crosses it is almost invisible and may appear to be just a scratch mark on the otherwise limpid rock.

Finally, a broad savannah on the top of the plateau is reached. In the distance, high mountains can be seen, some fifty miles to the west. The same river now crosses the savannah where enormous herds of milk-white cattle graze, and plunges into a chasm in the earth, emerging some hundred feet below.

Travellers to Watkinsland should visit the ruins of an abandoned city that can be seen on the high plateau. No one knows who built it or when or why it was abandoned. It stands on the edge of the plateau, overlooking the river and the forests and beaches below, built of stone and of bricks of time-hardened clay. The buildings are all roofless, perhaps because they were once roofed with thatch or tiles that could not withstand the force of rains and gales. All the walls are intact, as well as the floors made of delicate mosaics in blue, green and gold. Trees and flowering plants flourish among the empty buildings, presumably all that remain of the city's gardens. In the middle of the city is a large square of smooth stone, unbroken by the water channels that connect all buildings elsewhere. It is between seventy and one hundred yards across and an inner circle—perhaps fifty yards in diameter—enhances its geometric centre. Strange patterns are traced within the circle, suggestive of flowers and gardens, and of a certain correspondence with the movements of the sky.

The only people known to inhabit Watkinsland live in the forests that also grow on the plateau; they never seem to venture into the deserted city. The inhabitants are armed with bows and arrows and hunt the cattle of the plain. They eat the meat after roasting it on an open fire and drink the cattle's blood, which apparently inebriates them. Their meals are accompanied by singing and have an almost murderous, orgiastic quality.

The atmosphere of Watkinsland is calm and peaceful, and neither birds nor animals show any fear of men. Large cats, somewhat like leopards or panthers, have been seen near the coast but do not appear to be hostile.

The fauna of Watkinsland includes several curious species which have not been found elsewhere. A huge bird, with a wingspan of ten to twelve feet, and at least four feet high when perching, has been seen in the dusky woods. Apart from the yellow beak, which is perfectly straight and gives it an air of severity, it is completely white. A species of chimpanzee is often seen near the empty city, as well as a creature best described as a rat-dog. It has the head of a monkey, but the close brown fur of a dog and a long, scaly tail like that of a rat. It is as tall as a man when it walks on its hind legs, which it does most of the time. It seems, however, that it originally went on all fours and now has problems with its vision when walking erect, as its eyes do not focus in that position.

The rat-dogs communicate in barks and whistles and seem to be able to use sticks and stones as crude weapons. Their social organization does not appear to be highly developed. Usually they move in groups or packs, sometimes mixed and normally dominated by one individual, either male or female; because they quarrel and bicker constantly, the groups are always changing. A large number remain solitary and their attempts to join groups are not infrequently frustrated by the hostile group members.

The main activities of the rat-dogs are fighting, scuffling and mating. Their level of sexual activity is high, perhaps because the genitals are almost permanently displayed. The females are distinguished by a scarlet-edged strip from the anus to the lower belly; the sight of the female genitals is enough to arouse violent sexual excitement in the males. Much of the day is spent in sexual display, openly attracting the attention of others' partners, appropriating them and watching third parties mate. Although the rat-dogs seek privacy for sexual intercourse, the couple is inevitably followed by a crowd of spectators who become so stimulated themselves that they also begin to mate. One coupling is enough to spark off a sexual frenzy that may last for half a day or more.

The rat-dogs clearly consider themselves the dominant species, and this appears to be accepted by the other animals of Watkinsland. On the other hand, extremely violent battles have been observed between them and the chimpanzees. In the intoxication of the fight, members of the same species may even turn on each other. Cannibalism has been noted, but both species seem to practise primitive funeral rites and have been seen to drag corpses to the river and plunge them into the chasm.

Watkinsland is named after Charles Watkins, a professor of classics at Cambridge. According to his own account, he was brought here by a porpoise after having been shipwrecked in the south Atlantic.

Again according to the professor, a glowing disc of light, which he implies was a flying saucer, made use of the circle at the centre of the abandoned city as a kind of landing place. Though Professor Watkins' account has yet to be corroborated, travellers are advised to proceed with caution.

(Doris Lessing, *Briefing for a Descent into Hell*, London, 1971)

WEATHER HILLS, a range of hills on the north side of the road between BREE-LAND and the Mitheithel, a stream flowing across the ETTEN-MOORS. The Weather Hills rise in an undulating ridge to a height of almost one thousand feet and were at one time of great strategic importance.

The visitor who climbs to the top will be able to see much of the north of MIDDLE-EARTH, and on a clear day the peaks of the MISTY MOUNTAINS may be visible to the east.

The ruins in the hills testify to the historical importance of the area. At the summit of Weathertop, the tallest and southernmost hill, is a stone ring. This is all that remains of the great watch tower Amon Sûl, built in the early days of the vanished kingdom of ARNOR. Amon Sûl was the site of one of the *palantíri*, or Seeing-stones, that allowed the Men of the West to watch over their lands. And it was at Amon Sûl that their king, Elendil, awaited the arrival of his friend Gilgalad, last of the great Elven-kings, before they led their allied armies into battle against Sauron, Dark Lord of MORDOR. Both kings were slain by Sauron on ORODRUIN, a volcanic peak in Mordor.

Later, in the Third Age, the hills were fortified by the Men of the West during their struggle against Angmar, the kingdom of the Witch-king. The broken remains of the forts and walls built then can still be seen.

It was here on Weathertop that Frodo, perhaps the most famous of the hobbits of the SHIRE, was wounded by the Ringwraiths, or Nazgûl, during the War of the Ring. It is believed that the Lord of the Nazgûl was in fact the Witch-king of Angmar, in a new form. And this is one of the few areas where *athelas* (kingsfoil) grows. *Athelas* is a herb apparently brought to Middle-earth by the Men of the West, for it grows only in places where they lived or camped. It has a sweet pungent smell and is believed to have great powers for the healing of wounds.

(J.R.R. Tolkien, *The Fellowship of the Ring*, London, 1954; J.R.R. Tolkien, *The Return of the King*, London, 1955)

WEEPING ISLE, see EBUDA.

WELL AT THE WORLD'S END, LAND OF THE, to the north of UPMEADS, probably in northern Europe, a haven for those travellers who wish to improve their personal appearance.

The road to the Well itself is clearly marked. Beyond the mountains known as the Wall of the World, the traveller will reach a wide lava field. The way across this, indicated by signs carved in the rock (a sword crossed by a three-leaved bough), leads over a grassy plain and into a sec-

ond mountain range. Here stands the statue of a knight in armour, a sword in his hand, pointing towards a pass which eventually opens out onto small valleys.

The same sign of the sword and bough marks a cave where the traveller may rest. From here the road runs straight ahead, and after eight days' walk the traveller will reach the Land of the Innocent, which does not merit a prolonged visit. Another twelve days will bring him to a desolate wasteland, in which the only building is the House of the Sorcerers, inhabited by an old man and his grandsons who will provide hospitality. The House stands within a small woodland, beyond which lies a stony desert strewn with the bodies of those who have tried to cross it.

In spite of this warning, the traveller should proceed undaunted. Should he succeed in crossing, he will arrive in a valley shaped like an amphitheatre, which houses a dead, leafless tree growing in a pool of poisonous water, hung with the shields and weapons of many knights; the bodies of dead men, women and children mount guard on the slopes of the valley. Another two days' travel and he will reach a ridge of black rock on the River of Good Water.

A stairway cut into the cliff appears to lead only to the sea, but at low tide it gives access to a beach of black sand, and a large stone enclosure filled with water from a spring. An inscription reads: "Ye who have come a long way to look upon me, drink of me, if ye deem that ye be strong enough in desire to bear length of days; or else drink not; but tell your friends and the kindreds of the earth how you have seen a great marvel." The visitor will find a golden cup at hand, bearing the inscription "The strong of heart will drink of me." This is the Well at the World's End; those who drink from it are granted long lives and an unchangingly youthful appearance. All scars are removed from their bodies and they are said to look like the very gods that rule this earth. Not many travellers are known to have reached it.

(William Morris, *The Well at the World's End*, London, 1896) *Map on following page*

WENG, a remote and gloomy village in the Austrian Mountains. A railway station lies five kilometres down the mountain in the industrial valley,

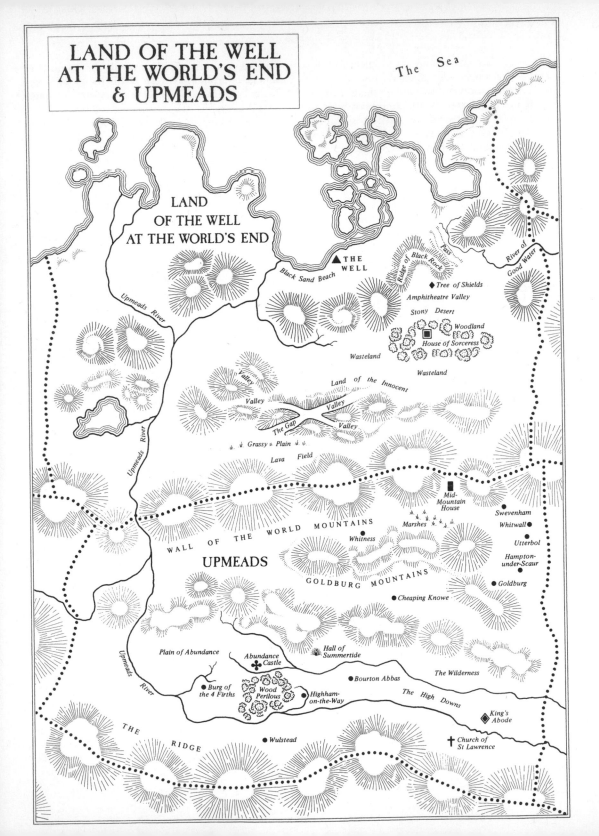

but the village itself can only be reached by foot. Travellers are greeted by howling dogs and a bleak, effaced landscape, said, however, to be more attractive than many of the beautiful landscapes of the world. The effect of this attraction is such that it can drive some people insane, and travellers are therefore advised to divert their attention by whoring, praying or drinking.

Weng is inhabited by a race of dwarf-like, feeble-minded people, no taller than 1.40 metres, all conceived in drunkenness, with high-pitched voices like those of children.

(Thomas Bernhard, *Frost*, Frankfurt, 1963)

WESTERN WILD, a mountainous region to the west of NARNIA. Among its high peaks lies a tranquil lake, the source of the Great River. On a grassy hill above the lake, crowned by a ring of turf, rise the golden gates that give access to one of the most marvellous gardens in the world.

Travellers can visit the gardens for one of three reasons: to atone for their sins, to seek personal gratification or to comply with an order from Aslan, creator of Narnia. They can either walk to the garden across mountains and river valleys or they can be brought here on Fledge, a flying horse which serves as transport between Narnia and the Western Wild.

The golden gates bear an inscription in silver letters that should not be disregarded:

> *Come in by the gold gates or not at all,*
> *Take of my fruits for others or forbear.*
> *For those who steal or those who climb my*
> *   wall*
> *Shall find their heart's desire and find*
> *   despair.*

The gates need only be touched slightly to be opened. Behind them rises the tree of silver apples. Should a traveller be given one of the apples, he will achieve great happiness; but should he steal one, he will be overcome by weariness and forevermore loathe the taste of the fruit.

Two animals are known to inhabit the garden: a talking mouse and a beautiful bird. The bird acts as a sentinel, watching those who arrive from its perch in the trees. It is larger than an eagle, with a saffron breast, a purple tail and a scarlet crest.

(C.S. Lewis, *The Magician's Nephew*, London, 1955; C.S. Lewis, *The Last Battle*, London, 1956)

WESTFARTHING, see The SHIRE.

WHERE-NOBODY-TALKS, a country located within the sound of our voice, right next to the country Where-People-Do-Talk. Streets and sidewalks, rooftops and automobile windshields are all covered with a thick, invisible snow which stifles everything.

The inhabitants are mute. But that does not mean that they do not understand the spoken word; on the contrary, they communicate better with each other than they could using words and sentences. They are like ants running along vines. They meet each other constantly, and tell each other things without ever being heard.

It is never cold in Where-Nobody-Talks, and indeed everything is mild and peaceful. To reach Where-Nobody-Talks, travellers must simply cross neighbouring Where-People-Do-Talk. They will find themselves surrounded by reverberating sounds that are painful to hear: cars, radios, wordmills. Gradually, however, the sounds will start to fight with each other, and finally they will cancel each other out.

(Jean-Marie-Gustave Le Clézio, *Voyages de l'autre côté*, Paris, 1975)

WHIMSIES, LAND OF THE, not far from NOMELAND. The Whimsies are a curious people, with large strong bodies, but extremely small heads, which means that they have very few brains. To compensate for the size of their heads and their lack of brains, the Whimsies habitually wear large pasteboard heads over their own, with pink, green and lavender sheep's wool attached for hair. Their artificial faces are painted in all sorts of strange fashions and the contrast between their large bodies and whimsical features gives these people their name.

The Whimsies are greatly feared because of their strength and ferocity in battle. It seems that they cannot be defeated, mainly because they do not have the sense to know when they have been beaten. They are ruled by a chief who is chosen simply because no one else is wiser or more capable of ruling.

A pasteboard head belonging to an inhabitant of the Land of the WHIMSIES.

(L. Frank Baum, *The Emerald City of Oz*, Chicago, 1910)

WHITE HOUSE, a small cottage in Kent, England, not far from Rochester. The house itself is not particularly distinctive, although the ironwork on the roof and coping has been described as an architect's nightmare. The main characteristic and advantage of the house is its isolation, standing as it does between a chalk quarry and a disused gravel pit, far away from any other building.

It was in the gravel pit that a group of five children on holiday at the White House discovered a Psammead, or sand fairy, while trying to dig a hole to take them to Australia. The Psammead appears to be the only one of its species in existence. Its eyes are on long horns, like those of a snail, and they can be moved in and out. The ears are like those of a bat and the plump body is similar to that of a spider. The Psammead is covered in thick fur; its hands and feet resemble a monkey's.

According to the Psammead, itself, it is thousands of years old. It seems that in prehistoric times the species was quite common. They lived in sand beaches where prehistoric children built them sandcastles to live in, but unfortunately the children also built moats around the castles and allowed the tide to flood them. As soon as the Psammeads got

wet they caught cold and usually died as a result. The specimen found in the gravel pit was luckier than most; it never really got wet—only the tip of its top left whisker had ever been in contact with water—and it survived by digging a deep hole in the sand, into which it retreated. For thousands of years it remained hidden from all living creatures.

Travellers are advised that the Psammead can grant wishes which come true, but which last only until sunset. To grant a wish it holds its breath until its eyes stand out and its whole body is puffed up; then it breathes out with a sigh. The wish is granted immediately. If the experience of the children who found it is typical, many of the wishes granted by a Psammead would appear to have embarrassing results. When they wished to be as beautiful as the day, their wish was granted but with the result that their family did not recognize them and actually turned them away from the house. A wish that the gravel pit become full of gold was also fulfilled, but the gold was not accepted currency in England and led to a difficult encounter with the police. A wish to have wings left them stranded on top of a church tower when the magic wore off at sunset.

(Edith Nesbit, *Five Children and It*, London, 1902)

WHITE MAN'S ISLAND, an island located at an unspecified point in the Irish Sea, where the ancient Druids live. Whenever sailors try to approach it, the island disappears. Only one man has ever been able to land, having sailed there on a small piece of rock taken from a cemetery. However, he never came back to tell of his experience, so nothing more is known about this island.

(Hersart de Villemarque, *Romans de anciens Bretons*, Paris, n/d)

WHITE MOUNTAINS, also known as **ERED NIMRAIS**. A range of snow-capped mountains in MIDDLE-EARTH, separating GONDOR and ROHAN. They run from west to east, from MINAS TIRITH almost to the sea. The major peaks are Mount Mindolluin, against which lies Minas Tirith, Starkhorn, which rises above Rohan's fortress at DUNHARROW, and the triple peak of THRIHYRNE above HELM'S DEEP. The subterranean passages called the PATHS OF THE DEAD lead beneath the mountains from Rohan to Gondor.

(J.R.R. Tolkien, *The Fellowship of the Ring*, London, 1954; J.R.R. Tolkien, *The Two Towers*, London, 1954; J.R.R. Tolkien, *The Return of the King*, London, 1955; J.R.R. Tolkien, *The Silmarillion*, London, 1977)

WHITE STONE, ISLAND OF THE, see Isle de la PIERRE BLANCHE.

WICKET, an island not far from CLERKSHIP, inhabited by a terrible tribe known as the Furrycats, who eat small children and live on marble stones. Their hair grows inwards and they have such long, strong, steel-tipped claws that nothing escapes them once they have got their claws into it. Some wear mortarboards, others caps ornamented with four spouts or codpieces, yet others wear modified headgear. All, however, carry as a badge or symbol an open pouch. They are ruled by Archduke Clawpuss, a monster with a harpy's claws, a muzzle like the bill of a raven, tusks like a boar and eyes like the throat of hell itself. He is habitually muffled in mortars and pestles, with only his claws showing. His usual seat is a new rack. When in court, he sits beneath a representation of Clawpussian justice: an old woman wearing spectacles, holding a sickle case in her left hand and the scales of justice in her right. The dishes of the scales are a pair of velvet pouches, one empty and the other full of bullion; this is an accurate representation of the justice of the country. The laws are like a spider's web, designed to catch all the little flies and pretty moths, but easily destroyed by great horseflies (robbers and tyrants). There are no restrictions on landing on Wicket, but the only way of escape is by order or discharge of the court. A hearing before the court almost inevitably involves interrogation, if not juridical torture. The usual (and only) way to avoid punishment is to pay large bribes to the Clawpuss. Indeed, bribery is the principal revenue of the Furrycats, who live extremely well by accepting bribes from all over the world. They are afraid of no one, and people happily pay bribes rather than forfeit their lives to the Furrycats' lust for human blood.

For the Furrycats, vice is virtue, wickedness is goodness and treason is loyalty, while thieving is termed "liberality." Plunder is their watchword. Travellers will know that plague, famine, wars and natural disasters in the whole world should not be attributed to the conjunction of the planets or any other cause, natural or supernatural; they all originate from the plotting and machinations contrived by the Furrycats, who are responsible for all the evil in the world. If they are not stopped by a powerful magistrate or Draconian laws, it is greatly to be feared that one day they will come to rule the world.

(François Rabelais, *Le cinquiesme et dernier livre des faicts et dicts du bon Pantagruel, auquel est contenu la visitation de L'Oracle de la dive Bacbuc, et le mot de la bouteille; pour lequel est enterpris tout ce long voyage*, Paris, 1564)

WILD BEASTS, LAND OF, see WAQ ARCHIPELAGO.

WILD ISLAND, perhaps in the Atlantic Ocean, linked to Tangerina Island by a string of rocks. Wild Island consists mostly of a jungle and a narrow strip of beach, almost cut in two by a river with swampy banks. The jungle is inhabited by wild boars, monkeys, tortoises, tigers that chew gum, rhinoceroses, lions, gorillas and also crocodiles that are fond of lollipops. A certain Elmer Elevator heard of the island from a stray cat he had adopted. He travelled here and rescued a helpless dragon that had fallen from a low cloud and was being used by other animals to ferry them and their goods across the river. On the bank a sign is still visible, reading: "To summon dragon, yank the crank. Report disorderly conduct to gorilla." The crank was attached to a rope, the other end of which was tied around the dragon's neck. Travellers today must use rafts to cross to the other side of the river.

(Ruth Stiles Gannet, *My Father's Dragon*, London, 1957) *Map on following page*

WILD WOOD, an extensive area of woodland on the edge of the water-meadows by RIVER BANK. Seen from a distance, Wild Wood is dense, compact and somewhat menacing. It is rarely visited by the inhabitants of River Bank and those who have strayed into it speak of "the Terror of Wild Wood." Visitors who venture into the wood soon have the feeling that they are being watched and may even see sharp-eyed, cruel faces staring at them from the thick undergrowth. Footsteps and whistling noises can be heard in the bushes, and it is considered inadvisable to go there without a knowledge of the passwords and signs used by the Wild Wooders, as

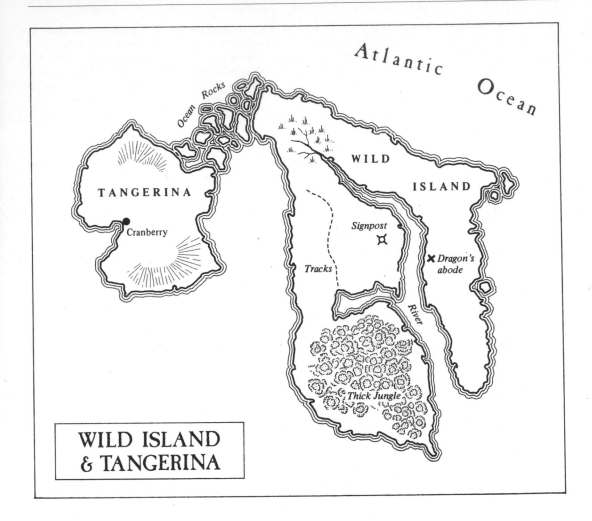

Atlantic Ocean

Ocean Rocks

TANGERINA

Cranberry

WILD ISLAND

Signpost

Tracks

✗ Dragon's abode

River

Thick Jungle

WILD ISLAND & TANGERINA

well as a supply of various plants that should be carried in the pocket as a precaution.

Wild Wood is inhabited by a variety of creatures. The squirrels, hedgehogs and rabbits are harmless (although the latter may be insolent as well as cowardly) but more sinister creatures like foxes, weasels, stoats and ferrets also lurk in dark places—they are not to be trusted.

It seems that Wild Wood was once a city of men but was abandoned for reasons which remain unknown, and that it gradually reverted to its original state; saplings sprang up, leaf-mould covered the ground, streams brought soil into the area, and finally the animals began to move back in.

At the centre of Wild Wood lies the under-

ground home of Mr. Badger, probably the wisest animal in the wood. He lives in an extensive maze of tunnels, many formed from the buried streets and squares of the derelict city. His tunnels and passages lead far and wide under the woods; a number of them have hidden entrances known to him alone, some even beyond the fringe of the woods. His home is warm and comfortable, with an impressive brick-walled kitchen. Oak settles stand on either side of the great hearth, its blazing fire guarded by an arm chair. The brick chimney-corners provide comfortable, draught-free seats. From the wooden rafters hang hams, bunches of herbs and long strings of onions. The other rooms of Mr. Badger's house vary in size;

some are little more than cupboards, others are almost as big as the great banqueting hall in TOAD HALL.

Although Mr. Badger has a reputation for being anti-social, he is in fact a good host as well as a loyal friend. In spite of this, the mother-weasels of the Wood often use his name to frighten and cow their fractious children, telling them that Mr. Badger will get them. As it happens, Badger is rather fond of children, but the warning inevitably has the desired effect.

(Kenneth Grahame, *The Wind in the Willows*, London, 1908)

WINDY ISLAND, see RUACH.

WINKFIELD'S ISLAND, off the east coast of North America. The precise location of the island is uncertain, but it is known to be close to the Island of the IDOL.

The island is named after Miss Unca Eliza Winkfield, who after several years of solitude on the Island of the Idol was able to convert the Indians from their traditional worship of the sun to Christianity. Some time afterwards she married her cousin, a priest who had searched for her and finally found her on the Island of the Idol. Between them, the two completed the conversion of the Indians and Winkfield's Island is now a flourishing Christian community which chooses not to have any relations with Europe or with other foreign countries. Visitors are unwelcome.

(Unca Eliza Winkfield [?], *The Female American; Or The Adventures Of Unca Eliza Winkfield. Compiled by Herself*, London, 1767)

WINTON POND, in a small estate in East Anglia, England, notable for an island of variable size under which lies a maze of tunnels. The pond, which appears sometimes to be as large as a lake, is reached by way of the Dark Walk, a laurel path in the gardens of the estate. The island is said to be the size of a table top but it too is known to become much larger at times. It can be reached either by swimming or wading the lake, or by paddling a raft.

Travellers reaching the island are advised to sleep at Camp Hope, a stopover so named by the area's first explorer, William Wilditch. Some three

hundred yards away rises a great oak of enormous age with roots that coil up above the ground. One of the roots forms an arch more than two feet high, and behind it lies Friday's Cave. From here onwards, the visitor must inch his way like a worm through a low tunnel, descending farther and farther underground. He will finally come to a room or series of rooms; on one of the walls is chiselled the outline of a gigantic fish and a few illegible letters.

This underground dwelling is inhabited by an old couple, a woman who quacks like a duck and a man prone to philosophizing. They live among wasted furniture and potato sacks, and drink a wholesome broth out of a dish marked "Fido." William Wilditch was detained by the old man who insisted that he read to him from the many old newspapers lying around the place. In order to escape, William took the old man by surprise while the woman was not looking and tied him up. His flight from their underground world, pursued by the quacking old woman, was a fearful experience.

The old couple are believed to have an immense treasure hidden underground, which travellers might find tempting: necklaces, bracelets, lockets, bangles, pins, rings, pendants, buttons, tourist mementoes, golden coins, birds made out of precious stones, hairpins with rubies turned into roses, toothpicks of gold, swizzle-sticks, golden spoons to dig the wax out of one's ears, cigarette-holders studded with diamonds, small boxes for pastilles and snuff, key-rings and portraits in gold and enamel. The treasure seems to consist of all the valuable rubbish that people have lost throughout the ages. Should the traveller, once he is back up on the surface, abandon his part of the treasure, it will lose its preciousness as if to efface all traces of its underground life.

The letter *W* seems to be important in this underground place, perhaps because it is the only one in the alphabet which takes on another meaning when upside down; while travellers who have already visited WONDERLAND may recognize in the discourse of the old man some of Wonderland's preaching characters.

(Graham Greene, "Under the Garden," in *A Sense of Reality*, London, 1963)

WISDOM, ISLES OF, an archipelago of some three to four hundred islands to the north and north-east of the Tuscarora Sound in the north

Pacific. Their total surface area is less than one thousand square miles. Their small size and their distance from any shipping lanes no doubt explains why they have remained hidden from the world so long. The Isles of Wisdom were first visited by an American expedition in the early 1920's. Not all the islands were visited and the reports brought back by the expedition are in some ways fragmentary.

Although isolated, the people of the Isles of Wisdom have for centuries sent out disguised citizens to study events in foreign countries and to bring back scientific and other information. Great quantities of books—many of them extremely rare in their countries of origin—have been brought back to the archipelago and the ideas expressed in them have formed the basis for the different cultures and civilizations found on the islands.

In terms of civilization the islands differ vastly, from the mechanized society of SARRA-GALLA to the culture of HELIKONDA, from the traditional Buddhism of VLÉHA to the deliberately cultivated bureaucracy of Atrocla. Despite their differences, the people of the archipelago are united by their common language and by their shared determination to remain independent of the outside world. (The major islands are described separately; apart from those already mentioned, see VORELA, KRADAK and BALEUTA.)

All the islands use the same currency: the *dragoma*, divided into one hundred *dragominas*, is roughly equivalent to twenty-five American cents, but in practice the exchange rate varies considerably. On Baleuta, for instance, the American expedition had to pay ten dollars per *dragoma*.

The island of Dubiaxo is inhabited by a sect of sceptics. They are, as a nation, obsessed with the idea that man cannot know anything with certainty and have expressed doubts as to their own existence. According to their philosophy, doubt is the sovereign of thought. The island is ruled by the Sceptophylax, whose role it is to ensure that scepticism, argument and doubt are instilled into everything. Particular attention is paid to introducing a degree of doubt and uncertainty into all subjects taught in the island's schools.

The contrast between Dubiaxo and the neighbouring island of Tivalera is typical of the archipelago. The people here have been familiar with the principles of relativity for more than four hundred years. The theory of relativity was first discovered by Olhazen, a contemporary of Copernicus, and is now so well known to the islanders that they are ac-

tually born with innate relative ideas. A child playing with a hoop, for example, has no difficulty in contemplating the idea that, in relative terms, his hoop may be stationary and the earth moving. The theory of relativity is reflected in the speech of the islanders, who when asked what the time is may well answer "six metres." In similar fashion, the sentence "This carriage moves along the road" is strictly equivalent to "The road moves inversely under the carriage"; "He beats about the bush" is equivalent to "The bush beats about him."

All public authorities and institutions, from marriage to government, are regarded as being of relative importance; officials, officers of state and marriage partners are therefore interchangeable.

The people of Tivalera are reported to be carrying out experiments in the reversal of time, using very fast-moving roundabouts.

Neighbouring Obalsa, by contrast, is ruled by the philosophy of "as if." The island was once a constitutional monarchy, with the king ruling "as if" he were bound by the constitution. He was subsequently dethroned, his erstwhile subjects behaving "as if" they had never had any monarchical feelings. Obalsa is now a republic, to which all its citizens pledge their allegiance "as if" they had always done so.

In Obalsa, divorce is as common as marriage. In the initial stages of their marriage, couples are convinced that they cannot live without their desired partner; this rapidly gives way to the equally strong conviction that life together is quite impossible. While they are still married, they live "as if" life were not designed to be lived in pairs, giving numerous parties, urgently pressing guests to stay until all hours as if they really did not want to see them go. Later on, they pretend that they are very much in love, when in fact they can hardly stand each other.

Art and literature are assiduously cultivated, and poets, writers and painters work away feverishly, as if something dreadful might happen to them if they even once put down their pens or brushes. It is typical of life on Obalsa that an excessive importance is given to symbols of all kinds; the national flag, for example, is much more important to the people than the ideal it represents.

Of all the lesser islands of the archipelago, the one to be avoided by visitors is Atrocla. This was once the wealthiest of all the islands, so much so that all citizens were paid a monthly allowance by the State instead of having to pay taxes to it. The

ISLES OF WISDOM

notion then emerged that if a man is too happy he will begin to degenerate, and ways were sought to introduce a balance of pain and pleasure into island life. Institutions were set up to determine how to achieve this end in accordance with the *Ars complicatoria,* the art of so complicating all the demands of life that not even a genius can disentangle them. An increasingly great torrent of obscure and difficult laws were promulgated, along with rules and regulations covering every aspect of day-to-day life. The result was that in a very short time virtually all islanders had been found guilty of breaking one or other of the laws and had been duly punished. Those who escaped punishment soon came to be regarded with great suspicion by their fellows.

All laws passed in Atrocla are recorded in the 350,000 volumes stored in the National Library. The catalogues are kept under lock and key to prevent any leakage of information. In order to further frustrate those seeking knowledge of the laws, there are now two categories of librarian—those who give no information at all and those who give only false and misleading information. The State assiduously cultivates the art of statistics, thereby ensuring that the population is perpetually occupied in filling in forms, a task which not infrequently takes all day and half the night. In order to process the statistics thus obtained, an army of officials—all enjoying opulent salaries—has grown to vast proportions.

Tax is levied on everything. Every word in the language is carefully assessed for its fiscal value to the State; vices, virtues and follies are all taxed. Even honesty itself is subject to taxation. The result is that the wheels of the State absorb all the gold that passes through them. On Atrocla, the State has finally achieved the minimum effect with the maximum possible effort.

The island of Delix is in many ways the direct opposite of Atrocla. Physically and climatically, the island enjoys all possible natural advantages, and its people are bent on enjoying themselves in every way. Their concern for pleasure is so great that they often imagine themselves to be living in the earthly paradises described by the classical writers. In reality, they lead a pleasant, urbane life, convinced that if they absorb enough pleasant things they will finally come to feel that they are leading perfectly happy lives.

In the past, the Ministry of Pleasure existed to provide feasts along the lines of those described by Epicurus. This, unfortunately, led to several deaths from over-indulgence and gave way to the cult of physical health, now seen as the true basis of happiness. Everything was scientifically calculated so as to prolong life as long as possible; even the motions of the jaw in eating were accurately measured and described. Health regulations covering almost every aspect of day-to-day life were issued, with particularly stern warnings against the dangers posed by the "kissing bacilli." It seems that this concern for health is now being abandoned and that many of the islanders are adopting the ideas of the Cynics, claiming that these represent the path of true happiness.

The political differences that can be observed to exist among the islands of the archipelago are well-illustrated by the "pacifist" islands of Allalina and O-Blaha. The former is more typical of the two. On Allalina, all laws are derived from a sacred book, the *Trismagest,* which states quite clearly that all sinners must be forgiven and that no man should be used as an object for revenge. On the other hand, the island's law also invokes the law of "an eye for an eye, a tooth for a tooth." In order to overcome the contradiction between the two systems, two sets of tribunals have been established, both with incorruptible judges. One set is extremely harsh, the other correspondingly mild; the choice of tribunal is settled by drawing lots. There are twelve levels of court and a convicted person may always appeal to the next court in the hierarchy. Finally, he may appeal to the nation as a whole, the final verdict being given by plebiscite. One of the peculiarities of the law of Allalina is that the intention is tried as well as the action. Thus, a virgin is known to be in prison for having tried to procure an abortion for herself; she believed she was pregnant and acted accordingly. Although she was of course innocent of *having* an abortion, she was guilty of intending to do so and was therefore imprisoned.

Relations between Allalina and O-Blaha have recently become very strained. Traditionally, both islands share the ideal of pacifism and of the suppression of all egotistical feelings by right-thinking and right-acting. Over the years they have made intensive studies of all known systems of ethics but have so far been unable to decide what the word "ethics" actually means. In time, Allalina became the home of the more idealistic "left" pacifists, while the more practical "rightists" came to predominate on O-Blaha. A joint conference was held to try and overcome their differences but while they could agree on demands for the abolition of war and for the human race becoming a single happy family, important disagreements arose over the possibility of a just war. The conference ended in great disarray, and a state of war was declared between the two pacifist islands. They are now reported to be arming themselves with advanced and dangerous weapons, both sides relying on Sarragalla for their supplies.

Finally, the lesser island of Zyundal, the homeland of the Pramites, deserves a mention. The Pramites are a race of unknown origin who traditionally wandered through the whole archipelago, often persecuted and scorned by the other islanders, until they finally settled peacefully on

Zyundal. But it now seems that anti-Pramitic feeling has begun to emerge there too. It also seems that many of the settlers wish to leave, as though they actually preferred their earlier wandering existence in spite of all the problems it posed.

(Alexander Moszkowski, *Die Inseln der Weisheit, Geschichte einer abenteuerlichen Entdeckungsfahrt*, Berlin, 1922)

WISDOM KINGDOM, reached via a tollbooth. Travellers wishing to visit the kingdom are given a kit containing maps, coins and a book of rules; results are not guaranteed but waste of time will be refunded.

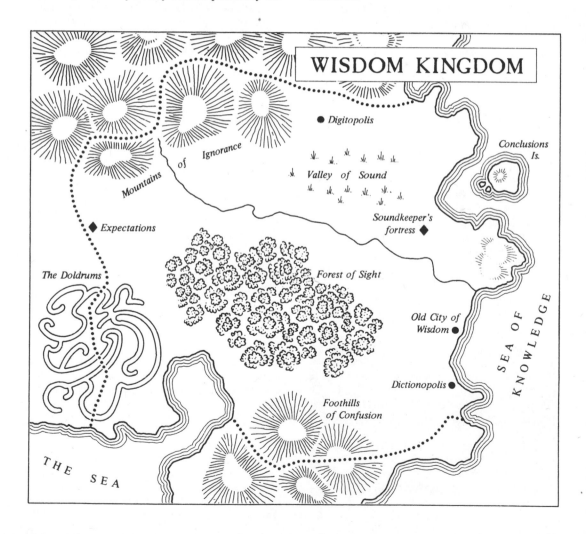

Wisdom Kingdom was once known as the Land of Null, a barren, frightening wilderness inhabited by the demons of darkness. History tells us that a young prince crossed the Sea of Knowledge in search of the future and laid claim to Null in the name of goodness and truth. The old city of Wisdom, constantly besieged by demons, monsters and giants, became under his rule a prosperous kingdom. The prince's two sons set out to found new towns, and established DICTIONOPOLIS in the south and DIGITOPOLIS in the north, at the foot of the Mountains of IGNORANCE. The new cities became rivals after an argument about whether words or numbers were more important than wisdom, and their constant bickering brought ruin to Wisdom Kingdom. However, the king's two adopted daughters, Rhyme and Reason, managed to assemble the armies of Wisdom, lead them into victorious battle and re-establish a peaceful reign.

(Norton Juster, *The Phantom Tollbooth*, London, 1962)

WISH HOUSE, see SMALLDENE.

WITLINGEN ISLAND, see LOONARIE.

WOLF'S GLEN, in Bohemia. Travellers who are keen sportsmen can obtain here seven magic bullets from Samiel, the wild huntsman, in exchange for their souls. Of these bullets, six will go true to their mark and the seventh wherever the huntsman wills it. The glen is cumbered with the ghosts of deceased parents who try to warn their children

A view of WOLF'S GLEN in Bohemia.

away. Cadavers and spooky-looking animals crawl among the caves in the rocks, spitting flames and sparks.

(Carl Maria, Freiherr von Weber & Johann Friedrich Kind, *Der Freischütz*, first performance, Berlin, 1821)

WOMEN'S ISLAND, a large island in the China Sea populated exclusively by women. Three days' travel separates the island from any other inhabited place. The women become pregnant either through seeds carried by the wind or by eating the fruit of a certain local tree. In either case, they give birth only to children of the female sex. Male visitors are warned that they will not be welcomed; they will be either put to death or set on a ship and forced to leave the island.

The most notable building on Women's Island is the House of the Sun, because the sun rises on its eastern side and sets behind its western wall. When this happens, all the inhabitants run out of their houses, shouting, "There it is! There it is!" and worship the sun with prayers and various genuflexions.

(Anonymous, *Le livre de merveilles de l'Inde*, transl. L.M. Devic, Leiden, 1883–86)

WONDER, LAND OF, far beyond the Mountains of Darkness, on the other side of the Sambatyon River, inhabited solely by red-haired Jews. Faithstone, the royal residence in the country's capital, is a high, white marble palace standing in a luxuriant green park, with hundreds of golden columns and thousands of diamond windows.

Land of Wonder is famous because it was here that a tribe of black dwarves made peace with Solomon XXVII, great-great-great-grandson of King Solomon himself. Nothing more is known about the country, except that travellers who have reached it have praised the song of its nightingales which perch in the royal gardens on branches laden with fruit.

(Isaac Lieb Peretz, *Ale Verk,* Vilna, 1912)

WONDERLAND, a kingdom under England, inhabited by a pack of cards and a few other creatures. Access is gained through a rabbit-hole possibly located on the banks of the Thames between Folly Bridge and Godstow, Oxford.

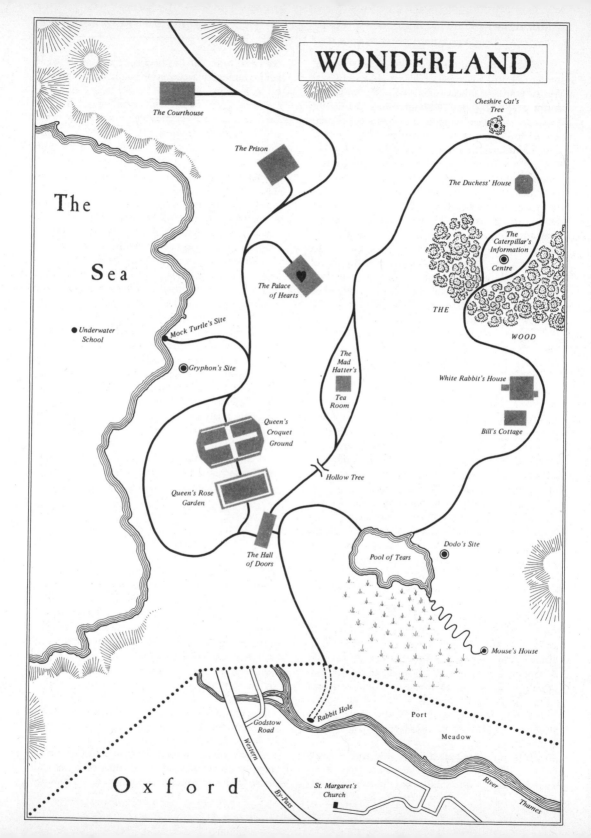

The visitor entering the hole will fall for quite a long way past a number of household articles and finally land on a heap of sticks and dry leaves. From here a long passage leads into a low hall lit by a row of lamps hanging from the roof. There are several doors along the hall but the visitor is advised to use the miniature door concealed behind a low curtain, through which the Queen's Rose Garden can be seen.

The door can be opened with a small golden key found on a solid glass table next to it. In order to fit through the door—if the visitor is larger than a medium-sized rat—it is best that he or she partake of a tonic or of some small cakes, also found on the aforementioned table. Visitors are advised that any food and drink consumed in Wonderland may cause immediate growing or shrinking of the consumer and should therefore be taken with caution.

Several places in Wonderland are worth a visit: the White Rabbit's dainty cottage; the Duchess' house with its spicy though somewhat neglected kitchen: and the Mad Hatter's outdoor tea-room, open all hours.

Wonderland kingdom is ruled by the Queen and King of Hearts, though power is mainly in the hands of the Queen. Death by decapitation is a common sentence but seldom carried out. The Royal sport is croquet, played with live flamingoes and hedgehogs; this makes the game interesting but difficult and visitors are not advised to attempt it.

There seems to be no organized system of education in Wonderland, except for some private tuition in underwater schools like those attended by gryphons and mock-turtles (a cross-breeding of calf and turtle used to make mock-turtle soup). A number of uncommon subjects are taught at these schools: reeling, writhing, the different branches of arithmetic (ambition, distraction, uglification and derision); mystery ancient and modern; seaography; art (drawling, stretching and fainting in coils) and the classics, laughing and grief. Also French, music and washing (extra). A peculiar school tradition is the lobster-quadrille, a dance in which gryphons, mock-turtles, seals, salmon and other fish take part, each with a lobster as a partner. When visiting the school, visitors must have a porpoise; in fact it is inadvisable for visitors to go *anywhere* without a porpoise.

The judiciary system in Wonderland is based on trial by jury. The King acts as judge and instructs the jury, who seldom take his advice. Spec-tators who persist in cheering are suppressed by being put into a large canvas bag which is then tied up with string.

Compared to the fauna, the flora of Wonderland is not very remarkable: a species of white rose, sometimes painted red, can be seen near the Queen's croquet ground. The fauna, on the other hand, is unique because most animals can speak English and some, like the mice, a little French. There are dogs, guinea-pigs, crabs, rabbits (in waistcoats), lizards, frogs, land-fish, dormice with a passion for treacle, March hares and a Cheshire cat. The latter, notable for his grin and witty remarks, can make himself invisible, leaving just the grin floating in mid-air. Pigs—or baby boys who have been turned into pigs—can also be found. Many birds have their habitat in Wonderland: ducks, dodos (elsewhere extinct), lories, pigeons, eaglets and flamingoes.

Few travellers have visited Wonderland. In the 1860's Alice Liddell is known to have spent several hours here. Agatha, sister to the Dowager Lady Monchensey, looked through the miniature door in the low entrance hall in 1937 and heard tiny voices in the distance, while a black raven— probably related to the monstrous crow of nearby LOOKING-GLASS LAND—flew frighteningly over her head.

Should a traveller lose his way in Wonderland, information can be obtained from a knowledgeable caterpillar smoking a hookah.

(Lewis Carroll [Charles Lutwidge Dodgson], *Alice's Adventures in Wonderland,* London, 1865; T.S. Eliot, *The Family Reunion,* London, 1939)

WOOD BETWEEN THE WORLDS, a quiet, dreamy place where there is no sound or movement, no birds or animals. All that can be heard is the sound of the trees growing. The Wood is so thickly knit that everything appears to be bathed in a warm green light, as if it were always morning.

Every few yards between the trees are pools which give access to innumerable other worlds. The water of these pools has the peculiarity of not wetting the skin of those who dive into them or emerge from them. These pools must be carefully distinguished from the ordinary puddles in the Woods, which contain ordinary water.

Travellers can enter the Wood by using certain magic rings, made from dust that originally came from the Wood itself. Yellow or "homeward" rings bring the traveller to the Wood: green or "outward" rings will take him to other worlds. The rings must be in direct contact with the skin of the traveller—the wearing of gloves will render them ineffective. People with the ring must be careful not to touch anyone else while wearing it, as by contact with the ring they will become a human magnet and will take others with them to other worlds.

It is extremely difficult to distinguish between the different pools and it is quite possible to end up in the wrong world. Travellers are therefore advised to be extremely cautious. To return to the Wood a traveller must put on a yellow ring and plunge back into the appropriate pool.

Travellers who have visited the Wood Between the Worlds say that it is intricately alive, despite the stillness, and "as rich as Plumcake." They also say that having arrived in the Wood they cannot recall with any clarity how they got there, and feel both that they have been there before and that their former lives were a dream which is now fading. Dante Gabriel Rossetti perhaps visited the Wood and wrote a short poem about it.

(Dante Gabriel Rossetti, "Sudden Light," in *Poems*, London, 1870; C.S. Lewis, *The Magician's Nephew*, London, 1955)

WOOD BEYOND THE WORLD, a country of gentle wooded hills to the north of the BEAR COUNTRY.

Most of the country is clad in a wide variety of deciduous trees, ranging from oak to hornbeam and from rowan to hazel and sweet chestnut. To the south, the land is bounded by a stony wilderness and by a range of mountains which end in a sheer cliff wall overlooking the sea.

There are only two buildings in the Wood Beyond the World. One is a simple thatched cottage in an enclosed garden of roses and flowers; the other is the elaborate Golden House. The latter is built of white marble with carved and painted figures in painted or gilded niches; images of men and beasts can be seen between the pillars of the porch. The golden roof gives its name to the building. The main hall is vaulted and lined with pillars; its walls are painted in gold and ultramarine, the floor is spangled with many colours and the windows are glazed with knots and pictures. A fountain of gold plays in the centre of the room.

The Golden House is the home of the ruler of the Wood, referred to simply as the Lady, who is regarded as a mother and goddess by her subjects; she is also worshipped in the neighbouring Bear Country. She has great magical powers and can transform the appearance of the people and things around her, control the weather and read men's thoughts. Lusty male travellers are warned that her magical powers will disappear with her maidenhead.

The Wood is also the home of a race of dwarves who swarm like rabbits in some areas; they have little intelligence. Sometimes, the dwarves walk upright; at other times on all fours.

(William Morris, *The Wood Beyond the World*, London, 1894)

WORDS, CITY OF, see DICTIONOPOLIS.

WORLD'S END ISLAND, so far to the east of NARNIA

that the very constellations in the sky are new and different and the sun appears much larger than it does in Narnia. The island is covered with fine springy turf, dotted with a plant that resembles heather.

The only "building" on the island is a roofless wide space paved with smooth stones and surrounded by grey pillars. A long table runs the length of this paved area, covered with a crimson cloth falling almost to the ground. On either side stand stone chairs, all richly carved and provided with silk cushions. The table was placed here by Aslan, creator of Narnia, and is kept stocked with the most delicious food for the refreshment of those who have travelled here. The food is brought and taken away each day by flocks of great white birds which fly in from the east. As they swoop down towards the island they sing in an unknown but recognizably human language.

The island is the home of Ramandu, a star who is undergoing rejuvenation until he can take his place in the heavens again. As in the sky above Narnia, the stars of this region are not balls of flaming gas but people who glimmer, with silver clothes and hair. When Ramandu became old and decrepit he was brought down from the sky to World's End Island. Each day the birds bring him a fire berry from the valleys of the sun. The berries reverse the process of aging and one day Ramandu will be young enough to become a star in the sky once more.

World's End Island lies in the waters of the

Last Sea. This sea is so perfectly clear that the shadow of a moving boat can be seen running across the sea bed. Its water is sweet and fresh and has been described as being like a strong yet light wine. It is extremely nourishing, making both food and sleep unnecessary to those that sail this sea. Through the clear water a submarine landscape can be seen; mountains, hills, forests and open parkland. The submarine valleys are dark and dangerous, the lair of wicked creatures like the squid, the sea-serpent and the kraken. But the hills of this submarine world are warm and peaceful; it is here that cities and castles are built, notably one described as the Throne of Death by an American journalist. The buildings are the colour of pearls or ivory, surmounted by numerous pinnacles, minarets and domes. The people of the sea (not to be confused with the inhabitants of MERKING'S KINGDOM) have skin the colour of old ivory and dark purple hair. The king and his entourage wear coronets and chains of pearls; streamers of emerald or orange material flutter from their shoulders in the current. One of their most popular pastimes is hunting, when the nobles ride on sea horses. Small fierce fish are used to hunt other species.

There are no waves or winds in this sea, only a current some forty feet wide which flows from west to east. As one travels east the light becomes brighter, so that eventually one can stare into the face of the sun without blinking and see the white birds as they prepare to fly to World's End Island.

The last reach of this sea is called the Silver Sea because it is covered with dazzlingly bright flowers, rather like lilies. The water gradually becomes more and more shallow, and a rowing boat has to be used to reach the End of the World itself. The End of the World is marked by what seems, from a distance, to be a wall. It is in fact a huge wave, perpetually frozen, behind which the sun rises. Beyond lies ASLAN'S COUNTRY.

(Edgar Allan Poe, "The City Under the Sea," in *The Raven and Other Poems*, New York, 1845; C.S. Lewis, *The Lion, the Witch and the Wardrobe*, London, 1950; C.S. Lewis, *Prince Caspian*, London, 1952; C.S. Lewis, *The Voyage of the "Dawn Treader,"* London, 1952)

WOTNEKST, see LOONARIE.

WRAITH-ISLAND, one of the many islands and swamps in an unnamed bush in Nigeria. The inhabitants are known for their hospitality; travellers are received with kindness and given a lovely house to live in. The inhabitants' only work is to plant their food; after that, they have no other occupations than music and dance. Though they are not human, their aspect is beautiful and, when they dress, travellers are led to believe that they are like ordinary men and women.

The island itself is very high and, like all islands, entirely surrounded by water, but this does not protect it from dangerous beasts. One is a strange vegetarian creature that destroys the crops. This animal is as big as an elephant, with long fingernails and a horned head ten times larger than its body. Its mouth is full of teeth a foot long and thick as a cow's horn, and its body is covered in long black hair like a horse's tail. If travellers do not make the appropriate sacrifice to it, it will force them to mount its hairy back and will take them to its house, where it will give the impious foreigners certain quick-germinating grains that must be planted to the creature's satisfaction. Another fearful creature is the so-called Spirit of Prey. As big as a hippopotamus, he walks upright like a human being. Both his legs have two feet each. His head is covered with hard scales the size of a shovel or hoe, all curved towards his body. If the Spirit of Prey wants to catch his prey, he will simply stand in one place and look at it. He will close his eyes and, before he opens them again, the prey will be dead. His eyes shed light the colour of mercury, which serves as a warning to travellers who venture out at night.

(Amos Tutuola, *The Palm-Wine Drinkard and His Dead Palm-Wine Tapster in the Dead's Town*, London, 1952)

X

X, a boundless city of uncertain location, yet from the fact that it lies three weeks away on foot from the nearest railway station one can infer that it is not located in Europe. Merely a partial and incomplete description has been provided by the only traveller known to have set foot in X: a certain A.G. of Budapest, who wrote his report in 1929.

A.G. left the train at the terminus (the name of which he forgets to give) and travelled four days in a donkey trap, guided by a kind railway man. From then on he travelled on foot through a grey, flat landscape blown by persistent winds. First he found vast zones where scraps of metal had been kept or thrown. For two days he saw only broken pipes and tangles of metallic cables; the next day he found nothing but large heaps of kitchen pots and pans, burnt saucepans, broken colanders, dented frying pans, forming mounds as high as a man; for another whole day he saw nothing but cogs. The next two days the whole country appeared to be covered with iron sheets of different thicknesses. Finally, approaching the city, he crossed a triple circle of war machinery, railroad gear and automobile parts.

The outskirts of X are in a state of utter ruin; for yet another three days A.G. crossed endless suburbs of abandoned and derelict houses and only on the fourth day did he meet a human being. At last, on the next day, he reached the inhabited section of X. According to his report, X has no centre—geographical, spiritual, commercial or historical. The city is as deceiving as if it were made of rubber, sometimes expanding and sometimes contracting. At one end is a sector that the inhabitants have for no known reason abandoned; at the other end a new section has risen, no one knows why since no one plans to live there. From time to time, without anyone noticing it, the city begins to become crowded again, so much so that even derelict buildings become inhabited. Throughout the whole of the city, the streets look the same—flanked by ruinous or semi-destroyed houses, interrupted constructions, heaps of sand and bricks obstructing the pavements, abandoned water-works, impoverished shops that sell odd merchandise—bread, shoes, anything—and with hardly more than a single sample.

Through the streets, night and day, streams a shapeless crowd dressed in dirty and tattered clothes. A small steam engine on a narrow gauge runs through the city but no one knows where to embark because the stops are arranged without any previous notice or any clear plan. There are taxi ranks, of course, but it is highly unlikely that one will see a taxi. In the restaurants, provided one can find them, the quality of the food deteriorates with each visit and restaurants can close any day without any explanation. As to the hotels, the most comfortable ones have old-fashioned, noisy plumbing systems running from wall to wall. The lamps are lit throughout the day and are switched off as soon as it gets dark; they are controlled from a central panel and there are no individual switches in the rooms. The lifts are extremely fast and have no control buttons; so the floor at which one wants to alight must be guessed at according to the time taken to go up or down.

A.G. tells us little of the political organization of X, except that the president is chosen according to the length of his arms. One of the best-beloved presidents was a certain Larra Senior, whose arms were almost two inches longer than all his predecessors'. He could, with hardly any effort, put his right hand in his left trouser pocket or his left hand in his right trouser pocket. According to A.G., the inhabitants of X have no goal in life and if they had one, he says, they would not know how to reach it. This mentality somehow corresponds to the architecture of their city; half in ruins and half unbuilt.

(Tibor Déry, *G.A. úr X.-ben*, Budapest, 1963)

XANADU, a kingdom on the coast of Asia where Kubla Khan ordered a stately pleasure dome to be constructed, described as "a miracle of rare device." The caves of ice beneath the sunny dome are particularly enchanting. The palace still stands— or at least what was built of it, for a person from Porlock prevented completion. It covers ten miles of fertile ground, surrounded by walls and towers, its gardens bright with small streams and blossoming incense-bearing trees.

It was in the nearby, ancient forests, in a savage, holy and enchanted place where women can be heard wailing for their demon lovers, that a mighty fountain of water, flung up violently from a deep chasm, was revealed to be the source of the sacred river Alph.

The River Alph in XANADU; in the background, the Pleasure Dome.

The river flows for some five miles through woods and valleys and then plunges into measureless caverns down towards a lifeless ocean. It is said that through the turmoil of this waterfall, the voices of Kubla Khan's great ancestors can be heard.

(Samuel Taylor Coleridge, *Kubla Khan, a Vision in a Dream*, London, 1816)

XEXOTLAND, the country of the yellow-skinned Xexots which lies in the south-west of the underground continent of PELLUCIDAR, beyond the Land of the Awful Shadow and the nameless strait that connects the KORSAR Az with the Sojar Az. The cultural development of the Xexots corresponds roughly to that of the Bronze Age on the surface of the earth. Unlike the majority of the people of Pellucidar, the Xexots live in walled cities. The houses are merely crude structures of clay bricks and the streets are narrow, winding lanes, but they still represent a higher level of development than that achieved by most of Pellucidar. The greatest architectural achievements of the Xexots are the domed temples in their cities, splendid constructions of bold design which no traveller should miss.

Xexotland has a crude monetary economy, based on the use of octagonal bronze coins. Their weapons are also of bronze. They wear leather aprons with bright designs painted on them, but both men and women go naked from the waist upwards; children and young people do not wear any clothes at all. The priests are distinguished by their long leather coats and the hideous masks they wear over their faces.

The Xexots are also one of the few peoples of Pellucidar to have anything approaching a systematic religion. Whereas most inhabitants of Pellucidar accept that their world floats on a burning sea, the Molop Az, and that evil-doers are carried down to it piece by piece by the wicked little men who live there, it appears that only the Xexots have developed the idea of a heaven, Karana, to which the virtuous will go after their deaths. Karana is also the home of an omnipotent God known as Pu.

(Edgar Rice Burroughs, *Return to Pellucidar*, New York, 1941; Edgar Rice Burroughs, *Men of the Bronze Age*, New York, 1942)

XIMEQUE, one of the largest and most powerful empires on the continent of GENOTIA in the south Atlantic. Travellers might visit the province of Phenacil, on the Gulf of Genotia, where the inhabitants have converted to the religion of Mithras.

(Louis Adrien Duperron de Castera, *Le Theatre Des Passions Et De La Fortune Ou Les Avantures Surprenantes de Rosamidor & de Theoglaphire. Histoire Australe*, Paris, 1731)

XIROS, an island in the Aegean Sea, which can be reached by a special boat from Rynos, or by the ferry that calls here once every five days to leave provisions and to collect the fishermen's catch. The people are Greek and their main occupation is the catching of octopuses.

From a distance, especially at midday, Xiros looks remarkably like a turtle with its legs in the air. The south coast is uninhabitable, but towards the west is a Lydian or Greco–Mycenaean colony. Visitors should note the two stone pillars supporting the pier, decorated with hieroglyphics and discovered by a certain Professor Goldmann.

The main characteristic of the island is that

once seen, even from afar, it cannot be forgotten. Its image will haunt the traveller throughout his life, he will pine for its white sand and scorching sun, and when at last he sets his feet on Xiros, he will enjoy the utter bliss of having reached a much-longed-for haven. However, this joy will be short-lived, and after a few hours of peaceful exultation death will overtake him.

This odd, haunting characteristic of Xiros is also found in an object called *zahir*, which can appear under one of several forms: a twenty-cent Argentine coin, a tiger, a blind man, an astrolabe, a small compass, a vein in one of the twelve hundred marble pillars of the Mosque of Cordova, the bottom of a well in Tetuan. Any of these things, once seen, cannot be torn from one's memory.

(Jorge Luis Borges, "El Zahir," in *El Aleph*, Buenos Aires, 1949; Julio Cortázar, "La isla a mediodia," in *Todos los fuegos el fuego*, Madrid, 1976)

XUJAN KINGDOM, a walled city in Africa inhabited by a tribe of madmen who revere parrots.

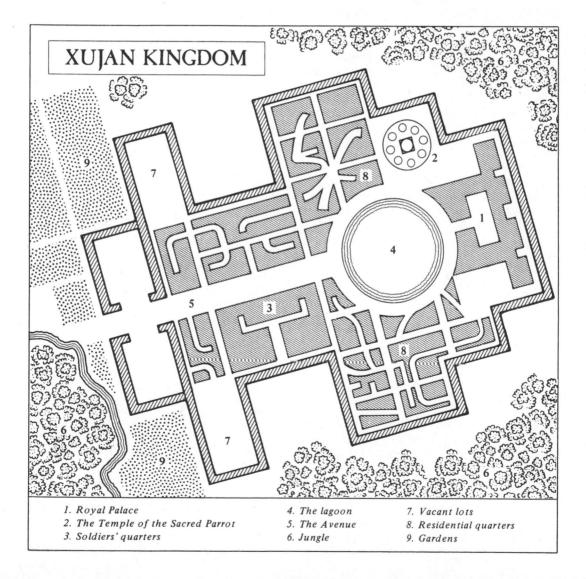

1. *Royal Palace*
2. *The Temple of the Sacred Parrot*
3. *Soldiers' quarters*
4. *The lagoon*
5. *The Avenue*
6. *Jungle*
7. *Vacant lots*
8. *Residential quarters*
9. *Gardens*

Their religious rites involving these birds are extremely revolting and may have brought the race to its present condition of imbecility. The Xujans are peculiar in many respects, not only in their form of worship but also in that they breed lions as other people breed cattle, some for their milk and some to fatten and eat. They never touch the flesh of birds or monkeys and keep boars, deer and antelopes to feed their lions.

The Xujans are strongly built. Their skin is yellow, of a leathery appearance; their hair is coal black and cut very short, growing stiffly at right angles to the scalp. Their upper canines are unusually long and sharp, their eyes closely set with black irises so that the white of the eye seems to cover the entire eye. They are beardless, with a heavy lower lip and a weak chin, as if their countenance had been degraded by filthy habits and indecent thoughts. Many have fits in the streets, uttering savage screams or attacking innocent children.

The city is a forest of domes and minarets. The outer walls, some three hundred feet high, form a long, narrow rectangle; the streets within are crooked and winding. The main street opens suddenly upon a wide avenue and a broad lagoon. The buildings in this section are higher and the houses are decorated with golden parrots, lions and monkeys. The highest and most pretentious building around the lagoon is the Royal Palace, some seven storeys high. It is approached by a wide flight of steps guarded by enormous stone lions; the entrance itself is flanked by two stone parrots.

Visitors should note the palace throne room, where the walls are entirely hidden by hangings on which thousands of parrots are embroidered; the floor is inlaid with golden parrots and the ceiling painted with flying parrots.

Travellers are advised that visiting the Xujan Kingdom can be extremely dangerous. Women are kidnapped by the king and then forgotten in one of the royal chambers; men are killed or used as slaves for hard labour. Escape is difficult. The houses have barred windows, the doors are guarded by eunuchs, the streets patrolled by soldiers, the outer wall protected by guards and by lions trained as watchdogs. It is said that in the sixteenth century a Spaniard visited the city and managed to escape but was hunted down in the desert beyond. Lord Greystoke, known to the natives as Tarzan, also visited the Xujan Kingdom and was able to leave it unharmed. No other travellers are known to have returned from it.

(Edgar Rice Burroughs, *Tarzan the Untamed*, New York, 1919)

Y

YALDING TOWERS, the stately home of Lord Yalding, close to the small market town of Liddlesby in Hampshire, England. The house stands in extensive grounds, laid out in the Italian style. An avenue of cypresses leads to a marble terrace overlooking an ornamental lake with a small island in the centre; the lake is fringed by weeping willows and swans can be seen gliding between its lily pads. To the left stands the Temple of Flora, a white marble pavilion sheltering a statue of the goddess. Temples to Phoebus and Dionysus can also be seen in the grounds and statues of the classical gods and goddesses are scattered throughout the gardens. To the right of the lake, an artificial waterfall tumbles down into its waters. From the terrace above the lake, the ornate towers and turrets of the house can be seen through the lime trees. The grounds also include a maze and a rose garden shaded by yew trees. In the mid-nineteenth century, shortly after the Great Exhibition, a collection of stone figures of prehistoric animals was added to the gardens. Similar to those seen at the Crystal Palace in London, they lurk among the trees and undergrowth in a somewhat sinister fashion.

Beyond the beech woods on the edge of the estate the ground rises to a flat hilltop where a circle of standing stones can be seen. One of them is pierced with a curious round hole, now worn smooth at the edges, probably erected by a precursor of Barbara Hepworth. In the middle of the circle lies a solitary flat stone, full of distant memories of old faiths and creeds.

Yalding Towers itself is noted mainly for its carved wall panelling and for the collection of arms in the dining room. The most unusual room in the house is a domed chamber with a blue roof on which golden stars have been painted.

Yalding Towers was built by an ancestor of the present owner, partly for love of a French woman and partly to practise his magic. The magic came from a ring handed down in the family, originally given to a mortal by a supernatural being. However, a price had to be paid for using the magic ring—and the French woman died before seeing her lover's work completed.

Should a visitor to Yalding Towers find the ring today, he or she will discover that it makes its wearer invisible. It also has the power to make the wearer see the garden's statues and prehistoric animals come to life. At a more practical level, it has, on one occasion at least, led to the discovery of a precious collection of jewellery.

Yalding Towers is open to the public only once a week; picnics may not be taken into the grounds.

(Edith Nesbit, *The Enchanted Castle,* London, 1907)

YAMS, ISLE OF, see VALAPEE.

YELDA, a kingdom to the south-east of the BEKLAN EMPIRE of which it was once a province. It is told that the kingdom was liberated from oppression by U-Deparioth, the son of the only person known to have survived the Streels of URTAH. Legends and ballads about this ancient hero are sung throughout the lands around the Beklan Empire and even in BEKLA itself.

(Richard Adams, *Shardik,* London, 1974)

YLUANA, an island in the River Plate, about four miles from the sea. The island is not marked on any map and its existence is known only to Jesuit missionaries in the surrounding area. Yluana is a beautiful, fertile island with pleasant wooded hills and gentle streams.

The original inhabitants came from the East and are followers of the great law-giver Zoroaster, known to them as Zar-Touche, who brought them to the island. Centuries later, people from the north reached Yluana—probably Peruvian Indians fleeing the cruelty of the Spanish. The two nations are completely integrated and profess the religion of Zoroaster. They regard themselves (and all men) as the children of one divine father.

The king is considered their earthly father and he sees his people as his children. Normally the king's son succeeds him to the throne, but if he is not sufficiently virtuous he may be set aside by a popular council. The same council also sits as a court, although crime is virtually unknown. The worst imaginable punishment for the Yluanais is shame.

Gold and silver are not highly valued by the Yluanais, although they are well aware of how much Europeans value them. Each individual is content with his own property and does not envy that of others. The Yluanais scorn the benefits of civilization, and having seen how the Jesuits exploit the native population and live in luxury at its expense, avoid all contact with them. Yearly visits to the mission lands are, however, made by royal ambassadors. Despite their scorn for civilization, the Yluanais are extremely hospitable. They detest the idea of war, but are ready to fight very bravely if they are attacked.

Marriage is encouraged in order to increase the population; men marry at nineteen and women at seventeen. Adultery, unknown now for many years, is in theory punishable by death. Flattery and lying are unknown; ingratitude is considered the worst of crimes. In Yluana, love, joy and friendship flourish.

The houses of the Yluanais are well built, with no pomp or superfluous ornaments. The palace of the king is distinguished by its size alone. Again, it is a simple, elegant building. The only sumptuous buildings to be found in Yluana are those dedicated to their god in heaven.

The men usually wear white garments and a red flowing mantle; members of the royal family wear blue mantles. The royal crown is a plain gold circle; the only other sign of the king's rank is a black wand, tipped with silver, that he carries. The women wear flowers in their hair, long, graceful robes, and sometimes garlands of purple flowers.

(Charles Searle [?], *The Wanderer: Or, Memoirs Of Charles Searle, Esq; Containing His Adventures by Sea and Land. With Many remarkable Characters, and interesting Situations in Real Life; and a Variety of surprizing Incidents*, London, 1776)

YOKA ISLAND, named after the village of Yoka, the seat of the island's government. A tropical island in the Pacific Ocean, it is fairly large and mountainous, with a steep coast and a few small coves, and is inhabited by fierce, primitive head-hunting natives. Some three hundred and fifty years ago the women married a group of Japanese samurai who had fled Japan just before the Ashikaga Dynasty of shoguns was overthrown. Their descendants, known today as Yoka Samurai, are small brown men with black beady eyes set in fleshy slits. They wear their hair shaved up to a broad strip along the top of their heads and then drawn back into an unbraided queue brought up from the neck to the top of the forehead. They

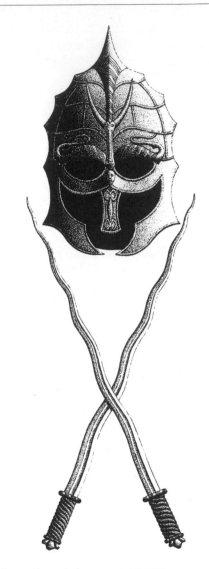

Helmet and swords from YOKA ISLAND.

wear medieval armour, and carry wicked-looking swords and helmets. They speak Japanese.

The village of Yoka is set high up in lofty mountains. The dwellings are half-buried cave-like rooms, with the upper walls and the thatched roof rising a maximum of four feet above the ground. Sometimes a second room is added to keep a few pigs or chickens. The natives have built granaries on stilts, dotted here and there across the mountains. The king of Yoka has absolute power and is much revered by the inhabitants of the village.

Yoka was first described by a gentleman boxer from Chicago, in the United States, who visited the island towards the beginning of the twentieth century.

(Edgar Rice Burroughs, *The Mucker,* New York, 1914)

YOUKALI, an island almost at the end of the world. Its only inhabitant is a fairy whose mission is to welcome desolate travellers. Any lost soul arriving at Youkali is invited to tour the island, which will assume the shape of that soul's keenest desires and most longed-for delights. Youkali has been described as the End of All Sorrow, the Land of Exchanged Vows and Reciprocated Love, the Hope That Lies at the Core of Every Human Heart. Certain travellers report that there is no such place and that Youkali is nothing but a desperate daydream; such reports are not, however, conclusive.

(Kurt Weill & Roger Fernay, "Youkali: Tango Habanera," New York, 1935)

YOUNG AND OLD, ISLE OF THE, see GREAT WATER.

YS, the ruins of a city in the Bay of Douarnenez, Finistère, France, near the town of Plomarch. Towards the end of the fourth century AD, Ys was protected from the sea by a strong dam, the gates of which were hidden; only the king possessed the key to these gates. The king's daughter was tempted by a mysterious stranger. To please him, she stole the key from her father's chamber; the gates were opened and the city was drowned.

To this very day, travellers can hear the bells of the churches of Ys sounding the hours, deep in the shadowed bay.

(Edouard Blau & Edouard Lalo, *Le Roi d'Ys,* first performance, Paris, 1888; Charles Guyot, *La Légende de la ville d'Ys d'après les anciens textes,* Paris, 1926)

YSPADDADEN PENKAWR, a castle somewhere in Wales, in the middle of a wide open plain. For unexplained reasons, the closer a traveller comes to it, the farther away the castle appears to be. The main hall of the castle—if reached—is entered via any one of nine doors, each guarded by a watchman with a guard dog.

(Anonymous, *The Mabinogion,* 14th–15th cen. AD)

Z

ZAK, see SOUTHERN SEA.

ZAKALON, an extensive kingdom some ten days' journey by horse to the east of the BEKLAN EM-PIRE, and ruled by His Ascendant Majesty King Luin. Zakalon is a highly developed and sophisticated society with a high level of culture and philosophy. Its cities are famed for their numerous flower gardens.

After the conclusion of the wars that divided the Beklan Empire, trade relations were established between the two countries. Zakalon now imports wine, gold, iron and various artifacts from the Empire. The embroidery made in the Empire is especially prized in Zakalon. It was from Zakalon that the first horses were introduced into the Beklan Empire; before the introduction of trading relations they had been unknown in that country.

(Richard Adams, *Shardik*, London, 1974)

ZANTHODON, a realm deep below the surface of the earth, covering a quarter of a million square miles, uncannily similar to PELLUCIDAR. The only known access is down the cone of an extinct volcano in the Ahaggar region of North Africa.

Zanthodon is thought to have been formed by a huge meteor which entered the volcano, and exploded inside the earth when it came in contact with solid matter. The explosion caused much of the solid matter to disintegrate, forming a huge bubble of molten rock, the shell of Zanthodon. The whole country is permanently bathed in an unnatural daylight thought to be produced by chemical photoluminescence sparked off by the substances released in the original explosion. As there are no stars or planets in Zanthodon's sky it is impossible to devise an astronomical system of directions. Similarly the permanent daylight means that there is no natural method of reckoning time—which effectively does not exist here. The climate of Zanthodon is warm and very humid, with frequent showers.

Little of this underground world has been explored, and most of the areas that have been visited are covered in thick jungle. The flora of Zanthodon closely resembles that found on the surface of the earth during prehistoric times. The swampy area around the bottom of the volcano's shaft is covered in forests typical of the early Cretaceous period: huge tree-ferns somewhat like feathery bamboo and trees with broad fan-shaped leaves and twisted boughs. Elsewhere conifers of the Jurassic period can be seen, and plants typical of the Devonian age on earth. The latter includes the slender psilothron, the lycopod or clubmoss, and a tree rather like a palm but with a cross-hatched trunk that looks like the outside of a pineapple. Tall waving grass covers the plains.

Two seas are known to exist in Zanthodon: the Sogar Jad or Great Sea and the smaller inland sea known as the Lugar Jad. The shores of the latter rise to a range of rolling hills and ultimately to the mountains known as the Peaks of Peril. The name is apt, as the mountains are the main breeding ground of one of the most vicious of Zanthodon's animals, the pterodactyl or *thakdal*, to give it its local name. These great flying reptiles nest and breed in the rugged crags of the Peaks of Peril. Although it is normally a scavenger, the *thakdal is* perfectly able to hunt for itself and has been known to carry off full-grown human beings. The size of these creatures varies; large specimens have an estimated wingspan of over thirty feet. The Peaks of Peril are also the home of the *omodon* or cave-bear, a species which has been extinct for thousands of years on the surface of the earth.

In the swamps of the jungle is a primitive type of crocodile; it reaches a length of three to four feet, and along its back are heavy armoured plates; its hide is green, apart from a yellowish patch on the throat, its eyes a bright scarlet. On the plains of Zanthodon visitors will see the *coelorosaur*, a lizardlike scavenger which grows to a length of three feet and can walk erect on its hind legs. The drier areas of the forests and the plains are the habitat of the *vander* or sabretoothed tiger, a tawny-coloured feline which can measure seventeen feet from nose to tail.

Virtually all the animals found in Zanthodon are savage predators, the exceptions being a small mammal—probably a remote ancestor of the horse—and the gigantic woolly mammoth which roamed the earth during the Ice Age. The mammoths are herbivorous and are not dangerous unless attacked or startled.

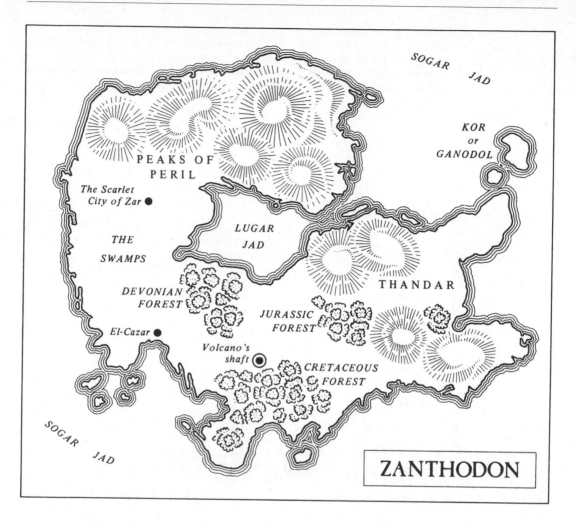

The origins and evolution of the fauna of Zanthodon remain a mystery, as animals thought to have existed normally in different geological periods are found together. It has been conjectured that many of the creatures came from the surface of the earth, migrating south across the land-bridge that once connected Europe and Africa as the glaciers of the Ice Age advanced, and then found their way down to Zanthodon where, for unexplained reasons, evolution did not pursue the same course as on the surface.

At least four different races are known to live in Zanthodon; their customs, however, have yet to be studied in any detail. The realm of Kor on Ganodol—a large island on the Sogar Jad—is the home of a race of Neanderthal ape-men, strong, ugly men covered in matted hair. They dress in badly tanned animal skins and wear ornaments made from seashells; their weapons are heavy clubs and crude spears tipped with stone. According to the other peoples of Zanthodon, the ape-men are cannibals. There is no definite proof of this, but the royal throne is not reassuring—it consists of a huge collection of human skulls, welded together with lead. The king lives in a cave-palace, lit by smoking torches, beneath the rocky hills of Kor. The ape-women—though never actually seen by visitors to the underground world—are said to be extremely ugly and merci-fully few. In order to procure more graceful mates, the ape-men make raids on the Cro-Magnon races of Thandar—a land of plains and rocky hills. These races represent a much higher stage of development than the ape-men, who are dismissively referred to as *drugars* or "ugly ones" by the Cro-Magnons.

The *panjani* or "smooth skins"—as the ape-men call the Cro-Magnons—have beautiful and totally unselfconscious women who dress in furs and do not trouble to cover their breasts. Both men and women are tall, with blue eyes and blonde hair. Like the ape-men they wear animal hides but their tanning and curing techniques are more advanced. Copper and bronze ornaments are often worn, together with polished pebbles hanging from thongs.

The *panjani* have an organized tribal existence and are ruled by a high chief or *omad*. His son and heir is known as the *jamad* and his daughter as the *gomad*. *Panjani* women have no right to choose their own mates and marriage is usually a matter of combat between rival men.

When on expeditions, the *panjani* use tents made of tanned hide. For the nightly halts, they surround their camp with a palisade of bound logs—a crude but effective defence against predators. The *panjani* are not known to be farmers and appear to live only by hunting and gathering.

Two other races live in Zanthodon, but very little is known of them. The people of the Scarlet City of Zar, which lies far inland from the Lugar Jad, appear to be highly civilized but their city has not yet been visited by anyone from the surface. Little more is known of the fourth race of Zanthodon. On the waters of the Sogar Jad oared galleys have been seen, built on the lines of the Barbary corsairs of the past and flying the green banner of Islam. These galleys are manned by pirates based at El-Cazar, a port which no foreigner has ever visited. It is thought that the pirates may be descended from corsairs, who were driven out of the Mediterranean by the French in the nineteenth century, and fled inland to the Ahaggar Mountains, where they somehow found the entrance to this subterranean world.

All the people of Zanthodon speak the same language, which has been dubbed proto-Aryan. It is believed that this is the common tongue which gave rise to Sanscrit and hence to all the Indo-European languages of the world. Proto-Aryan is quite simple, consisting of verbs, nouns and adjectives, and devoid of any complex system of tenses;

it is easily learnt. Those who have studied it say that it is like recalling a forgotten memory rather than studying a brand new tongue.

The existence of Zanthodon has been known in legend for centuries. To the Sumerians it was Na-an-Gub, the "great below"; ancient Hebrew myths speak of it as Tehom, "the great deep and the home of the giants." To the Egyptians it was Amenet, the "sacred land" or the "land in the west"; to the Muslims it is Shadukiam, the "underworld of the djinns," ruled by Al-Dimiryat. Its existence is also mentioned in the Enuman Elish, the ancient Babylonian creation epic.

Zanthodon remained unknown until the late 1960's, when Professor Percival Penthesilia Potter pieced together the existing evidence and located the entrance through the volcano in the Ahaggar. With a young American adventurer, Eric Carstairs, he descended the cone of the extinct volcano in a helicopter and collected what information we have.

(Lin Carter, *Journey to the Underground World*, New York, 1979)

ZARA'S KINGDOM, a South Sea island where the lazy subjects of King Paramount have established a prosperous nation thanks to the intervention of Zara, the king's daughter, who was educated in England. Visitors will notice the English influence both in the disposition of the palm groves around the royal palace, and in the decoration of the throne room, furnished in the style of one of Queen Victoria's drawing rooms.

When Zara returned to her island she brought with her six Englishmen, whom she dubbed "the six flowers of progress," representing the highest achievements of British culture as examples for the islanders to live up to. These comprised a Lord High Chamberlain, Censor of Plays; a company promoter; a county counsellor; a lawyer well versed in the science of philology, who could demonstrate that "yes" is but another and neater form of "no"; a navy captain, Corcoran K.C.B., formerly of *H.M.S. Pinafore*, who abandoned sail for steam; and finally Captain Fitzbattleaxe, First Life Guards. These six did their job so well and established laws so perfect that all the island's lawyers were out of work, all doctors were starving, all neighbouring nations disarmed and war an impossibility. Outraged by this state of affairs, the islanders rebelled, but then Princess Zara remembered one of Britain's most important political developments whereby her nation could be saved: the government by party. Thanks to this system, no political measure could endure, because one party would certainly undo what the other party did, and while grouse were shot and foxes worried to death, the legislative action of the country would come to a standstill. Much to the delight of the population, the government by party brought sickness in plenty, endless lawsuits, crowded jails, interminable confusion in the army and the navy, and in short, general and unrestrained prosperity.

(Sir William Schwenck Gilbert & Sir Arthur Sullivan, *Utopia Limited; or, The Flowers of Progress,* first performance, London, 1893)

ZAROFF'S ISLAND or **BARANKA ISLAND,** in the Caribbean. On old maps it is called Ship-Trap Island; sailors are known to have a superstitious dread of it and avoid it whenever possible. It is surrounded on all sides by jagged rocks, and a dense jungle comes down to the edge of the cliffs. There is some ridged, high ground in the centre of the island and, in the south-east corner, a mire of quicksand called Death Swamp. On a spur of rock at the northern extremity is a lighthouse which appears to indicate a safe channel; travellers should in fact ignore it, as it has been set up to lure ships onto the dangerous rocks and wreck them. Over the whole island looms Count Zaroff's castle, surmounted by many pointed towers. It stands high on a bluff, surrounded on three sides by the sea. The castle is furnished throughout in lavish baronial style; heads of game (including human heads) adorn the walls—the Count is a dedicated hunter.

Brought up in Russia, Count Zaroff was taught to handle a gun from earliest childhood and hunted all forms of game in all parts of the world. Eventually becoming bored with the fact that he could outwit the most cunning and ferocious of animals, he decided that man was the only game which could match him in wits. The Count retired to this island, and kept it stocked with human subjects. Survivors from wrecked ships, led astray by the false lighthouse, are his game. The courtyard and outer perimeter of the castle are guarded by fierce dogs used in the Count's hunts.

Visitors are certainly not advised to approach the island, but if they do it may be useful to know that the Count gives his prey a three hour head-start and then hunts him to the death. Any game that eludes him for three days is allowed to go free and is returned to the mainland, but no quarry has so far succeeded.

It has been reported that, in circumstances yet to be investigated, the Count met his death and was devoured by his own hounds. Visitors, however, are still advised to be on their guard.

(Richard Connell, "The Most Dangerous Game," in *Stories,* New York, 1927; *The Most Dangerous Game,* directed by Ernest Schoedsack & Irving Pichel, USA, 1932)

ZAVATTINIA, a small village (sometimes called a slum) in the outskirts of the large city of Bamba in capitalistic Europe. It consists of a number of poor huts well disposed along clean roads with instructive names, such as "1 + 1 = 2," or called after humble workers or unemployed people. In the central square, the inhabitants of Zavattinia have erected a cast-off statue that comes to life during the night.

Visitors are invited to attend, for a few lire, the spectacle of dusk: from a number of wooden seats set up to the west of Zavattinia, they can enjoy an uncluttered view of the setting of the sun.

The inhabitants make a living of begging in Bamba, in spite of the hostility of the Mobbis, hard-hearted creatures in fur coats who inhabit the nearby city. Zavattinia is governed by a young man, Totò, born from a cabbage, who is advised in political matters by a dove given to him by his mother's departed spirit.

(Cesare Zavattini, *Totò il Buono,* Milan, 1943)

ZAYANA, capital of MESZRIA and the seat of a ducal court. The town is surrounded by walls of old red sandstone and centres on the square known as the Piazza of the Winds. From the main gate of the town the Way of the Seven Hundred Pillars leads up towards the main gate of a citadel or palace, the Acrozayana, at the top of a stairway of green and purple *panteron* stone.

The most magnificent chamber in the luxurious palace-citadel is the throne room, with its walls of hammered mountain gold and its images of flowers, animals and birds. It is lined with columns four times taller than a man, of carved black onyx with white veins, forming towering snakes and supporting a frieze of jet carved with flowers. The roof is a tracery of ivory and gold. In each corner of the rectangular room, gold tripods support basins of moonstone filled with perfumes and sweet essences. The floor is of flags of Parian marble set in a lozenge pattern with topaz insets. The ducal throne stands on a dais of topaz, but the throne itself is quite plain, being carved from a block of dreamstone, grey with flecks and veins of silver. It is shaded by two golden wings, both inlaid with thousands of tiny peacocks. Visitors should note that the appearance of the duke in the throne room is signalled by a blast of trumpets and then by the entry of thirty peacocks, walking in pairs; they display their tails and then take up their positions on either side of the throne.

Visitors should not miss a chance to see the bedrooms, where the beds are made of gold and have bedposts in the form of golden hippogriffs with eyes of sapphire.

To the south of Zayana, the Darial hills slope gently down to the shores of Reisma Mere. In the centre of the mere is a small island known as Ambermere, with a small natural harbour of white sand at its south-eastern point. Ambermere is covered in cypress trees; on its north-western extremity is a small garden shaded by oaks, cedars and unique strawberry trees, used by the ducal court as a banqueting place and as a setting for open-air balls and masques.

(E.R. Eddison, *Mistress of Mistresses, A Vision of Zimiamvia*, London, 1935; E.R. Eddison, *A Fish Dinner in Memison*, London, 1941; E.R. Eddison, *The Mezentian Gate*, London, 1958)

ZEMRUDE, a city in Asia, whose form is given by the beholder's mood. If a traveller goes by whistling, his nose atilt behind the whistle, he will know the city from below: window sills, flapping curtains, fountains. If another traveller walks along hanging his head, his nails dug into the palms of his hands, his gaze will be held on the ground, in the gutters, the manhole covers, the fish scales, wastepaper. One cannot say that one aspect of the city is truer than the other, but one hears of the upper Zemrude chiefly from those who remember it, as they sink into the lower Zemrude, following every day the same stretches of street and finding again each morning the ill-humour of the day be-

fore, encrusted at the foot of the walls. For all people, sooner or later, the day comes when they bring their gaze down along the drainpipes and they can no longer detach it from the cobblestones. The reverse is not impossible, but it is more rare: and so the people of Zemrude continue walking through the city's streets with eyes now digging into the cellars, the foundations, the wells.

(Italo Calvino, *Le città invisibili*, Turin, 1972)

ZENDA, a small, placid, undisturbed country town in RURITANIA, some fifty miles from the capital, Strelsau, and about ten from the frontier. Zenda in itself is not unusually interesting—the focal points of the town are a telegraph office and a railway station where the Dresden train stops. A visit, however, should be made to the graveyard in Zenda where the charred body of King Rudolf V was laid to rest.

Lying as it does in a valley, Zenda is surrounded by wooded hills, on one of which stands the famous castle of Zenda; on the opposing hill, about five miles from the town centre, stands the Château of Tarlenheim, site of the ancient castle of Festenburg. Festenburg Castle was fortified by Count Nikolas until it threatened to surpass Zenda itself in both strength and magnificence. In a game of dice played between Rudolf III and the Count, the latter won Zenda Castle but was killed by Frederick of Hentzau, Bishop of Modenstein, in retaliation for the Count's kidnapping of the King's sister, Princess Osra. Festenburg Castle was then demolished and the moat filled in.

The Castle of Zenda is the country residence of the kings of Ruritania. In olden times it was a fortress and the ancient keep is still well preserved and appears very imposing. Behind it stands another portion of the original castle and behind that again (but separated by a deep and broad moat) is a handsome and modern château erected by the father of King Rudolf V, Black Michael.

The old and new portions of Zenda Castle are connected by a drawbridge, but a wide, handsome avenue leads to the modern château. The combination of old and modern allows for an ideal residence: if company is desired, the château serves the purpose; if not, one has merely to cross the bridge and draw it up, and nothing short of a regiment can enter.

Visitors can tell when the King or Queen is

The modern château seen from the back windows of
ZENDA CASTLE.

present because the royal standard is then flown
on the keep. When they are absent, parts of the
castle are open to the public.

(Anthony Hope [Anthony Hope Hawkins], *The
Prisoner of Zenda*, London, 1894; Anthony Hope
[Anthony Hope Hawkins], *Rupert of Hentzau*,
London, 1898; Anthony Hope [Anthony Hope

Hawkins], *The Heart of Princess Osra*, London,
1906)

ZENOBIA, a city in Asia. Though set on dry terrain it stands on high pilings, and the houses are of
bamboo and zinc, many platforms and balconies
placed on stilts at various heights, crossing one another, linked by ladders and hanging sidewalks,
surmounted by cone-roofed belvederes, barrels
storing water, weather-vanes, jutting pulleys and
fish poles and cranes.

No one remembers what need or command
or desire drove Zenobia's founders to give their
city this form, so there is no telling whether it was
satisfied by the city as one sees it today, which has
perhaps grown through successive superimposi-
tions from the first, now undecipherable plan. But
what is certain is that if a traveller asks an inhabitant of Zenobia to describe his vision of a happy
life, it is always a city like Zenobia that he imag-
ines, with its pilings and its suspended stairways, a
Zenobia perhaps quite different, aflutter with banners and ribbons, but always derived by combining
elements of that first model.

However, it is pointless trying to decide
whether Zenobia is to be classified among happy
cities or among the unhappy. It makes no sense to
divide cities into these two species, but rather into
another two: those that through the years and the
changes continue to give their form to desires, and
those in which desires either erase the city or are
erased by it.

(Italo Calvino, *Le città invisibili*, Turin, 1972)

ZERAY, a wild, wooded region in the north-east
of the BEKLAN EMPIRE. To the south Zeray is
bounded by the river Vrako which flows into the
Telthearna River near the Gorge of BEREEL. In
the past Zeray was regarded as the midden of the
Empire which, to all intents and purposes, ended
at the frontier town of KABIN. Zeray was a lawless
area, with no roads and no real villages or towns.
Even at the height of the Empire it was never
taxed and army patrols did not venture into it.
The whole area, consisting mostly of forest and
marsh, was a refuge for bandits and criminals of all
types. No one was safe here, where murder and
rape were daily occurrences. Men carried all their
wealth with them and murdered one another for

coins that could not even be used within Zeray. The town of Zeray itself was a collection of buildings rather than a real town; it had no definable streets and consisted merely of hovels and houses distributed as haphazardly as anthills in a field.

Zeray is now much more civilized than in the past and it is expected to develop as a frontier town for the new trade with ZAKALON. A ferry drawn by ropes has been established and a shanty town is growing up. The development of Zeray is closely and ironically connected with the history of the cult of Shardik, the bear once thought in BEKLA to represent the power of God.

The first known connection between Zeray and the cult of Shardik was the arrival here of Belka-Trazet, former High Baron of ORTELGA who had been driven out by the supporters of Shardik. He attempted to establish law and order in Zeray and began negotiations with the enemies of the Beklan Empire. Before anything could be concluded, he died of one of the diseases that were then rife in this area.

Some time later Kelderek, former Priest King of Bekla, arrived in Zeray in search of the bear Shardik. In Zeray he found the Tuginda or High Priestess of Shardik who had also left the island of QUISO in search of the sacred bear, and Melathys, one of the priestesses of the cult. By this time Kelderek was becoming convinced that the cult of Shardik was evil rather than good and that he had allowed it to become a perverted source of political power rather than a religious belief. He was even thinking of killing the bear if possible, but when he set out in search of it he was captured by a slave trader. He was acutely aware of the irony of the situation; it was he who, as Priest King, had allowed slavery to be reintroduced into the Empire. He found himself in a company of slave-children, and his sufferings with them were severe; like them he had his ear pierced so that a chain could be passed through it.

By a strange coincidence the children were freed by Shardik himself. The slaver met the great bear and tried to attack it with burning arrows. Both died in the struggle that ensued. Thus Shardik finally saved the children who had been enslaved as a result of the cult devoted to him.

Kelderek and the children were found by soldiers and taken to the river village of Tissarn, to the north of Zeray. Kelderek settled with Melathys, the former priestess, and under the terms of the armistice became governor of Zeray.

One of the peculiarities of Zeray is its extremely young population. Much of the fishing and agricultural work is carried out by children; it is a refuge for all those who were orphaned, lost or deserted during the wars that afflicted the Empire.

It was in Zeray that the cult of Shardik took on its final form; it is uncertain to what extent it is observed in other areas of the Empire. After the rescue of the children from the slaver, the bear became known as "Lord Shardik Die for Children." The body of the bear and that of a little girl killed by the slaver were placed on a burning raft and left to float down the river. This is now commemorated during the spring festival known, after the girl, as Shara's Day. A wooden raft, decked with flowers, is set on fire and sent floating down the river. At the same time clay bears are floated off on pieces of wood. Songs telling the story of Shardik and the children are often sung as shanties on the newly established ferry across the river.

(Richard Adams, *Shardik*, London, 1974)

ZURA, see SOUTHERN SEA.

ZURTLAND, a narrow valley in the underground continent of PELLUCIDAR, separated by the Terrible Mountains from the area around the city of SARI. A river, alive with crocodiles, flows down the valley to the KORSAR Az through pleasant countryside. Inland, the Zurtland valley narrows and rises to a tree-dotted plateau.

The valley takes its name from its inhabitants, a tribe known as the Zurts. They live in a fair-sized village some way up the valley, in houses built from bamboo poles, thatched with grass and raised ten feet above the ground on posts. The Zurts are dark-skinned people with raven-black hair. Travellers are warned that, according to Zurt customs, a foreign woman who reaches the village may stay for thirty sleeps (this being the only way to measure time in Pellucidar, where night is unknown) and then leave freely; but that if one of the Zurts takes her as his mate, she will not be allowed to leave.

Zurtland is one of the few regions of Pellucidar where the *jolok* is known to have been tamed. The *jolok* is a type of wolf-dog found throughout Pellucidar, the size of a leopard, but with longer legs. The back and flanks are covered with dark shaggy hair; the belly and breast are white. *Joloks* normally hunt in packs and are quite fearless—even the largest and fiercest animals of Pellucidar are not safe from them. In Zurtland they are used for hunting and for personal protection against human and other enemies. How or when the Zurts began to tame these notoriously vicious animals is not known.

(Edgar Rice Burroughs, *Savage Pellucidar*, New York, 1963)

ZUVENDIS, a vast territory in East Africa, about the size of France, and very difficult of access, surrounded by forests, marshes, deserts and impregnable mountains. The climate is mild and frequently cool because of the altitude; rains are infrequent. The land is fertile and rich in many minerals—gold, marble and coal are all found in the area. The name of the country derives from its gold mines; in the native language, Zuvendis means "yellow land." There are many important mountains and lakes; the largest lake extends in front of the capital city, MILOSIS.

The inhabitants are white and number over ten million. The origin of this white population is unknown.

The architecture of Zuvendis is vaguely reminiscent of ancient Egyptian or Assyrian architecture, but in manners the inhabitants are similar to the Syrians or Persians. Like the Persians, the inhabitants venerate the hippopotamus which they consider to be an animal sacred to the sun.

The population is extremely bellicose, constantly at war with other nations. Zuvendis is a monarchy but the power is truly in the hands of the priests and the aristocracy. The population is divided into distinct classes: landed gentry, like that of feudal Europe; courtesans; artisans and peasants. Theoretically polygamous, the inhabitants do not usually take more than one wife.

The laws of Zuvendis are strict and recommend three kinds of punishment: public flogging, forced labour and death. Criminals condemned to death are thrown into the furnace in the Temple of the Sun at Milosis; these include those convicted of high treason, of fraud against a widow or an orphan, of sacrilege or of trying to leave the country.

(Henry Rider Haggard, *Allan Quatermain*, London, 1887)

ZUY, a prosperous Elfin kingdom in the Netherlands. Zuy is one of the most well-regulated of the many Elfin kingdoms in Europe and probably the most wealthy. It has a substantial share in the East Indies Trade, importing spices, muslins and leopard skins, and exporting musical boxes, *marrons glacés*, starch, suppositories and religious pictures.

This commercialism is not much appreciated by other Elfin realms. BROCÉLIANDE, for instance, considers Zuy little more than a gilded grocery shop. In their turn, the elves and fairies of Zuy have little time for the formalism and traditionalism of Brocéliande and strongly resent the fact that Brocéliande's income is bolstered by the proceeds from gambling rather than by honest trade. Nor does Zuy have a particularly high opinion of the elves of the British Isles, Zuyans considering these elves to be barbarians not only because of their habit of living beneath hills, but also because they have green skin.

It was an expedition from Zuy that finally discovered the PERI KINGDOM, the almost legendary land from which all the elves and fairies of Europe are descended. As a result of this expedition, trade relations were established with the Middle East and Zuy's prosperity became even greater.

(Sylvia Townsend Warner, *Kingdoms of Elfin*, London, 1972)

ZYUNDAL, see Isles of WISDOM.

INDEX

All places in the Dictionary are listed here under the author's name, and printed in capital letters. The authors are listed alphabetically by surname; when an author is better known by a pseudonym, the proper name is cross-referenced. ("Author," in this instance, includes playwrights, film directors and composers.)

Titles are cross-referenced to the author. They are given in the original language, followed by an English translation in brackets. The English translation is also listed separately.

A

Abbott, Edwin A., *Flatland*, FLATLAND, LINELAND.

"Abdias," see Stifter, Adalbert.

Ablancourt, Jean Jacobé de Frémont d', *Supplément de l'Histoire Véritable de Lucien (Sequel to Lucian's "True History")*, ANIMAL REPUBLIC, Island of POETRY, PYRANDRIA.

Account of the First Settlement, Laws, Form of Government and Police of the Cessares, An, see Burgh, James.

Accounts of the Ten Continents, see Shuo Tung-Fang.

Acts of King Arthur and His Noble Knights, The, From the Winchester Manuscripts of Sir Thomas Malory and Other Sources, see Steinbeck, John.

Adam, Paul, *Lettres de Malaisie (Letters from Malaysia)*, ADAM'S COUNTRY.

Adams, Richard, *Shardik*, BEKLA, BEKLAN EMPIRE, DEELGUY, GELT MOUNTAINS, KABIN, ORTELGA, QUISO, TEREKENALT, The Streels of URTAH, YELDA, ZAKALON, ZERAY.

Address by the Founder of Icaria, see Cabet, Etienne.

Adresse du fondateur d'Icarie, see Cabet, Etienne.

"Adventure of the Creeping Man, The," see Doyle, Sir Arthur Conan.

"Adventure of the Lion's Mane, The," see Doyle, Sir Arthur Conan.

Adventures, And Surprizing Deliverances, Of James Dubourdieu, And His Wife, The, see Evans, Ambrose.

Adventures of Jacques Sadeur, see Foigny, Gabriel.

Adventures of King Pausole, The, see Loüys, Pierre.

Adventures of Pinocchio, The, see Collodi, Carlo.

Adventurous Simplicissimus Teutsch, The, see Grimmelshausen, von.

Aelianus, Claudius, *Varia Historia (Diverse History)*, ANOSTUS.

Aeneid, The, see Virgil.

"Aepyornis Island," see Wells, H.G.

Aethiopis, see Arctinus of Miletus.

Africa of Impressions, see Ferry, Jean.

Agraives, Jean d', *La Cité des sables (The City of Sand)*, City of SAND.

Alastor or The Spirit of Solitude, see Shelley, Percy Bysshe.

Alberny, Luc, *Le Mammouth Bleu (The Blue Mammoth)*, GRANDE EUSCARIE.

Alcina, see Handel, George Friederic & A. Marchi.

Aldiss, Brian W., & Mike Wilks, *Pile. Petals from St. Klaed's Computer*, PILE.

Ale Verk, see Peretz, Isaac Lieb.

Alexander, Lloyd, *The Black Cauldron*, CAER CADARN, CAER DALLBEN, CAER DATHYL, MONA, MORVA, PRYDAIN, The Barrow of RHITTA, SUMMER COUNTRY, TYLWYTH TEG.

————, *The Book of Three*, CAER DALLBEN, CAER DATHYL, MEDWYN'S VALLEY, MONA, PRYDAIN, The Barrow OF RHITTA, SUMMER COUNTRY, TYLWYTH TEG.

————, *The Castle of Llyr*, CAER DALLBEN, CAER DATHYL, MONA, PRYDAIN, The Barrow of RHITTA, SUMMER COUNTRY, TYLWYTH TEG.

————, *The High King*, CAER CADARN, CAER DALLBEN, CAER DATHYL, FREE COMMOTS, MEDWYN'S VALLEY, MONA, MORVA, PRYDAIN, The Barrow of RHITTA, SUMMER COUNTRY, TYLWYTH TEG.

————, *Taran Wanderer*, CAER CADARN, CAER DALLBEN, CAER DATHYL,

C

E

I

S

W